Sim

This book is a work of fiction. The characters, incidents, and dialogue
are drawn from the author's imagination and are not to be construed as
real. Any resemblance to actual events or persons, living or dead, is
entirely coincidental.

HarperCollins books may be purchased for educational,
business, or sales promotional use. For information please write:
Special Markets Department, HarperCollins Publishers,
10 East 53rd Street, New York, NY 10022.

FIRST EDITION

Printed on acid-free paper

Library of Congress Cataloging-in-Publication Data

Simmons, Dan.
    Olympos / Dan Simmons.—1st ed.
        p. cm.
    ISBN 0-380-97894-6 (hardcover)
    1. Mars (Planet)—Fiction. 2. Imaginary wars and battles—Fiction.
3. Mythology, Greek—Fiction. 4. Gods, Greek—Fiction. I. Title.

PS3569.I47292O49 2005
813'.54—dc22   2005040024

05 06 07 08 09 JTC/QW 10 9 8 7 6 5 4 3 2 1

OLYMPOS

DAN SIMMONS

An Imprint of HarperCollins*Publishers*

OLYMPOS

This novel is for Harold Bloom, who—in his refusal
to collaborate in this Age of Resentment—has given me great pleasure.

How could Homer have known about these things?
When all this happened he was a camel in Bactria!

—LUCIAN, *The Dream*

. . . the real-life history of the earth must in the last
instance be a history of a really relentless warfare. Neither
his fellows, nor his gods, nor his passions will leave a man alone.

—JOSEPH CONRAD, *Notes on Life and Letters*

O write no more the tale of Troy,
    If earth Death's scroll must be—
Nor mix with Laian rage the joy
    Which dawns upon the free:
Although a subtler Sphinx renew
Riddles of death Thebes never knew.

Another Athens shall arise,
    And to remoter time
Bequeath, like sunset to the skies,
    The splendor of its prime;
And leave, if naught so bright may live,
All earth can take or Heaven can give.

—PERCY BYSSHE SHELLEY, *Hellas*

PART

1

1

Helen of Troy awakes just before dawn to the sound of air raid sirens. She feels along the cushions of her bed but her current lover, Hockenberry, is gone—slipped out into the night again before the servants wake, acting as he always does after their nights of lovemaking, acting as if he has done something shameful, no doubt stealing his way home this very minute through the alleys and back streets where the torches burn least bright. Helen thinks that Hockenberry is a strange and sad man. Then she remembers.

My husband is dead.

This fact, Paris killed in single combat with the merciless Apollo, has been reality for nine days—the great funeral involving both Trojans and Achaeans will begin in three hours if the god-chariot now over the city does not destroy Ilium completely in the next few minutes—but Helen still cannot believe that her Paris is gone. Paris, son of Priam, defeated on the field of battle? Paris dead? Paris thrown down into the shaded caverns of Hades without beauty of body or the elegance of action? Unthinkable. This is *Paris*, her beautiful boy-child who had stolen her away from Menelaus, past the guards and across the green lawns of Lacedaemon. This is Paris, her most attentive lover even after this long decade of tiring war, he whom she had often secretly referred to as her "plunging stallion full-fed at the manger."

Helen slips out of bed and crosses to the outer balcony, parting the gauzy curtains as she emerges into the pre-dawn light of Ilium. It is midwinter and the marble is cold under her bare feet. The sky is still dark enough that she can see forty or fifty searchlights stabbing skyward, searching for the god or goddess and the flying chariot. Muffled plasma explosions ripple across the half dome of the moravecs' energy field that shields the city. Suddenly, multiple beams of coherent light—shafts of solid blue, emerald green, blood red—lance upward from Ilium's perimeter defenses. As Helen watches, a single huge explosion shakes the northern quadrant of the city, sending its shockwave echoing across the topless towers of Ilium and stirring the curls of Helen's long, dark hair from her shoulders. The gods have begun using physical bombs to penetrate the force shield in recent weeks, the single-molecule bomb casings quantum phase-shifting through the moravecs' shield. Or so Hockenberry and the amusing little metal creature, Mahnmut, have tried to explain to her.

Helen of Troy does not give a fig about machines.

Paris is dead. The thought is simply unsupportable. Helen has been prepared to die with Paris on the day that the Achaeans, led by her former husband, Menelaus, and by his brother Agamemnon, ultimately breach the walls, as breach they must according to her prophetess friend Cassandra, putting every man and boy-child in the city to death, raping the women and hauling them off to slavery in the Greek Isles. Helen has been ready for *that* day—ready to die by her own hand or by the sword of Menelaus—but somehow she has never really believed that her dear, vain, godlike Paris, her plunging stallion, her beautiful warrior-husband, could die first. Through more than nine years of siege and glorious battle, Helen has trusted the gods to keep her beloved Paris alive and intact and in her bed. And they did. And now they have killed him.

She calls back the last time she saw her Trojan husband, ten days earlier, heading out from the city to enter into single combat with the god Apollo. Paris had never looked more confident in his armor of elegant, gleaming bronze, his head flung back, his long hair flowing back over his shoulders like a stallion's mane, his white teeth flashing as Helen and thousands of others watched and cheered from the wall above the Scaean Gate. His fast feet had sped him on, "sure and sleek in his glory," as King Priam's favorite bard liked to sing. But this day they had sped him on to his own slaughter by the hands of furious Apollo.

And now he's dead, thinks Helen, *and, if the whispered reports I've overheard are accurate, his body is a scorched and blasted thing, his bones broken, his perfect, golden face burned into an obscenely grinning skull, his blue eyes melted to tallow, tatters of barbecued flesh stringing back from his scorched cheekbones like . . . like . . . firstlings—like those charred first bits of ceremonial meat tossed from the sacrificial fire because they have been deemed unworthy.* Helen shivers in the cold wind coming up with the dawn and watches smoke rise above the rooftops of Troy.

Three antiaircraft rockets from the Achaean encampment to the south roar skyward in search of the retreating god-chariot. Helen catches a glimpse of that retreating chariot—a brief gleaming as bright as the morning star, pursued now by the exhaust trails from the Greek rockets. Without warning, the shining speck quantum shifts out of sight, leaving the morning sky empty. *Flee back to besieged Olympos, you cowards,* thinks Helen of Troy.

The all-clear sirens begin to whine. The street below Helen's apartments in Paris's estate so near Priam's battered palace are suddenly filled with running men, bucket brigades rushing to the northwest where smoke still rises into the winter air. Moravec flying machines hum over the rooftops, looking like nothing so much as chitinous black hornets with their barbed landing gear and swiveling projectors. Some, she knows from experience and from Hockenberry's late-night rants, will fly what he calls air cover, too late to help, while others will aid in putting out the fire. Then Trojans and moravecs both will pull mangled bodies from the rubble for hours. Since Helen knows almost everyone in the city, she wonders numbly who will be in the ranks of those sent down to sunless Hades so early this morning.

The morning of Paris's funeral. My beloved. My foolish and betrayed beloved.

Helen hears her servants beginning to stir. The oldest of the servants—the old woman Aithra, formerly queen of Athens and mother to royal Theseus until carried away by Helen's brothers in revenge for the kidnapping of their sister—is standing in the doorway to Helen's bedchamber.

"Shall I have the girls draw your bath, my lady?" asks Aithra.

Helen nods. She watches the skies brighten a moment more—sees the smoke to the northwest thicken and then lessen as the fire brigades and moravec fire engines bring it under control, watches another moment as the rockvec battle hornets continue to fling themselves eastward in hopeless pursuit of the already quantum-teleported chariot—and then Helen of Troy turns to go inside, her bare feet whispering on the cold marble. She has to prepare herself for Paris's funeral rites and for seeing her cuckolded husband, Menelaus, for the first time in ten years. This also will be the first time that Hector, Achilles, Menelaus, Helen, and many of the other Achaeans and Trojans all will be present at a public event. Anything could happen.

Only the gods know what will come of this awful day, thinks Helen. And then she has to smile despite her sadness. These days, prayers to the gods go unanswered with a vengeance. These days, the gods share nothing with mortal men—or at least nothing except death and doom and terrible destruction carried earthward by their own divine hands.

Helen of Troy goes inside to bathe and dress for the funeral.

2

Red-haired Menelaus stood silent in his best armor, upright, motionless, regal, and proud between Odysseus and Diomedes at the forefront of the Achaean delegation of heroes gathered there at the funeral rites within the walls of Ilium to honor his wife-stealing enemy, Priam's son, that shit-eating pig-dog, Paris. Every minute he stood there Menelaus was pondering how and when to kill Helen.

It should be easy enough. She was just across the broad lane and up the wall a bit, less than fifty feet from him opposite the Achaean delegation at the heart of the huge inner court of Troy, up there on the royal reviewing stand with old Priam. With luck, Menelaus could sprint there faster than anyone could intercept him. And even without luck, if the Trojans *did* have time to get between him and his wife, Menelaus would hack them down like weeds.

Menelaus was not a tall man—not a noble giant like his absent brother, Agamemnon, nor an ignoble giant like that ant-pizzle Achilles—so he knew he'd never be able to leap to the reviewing ledge, but would have to take the stairs up through the crowd of Trojans there, hacking and shoving and killing as he went. That was fine with Menelaus.

But Helen could not escape. The reviewing balcony on the wall of the Temple of Zeus had only the one staircase down to this city courtyard. She could retreat into the Temple of Zeus, but he could follow her there, corner her there. Menelaus knew that he would kill her before he went down under the attacks of scores of outraged Trojans—including Hector leading the funeral procession now coming into sight—and then the Achaeans and Trojans would be at war with one another again, forsaking their mad war against the gods. Of course, Menelaus' life would almost certainly be forfeit if the Trojan War resumed here, today—as would Odysseus', Diomedes', and perhaps even the life of invulnerable Achilles himself, since there were only thirty Achaeans here at the pig Paris's funeral, and thousands of Trojans present all around in the courtyard and on the walls and massed between the Achaeans and the Scaean Gate behind them.

It will be worth it.

This thought crashed through Menelaus' skull like the point of a lance. *It will be worth it—any price would be worth it—to kill that faithless bitch.* Despite the weather—it was a cool, gray winter's day—sweat poured down under his helmet, trickled through his short, red beard, and dripped from his chin, spattering on his bronze breastplate. He'd heard that dripping, spattering-on-metal sound many times before, of course, but it had always been his enemies' blood dripping on armor. Menelaus' right hand, set lightly on his silver-studded sword, gripped the hilt of that sword with a numbing ferocity.

Now?

Not now.

Why not now? If not now, when?

Not now.

The two arguing voices in his aching skull—both voices his, since the gods no longer spoke to him—were driving Menelaus insane.

Wait until Hector lights the funeral pyre and then act.

Menelaus blinked sweat out of his eyes. He didn't know which voice this was—the one that had been urging action or the cowardly one urging restraint—but Menelaus agreed with its suggestion. The funeral procession had just entered the city through the huge Scaean Gate, was in the process of carrying Paris's burned corpse—hidden now beneath a silken shroud—down the main thoroughfare to the center courtyard of Troy, where ranks upon ranks of dignitaries and heroes waited, the women—including Helen—watching from the reviewing wall above. Within a very few minutes, the dead man's older brother Hector would be lighting the pyre and all attention would be riveted on the flames as they devoured the already burned body. *A perfect time to act—no one will notice me until my blade is ten inches into Helen's traitorous breast.*

Traditionally, funerals for such royal personages as Paris, son of Priam, one of the Princes of Troy, lasted nine days, with many of the days taken up by funeral games—including chariot races and athletic competitions, usually ending in spear-throwing. But Menelaus knew that the ritual nine days since Apollo blasted Paris into charcoal had been taken up by the long voyage of carts and cutters to the forests still standing on Mount Ida many leagues to the southeast. The little machine-things called moravecs had been called on to fly their hornets and magical devices along with the cutters, providing force-shield defenses against the gods should they attack. And they had attacked, of course. But the woodcutters had done their job.

It was only now, on the tenth day, that the wood was gathered and in

Troy and ready for the pyre, although Menelaus and many of his friends, including Diomedes standing next to him here in the Achaean contingent, thought that burning Paris's putrid corpse on a funeral pyre was an absolute waste of good firewood since both the city of Troy and the miles of Achaean camps along the shore had been out of fuel for campfires for many months, so picked-over were the scrub trees and former forests surrounding Ilium itself ten years into that war. The battlefield was a stubble of stumps. Even the branches had long since been scavenged. The Achaean slaves were cooking dinners for their masters over dung-fueled fires, and that didn't improve either the taste of meat or the foul mood of the Achaean warriors.

Leading the funeral cortege into Ilium was a procession of Trojan chariots, one by one, the horses' hooves wrapped in black felt and raising little noise on the broad stones of the city's thoroughfare and town square. Riding on these chariots, standing silent beside their drivers, were some of the greatest heroes of Ilium, fighters who'd survived more than nine years of the original war and now eight months of this more terrible war with the gods. First came Polydorus, another son of Priam's, followed by Paris's other half brother, Mestor. The next chariot carried the Trojan ally Ipheus, then Laoducus, son of Antenor. Following in their own jewel-bedecked chariots were old Antenor himself, down among the fighting men as always rather than up on the wall with the other elders, then the captain Polyphetes, then Sarpedon's famed charioteer, Thrasmelus, standing in for the Sarpedon himself, co-commander of the Lycians, killed by Patroclus months ago when Trojans still fought Greeks rather than gods. Then came noble Pylartes—not, of course, the Trojan killed by Great Ajax just before the war with the gods began, but this other Pylartes who so often fights alongside Elasus and Mulius. Also in this procession are Megas' son, Perimus, as well as Epistor and Melanippus.

Menelaus recognized them all, these men, these heroes, these enemies. He'd seen their contorted and blood-filled faces under bronze helmets a thousand times across the short deadly space of lance-thrust and sword-hack separating him from his twin goals—Ilium and Helen.

She's fifty feet away. And no one will expect my attack.

Behind the muffled chariots came groomsmen leading the potential sacrificial animals—ten of Paris's second-best horses and his hunting dogs, droves of fat sheep—a serious sacrifice these last, since both wool and mutton were growing scarce under the siege of the gods—and some old, shambling crooked-horned cattle. These cattle were not there for their pride of sacrifice—who was there to sacrifice to now that the gods were enemies?—but there for their fat to make the funeral pyre burn brighter and hotter.

Behind the sacrificial animals came thousands of Trojan infantry, all in polished armor this dull winter's day, their ranks running back out through the Scaean Gate and onto the plains of Ilium. In the midst of this mass of men moved Paris's funeral bier, carried by twelve of his closest comrades-in-arms, men who would have died for Priam's second-eldest son and who even now wept as they carried the massive palanquin for the dead.

Paris's body was covered by a blue shroud and that shroud was already buried in thousands of locks of hair—symbols of mourning from Paris's men and lesser relatives, since Hector and the closer relatives would cut their locks just before the funeral pyre was lighted. The Trojans had not asked the Achaeans to contribute locks for mourning, and if they had—and if Achilles, Hector's principal ally these mad days, had passed on that request, or worse yet, formed it as an order to be enforced by his Myrmidons—Menelaus would have personally led the revolt.

Menelaus wished that his brother Agamemnon were there. Agamemnon always seemed to know the proper course of action. Agamemnon was their true Argive commander—not the usurper Achilles and never the Trojan bastard Hector, who presumed to give orders to Argives, Achaeans, Myrmidons, and Trojans alike these days. No, Agamemnon was the Greeks' true leader, and if he were there today, he'd either stop Menelaus from this reckless attack on Helen or join him to the death in carrying it out. But Agamemnon and five hundred of his loyal men had sailed their black ships back to Sparta and the Greek Isles seven weeks earlier—they were expected to be gone another month, at least—ostensibly to round up new recruits in this war against the gods, but secretly to enlist allies in a revolt against Achilles.

Achilles. Now appeared that traitorous monster walking only a step behind weeping Hector, who kept pace just behind the bier, cradling his dead brother's head in his two huge hands.

At the sight of Paris's body, a great moan went up from the thousands of Trojans massed on the walls and within the square. Women on rooftops and the wall—lesser women, not the females in Priam's royal family or Helen—began a keening ululation. Despite himself, Menelaus felt goosebumps break out on his forearms. Funeral cries from women always affected him thus.

My broken and twisted arm, thought Menelaus, stoking his anger as one would stoke a fading bonfire.

Achilles—this same Achilles man-god passing now as Paris's bier was solemnly carried past this honor-contingent of Achaean captains— had broken Menelaus' arm just eight months earlier, on the day that the fleet-footed mankiller had announced to all the Achaeans that Pallas Athena had killed his friend Patroclus and carried the body to Olympos as a taunt. Then Achilles had announced that the Achaeans and Trojans would no longer make war on each other, but besiege holy Mount Olympos instead.

Agamemnon had objected to this—objected to everything: to Achilles' arrogance and usurpation of Agamemnon's rightful power as king-of-kings of all the Greeks assembled here at Troy, to the blasphemy of attacking the gods, no matter whose friend had been murdered by Athena—if Achilles was even telling the truth—and had objected most to the fact that tens and tens of thousands of Achaean fighters being put under Achilles' control.

Achilles' response that fateful day had been short and simple—he would fight any man, any Greek, who opposed his leadership and his declaration of war. He would fight them in single combat or take them all on at once. Let the last man standing rule the Achaeans from that morning forward.

Agamemnon and Menelaus, the proud sons of Atreus, had both attacked Achilles with spear, sword, and shield, while hundreds of the Achaean captains and thousands of the infantry watched in stunned silence.

Menelaus was a bloodied veteran though not counted amongst the first ranks of heroes at Troy, but his older brother was considered—at least while Achilles had sulked in his tent for weeks—the fiercest fighter of all the Achaeans. His spearcasts were almost always on target, his sword cut through reinforced enemy shields like a blade through cloth, and he showed no mercy to even the noblest enemies begging for their lives to be spared. Agamemnon was as tall and muscled and godlike as blond Achilles, but his body bore a decade's more battle scars and his eyes that day were filled with a demon's rage, while Achilles waited coolly, an almost distracted look on his boy-man's face.

Achilles had disarmed both brothers as if they were children. Agamemnon's powerful spearcast deflected from Achilles' flesh as if Peleus' and the goddess Thetis' son were surrounded by one of the moravecs' invisible energy shields. Agamemnon's savage sword swing—fierce enough, Menelaus had thought at the time, to cut through a block of stone—shattered on Achilles' beautiful shield.

Then Achilles had disarmed them both—throwing their extra spears and Menelaus' sword into the ocean—tossing them down onto the packed sand and ripping their armor from their bodies with the ease a great eagle might tear cloth away from a helpless corpse. The fleet-footed mankiller had broken Menelaus' left arm then—the circle of straining captains and infantry had gasped at the green-stick snap of the bone—and then Achilles broke Agamemnon's nose with a seemingly effortless flat thrust of his palm, finally kicking in the ribs of the king-of-kings. Then Achilles planted his sandal on the moaning Agamemnon's chest while Menelaus lay moaning next to his brother.

Only then had Achilles drawn his sword.

"Surrender and vow allegiance to me this day and I will treat you both with the respect due the sons of Atreus and honor you as fellow-captains and allies in the war to come," Achilles said. "Hesitate a second, and I'll send your dog-souls down to Hades before your friends can blink and scatter your corpses to the waiting vultures so that your bodies will never find burial."

Agamemnon, gasping and groaning, almost vomiting the bile rising within him, had given surrender and allegiance to Achilles. Menelaus, filled with the agony of a bruised leg, his own set of broken ribs, and a shattered arm, had followed suit a second later.

All in all, thirty-five captains of the Achaeans had chosen to oppose Achilles that day. All had been bested within an hour, the bravest of them decapitated when they refused to surrender, their corpses thrown to birds and fish and dogs just as Achilles had threatened, but the other twenty-eight had ended up swearing their service. None of the other great Achaean heroes of Agamemnon's stature—not Odysseus, not Diomedes, not Nestor, neither Big nor Little Ajax, not Teucer—had challenged the fleet-footed mankiller that day. All had vowed aloud—after hearing more about Athena's murder of Patroclus and, later, hearing the details of the same goddess's slaughter of Hector's baby son, Scamandrius—to declare war on the gods that very morning.

Now Menelaus felt his arm ache—the set bones had not healed straight and proper, despite the best ministrations of their famed healer, Podalirius, son of Asclepius, and the arm still bothered Menelaus on cool days like this—but he resisted the urge to rub that ache as Paris's funeral bier and Apollo proceeded slowly in front of the Achaean delegation.

Now the shrouded and lock-covered bier is set down next to the funeral pyre, below the reviewing stand on the wall of the Temple to Zeus. The ranks of infantry in the procession cease marching. The women's moans and ululation from the other walls cease. In the sudden silence, Menelaus can hear the horses' rough breathing and then the stream from one horse pissing on stone.

On the wall, Helenus, the old male seer standing next to Priam, the primary prophet and counselor of Ilium, shouts down some short eulogy that is lost on the wind that has just come in from the sea, blowing like a cold, disapproving breath from the gods. Helenus hands a ceremonial knife to Priam, who, though almost bald, has kept a few long strands of gray hair above his ears for just such solemn occasions. Priam uses the razor-sharp blade to sever a lock of that gray hair. A slave—Paris's personal slave for many years—catches that lock in a golden bowl and moves on to Helen, who receives the knife from Priam and looks at the blade for a long second as if contemplating using it on herself, plunging it into her breast—Menelaus feels a sudden alarm that she will do just that, depriving him of his vengeance that is now only moments away—but then Helen raises the knife, seizes one of her long side tresses, and slices off the end. The brunette lock falls into the golden bowl and the slave moves on to mad Cassandra, one of Priam's many daughters.

Despite the effort and danger of bringing the wood from Mount Ida, the pyre is a worthy one. Since they could not fill the city square with a traditional royal pyre a hundred feet on each side and still have room for people there, the pyre is only thirty feet to a side, but taller than usual, rising up to the level of the reviewing platform on the wall. Broad wooden steps, small platforms in themselves, have been built as a rampway to the apex of the pyre. Strong timber, reft from Paris's own palace walls, square and support the massive heap of firewood.

The strong pallbearers carry Paris's bier to the small platform at the top of the pyre. Hector waits below at the foot of the wide stairs.

Now the animals are quickly and efficiently killed by men who are experts at both butchery and religious sacrifice—and after all, thinks Menelaus, what's the difference between the two? The sheep and cattle's throats are cut, blood drained into more ceremonial bowls, hides skinned, and fat flensed in mere minutes. Paris's corpse is wrapped about in folds of animal fat like soft bread around burned meat.

Now the flayed animal carcasses are carried up the steps and laid around Paris's shrouded body. Women—virgins in full ceremonial gowns with their faces covered by veils—come forth from Zeus's temple carrying two-handled jars of honey and oil. Not allowed on the pyre itself, they hand these jars to Paris's bodyguards, now turned bier-bearers, who carry the jars up the steps and set them around the bier with great care.

Paris's favorite chariot horses are led forth, the four finest are chosen from the ten, and Hector cuts the animals' throats with his brother's long knife—moving from one to the next so quickly that even these intelligent, high-spirited, superbly trained war animals have no time to react.

It's Achilles who—with wild zeal and inhuman strength—flings the bodies of the four massive stallions onto the pyre, one after the next, each one higher onto the pyramid of timbers and logs.

Paris's personal slave leads six of his master's favorite dogs into the clearing next to the pyre. Hector moves from one dog to the next, patting and scratching them behind the ears. Then he pauses to think a moment, as if remembering all the times he had seen his brother feed these dogs from the table and take them on hunting expeditions to the mountains or the inland marshes.

Hector chooses two of the dogs, nods for the others to be led away, holds each affectionately for a minute by the loose skin at the back of its neck as if offering it a bone or a treat, and then cuts each dog's throat so violently that the blade almost severs the animal's head from its body. Hector himself flings the corpses of the two dogs onto the pyre—heaving them far above the bodies of the stallions so that they land at the foot of the bier itself.

Now a surprise.

Ten bronze-armored Trojans and ten bronze-armored Achaean spearmen lead forward a man-pulled cart. On the cart is a cage. In the cage is a god.

On the reviewing balcony high on the wall of Zeus's temple, Cassandra watched the funeral ceremony for Paris with a growing sense of doom. When the cart was pulled into the center courtyard of Troy—pulled by eight chosen Trojan spearmen, not by horses or oxen—the cart carrying its sole cargo of a doomed god, Cassandra came close to swooning.

Helen caught her elbow and held her up. "What is it?" whispered the Greek woman, her friend, who, with Paris, had brought all this pain and tragedy down on Troy.

"It's madness," whispered Cassandra, leaning back against the marble wall, although whether *her* madness, or the madness of sacrificing a *god* or the madness of this whole, long war, or the madness of Menelaus below in the courtyard—a madness which she had been sensing grow over the past hour like a terrible storm sent by Zeus—Cassandra did not make clear to Helen. Nor did she herself know which she meant.

The captured god, held not only behind the iron bars hammered into the cart but also within the clear egg of the moravec forcefield that had finally trapped him, was named *Dionysos*—or Dionysus, son of Zeus by Semele, god of fulfillment in wine and in sex and in release to rapture. Cassandra, whose personal Lord from childhood had been Apollo— Paris's killer—had nonetheless communed with Dionysos on more than one intimate occasion. This god had been the only divinity captured in combat so far in the new war, wrestled into submission by godlike Achilles, denied his quantum teleportation by moravec magic, talked into surrender by the wily Odysseus, and kept in thrall by the borrowed moravec forceshield now shimmering around him like heated air on a midsummer's day.

Dionysos was unprepossessing for a god—short of stature, a mere six feet tall, pale, pudgy even by mortal standards, with a mass of gold-brown curls and a boy's first attempt at a sketchy beard.

The cart stopped. Hector unlocked the cage and reached through the semipermeable forcefield to drag Dionysos up onto the first step of the pyre's staircase. Achilles also laid his hand on the small god's neck.

"Deicide," whispered Cassandra. "God murder. Madness and deicide."

Helen and Priam and Andromache and the others on the reviewing balcony ignored her. All eyes were on the pale god and the two taller, bronzed mortals on either side of him.

Unlike Seer Helenus' wispy voice, which had been lost to the cold wind and crowd murmur, Hector's booming shout rolled out over the crowded city center and echoed back from the tall towers and high walls of Ilium; it might have been clearly audible atop Mount Ida leagues to the east.

"Paris, beloved brother—we are here to say farewell to you and to say it so that you shall hear us even there where you now reside, deep in the House of Death.

"We send you sweet honey, rare oil, your favorite steeds, and your most loyal dogs—and now I offer to you this god from Olympos, Zeus's son, whose fat shall feed the hungry flames and speed your soul to Hades."

Hector drew his sword. The forcefield flickered and died, but Dionysos remained shackled in leg irons and wrist irons. "May I speak?" said the pale little god. His voice did not carry as far as Hector's had.

Hector hesitated.

"Let the god speak!" called down the seer Helenus from his place by Priam on the balcony of Zeus's temple.

"Let the god speak!" cried the Achaean seer Calchas from his place near Menelaus.

Hector frowned but nodded. "Say your last words, bastard son of Zeus. But even if they are a plea to your father, they will not save you today. Nothing will save you today. Today you are *firstling* for my brother's corpse fire."

Dionysos smiled, but it was a tremulous smile—tremulous for a mortal man, much less for a god.

"Trojans and Achaeans," called the flabby little god with the straggly bit of beard. "You can't kill one of the immortal gods. I was born from the womb of death, you fools. As a boy-god, Zeus's child, my toys were those prophesied as the toys of the new ruler of the world—dice, ball, top, golden apples, bullroarer, and wool.

"But the Titans, whom my Father had beaten and thrown down into Tartarus, the hell beneath hell, the nightmare kingdom below the kingdom of the dead where your brother Paris now floats like a forgotten fart, whitened their faces with chalk and came like the spirits of the dead and attacked me with their bare, white hands and tore me into seven pieces, and threw me into a cauldron standing over a tripod that stood above a fire much hotter than this puny pyre you build here today."

"Are you finished?" asked Hector, raising his sword.

"Almost," said Dionysos, his voice happier and stronger now, its power echoing back from the far walls that had sent Hector's voice bouncing back earlier.

"They boiled me and then roasted me over the fire on seven spits, and the smell of my cooking was so delicious that it drew my father, Zeus himself, down to the Titans' feast, hoping to be invited to the meal. But when he saw my boy's skull on the spit and my boy's hands in the broth, Father smote the Titans with lightning and hurled them back in Tartarus, where they reside in terror and misery unto this very day."

"Is that all?" said Hector.

"Almost," said Dionysos. He raised his face to King Priam and the royals on the balcony of Zeus's temple. The small god's voice was a bull-roar now.

"But others say that my boiled limbs were thrown into the earth where Demeter gathered them together—and thus came to man the first vines to give you wine. Only one boyish limb of mine survived the fire and the earth—and Pallas Athena brought that limb to Zeus, who entrusted my *kradiaios Dionysos* to Hipta, the Asian name for the Great Mother Rheaso, that she might carry it on her head. Father used that term, *kradiaios Dionysos* as a sort of pun, you seen, since *kradia* in the old tongue means 'heart' and *krada* means 'fig tree', so . . ."

"Enough," cried Hector. "Endless prattling will not prolong your dog's life. End this in ten words or fewer or I'll end it for you."

"Eat me," said Dionysos.

Hector swung his great sword with both hands, decapitating the god with one blow.

The crowd of Trojans and Greeks gasped. The massed ranks all took a step backward. Dionysos' headless body stood there on the lowest platform for several seconds, tottering but still upright, until it suddenly toppled like a marionette with its strings cut. Hector grabbed the fallen head, its mouth still open, lifted it by its thin beard, and threw it high up on the funeral pyre so that it landed between the corpses of the horses and the dogs.

Using his sword overhand like an axe now, Hector hacked away—cutting off Dionysos' arms, then legs, then genitals—throwing every bit onto a different section of the pyre. He took care not to throw them too near Paris's bier, however, since he and the others would have to sort the ashes later to separate Paris's revered bones from the unworthy bone-garbage of the dogs, horses, and god. Finally, Hector cut the torso into dozens of small, fleshy bits, throwing most onto the pyre, but lobbing others down to the pack of Paris's surviving dogs, who had been released into the square by the men who had been handling them since the funeral procession.

As the last bits of bone and gristle were hacked to bits, a black cloud seemed to rise from the pitiful remnants of Dionysos' corpse—rising like a swirling mass of invisible black gnats, like a small cyclone of black smoke—so fierce for a few seconds that even Hector had to stop his grim work and step back. The crowds, including the Trojan infantry in ranks and the Achaean heroes, also took another step back. Women on the wall screamed and covered their faces with their veils and hands.

Then the cloud was gone, Hector threw the last bits of pasty-white and pink flesh onto the pyre and kicked the rib cage and spine in among the faggots of heaped wood. Then Hector struggled out of his bloody bronze, allowing his attendants to carry away the soiled armor. One slave brought a basin of water and the tall man washed blood off his arms and hands and brow with it, accepting a clean towel from another slave.

Clean now, clad only in tunic and sandals, Hector lifted the golden bowl filled with fresh-cut locks of hair for mourning, ascended the broad steps to the summit of the pyre where the bier resided on its resin-and-wood platform, and poured the hair of his brother's loved ones and friends and comrades onto the shroud of Paris. A runner—the fastest runner in all the running games in Troy's recent history—entered through the Scaean Gate carrying a tall torch, jogged through the crowd of infantry and onlookers—a crowd that parted for him—and ran up the wide platform steps to where Hector waited at the top of the pyre.

The runner handed the flickering torch to Hector, bowed, and descended the stairs backward, still bowing.

Menelaus looks up as a dark cloud moves in over the city.

"Phoebus Apollo shrouds the day," whispers Odysseus.

A cold wind blows in from the west just as Hector drops the torch into the fat- and resin-soaked timber below the bier. The wood smokes but does not burn.

Menelaus, who has always been more excitable in battle than his brother Agamemnon or many other of the coolest killers and greatest heroes among the Greeks, feels his heart begin to pound as the moment for action approaches. It does not bother him so much that he may only have moments more to live, as long as that bitch Helen goes screaming down to Hades before him. If Menelaus, son of Atreus, had his way, the woman would be thrown down into the deeper hell of Tartarus where the Titans whom the dead god Dionysos had just been prattling about still scream and blunder about in the gloom and pain and roar.

Hector gestures, and Achilles carries two brimming goblets up to his former enemy and then goes back down the steps. Hector raises the goblets.

"Winds of the West and North," cries Hector, raising the goblets, "blustering Zephyr and cold-fingered Boreas, come with a strong blast and light the pyre where Paris lies in state, all the Trojans and even the honoring Argives mourning around him! Come Boreas, come Zephyr, help us light this pyre with your breath and I promise you splendid victims and generous, brimming cups of libation!"

On the balcony above, Helen whispers to Andromache, "This is madness. Madness. Our beloved Hector invoking the aid of the gods, with whom we war, to burn the corpse of the god he just slaughtered."

Before Andromache can reply, Cassandra laughs aloud from the shadows, drawing stern glances from Priam and the old men around him.

Cassandra ignores the reproachful stares and hisses at Helen and Andromache. "Madnesssss, yesssss. I *told* you all was madness. It's madness what Menelaussss is planning now, Helen, your slaughter, moments away, no less bloody than the death of Dionysos."

"What are you talking about, Cassandra?" Helen's whisper is harsh, but she has gone very pale.

Cassandra smiles. "I'm talking about your death, woman. And just minutes away, postponed only by the refusal of a corpse pyre to light."

"Menelaus?"

"Your worthy husband," laughs Cassandra. "Your *previous* worthy husband. The one who's not rotting away now like charred compost on a woodpile. Can't you hear Menelaus' ragged breathing as he prepares to cut you down? Can't you smell his sweat? Can't you hear his foul heart pounding? I can."

Andromache turns away from the funeral and steps closer to Cassandra, ready to lead her off the balcony into the temple, out of sight and earshot.

Cassandra laughs again and shows a short but very sharp dagger in her hand. "Touch me, bitch, and I'll carve you up the way you cut up that slave baby you called your own child."

"Silence!" hisses Andromache. Her eyes are suddenly wide with fury.

Priam and the other old men turn and scowl again. They obviously have not made out the words in their aged semi-deafness, but the tone of the angry whispers and hisses must be unmistakable to them.

Helen's hands are shaking. "Cassandra, you've told me yourself that all your predictions from all your years of casting doom were false. Troy still stands months after you predicted its destruction. Priam is alive, not cut down in this very temple of Zeus as you prophesied. Achilles and Hector are alive, when for years you said they would die before the city fell. None of us women have been dragged into slavery as you predicted, neither you to Agamemnon's house—where you told us Clytemnestra would slaughter that great king along with you and your infants—nor Andromache to . . ."

Cassandra throws back her head in a silent howl. Below them, Hector is still offering the wind gods sacrifices and honeyed wine if only they will light his brother's pyre. If theater had been created at this time, the attendees here today would think that this drama had slipped into farce.

"All that is *gone*," whispers Cassandra, slicing across her own forearm with the razor-sharp edge of her dagger. Blood trickles across her pale flesh and drips on marble, but she never looks down at it. Her gaze stays on Andromache and Helen. "The old future is no more, sisters. The Fates have abandoned us. Our world and its future have ceased to be, and some other one—some strange other *kosmos*—has come into being. But Apollo's curse of second sight has not abandoned me, sisters. Menelaus is seconds away from rushing up here and sticking his sword through your lovely tit, *Helen of Troy*." The last three words are spat out with total sarcasm.

Helen grabs Cassandra by the shoulders. Andromache wrestles away the knife. Together, the two shove the younger woman back between the pillars and into the cool shadows of the interior mezzanine of Zeus's temple. The clairvoyant young woman is pressed back against the marble railing, the two older women hovering over her like Furies.

Andromache lifts the blade to Cassandra's pale throat. "We've been friends for years, Cassandra," hisses Hector's wife, "but one more word out of you, you crazy cunt, and I'll cut your throat like a hog being hung up to bleed."

Cassandra smiles.

Helen puts one hand on Andromache's wrist—although whether to restrain her or be an accomplice to murder, it is hard to tell. Her other hand remains on Cassandra's shoulder.

"Is Menelaus coming to kill me?" she whispers into the tormented seer's ear.

"Twice he will come for you today, and each time he will be thwarted," replied Cassandra in monotone. Her eyes are not focused on either woman. Her smile is a rictus.

"When will he come?" asks Helen. "And who will thwart him?"

"First when Paris's pyre is lighted," says Cassandra, her tone as flat and disinterested as if she is reciting from an old children's tale. "And secondly when Paris's pyre burns out."

"And who shall thwart him?" repeats Helen.

"First shall Menelaus be stopped by Paris's wife," says Cassandra. Her eyes have rotated up in her head so that only the whites show. "Then by Agamemnon and the would-be Achilles-killer, Penthesilea."

"The *amazon* Penthesilea?" says Andromache, her surprised voice loud enough to echo in the Temple of Zeus. "She's a thousand leagues from here, as is Agamemnon. How can they be here by the time that Paris's funeral pyre burns out?"

"Hush," hisses Helen. To Cassandra, whose eyelids are fluttering, she says, "You say Paris's wife stops Menelaus from murdering me when the funeral pyre is lighted. How do I do that? How?"

Cassandra slumps to the floor in a swoon. Andromache slips the dagger into the folds of her gown and slaps the younger woman several times, hard. Cassandra does not awaken.

Helen kicks the fallen form. "Gods *damn* her. How am I to stop Menelaus from murdering me? We may be just minutes away from . . ."

From outside the temple a huge roar goes up from the Trojans and Achaeans in the square. Both women can hear the whoosh and roar.

The winds have obediently roared in through the Scaean Gate. The tinder and timber have caught the spark. The pyre is lighted.

4

Menelaus watched as the winds blew in from the west and fanned the embers of Paris's pyre first into a few flickering tongues of flame and then into a blazing bonfire. Hector barely had time to run down the steps and leap free before the entire pyre erupted in flames.

Now, thought Menelaus.

The ordered ranks of Achaeans had broken up as the crowd jostled back away from the heat of the pyre, and Menelaus used the confusion to hide his movements as he slid past his fellow Argives and through the ranks of Trojan infantry facing the flames. He edged his way around to the left, toward Zeus's temple and the waiting staircase. Menelaus noticed that the heat and sparks from the fire—the wind was blowing toward the temple—had driven Priam, Helen, and the others back off the balcony and—more important—the intervening soldiers off the stairs, so his way was clear.

It's as if the gods are helping me.

Perhaps they are, thought Menelaus. There were reports every day of contact between Argives and Trojans and their old gods. Just because mortals and gods were warring now didn't mean that the bonds of blood and old habit had been completely broken. Menelaus knew dozens of his peers who secretly offered sacrifices to the gods at night, just as they always had, even while fighting the gods by day. Hadn't Hector himself just called on the gods of the west and north winds— Zephyr and Boreas—to help him light his brother's pyre? And hadn't the gods complied, even though the bones and guts of Dionysos, Zeus's own son, had been scattered on the same pyre like inadequate *firstlings* that one tosses to dogs?

It's a confusing time to be alive.

Well, answered the other voice in Menelaus' mind, the cynical one that had not been ready to kill Helen this day, *you won't be alive for long, boyo.*

Menelaus paused at the bottom of the steps and slipped his sword from its scabbard. No one noticed. All eyes were on the funeral pyre blazing and crackling thirty feet away. Hundreds of soldiers raised their sword hands to shield their eyes and face from the heat of the flames.

Menelaus stepped up onto the first step.

A woman, one of the veiled virgins who had earlier carried the oil and honey to the pyre, emerged from the portico of Zeus's temple not ten feet from Menelaus and walked straight toward the flames. All eyes turned in her direction and Menelaus had to freeze on the lowest step, lowering his sword, since he was standing almost directly behind her and did not want to draw attention to himself.

The woman threw down her veil. The Trojan crowd opposite the pyre from Menelaus gasped.

"Oenone," cried a woman from the balcony above.

Menelaus craned to look up. Priam, Helen, Andromache, and some of the others had stepped back out onto the balcony at the sound of the crowd's gasps and shouts. It had not been Helen who spoke, but one of the attending female slaves.

Oenone? The name was vaguely familiar to Menelaus, something from before the last ten years of war, but he couldn't place it. His thoughts were on the next half minute. Helen was at the top of these fifteen steps with no men between him and her.

"I am Oenone, Paris's true wife!" shouted this woman called Oenone, her voice barely audible even at this proximity over the rage of wind and fierce crackling of the corpse fire.

Paris's true wife? In his puzzlement, Menelaus hesitated. There were more Trojans jostling out of the temple and adjoining alleys to watch this spectacle. Several men stepped up onto the stairs next to and above Menelaus. The red-haired Argive remembered now that the word in Sparta after the abduction of Helen had been that Paris had been married to a plain-looking woman—ten years older than he had been on their wedding day—and that he had put this wife aside when the gods helped him to abduct Helen. *Oenone.*

"Phoebus Apollo did not kill Priam's son, Paris," shouted this woman called Oenone. "I did!"

There were shouts, even obscenities, and some of the Trojan warriors on the near side of the fire stepped forward as if to grab this crazy women, but their comrades held them back. The majority wanted to hear what she had to say.

Menelaus could see Hector through the flames. Even Ilium's greatest hero was powerless to intercede here, since his brother's blazing corpse fire stood between him and this middle-aged woman.

Oenone was so close to the flames that her clothing steamed. She looked wet, as if she had doused herself in water in preparation for this stunt. Her full breasts were clearly visible as they drooped under her soaked gown.

"Paris did not die from flames by Phoebus Apollo's hands!" screamed the harpy. "When my husband and the god disappeared from sight into Slow Time ten days ago, they exchanged bowshots—it was an archer's duel, just as Paris had planned. Both man and god missed his mark. It was a mortal—the coward Philoctetes—who fired the fatal arrow that doomed my husband!" Here Oenone pointed into the group of Achaeans to where old Philoctetes stood near Big Ajax.

"Lies!" screamed the old archer, who had been rescued from his isle of exile and disease only recently by Odysseus, months after the war with the gods had begun.

Oenone ignored him and stepped even closer to the flames. The skin of her bare arms and face reddened in the heat. The steam from her garments became as thick as a mist around her. "When Apollo QT'd back to Olympos in frustration, it was the Argive coward Philoctetes, bearing old grudges, who fired his poison arrow into my husband's groin!"

"How could you know this, woman? None of us followed Priam's son and Apollo into Slow Time. None of us saw the battle!" bellowed Achilles, his voice a hundred times more clear than the widow's.

"When Apollo saw the treachery, he QT'd my husband to the slopes of Mount Ida, where I have lived in exile this decade and more . . ." continued Oenone.

There were a few shouts now, but for the most part the gigantic city square, filled with thousands of Trojan warriors, as well as the populated walls and rooftops above, were silent. Everyone waited.

"Paris begged me to take him back . . ." shouted the weeping woman, her wet hair now steaming as furiously as her clothes. Even her tears seemed to turn to steam. "He was dying of Greek poison, his balls and once-beloved member and lower belly already black from it, but he begged me to heal him."

"How could a mere harridan heal him from mortal poison?" shouted Hector, speaking up for the first time, his voice bellowing through the flames like a god's.

"An oracle had told my husband that only I could heal him from such a mortal wound," Oenone shouted back hoarsely, her voice either failing now or being defeated by the heat and roar. Menelaus could hear her words, but he doubted if most of the others in the square could.

"He implored me in his agony," cried the woman, "asking me to put balm on his poisoned wound.'Do not hate me now,' Paris begged me, 'I left you only because the Fates ordered me to go to Helen. I wish I had died before bringing that bitch to Priam's palace. I implore you, Oenone, by the love we bore each other and by the vows we once took, forgive me and heal me now.' "

Menelaus watched her take two more steps closer to the pyre, until flames licked around her, blackening her ankles and causing her sandals to curl.

"I refused!" she shouted, her voice hoarse but louder again. "He died. My only love and only lover and only husband died. He died in horrible pain, screaming obscenities. My servants and I tried to burn his body—to give my poor Fates-doomed husband the hero's funeral pyre he deserved—but the trees were strong and hard to cut, and we were women, and weak, and I failed to do even this simple task. When Phoebus Apollo saw how poorly we had honored Paris's remains, he took pity on his fallen foe a second time, QT'd Paris's desecrated body back to the battlefield, and let the charred corpse fall out of Slow Time as if he had been burned in battle.

"I'm sorry that I did not heal him," called Oenone. "I'm sorry for everything." She turned long enough to look up at the balcony, but it was doubtful if she could see the people there clearly through the heat haze and smoke and pain of her burning eyes. "But at least that cunt Helen never saw him alive again."

The ranks of Trojans began to murmur until the sound built into a roar.

Now, too late, a dozen Trojan guards ran toward Oenone to drag her back for further interrogation.

She stepped up onto the flaming pyre.

First her hair burst into flames, and then her gown. Incredibly, impossibly, she continued climbing the heaped wood, even as her flesh burned and blackened and folded back like charred parchment. Only in the last seconds before she fell did she visibly writhe in agony. But her screams filled the square for what seemed like minutes, stunning the crowd into silence.

When the massed Trojans spoke again, it was to shout for Philoctetes, demanding that the honor guard of Achaeans give him up.

Furious, confused, Menelaus looked up the staircase. Priam's royal guard had surrounded everyone on the balcony now. The way to Helen was blocked by a wall of circular Trojan shields and a picket of spears.

Menelaus jumped down from his step and ran across the empty space near the pyre, feeling the heat hitting his face like a fist and knowing that his eyebrows were being singed off. In a minute he had joined the ranks of his fellow Argives, his sword raised. Ajax, Diomedes, Odysseus, Teucer, and the others had made their own circle around Philoctetes and also had their weapons raised and ready.

The overwhelming mass of Trojans surrounding them lifted high their shields, raised their spears, and advanced on the two dozen doomed Greeks.

Suddenly Hector's voice roared everyone into immobility.

"Stop! I forbid this! Oenone's babblings—if this even *was* Oenone who killed herself here today, for I did not recognize the crone—mean nothing. She was mad! My brother died in mortal combat with Phoebus Apollo."

The furious Trojans did not seem convinced. Spearpoints and swords remained poised and eager. Menelaus looked around at his doomed band and noticed that while Odysseus was frowning and Philoctetes was cowering, Big Ajax was grinning as if anticipating the imminent slaughter that would end his life.

Hector strode past the pyre and put himself between the Trojan spears and the circle of Greeks. He still wore no armor and carried no weapons, but suddenly he seemed the most formidable foe on the field.

"These men are our allies and are my invited guests at the funeral of my brother," shouted Hector. "You shall *not* harm them. Anyone who defies my order will die by my hand. I swear this on the bones of my brother!"

Achilles stepped off the platform and raised his shield. He *was* still dressed in his best armor and was armed. He said nothing and made no move, but every Trojan in the city must have been aware of him.

The hundreds of Trojans looked at their leader, looked over at fleet-footed mankilling Achilles, looked a final time at the funeral pyre where the woman's corpse had been all but consumed by the flames, and they gave way. Menelaus could feel the fighting spirit slide out of the mobs surrounding them, could see the confusion on the tanned Trojan faces.

Odysseus led the Achaeans toward the Scaean Gates. Menelaus and the other men lowered their swords but did not sheath them. The Trojans parted like a reluctant but still-blood-hungry sea before them.

"By the gods . . ." whispered Philoctetes from the center of their circle as they went out through the gates and past more ranks of Trojans, "I swear to you that . . ."

"Shut the fuck up, old man," said powerful Diomedes. "You say one more word before we're back to the black ships, I'll kill you myself."

Beyond the Achaean pickets, past the defensive trenches and beneath the moravec forceshields, there was confusion along the coast even though the encampments there couldn't have heard about the near disaster in the city of Troy. Menelaus broke away from the others and ran down to the beach.

"The King has returned!" cried a spearman, running past Menelaus and wildly blowing a conch shell. "The commander has returned."

Not Agamemnon, thought Menelaus. *He won't be back for at least another month. Perhaps two.*

But it was his brother, standing at the prow of the largest of the thirty black ships in his small fleet. His golden armor flashed as the rowers drove the long, thin craft through the surf and in toward the beach.

Menelaus waded into the waves until the water covered the bronze greaves protecting his shins. "Brother!" he cried, waving his arms over his head like a boy. "What news is there from home? Where are the new warriors you swore to return with?"

Still sixty or seventy feet out from shore, water splashing about the bow of his black ship as it surfed in on the long, great swell, Agamemnon covered his eyes as if the afternoon sun hurt them and shouted back, "Gone, fellow son of Atreus. All are gone!"

5

The corpse fire will burn all through the night.

Thomas Hockenberry, B.A. in English from Wabash College, M.A. and Ph.D. from Yale in classical studies, formerly on the faculty of Indiana University—in truth, head of the classics department there until he died of cancer in A.D. 2006—and most recently, for ten years of the ten years and eight months since his resurrection, Homeric *scholic* for the Olympian gods, whose duties during that time included reporting daily and verbally to his Muse, Melete by name, on the progress of the Trojan War and how the tale was following or diverging from Homer's *Iliad*— the gods, it turns out, are as preliterate as three-year-olds—leaves the city square and Paris's flaming pyre shortly before dusk and climbs the second-tallest tower in Troy, damaged and dangerous though it is, to eat his bread and cheese and drink his wine in peace. In Hockenberry's opinion, it's been a long, weird day.

The tower he frequently chooses for solitude is closer to the Scaean Gate than to the center of the city near Priam's palace, but it's not on the main thoroughfare and most of the warehouses at its base are empty these days. Officially, the tower—one of the tallest in Ilium before the war, almost fourteen stories tall by Twentieth Century reckoning and shaped like a poppy reed or a minaret with a bulbous swelling near its top—is closed to the public. A bomb from the gods in the early weeks of the current war blasted off the top three floors and diagonally shattered the bulb, leaving the small rooms near the top open to the air. The main shaft of the tower shows alarming cracks and the narrow spiral staircase is littered with masonry, plaster, and dislodged stones. It took hours for Hockenberry to clear the way to the eleventh-floor bulb during his first venture up the tower two months earlier. The moravecs—at Hector's direction—have placed orange plastic tape across the entrances, warning people in graphic pictograms what harm they could come to—the tower itself could tumble over at any time according to the most alarming of the graphic images—and other symbols command them to stay out upon penalty of King Priam's wrath.

The looters had then emptied the place within seventy-two hours, and after that the locals *did* stay out—for what use was an empty building? Now Hockenberry slips between the bands of tape, clicks on his flashlight, and begins his long ascent with little worry about being arrested or robbed or interrupted here. He's armed with a knife and short sword. Besides, he's well known: Thomas Hockenberry, son of Duane, occasional friend . . . well, no, not friend, but interlocutor at least . . . of both Achilles and Hector, not to mention a public figure now with more than passing acquaintance with both the moravecs and rockvecs . . . so there are very few Greeks or Trojans who will move to harm him without thinking twice.

But the gods, now . . . well, that's another matter.

Hockenberry is panting by the third floor, actively wheezing and stopping to catch his breath by the tenth, and making noises like the 1947 Packard his father had once owned by the time he reaches the shattered eleventh floor. He's spent more than ten years watching these human demigods—Greek and Trojan alike—warring and feasting and loving and debauching like muscular ads for the most successful health club in the world, not to mention the gods, male and female, who are walking advertisements for the best health club in the *universe*, but Thomas Hockenberry, Ph.D., has never found time to get himself in shape. *Typical*, he thinks.

The stairway winds tightly up through the center of the circular building. There are no doorways and some evening light comes into the central stairwell through windows in the tiny, pie-shaped rooms on either side, but the ascent is still dark. He uses the flashlight to make sure that the stairs are where they should be and that no new debris has tumbled into the stairwell. At least the walls are clean of *graffiti*—one of the many blessings of a totally illiterate populace, thinks Professor Thomas Hockenberry.

As always when he reaches his little niche on what is now the top floor, long since swept clear of debris and the worst of the plaster dust by him but open to rain and wind, he decides that the climb has been worth the effort.

Hockenberry sits on his favorite block of stone, sets down his pack, puts away his flashlight—loaned to him months ago by one of the moravecs—and pulls out his small wrapped package of fresh bread and stale cheese. He also digs out his wineskin. Sitting there, feeling the evening breeze coming off the sea stir his new beard and long hair, idly cutting off chunks of cheese and slicing the slab of bread with his combat knife, Hockenberry gazes out at the view and lets the tension of the day seep out of him.

The view is a good one. Sweeping almost three hundred degrees, blocked from being circular by just a shard of wall left standing behind him, the view allows Hockenberry to see most of the city beneath him—Paris's funeral pyre just a few blocks east and seeming to be almost directly beneath him from this height—and the city walls all around, their torches and bonfires just being lighted, and the Achaean encampment strung out north and south along the coast for miles, the lights of the hundreds upon hundreds of cooking fires reminding Hockenberry of a view he'd once glimpsed from an aircraft descending above Lake Shore Drive in Chicago after dark, the lakefront bejeweled with its shifting necklace of headlights and countless lighted apartment buildings. And now, just visible against the wine-dark sea, are the thirty or so black ships just returned with Agamemnon, the long boats mostly still bobbing at anchor rather than pulled up on the beach. Agamemnon's camp—all but empty the last month and a half—is ablaze with fires and blurred with motion this evening.

The skies are not empty here. To the northeast, the last of the space-warp holes, Brane Holes, whatever they are—people have just called the remaining one the Hole for the last six months—cuts a disk out of the Trojan sky as it connects the plains of Ilium to the ocean of Mars. Brown Asia Minor soil leads directly to red Martian dust without so much as a crack in the earth to separate the two. It's a bit earlier in the evening on Mars, and a red twilight lingers there, outlining the Hole against the darker old-Earth sky here.

Navigation lights blink red and green on a score of moravec hornets flying night patrol above the Hole, over the city, circling out over the sea, and prowling as far away as the dimly glimpsed shadows that are the wooded peaks of Mount Ida to the east.

Even though the sun has just set—early on this winter's night—the streets of Troy are open for business. The last traders in the marketplace near Priam's palace have folded away their awnings and are trundling their wares away in carts—Hockenberry can hear the creaking wooden wheels over the wind even at this height—but the adjoining streets, filled with brothels and restaurants and bathhouses and more brothels, are coming alive, filling with jostling forms and flickering torches. As is the Trojan custom, every major intersection in the city, as well as every turn and angle on the broad walls around the city, are lighted every evening by huge bronze braziers in which oil or wood fires are kept burning all through the night, and the last of these are now being lighted by watchmen. Hockenberry can see dark forms pressing close to warm themselves around each of these fires.

Around all but one. In Ilium's main square, Paris's funeral pyre outshines all the other fires in and around the city, but only one dark form presses close to it as if for warmth—Hector, moaning aloud, weeping, calling to his soldiers and servants and slaves to pour more wood onto the howling flames while he uses a large, two-handed cup to dip wine from a golden bowl, constantly pouring it onto the ground near the pyre until the earth there is so drenched it looks to be oozing blood.

Hockenberry is just finishing his dinner when he hears the footsteps coming up the spiral staircase.

Suddenly his heart is pounding and he can taste the fear in his mouth. Someone *has* followed him up here—there can be little doubt. The tread on the steps is too light—as if the person climbing the stairs is trying to move stealthily.

Maybe it's some woman scavenging, thinks Hockenberry, but even as the hope rises, it's dashed; he can hear a faint metallic echo in the stairwell, as of bronze armor rattling. Besides, he knows, the women in Troy can be more deadly than most men he'd known in his Twentieth and Twenty-first century world.

Hockenberry rises as quietly as he can, sets the wineskin and bread and cheese aside, sheaths his knife, silently draws his sword, and steps back toward the only standing wall. The wind rises and rustles his red cape as he conceals the sword under its folds.

My QT medallion. He uses his left hand to touch the small quantum teleportation device where it hangs against his chest under his tunic. *Why did I think I had nothing valuable with me? Even if I can't use this any longer without being detected and pursued by the gods, it's unique. Invaluable.* Hockenberry pulls out the flashlight and holds it extended the way he used to aim his taser baton when he owned one. He wishes he had one now.

It occurs to him that it might be a god climbing the last of the eleven flights of steps just below him. The Masters of Olympos had been known to sneak into Ilium disguised as mortals. The gods certainly had reason enough to kill him and to take back their QT medallion.

The climbing figure comes up the last few stairs and steps into the open. Hockenberry flicks on the flashlight, shining the beam full on the figure.

It is a small and only vaguely humanoid form—its knees are backward, its arms are articulated wrong, its hands are interchangeable, and it has no face as such—barely a meter tall, sheathed in dark plastic and gray-black-and-red metal.

"Mahnmut," Hockenberry says in relief. He shifts the circle of the flashlight beam away from the little Europan moravec's vision plate.

"You carrying a sword under that cape," asks Mahnmut in English, "or are you just happy to see me?"

It's been Hockenberry's habit to carry some fuel in his backpack for a small fire when he's up here. In recent months, this has often meant dried cow chips, but tonight he's brought plenty of sweet-smelling kindling sold everywhere on the black market today by those woodcutters who had brought back the wood for Paris's pyre. Now Hockenberry has the little fire going while he and Mahnmut sit on blocks of stone on opposite sides of it. The wind is chill and Hockenberry, at least, is glad for the fire.

"I haven't seen you around for a few days," he says to the little moravec. Hockenberry notices how the flames reflect off Mahnmut's shiny plastic vision plate.

"I've been up at Phobos."

It takes Hockenberry a few seconds to remember that Phobos is one of the moons of Mars. The closer one, he thinks. Or maybe the smaller one. At any rate, a moon. He turns his head to see the huge Hole a few miles to the northeast of Troy: it's now night on Mars as well—the disk of the Hole is only barely visible against the night sky, and that is only because the stars look slightly different there, more brilliant, or clustered more tightly together, or maybe both. Neither of the Martian moons is visible.

"Anything interesting happen today while I was gone?" asks Mahnmut.

Hockenberry has to chuckle at that. He tells the moravec about the morning funeral services and Oenone's self-immolation.

"Whoa, doggies," says Mahnmut. The ex-scholic can only assume that the moravec deliberately uses idiomatic English he thinks is specific to the era Hockenberry had lived through on his Earth. Sometimes it works; sometimes, like now, it's laughable.

"I don't remember from the *Iliad* that Paris had an earlier wife," continues Mahnmut.

"I don't think it's mentioned in the *Iliad*." Hockenberry tries to remember if he'd ever taught that fact. He doesn't think so.

"That must have been pretty dramatic to watch."

"Yes," says Hockenberry, "but her accusations about Philoctetes really killing Paris were even more dramatic."

"Philoctetes?" Mahnmut cocks his head in a way that seemed almost canine to Hockenberry. For whatever reason, he's come to associate that movement with the idea that Mahnmut is accessing memory banks. "From the play by Sophocles?" asks Mahnmut after a second.

"Yeah. He was the original commander of the Thessalians from Methone."

"I don't remember him from the *Iliad*," says Mahnmut. "And I don't think I've met him here either."

Hockenberry shakes his head. "Agamemnon and Odysseus dumped him on the isle of Lemnos years ago, on their way here."

"Why'd they do that?" Mahnmut's voice, so human in timbre, sounds interested.

"Because he smelled bad, mostly."

"Smelled bad? Most of these human heroes smell bad."

Hockenberry has to blink at that. He remembers thinking just that ten years ago, when he'd first started as a scholic here shortly after his resurrection on Olympos. But somehow he hadn't noticed it after the first six months or so. Did *he* smell bad? he wonders. He says, "Philoctetes smelled especially bad because of his suppurating wound."

"Wound?"

"Snakebite. Bitten by a poisonous snake when he . . . well, it's a long story. The usual 'stealing stuff from the gods' story. But Philoctetes' foot and leg got so bad that it just poured pus, smelled bad all the time, and sent the archer into screaming and fainting fits at regular intervals. This was on the boat ride here to Troy ten years ago, remember. So finally Agamemnon, on Odysseus' advice, just dumped the old man on the island of Lemnos and literally left him to rot there."

"But he survived?" says Mahnmut.

"Obviously. Probably because the gods kept him alive for some reason, but he was in agony with that rotting foot and leg the whole time."

Mahmut cocks his head again. "All right . . . I'm remembering the Sophocles play now. Odysseus went to get him when the seer Helenus told the Greeks that they wouldn't defeat Troy without Philoctetes' bow—given to him by . . . who? . . . Heracles. Hercules."

"Yes, he inherited the bow," says Hockenberry.

"I don't remember Odysseus going to fetch him. In real life, I mean. During the past eight months."

Hockenberry shakes his head again. "It was very quietly done. Odysseus was gone for only about three weeks and no one made a big deal about it. When he returned, it was sort of like . . . oh, yeah, I picked up Philoctetes on my way back from getting the wine."

"In Sophocles' play," says Mahnmut, "Achilles' son, Neoptolemus, was a central figure. But he never met his father when Achilles was alive. Don't tell me he's here too?"

"Not that I know of," says Hockenberry. "Just Philoctetes. And his bow."

"And now Oenone's accused him rather than Apollo of killing Paris."

"Yep." Hockenberry tosses a few more sticks on the fire. Sparks spin in the wind and rise toward the stars. There is blackness out over the ocean where clouds are moving in. Hockenberry guesses that it might rain before morning. Some nights, he sleeps up here—using his pack as a pillow and his cape for a blanket—but not tonight.

"But how could Philoctetes shift into Slow Time?" asks Mahnmut. The moravec rises and walks to the broken edge of the platform in the dark, evidently having no fear of the hundred-foot-plus drop. "The nanotechnology that allows that shift was only injected into Paris before that single combat, right?"

"You should know," says Hockenberry. "You moravecs are the ones who injected Paris with the nanothingees so that he could fight the god."

Mahnmut walks back to the fire but remains standing. He holds out his hands as if to warm them by the flames. Maybe he *is* warming them, thinks Hockenberry. He knows that parts of moravecs are organic.

"Some of the other heroes—Diomedes, for example—still have Slow-Time nanoclusters left in their systems from when Athena or one of the other gods injected them," says Mahnmut. "But you're right, only Paris had them updated ten days ago for the single combat with Apollo."

"And Philoctetes wasn't here for the last ten years," says Hockenberry. "So it doesn't make any sense that one of the gods would have accelerated him with the Slow-Time nanomemes. And it *is* acceleration, not a slowing down of time, right?"

"Right," says the moravec. " 'Slow Time' is a misnomer. It seems to the Slow-Time traveler that time has stopped—that everything and everyone is frozen in amber—but in reality, the body's moved into hyperfast action, reacting in milliseconds."

"Why doesn't the person just burn up?" asks Hockenberry. He could have followed Apollo and Paris into Slow Time to watch the battle—in fact, if he'd been there that day, he would have. The gods had riddled his blood and bones with nanomemes for just that purpose, and many was the time he'd shifted into Slow Time to watch the gods prepare one of their Achaean or Trojan heroes for combat. "From friction," he added. "With the air or whatever . . ." He broke off lamely. Science wasn't his strong suit.

But Mahnmut nodded as if the scholic had said something wise. "The Slow-Time accelerator's body *would* burn up—from internal heat if nothing else—if the tailored nanoclusters didn't deal with that as well. It's part of the body's nano-generated forcefield."

"Like Achilles'?"

"Yes."

"Could Paris have burned up just because of that?" asks Hockenberry. "Some sort of nano-tech failure?"

"Very unlikely," says Mahnmut and sits on the smaller block of stone. "But why would this Philoctetes kill Paris? What motive would he have?"

Hockenberry shrugs. "In the non-Iliad, non-Homeric tales of Troy, it *is* Philoctetes who kills Paris. With his bow. And a poisoned arrow. Just as Oenone described. Homer even refers to fetching Philoctetes to bring about the prophecy that Ilium will fall only when Philoctetes joins the fray—in the second book, I think."

"But the Trojans and the Greeks are allies now."

Hockenberry has to smile. "Just barely. You know as well as I that there are conspiracies and incipient rebellions brewing in both camps. Nobody but Hector and Achilles is happy about this war with the gods. It's just a matter of time until there's another rebellion."

"But Hector and Achilles make for an almost unbeatable duo. And they have tens of thousands of Trojans and Achaeans loyal to them."

"So far," says Hockenberry. "But now maybe the gods themselves have been kibbitzing."

"Helping Philoctetes shift into Slow Time?" says Mahnmut. "But why? Occam's Razor suggests that if they wanted Paris dead, they could have just let Apollo kill him as everyone assumed he had. Until today. Until Oenone's accusation. Why have a Greek assassinate him . . ." He stops and then murmurs, "Ah, yes."

"Right," said Hockenberry. "The gods want to hurry up the next mutiny, get Hector and Achilles out of the way, break up this alliance, and get the Greeks and Trojans killing each other again."

"Thus the poison," says the moravec. "So that Paris can live just long enough to tell his wife—his first wife—who really killed him. Now the Trojans will want revenge and even the Greeks loyal to Achilles will be ready to fight to defend themselves. Clever. Has anything else of comparable interest happened today?"

"Agamemnon's back."

"No shit?" says Mahnmut.

I need to talk to him about his vernacular vocabulary, thinks Hockenberry. *This is like talking to one of my freshmen at IU.*

"Yes, correct, no shit," says Hockenberry. "He's back from his voyage home a month or two early and has some really surprising news."

Mahnmut leans forward expectantly. Or at least Hockenberry interprets the body language of the little humanoid cyborg as expressing expectation. The smooth metallic-plastic face shows nothing but reflection of the firelight.

Hockenberry clears his throat. "The people back home are gone," he says. "Missing. Disappeared."

Hockenberry had expected some sort of exclamation of surprise, but the little moravec waits silently.

"Everyone gone," continues Hockenberry. "Not just in Mycenae, where Agamemnon first returned—not just his wife Clytemnestra and his son Orestes and all the rest of that cast, but *everyone's* missing. Cities empty. Food sitting uneaten on tables. Horses starving in stables. Dogs pining on empty hearths. Cows unmilked in pastures. Sheep unshorn. Everywhere Agamemnon and his boats put in in the Peloponnese and beyond—Menelaus' kingdom of Lacedaemon, empty. Odysseus' Ithaca—empty."

"Yes," says Mahnmut.

"Wait a minute," says Hockenberry. "You're not in the least surprised. You *knew.* You moravecs knew that the Greek cities and kingdoms had been emptied out. How?"

"Do you mean how did we know?" asks Mahnmut. "Simple. We've been keeping tabs on these places from earth orbit since we arrived. Sending down remote drones to record data. There's a lot to be learned here on the earth of three thousand years before your day—three thousand years before the Twentieth and Twenty-first centuries, that is."

Hockenberry is stunned. He'd never thought of the moravecs paying attention to anything other than Troy, the surrounding battlefields, the connecting Hole, Mars, Mount Olympos, the gods, maybe a Martian moon or two . . . Jesus, wasn't that *enough?*

"When did they . . . disappear?" Hockenberry manages at last. "Agamemnon is telling everyone that some of the food left behind was fresh enough to eat."

"I guess that depends upon your definition of 'fresh,' " says Mahnmut. "According to our surveillance, the people disappeared about four and a half weeks ago. Just as Agamemnon's little fleet was approaching the Peloponnese."

"Jesus Christ," whispers Hockenberry.

"Yes."

"Did you see them disappear? On your satellite cameras or probes or whatever?"

"Not really. One minute they were there and the next minute they weren't. It happened about two a.m. Greek time, so there wasn't a lot of movement to monitor . . . in the Greek cities, I mean."

"In the Greek cities . . ." Hockenberry repeats dully. "Do you mean . . . I mean . . . is there . . . have other people disappeared as well? In . . . say . . . China?"

"Yes."

The wind suddenly whips around their eyrie and scatters sparks in all directions. Hockenberry covers his face with his hands during the spark storm and then brushes embers off his cloak and tunic. When the wind subsides, he throws the last of his sticks on the fire.

Other than Troy and Olympos—which, he discovered eight months ago, wasn't on Earth at all—Hockenberry had only traveled to one other place in this past-Earth, and that was to prehistoric Indiana, where he deposited the only other surviving scholic, Keith Nightenhelser, with the Indians there to keep him safe when the Muse had gone on a killing spree. Now, without consciously meaning to, Hockenberry touches the QT medallion under his shirt. *I need to check on Nightenhelser.*

As if reading his mind, the moravec says, "Everyone else is gone—everyone outside a five-hundred-kilometer radius of Troy. Africans. North American Indians. South American Indians. The Chinese and aborigines in Australia. Polynesians. Northern European Huns and Danes and Vikings-to-be. The proto-Mongols. Everyone. Every other human being on the planet—we estimated that there were about twenty-two million—has disappeared."

"That's not possible," says Hockenberry.

"No. It wouldn't seem so."

"What kind of power . . ."

"Godlike," says Mahnmut.

"But certainly not these Olympian gods. They're just . . . just . . ."

"More powerful humanoids?" said Mahnmut. "Yes, that's what we thought. There are other energies at work here."

"God?" whispers Hockenberry, who had been raised in a strict Indiana Baptist family before he had traded faith for education.

"Well, maybe," says the moravec, "but if so, He lives on or around planet Earth. Huge amounts of quantum energy were released from Earth or near-earth-orbit at the same time Agamemnon's wife and kids disappeared."

"The energy came from Earth?" repeats Hockenberry. He looks around at the night, the funeral pyre below, the city nightlife becoming active beneath them, the distant campfires of the Achaeans, and the more distant stars. "From here?"

"Not this Earth," says Mahnmut. "The other Earth. Yours. And it looks like we're going to it."

For a minute Hockenberry's heart pounds so wildly that he's afraid he's going to be sick. Then he realizes that Mahnmut isn't really talking about *his* Earth—the Twenty-first Century world of the half-remembered fragments of his former life before the gods resurrected him from old DNA and books and God knows what else, the slowly-returning-to-consciousness world of Indiana University and his wife and his students—but the concurrent-with-terraformed-Mars Earth of more than three thousand years *after* the short, not-so-happy first life of Thomas Hockenberry.

Unable to sit still, he stands and paces back and forth on the shattered eleventh floor of the building, walking to the shattered wall on the northeast side, then to the vertical drop on the south and west sides. A pebble scraped up by his sandal falls more than a hundred feet into the dark streets below. The wind whips his cape and his long, graying hair back. Intellectually, he's known for eight months that the Mars visible now through the Hole coexisted in some future solar system with Earth and the other planets, but he'd never really connected that simple fact with the idea that this other Earth was really *there*, waiting.

My wife's bones are mingled with the dust there, he thinks and then, on the verge of tears, almost laughs. *Fuck, my bones are mingled with the dust there.*

"How can you go to that Earth?" he asks and immediately realizes how stupid the question is. He's heard the story of how Mahnmut and his huge friend Orphu traveled to Mars from Jupiter space with some other moravecs who did not survive their first encounter with the gods. *They have* spaceships, *Hockenbush.* While most of the moravec and rock-vec spacecraft had appeared as if by magic through the quantum Holes that Mahnmut had helped bring into existence, they were still space-craft.

"We're building a ship just for that purpose on and near Phobos," the moravec says softly. "This time we're not going alone. Or unarmed."

Hockenberry can't stop pacing back and forth. When he gets to the edge of the shattered floor, he has the urge to jump to his death—an urge that has tempted him when in high places since he was a kid. *Is that why I like to come up here? Thinking about jumping? Thinking about suicide?* He realizes it is. He realizes how lonely he's been for the last eight months. *And now even Nightenhelser is gone—gone with the Indians probably, sucked up by whatever cosmic vacuum cleaner made all the humans on earth except these poor fucked Trojans and Greeks disappear this month.* Hockenberry knows that he can twist the QT medallion hanging against his chest and be in North America in no time at all, searching for his old scholic friend in that part of prehistoric Indiana where he'd left him eight months earlier. But he also knew that the gods might track him through the Planck-space interstices. It's why he hasn't QT'd in eight months.

He walks back to the fire and stands looming over the little moravec. "Why the hell are you telling me this?"

"We're inviting you to go with us," says Mahnmut.

Hockenberry sits down heavily. After a minute he is able to say, "Why, for God's sake? What possible use could I be to you on such an expedition?"

Mahnmut shrugs in a most human fashion. "You're from that world," he says simply. "If not that time. There are humans on this other Earth, you know."

"There are?" Hockenberry hears how stunned and stupid his own voice sounds. He'd never thought to ask.

"Yes. Not many—most of the humans appear to have evolved into some sort of post-human status and moved off the planet into orbital ring cities more than fourteen hundred years ago—but our observations suggest that there are a few hundred thousand old-style human beings left."

"Old-style human beings," repeats Hockenberry, not even trying not to sound stunned. "Like me."

"Exactly," says Mahnmut. He stands, his vision plate barely coming up to Hockenberry's belt. Never a tall man, Hockenberry suddenly realizes how the Olympian gods must feel around ordinary mortals. "We think you should come with us. You could be of tremendous help when we meet and talk to the humans on your future Earth."

"Jesus Christ," repeats Hockenberry. He walks to the edge again, realizes again how easy it would be to take one more step off this edge into the darkness. This time the gods wouldn't resurrect him. "Jesus Christ," he says yet again.

Hockenberry can see the shadowy figure of Hector at Paris's funeral pyre, still pouring wine into the earth, still ordering men to pile more firewood into the flames.

I killed Paris, thinks Hockenberry. *I've killed every man, woman, child, and god who's died since I morphed into the form of Athena and kidnapped Patroclus—pretending to kill him—in order to provoke Achilles into attacking the gods.* Hockenberry suddenly laughs bitterly, not embarrassed that the little machine-person behind him will think he's lost his mind. *I have lost my mind. This is nuts. Part of the reason I haven't jumped off this fucking ledge before tonight is that it would feel like a dereliction of duty . . . like I need to keep observing, as if I'm still a scholic reporting to the Muse who reports to the gods.*

I've absolutely lost my mind. He feels, not for the first or fiftieth time, like sobbing.

"Will you go with us to Earth, Dr. Hockenberry?" Mahnmut asks softly.

"Yeah, sure, shit, why not? When?"

"How about right now?" says the little moravec.

The hornet must have been hovering silently hundreds of feet above them but with its navigation lights off. Now the black and barbed machine swoops down out of the darkness with such suddenness that Hockenberry almost falls off the edge of the building.

An especially strong gust of wind helps him keep his balance and he steps back from the edge just as a staircase ramp hums down from the belly of the hornet and clunks on stone. Hockenberry can see a red glow from inside the ship.

"After you," says Mahnmut.

6

It was just after sunrise and Zeus was alone in the Great Hall of the Gods when his wife, Hera, came in leading a dog on a golden leash.

"Is that the one?" asked the Lord of the Gods from where he sat brooding on his golden throne.

"It is," said Hera. She slipped the leash off the dog. It sat.

"Call for your son," said Zeus.

"Which son?"

"The great artificer. The one who lusts after Athena so much that he humped her thigh just as this dog would if the dog had no manners."

Hera turned to go. The dog started to follow her.

"Leave the dog," said Zeus.

Hera motioned the dog to stay and it stayed.

The dog was large, gray, short-haired, and sleek, with mild brown eyes that somehow managed to look both stupid and cunning. It began to pace and its claws made scraping sounds on the marble as it wandered back and forth around Zeus's gold throne. It sniffed the sandals and bare toes of the Lord of Lightning, the Son of Kronos. Then it claw-clicked its way to the edge of the huge holovision pool, peered in, saw nothing that interested it in the dark videoswirl of the surface static, lost interest, and wandered toward a pillar many yards away.

"Come here!" ordered Zeus.

The dog looked back at Zeus, then looked away. It began to sniff at the base of the huge white pillar in a preparatory way.

Zeus whistled.

The dog's head came up and around, its ears shifted, but it did not come.

Zeus whistled again and clapped his hands.

The gray dog came quickly then, running in a rocking motion, tongue lolling, eyes happy.

Zeus stepped down from his throne and petted the animal. Then he pulled a blade from his robes and cut off the dog's head with a single swing of his massive arm. The dog's head rolled almost to the edge of the vision pool while the body dropped straight to the marble, forelegs stretched ahead of it as if it had been ordered to lie down and was complying in hopes of getting a treat.

Hera and Hephaestus entered the Great Hall and approached across acres of marble.

"Playing with the pets again, My Lord?" asked Hera when she drew near.

Zeus waved his hand as if dismissing her, sheathed the blade in the sleeve of his robe, and returned to his throne.

Hephaestus was dwarfish and stocky as gods go, a little under six feet tall. He most resembled a great, hairy barrel. The god of fire was also lame and dragged his left leg along as if it were a dead thing, which it was. He had wild hair, an even wilder beard that seemed to merge with the hair on his chest, and red-rimmed eyes that were always darting to and fro. He seemed to be wearing armor, but closer inspection showed the armor to be a solid covering made up from hundreds of tiny boxes and pouches and tools and devices—some forged of precious metal, some shaped of base metal, some tooled of leather, some seemingly woven of hair—all hanging from straps and belts that crisscrossed his hairy body. The ultimate metalworker, Hephaestus was famous on Olympos for once having created women made of gold, young clockwork virgins, who could move and smile and give men pleasure almost as if they were alive. It was said that from his alchemic vats he had also fashioned the first woman—Pandora.

"Welcome, artificer," boomed Zeus. "I would have summoned you sooner but we had no tin pots or toy shields to repair."

Hephaestus knelt by the dog's headless body. "You needn't have done this," he muttered. "No need. No need at all."

"It irritated me." Zeus raised a goblet from the arm of his golden throne and drank deeply.

Hephaestus rolled the headless body on its side, ran his blunt hand along its rib cage as if offering to scratch the dead dog's belly, and pressed. A panel of flesh and hair popped open. The god of fire reached into the dog's gut and removed a clear bag filled with scraps of meat and other things. Hephaestus pulled a sliver of wet, pink flesh from the gut-bag.

"Dionysos," he said.

"My son," said Zeus. He rubbed his temples as if weary of all this.

"Shall I deliver this scrap to the Healer and the vats, O Son of Kronos?" asked the god of fire.

"No. We shall have one of our kind eat it so that my son may be reborn according to his wishes. Such Communion is painful for the host, but perhaps that will teach the gods and goddesses here on Olympos to take better care when watching out for my children. "

Zeus looked down at Hera, who had come closer and was now sitting on the second stone step of his throne with her right arm laid affectionately along his leg, her white hand touching his knee.

"No, my husband," she said softly. "Please."

Zeus smiled. "You choose then, wife."

Without hesitation, Hera said, "Aphrodite. She's used to stuffing parts of men into her mouth."

Zeus shook his head. "Not Aphrodite. She has done nothing since she herself was in the vats to incur my displeasure. Shouldn't it be Pallas Athena, the immortal who brought this war with the mortals down on us with her intemperate murder of Achilles' beloved Patroclus? And of the infant son of Hector?"

Hera pulled her arm back. "Athena denies that she did these things, Son of Kronos. And the mortals say that Aphrodite was with Athena when they slaughtered Hector's babe."

"We have the vision-pool image of the murder of Patroclus, wife. Do you want me to play it again for you?" Zeus's voice, so low it resembled distant thunder even when he whispered, now showed signs of growing anger. The effect was of a storm moving into the echoing Hall of the Gods.

"No, Lord," said Hera. "But you know that Athena insists that it was the missing scholic, Hockenberry, who must have assumed her form and done these things. She swears upon her love for you that . . ."

Zeus stood impatiently and paced away from the throne. "The scholic morphing bands were not designed to grant a mortal the shape or power of a god," he snapped. "It's not possible. However briefly. Some god or goddess from Olympos did those deeds—either Athena or one of our family assuming Athena's form. Now . . . choose who will receive the body and blood of my son, Dionysos."

"Demeter."

Zeus rubbed his short white beard. "Demeter. My sister. Mother to my much-loved Persephone?"

Hera stood, stepped back, and showed her white hands. "Is there a god on this mount who is *not* related to you, my husband? I am your sister as well as your wife. At least Demeter has experience giving birth to odd things. And she has little to do these days since there is no grain crop being harvested or sewn by the mortals."

"So be it," said Zeus. To Hephaestus he commanded, "Deliver the flesh of my son to Demeter, tell her it is the will of her lord, Zeus himself, that she eat this flesh and bring my son to life again. Assign three of my Furies to watch over her until this birth is achieved."

The god of fire shrugged and dropped the bit of flesh into one of his pouches. "Do you want to see images from Paris's pyre?"

"Yes," said Zeus. He returned to his throne and sat, patting the step that Hera had vacated when she stood.

She obediently returned and took her place, but did not lay her arm on his leg again.

Grumbling to himself, Hephaestus walked over to the dog's head, lifted it by its ears, and carried it to the vision pool. He crouched there at pool's edge, pulled a curved metal tool from one of his chest-belts, and worried the dog's left eyeball out of its socket. There was no blood. He pulled the eye free easily, but red, green, and white strands of optic nerve ran back into the empty eye socket, the cords unreeling as the god of fire pulled. When he had two feet of the glistening strands exposed, he pulled yet another tool from his belt and snipped them.

Pulling mucus and insulation off with his teeth, Hephaestus revealed thin, glittering gold wires within. These he crimped and attached to what looked to be a small metal sphere from one of his pouches. He dropped the eyeball and colored nerve strands into the pool while keeping the sphere next to him.

Immediately the pool filled with three-dimensional images. Sound surrounded the three gods as it emanated from piezo-electric microspeakers set into the walls and pillars around them.

The images from Ilium were from a dog's point of view—low, many bare knees and bronze shin-guarding greaves.

"I preferred our old views," muttered Hera.

"The moravecs detect and shoot down all our drones, even the fucking insect eyes," said Hephaestus, still fast-forwarding through Paris's funeral procession. "We're lucky to have . . ."

"Silence," commanded Zeus. The word echoed like thunder from the walls. "There. That. Sound."

The three watched the last minutes of the funeral rites, including the slaughter of Dionysos by Hector.

They watched Zeus's son look right at the dog in the crowd when he said, "Eat me."

"You can turn it off," said Hera when the images were of Hector dropping the torch onto the waiting pyre.

"No," said Zeus. "Let it run."

A minute later, the Lord of Lightning was off his throne and walking toward the holoview pool with his brow furrowed, eyes furious, and fists clenched. "How *dare* that mortal Hector call upon Boreas and Zephyr to fan the fires containing a god's guts and balls and bowels! *HOW DARE HE!!*"

Zeus QT'd out of sight and there was a clap of thunder as the air rushed into the hole in the air where the huge god had been a microsecond earlier.

Hera shook her head. "He watches the ritual murder of his son, Dionysos, easily enough, but flies into a rage when Hector tries to summon the gods of the wind. The Father is losing it, Hephaestus."

Her son grunted, reeled in the eyeball, and set it and the metal sphere in a pouch. He put the dog's head in a larger pouch. "Do you need anything else from me this morning, Daughter of Kronos?"

She nodded at the dog's carcass, its belly panel still flopped open. "Take that with you."

When her surly son was gone, Hera touched her breast and quantum teleported away from the Great Hall of the Gods.

No one could QT into Hera's inner sleeping chamber, not even Hera. Long ago—if her immortal memory still served her, since all memories were suspect these days—she had ordered her son Hephaestus to secure her rooms with his artificer's skills: forcefields of quantum flux, similar but not identical to those the moravec creatures had used to shield Troy and the Achaean camps from divine intrusion, pulsed within the walls; the door to her chamber was flux-infused reinforced titanium, strong enough to hold even an angered Zeus at bay, and Hephaestus had hung it from quantum doorposts snug and tight, locking it all with a secret bolt of a telepathic password that Hera changed daily.

She mentally opened that bolt and slipped in, securing the seamless, gleaming metal barrier behind her and moving into the bathing chamber, discarding her gown and flimsy underthings as she went.

First the ox-eyed Hera drew her bath, which was deep and fed from the purest springs of Olympos ice, heated by Hephaestus's infernal engines tapping into the core of the old volcano's warmth. She used the ambrosia first, using it to scrub away all faint stains or shadows of imperfection from her glowing white skin.

Then the white-armed Hera anointed her eternally adorable and enticing body with a deep olive rub, followed by a redolent oil. It was said on Olympos that the fragrance from this oil, used only by Hera, would stir not only every male divinity within the bronze-floored halls of Zeus, but could and did drift down to earth itself in a perfumed cloud that made unsuspecting mortal men lose their minds in frenzies of longing.

Then the daughter of mighty Kronos arranged her shining, ambrosial curls along her sharp-cheeked face and dressed in an ambrosial robe that had been made expressly for her by Athena, when the two had been friends so long ago. The gown was wonderfully smooth, with many designs and figures on it, including a wonderful rose brocade worked into the weft by Athena's fingers and magic loom. Hera pinned this goddess material across her high breasts with a golden brooch, and fastened— just under her breasts—a waistband ornamented with a hundred floating tassels.

Into the lobes of her carefully pierced ears—just peeking out like pale, shy sea-things from her dark-scented curls—Hera looped her earrings, triple drops of mulberry clusters whose silver glint was guaranteed to cast hooks deep into every male heart.

Then back over her brow she veiled herself with a sweet, fresh veil made of suspended gold fabric that glinted like sunlight along her rosy cheekbones. Finally she fastened supple sandals under her soft, pale feet, crossing the gold straps up her smooth calves.

Now, dazzling from head to foot, Hera paused by the reflecting wall at the door to her bath chamber, considered the reflection for a silent moment, and said softly, "You still have it."

Then she left her chambers and entered the echoing marble hall, touched her left breast, and quantum teleported away.

Hera found Aphrodite, goddess of love, walking alone on the grassy south-facing slopes of Mount Olympos. It was just before sunset, the temples and gods' homes there on the east side of the caldera were limned in light, and Aphrodite had been admiring the gold glow on the Martian ocean to the north as well as on the icefields near the summit of three huge shield volcanoes visible far to the east, toward which Olympos threw its huge shadow for more than two hundred kilometers. The view was slightly blurred because of the usual forcefield around Olympos, which allowed them to breathe and survive and walk in near Earth-normal gravity here so close to the vacuum of space itself above ter-raformed Mars, and also blurred because of the shimmering *aegis* that Zeus had set in place around Olympos at the beginning of the war.

The Hole down there—a circle cut out of Olympos' shadow, glowing within from a sunset on a different world and filled with lines of busy lights from mortal fires and moving moravec transports—was a re-minder of that war.

"Dear child," Hera called to the goddess of love, "would you do something for me if I asked, or would you refuse it? Are you still angry at me for helping the Argives these ten mortal years past while you de-fended your beloved Trojans?"

"Queen of the Skies," said Aphrodite, "Beloved of Zeus, ask me any-thing. I will be eager to obey. Whatever I *can* do for one so powerful as yourself."

The sun had all but set now, casting both goddesses into shadow, but Hera noticed how Aphrodite's skin and ever-present smile seemed to glow of their own accord. Hera responded sensually to it as a female; she couldn't imagine how the male gods felt in Aphrodite's presence, much less the weak-willed mortal men.

Taking a breath—since her next words would commit her to the most dangerous scheme the scheming Hera had ever devised—she said, "Give me your powers to create Love, to command Longing—all the powers you use to overwhelm the gods and mortal men!"

Aphrodite's smile remained, but her clear eyes narrowed ever so slightly. "Of course I will, Daughter of Kronos, if you so request—but why does someone who already lies in the arms of mighty Zeus require my few wiles?"

Hera kept her voice steady as she lied. As most liars do, she gave too many details in her lie. "This war wearies me, Goddess of Love. The plotting and scheming among the gods and among the Argives and Tro-jans hurts my heart. I go now to the ends of the generous other earth to visit Okeanos, that fountain from which the gods have risen, and Mother Tethys. These two kindly raised me in their own house and took me from Rhea when thundering Zeus, he of the wide brows, drove Kronos deep beneath the earth and the barren salt seas and built our new home here on this cold, red world."

"But why, Hera," Aphrodite asked softly, "do you need my poor charms to visit Okeanos and Tethys?"

Hera smiled in her treachery. "The Old Ones have grown apart, their marriage bed grown cold. I go now to visit them and to dissolve their an-cient feud and to mend their discord. For too long have they stayed apart from each other and from their bed of love—I would lure them back to love, back to each other's warm bodies, and no mere words of mine will suffice in this effort. So I ask you, Aphrodite, as your loving friend and one who wishes two old friends to love again, loan me one of the secrets of your charms so that I can secretly help Tethys win back Okeanos to desire."

Aphrodite's charming smile grew even more radiant. The sun had set now behind the edge of Mars, the summit of Olympos had been plunged into shadow, but the love goddess's smile warmed them both. "It would be wrong of me to deny your warmhearted request, O Wife of Zeus, since your husband, our lord, commands us all."

With that, Aphrodite loosed from beneath her breasts her secret breastband, and held the thin web of cloth and microcircuits in her hand.

Hera stared at it, her mouth suddenly dry. *Dare I go forward with this? If Athena discovers what I'm up to, she and her fellow conspirators among the gods will attack me without mercy. If Zeus recognizes my treachery, he will destroy me in a way that no healing vat or alien Healer will ever hope to restore to even a simulacrum of Olympian life.* "Tell me how it works," she whispered to the goddess of love.

"On this band are all the beguilements of seduction," Aphrodite said softly. "The heat of Love, the pulsing rush of Longing, the sibilant slidings of sex, the urgent lover's cries, and the whispers of endearment."

"All on that little breastband?" said Hera. "How does it work?"

"It has in it the magic to make any man go mad with lust," whispered Aphrodite.

"Yes, yes, but how does it *work*?" Hera heard the impatience in her own words.

"How do I know?" asked the goddess of love, laughing now. "It was part of the package I received when . . . *he* . . . made us gods. A broad spectrum of pheromones? Nano-kindled hormone enactors? Microwaved energy directed directly at the sex and pleasure centers of the brain? It doesn't matter . . . although this is only one of my many tricks, it works. Try it on, Wife of Zeus."

Hera broke into a smile. She tucked the band between and under her high breasts, so that it was barely concealed by her gown. "How do I activate it?"

"Don't you mean how will you help Mother Tethys activate it?" asked Aphrodite, still smiling.

"Yes, yes."

"When the moment comes, touch your breast just as you would to activate the QT nanotriggers, but instead of imagining a far place to teleport, let one finger touch the circuited fabric in the breastband and think lustful thoughts."

"That's it? That's all?"

"That is all," said Aphrodite, "but it will suffice. A new world lies in this band's weaving."

"Thank you, Goddess of Love," Hera said formally. Laser lances were stabbing upward through the forcefield above them. A moravec hornet or spacecraft had come through the Hole and was climbing for space.

"I know you won't return with your missions unaccomplished," said Aphrodite. "Whatever your eager heart is hoping to do, I am sure it will be fulfilled."

Hera smiled at that. Then she touched her breast—careful not to touch the breastband nestled just beneath her nipples—and teleported away, following the quantum trail Zeus had made through folded space-time.

7

At dawn, Hector ordered the funeral fires quenched with wine. Then he and Paris's most trusted comrades began raking through the embers, taking infinite care to find the bones of Priam's other son while keeping them separate from the ashes and charred bones of dogs, stallions, and the weakling god. These lesser bones had all fallen far out near the edge of the pyre, while Paris's charred remains lay near the center.

Weeping, Hector and his battle-comrades gathered Paris's bones in a golden urn and sealed the urn with a double layer of fat, as was their custom for the brave and noble-born. Then, in solemn procession, they carried the urn through the busy streets and marketplaces—peasants and warriors alike stepping aside to let them pass in silence—and delivered the remains to the field cleared of rubble where the south wing of Priam's palace had stood before the first Olympian bombing run eight months earlier. In the center of the cratered field rose a temporary tomb made from stone blocks scattered during the bombing—Hecuba, Priam's wife, queen, and mother to Hector and Paris, had her few recovered bones in that tomb already—and now Hector covered Paris's urn with a light linen shroud and personally carried it into the barrow.

"Here, Brother, I leave your bones for now," said Hector in front of the men who'd followed him, "allowing the earth here to enfold you until I enfold you myself in the dim halls of Hades. When this war is over, we will build you and our mother and all those others who fall—most likely including myself—a greater tomb, reminiscent of the House of Death itself. Until then, Brother, farewell."

Then Hector and his men came out and a hundred waiting Trojan heroes covered over the temporary stone tomb with dirt and piled more rubble and rocks high upon it.

And then Hector—who had not slept for two nights—went in search of Achilles, eager now to re-engage in combat with the gods and hungrier than ever to spill their golden blood.

Cassandra awoke at dawn to find herself all but naked, her robe torn and in disarray, her wrists and ankles tied with silken ropes to the posts of a strange bed. *What mischief is this?* she wondered, trying to remember if she had once again gotten drunk and passed out with some kinky soldier.

Then she remembered the funeral pyre and fainting into the arms of Andromache and Helen at its fiery conclusion.

Shit, thought Cassandra. *My big mouth's got me in trouble again.* She looked around the room—no windows, huge stone blocks, a sense of underground damp. She might well be in someone's personal underground torture chamber. Cassandra struggled and thrashed against the silken cords. They were smooth, but they were tight and well tied and remained firm.

Shit, Cassandra thought again.

Andromache, Hector's wife, came into the room and looked down on the sybil. Andromache's hands were empty, but Cassandra could easily imagine the dagger in the sleeve of the older woman's gown. For a long moment, neither woman spoke. Finally, Cassandra said, "Old friend, please release me."

Andromache said, "Old friend, I should cut your throat."

"Then do it, you bitch," said Cassandra. "Don't talk about it." She had little fear, since even within the kaleidoscope of shifting views of the future in the past eight months since the old futures had died, she had never foreseen Andromache killing her.

"Cassandra, why did you say that about the death of my baby? You know that Pallas Athena and Aphrodite both came into my tiny son's chamber eight months ago and slaughtered him and his wet nurse, saying that his sacrifice was a warning—that the gods on Olympos had been ill pleased at my husband's failure to burn the Argive ships and that little Astyanax, whom his father and I had called Scamandrius, was to be their yearly heiffer chosen for sacrifice."

"Bullshit," said Cassandra. "Untie me." Her head hurt. She always had a hangover after the most vivid of her prophecies.

"Not until you tell me why you said that I had substituted a slave baby for Astyanax in that bloodied nursery," said cool-eyed Andromache. The dagger was in her hand now. "How could I do that? How could I know that the goddesses were coming? Why would I do that?"

Cassandra sighed and closed her eyes. "There were no *goddesses*," she said tiredly but with contempt. She opened her eyes again. "When you heard the news that Pallas Athena had killed Achilles' beloved friend Patroclus—news which still may turn out to be another lie—you decided, or conspired with Hecuba and Helen to decide—to slaughter the wet nurse's own child, who was the same age as Astyanax, and then kill the wet nurse as well. Then you told Hector and Achilles and all the others who assembled at the sound of your screams that it was the goddesses who killed your son."

Andromache's hazel eyes were as blue and cold and ungiving as ice on the surface of a mountain stream in spring. "Why would I do that?"

"You saw the chance to realize the Trojan Women's scheme," said Cassandra. "Our scheme of all these years. To somehow turn our Trojan men away from war with the Argives—a war I had prophesied as ending in all of our death or destruction. It was brilliant, Andromache. I applaud your courage for acting."

"Except, if what you say is true," said Andromache, "I've helped plunge us all into an even more hopeless war with the gods. At least in your earlier visions, some of us women survived—as slaves, but still among the living."

Cassandra shrugged, an awkward motion with her arms extended and tethered to the bedposts. "You were thinking only of saving your son, whom we know would have been foully murdered had the old past become the current present. I understand, Andromache."

Andromache extended the knife. "It's all of my family's death—even Hector's—if you were to ever speak of this again and if the rabble—Trojan and Achaean alike—were to believe you. My only safety is in your death."

Cassandra met the other woman's flat gaze. "My gift of foresight can still serve you, *Old Friend*. It may even save you—you and your Hector and your hidden Astyanax, wherever he is. You know that when I am in the throes of my visions that I cannot control what I cry aloud. You and Helen and whoever else is in on this conspiracy—stay with me, or assign murderous slave girls to stay with me, and shut me up if I start to babble such truth again. If I do reveal this to others, kill me then."

Andromache hesitated, lightly bit her lower lip, and then leaned forward and cut the silken cord that bound Cassandra's right wrist to the bed. While she was cutting the other cords, she said, "The Amazons have arrived."

Menelaus spent the night listening to and then talking to his brother and by the time Dawn spread forth her rosy fingertips, he was resolved to action.

All night he had moved from one Achaean and Argive camp to another around the bay and along the shoreline, listening to Agamemnon tell the horrifying story of their empty cities, empty farm fields, abandoned harbors—of unmanned Greek ships bobbing at anchor in Marathon, Eretria, Chalcis, Aulis, Hermione, Tiryns, Helos, and a score of other shoreside cities. He listened to Agamemnon tell the horrified Achaeans, Argives, Cretans, Ithacans, Lacadaemons, Calydnaeans, Buprasians, Dulichions, Pylosians, Pharisans, Spartans, Messeians, Thracians, Oechalians—all the hundreds of allied groups of varied Greeks from the mainland, from the rocky isles, from the Peloponnese itself—that their cities were empty, their homes abandoned as if by the will of the gods—meals rotting on tables, clothing set out on couches, baths and pools tepid and scummed over with algae, weapons lying unscabbarded. On the Aegean, Agamemnon described in his full, strong, booming voice—empty ships bellying against the waves, sails full but tattered, no sign of furling or storm—the skies were blue and the seas were fair coming and going in their month-long voyage, Agamemnon explained—but the ships were empty: Athenian ships full-loaded with cargo or still resplendent with rows of unmanned oars; great Persian scows empty of their clumsy crews and helmeted, hopeless spearmen; graceful, crewless Egyptian ships waiting to carry grain to the home islands.

"The world has been emptied of men and women and children," cried Agamemnon at each Achaean encampment, "except for us here, the wily Trojans and us. While we have turned our backs on the gods—worse, turned our hands and hearts against them—the gods have carried away the hopes of our hearts—our wives and families and fathers and slaves."

"Are they dead?" cried man after man in camp after camp. The cries always were made though moans of pain. Lamentations filled the winter night all along the line of Argive fires.

Agamemnon always answered with upraised palms and silence for a terrible minute. "There was no sign of struggle," he would say at last. "No blood. No decaying bodies feeding the starving dogs and circling birds."

And always, at every encampment, the brave Argive crews and · bodyguards and foot soldiers and captains who had accompanied

Agamemnon homeward were having their own private conversations with others of their rank. By dawn, everyone had heard the terrible news, and palsied terror was giving way to impotent rage.

Menelaus knew that this was perfect for their purpose—the Atridae brothers, Agamemnon and Menelaus—to turn the Acheaens not only against the Trojans once again and to finish this war, but to overthrow the dictatorship of fleet-footed Achilles. Within days, if not hours, Agamemnon would once again be commander in chief.

At dawn, Agamemnon had finished his duty of reporting to all the Greeks, the great captains had wandered away—Diomedes back to his tent, the Great Telamonian Ajax, who had wept like a child when he heard that Salamis had been found as empty as all the other homelands—and Odysseus, Idomeneus, and Little Ajax, who had cried out in pain with all his men from Locris when Agamemnon had told them the news, and even garrulous old Nestor—all had wandered away at dawn to catch a few hours' restless sleep.

"So tell me the news of the War with the Gods," said Agamemnon to Menelaus as the two brothers sat alone in center of their Lacadaemon encampment, surrounded by rings of loyal captains, bodyguards, and spearmen. These men stayed far enough away to let their lords converse in private.

Red-haired Menelaus told his older brother what news there was— the ignoble daily battles between moravec wizardry and the gods' divine weapons, the occasional single combat—the death of Paris and a hundred lesser names, both Trojan and Achaean—and about the funeral just finished. The corpse-fire smoke had ceased to rise and the flames above the wall of Troy had disappeared from sight only an hour earlier.

"Good riddance," said royal Agamemnon, his strong white teeth gnawing off a strip of the suckling pig they'd roasted for his breakfast. "I'm only sorry Apollo killed Paris . . . I wanted to do the job myself."

Menelaus laughed, ate some of the suckling pig himself, washed it down with breakfast wine, and told his dear brother about Paris's first wife, Oenone, appearing out of nowhere and of her self-immolation.

Agamemnon laughed at this. "Would that it had been your bitch of a wife, Helen, who'd been so moved to throw herself into the flames, Brother."

Menelaus nodded at this, but he felt his heart lurch at the sound of Helen's name. He told Agamemnon of Oenone's ravings about Philoctetes, not Apollo, being the cause of Paris's death, and about the anger that had swept through the Trojan ranks, causing the small contingent of Achaeans to beat a hasty retreat from the city.

Agamemnon slapped his thigh. "Wonderful! It's the penultimate stone set in place. Within forty-eight hours, I'll stir this discontent into action throughout the Achaean ranks. We'll be at war with the Trojans again before the week is out, Brother. I swear this on the stones and dirt of our father's barrow."

"But the gods . . ." began Menelaus.

"The gods will be as they were," he said with what sounded like complete confidence. "Zeus neutral. Some helping the mewling, doomed Trojans. Most allying themselves with us. But this time we'll finish the job. Ilium will be ashes within the fortnight . . . as sure as Paris is nothing but bones and ashes this morning."

Menelaus nodded. He knew that he should ask questions about how his brother hoped to mend the peace with the gods again, as well as overthrow the invincible Achilles, but he ached to discuss a more pressing topic.

"I saw Helen," he said, hearing his own voice stumble at his wife's name. "I was within seconds of killing her."

Agamemnon wiped grease from his mouth and beard, drank from a silver cup, and raised one eyebrow to show that he was listening.

Menelaus described his firm resolve and opportunity to get to Helen—and how both were ruined by Oenone's sudden appearance and her dying accusations against Philoctetes. "We were lucky to get out of the city alive," he said again.

Agamemnon squinted toward the distant walls. Somewhere a moravec siren wailed and missiles hurtled skyward toward some unseen Olympian target. The forcefield over the main Achaean camp hummed into a deeper tone of readiness.

"You should kill her today," said Menelaus' older and wiser brother. "Now. This morning."

"This morning?" Menelaus licked his lips. Despite the pig grease, they were dry.

"This morning," repeated the once and future commander in chief of all the Greek armies assembled to sack Troy. "Within a day or so, the opening rift between our men and those dog-spittle Trojans will be so great that the cowards will be closing and bolting their fucking Scaean Gate again."

Menelaus looked toward the city. Its walls were rose-colored in the light of the rising winter sun. He was very confused. "They won't allow me in by myself . . ." he began.

"Go in disguise," interrupted Agamemnon. The royal king drank again and belched. "Think as Odysseus would think . . . as some crafty weasel would think."

Menelaus, as proud a man as his brother or any other Achaean hero in his own way, wasn't sure he appreciated that comparison. "How can I disguise myself?"

Agamemnon gestured toward his own royal tent, its scarlet silk billowing again nearby. "I have the lion skin and old bore-tusk wraparound helmet that Diomedes wore when he and Odysseus attempted to steal the Palladian from Troy last year," he said. "With that strange helmet hiding your red hair and the tusks hiding your beard—not to mention the lion skin concealing your glorious Achaean armor—the sleepy guards at the gate will think you another barbarian ally of theirs and let you pass without challenge. But go quickly—before the guard changes and before the gates are locked to us for the duration of Ilium's doomed existence."

Menelaus had to think about this for only a few seconds. Then he rose, clasped his brother firmly on the shoulder, and went into the tent to gather his disguise and to arm himself with more killing blades.

The moon Phobos looked like a huge, grooved, dusty olive with bright lights encircling the concave end. Mahnmut told Hockenberry that the hollowed tip was a giant crater called Stickney and that the lights were the moravec base.

The ride up had not been without some adrenaline flow for Hockenberry. He'd seen enough of the moravec hornets at short range to notice that none of them seemed to have windows or ports, so he assumed the ride would be a blind one, except perhaps for some TV monitors. He'd underestimated asteroid-belt moravec technology—for all the hornets were from the rockvecs according to Mahnmut. Hockenberry had also assumed there would be acceleration couches or Twentieth Century space-shuttle-style chairs with huge straps and buckles.

There were no chairs. No visible means of support. Invisible forcefields enfolded Hockenberry and the small moravec as they seemed to sit on thin air. Holograms—or some sort of three-dimensional projections so real that there was no sense of projection—surrounded them on three sides and beneath them. Not only were they sitting on invisible chairs, the invisible chairs and their bodies were suspended over a two-mile drop as the hornet flashed through the Hole and climbed for altitude to the south of Olympus Mons.

Hockenberry screamed.

"Does the display bother you?" asked Mahnmut.

Hockenberry screamed again.

The moravec quickly touched holographic controls that appeared as if by magic. The drop below them shrank until it appeared to be set into the metal floor of the hull like a mere giant-screen TV. All around them, the panorama continued to unfold as the forcefield-shrouded summit of Olympus Mons flashed past—lasers or some sort of energy lances flickering at them and splashing against the hornet's own energy field—and then the blue Martian sky shifted to thin pink, then to black, and the hornet was above the atmosphere, pitching over—although the great limb of Mars seemed to rotate until it filled the virtual windows.

"Better," gasped Hockenberry, flailing for something to hang on to. The forcefield chair didn't fight him, but it didn't release him either. "Jesus Christ," he gasped as the ship did a one-hundred-eighty degree roll and fired its engines. Phobos tumbled into view, almost on top of them.

There was no sound. Not a whisper.

"I'm sorry," said Mahnmut. "I should have warned you. This is Phobos filling the aft windowscreen right now. It's the smaller of Mars' two moons, just about eight miles in diameter . . . although you can see it's not a sphere by any means."

"It looks like a potato that some cat's been clawing," managed Hockenberry. The moon was approaching *very* fast. "Or a giant olive."

"Olive, yes," said Mahnmut. "That's because of the crater at this end. It's named Stickney—after Asaph Hall's wife, Angeline Stickney Hall."

"Who was . . . Asaph . . . Hall?" managed Hockenberry. "Some astronaut . . . or . . . cosmonaut . . . or . . . who?" He'd found something to hang on to. Mahnmut. The little moravec didn't seem to mind his metal-plastic shoulders being clutched. The aft view-holo flared with flame as some silent thrusters or engines fired. Hockenberry was just barely succeeding in keeping his teeth from chattering.

"Asaph Hall was an astronomer with the United States Naval Observatory in Washington, D.C.," said Mahnmut in his usual soft, conversational tones. The hornet was pitching over again. And spinning. Phobos and the Stickney Crater hole were filling first one holographic window and then another.

Hockenberry was pretty sure that the thing was crashing and that he would be dead in less than a minute. He tried to remember a prayer from his childhood—damn all those years as an intellectual agnostic!—

but all he could bring back was the singsong "Now I lay me down to sleep . . ."

It seemed appropriate. Hockenberry went with it.

"I believe that Hall discovered both moons of Mars in 1877," Mahnmut was saying. "There is no record—none of which I am aware—of whether Mrs. Hall appreciated a huge crater being named after her. Of course, it was her maiden name."

Hockenberry suddenly realized why they were out of control and going to crash and die. No one was flying the goddamned ship. It was just the two of them in the hornet, and the only control—real or virtual—that Mahnmut had touched had been the one to adjust the holographic views. He considered mentioning this oversight to the little organic-robot, but since the Stickney Crater was filling all the forward windows now and approaching at a speed they had no chance of decreasing before impact, Hockenberry kept his mouth shut.

"It's a strange little moon," said Mahnmut. "A captured asteroid, really—as is Deimos, of course. They're quite different from each other. Phobos here orbits only three thousand seven hundred miles above the Martian surface—almost skimming the atmosphere, as it were—and is destined to crash into Mars in approximately eighty-three million years if no one does anything about it."

"Speaking of crashing . . ." began Hockenberry.

At that moment the hornet slowed to a hover, dropped into the flood-lit crater, and touched down near a complex network of domes, girders, cranes, glowing yellow bubbles, blue domes, green spires, moving vehicles, and hundreds of busy moravecs bustling around in vacuum. The landing, when it came, was so gentle that Hockenberry only just felt it through the metal floor and forcefield chair.

"Home again, home again," chanted Mahnmut. "Well, not really *home,* of course, but . . . watch your head when we get out. That door is a little low for human heads."

Before Hockenberry could comment or scream again, the door had swung out and down and all the air in the little compartment roared out into the vacuum of space.

Hockenberry had been a classics major and professor during his previous life, never very science literate, but he'd seen enough science-fiction movies in his time to know the fate of explosive decompression: eyes expanding until they were the size of grapefruits, eardrums bursting in great gouts of blood, flesh and skin boiling and expanding and ripping as internal pressures expanded when finding no resistance against the zero external pressure of hard vacuum.

None of that happened.

Mahnmut paused on the ramp. "Aren't you coming?" The little moravec's voice sounded tinny in the human's ears.

"Why aren't I dead?" said Hockenberry. It felt as if he'd suddenly been wrapped in invisible bubble wrap.

"Your chair's protecting you."

"My *chair*??" Hockenberry looked around him but there was not so much as a shimmer. "You mean I have to keep sitting here forever or die?"

"No," said Mahnmut, sounding amused. "Come on out. The forcefield-chair will come with you. It's already providing heat, cooling, osmotic scrubbing and recycling of your oxygen—good for about thirty minutes—and acting as a pressure suit."

"But the . . . chair . . . is part of the ship,"said Hockenberry, standing gingerly and feeling the invisible bubble wrap move with him. "How can it go outside the hornet?"

"Actually, the hornet is more a part of the chair," said Mahnmut. "Trust me. But watch your step out here. The chair-suit will give you a little down-thrust once you're on the surface, but the gravity on Phobos is so weak that a good jump would allow you to reach escape velocity. *Adios*, Phobos, for Thomas Hockenberry."

Hockenberry paused at the top stair of the ramp and clutched the metal door frame.

"Come on," said Mahnmut. "The chair and I won't let you float away. Let's get inside. There are other moravecs who want to talk to you."

After leaving Hockenberry with Asteague/Che and the other prime integrators from the Five Moons Consortium, Mahnmut left the pressurized dome and went for a walk in Stickney Crater. The view was spectacular. The long axis of Phobos constantly pointed at Mars and the moravec engineers had tweaked it so that the red planet was always hanging directly above Stickney, filling most of the black sky, since the steep crater walls blocked out the peripheral views. The little moon turned on its axis once every seven hours—precisely the same amount of time it took to orbit Mars—so the giant red disk with its blue oceans and white volcanoes rotated slowly above.

He found his friend Orphu of Io several hundred meters up amidst the spiderweb of cranes, girders, and cables tethering the Going-to-Earth ship to the launch crater. Deep-space moravecs, engineering bots, black-beetled rockvecs, and Callistan supervisors scuttled and clambered over the ship and connecting girders like glittering aphids. Searchlights and worklights played on the dark hull of the huge Earth-ship. Sparks fell in cascades from batteries of roving autowelders. Nearby, more secure in the mesh of a metal cradle, was *The Dark Lady*, Mahnmut's own deep-sea submersible from Europa. Months ago, the moravecs had salvaged the damaged and powerless vessel from its hiding place along the Martian coast of the north Tethys Sea, used tugs to lift it to Phobos, and then repaired, repowered, and modified the tough little sub for service on the Earth mission.

Mahnmut found his friend a hundred meters up, scuttling along steel cables under the belly of the spaceship. He hailed him on their old private band.

"Is that Orphu I spy? The Orphu formerly of Mars, formerly of Ilium, and always of Io? *That* Orphu?"

"The same," said Orphu. Even on the radio or tightbeam channels, Orphu's rumble seemed to border on the subsonic. The hardvac moravec used its carapace thrusters to jump thirty meters from the cables to the girder where Mahnmut was balancing. Orphu grabbed a girder with his manipulator pincers and hung there a few meters out.

Some of the moravecs—Asteague/Che, for example, the chitinous Belt moravecs for another, Mahnmut himself somewhat less so—were humanoid-looking enough. Not Orphu of Io. The moravec, designed and evolved to work in the sulfur-torus of Io in the magnetic, gravitational, and blinding radiation storms of Jupiter space, was about five meters long, more than two meters high, and slightly resembled a horseshoe crab, if horseshoe crabs were outfitted with extra legs, sensor packs, thruster pods, manipulators that almost—not quite—could serve as hands, and an aged, pitted shell-carapace so many times cracked and mended that it looked as if it had been cemented together by spackle.

"Is Mars still spinning up there, old friend?" rumbled Orphu.

Mahnmut turned his head skyward. "It is. Still rotating like some huge red shield. I can see Olympus Mons just coming out from the terminator."

Mahnmut hesitated a moment. "I'm sorry about the outcome of the most recent surgery," he said at last. "I'm sorry they couldn't fix it."

Orphu shrugged four articulated arm-legs. "It doesn't matter, old friend. Who needs organic eyes when one has thermal imaging, sniffy little gas chromatograph mass spectrometers on my knees, radar—deep and phased—sonar and a laser-mapper? It's just those useless, faraway things like stars and Mars that I can't quite make out with all these lovely sensory organs."

"Yes," said Mahnmut. "But I'm sorry." His friend had lost his organic optic nerve when he was almost destroyed during their first encounter with an Olympian god in Mars orbit—the same god who had blasted their ship and two comrades into gas and debris. Mahnmut knew that Orphu was lucky to be alive and repairable to the extent he had been, but still . . .

"Did you deliver Hockenberry?" rumbled Orphu.

"Yes. The prime integrators are briefing him now."

"Bureaucrats," rumbled the large Ionian. "Want a ride to the ship?"

"Sure." Mahnmut jumped to Orphu's shell, grabbed a handhold with his most serious gripping pincer, and held on as the hardvac moravec thrusted out away from the gantry, up to the ship, and then around. They were almost a kilometer above the crater floor here and the true size of the Earth-ship—tethered to the gantry like an ellipsoid helium balloon—became visible for the first time. It was easily five times the length of the spacecraft that had brought the four moravecs to Mars from Jupiter space more than a standard-year earlier.

"It's impressive, isn't it?" said Orphu. He'd been working with the Belt and Five Moons engineers for more than two months on the craft.

"It's big," said Mahnmut. And then, sensing Orphu's disappointment, he added, "And rather beautiful in a bumpy, bulgy, black, bulbous, sinister sort of way."

Orphu rumbled his deep laugh—tones that always made Mahnmut think of aftershocks from a Europan icequake or follow-on waves to a tsunami. "That's an awful lot of alliteration from an anxious astronaut," he said.

Mahnmut shrugged, felt bad for a second because his friend could not see the gesture, and then realized Orphu had seen it. The big moravec's new radar was a very fine instrument, lacking only the ability to see colors. Orphu had told him that he could make out subtle shifts on a human's face with the close-radar. *Useful if Hockenberry does come on this mission,* thought Mahnmut.

As if reading his mind and memory banks, Orphu said, "I've been thinking a lot about human sadness recently, and how it compares to our moravec style of dealing with loss."

"Oh, no," said Mahnmut, "you've been reading that French person again."

"Proust," said Orphu. "That 'French person's' name is Proust."

"I know. But why do you do that? You know that you always get depressed when you read *Remembrance of Things Past.*"

"*In Search of Lost Time,*" corrected Orphu of Io. "I've been reading the section called 'Grief and Oblivion.' You know, the part after Albertine dies and Marcel, the narrator, is trying to forget her, but he can't?"

"Oh, well," said Mahnmut. "*That* should cheer you up. How about if I loaned you *Hamlet* for a chaser?"

Orphu ignored the offer. They were high enough now to see the entire ship beneath them and to peer over the walls of Stickney Crater. Mahnmut knew that Orphu could travel many thousands of kilometers of deep space with no problem, but the sense that they were out of control and flying away from Phobos and the Stickney Base—just as he'd warned Hockenberry—was very strong.

"To cut the cords of connection to Albertine," says Orphu, "the poor narrator has to go back through his memory and consciousness and confront *all* of the Albertines—the ones from memory, as well as the imaginary ones he'd desired and been jealous of—all those *virtual* Albertines he'd created in his own mind when he was worrying about whether she was sneaking out to see other women behind his back. Not to mention the different Albertines of his desire—the girl he hardly knew, the woman he captured but did not possess, the woman he'd grown tired of."

"It sounds very tiring," said Mahnmut, trying to convey through his own tone over the radio band how tired he was of the whole Proust thing.

"That's not the half of it," said Orphu, ignoring the hint—or perhaps oblivious to it. "To move ahead in grieving, poor Marcel—the narrator-character has the same name as the author, you know . . . wait, you *did* read this, didn't you, Mahnmut? You assured me you had when we were coming in-system last year."

"I . . . *skimmed* it," said the Europan moravec.

Even Orphu's sigh bordered on the subsonic. "Well, as I was saying, poor Marcel not only has to confront this legion of Albertines in his consciousness before being able to let her go, he has to also confront all the Marcels who had perceived these multiple Albertines—the ones who had desired her beyond all things, the insanely jealous Marcels, the indifferent Marcels, the Marcels whose judgment had been distorted by desire, the . . ."

"Is there a point here?" asked Mahnmut. His own area of interest over the past standard century and a half had been Shakespeare's sonnets.

"Just the staggering complexity of human consciousness," said Orphu. He rotated his shell one hundred and eighty degrees, fired his thrusters, and they started back toward the ship, the gantry, Stickney Crater, and safety—such as it was. Mahnmut craned his short neck to look up at Mars as they pivoted. He knew it was an illusion, but it seemed closer. Olympus and the Tharsis volcanoes were almost out of sight now as Phobos hurtled toward the far limb of the planet.

"Do you ever wonder how our grieving differs from . . . say . . . Hockenberry's? Or Achilles'?" asked Orphu.

"Not really," said Mahnmut. "Hockenberry seems to grieve as much for the loss of memory of most of his previous life as he does for his dead wife, friends, students, and so forth. But who can tell with human beings? And Hockenberry is only a reconstituted human being—someone or something rebuilt him out of DNA, RNA, his old books, and who knows what kinds of best-guess programs? As for Achilles—when he gets sad, he goes out and kills someone. Or a bunch of someones."

"I wish I'd been there to see his Attack on the Gods during the first month of the war," said Orphu. "From the way you described it, the carnage was astounding."

"It was," said Mahnmut. "I've blocked random access to those files in my NOM because they're so disturbing."

"That's another element of Proust I've been thinking about," said Orphu. They touched down on the upper hull of the Earth-ship and the big moravec drove connecting micro-pitons into the sheath of insulating material there. "We have our non-organic memory to fall back on when our neural memories seem doubtful. Human beings have only that confusing mass of chemically driven neurological storage to rely on. They're all subjective and emotion-tinged. How can they trust any of their memories?"

"I don't know," said Mahnmut. "If Hockenberry goes with us to Earth, maybe we can get a glimpse of how his mind works."

"It's not as if we'll be alone with him with a lot of time to talk," said Orphu. "This will be a high-g boost and an even higher-g deceleration and there'll be quite a mob this time—at least three dozen Five Moons 'vecs and a thousand rockvec troopers."

"Prepared for anything this time, huh?" said Mahnmut.

"I doubt it," rumbled Orphu. "Although this ship carries enough weapons to reduce Earth to cinders. But so far, our planning hasn't kept up with the surprises."

Mahnmut felt the same sickness he'd been touched by when he'd learned their ship to Mars had been secretly armed. "Do you ever mourn for Koros III and Ri Po the way your Proust narrator mourns for his dead?" he asked the Ionian.

Orphu's fine radar antenna shifted slightly toward the smaller moravec, as if trying to read Mahnmut's expression the way he said he could a human's. Mahnmut, of course, had no expression.

"Not really," said Orphu. "We didn't know them before the mission and didn't travel in the same compartment with them during the mission. Before Zeus . . . got us. So mostly they were voices on the comm to me, although sometimes I access NOM to see their images . . . just to honor their memory, I guess."

"Yes," said Mahnmut. He did the same thing.

"Do you know what Proust said about conversation?"

Mahnmut resisted another sigh. "What?"

"He said . . . 'When we chat, it is no longer we who speak. . . . we are fashioning ourselves then in the likeness of other people, and not of a self that differs from them.' "

"So when I talk to you," Mahnmut said on their private frequency, "I'm really shaping myself into the likeness of a six-ton horseshoe crab with a beat-up shell, too many legs, and no eyes?"

"You can hope," rumbled Orphu of Io. "But your reach should always exceed your grasp."

Penthesilea swept into Ilium on horseback an hour after dawn with twelve of her finest sister-warriors riding two abreast behind her. Despite the early hour and the cold wind, thousands of Trojans were on the walls and lining the road that passed through the Scaean Gate to Priam's temporary palace, all of them cheering as if the Amazon queen were arriving with thousands of reinforcements rather than thirteen. The mobs waved kerchiefs, thumped spears against leather shields, wept, hurrahed, and threw flowers beneath the hooves of the horses.

Penthesilea accepted it all as her due.

Deiphobus, King Priam's son, Hector's and the dead Paris's brother, and the man whom the whole world knew would be Helen's next husband, met the Amazon queen and her warriors just outside the walls of Paris's palace, where Priam currently resided. The stout man stood in gleaming armor and red cape, his helmet brush stiff and golden, his arms folded until he extended one palm up in salute. Fifteen of Priam's private guardsmen stood at rigid attention behind him

"Hail, Penthesilea, daughter of Ares, Queen of the Amazons," cried Deiphobus. "Welcome to you and your twelve warrior women. All Ilium offers you thanks and honor this day, for coming as ally and friend to help us in our war with the gods of Olympos themselves. Come inside, bathe, receive our gifts, and know the true richness of Troy's hospitality and appreciation. Hector, our noblest hero, would be here to welcome you in person but he is resting for a few hours after tending our brother's funeral pyre all through the night."

Penthesilea swung down lightly from her giant war steed, moving with consummate grace despite her solid armor and gleaming helmet. She grasped Deiphobus by the forearm with both her strong hands, greeting him with a fellow-warrior's grip of friendship. "Thank you, Deiphobus, son of Priam, hero of a thousand single combats. I and my companions thank you, extend our condolences to you, your father, and all of Priam's people at the news of Paris's death—news that reached us two days ago—and we accept your generous hospitality. But I must tell you before I enter Paris's home, Priam's palace now, that I come not to fight the gods alongside you, but to end your war with the gods once and for all."

Deiphobus, whose eyes tended to protrude in a hypothalic way at the best of times, literally goggled now at this beautiful Amazon. "How would you do this, Queen Penthesilea?"

"This thing I have come to tell you, and then to do," said Penthesilea. "Come, take me in, friend Deiphobus. I need to meet with your father."

Deiphobus explained to the Amazon queen and her bodyguard-army that his father, royal Priam, was staying here in this wing of Paris's lesser palace because the gods had destroyed Priam's palace on the first day of the war eight months earlier, killing his wife and the city's queen, Hecuba.

"Again you have the Amazon women's condolences, Deiphobos," said Penthesilea. "Sorrow at the news of the queen's death reached even into our distant isles and hills."

As they entered the royal chamber, Deiphobos cleared his throat. "Speaking of your distant land, daughter of Ares, how is that you survived the gods' wrath this month? Word has spread through the city overnight that Agamemnon found the Greek Isles empty of human life during his voyage home. Even the brave defenders of Ilium are quaking this morning at the thought of the gods eliminating all peoples save for the Argives and us. How is that you and your race was spared?"

"My race hasn't been," Penthesilea said flatly. "We fear that the land of the brave Amazon women is as empty as the other lands we've passed through the last week of our travel. But Athena has spared us for our mission. And the goddess sent an important message to the people of Ilium."

"Pray tell us," said Deiphobus.

Penthesilea shook her head. "The message is for royal Priam's ears."

As if on cue, trumpets sounded, curtains were pulled back, and Priam entered slowly, leaning on the arm of one of his royal guardsmen.

Penthesilea had seen Priam in his own royal hall less than a year before when she and fifty of her women had braved the Achaean siege to bring words of encouragement and alliance to Troy—Priam had told her that the Amazon's help was not needed then, but had showered her with gold and other gifts. But now the Amazon queen was shocked into silence by Priam's appearance.

The king, always venerable but filled with energy, had seemed to age twenty years in the past twelve months. His back, always so straight, was now crooked. His cheeks, always ruddy with wine or excitement at the times Penthesilea had seen him over her five-and-twenty years, even when she was a child and she and her sister, Hippolyte, had hidden behind curtains in their mother's throne room when the royal party from Ilium visited to pay tribute, were now concave, as if the old man had lost all of his teeth. His salt-and-pepper hair and beard had gone a sad, straggly white. Priam's eyes were rheumy now, gazing at ghosts.

The old man almost collapsed into the gold-and-lapis throne.

"Hail, Priam, son of Laomedon, noble ruler in the line of Dardanus, father of brave Hector, pitiable Paris, and welcoming Deiphobus," said Penthesilea, going to one greaved knee. Her young-woman's voice, although melodious, was more than strong enough to echo in the huge chamber. "I, Queen Penthesilea, perhaps the last of the Amazon queens, and my twelve breasted and bronze-armored warriors bring you praise, condolences, gifts, and our spears."

"Your condolences and loyalties are your most precious gifts to us, dear Penthesilea."

"I also bring you a message from Pallas Athena and the key to ending your war with the gods," said Penthesilea.

The king cocked his head. Some of his retinue audibly gasped.

"Pallas Athena has never loved Ilium, beloved daughter. She always conspired with our Argive enemies to destroy this city and all within its walls. But the goddess is our sworn enemy now. She and Aphrodite murdered my son Hector's baby, Astyanax, young lord of the city— saying that we and our children were like mere offerings to them. Sacrifices. There will be no peace with the gods until their race or ours is extinguished."

Penthesilea, still on one knee but her head held high and her blue eyes flashing challenge, said, "The charge against Athena and Aphrodite is false. The war is false. The gods who love Ilium wish to love us and support us once again—including Father Zeus himself. Even gray-eyed Pallas Athena has come over to the side of Ilium because of the base treachery of the Achaeans—that liar Achilles most specifically, since he invented the calumny that Athena murdered his friend Patroclus."

"Do the gods offer peace terms?" asked Priam. The old man's voice was whispery, his tone almost wistful.

"Athena offers more than peace terms," said Penthesilea, rising to her feet. "She—and the gods who love Troy—offer you victory."

"Victory over whom?" called Deiphobus, moving to his father's side. "The Achaeans are our allies now. They and the artificed beings, the moravecs, who shield our cities and camps from Zeus's thunderbolts."

Penthesilea laughed. At that moment, every man in the room marveled at how beautiful the Amazon queen was—young and fair, her cheeks flushed and her features as animated as a girl's, her body under the beautifully molded bronze armor both lithe and lush at the same time. But Penthesilea's eyes and eager expression were not those of a mere girl's—they brimmed over with vitality, animal spirits, and sharp intelligence, as well as showing a warrior's fire for action.

"Victory over Achilles who has misled your son, noble Hector, who even now leads Ilium to ruin," cried Penthesilea. "Victory over the Argives, the Achaeans, who even now plot your downfall, the city's ruin, your other sons' and grandsons' death, and the enslavement of your wives and daughters."

Priam shook his head almost sadly. "No one can best fleet-footed Achilles in combat, Amazon. Not even Ares, who three times has been killed by Achilles' own hands. Not even Athena, who has fled at his attack. Not even Apollo, who was carried back to Olympus in golden-bloodied pieces after challenging Achilles. Not even Zeus, who fears to come down to do single combat with the man-god."

Penthesilea shook her head and her golden curls flashed. "Zeus fears no one, Noble Priam, pride of the Dardanus line. And he could destroy Troy—lo, destroy the entire earth on which Troy resides—with one flick of his *aegis*."

Spearmen went pale and even Priam flinched at the mention of the *aegis*, Zeus's most powerful and divine and mysterious weapon. It was understood by all that even the other Olympian gods could be destroyed in a minute if Zeus chose to use the *aegis*. This was no mere thermonuclear weapon such as the Thunder God dropped uselessly on moravec forcefields early in the war. The *aegis* was to be feared.

"I make this vow to you, Noble Priam," said the Amazon queen. "Achilles will be dead before the sun sets on either world today. I vow on the blood of my sisters and mother that . . ."

Priam held up his hand to stop her.

"Make no vow before me now, young Penthesilea. You are like another daughter to me and have been since you were a baby. Challenging Achilles to mortal combat is death. What made you come to Troy to find your death this way?"

"It is not death, My Lord," said the Amazon with strain audible in her voice. "It is glory."

"Often the two are the same," said Priam. "Come, sit down next to me. Talk to me softly." He waved his bodyguard and son, Deiphobus, back out of the range of hearing. The dozen Amazon women also took several steps away from the two thrones.

Penthesilea sat on the high-backed throne, once Hecuba's, recovered from the wreckage of the old palace and now kept empty here in Hecuba's memory. The Amazon set her shining helmet on the broad arm of the throne and leaned closer to the old man.

"I am pursued by Furies, Father Priam. For three months to this day I have been pursued by the Furies."

"Why?" asked Priam. He leaned closer, like some future-era priest to some yet unborn confessor. "Those avenging spirits seek to exact blood for blood only when no human avenger is left alive to do so, my daughter—especially when one family member has been injured by another. Surely you have hurt no member of your royal Amazon family."

"I killed my sister, Hippolyte," said Penthesilea, her voice quavering.

Priam pulled back. "You murdered Hippolyte? The former queen of the Amazons? Theseus' royal wife? We heard that she had died in a hunting accident when someone had seen movement and mistaken the Queen of Athens for a stag."

"I did not mean to murder her, Priam. But after Theseus abducted my sister—seduced her aboard his ship during a state visit, set sail, and carried her off—we Amazons set our mind to revenge. This year, while all eyes and attention in the home isles and Peloponnese were turned to your struggle here at Troy, with heroes away and Athens lying undefended, we made up a small fleet, set our own siege—though nothing so grand and immortal in the telling as the Argives' siege of Ilium—and invaded Theseus' stronghold."

"We heard this, of course," mumbled old Priam. "But the battle ended quickly in a treaty of peace and the Amazons departed. We heard that Queen Hippolyte died shortly after, during a grand hunt to celebrate the peace."

"She died by my spear," said Penthesilea, forcing every word out into the air. "Originally, the Athenians were on the run, Theseus was wounded, and we thought we had the city in our grasp. Our only goal was to rescue Hippolyte from this man—whether she wanted to be rescued or not—and we were close to doing so when Theseus led a counterattack that drove us a day's bloody retreat back to our ships. Many of my sisters were slain. We were fighting for our lives now, and once again Amazon valor won out—we drove Theseus and his fighters back a day's walk toward his walls. But my final spearcast, aimed for Theseus himself, found its deadly way into the heart of my sister, who—in her bold Athenian armor—looked like a man as she fought alongside her lord and husband."

"Against the Amazons," whispered Priam. "Against her sisters."

"Yes. As soon as we discovered whom I had killed, the battle stopped. The peace was made. We erected a white column near the acropolis in my noble sister's memory, and we departed in sorrow and shame."

"And the Furies hound you now, for your sister's shed blood."

"Every day," said Penthesilea. Her bright eyes were moist. Her fresh cheeks had gone flushed with the telling and now were pale. She looked extraordinarily beautiful.

"But what does Achilles and our war have to do with this tragedy, my daughter?" whispered Priam.

"This month, son of Laomedon and scion of the line of Dardanus, Athena appeared to me. She explained that no offering I could make to the Furies would ever appease the hell-beasts, but that I could make amends for Hippolyte's death by traveling to Ilium with twelve of my chosen companions and defeating Achilles in single combat, thus ending this errant war and restoring peace between gods and men."

Priam rubbed his chin where the gray stubble he'd let grow since Hecuba's death passed for a beard. "No one can defeat Achilles, Amazon. My son Hector—the finest warrior Troy has ever bred—tried for eight years and failed. Now he is ally and friend to the fleet-footed mankiller. The gods themselves have tried for more than eight months, and all have failed or fallen before the wrath of Achilles—Ares, Apollo, Poseidon, Hermes, Hades, Athena herself—all have taken on Achilles and failed."

"It's because none of them knew of his weakness," whispered the Amazon Penthesilea. "His mother, the goddess Thetis, found a secret way to confer invulnerability in battle to her mortal son when he was an infant. He cannot fall in battle except by injury to this one weak place."

"What is it?" gasped Priam. "*Where* is it?"

"I swore to Athena—upon pain of death—that I would reveal it to no one, Father Priam. But that I would use the knowledge to kill Achilles by my own Amazon hand and thus end this war."

"If Athena knows Achilles' weakness, then why did she not use it to end his life in their own combat, woman? A duel which ended with Athena fleeing, wounded, QTing back to Olympos in pain and fear."

"The Fates decreed when Achilles was an infant that his secret weakness would be found only by another mortal, during this battle for Ilium. But the work of the Fates has come undone."

Priam sat back in his throne. "So Hector was fated to kill fleet-footed Achilles after all," he murmured. "If we had not opened this war with the gods, that destiny would have come about."

Penthesilea shook her head. "No, not Hector. Another mortal—a

Trojan—would have taken Achilles' life after he had killed Hector. One of the Muses had learned this from a slave they called a scholic, who knew the future."

"A seer," said Priam. "Like our esteemed Helenus or the Achaeans' prophet Calchas."

The Amazon shook her golden curls again. "No, the scholics did not see the future—somehow, they came from the future. But they are all dead now, according to Athena. But Achilles' Fate awaits. And I will fulfill it."

"When?" said old Priam, obviously turning over all the ramifications of this in his mind. He had not been king of the grandest city on earth for more than five decades for no reason, to no purpose. His son, Hector, was blood ally to Achilles now, but Hector was not king. Hector was Ilium's noblest warrior, but while he might have once carried the fate of the city and its inhabitants in his sword arm, he had never imagined it in his mind. This was Priam's work.

"When?" asked Priam again. "How soon can you and your twelve Amazon warriors kill Achilles?"

"Today," promised Penthesilea. "As I promised. Before the sun sets on either Ilium or Olympos visible through that hole in the air we passed on the way in."

"What do you require, daughter? Weapons? Gold? Riches?"

"Only your blessing, Noble Priam. And food. And a couch for my women and me, for a short nap before we bathe, adorn ourselves again in armor, and go out to end this war with the gods."

Priam clapped his hands. Deiphobus, the many guards, his courtiers, and the twelve Amazon women stepped back into earshot.

He ordered fine food be brought to these women, then soft couches made available for their short sleep, then warm baths to be drawn and slave women to be ready to apply oils and unguents after their baths, and massages, and finally that the thirteen women's horses be fed and combed and resaddled when Penthesilea was ready to go forth to do battle that afternoon.

Penthesilea was smiling and confident when she led her twelve companions out of the royal hall.

10

Quantum teleportation through Planck space—a term the goddess Hera did not know—was supposed to be instantaneous, but in Planck space, such terms had little meaning. Transit through such interstices in the weave of space-time left trails, and the gods and goddesses, thanks to the nanomemes and cellular re-engineering that was part of their creation, knew how to follow such trails as effortlessly as a hunter, as easily as the goddess Artemis would track a stag through the forest.

Hera followed Zeus's winding trail through Planck nothing, knowing only that it was not one of the regular string channels between Olympos and Ilium or Mount Ida. It was somewhere else on the ancient earth of Ilium.

She QT'd into existence in a large hall that Athena knew well. A giant quiver of arrows and the outline of a giant bow was painted on one wall and there was a long, low table set with dozens of fine goblets, serving bowls, and golden plates.

Zeus looked up in surprise from where he was sitting at the table—he had reduced his size to a mere seven feet here in this human hall—and idly scratching behind the ears of a gray-muzzled dog.

"My Lord," said Hera. "Are you going to cut that dog's head off as well?"

Zeus did not smile. "I should," he rumbled. "As a mercy to it." His brow was still furrowed. "Do you recognize this place and this dog, wife?"

"Yes. It is Odysseus' home, on rugged Ithaca. The dog is named Argus, and was bred by the younger Odysseus shortly before he left for Troy. He trained the pup."

"And it waits for him still," said Zeus. "But now Penelope is gone, and Telemachus, and even the suitors who had just now begun to gather like carrion crows in Odysseus' home, seeking Penelope's hand and lands and wealth, have mysteriously disappeared along with Penelope, Telemachus, and all other mortals save for those few thousand at Troy. There is no one to feed this mutt."

Hera shrugged. "You could send it to Ilium and let it dine on Dionysos, your wastrel son."

Zeus shook his head. "Why are you so harsh with me, wife? And why have you followed me here when I want to be alone to ponder this strange theft of all the world's people?"

Hera stepped closer to the white-bearded God of Gods. She feared his wrath—of all the gods and mortals, only Zeus could destroy her. She feared for what she was about to do, but she was resolved to do it.

"Dread majesty, Son of Kronos, I stopped by only to say goodbye for a few sols. I did not want to leave our last discussion on its note of discord." She stepped even closer and covertly touched Aphrodite's breastband tucked under her right breast. Hera could feel the flow of sexual energy filling the room; sense the pheromones flowing from her.

"Where are you going for several sols when both Olympos and the war for Troy are in such turmoil, wife?" grumbled Zeus. But his nostrils flared and he looked up at her with a new interest, ignoring Argus the dog.

"With Nyx's help, I am off to the ends of this empty earth to visit Okeanos and Mother Tethys, who prefer this world to our cold Mars, as well you know, husband." She took three steps closer so that she was almost within touching distance of Zeus.

"Why visit them now, Hera? They've done well enough without you in the centuries since we tamed the Red World and inhabited Olympos."

"I'm hoping to end their endless feud," said Hera in her guileful way. "For too long have they held back from each other, hesitated to make love because of the anger in their hearts. I wanted to tell you where I would be so that you would not flare in godly anger at me, should you think I'd gone in secret to Okeanos' deep, flowing halls."

Zeus stood. Hera could sense the excitement stirring in him. Only the folds of his god-robe concealed his lust.

"Why hurry, Hera?" Zeus's eyes were devouring her now. His look made Hera remember the feel of her brother-husband-lover's tongue and hands upon her softest places.

"Why tarry, husband?"

"Going to see Okeanos and Tethys is a journey you can take tomorrow or the day after tomorrow or never," said Zeus, stepping toward Hera. "Today, here, we can lose ourselves in love! Come, wife . . ."

Zeus swept all the goblets, cutlery, and spoiled food from the long table with a blast of invisible force from his raised hand. He ripped a giant tapestry from the wall and tossed it onto the rough-plank table.

Hera took a step back and touched her breast as if she were going to QT away. "What are you saying, Lord Zeus? You want to make love here? In Odysseus' and Penelope's abandoned home, with that dog watching? Who is to say that all the gods will not be watching us through their pools and viewers and holowalls? If love is your pleasure, wait until I return from Okeanos' watery halls and we will make love in my own bedroom, made private by Hephaestus's craft . . ."

"No!" roared Zeus. He was growing in more ways than one now, his gray-curled head brushing the ceiling. "Don't worry about prying eyes. I will make a golden cloud so dense around the isle of Ithaca and Odysseus' home that the sharpest eyes in the universe, neither god nor mortal, not even Prospero or Setebos, could pierce the mist and see us while we're making love. Take your clothes off!"

Zeus waved his blunt-fingered hand again and the entire house vibrated with the energy of the surrounding forcefield and concealing golden cloud. The dog, Argus, ran from the room, his hair standing on end from the energies being unleashed.

Zeus grabbed Hera by the wrist and pulled her closer with his right hand, even while pulling her gown down away from her breasts with his free hand. Aphrodite's breastband fell away with the gown Athena had made for Hera, but it did not matter—the air was so thick with lust and pheromones that the queen thought she could swim in it.

Zeus lifted her with one arm and tossed her back on the tapestry-covered table. It was a good thing, thought Hera, that Odysseus had made his long dining table of thick, solid planks pulled from the deck of a ship run aground on Ithaca's treacherous rocks. He pulled the gown away from her legs, leaving her naked. Then he stepped out of his own robes.

As many times as Hera had seen her husband's divine phallus standing erect, it never ceased to stop her breath in her throat. All of the male gods were . . . well, *gods* . . . but in their almost-forgotten Transformation to Olympians, Zeus had saved the most impressive attributes for himself. This purple-knobbed staff now pressing between her pale knees was the only scepter this King of the Gods would ever need to create awe among mortals or envy among his fellow gods, and although Hera thought that he showed it too frequently—his lust was the equal of his size and virility—she still thought of this part of her Dread Majesty as hers alone.

But, at risk of bruising or worse, Hera kept her naked knees and thighs tight closed.

"You want me, husband?"

Zeus was breathing through his mouth. His eyes were wild. "I want you, wife. Never has such a lust for goddess or mortal woman flooded my pounding heart and prick and overwhelmed me so. Open your legs!"

"Never?" asked Hera, keeping her legs closed. "Not even when you bedded Ixion's wife, who bore you Pirithous, rival to all the gods in wisdom and . . ."

"Not even then, with Ixion's wife of the blue-veined breasts," gasped Zeus. He forced her knees wide and stepped between her white thighs, his phallus reaching to her pale, firm belly and vibrating with lust.

"Not even when you loved Ascrisius' daughter Danae?" asked Hera.

"Not even with her," said Zeus, leaning far forward to suckle at Hera's raised nipples, first the left, then the right. His hand moved between her legs. She was wet—from the breastband's work and from her own eagerness. "Although, by all the gods," he added, "Danae's ankles alone could make a man come!"

"It must have more than once with you, My Lord," gasped Hera as Zeus set his broad palm beneath her buttocks and lifted her closer. The broad, hot head of his scepter was batting at her thighs now, making them moist with his own anticipating wetness. "For she bore you a paragon of men."

Zeus was so excited that he could not find entry, but lunged around her warmth like a boy in his first time with a woman. When he released her breast with his left hand to guide himself home, Hera seized his wrist.

"Do you want me more than you wanted Europa, Phoenix' daughter?" she whispered urgently.

"More than Europa, yes," breathed Zeus. He grabbed her hand and set it on himself. She squeezed, but did not guide. Not yet.

"Do you want to lie with me more than you did with Semele, Dionysos' irresistible mother?"

"More than Semele, yes. Yes." He set her hand more firmly around himself and lunged, but he was so engorged that it was more a ram's head shoving than a penetration. Hera was pushed two feet up the table. He pulled her back. "And more than Alcmene in Thebes," he gasped, "although my seed that day brought invincible Herakles into the world."

"Do you want me more than you wanted fair-haired Demeter when . . ."

"Yes, yes, god damn it, more than Demeter." He pushed Hera's legs further apart and, with only his right palm, lifted her backside a foot off the table. She could not help opening for him now.

"Do you want me more than you wanted Leda on the day you took the shape of a swan to couple with her while you beat her down and held her with your great swan's wings and entered her with your great swan's . . ."

"Yes, yes," gasped Zeus. "Shut up, please."

He entered her then. Opening her like some great ram-headed battering engine would open the Scaean Gates had the Greeks ever won entrance to Ilium.

In the next twenty minutes, Hera almost swooned twice. Zeus was passionate, but not quick. He took his pleasure urgently, but waited for its climax with all the miserliness of a hedonist ascetic. The second time, Hera felt consciousness sliding away under the oiled and sweating pounding—the table shook and almost upended although it was thirty feet long, the chairs and couches tumbled away, dust fell from the ceiling, Odysseus' ancient home almost came down around them—and Hera thought, *This will not do—I must be conscious when Zeus climaxes or all my scheming is for naught.*

She forced herself to stay attentive even after four orgasms of her own. Odysseus' great quiver of arrows fell from the wall, scattering barbed and possibly poisoned arrows across tile in the last seconds of Zeus's heavy pounding. He had to hold Hera in place with one hand under her, pressing up so fiercely that she heard her divine hipbones creak, while his other gripped her shoulder, keeping her from sliding far down the quivering, straining table.

Then he erupted inside her. Hera did scream then and swooned for a few seconds, despite herself.

When her eyelids flickered opened, she felt his great weight upon her—he'd grown to fifteen feet in his involuntary last seconds of passion—his beard scratched against her breast, the top of his head—hair soaked with sweat—lay against her cheek.

Hera raised her treacherous finger with the injection ampule set in the false nail by crafty Hephaestus. Stroking his neck curls with her cool hand, she bent the nail back and activated the injector—there was barely a hiss, unheard over his ragged breathing and the pounding of both their divine hearts.

The drug was called Absolute Sleep and it lived up to its name within microseconds.

Almost instantly, Zeus was snoring and slobbering against her rubbed-red chest.

It took all of Hera's divine strength to shove him off, to remove his softening member from her folds, to slide out from under him.

Her unique, Athena-made gown was a torn mess. So was she, Hera realized. Bruised and scratched and pummeled in every muscle, outside and in. The divine seed from the King of the Gods ran down her thigh as she stood. Hera mopped it away with the tatters of her ruined gown.

Retrieving Aphrodite's breastband from the torn silk, Hera went into Odysseus' wife Penelope's dressing room, next to the bedroom where their great marriage bed had one post made of a living olive tree and a frame inlaid with gold, silver, and ivory, with thongs of oxhide dyed crimson stretched end to end to hold soft fleeces and rich coverlets. From camphor-lined trunks set by Penelope's bath, Hera pulled gown after gown—Odysseus' wife had been about her size, and the goddess could morph her shape enough to finish the tailoring—finally choosing a peach-colored silk shift with an embroidered band that would hold her bruised breasts high. But before dressing, Hera made her bath as best she could from the copper kettles of cold water set out days or weeks earlier for a hot bath Penelope never had.

Later, emerging into the dining hall again, dressed, walking gingerly, Hera stared at the great, bronzed, naked hulk snoring face-down on the long table. *Could I kill him now?* she wondered. It was not the first time—or the thousandth—that the queen had held this thought while looking at and listening to her snoring lord. She knew she was not alone in the wondering. How many wives—goddess and mortal woman, long dead and yet unborn—had felt this thought slipping across their minds like a cloud shadow over rocky ground? *If I could kill him, would I kill him? If it were possible, would I act now?*

Instead, Hera prepared to quantum teleport to the plains of Ilium. So far, the plot was unfolding according to plan. Poseidon, the Earth-Shaker, should be maneuvering Agamemnon and Menelaus into action at any minute. Within hours, if not sooner, Achilles might be dead—slain by the hands of a mere woman, although Amazon, his heel pierced by poison spearpoint—and Hector isolated. And if Achilles killed the woman who attacked him, Athena and Hera had plans for him still. The mortal revolt would be over by the time Zeus awoke, if Hera ever allowed him to awake at all—Absolute Sleep needed an antidote or it would work until these high walls of Odysseus' home would tumble down in rot. Or Hera might wake Zeus soon, if her goals were fulfilled earlier than planned, and the Lord of Gods would not even be aware that he had been felled by drugs rather than mere lust and a need to sleep. Whenever she chose to waken her husband, the war between gods and men would be over, the Trojan War resumed, that status quo restored, the *fait* chosen by Hera and her co-conspirators most decidedly *accompli*.

Turning her back on the sleeping Son of Kronos, Hera walked from Odysseus' house—for no one, not even a queen, could QT through the concealing forcefield Zeus had set around it—pressed through the watery wall of energy like an infant fighting from its caul, and teleported triumphantly back to Troy.

11

Hockenberry didn't recognize any of the moravecs who met him in the blue bubble inside Stickney Crater on the moon Phobos. At first, when the chair forcefield clicked off and left him exposed to the elements, he'd panicked and held his breath for a few seconds—still thinking he was in hard vacuum—but then he felt the air pressure against his skin and the comfortable temperature, so he'd taken a ragged breath just as little Mahnmut was introducing him to the taller moravecs who'd come forward like an official delegation. It was embarrassing, actually. Then Mahnmut had left and Hockenberry was on his own with these strange organic machines.

"Welcome, Dr. Hockenberry," said the closest of the five moravecs facing him. "I trust your trip up from Mars was uneventful."

For a second, Hockenberry felt a stab of something almost like nausea at hearing someone call him "Doctor." Except for Mahnmut using the honorific, it had been a long time since . . . no, it had been *never* in this second life, unless his scholic friend Nightenhelser had used his title jokingly once or twice in the past decade.

"Thank you, yes . . . I mean . . . I'm sorry, I didn't catch all your names," said Hockenberry. "I apologize. I was . . . distracted." *Thinking I was going to die when the chair deserted me,* thought Hockenberry.

The short moravec nodded. "I don't doubt," it said. "There's a lot of activity in this bubble and the atmosphere certainly conveys the noise."

That it did. And that there was. The huge blue bubble, covering at least two or three acres—Hockenberry was always poor at judging sizes and distances, a failure due to not playing sports, he'd always thought—was filled with gantry-structures, banks of machines larger than most buildings in his old stomping grounds of Bloomington, Indiana, pulsating organic blobs that looked like runaway blancmanges the size of tennis courts, hundreds of moravecs—all busy on one task or another—and floating globes shedding light and spitting out laser beams that cut and welded and melted and moved on. The only thing that looked even remotely familiar in the huge space, although completely out of place, was a round rosewood table sitting about thirty feet away. It was surrounded by six stools of varying heights.

"My name is Asteague/Che," said the small moravec. "I'm Europan, like your friend Mahnmut."

"European?" Hockenberry repeated stupidly. He'd been to France once on vacation and once to Athens for a classics conference, and while the men and women in both places had been . . . different . . . none of them resembled this Asteague/Che: taller than Mahnmut, at least four feet tall, and more humanoid—especially around the hands—but still covered with the same plasticky-metallic material as Mahnmut, although Asteague/Che was mostly a brilliant, slick yellow. The moravec reminded Hockenberry of a slick yellow-rubber raincoat he'd had and loved when he was a kid.

"Europa," said Asteague/Che with no hint of impatience. "The icy, watery moon of Jupiter. Mahnmut's home. And mine."

"Of course," said Hockenberry. He was blushing and knowing he was blushing made him blush again. "Sorry. Of course. I knew Mahnmut was from some moon out there. Sorry."

"My title . . . although 'title' is too formal and ostentatious a word, perhaps 'job function' would be a more appropriate translation," continued Asteague/Che, "is Prime Integrator for the Five Moons Consortium."

Hockenberry bowed slightly, realizing that he was in the presence of a politician. Or at least a top bureaucrat. He had no clue as to what the other four moons might be named. He'd heard of Europa in his other life and he seemed to recall that they were finding a new Jovian moon every few weeks—or so it seemed—back at the end of the Twentieth Century, beginning of the Twenty-first—but the names escaped him. Maybe they hadn't been named by the time he'd died, he couldn't remember. Also, Hockenberry had always preferred Greek over Latin and thought that the solar system's largest planet should have been called Zeus, not Jupiter . . . although in current circumstances that might be confusing.

"Allow me to reintroduce my colleagues," said Asteague/Che.

The moravec's voice had been reminding Hockenberry of someone and now he realized who—the movie actor James Mason.

"The tall gentleman to my right is General Beh bin Adee, commander of the Asteroid Belt contingent of combat moravecs."

"Dr. Hockenberry," said General Beh bin Adee. "A pleasure to meet you at last." The tall figure did not offer his hand to shake, since he had no hand—only barbed pincers with a myriad of fine-motor manipulators.

Gentleman, thought Hockenberry. *Rockvec.* In the last eight months, he'd seen thousands of the soldier rockvecs on both the plains of Ilium and the surface of Mars around Olympos—always tall, about two meters as this one was, always black, as the general was, and always a mass of barbs, hooks, chitinous ridges, and sharp serrations. *They obviously don't breed them . . . or build them . . . for beauty in the Asteroid Belt*, thought Hockenberry.

"My pleasure, General . . . Beh bin Adee," he said aloud, and bowed slightly.

"To my left," continued Prime Integrator Asteague/Che, "is Integrator Cho Li from the moon Callisto."

"Welcome to Phobos, Dr. Hockenberry," said Cho Li in a voice so soft it sounded absolutely feminine. *Do moravecs have genders?* wondered Hockenberry. He'd always thought of Mahnmut and Orphu as male robots—and there was no doubt about the testosteronic attitudes of the rockvec troopers. But these creations had distinct personalities, so why not genders?

"Integrator Cho Li," repeated Hockenberry and bowed again. The Callistan—Callistoid? Callistonian?—was smaller than Asteague/Che but more massive and far less humanoid. Less humanoid even than the absent Mahnmut. What disconcerted Hockenberry a bit were the glimpses of what looked to be raw, pink flesh between panels of plastic and steel. If Quasimodo—the Hunchback of Notre Dame—had been assembled out of bits of flesh and used car parts, with boneless arms, a wandering multitude of eyes in assorted sizes, and a narrow maw that looked like a mail slit, and then miniaturized—he might have been a sibling of Integrator Cho Li. Because of the names, Hockenberry wondered if these Callistoidonal moravecs had been designed by the Chinese.

"Behind Cho Li is Suma IV," said Asteague/Che in its, his, smooth, James Mason voice. "Suma IV is from the moon Ganymede."

Suma IV was very human in height and proportion, but not so human in appearance. Somewhere over six feet tall, the Ganymedan had properly proportioned arms and legs, a waist, a flat chest, and the proper number of fingers—all sheathed in a fluid, grayish, oil-like coating that Hockenberry had once heard Mahnmut refer to as buckycarbon. But that had been on the hull of a hornet. Poured over a person . . . or a person-shaped moravec . . . the effect was disconcerting.

Even more disconcerting were this moravec's oversized eyes with their hundreds upon hundreds of shining facets. Hockenberry had to wonder if Suma IV or his ilk had landed on Earth in his day . . . say at Roswell, New Mexico? Did Suma IV have some cousin on ice in Area 51?

No, he reminded himself, *these creatures aren't aliens. They're robotic-organic entities that human beings designed and built and scattered in the solar system. Centuries and centuries after I died.*

"How do you do, Suma IV," said Hockenberry.

"A pleasure to make your acquaintance, Dr. Hockenberry," said the tall Ganymedan moravec. No James-Masony or little-girl tones here . . . the shiny black figure with the glittering fly's eyes had a voice that sounded like boys pelting a hollow boiler with cinders.

"May I introduce our last representative from the Consortium," said Asteague/Che. "Retrograde Sinopessen from Amalthea."

"Retrograde Sinopessen?" repeated Hockenberry, stifling a sudden urge to laugh until he wept. He wanted to go lie down, take a nap, and wake up in his study in the old white house near Indiana University.

"Retrograde Sinopessen, yes," said Asteague/Che, nodding.

The thrice-identified moravec skittered forward on silver-spider legs. Hockenberry observed that Mr. Sinopessen was about the size of a Lionel train transformer, although much shinier in a polished-aluminum sort of way, and his eight legs were so thin as to be almost invisible. Eyes or diodes or tiny little lights glowed at various points on and in the box.

"A pleasure, Dr. Hockenberry," said the shiny little box in a voice so deep it rivaled Orphu of Io's near-subsonic rumble. "I've read all of your books and papers. All that we have in our archives, at least. They're brilliant. It's an honor to meet you in person."

"Thank you," Hockenberry said stupidly. He looked at the five moravecs, at the hundreds more working on other incomprehensible machines in the huge pressurized bubble, looked back at Asteague/Che, and said, "So now what?"

"Why don't we sit down around that table and discuss this imminent expedition to Earth and your possible participation in it," suggested the Europan Prime Integrator of the Five Moons Consortium.

"Sure," said Thomas Hockenberry. "Why not?"

12

Helen was alone and unarmed when Menelaus finally cornered her.

The day after Paris's funeral started bizarrely and grew only more bizarre as the day wore on. There was a smell of fear and apocalypse on the winter wind.

Early that morning, even as Hector was bearing his brother's bones to their barrow, Helen was summoned by Andromache's messenger. Hector's wife and a female servant, a slave from the isle of Lesbos, her tongue torn out many years earlier, now sworn to serve the secret society once known as the Trojan Women, were holding wild-eyed Cassandra prisoner in Andromache's secret apartments near the Scaean Gates.

"What's this?" asked Helen as she came into the apartment. Cassandra did not know about this house. Cassandra was supposed to never know about this house. Now Priam's daughter, the mad prophetess, sat sunk-shouldered on a wooden couch. The servant, whose slave name was Hypsipyle after Euneus' famous mother by Jason, held a long-bladed knife in her tattooed hand.

"She knows," said Andromache. Hector's wife sounded tired, as if she had been awake all night. "She knows about Astyanax."

"How?"

It was Cassandra who replied, without lifting her head. "I saw it in one of my trances."

Helen sighed. There had been seven of them at the height of their conspiracy—Andromache, Hector's wife, and her mother-in-law, Hecuba, Priam's queen, had begun the planning. Then Theano had joined the group—the horseman Antenor's wife, but also high priestess in Athena's temple. Then Hecuba's daughter, Laodice, was brought into the secret circle. Those four had trusted Helen with their secret and their purpose—to end the war, to save their husbands' lives, to save their children's lives, to save themselves from enslavement by the Achaeans.

Helen had been honored to become one of the secret Trojan Women—no Trojan, she knew, but only the source of the true Trojan Women's sorrows—and like Hecuba, Andromache, Theano, and Laodice, she had worked for years to find a third way—an end to the war with honor, but without such a terrible price.

They'd had no choice but to include Cassandra, Priam's prettiest but maddest daughter, in their plotting. The young woman had been given the gift of second sight by Apollo, and they needed her visions if they were to plan and plot. Besides, Cassandra had already found them out in one of her mad trances—babbling already about the Trojan Women and their secret meetings in the vault beneath Athena's temple—so they included her in order to silence her.

The seventh and final and oldest Trojan Woman was Herophile, "beloved of Hera," the oldest and wisest sibyl and priestess of Apollo Smintheus. As a sibyl, Herophile often interpreted Cassandra's wild dreams more accurately than Cassandra could.

So when Achilles had overthrown Agamemnon, the fleet-footed mankiller claiming that Pallas Athena herself had murdered his best friend, Patroclus, and then leading the Achaeans against the gods themselves in violent war, the Trojan Women had seen their chance. Excluding Cassandra from their planning—for the prophetess was too unstable in those final days before her prophesied fall of Troy—they had carried out the murder of Andromache's nurse and that nurse's child, Andromache then claiming—shouting, sobbing hysterically—that it had been Pallas Athena and the goddess Aphrodite who had slaughtered young Astyanax, Hector's child.

Hector, like Achilles before him, had gone mad with grief and anger. The Trojan War ended. The War with the Gods began. The Achaeans and Trojans marched through the Hole to besiege Olympos with their new allies, the minor-gods, the moravecs.

And in that first day of bombing from the gods—before the moravecs protected Ilium with their forcefields—Hecuba had died. And her daughter Laodice. And Theano, Athena's most beloved priestess.

Three of the seven Trojan Women dead that first day of the war they had brought about. Then hundreds of other warriors and civilians dear to them.

Now another? thought Helen, her heart sinking into some region of sorrow beneath sorrow. To Andromache, she asked, "Are you going to kill Cassandra?"

Hector's wife turned her cold gaze in Helen's direction. "No," she said at last, "I'm going to show her Scamandrius, my Astyanax."

Menelaus had no problem getting into the city in his clumsy disguise of boar-tusk helmet and lion-skin robe. He pushed in past the gate guards along with scores of other barbarians, Trojan allies all, after Paris's funeral procession and just before the much-heralded arrival of the Amazon women.

It was still early. He avoided the area around Priam's bombed-out palace since he knew that Hector and his captains would be there interring Paris's bones and too many of those Trojan heroes could recognize the boar-tusk helmet or Diomedes' lion skin. Wending his way past the bustling marketplace and through alleys, he came out by the small square in front of Paris's palace—King Priam's temporary quarters and still home to Helen. There were elite guards at the door, of course, and more on the walls and every terrace. Odysseus had once told him which set-back terrace was Helen's, and Menelaus watched those billowing curtains with a terrible intensity, but his wife did not appear. There were two spearmen there in glinting bronze, which suggested that Helen was not at home this morning—she had never allowed bodyguards in her private apartments back in their more modest palace in Lacedaemon.

There was a wine and cheese shop across the square from Paris's palace, rough tables set out into the sunny alley, and Menelaus broke his fast there, paying in the Trojan gold pieces he'd had the foresight to grab from Agamemnon's trunk while he was dressing. He tarried there for hours—slipping more triangular coins to the shopkeeper to keep him happy during his tarrying—and listened to the gab and gossip from crowds in the square and townsfolk at adjoining benches.

"Is her ladyship in today?" one old crone asked another.

"Not since this morning. My Phoebe said that her chinks had gone and left at first light, yes, but not to honor her hubby's bones bein' put in all right and proper, no."

"What then?" cackled the more toothless of the two old hags gumming their cheese. The old woman leaned closer as if ready to receive whispers, but the other old hag—as deaf as the first—fairly bellowed her response.

"Rumor has it that old priapic Priam insists that her Helenship—poxy foreign bitch that she is—marry his other son—not one of the army of Priam bastards roundabouts, you can't throw a dog-puking rock without hitting a bastard of Priam's, but that fat, stupid, rightful son, Deiphobus—and wed within forty-eight hours of Paris's barbecue party."

"Soon then."

"Aye, soon. Today, perhaps. Deiphobus has been waiting his turn in line to boink the poxy doxy since the week Paris dragged her bumpy ass here—gods curse the day—so he's probably well into the rites of Dionysos, if not of marriage, even as we speak, sister."

The old hags cackled up bits of cheese and bread.

Menelaus slammed up from his table and strode the streets, carrying his spear in his left hand, his right hand on the hilt of his sword.

Deiphobus? Where does Deiphobus live?

It had been easier before the War with the Gods began. All of Priam's unmarried sons and daughters—some in the fifties now—had lived in the huge palace in the center of the city—the Achaeans had carefully planned to carry the slaughter there first after breaching the Trojan walls—but that one lucky bomb on the first day of the new war had scattered the princes and their sisters to equally plush living quarters all over the huge city.

Thus, an hour after leaving the cheese shop, Menelaus was still striding the crowded streets when the Amazon Penthesilea and her dozen fighting women rode past while the crowds went wild.

Menelaus had to step back or be struck by the lead Amazon's warhorse. Her greaved leg almost brushed his cloak. She never looked down or to the side.

Menelaus was struck so hard by Penthesilea's beauty that he almost sat down then and there on the horse-dunged cobblestones. By Zeus, what frail beauty wrapped in such gorgeous, gleaming war armor! Those eyes! Menelaus—who'd never gone to war against or alongside the Amazon tribe—had never seen anything like it.

As if in a seer's trance, he stumbled along behind the procession, following the crowds and the Amazons back to Paris's palace. There the Amazon was greeted by Deiphobus, with no Helen in the retinue, so it seemed like the cheese hags had been wrong. At least about Helen's current whereabouts.

Watching the door where Penthesilea had disappeared, Menelaus, like some lovestruck teenage shepherd boy, finally pulled himself away and began wandering the streets again. It was almost noon. He knew he had little time—Agamemnon had planned to start the uprising against Achilles' rule by midday and have the battles fought by nightfall—and he recognized for the first time what a huge city Ilium was. What chance did he have of stumbling across Helen here in time to act? Almost none, he realized, since at first cry of battle amidst the Argive ranks, the great Scaean Gates would be closed and the guard on the walls doubled. Menelaus would be trapped.

He was headed for the Scaean Gates, filled with the triple nausea of failure, hatred, and love, almost running, half happy he had not found her and sick to his soul that he had not found and killed her, when he came upon a sort of riot near the gate.

He watched for a bit, seemingly unable to tear himself away from the spectacle, although the spectacle threatened to engulf him as it spiraled out of hand. Old women nearby babbled the tale.

It seemed the women of Troy had been somehow inspired by the mere arrival of Penthesilea and her egg-carton of Amazons—all sleeping now, presumably, on Priam's softest couches—word had leaked out of the temporary palace of Penthesilea's vow to kill Achilles—and Ajax, too, if she had the time, and any other Achaean captain who got in her way, since her Amazon eyes were full of business. This had stirred something dormant but certainly not passive in the women of Troy (as opposed to the surviving few Trojan Women), and they had rushed out into the street, to the walls, onto the very battlements, where the confused guards had given way to the screaming wives and daughters and sisters and mothers.

Then it seemed that a woman named Hippodamia, not the well-known wife of Pirithous, but rather the wife of Tisiphonus—such an unimportant Trojan captain that Menelaus had never faced him on the field nor heard of him around the campfire—now this Hippodamia was whipping the women of Troy into a killing frenzy with her shouted oratory. Menelaus had paused to blend into the crowd but stayed to listen and watch.

"Sisters!" screamed Hippodamia, a thick-armed and heavy-hipped woman not without appeal. Her tied-back hair had come loose and vibrated around her shoulders as she shouted and gestured. "Why haven't we been fighting alongside our men? Why have we wept about the fate of Ilium—wailed about the fate of our children—yet done nothing to change that fate? Are we so much weaker than the beardless boys of Troy who, in this past year, have gone out to die for their city? Are we not as supple and as serious as our sons?"

The crowd of women roared.

"We share food, light, air, and our beds with the men of our city," shouted full-hipped Hippodamia, "why have we failed to share their fates in combat? Are we so weak?"

"No!" roared a thousand women of Troy from the walls.

"Is there anyone here, any woman, who has not lost a husband, a brother, a father, a son, a kinsman in this war with the Achaeans?"

"No!"

"Does any among us doubt what would be our fate, as women, should the Achaeans have won this war?"

"No!"

"So let us not tarry and loiter here a moment longer," shouted Hippodamia above the roar. "The Amazon queen has vowed to kill Achilles before the sun sets today, and she has come from afar to fight for a city that is not her home. Can we vow less, do less, for our home, for our men, for our children, and for our own lives and futures?"

"No!" This time the roar went on and on and women began running from the square, jumping from the steps to the wall, some almost trampling Menelaus in their eagerness.

"Arm yourselves!" screamed Hippodamia. "Toss aside your weavings and your wools, leave your looms, don armor, gird yourselves, meet me outside these walls!"

The men on the walls and watching, men who had been leering and laughing during the first part of Tisiphonus' wife's tirade, slunk back into doorways and alleys now, getting out of the way of the rushing mob. Menelaus did the same.

He had just turned to leave, heading for the nearby Scaean Gate— still open, thank the gods—when he saw Helen standing on a nearby corner. She was looking the other way and did not see him. He watched her kiss two women goodbye and begin walking up the street. Alone.

Menelaus stopped, took a breath, touched the hilt of his sword, turned, and followed her.

*   *   *

"Theano stopped this madness," said Cassandra. "Theano spoke to the crowd and brought this mob of women to its senses."

"Theano is dead eight months and more," said Andromache in cold tones.

"In the other now," said Cassandra in that maddening monotone she assumed when half in trance. "In the other future. Theano stopped this. All heeded the chief priestess of Athena's Temple."

"Well, Theano is worm meat. Dead as Prince Paris's pizzle," said Helen. "No one stopped this mob."

Women were already returning to the square and filing out through the gate in a parody of military order. They had obviously scattered to their homes and girded themselves in whatever odd armor they could find around the house—a father's dull bronze helmet, its crest wilted or missing horsehair, a brother's cast-off shield, a husband's or son's spear or sword. All the armor was too large, the spears too heavy, and most of the women looked like children playing dress-up as they rattled and clank-banged by.

"This is madness," whispered Andromache. "Madness."

"Everything since the death of Achilles' friend Patroclus has been mere madness," said Cassandra, her pale eyes bright as with fever and their own madness. "Untrue. False. Unfirm."

For more than two hours in Andromache's sun-filled top-floor apartment by the wall, the women had spent time with eighteen-month-old Scamandrius, the "god-murdered" child the whole city had mourned, the babe for whom Hector had gone to war with all the Olympian gods to avenge. Scamandrius—Astyanax, "Lord of the City"—was healthy enough under the watchful eye of his new nurse, while at the door, loyal Cicilian guards brought from fallen Thebe stood twenty-four-hour watch. These men had tried to die for Andromache's fallen father, King Eetion, killed by Achilles when the city fell, and, spared not by their own choice but by Achilles' whims, now lived only for Eetion's daughter and her hidden son.

The babe, babbling words and toddling up a mile these days, recognized his Aunt Cassandra after all these months, almost half his short life, and came rushing toward her with his arms outspread.

Cassandra accepted the hug, returned it, wept, and for almost two hours the three Trojan Women and the two slaves—one a wet nurse, the other a Lesbos killer—talked and played with the little boy and talked more when he was laid down to nap.

"You see why you must not speak these trance words aloud again,"

Andromache said softly after the visit was done. "If the wrong ear hears them—if any ears other than ours hear this hidden truth—Scamandrius will die just as you once prophesied—thrown down from the highest point on the walls, his brains dashed out on the rocks."

Cassandra went whiter than her usual white and wept again briefly. "I will learn how to hold my tongue," she said at last, "even when I have no control over it. Your ever-watching servant will see to that." She nodded toward the expressionless Hypsipyle.

Then they had heard the growing commotion and women's screams from the nearby wall and city square and had gone out together, their veils pulled down, to see what all the fuss was about.

Several times during Hippodamia's harangue, Helen was tempted to intervene. She realized, after it was too late—when the women had scattered by the hundreds to their homes to fetch armor and weapons, fritting to and fro like a pack of hysterical bees—that Cassandra was right. Theano, their old friend, the high priestess of the still-revered Temple of Athena, would have stopped this nonsense. With her temple-trained voice, Theano would have boomed out "What folly!" and gotten the attention of the crowd and sobered the women with her words. Theano would have explained that this Penthesilea—who had done nothing for Troy yet except make promises to its aging king and sleep—was the daughter of the war-god. Were any of these women shouting in this city square daughters of a god? Could any claim Ares as their father?

What's more, Helen was sure Theano would have pointed out to the suddenly quieting crowd, the Greeks had not battled for almost ten years, equaling and sometimes besting such heroes as Hector, to submit this day to untrained female rabble. Unless you've secretly learned how to handle horses, manhandle chariots, cast spears half a league, deflect violent sword thrusts with your shield, and are prepared to separate men's screaming heads from their sturdy bodies, go home—Theano would have said all this, Helen was sure—trade in your borrowed spears for spindles and let your men protect you and decide the outcome of their men's war. And the mob would have dispersed.

But Theano was not there. Theano was—in Helen's sensitive phrase—as dead as Prince Paris's pizzle.

So the mobs of half-armored women marched out to war, heading for the Hole, going to the foothills of Olympos, sure they would slay Achilles even before the Amazon Penthesilea awoke from her beauty nap. Hippodamia rushed late through the Scaean Gates, her borrowed armor askew—it looked to be from some previous age, as from the time of the War with the Centaurs—its bronze breastplates poorly tied and clattering and banging against her large bosoms. The mob-arouser had lost control of her mob. Like all politicians, she was rushing—and fail-ing—to get ahead of the parade.

Helen and Andromache and Cassandra—with the killer-slave Hyp-sipyle already watching the red-eyed prophetess—had kissed goodbye and Helen had gone her way, knowing that Priam wanted to settle her marriage-date with gross Deiphobus before this day was out.

But on her way back to the palace she had shared with Paris, Helen stepped away from the mobs and went into Athena's Temple. The place was empty of course—these days few openly worshiped the goddess who had reportedly killed Astyanax and plunged the world of mortals into war with the Olympians—and Helen paused to step into the dark and incense-rich space, breathing in the calm, and to look up at the huge golden statue of the goddess.

"Helen."

For an instant, Helen of Troy was sure the goddess had spoken in her former husband's voice. Then she slowly turned.

"Helen."

Menelaus was there not ten feet from her, his legs wide, sandals firmly planted on the dark marble floor. Even by only the flickering of the vestal votive candles, Helen could see his red beard, his glowering aspect, the sword in his right hand, and a boar-tusk helmet held loose in his left hand.

"Helen."

It was as if this was all the cuckolded king and warrior could say now that his moment of vengeance was at hand.

Helen considered running and knew it would do no good. She could never get past Menelaus to the street, and her husband had always been one of the fleetest runners in all Lacedaemon. They had always joked that when they had a son, he would be too fast for either of them to catch for a spanking. They had never had a son.

"Helen."

Helen had thought she'd heard every sort of male groan—from or-gasm to death and everything in between—but she'd never heard such a surrender to pain from a man before. Certainly not sobbed out in one familiar but totally alien word like this.

"Helen."

Menelaus walked quickly forward, raising his sword as he came.

Helen made no move to run. In the full light of the candles and the golden goddess glow, she went to her knees, looked up at her rightful husband, lowered her eyes, and pulled her gown down, baring her breasts, waiting for the blade.

13

"To answer your last question," said Prime Integrator Asteague/Che, "we have to go to Earth because it appears that the center of all this quantum activity originates on or near the Earth."

"Mahnmut told me shortly after I met him that you'd sent him and Orphu to Mars precisely because Mars—Olympus Mons in particular—was the source of all this . . . quantum? . . . activity," said Hockenberry.

"That was what we believed when we tapped into the Olympians' QT ability to transit these Holes, coming from the Belt and Jupiter space into Mars and the Earth of Ilium's day. But our technology now suggests that Earth is the source and center of this activity, Mars the recipient . . . or target, perhaps would be the better word."

"Your technology has changed so much in eight months?" said Hockenberry.

"We've easily tripled our knowledge of unified quantum theory since we piggybacked in on the Olympians' quantum tunnels," said Cho Li. The Callistan seemed to be the expert on technical things. "Most of what we know about quantum gravity, for instance, we've learned in the last eight standard months."

"And what *have* you learned?" asked Hockenberry. He didn't expect to understand the science, but he was suspicious of the moravecs for the first time.

Retrograde Sinopessen, the transformer with spider legs, answered in his incongruous rumble. "Everything we've learned is terrifying. Absolutely terrifying."

That word Hockenberry understood. "Because the quantum whatsis is unstable? Mahnmut and Orphu told me that you knew that before you sent them to Mars. Is it worse than you thought?"

"Not just that factor," said Asteague/Che, "but our growing understanding of how the force or forces behind the so-called gods are using this quantum-field energy."

Force or forces behind the gods. Hockenberry noted that but did not pursue it at that moment. "How are they using it?" he asked.

"The Olympians actually use ripples—folds—in the quantum field to fly their chariots," said the Ganymedan, Suma IV. The tall creature's multifaceted eyes caught the light in a prism of reflections.

"Is that bad?"

"Only in the sense that it would be if you used a thermonuclear weapon to power a lightbulb in your home," said Cho Li in his/her soft tones. "The energies being tapped into are almost immeasurable."

"Then why haven't the gods won this war?" asked Hockenberry. "It seems that your technology has sort of stalemated them . . . even Zeus's *aegis.*"

Beh bin Adee, the rockvec commander, answered. "The gods use only the slightest fraction of the quantum energy in play on and around Mars and Ilium. We don't believe they understand the technology behind their power. It's been . . . loaned to them."

"By whom?" Hockenberry was suddenly very thirsty. He wondered if the moravecs had included any human-style food or drink in their pressurized bubble.

"That's what we're going to Earth to find out," said Asteague/Che.

"Why use a spaceship?" said Hockenberry.

"Pardon me?" asked Cho Li in soft tones. "How else could we travel between worlds?"

"The same way you got to Mars in your invasion," said Hockenberry. "Use one of the Holes."

Asteague/Che shook his head in a manner similar to Mahnmut's. "There are no quantum-tunnel Brane Holes between Mars and Earth."

"But you created your own Holes to come from Jupiter space and the Belt, right?" said Hockenberry. His head hurt. "Why not do that again?"

Cho Li answered. "Mahnmut succeeded in placing our transponder precisely at the quincunx locus of the quantum flux on Olympos. We have no one on Earth or in near-Earth orbit to do that for us now. That is one of the goals of our mission. We'll be bringing a similar, although updated, transponder with us on the ship."

Hockenberry nodded, but wasn't quite sure of what he was nodding in agreement to. He was trying to remember the definition of "quincunx." Was it a rectangle with a fifth point in the middle? Or something to do with leaves or petals? He knew it had to do with the number five.

Asteague/Che leaned closer over the table. "Dr. Hockenberry, may I give you a hint of why this frivolous use of quantum energy terrifies us?"

"Please." *Such manners,* thought Hockenberry, who had been around Trojan and Greek heroes too long.

"Have you noticed anything about the gravity on Olympos and the rest of Mars during your more than nine years shuttling between there and Ilium, Doctor?"

"Well . . . yeah, sure . . . I always felt a little lighter on Olympos. Even before I realized it was Mars, which was only after you guys showed up. So? That's right, isn't it? Doesn't Mars have less gravity than Earth?"

"Very much less," piped in Cho Li . . . and her voice *did* sound a lot like pipes to Hockenberry's ear. Pan's pipes. "It's approximately three seventy-two kilometers per second per second."

"Translate," said Hockenberry.

"It's thirty-eight percent of Earth's gravitational field," said Retrograde Sinopessen. "And you were moving—quantum teleporting, actually—between Earth's full gravity and Olympos' every day. Did you notice a sixty-two percent difference in gravity, Dr. Hockenberry."

"Please, everyone, call me Thomas," Hockenberry said while distracted. *Sixty-two percent difference? I'd almost be floating like a balloon on Mars . . . jumping twenty yards at a leap. Nonsense.*

"You didn't observe this gravitational difference," said Asteague/Che, not framing it as a question.

"Not really," agreed Hockenberry. It was always a little easier walking after the return to Olympos after a long day observing the Trojan War—and not just on the mountain, but in the scholics barracks at the base of the huge massif. A little easier—a little lighter in the walking and carrying loads—but sixty-two percent difference? No way in hell. "There was a difference," he added, "but not such a profound one."

"You didn't notice a profound difference, Dr. Hockenberry, because the gravity of the Mars you have been living on for the past ten years—and which we have been fighting on for the past eight Earth-standard months—is ninety-three point eight-two-one percent Earth normal."

Hockenberry thought about this for a moment. "So?" he said at last. "The gods tweaked the gravity while they were adding the air and oceans. They are, after all, *gods*."

"They're something," agreed Asteague/Che, "but not what they appear."

"Is changing the gravity of a planet such a big deal?" asked Hockenberry.

There was a silence, and while Hockenberry did not see any of the moravecs turn their heads or eyes or whatever to look at any of the other moravecs, he had the sense that they were all busy communing on some radio band or the other. *How to explain to this idiot human?*

Finally Suma IV, the tall Ganymedan, said, "It is a *very* big deal."

"Bigger even than the terraforming of a world like the original Mars in less than a century and a half," piped in Cho Li. "Which is impossible."

"Gravity equals mass," said Retrograde Sinopessen.

"It does?" said Hockenberry, hearing how stupid he sounded but not caring. "I always thought it was what held things down."

"Gravity is an effect of mass on space/time," continued the silver spider. "The current Mars is three point nine-six times the density of water. The original Mars—the pre-terraformed world we observed not much more than a century ago—was three point nine-four times the density of water."

"That doesn't sound like too much of a change," said Hockenberry.

"It is not," agreed Asteague/Che. "It in no way accounts for an increase in gravitation attraction of almost fifty-six percent."

"Gravity is also an acceleration," Cho Li said in her musical tones.

Now they'd lost Hockenberry completely. He'd come here to learn about the upcoming visit to Earth and to hear why they wanted him to join them, not to be lectured like a particularly slow eighth grade science student.

"So they—someone, not the gods—changed Mars' gravity," he said. "And you think it's a very big deal."

"It is a very big deal, Dr. Hockenberry," said Asteague/Che. "Whoever and whatever manipulated Mars' gravity this way is a master of quantum gravity. The Holes . . . as they've come to be called . . . are quantum tunnels that also bend and manipulate gravity."

"Wormholes," said Hockenberry. "I know about them." From *Star Trek*, he thought but did not say. "Black holes," he added. Then, "And white holes." He'd just exhausted his entire vocabulary on this subject. Even nonscience types like old Dr. Hockenberry at the end of the Twentieth Century had known that the universe was full of wormholes connecting distant places in this galaxy and others, and that to go through a wormhole, you went through a black hole and came out a white hole. Or maybe vice versa.

Asteague/Che shook his head in that Mahnmut way. "Not wormholes. *Brane Holes* . . . as in mem*brane*. It looks like the post-humans in Earth orbit used black holes to create very temporary wormholes, but the Brane Holes—and there is only one left connecting Mars and Ilium, you must remember; the others have lost stability and decayed away—are not wormholes."

"You'd be dead if you tried to go through a wormhole or a black hole," said Cho Li.

"Spaghettified," said General Beh bin Adee. The rockvec sounded as if he enjoyed the concept of spaghettification.

"Being spaghettified . . ." began Retrograde Sinopessen.

"I get the idea," said Hockenberry. "So this use of quantum gravity and these quantum Brane Holes makes the adversary much scarier even than you'd feared."

"Yes," said Asteague/Che.

"And you're taking this big spaceship to Earth to find out who or what created these Holes, terraformed Mars, and probably created the gods as well."

"Yes."

"And you want me along."

"Yes."

"Why?" said Hockenberry. "What possible contribution could I make to . . ." He paused and touched the lump under his tunic, the heavy circle against his chest. "The QT medallion."

"Yes," said Asteague/Che.

"Back when you guys first arrived, I loaned the medallion to you for six days. I was afraid you'd never give it back. You did tests on me as well . . . blood, DNA, the whole nine yards. I would have guessed that you'd replicated a thousand QT medallions by now."

"If we were able to replicate a dozen . . . half a dozen . . . one more," growled General Beh bin Adee, "the war with the gods would be over, Olympos occupied."

"It's not possible for us to build a duplicate QT device," said Cho Li.

"Why?" Hockenberry's headache was killing him.

"The QT medallion was customized to your mind and body," Asteague/Che said in his mellifluous James Mason way. "Your mind and body were . . . customized . . . to work with the QT medallion."

Hockenberry thought about this. Finally he shook his head and touched the heavy medallion under his tunic again. "That doesn't make any sense. This thing wasn't standard issue, you know. We scholics had to go to prearranged places to get back to Olympos—the gods QT'd us back. It was sort of a beam-me-up-Scotty thing, if you understand what I mean, which you can't."

"Yes, we understand perfectly," said the Lionel transformer box on its millimeter-thin silver-spider legs. "I love that program. I have all the episodes recorded. Especially the first series . . . I've always wondered if there was some sort of hidden physical-romantic liaison between Captain Kirk and Mr. Spock."

Hockenberry started to reply, stopped. "Look," he said at last, "the goddess Aphrodite gave me this QT medallion so that I could spy on Athena, whom she wanted to kill. But that was more than nine years after I started work as a scholic, shuttling between Olympos and Ilium. How could my body have been 'customized' to work with the medallion when nobody could have known that . . ." He stopped. A hint of nausea was creeping in under the headache. He wondered if the air was good in this blue bubble.

"You were originally . . . reconstructed . . . to work with the QT medallion," said Asteague/Che. "Just as the gods were designed to QT on their own. Of this we are sure. Perhaps the answer to why lies back on Earth or in Earth orbit in one of the hundreds of thousands of post-human orbital devices and cities there."

Hockenberry sat back in his chair. He'd noticed when they sat down at the table that his stool had been the only one with a back on it. The moravecs were very considerate that way.

"You want me along on the expedition," he said, "so that I could QT back here if things go wrong. I'm like one of those emergency buoys that nuclear submarines used to carry in my time on Earth. They only launched it when they knew they were screwed."

"Yes," said Asteague/Che. "This is precisely the reason we want you along on the voyage."

Hockenberry blinked. "Well, you're honest . . . I'll give you that. What are the goals of this expedition?"

"Goal One—to find the source of the quantum energy," said Cho Li. "And to shut it off if possible. It threatens the entire solar system."

"Goal Two—to make contact with any surviving humans or post-humans on or around the planet to interrogate them as to the motives behind this gods-Ilium connection and the dangerous quantum manip-ulation surrounding it," said the gray-oily Ganymedan, Suma IV.

"Goal Three—to map the existing and any additional hidden quan-tum tunnels—Brane Holes—and to see if they can be harnessed for in-terplanetary or interstellar travel," said Retrograde Sinopessen.

"Goal Four—to find the alien entities who entered our solar system fourteen hundred years ago, the real gods behind these midget Olympian gods, as it were, and to reason with them," said General Beh bin Abee. "And if reason fails, to destroy them."

"Goal Five," Asteague/Che said softly in his slow British drawl, "to return all of our moravec and human crewmen to Mars . . . alive and functioning."

"I like that goal, at least," said Hockenberry. His heart was pounding and the headache had become the kind of migraine he'd had when in graduate school, during the unhappiest period of his previous life. He stood.

The five moravecs quickly stood.

"How long do I have to decide?" asked Hockenberry. "Because if you're leaving in the next hour, I'm not going. I want to think about this."

"The ship won't be ready and provisioned for forty-eight hours," said Asteague/Che. "Would you like to wait here while you think it over? We've prepared a suitable habitation for you in a quiet part of the . . ."

"I want to go back to Ilium," said Hockenberry. "I'll be able to think better there."

Asteague/Che said, "We'll prepare your hornet for immediate departure. But I'm afraid it's getting rather hectic there today according to the updates I'm receiving from our various monitors."

"Isn't that the way?" said Hockenberry. "I leave for a few hours and miss all the good stuff."

"You may find evolving events at Ilium and on Olympos too interesting to leave behind, Dr. Hockenberry," said Retrograde Sinopessen. "I would certainly undersand an *Iliad* scholar's commitment to remaining and observing."

Hockenberry sighed and shook his aching head. "Wherever we are in what's going on at Ilium and Olympos," he said, "it's way the hell outside the *Iliad*. Most of the time, I'm at as much of a loss as that poor woman Cassandra."

A hornet came through the curving wall of the blue bubble, hovered over them, and set down silently. The ramp curled down. Mahnmut stood in the doorway.

Hockenberry nodded formally toward the moravec delegation, said, "I'll let you know before the forty-eight hours are up," and walked toward the ramp.

"Dr. Hockenberry?" said the James Mason voice behind him.

Hockenberry turned.

"We want to take one Greek or Trojan with us on this expedition," said Asteague/Che. "Your recommendation would be appreciated."

"Why?" said Hockenberry. "I mean, why take along someone from the Bronze Age. Someone who lived and died six thousand years before the time of the Earth you're visiting?"

"We have our reasons," said the Prime Integrator. "Just off the top of your mind, who would you nominate for the trip?"

Helen of Troy, thought Hockenberry. *Give us the honeymoon suite on the trip to Earth and this could be one hell of an enjoyable expedition.* He tried to imagine sex with Helen in zero-g. His headache stopped him from succeeding.

"Do you want a warrior?" asked Hockenberry. "A hero?"

"Not necessarily," said General Beh bin Adee. "We're bringing one hundred warriors of our own. Just someone from the Trojan War era who might be an asset."

Helen of Troy, he thought again. *She has a great . . .* He shook his head. "Achilles would be the obvious choice," he said aloud. "He's invulnerable, you know."

"We know," Cho Li said softly. "We covertly analyzed him and know why he is, as you say, invulnerable."

"It's because his mother, the goddess Thetis, dipped him in the River . . ." began Hockenberry.

"Actually," interrupted Retrograde Sinopessen, "it is because some-one . . . some *thing* . . . has warped the quantum-probability matrix around Mr. Achilles to a quite improbable extent."

"All right," said Hockenberry, not understanding a word of that sentence. "So do you want Achilles?"

"I don't believe Achilles would agree to go with us, do you, Dr. Hockenberry?" said Asteague/Che.

"Ah . . . no. Could you make him go?"

"I believe it would be a riskier proposition than all the rest of the dangers involved in the visit to the third planet combined," rumbled General Beh bin Adee.

A sense of humor from a rockvec? thought Hockenberry. "If not Achilles," he said, "who then?"

"We were wondering if you would suggest someone. Someone courageous but intelligent. An explorer, but sensible. Someone we could communicate with. A flexible personality, you might say."

"Odysseus," said Hockenberry with no hesitation. "You want Odysseus."

"Do you think he would agree to go?" asked Retrograde Sinopessen.

Hockenberry took a breath. "If you tell him that Penelope is waiting for him at the other end, he'll go to hell and back with you."

"We cannot lie to him," said Asteague/Che.

"I can," said Hockenberry. "I'd be glad to. Whether I go with you or not, I'll be your intermediary in conning Odysseus into joining you."

"We would appreciate that," said Asteague/Che. "We look forward to hearing your own decision on joining us within the next forty-eight hours." The Europan held out his arm and Hockenberry realized that there was a fairly humanoid hand on the end of it.

He shook the hand and got into the hornet behind Mahnmut. The ramp came up. The invisible chair grabbed him. They left the bubble.

14

Impatient, furious, pacing in front of his thousand best Myrmidons along the coastline at the base of Olympos, waiting for the gods to send down their champion for the day so that he could kill him, Achilles remembers the first month of the war—a time all Trojans and Argives still called "the Wrath of Achilles."

They had QT'd down from the Olympian heights in legions then, these gods, confident in their forcefields and blood-machines, ready to leap into Slow Time and escape any mortal wrath, not knowing that the little moravec clock-people, new allies to Achilles, had their own formulas and enchantments to counter such god-tricks.

Ares, Hades, and Hermes had leaped first, clicking into the Achaean and Trojan ranks while the sky exploded. Flame followed forcelines until both Olympos and the mortal ranks became domes and spires and shimmering waves of flame. The sea boiled. The Little Green Men scattered for their feluccas. Zeus's *aegis* shuddered and grew visible as it absorbed megatons of moravec assault.

Achilles had eyes only for Ares and his newly QT'd cohorts, Hades, red-eyed in his black bronze, and black-eyed Hermes in his barbed red-armor.

"Teach the mortals death!" screamed Ares, god of war, twelve feet tall, shimmering, attacking the Argive ranks at a run. Hades and Hermes followed. All three cast god-spears that could not miss their mark.

They missed their mark. Achilles' fate was not to die that day. Or any day by the hands of an immortal.

One immortal's spear grazed the fleet-footed mankiller's strong right arm but drew no blood. Another embedded itself in his beautiful shield, but the god-forged layer of polarized gold blocked it. A third glanced from Achilles' golden helmet without making a mark.

The three gods fired energy blasts from their god-palms. Achilles' own nano-bred fields shed the millions of volts the way a dog shakes off water.

Ares and Achilles crashed together like mountains colliding. The quake threw hundreds of Trojans and Greeks and gods off their feet even as the battle lines joined. Ares was the first to fall back. He raised his red sword and swung a decapitating blow at the upstart mortal, Achilles.

Achilles ducked the blade and ran the war god through, scooping a slice through divine armor and gut until Ares' belly opened, golden ichor covered mortal and immortal alike, and the war god's divine bowels spilled out on the red Martian gorse. Too surprised to fall, too outraged to die, Ares stared at his own insides still unraveling and uncoiling onto the dirt.

Achilles reached high, grabbed Ares by his helmet and jerked him down and forward until his human spittle splattered the god's perfect features. "*You* taste death, you gutless effigy!" Then, working like a marketplace butcher at the beginning of a long day's labor, he lopped off Ares' hands at the wrists, then his legs above the knee, and then his arms.

Screaming black whirling around the corpse, other gods gaping, Ares' head continued to scream even after Achilles cut it off at the neck.

Hermes, horrified but also ambidextrous and deadly, raised his second spear.

Achilles leaped forward so quickly that everyone assumed he had teleported. Grabbing the second god's spear, he jerked it toward him. Hermes tried to pull it back. Hades swung his black sword at Achilles' knees but the mankiller leaped high, avoiding the blur of dark carbon-steel.

Losing the tug of war for his spear, Hermes leaped back and tried to QT away.

The moravecs had cast their field around them. No one would be quantum teleporting out or in until this fight was finished.

Hermes pulled his sword, a curved and wicked thing. Achilles cut off the giant-killer's arm at the elbow, and the sword arm and the still-grasping hand fell to Mars' rich, red soil.

"Mercy!" cried Hermes, throwing himself to his knees and embracing Achilles' around the waist. "Mercy, I beg you!"

"There is none," said Achilles and then hacked the god into as many quivering, gold-bleeding bits.

Hades backed away from the slaughter, his red eyes filled with fear. More gods were flicking into the human-set trap by the hundreds, and Hector and his Trojan captains and Achilles' Mymidons and all the heroes of the Greeks were engaging them, the moravec forcefields not allowing the gods to QT away once they arrived. For the first time in the memory of anyone on the field, gods and heroes, demigods and mortals, legends and infantry grunts, all fought on something not unlike equal terms.

Hades shifted into Slow Time.

The world stopped turning. The air thickened. The waves froze in their curl against the rocky shore. Birds halted and hung in midflight. Hades panted and retched in relief. No mortal could follow him here.

Achilles shifted into Slow Time after him.

"This . . . is . . . not . . . possible," the ruler of the dead said through the syrup-slow air.

"Die, Death," shouted Achilles and drove his father Peleus' spear through the god's throat, just below where the black cheek-guards curved up again toward Hades' skull-like cheekbones. Golden ichor spurted in slow motion.

Achilles shoved aside Hades' black-ornamented shield and put his blade through the death god's belly and spine. Dying, Hades still returned the thrust with a blow that could have split a mountainside. The black blade slid off Achilles' chest as if it had not touched him. It was not Achilles' fate to die that day, and never by the hands of an immortal. Hades' fate was to die that day—however temporarily by human standards. He fell heavily and blackness swirled around him as he disappeared within an onyx cyclone.

Manipulating new nanotechnology without conscious effort, playing havoc with already-battered quantum fields of probability, Achilles flicked back out of Slow Time to rejoin the battle. Zeus had left the field. The other gods were fleeing, forgetting, in their panic, to raise the *aegis* behind them. More moravec magic, injected that very morning, allowed Achilles to push through their lesser energy fields and give pursuit up the cliffs of Olympos onto the lower ramparts.

Then his slaughter of gods and goddesses began in earnest.

But all this was in the early days of the war. Today—this day after Paris's funeral—no gods are coming down to fight.

So, with his ally Hector gone and the Trojans quiescent on their part of the front today, Hector's lesser-brother Aeneas in charge of the thousands of Trojans there, Achilles is meeting with his Achaean captains and moravec artillery experts to plan an imminent attack on Olympos.

The attack will be simple: while moravec energy and nuclear weapons activate the *aegis* on the lower slopes, Achilles and five hundred of his best captains and Achaeans in thirty transport hornets will punch through a lesser section of the energy shield almost a thousand leagues around the back of Olympos, make a dash for the summit, and carry the torch to the gods in their homes. For those Achaeans who are wounded or lose their nerve fighting in the very citadel of Zeus and the gods, the hornets will lift them out after the element of surprise fades.

Achilles plans to stay until the top of Mount Olympos has been turned into a charnel house and all its white temples and god-dwellings are blackened rubble. After all, he thinks, Herakles once pulled down the walls of Ilium all by himself when angered and took the city single-handedly—why should the halls of Olympos be sacrosanct?

All morning, Achilles has expected Agamemnon and his simpler sibling, Menelaus, to show up, leading a mob of their loyal men to try to take back control of the Achaean forces and to push the war backward into mortal-versus-mortal, befriending the murderous, treacherous gods again, but so far that dog-eyed, deer-hearted former commander in chief has not shown his face. Achilles has decided that he will kill him when he does attempt the revolt. Him and his red-bearded stripling Menelaus and anyone and everyone who follows the two Atrides. The news of the home cities being emptied of all life is—Achilles is sure—merely a ruse by Agamemnon to incite the restless and cowardly Achaeans to revolt.

So when moravec Centurion Leader Mep Ahoo, the barbed rockvec in charge of the artillery and energy bombardment, looks up from the map they are studying under the silk of a lean-to shelter and announces that his binocular vision has picked up an odd-looking army coming through the Hole from the direction of Ilium, Achilles is not surprised.

But a few minutes later he *is* surprised as Odysseus—the most sharp-eyed among their command group huddled under the flapping canopy—says, "They're women. Trojan women."

"Amazons, you mean?" says Achilles, stepping out into the Olympos sunshine. Antilochus, son of Nestor, Achilles' old friend from countless campaigns, had ridden his chariot into camp here an hour earlier, telling everyone of the arrival of the thirteen Amazons and Penthesilea's vow to kill Achilles in single combat. The fleet-footed mankiller had laughed easily, showing his perfect teeth. He had not fought and defeated ten thousand Trojans and scores of gods to be frightened by a woman's bluster.

Odysseus shakes his head. "There must be two hundred of these women, all dressed out in ill-fitting armor, son of Peleus. No Amazons these. They are too fat, too short, too old, some almost lame."

"Every day," grumbles dour Diomedes, son of Tydeus, lord of Argos, "it seems we descend into another level of madness."

Teucer, the bastard master-archer and Big Ajax's half brother, says, "Shall I advance the camp pickets, noble Achilles? Have them intercept these women, whatever the folly of their mission here, and frog-march them back to their looms?"

"No," says Achilles. "Let's go out and meet them, see what brings the first women to venture through the Hole to Olympos and an Achaean camp."

"Perhaps they're looking for Aeneas and their Trojan husbands leagues to our left," says Big Ajax, son of Telamon, leader of the Salamis army supporting the Myrmidons' left flank this Martian morning.

"Perhaps." Achilles sounds amused and mildly irritated, but not convinced. He walks out into the weaker Olympian sunlight, leading the group of Achaean kings, captains, subcaptains, and their most loyal fighting men.

It is indeed a rabble of Trojan women. When they are within a hundred yards, Achilles stops with his contingent of fifty or so heroes, and waits for the clanking band of shouting women to come on. It sounds like a gaggle of geese to the fleet-footed mankiller.

"Do you see any high-born among the women?" Achilles asks sharp-eyed Odysseus as they stand waiting for the rattling horde to cross the last hundred yards of red-gorse soil that separates them. "Any wives or daughters of heroes? Andromache or Helen or wild-eyed Cassandra or Medesicaste or venerable Castianira?"

"None of those," Odysseus responds quickly. "No one of worth, either born to or married into. I recognize only Hippodamia—the big one with the spear and the ancient long shield, like that which Great Ajax chooses to carry—and her only because she visited me in Ithaca once with her husband, the far-traveling Trojan Tisiphonus. Penelope took her for a tour of our gardens, but said later that the woman was as sour as a pre-season pomegranate and would take no pleasure in beauty."

Achilles, who can see the women clearly enough now, says, "Well, she herself is certainly no beauty to take pleasure in. Philoctetes, go forward, halt them, ask them what they are doing here on the our battleground with the gods."

"Must I, son of Peleus?" whines the older-archer. "After the libel spread about me yesterday at Paris's funeral, I hardly think that I should be the one . . ."

Achilles turns and silences the man with an admonishing glance.

"I'll go with you to hold your hand," rumbles Big Ajax. "Teucer, come with us. Two archers and a master spearman should answer for this prickless rabble, even if they turn uglier than they already are."

The three men walk forward from Achilles' contingent.

What happens next happens very quickly.

Philoctetes, Teucer, and Big Ajax stop some twenty paces from the obviously winded and gasping, loose-formed lines of armored women, and the former commander of the Thessalians and former castaway steps forward, holding Herakles' fabled bow in his left hand while he holds his right palm up in peace.

One of the younger women to the right of Hippodamia casts her spear. Incredibly, astonishingly, it catches Philoctetes—ten-year survivor of poison snakebite and the ire of the gods—full in the chest, just above his light archer's armor, and passes clean through, severing his spine and dropping him lifeless to the red soil.

"Kill the bitch!" screams Achilles, outraged, running forward and pulling his sword from its scabbard.

Teucer, under fire now from wild-cast women's spears and a hail of ill-aimed arrows, needs no such prompting. Faster than most mortal eyes can follow, he notches an arrow, goes to full pull, and sets a yard-long shaft through the throat of the woman who has cut Philoctetes down.

Hippodamia and twenty or thirty women close with Big Ajax, thrusting spears tentatively and trying to swing their husbands' or fathers' or sons' massive swords in awkward two-handed blows.

Ajax, son of Telamon, looks back at Achilles for just an instant, giving the other men a glance of something like amusement, and then he pulls his long blade, slams Hippodamia's sword and shield aside with an easy shrug, and lops off the woman's head as if he were cutting weeds in his yard. The other women, maddened beyond fear now, rush at the two standing men. Teucer puts arrow after arrow into their eyes, thighs, flopping breasts, and—within a few seconds—fleeing backs. Big Ajax finishes the rest who are foolish enough to linger, wading through them like a tall man among children, leaving corpses in his wake.

By the time Achilles, Odysseus, Diomedes, Nestor, Chromius, Little Ajax, Antilochus, and the others arrive, forty or so women are dead or dying, a few screaming their death agonies on the red-soaked red soil, and the rest are fleeing back toward the Hole.

"What in Hades' name was *that* all about?" gasps Odysseus as he comes up to Big Ajax and steps among the bodies thrown down in all the graceful and graceless—but all too familiar to Odysseus—attitudes of violent death.

The son of Telamon grins. His face is spattered and his armor and sword run red with Trojan-women blood. "That's not the first time I've killed women," says the mortal giant, "but by the gods, it was the most satisfying!"

Calchas, son of Thestor and their most able soothsayer, hobbles up from behind. "This is not good. This is bad. This is not good at all."

"Shut up," says Achilles. He shields his eyes and looks toward the Hole where the last of the women are disappearing, only to be replaced by a small group of larger figures. "What now?" says the son of Peleus and the goddess Thetis. "Those look like centaurs. Has my old friend and tutor Chiron come to join our effort?"

"Not centaurs," says sharp-eyed, keen-witted Odysseus. "More women. On horseback."

"Horse*back*?" says Nestor, his old eyes squinting to see. "Not in chariots?"

"Riding horses like the fabled cavalries of ancient days," says Diomedes, who sees them now. No one rides horses in these modern days, using them only to pull chariots—although both Odysseus and Diomedes himself escaped a Trojan camp on a midnight raid some months earlier, before the truce, by riding bareback on untethered chariot horses through Hector's half-awakened army.

"The Amazons," says Achilles.

Athena's Temple. Menelaus advancing, red-faced, breathing hard— Helen on her knees, pale face lowered, paler breasts bared. He looms over her. He raises his sword. Her pale neck seems thin as a reed, offered. The endlessly sharpened blade will not even pause as it slices through skin, flesh, bone.

Menelaus pauses.

"Do not hesitate, my husband," whispers Helen, her voice quavering only slightly. Menelaus can see her pulse beating wildly at the base of her heavy, blue-veined left breast. He seizes the hilt in both hands.

He does not yet bring the blade down. "Damn you," he breathes. "Damn you."

"Yes," whispers Helen, face still downcast. The golden idol of Athena looms over them both in the incense-thick darkness.

Menelaus grips the sword hilt with a strangler's fervor. His arms vibrate with the twin strain of preparing to behead his wife while simultaneously stopping the action.

"Why shouldn't I kill you, you faithless cunt?" hisses Menelaus.

"No reason, husband. I am a faithless cunt. It and I have both been faithless. Finish it. Carry out your rightful sentence of death."

"*Don't call me husband,* damn you!"

Helen lifts her face. Her dark eyes are precisely the eyes Menelaus has dreamt of for more than ten years. "You are my husband. You always were. My only husband."

He almost kills her then, so painful are these words. Sweat falls from his brow and cheeks and spatters on her simple robe. "You deserted me—you deserted me and our daughter," he manages, "for that . . . that . . . boy. That popinjay. That pair of spangled leotards with a dick."

"Yes," says Helen and lowers her face again. Menelaus sees the small, familiar mole on the back of her neck, right at the base, right where the edge of the blade will strike.

"Why?" manages Menelaus. It is the last thing he will say before he kills her or forgives her . . . or both.

"I deserve to die," she whispers. "For sins against you, for sins against our daughter, for sins against our country. But I did not leave our palace in Sparta of my own free will."

Menelaus grinds his teeth so fiercely that he can hear them cracking.

"You were gone," whispers Helen, his wife, his tormenter, the bitch who betrayed him, the mother of his child. "You were always gone. Gone with your brother. Hunting. Warring. Whoring. Plundering. You and Agamemnon were the true couple—I was only the breed sow left at home. When Paris, that trickster, that guileful Odysseus without Odysseus' wisdom, took me by force, I had no husband home to protect me."

Menelaus breathes through his mouth. The sword seems to be whispering to him like a living thing, demanding the bitch's blood. So many voices rage in his ears that he can barely hear her soft tones. The memory of her voice has tormented him for four thousand nights; now it drives him beyond madness.

"I am penitent," she says, "but that cannot matter now. I am suppliant, but that cannot matter now. Shall I tell you of the hundred times in the last ten years that I have lifted a sword or fashioned a noose from rope, only to have my tirewomen and Paris's spies pull me back, urging me to think of our daughter if not of myself? This abduction and my long captivity here have been Aphrodite's doing, husband, not my own. But you can free me now with one blow of your familiar blade. Do so, my darling Menelaus. Tell our child that I loved her and love her still. And know yourself that I loved you, and love you still."

Menelaus screams, drops the blade clattering to the temple floor and falls to his knees next to his wife. He is sobbing like a child.

Helen removes his helmet, puts her hand on the back of his head, and draws his face to her bare breasts. She does not smile. No, she does not smile, nor is she tempted to. She feels the scratch of his short beard and his tears and the heat of his breath on her breasts that have held the weight of Paris, Hockenberry, Deiphobus, and others since Menelaus last touched her. *Treacherous cunt, yes,* thinks Helen of Troy. *So are we all.* She does not consider the last minute a victory. She was ready to die. She is very, very tired.

Menelaus gets to his feet. He angrily wipes tears and snot from his red mustache, reaches down for his sword, and slides it back into his strap ring. "Wife, lay aside your fear. What's done is done—Aphrodite's and Paris's evil, not yours. On the marble over there is a temple-virgin's cloak and veil. Put them on and we'll leave this doomed city forever."

Helen rises, touches her husband's shoulder under the odd lion skin she once saw Diomedes wear while slaying Trojans, and silently dons the white cloak and laced white veil.

Together they go out into the city.

Helen cannot believe she is leaving Ilium like this. After more than ten years, to walk out through the Scaean Gate and put all this behind her forever? What of Cassandra? What of her plans with Andromache and the others? What of her responsibility for the war with the gods she—Helen—has helped start through their machinations? What, even, of poor sad Hockenberry and their little love?

Helen feels her spirits soar like a released temple dove as she realizes that none of these things are her problem anymore. She will sail home to Sparta with her rightful husband—she has missed Menelaus, the . . . simplicity . . . of him—and she will see their daughter, grown into a woman now, and will view the last ten years as a bad dream as she ages into the last quarter of her life, her beauty undimmed, of course, thanks to the will of the gods, not hers. She has been reprieved in every way possible.

The two are out in the street, walking as if both still in a dream, when the city bells ring, the great horns on the watchwalls blare, and criers begin to call. All of the city's alarums are sounding at once.

The shouts sort themselves out. Menelaus stares at her through the gap in his absurd boar-tusk helmet and Helen stares back through the thin slit of her temple-virgin veil and turban. In those seconds, their eyes somehow manage to convey terror, confusion, and even grim amusement at the irony of it all.

The Scaean Gate is closed and barred. The Achaeans are attacking again. The Trojan War has begun anew.

They are trapped.

16

"Could I see the ship?" asked Hockenberry. The hornet had emerged from the blue bubble in Stickney Crater and was climbing toward the red disk of Mars.

"The Earth-ship?" said Mahnmut. At Hockenberry's nod, he said, "Of course."

The moravec broadcast commands to the hornet and it came around and circled the Earth-ship gantry, then rose until it docked with a port on the upper reaches of the long, articulated spacecraft.

Hockenberry wants to tour the ship, Mahnmut tightbeamed to Orphu of Io.

There was only a second of background static before—*Well, why not? We're asking him to risk his life on this voyage. Why shouldn't he see all of the ship? Asteague/Che and the others should have suggested it to him.*

"How long is this thing?" Hockenberry asked softly. Through the holographic windows, the ship seemed to drop away beneath them for miles.

"Approximately the height of your Twentieth Century Empire State Building," said Mahnmut. "But a little rounder and lumpier in places."

He's certainly never been in zero-g, sent Mahnmut. *Phobos gravity will just disorient him.*

The displacement fields are ready, tightbeamed Orphu. *I'll set them to point-eight-g on ship lateral and go to Earth-normal internal pressure. By the time you two get in the forward airlock, everything will be breathable and comfortable for him.*

"Isn't this too large for the mission they were talking about?" said Hockenberry. "Even with hundreds of rockvec soldiers aboard, this seems like overkill."

"We may want to bring things back with us," said Mahnmut. *Where are you?* he sent to Orphu.

I'm on the lower hull now, but I'll meet you in the Big Piston Room.

"Like rocks? Soil samples?" said Hockenberry. He'd been a young man the week human beings had first set foot on the moon. Memories came back now of him sitting in the backyard of his parents' house and watching the ghostly black-and-white images from the Sea of Tranquility on a small TV on the picnic table, extension cord running to the summerhouse, while the half-full moon itself was visible above through the leaves of the oak tree.

"Like people," said Mahnmut. "Perhaps thousands or tens of thousands of people. Hang on, we're docking." The moravec silently commanded the holoports off; attaching at right angles more than one thousand feet up the vertical hull of a spacecraft was a view that would give anyone vertigo.

Hockenberry asked little and said less during his tour of the ship. He'd imagined technology beyond his imagining—virtual control panels that disappeared at the flick of a thought, more energy-field chairs, an environment built for zero-g with no sense of up or down—but what he saw felt like some gigantic Nineteenth or early-Twentieth Century steamship. What it felt like, he realized, was a tour of the RMS *Titanic*.

Controls were physical, made of metal and plastic. Couches were clunky, physical things—enough, it looked like, for a crew of about thirty moravecs—the couch proportions were never really right for humans—along with long storage bins with metal-and-nylon bunks along bulkheads. Entire levels were set aside with high-tech-looking racks and sarcophagi for a thousand rockvec troopers, Mahnmut explained, who would make the trip in a state somewhere above death but below consciousness. Unlike their trip to Mars, the moravec explained, this time they were going armed and ready for battle.

"Suspended animation," said Hockenberry, who'd not avoided all sci-fi movies. He and his wife had had cable there toward the end.

"Not really," said Mahnmut. "Sort of."

There were ladders and broad stairways and elevators and all sorts of anachronistic mechanical devices. There were airlocks and science rooms and weapons' lockers. The furniture—there was furniture—was large and clunky, as if weight were no problem. There were astrogation bubbles looking out toward the rim walls of Stickney and up toward Mars and down toward the gantry lights and moravec bustle. There were mess halls and cooking galleys and sleeping cubbies and bathrooms, all of which, Mahnmut hurriedly explained, were for human passengers, should they have any coming or going.

"How many human passengers?" asked Hockenberry.

"Up to ten thousand," said Mahnmut.

Hockenberry whistled. "So is this a sort of Noah's ark?"

"No," said the little moravec. "Noah's boat was three hundred cubits long by fifty cubits wide by thirty cubits tall. That translates to about four hundred fifty feet in length, seventy-five feet in width, and forty-five feet high. Noah's ark had three decks comprising a volume of about one million four hundred thousand cubic feet and a gross tonnage of thirteen thousand nine hundred and sixty tons. This ship is more than twice that long, half again that width in diameter—although you saw that some sections, like the habitation cylinders and holds, are more bulbous—and masses more than forty-six thousand tons. Noah's ark was a rowboat compared to this craft."

Hockenberry found that he had no response to this news.

Mahnmut led the way into a small steel-cage elevator, and they descended through level after level past the holds, where Mahnmut explained his Europan submersible *The Dark Lady* would go—and down through what the moravec described as "charge storage magazines." The word "magazine" had military connotations for Hockenberry, but he assured himself that it couldn't be that. He saved his questions for later.

They met Orphu of Io in the engine room, which the larger moravec called the Big Piston Room. Hockenberry expressed his pleasure at seeing Orphu with his full complement of legs and sensors—*sans* real eyes, he understood—and the two talked about Proust and grief for a few minutes before the tour resumed.

"I don't know," Hockenberry said at last. "You once described the ship you took in from Jupiter, and it sounded high tech beyond my understanding. Everything I'm looking at here seems . . . looks like . . . I don't know."

Orphu rumbled loudly. When he spoke, Hockenberry thought, not for the first time, that the huge moravec sounded Falstaffian.

"It probably looks like the engine room of the *Titanic* to you," said Orphu.

"Well, yes. *Should* it?" said Hockenberry, trying not to sound more ignorant of such things than he was. "I mean, your moravec technology must be three thousand years beyond the *Titanic*. Three thousand years beyond my end-time in the early Twenty-first Century even. Why this . . . this?"

"Because it's based largely on mid-Twentieth Century plans," rumbled Orphu of Io. "Our engineers wanted something fast and dirty that would get us to Earth in the least possible time. In this case, about five weeks."

"But Mahnmut and you once told me that you zipped in from Jupiter space in *days*," said Hockenberry. "And I remember you talked about boron solar sails, fusion engines . . . a lot of terms I didn't understand. Are you using those things in this ship?"

"No," said Mahnmut. "We had the advantage coming in-system of using the energy from Jupiter's flux tube and a linear accelerator in Jovian orbit—a device our engineers have been working on for more than two centuries. We don't have those things going for us here in Mars orbit. We had to build this ship from scratch."

"But why Twentieth Century technology?" asked Hockenberry, looking at the huge pistons and driveshafts gleaming up toward the ceiling sixty or seventy feet overhead in the giant room. It *did* look like the engine room in the *Titanic* in that movie, only more so—bigger, more pistons, more gleaming bronze and steel and iron. More levers. More valves. And there were things that looked like giant shock absorbers. And the gauges everywhere looked like they measured steam pressure, not fusion reactors or some such. The air smelled of oil and steel.

"We had the plans," said Orphu. "We had the raw materials, both brought from asteroids in the Belt and mined right on Phobos and Deimos. We had the pulse units . . ." He paused.

"What are pulse units?" asked Hockenberry.

Big mouth, sent Mahnmut.

What, do you want me to hide *their presence from him?* sent Orphu.

Well, yes . . . at least until we were a few million miles away from here toward Earth, preferably with Hockenberry on board.

He might notice the effect of the pulse units during our departure and get curious, sent Orphu of Io.

"The pulse units are . . . small fission devices," Mahnmut said aloud to Hockenberry. "Atomic bombs."

"Atomic bombs?" said Hockenberry. "Atomic *bombs*? Aboard this ship? How many?"

"Twenty-nine thousand seven hundred in the charge storage magazines you passed through on the way to the engine room," said Orphu. "Another three thousand and eight in reserve stored below the engine room here."

"Thirty-two thousand atomic bombs," Hockenberry said softly. "I guess you guys are expecting a fight when you get to Earth."

Mahnmut shook his red and black head. "The pulse units are for propellant. To get us *to* Earth."

Hockenberry raised his palms to show his lack of understanding.

"These huge piston things are . . . well . . . pistons," said Orphu. "On the way to Earth, we'll be kicking a bomb out through a hole in the center of the pusher-plate beneath us about once every second for the first few hours—then once an hour for much of the rest of the flight."

"For every pulse cycle," adds Mahnmut, "we eject a charge—you'd just see a puff of steam out in space—we spray oil on the pusher-plate out there to act as an anti-ablative for the plate and the ejection tube muzzle, then the bomb explodes, and there'd be a flash of plasma that slams against the pusher-plate."

"Wouldn't that destroy the plate?" said Hockenberry. "And the ship?"

"Not at all," said Mahnmut. "Your scientists worked all this out in the 1950s. The plasma event slams the pusher-plate forward and drives these huge reciprocating pistons back and forth. Even after just a few hundred explosions behind our butt, the ship will begin to pick up some real speed."

"These gauges?" said Hockenberry, putting his hand on one that looked like a steam pressure gauge.

"That's a steam pressure gauge," said Orphu of Io. "The one next to it is an oil pressure gauge. The one above you there is a voltage regulator. You were right, Dr. Hockenberry . . . this room would be more quickly understood and manned by an engineer from the *Titanic* in 1912 than by a NASA engineer from your era."

"How powerful are the bombs?"

Shall we tell him? sent Mahnmut.

Of course, tightbeamed Orphu. *It's a little late to start lying to our guest now.*

"Each propellant charge packs a little more than forty-five kilotons," said Mahnmut.

"Forty-five kilotons each—twenty-four thousand-some bombs," muttered Hockenberry. "Are they going to leave a trail of radioactivity between Mars and Earth?"

"They're fairly clean bombs," said Orphu. "As fission bombs go."

"How big are they?" asked Hockenberry. He realized that the engine room must be hotter than the rest of the ship. There was sweat beaded on his chin, upper lip, and brow.

"Come up a level," said Mahnmut, leading the way to a spiral stairway broad enough for Orphu to repellor up the wide steps with them. "We'll show you."

Hockenberry guessed the room to be about a hundred and fifty feet in diameter and half that tall. It was almost completely filled with racks and conveyor belts and metal levels and ratcheting chains and chutes. Mahnmut pushed an oversized red button and the conveyor belts and chains and sorting devices began whirring and moving, shunting along hundreds or thousands of small silver containers that looked to Hockenberry like nothing so much as unlabeled Coke cans.

"It looks like the inside of a Coca-Cola dispenser," said Hockenberry, trying to lighten the sense of doom he was feeling with a bad joke.

"It *is* from the Coca-Cola company, circa 1959," rumbled Orphu of Io. "The designs and schematics were from one of their bottling plants in Atlanta, Georgia."

"You put in a quarter and it dispenses a Coke," managed Hockenberry. "Only instead of a Coke, it's a forty-five-kiloton bomb set to explode right behind the tail of the ship. Thousands of them."

"Correct," said Mahnmut.

"Not quite," said Orphu of Io. "Remember, this is a 1959 design. You only have to put in a dime."

The Ionian rumbled until the silver cans in the moving conveyor belt rattled in their metal rings.

Back in the hornet, just Mahnmut and him, climbing toward the widening disk of Mars, Hockenberry said, "I forgot to ask . . . does it have a name? The ship?"

"Yes," said Mahnmut. "Some of us thought it needed a name. We were first considering *Orion* . . ."

"Why *Orion*?" said Hockenberry. He was watching the rear window where Phobos and Stickney Crater and the huge ship were fast disappearing.

"That was the name your mid-Twentieth Century scientists gave the ship and the bomb-propellant project," said the little moravec. "But in the end, the prime integrators in charge of the Earth voyage accepted the name that Orphu and I finally suggested."

"What's that?" Hockenberry settled deeper into his forcefield chair as they began to roar and sizzle into Mars' atmosphere.

"*Queen Mab*," said Mahnmut.

"From *Romeo and Juliet*," said Hockenberry. "That must have been your suggestion. You're the Shakespeare fan."

"Oddly enough, it was Orphu's," said Mahnmut. They were in atmosphere now and flying over the Tharsis volcanoes toward Olympus Mons and the Brane Hole to Ilium.

"How does it apply to your ship?"

Mahnmut shook his head. "Orphu never answered that question, but he did cite some of the play to Asteague/Che and the others."

"Which part?"

MERCUTIO: O then I see Queen Mab hath been with you.
BENVOLIO: Queen Mab, what's she?
MERCUTIO: She is the fairies' midwife, and she comes
           In shape no bigger than an agate stone
           On the forefinger of an alderman,
           Drawn with a team of little atomi
           Athwart men's noses as they lie asleep,
           Her wagon spokes made of long spinners' legs;
           The cover, of the wings of grasshoppers;

Her traces, of the moonshine's wat'ry beams;
Her collars, of the smallest spider web;
Her whip, of cricket's bone, the lash of film;
Her wagoner, a small grey-coated gnat
Not half so big as a round little worm
Pricked from the lazy finger of a maid.
Her chariot is an empty hazelnut
Made by the joiner squirrel or old grub,
Time out o' mind the fairies' coachmakers.
And in this state she gallops night by night
Through lovers' brains, and then they dream of love;
O'er courtiers' knees, that dream on curtsies straight;
O'er ladies' lips, who straight on kisses dream,
Which oft the angry Mab with blisters plagues . . .

. . . and so on and so forth," said Mahnmut.

"And so on and so forth," repeated Dr. Thomas Hockenberry, Ph.D. Olympus Mons, the gods' Olympos, was filling all the forward windows. According to Mahmut, the volcano was a mere 69,841 feet above Martian sea level—more than 15,000 feet shorter than people in Hockenberry's day had thought, but tall enough.'Twil serve, thought Hockenberry.

And up there, on the summit—the grassy summit—under the glowing *aegis* now catching the late-morning light—there were living creatures. And not just living creatures, but gods. *The* gods. Warring, breathing, fighting, scheming, mating creatures, not so unlike the humans Hockenberry had known in his previous life.

At that moment, all the clouds of depression that had been gathering around Hockenberry for months blew away—like the streamers of white cloud he could see blowing south from Olympos itself as the afternoon winds picked up from the northern ocean called the Tethys Sea—and at that moment, Thomas C. Hockenberry, Ph.D. in classics, was simply and purely and totally happy to be alive. Whether he chose to go on this Earth expedition or not, he realized, he would change places right then with no one in any other time or at any other place.

Mahnmut banked the hornet to the east of Mons Olympus and headed for the Brane Hole and Ilium.

17

Hera jumped from outside the exclusion field around Odysseus' home on Ithaca directly to the summit of Olympos. The grassy slopes and white-columned buildings spreading out from the huge Caldera Lake all gleamed in the lesser light from the more distant sun.

Poseidon, the Earth-Shaker, QT'd into existence nearby. "It is done? The Thunderer sleeps?"

"The Thunderer makes thunder now only through his snores," said Hera. "On Earth?"

"It is as we planned, Daughter of Kronos. All these weeks of whispering and advising Agamemnon and his captains have come to the moment. Achilles is absent—as always—below us on the red plain, so the son of Atreus is even now raising his angry multitudes against the Myrmidons and other of Achilles' loyalists who stayed behind in camp. Then straight they march against the walls and open gates of Ilium."

"And the Trojans?" said Hera.

"Hector still sleeps after his night's vigil by his brother's burning bones. Aeneas is below Olympos here, but taking no action against us in Hector's absence. Deiphobus is still with Priam, discussing the Amazons' intentions."

"And Penthesilea?"

"Just within this hour did she awake and gird herself—and so did her twelve companions—for this mortal combat to come. They rode out of the city to cheers only a short time ago and just passed the Brane Hole."

"Is Pallas Athena with her?"

"I'm here." Athena, glorious in her golden battle armor, had just QT'd into instant solidity next to Poseidon. "Penthesilea has been sent off to her doom . . . and Achilles'. The mortals everywhere are in a state of shrill confusion."

Hera reached out to touch the glorious goddess's metal-wrapped wrist. "I know this was hard for you, sister-in-arms. Achilles has been your favorite since he was born."

Pallas shook her bright, helmeted head. "No longer. The mortal lied about me killing and carrying off his friend Patroclus. He lifted his sword against me and all my Olympian kin and kind. He can't be sent down to the shady halls of Hades too soon for my pleasure."

"It's Zeus whom I still fear," interrupted Poseidon. His battle armor was a deep-sea verdigris, with elaborate loops of waves, fishes, squids, leviathans, and sharks. His helmet bracketed his eyes with the raised fighting pincers of crabs.

"Hephaestus' potion will keep our dreaded majesty snoring like a pig for seven days and seven nights," said Hera. "It's vital that we achieve all of our goals within that time—Achilles dead or exiled, Agamemnon returned as leader of the Argives, Ilium overthrown or at least the ten-year-war resumed beyond hope of peace. Then Zeus will be confronted with facts he cannot change."

"His wrath will be terrible still," said Athena.

Hera laughed. "You deign to tell *me* about the son of Kronos' wrath? Zeus's anger makes mighty Achilles' wrath look like the stone-kicking pouts of a sullen and beardless boy. But leave the Father to me. I will handle Zeus when all our ends are met. Now, we must . . ."

Before she could finish, other gods and goddesses began winking into existence there on the long lawn in front of the Hall of the Gods on the shore of Caldera Lake. Flying chariots, complete with holograms of their straining steeds pulling them, zoomed in from each point of the compass and landed nearby until the lawn filled up with cars. The gods and goddesses gravitated into three groups: those pressing close to Hera, Athena, Poseidon, and the other champions of the Greeks; those others filling in the ranks behind glowering Apollo—principal champion of the Trojans—Apollo's sister Artemis, then Ares, his sister Aphrodite, their mother Leto, Demeter, and others who had also long fought for the triumph of Troy; and the third group, who had not yet taken sides. The quantum and chariot-borne convergence continued until there were hundreds of immortals clustered on the long lawn.

"Why is everyone here?" cried Hera, amusement in her voice. "Is there no one guarding the ramparts of Olympos today?"

"Shut up, schemer!" shouted Apollo. "This plot to overthrow Ilium today is yours. And no one can find Lord Zeus to stop it."

"Oh," said white-armed Hera, "is the Lord of the Silver Bow so frightened by unseen events that he must run to his father?"

Ares, the war god, fresh from the healing and resurrection vats three times now after his ill-considered combats with Achilles, stepped up next to Phoebus Apollo. "Female," gritted the tempestuous god of battle, growing to his full fighting height of more than fifteen feet, "we continue to suffer your existence because you're the incestuous wife of our Lord Zeus. There is no other reason."

Hera laughed her most calculatingly maddening laugh. "Incestuous *wife*," she taunted. "Ironic talk from a god who beds his sister more than any other woman, goddess or mortal."

Ares lifted his long killing spear. Apollo drew his powerful bow and notched an arrow. Aphrodite unlimbered her smaller but no less deadly bow.

"Would you incite violence against our queen?" asked Athena, stepping between Hera and the bows and spear. Every god on the summit had brought their personal forcefields up to full strength at the sight of the weapons being readied.

"Don't speak to me of inciting violence!" shouted red-faced Ares at Pallas Athena. "What insolence. Do you remember only months ago when you spurred on Tydeus' son, Diomedes, to wound me with his lance? Or how you cast your own immortal's spear at me, wounding me, thinking yourself safely cloaked in your concealing cloud?"

Athena shrugged. "It was on the battlefield. My blood was up."

"*That's* your excuse for trying to kill me, you immortal bitch?" roared Ares. "*Your blood was up?*"

"Where is Zeus?" demanded Apollo, speaking to Hera.

"I am not my husband's keeper," said white-armed Hera. "Although he needs one at times."

"Where is Zeus?" repeated Apollo, Lord of the Silver Bow.

"Zeus will have nothing to do with the events of men or gods for many days more," said Hera. "Perhaps he will never return. What happens next in the world below, we on Olympos shall determine."

Apollo notched the heavy, heat-seeking arrow back, but did not yet lift the bow.

Thetis, sea goddess, Nereid, daughter of Nereus—the true Old Man of the Sea—and Achilles' immortal mother by the mortal man Peleus, stepped between the two angry groups. She wore no armor, only her elaborate gown sewn to look like patterns of seaweed and shells.

"Sister, brothers, cousins all," she began, "stop this show of petulance and pride before we harm ourselves and our mortal children, and fatally offend our Almighty Father, who will return—no matter where he is, he will return—carrying the wrath at our defiance on his noble brow and death-dealing lightning in his hands."

"Oh, shut up," cried Ares, shifting the long killing spear in his right hand to throwing position. "If you hadn't dipped your wailing, mortal brat in the sacred river to make him near-immortal, Ilium would have triumphed ten years ago."

"I dipped no one in the river," said Thetis, drawing herself up to her full height and folding her slightly scaly arms across her breasts. "My darling Achilles was chosen by the Fates for his great destiny, not by me. When he was newborn—and following the Fates' imperious advice sent through thoughts alone—I nightly laid the infant in the Celestial Fire itself, purging him, through his own pain and suffering—(but even then, though only a baby, my Achilles did not cry out!)—of his father's mortal parts. By night I scarred and burned him terribly. By day I healed his scorched and blackened baby flesh with the same ambrosia we use to freshen our own immortal bodies—only this ambrosia was made more effective by the Fates' secret alchemy. And I *would* have made my babe immortal, succeeded in insuring Achilles' pure divinity, had I not been spied on by my husband, the mere human man Peleus, who, seeing our only child twitching and searing and writhing in the flames, seized him by the heel and pulled him free from the Celestial Fire only minutes before my process of deification would have been finished and done with.

"Then, ignoring my objections as all husbands will, the well-meaning but meddling Peleus carried our babe off to Chiron, the wisest and least man-hating of all the centaur race, rearer of many heroes himself, who tended Achilles through childhood, healing him by herbs and salves known only to the centaur savants, then growing him strong by nourishing him with the livers of lions and the marrow of bears."

"Would that the little bastard had died in the flames," said Aphrodite.

Thetis lost her mind at that and rushed at the goddess of love, wielding no weapons but the long fishbone-nails at the ends of her fingers.

As calmly as if shooting for a prize during a friendly picnic game, Aphrodite raised her bow and shot an arrow through Thetis' left breast. The Nereid fell lifeless to the grass and the black pregoddess essence of her whirled around her corpse like a swarm of black bees. No one rushed to claim and capture the body for repair by the Healer in the blue-wormed vats.

"Murderess!" cried a voice from the depths, and Nereus himself—the Old Man of the Sea—rose from the trackless depths of Olympos' Caldera Lake, the self-same lake he'd banished himself to eight months earlier when his earthly oceans had been invaded by moravecs and men.

"Murderess!" boomed the giant amphibian again, looming fifty feet above the water, his wet beard and braided locks looking like nothing so much as a mass of writhing, slithering eels. He cast a bolt of pure energy at Aphrodite.

The goddess of love was thrown a hundred feet backward across the lawn, her god-blood-generated forcefield saving her from total destruction, but not from flames and bruises as her lovely body smashed through two huge pillars in front of the Hall of the Gods and then through the thick granite wall itself.

Ares, her loving brother, cast his spear through Nereus' right eye. Roaring so loudly that his pain could be heard in Ilium an infinite distance below, the Old Man of the Sea pulled out both spear and eyeball and disappeared beneath the red-frothed waves.

Phoebus Apollo, realizing that the Final War had begun, raised his bow before Hera or Athena could react and fired two heat-seeking arrows that honed on their hearts. His drawing and firing were faster than even immortal eye could follow.

The arrows—unbreakable titanium both, coated with their own quantum fields to penetrate other forcefields—nonetheless stopped in midflight. And then melted.

Apollo stared.

Athena threw back her helmeted head and laughed. "You've forgotten, upstart, that when Zeus is well and truly gone, the *aegis* is programmed to obey our commands, Hera's and mine."

"You started this, Phoebus Apollo," white-armed Hera said softly. "Now feel the full force of Hera's curse and Athena's anger." She gestured ever so slightly and a boulder weighing at least a half a ton, lying at water's edge, tore itself loose from Olympos' soil and hurtled at Apollo at such speeds that it twice broke the sound barrier before striking the archer in the side of his head.

Apollo flew backward with a great crash and clatter of gold and silver and bronze, tumbling head over heel for seven rods in his fall, his tightly curled locks now covered with dust and soiled with lake mud.

Athena turned, cast a war lance, and when it fell some miles across the Caldera Lake, Apollo's white-columned home there exploded in a mushroom of fire, the million bits of marble and granite and steel rising two miles toward the humming forcefield above the summit.

Demeter, Zeus's sister, cast a shock wave at Athena and Hera that only folded air and blast around their pulsing *aegis,* but which lifted Hephaestus a hundred yards into the air and slammed him far across the summit of Olympos. Red-armored Hades answered back with a cone of black fire that obliterated all temples, ground, earth, water, and air in its wake.

The nine Muses screamed and joined Ares' rallying pack. Lightning leaped down from chariots that QT'd in from nowhere and the shimmering *aegis* lashed up from Athena. Ganymede, the cup bearer and only nine-tenths immortal, fell in the no-man's-land and howled as his divine flesh burned away from mortal bones. Eurynome, daughter of Okeanos, cast her lot with Athena but was immediately set upon by a dozen Furies, who flapped and flocked around her like so many huge vampire bats. Eurynome screamed once and was borne away over the battlefield and beyond the burning buildings.

The gods ran for cover or for their chariots. Some QT'd away, but most massed in war groups on one side of the great Caldera or the other. Energy fields flared in red, green, violet, blue, gold, and a myriad of other colors as individuals melded their personal fields into focused fighting shields.

Never in the history of these gods had they fought like this—with no quarter, no mercy, no professional courtesy of the sort one god always gave another, with no assurance of resurrection at the many, many hands of the Healer or hope of the healing vats—and worst of all, with no intervention from Father Zeus. The Thunderer had always been there to restrain them, cajole them, threaten them into something less than a killing rage against their fellow immortals. But not this day.

Poseidon QT'd down to Earth to oversee the Achaean destruction of Troy. Ares rose, trailing bloody golden ichor, and rallied threescore of outraged gods—Zeus loyalists all, Trojan supporters all—to his side. Hephaestus QT'd back from where he had been blasted and spread a poison black fog across the battlefield.

The War between the Gods began that hour and spread to all Olympos and down to Ilium in the hours that followed. By sunset, the summit of Olympos was on fire and parts of the Caldera Lake had boiled away to be replaced by lava.

18

Riding out to meet Achilles, Penthesilea knew without doubt that every year, month, day, hour, and minute of her life up to this second had been nothing more than prelude to today's sure pinnacle of glory. Everything that had come before, each breath, every bit of training, each victory or loss on the battlefield, had been but preparation. In the coming hours her destiny would be fulfilled. Either she would be triumphant and Achilles dead, or she would be dead and—infinitely worse—cast down in shame and forgotten to the ages.

The Amazon Penthesilea did not plan on being cast down in shame and forgotten to the ages.

When she awoke from her nap in Priam's palace, Penthesilea had felt strong and happy. She had taken time to bathe, and when she was dressing—standing in front of the polished metal mirror in her guest quarters—she paid attention to her own face and body in a way she rarely if ever did.

Penthesilea knew that she was beautiful as judged by the highest standards of men, women, and gods. She did not care. It simply was not important to her warrior soul. But this day, while unhurriedly donning her cleaned garments and shining armor, she allowed herself to admire her own beauty. After all, she thought, she would be the last thing that fleet-footed mankilling Achilles would ever see.

In her midtwenties, the Amazon had a child-woman's face and her large green eyes seemed even larger when framed, as they were now, by her short blond curls. Her lips were firm and rarely given to smiling, but they were also full and rosy. The body reflected in the burnished metal was muscled and tanned from hours of swimming, training, and hunting in the sun, but not lean. She had a woman's full hips and behind, which she noticed with a slight pout of disapproval as she buckled her silver belt around her thin waist. Penthesilea's breasts were higher and rounder than most women's, even those of her fellow Amazons, and her nipples were pink rather than brown. She was still a virgin and planned to stay that way for the rest of her life. Let her older sister—she winced at the thought of Hippolyte's death—be seduced by men's tricks and carried away to captivity to be used as breeding stock by some hairy man; this would never be Penthesilea's choice.

As she dressed, Penthesilea removed the magical perfumed balm from a silver, pomegranate-shaped vase and rubbed it above her heart, at the base of her throat, and above the vertical line of golden hair that rose from her sex. Such were the instructions of the goddess Aphrodite, who had appeared to her the day after Pallas Athena had first spoken to her and sent her on this mission. Aphrodite had assured her that this perfume—more powerful than ambrosia—had been formulated by the goddess of love herself to affect Achilles—and only Achilles—driving him into a state of overwhelming lust. Now Penthesilea had two secret weapons—the spear Athena had given her, which could not miss its mark, and Aphrodite's perfume. Penthesilea's plan was to deliver Achilles' death blow while the mankiller stood there overcome with desire.

One of her Amazon comrades, probably her faithful captain Clonia, had polished her queen's armor before allowing herself to nap, and now the bronze and gold gleamed in the metal mirror. Penthesilea's weapons were at hand: the bow and quiver of perfectly straight arrows with their red feathers, the sword—shorter than a man's, but perfectly balanced and just as deadly at close quarters as any man's blade—and her double-bladed battle-axe, usually an Amazon's favorite weapon. But not this day.

She hefted the spear Athena had given her. It seemed almost weightless, eager to fly to its target. The long, barbed killing tip was not bronze, nor even iron, but some sharper metal forged on Olympos. Nothing could dull it. No armor could stop it. Its tip, Athena had explained, had been dipped in the deadliest poison known to the gods. One cut in Achilles' mortal heel and the poison would pump its way to the hero's heart, dropping him within seconds, sending him down to Hades a few heartbeats after that. The shaft hummed in Penthesilea's hand. The spear was as eager as she was to pierce Achilles' flesh and bring him down, filling his eyes and mouth and lungs with the blackness of death.

Athena had whispered to Penthesilea about the source of Achilles' near-invulnerability—had told her all about Thetis' attempt to make the baby an immortal, thwarted only by Peleus pulling the infant from the Celestial Fire. *Achilles' heel is mortal,* whispered Athena, *its quantum probability set hasn't been tampered with . . .* whatever that meant. To Penthesilea, it meant that she was going to kill the mankiller Achilles—and womankiller and rapist as well, she knew, a scourge of women in his conquest of almost a score of cities taken by Achilles and his rampaging Myrmidons while the other Achaeans rested on their laurels and asses here on the coast. Even in her distant Amazon lands to the north, the young Penthesilea had heard how there had been two Trojan Wars—the Achaeans with their single-minded fighting here at Ilium, followed by long periods of sloth and feasting, and Achilles with his city-destroying, decade-long swath of destruction around all of Asia Minor. Seventeen cities had fallen to his relentless attacks.

And now it is his turn to fall.

Penthesilea and her women rode out through a city filled with confusion and alarms. Criers were calling out from the walls that the Achaeans were gathering behind Agamemnon and his captains. The rumor was that the Greeks were planning a treacherous assault while Hector slept and brave Aeneas was at the front on the other side of the Hole. Penthesilea noticed groups of women in the streets wandering aimlessly in ragtag bits of men's armor, as if pretending to be Amazons. Now the watchmen on the walls were blowing trumpets and the great Scaean Gates were slammed shut behind Penthesilea and her warriors.

Ignoring the scurrying Trojan fighters falling into ranks on the plain between the city and the Achaean camps, Penthesilea led her dozen women east toward the looming Hole. She'd seen the thing during her ride in, but it still made her heart pound with excitement. More than two hundred feet tall, it was a perfect three-quarters circle sliced out of the winter sky and anchored in the rocky plains east of the city. From the north and east—she knew, since they'd approached from that direction—there was no Hole. Ilium and the sea were both visible and there was no hint of this sorcery. Only when approached from the southwest did the Hole become visible.

Achaeans and Trojans—staying separate but not fighting—were scurrying out through the Hole on foot and in chariots in long columns, as if some evacuation had been ordered. Responding to messages from Ilium and from Agamemnon's camp, Penthesilea imagined, ordered to leave their front lines against the gods and to make haste home to prepare for renewed hostility against one another.

It did not matter to Penthesilea. Her goal was Achilles' death and woe to any Achaean—or Trojan—who made the mistake of getting between her and that goal. She had sent legions of men in battle down to Hades before, and she would do it again today if she had to.

She actually held her breath as she led her double column of Amazon cavalry through the Hole, but all she felt upon emerging on the other side was a strange sense of lightness, some subtle shift in the light itself, and a momentary shortness of breath—when she did bother to inhale again—as if she were suddenly on a mountaintop where the air was thinner. Penthesilea's horse also seemed to sense the change and pulled hard against the reins, but she forced him to his course.

She could not take her eyes off Olympos. The mountain filled the western horizon . . . no, it filled the world . . . no, it *was* the world. Straight ahead of her, beyond the small bands of men and moravecs and what looked like bodies on the red ground to the Amazon who had suddenly lost all interest in anything that was not Olympos, rose first the two-mile-high vertical cliffs at the base of the home of the gods, and then ten miles more of mountain, its slopes rising up and up and up . . .

"My Queen."

Penthesilea heard the voice only distantly, recognized it at last as belonging to Bremusa, her second lieutenant after faithful Clonia, but ignored it as surely as she did the sight of the limpid ocean to their right or the great stone heads that lined the shore. These things meant nothing when compared to the looming reality of Olympos itself. Penthesilea leaned back in her thin saddle to follow the line of the shoulder of the mountain higher and then higher and then endlessly higher as it rose into and above the light blue sky . . .

"My *Queen*."

Penthesilea swiveled to rebuke Bremusa only to find that the other women had reined their horses to a stop. The Amazon queen shook her head as if emerging from a dream and rode back to them.

She realized now that all the time she had been enraptured by Olympos, they had been passing women on this side of the Hole— women running, screaming, bleeding, stumbling, weeping, falling. Clonia had dismounted and had propped the head of such a wounded woman on her knee. The woman appeared to be wearing a bizarre crimson robe.

"Who?" said Penthesilea, looking down as if from a great height. She realized now that they had been following a trail of abandoned and bloody armor for the last mile or so.

"The Achaeans," rasped the dying woman. "Achilles . . ." If she had been wearing armor, it had not helped. Her breasts has been cut off. She was almost naked. The crimson robe was actually her own blood.

"Take her back to . . ." began Penthesilea but stopped. The woman had died.

Clonia mounted and fell in to the right and rear of Penthesilea, where she always rode. The queen could feel the rage coming off her old comrade like heat from a bonfire.

"Forward," said Penthesilea and spurred her war mount. Her war axe was strapped balanced across her pommel. Athena's spear was in her right hand. They galloped the last quarter mile to the band of men ahead. The Achaeans were standing and bending over more bodies— looting them. The sound of the Greeks' laughter was clear in the thin air.

Perhaps forty women had fallen here. Penthesilea slowed her steed to a walk, but the two lines of Amazon cavalry had to break ranks. Horses—even warhorses—do not like to step on human beings, and the bloodied corpses here—women all—had fallen so close that the horses had to pick their way carefully, setting their heavy hooves down in the few open spaces between the bodies.

The men looked up from their looting and pawing. Penthesilea estimated that there were about a hundred Achaeans standing around the women's bodies, but none of these men was recognizable. There were none of the Greek heroes there. She looked five or six hundred yards farther on and saw a nobler group of men walking back to the main Achaean army.

"Look, more women," said the mangiest of the men stripping the female corpses of their armor. "And this time they brought us horses."

"What is your name?" asked Penthesilea.

The man grinned, showing missing and rotted teeth. "My name is Molion and I'm trying to decide whether to fuck you before or after I kill you, woman."

"It must be a hard decision for such a limited mind," Penthesilea said calmly. "I met a Molion once, but he was a Trojan, comrade to Thymbraeus. Also, that Molion was a living man, and you are a dead dog."

Molion snarled and pulled his sword.

Without dismounting, Penthesilea swung her two-bladed axe and beheaded the man. Then she spurred her huge warhorse and rode down three others who barely had time to raise their shields before being trampled.

With an unearthly cry, her dozen Amazon comrades spurred into battle beside her, trampling, slashing, hacking, and spearing Achaeans as surely as if they were harvesting wheat with a scythe. Those men who stood to fight, died. Those who ran, died. Penthesilea herself killed the last seven men who had been stripping corpses alongside Molion and his three trampled friends.

Her comrades Euandra and Thermodoa had run down the last of the sniveling, groveling, begging Achaeans—an especially ugly, whining bastard who announced that his name was Thersites as he pleaded for mercy—and Penthesilea astounded her sisters by ordering them to let him go.

"Take this message to Achilles, Diomedes, the Ajaxes, Odysseus, Idomeneus, and the other Argive heroes I spy staring at us from yonder hill," she boomed at Thersites. "Tell them that I, Penthesilea, Queen of the Amazons, daughter of Ares, beloved of Athena and Aphrodite, have come to end Achilles' miserable life. Tell them that I will fight Achilles in single combat if he agrees, but that I and my Amazon comrades will kill all of them if they insist. Go, deliver my message."

Ugly Thersites scampered away as fast as his shaking legs could take him.

Her good right arm, unbeautiful but totally bold Clonia, rode up next to her. "My Queen, what are you saying? We can't fight all of the Achaean heroes. Any one of them is legend . . . together they are all but invincible, more than a match for any thirteen Amazons who have ever lived."

"Be calm and resolute, my sister," said Penthesilea. "Our victory is as much in the will of the gods as in our own strong hands. When Achilles falls dead, the other Achaeans will run—as they've run from Hector and mere Trojans when far lesser leaders of theirs have fallen or been wounded. And when they run, we will swing about, ride hard, pass back through that accursed Hole, and burn their ships before these so-called heroes can rally."

"We will follow you into death, My Queen," murmured Clonia, "just as we have followed you to glory in the past."

"To glory again, my beloved sister," said Penthesilea. "Look. That rat-faced dog Thersites has delivered our message and the Achaean captains are walking this way. See how Achilles' armor gleams more brightly than any other's. Let us meet them on the clean battlefield there."

She spurred her huge horse and the thirteen Amazons galloped forward together toward Achilles and the Achaeans.

19

"What blue beam?" said Hockenberry.

They had been discussing the disappearance of this Ilium-era Earth's population—all those outside a two-hundred-mile-radius of Troy—as Mahnmut guided the hornet down toward Mars, Olympos, and the Brane Hole.

"It's a blue beam stabbing up from Delphi, in the Peloponnesus," said the moravec. "It appeared the day the rest of the human population here disappeared. We thought it was composed of tachyons, but now we're not sure. There's a theory—just a theory—that all of the other humans were reduced to their basic Calabi-Yau string components, encoded, and fired into interstellar space on that beam."

"It comes from Delphi?" repeated Hockenberry. He didn't know a thing about tachyons or Calabi-Whatsis strings, but he knew quite a bit about Delphi and its oracle.

"Yes, I could show it to you if you have another ten minutes or so before you have to get back," said Mahnmut. "The odd thing is that there's a similar blue beam coming up from our present-day Earth, the one we're headed for, but it's coming from the city of Jerusalem."

"Jerusalem," repeated Hockenberry. The hornet was rocking and pitching as it nosed down toward the Hole and Hockenberry was gripping the invisible arms of the invisible forcefield chair. "The beams go up into the air? Into space? To where?"

"We don't know. There doesn't seem to be any destination. The beams stay on for quite a long time and rotate with the Earth, of course, but they pass out of the solar system—both Earth solar systems—and neither one seems to be aimed at any particular star or globular cluster or galaxy. But the blue beams are two-way. That is, there is a flow of tachyonic energy *returning* to Delphi—and presumably to Jerusalem—so that . . ."

"Wait," interrupted Hockenberry. "Did you see that?"

They had just passed through the Brane Hole, skimming just under its upper arc.

"I did," said Mahnmut. "It was just a blur, but it looked as if humans were fighting humans back there where the Achaeans generally keep their front lines near Olympos. And look—up ahead." The moravec magnified the holographic windows and Hockenberry could see Greeks and Trojans fighting outside the walls of Ilium. The Scaean Gates—open these eight months of the alliance—were closed.

"Jesus Christ," whispered Hockenberry.

"Yes."

"Mahnmut, can we go back to where we saw the first signs of fighting? On the Mars side of the Brane Hole? There was something strange about that."

What Hockenberry had seen was mounted cavalry—a very small troop—apparently attacking infantry. Neither the Achaeans nor the Trojans used cavalry.

"Of course," said Mahnmut, bringing the hornet around in a swooping bank. They accelerated back toward the Hole again.

Mahnmut, are you still copying me? came Orphu's voice on the tightbeam, relayed through the Hole by the transponders they'd buried there.

Loud and clear.

Is Dr. Hockenberry still with you?

Yes.

Stay on tightbeam then. Don't let him know we're talking. Do you see anything strange there?

We do. We're going back to investigate it. Cavalry fighting Argive hoplites on the Mars side of the Brane, Argives against Trojans on the Earth side.

"Can you cloak this thing?" asked Hockenberry as they approached about two hundred feet above the dozen or so mounted figures who were approaching fifty-some Achaean foot soldiers. The hornet was still about a mile from the apparent confrontation. "Can you camouflage it? Make us less obvious somehow?"

"Of course." Mahnmut activated full-stealth and slowed the hornet.

No, I'm not talking about what the humans are doing, sent Orphu. *Can you see anything odd about the Brane Hole itself?*

Mahnmut not only looked with his eyes on broad-spectrum, but he interfaced with all of the hornet's instruments and sensors. *The Brane seems normal,* he sent.

"Let's land behind Achilles and his men there," said Hockenberry. "Can we do that? Quietly? "

"Of course," said Mahnmut. He brought the hornet around and set it down silently about thirty yards behind the Achaeans. More Greeks were coming toward them from the army at the rear. The moravec could see some rockvecs in the approaching group, and could make out Centurion Leader Mep Ahoo. ◦

No, it's not normal, sent Orphu of Io. *We're picking up wild fluctuations in the Brane Hole and the rest of the membrane space. Plus something's going on atop Olympos—quantum and graviton readings are off the scale. We have evidence of fission, fusion, plasma, and other explosions. But the Brane Hole is our immediate worry.*

What are the anomaly parameters? asked Mahnmut. He'd never bothered himself with learning much W-theory or its various historical precursors, M-theory or string-theory, while driving his submersible under the ice of Europa. Most of what he knew now he'd downloaded from Orphu and the main banks on Phobos to catch up with the current thinking about the Holes he'd accidentally helped create to connect the Belt with Mars—and with this alternate Earth—and to understand why all but one of the Branes had disappeared in the last few months.

The Strominger-Vafa-Susskind-Sen sensors are giving us BPS rates showing increasing disparity between the Brane's minimum mass and its charge, sent Orphu.

BPS? sent Mahnmut. He knew the mass-charge disparity had to be bad, but wasn't sure why.

Bogomol'nyi, Prasard, Sommerfield sent Orphu in his oh-what-a-moron-but-I-like-you-anyway voice. *The Calabi-Yau space near you there is undergoing a space-tearing conifold transition.*

"Great, perfect," said Hockenberry, slipping out of the invisible chair and rushing toward the lowering ramp. "What I wouldn't give to have my old scholic gear back—morphing bracelet, shotgun mike, levitation harness. Are you coming?"

"In a second," said Mahnmut. *Are you telling me the Brane Hole is going unstable?*

I'm telling you it's going to collapse any minute, sent Orphu. *We've ordered the moravecs and rockvecs around Ilium and along the coast there to get the hell out. We think they have time to load up their gear, but the hornets and shuttles should be coming out of there within the next ten minutes at about Mach 3. Be prepared for sonic booms.*

That'll leave Ilium open to air attack and QT invasion from Olympos, sent Mahnmut. He was horrified at the thought. They were abandoning their Trojan and Greek allies.

That's not our problem anymore, rumbled Orphu of Io. *Asteague/Che and the other prime integrators have ordered the evacuation. If that Brane Hole closes—and it will, Mahnmut, trust me on that—we lose all eight hundred of the technicians, missile battery vecs, and others stationed on the Earth side. They've already been ordered out. They're risking their lives even taking the time to pack up their missiles, energy projectors, and other heavy weapons, but the integrators don't want those things left behind, even if disabled.*

Can I help? Mahnmut looked out the open hatch to where Hockenberry was jogging toward Achilles and his men. He felt useless—if he left Hockenberry behind, the scholic might die in the fight here. If he didn't get the hornet airborne and through the Hole immediately, other moravecs might be sealed away from their real universe forever.

Stand by, I'll check with the integrators and General Beh bin Adee, sent Orphu. A few seconds later the tightbeam channel crackled again. *Stay where you are right now. You're the best camera angle we have on the Brane at the moment. Can you hook all your feeds to Phobos and get outside the ship to add your own imaging to the link?*

Yes, I can do that, sent Mahnmut. He de-stealthed the hornet—he didn't want the approaching mob of Achaeans and rockvecs to bump into it—and hurried down the ramp to join Hockenberry.

Walking up to the cluster of Achaeans, Hockenberry felt a growing sense of unreality tinged with guilt. *This is my doing. If I hadn't morphed myself into Athena's form and kidnapped Patroclus eight months ago, Achilles wouldn't have declared war on the gods and none of this would have happened. If anyone dies here today, it's all my fault.*

It was Achilles who turned his back on the approaching cavalry and greeted him. "Welcome, Hockenberry, son of Duane."

There were about fifty of the Achaean leaders and their captains and spearmen standing there waiting for the women on horseback to arrive—from the rapidly closing distance, Hockenberry could see that they were indeed women decked out in resplendent armor—and among the top men here he recognized Diomedes, Big and Little Ajax, Idomeneus, Odysseus, Podarces, and his younger friend Menippus, Sthenelus, Euryalus, and Stichius. The former scholic was surprised to see the leering camp-lawyer Thersites standing by Achilles' side—normally, Hockenberry knew, the fleet-footed mankiller would not have allowed the corpse-robber within a mile of his person.

"What's going on?" he asked Achilles.

The tall, blond god-man shrugged. "It's been a bizarre day, son of Duane. First the gods refused to come down to fight. Then a motley group of Trojan women attacked us, killing Philoctetes with a lucky spearcast. Now these Amazons approach after killing more of our men, or so this rat by my side tells us."

Amazons.

Mahnmut came hurrying up. Most of the Achaeans were used to the little moravec now and gave the metal-plastic creature only a passing glance before returning their gazes to the fast-approaching Amazons.

"What's happening?" Mahnmut had spoken to Hockenberry in English. Rather than answer in the same language, Hockenberry recited—

> "Ducit Amazonidum lunatis agmina peltis
> Penthesilea furens, mediisque in milibus ardet,
> aurea sunectens exwerta cingula mammae
> bellatrix, audetque viris concurrere virgo."

"Don't make me download Latin," said Mahnmut. He nodded toward the huge horses being reined to a stop not five yards in front of them all, throwing up a cloud of dust that rolled over the Achaean captains.

"Furious, Penthesilea leads a battleline of Amazons," translated Hockenberry. "With crescent shields, and she glows in the middle of thousands, fastening golden belts around the exposed breast, female warrior, and the maiden dares run with men."

"That's just great," the little moravec said sarcastically. "But the Latin . . . it's not Homer, I presume?"

"Virgil," whispered Hockenberry in the sudden silence in which the paw of a horse's hoof sounded crashingly loud. "Somehow we're in the Aeneid here."

"That's just great," repeated Mahnmut.

The rockvec techs are almost loaded and will be ready to lift off from the Earth side in five minutes or less, sent Orphu. And there's something else you have to know. We're pushing up the launch time for the Queen Mab.

How soon? sent Mahnmut, his mostly organic heart sinking. We promised Hockenberry forty-eight hours to make up his mind and try to talk Odysseus into going with us.

Well, he has less than an hour now, sent Orphu of Io. Maybe forty minutes if we can get these damned rockvecs tranked and shelved and their weapons stored. You'll have to get back up here by then or stay behind.

But The Dark Lady, sent Mahnmut, thinking of his submersible. He'd not even run the last checks on the sub's many systems.

They're stowing her in the hold right now, sent Orphu from the Mab. I can feel the bumps. You can do your checklist when we're in flight. Don't dally down there, old friend. The tightbeam went from crackle to hiss as Orphu signed off.

Only one row back from the thin front line here, Hockenberry saw that the Amazons' horses were huge . . . as big as Percherons or those Budweiser horses. There were thirteen of them and Virgil, bless his heart, had been right—the Amazon women's armor left each of their left breasts bare. The effect was . . . distracting.

Achilles took three steps in front of the other men. He was so close to the blonde Amazon's horse that he could have stroked its nose. He didn't.

"What do you want, woman?" he asked. For such a huge, heavily muscled man, Achilles' voice was very soft.

"I am Penthesilea, daughter of the war god Ares and the Amazon queen Otrere," said the beautiful woman from high on her armored horse. "And I want you dead, Achilles, son of Peleus."

Achilles threw back his head and laughed. It was an easy, relaxed laugh, and all the more chilling to Hockenberry because of that. "Tell me woman," Achilles said softly, "how do you find the courage to challenge us, the most powerful heroes of this age, fighters who have laid siege to Olympos itself? Most of us are sprung from the blood of the Son of Kronos himself, Lord Zeus. Would you really do battle with us, woman?"

"The others can go if they want to live," called down Penthesilea, her voice as calm as Achilles' but louder. "I have no fight with Ajax, son of Telamon, or with the son of Tydeus or the son of Deucalion or the son of Laertes or the others gathered here. Only with you, son of Peleus."

The men listed—Big Ajax, Diomedes, Idomeneus, and Odysseus— looked startled for a second, glanced at Achilles, and then laughed in unison. The other Achaeans joined in the laughter. Fifty or sixty more Argive fighters were coming up from the rear, the rockvec Mep Ahoo in their ranks.

Hockenberry didn't notice as Mahnmut's black-visored head swiveled smoothly around, and Hockenberry had no idea that Centurion Leader Mep Ahoo was tightbeaming the smaller moravec about the imminent collapse of the Brane Hole.

"You have offended the gods by your feeble attack on their home," cried Penthesilea, her voice rising until it could be heard by the men a hundred yards away. "You have wronged the peaceful Trojans by your failed attack on *their* home. But today you die, womankiller Achilles. Prepare to do battle."

"Oh, my," said Mahnmut in English.

"Jesus Christ," whispered Hockenberry.

The thirteen women screamed in their Amazon language, kicked their warhorses' sides, the giant mounts leaped forward, and the air was suddenly filled with spears, arrows, and the clatter of bronze points slamming into armor and onto hastily raised shields.

20

Along the coast of the northern Martian sea, called the Northern Ocean
or the Tethys Sea by the inhabitants of Olympos, the Little Green Men—
also known as *zeks*—have erected more than eleven thousand great
stone heads. Each of the heads is twenty meters tall. They are identical—
each showing an old man's face with a fierce beak of a nose, thin lips,
high brow, frowning eyebrows, bald crown, firm chin, and a fringe of
long hair streaming back over his ears. The stone for the heads comes
from giant quarries gouged into the cliffs of the geologic tumble known
as Noctis Labyrinthus on the westernmost end of the four-thousand-
two-hundred-kilometer-long inland sea filling the rift known as Valles
Marineris. From the quarries at Noctis Labyrinthus, the little green men
have loaded each uncarved block of stone onto broad-beamed barges
and floated them the length of Valles Marineris. Once out into the
Tethys, *zek*-crewed feluccas with lanteen sails have guided the barges
into position along the coast, where hundreds of thronging LGM unload
each stone and carve the head in place as it lies on the sand. When the
carving is finished except for the hair on the back of the head, the mob
of *zeks* roll each head to a stone basepad prepared for it, sometimes having to lift the head up cliffs or transport it across bogs and marshes, and
then they pull it upright using a combination of pulleys, tackle, and
shifting sand. Finally they set a stone stem from the neck into the base
stone niche and rock the huge head into place. Then a dozen LGM finish the carving of the wavy hair while the majority of the little beings
move on to work on the next head.

The identical faces all look out to sea.

The first head was erected almost an Earth-measured century and a
half ago, at the base of Olympus Mons near where the surf of the Tethys
Sea rolls in, and since then the little green men have placed another head
every kilometer of the way, traveling east, around the great mushroom-
shaped peninsula called Tempe Terra, then curving back south and into
the estuary of Kasei Valles, then southeast along the marshes of Lunae

Planum, then to both sides of the huge estuary and sea-within-a-sea of Chryse Planitia, then on both cliff-faced shores of the broad estuary of Valles Marineris, and finally—in just the last eight months—northeast along the steep cliffs of Arabia Terra toward the northernmost archipelagoes of Deuteronilus and Protonilus Mensae.

But this day all work on the heads has ceased and more than a hundred feluccas have carried the LGM—meter-tall green photosynthesizing hominids with transparent flesh, no mouth or ears and coal-black eyes—to a point on the broad beaches of Tempe Terra some two hundred kilometers across the curve of water from Olympus Mons. From here the island volcano of Alba Patera can be seen far out in the sea to the west and the incredible massif of Olympus Mons rises up over the shoulder of the world far to the southwest.

The stone heads line a cliff face here some several hundred meters back from the water, but the beach is broad and flat and it is here that all seven thousand three hundred and three *zeks* have gathered, creating a solid mass of green along the beach except for an empty semicircle of sand some fifty-one meters across. For several Martian hours, the little green men stand silent and motionless, their black coal-button eyes trained on the empty sand. Feluccas and barges bob slightly to the very low Tethys surf. The only sound is wind blowing in from the west, occasionally lifting sand and pelting it against transparent green skin or whistling very slightly among the low gorse plants beyond the beach and below the cliffs.

Suddenly the air smells of ozone—although the *zeks* have no noses to pick up this scent—and repeated thunderclaps explode close above the beach. Although the LGM have no ears, they feel these explosions of sound through their incredibly sensitive skin.

Two meters above the beach, there suddenly appears a three-dimensional red rhomboid about fifteen meters wide. This rhomboid widens but then grows pinched at the waist, until it resembles two red candy kisses. At the points of these kisses, a tiny sphere emerges and then grows into a three-dimensional green oval, which appears to have swallowed the original red rhomboid. The oval and rhomboid begin to spin in opposite directions until sand is thrown a hundred meters into the air.

The LGM stand in the growing storm and stare impassively.

The three-dimensional oval and rhomboid spin themselves into a sphere, completing the original shape's flop-transition mirror rephrasing. A circle ten meters across appears in midair and seems to sink into the sand until a Brane Hole cuts a slice out of space and time. Because this Brane Hole is newborn, its protective world-sheet is still visible, petals and layers of eleven-dimensional energy protecting the sand, the air, Mars, and the universe from this deliberate degeneration of space-time fabric.

From the hole emerges a puffing, chugging sort of steam-powered carriole, hidden gyroscopes balancing the metal and wooden mass on its single rubber wheel. The vehicle clears the Hole and comes to a stop precisely in the center of the space the *zeks* have left clear on the sand. An intricately carved door opens on the vehicle and wooden steps lower and unfold like some carefully contrived puzzle.

Four voynix—two-meter-tall metallic bipeds with barrel chests, no necks, and heads looking like mere humps on their bodies—emerge from the carriole and, using their manipulator hands rather than their cutting-blade hands, begin to assemble a complex apparatus that includes silver tentacles ending in small parabolic projectors. When they are finished, the voynix step back toward the now-silent steam vehicle and freeze into immobility.

A man or a projection of a man shimmers first into visiblity and then into apparent solidity there on the sand between the projector's tentacle-filaments. He is an old man in a blue robe covered with marvelously embroidered astronomical icons. He carries a tall wooden staff to help him walk. His gold-slippered feet are solid enough and his flickering mass heavy enough to make impressions in the sand. His features are precisely the same as the face of the statues on the cliff.

The magus walks to the edge of the limpid sea and waits.

Before long the sea stirs and something huge rises from the water just beyond the line of desultory surf. The thing is large and it comes up slowly, more like an island rising from the sea than like any organic creature such as a whale or dolphin or sea serpent or sea god. Water streams from its folds and fissures as it moves in toward the beach. The *zeks* step back and to the side, making a larger space for the thing.

In its shaping and color, it is most like a gigantic brain. The tissue is pink—like a living human brain—and the convolutions most resemble the maximized folded surface area of a brain, but there the resemblance to mind matter ends since this thing has multiple pairs of yellow eyes set in the folds between pink tissue and a surfeit of hands: small grasping hands with different numbers of fingers arising from the folds and waving like sea anemones stirred by cold currents, larger hands on longer stalks set on either side of the various inset eyes, and—as becomes more apparent as the house-sized thing emerges from the water and shuffles to the sand—multiple sets of huge hands on its underside and edges to propel it, each grub-white or dead-gray hand the size of a headless horse.

Moving crablike, darting sideways onto the sodden sand, the huge thing scatters LGM farther back and then comes to a stop less than five feet from the blue-robed old man, who—after an initial backing away to give the thing room to find fingerhold on the dry beach—now stands his ground, holding his staff and looking up calmly at the multiple sets of cold yellow eyes.

What have you done with my favorite worshiper? asks the many-handed in a voice without sound.

"He is loosed upon the world again, it pains me to say," sighs the old man.

Which world? There are too many.

"Earth."

Which Earth? There are too many.

"My Earth," said the old man. "The true one."

The brain with hands makes a sound through holes and apertures in its folds, a mucousy noise like a whale snorting thick seawater. *Prosper, where is my priestess? My child?*

"Which child?" asks the man. "Dost thou seek after your blue-eyed sow-raven whore, malignant thing, or after the hag-born freckled whelp bastard, never honored with a human shape, that she did litter there on the shore of my world?"

The magus had used the Greek word *sus* for "raven" and *korax* for "sow," obviously enjoying his little pun, just as he had with the "litter."

Sycorax and Caliban. Where are they?

"The bitch is missing. The lizard-pup is free."

My Caliban has escaped the rock on which you confined him these long centuries?

"Have I not just said so? You need to trade some of your excess eyes for ears."

Has he eaten all your puny mortals on that world yet?

"Not all. Not yet." The magus gestures with his staff toward the stone versions of his own face that look out from atop the cliff behind him. "Have you enjoyed being watched, Many-Handed?"

The brain snorts brine and mucus once again. *I'll allow the green men to labor some more and then send a tsunami to drown all of them at the same time it knocks down your pathetic spy-stone effigies.*

"Why not do it now?"

You know I can. The nonvoice somehow conveys a snarl.

"I know you can, malignant thing," says Prospero. "But drowning this race would be a crime greater than many of your other great crimes. The *zeks* are close to compassion perfected, loyalty personified, not altered from their former state as you did the gods here on your monstrous whim, but truly creatures that are mine. I new-formed them."

And for that alone it will give me more pleasure to kill them. What use are such mute, chlorophyllic ciphers? They're like ambulatory begonias.

"They have no voice," says the old magus, "but they are far from mute. They communicate with one another through genetically altered packages of data, passed cell to cell by touch. When they must communicate with someone outside their race, one of them volunteers his heart up to touch, dying as an individual but then being absorbed by all the others and thus living on.'Tis a beautiful thing."

Manesque exire sepulcris, thinks-hisses the many-handed Setebos. *All you've done is call up the dead men from their graves. You play Medea's game*

Without warning, Setebos pivots on his walking hands and sends a smaller hand from his brainfolds shooting out twenty meters on a snake-like stalk. The gray-grub fist slams into a little green man standing near the surf, penetrates his chest, seizes his floating green heart, and rips it out. The *zek's* body falls lifeless to the sand, leaking out all its internal fluids. Another LGM instantly kneels to absorb what it can of the dead *zek's* cellular essence.

Setebos retrieves his retractable armstalk, squeezes the heart into a dry husk as one would squeeze moisture out of a sponge, and flings it away. *Its heart was as empty and voiceless as its head. There was no message there.*

"Not to you," agrees Prospero. "But the sad message now to me is not to speak so openly to my enemies. Others always suffer."

Others are meant to suffer. That's why we create them, you and I.

"Aye, to that end we have the key of both officer and office, to set all hearts in the state to what tune that pleases our ear. But your creations offend all, Setebos—especially Caliban. Your monster child is the ivy that hid my princely trunk and sucked my verdure out on it."

And so was he born to do.

"Born?" Prospero laughs softly. "Your hag-seed's bastard oozed into being amidst all the panoply of a true whore-priestess's charms—toads, beetles, bats, pigs who once were men—and the lizard-boy would have made a sty of mine own Earth had not I taken the traitorous creature in, taught it language, lodged it in my own cell, used it with humane care, and showed to it all the qualities of humankind . . . for all the good it did me or the world or the lying slave itself."

All the qualities of humankind, snorts Setebos. It moves five paces forward on its huge walking hands until its shadow falls over the old man. *I taught him power. You taught him pain.*

"When it did, like your own foul race, forget his own meaning and begin to gabble like a thing most brutish, I deservedly confined it into a rock where I kept it company in a form of myself."

You exiled Caliban to that orbital rock and sent one of your holograms there so that you could bait and torture him for centuries, lying magus.

"Torture? No. But when it disobeyed, I racked the foul amphibian with cramps, filled his bones with ache, and made him roar so as to make the other beasts of that now-fallen orbital isle tremble at his din. And I shall do so again when I capture him."

Too late. Setebos snorts. His unblinking eyes all turn to look down at the old man in the blue robe. Fingers twitch and sway. *You said yourself that my son, with whom I am well pleased, is loosed upon your world. I knew this, of course. I will be there soon to join him. Together, along with the thousands of little* calibani *you were so obliging as to create when you still dwelt among the post-humans there and thought that doomed world good, father and son-grandson will soon scour your green orb into a more pleasing place.*

"A swamp, you mean," says Prospero. "Filled with foul smells, fouler creatures, all forms of blackness, and all infections that fetch up from bogs, fens, flats, and the stink from Prosper's fall."

Yes. The huge, pink-brain thing seems to dance up and down on its long fingerlegs, swaying as if to unheard music or pleasing screams.

"Then Prosper must not fall," whispers the old man. "Must not fall."

You will, magus. You are but a shadow of a rumor of a hint of a noosphere—a personification of a centerless, soulless pulse of useless information, senseless mumbles from a race long fallen into dotage and decay, a cyber-sewn fart in the wind. You will fall and so shall your useless bio-whore, Ariel.

Prospero lifts his staff as if to strike the monster. Then he lowers it and leans on it as though suddenly drained of all energy. "Ariel is still our Earth's good and faithful servant. She shall never serve you or your monster son or your blue-eyed witch."

She will serve us by dying.

"Ariel *is* Earth, monster," breathes Prospero. "My darling grew into full consciousness from the noosphere interweaving itself with the self-aware biosphere. Would you kill a whole world to feed your rage and vanity?"

Oh, yes.

Setebos leaps forward on its giant fingertips and seizes up the old man in five hands, lifting him close to two of its sets of eyes. *Where is Sycorax?*

"She rots."

Circe is dead? Setebos' daughter and concubine cannot die.

"She rots."

Where? How?

"Age and envy did turn her into a hoop, and I rolled her into the form of a fish, which now rots from the head down."

The many-handed makes its mucus-snort and tears Prospero's legs off, casting them into the sea. Then the thing rips away the magus's arms, feeding them into a maw that opens from the deepest orifice of its folds. Finally, it pulls the old man's entrails out, slurping them up as it would a long noodle.

"Does this amuse you?" asks Prospero's head before that, too, is crunched by gray finger-thumbs and fed into the many-handed's maw.

Silver tentacles on the beach flicker and the parabolic suckers at the end shine. Prospero flicks back into solidity farther away on the beach.

"You are a dull thing, Setebos. Ever angry, ever hungry, but tiresome and dull."

I will find your true corporeal self, Prospero. Trust this. On your Earth or in its crust or under its sea or on its orbit, I will find the organic mass that once was you and I will chew on you slowly. There is no doubt of this.

"Dull," says the magus. He looks weary and sad. "Whatever the fate of your clay-made gods and my *zeks* here on Mars—and my beloved men and women on the Earth of Ilium—you and I will meet again soon. On Earth this time. And this, our long war, will soon and finally end for the better or for the worse."

Yes. The many-handed thing spits bloody shreds out onto the sand, pivots on its under-hands, and scuttles back into the sea until all that can be seen of it is a bloody spouting from its half-submerged tophole.

Prospero sighs. He nods to the voynix, crosses to the nearest LGM, and hugs one of the little green men.

"As much as I want to speak with you and hear your thoughts, my beloveds, my old heart can bear to see no more of your kind die today. So until I venture here again, in happier times, I pray thee, *corragio!* Have courage! *Corragio!*

The voynix come forward and flick off the projector. The magus vanishes. The voynix carefully fold up the silver tentacles, carry the projecting machine to the steam carriole, and disappear up its steps into its red-lighted interior. The steps fold up. The steam engine chugs more loudly.

The carriole puffs around in a lumbering, sand-spitting circle on the beach, the *zeks* silently stepping aside, and then the unwieldy machine lumbers through the Brane Hole and disappears.

A few seconds later, the Brane Hole itself shrinks, shrivels back into its eleven-dimensional world sheet of pure colored energy, shrinks again, and flicks out of existence.

For a while, the only sound or movement comes from the lethargic waves sliding into the red beach. Then the LGM disperse to their feluccas and barges and set sail back to their stone heads yet to be carved and raised.

21

Even as she spurred her horse forward and lifted Athena's spear for the killing throw, Penthesilea realized that she'd overlooked two things that might seal her fate.

First of all—incredibly—she realized that Athena had never told her, nor had she asked the goddess, which heel of the mankiller's was mortal. Penthesilea had assumed it was the right heel—that had been her image of Peleus pulling the baby from the Celestial Fire—but Athena had not specified, saying only that *one* of Achilles' heels was mortal.

Penthesilea had imagined the difficulty of striking the hero's heel, even with Athena's charmed spear—feeling safe in assuming that Achilles would not be running away from her—but she'd instructed her Amazon comrades to strike down as many Achaeans to the rear of Achilles as possible. Penthesilea planned to throw at the fleet-footed mankiller's heel the instant he turned to see who was wounded and who was dead, as any loyal captain would do. But to make this strategy work, Penthesilea had to hold back on her part of the attack, allowing her sisters to strike down these others so that Achilles would be made to turn. It went against Penthesilea's warrior nature not to lead, not to be the first to make killing contact, and even though her sisters understood this attack plan was necessary for the mankiller to be brought down, it caused the Amazon queen to flush with shame as the line of horses closed with the line of men as Penthesilea's huge steed hung a few seconds behind the others.

Then she realized her second mistake. The wind was blowing in from behind Achilles, not toward him. Part of Penthesilea's plan depended upon the confusing effect of Aphrodite's perfume, but the muscled male idiot had to *smell* it for the plan to work. Unless the wind changed—or unless Penthesilea closed the distance until she was literally on top of the blond Achaean warrior—the magical scent would not be a factor.

Fuck it, thought the Amazon queen as her comrades began to fire arrows and hurl spears. *Let the Fates have their way and Hades take the hindmost! Ares—Father!—be with me and protect me now!*

She half-expected the god of war to appear at her side then, and per-haps Athena and Aphrodite as well since it was their will that Achilles should die this day, but no god or goddess showed up in the few sec-onds before horses impaled themselves on hastily raised spears and thrown lances thunked down onto hurriedly raised shields and the un-stoppable Amazons collided with the immovable Achaeans.

At first, both luck and the gods seemed to be with the Amazons. Al-though several of their horses were impaled on spearpoint, the huge steeds crashed on through Argive lines. Some of the Greeks fell back; others simply fell. The Amazon warriors quickly encircled the fifty or so men around Achilles and began slashing downward with their swords and spears.

Clonia, Penthesilea's favorite lieutenant and the finest archer of all the living Amazons, was firing arrows as quickly as she could notch and release. Her targets were all behind Achilles, forcing the mankiller to turn as each man was hit. The Achaean Menippus went down with a long shaft through his throat. Menippus' friend, the mighty Podarces, son of Iphiclus and brother of the fallen Protesilaus, leaped forward in rage, trying to pierce the mounted Clonia through the hip with his lance, but the Amazon Bremusa slashed the lance in half and then cut off Po-darces' arm at the elbow with a mighty downward slash.

Penthesilea's sisters-in-arms, Euandra and Thermodoa, had been dismounted—their warhorses crashing to the ground, pierced through the heart by Achaean long lances—but the two women were on their feet in an instant, armored back to armored back, their crescent shields flashing—as they held off a circle of screaming, attacking Greek men.

Penthesilea found herself crashing through Argive shields in the sec-ond wave of Amazon attack, her comrades Alcibia, Dermachia, and Derione by her side. Bearded faces snarled up at them and were slashed down. An arrow, fired from the Achaeans' rear ranks, ricocheted off Penthesilea's helmet, causing her vision to blur red for an instant.

Where is Achilles? The confusion of battle had disoriented her for a moment, but then the Amazon queen saw the mankiller twenty paces to her right, surrounded by the core of Achaean captains—the Ajaxes, Idomeneus, Odysseus, Diomedes, Sthenelus, Teucer. Penthesilea gave out a loud Amazon war cry and kicked her horse in the ribs, urging it toward the core of heroes.

At that second the mob seemed to part for an instant just as Achilles turned to watch one of his men, Euenor of Dulichium, fall with one of Clonia's arrows in his eye. Penthesilea could easily see Achilles' exposed calf under the greaves' straps, his dusty ankles, his calloused heels.

Athena's spear seemed to hum in her hand as she drew back and threw with all her might and strength. The lance flew true, striking the fleet-footed mankiller in his unprotected right heel . . . and glancing away.

Achilles' head snapped around and came up until his blue-eyed gaze locked on Penthesilea. He grinned a horrible grin.

The Amazons were engaged with the core group of Achaean men now, and their luck began to turn.

Bremusa cast a spear at Idomeneus, but Deucalion's son raised his round shield almost casually and the lance broke in two. When he cast his longer spear, it flew deadly true, piercing the red-haired Bremusa just below the left breast and coming out through her spine. She tumbled backward off her lathered horse and half a dozen lesser Argives raced to strip her of her armor.

Screaming rage at their sister's fall, Alcibia and Dermachia drove their horses at Idomeneus, but the two Ajaxes grabbed the steeds' reins and wrestled them to a stop with their awful strength. When the two Amazons leaped down to carry the battle on foot, Diomedes, son of Tydeus, decapitated both of them with one wide sweep of his sword. Penthesilea watched in horror as Alcibia's head rolled, still blinking, to a dusty stop, only to be lifted up by the hair by a laughing Odysseus.

Penthesilea felt her leg raked by some grasping unnamed Argive and she plunged her second spear down through the man's chest until it pierced his bowels. He fell away, mouth gaping, but took her spear with him. She freed her battle-axe and spurred her horse forward, riding with only her knees holding her on to her steed.

Derione, riding to the Amazon queen's right, was pulled off her horse by Little Ajax, son of Oileus. On her back, her breath knocked out of her, Derione was just reaching for her sword when Little Ajax laughed and slammed his spear through her chest, twisting it until the Amazon stopped writhing.

Clonia fired an arrow at Little Ajax's heart. His armor deflected it. That is when Teucer, bastard son of Telamon, master archer of all archers, shot three fast arrows into the grunting Clonia—one in her throat, one through her armor into her stomach, a last one so deep into her bared left breast that only the feathers and three inches of the end of the shaft stayed visible. Penthesilea's dear friend fell lifeless from her bleeding horse.

Euandra and Thermodoa were still standing and fighting back to back—though wounded and bleeding and almost falling over from weariness—when the press of Achaeans around them fell away and Meriones, son of Molus, friend of Idomeneus and second in command of the Cretans, cast two spears at once—one from each hand. The heavy spears cut through all layers of the Amazon women's light armor and Thermodoa and Euandra fell dead in the dust.

All the other Amazons were down now. Penthesilea was wounded with a hundred scratches and slashes, but none of them mortal. Her axe blades were covered with blood and Argive gore, but the weapon was too heavy for her to lift now, so she set it aside and pulled her short sword. The space between her and Achilles opened wider.

As if the goddess Athena had ordained it, the unbroken spear she'd cast at Achilles' right heel was on the ground near her exhausted horse's right hoof. Normally, the Amazon queen could have bent low from a galloping horse to swoop up the magical weapon, but she was too exhausted, her armor was too heavy on her, and her wounded steed had no strength left to move, so Penthesilea slipped sideways on her saddle and slid down, bending low to retrieve the spear just as two of Teucer's arrows whizzed over her helmet top.

When she stood, there was no one left in her focused vision except Achilles. The rest of the surging throngs of screaming Achaeans were unimportant blurs.

"Throw again," said Achilles, still grinning his horrible grin.

Penthesilea put every ounce of strength left to her in the spearcast, throwing low where Achilles' bare, muscular thighs were visible below the circle of his beautiful shield.

Achilles crouched as quickly as any panther. Athena's spear struck his shield and splintered.

Now Penthesilea could only stand there and grasp her axe again as Achilles, still grinning, lifted his own lance, the legendary spear that the centaur Chiron had made for his father, Peleus, the lance that never missed its mark.

Achilles threw. Penthesilea raised her crescent shield. The lance smashed through the shield without slowing, pierced her armor, tore through her right breast and out her back, and went through her horse standing behind her, piercing its heart as well.

Amazon queen and her war steed fell into the dust together, Penthesilea's legs and feet flying high on the pendulum of the rising spear embedded in both their chests. As Achilles approached, sword in hand, Penthesilea strained to hold him in her sight as her vision dimmed. The axe fell from her nerveless fingers.

"Holy shit," whispered Hockenberry.

"Amen," said Mahnmut.

The ex-scholic and little moravec had been next to Achilles during the

entire brawl. They walked forward now as Achilles stood next to
Penthesilea's twitching body.

"*Tum saeva Amazon ultimus cecidit metus,*" murmured Hockenberry.
Then the savage Amazon fell, our greatest fear.

"Virgil again?" said Mahnmut.

"No, Pyrrhus in Seneca's tragedy, *Troades.*"

Now a strange thing happened.

As various Achaeans crowded around to strip the dead or dying
Penthesilea of her armor, Achilles folded his arms and stood above her,
his nostrils flaring as if taking in the stink of blood and horse sweat and
death. Then the fleet-footed mankiller raised his huge hands to his face,
covered his eyes, and began to weep.

Big Ajax, Diomedes, Odysseus, and several other captains who had
pressed close to see the dead Amazon queen stepped back in amazement. Rat-faced Thersites and some lesser Achaeans ignored the weeping man-god and persisted in their stripping of Penthesilea's armor,
pulling her helmet from her lolling head, allowing the dead queen's
golden locks to tumble down.

Achilles threw his head back and moaned as he had on the morning of
Patroclus' murder and kidnapping by Hockenberry disguised as Athena.
The captains stepped farther back from the dead woman and horse.

Thersites used his knife to cut away the straps on Penthesilea's
chestplate armor and belt, slashing into the dead queen's fair flesh in his
hurry to gather his unearned spoils. The queen was all but naked now—
only one dangling greave, her silver belt, and a single sandal remaining
on her slashed and bruised but somehow still-perfect body. Peleus' long
lance still pinned her to the carcass of the horse and Peleus' son made no
move to retrieve the spear.

"Step away," said Achilles. Most of the men obeyed at once.

Ugly Thersites—Penthesilea's armor under one arm and the queen's
bloodied helmet under his other arm—laughed over his shoulder as he
continued to strip her of her belt. "What a fool you are, son of Peleus, to
weep so for this fallen bitch, standing there sobbing for her beauty. She's
a meal for worms now, worth no more than that."

"Step away," said Achilles in his terrible monotone. Tears continued
to streak down his dusty face.

Emboldened by the mankiller's show of womanly weakness, Thersites ignored the command and tugged the silver belt from around dead
Penthesilea's hips, raising her body slightly to free the priceless band
and making the motion an obscenity by moving his own hips as if copulating with the corpse.

Achilles stepped forward and struck Thersites with his bare fist,
smashing his jaw and cheekbone, knocking every one of the rat-man's

yellow teeth out of his mouth, and sending him flying over the horse and dead queen to lie in the dust, vomiting blood from both mouth and nose.

"No grave or barrow for you, you bastard," said Achilles. "You once sneered at Odysseus, and Odysseus forgave you. You sneered at me just now, and I killed you. The son of Peleus will not be taunted without a reckoning. Go now, go on down to Hades and taunt the shadows there with your mocking wit."

Thersites choked on his own blood and vomit and died.

Achilles pulled Peleus' spear slowly—almost lovingly—from the dust, the horse's corpse, and up and out through Penthesilea's softly rocking corpse. All the Achaeans stepped farther back, not understanding the mankiller's moans and weeping.

"*Aurea cui postquam nudavit cassida frontem, vicit victorem candida forma virum,*" whispered Hockenberry to himself. "*After her gilded metal helmet was removed, her forehead exposed, her brilliant form conquered the man . . . Achilles . . . the victor.*" He looked down at Mahnmut. "Propertius, Book Three poem Eleven of his *Elegies*."

Mahnmut tugged at the scholic's hand. "Someone's going to be writing an elegy for us if we don't get out of here. And I mean *now*."

"Why?" said Hockenberry, blinking as he looked around.

Sirens were going off. The rockvec soldiers were moving among throngs of retreating Achaeans, urging them with alarms and amplified voices to get through the Hole at once. A huge retreat was under way, with chariots and running men pouring toward and through the Hole, but it wasn't the moravec loudspeakers that were creating the retreat— Olympos was erupting.

The earth . . . well, the Mars earth . . . shook and vibrated. The air was filled with the stink of sulfur. Behind the retreating Achaean and Trojan armies, the distant summit of Olympos glowed red beneath its *aegis* and columns of flame were leaping miles into the air. Already, rivers of red lava could be seen on the upper reaches of Olympus Mons, the largest volcano in the solar system. The air was full of red dust and the stink of fear.

"What's going on?" asked Hockenberry.

"The gods caused some sort of eruption up there and the Brane Hole is going to disappear any minute," said Mahnmut, leading Hockenberry away from where Achilles had knelt next to the fallen Amazon queen. The other dead Amazons had also been stripped of all their armor, and except for the core of captain-heroes, most of the men were hurrying toward the Hole.

You need to get out of there, came Orphu of Io's voice over the tight-beam to Mahnmut.

Yes, sent Mahnmut, *we can see the eruption from here.*

Worst than that, came Orphu's voice on the tightbeam. *The readings show the Calabi-Yau space there bending back toward a black hole and wormhole. String vibrations are totally unstable. Olympus Mons may or may not blow that part of Mars to bits, but you have minutes, at most, before the Brane Hole disappears. Get Hockenberry and Odysseus back to the ship here.*

Looking between the moving armor and dusty thighs, Mahnmut caught sight of Odysseus standing speaking to Diomedes thirty paces away. *Odysseus?* he sent. *Hockenberry hasn't had time to talk to Odysseus, much less convince him to come with us. Do we really need Odysseus?*

The Prime Integrator analysis says we do, sent Orphu. *And by the way, you had your video on during that entire fight. That was one hell of a thing to see.*

Why do we need Odysseus? sent Mahnmut. The ground rumbled and quaked. The placid sea to their north was no longer placid; great breakers rolled in against red rocks.

How am I supposed to know? rumbled Orphu of Io. *Do I look like a prime integrator to you?*

Any suggestions on how I'm going to persuade Odysseus to leave his friends and comrades and the war with the Trojans to come join us? sent Mahnmut. *It looks like he and the other captains—except for Achilles—are going to get into their chariots and head back through the Hole in about one minute. The smell from the volcano and all the noise are driving the horses crazy—and the people, too. How am I going to get Odysseus' attention at a time like this?*

Use some initiative, sent Orphu. *Isn't that what Europan sub-drivers are famous for? Initiative?*

Mahnmut shook his head and walked over to Centurion Leader Mep Ahoo where the rockvec stood using his loudspeaker to urge the Achaeans to return through the Brane Hole at once. Even his amplified voice was lost under the volcano rumble and the pounding of hooves and sandaled feet as the humans ran like hell to get away from Olympos.

Centurion Leader? sent Mahnmut, connecting directly via tactical channels.

The two-meter-tall black rockvec turned and snapped to attention. *Yes, sir.*

Technically, Mahnmut had no command rank in the moravec army, but in practical terms, the rockvecs understood that Mahnmut and Orphu were on the level of commanders such as the legendary Asteague/Che.

Go over to my hornet there and await further orders.

Yes, sir. Mep Ahoo left the evacuation shouts to one of the other rockvecs and jogged to the hornet.

"I have to get Odysseus over to the hornet," Mahnmut shouted to Hockenberry. "Will you help?"

Hockenberry, who was looking from the convulsions high on the shoulder of Olympos back at the quivering Brane Hole, gave the little moravec a distracted look but nodded and walked with him toward the cluster of Achaean captains.

Mahnmut and Hockenberry strode briskly past the two Ajaxes, Idomeneus, Teucer, and Diomedes to where Odysseus stood frowning at Achilles. The tactician seemed lost in thought.

"Just get him to the hornet," whispered Mahnmut.

"Son of Laertes," said Hockenberry.

Odysseus' head whipped around. "What is it, son of Duane?"

"We have word from your wife, sir."

"What?" Odysseus scowled and put his hand on his sword hilt. "What are you talking about?"

"I'm talking about your wife, Penelope, mother of Telemachus. She has sent a message to you through us, conveyed by moravec magic."

"Fuck your moravec magic," snarled Odysseus, scowling down at Mahnmut. "Go away, Hockenberry, and take that little abomination with you, before I open both of you from crotch to chin. Somehow . . . I don't know how, but somehow . . . I've always sensed that these new misfortunes rode in with you and these cursed moravecs."

"Penelope says to remember your bed," said Hockenberry, improvising and hoping he remembered his Fitzgerald correctly. He had tended to teach the *Iliad* and let Professor Smith handle the *Odyssey*.

"My bed?" frowned Odysseus, stepping away from the other captains. "What are you prattling about?"

"She says to tell you that a description of your marriage bed will be our way of letting you know that this message is truly from her."

Odysseus pulled his sword and set the side of the razored blade against Hockenberry's shoulder. "I am not amused. Describe the bed to me. For every error in your description, I will lop off one of your limbs."

Hockenberry resisted the urge to run or piss himself. "Penelope says to tell you that the frame was inlaid with gold, silver, and ivory, with thongs of oxhide stretched end to end to hold the many soft fleeces and coverlets."

"Bah," said Odysseus, "that could describe any great man's couch. Go away." Diomedes and Big Ajax had gone over to urge the still-kneeling Achilles to abandon the Amazon queen's corpse and come with them. The Brane Hole was visibly vibrating now, its edges blurry. The roar from Olympos was so loud now that everyone had to shout to be heard.

"Odysseus!" cried Hockenberry. "This is important. Come with us to hear your message from fair Penelope."

The short, bearded man turned back to glower at the scholic and moravec. His sword was still raised. "Tell me where I moved the bed after my bride and I moved in, and I may let you keep your arms."

"You never moved it," said Hockenberry, his raised voice steady despite his pounding heart. "Penelope says that when you built your palace, you left a strong, straight olive tree where the bedroom is today. She says that you cut away the branches, set the tree into a ceiling of wood, carved the trunk, and left it as one post of your marriage bed. These were words she said to tell you so that you would know that it was truly she who sent her message."

Odysseus stared for a long minute. Then he slid his sword back in its belt-sheath and said, "Tell me the message, son of Duane. Hurry." The man glanced at the lowering sky and roaring Olympos. Suddenly a flight of twenty hornets and dropship transports flew out through the Hole, hauling the moravec techs to safety. A series of sonic booms pounded the Martian earth and made running men duck and raise their arms to cover their heads.

"Let's go over by the moravec machine, son of Laertes. It is a message best delivered in private."

They walked through the milling, shouting men to where the black hornet crouched on its insectoid landing gear.

"Now, speak, and hurry," said Odysseus, grasping Hockenberry's shoulder in his powerful hand.

Mahnmut tightbeamed Mep Ahoo. *You have your taser?*

Yes, sir.

Taser Odysseus unconscious and load him into the hornet. Take the controls. We're going up to Phobos immediately.

The rockvec touched Odysseus on the neck, there was a spark, and the bearded man collapsed into the moravec soldier's barbed arms. Mep Ahoo slid the unconscious Odysseus into the hornet and jumped in, firing up the repellors.

Mahnmut looked around—none of the Achaeans had seemed to notice the kidnapping of one of their captains—and then jumped in next to Odysseus. "Come on," he said to Hockenberry. "The Hole's going to collapse any second. Anyone on this side stays on Mars forever." He glanced up at Olympos. "And forever may be measured in minutes if that volcano blows."

"I'm not going with you," said Hockenberry.

"Hockenberry, don't be crazy!" shouted Mahnmut. "Look over there. All the Achaean top brass—Diomedes, Idomeneus, the Ajaxes, Teucer—they're all running for the Hole."

"Achilles isn't," said Hockenberry, leaning closer to be heard. Sparks were falling all around, rattling on the roof of the hornet like hot hail.

"Achilles has lost his mind," shouted Mahnmut, thinking *Shall I have Mep Ahoo taser Hockenberry?*

As if reading his mind, Orphu came on the tightbeam. Mahnmut had forgotten that all this real-time video and sound was still being relayed up to Phobos and *Queen Mab*.

Don't zap him, sent Mahnmut. *We owe Hockenberry that. Let him make up his own mind.*

By the time he does, he'll be dead, sent Orphu of Io.

He was dead once, sent Mahnmut. *Perhaps he wants to be again.*

To Hockenberry, Mahnmut shouted, "Come on. Jump in! We need you aboard the Earth-ship, Thomas."

Hockenberry blinked at the use of his first name. Then he shook his head.

"Don't you want to see Earth again?" shouted the little moravec. The hornet was shaking on its gear as the ground vibrated with marsquake tremors. The clouds of sulfur and ash were swirling around the Brane Hole, which seemed to be growing smaller. Mahnmut realized that if he could keep Hockenberry talking another minute or two, the human would have no choice but to come with them.

Hockenberry took a step away from the hornet and gestured toward the last of the fleeing Achaeans, the dead Amazons, the dead horses, and the distant walls of Ilium and warring armies just visible through the now vibrating Brane Hole.

"I made this mess," said Hockenberry. "Or at least I helped make it. I think I should stay and try to clean it up."

Mahnmut pointed toward the war going on beyond the Brane Hole. "Ilium is going to fall, Hockenberry. The 'vec forcefields and air defenses and anti-QT fields are gone."

Hockenberry smiled even while shielding his face from the falling embers and ash. *"Et quae vagos vincina prospiciens Scythas ripam catervis Ponticam viduis ferit excisa ferro est, Pergannum incubuit sibi,"* he shouted.

I hate Latin, thought Mahnmut. *And I think I hate classics scholars.* Aloud, he said, "Virgil again?"

"Seneca," shouted Hockenberry. *"And she* . . . he meant Penthesilea . . . *the neighbor of the wandering Scythians, keeping watch, leads her destitute band toward the Pontic banks, having been cut down by iron, Pergamum* . . . you know, Mahnmut, Ilium, Troy . . . *itself stumbled."*

"Get your ass in the hornet, Hockenberry," shouted Mahnmut.

"Good luck, Mahnmut," said Hockenberry, stepping back. "Give my regards to Earth and Orphu. I'll miss them both."

He turned and slowly jogged past where Achilles was kneeling and weeping over Penthesilea's body—the mankiller was alone now except for the dead, the other living humans having all fled—and then, as Mahnmut's hornet lifted off and clawed toward space, Hockenberry ran as hard as he could toward the visibly shrinking Hole.

PART

2

22

After centuries of semitropical warmth, real winter had come to Ardis Hall. There was no snow, but the surrounding forests were free of all but the most stubbornly clinging leaves, frost marked the area of the great manor's shadow for an hour after the tardy sunrise—each morning Ada watched the line of white-tinged grass on the sloping west lawn retreating slowly back up toward the house until it became only the thinnest moat of frost—and visitors reported that the two small rivers that crossed the road in the one-and-one-quarter miles between Ardis Hall and the faxnode pavilion both showed scrims of ice on their surface.

This evening—one of the shortest of the year—Ada went through the house lighting the kerosene lamps and many candles, moving gracefully despite the fact that she was in the fifth month of her pregnancy. The old manor house, built more than eighteen hundred years earlier, before the Final Fax, was comfortable enough; almost two dozen fireplaces—used mostly for decorative and entertainment purposes during the previous centuries—now warmed most of the rooms. In the other chambers in the sixty-eight-room mansion, Harman had sigled the plans for and then built what he called Franklin stoves, and this evening these radiated enough heat to make Ada sleepy as she moved from the lower hall to rooms and then to the staircase and upper halls and rooms, lighting the lamps.

She paused at the large arched window at the end of the hall on the third floor. For the first time in thousands of years, thought Ada, forests were falling to human beings wielding axes—and not just for the firewood. In the last of the wan winter twilight flowing through the gravity-warped panes, she could see the view-blocking but reassuring gray wall of the wooden palisade down the hill on the south lawn. The palisade stretched all around Ardis Hall, sometimes as close as thirty yards from the house, sometimes as far away as a hundred yards behind the house to the edge of the forest. More trees had been felled to build the watchtowers rising at all the corners and angles of the palisade, and then even more to turn the scores of summer tents into homes and barracks for the more than four hundred people now living on the grounds of Ardis.

Where is Harman? Ada had been trying to block the urgency of that thought for hours—busying herself with a score of domestic tasks—but now she couldn't ignore her concern. Her lover—"husband" was the archaic word that Harman liked to use—had left with Hannah, Petyr, and Odysseus—who insisted upon being called Noman these days—a little after dawn that morning, leading an oxen-pulled droshky, sweeping up through the forests and meadows ten miles and more from the river hunting for deer and searching for more of the lost cattle.

They should have been home by now. He promised me he'd be home long before dark.

Ada returned to the first floor and went into the kitchen. For centuries the preserve only of servitors and the occasional voynix bringing in meat from their slaughter grounds, the huge kitchen was now alive with human activity. It was Emme and Reman's night to plan the meal—usually about fifty people ate in Ardis Hall itself—and there were almost a dozen men and women bustling around baking bread, preparing salads, roasting meat on the spit in the huge old fireplace, and generally producing a genial chaos that would soon resolve itself into a long table filled with food.

Emme caught Ada's eye. "Are they back yet?"

"Not yet," said Ada, smiling, attempting to make her voice sound totally unconcerned.

"They will be," said Emme, patting Ada's pale hand.

Not for the first time, and not with anger—she liked Emme—Ada wondered why people seemed to feel that they had a greater right to touch and pat you when you were pregnant. She said, "Of course they will. And I hope with some venison and at least four of those missing head of cattle . . . or better yet, two of the cattle and two cows."

"We need the milk," agreed Emme. She patted Ada's hand again and returned to her duties by the fire.

Ada slipped outside. For a second the cold took her breath away, but she'd brought her shawl and now she hitched it higher around her shoulders and neck. The cold air felt like needles against her cheeks after the warmth of the kitchen and she paused a moment on the back patio to let her eyes adjust to the dark.

To heck with it, she thought, raising her left palm and invoking the proxnet function by visualizing a single yellow circle with a green triangle in it. It was the fifth time she'd tried the function in the last two hours.

The blue oval coalesced into existence above her palm but the holographic imagery was still blurred and static-lashed. Harman had suggested that these occasional failures of proxnet or farnet or even of the old finder function had nothing to do with their bodies—the nanomachinery was still there in their genes and blood, he'd said with a laugh—but may have something to do with the satellites and relay asteroids in either the p-ring or e-ring, perhaps due to interference caused by the nightly meteor showers. Looking up at the darkening evening sky, Ada could see those polar and equatorial rings shifting and turning overhead like two crisscrossing bands of light, each ring composed of thousands of discrete glowing objects. For almost all of her twenty-seven years, those rings had been reassuring—the friendly home of the Firmary where their bodies would be renewed every Twenty, the home of the post-humans who watched over them and whose ranks they would ascend to on each person's Fifth and Final Twenty—but now, Ada knew from Harman and Daeman's experience there, the rings were empty of post-humans and a terrible threat. The Fifth Twenty had been a lie these long centuries—a final fax up to unconscious death by cannibalism from the thing called Caliban.

The falling stars—actually chunks of the two orbital objects that Harman and Daemon had helped to collide eight months earlier—were streaking from west to east, but this was a tiny meteor shower, nothing like the terrible bombardment of those first weeks after the Fall. Ada mused on that phrase they'd all used in the past months. *The Fall.* Fall of what? Fall of the chunks of the orbital asteroid Harman and Daemon had helped Prospero destroy, fall of the servitors, fall of the electrical grid, the end of the service from the voynix who had fled human control that very night . . . the night of the Fall. Everything had fallen that day a little more than eight months ago, Ada realized—not just the sky, but their world as they and preceding generations of old-style humans had known it for more than fourteen Five Twenties.

Ada began to feel the queasiness of the nausea she'd suffered the first three months of pregnancy, but this was anxiety, not morning sickness. Her head ached from tension. She thought *off* and the proxnet flicked off, tried farnet—it wasn't working either—tried the primitive finder function, but the three men and one woman she wanted to find weren't close enough for it to glow red, green, or amber. She blinked off all the palm functions.

Invoking any function made her want to read more books. Ada looked up at the glowing windows of the library—she could see the heads of others in there now, sigling away—and she wished she was with them, running her hands across the spines of the new volumes brought in and stacked in recent days, watching the golden words flow down her hands and arms into her mind and heart. But she'd read fifteen thick books already this short winter day, and even the thought of more sigling made her nausea surge.

Reading—or at least sigl-reading—is a lot like being pregnant, she thought, rather pleased with the metaphor. *It fills you with feelings and reactions you're not ready for . . .it makes you feel too full, not quite yourself, suddenly moving toward some destined moment that will change everything in your life forever.* She wondered what Harman would say about her metaphor—he was brutal in critiquing his own metaphors and analogies, she knew—and then she felt the nausea in her belly move to her heart as the concern flooded back in. *Where are they? Where is he? Is my darling all right?*

Ada's heart was pounding as she walked out toward the glowing open hearth and web of wooden scaffolding that was Hannah's cupola, manned twenty-four hours a day now that bronze and iron and other metals were being shaped for weapons.

Hannah's friend Loes and a group of the younger men were stoking and maintaining the fires tonight. "Good evening, Ada *Uhr,*" called down the tall, thin man. He'd known her for years, but always preferred the formality of the honorific.

"Good evening, Loes *Uhr.* Any word from the watchtowers?"

"None, I'm afraid," called down Loes, stepping away from the opening at the top of the cupola. Ada noticed in her distraction that the man had shaved his beard and that his face was red and sweaty from the heat. He was working bare-chested up there on a night when it might snow.

"Is there a pour tonight?" asked Ada. Hannah always informed her of such things—and night pours were dramatic to watch—but the metal furnace was not one of Ada's responsibilities and a fact of their new life that was only of passing interest to her.

"In the morning, Ada *Uhr.* And I'm sure that Harman *Uhr* and the others will be back soon. They can find their way easily enough in ring-light and starlight."

"Oh, yes, of course," called Ada. Then, as an afterthought, she asked, "Have you seen Daeman *Uhr?*"

Loes mopped his brow, spoke softly to one of the other men who ran to get firewood, and then called down, "Daeman *Uhr* left for Paris Crater this evening, do you remember? He's fetching his mother here to Ardis Hall."

"Ah, yes, of course," said Ada. She bit her lip, but had to ask, "Did he leave before dark? I certainly hope he did." The voynix attacks between Ardis and the faxnode had increased in recent weeks.

"Oh, yes, Ada *Uhr.* He left with plenty of time to get to the pavilion before dark. And he was carrying one of the new crossbows. He'll wait until after sunrise here to return with his mother."

"That's good," said Ada, looking north toward the wooden wall and the forest beyond it. It was already dark here on the open hillside, the last of the light fled from the western sky where dark clouds were massing, and she could imagine how very dark it must be under the trees out there. "I'll see you at dinner, Loes *Uhr*."

"A good evening to you until then, Ada *Uhr*."

She pulled her shawl up over her head as the wind came up. She was walking toward the north gate and the watchtower there, but she knew she wouldn't call up to distract the guards there with her anxiety. Besides, she'd spent an hour out there in late afternoon, watching the northern approaches, waiting almost happily. That was before the anxiety had set in like nausea. Ada walked aimlessly around the eastern side of Ardis Hall, nodding to the guards leaning on their spears near the circular driveway. The torches along the drive had been lit.

She couldn't go inside. Too much warmth, too much laughter, too much conversation. She saw young Peaen on the porch, talking earnestly with one of her young admirers who had moved to Ardis from Ulanbat after the Fall—one of the many disciples of Odysseus back when the old man had been a teacher, before he had become Noman and taciturn—and Ada turned back into the relative darkness of the side yard, not wishing to be drawn into so much as a greeting.

What if Harman dies? What if he is dead already somewhere out there in the dark?

Putting the thought into words made her feel better, made the nausea recede. The words were like objects, making the idea more solid—less a poisonous gas and more a loathsome cube of crystallized thought that she could rotate in her hands, studying its terrible facets.

What if Harman dies? She would not die herself—Ada, always a realist, knew that. She would live on, have the child, perhaps love again.

That last thought made the nausea return and she sat on a cold stone bench where she could look at the blazing cupola and at the closed north gate beyond it.

Ada knew that she had never really been in love before Harman—even when she had wanted to be, she'd known as both girl and young woman that the flirtations and dalliances had not been love, in a world before the Fall that had amounted to little more than flirtations and dalliances—with life and others and oneself.

Before Harman, Ada had never known the deep soul-satisfying pleasure of sleeping with one's beloved—and here she did not use a euphemism, but was thinking of *sleeping* next to him, waking next to him in the night, feeling his arm around her as she fell asleep and often first thing when she woke in the morning. She knew Harman's least self-conscious sounds and his touch and his scent—an outdoor and masculine scent, mixing the smell of leather of the tack in the stables visible there beyond the cupola and the autumn richness of the forest floor itself.

Her body had imprinted itself on his touch—and not just the intimate touch of their frequent lovemaking, but the slightest pressure of his hand on her shoulder or arm or back as he passed. She knew that she would miss the pressure of his gaze almost as much as she would miss his physical touch—indeed, his awareness of her and attention to her had become a sort of constant touch to Ada. She closed her eyes now and allowed herself to feel his large hand enclosing her cold, smaller hand— her fingers had always been long and thin, his were blunt and wide, his calloused palm always warmer than hers. She would miss his warmth. Ada realized that what she would miss most if Harman were dead— miss as much as the *essence* of her beloved—was his embodiment of her future. Not her fate, but her future—the ineffable sense that *tomorrow* meant seeing Harman, laughing with Harman, eating with Harman, discussing their unborn child with Harman, even disagreeing with Harman— she would forevermore miss the sense that the continuation of her life was more than another day of breathing, but was the gift of another day of engagement with her beloved across the spectrum of all things.

Sitting there on the cold bench with the rings revolving overhead and the nightly meteor shower increasing in intensity, her shadow thrown across the frost-whitened lawn by the glow of that light and the cupola, Ada realized that it was easier to contemplate one's own mortality than the death of one's beloved. This wasn't a total revelation to her—she had *imagined* such a perspective before, Ada was very, very good at imagining—but the reality and totality of the feeling itself was a revelation. As with the sense of the new life within her, the sensation of loss and love for Harman infused her—it was somehow, impossibly, larger not only than herself but than her capacity for such a thought or feeling.

Ada had expected to love making love with Harman—with sharing her body with him and learning the pleasure his body could bring her— but she had been amazed to find that as their closeness grew, it was as if each of them had discovered another body—not hers, not his, but something shared and inexplicable. Ada had never discussed this with anyone— not even with Harman, although she knew that he shared the feeling—and it was her opinion that it had taken the Fall to liberate this mystery in human beings.

These last eight months since the Fall should have been a hard, sad time for Ada—the servitors crashed to uselessness, her life of ease and partying gone forever, the world that she had known and grown up in gone forever, her mother—who had refused to come back to the danger of Ardis Hall, staying at the Loman Estate near the eastern coast with two thousand others, dead along with all the others there in the massed voynix attack in the autumn—the disappearance of Ada's cousin-friend Virginia from her estate outside of Chom above the Arctic Circle, the unprecedented worries about food and warmth and safety and survival, the terrible knowledge that the Firmary was gone forever and that the certainty of ascension to the heaven of the p-ring and e-ring was all a vicious myth, the sobering knowledge that only death awaited them someday and that even the Five Twenties lifespan was not their birthright any more, that they could die at any time . . . it all should have been terrifying and oppressive to the twenty-seven-year-old woman.

She had been happy. Ada had been happier than at any time in her life. She had been happy with the new challenges and with the need to find courage as well as the need to trust and depend on others for her life. Ada had been happy learning that she loved Harman and that he loved her in some way that their old world of fax-in parties and servitor luxuries and temporary connections between men and women would never have allowed. As unhappy as she was each time he left on a hunting trip or to lead an attack on voynixes or on a sonie voyage to the Golden Gate at Machu Picchu or to another ancient site, or on one of his teaching fax-journeys to any of the three-hundred-some other communities of survivors—*at least half the humans on Earth dead since the Fall, and there were never a million of us we know now, that number the post-humans had given us centuries ago had always been a lie*—she was equally happy every time he returned and gloriously happy every cold, dangerous, uncertain day that he was there at Ardis Hall with her.

She would go on if her beloved Harman was dead—she knew in her heart that she would go on, survive, fight, birth and raise this child, perhaps love again—but she also knew this night that the fierce, gliding joy of the past eight months would be gone forever.

Quit being an idiot, Ada commanded herself.

She rose, adjusted her shawl, and had turned to go into the house when the bell in the gate watchtower rang out, as did the voice of one of the sentries.

"Three people approaching from the forest!"

All the men at the cupola dropped their work, grabbed spears or bows or crossbows, and ran to the walls. The roving sentries from the east and west yards also ran to the ladders and parapets.

Three people. For a moment, Ada stood frozen where she was. Four had left that morning. And they'd had a converted droshky pulled by an ox. They wouldn't return without the droshky and ox unless something terrible had happened, and if it was just that someone had been injured—

say, a twisted ankle or broken leg—they would have used the droshky to transport him or her.

"Three people approaching the north gate," cried the watchtower guard again. "Open the gate. They're carrying a body."

Ada dropped her shawl and ran as fast as she could for the north gate.

23

Hours before the voynix attacked, Harman had the sense that something terrible was going to happen.

This outing hadn't really been necessary. Odysseus—Noman now, Harman reminded himself, although to him the sturdy man with the salt-and-pepper beard would always be Odysseus—had wanted to bring in fresh meat, track down some of the missing cattle, and reconnoiter the hill country to the north. Petyr suggested that they just use the sonie, but Odysseus argued that even with the leaves off the trees, it was still difficult to see even something as large as a cow from a low-flying sonie. Besides, he wanted to *hunt*.

"The voynix want to hunt too," Harman had said. "They're getting bolder every week."

Odysseus—Noman—had shrugged.

Harman had come along despite his sure knowledge that everyone on this little expedition had better things to do. Hannah had been working toward an early morning iron pour for the following day and her absence might throw that plan behind schedule. Petyr had been cataloging the hundreds of books brought in during the last two weeks, setting priorities on which should be sigled first. Noman himself had been talking about finally going on his long-delayed solo sonie search for the elusive robotic factory somewhere along the shores of what had once been called Lake Michigan. And Harman would have probably devoted the entire day to his obsessive attempt to penetrate the allnet and discover more functions, although he'd also been considering going to Paris Crater with Daemon to help fetch his friend's mother.

But Noman—who constantly went on solo hunting expeditions—had wanted to go out with others this time. And poor Hannah, who had been in love with Noman-Odysseus since the day she'd met him on the Golden Gate Bridge at Machu Picchu more than nine months earlier, insisted on coming along. Then Petyr, who had first come to Ardis Hall as a disciple of Odysseus' before the Fall, back when the old man was still teaching his strange philosophy, but who was now a disciple only of Hannah in the sense that he was helplessly in love with her, had also insisted on going. And finally Harman had agreed to join them because . . . he wasn't sure why he had agreed to join them. Perhaps he didn't want three such star-crossed lovers alone in the woods all day with their weapons.

Later, while walking behind those three in the cold forest and thinking these words, Harman had to smile. He'd run across that phrase—"star-crossed lovers"—only the previous day while reading—visually reading, not function-sigling—Shakespeare's *Romeo and Juliet*.

Harman was drunk on Shakespeare that week, having read three plays in two days. He was surprised he could walk, much less hold a conversation. His mind was filled to overflowing with incredible cadences, a torrent of new vocabulary, and more insight into the complexity of what it meant to be human than he'd ever hoped to achieve. It made him want to weep.

If he wept, he knew with some shame, it would not be for the beauty and power of the plays—the entire concept of staged drama was new to Harman and his postliterate world. No, he'd be weeping because of selfish sorrow over the fact that he'd not encountered such things as Shakespeare until less than three months before his allotted fivescore years was up. Even though he was certain, since he'd helped to destroy it, that the orbital Firmary would be faxing no more old-style humans up to the e-ring on their Fifth Twenty—or on any other Twenty for that matter—ninety-nine years of thinking that his life on earth would end on the stroke of midnight marking his hundredth birthday was a hard mind-set to escape.

As dusk approached, the four of them walked slowly along a cliff's edge, returning from their fruitless day. Their pace was never faster than the lumbering ox they'd brought along to pull the droshky. Before the Fall, the conveyances had been balanced on one wheel by internal gyroscopes and pulled by voynix, but without internal power now, the damned things couldn't balance, so the machine-guts and moving parts of each vehicle had been ripped out, the tongues moved farther apart, and a yoke rigged for the ox, while the single, slender center wheel had been replaced by two broader wheels on a newly forged axle. Harman thought the jury-rigged droshkies and carrioles were pathetically crude, but they did represent the first human-built wheeled vehicles in more than fifteen hundred years of nonhistory.

That thought also made him want to weep.

They'd headed about four miles north, walking mostly along the low bluffs overlooking a tributary to the river Harman now knew had once been named the Ekei, and before that the Ohio. The droshky was necessary to transport any deer carcasses they managed to accumulate—although Noman was notorious for walking miles with a dead deer draped over his shoulders—so their progress was slow in the way that only an ox's progress could be slow.

At times, two of them would stay with the cart while two went into the woods with bows or crossbows. Petyr was carrying a flechette rifle—one of the few firearms at Ardis Hall—but they preferred to hunt with less noisy weapons. Voynix did not have ears, as such, but somehow their hearing was excellent.

All during the morning, the three old-style humans had monitored their palms. For whatever reason, voynix did not show up on the finders, farnet, or the rarely used allnet functions, but they usually did on proxnet. But then again, as Harman and Daeman had learned with Savi nine months earlier in a place called Jerusalem, voynix also used proxnet—to locate humans.

It didn't matter this day. By noon, all of the functions were down. The four trusted to their eyes, being more careful in the forest, watching the edge of the tree line when moving through meadows and along the line of low bluffs.

The wind out of the northwest was very cold. All of the old distributories had quit working on the day of the Fall, and there had been few heavy garments needed before then anyway, so the three old-style humans were wearing rudely fashioned coats and cloaks of wool or animal hides. Odysseus . . . Noman . . . seemed impervious to the cold and wore the same chest armor and short-skirt sort of girdle he always wore on his expeditions, with only a short red blanket-cape draped around his shoulders for warmth.

They found no deer, which was odd. Luckily they ran across no allosauruses or other RNA-returned dinosaurs either. The consensus at Ardis Hall was that the few dinos that still hunted this far north had migrated south during this unusual cold spell. The bad news was that the sabertoothed tigers that had shown up the previous summer had *not* migrated with the large reptiles. Noman showed them fresh pugmarks not far from the cattle tracks they'd been following for much of the day.

Petyr made sure that the power rifle had a fresh magazine of crystal flechettes locked in.

They turned back after they found the rib cages and scattered, bloody bones of two of the missing cattle along a rocky stretch of cliff. Then ten minutes later, they found the hide, hair, vertebrae, skull, and amazing curved teeth of a sabertooth.

Noman's head had come up and he'd turned three hundred and sixty degrees, scrutinizing every distant tree and boulder. He kept both hands on his long spear.

"Did another sabertooth do this?" asked Hannah.

"Either that or voynix," said Noman.

"Voynix don't eat," said Harman, realizing how silly his comment was as soon as he'd said it.

Noman shook his head. His gray curls stirred in the wind. "No, but this sabertooth might have attacked a pack of voynix. Scavengers or other cats ate this one afterward. See those other pugmarks in the soft soil there? Right next to them are voynix padmarks."

Harman saw them, but only after Noman actually pointed again.

They'd turned back then, but the stupid ox walked more slowly than ever, despite Noman's encouragement to it with the shaft of his spear and even the sharp end on occasion. The wheels and axle squeaked and creaked and once they had to repair a loose hub. The low clouds moved in with an even colder wind and the daylight began to fade when they were still two miles from home.

"They'll keep our dinner warm," said Hannah. Until her recent bout of lovesickness, the tall, athletic young woman had always been the optimist. But now her easy smile seemed strained.

"Try your proxnet," said Noman. The old Greek had no functions. But on the other hand, his ancient-style body, devoid of the last two millennia's nanogenetic tampering, didn't register on finder, farnet, or proxnet on the voynix's functions.

"Just static," said Hannah, looking at the blue oval floating above her palm. She flicked it off.

"Well, now they can't see us either," said Petyr. The young man had a lance in one hand, the flechette rifle slung over his shoulder, but his gaze remained on Hannah.

They resumed trudging across the meadow, the high, brittle grass scraping against their legs, the repaired droshky squeaking louder than usual. Harman glanced at Noman-Odysseus' bare legs above the high-strapped sandals and wondered why his calves and shins weren't a maze of welts.

"It looks like our day was sort of useless," said Petyr.

Noman shrugged. "We know now that something large is taking the deer near Ardis," he said. "A month ago, I would have killed two or three on a long day's hunt like this."

"A new predator?" said Harman. He chewed his lip at the idea.

"Could be," said Noman. "Or perhaps the voynix are killing off the wild game and driving the cattle away in an attempt to starve us out."

"Are the voynix that smart?" asked Hannah. The organic-mechanical things had always been looked down upon as slave labor by the old-style humans—mute, dumb except to orders, programmed, like the servitors, to care for, take orders from, and protect human beings. But the servitors had all crashed on the day of the Fall and the voynix had fled and turned lethal.

Noman shrugged again. "Athough they can function on their own, the voynix take orders. Always have. From who or what, I'm not quite sure."

"Not from Prospero," Harman said softly. "After we were in the city called Jerusalem, which was crawling with voynix, Savi said that the noosphere thing named Prospero had created Caliban and the *calibani* as protection against the voynix. They're not from this world."

"Savi," grunted Noman. "I can't believe the old woman is dead."

"She is," said Harman. He and Daeman had watched the monster Caliban murder her and drag her corpse away, up there on that orbital isle. "How long did you know her, Odysseus . . . Noman?"

The older man rubbed his short, gray beard. "How long did I know Savi? Just a few months of real time . . . but spread out over more than a millennium. Sometimes we slept together."

Hannah looked shocked and actually stopped walking.

Noman laughed. "She in her cryo crèche, I in my time sarcophagus on the Golden Gate. It was all very proper and parallel. Two babies in separate cribs. If I were to take the name of one of my countrymen in vain . . . I would say it was a *platonic* relationship." Noman laughed heartily even though no one joined in. But when he was finished laughing, he said, "Don't believe everything that old crone told you, Harman. She lied about much, misunderstood more."

"She was the wisest woman I've ever met," said Harman. "I won't see her like again."

Noman flashed his unfriendly smile. "The second part of that statement is correct."

They encountered a stream that ran down into the larger stream, balancing precariously on rocks and fallen logs as they crossed. It was too cold to get their feet and clothes wet unless necessary. The ox lumbered through the chill water, bouncing the empty droshky behind him. Petyr crossed first and stood guard with the flechette rifle ready as the other three came over. They were not following the same cattle tracks home, but were within a few hundred yards of the way they'd come. They knew they had one more rolling, wooded ridge to cross, then a long rocky meadow, then another bit of meadow before Ardis Hall, warmth, food, and relative safety.

The sun had set behind the bank of dark clouds to the southwest. Within minutes, it was dark enough that the rings were providing most of the light. There were two lanterns in the droshky and candles in the pack that Harman carried, but they wouldn't need them unless the clouds moved in to obscure the rings and stars.

"I wonder if Daeman got off to go get his mother," said Petyr. The young man seemed uncomfortable in long silences.

"I wish he'd waited for me," said Harman. " Or at least until daylight on the other end. Paris Crater isn't very safe these days."

Noman grunted. "Of all of you, Daeman—amazingly—seems the best fitted to take care of himself. He's surprised you, hasn't he, Harman?"

"Not really," said Harman. Instantly he realized that this wasn't the truth. Less than a year ago, when he'd first met Daeman, he'd seen a whining, pudgy momma's boy whose only hobbies were capturing butterflies and seducing young women. In fact, Harman was sure that Daeman had come to Ardis Hall ten months ago to seduce his cousin Ada. In their first adventures, Daeman had been timid and complaining. But Harman had to acknowledge to himself that events had changed the younger man, and much more for the better than they'd changed Harman. It had been a starved but determined Daeman—forty pounds lighter but infinitely more aggressive—who had taken on Caliban in single combat in the near zero-gravity of Prospero's orbital isle. And it had been Daeman who had gotten Harman and Hannah out alive. Since the Fall, Daeman had been much quieter, more serious, and dedicated to learning every fighting and survival skill that Odysseus would teach.

Harman was a little envious. He'd thought of himself as the natural leader of the Ardis group—older, wiser, the only man on earth nine months ago who could read, or wanted to, the only man on earth who knew then that the earth was round—but now Harman had to admit that the ordeal that had strengthened Daeman had weakened him in both body and spirit. *Is it my age?* Physically, Harman looked to be in his healthy late thirties or early forties, like any Four Twenties-plus male before the Fall. The blue worms and bubbling chemicals he'd seen in the Firmary tanks up there had renewed him well enough during his first four visits. *But psychologically?* Harman had to worry. Perhaps old was old, no matter how skillfully one's human form had been reworked. Adding to this feeling was the fact that Harman was still limping from injuries to his leg received up there on Prospero's hellish isle eight months earlier. No Firmary tank now waited to undo every bit of damage done, no servitors floated forth to bandage and heal the result of every little careless accident. Harman knew his leg would never be right, that he'd limp until the day he died—and this thought added to his odd sadness this day.

They trudged on through the woods in silence. Each of them seemed to the others to be lost in his or her own thoughts. Harman was taking his turn to lead the ox by its halter, and the ox was getting more stubborn and willful as the evening grew darker. All it would take was for the stupid animal to lurch the wrong way, bash the droshky against one of these trees, and they'd have to either stay out all night repairing the goddamned thing or just leave it out here and lead the ox home without it. Neither alternative was appealing.

He glanced at Odysseus-Noman walking easily along, shortening his stride to keep pace with the slow ox and limping Harman, and then he looked at Hannah staring wistfully at Noman and Petyr staring wistfully at Hannah, and he just wanted to sit down on the cold ground and weep for the world that was too busy surviving to weep. He thought of the incredible play he'd just read—*Romeo and Juliet*—and wondered if some things and follies were universal to human nature even after almost two millennia of self-styled evolution, nano-engineering, and genetic manipulation.

Perhaps I shouldn't have allowed Ada to get pregnant. This was the thought that haunted Harman the most.

She had wanted a child. He had wanted a child. More than that, uniquely after all these centuries, they had both wanted a family—a man to stay with the woman and child, the child to be raised by them and not by servitors. While all pre-Fall old-style humans knew their mothers, almost no one had known—or wanted to know—who his or her father was. In a world where males stayed young and vital until their Fifth and Final Twenty, in a small population—perhaps fewer than three hundred thousand people worldwide—and in a culture comprised of little more than parties and brief sexual liaisons where youthful beauty was prized above all else, it was almost certain that many fathers would unknowingly couple with their daughters, young men with their mothers.

This bothered Harman after he had taught himself to read and got his first glimpses of previous cultures, long-lost values—*too late, too late*—but the incest would have bothered no one else nine months ago. The same genetically engineered nano-sensors in a woman's body that allowed her to choose from carefully stored sperm packets months or years after intercourse, would have never allowed the woman to choose someone from her immediate family as a breeding mate. It simply couldn't happen. The nanoprogramming was foolproof, even if the coupling humans were fools.

But now everything is different, thought Harman. They would need families to survive—not just to make it through the voynix attacks and hardships after the Fall, but to help them organize for the war that Odysseus had sworn was coming. The old Greek wouldn't say anything else about his Fall-night prophecy, but he had said that night that some large war was coming—some speculated a war related to the siege of Troy they'd all vicariously enjoyed under their turin cloths before those embedded microcircuits also ceased to function. "New worlds will appear on your lawn," he'd told Ada.

As they came out into the last broad meadow before the final rim of forest, Harman realized that he was tired and scared. Tired of always trying to decide what was right—who was he to have destroyed the Firmary, possibly freed Prospero, and now always to be lecturing on family and the need to organize into protective groups? What did he know—ninety-nine-year-old Harman who had wasted almost all of his lifetime without learning wisdom?

And he was scared not so much of dying—although they all shared that fear for the first time in a millennium and half of human experience—but of the very change he'd helped bring about. And he was afraid of the responsibility.

Were we right to allow Ada to get pregnant now? In this new world, the two had decided that it made more sense—even in the midst of hardships and uncertainty—to begin a family, though "begin a family" was a strange phrase since it took a great effort even to think of having more than one child. Only one child had been permitted to each old-style human woman during the millennium-and-a-half rule of the absent post-humans. It had been disorienting to the point of vertigo for Ada and Harman to realize that they could have several children if they so chose and if their biology agreed. There was no waiting list, no need for post-human approval signaled through the servitors. On the other hand, they didn't know if a human *could* have more than one child. Would their altered genetics and nanoprogramming allow it?

They'd decided to have the baby now, while Ada was still in her twenties and they thought they could show the others, not just at Ardis but in all the other surviving faxnode communities, what a family with a father present could be like.

All this frightened Harman. Even when he felt sure he was right, it frightened him. First there was the uncertainty of mother and child surviving a non-Firmary birth. There was not an old-style human alive who had seen a human baby being born—birth was, like death, something one had been faxed up to the e-ring to experience alone. And as with pre-Fall humans suffering serious injury or premature death, as Daeman once experienced upon being eaten by an allosaurus, Firmary birth was something so traumatic that it had to be blocked from memory. Women remembered no more about the Firmary birth experience than did their infants.

At the appointed time in her pregnancy, a time announced by servitors, the woman was faxed away and returned healthy and thin two days later. For many months afterward, the babies were fed and cared for exclusively by servitors. Mothers tended to keep in touch with their children, but they had little hand in raising them. Before the Fall, fathers not only did not know their children—they never knew they'd fathered a child, since their sexual contact with that woman may have occurred years or decades earlier.

Now Harman and the others were reading books about the ancient habit of childbirth—the process seemed unbelievably dangerous and barbaric, even when carried out in hospitals, which seemed to be crude pre-Firmary versions of the Firmary, and even when supervised by professionals—but now there wasn't a single person on the planet who had seen a baby being born.

Except for Noman. The Greek had once admitted that in his former life, in that unreal age of blood and warfare shown in the turin-cloth adventure, he had seen at least part of the process of a child being born, including his own son, Telemachus. He was Ardis's midwife.

And in a new world where there were no doctors—no one who understood how to heal the simplest injury or health problem—Odysseus-Noman was a master of the healing art. He knew poultices. He know how to stitch up wounds. He knew how to set broken bones. In his near-decade of travels through time and space after escaping someone named Circe, he'd learned about modern medical techniques such as washing one's hands and one's knife before cutting into a living body.

Nine months ago, Odysseus had talked about staying at Ardis Hall for only a few weeks before moving on. Now, if the old man tried to leave, Harman suspected that fifty people would jump on him and tie him down, just to keep him there for his expertise—making weapons, hunting, dressing out game, cooking over open flames, forging metal, sewing garments, programming the sonie for flight, healing, and dealing with wounds—helping a baby to be born.

They could see the meadow beyond the forest now. The rings were being swallowed by clouds and it was getting very dark.

"I wanted to see Daeman today . . ." began Noman.

It was the last thing he had time to say.

The voynix dropped down out of the trees like huge, silent spiders. There were at least a dozen of them. They all had their killing blades extended.

Two landed on the ox's back and cut its throat. Two landed near Hannah and slashed at her, sending blood and fabric flying. She leaped back, trying to raise her crossbow and ratchet back the bolt, but the voynix knocked her down and leaned closer to finish the job.

Odysseus screamed, activated his sword—a gift from Circe, he'd told them long ago—to a vibrating blur, and leaped forward swinging. Bits of voynix shells and arms flew into the air and Harman was spattered by white blood and blue oil.

A voynix landed on Harman, knocking the wind out of him, but he rolled away from its fingerblades. A second voynix landed on all fours and snapped upright, moving like something in a speeded-up nightmare. Getting to his feet, fumbling his spear up, Harman stabbed at the second creature at the same instant the first one slashed at his back.

There was a ratcheting explosion as Petyr brought the rifle into play. Crystal flechettes whizzed by Harman's ear as the voynix behind him spun and fell away under the impact of a thousand shining slivers. Harman turned just as the second voynix jumped. He rammed the spear through its chest and watched as the whirling thing went down, but cursed as it pulled the spear out of his hands in its falling. Harman reached for the shaft, but then jumped back and pulled his bow from his shoulder as three more voynix turned his way and attacked.

The four humans set their backs to the droshky as the eight remaining voynix made a circle and closed in on them, fingerblades gleaming in the dying light.

Hannah fired two crossbow quarrels deep into the chest of the one closest to her. It went down, but continued its attack on all fours, dragging itself forward with its blades. Odysseus-Noman stepped forward and sliced the thing in two with his Circe sword.

Three voynix rushed Harman. He had nowhere to run. He fired his single arrow, saw it glance off the lead voynix's metal chest, and then they were on him. Harman ducked, felt something slash his leg, and now he was rolling under the droshky—he could smell the ox's blood, a copperish taste in his mouth and nose—and then he was up and on his feet on the other side. The three voynix leaped up and over the droshky.

Petyr whirled, crouched, and fired an entire magazine of several thousand flechettes at the leaping figures. The three voynix flew apart and landed in a gout of organic blood and machine oil.

"Cover me while I reload!" shouted Petyr, reaching into his cape's pocket to pull out another flechette magazine and slap it into place.

Harman dropped his bow—the things were too close—pulled out a short sword forged in Hannah's furnace only two months ago, and began hacking away at the two closest metallic shapes. They were too fast. One dodged. The other batted Harman's sword out of his hands.

Hannah jumped up into the droshky and fired a crossbow bolt into the back of the voynix that was slashing at Harman. The monster whirled but then spun back to the attack, metallic arms raised, blades swinging. It had no mouth or eyes.

Harman ducked beneath the killing blow, landed on his hands, and kicked at the thing's knees. It was like kicking at thick metal pipes embedded in concrete.

All five of the remaining voynix were on Harman's side of the cart now, rushing at Petyr and him before the younger man could raise the flechette rifle.

At that second, Odysseus came around the cart with a berserker scream and waded into them, his short sword a blur within a blur. All five voynix turned on him, their arms and rotating blades also spinning into motion.

Hannah raised the heavy crossbow but had no clear shot. Odysseus was in the middle of that whirling mass of violence and everything was moving too fast. Harman leaned into the droshky and pulled out one of the extra hunting spears.

"Odysseus, drop!" screamed Petyr.

The old Greek went down, although due to heeding the shout or just from the voynix attack, they couldn't tell. He'd sliced two of the things apart, but the final three were still functional and lethal.

BRRPPPPPPPPPPPPPPRRRRRRRRRBRRRRRPPPPPBRPPPPPP.

The flechette rifle on full automatic sounded like someone sticking a wooden paddle into the blades of a swiftly turning fan. The final three voynix were thrown six feet backward, their shells riddled with over ten thousand crystal flechettes all glittering like a mosaic of broken glass in the dying ringlight.

"Jesus Christ," gasped Harman.

The voynix that Hannah had wounded rose up behind her on the other side of the droshky.

Harman threw his spear with every ounce and erg of energy left in his body. The voynix staggered back, pulled the spear free, and snapped its shaft.

Harman jumped into the droshky and grabbed up another spear from the bed of the vehicle. Hannah fired two quarrels into the voynix. One of the bolts deflected off into the darkness under the trees, but the other sank deep. Harman leaped from the droshky and drove the remaining spear into the last voynix's chest. The creature twitched and staggered back another step.

Harman wrenched the lance out, drove it home again with the pure violence of madness, twisted the barbed tip, pulled it free, and drove it home again.

The voynix fell backward, clattering onto the roots of an ancient elm.

Harman straddled the voynix, unmindful of its still-twitching arms and blades, lifted the blue-milked spear straight up, drove it down, twisted it, ripped it out, lifted it, drove it down lower on the thing's shell, ripped it free, drove it in where a human's groin would be, twisted the barbs to do maximum damage to the soft parts inside, lifted it out—part of the shell ripping away—and drove it home again so fiercely that he could feel the speartip hit soil and root. He pulled the spear free, lifted it, drove it deep, lifted it . . .

"Harman," said Petyr, setting a hand on the older man's shoulder. "It's dead. It's dead."

Harman looked around. He didn't recognize Petyr and couldn't get enough air into his lungs. He heard a violent noise and realized that it was his own labored breathing.

It was too fucking damned dark. The clouds had covered the rings and it was too fucking damned dark here under the trees. There could be fifty more voynix there in the shadows, waiting to leap.

Hannah lighted the lantern.

There were no more voynix visible in the sudden circle of light. The fallen ones had ceased twitching. Odysseus was still down, one of the voynix fallen across him. Neither voynix nor man moved.

"Odysseus!" Hannah leaped from the droshky with the lantern, kicking the voynix corpse aside.

Petyr rushed around and went to one knee next to the fallen man. Harman limped over as quickly as he could, leaning on his spear. The deep scratches on his back and legs were just beginning to hurt.

"Oh," said Hannah. She was on her knees, holding the lantern over Odysseus. Her hand was shaking. "Oh," she said again.

Odysseus-Noman's armor had been knocked off his body, the leather straps slashed apart. His broad chest was a latticework of deep wounds. A single slash had taken off part of his left ear and a section of scalp.

But it was the damage to the old man's right arm that made Harman gasp.

The voynix—in their wild attempt to make Odysseus drop the Circe sword, which he had never done, it was still humming in his hand—had ripped the man's arm to shreds and then all but torn the arm from his body. Blood and mangled tissue shone in the harsh lantern light. Harman could see white bone glistening. "Dear God," he whispered. In the eight months since the Fall, no one at Ardis Hall or at any of the survivors' communes Harman knew of had suffered such wounds and survived.

Hannah was pounding the earth with one fist while her other hand pressed palm downward on Odysseus' bloody chest. "I can't feel a heartbeat," she said almost calmly. Only her wild white eyes in the lantern's gleam belied that calm. "I can't feel a heartbeat."

"Put him in the droshky . . ." began Harman. He felt the post-adrenaline shakiness and nausea that he'd experienced once before. His bad leg and lacerated back were bleeding fiercely.

"Fuck the droshky," said Petyr. The young man twisted the hilt of the Circe sword and the vibration ceased, the blade becoming visible again. He handed Harman the sword, the flechette rifle, and two extra magazines. Then he bent, went to one knee, lifted the unconscious or dead Odysseus over his shoulder, and stood. "Hannah, lead the way with the lantern. Reload your crossbow. Harman, bring up the rear with the rifle. Shoot at anything that even looks like it might move." He staggered off toward the last meadow with the bleeding figure over his shoulder, looking ironically, horribly, much like Odysseus often had when hauling home the carcass of a deer.

Nodding dumbly, Harman cast aside the spear, tucked the Circe sword in his belt, lifted the flechette rifle, and followed the other two survivors out of the forest.

As soon as he faxed into Paris Crater, Daeman wished that he'd arrived in daylight. Or at least waited until Harman or someone else could have come with him.

It was about five p.m. and the light had been fading when he'd reached the fax pavilion palisade a little more than a mile from Ardis Hall, and now it was one in the morning, very dark, and raining hard here in Paris Crater. He'd faxed to the node closest to his mother's domi—a fax pavilion called Invalid Hotel for no reason understood by any living person—and he came through the fax portal with his crossbow raised, swiveling and ready. The water pouring off the roof of the pavilion made looking out into the city feel like peering out through a curtain or waterfall.

It was irritating. The survivors in Paris Crater didn't guard their faxnodes. About a third of the survivor communities, with Ardis leading the way, had put a wall around their fax pavilions and posted a full-time guard, but the remaining residents of Paris Crater just refused to do so. No one knew if voynix faxed themselves from place to place—there seemed to be enough of them everywhere without them having to do that—but the humans would never know if places like Paris Crater refused to monitor their nodes.

Of course, that guarding had begun at Ardis not as an attempt to prevent voynix from faxing, but as a way to limit the number of refugees streaming in after the Fall. The first reaction when the servitors crashed and the power failed was to flee toward safety and food, so tens and tens of thousands had been faxing almost randomly in those early weeks and months, flicking to fifty locations around the planet within a dozen hours, depleting food supplies and then faxing away again. Few places had their own store of food then; no place was really safe. Ardis had been one of the first colonies of survivors to arm itself and the first to turn away fear-crazed refugees, unless they had some essential skill. But almost no one had any important skill after more than fourteen hundred years of what Savi had called "sickening *eloi* uselessness."

A month after the Fall and that early confusion, Harman had insisted at the Ardis Council meetings that they make up for their selfishness by faxing representatives to all the other communities, giving advice on how to raise crops, tips on how to improve security, demonstrations of how to slaughter their own meat animals, and—once Harman had discovered the reading sigl-function—seminars to show the scattered survivors how they could also pull crucial information from old books. Ardis had also bartered weapons and handed out the plans for making crossbows, bolts, bows, arrows, lances, arrowheads, speartips, knives, and other weapons. Luckily, most of the old-style humans had been using the turin cloths for entertainment for half a Twenty, so they were familiar with everything less complicated than a crossbow. Finally, Harman had sent Ardis residents faxing to all of the three hundred-plus nodes, asking every survivor's help in finding the legendary robotic factories and distributories. He would demonstrate one of the few guns he'd brought back from his second visit to the museum at the Golden Gate at Machu Picchu and explain that if they were to survive the voynix, human communities needed thousands of these weapons.

Staring out into the darkness through the rain and runoff, Daeman realized that it would have been difficult to guard all this city's fax-nodes; Paris Crater had been one of the largest cities on the planet just eight months earlier, with twenty-five thousand residents and a dozen working fax portals. Now, if his mother's friends were to be believed, there were fewer than three thousand men and women left here. The voynix roamed the streets and skittered and scrabbled across the old skywalks and residential towers at will. It was past time to get his mother out of this town. Only a lifetime—almost two Twenties—of habit obeying his mother's every wish and whim had caused Daeman to acquiesce to her insistence on staying here.

Still, it seemed relatively safe. There were more than a hundred survivors, mostly men, who had secured the tower complex near the west side of the crater where Marina, Daeman's mother, had her extensive domi apartments. They had water because of rainfall accumulators stretched from rooftop to rooftop, and it rained most of the time in Paris Crater. They had food from terrace gardens and from the livestock they'd driven in from the old voynix-tended fields and then penned in the grassy swards around the crater. Every midweek there was an open market in the nearby Champs Ulysses with all of the survivor camps in West Paris Crater meeting to barter food, clothing, and other survival essentials. They even had wine faxed in from the far-flung vineyard-estate communities. They had weapons—including crossbows purchased from Ardis Hall, a few flechette guns, and an energy-beam projector one of the men had brought up from an abandoned underground museum someone had found after the Fall. Amazingly, the energy-beam weapon worked.

But Daeman knew that Marina had really stayed in Paris Crater because of an old bastard here named Goman who had been her primary lover for almost a full Twenty. Daeman had always disliked Goman.

Paris Crater had always been known as the "City of Light"—and it had been in Daeman's experience growing up there, with floating glow globes on every street and boulevard, entire towers illuminated by electric lights, thousands of lanterns, and the lighted, thousand-foot-tall structure that symbolized the city towering over everything—but now the glow globes were dark and fallen, the electrical grid gone, most of the lanterns were dark or hidden behind shuttered windows, and the Enormous Whore had gone dark and inactive for the first time in two thousand years or more. Daeman glanced up at her as he ran, but her head and breasts—usually filled with bubbling photoluminescent red liquid—were invisible against or perhaps *in* the dark storm clouds and the famous thighs and buttocks were just black-iron armatures now, drawing the lightning that crackled over the city.

Actually, it was the lightning that helped Daeman traverse the three long city blocks between the Invalid Hotel faxnode and Marina's domi tower. With the hood of his anorak up to give him at least an illusion of staying dry in the downpour, Daeman would wait at each intersection, crossbow raised, and then sprint across open areas when the lightning revealed the shadows in doorways and under arches to be free of voynix. He had tried proxnet and farnet when waiting in the pavilion, but both were down. This was good for him since the voynix were using both functions these days to seek out humans. Daeman didn't need to bring up the finder function—this was his home, after all, despite the weaselly Goman's usurpation of his place next to his mother.

There were abandoned altars in some of the lightning-illuminated empty courtyards. Daeman caught sight of crudely modeled papier-mâché statues of what had been meant to be robed goddesses, naked archers, and bearded patriarchs as he sprinted by these sad testaments to desperation. The altars were for the Olympian gods of the turin drama—Athena, Apollo, Zeus, and others—and that craze for propitiation had begun even before the Fall here in Paris Crater and in other node communities on the continent that Harman, Daeman, and the other readers at Ardis Hall now knew as Europe.

The papier-mâché effigies had melted in the constant rain, so the once-again-abandoned gods on the windstrewn altars looked like humpbacked monstrosities from some other world. *That's more appropriate than worshiping the turin gods,* thought Daeman. He had been on Prospero's Isle in the e-ring and heard about the Quiet. Caliban himself—itself—had bragged to his three captives about the power of his god, the many-handed Setebos, before the monster killed Savi and dragged her away into the sewage-swamps there.

Daeman was only half a block from his mother's tower when he heard a scrabbling. He faded back into the darkness of a rain-filled doorway and clicked off the safety on the crossbow. Daeman had one of the newer weapons that fired two sharp, barbed quarrels with each snap of the powerful steel band. He raised the weapon against his shoulder and waited.

Only the lightning allowed him to see the half-dozen voynix as they scrabbled by half a block away, heading west. They weren't walking, but racing along the sides of old stone buildings here like metallic cockroaches, finding grip with their barbed fingerblades and horned footpeds. The first time Daeman had seen voynix scramble along walls like that had been in Jerusalem some nine months ago.

He knew now that the things could see in the infrared, so darkness alone would not hide him, but the creatures were in a hurry—scrabbling in the opposite direction from Marina's tower—and none of them turned the IR-sensors on their chests in his direction in the three seconds it took them to scuttle out of sight.

Heart pounding, Daeman sprinted the last hundred yards to his mother's tower where it rose above the west curve of the crater. The hand-cranked elevator basket wasn't at street level, of course—Daeman could just make it out some twenty-five stories higher along the column of scaffolding, where the residential stacks began above the old shopping esplanade. There was a bell rope hanging at the bottom of the elevator scaffolding to alert the tower residents to a guest's presence, but a full minute of pulling on Daeman's part showed no lights coming on up there nor any answering tugs.

Still gasping from his run through the streets, Daeman squinted up into the rain and considered returning to Invalid Hotel. It would be a twenty-five-floor climb—much of it in the old dark stairwells—with absolutely no guarantee that the fifteen stories below the abandoned esplanade would be free of voynix.

Many of the former faxnode communities based in the ancient cities or high towers had to be abandoned after the Fall. Without electricity—old-style humans didn't even know where the current had been generated or how it was distributed—the lift shafts and elevators wouldn't work. No one was going to climb and descend two hundred and fifty feet—or much more for some tower communities such as Ulanbat, with its two-hundred-story Circles to Heaven—every time they needed to seek food or water. But, amazingly, some survivors still lived in Ulanbat, even though the tower rose in a desert where no food could be grown and no edible animals wandered as game. The secret there was the tower-core faxnodes every six floors. As long as other communities continued to barter food for the lovely garments that Ulanbat had always been famous for—and which they had in surplus after one-third of their population was killed by voynix before they learned how to seal off the upper floors—the Circles to Heaven would continue to exist.

There were no faxnodes in Marina's tower, but the survivors up there had shown amazing ingenuity in adapting a small exterior servitor elevator to occasional human use, rigging the cables to a system of gears and cranks so that as many as three people could be lifted up from the street in a sort of basket. The elevator only went to the esplanade level, but that made the last ten stories more climbable. This wouldn't work for frequent trips—and the ride itself was hair-raising, with startling jerks and occasional dips—but the hundred or so residents of his mother's tower had more or less seceded from the surface world, relying on their high terrace gardens and water accumulators, sending their representatives down to market twice a week and having little other intercourse with the world.

Why don't they respond? He pulled on the bell rope another two minutes, waited another three.

There was a scrabbling echo from two blocks south, toward the wide boulevard there.

Make up your mind. Stay or go, but decide. Daeman stepped farther out into the street and looked up again. Lightning illuminated the spidery black buckylace supports and gleaming bamboo-three structures on the towers above the old esplanade. Several windows up there were illuminated by lanterns. From this vantage point, he could see the signal fires that Goman kept burning on his mother's city-side terrace, in the shelter of the bamboo-three roof.

Scrabbling noises came from alleys to the north.

"To hell with it," said Daeman. It was time to get his mother out of here. If Goman and all his pals tried to stop him from taking her to Ardis tonight, he was prepared to throw all of them over the terrace railing into the Crater if he had to. Daeman set the safeties on the crossbow so he wouldn't put two pieces of barbed iron into his foot by mistake, went into the building, and began climbing the dark stairway.

He knew by the time he reached the esplanade level that something was terribly wrong. The other times he'd come here in recent months—always arriving in daylight—there were guards here with their primitive pikes and more sophisticated Ardis bows. None tonight.

Do they drop their esplanade guard at night? No, that made no sense— the voynix were most active at night. Besides, Daeman had been here visiting his mother on several occasions—the last time more than a month ago—when he'd heard the guards changing through the night. He'd even stood guard once on the two a.m. to six a.m. shift, before faxing back to Ardis blurry-eyed and tired.

At least the stairway here above the esplanade was open on the sides; the lightning showed him the next rise or landing before he sprinted up the stairs or crossed a dark space. He kept the crossbow raised and his finger just outside the trigger guard.

Even before he stepped out onto the first residential level where his mother lived, he knew what he'd find.

The signal flames in the metal barrel on the city-side terrace were burning low. There was blood on the bamboo-three of the deck, blood on the walls, and blood on the underside of the eaves. The door was open to the first domi he came to, not his mother's.

Blood everywhere inside. Daeman found it hard to believe that there had been this much blood in all the bodies of all the hundred-some members of the community combined. There were countless signs of panic—doors hastily barricaded, then the doors and barricades splintered, bloody footprints on terraces and stairways, shreds of sleeping clothes thrown here and there—but no real signs of resistance. No bloodied arrows or lances stuck in wooden beams after being thrown, their targets missed. There were no signs that weapons had been reached or raised.

There were no bodies.

He searched three other domis before working up the nerve to enter

his mother's. In each domi he found blood spattered, furniture shattered, cushions torn, tapestries ripped down, tables overturned, furniture stuffing strewn everywhere—blood on white feathers and blood on
pale foam—but no bodies.

His mother's door was locked. The old thumb locks had failed with
the Fall, but Goman had replaced the automatic lock with a simple bolt
and chain that Daeman had thought was too flimsy. It proved to be now.
After several soft knocks with no answer. Daeman kicked hard three
times and the door splintered and came out of its groove. He squeezed
into the darkness, crossbow first.

The entryway smelled of blood. There was a light in the back rooms
facing the crater, but almost none here in the foyer, hallway, or public anteroom. Daeman moved as silently as he could, his stomach convulsing
at the stench of blood and slight ripples under his feet as he moved
through unseen pools. He could see just well enough here to make sure
there was nothing or no one waiting, and that there were no bodies un-
derfoot.

"Mother!" His own cry alarmed him. Again. "Mother! Goman?
Anyone?"

Wind stirred the chimes on the terrace beyond the living area, and although the crater and the city beyond the crater were mostly dark, lightning flashes illuminated the main sitting area. The blue and green silk
tapestries he'd never loved but had grown so used to on the south wall
had gained red-brown streaks and spatters. The nesting chair he'd always claimed when he was home—a body-molded womb of corrugated
paper—had been shredded. There were no bodies. Daeman could only
wonder if he was ready to see what he had to see here.

Swirls, trails, and smears of blood came in from the terrace and led
from the common sitting room into the dining room where Marina loved
to entertain at the long table. Daeman waited for the next flash of
lightning—the storm had moved east and there were more seconds between each flash and the following thunder—and then he lifted the
crossbow back to his shoulder and moved into the large dining room.

Three successive bolts of lightning showed him the room and its contents. There were no bodies as such. But on his mother's twenty-foot-
long mahogany table, a pyramid of skulls rose almost to the ceiling
seven feet above Daeman's head. Scores of empty eye sockets stared at
him. The white of bone was like a retinal after-image between each lightning flash.

Daeman lowered the heavy crossbow, clicked on the safety, and came
closer to the pyramid. There was blood everywhere in the room except
atop the table, which was pristine. In front of the pyramid of grinning,

gaping skulls was an old turin cloth, spread wide with its embroidered circuitry centered in line with the topmost skull.

Daeman stepped up onto the chair he'd always sat in when at his mother's table, and then stepped on the table itself, bringing his face up to the level of that highest skull of these hundred skulls. In the white flashes from the receding storm, he could see that all of the other skulls were picked clean, pure white, holding no fleshly remains of their victims. This top skull was not so clean. Several strands of curly red hair had been left—oh so deliberately left—like a topknot and more at the back of the skull.

Daeman had reddish hair. His mother had red hair.

He jumped down from the table, threw open the window wall, and staggered out onto the terrace, retching over the side into the single, red eye of the crater magma fifty miles directly below. He vomited again, and then again, and then several more times, even though he had nothing left in him to throw up. Finally he turned, dropped the heavy crossbow onto the floor of the terrace, rinsed his face and mouth with water from the copper basin his mother left hanging there from ornamental chains as a birdbath, and then he collapsed with his back to the bamboo-three railing, staring in through the open sliding window-door of the dining room.

The lightning was growing dimmer and less frequent, but as Daeman's eyes adjusted, the red glow from the crater illuminated the curved backs of countless skulls. He could see the red hair.

Nine months ago, Daeman would have wept like the thirty-seven-year-old child he was. Now, though his stomach churned and some black emotion folded itself into a fist in his chest, he tried to think coolly.

He had no question about who or what had done this thing. Voynix did not feed, nor did they carry off their victims' bodies. This was not random voynix violence. This was a message to Daeman, and only one creature in all of dark creation could send such a message. Everyone in this domi tower had died and been filleted like fish, skulls stacked like white coconuts, just so the message could be delivered. And from the stench-freshness of the blood, it had occurred only hours earlier, perhaps even more recently.

Leaving his crossbow lying where it fell for now, Daeman got to his hands and knees, and then to his feet—only because he did not want to further smear his hands in the gore on the terrace floor—and he walked into the dining room again, circling the long table, finally climbing to take down his mother's skull. His hands were shaking. He did not feel like weeping.

Humans had only just recently learned how to bury their fellow humans. Seven had died at Ardis in the past eight months, six from voynix, one from some mysterious illness that had carried the young woman away in one feverish night. Daeman hadn't known it was possible for old-style humans to contract illness or disease.

Should I take her back with me? Have some burial service out by the wall where Noman and Harman had directed us to create the cemetery for our dead?

No. Marina had always loved her domis here in Paris Crater better than anyplace else in the faxable world.

But I can't leave her here with these other skulls, thought Daeman, feeling wave after wave of indescribable emotion surge through him. *One of these other skulls is that bastard Goman.*

He carried the skull back out onto the terrace. The rain had grown much more fierce, the wind had dropped off, and Daeman stood a long minute at the railing, letting the raindrops wet his face and further clean the skull. Then he dropped the skull over the edge of the railing and watched it fall toward the red eye below until the tiny white speck was gone.

He lifted the crossbow and started to leave—back through the dining room, the common area, the inner hall—then he paused.

It hadn't been a sound. The pounding of the rain was so loud that he couldn't have heard an allosaurus if it was ten feet behind him. He'd forgotten something. *What?*

Daeman went back into the dining room, trying to avoid the accusatory stares of the dozens of skulls—*What could I have done?* he asked silently. *Died with us,* they silently responded—and swept up the turin cloth.

He—*it*—had left the cloth here for some purpose. It and the table were the only things in the domi complex not smeared and spattered with human blood. Daeman stuffed the cloth into the side pocket of his anorak and went out of that place.

It was dark in the stairway down to the esplanade and even darker in the enclosed stairway for fifteen stories beneath the esplanade. Daeman did not even raise his crossbow to the ready. If it—*he*—was waiting for him here, so be it. It would be a contest of teeth and fingernails and rages.

Nothing waited there.

Daeman was halfway back to the Invalid Hotel fax pavilion, walking stolidly down the center of the boulevard in the pounding rain, when there came a crackling and crashing behind him.

He turned, went to one knee, and raised the heavy weapon to his shoulder. This was not *its* sound. *It* was silent on its horn-padded and yellow-taloned webbed feet.

Daeman raised his face and stared, jaw going slack. A spinning had appeared in the direction of the crater, somewhere between him and his mother's domi tower. The thing was some hundreds of meters across and spinning rapidly. A form of lightning crackled around it like a crown of electrical thorns and rays of random light stabbed out from the sphere. The wet air was filled with rumbles that made the pavements shake. Shifting fractal designs filled the sphere until the sphere became a circle and the circle sank, ripping a building apart as it settled to the earth and then partially beneath the earth.

Sunlight flooded out of the circle now, but it was not any sunlight as ever seen from Earth. The circle stopped sinking with only one-fourth of it wedged into the ground like some giant portal. It was only two blocks away, filling the sky to the east. Air rushed toward it from behind Daeman at near-hurricane speeds, almost knocking him down in its loud, wailing rush.

There was a daylit world visible through that still vibrating three-quarters circle—a world of a tepidly lapping blue sea, red soil, rocks, and a mountain—no, a volcano, rising to impossible heights in front of an off-blue sky. Something very large and pink and gray and moist emerged from that tepid sea and appeared to scuttle toward the open hole on centipede-fast feet that looked like giant hands to Daeman's eyes. Then the air in front of that view was filled with debris and dust as the winds raged, mixed, were absorbed, and died away.

Daeman stood there another minute, peering through the obscuring dust, holding his hand up to shield his eyes from the diffused but still blinding sunlight streaming from the hole. The buildings of Paris Crater west of the hole—and the iron-armature thighs and emptied belly of the Enormous Whore—glinted in the cold, alien sunlight and then disappeared in the dust cloud broiling out of the hole. Other parts of the city remained invisible and wet, wrapped in night.

There came voynix scrabblings—urgent, many-clawed—from streets to the north and south.

Two voynix exploded out of a dark doorway on Daeman's boulevard and rushed him on all fours, killing blades clattering.

He tracked them with his crossbow sight, led them, fired the first bolt into the leathery hood of the second voynix—it fell—and then fired his second bolt into the chest of the leading one. It fell but kept pulling itself closer.

Daeman carefully pulled two barbed, iron bolts from the pouch slung over his shoulder, reloaded, recocked, and shot both bolts into the thing's nerve-center hump at a distance of ten feet. It quit crawling.

More scrabblings to the west and south. The reddish daylight from the hole was revealing everything on the street here. Daeman's concealment of darkness was gone. Something bellowed from that rising dust cloud—making a sound like nothing Daeman had ever heard—deeper, more malignant, the incomprehensible growls sounding like some terrible language being bellowed in reverse.

Not hurrying, Daeman reloaded again, looked one last time over his shoulder at the red mountain visible through the hole in Paris Crater's sky and cityscape, and then he jogged west—not in panic—toward Invalid Hotel.

Noman was dying.

Harman went in and out of the small room on the first floor of Ardis Hall that had been converted into a makeshift—and largely useless—infirmary. There were books in there from which they could sigl anatomy charts and instructions for simple surgery, mending broken bones, etc., but no one but Noman had been proficient in dealing with serious wounds. Two of those buried in the new cemetery near the northwest corner of the palisade had died after days of pain in this same infirmary.

Ada stayed with Harman, had been by his side since he'd staggered through the north gate more than an hour earlier, often touching his arm or taking his hand as if reassuring herself he was really there. Harman had been treated for his wounds on the cot next to where Noman lay now—Harman's wounds had been deep scratches, requiring a painful few stitches and an even more painful administration of their crude, homemade versions of antiseptic—including raw alcohol. But the unconscious Noman's terrible wounds to his arm and scalp were too serious to be treated with only these few inadequate measures. They'd cleaned him as best they could, applied stitches to his scalp, used their antiseptics on the open wounds—Noman did not even return to consciousness when the alcohol was poured on—but the arm was too mauled, connected to his torso only by ragged strings of ligament, tissue, and shattered bone. They had stapled and bandaged, but already the bandages were soaked through with blood.

"He's going to die, isn't he?" asked Hannah, who'd not left the infirmary even to change her bloody clothes. They'd treated her for slashes to her left shoulder and she'd never taken her eyes off Noman as the stitches and antiseptic were applied to her.

"Yes, I think so," said Petyr. "He won't survive."

"Why is he still unconscious?" asked the young woman.

"I think that's a result of the concussion he received," said Harman, "not the claw wounds." Harman wanted to curse at the simple fact that sigling a hundred volumes on neuroanatomy did not teach one how to actually open a skull and relieve pressure on the brain. If they tried it with their current rough instruments and almost nonexistent level of experience as surgeons, Noman would certainly die sooner than if they left things to nature's way. Either way, Noman-Odysseus was going to die.

Ferman, who was the usual keeper of the infirmary and who had sigled more books on the subject than Harman, looked up from sharpening a saw and cleaver in case they decided to remove the arm. "We'll have to decide soon about the arm," he said softly and returned to working his whetstone.

Hannah turned to Petyr. "I heard him mumble a few times while you were carrying him but couldn't hear what he said. Did it make any sense?"

"Not really. I couldn't make most of it out. I think it was in the language the other Odysseus used in the turin drama . . ."

"Greek," said Harman.

"Whatever," said Petyr. "The couple of words I could make out in English weren't important."

"What were they?" asked Hannah.

"I'm sure he said something that ended in 'gate.' And then 'crash' . . . I think. He was mumbling, I was panting loudly, and the guards on the wall were shouting. It was when we were approaching the north gate of the palisade, so he must have been saying 'crash it' if they don't open it."

"That doesn't make much sense," said Hannah.

"He was in pain and lapsing into coma," said Petyr.

"Maybe," said Harman. He left the infirmary, Ada still holding his arm, and began to pace through the manor house.

About fifty of Ardis's population of four hundred were eating in the main dining room.

"You should eat," said Harman, touching Ada's stomach.

"Are you hungry?"

"Not yet." In truth, the pain to Harman's bad leg from the new slashes was bad enough to make him a little nauseated. Or perhaps it was the mental image of Noman lying there bleeding and dying.

"Hannah will be so upset," whispered Ada.

Harman nodded distractedly. Something was gnawing at the subconscious and he was trying to let it have its way.

They went through the former grand ballroom where dozens of people were still working at long tables, applying bronze arrowheads to wooden shafts, then adding the prepared feathers, crafting spears, or carving bows. Many looked up and nodded as Ada and Harman went by. Harman led the way out back into the overheated blacksmithing annex where three men and two women were hammering bronze sword and knife blades, adding edges and sharpening on large whetstones. In the morning, Harman knew, this room would be insufferably hot as they carried in the molten metal from the next pour to be molded and hammered into shape. He paused to touch a sword blade and hilt that was finished except for the last of the leather to be wrapped around the hilt.

So crude, he thought. *So unspeakably crude compared to the craft and artistry not only of Noman's Circe sword—wherever that came from—but from the weapons in the old turin drama. And how sad that the first pieces of technology we old-style humans pour and cast and worry into a shape after two millennia or more are these rough weapons, their time come round again at last.*

Reman came bursting into the blacksmith annex on the way to the main house.

"What is it?" said Ada.

"Voynix," said Reman, who'd gone out to guard duty after finishing his chores in the kitchen. He was wet from the rain that had been falling since nightfall and his beard was icy. "A lot of voynix. More than I've ever seen at once."

"Out of the woods yet?" asked Harman.

"Massing under the trees. But scores and scores of them."

Outside, from the ramparts on all parts of the palisades the bells began to sound the alarm. The horns would blow if and when the voynix actually began their attack.

The dining hall emptied as men and women grabbed their coats and weapons and ran to their fighting stations on the walls, in the yard, and at windows, doorways, gables, porches, and balconies in the house itself.

Harman did not move. He let the running shapes flow around him like a river.

"Harman?" whispered Ada.

Turning against the current, he led her back into the infirmary where Noman lay dying. Hannah had pulled on her coat and found a lance, but seemed unable to leave Noman's side. Petyr was half out the door but returned when Harman and Ada went in to stand by Noman's bloodied cot.

"He didn't say crash the gate," whispered Harman. "He said Golden Gate. The crèche at Golden Gate."

Outside, the horns began to blow.

26

Daeman knew that he should fax straight back to the Ardis node to report on what he'd seen, even if he had to make the mile-and-a-quarter-walk from the palisaded faxnode pavilion to Ardis Hall in the dark, but he couldn't. As important as his news about the hole in the sky was, he wasn't ready to go back.

He faxed to a previously unknown code he'd discovered when they were doing their node survey six months earlier, mapping out the four hundred and nine known nodes—hunting for survivors of the Fall—and looking for unnumbered destinations. This place was hot and in sunlight. The pavilion was on a knoll among palm trees stirring in soft breezes from the sea. Just down the hill began the beach—a white crescent almost encircling a lagoon so clear he could see the sandy bottom forty feet down out where the reef began. There were no people around, either old-style human or post-human, although Daeman had found the overgrown ruins of what had once been a pre–Final Fax city just inland on the north side of the crescent beach.

He'd seen no voynix in the dozen or so times he'd come here to sit and think. On one trip, some huge, legless, flippered saurian thing had risen out of the surf just beyond the reef, then crashed back into the water with a thirty-foot shark in its mouth, but other than that one disconcerting sighting, he'd seen nothing threatening here.

Now he trudged down to the beach, dropped his heavy crossbow onto the sand, and sat down next to it. The sun was hot. He pulled off his bulky backpack, anorak, and shirt. There was something hanging out of the pocket of his anorak and he pulled it out—the turin cloth from the table of skulls. He tossed it away on the sand. Daeman removed his shoes, trousers, and underwear and staggered naked toward the water's edge, not even glancing toward the jungle's edge to make sure he was alone.

My mother is dead. The fact hit him like a physical blow and he thought he might be sick again. *Dead*.

Daeman walked naked toward the surf. He stood at the edge of the lagoon and let the warm waves lap at his feet, move the sand from under his toes. *Dead*. He would never see his mother or hear her voice again. Never, never, never, never, never.

He sat down heavily on the wet sand. Daeman had thought himself reconciled to this new world where death was a finality; he thought he'd come to terms with this obscenity when he'd faced his own death eight months earlier up there on Prospero's Isle.

I knew that I had to die someday . . . but not my mother. Not Marina. That's not . . . fair.

Daeman sobbed a laugh at the absurdity of what he was thinking and feeling. Thousands dead since the Fall . . . he knew there were thousands dead, because he'd been one of Ardis's envoys to the hundreds of other nodes, he'd seen the graves, even taught some communities how to dig graves and set the bodies in them to rot away . . .

My mother! Had she suffered? Had Caliban played with her, tormented her, tortured her before slaughtering her?

I know it was Caliban. He killed them all. It doesn't matter if that's impossible— it's true. He killed them all, but only to get to my mother, to set her skull on top of the pyramid of skulls, wisps of her red hair remaining to show me that it was indeed my mother. Caliban. You whoremongering gill-slitted motherfucking sonofabitching asshole-licking freakshit murderous gape-mawed goddamned fucking . . .

Daeman couldn't breathe. His chest simply locked up. He opened his mouth as if to retch again, but he couldn't move air in or out.

Dead. Forever. Dead.

He stood, waded into the sun-warmed water, and then dove, striking out and swimming hard, swimming toward the reef where the waves lifted white and where he'd seen the giant beast with the shark in its jaws, swimming hard, feeling the sting of saltwater in his eyes and on his cheeks . . .

The swimming allowed him to breathe. He swam a hundred yards to where the lagoon opened onto the sea and then treaded water, feeling the cold currents tugging at him, watching the heavy waves beyond the reef, listening to the wonderful violence of their crashing, almost surrendering then to the undertow beckoning him out, farther, farther— there was no Pacific Breach as there was in the Atlantic, his body might drift for days—and then he turned and swam back into the beach.

He came out of the water oblivous of his nakedness but no longer oblivious to his safety. He lifted his salt-crusted left palm and invoked the farnet function. He was on this island in the South Pacific—Daeman almost laughed at this thought, since nine months ago, before he'd met Harman, he hadn't known the names of the oceans, hadn't even known the world was round, hadn't known the landmasses, didn't know there was more than one ocean—and what goddamn good had it done him since to know these things? None, as far as he could tell.

But the farnet showed him that there were no old-style humans or voynix around. He walked up the beach to his clothes and dropped onto the anorak, using it as a beach blanket. His tanned legs were covered with sand.

Just as he went to his knees, a gust of wind from the land caught the tumbling turin cloth and blew it over his head, toward the water. Acting on pure reflex, Daeman reached high and caught it. He shook his head and used the borders of the elaborately embroidered cloth to dry his hair.

Daeman flopped onto his back, the wadded cloth still in his hand, and stared up at the flawless blue sky.

She's dead. I held her skull in my hands. How had he known for sure that this one skull out of a hundred—even with the obscene hint of the strands of short, red hair—had been his mother? He was sure. *Perhaps I should have left her there with the others.* Not with Goman, whose stubbornness at staying in Paris Crater killed her. No, not with him. Daeman had a clear image of the small, white skull tumbling toward the red-magma eye of the crater.

He closed his eyes, wincing. The pain of this night was a physical thing, lurking behind his eyes like lancets.

He had to get back to Ardis to tell everyone about what he'd seen— about the certainty of Caliban's return to earth and about the hole in the night sky and about the huge thing that had come through the hole.

He imagined Harman's or Noman's or Ada's or some of the other people's questions. *How can you be certain it was Caliban?*

Daeman was certain. He *knew.* There had been a connection between him and the monster since the two tumbled in near zero-gravity in the great ruined cathedral space of Prospero's orbital isle. He'd known since the Fall that Caliban was still alive—had probably, somehow, impossibly, certainly, escaped the isle and returned to Earth.

How could you know?

He knew.

How could one creature, smaller than a voynix, kill a hundred of the Paris Crater survivors—most of them men?

Caliban could have used the clone things from the Mediterranean Basin—the *calibani* that Prospero had created centuries ago to keep the

Setebos' voynix at bay—but Daeman suspected the monster had not. He suspected that Caliban alone had slaughtered his mother and all the others. *Sending me a message.*

If Caliban wants to send you a message, why didn't he come to Ardis Hall and kill us all—saving you for last?

Good question. Daeman thought he knew the answer. He'd seen the Caliban-creature play with the eyeless lizard-things he'd caught up from the rank pools in his sewage ponds under the orbital city—play with them and tease them before swallowing them whole. He'd also seen Caliban play with them—Harman, Savi, and him—taunting them before leaping with lightning speed to bite through the old woman's neck, dragging her under the water to devour. *I'm being played with. We all are.*

What did you see coming through the hole above Paris Crater?

Another good question. What *had* he seen? It had been dusty, the air filled with debris from the hurricane winds, and the light from the hole had been all but blinding. *A huge, mucousy brain propelling itself on its hands?* Daeman could imagine the reaction from the others at Ardis Hall—at any of the survivor communities—when he told them that.

But Harman would not laugh. Harman had been there with Daeman—and with Savi, who had only minutes more to live—when Caliban had cackled and hissed and huffed its odd litany to and about his father-god, Setebos—*"Setebos, Setebos, and Setebos!"* the monster had cried. *"Thinketh, He dwelleth i' the cold o' the moon."* And later, *". . . Thinketh, though, that Setebos, the many-handed as a cuttlefish, who, making Himself feared through what He does, looks up, first, and perceives he cannot soar to what is quiet and happy in life, but makes this bauble-world to ape yon real. These good things to match those as hips do grapes."*

Daeman and Harman had later decided that the "bauble-world" was Prospero's orbital isle, but it was Caliban's god Setebos he was thinking of now—"the many-handed as a cuttlefish."

How big was this thing you saw come through the hole?

How big indeed? It had seemed to dwarf the smaller buildings. But the light, the wind, the mountain gleaming behind the scuttling thing—Daeman had no idea how large it had been.

I have to go back.

"Oh, Jesus Christ," moaned Daeman, knowing now that this easy epiphet so many had used since childhood related to some lost god from the Lost Age. "Oh, Jesus Christ." He didn't want to go back to Paris Crater tonight. He wanted to stay here in the warmth and sunlight and safety of this beach.

What did the giant cuttlefish thing do when it entered the city of Paris Crater? Was it coming to meet Caliban?

He had to go back and reconnoiter before faxing home to Ardis. But not this second. Not this very minute.

Daeman's head was aching from the spikes of agony-sorrow behind his eyes. The goddamned sun was far too bright here. First he set his left palm across his eyes—fleshly light, too much—and then he lifted the turin cloth and set it over his face as he'd done many times before. He'd never been very interested in the turin drama—seducing young women and collecting butterflies had been his two interests in life—but he'd gone under the turin more than a few times out of boredom or mild curiosity. Simply out of habit, knowing all the turins were as dead and inoperative as the servitors and electric lights, he aligned the embroidered microcircuits in the cloth with the center of his forehead.

The images and voices and physical impressions flowed in.

Achilles kneels next to the dead body of the Amazon Penthesilea. The Hole has closed—red Mars stretches away east and south along the coast of the Tethys with no sign left of Ilium and the Earth—and most of the captains who had fought the Amazons with Achilles have escaped through it in time. Big and Little Ajax are gone, as are Diomedes, Idomeneus, Stichius, Sthenelus, Euryalus, Teucer—even Odysseus has disappeared. Some of the Achaeans—Euenor, Pretesilaus and his friend Podarces, Menippus—lay dead among the bodies of the defeated Amazons. In the confusion and panic as the Hole closed, even the Myrmidons, Achilles' most faithful followers, have fled with the others, thinking their hero Achilles was with them.

Achilles is alone here with the dead. The Martian wind blows down from the steep cliffs at the base of Olympos and howls among scattered, hollow armor, stirring the bloodied pennants on the shafts of spears pinning the dead to the red ground.

The fleet-footed mankiller cradles the body of Penthesilea, lifting her head and shoulders to his knee. He weeps at the sight of what he has done—her pierced breast, her no-longer-bleeding wounds. Five minutes earlier, Achilles had been triumphant in his victory, crying at the dying queen—"I don't know what riches Priam promised you, foolish girl, but here is your reward! Now the dogs and birds will feed on your white flesh."

Achilles can only weep more fiercely at the memory of his own words. He cannot take his eyes from her fair brow, her still-pink lips. The Amazon's golden curls stir to the rising breeze and he watches her eyelashes, waiting for them to flicker, for her eyes to open. His tears fall onto the dust of her cheek and brow, and he takes the hem of his tunic to wipe the mud from her face. Her eyelids do not flicker. Her eyes do not open.

His spearcast passed through her body and pierced her horse as well, so fierce had been the force of his throw.

"You should have married her, son of Peleus, not murdered her."

Achilles looks up through his tears at the tall form standing between him and the sun.

"Pallas Athena, goddess . . ." begins the mankiller and then can only choke his words back or sob. He knows that among all the gods, Athena is his most sworn enemy—that it was she who appeared in his tent eight months earlier and murdered his dearest friend, Patroclus, that it is she whom he'd most longed to slaughter as he fought and wounded dozens of other gods in the past months—but Achilles can find no rage in his heart right now, only bottomless sorrow at the death of Penthesilea.

"How very strange," says the goddess, looming over him in her golden armor, her tall golden lance catching the low sunlight. "Twenty minutes ago you were willing—nay, *eager*—to leave her body to the birds and dogs. Now you weep for her."

"I did not love her when I killed her," manages Achilles. He brushes at the muddy streaks on the dead Amazon's fair face.

"No, and you have never loved thus before," says Pallas Athena. "Never a woman."

"I have bedded many a woman," says Achilles, unable to take his eyes off Penthesilea's dead face. "I have refused to fight for Agamemnon for the love of Briseis."

Athena laughs. "Briseis was your slave, son of Peleus. All the women you have ever bedded—including the mother of your son, Pyrrhus, whom the Argives will someday call Neoptolemus—were your slaves. Slaves of your ego. You have never *loved* a woman before this day, fleet-footed Achilles."

Achilles wants to stand and fight the goddess—she is, after all, his worst enemy, the murderer of his beloved Patroclus, the reason he led his people into war with the gods—but he finds that he cannot take his arms from around the corpse of Penthesilea. Her deadly spearcast had failed, but his heart has been pierced nonetheless. Never—not even at the death of his dearest friend Patroclus—has the mankiller felt such terrible sorrow. "Why . . . now?" he gasps between wracking sobs. "Why . . . her?"

"It is a spell put on you by the witch goddess of lust, Aphrodite," says Athena, moving around him and the fallen horse and Amazon so that he can see her without moving his head. "It was always Aphrodite and her incestuous brother Ares who confounded your will, killed your friends, and murdered your joys, Achilles. It was Aphrodite who killed Patroclus and carried away his body these eight months past."

"No . . . I was there . . . I saw . . ."

"You saw Aphrodite take my form," interrupts Pallas Athena. "Do you doubt that we gods can take any form we wish? Shall I make myself into the form and shape of the dead Penthesilea so you can slake your lust with a living body rather than a dead one?"

Achilles stares up at her, his jaw hanging slack. "Aphrodite . . ." he says after a minute, his tone that of a deadly curse. "I will kill the cunt."

Athena smiles. "An act most worthy and long overdue, fleet-footed mankiller. Let me give you this . . ." She hands him a small jewel-encrusted dagger.

Still cradling Penthesilea in his right arm, he accepts the thing with his left hand. "What is it?"

"A knife."

"I *know* it's a knife," snarls Achilles, his tone showing no respect for the fact that he's speaking to a goddess, third-born of all the gods sired by Zeus. "Why in Hades' name would I want this girl's toy of a blade when I have my own sword, my own gutting knife? Take this back."

"This knife is different," says the goddess. "This knife can kill a god."

"I've cut down gods with my regular blade."

"Cut them down, yes," says Athena. "Killed them, no. This blade does for immortal flesh what your mere human sword does for your puny fellow mortals."

Achilles stands, easily shifting the body of Penthesilea to his right shoulder. He holds the short blade in his right hand. "Why would you give me such a thing, Pallas Athena? We have opposed each other across this battlefield for months now. Why would you aid me now?"

"I have my reasons, son of Peleus. Where is Hockenberry?"

"Hockenberry?"

"Yes, that former scholic who became Aphrodite's agent," says Pallas Athena. "Does he still live? I have business with this mortal, but do not know where to seek him out. The moravec forcefields have clouded our godly vision of recent."

Achilles looks around him, blinking as if noticing for the first time that he is the only living human being left on the red Martian plain. "Hockenberry was here only a few minutes ago. I spoke to him before I slew . . . her." He begins weeping again.

"I look forward to meeting this Hockenberry again," says Athena, muttering as if to herself. "Today is a time of reckonings, and his is long overdue." She reaches out and takes Achilles' chin in her powerful, slender hand, raising his face, locking her gaze to his. "Son of Peleus, do you wish this woman . . . this Amazon . . . alive again, to be your bride?"

Achilles stares. "I wish to be released from this spell of love, noble goddess."

Athena shakes her golden-helmeted head. The red sun glints everywhere on her armor. "There is no release from this particular spell of Aphrodite—the pheromones have spoken and their judgment is final. Penthesilea will be your only love for this life, either as a corpse or as a living woman . . . do you want her alive?"

"*Yes!!*" cries Achilles, stepping closer with the dead woman in his arms and bright madness in his eyes. "Return her to life!"

"No god or goddess can do that, son of Peleus," Athena says sadly. "As you once said to Odysseus—'*Of possessions cattle and fat sheep are things to be had for the lifting, and tripods can be won, and the tawny high heads of horses, but a man's life*—nor a woman's, Achilles—*cannot come back again, it cannot be lifted nor captured again by force, once it has crossed the teeth's barrier.* Not even Father Zeus has this power of resurrection, Achilles."

"Then why the fuck did you offer it to me?" snarls the mankiller. He feels the rage flow in next to the love now—oil and water, fire and . . . not ice—but a different form of fire. He is very aware of both his rage and the god- and goddess-killing knife in his hand. To keep himself from doing something rash, he sets the blade in his broad warbelt.

"It is possible to return Penthesilea to life," says Athena, "but I do not have that power. I will sprinkle her with a form of ambrosia which will preserve her from all decay. Her dead body will forevermore carry the blush on her cheeks and the hint of fading warmth you feel now. Her beauty will never depart."

"What good does that do me?" snarls Achilles. "Do you really expect me to celebrate my love with an act of necrophilia?"

"That's your personal choice," says Pallas Athena with a smirk that almost makes Achilles pull the dagger from his belt. She continues, "But if you are a man of action, I expect you to carry your love's body to the summit of Mount Olympos. There, in a great building near a lake, is our godly secret—a hall of clear, fluid-filled tanks where strange creatures tend to our wounds, repairing all damage, assuring that we return—as you put it so well—across the teeth's barrier."

Achilles turns and stares up at the endless mountain catching the sunlight. It rises forever. The summit is not in sight. The vertical cliffs at its base, a mere beginning to the giant massif, are more than fourteen thousand feet tall. "Climb Olympos . . ." he says.

"There was an escalator . . . a staircase," says Pallas Athena, pointing with her long lance. "You see the ruins there. It is still the easiest way up."

"I'll have to fight my way up, every foot of the way," says Achilles, grinning horribly. "I am still at war with the gods."

Pallas Athena also grins. "The gods are now at war with each other, son of Peleus. And they know the Brane Hole has closed forever. Mortals no longer threaten the halls of Olympos. I would guess that you will climb undetected, unopposed, but once you are there they will surely sound the alarm."

"Aphrodite," whispers the fleet-footed mankiller.

"Yes, she will be there. And Ares. All the architects of your personal hell. You have my permission to kill them. I ask you only one favor in return for my ambrosia, my guidance, and my love."

Achilles turns back to her and waits.

"Destroy the healing tanks after they have brought your Amazon love back to life. Kill the Healer—a great monstrous centipede thing with too many arms and eyes. Destroy everything in the Healer's Hall."

"Goddess, would that not destroy your own immortality?" asks Achilles.

"I will worry about that, son of Peleus," says Pallas Athena. She extends her arms, palms downward, and golden ambrosia falls on the bloody, pierced body of Penthesilea. "Go now. I must return to my own wars. The issue of Ilium will be decided soon. Your fate will be settled there, on Olympos." She points to the mountain rising endlessly above them.

"You goad me as if I have the power of a god, Pallas Athena," whispers Achilles.

"You have always had the power of a god, son of Peleus," says the goddess. She raises her free hand in benediction and QT's away. The air rushes into the vacuum with a soft thunderclap.

Achilles lays Penthesilea's body down among the other corpses only long enough to wrap it in clean white cloth retrieved from his battle tent. Then he seeks out his own shield, lance, helmet, and a single bag of bread and wineskins he'd brought along so many hours earlier. Finally, his weapons securely lashed to him, he kneels, lifts the dead Amazon, and begins walking toward Mount Olympos.

"Holy shit," says Daeman, pulling the turin cloth away from his face. Long minutes have passed. He checks his proxnet palm—no voynix nearby. They could have deboned him like a fish while he lay under the turin's spell. "Holy shit," he says again.

There is no reply except for the low waves lapping along the beach.

"Which is more important?" he mutters to himself. "Getting this working turin cloth back to Ardis as quickly as possible—and figuring out why Caliban or his master left it for me? Or going back to Paris Crater to see what the many-handed-as-a-cuttlefish is up to there?"

He stays on his knees in the sand for a minute. Then he pulls on his clothes, stuffs the turin cloth into his backpack, sets his sword back on his belt, lifts the crossbow, and slogs up the hill to the waiting fax pavilion.

27

Ada awoke in the dark to find three voynix in her room. One of them was holding Harman's severed head in its long fingerblades.

Ada awoke in the diffused light just before dawn with her heart pounding. Her mouth was open as if already forming a scream.

"Harman!"

She rolled out of bed, sitting on the edge, her head in her hands, her heart still pounding so fiercely that it gave her vertigo. She couldn't believe that she'd come up to her bedroom and fallen asleep while Harman was still awake. This pregnancy was a stupid thing, she thought. It made her body a traitor at times.

She'd slept in her clothes—tunic, vest, canvas trousers, thick socks— and she pressed her hair and long shirt down as well as she could to calm the worst of the wildness, considered using some of the precious hot water for a standing bath at the basin—her birdbath, Harman always called it—and rejected the idea. Too much might have happened in the hour or two since she fell asleep. Ada pulled on her boots and hurried downstairs.

Harman was in the front parlor where the wide window doors had been unshuttered, allowing a view down the south lawn to the lower palisade. There was no sunrise—the morning was too cloudy—and it had begun to snow. Ada had seen snow before in her life, but only once here at Ardis Hall, when she was very young. About a dozen men and women, including Daeman—who looked oddly flushed—were standing by the windows, watching the snow fall and talking softly.

Ada gave Daeman a quick hug and moved close to Harman, slipping her arm around him. "How is Ody . . ." she began.

"Noman's still alive, but only barely," Harman said softly. "He's lost too much blood. His breathing is becoming more and more difficult. Loes thinks that he'll die within the next hour or two. We're trying to decide what to do." He touched her lower back. "Ada, Daeman has brought us some terrible news about his mother."

Ada looked at her friend, wondering if his mother had simply re-fused to come to Ardis. She and Daeman had visited Marina twice in the past eight months, and neither time had they come close to convincing the older woman.

"She's dead," said Daeman. "Caliban killed her and everyone else in the domi tower."

Ada bit her knuckle until it almost bled and then said, "Oh, Daeman, I am so, so sorry . . ." And then, realizing what he'd said, she whispered, *"Caliban?"* She had convinced herself from Harman's stories about Pros-pero's Isle that the creature had died up there. "Caliban?" she repeated stupidly. Her dream was still with her like a weight on her neck. "You're sure?"

"Yes," said Daeman.

Ada put her arms around him, but Daeman's body was as tight and rigid as a rock. He patted her shoulder almost absently. Ada wondered if he was in shock.

The group resumed discussing the night's defense of Ardis Hall.

The voynix had attacked just before midnight—at least a hundred of them, perhaps a hundred and fifty; it was hard to tell in the dark and rain—and they had rushed at least three out of the four sides of the pal-isade perimeter. It was the largest and certainly the most coordinated at-tack the voynix had ever carried out against Ardis.

The defenders had killed them until just before dawn—first setting the huge braziers alight, burning the precious kerosene and naphtha saved for that purpose, illuminating the walls and fields beyond the walls—and then showering volley upon volley of aimed bow-and-crossbow fire onto the rushing forms.

Arrows and bolts didn't always penetrate a voynix's carapace or leathery hood—more often than not they didn't—so the defenders ex-pended a huge percentage of their arrows and bolts. Dozens of the voynix had fallen—Loes reported that his team had counted fifty-three voynix corpses in the fields and woods at first light.

Some of the things had gotten to the walls and leapt to the ramparts—voynix could jump thirty feet and more from a standing start, like huge grasshoppers—but the mass of pikes and reserve fighters with swords had stopped any from getting to the house. Eight of Ardis's people had been hurt, but only two seriously: a woman named Kirik with a badly broken arm, and Laman, a friend of Petyr's, with four fingers lopped off—not by a voynix's blades, but from a fellow defender's ill-timed swing of a sword.

What had turned the tide was the sonie.

Harman launched the oval disk from the ancient jinker platform high on Ardis Hall's gabled rooftop. He flew it from its center-forward niche.

The flying machine had six shallow, cushioned indentations for people lying prone, but Petyr, Loes, Reman, and Hannah had knelt in their niches, shooting down from the sonie, the three men wielding all of Ardis's flechette rifles and Hannah firing the finest crossbow she'd ever crafted.

Harman couldn't go lower than about sixty feet because of the voynix's amazing leaping abilities. But that was close enough. Even in the dark and the rain, even with the voynix scuttling as fast as cockroaches and leaping like giant grasshoppers on a griddle, the sustained flechette and crossbow fire dropped the creatures in their tracks. Harman flew the sonie in among the tall trees at the bottom and top of the hill, the defenders on the palisade ramparts shot flaming arrows and catapult-launched balls of burning, hissing naphtha to illuminate the night. The voynix scattered, regrouped, and attacked six more times before finally disappearing, some toward the river far down the hill from Ardis and the rest into the hills to the north.

"But why did they stop attacking?" asked the young woman named Peaen. "Why'd they leave?"

"What do you mean?" said Petyr. "We killed a third of them."

Harman crossed his arms and glared out at the softly falling snow. "I know what Peaen means. It's a good question. Why did they break off the attack? We've never seen a voynix react to pain. They die . . . but they don't complain about it. Why didn't they all keep coming until they overran us or died?"

"Because someone or something recalled them," Daeman said.

Ada glanced at him. Daeman's face was almost slack, his voice dull, his eyes not quite focused on anything. For the last nine months, Daeman's energy and determination had deepened and visibly increased daily. Now he was listless, seemingly indifferent to the conversation and the people around him. Ada felt sure that his mother's death had almost undone him—perhaps it would yet do so.

"If the voynix were recalled, who recalled them?" asked Hannah.

No one spoke.

"Daeman," Harman said, "please tell your story again, for Ada. And add any detail you left out the first time." More men and women had gathered in the long room. Everyone looked tired. No one spoke or asked questions as Daeman gave his story again, his voice a dull monotone.

He told of the slaughter at his mother's domi, the stack of skulls, the presence of the turin cloth on the table—the only thing not splattered with blood—and how he activated it later when he'd faxed somewhere else; he didn't specify where exactly. He told of the appearance of the hole above the city of Paris Crater and about his glimpse of something large emerging from it—something that seemed to scuttle about on impossible sets of giant hands.

He explained how he had faxed away to regain his composure, then faxed to the Ardis node—the guards at the small fort there told him of the movement of voynix they'd glimpsed all night, the torches were lit and every man was at the walls, and about the sounds of fighting and flashes of torches and naphtha they'd seen from the direction of Ardis Hall. Daeman had been tempted to start toward Ardis on foot but the men at the barricades there at the fax pavilion were positive it'd be certain death to try that walk in the dark—they'd counted more than seventy voynix slipping past across meadows and into the woods, headed toward the great house.

Daeman explained how he'd left the turin cloth with Casman and Greogi, the two captains of the guard there, and directed one of them to fax to Chom or somewhere safe with the turin if the voynix overran the fax pavilion before he got back.

"We plan to fax out if those bastards attack us," said Greogi. "We've made plans on who goes when and in which order, while others provide covering fire until it's their turn. We're not planning to die to protect this pavilion."

Daeman had nodded and faxed back to Paris Crater.

He told the others now that if he had chosen the closer-in Invalid Hotel node to the more distant Guarded Lion, he would have died. All the center of Paris Crater had been transformed. The hole in space was still there—weak sunlight streaming out—but the center of the city itself had been encased in a webbed glacier of blue ice.

"Blue ice?" interrupted Ada. "It was that cold?"

"Very cold near the stuff," said Daeman. "But not so bad just a few yards away. Just chilly and raining, It wasn't really ice, I don't think. Just something chill and crystalline—cold but organic, like spiderwebs rising out of icebergs—and the blocks and webs of the stuff covered the old domi towers and boulevards all around the crater in the heart of Paris Crater."

"Did you see that . . . thing . . . you saw come through the hole?" asked Emme.

"No. I couldn't get close enough. There were more voynix than I'd ever seen before. The Guarded Lion building itself—it used to be some sort of transport center, you know, with rails running in and out and landing pads on the roof—was alive with voynix." Daeman looked at Harman. "It reminded me of Jerusalem last year."

"That many?" said Harman.

"That many. And there was something else. Two things that I haven't talked about yet."

Everyone waited. Outside, the snow fell. There was a moan from the infirmary, and Hannah slipped away to check on Noman-Odysseus again.

"There's a blue light shining from Paris Crater now," said Daeman.

"A blue light?" asked the woman named Loes.

Only Harman, Ada, and Petyr registered comprehension—Harman because he'd been there in Jerusalem with Daeman and Savi nine months earlier; Ada and Petyr because they'd heard the stories.

"Does it shoot skyward like the one we saw in Jerusalem?" asked Harman.

"Yes."

"What the hell are you talking about?" asked the redheaded woman named Oelleo.

Harman answered. "We saw a similar beam in Jerusalem last year—a city near the drained Mediterranean Basin. Savi, the old woman with us, said that the beam was made of . . .what was it, Daeman? Tachyons?"

"I think so."

"Tachyons," continued Harman. "And that it contained the captured codes of all of her race from before the Final Fax. That beam *was* the Final Fax."

"I don't understand," said Reman. He looked very tired.

Daeman shook his head. "Neither do I. I don't know if the beam came with the creature I saw come through the hole, or if the beam somehow brought that thing to Paris Crater. But there's more news—and it's worse."

"How could it be?" asked Peaen with a laugh.

Daeman did not smile. "I had to get out of Paris Crater quickly—the Guarded Lion node would be death by now, voynix everywhere—and I knew it wouldn't be light here yet, so I faxed to Bellinbad, then Ulanbat, then Chom, then Drid, then Loman's Place, then Kiev, then Fuego, then Devi, then Satle Heights, then to Mantua, finally to Cape Town Tower."

"To warn them all," said Ada.

"Yes."

"Why is that bad news?" asked Harman.

"Because the holes have opened at both Chom and Ulanbat," said Daeman. "The community cores there are webbed with blue ice. The blue beams rise from both of those survivor colonies. Setebos has been there."

28

The forty or so people in the room simply stared at each other. Then there was a babble-chorus of questions. Daeman and Harman explained what Caliban on the orbital isle had said about his god, Setebos, the "many-handed like a cuttlefish."

They asked about Ulanbat and Chom. Chom he'd seen only from a distance—a growing web of blue ice. In Ulanbat, he told them, he'd faxed to the seventy-ninth floor of the Circles of Heaven and seen from the ring terrace there that the hole was a mile out over the Gobi Desert, the web of ice-stuff connecting the low outbuildings to the bottom levels of the Circles. The seventy-ninth floor seemed to be above the ice—for now.

"Did you see any people there?" asked Ada.

"No."

"Voynix?" asked Reman.

"Hundreds. Scuttling in and under and around the ice web. But not in the Circles."

"Then where are the people?" asked Emme in a small voice. "We know Ulanbat had weapons—we bartered them for their rice and textiles."

"They must have faxed out when the hole appeared," said Petyr. It sounded obvious to Ada that the young man was putting more certainty in his voice than he felt.

"If they faxed out," said Peaen, "I mean the people in both Ulanbat and Chom, why haven't they shown up here as refugees? Those three node cities—Paris Crater, Chom, Ulanbat—still house tens of thousands of old-style humans like us. Where are they? Where did they go?" She looked at Greogi and Casman, who'd just come in from their overnight guard duty at the fax pavilion. "Greogi, Cas, have people been faxing in overnight? Fleeing something?"

Greogi shook his head. "The only traffic was Daeman *Uhr* here—late last night and then again this morning."

Ada stepped into the middle of the circle. "Look . . . we'll meet to talk about this later. Right now you're all exhausted. Most of you were up all night. A lot of people hadn't eaten when all this started. Stoman, Cal, Boman, Elle, Anna, and Uru have been cooking up a huge breakfast. Those of you who need to go on guard duty—you're first in line in the dining hall. Make sure you get plenty of coffee. The rest of you should also eat before you catch some sleep. Reman wanted me to mention that the iron pour will be at ten a.m. We'll all get together in the old ballroom at three p.m. for a full community meeting."

People milled, stirred, buzzed with conversation, but left to get their breakfasts and to go about their duties.

Harman walked toward the infirmary, caught Ada's and Daeman's eye, nodded in that direction. The two joined him as the last of the crowd dispersed.

Ada quietly told Siris and Tom, who'd been working as medical attendants, applying first aid to the wounded and watching over Noman during the night, that they should go get something to eat. The two slipped out, leaving Hannah sitting next to the bed and Daeman, Ada, and Harman standing.

"This is like old times," said Harman, referring to when the five of them had traveled together, and then with Savi, nine months earlier. They'd rarely had time to be alone together since then.

"Except that Odysseus is dying," said Hannah, her voice flat and ragged. She was holding the unconscious man's left hand and squeezing it so tightly that all the interlaced fingers, his and hers, were white.

Harman stepped closer and studied the unconscious man. His bandages—just replaced an hour earlier—were soaked through with blood. His lips were as white as his fingertips and his eyes no longer moved beneath their closed eyelids. Noman's mouth was open slightly and the breath that rattled there was swift, shallow, and unsure.

"I'm going to take him to the Golden Gate at Machu Picchu," said Harman.

Everyone stared at him. Finally Hannah said, "You mean when he . . . dies? To bury him?"

"No. Now. To save him."

Ada gripped Harman's upper arm so fiercely that he almost flinched away. "What are you talking about?"

"What Petyr said—Noman's last words before losing consciousness near the wall yesterday evening—I think he was trying to tell him to take him back to the crèche at Golden Gate."

"What crèche?" said Daeman. "I only remember the crystal coffins."

"Cryotemporal sarcophagi," said Hannah, enunciating each syllable with care. "I remember them in the museum there. I remember Savi talking about them. It's where she slept some of the centuries away. It's where she said she found Odysseus sleeping three weeks before we met here."

"But Savi didn't always tell the truth," said Harman. "Perhaps she never did. Odysseus has admitted that he and Savi had known each other for a long, long time—that it was the two of them who distributed the turin cloths almost eleven years ago."

Ada held up the turin cloth that Daeman had left behind in the other room.

"And Prospero told us . . . up there . . . that there was more to this Odysseus than we could understand. And on a couple of occasions, after a lot of wine, Odysseus has mentioned his crèche at the Golden Gate— joked about returning to it."

"He must have meant the crystal coffins . . . the sarcophagi," said Ada.

"I don't think so," said Harman, pacing back and forth past the empty beds. All of the other victims of last night's fighting had decided to recuperate in their rooms in Ardis Hall or the outlying barracks. Only Noman was still here this morning. "I think there was another thing there at Golden Gate, a sort of healing crèche."

"Blue worms," whispered Daeman. His pale face grew even paler. Hannah was so shocked at the image—her cells remembered her hours in the worm-filled tanks up there in the Firmary on Prospero's orbital isle even if her mind did not—that she released Odysseus' hand.

"No, I don't think so," Harman said quickly. "We didn't see anything that resembled the Firmary healing tanks when we were at the Golden Gate. No blue worms. No orange fluid. I think the crèche is something else."

"You're just guessing," Ada said flatly, almost harshly.

"Yes. I'm just guessing." He rubbed his cheeks. He was so very tired. "But I think that if Noman . . . Odysseus . . . survives the sonie flight, there might be a chance for him at the Golden Gate."

"You can't do that," said Ada. "No."

"Why not?"

"We need the sonie here. To fight the voynix if they come back tonight. *When* they come back tonight."

"I'll be back before dark," said Harman.

Hannah stood. "How can that be? When we flew from the Golden Gate with Savi it took more than a day of flying."

"It can fly faster than that," said Harman. "Savi was flying slowly so as not to scare us."

"How much faster?" asked Daeman.

Harman hesitated a few seconds. "Much faster," he said at last. "The sonie tells me that it can get to the Golden Gate at Machu Picchu in thirty-eight minutes."

"Thirty-eight minutes!" cried Ada, who had also been on that long, long flight up with Savi.

"The *sonie* told you?" said Hannah. She was upset. "When did the sonie tell you? I thought the machine couldn't answer questions about destinations."

"It hasn't until this morning," said Harman. "Just after the fighting. I had a few minutes alone up on the jinker platform with the sonie and I figured out how to interface my palm functions with its display."

"How did you discover that?" asked Ada. "You've been trying to find some function interface for months."

Harman rubbed his cheek again. "I finally just asked it how to start the function interface. Three green circles within three larger red circles. Easy."

"And it told you how long it would take to get to Golden Gate?" said Daeman. He sounded dubious.

"It *showed* me," Harman said softly. "Diagrams. Maps. Airspeed. Velocity vectors. All superimposed on my vision—just like farnet or . . ." He paused.

"Or allnet," said Hannah. They'd all experienced the vertigo-inducing confusion of allnet since Savi had shown them how to access it the previous spring. None of them had mastered its use. It was just too much information to process.

"Yeah," said Harman. "So I figure if I take Odysseus . . . Noman . . . this morning, I can see if there's some sort of a healing crèche there for him . . . install him in one of the crystal coffins if there's not—and be back here before the three p.m. meeting. Heck, I could be back here for lunch."

"He probably wouldn't survive the trip," said Hannah, her voice wooden. She was staring at the gasping unconscious man whom she loved.

"He definitely won't survive another day here at Ardis without medical care," said Harman. "We're just . . . too . . . fucking . . . ignorant." He slammed his fist down on a wooden cabinet top and then pulled it back, knuckles bleeding. He was embarrassed by the outburst.

Ada said, "I'll go with you. You can't carry him into the Bridge bubbles by yourself. You'll have to use a stretcher."

"No," said Harman. "You shouldn't go, my dear."

Ada's pale face came up quickly and her black eyes flashed with anger. "Because I'm . . ."

"No, not because you're pregnant." Harman touched her fingers that she'd folded into a fist, setting his large, rough fingers around her slender, softer ones. "You're just too important here. This news that Daeman brought is going to spread through the entire community in the next hour. Everyone's going to be near panic."

"Another reason that *you* shouldn't go," whispered Ada.

Harman shook his head. "You're the leader here, my darling. Ardis is your estate now. We're all guests here at your home. The people will need answers—not just at the meeting, but in the coming hours—and you need to be here to calm them."

"I don't have any answers," Ada said in a small voice.

"Yes, you do," said Harman. "What would you suggest we do about Daeman's news?"

Ada turned her face toward the window. There was frost on the panes, but it had quit snowing and raining outside. "We need to see how many of the other communities have been invaded by the holes and blue ice," she said softly. "Send about ten messengers out to fax to the remaining nodes."

"Just ten?" said Daeman. There were more than three hundred remaining faxnodes that had survivor communities.

"We can't spare more than ten, in case the voynix return during the daylight," Ada said flatly. "They can each take thirty codes and see how many nodes they can cover before nightfall in this hemisphere."

"And I'll look for more flechette magazines at the Golden Gate," said Harman. "Odysseus brought back three hundred magazines with him when he found the three rifles last fall, but we're almost out after last night."

"We have teams pulling crossbow bolts from the voynix carcasses," said Ada, "but I'll tell Reman that we'll need to cast as many new ones as we can today. I'll have the workshop double up on that work today. The arrows take so much longer, but we can put more bows on the ramparts by darkfall."

"I'm going with you," Hannah said to Harman. "You *will* need someone else to carry Odysseus in on the stretcher, and no one here has explored the green bubble city on the Golden Gate more than I have."

"All right," said Harman, seeing his wife—what a strange word and thought, "wife"—throw the younger woman a sharp glance that considered jealousy and then rejected it. Ada knew that Hannah's only love—as hopeless and unrequited as it had been—was for Odysseus.

"I'll go, too," said Daeman. "You could use an extra crossbow there."

"True," said Harman, "but I think it would be more useful if you'd be in charge of choosing the fax-messenger teams, briefing them on what you saw, and sorting out their destinations."

Daeman shrugged. "All right. I'll take thirty nodes myself. Good luck." He nodded toward Hannah and Harman, touched Ada's arm, and left the infirmary.

"Let's eat very quickly," Harman said to Hannah, "and then grab some clothes and weapons and get going. We'll get some strong young guys to help us carry Odysseus outside. I'll bring the sonie down."

"Couldn't we eat in the sonie?" said Hannah.

"I think it'd be better if we grabbed a fast bite first," said Harman. He was remembering the impossible trajectories the sonie had shown him—the launch from Ardis almost vertical, leaving the atmosphere, arcing up into outer space, then reentering like a bullet dropped from heaven. Just the memory of the trajectory graphic made his heart pound.

"I'll go get my stuff and see if Tom and Siris can help me get Odysseus ready for the trip," said Hannah. She kissed Ada on the cheek and hurried out.

Harman took a last look at Odysseus—the strong man's face was gray—and then took Ada by the elbow and led her down the hall to a quiet place by the rear door.

"I still think I should go," said Ada.

Harman nodded. "I wish you could. But when the people digest Daeman's news—when they get the sense that Ardis may be the last free node left and that someone or something is gobbling up all the other cities and settlements—there's liable to be a real panic."

"Do you think we're the last ones left?" whispered Ada.

"I have no idea. But if this thing Daeman glimpsed coming through the hole is the Setebos god-thing that Caliban and Prospero talked about, I think we're in big trouble."

"And you think Daeman's right . . . that Caliban himself is on Earth?"

Harman chewed his lip for a moment. "Yes," he said at last. "I think Daeman's right in thinking that the monster slaughtered everyone in the Paris Crater domi tower just to get to Marina, Daeman's mother—to send Daeman a message."

The clouds had covered the sun again and it grew darker outside. Ada seemed intent on watching the feverish activity on the cupola scaffolding. A team of a dozen men and women were laughing as they walked to relieve the guards on the north wall.

"If Daeman's right," Ada said softly, never turning to look at Harman, "what's to keep Caliban and his creatures from coming here while you're gone? What's to prevent you from returning from this trip to save Odysseus only to find stacks of skulls in Ardis Hall? We wouldn't even have the sonie to escape in."

"Oh . . ." said Harman and it came out as a moan. He took a step away from her and brushed sweat from his forehead and cheeks, realizing how cold and clammy his skin was.

"My love," said Ada, whirling, taking two fast steps, and hugging him fiercely. "I'm sorry I said that. Of course you have to go. It's terribly important that we try to save Odysseus—not just because he's our friend, but because he's the only one who might know what this new threat is and how to counter it. And we need the flechette ammunition. And I wouldn't flee Ardis in a sonie under any circumstances. It's my home. It's our home. We're lucky to have four hundred others to help us defend it." She kissed him on the mouth, then hugged him fiercely again and spoke into the leather of his tunic. "Of course you have to go, Harman. You do. I'm sorry. I shouldn't have said that. Just come back soon."

Harman tried to speak but found no words. He hugged her to him.

When Harman flew the sonie down from the jinker platform to let it hover three feet off the ground near Ardis Hall's main back door, it was Petyr who met him there.

"I want to go," said the younger man. He was wearing his travel cape and weapons belt—a short sword and killing knife were slung on the belt—and his handmade bow and arrow-filled quiver were slung over his shoulder.

"I told Daeman . . ." began Harman, propping himself on an elbow and looking up as he lay in the forward-center open niche on the surface of the oval flying machine.

"Yes. And that made sense . . . to tell Daeman. He's still in shock from his mother's death and organizing the messengers might help him come out of it. But you need someone with you on the Bridge. Hannah's strong enough to carry the litter with Noman on it, but you need someone to cover both your backs while you do it."

"You're needed here . . ."

Petyr interrupted again. His voice was quiet, firm, calm, but his gaze was intense. "No, I'm not, Harman *Uhr*," said the bearded man. "The flechette rifle's needed here, and I'm leaving it with the few flechette magazines left to it, but *I'm* not needed here. Like you, I've been up for more than twenty-four hours—I have a six-hour sleep period coming before I have to return to duty on the walls. I understand that you told Ada *Uhr* that you and Hannah will be back in a few hours."

"We should be . . ." began Harman and stopped. Hannah, Ada, Siris, and Tom were carrying Odysseus-Noman's stretcher out the door. The dying man was wrapped in thick blankets. Harman slid out of the hovering sonie and helped lift the old man into the cushioned rear-center niche. The sonie used directed forcefields as safety restraints for its passengers, but there was also a silk-webbed netting built into the periphery of each niche for gear or inanimate objects, and Harman and Hannah pulled this over the comatose Noman and secured it. Their friend might well be dead before they reached the Golden Gate and Harman didn't want the body tumbling out.

Harman clambered forward and dropped into the piloting niche. "Petyr's coming with us," he told Hannah. Her gaze was on the dying Odysseus and she showed no flicker of interest at the news. "Petyr," he continued, "left rear. And keep your bow and quiver handy. Hannah, right rear. Web in."

Ada came around, leaned over the metal surface, and gave him a quick kiss. "Be back before dark or you'll be in big trouble with me," she said softly. She walked back into the manor house with Tom and Siris.

Harman checked to make sure that all were wearing their webnets, including himself, and then he thrust both palms under the sonie's forward rim, activating the holographic control panel. He visualized three green circles set within three larger red circles. His left palm glowed blue and his vision was overlaid with impossible trajectories.

"*Destination Golden Gate at Machu Picchu?*" came the machine's flat voice.

"Yes," said Harman.

"*Fastest flight path?*" asked the machine.

"Yes."

"*Ready to initiate flight?*"

"Ready," said Harman. "Go."

The restraint forcefields pressed down on all of them. The sonie accelerated over the palisade and trees, went nearly vertical, and broke the sound barrier before it reached two thousand feet of altitude.

Ada didn't watch the sonie leave and when the sonic boom slammed the house—she'd heard hundreds of them during the meteor bombardment at the time of the Fall—her only reaction was to ask Oelleo, who was on housekeeping duty that week, to check for broken panes and mend them as needed.

She pulled a wool cape from her peg in the main hall and went out into the yard, then through the front gate of the palisade. The grass here—formerly her beautiful front lawn that ran downhill for a quarter of a mile, now Ardis's pasture and killing ground—had been churned up by hooves and voynix peds and then refrozen. It was difficult to walk without spraining an ankle. Several oxen-pulled, long-bed droshkies rumbled along the edge of the tree line where men and women lifted voynix carcasses onto the cargo bed. The metal of their carapaces would be recycled into weapons. Their leatherish hoods would be cut and sewn into clothing and shields. Ada paused to watch Kaman, one of Odysseus' earliest disciples last summer, use special tongs that Hannah had designed and forged to pull crossbow bolts out of voynix bodies. These went into buckets on the droshky and would be cleaned and re-sharpened. The droshky bed, Kaman's gloved hands, and the frozen soil were blue with voynix blood.

Ada moved around the palisade, strolling in and out of the gates, chatting with other work groups, urging those who had been on the wall all morning to go in for breakfast, and finally climbing up on the furnace cupola to talk with Loes and watch the last preparations for the morn-ing's iron pour. She pretended not to notice Emme and three young men with crossbows casually walking thirty paces behind her all the way, watching the woods for movement, their crossbows cocked and double-loaded.

Ada came back into the house through the kitchen and checked her palm time function—thirty-nine minutes since Harman had left. If his silly sonie timetable was right—and she could hardly believe it, since she remembered so clearly the long, long day of flying up from the Golden Gate nine months ago, with the stop in what she now knew was a redwood forest in the area once called Texas—but if his timetable was right, they'd be there now. Assume an hour to find this mythical healing crèche, or at least to stow the dying Noman in one of the temporal sar-cophagi, and her beloved would be home before lunch would be served. She reminded herself that tomorrow was her day on cooking duty for dinner.

She hung her shawl on its peg and went up to her room—the room she now shared with Harman—closing the door. She'd folded the turin cloth Daeman had brought back with him and slipped it into her largest tunic pocket during the conversations, and now she removed the cloth and unfolded it.

Harman had almost never gone under the turin. She remembered that Daeman also rarely indulged—seducing young women had been his idea of recreation before the Fall, although, to be fair, she also re-membered that he had worked hard to collect butterflies in the fields and forests when he'd visited her at Ardis when she was a girl. They were technically cousins, although the phrase meant little in terms of blood relationship in that world that had ended nine months earlier. Like the term "sister," the idea of "cousin" was an honorific given among female adults who had been friends for years, offering at least the idea of a special relationship between their children. Now, as an adult herself, and a pregnant one at that, Ada realized that the honorific "cousin" might have been a sign that her late mother and Daeman's mother—also dead now, she realized with a pang—had chosen to be impregnated by the same father's sperm packet at different times in their lives. She had to smile at that, and be thankful that the pudgy, lecherous young man Daeman had once been had never succeeded in seducing her.

No, Harman and Daeman had never spent much time under the turin cloth. But Ada had. She'd escaped to the gory images of the siege of Troy almost daily for the almost eleven years that the turins had functioned. Ada had to confess to herself that she had loved the violence and the energy of those imaginary people—at least they had been presumed to be imaginary until they met the older Odysseus at the Golden Gate—and even the barbaric language, somehow translated by the turin, had been like an intoxicating drug to her.

Now Ada lay back on the bed, lifted the turin cloth over her face, set the embroidered microcircuits against her forehead, and closed her eyes, not really expecting the turin to work.

It is night. She is in a tower in Troy.

Ada knows it's Troy—Ilium—because she's seen the nighttime silhouette of the city's buildings and walls during her hundreds of times under the turin over the past decade, but she's never seen it from this perspective before. She realizes that she's in a shattered, circular tower with a wall missing on the south side of the building and that two people are huddled a few feet away, holding a low blanket over a fire consisting of little more than embers. She recognizes them at once—Helen and her former husband Menelaus—but she has no idea of why they're together here, inside the city, looking out over the wall and the Scaean Gate at a night battle in full progress. What's Menelaus doing here and how can he be sharing a blanket—no, she realizes, it's a red warrior's cape—with Helen? For almost ten years, Ada has watched Menelaus and the other Achaeans battling to get inside the city, presumably to capture or kill this very woman.

It's obvious that the Achaeans are battling to get inside the city at this very moment.

Ada turns her nonexistent head to change her field of vision—this turin-cloth experience is different from all her other ones—and stares in awe out toward the Scaean Gate and the high wall.

* * *

This is much like our battle last night here at Ardis, she thinks, but then almost laughs at the comparison. Instead of a twelve-foot-tall rickety wooden palisade, Ilium is surrounded by its hundred-foot-high, twenty-foot-thick wall, its defense further augmented by its many towers, sally ports, embrasures, trenches, rows of sharpened stakes, moats, and parapets. Instead of an attacking army of a hundred-some silent voynix, this great city is being attacked by tens of thousands of cheering, roaring, cursing Greeks—torches and campfires and flaming arrows illuminate mile upon mile of the surging horde of heroes—each group complete with its own kings, captains, siege ladders, and chariots, each group intent upon its own battle-within-the-larger-battle. Instead of Ardis Hall with its four hundred souls, the defenders here—she can see thousands of archers and spearmen on just the parapets and stairways of the long south wall visible from this tower—are defending the lives of more than a hundred thousand terrified kinsmen, including their children, wives, daughters, young sons, and helpless elders. Instead of Harman's one silent sonie flying over a backyard battlefield, Ada sees the air here filled with dozens of flying chariots, each protected by its own force bubble, its divine occupants launching shafts of energy and bolts of lightning either into the city or out toward the attacking hordes.

In all of her previous times under the turin, Ada has never seen so many of the Olympian gods so personally involved in the fighting. Even from this distance she can make out Ares, Aphrodite, Artemis, and Apollo flying and fighting in defense of Troy, and Hecuba, Athena, Poseidon, and other rarely seen gods raging on the side of the attacking Achaeans. There is no sign of Zeus.

Things have certainly changed during the nine months I've been away from the turin, thinks Ada.

"Hector has not come out of his apartments to lead the fight," Helen whispers to Menelaus. Ada turns her attention back to the couple. They are huddled together over the tiniest of campfires up here on the broken, open-air platform, the red soldier's cape shielding the embers from anyone's view from below.

"He's a coward," says Menelaus.

"You know better than that. There has been no braver man in this mad war than Hector, son of Priam. He's in mourning."

"For whom?" laughs Menelaus. "Himself? His life span can now be counted in hours." He gestures out toward the hordes of Achaeans attacking Troy from all directions.

Helen also looks. "Do you think this attack will succeed, my husband? It seems uncoordinated to me. And there are no siege engines."

Menelaus grunts. "Yes, perhaps my brother led them to the attack too quickly—there is too much confusion. But if tonight's attack fails, tomorrow's will succeed. Ilium is doomed."

"It seems so," Helen says softly. "But it has always been, has it not? No, Hector is not grieving for himself, noble husband. He grieves for his murdered son, Scamandrius, and for the end of the war with the gods that might have avenged the baby."

"The war was pure folly," grumbles Menelaus. "The gods would have destroyed us or banished us from the earth, just as they stole our families back home."

"You believe Agamemnon?" whispers Helen. "Everyone is gone?"

"I believe what Poseidon and Hera and Athena told Agamemnon— that our families and friends and slaves and everyone else in the world will be returned by the gods when we Achaeans put Ilium to the torch."

"Could even the immortal gods do such a thing, my husband— remove all humans from our world?"

"They must have," says Menelaus. "My brother does not lie. The gods told him it had been their work and lo, our cities are empty! And I've talked to the others who sailed with him. All of the farms and homes in the Peloponnesus are . . . shhh, someone's coming." He kicks the embers apart, rises, thrusts Helen into the deepest shadows of the broken wall, and stands in the blind side of the opening to the circular staircase, his sword out and ready.

Ada can hear the shuffle of sandals on the stairs.

A man Ada has never seen before—dressed in Achaean infantry armor and cape but less fit, milder-looking than any soldier she's ever noticed while under the turin—steps up onto the open area where the stairway abruptly ends.

Menelaus springs, pins the man so he can't raise his arms, and sets his blade across the startled intruder's throat, ready to open his jugular with a single slash.

"No!" cries Helen.

Menelaus pauses.

"It is my friend Hock-en-bear-eeee."

Menelaus waits a second, his expression set and forearm flexing as if still planning to cut the thinner man's throat, but then he pulls the man's sword out of its sheath and tosses it away. He shoves the thinner man down onto the floor and stands almost astride of him. "Hockenberry? The son of Duane?" growls Menelaus. "I've seen you with Achilles and Hector many times. You came with the machine-beings."

Hockenberry? thinks Ada. She's never heard a name like that in the turin tale.

"No," says Hockenberry, rubbing both his throat and his bruised bare knee. "I've been here for years, but always observing until nine months ago when the war with the gods began."

"You're a friend of that dog-fucker Achilles," snarls Menelaus. "You're a lackey of my enemy, Hector, whose doom is sealed this day. And so is yours . . ."

"No!" Helen cries again and steps forward, grasping her husband's arm. "Hock-en-bear-eeee is a favorite of the gods. And my friend. He is the one who told me of this tower platform. And you remember that he used to bear Achilles invisibly away, using the medallion at his throat to travel like the gods themselves."

"I remember," says Menelaus. "But a friend of Achilles and Hector is no friend of mine. He's found us out. He'll tell the Trojans where we're hiding. He must die."

"No," says Helen a third time. Her white fingers look very small on Menelaus' tanned and hairy forearm. "Hock-en-bear-eeee is the solution to our problem, my husband."

Menelaus glares at her, not understanding.

Helen points to the battle going on out beyond the walls. The archers firing hundreds—thousands—of arrows in deadly volleys. The disorganized Achaeans first surging to the wall with ladders, then falling back as the archers' crossfire thins their ranks. The last of the Trojan defenders outside the wall fighting valiantly on their side of the stakes and trenches—Achaean chariots crashing, wood splintering, horses screaming in the night as stakes pierce their lathered sides—and even the Achaean-loving goddesses and gods Athena, Hera, and Poseidon are falling back under the berserker counterassault of Troy's principal defending gods, Ares and Apollo. The violet energy-arrows of the Lord of the Silver Bow are falling everywhere among the Achaeans and their immortal allies, dropping men and horses like saplings under the axe.

"I don't understand," growls Menelaus. "What can this scrawny bastard do for us? His sword doesn't even have an edge."

Still touching her husband's forearm, Helen kneels gracefully and lifts the heavy gold medallion on its thick chain around Hockenberry's neck. "He can carry us instantly to your brother's side, my darling husband. He is our escape. Our only way out of Ilium."

Menelaus squints, obviously understanding. "Stand back, wife. I'll cut his throat and we'll use the magic medallion."

"It only works for me," Hockenberry says softly. "Even the moravecs with their advanced engineering couldn't duplicate it or make it work for them. The QT medallion is cued to my brainwaves and DNA."

"It's true," says Helen, almost whispering. "This is why Hector and Achilles always held Hock-en-bear-eeee's arm when they used the god magic to travel with him."

"Stand up," says Menelaus.

Hockenberry stands. Menelaus is not a tall man like his brother, nor a barrel-chested ox of a man like Odysseus or Ajax, but he is almost godlike in his muscle and mass compared to this thin, potbellied Hockenberry.

"Take us there now, son of Duane," commands Menelaus. "To my brother's tent on the sands."

Hockenberry shakes his head. "For months I've not used the QT medallion myself, son of Atreus. The moravecs explained that the gods could track me through something called Planck space in the Calabi-Yau matrix—follow me through the void that the gods use for travel. I betrayed the gods and they would kill me if I quantum teleport again."

Menelaus smiles. He lifts the sword, pokes it into Hockenberry's belly until it draws blood through the tunic. "I'll kill you now if you don't, you pig's arse. And draw your bowels out slow in the killing."

Helen sets her free hand on Hockenberry's shoulder. "My friend, look at the warring there—there beyond the wall. The gods are all engaged in bloodletting this night. There, see Athena falling back with a host of her Furies? See mighty Apollo in his chariot, firing down death into the retreating Greek ranks. No one will notice you if you QT this night, Hock-en-bear-eeee."

The meek-looking man bites his lip, looks again at the battle—the Trojan defenders clearly have the upper hand now, with more soldiers flowing out of sally ports and man doors near the Scaean Gate—Ada can see Hector, come at last, leading his core of crack troops.

"All right," says Hockenberry. "But I can only QT one of you at a time."

"You will take us both at once," growls Menelaus.

Hockenberry shakes his head. "I can't. I don't know why, but the QT medallion allows me to teleport only one other person that I'm in contact with. If you remember me with Achilles and Hector, you remember that I never QT'd away with more than one of them, returning for the other a few seconds later."

"It's true, my husband," says Helen. "I have seen this myself."

"Take Helen first then," says Menelaus. "To Agamemnon's tent on the beach, near where the black ships are drawn up on the sand." There are shouts on the street below, and all three step back from the edge of the shattered platform.

Helen laughs. "My husband, darling Menelaus, I can't go first. I am the most hated woman in the memory of the Argives and Achaeans. Even in the few seconds it would take for my friend Hock-en-bear-eeee to come back here and return with you, Agamemnon's guards or the other Greeks there—recognizing me as the bitch I am—would pierce me with a dozen lances. You must go first. You are my only protector."

Menelaus nods and seizes Hockenberry by the bare throat. "Use your medallion . . . *now*."

Before touching the gold circle, Hockenberry says, "Will you let me live if I do this? Will you let me go free?"

"Of course," growls Menelaus, but even Ada can see the glance he gives Helen.

"You have my word that my husband Menelaus will not harm you," says Helen. "Now go, QT quickly. I think I hear footsteps on the stairway below."

Hockenberry grasps the gold medallion, closes his eyes, twists something on its surface, and he and Menelaus disappear with a soft *plop* of inrushing air.

For a minute, Ada is alone on the shattered platform with Helen of Troy. The wind rises, whistling softly through the broken masonry up here and bringing the shouts of the retreating Greeks and pursuing Trojans up from the torchlit plain below. People in the city are cheering.

Suddenly Hockenberry reappears. "Your turn," he says, touching Helen's forearm. "You're right that no god pursued me. There's too much chaos tonight." He nods toward the sky filled with swooping chariots and slashing bolts of energy.

Hockenberry pauses before touching his medallion again. "You're sure that Menelaus won't hurt me when I bring you there, Helen?"

"He will not hurt you," whispers Helen. She seems almost distracted, as if listening for the footsteps on the stairs.

Ada can hear only the wind and distant shouts.

"Hock-en-bear-eeee, wait a second," says Helen. "I need to tell you that you were a good lover . . . a good friend. I am very fond of you."

Hockenberry visibly swallows. "I'm . . . fond . . . of you, Helen."

The black-haired woman smiles. "I'm not going to join Menelaus, Hock-en-bear-eeee. I hate him. I fear him. I will never submit to him again."

Hockenberry blinks and looks out toward the now-distant Achaean lines. They are regrouping beyond their own staked trenches two miles away, near the endless line of tents and bonfires where the countless black ships are drawn up on the sand. "He'll kill you if they take the city," he says softly.

"Yes."

"I can QT you away. Somewhere safe."

"Is it true, my darling Hock-en-bear-eeee, that all the world is empty now? The great cities? My Sparta? The stony farms? Odysseus' isle of Ithaca? The golden Persian cities?"

Hockenberry chews his lip. "Yes," he says at last, "it's true."

"Then where could I go, Hock-en-bear-eeee? Mount Olympos? Even the Hole has disappeared, and the Olympians have gone mad."

Hockenberry shows his palms. "Then we'll just have to trust that Hector and his legions hold them off, Helen . . . my darling. I swear to you that whatever happens, I'll never tell Menelaus that you chose to stay behind."

"I know," says Helen. From her wide sleeve, a knife slips into her hand. She swings her arm, bringing the short but very sharp blade up under Hockenberry's ribs, piercing to the hilt. She twists the blade to find the heart.

Hockenberry opens his mouth as if to cry out but can only gasp. Grasping his bloody midsection, he collapses in a heap.

Helen has pulled the knife free as he fell. "Goodbye, Hock-en-bear-eeee." She goes quickly down the steps, her slippers making almost no noise on the stone.

Ada looks down at the bleeding, dying man wishing she could do something, but she is, of course, invisible and intangible. On impulse, remembering how Harman had communicated with the sonie, she raises her hand to the turin cloth, feels the embroidery under her fingers, and visualizes three blue squares centered in three red circles.

Suddenly Ada is *there*—standing on that shattered, exposed platform in the topless tower in Ilium. She's not turin-viewing something from there, she is *there*. She can feel the cold wind tugging at her blouse and skirt. She can smell the alien cooking scents and smell of livestock floating up from the marketplace visible below in the night. She can hear the roar of the battle just beyond the wall and feel the vibration in the air from the great bells and gongs ringing along the Trojan walls. She looks down and can see her feet firmly planted on the cracked masonry.

"Help . . . me . . . please," whispers the bleeding, dying man. He has spoken in Common English. Eyes widening in horror, Ada realizes that he can *see* her . . . he is staring right *at* her. He uses the last of his strength to lift his left hand toward her, imploring, beseeching.

Ada flung the turin cloth from her brow.

She was in her bedroom at Ardis Hall. Panicked, her heart pounding, she called up the time function from her palm.

Only ten minutes had passed since she first lay down with the turin cloth, forty-nine minutes since her beloved Harman had left in the sonie. Ada felt disoriented and slightly nauseated again, as if the morning sickness were returning. She tried to shake the feeling away and replace it with resolve, but only ended up with a resolvedly stronger conviction of nausea.

Folding the turin cloth and hiding it in her underwear drawer, Ada hurried down to see what was happening in and around Ardis.

30

The sonie ride was even more exciting than Harman had imagined, and Harman knew that he had a damned good imagination. He was also the only one onboard the sonie who'd ridden a wooden chair up a cyclone of lightning all the way from the Mediterranean Basin to an asteroid on the equatorial ring, and he assumed that nothing could match the thrill and terror of that ride.

This ride came in a close second.

The sonie smashed through the sound barrier—Harman had learned about the sound barrier in a book he'd sigled just last month—before it reached two thousand feet of altitude above Ardis, and by the time the machine ripped out of the top layer of clouds into bright sunlight, it was traveling almost vertically and outrunning its own sonic booms, although the ride was far from silent. The hiss and rush of air roaring over the force-field was loud enough to drown out any attempts at conversation.

There were no attempts at conversation. The same forcefield that saved them from the roaring wind kept the four of them pinned belly-down in their cushioned niches; Noman remained unconscious, Hannah had one arm thrown over him, and Petyr was staring wide-eyed back over his shoulder at the clouds receding fast so far below.

Within minutes, the roaring lessened to a teakettle hiss and then faded away to a sigh. The blue sky grew black. The horizon arched like a white bow drawn to full pull and the sonie continued to shoot skyward—the silver tip of an invisible arrow. Then the stars suddenly became visible, not emerging gradually as they do at sunset, but all appearing in an instant, filling the black sky like silent fireworks. Directly above them, the slowly revolving e- and p-rings glowed frighteningly bright.

For a terrible moment, Harman was sure that the sonie was taking them back up to the rings—this same machine had brought Daeman, the unconscious Hannah, and him down from Prospero's orbital asteroid, after all—but then the sonie began to level off and he realized that they were still thousands of miles from the orbital rings, just barely above the atmosphere. The horizon was curved, but the Earth still filled the view beneath them. When he and Savi and Daeman had ridden the lightning vortex up to the e-ring nine months ago, the Earth had seemed much farther below.

"Harman . . ." Hannah was calling from the rear niche as the sonie pitched over until it was upside down, the blinding sweep of the cloud-white planet now above them. "Is everything all right? Is this the way it should be?"

"Yes, this is normal," called back Harman. Various forces, including fear, were trying to lift his prone body off the cushions, but the forcefield pressed him back down. His stomach and inner ears were reacting to the lack of gravity and horizon. In truth, he had no idea whether this was normal or whether the sonie had tried to perform some maneuver it wasn't capable of and they were all seconds away from dying.

Petyr caught his eye and Harman saw that the younger man knew he was lying.

"I may throw up," said Hannah. Her tone was completely matter-of-fact.

The sonie surged forward and down, propelled by invisible thrusters and forces, and the Earth began to spin. "Close your eyes and hang on to Odysseus," called Harman.

The noise returned as they re-entered the Earth's atmosphere. Harman found himself straining to look back up in the rings, wondering if much of Prospero's orbital island had survived, wondering if Daeman was correct in his certainty that it was Caliban who had murdered the young man's mother and slaughtered the others in Paris Crater.

Minutes passed. It seemed to Harman that they were re-entering above the continent he knew had once been called South America. There were clouds in both hemispheres, swirling, crenellated, rippled, flattened and towering, but he also caught a glimpse through the gaps in the cloud cover of the broad, watery strait that Savi told them had once been a continuous isthmus connecting the two continents.

Then fire surrounded them and the screech and roar grew louder even than during their ascent. The sonie spiraled into thicker atmosphere like a spinning flechette dart.

"It'll be all right!" Harman shouted to Hannah and Petyr. "I've been through this before. It'll be all right."

They couldn't hear him—the roaring was already too loud—so Harman didn't add the "I've been through it before . . . *once*" disclaimer that he was thinking. Hannah had been aboard when this same sonie had brought Daeman, Harman, and her down from Prospero's disintegrating orbital isle, but she hadn't been fully conscious and had no real memory of the event.

Harman decided that closing his eyes as the sonie hurtled Earthward again within its womb of plasma was the best choice for him as well.

What the hell am I doing? Doubts filled him again. He was no leader—what did he think he was doing taking this sonie and two trusting lives and risking them this way? He'd never flown the sonie this way, why did he think it was going to make the trip successfully? And even if it did, how could he justify taking the sonie away from Ardis Hall at the community's time of maximum danger? Daeman's report of the Setebos creature's entombing of Paris Crater and the other faxnode communities should have taken top priority, not this running off to the Golden Gate and Machu Picchu just to save Odysseus. How dare Harman leave Ada when she was pregnant and depending upon him? Noman was almost certainly going to die anyway, why risk several hundred lives—perhaps tens of thousands if their warning didn't get out to the other communities—on this almost surely hopeless attempt to save the wounded old man?

Old man. As the wind shrieked and the sonie bucked, Harman held on for dear life and grimaced. *He* was the old man of the group, less than two months to go before his Fifth and Final Twenty. Harman realized that he was still expecting to disappear when his final birthday rolled around, and then be faxed up to the rings even if there were no healing tanks left there to receive him. *And who knows that won't be the case?* he thought. Harman believed himself to be the oldest man on Earth, with the possible exception of Odysseus-Noman, who could be any age. But Noman probably would be dead in minutes or hours anyway. *So might we all,* thought Harman.

What the hell was he thinking, having a child with a woman only seven years beyond her First Twenty? What right did he have to urge others to return to the idea of Lost Era–type families? Who was he to say that the new reality demanded that fathers of children be known to the mother and to others and that the man should stay with the woman and children? What did the old man named Harman *really* know about the old idea of family—about duty—about anything, and who was he to lead anyone? The only thing unique about himself, Harman realized, was that he'd taught himself to read. He'd been the only person on Earth who could do that for many years. *Big deal.* Now everyone who wanted it had the sigl function and many others at Ardis had also learned how to decode the words and sounds from the squiggles in the old books.

I'm not so special after all.

The plasma shield around the sonie faded and the spinning ceased, but tongues of flame still licked past on either side.

If the sonie is destroyed—or just runs out of fuel, energy, whatever it runs on—Ardis is doomed. No one will ever know what happened to us—we'll simply disappear and Ardis will be without its only flying machine. The voynix will attack again or Setebos would show up, and without the sonie to fly between the Hall and the faxnode pavilion, there will be no retreat for Ada and the others. I've endangered their only hope of escape.

The stars disappeared, the sky grew deep blue, then pale blue, and then they were entering a high cloud layer as the sonie bled off velocity.

If I get Noman into some sort of crèche, I'm heading straight back, thought Harman. *I'm going to stay with Ada and let Daeman or Petyr or Hannah and the younger people make the decisions and go on their voyages. I have a baby to think of.* That last thought was more terrifying than the violent leaping and bucking of the sonie.

For long minutes, the descending flying machine was wrapped in clouds that flowed over the sonie's still-humming forcefield like whirling smoke, first mixing with the snow flying by and then just rushing by like the rising souls of all those billions of humans who had lived and died before Harman's century on the still-shrouded Earth. Then the sonie broke out of the cloud cover about three thousand feet above the steep peaks and once again, Harman looked down on the Golden Gate at Machu Picchu.

The plateau was high, steep, green, and terraced, bordered by jagged peaks and deep, greener canyons. The ancient bridge, its rusted towers more than seven hundred feet tall, was almost-but-not-quite connected to the two jagged mountains on either side of the terraced plateau, which showed outlines of even more ancient ruins. What had once been buildings on the plateau were just stone outlines against the green now. At places on the huge bridge itself, paint that must once have been orange glowed like patches of lichen, but rust had turned most of the structure a deep, dried-blood red. The suspended roadbed had fallen away here and there, some suspension cables had collapsed, but the Golden Gate was most visibly still a bridge . . . but a bridge that started nowhere and went nowhere.

The first time Harman had seen the ruined structure from a distance, he'd thought the huge towers and heavy horizontal connecting cables were wrapped about with bright green ivy, but he knew now that these green bubbles, hanging vines, and connecting tubules were the actual habitation structures, probably added centuries after the bridge itself was built. Savi had said, perhaps not all in jest, that the green buckyglas globes and globs and spiraling strands were the only thing holding the older structure up.

Harman, Hannah, and Petyr all rose to their elbows to stare as the sonie slowed, leveled off briefly, and then began a long, descending turn that would bring them to the plateau and bridge from the south. The view was even more dynamic than the first time Harman had seen it since the clouds were lower now, rain was falling on the boundary peaks, and lightning was flashing behind the higher mountains to the west even while itinerant beams of sunlight shafted down through gaps in the flying clouds to illuminate the bridge, roadbed, green buckyglas helixes, and the plateau itself. Scudding clouds dragged black curtains of rain between the sonie and the bridge, obscuring their view for a minute, but then quickly moved past them toward the east as more tatters of clouds and shafts of sunlight kept the entire scene in apparent motion.

No, not just apparent motion, Harman realized . . . things were moving on the hill and bridge. Thousands of things were moving. At first Harman thought it was an optical trick of the quickly moving clouds and shifting light, but as the sonie swooped toward the north tower to land, he realized that he was looking at thousands of voynix—perhaps tens of thousands. The eyeless, gray-bodied, leather-humped creatures covered the old ruins and green summit and swarmed up the bridge towers, jostled against each other on the broken roadbed, and skittered and scuttled like six-foot-tall cockroaches along the rusted suspension cables. There were a score of the things on the flat north tower where Savi had landed them last time and where the sonie seemed intent upon landing now.

"Manual or automatic approach?" asked the sonie.

"Manual!" shouted Harman. The holographic virtual controls blinked into existence and he twisted the omni controller to turn the sonie away from the north tower just a few seconds and fifty feet before they would have landed amongst the voynix. Two of the voynix actually leaped at them, one of them coming within ten feet of the sonie before silently falling more than seventy stories to the rocks below. The dozen or so remaining voynix on the flat tower top followed the sonie with their eyeless, infrared gazes and dozens more streamed up the scabrous towers to the tops, their bladed fingers and sharp-edged peds cutting into cement as they clambered.

"We can't land," said Harman. The bridge and hillsides and even the surrounding peaks were alive with the scuttling things.

"There aren't any voynix on the green bubbles," called Petyr. He was up and on his knees, his bow in his left hand and an arrow notched. The forcefield had flicked off and the air was both chill and humid. The smell of rain and rotting vegetation was very strong.

"We can't land on the green bubbles," said Harman, circling the sonie about a hundred feet out from the suspension cables. "There's no way in. We have to turn back." He swung the sonie back north and began to gain altitude.

"Wait!" called Hannah. "Stop."

Harman leveled off and set the sonie in a gentle, banking circle pattern. To the west, lightning flickered between the low clouds and high peaks.

"When we were here ten months ago, I explored the place while you and Ada were out hunting Terror Birds with Odysseus," said Hannah. "One of the bubbles . . . on the south tower . . . had other sonies in it, like a sort of . . . I don't know. What was that word we sigled from the gray-bound book? 'Garage?' "

"Other sonies!" cried Petyr. Harman also wanted to shout aloud. More flying machines could decide the fate of everyone at Ardis Hall. He wondered why Odysseus had never mentioned the extra sonies when he came back with the flechette guns after his solo return trip to the Bridge some months ago.

"No, not sonies . . . I mean, not complete sonies," Hannah said hurriedly, "but *parts* of them. Shells. Machine parts."

Harman shook his head, feeling his eagerness deflate. "What does this have to do with . . ." he began.

"It looked like a place where they could *land*," said Hannah.

Harman banked the sonie past the south tower, taking care to stay far out. There were over a hundred voynix atop the towers, but none on the scores of green bubbles that clustered and twisted around the bridge tower like grapes of various sizes. "There's no opening anywhere," called back Harman. "And so many bubbles . . . you'd never remember which one you were in from out here." He remembered from their first visit that although the glass of the buckyglas globules was clear and color-free while inside looking out, the bubbles were opaque to an outside viewer.

Lightning flashed. It began to rain on them and the forcefield flickered up again. The voynix on the tops of the tower and the hundreds more clinging to the vertical tower itself turned their eyeless bodies to follow their circling.

"I can remember," said Hannah from the rear niche. She was also on her knees, holding the unconscious Odysseus' hand in hers. "I have a good visual memory . . . I'll just retrace my steps from that afternoon I was there, look at the landscape from different angles, and figure out which bubble I was in." She glanced around and then closed her eyes for a minute.

"There," said Hannah, pointing to a green bubble protruding about sixty feet out from the south tower, two-thirds of the way up the orange-red monolith. It was just one of hundreds of green-glass bumps on that tower.

Harman flew lower.

"No opening," he said as he twisted the virtual omnicontroller, bringing the sonie to a hover about seventy-five feet out from the bubble. "Savi landed us on the top of the north tower."

"But it makes sense that they would have *flown* the sonies into that . . .

garage," said Hannah. "The bottom of it was flat, and a different substance than most of the green globes."

"You two told me once that Savi said it was a museum," said Petyr, "and I've sigled that word since then. They probably brought the sonie parts in piece by piece."

Hannah shook her head. Harman thought, not for the first time, that the pleasant young woman could be stubborn when she wanted to be.

"Let's go closer," she said.

"The voynix . . ." began Harman.

"They aren't out on the bubble, so they'd have to leap from the tower," argued Hannah. "We can get all the way to the bubble and they can't reach us by jumping."

"They can be out on the green stuff in a minute . . ." began Petyr.

"I don't think they can," said Hannah. "Something's keeping them off the glass."

"That doesn't make any sense," said Petyr.

"Wait," said Harman. "Maybe it does." He told them both about the crawler they'd been in when Savi drove Daeman and him into the Mediterranean Basin ten months earlier. "The top of the machine was like this glass," he said, "tinted from the outside but clear when looking out. But nothing stuck to it. Not rain, not even voynix when they tried to jump on the crawler in Jerusalem. Savi said that the glass had some sort of forcefield just above the glass material that made it frictionless. I can't remember if she said it was buckyglas, though."

"Let's go closer," said Hannah.

Twenty feet from the bubble and Harman saw the way to get in. It was subtle, and if he hadn't been to Prospero's Isle, where both the airlock to the orbital city and the entrance to the Firmary worked with this same technology, he never would have noticed it. A barely visible rectangle on the edge of the elongated bubble was a slightly lighter green than the rest of the buckyglas. He told the other two about what Savi had called "semipermeable membranes" on Prospero's airlock and Firmary.

"What if this isn't one of those semiwhatsit membranes," said Petyr. "Just a trick of the light?"

"I guess we crash," said Harman. He nudged the omnicontroller and the sonie slid forward.

"If you couch him there, he shall die," said a voice from the darkness. Then Ariel stepped into the light.

The semipermeable molecular membrane had been quite permeable enough, the rectangle had solidified behind them, Harman had landed the sonie on the metal deck amongst the cannibalized parts of the machine's own kind, and the three of them had wasted no time getting Odysseus-Noman onto the stretcher and out of the garage. Hannah had grabbed the front of the stretcher, Harman had taken the rear, Petyr provided security, and they were into the green-bubble helix maze at once, traversing corridors, climbing unmoving escalators, and heading for the bubble filled with crystal coffins where Savi had said both she and Odysseus had slept their long cryosleeps.

Within minutes, Harman was impressed not only with Hannah's memory—she never hesitated when they came to a junction of bubble corridors or stairs—but with her strength. The thin young woman wasn't even breathing hard, but Harman would have welcomed a break. Odysseus-Noman wasn't that tall, but he was *heavy*. Harman caught himself glancing at the unconscious man's chest to make sure he was still breathing. He was . . . but only just.

When they reached the main bubble helix rising around the bridge tower, all three of them hesitated and Petyr raised his readied bow.

Scores of voynix were hanging from the bridge metal, apparently looking down at them with their eyeless carapaces.

"They can't see us," said Hannah. "The bubble's dark from the outside."

"No, I think they can see us," said Harman. "Savi said their hood receptors see three hundred and sixty degrees in the infrared . . . the range of light that's more heat than vision, our eyes don't see into it . . . and I have the feeling they're looking at us right through the opaque buckyglas."

They advanced down the curved corridor another thirty paces and the voynix shifted their clinging postures to follow their advance. Suddenly half a dozen of the heavy creatures leaped down onto the glass.

Petyr raised his nocked bow and Harman was sure that the voynix would come crashing through the buckyglas, but there was only the softest of thumps as each voynix struck the millimeter-thin forcefield and slid off, falling away. The humans happened to be in a stretch of the bubble corridor where the floor was almost transparent—an unnerving experience, but at least Harman and Hannah had seen it before and trusted the near-transparent floor to hold them. Petyr kept glancing at his feet as if he were going to fall any second.

They passed through the largest room—museum, Savi had called it—and entered the long bubble with the crystal coffins. Here the buckyglas was almost opaque and very green. It reminded Harman of the time—could it only have been a year and a half ago—when he had walked miles out into the Atlantic Breach and peered in through towering walls of water on each side to see huge fish swimming higher than his head. The light had been dim and green like this.

Hannah set down the stretcher, Harman hurried to lower it with her, and she looked around. "Which cryo-crèche?"

There were eight crystal coffins in the long room, all empty and gleaming dully in the low light. Tall boxes of humming machines were connected to each coffin and virtual lights blinked green, red, and amber above metal surfaces.

"I have no idea," said Harman. Savi had talked to Daeman and him about her sleeping for centuries in one or more of these cryo-crèches, but that conversation had taken place more than ten months ago while they were entering the Mediterranean Basin in the crawler and he didn't remember the details well. Perhaps there had been no details to remember.

"Let's just try this closest one," said Harman. He took hold of the unconscious Odysseus under the man's bandaged arms, waited for Petyr and Hannah to find a grip, and they started lifting him into the coffin closest to a spiral staircase that Harman remembered going up into another bubble corridor.

"If you couch him there, he shall die," said a soft, androgynous voice from the darkness.

All three hurried to lower Odysseus back onto the stretcher. Petyr raised his bow. Harman and Hannah set their hands to their sword hilts. The figure emerged from the darkness beyond the monitoring machines.

Harman instantly knew that this was the Ariel of whom Savi and Prospero had spoken, but he did not know how he knew this. The figure was short—barely five feet tall—and not-quite-human. He or she had greenish-white skin that was not really skin—Harman could see right through the outer layer to the interior, where sparkling lights seemed to float in emerald fluid—and a perfectly formed face so androgynous that it reminded Harman of pictures of angels he had sigled from some of Ardis Hall's oldest books. He or she had long slender arms and normal hands except for the length and grace of the fingers, and appeared to be wearing soft green slippers. At first Harman thought that the Ariel figure was wearing clothes—or not so much clothes as a series of pale, leaf-embroidered vines running round and round its slim form and sewn into a tight bodysuit—but then he realized that pattern lay *in* the creature's skin rather than atop it. There was still no sign of gender.

Ariel's face was human enough—long, thin nose, full lips curved in a slight smile, black eyes, hair curling down to his or her shoulders in greenish-white strands—but the effect of looking right through Ariel's transparent skin to the floating nodes of light within diminished any sense that one was looking at a human being.

"You're Ariel," said Harman, not quite making it a question.

The figure dipped its head in acknowledgment. "I see that Savi herself has told thee of me," he or she said in that maddeningly soft voice.

"Yes. But I thought that you would be . . . intangible . . . like Prospero's projection."

"A hologram," said Ariel. "No. Prospero assumes substance as he pleases, but rarely does it please him to do so. I, on the other hand, whilst being called a spirit or sprite for so very long by so very many, yet love to be corporeal."

"Why do you say that this crèche will kill Odysseus?" asked Hannah. She was crouching next to the unconscious man, trying to find his pulse. Noman looked dead to Harman's eye.

Ariel stepped closer. Harman glanced at Petyr, who was staring at the figure's translucent skin. The younger man had lowered the bow but continued to look shocked and suspicious.

"These are crèches such as Savi used," said Ariel, gesturing toward the eight crystal coffins. "Therein all activity of the body is suspended or slowed, it is true, like an insect in amber or a corpse on ice, but these couches heal no wounds, no. Odysseus has for centuries kept his own time-ark hidden here. Its abilities surpasseth my understanding. "

"What are you?" asked Hannah, rising. "Harman told us that Ariel was an avatar of the self-aware biosphere, but I don't know what that means."

"No one does," said Ariel, making a delicate motion part bow, part curtsy. "Wilst thou follow me then to Odysseus' ark?"

Ariel led them to the spiral staircase that helixed up through the ceiling, but rather than climbing, she laid her right palm against the floor and a hidden segment of the floor irised open, showing more spiral staircase continuing downward. The stairs were wide enough to accommodate the stretcher, but it was still hard and tricky work to carry the heavy Odysseus down the stairway. Petyr had to go ahead with Hannah to keep the unconscious man from sliding off.

Then they followed a green bubble corridor to an even smaller room, this one allowing in even less light than the crystal coffin chamber above. With a start, Harman realized that this space was not in one of the buckyglas bubbles, but had been carved out of the concrete and steel of the actual Bridge tower. Here there was only one crèche, wildly different from the crystal boxes—this machine was larger, heavier, darker, an onyx coffin with clear glass only above where the man or woman's face would be. It was connected by a myriad of cables, hoses, conduits, and pipes to an even larger onyx machine that had no dials or readouts of any sort. There was a strong smell which reminded Harman of the air just before a serious thunderstorm.

Ariel touched a pressure plate on the side of the time-ark and the long lid hissed open. The cushions inside were frayed and faded, still impressed with the outline of a man just Noman's size.

Harman looked at Hannah, they hesitated only a second, and then they set Odysseus-Noman's body inside the ark.

Ariel made a motion as if to shut the lid, but Hannah quickly stepped closer, leaned into the ark, and kissed Odysseus gently on the lips. Then she stepped back and allowed Ariel to close the lid. It sealed shut with an ominous hiss.

An amber sphere immediately flicked into existence between the ark and the dark machine.

"What does that mean?" asked Hannah. "Will he live?"

Ariel shrugged—a graceful motion of slim shoulders. "Ariel is the last of all living things to know the heart of a mere machine. But this machine decides its occupants' fates within three revolutions of our world. Come, we must depart. The air here will soon grow too thick and foul to breathe. Up into the light again, and we shall speak to one another like civil creatures."

"I'm not leaving Odysseus," said Hannah. "If we'll know if he'll live or die within seventy-two hours, then I'll stay until we know."

"You can't stay," said an indignant Petyr. "We have to hunt for the weapons and get back to Ardis as quick as we can."

The temperature in the stuffy alcove was rising quickly. Harman felt sweat trickle down his ribs under his tunic. The thunderstorm burning smell was very strong now. Hannah took a step away from them and folded her arms across her chest. It was obvious that she intended to stay near the crèche.

"You will die here, cooling this fetid air with your sighs," said Ariel. "But if thee wishes to monitor your beloved's life or death, step closer here."

Hannah stepped closer. She towered over the slightly glowing form that was Ariel.

"Give me your hand, child," said Ariel.

Hannah warily extended her palm. Ariel took the hand, set it against his or her chest, and then pushed it *into* its green chest. Hannah gasped and tried to pull away, but Ariel's strength was too much for her.

Before Harman or Petyr could move, Hannah's hand and forearm were free again. The young woman stared in horror at a green-gold blob that remained in her fist. As the three humans watched, the organ deliquesced, seeming to flow into Hannah's palm until it was gone.

Hannah gasped again.

"It is only a telltale," said Ariel. "When your lover's condition changeth, thee shall know it now."

"How will I know it?" asked Hannah. Harman saw that the girl was pale and sweating.

"Thee shall know it," repeated Ariel.

They followed the palely glowing figure out into the green buckyglas corridor and then up the stairs again.

*   *   *

No one spoke as they followed Ariel through corridors and up frozen escalators and then along a helix of globules attached to the underside of the great suspension cable. They stopped in a glass room attached to the concrete and steel cross-support high on the south tower. Just beyond the glass, voynix on this horizontal segment of the Bridge silently threw themselves at the green wall, clawing and scrabbling but finding neither entry nor purchase. Ariel paid them no heed as he or she led them to the largest room along this string of globules. There were tables and chairs here, and machines set into countertops.

"I remember this place," said Harman. "We ate dinner here our one night at the Bridge. Odysseus cooked his Terror Bird right outside there on the Bridge . . . during a lightning storm. Do you remember, Hannah?"

Hannah nodded, but her gaze was distracted. She was chewing her lower lip.

"I thought all of you might wish to eat," said Ariel.

"We don't have time . . ." began Harman, but Petyr interrupted.

"We're hungry," he said. "We'll take time to eat."

Ariel waved them to the round table. She or he used a microwave to heat three bowls of soup in wooden bowls, then brought the bowls to the table and set out spoons and napkins. She or he poured cold water into four glasses, set the glasses in place, and joined them at the table. Harman tasted the soup warily—found it delicious, filled with fresh vegetables—and ate it with pleasure. Petyr tasted his and ate slowly, suspiciously, keeping one eye on Ariel as the biosphere avatar stood by the counter. Hannah didn't touch her soup. She seemed to have flowed into herself, out of reach, much as the green-gold glob from Ariel had.

This is madness, thought Harman. *This greenish . . . creature . . . has one of our party reach into his or her chest and remove a golden organ, and the three of us come up to have hot soup while the voynix scrabble at the glass ten feet away and the self-aware avatar of the planetary biosphere acts as our servitor. I've gone mad.*

Harman acknowledged to himself that he may have gone mad, but the soup was good. He thought of Ada and continued eating.

"Why are you here?" asked Petyr. He'd pushed the wooden bowl away from him and was staring intently at Ariel. His bow was by his chair.

"What would thee have me tell you?" asked Ariel.

"What the hell is going on?" asked Petyr, never one for small talk or subtleties. "Who the hell are you, *really*? Why are the voynix here and why are they attacking Ardis? What is that goddamned thing that Daeman saw in Paris Crater? Is it a threat . . . and if so, how can we kill it?"

Ariel smiled. "Always among the first questions of thy kind . . . what is it and how can I kill it?"

Petyr waited. Harman lowered his spoon.

"It *is* a good question," said Ariel, " for if thee were the first men to leap up, instead of the last, thou shoulds't cry, 'Hell is empty, and all the devils are here!' But it is a long tale, as long as dying Odysseus', I think, and hard to tell over cold soup."

"Then start by telling us again who you are," said Harman. "Are you Prospero's creature?"

"Aye, I was once. Not quite slave, not quite servant, but indentured to him."

"Why?" asked Petyr. It had begun to rain hard, but the water droplets found no more purchase on the curved buckyglas than had the leaping voynix. Still, the pounding of the showers on the Bridge and girders made a background roar.

"The magus of the logosphere saved me from that damned witch Sycorax," said Ariel, "whose servant then I was. For it was she who had mastered the deep codes of the biosphere, she who summoned Setebos, her lord, but when I showed myself too delicate to act her earthy and abhorred demands, she—in her most unmitigable rage—anchored me to a single, cloven pine, in which rift I did remain a dozen times a dozen years before being released by Prospero."

"Prospero saved you," said Harman.

"Prospero released me to do his bidding," said Ariel. The thin, pale lips curved upward slightly. "And then demanded my service for another dozen times a dozen years."

"And did you serve him?" asked Petyr.

"I did."

"Do you serve him now?" asked Harman.

"I serve no man or magus now."

"Caliban served Prospero once," said Harman, trying to remember everything Savi had said, everything that the hologram named Prospero had told him up there on that orbital isle. "Do you know Caliban?"

"I do," said Ariel. "A villain I do not love to look on."

"Do you know if Caliban is back on Earth?" pressed Harman. He wished Daeman were here.

"Thou know'st it is truth," said Ariel. "He seeks to turn all Earth into his old filthy-mantled pool, make the frozen sky his cell."

The frozen sky his cell, thought Harman. "So Caliban is ally of this Setebos?" he asked aloud.

"Aye."

"Why did you show yourself to us?" asked Hannah. The beautiful young woman's gaze was still distracted by sorrow, but she had turned her head to look at Ariel.

Ariel began to sing—

> "Where the bee sucks, there suck I
> In a cowslip's bell I lie;
> There I crouch when owls do cry.
> On the bat's back I do fly
> After summer merrily:
> Merrily, merrily, shall I live now
> Under the blossom that hangs on the bough."

"The creature's mad," said Petyr. He stood abruptly and walked to the bridge-side wall. Three voynix leapt at him, struck the field above the buckyglas, and dropped away. One of them managed to sink its bladed hands into the Bridge concrete and arrested its fall. The other two disappeared in the clouds below.

Ariel laughed softly. Then he or she wept. "Our shared Earth is under siege. The war has come here. Savi is dead. Odysseus is dying. Setebos would fain kill everything I am and come from and exist to protect. You old-style humans are either enemies or allies . . . I choose the latter. You have no vote in the matter."

"You'll help us fight the voynix, Caliban, and this Setebos creature?" asked Harman.

"No, thee shall help *me*."

"How?" said Hannah.

"I have tasks for thee. First, you came for weapons . . ."

"Yes!" said Hannah, Petyr, and Harman in unison.

"Those two who stay shall find them in a secret room at the bottom of the south tower, behind the old, dead computing machines. You will see a circle on the opaque, greenglass wall, having then a pentacle inscribed within. Say merely 'open' and you will find the room where sly Odysseus and poor, dead Savi did conceal their little Lost-Era toys."

"You said the *two* who stay?" said Petyr.

"One of thee three should take the sonie home to Ardis Hall before yon Ardis falls," said Ariel. "The second of thee should stay here and tend to Odysseus if he does not die, for he alone knows the secrets of Sycorax, since once he did lie with her—and no man lies with Sycorax without suffering a change. The third of thee shall come with me."

The three people looked at each other. With the heavy rain and cloudy light, it was as if they were deep underwater, staring at each other through cold green gloom.

"I'll stay," said Hannah. "I'd decided to stay anyway. If Odysseus awakes, someone should be here."

"I'll take the sonie home," said Harman, cringing at his own cowardice but not caring at the same time. He had to get home to Ada.

"I'll go with you, Ariel," said Petyr, stepping closer to the delicate little figure.

"No," he or she said.

The three humans glanced at each other and waited.

"No, it must be Harman who comes with me," said Ariel. "We will tell the sonie to take Petyr straight home, but at half the speed thee came. It is an old machine and should not suffer the spur without dire cause. Harman must come with me."

"Why?" said Harman. He wasn't going anywhere but home to Ada—of this he was sure.

"Because drowning is thy destiny," said Ariel, "and because thy wife's life and thy child's life depend upon this destiny. And Harman's destiny this day is to come with me." Ariel rose from the ground then, weightless, floating above them, floating six feet above the table, his or her black gaze never leaving Harman's face as she or he sang again—

> "Full fathom five our Harman lies,
> Of his bones are coral made:
> Those are pearls that were his eyes:
> Nothing of him that doth fade,
> But doth suffer a sea-change
> Into something rich and strange.
> Ding dong, ding dong."

"No," said Harman. "I'm sorry, but . . . no."

Petyr set an arrow to his string and drew back the bow.

"Are you going bat-fowling?" asked Ariel, twenty feet away now as she/he drifted in the green-gloomed air, but smiling at Petyr.

"Don't . . ." said Hannah, but whether she was talking to Ariel or Petyr he never found out.

"Time to go," said Ariel, almost laughing.

The lights went out. In the absolute darkness, there came a fluttering, rushing sound—as of an owl swooping—and in the darkness, Harman felt something lift him off the floor as effortlessly as a hawk would lift a baby rabbit, flinging and carrying him backward through the darkness, sending him flailing and falling down into the sudden blackness between the tall pillars of the Golden Gate at Machu Picchu.

31

The first day out from Mars and Phobos.

The thousand-foot-long, moravec-built atomic spaceship *Queen Mab* moves up out of Mars' gravity well with a series of brilliant explosions literally kicking it in the butt.

Escape velocity from the moon Phobos is a mere 10 cm/sec, but the *Queen Mab* quickly kicks herself up to 20 km/sec acceleration in order to start the process of climbing up and out of Mars' gravity. While the three-hundred-meter-long spacecraft could travel to Earth at that velocity, it's too impatient to do so; the *Queen Mab* plans to keep accelerating until its thirty-eight thousand tons of mass are moving at a brisk 700 km/sec. On the pulse-unit storage decks, well-oiled chains and ratchets and chutes guide the Coke-can-sized forty-five-kiloton bombs down and into the ejector mechanism that runs out through the center of the pusher plate at the rear end of the spacecraft. During this part of the voyage, a bomb-can is ejected every twenty-five seconds and is then detonated six hundred meters behind the *Queen Mab*. On each pulse-unit ejection, the muzzle of the ejection tube is sprayed by anti-ablation oil, which also coats the pusher after each detonation. The heavy pusher plate is driven backward into the ship on thirty-three-meter-long shock absorbers, and then its huge pistons drive it back into place for the next plasma flash. The *Queen Mab* is soon moving toward Earth at a comfortable and steady 1.28-g's, its actual acceleration increasing with every blast. The moravecs, of course, could withstand hundreds or even thousands of times that g-force for short periods, but there is one human aboard—the shanghaied Odysseus—and the moravecs were unanimous in not wanting him to end up as raspberry jam on a deck floor.

On the engineering level, Orphu of Io and other technical 'vecs watch steam pressure and oil-level gauges while also monitoring voltage and coolant levels. With atom bombs going off behind it every thirty seconds, the spacecraft has much use for lubricant, so oil reservoirs the size of small oceangoing oil tankers from the Lost Era ring the bottom ten decks. The engine-room deck with its myriad of pipes, valves, meters, reciprocating pistons, and huge pressure gauges still looks to all concerned like something out of an early-Twentieth Century steamship.

Even with its gentle 1.28-g-load, the *Queen Mab* will be accelerating briskly enough, for long enough, and then decelerating quickly enough, that it plans to reach the Earth-Moon system in just a little over thirty-three standard days.

Mahnmut is busy this first day out checking systems in his submersible the *Dark Lady*. The sub is not only fitted snugly into one of the holds of the *Queen Mab*, but is also attached to a winged reentry shuttle for its drop into the Earth's atmosphere in a month or so, and Mahnmut is making sure that the new controls and interfaces for these new parts are all in working order. Although a dozen decks apart while they work, Mahnmut and Orphu chat with each other via private tightbeam while they watch on separate ship video and radar links as Mars falls farther and farther behind. The cameras showing Mahnmut this stern-view require sophisticated computerized filters to be able to peer through the near-continuous flash-blast of the constantly erupting "pulse-units" . . . aka bombs. Orphu, while blind to the visible spectrum of light, "watches" Mars recede through a series of radar plots.

It feels weird to be leaving Mars after all the trouble we went through to get there, sends Mahnmut on the tightbeam.

Indeed, answers Orphu of Io. *Especially now that the Olympian gods are warring so furiously together.* To illustrate his point, the deep space moravec zooms Mahnmut's video of retreating Mars, focusing on the icy slopes and green summit of Olympus Mons. Orphu of Io sees the activity as a series of infrared data columns, but Mahnmut can see it clearly enough. Bright explosions flash here and there and the caldera—a lake only twenty-four hours ago—now glows yellow and red on the infrared, showing that it is filled with lava once again.

Asteague/Che, Retrograde Sinopessen, Cho Li, General Beh bin Adee, and the other prime integrators seemed actively frightened, sends Mahnmut as he runs checks on the submersible's power systems. *Their explanation to Hockenberry about the gravity of Mars being wrong—how whoever or whatever changed it to near Earth-normal—also frightened me.* This is the first time that he and Orphu have found to speak privately since the launch of the *Queen Mab* and Mahnmut welcomes the chance to share his anxiety.

That's not even the tip of the merde *iceberg*, sends Orphu.

What do you mean? Mahnmut's organic parts feel a sudden chill.

That's right, rumbles Orphu, *you were so busy shuttling around Mars and Ilium, you didn't hear all of the Prime Integrators Commission findings, did you?*

Tell me.

You'll be happier not knowing, my friend.

Shut up and tell me . . . you know what I mean. Talk.

Orphu sighs—an odd noise over the tightbeam, sounding like the entire one thousand and thirty feet of the *Queen Mab* has suddenly depressurized. *First of all, there's the terraforming . . .*

So? In their many weeks of traveling across Mars by submersible, felucca, and balloon, Mahnmut had grown accustomed to the blue sky, blue sea, lichen, trees, and abundant air.

All that water and life and air wasn't there a mere century and a quarter ago, sends Orphu.

I know. Asteague/Che explained that during our first briefing on Europa, almost a standard year ago. It almost seemed impossible that the planet could have been terraformed that quickly. So?

So it was *impossible,* sends Orphu of Io. *While you were schmoozing with the Greeks and Trojans, our science 'vecs, both Five Moons and Belt, have been studying terraformed Mars. It wasn't done by magic, you know . . . asteroids were used to melt the ice caps and free the CO_2, more asteroids were targeted on the huge underground frozen water deposits and crashed into the Martian crust to set H_2O flowing on the surface after millions of years, lichen, algae, and earthworms were seeded to prepare the soil for larger plants, and all that could happen only after fusion-fired oxygen and nitrogen generating plants had thickened the Martian atmosphere by a factor of ten.*

In his submersible control crèche, Mahnmut quits tapping at his computer screen. He unjacks from virtual ports and lets the schematics and images of the sub and its reentry shuttle fade away. *That would mean . . .* he sends hesitantly.

Yep. That means that it took almost eight thousand standard years to terraform Mars to its present stage.

But . . . but . . . Mahnmut is sputtering on the tightbeam line, but he can't help it. Asteague/Che had shown them astronomical photos of the old Mars, the airless, cold, lifeless Mars, taken from Jupiter and Saturn space only a standard century and a half ago. And the moravecs themselves had been seeded in the Outer System by human beings less than three thousand years earlier. Mars certainly hadn't been terraformed then—except for a few domed Chinese colonies on Phobos and the surface, it was exactly as the early probes from Earth had first photographed it in the Twentieth or Twenty-first century or whenever.

But . . . sends Mahnmut again.

I love it when you're speechless, sends Orphu, but there is none of the accompanying rumble that usually means the hard-vac moravec is amused.

You're saying that we're either talking magic or real gods here . . . a God-type god . . . or . . . Mahnmut's tone on the tightbeam is approaching anger.

Or?

That's not the real Mars.

Exactly, sends Orphu. *Or rather, it's the real Mars, but not* our *real Mars. Not the Mars that's been in our solar system for lo, these billions of years.*

Someone . . . something . . . swapped . . . our Mars . . . for . . . another . . . one?

It appears that way, sends Orphu. *The Prime Integrators and their top science 'vecs didn't want to believe it either, but that's the only answer that fits the facts. The sol-day thing cinched it.*

Mahnmut realizes that his hands are shaking. He clasps them, shuts off his vision and video feeds so he can concentrate, and sends—*Sol-day thing?*

A small matter, but important, sends Orphu. *Did you happen to notice during your travels through the Brane Hole between Mars and the Earth with Ilium that the days and nights were the same length?*

I guess so but . . . Mahnmut stops. He doesn't have to access his nonorganic memory banks to know that the Earth rotates once every twenty-three hours and fifty-six minutes, Mars every twenty-four hours and thirty-seven minutes. A small difference, but one whose disparity would have accumulated during the months of their stay on both Mars and the Hole-connected Earth where the Greeks were battling the Trojans. But it hadn't. The days and nights on both worlds had been the same length, synchronized.

Jesus Christ, whispers Mahnmut on the tightbeam. *Jesus Christ.*

Maybe, sends Orphu, and this time the rumble is there. *Or at least someone with comparable God-powers.*

Someone or something from Earth punched holes in multidimensional Calabi-Yau Space, connected Branes across different universes, swapped our Mars for theirs . . . whoever and wherever "theirs" is . . . and left that other Mars . . . the terraformed Mars with gods on top of Olympos . . . still connected to the Ilium-Earth with quantum Brane Holes. And while they were at it, they changed the gravity and rotational period of Mars. Jesus, Mary, Joseph, and holy crap!

Yes, sends Orphu. *And the Prime Integrators now think that whoever or whatever did this little trick is on Earth or in near-Earth orbit. Still want to go on this trip?*

I . . . I . . . if . . . I . . . begins Mahnmut and falls silent. Would he have volunteered for this trip if he'd known all this? After all, he already knew how dangerous it was, had known since he'd volunteered to go to Mars after being briefed on Europa. Whatever these beings were—these evolved post-humans or creatures from some other universe or dimension—they'd already shown themselves capable of controlling and playing with the very quantum fabric of the universe. What's a couple of moved-around planets and altered rotation periods and gravitational fields compared to that? And what the hell was he doing on the *Queen Mab* hurtling toward Earth and its waiting god-monsters at a velocity of 180 km/sec and climbing? The unknown enemy's control of the quantum underpinnings of the universe—of all universes—made this spaceship's puny weapons and the thousand sleeping rockvec soldiers on board seem like a joke.

This is sort of sobering, he finally sends to Orphu.

Amen, sends his friend.

At that moment alarm bells begin ringing all over the ship, while alarm lights and klaxons override tightbeams and flash and clang across all other shared virtual and comm channels.

"Intruder! Intruder!" sounds the ship's voice.

Is this a joke? sends Mahnmut.

No, replies Orphu. *Your friend Thomas Hockenberry just . . . appeared . . . on the deck of the engine room here. He must have quantum teleported in.*

Is he all right?

No. He's bleeding profusely . . . there's already blood all over the deck. He looks dead to me, Mahnmut. I've got him in my manipulators and I'm moving toward the human-hospital as fast as my repellors can get me there.

The ship is huge, the gravity is greater than anything he's operated in before, and it takes Mahnmut several minutes to get out of his submersible, then out of the hold, and then up to the decks that he thinks of as the "human levels" of the ship. Besides enough sleeping and cooking quarters and toilets and acceleration couches to accommodate five hundred human beings, besides an oxygen-nitrogen atmosphere set at sea-level pressure to be harmonious for humans, Deck 17 has a working medical infirmary outfitted with state-of-the-art early Twenty-second Century surgical and diagnostic equipment—ancient, but based on the most updated schematics that the Five Moons moravecs had on file.

Odysseus—their reluctant and angry human passenger—has been the only occupant of Deck 17 for this first day out from Phobos, but by the time Mahnmut arrives, he sees that a majority of the moravecs on the ship have gathered. Orphu is here, filling the corridor, as is the Ganymedan Prime Integrator Suma IV, the Callistan Cho Li, rockvec General Beh bin Adee, and two of the pilot techs from the bridge. The door to the medlab surgery is closed, but through the clear glass, Mahnmut can see Prime Integrator Asteague/Che watching as the spidery Amalthean, Prime Integrator Retrograde Sinopessen, works frantically over Hockenberry's bloody body. Two smaller tech 'vecs are taking Sinopessen's orders, wielding laser scalpels and saws, connecting tubes, fetching gauze, and aiming virtual imaging equipment. There is blood on Retrograde Sinopessen's small metal body and elegant silver manipulators.

Human blood, thinks Mahnmut. *Hockenberry's blood.* There is more blood spattered here on the floor of the wide access corridor, some on the walls, and more on the pitted carapace and broad manipulators of his friend Orphu of Io.

"How is he?" Mahnmut asks Orphu, vocalizing the words. It is considered impolite to tightbeam in the company of other 'vecs.

"Dead when I got him here," says Orphu. "They're trying to bring him back."

"Is Integrator Sinopessen a student of human anatomy and medicine?"

"He's always had an interest in Lost Era human medicine," says Orphu. "It was his hobby. Sort of like you with Shakespeare's sonnets and me with Proust."

Mahnmut nods. Most of the moravecs he'd known on Europa had some interest in humanity and their ancient arts and sciences. Such interests had been programmed into the early autonomous robots and cyborgs seeded in the Asteroid Belt and Outer System, and their evolved moravec descendants retained the fascination. *But does Sinopessen know enough human medicine to bring Hockenberry back from the dead?*

Mahnmut sees Odysseus emerging from the cubby where he's been sleeping. The barrel-chested man stops when he sees the crowd in the corridor and his hand automatically goes to the hilt of his sword—or rather, to the empty loop on his belt, for the moravecs had relieved him of his sword while he was unconscious on the hornet trip up to the ship. Mahnmut tries to imagine how strange this all must look to the son of Laertes—this metal ship they've described to him, sailing on the ocean of space he cannot see, now this motley assortment of moravecs in the corridor. No two 'vecs are quite the same in size or appearance, ranging from Orphu's two-ton hulking presence to the blackly smooth Suma IV to the chitinous and warlike rockvec General Beh bin Adee.

Odysseus ignores all of them and goes straight to the med lab window to stare in at the surgery, his face expressionless. Again, Mahnmut wonders what the bearded, barrel-chested warrior is thinking, seeing this long-legged silver spider and the two black-shelled techvecs hunched over Hockenberry—a man whom Odysseus has seen and spoken to many times in the last nine months—Odysseus and the group of moravecs in the corridor all staring at Hockenberry's blood and opened chest and spread ribs splayed like something in a butcher shop. *Will Odysseus think that Retrograde Sinopessen is eating him?* wonders Mahnmut.

Without turning his gaze away from the operation, Odysseus says to

Mahnmut in ancient Greek, "Why did your friends kill Hockenberry, son of Duane?"

"They didn't. Hockenberry suddenly appeared here in our ship . . . you remember how he can use the gods' abilities to travel instantly from place to place?"

"I remember," says Odysseus. "I've watched him transport Achilles to Ilium, disappearing and appearing again as do the gods themselves. But I never believed that Hockenberry was a god or a son of a god."

"No, he's not, and has never claimed to be," says Mahnmut. "And now it looks as if someone has stabbed him, but he was able to QT . . . to travel like the gods travel . . . here for help. The silver moravec you see in there and its two assistants are trying to save Hockenberry's life."

Odysseus turns his gray-eyed gaze down on Mahnmut. "Save his life, little machine-man? I can see that he is dead. The spider is lifting out his heart."

Mahnmut turns to look. The son of Laertes is right.

Unwilling to distract Sinopessen, Mahnmut contacts Asteague/Che on the common channel. *Is he dead? Irretrievably dead?*

The Prime Integrator standing near the surgical table watching the procedure does not lift his head as he answers on the common band. *No. Hockenberry's life functions ceased for only a little over a minute before Sinopessen froze all brain activity—he believes that there was no irreversible damage. Integrator Sinopessen informs me that normally the procedure would be to inject several million nanocytes to repair the human's damaged aorta and heart muscle, then insert more specialized molecular machines to replenish his blood supply and strengthen his immune system. The Integrator discovered that this is not possible with scholic Hockenberry.*

Why not? asks the Callistan integrator, Cho Li.

Scholic Hockenberry's cells are signed.

Signed? says Mahnmut. He'd never had much interest in biology or genetics—human or moravec—although he had long studied the biology of kraken, kelp, and other creatures of the Europan ocean where he'd driven his submersible for the last standard century and more.

Signed—copyrighted and copy-protected, sends Asteague/Che on the common band. Everyone on the ship except Odysseus and the unconscious Hockenberry is listening. *This scholic was not born, he was . . . built. Retroengineered from some starter DNA and RNA. His body will accept no organ transplants, but more important than that, it will not accept new nanocytes, since it is already filled with very advanced nanotechnology.*

What kind? asks the buckycarbon-sheathed Ganymedan, Suma IV. *What does it do?*

We don't know yet. This answer comes from Sinopessen himself, even as his thin fingers wield laser scalpel, sutures, and micro-scissors while one of his other hands holds Hockenberry's heart. *These nanomemes and microcytes are much more sophisticated and complex than anything this surgery has or anything we've designed for moravec use. The cells and subcellular machinery ignore our own nano-interrogation and destroy any alien intrusion.*

But you can save him anyway? asks Cho Li.

I believe so, says Retrograde Sinopessen. *I'll finish replenishing Scholic Hockenberry's blood supply, complete the cell-repair and sewing up, allow neural activity to resume, initiate Grsvki-field stimulus to accelerate recovery, and he should be all right.*

Mahnmut turns to share this prognosis with Odysseus, but the Achaean has turned and walked away.

The second day out from Mars and Phobos.

Odysseus walks the hallways, climbs the stairways, avoids the elevators, searches the rooms, and ignores the Hephaestan artifices called moravecs as he seeks a way out of this metal-halled annex to Hades.

"O Zeus," he whispers in a long chamber empty and silent except for humming boxes, whispering ventilators, and gurgling pipes, "Father wide-ruling over gods and men alike, Father whom I disobeyed and rashly warred with, He who hast thundered forth from starry heaven for all the length of my life, He who once sent his beloved daughter Athena to favor me with her protection and love, Father, I ask thee now for a sign. Lead me out of this metal Hades of shadows and shades and impotent gestures to which I have come before my time. I ask only for my chance to die in battle, O Zeus, O Father who rules over the firm earth and the wide sea. Grant me this final wish and I shall be thy servant for all the days remaining to me."

There is no answer, not even an echo.

Odysseus, son of Laertes, father of Telemachus, beloved of Penelope, favorite of Athena, clenches his fists and teeth against his fury and continues to pace the metal tunnels of this shell, this hell.

The artifices have told him that he is in a metal ship sailing the black sea of the *kosmos,* but they lie. They have told him that they took him from the battlefield on the day the Hole collapsed because they seek to help him find his way home to his wife and son, but they lie. They have told him that they are thinking objects—like men—with souls and hearts like men, but they lie.

This metal tomb is huge, a vertical labyrinth, and it has no windows. Here and there Odysseus finds transparent surfaces through which he can peer into yet another room, but he finds no windows or ports to look out onto this black sea of which they speak, only a few bubbles of clear glass that show him an eternally black sky holding the usual constellations. Sometimes the stars wheel and spin as if he's had too much to drink. When none of the moravec machine toys are around, he pounds the windows and the walls until his massive, war-calloused fists are bloody, but he makes no marks on the glass or metal. He breaks nothing. Nothing opens to his will.

Some chambers are open to Odysseus, many are locked, and a few—like the place called the bridge, which they showed him on that first day of his exile in this right-angled Hades—are guarded by the black and thorny artifices called rockvecs or battle 'vecs or Belt troopers. He has seen these black-thorned things fight during the months they helped protect Ilium and the Achaean encampments against the fury of the gods, and he knows that they have no honor. They are only machines using machines to fight other machines. But they are larger and heavier than Odysseus, armed with their machine weapons, and armored with their built-in blades and metal skin, whereas Odysseus has been stripped of all his weapons and armor. If all else fails, he will try to wrest a weapon away from one of the battle 'vecs, but only after he has exhausted all his other choices. Having held and wielded weapons since he was a toddler, Odysseus, son of Laertes, knows that they must be learned—practiced with—their function and form understood as any artist understands his tools—and he does not know these blunt, scalloped, heavy, pointless weapons that the rockvecs carry.

In the room with all the roaring machines and the huge, plunging cylinders, he talks to the huge metal crab of a monster. Somehow, Odysseus knows the thing is blind. Yet somehow, he also knows, it finds its way around without the use of its eyes. Odysseus has known many brave men who were blind, and has visited blind seers, oracles, whose human sight had been replaced with second sight.

"I want to go back to the battlefields of Troy, Monster," he says. "Take me there at once."

The crab rumbles. It speaks Odysseus' language, the language of civilized men, but so abominably that the words sound more like the crash of harsh surf on rocks—or the plunge and hiss of the huge pistons above—rather than true human speech.

"We have . . . long trip . . . in front of me . . . us . . . noble Odysseus, honored son of Laertes. When that is dead . . . finished . . . over . . . we hope to remove you . . . return you . . . to Penelope and Telemachus."

How dare this animated metal hulk touch the names of my wife and child with its hidden tongue, thinks Odysseus. If he had even the dullest of swords or the crudest of clubs, he would bash this thing to pieces, tear open its shell, and find and rip out that tongue.

Odysseus leaves the crab-monster and seeks the bubble of curved glass where he can see the stars.

They are not moving now. They do not blink. Odysseus sets his scarred palms against the cold glass.

"Athena, goddess . . . I sing the glorious Power with azure eyes, Pallas Athena, tameless, chaste, and wise . . . hear my prayer.

"Tritogenia, goddess . . . town-preserving Maid, revered and mighty; from his awful head whom Zeus himself brought forth . . . in warlike armor dressed . . . Golden! All radiant! . . . I beseech thee, hear my prayer.

"Wonder, goddess, strange possessed . . . the everlasting Gods that Shape to see . . . shaking a javelin keen . . . impetuously rush from the crest of Aegis-bearing God, Father Zeus . . . so fearfully was heaven shaken . . . and did move beneath the might of the Cerulean-eyed. . . . hear my prayer.

"Child of the Aegis bearer, Third Born . . . sublime Pallas whom we rejoice to view . . . wisdom personified whose praise shall never unremembered be . . . hail to thee . . . please hear my prayer."

Odysseus opens his eyes. Only the unblinking stars and his own reflection return his gray-eyed gaze.

The third day out from Phobos and Mars.

To a distant observer—say, someone watching through a powerful optical telescope from one of the orbital rings around Earth—the *Queen Mab* would appear as a complicated spear-shaft of girder-wrapped spheres, ovals, tanks, brightly painted oblongs, many-belled thruster quads, and a profusion of black buckycarbon hexagons, all arranged around the core stack of cylindrical habitation modules, all of which, in turn, are balanced atop a column of increasingly brilliant atomic flashes.

Mahnmut goes to see Hockenberry in the infirmary. The human is healing quickly, thanks in part to the Grsvki-process, which fills the ten-bed recovery room with the smell of a thunderstorm. Mahnmut has brought flowers from the *Queen Mab*'s extensive greenhouse—his memory banks had told him that this was still proper protocol in the prerubicon Twenty-first Century from which Hockenberry, or at least Hockenberry's DNA, had come. The scholic actually laughs at the sight of them and allows that he's never been given flowers before, at least as best he can recall. But Hockenberry adds that his memory of his life on Earth—his real life, his life as a university scholar rather than as a scholic for the gods—is far from complete.

"It's lucky that you QT'd to the *Queen Mab*," says Mahnmut. "No one else would have had the medical expertise or the surgical skills with which to heal you."

"Or the spidery moravec surgeon," says Hockenberry. "Little did I know when I met Retrograde Sinopessen that he'd end up saving my life within twenty-four hours. Funny how life works."

Mahnmut can think of nothing to say to that. After a minute, he says, "I know you've talked to Asteague/Che about what happened to you, but would you mind discussing it again?"

"Not at all."

"You say that Helen stabbed you?"

"Yes."

"And the motive was just to keep her husband—Menelaus—from ever discovering that it was she who betrayed him after you quantum teleported him back to the Achaean lines?"

"I think so." Mahnmut was not an expert at reading human facial expressions, but even he could tell that Hockenberry looked sad at the thought.

"But you told Asteague/Che that you and Helen had been intimate . . . were once lovers."

"Yes."

"You'll have to excuse my ignorance about such things, Dr. Hockenberry, but it would appear that Helen of Troy is a very vicious woman."

Hockenberry shrugs and smiles, albeit sadly. "She's a product of her era, Mahnmut—formed by harsh times and motives beyond my understanding. When I used to teach the *Iliad* to my undergraduate students, I'd always emphasize that all of our attempts to humanize Homer's tale—to make it into something explicable by modern humanist sensibilities— were destined to fail. These characters . . . these *people* . . . while completely human, were poised at the very beginning of our so-called civilized era, millennia before our current humanist values would begin to emerge. Viewed in that light, Helen's actions and motivations are as hard for us to fathom as, say, Achilles' almost complete lack of mercy or Odysseus' endless guile."

Mahnmut nods. "Did you know that Odysseus is on this ship? Has he come to see you?"

"No, I haven't seen him. But Prime Integrator Asteague/Che told me he was aboard. Actually, I'm afraid he'll kill me."

"Kill you?" says Mahnmut, shocked.

"Well, you remember you used me to help kidnap him. I was the one who convinced him that you had a message from Penelope for him—all that garbage about the olive tree trunk as part of his bed back home in Ithaca. And when I got him to the hornet . . . zap! Mep Ahoo coldcocked him and loaded him aboard the hornet. If I were Odysseus, I'd sure carry a grudge against one Thomas Hockenberry."

Coldcocked, thinks Mahnmut. He loved it when he encountered a new English word. He runs it through his lexicon, finds it, discovers to his surprise that it isn't an obscenity, and files it away for future use. "I'm sorry I put you in a position of possible harm," says Mahnmut. He considers telling the scholic that in all the confusion of the Hole closing forever, Orphu had tightbeamed him an order from the prime integrators—get Odysseus—but then he thinks better of using that as an excuse. Thomas Hockenberry, Ph.D., had been born into the century when the excuse of *I was only following orders* went out of style once and for all.

"I'll talk to Odysseus . . ." begins Mahnmut.

Hockenberry shakes his head and smiles again. "I'll talk to him sooner or later. In the meantime, Asteague/Che posted one of your rockvecs as a guard."

"I wondered what the Belt moravec was doing outside the medlab," says Mahnmut.

"If worse comes to worse," says Hockenberry, touching the gold medallion visible through the opening in his pajama tops, "I'll just QT away."

"Really?" says Mahnmut. "Where would you go? Olympos is a war zone. Ilium may have been put to the torch by now."

Hockenberry's smile disappears. "Yeah. There is that problem. I could always go look for my friend Nightenhelser where I left him—in Indiana, circa 1000 B.C."

"Indiana . . ." Mahnmut says softly. "On which Earth?"

Hockenberry rubs his chest where, less than seventy-two hours earlier, Retrograde Sinopessen had been holding his heart. *"Which Earth,"* repeats the scholic. "You have to admit, that sounds odd."

"Yes," says Mahnmut, "but I suspect we'll all have to get used to thinking that way. Your friend Nightenhelser is on the Earth you QT'd away from—Ilium-Earth, we might call it. This spacecraft is headed toward an Earth that exists three thousand years after you first lived and . . . mmm . . ."

"Died," says Hockenberry. "Don't worry, I'm used to that concept. It doesn't bother me . . . too much."

"It's amazing that you were able to visualize the engine room of the *Queen Mab* so clearly after you were stabbed," says Mahnmut. "You arrived here unconscious, so you must have activated the QT medallion just as you were on the verge of passing out."

The scholic shakes his head. "I don't remember twisting the medallion or visualizing anything."

"What's the last thing you remember, Dr. Hockenberry?"

"A woman standing over me, looking down at me with an expression of horror," says the man. "A tall woman, pale skin, dark hair."

"Helen?"

Hockenberry shakes his head. "She'd left already, gone down the steps. This woman just . . . appeared."

"One of the Trojan women?"

"No. She was dressed . . . strangely. In a sort of tunic and skirt, more like a woman of my era than like any female outfit I've seen in the last ten years on Ilium or Olympos. But not like my era either . . ." He trailed away.

"Could she have been an hallucination?" asks Mahnmut. He doesn't add the obvious—that Helen's knife blade had nicked Hockenberry's heart, spilling blood into his chest and denying it to the human's brain.

"She could have been . . . but she wasn't. But I had the strangest sense when I stared at her and saw her looking back at me . . ."

"Yes?"

"I don't know how to describe it," says Hockenberry. "A sense of certainty that she and I were going to meet again soon, somewhere else. Somewhere far away from Troy."

Mahnmut thinks about this and the two—moravec and human—sit in comfortable silence for a long moment. The thud of the great pistons—a pounding that went through the very bones of the ship every thirty seconds followed by half-felt, half-heard hisses and sighs of the huge reciprocating cylinders—has become accustomed background noise, like the soft hiss of the ventilation system.

"Mahnmut," says Hockenberry, touching his chest through the gap in his pajama shirt, "do you know why I didn't want to come along on your voyage to Earth?"

Mahnmut shakes his head. He knows that Hockenberry can see his own reflection in the polished black plastic vision strip that runs around the front of Mahnmut's red metal-alloy skull.

"It's because I understood enough about the ship—this *Queen Mab*— to know her real reason for going to Earth."

"The prime integrators told you the real reason," says Mahnmut. "Didn't they?"

Hockenberry smiles. "No. Oh—the reasons they gave are true enough, but they're not the real reason. If you moravecs wanted to travel to Earth, you didn't have to build this huge monstrosity of a ship to make the voyage in. You had sixty-five combat spacecraft in orbit around Mars already, or shuttling between Mars and the Asteroid Belt."

"Sixty-five?" repeats Mahnmut. He'd known there had been ships in space, some of them hardly larger than the shuttle hornets, others large enough to haul heavy loads all the way from Jupiter space if necessary. He had no idea there were so many. "How do you know there were sixty-five, Dr. Hockenberry?"

"Centurion Leader Mep Ahoo told me while we were still on Mars and Ilium-Earth. I was curious about the ships' propulsion and he was vague—spacecraft engineering isn't his specialty, he's a combat 'vec—but I got the impression these other ships had fusion drives or ion drives . . . something much more sophisticated than atomic bombs in cans."

"Yes," says Mahnmut. He didn't know much about spacecraft either—the one that had brought Orphu and him to Mars had been a jury-rigged combination of solar sails and disposable fusion thrusters, all flung initially across the solar system by the two-trillion-watt moravec-built trebuchet of Jupiter's accelerator-scissors—but even he, a modest submersible driver from Europa, knew that the *Queen Mab* was primitive and much larger than its stated mission would demand. He thought he knew where Hockenberry was headed with this, and he wasn't sure he wanted to hear it.

"An atom bomb going off every thirty seconds," the human says softly, "behind a ship the size of the Empire State Building, as all the prime integrators and Orphu were eager to point out. And the *Mab* doesn't have any of the exterior stealth material that even the hornets are covered with. So you have this gigantic object with a bright what do you call it? . . . albedo . . . atop a series of atomic blasts that will be visible from the surface of the Earth in daytime by the time you arrive in Earth orbit . . . hell, it might be visible to the naked eye there now, for all I know."

"Which leads you to conclude . . ." says Mahnmut. He is tightbeaming this conversation to Orphu, but his Ionian friend has remained silent on their private channel.

"Which leads me to believe that the real purpose of this mission is to be seen as soon as possible," says Hockenberry. "To appear as threatening as possible so as to evoke a response from the powers on or around Earth—those very powers who you claim have jiggery-pokered the very fabric of quantum reality itself. You're trying to draw fire."

"Are we?" says Mahnmut. Even as he says it, he knows that Dr. Thomas Hockenberry is right . . . and that he, Mahnmut of Europa, has suspected this all along but not confronted his own certainty.

"Yes, you are," says Hockenberry. "My guess is that this ship is just loaded with recording devices, so that when the Unknown Powers in orbit around Earth—or wherever they're hiding—blast the *Queen Mab* to atoms—all the details of that power, the nature of those superweapons, will be transmitted back to Mars, or the Belt, or Jupiter Space, or wherever. This ship is like the Trojan Horse that the Greeks haven't yet thought to build back on Ilium-Earth—and may never build, since I've screwed up the flow of events and since Odysseus is your captive here on the ship. But this is a Trojan Horse that you know . . . or are fairly certain . . . that the other side is going to burn. With all of us in it."

On the tightbeam, Mahnmut sends, *Orphu, is this the truth of it?*

Yes, my friend, but not all of it, comes the grim reply.

To the human, Mahnmut says, "Not with all of *us* in it, Dr. Hockenberry. You still have your QT medallion. You can leave at any time."

The scholic quits rubbing his chest—the scar is just a line on his flesh, livid still but fading where the molecular glue is healing the incision—and now he touches the heavy QT medallion hanging there. "Yes," he says. "I can leave at any time."

Daeman had selected nine other people at Ardis—five men and four women—to help him with the warning trip, faxing to all three hundred known faxnode portals to see if Setebos had been there and to warn the inhabitants there if Setebos had not—but he decided to wait until Harman, Hannah, and Petyr returned with the sonie. Harman had told Ada that they'd be back by the lunch hour or shortly after.

The sonie wasn't back by lunchtime or by an hour after that.

Daeman waited. He knew that Ada and the others were nervous—scouts and firewood teams had noted shadowy movement of many voynix in the forests north, east, and south of Ardis, as if they were gathering for a major attack—and he didn't want to pull ten people off their duties before Harman and the other two returned.

They didn't return by midafternoon. Lookouts on the guard towers and palisades kept glancing toward the low, gray clouds, obviously hoping to see the sonie.

Daeman knew that he should leave—that Harman had been right, that the fax reconaissance and warning trip had to be done quickly—but he waited another hour. Then two. However illogical it might be, he felt that he would be abandoning Ada if he left before Harman and the sonie returned. If something had happened to Harman, Ada would be devastated but the community at Ardis might survive. Without the sonie, the fate of everyone might well be sealed during the next voynix attack.

Ada had been busy all afternoon, only coming outside occasionally to stand alone on Hannah's cupola tower to watch the skies. Daeman, Tom, Siris, Loes, and a few others stood nearby but did not speak to her. The clouds grew grayer and it began to snow again. All of the short afternoon felt more and more like some terrible twilight.

"Well, I have to go in to work in the kitchen," said Ada at last, pulling her shawl higher around her shoulders. Daeman and the others watched her go. Finally he went into the house, up to his small third-floor cubby under the eaves, and dug through his clothing chest until he found what he needed—the green thermskin suit and osmosis mask given to him by Sari more than ten months earlier.

The suit had been ripped and soiled—rent by Caliban's claws and teeth, smeared by his blood and Caliban's, then by the mud of their forced sonie landing the previous spring—and while cleaning had removed the stains, the suit had tried to heal all of its own rips and tears. It had almost succeeded. Here and there the green insulating overfabric was all but invisible, revealing the silver sheen of the molecular layer itself, but its heating and pressure-sealing faculties were almost intact— Daeman had faxed to an empty node at fourteen thousand feet above sea level, an uninhabited, wind-ravaged, snow-pelted node known only as Pikespik, to test it. The thermskin had kept him alive and warm and the osmosis mask had also worked, providing him with enough enhanced atmosphere to breathe easily.

Now, in his room under the eaves, he laid the almost weightless thermskin and mask in his pack next to the extra crossbow bolts and water bottles and went downstairs to assemble his waiting team.

A cry went up from outside. Daeman ran outdoors at the same time Ada and half the household did.

The sonie was visible about a mile away. It had come out through the clouds smoothly enough, circling around from the southwest, but suddenly it wobbled, dived, righted itself, then wobbled again, suddenly diving steeply toward earth just beyond the stockade on the south lawn. The silvery disk pulled up at the last minute, actually struck the top of the wooden palisade—making three guards there throw themselves to the ground to avoid the machine—and then it plowed into the frozen ground, bounced thirty feet, hit again, threw sod high into the air, bounced once more, and slid to a halt, plowing a shallow furrow into the rising lawn.

Ada led the rush from the front porch as everyone ran to the downed machine. Daeman reached it just seconds after Ada.

Petyr was the only person in the machine. He lay stunned and bleeding in the forward-center position. The other five cushioned passenger niches were filled with . . . guns. Daeman recognized variations on the flechette rifles that Odysseus had brought back, but also handguns and other weapons he'd never seen before.

They helped Petyr out of the sonie. Ada tore a clean strip of cloth from her tunic and pressed it against the young man's bleeding forehead.

"I hit my head when the forcefield went off . . ." said Petyr. "Stupid. I should have let it land itself . . . I said 'manual' when it came off auto-pilot just after it came out of the clouds . . . thought I knew how to fly it . . . didn't."

"Hush," said Ada. Tom, Siris, and others helped support the wobbly man. "Tell us about it when we get you in the house, Petyr. You guards . . . back to your posts, please. The rest of you, back to whatever you were doing. Loes, perhaps you and some of the men could bring in those weapons and ammunition magazines. There may be more in the sonie's storage compartments. Put everything in the main hall. Thank you."

In the parlor of Ardis Hall, Siris and Tom brought disinfectant and bandages while Petyr told his story to at least thirty people.

He described the Golden Gate under voynix siege and the meeting with Ariel. "Then the bubble went dark for several minutes, the glass gone opaque to sunlight, and when the buckyglas became transparent again, Harman was gone."

"Gone where, Petyr?" Ada's voice was steady.

"We don't know. We spent three hours searching the whole complex—Hannah and I—and we found the weapons in a sort of museum room in a bubble she'd never been in before—but there was no sign of Harman or this green thing, Ariel."

"Where is Hannah?" asked Daeman.

"She stayed behind," said Petyr. He was bent over, holding his band-aged head. "We knew we had to get the sonie and as many of the weapons back to Ardis as quickly as possible—Ariel had said that he, she, had reprogrammed the sonie to return more slowly than we'd gone—it took about four hours on the return trip. Ariel had said that Odysseus would be out of his crèche in seventy-two hours if the ma-chine could save his life, and Hannah said she was going to stay there until she knew . . . knew whether he'd made it or not. Besides, we found scores more weapons—we'll have to go back with the sonie—and Han-nah said we could pick her up then."

"Were the voynix on the verge of getting into the bubbles?" asked Loes.

Petyr shook his head and then grimaced at the pain. "We didn't think so. They slid right off the buckyglas and there were no exits or entrances functioning except the semipermeable garage door that sealed behind me when I flew out."

Daeman nodded thoughtfully. He remembered both the friction-free buckyglas of the crawler canopy during their drive into the Mediterranean Basin with Savi and the semipermeable membrane doors up on Prospero's orbital isle.

"Anyway, Hannah has about fifty flechette weapons," said Petyr with a wry grin, "we carried them out of the museum in chests and blankets. She could kill a lot of voynix if they do get in. Plus, the room that Odysseus' crèche is in is sort of hidden from the rest of the complex."

"We're not sending the sonie back tonight, are we?" asked the woman named Salas. "I mean . . ." She glanced out the windows at the dimming afternoon.

"No, we're not sending the sonie back today," said Ada. "Thank you, Petyr. Go on to the infirmary and get some rest. We'll bring the sonie up to the house and inventory the weapons and ammunition you brought back. You may have saved Ardis."

People went about their business. Even out on the far lawn, there was the buzz of excited conversation. Loes and others who had fired the flechette guns originally brought back by Odysseus, tested the new weapons—all those flechette guns they tried worked—and set up an ad hoc firing range behind Ardis where they could begin training others. Daeman himself oversaw the brushing off of the sonie. It hummed back to life when the controls were reactivated and resumed its hover three feet off the ground. Half a dozen men walked it back to the house. The storage compartments at the rear and sides of the machine—where Odysseus had once stored his spears while going on a hunt for Terror Birds—had indeed been filled with more guns.

Finally, by late afternoon, with the winter twilight fading the day from the sky, Daeman went out to see Ada where she was standing by Hannah's flaming hearth tower. He started to speak, then found he didn't know what to say.

"Go," said Ada. "Good luck." She kissed Daeman on the cheek and pushed him back toward the house.

In the last gray light of the snowy afternoon, Daeman and the nine others loaded their packs with more crossbow bolts, biscuits, cheese, and water bottles—they considered taking some of the new flechette pistols, but decided to stay with the crossbows and knives, weapons they were familiar with—and then they quickly walked the mile and a quarter of road between the Ardis Hall stockade and the fax pavilion. At times they jogged. Shadows were moving within the deeper shade of the forest, although the ten couldn't see any voynix in the open. There was no bird sound from the trees—not even the sparse flutters and calls common in deep winter. At the fax pavilion stockade, the nervous men and women keeping guard there—twenty of them—first welcomed them as their relief come early, then showed their displeasure when they learned the group was faxing out. No one had faxed in or out in the past twenty-four hours and the guard team had seen voynix—scores of them—moving west in the forest. They knew the faxnode pavilion was not really defensible should the voynix attack en masse and all of them wanted to be back at Ardis before nightfall. Daeman told them that Ardis was not the place they wanted to be this night—that a relief crew might not make it down to the fax pavilion before nightfall because of the voynix activity, but that someone would fly down in the sonie and check on them within the next few hours. If there was an attack here at the pavilion and the defenders here could get one messenger back to Ardis, the sonie could bring in reinforcements, five at a time.

Daeman looked at the team he'd put together—Ramis, Caman, Dorman, Caul, Edide, Cara, Siman, Oko, and Elle—and then he briefed the nine volunteers on their mission a final time: each had been assigned a list of thirty faxnode codes, codes simply rising in numerical order since distance from Ardis made no difference in the fax world, and explained again how they were to flick to all thirty sites before returning. If there was sign of the blue ice-web and the many-handed Setebos, they were to note it, see what they could from the fax pavilion there, and get the hell out. Their job was not to fight. If the community there looked normal, they were to spread the word to whoever was in charge, then fax on to the next node as quickly as possible. Even with delays in delivering their messages, Daeman hoped that each could complete his or her mission in less than twelve hours. Some of the nodes were sparsely inhabited—little more than a cluster of homes around a fax pavilion—so the stays should be short, even shorter if the humans had fled. If any of the messengers didn't return to Ardis Hall in twenty-four hours, he or she would be presumed lost and someone sent in his or her place to notify those thirty nodes. They were to return early—before completing their circuit of thirty nodes—only if they were seriously injured or if they learned something that was important to the survival of everyone at Ardis. In that case, they were to come straight back.

The man named Siman looked anxiously at the surrounding hills and meadows. It was already growing dark. The man said nothing, but Daeman could read his mind—*What chance would they have trying to make the mile and a quarter in the dark, with the voynix on the move?*

Daeman called the fax pavilion defenders into their circle. He explained that if any of these people faxed back with important news and the sonie was not available, fifteen of the guard troop would accompany the messenger back to Ardis Hall. In no case was the fax pavilion to be left undefended.

"Any questions?" he asked the group. In the dying light, their faces were white ovals turned toward him. No one had a question.

"We'll leave in fax code order," he said. He did not waste time wishing them luck. One by one they faxed out, tapping the first of their codes onto the diskplate pad on the column in the center of the pavilion and flicking out of sight. Daeman had taken the last thirty codes, primarily because Paris Crater was one of these high numbers, as were the nodes he'd checked. But when he faxed out, he tapped none of these codes in. Instead, he set in the little-known high-number code for the uninhabited tropical isle.

It was still bright daylight when he arrived. The lagoon was light blue, the water beyond the reef still a deeper color. Storm clouds were piled high on the western horizon and morning sunlight illuminated the tops of what he'd recently learned were called stratocumulus.

Glancing around to make sure he was alone, Daeman stripped naked and pulled on the thermskin, allowing the hood to lie loose at his neck and the osmosis mask to hang on a strap beneath his tunic. Then he pulled on his trousers, tunic, and shoes, stuffing his underwear into his pack.

He checked the other items in his rucksack—strips of yellow cloth he'd cut up at Ardis, the two crude clawhammers he'd had Reman forge—Reman was the best ironworker at Ardis when Hannah was gone. Coils of rope. Extra crossbow quarrels.

He wanted to go back to Paris Crater first, but it was the middle of the night there and to see what he had to see, Daeman needed daylight. He knew that he had about seven hours before sunrise at Paris Crater and he was pretty sure that he could visit most of his other twenty-nine nodes by then. Some of those on his list were the ones he'd faxed to after fleeing from Paris Crater last time—Kiev, Bellinbad, Ulanbat, Chom, Loman's Place, Drid, Fuego, Cape Town Tower, Devi, Mantua, and Satle Heights. Only Chom and Ulanbat had been infected with the blue ice then, and he hoped it would still be that way. Even if it took a full twelve hours to warn the people in the other cities and nodes, it would be full daylight when he faxed last to Paris Crater.

And Paris Crater is where he planned to do what he had to do.

Daeman tugged on his heavy pack, lifted the crossbow, walked back to the pavilion, said a silent goodbye to the tropical breezes and rustle of palm fronds, and tapped in the first code on his list.

33

Achilles has carried the dead but perfectly preserved corpse of the Amazon Penthesilea more than thirty leagues, almost ninety miles, up the slope of Mount Olympos and is prepared to carry her another fifty leagues more—or a hundred more if it comes to that, or a thousand—but somewhere on this third day, somewhere around the altitude of sixty thousand feet, the air and warmth disappear completely.

For three days and nights, with only short breaks for rest and cat-naps, Achilles, son of Peleus and the goddess Thetis, grandson of Aeacus, has climbed within the glass-shrouded tube of the crystal escalator that rises to the summit of Olympos. Shattered on the lower slopes in the first days of fighting between the forces of Hector and Achilles and the immortal gods, most of the escalator had retained its pressurized atmosphere and its heating elements. Until the sixty-thousand-foot level. Until here. Until now.

Here some lightning bolt or plasma weapon has severed the escalator tube completely, leaving a gap of a quarter mile or more. It makes the crystal escalator on the red volcanic slope look like nothing so much as a snake chopped in half with a hoe. Achilles presses through the force-field on the open end of the tube and crosses that terrible openness, carrying his weapons, his shield, and the body of Penthesilea—the Amazon's corpse anointed in Pallas Athena's preserving ambrosia and bound in once-white linen he'd taken from his own command tent—but when he does reach the other side, his lungs bursting, eyes burning and ears bleeding from the low pressure, his skin scored by the burning cold, he sees that the tube beyond is shattered for miles more, the wreckage rising up over the ever-receding curving slope of Olympos, its interior without air or heat. Instead of a staircase he can climb, the escalator is now a series of shattered shards showing jagged metal and twisted glass for as far as he can see. Airless, freezing, it does not even offer shelter from the howling jet-stream winds.

Cursing, gasping, Achilles staggers back down the open slope, presses back through the humming forcefield at the opening to the crystal tube, and collapses on the metal steps, setting his wrapped burden gently on the stairs. His skin is raw and cracked from the cold—*How can it be* cold *this close to the sun?* he wonders. Fleet-footed Achilles feels sure that he has climbed higher than Icarus flew, and the wax on the wings of the boy-who-would-be-bird had melted from the heat of the sun. Had it not? But the mountaintops in the land of his childhood—Chiron's land, the country of the centaurs—were cold, windy, inhospitable places where the air grew thinner the higher one climbed. Achilles realizes that he expected more from Olympos.

He takes a leather bag from his cape, removes a small wineskin from the pouch, and squirts the last of his wine between his parched and cracked lips. Achilles ate the last of his cheese and bread ten hours earlier, confident that he would soon reach the summit. But Olympos seems to have no summit.

It seems now like months since the morning of the day he'd begun this quest three days earlier—the day he'd killed Penthesilea, the day the Hole closed, sealing him away from Troy and his fellow Myrmidons and Achaeans, not that he cared that the Hole was gone, since he had no intention of going back until Penthesilea lived again and was his bride. But he hadn't planned this expedition. On that morning three days earlier when Achilles had set out from his tent on the battlefield near the base of Olympos, he'd carried only a few scraps of food into the battle with the Amazons, not planning to be gone for more than a few hours. His strength that morning had seemed as limitless as his wrath.

Now Achilles wonders if he has the strength to descend the thirty leagues of metal staircase.

Maybe if I leave the woman's corpse behind.

Even as the thought slides through his exhausted mind, he knows that he won't do it . . . he can't do it. What had Athena said? *"There is no release from this particular spell of Aphrodite—the pheromones have spoken and their judgment is final. Penthesilea will be your only love for this life, either as a corpse or as a living woman . . ."*

Achilles, son of Peleus, has no idea what pheromones might be, but he knows that Aphrodite's curse is real enough. The love for this woman he so brutally killed chews at his guts more fiercely than the hunger pangs that make his belly growl. He'll never turn back. Athena had said that there were healing tanks at the summit of Olympos, the gods' secret, the source of their own physical repair and immortality—a secret path around the inviolate line between the light and dark that is Death's teeth's barrier. The healing tanks . . . this is where Achilles will take Penthesilea. When she breathes again, she will be his bride. He defies the Fates themselves to oppose him on this mission.

But now his exhaustion makes his powerful, tanned arms shake and he leans forward, resting those arms on his bloodied knees just above his greaves. He looks out through the crystal roof and sides of the enclosed metal staircase and—for the first time in three days—really takes in the view.

It is almost sunset and the shadow of Olympos stretches far out over the red landscape below. The Hole is gone and there are no longer any battlefield campfires visible on the red plain below. Achilles can see the winding line of the crystal escalator for much of the thirty leagues he has climbed, its glass catching more light than the dark slopes beneath it. Farther out, the shadow of the mountain falls across shoreline, distant hills, and even the blue sea that rolls in so tepidly from the north. Farther to the east now, Achilles can see the white summits of three other tall peaks, rising above low clouds, catching the red sunset glow. The edge of the world is curved. This strikes Achilles as a very strange thing, since everyone knows that the world is either flat or saucer-shaped, with the far walls curving upward, not downward as the edge of this world is now in the evening light. This is obviously not the Mount Olympos in Greece, but Achilles has been aware of this for many months. This red-soil, blue-sky world with this impossibly tall mountain is the true home of the gods, and he suspects that the horizon can curve downward here or do anything else it pleases.

He turns to look back uphill just as a god QT's into sight.

He's a small god by Olympian standards, a dwarf—just six feet tall—bearded, ugly, and, as he staggers around viewing the damage to his escalator—Achilles can see that he is crippled, almost hunchbacked. As familiar with the Olympian Pantheon as the next Argive hero, Achilles knows at once who this is—Hephaestus, god of fire and chief artificer to the gods.

Hephaestus appears to be almost finished surveying the damage to his artificing—standing out there in the freezing cold and howling jet stream, his back to Achilles, scratching his beard and muttering while he surveys the wreckage—and it looks as if he hasn't noticed Achilles and his linen-wrapped bundle.

Achilles doesn't wait for him to turn. Running through the forcefield at top speed, the fleet-footed mankiller tackles the god of fire and uses his favorite wrestling moves on him—first using the famous "body hold" that has won Achilles countless prizes in wrestling games, grabbing the god by his burly waist, flipping him upside down, and hurling him headfirst into the red rock. Hephaestus howls a curse and tries to rise. Achilles grabs the gnome-god by his burly forearm and uses the "flying mare" move—hurling Hephaestus over his shoulder in a complete flip and slamming him to the ground on his back.

Hephaestus moans and shouts a truly obscene curse.

Knowing that the god's next move will be to teleport away, Achilles throws himself on the shorter, bulkier figure, wrapping his legs around Hephaestus's waist in a rib-crunching scissors hold, setting his left arm around the bearded god's neck, and pulling the short god-killing knife from his belt and holding it under the fire god's chin.

"You fly away, I go with you and kill you at the same time," hisses Apollo in the artificer's hairy ear.

"You . . . can't . . . kill . . . a fucking . . . god," gasps Hephaestus, using his blunt, calloused god-fingers to try to pry Achilles' forearm away from his throat.

Achilles uses the Athena-blade to draw a three-inch cut—long but shallow—under Hephaestus' chin. Golden ichor spills onto the ratty beard. At the same instant, Achilles closes his legs tighter around the god's creaking ribs.

The god shoots electricity through his body and into Achilles' thighs. Achilles grimaces at the high voltage but does not release his grip. The god exerts superhuman strength to escape—Achilles counters with even more superhuman strength and holds him tight, increasing the pressure of his scissoring legs. Achilles brings the blade up more sharply under the red-faced god's chin.

Hephaestus grunts, woofs, and goes limp. "All right . . . enough," he gasps. "You win this match, son of Peleus."

"Give me your word that you will not flick away."

"I give you my word," gasps Hephaestus. He groans as Achilles tightens his powerful thighs.

"And know that I will kill you when you break your word,"growls Achilles. He rolls away, aware that the air is too thin for him to stay conscious more than a few more seconds. Grabbing the fire god by his tunic and tangled hair, he drags him through the forcefield into the warmth and thick air of the enclosed crystal staircase.

Once inside, Achilles throws the god down on the metal steps and wraps his legs around Hephaestus' ribs again. He knows through watching Hockenberry and the gods themselves that when they QT away to wherever they're going, they transport with them anyone who is in physical contact.

Wheezing, moaning, Hephaestus glances at the linen-wrapped body of Penthesilea and says, "What brings you up to Olympos, fleet-footed Achilles? Bringing your laundry up to be washed?"

"Shut up," gasps Achilles. The three days without food and the exertions of climbing sixty thousand feet on an airless mountain have taken too much out of him. He can feel his superhuman strength ebbing like water out of a sieve. Another minute and he'll have to release Hephaestus—or kill him.

"Where did you get that knife, mortal?" asks the bearded and ichor-bleeding god.

"Pallas Athena entrusted me with it." Achilles sees no reason to lie and unlike some—crafty Odysseus for one—he never lies anyway.

"Athena, eh?" grunts Hephaestus. "She is the goddess I love above all others."

"Yes, I have heard this," says Achilles. Actually, what Achilles has heard is that Hephaestus pursued the virgin goddess for centuries, trying to have his way with her. At one point he came close enough that Athena was batting Hephaestus' turgid member away from her thighs—and Greeks coyly used the word for "thighs" to mean a woman's pudenda—when, dry humping for all he was worth, the bearded cripple of a god ejaculated all over her upper legs just as the more powerful goddess shoved him away from her. As a child, Achilles' stepfather, the centaur Chiron, had told him many tales in which the wool, *erion,* that Athena used to wipe away the semen, or the dust in which that semen fell, all played interesting roles. As a man and the world's greatest warrior, Achilles had heard the poet-minstrels sing of "bridal dew"—*herse* or *drosos* in the language of his home isle—but these words also meant a newborn child itself. It was said that various human heroes—some included Apollon—had been born of this semen-impregnated wool or dust.

Achilles decides not to mention either tale right now. Besides, he's almost out of strength—he needs to conserve his breath.

"Release me and I will be your ally," says Hephaestus, gasping again. "We are like brothers anyway."

"How are we like brothers?" manages Achilles. He has decided that if he has to release Hephaestus, he will drive the god-killing Athena dagger up through the god's underjaw and into his skull, skewering the artificer's brain and pulling it free like spearing a fish from a stream.

"When I was flung into the sea not long after the Change, Eurynome, daughter of Okeanos, and your mother, Thetis, received me on their laps," gasped the god. "I would have drowned had not your mother—dearest Thetis, daughter of Nereus—caught me up and cared for me. We are like brothers."

Achilles hesitates.

"We are more than brothers," gasps Hephaestus. "We are allies."

Achilles does not speak because to do so would be to reveal his approaching weakness.

"Allies!" cries Hephaestus, whose ribs are snapping one after the other, like saplings in the cold. "My beloved mother, Hera, hates the immortal bitch Aphrodite, who is your enemy. My adored beloved, Athena, sent you on this task, you say, so it is my will to aid you in your quest."

"Take me to the healing tanks," manages Achilles.

"The healing tanks?" Hephaestus breathes deeply as Achilles relinquishes the pressure a bit. "You'll be found out there now, son of Peleus and Thetis. Olympos is in the thrall of *kaos* and civil war this day—Zeus has disappeared—but there are still guards at the healing tanks. It is not yet dark. Come to my quarters, eat, drink, refresh yourself, and I will then take you directly to the healing tanks in the dead of night, when only the monstrous Healer and a few sleepy guards are there."

Food? thinks Achilles. It's true, he realizes, that he will hardly be able to fight—much less command others to bring Penthesilea back to life—unless he gets something to eat soon.

"All right," grunts Achilles, pulling his legs from around the bearded god's middle and pushing the Athena-blade back in his belt. "Take me to your quarters on the summit of Olympos. No tricks, now."

"No tricks," growls Hephaestus, scowling and feeling his bruised and broken ribs. "But it is an ill day when an immortal can be treated this way. Take hold of my arm and we will QT there now."

"A minute," says Achilles. He can barely lift Penthesilea's body to his shoulder, he is so weak. "All right," he says, grabbing the god's hairy forearm, "we can go now."

34

The voynix attacked a little after midnight.

After helping to make and serve dinner to the Ardis Hall multitudes, Ada had joined in the evening heavy outside work of reinforcing Ardis's defenses. Despite requests from Peaen, Loes, Petyr, and Isis—all of whom knew she is pregnant—she stayed outside in the cold and light snow, helping to dig the ditches about a hundred feet inside the fences of the palisade. It had been Harman and Daeman's idea—fire ditches, filled with their precious lantern oil and ignited if the voynix managed to break through the palisade—and Ada wished that Harman and Daeman were there that night to help dig.

The earth was frozen and Ada found that she was too weary to break through the soil, even though she had one of the sharper shovels. This frustrated her so much that she had to wipe away the tears and snot as she waited for Greogi and Emme to break through the frozen dirt before she could lift and shovel it away. Luckily, it was dark and no one was looking at her. The embarrassment of being seen crying would have made her blubber harder. When Petyr came from where he was working in the hall to finish first-floor defenses and asked her again to come in the house, at least, she told him truthfully that she loved working on the line out here with the hundreds of other laborers. The manual labor and the proximity of so many made her feel better and kept her from thinking about Harman, she said. It was the truth.

Some time after ten p.m., the ditches were finished. They were crude things, at best—five feet across, less than two feet deep, lined with plastic bags scavenged from Chom in previous weeks. Cans of the precious lamp oil—kerosene, Harman had called it—were in the hallway, ready to be carried out, poured, and ignited if the palisade defenders had to fall back.

"What happens after we use a year's worth of lighting fuel in a few minutes?" Anna had asked.

"We sit in the dark," had been Ada's response. "But we'll be alive."

In truth, she had reservations about that assessment. If the voynix got past the outer perimeter, she doubted if a little wall of flame—if they even had time to ignite it—could hold them back. Harman and Daeman had helped draw up the plans for reinforcing Ardis's doorways and attaching the heavy shutters on the inside of all the first- and second-floor windows—the work had been going on for three days and was almost completed, according to Petyr—but Ada had her doubts about that line of defense as well.

When the ditches were finished, guards doubled on the palisades, cans of kerosene set in the outer hall and people assigned to deliver them to the trenches in case of attack, the new flechette rifles and pistols distributed—there were enough to arm one out of every six persons at Ardis, a far cry from the two flechette rifles they'd had before—and Greogi was circling overhead in the sonie, keeping watch, Ada went inside to help Petyr with the interior defenses.

The heavy shutters were almost finished—large, solid planks of wood set deep into the ancient oak frames of Ardis Hall's windows and ready to be swung shut and latched with iron locks forged in Hannah's cupola out back. It looked so ugly that Ada just nodded her approval and then turned away to weep.

She remembered how beautiful and gracious Ardis Hall had been less than a year ago—part of a tradition that stretched back almost two thousand years. It had always been a wonderful place to live and to entertain—sophisticated, gracious, elegant. Less than a year ago they had celebrated Harman's ninety-ninth birthday here in comfort with a huge feast out under the spreading elm and oak trees—lighted lanterns in the trees, food from all over the planet being served by floating servitors, docile voynix pulling carrioles and droshkies up the crushed-stone drive to the lighted front porch, with men and women from everywhere showing up in their finest robes and linens and elegant hairdos. Looking around at the scores of people in rough tunics milling in the cluttered main parlor, lanterns hissing and spitting in the dark, bedrolls on the floor and flechette rifles and crossbows stacked close to hand, fires burning in the fireplace not for ambience but for survival warmth with a score of exhausted and grimy men and women snoring near the hearth, muddy bootprints everywhere and heavy wooden shutters where her mother's beautiful drapes once hung, Ada thought *Has it come to this?*

It had.

There were four hundred people living in and around Ardis now. It was no longer Ada's home. Or rather, now it was the home to everyone willing to live here and fight for it.

Petyr showed her the shutters and other additions—slits cut into the first- and second-floor window shutters through which the defenders could continue to fire arrows, crossbow bolts, and flechettes at the voynix if they made it through the palisade, into the grounds—boiling water in huge vats on the third floor and raised by winches to the high gable terraces above, from which last-ditch defenders could pour the hot liquid down on the voynix. Harman had sigled that idea from one of his old books. Now the large vats of water and oil bubbled and boiled on makeshift stoves hauled up into Ada's family's former private quarters. It was all ugly, but it looked as if it might work.

Greogi came in.

"The sonie?" asked Ada.

"Up on the jinker platform. Reman and the others are preparing to take it up with archers."

"What did you see?" asked Petyr. They'd quit sending reconnaissance parties out into the forest after sunset—the voynix could see better than humans in the dark and it was just too risky on such a cloudy night without moonlight or ringlight—so the sonie forays had become their eyes.

"It's hard to see in the dark and sleet," said Greogi. "But we dropped flares into the woods. There are voynix everywhere—more than we've ever seen before . . ."

"Where do they *come* from?" asked the older woman named Uru, rubbing her own elbows as if cold. "They're not *faxing* in. I was on guard duty yesterday and . . ."

"That's not our worry right now," interrupted Petyr. "What else did you see, Greogi?"

"They're still carrying rocks up from the river," said the short, red-headed man.

Ada winced at this. The foot patrols had reported that as early as midday, voynix were seen carrying heavy stones and stacking them in the woods. It was a behavior the people of Ardis had never seen before, and any new behavior from the voynix made Ada sick with anxiety.

"Do they seem to be building something?" asked Casman. His voice sounded almost hopeful. "A wall or something? Shelters?"

"No, just stacking the rocks in rows and heaps near the edge of the woods," said Greogi.

"We have to assume they'll use them as missiles," Siris said quietly.

Ada thought of all the years—centuries—that the voynix were powerful but passive, silent servants, doing all the tasks that old-style humans had abandoned—herding and slaughtering their animals for them, standing guard against ARNied dinosaurs and other dangerous replicant creatures, pulling droshkies and carrioles like beasts of burden. For centuries before the Final Fax fourteen hundred years earlier, it was said that voynix were everywhere but were immobile, unresponsive—simply headless statues with leathery humps and metal carapaces. Until the Fall nine months earlier, when Prospero's Isle came flaming down from the e-ring in ten thousand meteoric pieces, no one in living memory had ever seen a voynix do something unexpected, much less act on its own initiative.

Times had changed.

"How do we defend against thrown rocks?" asked Ada. Voynix had powerful arms.

Kaman, one of Odysseus' earliest disciples, stepped forward, closer to the center of the circle that had formed here in the second-floor parlor. "I sigled a book last month that told of ancient siege engines and pre–Lost Era machines that could fling huge rocks, boulders, for miles."

"Did the book have diagrams?" asked Ada.

Kaman chewed a lip. "One. It wasn't all that clear how it worked."

"That's not a defense anyway," said Petyr.

"It would allow us to throw rocks back at them," said Ada. "Kaman, why don't you find that book and get it to Reman, Emme, Loes, Caul, and some of the others who help Hannah with the cupola and who are especially good at building things . . ."

"Caul's gone," said the woman with the shortest hair at Ardis, Salas. "He left today with Daeman and that group."

"Well, get it to everyone left good at building things," Ada said to Kaman.

The thin, bearded man nodded and jogged toward the library.

"We going to throw their rocks back at them?" asked Petyr with a smile.

Ada shrugged. She wished Daeman and the nine others weren't gone. She wished Hannah had come back from the Golden Gate. Most of all, she wished Harman were home.

"Let's go finish our work, people," said Petyr. The group broke up with Greogi leading some people upstairs to the jinker platform to re-launch the sonie. Others went off to bed.

Petyr touched Ada's arm. "You have to get some sleep."

"Stand guard . . ." mumbled Ada. There seemed to be a loud buzz in the air, as if the cicadas of summer had returned.

Petyr shook his head and led her down the hall toward her room. *Harman and my room,* she thought.

"You're exhausted, Ada. You've been going for twenty hours straight. All the day-shift people are asleep now. We have extra people on the walls and watching from above. We've done all we can do for today. You need to get some sleep. You're special."

Ada pulled her arm away in shock. "I'm not special!"

Petyr stared at her. His eyes were dark in the flickering lantern light of the hallway. "You are, whether you acknowledge it or not, Ada. You're part of Ardis. To so many of us, you're the living embodiment of this place. You're still our hostess, whether you admit it or not. People wait for your decision on things, and not just because Harman's been our de facto leader for months. Besides, you're the only pregnant woman here."

Ada couldn't argue with that. She allowed herself to be led off to her bedroom.

Ada knew she should sleep—she had to sleep if she was to be any good to Ardis or herself—but sleep evaded her. All she could do was worry about the defenses and think of Harman. Where was he? Was he alive? Was he all right? Would he return to her?

As soon as this current voynix threat was past, she was flying to the Golden Gate at Machu Picchu—no one could stop her—and she would find her lover, her *husband,* if it was the last thing she ever did.

Ada got up in the dark room, crossed to her dresser, and withdrew the turin cloth, carrying it back to bed with her. She had no urge to use a function to interact with the images again—her memory of the dying man in the tower looking up at her, *seeing* her, was too terribly fresh—but she did want to see the images of ancient Troy again. *A city under siege—someone's home under siege.* It might give her hope.

She lay back, set the embroidered microcircuits in the cloth to her forehead, and closed her eyes.

It is morning in Ilium. Helen of Troy enters the main hall of Priam's temporary palace—Paris and Helen's former mansion—and hurries to join Cassandra, Andromache, Herophile, and the huge Lesbos slave-woman Hypsipyle, who stand in a cluster of royal women to the left and rear of King Priam's throne.

Andromache shoots Helen a glance. "We sent servants to search for you in your quarters," she whispers. "Where have you been?"

Helen has just had time to bathe and put on clean clothes since she escaped Menelaus and left the dying Hockenberry in the tower. "I was walking," she whispers back.

"Walking," says beautiful Cassandra in the inebriated tone that often accompanies her trances. The blonde woman smirks. "Walking . . . with your blade, dear Helen? Have you wiped it off yet?"

Andromache hushes Priam's daughter. The slave woman Hypsipyle leans closer to Cassandra and now Helen can see that Hypsipyle has a grip on the prophetess's pale arm. Cassandra winces from the pressure—Hypsipyle's fingers are sinking into the pale flesh upon the command of Andromache's nod—but then Cassandra smiles again.

We'll have to kill her, thinks Helen. It seems like months since she has seen the other two surviving members of the original Trojan Women, as they had called themselves, but it has been less than twenty-four hours since she said goodbye to them and was kidnapped by Menelaus. The fourth and final surviving secret Trojan Women—Herophile, "beloved of Hera," the oldest sibyl in the city—is here now in the cluster of important women, but Herophile's gaze is vacant and she looks to have aged twenty years in the past eight months. As with Priam, Helen realizes, Herophile's day is done.

Returning her thoughts now to the mindset of Ilium's internal politics, Helen is amazed that Andromache has allowed Cassandra to stay alive—if Priam and the people learn that Andromache and Hector's baby, Astyanax, is still alive, that the death of the child had been only a ruse for war with the gods, Hector's wife would be ripped limb from limb. In fact, Helen realizes, Hector would kill her.

Where is Hector? Helen realizes that this is whom everyone is waiting for.

Just as she is about to whisper the question to Andromache, Hector enters, accompanied by a dozen of his captains and closest comrades. Even though the king of Troy—ancient Priam—is sitting on his throne, Queen Hecuba's throne empty next to him, it is as if the true king of all Ilium has just entered the room. The red-crested spearmen standing guard snap to even greater attention. The weary war captains and heroes, many still covered with dust and blood from the night's battle, stand straighter. Everyone, even the women of the royal family, hold their heads up higher.

Hector is here.

Even after ten years of admiring his presence and heroism and wisdom, even after ten years of being a plant curling toward the sunshine that is Hector's charisma, Helen of Troy feels her pulse race for the ten thousandth time as Hector, son of Priam, true leader of the fighters and people of Troy, enters the hall.

Hector is wearing his battle armor. He is clean—obviously risen from a bed rather than a battlefield, his armor is freshly polished, his shield unmarked, even his hair is freshly shampooed and plaited—but the young man looks tired, wounded by a pain of the soul.

Hector salutes his royal father and sits easily in his dead mother's throne while his captains take their place behind him.

"What is the situation?" asks Hector.

Deiphobus, Hector's brother, bloodied by the night's fighting, answers, looking at King Priam as if reporting to him but actually speaking to Hector. "The walls and great Scaean Gate are secure. We were almost taken by surprise by Agamemnon's sudden attack and we were undermanned with so many of the fighters away through the Hole fighting the gods, but we repulsed the Argives, drove the Achaeans back to their ships by dawn. But it was a close thing."

"And the Hole is closed?" asks Hector.

"Gone," says Deiphobus.

"And all of our men made it back through the Hole before it disappeared?"

Deiphobus glances at one of his captains, receives some subtle signal. "We believe so. There was much confusion as thousands retreated back to the city, the moravec artifices fled in their flying machines, and Agamemnon launched his sneak attack—many of our bravest fell outside the walls, caught between our archers and the Achaeans—but we believe that no one was left behind on the other side of the Hole except Achilles."

"Achilles did not return?" asks Hector, raising his head.

Deiphobus shakes his head. "After slaying all the Amazon women, Achilles stayed behind. The other Achaean captains and kings fled back to their own ranks."

"Penthesilea is dead?" asks Hector. Helen realizes now that Priam's greatest son has been out of touch for more than twenty hours, sunk in his own misery and disbelief that his war with the gods had ended.

"Penthesilea, Clonia, Bremusa, Euandra, Thermodoa, Alcibia, Derma-chia, Derione—all thirteen of the Amazons were slaughtered, my lord."

"What now of the gods?" asks Hector.

"They war amongst themselves most fiercely," says Deiphobus. "It is like the days before . . . before our war against them."

"How many are here?" asks Hector.

"For the Achaeans," says Deiphobus, "Hera and Athena are their principal allies and patrons. Poseidon, Hades, and a dozen more of the immortals have been seen on the battlefield this night, urging on Agamemnon's hordes, casting bolts and lightning at our walls."

Old Priam clears his throat. "Then why do our walls still stand, my son?"

Deiphobus grins. "As in the old days, my father, for every god who wishes us ill, we have our protectors. Apollo is here with his silver bow. Ares led our counterattack at dawn. Demeter and Aphrodite . . ." He stops.

"Aphrodite?" says Hector. His voice is cold and flat, like a knife dropped on marble. Here was the goddess Andromache had said had killed Hector's babe. Here was the name that forged the alliance between the greatest enemies in history—Hector and Achilles—and began their war against the gods.

"Yes," says Deiphobus. "Aphrodite fights alongside the other gods who love us. Aphrodite tells us that it was not she who slayed our beloved Scamandrius, our Astyanax, our young lord of the city."

Hector's lips are white. "Continue," he says.

Deiphobus takes a breath. Helen looks around the great hall. The scores of faces are white, intense, rapt with the force of the moment.

"Agamemnon and his men and their immortal allies are regroup-ing near their black ships," says Hector's balding brother. "They got close enough in the night to throw their ladders against our walls and send many a brave son of Ilium down to Hades, but their attacks were not well coordinated and came too soon—before the bulk of their captains and men were back through the Hole—and with Apollo's help and Ares' leadership, we threw them back beyond Thicket Ridge, back beyond their own old trenches and the aban-doned moravec revetments."

For a long moment there is total silence in the hall as Hector sits there, gaze lowered, seemingly lost in thought. His polished helmet in the crook of his arm gleams and throws a distorted reflection of the near-est watching faces.

Hector stands, walks to Deiphobus, clasps his brother's shoulder a second, and turns to his father.

"Noble Priam, beloved Father, Deiphobus—dearest of all my brothers—

has saved our city while I sulked in my apartments like an old woman lost in sour memories. But I ask now that I may be forgiven and that I might enter the ranks again in the defense of our city."

Priam's rheumy eyes seem to gain a faint glimmer of life. "You would put aside your fight with the gods who help us, my son?"

"My enemy is the enemy of Ilium," says Hector. "My allies are those who kill the enemies of Ilium."

"You will fight alongside Aphrodite?" presses old Priam. "You will ally yourself with the gods you've tried to kill these last many months? Kill those Achaeans, those Argives, whom you've learned to call friend?"

"My enemy is the enemy of Ilium," repeats Hector, his jaw set. He lifts the golden helmet and sets it on. His eyes are fierce through the circles in polished metal.

Priam rises, hugs Hector, kisses his hand with infinite gentleness. "Lead our armies to victory this day, Noble Hector."

Hector turns, clasps Deiphobus' forearm for a second, and speaks loudly, addressing all the ranked and weary captains and their men.

"This day we bring fire to the enemy. This day we roar with war cries, all together! Zeus has handed us this day, a day worth all the rest in our long lives. This is the day we seize the ships, kill Agamemnon, and end this war forever!"

The silence echoes for a long pause and then suddenly the great hall is filled with a roar that frightens Helen, makes her step back behind Cassandra, who is smiling ear to ear in a sort of death rictus.

The hall empties then as if the people in it have been carried off by the roar—a roar that does not die but that begins anew and then grows even louder as Hector leaves Helen's former palace and is cheered by his thousands of men waiting outside.

"Thus it begins again," whispers Cassandra, her terrible grin frozen in place. "Thus the old futures come 'round again to be born in blood."

"Shut up," hisses Helen.

"Get up, Ada! Get up!"

Ada threw the turin cloth aside and sat up in bed. It was Emme in her room, shaking her. Ada raised her left palm and saw that it was only a little after midnight.

Outside there came shouts, screams, the rip-crack of flechette rifles and the twang-thud of heavy crossbows firing. Something heavy smashed into the wall of Ardis Hall and a second later a window in the room next door exploded inward. There were flames lighting the window—flames outside and below.

Ada jumped out of bed. She hadn't even taken her boots off, so she tugged her tunic straight and followed Emme out into a hallway filled with running figures. Everyone had a weapon and was heading for his or her assigned positions.

Petyr met her at the base of the stairs.

"They've broken through the west wall. We have a lot of people dead. The voynix are in the compound."

Ada emerged from Ardis Hall into confusion, darkness, death, and terror.

She and Petyr and a group of others had rushed out through the front door onto the south lawn, but the night was so dark that she could see only torches on the palisades and the vague shapes of people running toward the Hall, hear only shouts and screams.

Reman jogged up to them. The powerfully built bearded man—one of the earliest of those who came to Ardis to hear Odysseus' teachings while he was still teaching—was carrying a crossbow with no bolts left in it. "The voynix came in over the north wall first. Three or four hundred of them at once, concentrated, *en masse* . . ."

"Three or four hundred?" whispered Ada. The previous night's attack had been the worst, and they'd estimated that no more than a hundred and fifty of the creatures, spread out, had attacked all four sides of the compound.

"There are at least a couple of hundred coming over each wall," gasped Reman. "But they came over the north wall first, behind a fusillade of stones. A lot of our people were hit . . . we couldn't see the rocks in the dark . . . and when our numbers on the ramparts dropped, we had to keep our heads down, some ran, the voynix came leaping over, using each other's backs as springboards. They were in among the cattle before we could bring up the reserves. I need more quarrels for the crossbow and a new spear . . ."

He started to brush past them into the foyer where the weapons were being dispensed, but Petyr caught his arm.

"Did you get the injured back from the wall?"

Reman shook his head. "It's crazy up there. The voynix butchered those that fell, even those with just light head wounds or bruises from the rocks. We couldn't . . . we couldn't . . . get to them." The big man turned away to hide his face.

Ada ran around the house toward the north wall.

The huge cupola was on fire and the flames illuminated the confusion. The temporary wooden barracks and tents where more than half the people at Ardis slept were also on fire. Men and women were running back toward Ardis Hall in total panic. The cattle were lowing as shadowy, flick-fast shapes of voynix slaughtered them—that was what voynix once did, Ada well knew, slaughter animals for humans, and they still had their deadly manipulator blades at the ends of those powerful steel arms. More cows went down in the mud and snow as Ada watched in horror, and then the voynix began hopping and leaping her way, quickly covering the hundred yards toward the house in giant grasshopper bounds.

Petyr grabbed her. "Come on, we have to fall back."

"The fire trenches . . ." said Ada, pulling out of his grasp. She made her way across the current of running people until she reached one of the torches along the back patio, caught it up, and ran back toward the nearest trench. She had to dodge and weave her way against the crowd of men and women running toward the house—she could see Reman and others trying to stem the flight, but the panicked, defeated mob ran on, many of them throwing down their crossbows, bows, and flechette weapons. The voynix were past the burning cupola now, their silvery forms leaping across the burning scaffolding, striking down men and women trying to put out the fire. More voynix—scores of them—were hopping, scuttling, and running toward Ada. The trench was fifty feet away, the voynix less than eighty.

"Ada!"

She ran on. Petyr and a small group of men and women followed her to the trenches, even as the leading voynix leaped across the first ditch.

The kerosene drums were in place, but no one had poured the fluid into the trench. Ada pried the top off and kicked a heavy drum over, then rolled it along the edge of the trench as the strong-smelling fuel poured sluggishly into the shallow ditch. Petyr, Salas, Peaen, Emme, and others seized more of the heavy drums of lamp oil and began tipping and pouring them.

Then the voynix were on them. One of the creatures leaped the ditch and slashed Emme's arm off at the shoulder. Ada's friend did not even scream. She looked down at her missing arm in silent astonishment, her mouth hanging open. The voynix raised its arm and its cutting blades flashed in the light.

Ada dropped the torch into the trench, picked up a fallen crossbow, and fired a bolt into the voynix's leather hump. The creature turned away from Emme and coiled, crouching, ready to leap at Ada. Petyr sloshed half a can of kerosene across its carapace at almost the same time that Loes threw his torch at the thing.

The voynix exploded into flame and staggered in circles, its infrared sensors overloaded, metal arms flapping. Two men near Petyr fired clouds of flechettes into it. Finally it fell into the ditch and ignited that entire section of the trench. Emme collapsed and Reman caught her, lifting her easily, and turned to carry her back to the house.

A fist-sized rock came hurtling out of the darkness, fast as a flechette and almost as invisible, and smashed in the back of Reman's head. Still holding Emme, he tumbled backward into the burning ditch. Their bodies burst into flame.

"Come on!" shouted Petyr, grabbing Ada's arm. A voynix leaped through the flames and landed between them. Ada fired the remaining crossbow bolt into the voynix's belly, grabbed Petyr's wrist, dodged past the staggered voynix, and turned to run.

There were fires all over the compound now, and Ada could see voynix everywhere—many past the flame trenches already, all of them within the walls. Some fell to flechette fire or were slowed by well-placed crossbow bolts and arrows, others were flung back when hit by flechette bursts, but the human firing was sporadic, individual, and poorly aimed. People were panicked. Discipline was not holding. The hail of flung rocks from the unseen voynix beyond the walls, on the other hand, was incessant—a constant and deadly barrage out of the darkness. Ada and Petyr tried to help a very young redheaded woman to her feet before the voynix overran them all. The woman had been struck in the side by a rock and was coughing blood onto her white tunic. Ada threw down her empty crossbow and used both hands to help the woman get to her feet and begin staggering back toward the Hall.

Flame trenches were being ignited on all four sides of Ardis Hall now by the retreating humans, but Ada saw the voynix run through the fire or leap over it. Wild shadows leaped everywhere on the lawn and the temperature rose a dozen degrees or more in a few seconds.

The woman sagged against Ada and almost pulled her down as she fell. Ada crouched next to her—amazed at the amount of blood the red-headed girl was vomiting onto her tunic—but Petyr was trying to pull her to her feet, guide her away. "Ada, we have to *go*!"

"No."

Ada bent low, got the bleeding girl over her shoulder, and managed to stand. There were five voynix surrounding them.

Petyr had lifted a broken spear from the ground and was holding them back with feints and stabs, but the voynix were faster. They dodged back and lunged forward more quickly than Petyr could turn and thrust. One of the creatures grabbed the spear and wrenched it out of his hands. Petyr fell onto his stomach almost at the voynix's feet. Ada looked around wildly for any weapon she could grab or use. She tried to set the girl on her feet so she could free her own hands, but the redhead's knees buckled and she fell again. Ada rushed at the voynix standing over Petyr, ready to use her bare hands on it.

There came a rip of flechette fire and two of the voynix, including the one ready to behead Petyr, went down. The other three creatures whirled to meet the attack.

Petyr's friend Laman—who had lost four fingers on his right hand in the last voynix attack—was firing a flechette pistol with his left hand. His right arm held up a wood-and-bronze shield and rocks ricocheted off it. Behind Laman came Salas, Oelleo, and Loes—all friends of Hannah's and disciples of Odysseus—also using shields for defense and flechette weapons to kill. Two of the voynix went down and the third leaped back across the flaming ditch. But dozens more were running, leaping, and scrabbling around Ada's group.

Petyr staggered to his feet, helped Ada lift the girl, and they headed toward the house still more than a hundred feet away, with Laman leading the way and Loes, Salas, and the petite Oelleo giving them protection on each side with their shields.

Two voynix landed on Salas's back, driving her into the muddy, churned-up soil and tearing her spine away. Laman turned and shot the voynix in the hump with a full spread of flechettes. The creature was blasted sideways across the frozen ground, but Ada could see that Salas was dead. At that instant, a rock caught Laman in the temple and he fell lifeless.

Ada let Petyr support the girl's weight while she snatched up the heavy flechette pistol. A solid volley of rocks came flying out of the darkness, but the humans crouched behind Loes's and Oelleo's shields. Petyr grabbed the fallen Laman's shield and added it to the defensive barricade. One of the larger stones smashed Oelleo's left arm through the wood and leather shield, and the woman—the absent Daeman's close friend—threw back her head and screamed with the pain.

There were scores—hundreds—of voynix around them now, scrabbling, leaping, killing the wounded humans on the ground, with more rushing toward Ardis Hall.

"We're cut off!" cried Petyr. Behind them, the flames in the trenches had lost much of their intensity and the voynix were leaping across without problem. The ground was littered with more human bodies than voynix corpses.

"We have to try!" shouted Ada. One arm around the unconscious girl, firing the flechette pistol with her right hand, she yelled for Oelleo to raise her shield with her right arm and to set it next to Loes's. Behind that flimsy barricade, the five of them ran toward the house.

More voynix saw them coming and leaped to join the twenty or thirty blocking the way. Some of the creatures had crystal flechette darts lodged in their carapaces and leather humps; the light from the flames caught the crystal and danced in red and green flashes. A voynix grabbed Oelleo's shield, pulled her off her feet, and cut her throat with a powerful slash of its left arm. Another pulled the girl away from Ada, who set the muzzle of the flechette pistol against the thing's hump and squeezed the trigger four times. The blast blew out the front of the voynix's carapace and it collapsed on top of the unconscious girl in a flood of its own blue-white blood-fluid, but Ada could hear the pistol click on an empty chamber as a dozen more voynix leapt closer.

Petyr, Loes, and Ada were kneeling now, trying to protect the fallen girl with the shield, Loes firing with the one remaining flechette gun, Petyr holding out the shortened, broken spear against the next attack, but there were scores of voynix converging.

Harman, Ada had time to think. She realized that she said his name with a mixture of total love and total anger. Why wasn't he here? Why had he insisted on going away on her last day of life? Now the child growing in her belly was as doomed as Ada was, and Harman was not here to protect either of them. At that second she loved Harman beyond words and hated him at the same time. *I'm sorry,* she thought—not to Harman, not to herself, but to the fetus inside her. The closest voynix leaped at her and she threw her empty flechette pistol at its metal carapace.

The voynix flew backward, smashed to bits. Ada blinked. The five voynix on either side either fell or were flung backward. The dozen voynix around them crouched, raising their arms, as a withering hail of flechette fire rained down on them from the sonie. There were at least eight humans on the disk, overloading it, firing wildly.

Greogi brought the machine lower, chest height—*Foolish!* thought Ada. The voynix could leap on it, drag it down. If they lost the sonie, Ardis was lost.

"Hurry!" shouted Greogi.

Loes shielded them with his body as Petyr and Ada extricated the unconscious redheaded girl from the voynix carcass and tossed her into the center of the crowded sonie. Hands pulled Ada up. Petyr crawled on. Rocks were pelting around them. Three voynix leaped, higher than the heads of the people on the sonie, but someone—the young woman named Peaen—fired a flechette rifle and two of them were knocked aside. The last one landed on the front of the disk, directly in front of

Greogi. The bald pilot stabbed the thing in the chest. The voynix pulled the sword with it when it fell away.

Loes turned and jumped aboard. The sonie wobbled from the weight, staggered, dropped, hit the frozen earth. Voynix were rushing from all sides now and they seemed much larger than usual from Ada's perspective lying on the bloodied surface of the downed sonie.

Greogi did something with the virtual controls and the sonie bobbed, then rose vertically. Voynix leaped at them but those with rifles in the outer niches blasted them away.

"We're almost out of flechettes!" shouted Stoman from the rear.

"Are you all right?" asked Petyr, leaning over Ada.

"Yes," she managed. She'd been trying to stem the girl's bleeding, but it was internal. Ada couldn't find a pulse on the girl's throat. "I don't think . . ." she began.

The rocks hit the underside and edges of the sonie like a sudden hailstorm. One caught Peaen in the chest and knocked her backward, across the girl's body. Another caught Petyr behind the ear, snapping his head forward.

"Petyr!" cried Ada, rising to her knees to grab him.

He lifted his face, looked at her quizzically, smiled slightly, and fell backward off the sonie, dropping into the scuttling mass of voynix fifty feet below.

"Hang on!" cried Greogi.

They circled high once, flew around Ardis Hall. Ada leaned out to see the voynix at every door, scuttling over the porch, beginning to climb every wall, smashing at every shuttered window. The Hall was surrounded by a giant rectangle of flame, and the burning cupola and barracks added to the light. Ada was never good at numbers and estimating, but she guessed that there were a thousand voynix inside the walls down there, all converging on the main house.

"I'm out of flechettes," cried the man at the right front of the sonie. Ada recognized him—Boman—he'd cooked breakfast for her yesterday.

Greogi looked up, his face white behind streaks of blood and mud. "We should fly to the faxnode pavilion," he said. "Ardis is lost."

Ada shook her head. "You go if you want. I'm staying. Let me out there." She pointed at the ancient jinker platform up between the gables and skylights on the roof. She remembered the day when she was a young teenager, leading her "cousin" Daeman up the ladders to show him that platform—he'd peeked up her skirt and discovered that she didn't wear underwear. She'd done it deliberately, knowing what a lecherous boy-man her older cousin was in those days.

"Let me out," she said again. Men and women—hunched shadows like lean and leaning gargoyles—were firing down from the gables, broad gutters, and the jinker platform itself, firing flechettes and bolts and arrows into the growing mob of skittering voynix below. Ada realized that it was like trying to stop an ocean's tide by throwing pebbles at it.

Greogi hovered the sonie over the crowded platform. Ada jumped out and they lowered the girl's body to her—Ada couldn't tell if she was alive or dead. Then they handed her the unconscious but moaning Peaen. Ada lowered both bodies to the platform. Boman jumped down just long enough to throw four heavy bags of flechette magazines into the sonie and clamber back aboard. Then the machine pivoted silently on its axis and dived away, Greogi's hands working the virtual controls gracefully, his face rapt with attention, reminding Ada of her mother's focus when she used to play the piano in the front parlor.

Ada staggered to the edge of the jinker platform. She was very dizzy, and if someone in the dark hadn't steadied her, she would have fallen. The dark figure who'd saved her moved away, back to the edge of the platform, and continued firing a flechette rifle with its heavy *thunk-thunk-thunk*. A rock flew up out of the darkness and the man or woman fell backward off the jinker platform, the body sliding down the steep roof and dropping away. Ada never saw who it was who had saved her.

Now she stood at the edge of the platform and looked down with a detachment almost approaching disinterest. It was as if what she was watching now was part of the turin-cloth drama—something vulgar and unreal she would view on a rainy autumn afternoon to pass the time away.

The voynix were climbing straight up the outside walls of Ardis Hall. Some of the window shutters had been smashed inward and the creatures were scrabbling in. Light from the front doors spilled down the voynix-crowded front steps and told Ada that the main doors had been breached—there must be no human defenders left alive in the front hall or foyer. The voynix moved with impossible insect-speed. They'd be up here on the roof in seconds, not minutes. Part of the west wing of Ada's home was on fire, but the voynix were going to reach her long before the flames would.

Ada turned, groping in the dark along the jinker platform, feeling wet bodies there, searching for the flechette rifle her savior had dropped. She had no intention of dying with empty hands.

36

Daeman had expected it to be cold when he faxed to the Paris Crater node, but not this cold.

The air inside the Guarded Lion fax pavilion was too cold to breathe. The pavilion itself was sheathed in cords of thick, blue ice, the strands overlapping and attached to the circular faxnode structure like tendons wrapped tight to a bone.

It had taken him more than thirteen hours to fax to the other twenty-nine nodes and warn them of the coming of Setebos and the blue ice. Rumors had preceded him—people from other warned nodes had faxed in ahead of him, filled with panic—and everyone had questions. He'd told them what he knew and then faxed on as quickly as possible, but there were always more questions—where was it safe? All of the node communities had voynix gathering. Several had suffered small raiding attacks, but few had experienced the kind of serious attack that Ardis had fought off the night before Daeman left. *Where to go?* they all wanted to know. *Where was safe?* Daeman told them about what he knew of Setebos, Caliban's many-handed god, and about the blue ice, and then he faxed on—although twice he'd had to brandish his crossbow to get away.

Chom, seen from its hilltop fax pavilion half a mile away, was a dead, blue bubble of ice. The Circles at Ulanbat were now completely enclosed in the strange blue strands and Daeman had faxed away at once before the cold seized him there, tapping in the code for Paris Crater, not knowing what to expect there.

Now he knew. Blue cold. The Guarded Lion faxnode buried in Setebos' strange ice. Daeman hurriedly pulled up his thermskin hood and fixed the osmosis mask in place—and even then the air was so cold that it burned his lungs. He slung the crossbow over a shoulder already burdened with his heavy rucksack and considered his options.

No one—not even himself—would blame him for turning back now, faxing back to Ardis and reporting what he'd seen and heard. He'd completed his work. This fax pavilion was entombed in blue ice. The largest opening of the dozen or so visible was not more than thirty inches across and it curved away in an ice tunnel that might well lead nowhere. And if he did enter this ice-labyrinth that Setebos had created over the bones of a dead city, what if he didn't get back? They might need him at Ardis. They certainly needed the information he'd gathered in the past thirteen hours.

Daeman sighed, unslung his pack and crossbow, crouched by the largest opening—it was low, near the floor—shoved the pack in ahead of him, nudged it forward with the cocked crossbow, and began crawling on the ice, feeling the deep-space cold through his thermskinned hands and knees.

The shuffling along was tiring and eventually painful. Less than a hundred yards in, the tunnel forked; Daeman took the left branch because there seemed to be more sunlight in it. Fifty yards beyond that, the tunnel dipped slightly, widened considerably, and then continued almost straight up.

Daeman sat back—feeling the cold reaching his butt through his clothing and thermskin—and then took a water bottle from his backpack. He was exhausted and dehydrated after his hours of faxing and the anxious confrontations with frightened people. He'd rationed his water, but he still had half this bottle left. It didn't matter though, because the water was firmly frozen. He set the bottle inside his tunic, next to the molecular thermskin, and looked at the ice wall.

It wasn't perfectly smooth—none of the blue ice was. All of it was striated, and here some of the striations ran horizontally or diagonally in such a way that he thought he might find fingerholds or footholds on it. But it continued rising for at least a hundred feet, angling slowly away from the vertical until it pitched out of sight above. But the sunlight seemed stronger up there.

He withdrew from his pack the two ice hammers he'd had Reman forge for him the long day before this one. Until he'd sigled the word from one of Harman's old books, Daeman had never heard the word "hammer." If he had heard the word before the Fall, the idea of such a tool would have bored him silly. Human beings did not use tools. Now his life depended upon these things.

The twin hammers were each about fourteen inches long, with one side of the ice hammer straight and sharp, the other curved and serrated. Reman had helped him tightly wrap the handles with cross-hatched leather—something he could find a grip with even through his thermskin gloves. The points had been sharpened as well as Hannah's grindstone at Ardis had permitted.

Standing, craning his head back, setting the osmosis mask more firmly in place over his mouth and nose, Daeman shouldered his pack again, made sure the crossbow strap was firmly secure over his left shoulder—the heavy weapon lying diagonally over the pack on his back—and then he raised one of the hammers, slammed it into the ice, slammed it again, and pulled himself four feet up the wall. The tunnel was not much wider than the main chimney at Ardis, so Daeman braced himself across it with a straight leg while he set his left knee on the ice wall to rest there a minute. Then he raised the second hammer as high as he could reach and slammed it into the ice, pulling himself until he was hanging there from one hammer, supporting his weight on the other. *Next time,* he thought, *I'm going to rig some sharp spikes for my boots.*

Panting, laughing at the idea of ever doing this a second time, his breath icing the air even through the filtering osmosis mask, his pack threatening to pull him off his precarious perch, Daeman hacked and chipped toeholds, lifted himself, wedged the tips of his boots in, slammed the right hammer in higher, pulled himself up, hacked footholds with the left. After another twenty feet gained, he hung from both hammers embedded in the ice and leaned back to look up the ice chimney. *So far so good,* he thought. *Only ten or fifteen more moves like that and I'll reach the bend a hundred feet up.* Another part of his mind whispered, *And find that it's a dead end.* An even darker part of his mind muttered, *Or you'll fall and die.* He shook all of the voices out of his head. His arms and legs were beginning to shake from the tension and fatigue. Next stop, he'd chip in a deeper foothold so he could rest more easily. If he had to come back down the ice chimney, he had the rope in his rucksack. Soon he'd find out if he'd packed enough.

Above the ice chimney, the tunnel leveled out for sixty feet or so, forked twice more, and then opened up to a canyon-wide crevasse in the blue ice. Daeman packed away the ice hammers with shaking hands and unlimbered his crossbow. When he reached the opening into the wide crevasse, he looked up and saw bright afternoon sunlight and blue sky. The crevasse stretched away to his right and left, the striated floor sometimes dropping away thirty, forty feet and more, the bottom of the gap connected only by ice bridges, the walls riddled with stalactites and stalagmites and spanned here and there above him by bridges of thick ice. Sections of buildings emerged from the icy blue matrix and then were swallowed again; he could see protruding segments of masonry, broken windows and windows blind with frost, bamboo-three towers and buckyfiber additions to the older, Lost Era buildings below, all equal now in the grip of the blue ice. Daeman realized that he was on the rue de Rambouillet near the Guarded Lion faxnode, but six stories above the street he'd walked down and ridden on in voynix-pulled droshkies and carrioles his whole life.

Ahead, to the northwest, the floor of the crevasse descended slowly until it was almost down at the original street level. Daeman fell twice on the slippery slope, but he'd taken one of the ice hammers out of the pack and both times he arrested his fall with the curved iron claw.

Lower now, the light bright and the air still burning his lungs, at the bottom of a two-hundred-foot crevasse whose ice walls were made of countless strands of what Daeman began more and more to think were some sort of living tissue, he saw a second crevasse-tunnel crossing his on the diagonal and he recognized it at once. *Avenue Daumesnil.* He knew this area well—he'd played here as a child, seduced girls here as a teenager, taken his mother for countless walks here as an adult.

If he followed the other crevasse to his right, the southeast, it would take him away from the crater and the city center, out toward the forest called Bois de Vincennes. But he didn't want to head away from the center of Paris Crater—he'd seen the Hole appear to the northwest, very near his mother's domi tower right on the Crater. To go that way, he would have to head up the Avenue Daumesnil crevasse toward the bamboo-three marketplace called the Oprabastel just opposite an ancient heap of overgrown rubble called the Bastille. He'd had rock fights there as a boy, with the few children from his domi tower flinging rocks and clods at those boys from the west, kids that his neighborhood group had always insultingly called the "radioactive bastillites" for some reason known to no one, adults or children.

The blue ice seemed thicker and more ominous in the direction of the Oprabastel, but Daeman realized he had no choice. He'd caught that first glimpse of Setebos in that direction, back toward the Crater.

The trench he was in angled around to the east again before intersecting Avenue Daumesnil. This larger crevasse was too deep to enter directly, so Daeman crossed it on an ice bridge. Looking down, he saw the bamboo-three and everplas-sealed ruins of the street and avenue he'd known his whole life, but the trench continued lower than that, revealing layers of ruins of some old steel-and-masonry city beneath the Paris Crater he was familiar with. He had the horrible image of the gray-and-pink brain Setebos scrabbling in the earth with its many hands, uncovering the bones of the city under the city. *What was he hunting for?* And then an even more horrible thought occurred to Daeman. *What could he be burying?*

The ropes and stalagmites of blue on regular street level were too thick to allow him to proceed northwest up Avenue Daumesnil itself, but, amazingly, there was a stretch of green pathway down there paralleling the avenue. He rigged a bent quarrel driven into the blue ice to secure his thirty-foot descent, looping a rope over it and lowering himself carefully, knowing that a broken leg now would probably mean his death. There was an icy overhang near the bottom and he had to swing free, then slide down the rope the last ten feet to the absurdly grassy floor of the trench.

There were a dozen voynix waiting in the darkness under the overhang.

Daeman was so surprised that he let go of the rope at the same instant he started fumbling for the crossbow strung across his back. He fell four feet, lost his footing on the grass, and tumbled backward without extricating the heavy crossbow. He half lay there on his back, hands empty, looking at the raised steel arms, sharp killing blades, and emerging carapaces of the mob of voynix frozen in the act of leaping at him from only eight feet away.

Frozen. All twelve of the creatures were mostly entombed in the blue ice with only bits of blade or arm or leg or shell protruding. None of their peds were fully on the ground and it was obvious that the ice had caught them in the act of running and leaping. Voynix were fast on their peds. *How could this blue ice form quickly enough to catch them thus?*

Daeman had no answer, only thankfulness that it had. He got to his feet, felt his back and ribs ache where he'd fallen on the crossbow and lumpy pack, and pulled the rope down. He could have left it fixed in place—he had more than a hundred feet more and he might need to ascend that ice cliff quickly on his return rather than laboriously chipping footholds with his ice hammers—but he might need all the rope before this day was done. Heading northwest now, parallel to the Avenue Daumesnil on what he still thought of as the *Promenade Plantee*—the familiar bamboo-three elevated walkway frozen in ice sixty feet above him now—Daeman freed the crossbow, made sure again that the heavy weapon was cocked and ready, and followed the impossible path of green grass toward the heart of Paris Crater.

Promenade Plantee, everyone in Paris Crater had called the walkway above. It was one of those rare old names, in words that seemed to predate the world's common language, and no one Daeman knew had ever asked its meaning. He wondered now as he followed the green strip down the darkening and ever-deeper canyon through blue ice and excavated ruins if the walkway he'd known had been named after this older, forgotten path, buried until Setebos had seen fit to dig it up with his many hands.

Daeman advanced cautiously and with a growing sense of anxiety. He didn't know what he thought he'd find here—his main goal had been to get one clear look at Setebos, if Setebos it was, and perhaps be able to report to everyone at Ardis Hall on just what this blue-ice city was like after its invasion—but as he saw other things frozen in the organic blue ice on either side of the *Promenade,* half a dozen more voynix, stacks of human skulls, more ruins that had not seen the light of day for centuries, his palms grew more moist even as his mouth dried up.

He wished he'd taken one of the flechette pistols or rifles that Petyr had brought back from the Bridge. Daeman clearly remembered Savi firing a full cloud of flechettes into Caliban's chest at almost zero range up there in the subterranean grotto on Prospero's orbital isle. It hadn't killed the monster; Caliban had howled and bled, but had also lifted Savi in his long arms and bitten through her neck with one horribly audible snap of his jaws. Then the creature had hauled her body away, diving into the swamp and carrying her corpse off through the system of sewage pipes and flooded tunnels.

I came to find Caliban, thought Daeman, clearly acknowledging that as fact for the first time. Caliban was his enemy—his *nemesis.* Daeman had learned the word only the previous month and knew at once that in his life, the term "nemesis" applied only to Caliban. And—after his trying to kill the creature up there on Prospero's isle, then leaving it to die there after maneuvering the orbiting black-hole machine into the island—it was all too possible that Caliban considered Daeman *his* nemesis.

Daeman hoped so, though the thought of fighting the creature again made his mouth drier and his palms wetter. But then Daeman would remember holding his mother's skull, remember the taunting insult of that pyramid of skulls—an insult that could have come only from Caliban, Sycorax's child, Prospero's creature, worshiper of that god of arbitrary violence, Setebos—and he kept on walking, his crossbow with its two inadequate but sharpened and barbed bolts cocked and ready.

He was in the deep shadow of another larger overhang when he saw the forms emerging from the blue ice. These weren't frozen voynix; they appeared to be humans, giants, heavily muscled and contorted, with blue-gray flesh and vacant, upturned eyes.

Daeman had his crossbow leveled and was frozen in his tracks for thirty seconds before he understood what he was looking at.

Statues. He'd first learned the real meaning of the word from Hannah—stone or some other material shaped into human form. There had been no "statues" in the Paris Crater and faxworld of his youth and the first time he'd actually seen one had been at the Golden Gate at Machu Picchu just ten months or so before. That place, or at least the green habitation globes clinging to it like ivy, was a museum more than a bridge, but it had taken Hannah—always interested in making and pouring molten metal into shapes—to explain that the human forms they were looking at there were "statues," works of art—also an alien idea. Evidently these statues had no other reason for existence than to please the eye. Daeman had to smile even now at one memory from the Bridge—they'd thought that Odysseus, Noman now, had been one of those museum statues until he'd moved and spoken to them.

These shapes weren't moving. Daeman stepped closer and lowered the crossbow.

The figures were huge—more than twice life-sized—and leaning out of the ice because the ancient building they were part of had tilted forward. Each stone or concrete gray shape was the same—a man, beardless, with curls around the gray mass that stood for his hair, nude except for a small sleeveless shirt that was pulled up above his midriff. The figure's left arm was raised and bent, its hand set on the back of his head. The right arm was massive, muscular, bent at elbow and wrist, with his huge right hand resting on the man's bare belly just under its chest, actually pushing up the gray, concrete folds of the shirt. The man's right leg was the only other limb visible, curving out of the façade of the building, a shelf or ridge of some sort above small windows running through the line of identical male statues like something piercing their hips.

Daeman stepped closer, his eyes adapting to the darkness under the blue-ice overhang. The man's—the "statue's"—head was tilted to the right, the gray cheek almost touching the gray shoulder, and the expression on the sculpted face was hard for Daeman to describe—eyes closed, bow of lips pursed upward. Was it agony? Or some sort of orgasmic pleasure? It could be either—or perhaps some more complicated emotion known to humans then and lost to Daeman's era. The long line of identical shapes emerging from both the façade of the ancient ruin and the wall of blue ice made Daeman think of a dancing line of simpering men undressing for some unseen audience. *What had this building been? What use had the Ancients put it to? Why this decoration?*

Nearby on the façade were letters—Daeman recognized them as such now after his months with Harman and his own learning the sigl-function.

SAGI

M YUNEZ

YANOWSKI

1991

Daeman had never learned to read, but out of habit he set his thermskinned hand on the cold stone and brought up the mental image of five blue triangles in a row. Nothing. He had to laugh at himself—you couldn't sigl stone, only books, and only certain books at that. Besides, would the sigl-function work through molecular thermskin? He had no way of knowing.

However, Daeman could read the numerals. One-nine-nine-one. No faxnode code ran that high. Could it be some sort of explanation of the statues? Or some ancient attempt to set the figures more firmly in time, just as the human likenesses had been set in stone? *How does one number time?* he wondered. Daeman tried for a moment to imagine what one-nine-nine-one might stand for in years . . . the years since the reign of some ancient king, such as Agamemnon or Priam in the turin drama? Or perhaps it was part of the way the artist of these disturbing statues proclaimed his or her own identity. Was it possible that everyone in the Lost Era identified themselves through numerals rather than names?

Daeman shook his head and left the blue-ice grotto. He was wasting time and the strangeness of these things—these buildings and "statues" that should have remained buried, these thoughts of people unlike those he'd always known, of someone trying to put a numerical value to time itself—were as alien and unsettling to him as the memory of Setebos coming through the Hole, a swollen, disembodied brain being carried by scuttling rats.

If he was to find Caliban and Setebos—or allow them to find him—he'd find them in this dome-cathedral.

It was not a true cathedral, of course—Daeman had only known that word, "cathedral," for a few months, sigling it in a book of Harman's from which he'd learned many words and understood almost nothing— but the inside of this huge dome seemed much like Daeman imagined a cathedral to be. But certainly no cathedral like this had ever stood in the city now called Paris Crater.

That was after dark. While the light still lasted, he'd followed the green slash of the *Promenade Plantee* along the trench of the Avenue Daumesnil until that dead-ended in an ice mass he guessed to be the Operbastel. Although the crevasse had closed overhead, he followed a tunnel that seemed to follow the Rude Lyon up to the juncture that was the Bastille. Here more tunnels and open, narrow crevasses—in one he could extend his arms and touch both ice walls at once—led to his left toward the Seine.

In Daeman's lifetime and for a hundred Five-Twenty lifetimes before him, the Seine had been dried up and paved with human skulls. No one knew why the skulls were there, only that they always had been—they looked like white and brown paving stones from any of the many bridges one would cross in a droshky, barouche, or carriole—and no one in Daeman's experience had ever wondered where the water in the river had disappeared to, since the mile-wide Crater itself bisected the old riverbed. Now there were more skulls—skulls recently liberated from living human bodies—lining the walls of the crevasse he was following toward the Île de la Cité and the east rim of the crater.

According to what little legend remained in a culture largely devoid of history, oral or otherwise, Paris Crater was said to have gained its crater more than two millennia ago when post-humans lost control of a tiny black hole they'd created during a demonstration at a place called the Institut de France. The hole had bored its way through the center of the earth several times but the only crater it had left in the planet's surface was right here between the Invalids Hotel faxnode and the Guarded Lion node. Legends persisted that right where the north rim of the crater was now, a huge building called the Luv—or sometimes "the Lover"—had been sucked down to the center of the earth with the runaway hole, taking with it a lot of old-style human "art." Since the only "art" that Daeman had ever encountered were these few "statues," he couldn't imagine that the loss of the Luv amounted to much if everything in it had been as stupid as the dancing naked men in the Avenue Daumesnil crevasse now behind him.

Daeman couldn't see anything from the one open crevasse leading to Île St-Louis and Île de la Cité, so he spent the better part of an hour climbing an ice wall—laboriously chipping steps, driving in heavy bolts to loop his rope around, frequently hanging from one or both of his ice hammers to let the sweat run out of his eyes and to allow his pounding heart to slow. One good thing about the incredible exercise of the climb—he was no longer cold.

He came out atop the blue-ice crust over the city right about where the west end of Île de la Cité used to be. The ice was a hundred feet deep here and Daeman had expected to look west across the Crater and see at least the tops of the skyline he was used to—the tall buckylace and bamboo-three domi towers ringing the crater itself, his mother's tower just across the way, and farther west the thousand-foot-high *La putain énorme*, the giant naked woman made of iron and polymer. *A* statue, *just a big statue,* he thought now, *but I never knew the word before.*

None of these things were visible. Straight ahead of Daeman, looking west, an enormous dome of organic blue ice rose at least two thousand feet above the level of the old city. Only corners, edges, shadows, and an occasional extruding terrace showed where the ring of once-proud towers had circled the crater. His mother's tall domi was not visible. Nor was the *putain* farther west. Besides the huge blue dome itself—both blocking and absorbing what Daeman realized was late-evening light— the area around the crater was now a mass of airy ice towers, flying buttresses, complex tessellations, and blue ice stalagmites rising a hundred stories and more. All these soaring towers and protrusions surrounding the dome were connected through the air by webs of the blue ice that looked delicate but which—Daeman realized—must each be wider across than any of the city's broad avenues. Everything glittered in the rich, low sunlight, and there appeared to be jolts and jots of light moving within the towers and webs and the dome itself.

Jesus Christ, whispered Daeman.

For all the scrotum-tightening impressiveness of glowing ice towers leaping sixty, eighty, a hundred stories above the lower cap of ice covering the old city, the dome was most impressive of all.

At least two hundred stories tall—Daeman could judge its height and staggering mass only by the glimpses of the old domi towers low on the dome's flank—the dome stretched more than a mile in radius, from his position here on the Île de la Cité south to the huge garbage dump his mother used to call the Luxembourg Gardens, north past the greensward called boulevard Haussmann, enveloping the domi tower at Gare St-Lazare where his mother's most recent lover used to live, and then west almost to the Champs de Mars, where the straddle-legged *putain* was always visible. But not visible this day. The dome blocked even a thousand-foot-tall woman from view.

If I'd faxed in to the Invalid Hotel node, I would have ended up inside the dome, he thought.

The idea made his heart pound more wildly than the ice climb had, but then he had two more terrifying thoughts in rapid succession.

His first thought was—*Setebos built this thing* across *the Crater.* That was impossible, but it had to be true. In fact, with the orange sunset glow lessening slightly on the towers and Dome itself, Daeman could now see a red glow coming up through the ice—a red pulsing that could be coming only from the Crater.

His second thought was—*I have to go in there.*

If Setebos was still here in Paris Crater, *there* is where he would be waiting. If Caliban was here, the Dome is where he would be.

Hands shaking from the cold—*from the cold,* he told himself—Daeman went back to the wall of ice, secured the rope around a bamboo-three girder emerging from the blue ice, and lowered himself back into the waiting crevasse.

It was already dark at the bottom of the narrow ice canyon—he could look up and see stars in the paling sky—and the only way forward from Île de la Cité was into one of the many small tunnels opening like eyes in the ice, tunnels in which it would be darker still.

Daeman found one tunnel opening about chest high above the floor of the crevasse and he crawled in, feeling the even deeper cold come up through the ice into his knees and palms. Only the thermskin kept him alive here. Only the osmosis mask kept his breath from freezing in his throat.

Scooting on his knees when he could, his rucksack scraping the lowering ice ceiling above him, his crossbow extended before him, he crawled on his belly toward the red glow in the dome-cathedral ahead.

37

Hockenberry comes to the astrogation bubble to confront Odysseus, perhaps to be beaten up by him, but he stays to get drunk with him.

It has taken Hockenberry more than a week to work up the courage to go talk to the only other human being on board, and by the time he does, the *Queen Mab* has reached its turn-around point and the moravecs have warned him that there will be twenty-four hours of zero-gravity before the ship rotates stern-first toward the Earth, the bombs begin detonating again, and the 1.28 Earth-gravity will return during the deceleration phase. Mahnmut and Prime Integrator Asteague/Che both came by to make sure that his cubby would be freefall-proofed—i.e., all sharp corners padded, loose things stowed so they wouldn't float away, velcro slippers and mats provided—but no one warned Hockenberry that a common reaction to zero-g is to get violently seasick.

Hockenberry does. Repeatedly. His inner ear keeps telling him that he is falling out of control and there certainly is no horizon to focus on— his cubby doesn't have a window or a porthole or anything to peer out of—and while the bathroom facilities were designed to operate in the predominant 1.28-g gravity environment, Hockenberry soon learns how to use the in-flight bags that Mahnmut brings him whenever he announces that he's beginning to feel sick again.

But six hours of nausea is enough, and eventually the scholic begins to feel better and even starts to enjoy kicking around the padded cubby, floating from his bolted-down couch to his well-secured writing desk. Finally he asks permission to leave his room, permission is granted at once, and then Hockenberry has the time of his life floating down long corridors, kicking down the broad ship's stairways that look so silly now in a truly three-dimensional world, and pulling his way from one hand-hold to the next in the wonderfully byzantine engine room. Mahnmut remains his faithful assistant during all this, making sure that Hockenberry doesn't grab an unfortuitous lever in the engine room or forget that things still have mass here even while they show no weight.

When Hockenberry announces that he wants to visit Odysseus, Mahnmut tells him that the Greek is in the forward astrogation bubble and leads him there. Hockenberry knows that he should send the little moravec away—that this is to be a private apology and conversation, and possible beating, between the two men—but perhaps it is the craven part of the scholic that lets Mahnmut tag along. Surely the moravec won't let Odysseus tear him limb from limb, whatever right the kid-napped Greek might have to do so.

The astrogation bubble consists of a round table anchored amidst an ocean of stars. There are three chairs connected to the table, but Odysseus merely uses one to anchor himself, hooking his bare foot be-tween the slats. When the *Queen Mab* spins or pivots—which it seems to be doing a lot of in its twenty-four hours without thrust—the stars swing past in a way that would have sent Hockenberry running for the zero-g bag a few hours earlier, but which now doesn't bother him. It's as if he has always existed in freefall. Odysseus must feel the same way, Hock-enberry thinks, for the Achaean has emptied three wine gourds of the nine or ten tied to the table by long tethers. He passes one to Hocken-berry by propelling it through the air with a flick of his fingers, and even though Hockenberry's stomach is empty, he can't refuse the wine of-fered as a gesture of reconciliation. Besides, it's excellent.

"The artifactoids ferment it and put it up somewhere here on this godless ship," says Odysseus. "Drink up, human artifact. Join us, moravec." This last is to Mahnmut, who has pulled himself down into one of the chairs but who declines the drink with a shake of his metallic head.

Hockenberry apologizes for deceiving Odysseus, for bringing him to the hornet so that the moravecs could shanghai him. Odysseus waves away the apology. "I thought of killing you, son of Duane, but to what purpose? Obviously the gods have ordained that I come on this long voyage, so it is not my place to defy the will of the immortals."

"You still believe in the gods?" asks Hockenberry, taking a long sip of the powerful wine. "Even after going to war with them?"

The bearded war planner frowns at this, then smiles and scratches his cheek. "Sometimes it may be difficult to believe in one's friends, Hock-enberry, son of Duane, but one must *always* believe in one's enemies. Es-pecially if you are privileged to count the gods amongst your enemies."

They drink a minute in silence. The ship rotates again. Bright sun-light blots out the stars for a moment and then the ship turns into its own shadow once more and the stars reappear.

The powerful wine hits Hockenberry in a wave of warmth. He's happy to be alive—he raises his hand to his chest, touching not only the QT medallion there but the thin line of disappearing scar under his tunic—and he realizes that after ten years of living amongst the Greeks and Trojans, this is the first time he's sat down to drink wine and schmooze with one of the serious heroes and major characters of the *Iliad*. How strange, after teaching the tale to undergraduates for so many years.

For a while the two men talk about the events they'd seen just before leaving Earth and the base of Olympos—the Hole between the worlds closing, the one-sided battle between the Amazons and Achilles' men. Odysseus is surprised that Hockenberry knows so much about Penthe-silea and the other Amazons, and Hockenberry doesn't find it necessary to tell the warrior that he'd read about them in Virgil. The two men spec-ulate on how quickly the real war will resume and whether the Achaeans and Argives under the leadership of Agamemnon again will finally bring down the walls of Troy.

"Agamemnon may have the brute strength to destroy Ilium," says Odysseus, his eyes on the turning stars, "but if strength and numbers fail him, I doubt he has the craft."

"The craft?" repeats Hockenberry. He has been thinking and com-municating in this ancient Greek for so long that he rarely has to pause to consider a word, but he does so now. Odysseus has used the word *dolos* for craft—which could mean "cleverness" in a way that would draw either praise or abuse.

Odysseus nods. "Agamemnon is Agamemnon—all see him for what he is, for he is capable of nothing more. But I am Odysseus, known to the world for every kind of craft."

Again Hockenberry hears this *dolos* and realizes that Odysseus is bragging of the very same character trait of cleverness and guile that made Achilles say of him—Hockenberry had been there to hear this dur-ing their embassy to Achilles months ago—"I hate that man like the very Gates of Death who . . . stoops to peddling lies."

Odysseus had obviously understood Achilles' implied insult that night, but had chosen not to take offense. Now, after four gourds of wine, the son of Laertes was showing pride in his cleverness. Not for the first time, Hockenberry wonders—*Will they be able to bring down Troy without Odysseus' wooden horse?* He thinks of the layers of this word, *dolos,* and has to smile to himself.

"Why are you grinning, son of Duane? Did I say something funny?"

"No, no, honored Odysseus," says the scholic. "I was just thinking about Achilles . . ." He lets his voice drift off before he says something that will anger the other man.

"I dreamt of Achilles last night," says Odysseus, rotating easily in the air to look at the near-sphere of stars around them. The astrogation bubble looks both ways along the *Queen Mab*'s hull, but the metal and plastic there mostly reflect the starlight. "I dreamed that I talked to Achilles in Hades."

"Is the son of Peleus dead then?" asks Hockenberry. He opens another gourd of wine.

Odysseus shrugs. "It was just a dream. Dreams do not accept time as a boundary. Whether Achilles breathes now or already shuffles amongst the dead, I do not know, but it's certain that Hades will someday be his home—as it will be all of ours."

"Ah," says Hockenberry. "What did Achilles say to you in the dream?"

Odysseus turns his dark-eyed stare back on the scholic. "He wanted to know about his son, Neoptolemus, about whether the boy had become a champion at Troy."

"And did you tell him?"

"I told him I did not know, that my own fate has carried me far from the walls of Ilium before Neoptolemus could enter battle there. This did not satisfy the son of Peleus."

Hockenberry nods. He can imagine Achilles' petulance.

"I tried to comfort Achilles," continues Odysseus. "To tell him how the Argives honored him as a god now that he was dead—how living men would always sing of his feats of bravery—but Achilles would have none of it."

"No?" The wine was not only good, it was wonderful. It sent liquid heat blossoming out from Hockenberry's belly and made him feel as if he were floating more freely even than zero-g would allow.

"No. He told me to stuff those songs of glory up my ass."

Hockenberry splutters a sort of laugh. Bubbles and beads of red wine float free. The scholic tries to bat them away, but the red spheres burst and make his fingers sticky.

Odysseus still stares out at the stars. "The shade of Achilles told me last night that he'd rather be a peasant sod buster, his hands covered with calluses not from the sword but from the plow, staring up an oxen's ass ten hours a day, than to be the greatest hero in Hades, or even the king there, ruling over the breathless dead. Achilles doesn't like being dead."

"No," says Hockenberry, "I could see that he would not."

Odysseus pirouettes in zero-g, grabs the back of the chair, and looks at the scholic. "I've never seen you fight, Hockenberry. Do you fight?"

"No."

Odysseus nods. "That's smart. That's wise. You must come from a long line of philosophers."

"My father fought," says Hockenberry, surprised at the memories flooding in. As far as he can tell, he's not thought of or remembered his father in the last ten years of his second life.

"Where?" asks Odysseus. "Tell me the battle. I may have been there."

"Okinawa," says Hockenberry.

"I don't know of this battle."

"My father survived it," says Hockenberry, feeling his throat tightening. "He was very young. Nineteen. He was in the Marines. He came home later that same year and I was born three years after that. He never spoke of it."

"He didn't brag of his bravery or describe the battle to his boy?" asks Odysseus, incredulous. "No wonder you grew up to be a philospher rather than a fighter."

"He never mentioned it at all," says Hockenberry. "I knew he was in the war, but I found out about his actions on Okinawa only years later, by reading old letters of commendation from his commanding officer, a lieutenant not much older than my father when they fought. I found the letters, and medals, in my father's old Marine trunk after he died. I was already close to having my Ph.D. in classics then, so I used my research skills to learn something about the battle in which my father received a Purple Heart and a Silver Star."

Odysseus doesn't ask about these odd-sounding prizes. Instead, he says, "Did your father do well in battle, son of Duane?"

"I think he did. He was wounded twice on May 20, 1945, during a fight for a place called Sugar Loaf Hill on the island of Okinawa."

"I don't know this island."

"No, you wouldn't," said Hockenberry. "It's far away from Ithaca."

"Were there many men in this fight?"

"My father's side had one hundred and eighty-three thousand men ready to be thrown into the battle," says Hockenberry. He is also looking out at the stars now. "His army was carried to the island of Okinawa in a fleet of more than sixteen hundred ships. There were a hundred and ten thousand of the enemy waiting for them, dug into rock and coral and caves."

"No city to lay siege to?" asks Odysseus, looking at the scholic with an expression of interest for the first time since their conversation began.

"No real city, no," says Hockenberry. "It was just one battle in a bigger war. The other side wanted to kill our people to prevent an invasion of their home island. Our side ended up killing them any way they could—they poured flame into their caves, entombed them alive. My father's comrades killed more than a hundred thousand of the hundred and ten thousand Japanese on the island." He takes a drink. "The Japanese were our enemies then."

"A glorious victory," says Odysseus.

Hockenberry makes a soft noise.

"The numbers involved—men, ships—reminds me of our war for Troy," says the Argive.

"Yes, very similar," says Hockenberry. "As was the ferocity of the fighting. Hand-to-hand in rain and mud, day and night."

"Did your father return with much plunder? Slave girls? Gold?"

"He brought home a samurai sword—the sword of an enemy officer—but put it away in a trunk and never even showed it to me when I was a boy."

"Were many of your father's comrades sent down to the House of Death?"

"Counting both the men fighting on land and at sea, 12,520 Americans were killed," says Hockenberry, his scholar's mind—and his son's heart—having no trouble recalling the figures. "There were 33,631 wounded on our side. The enemy, as I said, lost more than a hundred thousand dead, thousands and thousands burned to death and entombed in the caves and holes where they dug in to fight."

"We Achaeans have lost more than twenty-five thousand comrades in front of the walls of Ilium," says Odysseus. "The Trojans have built funeral pyres to at least that many of their own."

"Yes," says Hockenberry with a slight smile, "but that's over a period of ten years. My father's battle on the island of Okinawa lasted only *ninety days.*"

There is a silence. The *Queen Mab* rotates again, as smoothly and majestically as some giant marine mammal rolling over as it swims. Brilliant sunlight pours over them briefly, causing each man to raise his hand to shield his eyes, and then the stars return.

"I'm surprised I've never heard of this war," says Odysseus, handing the scholic a fresh gourd of wine. "But still, you must be proud of your father, son of Duane. Your people must have treated the victors in that battle like gods. Songs will be sung of it for centuries around your hearths. The names of the men who fought and died there will be known to the grandsons of the grandsons of the heroes, and the details of every individual combat will be sung by minstrels and poets."

"Actually," says Hockenberry, taking a long drink, "almost everyone in my country has forgotten that battle already."

Are you hearing this? sends Mahnmut on tightbeam.

Yes. Orphu of Io is outside on the hull of the *Queen Mab,* scuttling around with the other hard-vac moravecs during the twenty-four hours that the ship is not under acceleration or deceleration, doing inspections and carrying out repairs on minor damage from micrometeorite hits, solar flares, or the effects of the fission bombs they have been detonating behind them. It is possible to work on the hull while the ship is under way—Orphu has been outside several times in the last two weeks, moving along the system of catwalks and ladders rigged for that purpose—but the big Ionian is already on record as saying he prefers the zero-gravity to what he's described as working on the face of a hundred-story building while under acceleration, with an all-too-real sense of the stern and pusher plate of the ship being *down*.

Hockenberry sounds quite drunk, sends Orphu.

I think he is, responds Mahnmut. *This wine that Asteague/Che had the galley replicate is powerful stuff, based on a sample of Medean wine from an amphora "borrowed" from Hector's wine cellar. Hockenberry has been drinking lesser versions of this red Medean for years with the Greeks and Trojans, but almost certainly in moderation—the Greeks mix more water than wine into their cups. Sometimes they add saltwater or perfumes like myrrh.*

Now that *sounds barbarous*, tightbeams Orphu.

At any rate, sends Mahnmut, *the scholic hasn't eaten since he was spacesick earlier today, so his empty stomach isn't any help in keeping him sober.*

It sounds as if he'll be spacesick again later today.

If he is, sends Mahnmut, *it's your turn to bring him more spacesickness bags. I've held his head over them enough for one twenty-four-hour cycle.*

Darn, sends Orphu of Io, *I'd really love to take my turn at that, but I don't think the doorways there in the human-cubby level of the ship are wide enough for me.*

Wait, sends Mahnmut. *Listen to this.*

"Do you like to play games, son of Duane?"

"Games?" said Hockenberry. "What kind of games?"

"The kinds of game one would play during a celebration, or a funeral," says Odysseus. "The games we would have had at Patroclus' funeral, if Achilles had acknowledged his friend's death and allowed us to put on a funeral after Patroclus' disappearance."

Hockenberry is quiet for a minute and then says, "You mean discus, javelin . . . that sort of thing."

"Aye," says Odysseus. "And chariot races. Footraces. Wrestling and boxing."

"I've seen your boxing matches there at your camps near where the black ships are drawn up," says Hockenberry, slurring only slightly. "The men fight with just rawhide thongs wrapped around their hands."

Odysseus laughs. "What else should they wear on their hands, son of Duane? Great soft pillows?"

Hockenberry ignores the question. "Last summer in your camp I watched Epeus beat a dozen men bloody, smashing their ribs, breaking their jaws. He took on all comers and fought from early afternoon to late after moonrise."

Odysseus is grinning. "I remember those matches. No one could stand up to Panopeus' son that day, although many men tried."

"Two men died."

Odysseus shrugs and sips more wine. "Diomedes was training and backing Euryalus, son of Mecisteus, third in command of the Argolid fighters. He had him out running every morning before dawn, hardening his fists by slugging oxen halves fresh from the slaughter pens. But Epeus coldcocked him that evening in only twenty rounds. Diomedes had to drag his man out of the circle with poor Euryalus' toes leaving ten furrows in the sand. But he lived to fight another day—and the next time he won't drop his fucking guard, that's for sure."

"Boxing is a filthy enterprise," quotes Hockenberry, "and if you stay in it long enough, your mind will become a concert hall where Chinese music never stops playing."

Odysseus brays a laugh. "That's funny. Who said it?"

"A wise man by the name of Jimmy Cannon."

"But what is Chinese music?" asks Odysseus, still chuckling. "And what exactly is a concert hall?"

"Never mind," says Hockenberry. "You know, in all the years of watching the war, I don't remember your boxing champion, Epeus, ever distinguishing himself in *aristeia*—single combat for glory."

"No, that's true," agrees Odysseus. "Epeus himself acknowledges that he's no great man of war. Sometimes the courage it takes to face another man bare-fisted is not the kind required to run an enemy through the belly with your spearpoint, and then twist the blade out, spilling the man's guts like so much offal in the dirt."

"But you can do that." Hockenberry's voice is flat.

"Oh, yes," laughs Odysseus. "But the gods have willed it so. I'm of a generation of Achaeans whom Zeus has decreed, from youth to old age, must wind down our brutal wars to the bitter end until we ourselves drop and die, down to the last man."

Odysseus is quite the optimist, sends Orphu.

A realist, says Mahnmut on the tightbeam.

"But you were talking about games," says Hockenberry. "I've seen you wrestle. And win. And you've won camp footraces as well."

"Yes," says Odysseus, "more than one time I've carried off the cup at the running race while Ajax has had to settle for the ox. Athena has helped me there—tripping up the big oaf to let me cross the finish line first. And I've bested Ajax in wrestling as well, clipping the hollow of his knee, throwing him backward, and pinning him before the dull-witted giant noticed that he'd been thrown."

"Does that make you a better man?" asks Hockenberry.

"Of course it does," booms Odysseus. "What would the world be without the *agon*—the agonistics of one man against another—to show everyone the order of precedence among men, just as no two other things on earth are alike? How could any of us alive know quality if competition and personal combat did not let all the world know who embodies excellence and who merely manages mediocrity? What games do you excel in, son of Duane?"

"I went out for track my freshman year at college," says Hockenberry. "I didn't make the team."

"Well, I have to admit that I'm not half bad in the world of games where men compete," says Odysseus. "I know how to handle a well-carved, fine-polished bow and will be the first among my comrades to hit my man in a moving mass of enemies, even with my friends jostling against me, everyone trying to take aim at once. One reason I was willing to follow Achilles and Hector into a war with the gods was my eagerness to test my prowess as an archer against Apollo's skill—although in my heart, I knew this was folly. Whenever mortal man rivals the gods in archery—look at poor Eurytus of Oechalia—that man can bet he'll die a sudden death, not pass away from old age within the halls of his own home. And I don't think I'd go up against the Lord of the Silver Bow unless I had my best bow with me, and I never take it to war when I sail off in the black ships. That bow is on the wall of my great hall even now. Iphitus gave me that bow as a sign of friendship when we first met—the bow belonged to his father, the archer Eurytus himself. I liked Iphitus a lot, and I'm sorry I gave him only a sword and rough-hewn spear in exchange for the finest bow on earth. Heracles murdered Iphitus before I really had time to get to know the man.

"As for spears, I can fling a lance as far as the next man can shoot an arrow. And you've seen me box and wrestle. As for sprinting—yes, you saw me beat Ajax, and I can run for hours without vomiting up my breakfast, but in the short sprint, many runners will leave me behind in the dust unless Athena intervenes on my behalf."

"I could have qualified for track," says Hockenberry, almost muttering to himself now. "Long distance was my thing. But there was this guy named Brad Muldorff—the Duck we used to call him—who squeezed me out for the last position on the team."

"Failing tastes of bile and dog vomit," says Odysseus. "Shame on any man who gets used to that taste." He gulps some wine, throwing his head back to swallow, then wipes droplets from his brown beard. "I dream of talking to dead Achilles in the shaded halls of Hades, but it's my son Telemachus whom I really want to know about. If the gods are going to send me dreams, why not dreams of my son? He was a boy when I left—timid and untested—and I'd like to know if he's turned into a man or become one of those pantywaists who hang around better men's halls, seeking a rich wife, buggering boys, and playing the lyre all day."

"We never had any children," says Hockenberry. He rubs his forehead. "I don't *think* we did. Memories of my real life are mixed up and murky. I'm like a sunken ship that someone refloated for their own reasons, but didn't bother to pump all the water out—just enough to make it float. Too many compartments are still flooded."

Odysseus looks at the scholic, obviously not understanding and obviously not interested enough to ask a question.

Hockenberry looks back at the Greek captain-king, his gaze suddenly focused and intense. "I mean, answer me this if you can . . . I mean, what does it *mean* to be a man?"

"To be a man?" repeats Odysseus. He opens the last two gourds of wine and hands Hockenberry one.

"Yess . . . excuse me, yes. To *be* a man. To *become* a man. In my country, the only rite of passage is when you get the car keys . . . or get laid for the first time."

Odysseus nods. "Getting laid for the first time is important."

"But certainly that can't be *it,* son of Laertes! What does it take to be a man—or a human being, for that matter?"

This should be good, Mahnmut sends to Orphu on the tightbeam. *I've wondered this myself more than a few times—and not just when I'm trying to understand Shakespeare's sonnets.*

We've all wondered it, replies Orphu. *All of us obsessed with things human. Which is to say, all of us moravecs, since our programming and designed DNA lead us back to studying and trying to understand our creators.*

"Being a man?" repeats Odysseus, his voice serious, almost distracted. "Right now I have to piss. Do you have to piss, Hockenberry?"

"I mean," continues the scholic, "maybe it has something to do with consistency." He has to try the word twice before getting it right. "Consistency. I mean, look at your Olympics versus ours. Just look at that!"

"That other moravec told me how to piss in that latrine in the room, it has some sort of vacuum that sucks it in even in this floating time, but I find it damned hard not to send blobs everywhere, don't you, Hockenberry?"

"Twelve hundred years you ancient Greeks kept your Games going," says Hockenberry. "Five days of games, every four years, for *twelve hundred years,* until some pissant Christian emperor of Rome abolished them. *Twelve hundred years!* Through drought and famine, pestilence and plague. Every four years, the wars would be brought to a halt, and your athletes would travel from all over their world to Olympia, to pay homage to the gods and to compete in the chariot races, footraces, wrestling, discus, and javelin, and *pankration*—that weird mixture of wrestling and kickboxing that I've never seen and I bet you haven't either. Twelve hundred years, son of Laertes! When my own people brought the Games back, they couldn't keep them going for much more than a hundred years without three of them being canceled for war, countries refusing to show up because they were pissed off by this or that slight or offense, and we even had terrorists kill Jewish athletes . . ."

"Pissed off, yes," says Odysseus, releasing the gourd on its tether and spinning around, ready to kick back to his cubby. "Have to piss. Be right back."

"Maybe the only thing that's really consistent is what Homer said— *'Dear to us ever is the banquet and the harp and the dance and changes of raiment and the warm bath and love, and sleep.' "*

"Who's Homer?" asks Odysseus, pausing in midair at the irised door to the astrogation bubble.

"No one you'd know," says Hockenberry, drinking more wine. "But you know what . . ."

He stops. Odysseus is gone.

Mahnmut goes out through the medical deck airlock, tethers himself even though he has reaction-thruster fuel in his backpack, and follows catwalks, ladders, and ship lines around and up the *Queen Mab*. He finds Orphu of Io welding a patch on the cargo bay doors in which *The Dark Lady* is stored, cradled under the folding wings of the reentry shuttle.

"That could have been more enlightening," says Mahnmut on their private radio frequency.

"Most conversations share that particular quality," says Orphu. "Even ours."

"But we're not usually drunk during our conversations."

"Since moravecs don't ingest alcohol for stimulative or depressive purposes, you are technically correct," says Orphu, his shell, legs, and sensors brightly illuminated by the shower of sparks from his welding. "But we've discussed things while you've been hypoxic, drugged with fatigue toxins, and—as the humans would say—scared shitless, so Odysseus' and Hockenberry's disjointed conversation did not sound unfamiliar to my ears . . . if I had ears."

"What would Proust say about what it takes to be human . . . or a man, for that matter?" asks Mahnmut.

"Ah, Proust, that tiresome fellow," says Orphu. "I was reading him again just this morning."

"You once tried to explain to me his steps to truth," says Mahnmut. "But first you said he had three steps, then four, then three, then back to four. I don't think you ever told me what they were, either. In fact, I think you lost track of what you were talking about."

"Just testing you," says Orphu with a rumble. "Seeing if you were listening."

"So you say," says Mahnmut. "I think you were having a moravec moment."

"It wouldn't be the first," says Orphu of Io. Data overload from both their organic brains and cybernetic memory banks was an increasing problem as moravecs moved into their second or third century.

"Well," says Mahnmut, "I doubt if Proust's ideas about the essence of being human connect too well with Odysseus'."

Four of Orphu's multiply jointed arms are busy with the welding, but he shrugs two others. "You remember that he tried friendship—even as a lover—as being one of those paths," says the Ionian. "So he has that in common with both Odysseus and our scholic in there. But Proust's narrator discovers that his own calling to truth is writing, examining the nuances wrapped within the other nuances of his life."

"But he'd rejected art earlier as a path to the deepest humanity," says Mahnmut. "I thought you told me that he decided that art wasn't the way to truth after all."

"He discovers that real art is an actual form of *creation*," says Orphu. "Here, listen to this passage from an early section of *The Guermantes Way*—

" 'People of taste tell us nowadays that Renoir is a great eighteenth-century painter. But in so saying they forget the element of Time, and that it took a great deal of time, even at the height of the nineteenth century, for Renoir to be hailed as a great artist. To succeed thus in gaining recognition, the original painter or the orginal writer proceeds on the lines of the oculist. The course of treatment they give us by their painting or by their prose is not always pleasant. When it is at an end the practitioner says to us: "Now look!" And, lo and behold, the world around us (which was not created once and for all, but is created afresh as often as an original artist is born) appears to us entirely different from the old world, but perfectly clear. Women pass in the street, different from those we formerly saw, because they are Renoirs, those Renoirs we persistently refused to see as women. The carriages, too, are Renoirs, and the water, and the sky; we feel tempted to go for a walk in the forest which is identical with the one which when we first saw it looked like anything in the world except a forest, like for instance a tapestry of innumerable hues, but lacking precisely the hues peculiar to forests. Such is the new and perishable universe which has just been created. It will last until the next geological catastrophe is precipitated by a new painter of original talent.' And he goes on to explain how writers do the same thing, Mahnmut—bring new universes into existence."

"Surely he doesn't mean that in a literal sense," says Mahnmut. "Not bringing *real* universes into existence."

"I think he is speaking literally," replies Orphu, his tone on the radio band as serious as Mahnmut has ever heard it. "Have you been following the quantum flux sensor readings that Asteague/Che has been putting on the common band?"

"No, not really. Quantum theory bores me."

"This isn't theory," says Orphu. "Every day we've been making this Mars-Earth transit, the quantum instability between the two worlds, within our entire solar system, has grown larger. The Earth is at the center of this flux. It's as if all of its space-time probability matrices have entered some vortex, some region of self-induced chaos."

"What does that have to do with Proust?"

Orphu shuts off the welding torch. The large patch-plate on the cargo-bay doors is perfectly joined. "Somebody or something is screwing around with worlds, perhaps with entire universes. Break down the math of the quantum data flowing in, and it's as if different quantum Calabi-Yau spaces have somehow attempted to coexist on one Brane. It's almost as if new worlds are trying to come into existence—as if they've been willed into existence by some singular genius, just as Proust suggests."

Somewhere on the *Queen Mab*, invisible thrusters fire and the long, inelegant-but-beautiful black buckycarbon and steel spacecraft rotates and tumbles. Mahnmut grabs a clutch-bar, his feet flying out away from the ship, as three hundred meters of atomic spacecraft twist and tumble like a circus acrobat. Sunlight slides across the two moravecs and then sets behind the bulky pusher plates at the stern. Mahnmut readjusts his polarized filters, sees the stars again, and knows that while Orphu can't see them on the visible spectrum, he's listening to their radio squawks and screeches. *That thermonuclear choir*, the Ionian once had called it.

"Orphu, my friend," Mahnmut says, "are you getting religious on me?"

The Ionian rumbles in the subsonic. "If I am—and if Proust is right and real universes are created when those rare, almost unique genius-level minds concentrate on creating them—I don't think I want to meet the creators of this current reality. There's something malignant at work here."

"I don't see why this . . ." begins Mahnmut and then pauses, listening to the common band. "What's a twelve-oh-one alarm?"

"The mass of the *Mab* has just decreased by sixty-four kilograms," says Orphu.

"Waste and urine dump?"

"Not quite. Our friend Hockenberry has just quantum teleported away."

Mahnmut's first thought is—*Hockenberry's in no condition to QT anywhere—we should have stopped him. Friends don't let friends teleport drunk—*but he decides not to share this with Orphu.

A second later, Orphu says, "Do you hear that?"

"No, what?"

"I've been monitoring the radio bands. We just brought the high-gain antenna around to aim it at Earth—or actually, the polar orbital ring around Earth—and it's just picked up a modulated radio broadcast being masered right at us."

"What does it say?" Mahnmut feels his organic heart beginning to pump faster. He doesn't override the adrenaline, but lets it pump.

"It's definitely from the polar ring," says Orphu, "about thirty-five thousand kilometers above Earth. The message is in a woman's voice. And it just says, over and over—'Bring Odysseus to me.' "

Daeman entered the blue-ice dome-cathedral to an echoing susurration of whispers and chants.

"Thinketh, He made it, with the fire to match, one fire-eye in a ball of foam, that floats and feeds! Thinketh, He hath watched hunt with that slant white-wedge eye by moonlight; and the pie with the long tongue, that pricks deep into oakwarts for a worm, and says a plain word when she finds her prize, but will not eat the ants; the ants themselves that built a wall of seeds and settled stalks about their hole—He made all these and more, made all we see, and us, in spite: how else?"

Daeman recognized the voice at once—Caliban. The sibilant whispers echoed off blue-ice wall and blue-ice tunnel, seeming to come from everywhere, reassuringly distant, terrifyingly close. And somehow that single Caliban voice was a chorus, a choir, a multitude of voices in terrible harmony. More frightened than he thought he'd be—much, much more frightened than he'd hoped he would be—Daeman bent his head low and moved forward out of the ice tunnel onto the ice mezzanine.

After an hour's crawling, often backtracking as some blue-ice tunnel narrowed and closed at a dead end, sometimes emerging into corridors ten yards across only to come up against a wall or vertical shaft far too high to climb, sometimes crawling on his belly so that his back scraped the ice ceiling, shoving his pack ahead of him along with the crossbow, Daeman had emerged into what he thought of as the center of the ice-dome cathedral.

Daeman had none of the ancient words to describe this space he had stepped out into, standing as he was on one of what looked to be hundreds of shadowy ice-mezzanines in the inner, curved wall of the vast structure, but if he had sigled the words, he would have fumbled through them now—spires, dome, arches, flying buttresses, apse, nave, basilica, choir loft, porch, chapel, rose window, alcove, pillar, altar. They all would have applied to one or more parts of what he was looking at now, and he would have needed more words. Many more words.

As best as Daeman could estimate, the interior of this space was just a little over a mile across and about two thousand feet from the red-glowing floor to the blue-ice apex of the dome. As he'd guessed earlier from the outside, Setebos had covered over the entire crater at the heart of Paris Crater and the vast circle now glowed red, pulsing as if from some huge heartbeat. Daeman had no idea whether this was due to some natural volcanic activity in the crater, some magma rising from miles below where the black hole had once torn at the heart of the Earth, or whether Setebos was somehow summoning and using that heat and light. The rest of the dome glowed in shades of colors Daeman could not describe—from all the varieties of red at the base, through iridescent and then subtle oranges along the periphery of the crater and lower reaches of the dome, veins of red branching up through orange-yellow but-tresses and stalagmites and then the hotter colors fading into the cool glow of the immense blue pillars. The blue-ice walls, columns, tendons, and towers were shot through with pulses of green light and yellow sparks, ordered columns of red pulses moving along hidden channels like surges of electricity, open sparks connecting brachiated sections of the cathedral like dendrites firing.

The shell of the dome was thin enough in places that the last evening light from outside illuminated rose circles on the west side. The highest point on the ceiling was as thin as glass and showed an oval of darken-ing sky and an only slightly blurred view of the emerging stars. Most cu-rious though, low on the inner walls of the dome were hundreds of cross-shaped impressions, each about six feet high. They circled the space, and by leaning out from his rough mezzanine slab, Daeman could see more of these cross-niches below him, indented as if burned into the blue-ice. They seemed to be made of metal and were empty, their steel interiors reflecting the red glow from the center of the crater.

The red-hued floor of the crater itself was not empty. Everywhere rose thorned stalagmites and craggy spires, with some rising all the way to the ceiling—creating neat rows of blue-ice pillars—while others remained freestanding. Nor was the floor of the crater smooth; every-where were smaller craters and raised fumaroles. Gases, steam, and smoke curled out of most of these and Daeman caught the stink of sul-fur on the tepid, overheated air currents. In the center of the red-glowing circle was a raised and raw-rimmed crater ringed with blue-ice stairways and lesser fumaroles. This crater above the crater appeared to be filled almost to the rim with round, white stones, until Daeman real-ized that the stones were the tops of human skulls—tens of thousands of human skulls, most lying beneath the mass that almost filled the crater. This raised crater looked very much like a nest and the impres-sion was reinforced by the thing that filled it—gray brain tissue, convo-luted ridges, multiple pairs of eyes, mouths, and orifices opening and shutting in no unison, a score of huge hands beneath it—these hands occasionally rearranging the huge form's mass on its nest, settling it more comfortably—and he saw other hands, each larger than the room Daeman occupied at Ardis Hall, that had emerged from the brain on stalks and were pulling themselves and their trailing tentacles across the glowing floor. Some of the hands were close enough that Daeman could see a myriad of curved, barbed, black hair spikes or hooks emerg-ing from the ends of those huge fingers. Each barb—some sort of evolved hair?—was longer than the killing knife that Daeman wore on his belt, and the fingers used the filaments to sink into the blue-ice. The hands could climb anywhere, pull themselves along any surface—masonry, ice, or steel—by sinking those black, hooked blades into what-ever lay underhand.

The brain-shape of Setebos itself was much larger than Daeman re-membered from its emergence through the Hole in the sky less than two days before—if that thing had been a hundred feet along its axis, it was now at least a hundred yards long and thirty yards high in the center, where the convoluted tissue was separated by a deep, glowing groove. It filled its nest and whenever it resettled its bulk, there came the crunch of skulls like the snapping and settling of straw.

"Thinketh, such glory shows nor right nor wrong in Him, nor kind, nor cruel: He is strong and Lord. 'Saith, He is terrible: watch His feats in proof!"

Caliban's sibilant hiss slid off the dome in some show of perfect acoustics, echoed off fumaroles and ziggurats, echoed again down the labyrinth of ice tunnels, and seemed to come at Daeman from front, back, and side—a murderous whisper.

As Daeman's eyes adjusted to the red-glow gloom and the scale of the vast hollowed-out dome, he could see smaller objects moving now—scuttling around the base of Setebos' nest, scurrying on all fours up the blue-ice steps to the base of the brain-shape and then trudging back down on hind legs only, carrying large oval pods that glowed with a sick and slick milkiness.

For a minute, Daeman thought they were voynix—he'd seen the remains of dozens of voynix during his long crawl in through the ice-maze, not voynix frozen in the ice as he'd encountered in the outside crevasse, but gutted remains of voynix, a hollowed-out carapace here, a torn ped or lacerated leather hump there, a set of claw-hands lying alone—but now looking through the stream and fog from the fumaroles, he could see that these attending shapes were not voynix. They had the form of Caliban.

Calibani, thought Daeman. He'd encountered them in the Mediterranean Basin with Savi and Harman almost a year earlier, and he realized now the significance of the cross shapes in the wall of the dome. *Recharging cradles*, Savi had called the hollowed-out crosses, and Daeman himself had stumbled across a single naked *calibani* lolling in one such vertical cross, arms spread, and he'd thought it dead until the yellow cat's-eyes had flickered open.

Savi had told them that Prospero and the unmet biosphere entity named Ariel had evolved a strain of humanity into the *calibani* in order to stop the voynix from invading the Mediterranean Basin and other areas Prospero wanted to keep private. Daeman thought now that this was either a lie or Savi's own mistake—the *calibani* weren't evolved from any human strain, but rather cloned from the original and much more terrible Caliban, as Prospero had admitted up on his orbital isle—but at the time, Harman had asked the old Jewish woman why the post-humans had created the voynix in the first place if they—or Prospero—then had to create some other form of monster to contain them.

"Oh, they didn't create the voynix," the old woman had said. *"The voynix came from somewhere else, serving someone else, with their own agenda."*

Daeman did not understand then and he understood less now. These *calibani* he watched scuttling like obscenely pink ants across the crater floor, carrying those milky eggs, were clearly not serving Prospero—they served Setebos.

Then who brought the voynix to Earth? he wondered. *Why are the voynix attacking Ardis and the other old-style human communities if they're not serving Setebos? Who do the voynix serve?*

All Daeman knew for sure right now was that the coming of Setebos to Paris Crater had been a disaster for the voynix here—those not frozen in the rapidly expanding blue-ice had been caught and shelled like tasty crabs. *Shelled by whom? Or by what?* Two answers came to mind, and neither one was reassuring—the voynix had been crunched open either by the teeth and claws of the *calibani* or by Setebos' own hands.

Daeman realized now that what he'd thought were gray-pink ridges running along the floor of the crater were actually more arm-stalks emanating from Setebos. The fleshy stalks disappeared into openings in the dome wall and . . .

Daeman whirled around, raising his crossbow, finger on the trigger. There had been a sliding sound in the ice tunnel behind him. *One of Setebos' hands, three times my size, squeezing through the tunnel behind me.*

Daeman crouched there waiting, arms finally shaking from holding the weight of the raised crossbow, but no silent hand emerged. But the corridor of ice hissed and slithered to echoed noises.

The hands are in the walls and probably outside in the crevasses by now, thought Daeman, trying to slow his hammering heart. *It's dark in the tunnels and outside. What do I do if I run into one or more of the hands in there?* He'd seen the pulsing feeding orifice in the palms of the hands below— a group of *calibani* had been feeding them large chunks of raw red meat, either voynix or human.

Finally he lay back on his belly on the blue-ice balcony, feeling the cold of the ice—a substance he now believed to be living tissue extruded by Setebos himself—flow up through his thermskin.

I can get out of here now. I've seen enough.

Lying there on his belly, the silly crossbow ahead of him, keeping his head down as a group of *calibani* scuttled across the crater floor on all fours not a hundred yards below and in front of him, Daeman waited for strength to return to his cowardly arms and legs so he could get the hell out of this unholy cathedral.

I need to report back to Ardis, came the reasonable voice in his mind. *I've done all I can here.*

No, you haven't, answered the honest part of Daeman's mind—the part that would get him killed someday. *You have to see what those slick, gray egg shapes are.*

The *calibani* had stowed some of those gray pods in a steaming fumarole not a hundred yards from him, below and to the right of his low mezzanine.

I can't possibly climb down there. It's too far.

Liar. It's less than a hundred feet. You still have most of your rope and the spikes. And the ice hammers. Then it would just be a fast sprint out to look at the pod-shapes—grab one to bring back if you can—and then back to your balcony here and out.

That's crazy. I'd be exposed the whole time I was on the crater floor. Those calibani *were between me and that nest. If I'd been out there when they appeared, they would have grabbed me. Eaten me there or taken me to Setebos.*

They're gone now. Now is your chance. Get down there now.

"No," said Daeman, realizing that he'd whispered the terrified syllable aloud.

But a minute later he was driving a spike into the blue-ice floor of his balcony, tying the rope securely around it, setting the crossbow over his shoulder next to his pack, and beginning the laborious process of lowering himself to the crater floor.

This is good. You're showing some courage for a change and . . .

Shut the fuck up, Daeman ordered that brave, totally stupid part of his mind.

His mind obeyed.

"Conceiveth all things will continue thus, and we shall have to live in fear of Him," came the hymn-chant-hiss of Caliban—not from the *calibani,* Daeman was sure, but from Caliban himself. The original monster must be somewhere here in the dome, perhaps on the other side of Setebos and the crater nest.

"Thinketh this, that some strange day, Setebos, Lord, He who dances on dark nights, shall come to us like tongue to eye, like teeth to throat—or suppose, grow into it, as grub grow butterflies: else, here are we, and there is He, and nowhere help at all."

Daeman continued sliding down the slippery rope.

39

The first thing Dr. Thomas Hockenberry, Ph.D., had to do after quantum teleporting into Ilium was find an alley he could puke in.

That wasn't hard, even in his inebriated state, since the ex-scholic had spent almost ten years in and around Troy and he'd QT'd back to a minor street off the square near Hector and Paris's apartments where he'd been a thousand times. Luckily, it was night in Ilium, the shops, market stalls, and little restaurants around the square were closed and shuttered, and no spearman or night guard noticed his silent arrival. Still, he needed an alley and found it fast, was sick until the dry heaves passed, and then he needed an even darker and less traveled alley. Luckily the lanes were many and narrow near the dead Paris's palace—now Helen's home and the temporary palace of Priam—and Hockenberry quickly sought out the darkest and narrowest lane, barely four feet across, where he curled up on some straw, wrapped the blanket he'd brought from his cubby on the *Queen Mab* around him, and slept heavily.

He awoke a little after dawn, aching, surly, profoundly hungover, and acutely aware of both the noise in the square near the palace and the fact that he'd brought the wrong clothes from the *Queen Mab*; he was dressed in a soft gray cotton jumpsuit and zero-g slippers, something the moravecs had thought suitable for a Twenty-first Century man. The outfit didn't blend in too well with the robes, leather greaves, sandals, tunics, togas, capes, furs, bronze armor, and rough homespun seen in Ilium.

When he did get to the public square—brushing off the worst of the alley filth even while noticing the real difference between the 1.28-g acceleration load he'd been living under and the single gravity of Earth, he felt bouncy and strong now despite his hangover—Hockenberry was surprised to see how *few* people were in the square. Just after dawn was the busiest time in this market, but most of the stalls were attended only by their owners, tables at the outdoor eating establishments were all but empty, and the only people at the far side of the square, in front of Paris's, Helen's, and now Priam's palace, were the few guards by the doors and gates.

He decided that proper clothes should precede even breakfast, so he stepped into the shadows under the loggia and began bartering with a one-eyed, one-toothed ancient in a red-rag turban. This old man had the largest cart with the widest variety of goods—mostly discards or rags stolen from fresh corpses—but he haggled like a dragon loath to part with his gold. Hockenberry's pockets were empty, so all he had to bargain with were the ship clothes and the blanket he'd brought along, but these were exotic enough—he had to tell the old man that he'd come all the way from Persia—that he ended up with a toga, high-lace sandals, some unlucky commander's fine red wool cape, a regular tunic and skirt, and under linens—Hockenberry chose the cleanest ones in the bin, and when he couldn't manage clean, he settled for louse-free. He left the plaza with a broad leather belt that held a sword that had seen much action but was still sharp, and two knives, one that he'd carry tucked into the belt and the other that slipped into a specially sewn fold inside the red cape. He also received a handful of coins. One glance back at the old man's gaping, one-toothed grin let Hockenberry know that the geezer had made out well, that the unusual jumpsuit would probably trade for a horse or gold shield or better. *Ah, well.*

Hockenberry hadn't asked the old man or the few other drowsy merchants what was going on—why the mostly empty square, why the absence of soldiers and families, why the strange quiet over the city—but he knew he'd find out soon enough.

When he'd been changing clothes behind the seller's cart, the old man and two of his neighbors had offered him gold for his QT medallion, the fat man behind the fruit cart topping the bidding at 200 weight of gold and 500 silver Thracian coins, but Hockenberry had said no, glad that he'd taken possession of the sword and two daggers before stripping.

Now, after spending some of his new coins for a stand-up breakfast of fresh bread, dried fish, some cheese, and a hot-tea sort of substance infinitely less satisfying than coffee, he stepped back into the shadows and looked at Helen's palace across the way.

He could QT into her private chambers. He'd certainly done it before. *And if she's there, then what?*

A fast thrust with his sword and then QT away again, the perfect invisible assassin? But who was to say that the guards wouldn't see him? For the ten thousandth time in the last nine months, Hockenberry mourned the loss of his morphing bracelet—the gods' essential basic for all of their scholics, allowing them to shift quantum probability to the point that Hockenberry, Nightenhelser, of any of the other ill-fated scholics could instantly displace any man or woman in or around Ilium, not only taking their form and clothing, but truly replacing them on the quantum level of things. This had allowed even the massive Nightenhelser to morph into a boy a third his weight without defying the rule that one of the scientific-oriented scholics years ago had described to Hockenberry as the conservation of mass.

Well, Hockenberry had no morphing capability now—the morphing bracelet had been left behind on Olympos along with his taser baton, shotgun microphone, and impact armor—but he still had the QT medallion.

Now he touched that gold circle against his chest and . . . hesitated. What *would* he do when he faced Helen of Troy? Hockenberry had no idea. He'd never killed anyone—much less the most beautiful woman he'd ever made love to, the most beautiful woman he'd ever seen, a rival to the immortal goddess Aphrodite—so he hesitated.

There was a commotion toward the Scaean Gate. He walked that way, nibbling on the last of his bread, a newly purchased goatskin of wine slung over his shoulder, thinking about the situation here in Ilium.

I've been gone more than two weeks. On the night I left—on the night Helen tried to kill me—it appeared that the Achaeans were going to overrun the city.

Certainly Troy and its few allied gods and goddesses—Apollo, Ares, Aphrodite, lesser deities—didn't seem capable of defending the city against the determined attack by Agamemnon's armies supported by Athena, Hera, Poseidon, and the rest.

Hockenberry had seen enough of this war to know that nothing was certain. Of course, that had been Homer's vision—the events here in this real past, on this real Earth, in and around this real Troy, had usually paralleled, if not always directly followed, Homer's great tale. Now, with events diverging so dramatically in the past months—thanks, he knew, to the meddling of one Thomas Hockenberry—all bets were off. So he hurried to follow the tail end of crowds that obviously were headed straight toward the main city gates at first light.

He found her on the wall above the Scaean Gate, with the rest of the royal family and a bunch of dignitaries all crowded onto the wide reviewing platform where he'd watched her match faces to names during the gathering of the Achaean army for the Trojans ten years earlier. That day, she'd whispered the names of the various Greek heroes to Priam, Hecuba, Paris, Hector, and the others. Today Hecuba and Paris were dead—along with so many thousand others—but Helen still stood at Priam's right, along with Andromache. The old king had been standing for the review of the armies ten years ago, but now he was half-reclining in the throne-cum-litter in which he was carried these days. Priam looked a lot more than ten years older than the vital king Hockenberry had watched here a mere decade ago—the old man was a shrunken, wizened caricature of powerful Priam.

But today the mummy seemed happy enough.

"Until this day I had pitied me," cried Priam, addressing the dignitaries around him and a few hundred royal guardsmen on the stairs and plain below them. There was no army in sight—Thicket Ridge and the approaches to Ilium were clear of soldiers—but by straining and following Helen's gaze, Hockenberry could see a huge mob almost two miles away, where the Greek black ships were drawn up. It looked as if the Trojan army had surrounded the Achaeans, overrun their moat and horse-staked trenches, and reduced the miles of Achaean camps to a rough semicircle hardly more than a few hundred yards across. If this was so, the Greeks had their backs to the sea and were surrounded by a powerful Trojan force just waiting to pounce.

"I pitied me," repeated Priam, his cracked voice growing stronger, "and asked too many of you to pity me as well. Since my queen's death by the hands of the gods, I have been but a harrowed, broken old man marked for doom . . . worse than old, past the threshold of decrepitude . . . certain that Father Zeus had singled me out to be wasted by a terrible fate.

"In the last ten years, I had seen too many of my sons laid low and I was certain that Hector would join them in the halls of Hades even before his father's spirit traveled there. I was prepared to watch my daughters dragged away, my treasure vaults looted, the Paladion stolen from Athena's temple, and helpless babies hurled from our parapets to the red-blooded end of barbarous war.

"A month ago, friends and family, warriors and wives, I waited to watch my sons' wives be hauled off by the Argives' bloody hands, Helen struck down by murderous Menelaus, my daughter Cassandra raped, so that I would be willing—nay, eager—to greet the Argive dogs before my doors, urge them to eat me raw, after the spear of Achilles or Agamemnon or crafty Odysseus or unforgiving Ajax or terrible Menelaus or powerful Diomedes would bring me down. Splitting me with a spear, wrenching and tearing my old life out of my old body, feeding my guts to my own dogs—yes, those faithful hounds who guarded my gates and chamber door—letting these suddenly rabid friends lap their master's blood and eat their master's heart in front of everyone.

"Yes, this was my lament ten months ago, two weeks ago . . . but look at the world born anew this morning, my beloved Trojans. Zeus took away all the gods—those who wished to save us, those who wished to destroy us. The Father of the Gods struck down his own Hera in a blast of his thunder. Mighty Zeus has burned the Argives' black ships and ordered all immortals to return to Olympos to face his punishment for disobedience. With the gods no longer filling the days and nights with fire and noise, my son Hector led our troops to victory after victory. Without Achilles to stop the noble Hector, the Achaean pigs have been driven back to the burned hulls of their black ships, their southern camps shredded, their northern camps put to the torch. And now they are bound in tight from the west by Hector and our Ilium-born, by Aeneas and his Dardanians, by Antenor's two surviving sons, Acamas and Archelochus.

"To the south, they are shut off from retreat by the shining sons of Lycaon and our faithful allies from Zelea, under the foot of Ida where Zeus oft makes his throne.

"To the north, the Greeks are stymied by Adrestus and Amphius, trim in their linen corsets, leading the Apaesians and the Adestrians, marvelous in their new-acquired gold and bronze, wrenched from the dead Achaeans who fell in their panicked flight.

"Our beloved Hippothous and Pylaeus, who survived the ten years of carnage and were ready to die this month with us, with their Trojan friends and brothers, but instead, this day, who lead their dark-skinned

Plasgian warriors alongside the captains of Abydos and gleaming Arisbe. Instead of ignoble death and defeat this day, our sons and allies are but hours away from seeing the head of our enemy, Agamemnon, lifted high on a spike, while our Thracians and Trojans and Pelasgians and Cicones and Paeonians and Paphlagonians and Halizonians have lived to watch the end of this long war at last, and soon will be raking up the gold of defeated Argives, soon will be sweeping up the well-earned armor of Agamemnon and his men. This day, unable to flee to their black ships, all the Greek kings who came to kill and loot will be killed and looted.

"This day, all the gods willing—and Zeus has already spoken it into being—let my friends and family—and our foes—witness our final victory. Let us see the end to this war. Let us prepare now—before this beginning day ends—to welcome home Hector and Deiphobus in a victory celebration that will last a week—no, a month!—a party of celebration and deliverance that will let your faithful servant Priam of Ilium die a happy man!"

So spake Priam, King of Ilium, Father of Hector, and Hockenberry couldn't believe his ears.

Helen slipped away from the side of Andromache and the other women, then descended the wide steps back down to the city, with only Andromache's warrior slave-woman, Hypsipyle, at her side. Hockenberry hid behind the broad back of an imperial spearman until Helen was out of sight on the steps, and then he followed.

The two women turned down a narrow alley almost in the shadow of the west wall, then east up an even more narrow lane, and Hockenberry knew where they were going. Months ago, during his jealous phase after Helen had quit seeing him, he'd trailed Andromache and her here, discovering their secret. This was where Hector's wife, Andromache, kept her secret apartment where Hypsipyle and another nurse watched over Andromache's son, Astyanax. Not even Hector knew that his son was alive, that the baby's murder by the hands of Aphrodite and Athena was a ruse by the few Trojan Women to end the war between the Argives and Trojans, turning Hector's wrath toward the gods themselves.

Well, Hockenberry thought now, staying back at the head of the smaller alley so the two women would not notice they were being followed, that ruse had worked wonderfully well. But now the war with the gods was over and it looked as if the Trojan War was in its final hour.

Hockenberry didn't want them to reach the apartment itself; there had been male Cicilian guards there as well. Now he bent and lifted a heavy, smooth, oval stone, just the size of his palm, and curled his fist around it.

Am I really going to kill Helen? He had no answer to that. Not yet.

Helen and Hypsipyle were pausing at the gate that led into the courtyard to the secret house when Hockenberry moved up quietly behind them and tapped the big Lesbos slave-woman on her brawny shoulder.

Hypsipyle whirled.

Hockenberry hit her in the jaw with a roundhouse uppercut. Even with the heavy rock in his fist, the big woman's bony jaw almost broke his fingers. But Hypsipyle went backward like a toppled statue, her head striking the courtyard door on the way down. She stayed down, clearly unconscious, her big jaw looking broken.

Great, thought Hockenberry, *after ten years in the Trojan War, you finally joined the fighting—by suckerpunching a woman.*

Helen stepped back, the little hidden dagger that had once found Hockenberry's heart already sliding down from her sleeve into her right hand. Hockenberry moved fast, clutching Helen's wrist, forcing her hand and arm back against the rough-hewn door, and—his bleeding, bruised right hand barely working—pulling his own long knife from his belt and thrusting the point of it into the softness under her chin. She dropped her knife.

"Hock-en-bear-eeee," she said, her head back but his knife drawing blood already.

He hesitated. His right arm was shaking. If he was going to do this, he needed to do it quickly, before the bitch began to speak. She had betrayed him, stabbed him in the heart and left him for dead, but she had also been the most amazing lover he'd ever had.

"You *are* a god," whispered Helen. Her eyes were wide, but she showed no fear.

"Not a god," gritted Hockenberry. "Just a cat. You took one of my lives. I'd already been given one extra. I must have seven left."

Despite the knife point cutting into her underjaw, Helen laughed. "A cat having nine lives. I like that conceit. You always did have a way with words . . . for a foreigner."

Kill her or not, but decide now . . . this is absurd, thought Hockenberry.

He pulled the point of the blade away from her throat, but before Helen of Troy could move or speak, he grabbed a fistful of her black hair in his left hand, held the dagger to her ribs, and pulled her down the alley with him, away from Andromache's apartment.

They'd come full circle—back to the abandoned tower overlooking the Scaean Gate wall where he'd discovered Menelaus and Helen hiding, where Helen had stabbed him after he'd QT'd her husband to Agamemnon's camp. Hockenberry shoved Helen up the narrow, winding staircase all the way to the top, to the mostly open level now atop the tower that had been shattered by the gods' bombing months ago.

He pushed her toward the open edge, but out of view of anyone on the wall below. "Strip," he said.

Helen brushed the hair out of her eyes. "Are you going to rape me before you throw me over the edge, Hock-en-bear-eeee?"

"Strip."

He stood back with his knife ready as Helen slipped out of her few layers of silky garments. This morning was warmer than the day on which he'd left—the wintry day when she'd stabbed him—but the breeze up this high was still cool enough to cause Helen's nipples to stand on end and to bring out goosebumps on her pale arms and belly. As she let each layer fall away, he told her to kick them over to him. Watching her carefully, he felt through the soft robes and silky undershift. No other hidden daggers.

She stood there in the morning light, legs slightly apart, not covering her breasts or pubic region with her hands but just letting her arms hang naturally at her sides. Her head was high and there was the slightest line of blood visible under her chin. Her gaze seemed to mix calm defiance with a mild curiosity about what was going to happen next. Even now, filled with fury as he was, he saw how she could have set these hundreds of thousands of men to killing one another. And it was a revelation to him that he could be so angry—close-to-killing angry—and still feel sexual desire for a woman. After the seventeen days in the 1.28-Earth-gravity acceleration field, he felt strong here on Earth, muscular, powerful. He knew that he could lift this beautiful woman in one arm and carry her wherever he wanted to, do whatever he wanted for as long as he wanted.

Hockenberry threw her clothes back to her. "Get dressed."

She watched him warily as she picked up her soft garments. From the wall and Scaean Gate below came shouts, applause, and the banging of wooden spear shafts on bronze-and-leather shields as Priam ended his speech.

"Tell me what's happened in the seventeen days I've been gone," he said gruffly.

"That's all you've come back for, Hock-en-bear-eeee? To ask me about recent events?" She was securing the low bodice across her white breasts.

He gestured her to the fallen piece of stone and when she'd taken a seat, he found another slab for himself about six feet away. Even with a knife in his hand, Hockenberry did not want to get too close to her.

"Tell me about the last weeks since I left," he said again.

"Don't you want to know why I stabbed you?"

"I know," Hockenberry said tiredly. "You'd had me QT Menelaus out of the city but you decided not to follow him. If I was dead, and the

Achaeans overran the city—which you were sure they were going to do—you could always tell Menelaus I refused to take you with me. Or something like that. But he would have killed you anyway, Helen. Men—even Menelaus, who's not the sharpest sword in the armory—can rationalize being betrayed once. Not twice."

"Yes, he would have killed me. But I hurt you, Hock-en-bear-eeee, so that *I* would have no choice . . . so that I *had* to stay in Ilium."

"Why?" This didn't make any sense to the former scholic. And his head hurt.

"When Menelaus found me that day, I realized that I was happy to go with him. Happy almost to be killed by him, if that had been his pleasure. My years here in Ilium as a harlot, as Paris's false wife, as the reason for all this death, had made me mean in every sense of the word. Base, brittle, empty inside—common."

You're many things, Helen of Troy, he was tempted to say, *but common is not one of them.*

"But with Paris dead," continued Helen, "I had no husband, no master, for the first time since I was a young girl. My first reaction of being glad to see Menelaus here in Ilium that day, I soon recognized as a slave's happiness at seeing his chains and shackles again. By the time you joined us here in this very tower that night, all I wanted to do was stay in Ilium, alone, not as Helen, wife of Menelaus, not as Helen, wife of Paris, but just as . . . Helen."

"That doesn't explain why you stabbed me," said Hockenberry. "You could have just told me you were staying after I delivered Menelaus to his brother's camp. Or you could have asked me to transport you anywhere in the world—I would have obeyed."

"That is the real reason I tried to kill you," Helen said softly.

Hockenberry could only frown at her.

"That day, I decided to wed my fate not to any man's, but to the city's . . . to Ilium," she said. "And I knew that as long as you were here and alive, I could make you use your magic to carry me anywhere . . . to safety . . . even as Agamemnon and Menelaus entered the city and put it to flames."

Hockenberry thought about this for a long minute. It made no sense. He knew it never would. He set it aside. "Tell me about the last couple of weeks and what has happened," he said for the third time.

"The days after I left you here for dead were dark ones for the city," said Helen. "Agamemnon's attack almost overwhelmed us that very night. Hector had been sulking in his apartments since before the Amazons went out to their doom. After the Hole had closed and it was certain that it wasn't opening again, Hector stayed in his apartment, his thoughts his own, closed even to Andromache—I know she considered telling him the secret that their son still lived, but held off, not knowing how to explain the deception in any way that would not cause her own life to be forfeit—and during the next days' battles, Agamemnon's armies and their supporting gods killed many Trojans. Only the city's Protector—Phoebus Apollo, Lord of the Silver Bow—firing his always unerring arrows into the Argive multitudes kept us from being overrun and destroyed on those dark days before Hector rejoined the fray.

"As it was, Hock-en-bear-eeee, the Argives, under Diomedes, did breach our walls at their lowest point—where the wild fig tree stands. Three times before in the ten years that did proceed our ill-fated war with the gods had the Argives tried that same spot, our weakness, perhaps revealed to them by some skilled prophet, but three times before, Hector, Paris, and our champions had beat them back—Great and Little Ajax in their attempts, then Atreus' sons, the third time Diomedes himself—but this time, four days after I tried to kill you and left your body here for the carrion birds, Diomedes led his warriors from Argos on the fourth assault on the point where the wild fig tree stands. Even while Agamemnon's ladders were rising to the western wall and battering rams the size of great trees were splintering the Scaean Gate in its huge hinges, Diomedes attacked the low point on our wall by stealth and strength, and by sunset that fourth day, the Argives were inside the wall.

"Only the courage of Deiphobus, Hector's brother, Priam's other son, the man who has been chosen by the royal family to be my next husband—only Deiphobus saved the city through his courage. Seeing the threat when others were despairing about Agamemnon's ladders and rams, Deiphobus swept up survivors of his old battalion, and Helenus', and the captain named Asisu, son of Hyrtacus, and a few hundred of Aeneas' fleeing men, and with the combat veteran Asteropaeus at his side, Deiphobus formed a counterattack through the overrun city streets, turning the nearby marketplace into a second line. In terrible battle with the winning Diomedes, Deiphobus fought godlike—parrying even Athena's spearcast, for the gods were battling here with as much violence as the men—more!

"At dawn that day, the Argive line was stopped temporarily—our wall by the wild fig tree breached, a dozen city blocks burned and occupied by the raging Argives, Agamemnon's hordes still trying to scale our western and northern walls, the great Scaean Gate hanging by splinters and holding only by its iron bands—and that was the morning that Hector announced to Priam and the other despairing royals that he would re-enter the battle."

"And did he?" asked Hockenberry.

Helen laughed. "*Did* he? Never has there been such a glorious *aristeia*, Hock-en-bear-eeee. On the first day of his wrath, Hector—protected by Apollo and Aphrodite from Athena's and Hera's bolts—met Diomedes in a fair fight and killed him, casting his finest spear all the way through the son of Tydeus and sending his Argus' fighters fleeing. By sunset that day, the city was whole again and our masons were building up the wall by the old fig tree, making it as tall as the wall near the Scaean Gate."

"Diomedes dead?" said Hockenberry. He was shocked. Ten years watching the fighting here and the scholic had begun to think that Diomedes was as invulnerable as Achilles or one of the gods. In Homer's *Iliad*, Diomedes' exploits—his excursus, his glorious single-combat or *aristeia*—had filled Book 5 and the beginning of Book 6, second only in length and ferocity in Homer's tale to that of Achilles' unleashed wrath in Books 20–22 . . . a wrath that was never to be realized here now, thanks to Hockenberry's own tampering with events.

"Diomedes is dead," repeated Hockenberry, stunned.

"And Ajax as well," said Helen. "For on the next day, Hector and Ajax met again—you remember that they had once fought in single combat but parted friends, so valiant was each of their struggles. But this time, Hector cut down the son of Telamon, using his sword to beat down the big man's huge, rectangular shield, bending its metal back on itself, and when Great Ajax cried out 'Mercy! Show mercy, son of Priam!,' Hector showed him none, but drove his sword through the hero's spine and heart, sending him down to Hades before the sun had risen a hand's breadth above the horizon that morning. Ajax's men, those famed fighters from Salamis, wept and rent their clothes in mourning that day, but they also fell back in confusion, crashing into Agamemnon and Menelaus' armies as they surged over Thicket Ridge—you know that ridge just beyond the city to the west that the gods call the Amazon Myrine's mounded tomb?"

"I know it," said Hockenberry.

"Well, this is where the dead Ajax's fleeing army crashed into the attacking men from Agamemnon and Menelaus' corps. It was confusion. Pure confusion.

"And into the melee swept Hector, leading his Trojan and Allied captains—Deiphobus now following his brother, Acamas and old Pirous leading the Thracians close behind, Mesthles and Antiphus' son driving the Maeonians on with shouts—all the remaining and surviving Trojan heroes, thought beaten just two days before, were part of that charge. I stood on the wall just below here that morning, Hock-en-bear-eeee, and for three hours none of us—Trojan women, old Priam, no longer able to walk but who had been carried there in his litter, we wives and daughters and mothers and sisters and the boys and old men—none of us could see a thing for three hours, so great was the dust cloud kicked up by the thousands of warriors and hundreds of chariots. Sometimes volleys of arrows from one side or the other would shield the sun.

"But when the dust settled and the gods retreated to Olympos after that morning's fighting, Menelaus had joined Diomedes and Ajax in the House of Death, and . . ."

"Menelaus is dead? Your husband is dead?" said Hockenberry. Again, he was deeply shocked. These men had fought and prevailed for ten years against each other, another ten months against the gods.

"Didn't I just say that he was?" asked Helen, irritated at being interrupted. "Hector didn't kill him. He was brought down by an arrow in the air, an arrow shot by dead Pandarus' son, young Palmys, Lycaon's grandson, using the same god-blessed bow that Pandarus had used to wound Menelaus in the hip just a year ago. But this time, there was no invisible Athena to flick aside the shaft, and Menelaus received the arrow through the eye-circle in his helmet and it passed through his brain and out the back of the bronze head-sheath."

"Little Palmys?" said Hockenberry, aware that he was repeating names like an idiot. "He can't be more than twelve years old . . ."

"Not yet eleven," said Helen with a smile. "But the boy used a man's bow—his dead father's, Pandarus, brought low by Diomedes a year ago—and the arrow settled all my husband's debts and resolved all our marital doubts. I have Menelaus' blood-splashed helmet in my rooms at the palace if you would like to see it—the boy Palmys kept his shield."

"My God," said Hockenberry. "Diomedes, Big Ajax, and Menelaus dead in a single twenty-four-hour period. No wonder you've driven the Argives back to their ships."

"No," said Helen, "the day might well still have gone to the Achaeans if Zeus had not appeared."

"Zeus!"

"Zeus," said Helen. "On the day that had begun with glorious victory, the gods and goddesses on the side of the Argives were so infuriated by the deaths of their champions that Hera and Athena alone murdered a thousand of our valiant Trojans with their fiery bolts. Poseidon, the old Earth-Shaker himself, bellowed so in anger that a score of strong buildings in Ilium crashed to the ground. Archers tumbled from our walls like falling leaves. Priam was thrown from his throne-litter.

"All our gains that day were lost in minutes—Hector falling back, still fighting, his men falling around him, Deiphobus wounded in the leg, finally having to be carried by his brother even while our Trojan men beat a retreat back to Thicket Ridge, then from Thicket Ridge to and through the Scaean Gates.

"We women actually rushed down to help set the great bar across the splintered gates, so wild was the fighting—scores of raging Argives had come through into the city with our retreating heroes—and again Poseidon shook the earth, knocking everyone to their knees even as Athena neutralized Apollo in their sky battles, their chariots whirling and flashing through the sky, while Hera herself cast explosive bolts of energy at our walls.

"Then Zeus appeared in the east. Larger and more impressive than any living mortal has ever seen . . ."

"More impressive than the day he appeared as a face in the atomic mushroom cloud?" asked Hockenberry.

Helen laughed. "*Much* more impressive, my Hock-en-bear-eeee. This Zeus was a colossus, his legs rising higher than Mount Ida's snowy summit in the east, his huge chest above the clouds, his giant brow so high above us as to be almost invisible, taller than the tops of the tallest stratocumulus piled high, one upon another, on a summer day before a storm."

"Whoa," said Hockenberry, trying to imagine it. He'd once tussled with Zeus—well, not tussled exactly, more just a sort of general scuttling away from him during an earthquake on Olympos, culminating in sliding between the Lord of All Gods' legs to grab the dropped QT medallion so he could teleport away right at the beginning of the human-god war—and the Father of the Gods had been wildly impressive when he was just his usual fifteen feet tall. He tried to imagine this ten-mile-high colossus. "Go on," he said.

"So when this giant Zeus appeared, the armies stopped in their tracks, froze like statues, swords raised, spears poised back, shields high—even the chariots of the gods froze in the sky, Athena and Phoebus Apollo as motionless as all the thousands of mortals below—and Zeus thundered forth—I cannot imitate his voice, Hock-en-bear-eeee, for it was all thunder and all earthquake and volcanoes erupting at once— but Zeus thundered—*UNCONTROLLABLE HERA—YOU AND YOUR TREACHERY YET AGAIN!—I WOULD BE SLEEPING YET HAD NOT YOUR CRIPPLED SON AND A MORTAL AWAKENED ME. HOW DARE YOU BETRAY ME WITH YOUR WARM EMBRACE, SEDUCE ME BLIND, SO THAT YOU CAN HAVE YOUR WAY, PURSUE YOUR WILL OF DESTROYING TROY IN DEFIANCE OF YOUR LORD'S COMMAND!*"

"Your crippled son and a mortal?" repeated Hockenberry. The crippled son would be Hephaestus, god of fire. The mortal?

"That's what he bellowed," said Helen, rubbing her pale neck as if her imitation of the bass earthquake-rumble had hurt her throat.

"And then?" prompted Hockenberry.

"And then, before Hera could speak in her own defense, before any of the gods could move, Zeus, the King of the Black Cloud, struck her down with a thunderbolt. It must have killed her, immortal as we all thought she was."

"The gods have a way of returning after they are 'killed,' " muttered Hockenberry, thinking of the huge healing tanks and their roiling blue worms up in the great, white building on Olympos, tanks tended by the giant insectoid Healer.

"Yes, we all know that," Helen said in a disgusted tone. "Didn't our own Hector kill Ares half a dozen times in the past eight months? Only to face him again a few days later? But this was different, Hock-en-bear-eeee."

"How so?"

"Zeus's lighting bolt *destroyed* Hera—threw bits of her golden chariot for miles, raining melted gold and steel on the rooftops of Troy. And gibbets of the goddess herself fell in a swath from the ocean to dead Paris's palace—scorched shards of pink flesh, which none of us were brave enough to touch, but which simmered and smoked for days."

"Jesus," whispered Hockenberry.

"And then the mighty Zeus struck down Poseidon, opening a great yawning pit under the fleeing Sea God and dropping him into it, screaming. The screams echoed for hours, until all mortals—Argives and Trojans alike—wept from the sound."

"Did Zeus say anything when he opened this pit?"

"Yes," said Helen, "he cried—*I AM ZEUS WHO DRIVES THE STORM CLOUDS, SON OF KRONOS, FATHER OF MEN AND GODS, MASTER OF PROBABILITY SPACE BEFORE YOU WERE CHANGED FROM YOUR PUNY POST-HUMAN FORMS! I WAS THE MASTER AND KEEPER OF SETEBOS BEFORE YOU DARED TO DREAM OF BEING IMMORTALS! YOU, POSEIDON, SHAKER OF THE EARTH, MY BETRAYER, DO YOU THINK I DON'T KNOW THAT YOU PLOTTED WITH MY OX-EYED QUEEN FOR MY OVERTHROW? I BANISH YOU TO TARTARUS, DEEP BENEATH HADES ITSELF, I SEND YOU PLUNGING DOWN TO THE PIT OF EARTH AND SEA WHERE KRONOS AND IAPETOS MAKE THEIR BEDS OF PAIN, WHERE NOT A RAY OF THE SUN CAN WARM THEIR HEARTS, DOWN TO THE DEPTHS OF TARTARUS WALLED ALL AROUND BY THE BLACK-HOLED ABYSS ITSELF!*"

Hockenberry waited while Helen paused to clear her throat again.

"Do you have any water, Hock-en-bear-eeee?"

He handed her the wineskin he'd filled with water from the plaza fountain and waited in silence while she drank.

"And this is what Zeus spoke as he opened up a pit beneath Poseidon and sent the Shaker of the Earth screaming into Tartarus. Those soldiers on the wall who saw into the pit could not speak for days, only mumble or scream."

Hockenberry waited.

"And then the Father of the Gods ordered all the other gods back to Olympos to face their punishment—you will pardon me, Hock-en-bear-eeee, if I do not try to imitate Zeus's bellow—and in an instant the flying chariots were gone, the Lord of the Silver Bow was gone, Athena was gone, red-eyed Hades was gone, that bitch Aphrodite was gone, blood-thirsty Ares was gone—all our Pantheon disappeared, QTing back to Olympos like guilty children waiting for their displeased father to use the rod on them."

"Did Zeus disappear then, too?" asked Hockenberry.

"Oh, no, the Son of Kronos had just begun to play. His towering form strode over Ilium and walked across the miles between here and the shore like Astyanax playing in his sandbox, striding over his toy soldiers. Hundreds of Trojans and Argives died under the giant feet of Zeus that day, Hock-en-bear-eeee, and when he reached Agamemnon's camp, Zeus reached out his palm and burned all the the hundreds of black ships pulled up on the sand there. And for those Argive ships still at anchor, or the convoy pulling in from Lemnos bringing wine sent across by Euneus, Jason's son, carrying gifts to Atrides Agamemnon and the dead Menelaus, Zeus closed his flaming hand into a fist and a great wave rose up, dashing the Lemnos ships and the anchored Argive ships ashore— again like toys, like Astyanax splashing in his bath, sinking his slave-carved balsawood toy boats in petulance divine."

"Holy God," whispered Hockenberry.

"Yes, exactly," said Helen. "And then Zeus disappeared in a crack of the loudest thunder yet, louder even than his voice that had deafened hundreds, and the wind howled into the place where giant Zeus had been, ripping up the Achaean tents and swirling them thousands of feet into the air, swirling strong Trojan stallions from their stalls and over our highest walls."

Hockenberry looked to the west where the armies of Troy had surrounded the diminished army of the Argives. "That was almost two weeks ago. Have the gods returned at all? Any of them? Zeus?"

"No, Hock-en-bear-eeee. We have seen no immortals since that day."

"But that was two weeks ago," said Hockenberry. "Why has it taken so long for Hector to besiege the Argive army? Surely with the deaths of Diomedes, Big Ajax, and Menelaus, the Achaeans must have been demoralized."

"They were," agreed Helen. "But both sides were in shock. Many of us could not hear for days. As I said, those on the wall or those Argives too close to the opening pit of Tartarus were little more than drooling idiots for a week. A truce was called without either side declaring it. We gathered our dead—for we had suffered terribly during Agamemnon's assaults, you remember—and for almost a week, corpse fires burned both here in the city and along the miles of shore where the terrified Argives still had their camps. Then, in the second week, when Agamemnon ordered men to the forests at the base of Mount Ida to begin felling trees—to make new ships, of course—Hector began the assault. The fighting has been slow and heavy work. With their backs to the sea and no ships for their flight, the Argives fight like cornered rats. But this morning, you see, the few thousands left are encircled there at the edge of the water and today Hector will unleash our final assault. Today ends the Trojan War, with Ilium still standing, Hector the hero of all heroes, and Helen free."

For a while the man and woman just sat on their respective great stones and stared out to the west, where sunlight glinted on armor and spears and where horns were sounding.

Finally Helen said, "What will you do with me now, Hock-en-bear-eeee?"

He blinked, looked at the knife still in his hand, and set it in his belt. "You can go," he said.

Helen looked at his face but she did not move.

"*Go!*" said Hockenberry.

She left slowly. The sound of her slippers came up the circular staircase—he remembered the same soft sound from when he lay dying here two and a half weeks ago.

Where do I go now?

Trained as a scholic in his second life, he had the loyal urge to report these variances from the *Iliad* to the Muse, and thence to all the gods. This thought made him smile. How many of the gods still existed in that other universe where Olympus Mons on Mars had been turned into Olympos? How extensive had Zeus's wrath really been? Had there been a genocidal deicide up there? He might never know. He didn't have the courage to quantum teleport to Olympos again.

Hockenberry touched the QT medallion under his tunic. Back to the ship? He wanted to see the Earth—*his* Earth, even one three thousand years or so in his future—and he wanted to be with the moravecs and Odysseus when they saw it. He had no duty or role here in this Ilium-universe now.

He brought the QT medallion out and ran his hand over the heavy gold.

Not back to the *Queen Mab*. Not yet. He might not be a scholic any longer—the gods may have abandoned him just as he had betrayed them—but he was still a *scholar*. Decades of teaching the *Iliad*, all those memories of wonderful dusty classrooms and very young college students, all those faces—pale, pimply, healthy, tanned, eager, indifferent, inspired, insipid—came flowing back now, filling in the gaps. How could he not see the last act in this new and absurdly revised version?

Twisting the medallion, Dr. Thomas Hockenberry, Ph.D., quantum teleported to the center of the besieged and doomed Achaean encampment.

Later, Daeman wasn't sure when he decided to steal one of the eggs.

It wasn't while he was sliding down the rope to the floor of the dome-crater, since he was too busy hanging on and trying not to be seen to plan anything then.

It wasn't while he was scurrying across the hot, cracked floor of the crater, since his heart was pounding too loudly during that sprint to allow him to think of anything except reaching the fumarole where he'd seen the eggs. Twice he saw groups of *calibani* scuttling along beyond the nearest smoking vents and both times Daeman threw himself down and lay still until they had hurried off on their business toward the main Setebos nest. The floor of the crater was hot enough that it would have burned his hands if he hadn't been wearing the thermskin under his regular clothes. As it was, a minute lying on his belly caused his shirt and trousers to singe. He sprinted forward and reached the side of the fumarole, crouching and panting in the heat—the walls of the fumarole were about twelve feet high, but rough, made of the same blue-ice as everything else. Daeman found enough fingerholds and footholds to climb it without using his ice hammers.

The fumarole—a hissing crater within the larger crater, one of dozens inside the dome-cathedral—was filled with human skulls. These were so heated that some glowed red even while sulfurous vapors hissed around them and rose into the stinking air. At least the steam and vapors gave Damean some cover as he dropped onto the mound of skulls and looked at the Setebos eggs.

Oval, gray-white, each pulsing with some internal energy or life, the things were each about three feet long. Daeman counted twenty-seven in this nest. Besides the cradling heap of hot skulls, the eggs themselves were surrounded by a ring of sticky, blue-gray mucus. Daeman crawled closer, fingers and feet scrabbling on skulls, and looked at the tall heap of eggs from as close as he could get without lifting his head above the level of the fumarole crater rim.

The shells were thin, warm, almost translucent. Some already glowed brightly, others had only a white gleam at their center. Daeman reached out and gingerly touched one—a mild heat, a strange sense of vertigo as if some instability in the egg itself flowed through his thermskinned finger. He tried to lift one and found it weighed about twenty pounds.

Now what?

Now he had to beat a retreat, get up the rope, out through the tunnels, back to the Avenue Daumesnil crevasse, and back to the Guarded Lion faxnode. He had to report all this to everyone at Ardis as soon as possible.

But why come all this way and risk exposure on the crater floor without taking a souvenir?

By dumping everything out of his rucksack except the extra crossbow bolts, he made room for the egg. At first it wouldn't fit, but by pushing gently but insistently he managed to get the broad end of the oval through the opening and wedge the bolts in around the side of the egg. *What if it breaks?* Well, he'd have a messy pack, he thought, but at least he'd know what was inside the damned things.

I don't want to break one of the eggs here, so close to Setebos and the calibani. *We'll inspect it back at Ardis.*

Amen, thought Daeman. He was finding it very hard to breathe. He'd had his osmosis mask on all this time, but the sulfurous vapors from the fumarole vent and the overwhelming heat made him dizzy. He knew that if he'd come into the dome without the thermskin and mask, he would have lost consciousness long ago. The air in here was poisonous. *Then how do the* calibani *breathe?*

To hell with the *calibani,* thought Daeman. He waited until the steam and vapors were thick as a smoke screen and slid down the side of the fumarole, dropping the last five feet. The egg shifted heavily in his rucksack, almost causing him to fall.

Easy, easy.

" 'Saith, what He hates be consecrate, all come to celebrate Thee and Thy state! Thinketh, what I hate be consecrate to celebrate Him and what He ate!" Caliban's chant-hymn was much louder down here. Somehow the acoustics of the giant dome-cathedral amplified as well as directed the monster's voice. Either that or Caliban was closer now.

Running in a crouch, dropping to one knee at any hint of motion through the shifting vapors, Daeman made it the hundred yards to his rope still dangling from the blue-ice balcony. He looked up at the rope hanging free.

What was I thinking? It must be eighty feet to the balcony. I can never climb that—especially not with this weight on my back.

Daeman looked around for another tunnel entrance. The nearest one was three or four hundred feet away around the curve of the dome wall to his right, but it was filled with the huge arm-stalk of one of Setebos' crawling hands.

That hand's up there in the ice tunnels, waiting for me . . . with the others. He could see other arm stalks disappearing into tunnel openings now, the slick gray flesh of the tentacles almost obscene in their wet physicality. Some of them rose three or four hundred feet up the curving wall, hanging down like fleshy tubules, some visibly writhing in a sort of peristalsis as the hands pulled more arm-stalk in after them.

How many hands and arms does this motherfucking brain have?

" 'Believeth that with the end of life, the pain will stop? Not so! He both plagueth enemies and feasts on friends. He doth His worst in this our life, giving respite only lest we die through pain, saving last pain for worst!"

It was climb or die. Daeman had lost almost fifty pounds in the last ten months, converting some weight to muscle, but he wished now that he'd been on Noman's obstacle course in the forest beyond Ardis's north wall every single day of the last ten months, lifting weights in his spare time.

"Fuck it," whispered Daeman. He jumped, grabbed the rope, got his legs and shins around it, reached higher with his thermskinned left hand, and began dragging himself up, shinnying when he could, resting when he had to.

It was slow. It was agonizingly slow. And the slowness was the least part of the agony. A third of the way up and he knew he couldn't make it—knew he probably did not have the strength even to hang on while sliding down. But if he jumped, the egg would break. Whatever was inside would get out. And Setebos and Caliban would know at once.

Something about this image made Daeman giggle until his eyes were filled with tears, fogging the clear lenses on the osmosis mask hood. He could hear his breath rasping in the osmosis mask. He could feel the thermskin suit tightening as it labored to cool him off. *Come on, Daeman, you're almost halfway. Another few feet and you can rest.*

He didn't rest after ten feet. He didn't rest after thirty feet. Daeman knew that if he tried to just hang here, if he paused to wrap the rope around his hands to just cling, he'd never get moving again.

Once the rope shifted on its belay pin and Daeman gasped, his heart leaping into his throat. He was more than halfway up the eighty-foot rope. A fall now would break a leg or arm and leave him crippled on the steaming, hissing crater floor.

The pin held. He hung there a minute, knowing how visible he was to *calibani* anywhere on this side of the crater. Perhaps dozens of the things were standing below him right now, waiting for him to fall into their scaly arms. He did not look down.

Another few feet. Daeman raised his aching, shaking arm, wrapped rope around his palm, and pulled himself up, his legs and ankles seeking traction. Again. Again. No pause allowed. Again.

Finally he couldn't climb anymore. The last of his energy was done. He hung there, his entire body shaking, the weight of his crossbow and the giant egg in his pack pulling him backward, off balance. He knew that he would fall any second. Blinking madly, Daeman freed one hand to wipe the mist from his thermskin lenses.

He was at the overhang of the balcony—a foot beneath its edge.

One last impossible surge and he was up and over, lying on his belly, pulling himself up to the belaying pin and lying on it, lying on the rope, spread-eagled on the blue-ice balcony.

Don't throw up . . . don't throw up! Either the vomit would drown him in his own osmosis mask or he'd have to tug the mask off and the vapors would render him unconscious in seconds. He'd die here and no one would even know that he'd been able to climb eighty feet of rope—no, more, perhaps ninety feet—he, pudgy Daeman, Marina's fat little boy, the kid who couldn't do a single chin-up on the buckycarbon struts.

Some time later, Daeman returned to full consciousness and willed himself to move again. He pulled off the crossbow, checked to make sure it was still cocked and loaded, safety off now. He checked the egg—pulsing more whitely and brightly than before, but still in one piece. He set the ice hammers on his belt and pulled up the hundred feet of rope. It was absurdly heavy.

He got lost in the tunnels. It had been twilight when he'd come in, the last of daylight filtering through the blue-ice, but it was deep night outside now and the only illumination was from the yellow electrical discharges surging through the living tissue all around him—Daeman was sure the blue-ice was organic, somehow part of Setebos.

He had left yellow fabric markers at the intersections, nailed into the ice, but somehow he missed one of those and found himself crawling to new junctions, tunnels he'd never seen before. Rather than backtrack— the tunnel was too narrow to turn around in and he dreaded trying to crawl backward in it—he chose the tunnel that seemed to head upward and crawled on.

Twice the tunnels ended or pitched steeply downward and he did have to backtrack to the junction. Finally a tunnel both rose and widened, and it was with infinite relief that he got to his feet and began moving up the gently sloping ice ramp on his feet, crossbow in his hands.

He stopped suddenly, trying to control his panting.

There was a junction less than ten feet ahead, another one thirty feet behind, and from one or the other or both came a scratching, scrabbling sound.

Calibani, he thought, feeling the terror like the cold of outer space seeping through the thermskin, but then a colder thought came. *One of the hands.*

It was a hand. Longer than Daeman, thicker through the middle, pulling itself along on fingernails emerging from the gray flesh like ten inches of sharpened steel, with black-barbed fiber hairs at the ends of the fingers grabbing ice, the pulsating hand pulled itself into the junction less than ten feet in front of Daeman and paused there, the palm rising— the orifice in the center of that palm visibly fluttering open and shut.

It's searching for me, thought Daeman, not daring to breathe. *It senses heat.*

He did not stir, not even to raise the crossbow. Everything depended upon the slashed and worn old thermskin suit. If he was radiating heat from it, the hand would be on him in a millisecond. Daeman lowered his face to the ice floor, not out of fear but to mask any heat emissions that might be leaking from his osmosis mask.

There was a wild scrabbling and when Daeman jerked his head up, he saw that the hand had taken a tunnel to his right. The fleshy, moving arm-stalk filled the tunnel ahead, almost blocking the junction.

I'll be goddamned if I'm going backwards, thought Daeman. He crawled forward to the junction, moving as quietly as he could.

The arm-stalk was sliding through the junction; a hundred yards of it had already flowed past but it seemed endless. He could no longer hear the scrabbling of the hand itself.

It's probably circled around through the tunnels and is behind me.

"'Listen! White blaze—a tree's head snaps—and there, there, there, there, there, His thunder follows! Fool to give at Him! Lo! 'Lieth flat and loveth Setebos!"

Caliban's chant was muffled by distance and ice, but it flowed up the tunnel after him.

Inches from the sliding arm-stalk, Daeman weighed the possibilities.

The tunnel it slid through was about six feet across and six feet high. The arm-stalk filled the width of the junction and tunnel—at least six feet, compressed by the blue-ice, but it was broader than it was tall. There was at least three feet of air between the top of the endless, sliding mass and the tunnel ceiling. On the other side, the tunnel Daeman had been following broadened and headed gradually toward the surface. Through the thermskin, he thought his skin could feel a movement of air from the outside. He might be only a few hundred feet from the surface here.

How to get past the arm-stalk?

He thought of the ice hammers—useless, he couldn't hang from the ceiling and cross that six feet. He thought of going back, back into the labyrinth that he'd been crawling through for what seemed like hours, and he put that thought from his mind.

Maybe the arm-stalk will slide past. That thought showed him how tired and stupid he was. This thing ended in the brain-mass that was Setebos, the better part of a mile away in the center of the crater.

It's going to fill all these tunnels up with its arms and its scrabbling hands. It's searching for me!

Part of Daeman's mind noted that pure panic tasted like blood. Then he realized that he'd bitten through the lining of his cheek. His mouth filled with blood, but he couldn't take time to slide the osmosis mask off to spit, so he swallowed instead.

To hell with it.

Daeman made sure the safety was on and then he tossed the heavy crossbow across the sliding mass of arm-stalk. It missed the oily gray flesh by inches and skittered on the ice of the tunnel opposite. The pack and egg were more difficult.

It'll break. It will smash open and the milky glow inside—it's brighter now, I'm sure it's brighter—will spill out and it'll be one of these hands, small and pink rather than gray, and its orifice will open and the little hand will scream and scream, and the huge gray hand will come scuttling back, or perhaps straight down the tunnel ahead, trapping me . . .

"God damn you," Daeman said aloud, not worrying about the noise. He hated himself for the coward he was, for the coward he'd always been. Marina's pudgy little baby, capable of seducing the girls and catching butterflies and nothing else.

Daeman slipped the pack off, wrapped the top around the egg as best he could, and heaved it sideways over the sliding mass of oily arm.

It landed on the pack side rather than the exposed eggshell and slid. The egg looked intact as best Daeman could tell.

My turn.

Feeling light and free without the rucksack and heavy crossbow, he backed up thirty feet down the almost-horizontal tunnel and then broke into a sprint before he could give himself time to think about it.

He almost slipped, but then his boots found purchase and he was moving fast when he reached the arm. The top of his thermskin hood brushed the ceiling as he dove as high as he could, his arms straight ahead of him, his feet coming up—but not quite enough, he felt the toes of his boots grazing the thick slithering arm—*Don't come down on the pack and egg!*—and then he was landing on his hands, rolling forward, crashing down—the blue-ice knocking the wind out of him, rolling over the crossbow but not firing it by accident because the safety was on.

Behind him the endless arm stopped moving.

Not waiting to get his breath back, Daeman grabbed the rucksack and crossbow and began running up the gently rising ice slope toward fresh air and the darkness of the exit.

He emerged into the fresh, cold night air a block or two south of the Île de la Cité crevasse he'd followed into the dome. There was no sight of any of the hands or *calibani* in the starlight and electric glow from the blue-ice nerve flashes.

Daeman pulled off the osmosis mask and gasped in huge draughts of fresh air.

He wasn't out yet. With the pack on his back and the crossbow in his hands again, he followed this crevasse until it ended somewhere near where the Île St-Louis should be. There was an ice wall to his right, tunnel entrances to his left.

I'm not going in a tunnel again. Laboriously, his arms shaking with fatigue even before he did anything, Daeman took the ice hammers out of his belt, slammed one into the flickering blue-ice wall, and began to climb.

Two hours later, he knew he was lost. He'd been navigating by the stars and rings and by glimpses of buildings rising from the ice or the shapes of masonry half-glimpsed in the shadows of crevasses. He thought he'd been paralleling the crevasse that ran along Avenue Daumesnil, but he knew now that he must be mistaken—nothing lay before him but a wide, black crevasse, dropping into absolute darkness.

Daeman lay on his stomach near the edge, feeling the egg shifting in his rucksack as if it were alive, wanting to hatch, and he had to concentrate on not weeping. There had been scrabblings in the tunnel openings and crevasses he'd passed—more hands searching, he was sure. He'd seen none up here in the starlight and ringlight atop the ice mass, but the dome behind him was glowing more brightly than ever.

Setebos is missing his egg.

His? thought Daeman, resisting the urge to laugh since hysteria might be right behind the softest giggle.

Something at the edge of the bottomless abyss ahead of him caught his eye. Daeman pulled himself forward on his elbows.

One of his nails with a tatter of yellow cloth attached.

This was the ice chimney only a hundred and fifty yards from the Guarded Lion node where he'd faxed in to Paris Crater.

Weeping openly now, Daeman hammered in the last of his ice nails, bent it, secured the rope—not even bothering to knot it in the rappelling knot he'd learned so he could slide it free when he reached the bottom—and heaving himself over the edge, he let himself down into the darkness.

Leaving the rope behind, Daeman staggered and crawled the last hundred yards or so. There was one last junction, marked by his yellow tatters of cloth, then he had to crawl, and then he was out and sliding into the Guarded Lion fax pavilion where he could stand up on a solid floor. The faxpad glowed softly on its pedestal in the center of the circular node.

The naked shape hit him from the side, sending him sliding across the floor, his crossbow skittering on tile.

The thing—Caliban or *calibani*, he couldn't tell in the blue darkness—wrapped long fingers around Daeman's throat even as yellow teeth snapped at his face.

Daeman rolled again, tried to throw the clinging shape off, but the naked form hung on with its legs and spatulate, prehensile toes even as it clung tight with its long arms and powerful hands.

The egg! thought Daeman, trying not to land on his back as the two surged back and forth, crashing into the faxpad pedestal.

Then he was free for a second and leaping for the crossbow against the far wall. The amphibian man-shape snarled and grabbed him, throwing Daeman up against the ice. The yellow eyes and yellow teeth glowed in the blue gloom.

Daeman had fought Caliban before and this wasn't Caliban—this fiend was smaller, not quite as strong, not quite as fast, but terrible enough. The teeth snapped at Daeman's eyes.

The human got his left palm under the *calibani*'s chin and forced the jaw up, the scaly face with its flat nose arching up and back, the yellow eyes glaring. Daeman felt strength flowing in with the rush of the last of his adrenaline, and he tried to snap the creature's neck by forcing its head back.

The *calibani*'s head whipped like a snake and it bit off two of the fingers on Daeman's straining left hand.

The man howled and fell away. The *calibani* swung its arms wide, paused to swallow fingers, and leaped.

Daeman swept the crossbow up with his good right hand and fired both bolts. The *calibani* was thrown backward, impaled on the ice wall with one of the long, iron, barbed bolts protruding through its upper shoulder into the ice and the other through its palm, its hand raised next to its howling face. The naked creature writhed, pulled, snarled, and snapped one of the bolts free.

Daeman also howled. He leaped to his feet, pulled the knife from his belt, and rammed the long blade up through the *calibani*'s underjaw, up through its soft palate and into its brain. Then he pressed against the length of the *calibani*'s long body like a lover and twisted the blade around—twisted again, again, and then again—and kept twisting until the obscene writhing against him stopped.

He fell back onto the tile, cradling his mangled hand. Incredibly, there was no bleeding. The thermskin glove had closed around the stumps of the two amputated fingers, but the pain made him want to vomit.

He could do that, and he did, kneeling and throwing up until he could vomit no more.

There was a scrabbling from one or more of the tunnels on the opposite wall.

Daeman stood, jerked the long knife from the *calibani*'s underjaw—the creature's body sagged but was held up by the bolt through its shoulder—and then he retrieved the other bolt, rocking it loose, picked up the crossbow, and crossed to the faxpad.

Something surged out of the glowing tunnel entrance behind him.

Daeman faxed into daylight at the Ardis Hall node. He staggered away from the faxpad there, fumbled a bolt out of his pack, dropped it in the groove in his crossbow, and used his foot to cock the massive mechanism. He aimed the crossbow at the faxpad node and waited.

Nothing came through.

After a long minute, he lowered the weapon and staggered out into the sunlight.

It looked to be early afternoon here at the Ardis node. There were no guards around. The palisade wall here had been pulled down in a dozen places. The carcasses of at least a score of dead voynix lay all around the fax pavilion, but other than streaks and smears and trails of human blood leading off to the meadow and into the forest, there was no sign of the humans who had been left behind to guard the pavilion.

Daeman's hand hurt so terribly that his entire body and skull became only an echo to that throbbing pain, but he cradled his hand to his chest, set another bolt in the crossbow, and staggered out to the road. It was a little less than a mile and a half to Ardis Hall.

Ardis Hall was gone.

Daeman had approached cautiously, staying off the road and moving through the trees most of the way, wading the narrow river upstream from the bridge. He had approached the palisade and Ardis from the northeast, through the woods, ready to call out quickly to the sentries rather than be shot as a voynix.

There were no sentries. For half an hour, Daeman crouched at the edge of the woods and watched. Nothing moved except the crows and magpies feeding on the remnants of human bodies. Then he moved carefully around to the left, coming as close to the barracks and east entrance to the Ardis palisade as he could before coming out of the cover of the trees.

The palisade had been breached in a hundred places. Much of the wall was down. Hannah's beautiful cupola and hearth had been burned and then knocked over. The line of barracks and tents where half of the four hundred people of Ardis had lived had all burned down. Ardis Hall itself—the grand hall that had weathered more than two thousand winters—had been reduced to a few carbon-smeared stone chimneys, burned and tumbled rafters, and heaps of collapsed stone.

The place stank of smoke and death. There were scores of dead voynix on what had been Ada's front yard, more piled where the porch had stood, but mixed in with the shattered carapaces were remains of hundreds of men and women. Daeman couldn't identify any of the corpses he could see around the burned ruins of the house—there a small charred corpse, seemingly too small to be an adult, burned black, the charred and flaking arms raised in a boxer's posture, here a rib cage and skull picked almost clean by the birds, there a woman lying seemingly unharmed in the sooty grass, but—when Daeman rushed to her and rolled her over—missing a face.

Daeman knelt in the cold, bloodied grass and tried to weep. The best he could do was wave his arms to chase away the heavy crows and hopping magpies that kept trying to return to the corpses.

The sun was going down. The light was fading from the sky.

Daeman rose to look at the other bodies—flung here and there like bundles of abandoned laundry on the frozen earth, some lying under voynix carcasses, others lying alone, some fallen in clumps as if the people had huddled together at the end. He had to find Ada. Identify and bury her and as many of the others as he could before trying to make his way back to the fax pavilion.

Where can I go? Which community will take me in?

Before he could answer that or reach the other bodies in the quickly falling twilight, he saw the movement at the edge of the forest.

At first Daeman thought that the survivors of the Ardis massacre were coming out of the trees, but even as he raised his good hand to hail them, he saw the glint on gray carapaces and knew that he was wrong.

Thirty, sixty, a hundred voynix moved out of the forest and across the grass toward him from the road and forest to the east.

Sighing, too tired to run, Daeman staggered a few yards toward the woods to the southwest and then saw the movement there. Voynix scuttling out of the darkness there, more voynix dropping from the trees and moving out into the open on all fours. They'd be on him in a few seconds.

He knew that it was no use running around the smoldering ruins of the Great Hall toward the north. There would just be more voynix there.

Daeman went to one knee, noticed that the egg in his rucksack was glowing brightly enough now to throw his shadow across the frozen grass, and then pulled the last of the crossbow quarrels out.

Six. He had six bolts left. Plus the two already loaded.

Smiling grimly, feeling something like a terrible elation rise in him, he stood and leveled the weapon at the closest cluster of advancing shapes. They were sixty feet away. He'd let them get closer, knowing that they could close the gap in seconds running at full voynix speed. His mangled hand was good enough to level the crossbow with his thumb and remaining two fingers.

Something cracked and slapped behind him. Daeman whirled, ready to meet the attack, but it was the sonie, flying in low from the west. Two people were firing flechette rifles from the rear niches. Voynix leaped at it but were slapped away by clouds of flickering flechettes.

"Jump!" yelled Greogi as the sonie flew in at head height and then hovered next to Daeman.

The voynix rushed in from every side, bouncing and leaping like giant silver grasshoppers. A man Daeman vaguely recognized as Boman and a woman with dark hair—not Ada, but the woman named Edide who had gone with Daeman on the fax-warning expedition—were firing their flechette rifles in opposite directions on full automatic, pouring out a cloud of crystal darts.

"Jump!" Greogi yelled again.

Daeman shook his head, retrieved the rucksack with the egg, tossed it up into the sonie, tossed in his crossbow, and only then jumped. The sonie began to climb even as he leaped.

He didn't quite make it. His good hand found a grip on the inner edge of the sonie, but his mangled left hand banged against metal, the pain blinded him, he released his grip and began to slide away toward the mass of silent voynix below.

Boman grabbed him by the arm and pulled him aboard.

Daeman couldn't speak for most of the fast flight northeast, hurtling several miles above the dark forest, finally circling toward a bare spur of rock rising two hundred feet above the skeletal trees. Daeman had seen this granite knob years earlier, when he'd first visited Ada and her mother here at Ardis Hall. He'd been hunting for butterflies then and at the end of a long afternoon of meandering, Ada had pointed out the rocky point rising almost vertically from a brambled meadow beyond the forest. "Starved Rock," she'd said, her teenager's voice sounding almost proud and possessive.

"Why do they call it that?" he'd asked.

Young Ada had shrugged.

"Do you want to climb it?" he'd said, thinking that if he got her up there, he might be able to seduce her on a grassy summit.

Ada had laughed. "No one can climb Starved Rock."

Now, in the last of the twilight and the first of the bright ringlight, Daeman saw what they had done. The summit was not grassy after all—bare rock stretched a flat hundred feet or so, broken by the occasional boulder, and crowded onto that summit were crude tarps and a half-dozen campfires. Dark figures huddled by those fires and more figures were posted at all the edges of the granite monolith . . . sentries, no doubt.

The field below Starved Rock seemed to be moving in the shadows. It *was* moving. Voynix shuffled and stirred there, stepping over hundreds of shattered carcasses of their own kind.

"How many people made it from Ardis?" asked Daeman as Greogi circled to land.

"About fifty," said the pilot. His face was soot-streaked and looked infinitely weary in the glow from the virtual controls.

Fifty out of more than four hundred, thought Daeman numbly. He realized that his body was in shock from losing fingers, and his mind was going into something like shock after seeing what he'd seen back at Ardis. The numbness and disinterest were not unpleasant.

"Ada?" he said hesitantly.

"She's alive," said Greogi. "But she's been unconscious for almost twenty-four hours. The Great Hall was burning and she wouldn't leave until everyone else who could be carried off had been . . . and even then, I don't think she would have left if that section of the burning roof hadn't collapsed and a rafter hadn't knocked her out. We don't know if her baby is still . . . viable . . . or not."

"Petyr?" said Daeman. "Reman?" He was trying to think of who would lead them with Harman gone, Ada injured, and so many lost.

"Dead." Greogi hovered the sonie and lowered it toward the dark mass of the granite summit. It bumped to a stop. Dark forms from one of the campfires rose and walked toward them.

"Why are you still here?" Daeman asked Greogi, holding him by his shirtfront as the others stepped off the grounded sonie. "Why are you still here with the voynix down there?"

Greogi easily pulled Daeman's hand free. "We tried the faxnode, but the voynix were on us before we could get people inside. We lost four people there before we could get away. And we don't have anywhere else to fly . . . with Ada injured so severely and a dozen others badly hurt, we could never get them all off Starved Rock in time, before those fucking animals come up the cliff. We need everyone here just to hold off the voynix . . . If we start flying out a few at a time, those staying behind will be overrun. We probably don't have enough flechette ammunition to hold out another night as it is."

Daeman looked around. The campfires were low, pitiful things—mere burning moss or lichen and a few twigs, nothing more. The brightest thing on the dark rock was the Setebos egg still glowing milkily in his rucksack.

"Has it come to this?" Daeman asked, speaking to himself.

"I guess it has," said Greogi, sliding off the sonie and staggering slightly. The man was obviously in some state beyond exhaustion. "It's full dark now. The voynix will be coming up the sides any minute."

PART

3

41

Harman fell through darkness with Ariel for what seemed an impossible length of time.

When they landed, it wasn't with a fatal crash at the base of the Golden Gate at Machu Picchu, but with a soft thump on a jungle floor covered with centuries' buildup of leaves and other humus.

For a stunned second Harman couldn't believe that he wasn't dead, but then he stumbled to his feet, shoved the small Ariel figure away—though Ariel had already danced out of range—and then stood, blinking in the darkness.

Darkness. It had been daytime at the Golden Gate. He was . . . somewhere else. Wherever the somewhere else might be, besides on the dark side of the planet, Harman knew that it was in deep jungle. The night smelled of richness and rot, the thick, humid air clung to his skin like a soaked blanket, Harman's shirt immediately soaked through and lay limp against him, and all around in the seemingly impenetrable night came the buzz of insects and the rustle of fronds, palms, undergrowth, insects, small creatures and large. Letting his eyes adapt, his hands raised into fists, hoping that Ariel would come back into striking range, Harman craned his head back and saw the hint of starlight between tiny gaps in foliage far, far above.

In another minute, he could see the pale, almost spectral, genderless figure of Ariel glowing slightly ten feet or so from him across the jungle floor.

"Take me back," growled Harman.

"Take thee back where?"

"To the Bridge. Or to Ardis. But do it *now*."

"I cannot." The genderless voice was maddening, insulting.

"You *will*," growled Harman. "You will *right now*. However you got me here, undo it, take me back. *Now*."

"Or what consequence ensues?" asked the glowing figure in the jungle dark. Ariel's voice sounded mildly amused.

"Or I'll kill you," Harman said flatly. He realized that he meant it. He would strangle this green-white flop of a thing, choke the life out of it, and spit on the corpse. *And then you'll be left lost in an unknown jungle* warned the last sensible part of Harman's mind. He ignored it.

"Oh, my," said Ariel, feigning terror, "I shall be pinched to death."

Harman leaped, arms extended. The little figure—not much more than four feet tall—caught him in midleap and threw him thirty feet through ripping fronds and tearing vines into the jungle.

It took Harman a minute or two to get his breath back and another minute to get to his knees. He realized at once that if Ariel had done that to him elsewhere—say, on the Golden Gate at Machu Picchu where they'd been a minute before—it would have broken his back. Now he stood again on deep humus, willed his vision to see through the encroaching darkness, and shoved and tore his way back through vines and thick vegetation to the small clearing where Ariel waited.

The sprite was no longer alone.

"O look," Ariel said in happy, conversational tones, "here is more of us!"

Harman paused. He could see better now by the starlight filtering down into this little clearing in the jungle and what he saw made him stare.

There were at least fifty or sixty other shapes in the clearing and under the trees and amidst the ferns and vines beyond. They were not human, but neither were they voynix or *calibani* or any other bipedal form that Harman had seen in his ninety-nine years and nine months of life. These humanoid shapes were like rough sketches of people—short, not much taller than little Ariel, and, like Ariel, with transparent skin and organs floating in greenish liquid. But where Ariel had lips, cheeks, a nose, and the eyes of a young man or woman, with physical features and muscles one associated with the human body, these short, green forms had neither mouths nor human eyes—they looked back at Harman in the starlight from black dots in their faces that could have been lumps of coal—and from their boneless-looking frames to their three-fingered hands, the forms seemed to lack all identity.

"I don't believe you've met my fellow ministers," Ariel said softly, gesturing with a feminine turn of hand toward the mob of shapes in the shadows. "Instruments to this lower world, they were belched up before your kind was born. They have different names—his Prosperousness doth fain to call them this and that, as takes his pleasure—but they are more like me than not, descended from chlorophyll and the motes set there in the forest to measure it in time before post-humans. They are the *zeks*—helpers and workers and prisoners all, and who of us is not all these things?"

Harman stared at the greenish shapes. They stared unblinking back.

"Seize him," lisped Ariel.

Four of the *zeks* came forward—they moved with a smooth grace that Harman wouldn't have expected from such gingerbread shapes—and before he could run or fight, two of them seized him with three-fingered grips of iron. The third *zek* leaned in close, unbreathing, until its feature-less chest touched the tunic above Harman's chest, and the fourth seized Harman's hand—just as Ariel had seized Hannah's only a short while before—and thrust it through the yielding green-skin membrane of the third *zek*'s chest. Harman felt the soft heart-organ in his hand, almost coming to him like a pet, and then the unspoken words echoed in his brain—

DO NOT IRRITATE

ARIEL

HE WILL KILL

YOU

ON A WHIM.

COME

WITH US

AND MAKE NO EFFORT

TO

RESIST.

IT IS TO YOUR BENEFIT

AND TO

YOUR LADY'S

ADA'S

TO COME WITH US

NOW.

"How do you know about Ada?" Harman shouted aloud.

COME

That was the last word transmitted through Harman's pulsing hand into his aching skull before his hand was wrenched free, the *zek*'s soft heart still in it, shriveling, dying, and then the *zek* itself pitched over backward, falling silently to the jungle floor, there to shrivel and desic-cate and die. Ariel and the other *zeks* ignored the corpse of the commu-nicator as Ariel turned and led the way down the slightest of trails along the dark jungle floor.

The *zeks* on either side of Harman still clung to his arm, but lightly now, and Harman made no effort to resist, only to keep up as the line of forms moved through the dark wood.

*   *   *

Harman's mind was racing faster than his feet as he stumbled to keep up through the dark jungle. At times, when the foliage overhead was too thick, he couldn't see anything—not even his legs or feet beneath him in the near absolute darkness—so he let the *zeks* guide him as if he were blind and concentrated on thinking. He knew that if he was ever going to see Ada and Ardis Hall again, he'd have to be a lot smarter in the coming hours than he'd been in the last many months.

First question—where was he? It had been a stormy morning when he'd been at the Golden Gate at Machu Picchu, but it felt very late here in this jungle. He tried to remember his self-taught geography, but the maps and spheres blurred in his mind now—words like Asia and Europe meaning almost nothing. But the darkness here suggested that Ariel hadn't just whisked him to some jungle on the same southern continent that held the Bridge. He couldn't *walk* back to Machu Picchu and Hannah and Petyr and the sonie.

Which led to the second question—how had Ariel brought him here? There had been no visible faxnode pavilion in the Golden Gate green globules. If there had been—if Savi had ever suggested a fax connection to the Bridge—he certainly wouldn't have flown the sonie there to get the weapons and ammunition and try to get Odysseus to the healing crèche. No . . . Ariel had used some other means to transport him through space to this dark, rot-smelling, muggy, insect-filled place.

Since he was being dragged through the darkness not ten paces behind the biosphere avatar—or so Prospero had once identified Ariel—Harman realized he could just ask these questions. The worst the pale sprite—his/her body visibly glowing in starlight as they crossed the occasional small opening in the jungle—could do was not answer.

Ariel answered both questions, the second one first.

"I shall have thy company for only a few hours more," said the small form. "Then I must deliver thee to my master, not long after we hear the strain of the strutting chanticleer—if strutting chanticleer there were in this wretched place."

"Your master Prospero?" asked Harman.

Ariel did not answer.

"So what is the name of this wretched place?" Harman asked.

The sprite laughed, a sound like the tinkling of small bells, but not altogether a pleasant noise. "They should call this wood Ariel's Nursery, for here ten times two hundred years ago, I came to be—rising into consciousness from a billion little sensor-transponders the old-old-style humans—your very ilk, guest—called motes. Trees were talking to their human masters and to each other, chatting in the mossy old net that had become the nascent noosphere, gabbling on about temperatures and birds' nests and hatchlings and pounds per square inch of osmotic pressure and trying to quantify photosynthesis the way a rheumy clerk counts his beads and bangles and thinks them treasure. The *zeks*—my beloved instruments of action, too many stolen from me for wasteful duty on the red world by that monster-magus master—rose likewise, yea, but not here, honored guest, not here, no."

Harman understood almost none of that, but Ariel was talking—babbling—and he knew that if he could keep the creature engaged in conversation, he'd learn something important sooner or later.

"Prospero, your master, called you the avatar of the biosphere when I spoke to him, your master, nine months ago on his orbital isle," said Harman.

"Aye," said Ariel, laughing again, "and I call Prospero, whom you call my master, Tom Shit." Ariel looked back at him, the small, greenish-white face glowing like some phosphorescent tropical plant as they plunged into a section of trail in total darkness under the encroaching leaves. "Harman, husband of Ada, friend of Noman, thou art, to mine eyes, a man of sin, a man whose destiny has import, in this lower world at least, less for what is in't than for its pallid shape. Thou, 'mongst all men, being most unfit to live—much less to live your full Five Twenty so like one of brother Caliban's long-baked meals—since time and tides of time hath made you mad. And even with such valour, you know, men hang and drown their proper selves."

Harman understood none of this and despite his asking many more questions, Ariel did not reply or speak again until dawn some three hours and many miles later.

An hour after Harman was sure that he had no energy left, they allowed him to stop and lean against a huge boulder to catch his breath. As the light came up, he realized that it was no boulder.

The boulder was actually a wall, the wall was part of a large building with levels set back as it rose, and the building was something that he guessed from his sigling was called a temple. Then Harman realized what his hands were touching and what his eyes were seeing.

Every inch of the large temple was carved. Some of the carvings were large—as wide as the length of Harman's arm—but most were small enough that he could cover them with the palm of his hand.

In the carvings—each one becoming more clear as the tropical sunrise bled light through the jungle overhead—men and women were making love—having sex—as were men and more than one woman, men and men, women and women, women and men and what looked to be horses, men and elephants, women and bulls, women and women and monkeys and men and men and men. . . .

Harman could only stare. He'd never seen anything like this in his ninety-nine years. On one level of carvings just at eye height, he could see a man with his head between a woman's legs while another man, straddling the first, offered his erect penis to the straining woman's open mouth, while behind her, a second woman wearing some sort of artificial penis was entering the first woman from behind while the first woman, servicing the two men and the woman behind her, was reaching her arm out to an animal Harman recognized from the turin drama as a horse, masturbating the excited stallion. Her other free hand was massaging the genitals of a human male figure standing next to the horse.

Harman stepped away from the temple wall, looking up at the vine-encrusted stone structure. There were thousands—perhaps tens of thousands—of variations on this theme, showing Harman aspects of sex he'd never imagined, *could* never have imagined. Just some of the elephant images alone. . . . The human figures were stylized, faces and breasts oval, eyes almond-shaped, the women's and men's mouths curling in pleased and decadent smiles.

"What is this place?" he asked.

Ariel sang in a falsetto—

> *"Above, half seen, in the lofty gloom,*
> *Strange works of a long dead people loom,*
> *What did they mean to those who now are dust,*
> *These rioting figures of love and lust?"*

Harman tried again. "What *is* this place?"

For once Ariel answered simply. "Khajuraho." The word meant nothing to Harman.

The biosphere sprite gestured, two of the little, green, largely transparent *zeks* touched Harman's arm, and the procession moved away from the temple, following a barely discernible path through the jungle. Looking back, Harman caught a final glimpse of the stone building—*buildings* he realized now, there was more than one temple there, all of them carved with erotic friezes—and he noticed again how the jungle had all but reclaimed the structures. The coupling figures were bound about by vines, partially obscured by grass, and tightly constricted by roots and green feelers.

Then the place called Khajuraho disappeared in the green growth and Harman concentrated on plodding along behind Ariel.

As the sunlight illuminated the wild density of the jungle around them—ten thousand shades of green, most of which Harman had never imagined—all he could think of was how to get back to Ardis and Ada, or at least back to the Bridge before Petyr flew off in the sonie. He didn't want to wait three days for Petyr's return to pick up Hannah and the restored—if that crèche could restore life and health—Noman/Odysseus.

"Ariel?" he said suddenly to the small form that seemed to be floating at the front of the line of *zeks* ahead of him.

"Ay, sir?" The androgynous quality of the otherwise pleasant voice disturbed Harman.

"How did you transport me from the Golden Gate to this jungle?"

"Did I not do my spriting gently enough, O Man?"

"Yes," said Harman, fearing that the pale figure was going to launch into more nonsense babble. "But *how*?"

"How dost thou travel from place to place, when you are not lying abelly in your sonie saucer?"

"We fax," said Harman. "But there was no fax pavilion at the Golden Gate . . . no faxnode."

Ariel floated higher, brushing branches and sending a shower of droplets down onto the *zeks* and Harman. "Did your friend Daeman go to a fax pavilion when the allosaurus ate him ten months ago?"

Harman stopped in his tracks. The *zeks* still holding his arms stopped with him, not yet pulling him on.

Of course, thought Harman. It had been in front of him all his life. He'd seen it all his life—but he'd been blind. When someone faxed up to the rings on any of his or her normal four Twenties of life, you went to the nearest fax pavilion. When someone wanted to fax anywhere, you went to the nearest faxnode pavilion. But when someone was injured—or killed, devoured as Daeman had been, torn apart in some freak accident—the *rings* faxed you up.

Harman had been there, on Prospero's Isle, in the Firmary tanks where naked bodies arrived, were fixed by the bubbling nutrient and blue worms, and were faxed back. Harman and Daeman had done the faxing themselves, on Prospero's instructions, destroying the servitors and setting the virtual dials and levers to fax as many of the bodies-under-repair home as they could.

Humans could be faxed without going to a fax pavilion, without starting from one of the three-hundred-some known faxnodes. Harman had seen this his entire life—almost one hundred years—but had never *seen* what he could see. The thought was too entrenched that the post-humans were calling you home when you were injured or killed before your Fifth Twenty. Faxnodes were science; going to the Firmary for emergency repair was something like religion.

But the Firmary on Prospero's Isle had machinery that could fax anyone from anywhere without relying on nodes and pavilions.

And Harman and Daeman had destroyed the Firmary and Prospero's Isle.

The *zeks* tugged at Harman's arms to get him moving again, but gently. Harman did not move quite yet. The intensity of his thoughts made him dizzy; if the *zeks* had not been clutching him, he might have fallen to the jungle floor.

Prospero's Isle was destroyed—he and all the old-style humans had watched the pieces burn through the night sky for months—but Ariel could still fax—a sort of free-fax, independent from nodes, portals, and pavilions. Something up on the rings—or on Earth itself—found the sprite, coded him, and faxed him, and today Harman with him, from the Bridge to here, wherever here and Khajuraho were. On the opposite side of the Earth if nothing else.

Harman might yet be able to fax home to Ada, if he could only get Ariel to reveal the secret of this free-faxing.

The *zeks* pulled again, gently but insistently. Ariel was far ahead, floating toward a patch of bright sunlight in the jungle. Harman did not want to get the *zeks* in trouble. Nor did he want to lose sight of Ariel—the sprite was his fax-ticket home.

Harman rushed, stumbling, to catch up with the avatar of Earth's biosphere.

When they first emerged into the clearing the sun was so bright that Harman squinted and covered his eyes, not seeing the structure looming above him for several seconds. When he did see it, he froze in his tracks.

The thing—structure—it wasn't quite a building—was gigantic, rising up for what Harman estimated—and his estimates on the size of things had always been uncannily good—for at least a thousand feet. Perhaps a little more. It had no skin; that is, the entire structure was a lacy, open-latticework skeleton of dark metal girders, rising inward from a huge square base that connected via semicircular metal arches at tree-top level, then continuing to curve inward until it became a pure spire, its dark knob of a summit far, far above. A phrase that the metal-working Hannah had once described came to his mind—*wrought iron*. Harman felt sure that the trusses, arches, girders, and open latticework he was staring at here in the hot, jungle sun were all made of some sort of iron.

"What is it?" he breathed. The *zeks* had released him and stepped back into the shade of the jungle, as if afraid to go closer to the base of the incredible tower. Harman realized that nothing grew on the acre or more at the base of the tower except for low, perfectly manicured grass. It was as if the strength of the structure itself was keeping the jungle at bay.

"It's seven thousand tons," said Ariel in a voice much more masculine than any the biosphere sprite had used before. "Two and a half million rivets. Four thousand three hundred and eleven years old—or at least the original of this was. There are more than fourteen thousand of these in Khan Ho Tep's *eiffelbahn*."

"*Eiffelbahn* . . ." repeated Harman. "I don't . . ."

"Come," snapped Ariel. His voice was powerfully masculine now, deep, threatening, not to be disobeyed.

There was a sort of wrought-iron cage at the base of one of the arched legs.

"Get in," said Ariel.

"I need to know . . ."

"Get in and you'll learn everything you need to know," said the biosphere avatar. "Including how to get back to your precious Ada. Stay here and you die."

Harman stepped into the cage. An iron grating slid shut. Gears clanked, metal screeched, and the cage began rising on the curve, following a series of cables and iron tracks.

"Aren't you coming?" Harman called down to Ariel.

The sprite did not answer. Harman's elevator continued rising into the tower.

42

The tower seemed to have three major landings. The first and broadest was just above the level of the jungle treetops. Harman looked across at a solid carpet of green. The elevator did not stop.

The second landing was high enough that the elevator was traveling almost vertically and Harman had moved to the center of the small cage. Looking up and out, he could see that a series of cables ran from the top of this tower and disappeared far to the east and west, sagging a bit in the distance. The elevator did not stop at the second landing.

The third and final landing was a thousand feet above the ground, just below the domed top of the tower with its spike of antennae. Here the elevator slowed and stopped—ancient gears ground and slipped, the elevator cage slipped back six feet, and Harman grabbed the wrought-iron bars of the cage and prepared to die.

A brake stopped the cage. The wrought-iron door slid back. Harman shakily crossed five or six feet of iron bridge with rotted wood planks. Ahead of him, a much more elaborate door—polished sections of mahogany set into a filagree of wrought iron—clanked, stirred, and then hissed open. Harman paused only a second before entering the darker interior. Any place was preferable to that exposed little bridge a thousand feet above the latticework of girders disappearing in a vertigo of iron below.

He was in a room. When the door hissed and clanked shut behind him, Harman realized that it was twenty or thirty degrees cooler here in the large room than outside in the sun. He stayed where he was for a few seconds, allowing his eyes to adapt to the relative dimness.

He was standing on a small, carpeted and booklined entry mezzanine as part of a larger room. From the mezzanine, a wrought-iron staircase spiraled down to the main floor of the room and up through the ceiling to what presumably was a second story.

Harman descended.

He'd never seen furnishings like this—oddly styled furniture, tufted, with red-velour fabric, thick drapes over a wall of windows on the south side of the room, the drapes dragging their gold tassels onto the elaborately designed red and brown carpet. There was a fireplace in the north wall—Harman stared at the design of black iron and green ceramics. A long table with elaborately carved legs ran for at least eight feet of the fifteen feet of window wall where the panes near the corners of the window were as complicated as the silk of a spider's web. Other furniture consisted of overstuffed single chairs with overstuffed ottomans, carved chairs of gleaming dark wood with gold metal inlays, and everywhere examples of what Hannah had once told him was polished brass.

There was a strange firehose of a speaking tube with a bell-shaped polished brass snout; there were levers of polished brass set into cherry-colored wooden boxes on the walls; on the long plank table rose several brass instruments—some with brass keys to punch and slowly turning gears, farther down the table an astrolabe with circles of brass turning within larger circles of brass, a polished brass lamp glowing softly with light. There were maps laid out on the table with small hemispheres of brass holding them down, more maps curled into a brass basket on the floor.

Harman ran forward and stared hungrily at the maps, pulling more out and unfurling them, laying brass hemispheres on them.

He'd never seen maps like these before. Everything was on a grid but within those grid boxes were ten thousand wriggly parallel lines—some close together where the map ran brown or green, some lines far apart where the map showed expanses of white. There were irregular blobs of blue that Harman guessed were lakes or seas and longer, wigglier blue lines that he guessed were rivers with unlikely names penned next to them—Tungabhadra, Krishna, Godavari, Normada, Mahanadi, and Ganga.

On the east and west wall of the room, surrounding smaller but still multipaned windows, were more bookshelves, more books, more brass trinkets, jade statues, brass machines.

Harman ran to the shelf and pulled down three books, smelling the scent of centuries rising from the ancient but still firm paper and the thick leather covers. The titles made his heart pound—*The Third Dynasty of Khan Ho Tep*—A.D. *2601–2939* and *Ramayana and Mahabharata Scripture Revised According to Ganesh the Cyborg* and Eiffelbahn *Maintenance and AI Interface.* Harman laid his right palm on the top book, closed his eyes to bring up the sigl function, and then hesitated. If he had time, he would prefer to *read* these books—sounding out each word and guessing at the definitions of the words from context. It was slow, laborious, painful, but he always gained more from reading than from sigling.

He laid the three books reverently on the polished, dust-free tabletop, and bounded up the circular stairs to the high second floor.

This was a bedroom—the head of the bed made of cylinders of polished brass, the bedspread a rich red velvet with fringes of elaborate, swirling designs. There was another chair set next to a brass floor lamp—a broader, comfortable-looking chair with floral designs, a high tufted leather ottoman pushed against it. There was a smaller room—a bathroom with a strange porcelain toilet under a porcelain tank and a hanging chain with a brass pull, panes of stained glass on the west wall, brass fixtures on faucets and spigots on the sink, a huge, clawfooted white porcelain bathtub with more brass fixtures. Back out in the bedroom again, the north wall here was also made up of windows—no, paned-glass doors with wrought-iron doorhandles.

Harman opened two of the doors and stepped out onto a wrought-iron balcony a thousand feet above the jungle. The sun and heat hit him like a hot fist. Blinking, he did not trust himself to stand on the iron—he could see the latticework of the tower beneath, but it would take no more than a gentle push to send him out and into nothing but air, a thousand feet of air.

Still gripping the door, he leaned out far enough to see some iron furniture, red cushions strapped on, a table on the ten-foot-wide balcony. Looking up, he saw the bulge of iron above the two-story room, a huge metal flywheel just under the gold-mica dome at the top of the tower, cables thicker than his forearm and thigh running out to the east and west.

Squinting to the east, Harman could see another vertical line of a dark tower there—how far away?—forty miles at least, seen from this height. He looked to the west to where the dozen or so cables disappeared, but there were only blue-black clouds of a storm visible there on the horizon.

Harman stepped back into the bedroom, shut the doors carefully, and walked back to the staircase and down and around, wiping the sweat from his forehead and neck with the sleeve of his tunic. It was so delightfully cool in here that he had no urge to go back down to the jungle yet.

"Hello, Harman," said a familiar voice from the gloom near the table and dark drapes.

Prospero was far more solid than Harman remembered from their meeting months earlier on the orbital rock high in the e-ring. The magus's wrinkled skin was no longer slightly transparent as his hologram had been. His robe of blue silk and wool, embroidered all about with gold planets, gray comets, and burning stars of red silk, hung in heavier folds now and dragged behind him on the Turkish carpet. Harman could see the long silver-white hair cascading behind the old man's sharp ears and noted the age marks on his brow and his hands as well as the slight, clawlike yellowing to his fingernails. Harman noted the seeming solidity of the carved, twined staff that the old magus clutched in his right hand, and how Prospero's blue slippers seemed to have weight as they shuffled across the wooden floor and thick carpet.

"Send me home," demanded Harman, stepping toward the old man. *"Now."*

"Patience, patience, human named Harman, friend of Noman," said the magus, showing his yellowed teeth in a slight smile.

"Fuck patience," said Harman. He'd had no idea until this instant how deep the fury in him went from being kidnapped from the Bridge by Ariel, taken away from Ardis and Ada and his unborn child, almost certainly on the orders of this shuffling figure in the blue robe. He took a step closer to the old man, reached out, grabbed a bit of the magus's flowing sleeve . . .

And was thrown eight feet backward across the room, finally sliding from the carpet to the polished floor and coming to rest on his back, blinking away retinal after-images of orange circles.

"I suffer no one's touch," Prospero said softly. "Do not make me remonstrate with this old man's stick." He raised his magus's staff ever so slightly.

Harman got to one knee. "Send me back. Please. I can't leave Ada alone. Not now."

"You already have chosen that course, have you not? No man made you take Noman to Machu Picchu, yet no man stopped you, either."

"What do you want, Prospero?" Harman got to his feet, tried unsuccessfully to blink away the last of the red-orange circles in his vision, and sat in the nearest wooden chair. "And how did you survive the destruction of the orbital asteroid? I thought your hologram was trapped there along with Caliban."

"Oh, it was," said Prospero, pacing back and forth. "A small part of my self, perhaps, taken all for all, but a vital small part. You brought me back to Earth."

"I . . ." began Harman. "The sonie? Somehow you loaded your hologram into the sonie's memory?"

"Aye."

Harman shook his head. "You could have called that sonie up to the orbital isle any time."

"Not true," said the magus. "It was Savi's machine and only makes orbital housecalls for humankind passengers. I do not qualify . . . quite."

"Then how did Caliban escape?" asked Harman. "I know that *it* wasn't in the sonie with Daeman, Hannah, and me."

Prospero shrugged. "Caliban's adventures are now solely Caliban's concerns. The wretch no longer serves me."

"He serves Setebos again," said Harman.

"Yes."

"But Caliban *did* survive and return to Earth after centuries."

"Yes."

Harman sighed and rubbed his hand over his face. He suddenly felt very tired and very thirsty.

"The wooden box beneath the mezzanine is a sort of cold-keeper," said Prospero. "There is food in there . . . and bottles of pure water."

Harman sat up straight. "Are you reading my mind, Magus?"

"No. Your face. There is no more obvious map than the human face. Go—get a drink. I will take a seat here by the window and await your return, refreshed, as interlocutor."

Harman felt how shaky his legs and arms were as he walked to the large wooden box with the brass handle, then stared into the cold a minute at all the bottles of water and heaps of clear-wrapped food. He drank deeply.

Returning to the center of the red and tan carpet where Prospero sat at the table with the sunlight behind him, he said, "Why did you have Ariel bring me here?"

"Actually, in deference to accuracy, I had my biosphere sprite bring you to the jungle near Khajuraho since no faxing is allowed within twenty kilometers of the *eiffelbahn*."

"Eiffelbahn?" repeated Harman, still sipping from the ice-cold water bottle. "Is that what you and Ariel call this tower?"

"No, no, my dear Harman. That is what we—or Khan Ho Tep, to be precise, since that gentleman built the *eiffelbahn* some millennia ago—called this *system.* This is just one of . . . oh, let me see . . . fourteen thousand eight hundred towers just like this."

"Why so many?" asked Harman.

"It pleased the Khan," said the magus. "And it takes that many Eiffel Towers to connect the cables from the east coast of China to the Atlantic Breach on the coast of Spain, what with all the trunk lines, spurs, side branches, and so forth."

Harman had no idea what the old man was talking about. "The *eiffelbahn* is some sort of transport system?"

"An opportunity for you to travel in style for a change," said Prospero. "Or I should say—for *us* to travel in style, for I shall travel with you for a small part of the way."

"I'm not traveling anywhere with you until . . ." began Harman. Then he stopped, dropped the water bottle to the floor, and clutched the heavy table with both hands.

The entire two-story platform one thousand feet atop the tower had lurched. There was a grinding and tearing of metal, an horrendous screech, and then the entire structure tilted, lurched again, tilted further.

"The tower's falling!" cried Harman. Beyond the many panes of glass in their elaborate iron frames, he could see the distant green horizon tilt, wobble, then tilt again.

"Not at all," said Prospero.

The two-story living unit was falling—sliding right out of the tower, screeching and rending across dry metal as if giant metal hands were pushing it out into thin air.

Harman leaped to his feet, decided to run for the doorway on the mezzanine, but then fell to his hands and knees as the two-story unit fell free of the tower, dropped at least fifteen feet, and then jerked violently before beginning a slide to the west.

Heart pounding, Harman stayed on his knees while the huge living unit rocked perilously back and forth on its long axis, then steadied. Above them, the screeching turned into a high-decibel hum. Harman stood, found his balance, staggered to the table, and looked out the window.

The tower was to their left and receding, an open patch of sky visible where this two-story, one-thousand-foot-level apartment had been. Harman could see the cables overhead and now understood the hum to be connected with some sort of flywheel in the housing above them. The *eiffelbahn* was some sort of cablecar system and this large iron house of a structure was the car. The vertical line he'd seen to the east earlier had been another tower, just like the one they'd just left. And the car was moving quickly to the west.

He turned to Prospero and took a step closer but stopped before coming within range of the magus's solid staff. "You have to let me get back to Ada," he said, trying for firmness but hearing the detestable pleading whine in his voice. "The voynix are all around Ardis Hall. I can't let her stay there in danger . . . without me. Please, Lord Prospero. Please."

"It is too late for you to intercede there, Harman, friend of Noman," said Prospero in his throaty, old-man's voice. "What's done is done at Ardis Hall. But let us put aside our sea-sorrow, sir, and not burden our remembrances with a heaviness that is gone. For we are embarked upon a new voyage now—surely the stuff of sea-change, friend of Noman— and one of us shall soon be the wiser, the deeper, fuller man, whilst our enemies—namely that darkness I bred and harbored out of Sycorax— shall drink of seawater and be forced to eat the withered roots of failure and the husks of scorn."

There was a storm brewing on and around Mount Olympos. A planetary dust storm had blanketed Mars in a red shroud, the howling winds swirling around the forcefield *aegis* that the absent Zeus had left in place around the home of the gods. Electrostatic particles so excited the shield that lightning flashed day and night around the summit of Olympos and thunder rumbled in the subsonic. Sunlight near the top of the mountain was diffused into a dull, bloody glow, punctuated by sheets of lightning and the ever-present rumble of the wind and thunder.

Achilles—still carrying his beloved but dead Amazon queen, Penthesilea—had quantum teleported to the home of his captive, Hephaestus, god of fire, chief Artificer to all the gods, husband of Aglaia, also known as Charis—the "delightfulness of art," one of the loveliest of Graces. Some said that the Artificer had built his wife as well.

Hephaestus had quantum teleported not directly into his home, but to its front door. To the casual glance the front of the crippled fire god's home looked like other dwelling places of the immortals—white stone, white pillars, white portico—but this was only the entrance; in truth Hephaestus had built his house and extensive workshops into the steep south slope of Olympos, far from Caldera Lake and the cluster of so many of the gods' huge temple-houses. He lived in a cave.

It was quite a cave, Achilles saw, as the foot-dragging Hephaestus led the way in and secured multiple iron doors behind them.

The cave had been carved out of the solid black stone of Olympos and this one room stretched away for hundreds of yards into the gloom. Everywhere were tables, arcane devices, magnifying lenses, tools, and machines in various stages of creation or dismembering. Deep in the cave roared an open hearth with liquid steel bubbling like orange lava. Closer to the front, where various stools, couches, low tables, a bed and braziers showed Hephaestus's actual living space carved out of the endless workshop, stood, sat, and walked some gold women—Hephaestus's infamous *attendants*—machine women with rivets, human eyes, metal breasts, and soft synthetic-flesh vaginas but also—so the tales said—with the stolen souls of human beings.

"You can lay her down here," said the dwarf-god, gesturing to a littered benchtop. With one swipe of his hairy forearm, Hephaestus cleared the table.

Releasing his grip on the dwarf-god, Achilles laid his linen-wrapped burden down with the utmost gentleness and reverence.

Penthesilea's face was visible and Hephaestus stared down for a minute. "She was beautiful, all right. And I can see Athena's work in the preservation of the corpse. Several days since death obviously and no rot or discoloration at all. The Amazon still has a flush to her cheeks. Do you mind if I roll the linen down just to take a peek at her tits?"

"If you touch her or her shroud," said Achilles, "I will kill you."

Hephaestus held up his palms. "All right, all right. Just curious." He slapped his palms together. "Food," he said. "Then strategy to bring your lady back."

The golden female attendants began bringing trays of hot food and large cups of wine to the round table at the center of Hephaestus' circle of couches. Fleet-footed Achilles and hairy Hephaestus both dug in with a will, not speaking except to demand more food or for the communal wine cup to be passed.

The attendants brought steaming fried liver wrapped in lamb intestines as an appetizer—one of Achilles' favorites. They carried in a complete roast piglet stuffed with the flesh of many small birds, raisins, chestnuts, egg yolks, and spiced meats. They set out bowls of pork stewed with bubbling apples and pears. They brought in pure delicacies such as roasted sow's womb and olives with mashed chickpeas. For the main course they served huge fish fried to a crispy, flaky brown on the outside.

"Netted in Zeus's own Caldera Lake atop Olympos," Hephaestus said with his mouth full.

For dessert and to cleanse the palate between courses they had a variety of fruits, sweetmeats, and nuts. The golden metal women set out bowls of figs and heaps of almonds, more bowls of fat dates and flat plates of the kind of delicious honeycakes that Achilles had tasted only once before when visiting the small city of Athens. Finally came that dessert most loved by Agamemnon, Priam, and other kings of kings—cheesecake.

After the meal, the robot attendants swept the table and floor and brought in more casks and double-handed goblets of wine—ten types of wine at least. Hephaestus did the honor of mixing the water with the wine and passing the huge cups.

The dwarf-god and god-man drank for two hours but neither entered the state that Achilles' people called *paroinia*—"intoxication frenzy."

The two males were mostly silent, but the naked, golden, female attendants celebrated for them—lining up and dancing around the table in the sensuous conga line that aesthetes such as Odysseus called the *komos*.

The man and god took turns going off to use the cave's toilet facilities, and when they were drinking wine again, Achilles said, "Is it night yet? Is it time for you to spirit me to the Healer's Hall?"

"Do you really think that Olympos' healing tanks will bring your Amazon doxie back to life, son of wet-breasted Thetis? Those tanks and worms were designed to repair immortals, not some human bitch—however beautiful."

Achilles was too drunk and too distracted to take offense. "Goddess Athena told me that the tanks would renew life to Penthesilea and Athena does not lie."

"Athena does nothing *but* lie," snorted Hephaestus, lifting the huge two-handled cup and drinking deeply. "And a few days ago you were waiting at the foot of Olympos, throwing rocks at Zeus's impenetrable *aegis*, howling for Athena to come down to fight so you could kill her just as surely as you stuck a spear through this Amazon's lovely tit. What changed, O Noble Mankiller?"

Achilles frowned at the god of fire. "This Trojan War has been . . . complicated, Cripple."

"I'll drink to that," laughed Hephaestus and lifted the big goblet again.

When they were ready to QT to the Healer's Hall, Achilles dressed in full armor again, his sword sharpened on the fire god's wheel and his shield polished, the son of Peleus walked to the bench to lift Penthesilea's body to his shoulder.

"No, leave her," said Hephaestus.

"What are you talking about?" growled Achilles. "She's the reason we're going to the Healer's Hall. I can't leave her here."

"We don't know which of the gods or guards will be there tonight," said the artificer. "You may have to fight your way through a phalanx. Do you want to do that with an Amazon's corpse on your shoulder? Or were you planning to use her beautiful body as a shield?"

Achilles hesitated.

"There's nothing here to harm her body," said Hephaestus. "I used to have rats and bats and roaches, but I built mechanical cats and falcons and praying mantises to rid the cave of them."

"Still . . ."

"If the Healer's Hall is empty, it'll take us three seconds to QT back here and fetch her corpse. In the meantime, I'll have the golden girls watch over her," said the artificer god. He snapped his stubby fingers and six of the metal attendants took up positions around the Amazon's body. "Are you ready now?"

"Yes."

Achilles gripped Hephaestus' heavily scarred upper arm and the two men popped out of existence.

The Healer's Hall was empty. No immortals were posted as guards. More surprising—even to Hephaestus—was that the many glass cylinders were empty. No gods were being healed and resurrected here tonight. In the huge space, lighted by only a few low-burning braziers and the violet light of the bubbling tanks themselves, nothing moved except the shuffling Hephaestus and the fleet-footed Achilles, shield held high.

Then the Healer emerged from the shadows of the bubbling vats.

Achilles raised his shield higher.

Athena had said to him over the corpse of Penthesilea—"Kill the Healer—a great, monstrous, centipede thing with too many arms and eyes. Destroy everything in the Healer's Hall"—but Achilles had assumed that Athena was calling the healer a centipede out of insult, not as a literal description.

This thing had the segmented body of a centipede, but it rose thirty feet high, its segmented body swaying, its body-circling rings of black eyes on the top segment locked on Achilles and Hephaestus. The Healer had feelers and segmented arms—too many—and spindly hands with spidery fingers on the ends of half a dozen of those upper arms. One body segment near the top wore a vest of many pockets, bulging with tools, and there were straps and bands and black belts holding other tools on other segments of the swaying torso.

"Healer," called Hephaestus, "where is everybody?"

The huge centipede swayed, waggled arms, and erupted in a stutter of noise from unseen mouths.

"Did you understand that?" Hephaestus asked Achilles.

"Understand what? It sounded like a boy running a stick along the rib cage of a skeleton."

"It's all good Greek," said Hephaestus. "You just have to slow it down in your mind, listen more carefully." To the Healer, the dwarf-god cried, "My mortal friend did not understand you. Could you repeat that, O Healer?"

"LordGodZeus'sOrdersAreThatNoMortalShallEverBePlaced InOneOfTheRegenerationTanksWithoutHisExpressCommand.The LordGodMasterZeusIsNowhereToBeFound.AndSinceHisCommand OnlyOnOlymposDoesTheHealerObeyICannotAllowAMortalToPass UntilZeusReturnsToHisThroneOnOlympos."

"Did you understand *that*?" the artificer asked Achilles.

"Something about this thing obeying only Zeus and not allowing Penthesilea to be put into one of the vats without Zeus's express command?"

"Precisely."

"I can kill this big bug," said Achilles.

"Perhaps so," said Hephaestus. "Although the Healer is whispered to be even more immortal than we johnny-come-lately gods. But if you kill it, Penthesilea will never be brought back to life. Only the Healer knows how to operate the machinery and command the blue and green worms that are part of the healing process."

"You're the Artificer," said Achilles, tapping his sword against the rim of his golden shield. "You must know how to operate this machinery."

"The fuck I do," growled Hephaestus. "This isn't simple technology like we used when we were mere post-humans. I could never figure out the Healer's quantum machines . . . and if I did, I still couldn't order the blue worms to work. I think they respond only to telepathy and only to the Healer."

"This bug said that he only obeyed Zeus *on Olympos*," said Achilles, who was perilously close to losing his temper and killing the god of fire, the giant centipede, and every god still left on Olympos. "Who else can command it?"

"Kronos," said Hephaestus with a maddening smile. "But Kronos

342 DAN SIMMONS

and the other Titans have been banished to Tartarus forever. Only Zeus in this universe can tell the Healer what to do."

"Then where is Zeus?"

"No one knows," growled Hephaestus, "but in his absence the gods are warring with one another for control. The fighting is now mostly centered down on Ilium's Earth, where the gods still support their Trojans or their Greeks, and Olympos is largely empty and peaceful now—it's why I ventured out onto this fucking volcano's slopes to survey the damage to my escalator."

"Why would Athena give me this god-killing knife and order me to kill the Healer after the thing brings Penthesilea back to life?" asked Achilles.

Hephaestus' eyes widened. "She told you to kill the Healer?" The bearded dwarf-god's voice was low and puzzled. "I have no idea why she would order such a thing. She has some scheme, but it must be a mad one. With the Healer dead, the vats here would be useless . . . all of our immortality would be a joke. We could live a very long time, but we would suffer, son of Peleus. Suffer terribly without nano-rejuvenation."

Achilles strode toward the Healer, pulling his famous shield tight until his eyes blazed through the slits of his shining war helmet. He pulled back his sword. "I'll make this thing activate the vats for Penthesilea."

Hephaestus hurried forward to grab Achilles' arm. "No, my mortal friend. Believe me when I say that the Healer does not fear death and it will not be moved. It obeys only Zeus. Without the fucking Healer, the blue worms will not perform. Without the fucking blue worms, the vats are useless. Without the fucking vats, your Amazon queen will stay fucking dead forfuckingever."

Achilles angrily shook off the artificer's hand. "This . . . bug . . . *has* to put Penthesilea in the healing vats." Even while he was saying this, Achilles again is reminded of Athena's command for him to kill the Healer. *What is that bitch-goddess up to? How is she using me? To what purpose? She's not insane and she certainly has no intention of killing the one creature who can preserve her immortality.*

"The Healer does not fear you, son of Peleus. You can kill it, but that only means you will never see your queen alive again."

Achilles walked away from the dwarf-god, brushed past the huge Healer, and slammed his beautiful shield—with all its hammered concentric circles of symbols—hard into the clear plastic of the huge regeneration tank. The sound echoed in the dim darkness of the hall.

He swung back to Hephaestus. "All right. This bug obeys Zeus. Where is Zeus?"

The god of fire began to laugh and then stopped when he saw

Achilles' eyes blazing out through his helmet's eyeslits. "You're serious? Your plan is to bend the God of Thunder, the Father of All Gods to your will?"

"*Where* is Zeus?"

"No one knows," repeated Hephaestus. The crippled god walked toward the tall doors, dragging his shorter leg behind. Lightning flashed outside as the dust storm made the forcefield *aegis* spark in a thousand places. The pillars cut columns of black out of the silver-white light flooding into the Hall of the Healer. "Zeus has been absent these two weeks and more," shouted the fire god over his shoulder. He tugged at his tangled beard. "Most of us suspect some fucking plot of Hera's. Maybe she threw her husband down into the hellpit of Tartarus to join his vanished father Kronos and mother Rhea."

"Can you find him?" Achilles turned his back on the Healer and slid his sword into its loop on his broad girdle. He swung his heavy shield over his back. "Can you take me to him?"

Hephaestus could only stare. "You'd go down into Tartarus to try to bend the God of Gods to your mortal will? There's only one life form in the pantheon of the original gods besides Zeus who might know where he is. That terrible power also is the only other immortal here on Mars who could send us to Tartarus. You would *go* to Tartarus if you had to?"

"I'd pass through the teeth of death and back again to bring life back to my Amazon," Achilles said softly.

"You'd find Tartarus a thousand times worse than death and the shaded halls of Hades, son of Peleus."

"Take me to this immortal of which you speak," commanded Achilles. His eyes through the eyeslits of his helmet were not quite sane.

For a long minute the bearded artificer stood hunched over, panting slightly, eyes unfocused, his hand still tugging absently at his tangled beard. Then he said, "So be it," dragged his bad leg across the polished marble more rapidly than seemed possible, and clasped both huge hands around Achilles' forearm.

44

Harman hadn't meant to sleep. As exhausted as he was, he'd agreed only to eat and drink something, warming up an excellent stew and eating it at the table by the window while Prospero sat silently in the overstuffed armchair. The magus was reading out of a huge, worn, leatherbound book.

When Harman turned to talk to Prospero again, to demand in stronger terms that he be returned to Ardis, the old man was gone and so was the book. Harman had sat at the table for some minutes, only half-aware of the jungle rolling by nine hundred feet below the moving, creaking, house-sized cablecar. Then—just to look at the upstairs again, he told himself—he'd dragged himself up the iron spiral staircase, stood looking at the large bed for a minute, and then had collapsed on it face-first.

When he awoke it was night. Moonlight and ringlight flooded through the panes into the strange bedroom, painting velvet and brass in light so rich it appeared to be stripes of white paint. Harman opened the doors and stepped out onto the bedroom terrace.

The air was cool almost a thousand feet above the jungle floor, the breeze constant due to the motion of the cablecar, but he still was struck by the humidity, heat, and organic scents of all the green life below. The top of the jungle canopy was almost unbroken, whitewashed with ringlight and moonlight from the three-quarters moon, and occasional strange sounds wafted up, audible even over the steady hum of the flywheels above and the creak of the long cable. Harman took a minute to orient himself by the e- and p-rings.

He was sure that the car had been headed west when they'd left the first tower hours earlier—he'd slept for ten hours, at least—but now there was no doubt that the cablecar was lumbering north-northeast. He could see the moonlight-illuminated tip of one of the *eiffelbahn* towers just showing over the horizon to the southwest, from the direction he must have come, and another coming closer less than twenty miles to the northeast. Somewhere, while he slept, the car he was traveling in must have changed direction at a tower junction. Harman's knowledge of geography was all self-taught, gleaned from books he'd taught himself to read—and he was quite sure that until recent months he was the *only* old-style human on Earth who had *any* sense of geography, any knowledge that the earth was a globe—but he'd never paid much attention to this arrow-shaped subcontinent south of what used to be called Asia. Still, it didn't take a cartographer's knowledge to know that if Prospero had been telling the truth—if his destination was the coast of Europe where the Atlantic Breach began along the 40th Parallel—then he was going the wrong way.

It didn't matter. Harman had no intention of staying in this odd device the necessary weeks or months it would take to travel all that distance. Ada needed him *now*.

He paced the length of the balcony, occasionally grabbing the railing when the cablecar-house rocked slightly. It was on his third turn that he noticed an iron-rung ladder running up the side of the structure just beyond the railing. Harman swung out, grasped a rung, and pulled himself onto the ladder. There was nothing beneath him and the ground now but a thousand feet of air and jungle canopy.

The ladder led onto the roof of the cablecar. Harman swung himself up, legs pinioning for a second before he found a handhold and pulled himself onto the flat roof.

He stood carefully, arms extended for balance when the cablecar rocked as it began climbing a ridgeline toward the blinking lights of an *eiffelbahn* tower now only ten miles or so ahead. Beyond the next tower, a range of mountains had just become visible on the horizon, their snowy peaks almost brilliant in the moonlight and ringlight.

Exhilarated by the night and sense of speed, Harman noticed something. There was a faint shimmering about three feet out from the leading edge of the cable car, a slight blurring of the moon, rings, and vista below. He walked to that edge and extended his hand as far as possible.

There was a forcefield there, not a powerful one—his fingers pressed through it as if pushing through a resistant but permeable membrane, reminding Harman of the entrance to the Firmary on Prospero's orbital isle—but strong enough to deflect the wind from the blunt and non-aerodynamic side of the cablecar-house. With his fingers beyond the forcefield, he could feel the true force of the wind, enough to bend his hand back. This thing was moving faster than he'd thought.

After a half hour or so of pacing and standing on the roof, listening to the cables hum, watching the next *eiffelbahn* tower approach, and working out strategies to get back to Ada, Harman went hand over hand down the rung-ladder, jumped onto the balcony, and reentered the house.

Prospero was waiting for him on the first floor. The magus was in the same armchair, his robed legs not up on the ottoman, the large book open on his lap and his staff near his right hand.

"What do you want from me?" asked Harman.

Prospero looked up. "I see, young sir, that you are as disproportionate in your manners as our mutual friend Caliban is in his shape."

"What do you want of me?" repeated Harman, his hands balling into fists.

"It is time for you to go to war, Harman of Ardis."

"Go to war?"

"Yes. Time for your kind to fight. Your kind, your kin, your species, your ilk—yourself."

"What are you talking about? War with whom?"

"With *what* might be a better phrasing," said Prospero.

"Are you talking about the voynix? We're already fighting them. I brought Noman-Odysseus to the Bridge at Machu Picchu primarily to fetch more weapons."

"Not the voynix, no," said Prospero. "Nor the *calibani,* although all these slave-things have been tasked to kill your kin and kind, the minutes of their plot come 'round at last. I am speaking of the Enemy."

"Setebos?" said Harman.

"Oh, yes." Prospero placed his aged hand on the broad page of the book, set a long leaf in as a bookmark, closed the book gently, and rose, leaning on his staff. "Setebos, the many-handed as a cuttlefish, is here at last, on your world and mine."

"I know that. Daeman saw the thing in Paris Crater. Setebos has woven some blue-ice web over that faxnode and a dozen others, including Chom and . . ."

"And do you know why the many-handed has come now to Earth?" interrupted Prospero.

"No," said Harman.

"To feed," Prospero said softly. "To feed."

"On us?" Harman felt the cablecar slow, then bump, and he noticed the next *eiffelbahn* tower surrounding them for a second, the two-story structure of the car fitting into the landing on the thousand-foot level just as it had on the first tower. He felt the car swivel, heard gears grind and clank, and they slid out of the tower on a different heading, traveling more east than north now. "Has Setebos come to feed on us?" he asked again.

Prospero smiled. "Not exactly. Not directly."

"What the hell does that mean?"

"It means, young Harman human, that Setebos is a ghoul. Our many-handed friend feeds on the residues of fear and pain, the dark energy of sudden terror and rich residue of equally sudden death. This memory of terror lies in the soil of your world—of any warlike sentient creatures' world—like so much coal or petroleum, all of a lost era's wild energy sleeping underground."

"I don't understand."

"It means that Setebos, the Devourer of Worlds, that Gourmet of Dark History, has secured some of your faxnodes in blue stasis, yes—to lay his eggs, to send his seed out across your world, to suck the warmth out of these places like a succubus sucking breath from a sleeping soul—but it's your memory and your history that will fatten him like a many-handed blood tick."

"I still don't understand," said Harman.

"His nest now is in Paris Crater, Chom, and these other provincial places where you humans party and sleep and waste your useless lives away," said Prospero, "but he will feed at Waterloo, HoTepsa, Stalingrad, Ground Zero, Kursk, Hiroshima, Saigon, Rwanda, Cape Town, Montreal, Gettysburg, Riyadh, Cambodia, Khanstaq, Chancellorsville, Okinawa, Tarawa, My Lai, Bergen Belsen, Auschwitz, the Somme—do any of these names mean anything to you, Harman?"

"No."

Prospero sighed. "This is our problem. Until some fragment of your human race regains the memory of your race, you cannot fight Setebos, you cannot understand Setebos. You cannot understand yourselves."

"Why is that your problem, Prospero?"

The old man sighed again. "If Setebos eats the human pain and memory of this world—an energy resource I call *umana*—this world will be physically alive but spiritually dead to any sentient being . . . including me."

"*Spiritually* dead?" repeated Harman. He knew the word from his reading and sigling—spirit, spiritual, spirituality—vague ideas having to do with ancient myths of ghosts and religion—it just made no sense coming from this hologram of a logosphere avatar, the too-cute construct of some set of ancient software programs and communication protocols.

"Spiritually dead," repeated the magus. "Psychically, philosophically, organically dead. On the quantum level, a living world records the most sentient energies its inhabitants experience, Harman of Ardis—love, hate, fear, hope. Like particles of magnetite aligning to a north or south pole. The poles may change, wander, disappear, but the recordings remain. The resulting energy field is as real—although more difficult to measure and locate—as the magnetosphere a planet with a hot spinning core produces, protecting the living inhabitants with its forcefield from the harshest realities of space. So does the memory of pain and suffering protect the future of a sentient race. Does *this* make sense to you?"

"No," said Harman.

Prospero shrugged. "Then take my word for it. If you ever want to see Ada alive again, you will have to learn . . . much. Perhaps too much. But after this learning, you will at least be able to join the fight. There may be no hope—there usually is none when Setebos begins devouring a world's memory—but at least we can fight."

"Why do you care?" asked Harman. "What difference does it make to you whether human beings survive? Or their memories?"

Prospero smiled thinly. "What do you take me for? Do you think I am a mere function of old e-mails, the icon of an ancient Internet with a staff and robe?"

"I don't know what the hell you are," said Harman. "A hologram."

Prospero took a step closer and slapped Harman hard across the face.

Harman took a step back, gaping. He raised his hand to his stinging cheek, balled that hand into a fist.

Prospero smiled and held his staff between them. "If you don't want to wake up on the floor ten minutes from now with the worst headache of your life, don't think about it."

"I want to go home to Ada," Harman said slowly.

"Did you try to find her with your functions?" asked the magus.

Harman blinked. "Yes."

"And did any of your functions work here on the cablecar, or in the jungle before it?"

"No," said Harman.

"Nor will they work until you've mastered the rest of the functions you command," said the old man, returning to his chair and carefully lowering himself into it.

"The rest of the functions . . ." began Harman. "What do you mean?"

"How many functions have you mastered?" asked Prospero.

"Five," said Harman. One had been known to everyone for ages—the Finder Function, which included a chronometer—but Savi had taught them three others. Then he had discovered the fifth.

"Recite them."

Harman sighed. "Finder function—proxnet, farnet, allnet, and sigling—reading through one's palm."

"And have you mastered the allnet function, Harman of Ardis?"

"Not really." There was too much information, too much *bandwidth,* as Savi had said.

"And do you think that old-style humans—the *real* old-style humans, your undesigned and unmodified ancestors—had five such functions, Harman of Ardis?"

"I . . . I don't know." He'd never thought about it.

"They did not," Prospero said flatly. "You are the result of four thou-

sand years of gene-tampering and nanotech splicing. How did you discover the sigl function, Harman of Ardis?"

"I . . . just experimented with mental images, triangles, squares, circles, until one worked," said Harman.

"That's what you told Ada and the others," said Prospero, "but that
is a lie. How did you *really* learn to sigl?"

"I dreamt the sigl function code," admitted Harman. It had been too
strange—too *precious*—to tell the others.

"Ariel helped you with that dream," said Prospero, his thin-lipped
smile showing again. "We grew impatient. Would you like to guess how
many functions each of you—every one of you 'old-style humans'—has
in your cells and blood and brainstuff?"

"More than five functions?" asked Harman.

"One hundred," said Prospero. "An even hundred."

"Teach them to me," said Harman, taking a step toward the magus.

Prospero shook his head. "I cannot. I would not. But you need to
learn them nonetheless. On this voyage you will learn them."

"We're going the wrong way," said Harman.

"What?"

"You said the *eiffelbahn* would take me to the coast of Europe where
the Atlantic Breach begins, but we're heading east now, away from Europe."

"We will swing north again two towers hence," said Prospero. "Are
you impatient to arrive?"

"Yes."

"Don't be," said the magus. "All the learning will happen during the
trip, not after it. Yours will be the sea change of all sea changes. And trust
me, you do not want to take the short route—over the old Pakistan
passes into the waste called Afghanistan, south along the Mediterranean
Basin and across the Sahara Marshes."

"Why not?" said Harman. He and Savi and Daeman had flown east
across the Atlantic and then over the Sahara Marshes to Jerusalem, then
taken a crawler into the dry Mediterranean Basin. It was a place on Earth
he knew. And he wanted to see if the blue tachyon beam still rose from
the Temple Mount in Jerusalem. Savi had said it carried all of the coded
information of all her lost contemporaries from fourteen hundred years
ago.

"The *calibani* are loosed," said Prospero.

"They've left the Basin?"

"They are freed of their old restraints, the center cannot hold. Mere
anarchy is loosed upon the world. Or at least upon that part of it."

"Then where are we going?"

"Patience, Harman of Ardis. Patience. Tomorrow we cross a mountain range I believe you will find most enlightening. Then into Asia—where you may behold the works of the mighty and the dead—and then west and west enough again. The Breach will wait."

"Too slow," said Harman, pacing back and forth. "Too long. If the functions don't work here, I don't have any way of knowing how Ada is. I need to go. I need to get home."

"You want to know how your Ada fares?" asked Prospero. He was not smiling. The magus pointed to a red cloth draped over the couch. "Use that. This one time only."

Harman frowned, went to the cloth, studied it. "A turin cloth?" he said. It was red—all turin cloths were tan. Nor was the microcircuit embroidery the same.

"There are a myriad of turin-cloth receivers," said Prospero. "Just as there are a myriad of sensory transmitters. Every person can be one."

Harman shook his head. "I don't give a damn about the turin drama—Troy, Agamemnon, all that nonsense. I'm not in the mood for amusements."

"This cloth tells you nothing of Ilium," said Prospero. "It will show you your Ada's fate. Try it."

Trembling, Harman sat back on the couch, adjusted the red cloth over his face, touched the embroidery to his forehead, and closed his eyes.

The *Queen Mab* decelerated toward Earth on a column of nuclear explosions, the ship kicking out a Coke-can-sized fission bomb every thirty seconds, the bomb exploding and driving the pusher plate back up to the stern of the thousand-foot-long ship, the huge pistons and cylinders in the clockwork engine room cycling back and forth, the next can-bomb being ejected . . .

Mahnmut was watching on the stern video channel. *If anyone on Earth didn't know we were coming, they must know now,* he said to Orphu on their tightbeam channel. The two had been invited to the bridge for the first time on the voyage and they were in the largest lift now, rising toward the bow of the ship—which during deceleration, of course, was aiming back toward space rather than at the rapidly growing Earth.

I don't think the idea is to be subtle, tightbeamed Orphu.

Obviously not. But this is about as subtle as a stomach pump, about as subtle as a pay toilet in the diarrhea ward, about as subtle as . . .

Do you have a point? rumbled Orphu.

It's too *unsubtle,* said Mahnmut. *Too obvious. Too visible. Too precious— I mean, mid-Twentieth Century spaceship designs, for God's sake. Fission bombs. Ejection mechanisms from the Atlanta, Georgia, Coca-Cola bottling plant circa 1959 . . .*

So your point is? interrupted Orphu. In the old days, his eye-stalks and video cameras would have tracked toward Mahnmut—some of them, at least—but those had not been replaced since his optic nerves had been burned out.

I have to assume that less obvious moravec ships—modern ships, stealth-activated and stealth-propelled ships—are following us, sent Mahnmut.

That has been my assumption as well, said the big hard-vac moravec.

You never mentioned it.

Nor have you, until now, said Orphu.

Why didn't Asteague/Che and the other Prime Integrators tell us? asked Mahnmut. *If we're being put out ahead of the real fleet as the obvious target, we have a right to know.*

Orphu sent a subsonic rumble that Mahnmut had learned was the Ionian's equivalent of a shrug. *It wouldn't make any difference, would it?* said the big moravec. *If the Earth defenses fire on us and breach our rather modest forcefield defenses, we'll be dead before we have time to complain.*

Speaking of Earth defenses, has the voice from the orbital city said anything else since the message two weeks ago? The maser broadcast had been succinct; the recorded female-human voice had simply said "Bring Odysseus to me" over and over for twenty-four hours and then had cut off as quickly as it had begun. The message had not been broadcast at random—it had been aimed precisely at the *Queen Mab.*

I've been monitoring the incoming channels, said Orphu, *and I haven't heard anything new.*

The lift whirred and stopped. The broad cargo doors opened. Mahnmut stepped onto the bridge for the first time since before their launch from Phobos and Orphu repellored after him.

The bridge was circular with a diameter of thirty meters, the ceiling dome-shaped and ringed with thick windows and holographic screens serving as windows. From a spaceship-spaceship point of view, it was almost completely satisfying to Mahnmut. Although the unnamed spacecraft that had brought Orphu, the late Koros III and Ri Po, and him to Mars had been centuries more advanced—accelerated to one-fifth light speed by magnetic scissors accelerator wickets, carrying a boron light sail, fusion engines, and other modern moravec devices—this strangely retro atomic spaceship and spaceship grid looked . . . *right*. Instead of purely virtual controls and simple jack-in stations, more than a dozen tech moravecs sat in old-fashioned acceleration chairs at even more old-fashioned metal and glass monitoring stations. There were actual switches, real toggles, physical dials—*dials!*—and a hundred other eye- and vid-camera-pleasing details. The floor looked to be of textured steel, perhaps lifted straight out of the hull of some World War II–era seagoing battleship.

The usual suspects—Orphu's irreverent term—stood awaiting them near the central navigation table: Asteague/Che their central Prime Integrator from Europa, General Beh bin Adee representing the Belt fighter-moravecs, Cho Li their Callistan navigator (looking and sounding far too much like the dead Ri Po for Mahnmut's comfort), Suma IV the brawny, buckycarbon-sheathed fly-eyed Ganymedan, and the spidery Retrograde Sinopessen.

Mahnmut walked closer to the map table and stepped up onto the metal ledge that allowed smaller moravecs to look down upon the glowing table surface. Mahnmut floated over.

"We have a little less than fourteen hours until low-Earth orbital insertion," said Asteague/Che without greetings or introductions. His voice—that James Mason voice to Mahnmut's Lost Era history-vid-trained ears and audio receivers—was smooth but businesslike. "We have to decide what to do."

The Prime Integrator was vocalizing rather than transmitting on the common band. The bridge was pressurized to Earth normal—an atmospheric content the Europan moravecs liked and the others could tolerate—and audible speech was more private than common band chatter and less conspiratorial than tightbeaming.

"Have there been any more broadcasts from that woman asking us to deliver Odysseus?" asked Orphu.

"No," said Cho Li, the bulky Callistan navigator. Cho Li's voice, as always, was very, very soft. "But the orbital construction that was the source of that broadcast is our destination."

Cho Li ran a manipulator tentacle over the map table and a large hologram of Earth appeared. The equatorial and polar rings were very bright, countless specks of light moving west to east along the equator and north to south around the poles.

"This is a live video feed," said the tiny little silver box amidst the skinny little silver legs that comprised the Amalthean Retrograde Sinopessen.

"I can read the data bars via the common channel," said Orphu of Io. "And I can 'see' all of you on my radar return and infrared scans. But there may be subtle aspects of the holo projections that I miss—being blind and all."

"I'll give a description via tightbeam of everything I see," said Mahnmut. He connected via tightbeam and set up a high-speed squirt feed to the Ionian, describing the holographic image of the blue and white Earth hanging in space above the chart table, the bright polar and equatorial rings crisscrossing above the oceans and clouds. The rings were close enough that countless discrete objects could be seen gleaming against the black of space.

"Magnification?" asked Orphu.

"Just ten," said Sinopessen. "Small binoculars level. We're approaching the orbit of Earth's Moon—although right now Luna is on the backside of the planet from us. We'll cease use of the fission bombs and switch to ion drive as we enter their cislunar space—no reason to antagonize anyone there. Our velocity is down to ten kilometers per second and dropping. You may have noticed our one-point-two-five Earth-g deceleration the last two days."

"How has Odysseus been taking the added g-load?" asked Mahnmut. He'd not seen their only remaining human passenger over the past week. Mahnmut had hoped that Hockenberry would QT back to the *Queen Mab,* but so far he hadn't.

"Fine," rumbled Suma IV, the tall Ganymedan. "He tends to stay in his bunk and quarters more than usual, but he was doing that before we raised the deceleration g-load."

"Has he said anything about the female voice on the maser—or the 'Bring Odysseus to me' message?" asked Orphu.

"No," said Asteague/Che. "He has told us that he doesn't recognize the voice—that he's sure it doesn't belong to Athena, Aphrodite, or any of the Olympian immortals he's met."

"Where did the broadcast come from?" Mahnmut asked.

Cho Li activated a laser pen embedded in one of his manipulators and pointed out the speck in the polar ring, currently approaching the south pole on the backside of the transparent Earth holo. "Magnify," the navigator ordered the *Mab*'s main AI.

The speck seemed to leap forward until it replaced the entire Earth hologram. It was a roughly dumbbell-shaped city of metal girders, opaque orange glass and light: tall glass towers, glass bubbles, glass domes, convoluted glass spires and arches. Mahnmut summarized it all in his tightbeam descriptions to Orphu.

"This is one of the larger artificial objects in Earth orbit," said Retrograde Sinopessen. "About twenty kilometers long, roughly the size of their Lost Era city of Manhattan before it was flooded. It seems to be built around a stone and heavy metal core—probably a captured asteroid—that gives—or gave—a little gravity to the inhabitants."

"How much?" asked Orphu or Io.

"Roughly ten centimeters per second," said the Almathean. "Enough that a human—or unmodified post-human—wouldn't float away or be able to achieve escape velocity by jumping, but light enough to float pretty much where you want to."

"Pretty close to Phobos' size and gravity," said Mahnmut. "Any clue who the voice belongs to or who lives there?"

"The post-humans built these orbital environments more than two thousand standard years ago," said Prime Integrator Asteague/Che. "You both know that we assumed the post-humans had died out—their radio chatter stopped more than a millennia ago even as the quantum flux between Earth and Mars began to build, we haven't seen their ships in cislunar space through our telescopes, there's been no sign of them on Earth itself—but we can't preclude the possibility that a few have survived. Or evolved."

"Into what?" asked Orphu.

Asteague/Che performed that most archaic, arcane, yet expressive of human motions—he shrugged. Mahnmut started to describe the other Europan's shrug to his friend but Orphu tightbeamed that he'd picked it up on both radar and infrared sensors.

"Let me show you some recent activity before we decide if you're going to drop *The Dark Lady* into Earth's atmosphere," continued Asteague/Che. He set one very humanoid hand above the chart table.

The orbital island hologram was replaced with holos showing Earth and Mars, in scale of size but not in distance, with a myriad of blue, green, and white strands connecting Near-Earth-Orbit and the surface of Mars. Columns of holographic data misted into existence. The two planets looked as if they'd been woven into a spider's frenzied web, except in this case the web itself pulsed and grew, strands contracting and expanding, extruding new strands and nodes as if of their own volition. Mahnmut rushed to describe it all on the tightbeam channel.

It's all right, transmitted Orphu. *I'm reading the databands. It's almost as good as seeing the graphics.*

"This is quantum activity of the past ten standard days," said Cho Li. "You'll note that it's almost ten percent more volatile and active than when we launched from Phobos. The instability is reaching a critical stage . . ."

"How critical?" asked Orphu of Io.

Asteague/Che turned his visored face toward the big Ionian. "Critical enough that we have to make a decision in the next week or so. Less time if the volatility continues to grow. This level of quantum instability threatens the entire solar system."

"What decision?" asked Mahnmut.

"Whether to destroy the Earth's polar and equatorial rings where the quantum flux originated, also whether to cauterize Olympus Mons and the other quantum nodes on Mars," said General Beh bin Adee. "And to sterilize the Earth itself if need be."

Orphu whistled, an odd sound on the echoing bridge. "Does the *Queen Mab* have such a military capability?" the Ionian asked softly.

"No," said the general.

I guess I was right about the invisible moravec ships shadowing us, thought Mahnmut.

On the tightbeam, Orphu sent—*I guess we were right about the invisible moravec ships shadowing us.* If Mahnmut had had eyelids, he would have blinked at this similarity in their thought patterns

A silence descended. None of the six moravecs around the chart table spoke or transmitted again for almost a minute.

"There are more developments to share with you," Suma IV said at last. The buckycarbon-sheathed Ganymedan touched controls and a different, magnified telescopic view of Earth leapt into place. Mahnmut recognized what had once been called the British Isles—Shakespeare!—and then the view zoomed in on the continent of Europe. Two images filled the holocube—an odd city radiating out from a black crater and then what might have been the same city, sheathed in a blue web not so dissimilar from the view of the quantum displacement between Earth and Mars. He described the blue mass to his friend.

"What the hell is it?" asked Orphu.

"We don't know," said Suma IV, "but it's appeared in the last seven standard days. These coordinates match those of the ancient city of Paris in the nation of France, but where our astronomers from Phobos and Martian space had been observing old-style human activity—primitive but visible—now there is just this blue dome, blue webs, blue spires surrounding what was obviously an old black-hole crater."

"What could be spinning that web?" asked Mahnmut.

"Again, we don't know," said Suma IV. "But look at the measurements coming from inside it."

Orphu did not whistle this time, but Mahnmut felt the urge to. Temperatures in the blue-webbed parts of Paris had dropped below minus 100 degrees Celsius, where, just meters away, the temperatures still hovered near Earth normal for that region and time of the year, while just meters away from *that*, the temperature spiked to levels where lead would melt.

"Could this be a natural phenomenon?" asked Mahnmut. "Something the post-humans brought about during the Demented Times when they were fooling with Earth's ecology and life forms?"

"We've never seen or recorded anything like this before," said Asteague/Che. "And we've never stopped monitoring Earth from Consortium space. But look at this."

A dozen other blue-marked locations appeared in the holocube map, which pulled back until it was a large Earth sphere again. Blue-webbed sites were marked elsewhere in Europe, in Asia, in what had been South America, southern Africa—a dozen in total. Next to the blue circles were data cubes recording measurements similar to the Paris phenomenon, with notes on the day, hour, minute, and second that the blue web had appeared to moravec sensors. Mahnmut raced to tightbeam the image descriptions to Orphu.

"And this," said Asteague/Che.

Another sphere of Earth appeared showing straight blue lines rising from Paris and the other blue nodes, including one city marked Jerusalem. The thin blue shafts continued straight into space, disappearing beyond the solar system.

"Well, we've seen that before," said Orphu of Io after Mahnmut described it to him. "It's the same kind of tachyon beam that appeared at Delphi on the other Earth, the ancient Earth of Ilium, when the population disappeared."

"Yes," said Prime Integrator Asteague/Che.

"That beam didn't seem to be aimed at anything in deep space," said Mahnmut. "Are these?"

"Not unless you count grazing the Lesser Magellanic Clouds," said Cho Li. "Plus, there is a quantum component to these tachyon beams."

"What does that mean—'quantum component'?" asked Orphu.

"The beams phase-shift on the quantum level, existing more in Calabi-Yau space than in four-dimensional Einsteinian spacetime," said the Callistan navigator.

"You mean," said Mahnmut, "they're shifting into a different universe."

"Yes."

"The Ilium-Earth's universe?" asked Mahnmut. His tone was hopeful. When the last Brane Hole that had connected the current-Mars and Ilium-Earth universes had collapsed weeks earlier, the moravecs had lost all communication with that ancient Earth of Troy and Agamemnon, but Hockenberry had been able to quantum teleport across the Calabi-Yau universe-membrane to the *Queen Mab*—and presumably to QT back, although no one knew where he'd gone when he'd teleported off the atomic spaceship. Mahnmut, who knew many of the Greeks and Trojans, had hopes of reconnecting to that universe once again.

"We don't think so," said Cho Li. "The reasons are as complicated as the multiple-membrane Calabi-Yau space math our assumptions are based on and are guided by what we learned from the Device you successfully activated on Mars eight months ago, but we think the tachyon beam's phase-shifting is to one or more different universes, not that of the Ilium-Earth."

Mahnmut spread his hands. "So what does all this have to do with our mission to Earth? I was supposed to pilot *The Dark Lady* in Earth's seas or oceans, bringing Suma IV down for his mission—just as I was supposed to bring the late Ri Po to Olympus Mons last year. Does the blue-web stuff and the tachyon beams change that plan?"

There was another silence.

"The dangers and cautionary unknowns of an atmospheric penetration are proliferating," said Suma IV.

"Could you translate that?" said Orphu of Io.

"Observe, please," said the tall Ganymedan.

A holographic astronomical recording began running above the chart table. Mahnmut described the visuals to Orphu on tightbeam.

"Please note the date," said Prime Integrator Asteague/Che.

"That's more than eight months ago," said Mahnmut.

"Yes," said the Europan Integrator. "Shortly after we used the Brane Holes to transit to Mars-Ilium space. You notice that the resolution is relatively poor compared to today's observations of the orbital rings. This is because we were observing from Phobos Base."

The visuals showed an orbital object similar to the one that had broadcast the message to the *Queen Mab*, but not quite the same. This asteroid was visible as a slowly rotating rock, albeit one with glowing glass towers, domes, and structures. This orbital object was smaller—less than two kilometers in length. Suddenly another object came into the visual range of the recording—a three-kilometer-long metal construct rather like a long silver wand, clustered about with girders, storage tanks, and fuel cylinders, the column ending in a bulbous, shimmering sphere. Thrusters were firing but Mahnmut didn't believe the thing was merely a spacecraft.

"What the hell is that?" asked Orphu after hearing Mahnmut's description and reading the data.

"An orbital linear accelerator with a wormhole collector at its snout," said Asteague/Che. "Notice that someone—or something—on the asteroid city has sent masered commands to this unmanned linear accelerator, overriding countless safety protocols, and is driving it right toward the asteroid."

"Why?" asked Orphu.

No one answered. The five moravecs watched and Orphu listened as the long, girdered orbital machine continued accelerating until it crashed into the asteroid island. Asteague/Che slowed the recording. The glowing towers and domes exploded and flew apart in extreme slow motion, then the asteroid itself broke up as the wormhole accumulator at the end of the linear accelerator exploded with the force of countless hydrogen bombs. There came a final series of slow-motion, silent explosions as the fuel tanks, thrusters, and main drive engines of the linear accelerator ignited themseves.

"Now watch," said Suma IV.

A second telescopic view, then a radar plot, joined the holographic explosions. Mahnmut tightbeamed a description of the blaze of thruster tails from throughout the plane of the equatorial orbital ring as dozens, then hundreds of small spacecraft hurried toward the exploding orbital asteroid.

"What's the scale on those?" asked Orphu.

"They're each about six meters long by three meters wide," said Cho Li.

"Unmanned," said Orphu. "Moravecs?"

"More like the servitors the humans used centuries ago," said Asteague/Che. "Simple AI's with one purpose, as you will see."

Mahnmut saw. And he described what he saw to Orphu. The hundreds, then thousands of tiny devices rushing toward the expanding asteroid and accelerator debris field were little more than high-powered lasers each with a brain and aiming device. The recording fast-forwarded through the next hours with the servitor-lasers scooting through, under, and over the debris field, zapping every piece of asteroid or accelerator that posed a serious threat of surviving reentry through the Earth's atmosphere.

"The post-humans weren't fools," said Asteague/Che. "At least when it came to engineering. The mass they accumulated in the two rings they built around Earth, if gathered together, would build a sizeable fraction of another Luna—more than a million separate objects, some like the one that hailed us, almost as massive as Phobos. But they had near foolproof failsafes for keeping them in orbit and a defense in depth if they threatened to fall—these high-boost laser hornets that break up any debris are the last line of that defense. Meteors are still falling on Earth more than eight standard months later, but there have been no catastrophic impacts."

"Orbital leukocytes," said Orphu of Io.

"Precisely," said the Prime Integrator of the Five Moons Consortium.

"I understand," Mahnmut said at last. "You're afraid that if we use the dropship carrying *The Dark Lady* the way we planned, these little robot leukocytes will scurry out and zap us as well."

"The mass of the dropship and your submersible combined would be

a threat to Earth," agreed Asteague/Che. "We watched the . . . leukocytes, as Orphu put it . . . laser to plasma or boost uphill much smaller
pieces of the destroyed asteroid."

Mahnmut shook his metal-and-plastic head. "I don't get it. You've
had this recording and this knowledge for more than eight months, yet
you hauled the *Lady* and us all this way . . . what's changed?"

General Beh bin Adee pointed to something in the rerunning holo
recording of the asteroid breakup.

The image zoomed. The computers enhanced the grainy, pixilated
image.

What? tightbeamed Orphu.

Mahnmut described the enhanced image. There in the midst of all the
explosions and zapped debris was a small craft with three human figures lying prone in what appeared to be an open cockpit. Only the slight
shimmer of a forcefield showed why the three were not dying in a vacuum.

"What is that thing?" asked Mahnmut after he had described it to
Orphu.

It was Orphu who answered. "An ancient flying vehicle used by both
old-style humans and post-humans millennia ago. It was called an
AFV—All Function Vehicle—or sometimes they just called it a sonie.
The post-humans used them to shuttle to and from the rings."

The recording sped up, paused, sped up again. Mahnmut described
to Orphu the image of the sonie twisting and turning as segments of the
asteroid exploded—were lasered—all around it.

The holo showed the trajectory of the sonie as it entered the atmosphere, spiraled across the center of North America, and landed in a region below one of the Great Lakes.

"That was one of our destinations," said Asteague/Che. He tapped
some icons and telescopic still images appeared of a large human home
on a hill. The huge house was surrounded by outbuildings and what
looked to be a defensive wooden wall. Human beings—or what appeared to be human beings—were visible near the walls and house. Several dozen could be seen in the still photograph.

"That was one week ago as we began decelerating," said General Beh
bin Adee. "These were taken yesterday."

Same telescopic view, but now the house and wall were in ruins,
burned. Corpses were visible scattered across a charred landscape.

"I don't understand," said Mahnmut. "It looks as if the humans are
being massacred there where the sonie landed eight months ago. Who or
what killed them?"

Beh bin Adee brought up an another telescope image, then magnified
it. Scores of non-human bipeds were visible between bare branches of

trees. The things were a dull silver-gray, essentially headless, with a dark hump. The arms and legs were articulated wrong to be either human or known moravecs.

"What are those?" asked Mahnmut. "Servitors of some kind? Robots?"

"We don't know," said Asteague/Che. "But these creatures are killing old-style human beings in their small communities all over Earth."

Mahnmut said, "This is terrible but what does it have to do with canceling our mission?"

"I understand," said Orphu of Io. "The issue is how do you get to the surface to see what's going on. And the question is—why didn't the laser leukocytes fire on the sonie in the first place? It was large enough that it might survive reentry and pose a threat to those on the ground. Why was it spared?"

Mahnmut thought for several seconds. "There were humans on board," he said at last.

"Or post-humans," said Asteague/Che. "The resolution isn't fine enough for us to tell which."

"The leukocytes allow a ship with human or post-human life aboard to pass into the atmosphere," Mahnmut said slowly. "You've known this for more than eight months. *That's* why you had me kidnap Odysseus for this mission."

"Yes," said Suma IV. "The human was going down to Earth with us. His human DNA was to be our passkey."

"But now the voice from the other orbital isle is demanding that we deliver Odysseus to her or it," said Orphu with a deep rumble that may have signified irony or humor or indigestion.

"Yes," said Asteague/Che. "We have no idea if our dropship and your submersible will be allowed to enter Earth's atmosphere if there is no human life on board."

"We can always just ignore the invitation from the asteroid-city in the polar ring," said Mahnmut. "Bring Odysseus down to Earth with us, maybe send him back up in the dropship . . ." He thought another few seconds. "No, that won't work. Odds are that the asteroid-city will fire on us if the *Queen Mab* doesn't rendezvous as requested."

"Yes, it seems a real possibility," said Asteague/Che. "This imperative to deliver Odysseus to the orbital city and the views of a massacre of humans on Earth by non-human creatures are new factors since we planned your dropship excursion."

"Too bad Dr. Hockenberry QT'd away on us," said Mahnmut. "His DNA may have been rebuilt by the Olympian gods or whomever, but it probably would have gotten us through the orbital leukocytes."

"We have a little less than eleven hours to decide," said Asteague/Che. "At that point we'll be rendezvousing with the orbital city in the polar ring and it will be too late to deploy the dropship and submersible. I suggest we reconvene here in two hours and make a final decision."

As the two stepped and repellored into the cargo elevator, Orphu of Io set one of his larger manipulator pads on Mahnmut's shoulder.

Well, Stanley, sent the Ionian, *this is another fine mess you've gotten us into.*

46

Harman experienced the attack on Ardis Hall in real time.

The turin-cloth experience—seeing, hearing, watching from the eyes of some unseen other—had always been a dramatic but irrelevant entertainment for him before this. Now it was a living hell. Instead of the absurd and seemingly fictional Trojan War, it was an attack on Ardis that Harman felt—*knew*—was real, either happening simultaneously to his viewing of it or very recently recorded.

Harman sat under the cloth, lost to the real world, for more than six hours. He watched from the time the voynix attacked a little after midnight until just before sunrise, when Ardis was ablaze and the sonie flew away to the north after his wounded, bleeding, unconscious, beloved Ada had been dragged aboard like a sack of suet.

Harman was surprised to see Petyr there at Ardis with the sonie— where were Hannah and Odysseus?—and he cried aloud in pain when he watched as Petyr was struck by a voynix-thrown rock and fell to his death. So many of his Ardis friends dead or dying—young Peaen falling, beautiful Emme having her arm torn off by a voynix and then burning to death in a ditch with Reman, Salas dead, Laman struck down. The weapons Petyr had brought from the Golden Gate at Machu Picchu had not turned the tide against the rampaging voynix.

Harman moaned under the blood-red turin cloth.

Six hours after he activated the microcircuit embroidery, the turin images ended and Harman rose and flung the cloth from him.

The magus was gone. Harman went into the small bathing room, used the strange toilet, flushed it with the porcelain handle on the brass chain, splashed water on his face and then drank prodigously, gulping handfuls of tap water. He came back out and searched the two-story cablecar-structure.

"Prospero! *PROSPERO!!*" His bellow echoed in the metal structure.

On the second floor, Harman threw open the doors to the balcony and stepped out. He jumped to the rungs—indifferent to the long fall beneath him—and climbed quickly to the roof of the moving, rising car.

The air was freezing. He'd turined away the night and a cold, gold sun was just rising to his right. The cables stretched away due north and they were rising. Harman stood at the edge of the roof and looked straight down, realizing that both the cablecar and the *eiffelbahn* must have been rising—climbing in altitude—for hours. He'd left the jungle and the plains behind in the night and climbed first into foothills and now into real mountains.

"*Prospero!!!!*" Harman's shout echoed from the rocks hundreds of feet below.

He stood atop the cablecar until the sun was two handspans above the horizon, but no warmth came with the rising sun. Harman realized he was freezing. The *eiffelbahn* was carrying him into a region of ice, rock, and sky—all green and growing things had been left behind. He looked over the edge and saw a huge river of ice—he knew the word from his sigling, *glacier*—winding like a white serpent between rock and ice peaks, the sunlight blinding from it, the great white mass wrinkled with black fissures and pocked with rocks and boulders it was carrying downhill.

Ice fell from the cables above him. The turning wheels took on a new, cold hum. Harman saw that ice had formed on the roof of the rocking car, lined the rungs going down the outside wall, gleamed on the cables themselves. Crawling to the edge, hands aching, body shaking, he made his way carefully down the rung ladder, swung to the ice-encrusted balcony, and staggered into the heated room.

There was a fire in the iron fireplace. Prospero stood there, warming his hands.

Harman stood by the ice-latticed doorpanes for several minutes, shaking as much from rage as from the cold. He resisted the urge to rush the magus. Time was precious; he did not want to wake up on the floor ten minutes from now.

"Lord Prospero," he said at last, forcing his voice to be sweet with reason, "whatever you want me to do, I will agree to do it. Whatever you want me to become, I agree to become—or to try my best to do it. I swear this to you on the life of my unborn child. *But please allow me to return to Ardis now—my wife is injured, she may be dying. She needs me."*

"No," said Prospero.

Harman ran at the old man. He would beat the fucking old fool's bald head in with his own walking staff. He would . . .

This time Harman did not lose consciousness. The high voltage threw him back across the room, bounced him off the strange sofa, sent him falling to his hands and knees on the elaborate carpet. His vision still blinded by red circles, Harman growled and rose again.

"Next time I will burn your right leg off," the magus said in a flat, cold, completely convincing tone. "If you ever get home to your woman, you'll do so hopping."

Harman stopped. "Tell me what to do," he whispered.

"Sit down . . . no, there at the table where you can see outside."

Harman sat at the table. The sunlight was very bright as it reflected from vertical ice walls and the rising glacier; much of the ice had melted from the glass panes. The mountains were growing taller—a profusion of the tallest peaks Harman had ever seen, much more dramatic than the mountains near the Golden Gate at Machu Picchu. The cablecar was following a high ridgeline, a glacier dropping farther and farther below to their left. At that moment the car rumbled through another *eiffelbahn* tower and Harman had to grab the table as the two-story car rocked, bounced, ground against ice, and then continued creaking upward.

The tower fell behind. Harman leaned against the cold glass to watch it recede—this tower was not black like the others, but resplendently silver, gleaming in the sunlight, its iron arches and girders standing out like a spider's web in morning dew. *Ice,* thought Harman. He looked the other way, to his right, in the direction the cables were climbing and rising, and could see the white face of the most amazing mountain imaginable—no, beyond imagination. Clouds massed to the west of it, piling against a ridge as serrated and merciless looking as a bone knife. The face they were rising toward was striated with rock, ice, more rock, a summit pyramid of white snow and gleaming ice. The cablecar was grinding and slipping on icy cables following a ridgeline to the east of this incredible peak. Harman could see another tower on a swooping ridge high above, the rising cables connecting this mountain ridge to the higher peak. High above that—on and around the summit of the impossibly tall mountain—rose the most perfect white dome imaginable, its surface tinted a light gold from the morning sun, its central mass surrounded by four white *eiffelbahn* towers, the entire complex set on a white base cantilevered out over the sheer face of the mountain and connected to surrounding peaks by at least six slender suspension bridges arching out into space to other peaks—each of the bridges a hundred times higher, slimmer, and more elegant than the Golden Gate at Machu Picchu.

"What is this place?" Harman whispered.

"Chomolungma," said Prospero. "Goddess Mother of the World."

"That building at the top . . ."

"Rongbok Pumori Chu-mu-lang-ma Feng Dudh Kosi Lhotse-Nuptse Khumbu aga Ghat-Mandir Khan Ho Tep Rauza," said the magus. "Known locally as the Taj Moira. We'll be stopping there."

47

The voynix didn't come scuttling up Starved Rock by the hundreds or thousands that first cold, rainy night Daeman was there. Nor did they attack on the second night. By the third night everyone was weak from hunger or seriously sick with colds, flu, incipient pneumonia, or wounds—Daeman's left hand ached and throbbed with a sick heat where the *calibani* at Paris Crater had bitten off two of his fingers and he felt light-headed much of the time—but still the voynix did not come.

Ada had regained consciousness that second day on the Rock. Her injuries had been numerous—cuts, abrasions, a broken right wrist, two broken ribs on her left side—but the only ones that had been life threatening had been a serious concussion and smoke inhalation. She'd finally awakened with a terrible headache, a rough cough, and hazy memories of the last hours of the Ardis Massacre, but her mind was clear. Voice flat, she had gone through the list of friends she was not sure she'd dreamt she'd seen die or actually watched die, only her eyes reacting when Greogi responded with his litany.

"Petyr?" she said softly, trying not to cough.

"Dead."

"Reman?"

"Dead."

"Emme?"

"Dead with Reman."

"Peaen?"

"Dead. A thrown rock crushed her chest and she died here on Starved Rock."

"Salas?"

"Dead."

"Oelleo?"

"Dead."

And so on for another twoscore names before Ada sagged back onto the dirty rucksack that was her pillow. Her face was parchment white beneath the streaked soot and blood.

Daeman was there, kneeling, the Setebos Egg glowing unseen in his own backpack. He cleared his throat. "Some important people survived, Ada," he said. "Boman's here . . . and Kaman. Kaman was one of Odysseus' earliest disciples and has sigled everything he could find on military history. Laman lost four fingers on his right hand defending Ardis but he's here and still alive. Loes and Stoman are here, as well as some of the people I sent on my fax-warning expedition—Caul, Oko, Elle, and Edide. Oh, and Tom and Siris both made it."

"That's good," said Ada and coughed. Tom and Siris were Ardis's best medics.

"But none of the medical gear or medicines made it here," said Greogi.

"What did?" asked Ada.

Greogi shrugged. "Weapons we were carrying but not enough flechette ammunition. The clothes on our back. A few tarps and blankets we've been huddling under during the last three nights of cold rain."

"Have you gone back to Ardis to bury those who fell?" asked Ada. Her voice was steady except for the rasp and cough.

Greogi glanced at Daeman and then looked away, out over the edge of the tall rock summit on which they all huddled. "Can't," he said, voice full. "We tried. Voynix wait for us. Ambush."

"Were you able to get any more stores from Ardis Hall?" asked the injured woman.

Greogi shook his head. "Nothing important. It's gone, Ada. Gone."

Ada only nodded. More than two thousand years of her family history and pride, burned down and gone forever. She was not thinking of Ardis Hall now, but of her surviving people injured, cold, and stranded on this miserable Starved Rock. "What have you been doing for food and water?"

"We've caught rainwater on plastic tarps and have been able to zip away on the sonie for some fast hunting," said Greogi, obviously glad to change the subject from those who had died. "Mostly rabbits, but we got an elk yesterday evening. We're still picking flechettes out of it."

"Why haven't the voynix finished us off?" asked Ada. Her voice sounded only mildly curious.

"Now *that*," said Daeman, "is a good question." He had his own theory about it, but it was too early to share it.

"It's not that they're afraid of us," said Greogi. "There must be two or three thousand of the damned things down there in the woods and we don't have enough flechette ammunition to kill more than a few hundred. They can come up the rock anytime they want. They just haven't."

"You've tried the faxnode," said Ada. It wasn't really a question.

"The voynix ambushed us there," said Greogi. He squinted up at the blue sky. This was the first sunny day they'd had and everyone was trying to dry clothes and blankets, laying them out like signal sheets on the flat acre of rock that was the summit of Starved Rock, but it was still a bitter winter, worse than any in Ardis-dwellers' memory, and everyone was shivering in the thin sunlight.

"We've done tests," said Daeman. "We can stack twelve people in the sonie—twice what it's designed for—but more than that and the machine's AI refuses to fly. And it handles like a pig with twelve."

"How many of us did you say made it up here?" asked Ada. "Only fifty?"

"Fifty-three," said Greogi. "Nine of those—including you until this morning—were too sick or injured to travel."

"Eight now," Ada said firmly. "That would be five trips on the sonie to evacuate everyone—assuming that the voynix don't attack as soon as we start the evacuation and also assuming we had somewhere to go."

"Yes, assuming we had somewhere to go," said Greogi.

When Ada had fallen asleep again—sleep, Tom assured them, not the semicoma she'd been in—Daeman took his own rucksack, carrying it gingerly away from his body, and walked to the edge of Starved Rock's summit. He could see the voynix down there, their leathery humps and headless, silvery bodies moving between the trees. Occasionally a group of them would move—seemingly with purpose—across the broad meadow on the south side of Starved Rock. None of them looked up.

Greogi, Boman, and the dark-haired woman Edide came over to see what he was doing.

"Thinking of jumping?" asked Boman.

"No," said Daeman, "but I'm curious about whether you have any rope up here . . . enough to lower me to just out of reach of the voynix?"

"We have about a hundred feet of rope," said Greogi. "But that leaves you seventy or eighty feet above the bastards—not that that would slow them down if they want to scramble up and grab you. Why the hell do you want to go down among 'em?"

Daeman squatted, set the rucksack on the rock, and pulled the Setebos egg out. The others squatted to stare at it.

Even before they could ask, Daeman told them where he'd gotten it.

"*Why?*" asked Edide.

Daeman had to shrug at that. "It was one of those 'It seemed like a good idea at the time' things."

"I always end up paying for those," said the small, dark-haired woman. Daeman thought that she might have seen four Twenties. It was hard to tell because of the Firmary rejuvenations, of course, but older old-style humans tended to have a greater sense of confidence than the younger ones.

Daeman lodged the glowing, slightly pulsing silver-white egg in a crevice in the rock so that it wouldn't roll away and said, "Touch it."

Boman tried first. He set his palm flat on the curved shell as if welcoming the warmth they could all feel flowing from it, but the blond man pulled his hand away quickly—as if he'd been shocked or nipped. "What the hell?"

"Yeah," said Daeman. "I feel it too when I touch it. It's like the thing sucks some energy out of you—is pulling something out of your heart. Or soul."

Greogi and Edide tried touching it—they both pulled their hands away quickly and then moved farther from it.

"Destroy it," said Edide.

"What if Setebos comes looking for it?" said Greogi. "Mothers do that, you know, when you steal their eggs. They take it personally. Especially when the mother is a monster-sized brain with yellow eyes and dozens of hands."

"I thought of that," said Daeman. He fell silent.

"And?" said Edide. Even in the few months he'd known her at Ardis Hall, she'd always seemed like a practical, competent person. It was one of the reasons he'd chosen her as part of his fax-to-three-hundred-nodes warning expedition. "Do you want me to destroy it?" she asked, standing and pulling on leather gloves. "We'll see how far I can hurl the damned thing and whether I can hit a voynix."

Daeman chewed his lip.

"We damned sure don't want it hatching up here on the top of Starved Rock," said Boman. The man actually had his crossbow out and was aiming it at the milky egg. "Even a little Setebos-thing, from your description of what the mommy-daddy thing did at Paris Crater, might kill us all up here."

"Wait," said Daeman. "It hasn't hatched yet. The cold may not be enough to kill it here—to make it nonviable—but it may be slowing its gestation . . . or whatever the hell you call the hatching period with a monster's egg. I want to try something with it before we destroy it."

They used the sonie. Greogi drove. Boman and Edide knelt in the rear niches, flechette rifles ready. The forcefield was off.

Voynix stirred in the shadows under the trees at the far end of the meadow, less than a hundred yards away. They hovered a hundred feet above the meadow, out of voynix leaping range. "Are you sure?" said Greogi. "They're faster than we are."

Not quite sure that he could speak properly, Daeman nodded.

The sonie swooped down. Daeman jumped out. The sonie went up vertically, like a silver-disk elevator.

Daeman had a fully loaded flechette rifle hitched over his shoulder, but it was the rucksack he removed, sliding the Setebos egg part of the way out, taking care not to touch it with his bare hands. Even in the bright sunlight the thing glowed like radioactive milk.

As if offering them a gift, Daeman began walking toward the voynix at the far end of the meadow. The things were obviously watching him via the infrared sensors in their metallic chests. Several of them pivoted to keep him centered in their sensor range. More voynix moved out of the forest shadows to stand at the edge of the meadow.

Daeman glanced up, seeing the sonie sixty feet above him, seeing Boman's and Edide's flechette rifles raised and ready, but also knowing that a voynix running moved at more than sixty miles per hour. The things could be on him before the sonie could drop and hover and if there were enough of the creatures in the charge, no amount of covering fire would save him.

Daeman walked on with the glowing Setebos egg half out of his rucksack, like some Twenty present peeking out of its gift wrapping. Once the egg shifted—Daeman was so shocked at the internal movement and brighter glow that he almost dropped the thing, but hung on through the torn and dirty fabric of his rucksack—but after fumbling for a minute, he continued walking. He was close enough to the massed voynix now that he could almost smell the old-leather and rust stench of the things.

Daeman was ashamed to realize that his legs and arms were shaking slightly. *I just wasn't smart enough to think of another way,* he thought. But there wasn't another way. Not with the serious condition that so many of the Ardis survivors were in—not with starvation and dehydration looming.

He was less than fifty feet from the cluster of thirty or more voynix now. Daeman lifted the Setebos egg like a talisman and walked straight toward them.

At thirty feet, the voynix began to fade back into the forest.

Daeman picked up his pace, almost running now. Voynix on all sides were moving away.

Afraid that he might stumble and smash the egg—he had the sickening mental image of the egg splitting and a small Setebos brain scuttling out on its dozens of baby-hands and stalks, then the thing leaping for his face—he still forced himself to run toward the retreating voynix.

The voynix dropped to all fours and loped away—hundreds of them fleeing out in all directions like frightened grazers freeing predators on some prehistoric plain—and Daeman ran until he could run no more.

He dropped to his knees, hugging the rucksack to his chest, feeling the Setebos egg stirring and shifting, feeling energy flowing from him toward the evil thing until he pushed it away from himself, setting it on the ground like the toxic thing it was.

Greogi landed the sonie. "My God," said the bald pilot. "My God."

Daeman nodded. "Take me back to the base of Starved Rock. I'll wait there with the egg while you ferry down those who can walk the mile or so to the faxnode pavilion. I'll lead that procession. You can load the weak and wounded and follow us by air."

"What . . ." began Edide and fell silent. She shook her head.

"Yeah," said Daeman. "I remembered the bodies of the voynix frozen in the blue ice at Paris Crater. They had all been frozen in the act of running *away* from Setebos."

He sat on the edge of the sonie, the rucksack on his lap, as they floated back to Starved Rock a comfortable six feet above the ground. There were no voynix in the trees or meadows.

"Where are we going to fax to?" asked Boman.

"I don't know," said Daeman. He felt very tired. "I'll figure that out as we walk there down the road from Ardis."

48

You'll need a thermskin," said Prospero.

"Why?" Harman's voice was distracted. He was staring out the glass doors at the beautiful triple-dome and marble arches of the Taj Moira. The cablecar house had clicked into place in the southeast *eiffelbahn* tower—one of four set at the corners of the giant square of cantilevered marble that held this magnificent building above the summit of Chomo-lungma. Harman had estimated the *eiffelbahn* tower to be about one thousand feet tall and the apex of the onion-domed white building was half again taller.

"The altitude here is eight thousand eight hundred forty-eight me-ters," said the magus. "More vacuum than air. The temperature out there in the sunlight is thirty degrees below zero Fahrenheit. That gentle breeze is blowing at fifty knots. There's a blue thermskin in the wardrobe next to the bed. Go up and put it on. You'll need your outer clothes and boots. Call down when you have your osmosis mask in place—I need to lower the pressure in the car here before we open the mezzanine door."

They took the elevator down from the thousand-foot-level platform. Harman looked at the tower struts, arches, and girders as they passed them on the way down and had to smile. The secret of the whiteness of this tower was as prosaic as white paint over the same dark iron and steel as the other *eiffelbahn* structures. He could feel the elevator and the entire tower shaking to the howling winds and realized that the paint must be scoured away in months or weeks here rather than years; he tried to imagine the kind of painting crew that would be always at work up here, then gave it up as a silly effort.

He was obeying the magus now because it got him out of the prison of the cablecar. Somehow here in this insane temple or palace or tomb or whatever it was on this insanely tall mountain, he would find a way back to Ada. If Ariel could fax without faxnode pavilions, so could he. Somehow.

Harman followed Prospero from the elevator at the base of the tower across the wide expanse of red sandstone and white marble leading to the front door of the domed building. The wind threatened to blow him off his feet but for some reason there was no ice on the exposed sandstone and marble.

"Don't maguses feel the cold or need air?" he shouted at the old man in the trailing blue robe.

"Not in the least," said the magus. The jet-stream-strong wind was blowing his robe to one side and sending his fringe of long, gray hair trailing sideways from his mostly bald skull. "One of the perquisites of old age," he cried over the wind howl.

Harman veered to his right, arms extended for balance against the wind, and walked toward the low marble railing—not more than two feet high—that ran around the huge square of sandstone and marble like a low bench around a skating rink.

"Where are you going?" called Prospero. "Be careful there!"

Harman reached the edge and looked over.

Later, studying maps, Harman realized that he must have been looking north from this mountain called Chomolungma or Chu-mu-lang-ma Feng or Qomolangma Feng or HoTepma Chini-ka-Rauza or Everest, depending upon the age and origin of the map, and that when he stood at the railing he was staring out for hundreds of miles—and six miles straight down—into lands that had once been called Khan's Ninth Kingdom or Tibet or China.

It was the *down* part that struck Harman viscerally.

The Taj Moira was essentially a sandstone-marble city block stuck on the summit of the Goddess Mother of the World like a tray embedded on a sharp stone, like a piece of paper slammed down onto a spike. As an engineering feet, the buckycarbon cantilevering was impressive to the point of impossibility—a god-child's form of showing off.

Harman stood by the two-foot-high, ten-inch-wide marble "railing" and stared straight down for more than twenty-nine thousand feet with the full force of the jet stream at his back, trying to shove him off into the endless empty air. Later, maps would tell him that he had been looking at other mountains with names and the east and west Rongbuk Glaciers with the brown plains of China far beyond toward the curve of the earth, but none of that mattered now. Shoved by the strong arms of the howling wind, windmilling his arms to keep his balance, Harman was looking *six miles straight down—from an overhang*!

He dropped to his hands and knees and began crawling back toward the temple-tomb and the waiting magus. Thirty feet in front of the huge doorway, a small, sharp boulder—no more than five feet tall—rose from the marble squares, ending in a thirty-inch pyramid of ice. With Prospero watching—arms crossed and a small smile on his face—Harman wrapped his arms around the decorative boulder and used its imperfections to pull himself back to his feet. He continued to lean on the boulder, arms wrapped around it, his chin resting on the icy point, afraid that if he looked back over his shoulder at the distant low wall and vertiginous drop, the urge to run toward that wall and leap would be overpowering. He closed his eyes.

"Are you going to stay there all day?" asked the magus.

"I might," said Harman, eyes still closed. After another minute, he shouted over the rising wind, "What is this rock anyway? Some sort of symbol? A monument?"

"It's the summit of Chomolungma," said Prospero. The magus turned and walked into the open, elegantly arched entrance of the structure he'd called Rongbok Pumori Chu-mu-lang-ma Feng Dudh Kosi Lhotse-Nuptse Khumbu aga Ghat-Mandir Khan Ho Tep Rauza. Harman saw that a semipermeable membrane was guarding that entrance—it had rippled as the magus passed through, another sign that Harman wasn't dealing with just a hologram this time.

Several minutes later, still hugging his boulder-summit, the eyepieces and osmosis mask of his thermskin hood almost completely frosted over because of the pelting snow squalls that struck his body like icy missiles, Harman considered the fact that it was probably warm inside that building, warm beyond that semipermeable forcefield.

He did not crawl the last thirty feet to the door, but he walked hunched over, face lowered, palms down and extended, *ready* to crawl.

Inside the single huge room under the dome, marble steps rose to a series of mezzanines—each in turn connected to the next mezzanine by another marble staircase—that lined the interior of the inward curving dome for a hundred levels, a hundred stories, until mist and distance above obscured the apex of the dome itself. What had appeared like tiny apertures in the dome from the cablecar during the approach and from the *eiffelbahn* tower—hardly more than decorative elements in the white marble—now proved to be hundreds of perspex windows that sent shafts of light down to illuminate the rich-bound books with slowly moving squares and rectangles and trapezoids of brightness.

"How long do you think it would take you to sigl all that?" asked Prospero, leaning on his staff and turning in a circle to take in the many mezzanines of books.

Harman opened his mouth to speak and then shut it. Weeks?

Months? Even moving from book to book, just setting his palm in place long enough to see the golden words move down his fingers and arms, it might take years to sigl this library. Finally he said, "You told me that the functions didn't work in and around the *eiffelbahn*. Have the rules changed?"

"We shall see," said the magus. He moved deeper into the dome, his staff tapping the white marble and the sound echoing up and around the acoustically perfect dome.

Harman realized that it was *warm* in this place. He pulled back the thermskin hood and gloves.

The interior of the domed building was broken into discrete spaces, if not actual rooms, by a maze of white marble screens that rose only eight feet high and were not a complete barrier to sight because of their latticeworked, filigreed construction and countless elegant oval, heart- and leaf-shaped openings. Harman noticed that the walls around the base of the dome up to a height of forty feet or so, where the first mezzanine began, were completely covered with carved designs of flowers, vines, elaborate and impossible plants, all brightened by the presence of inlaid jewels. So were the marble screens. Harman set his hand against one of the marble partitions as Prospero led the way through the maze— and it was a real maze—and he realized that anywhere he could set his hand, it would cover two or three of the designs at once, that there would always be several precious stones under his fingers. Some of the flower designs were less than an inch square and looked to contain fifty or sixty tiny inlays.

"What are these rocks?" asked Harman. His people had enjoyed wearing precious stones for decoration, baubles always fetched by the robotic servitors, but he'd never wondered where they came from.

"These . . . rocks . . ." said Prospero, "include agate, jasper, lapis lazuli, bloodstone, and cornelians—there are more than thirty-five varieties of cornelian in this simple little carnation leaf where I set my hand on this screen, do you see?"

Harman saw. The place made him dizzy. Trapezoids of light moving on the west wall below the books made the marble sparkle, gleam, and shimmer from the thousands of precious stones inlaid there.

"What is this place?" asked Harman. He realized that he was whispering.

"It was built as a mausoleum . . . a tomb," said the magus, sweeping around another junction of white marble screens and leading the way to the center of the great place as if the maze had yellow arrows painted on the floor. They stopped before an arched entrance to an inner rectangle at the center of the maze of hundreds of screens. "Can you read this stele, Harman of Ardis?"

Harman peered at it in the milky light. The letters in the marble were carved strangely—they were swirly and elaborate rather than the straight lines he was used to from books—but it was written in Standard World English.

"Read it aloud," said the magus.

" 'Enter with awe the illustrious sepulchre of Khan Ho Tep, Lord of Asia and Protector of Earth, and his bride and beloved Lias Lo Amumja, adored by all the world. She left this transient world on the fourteenth night of the month of Rahab-Septem in the year of the Khanate 987. She and her Lord dwell now in the starry Heaven and watch over you who enter here.' "

"What do you think?" asked Prospero, standing under the elaborate arch where the center of the maze opened to the yet-unseen interior.

"Of the inscription or this place?"

"Both," said the magus.

Harman rubbed his chin and cheek, feeling the stubble there. "This place is . . . *wrong*. Too big. Too rich. Out of scale. Except for the books."

Prospero laughed and the noise echoed and then re-echoed. "I agree with you, Harman of Ardis. This place was stolen—the idea, the design, the inlays, the chessboard design of the courtyard outside—everything stolen except for the mezzanines and books, which were placed there six hundred years later by Rajahar the Silent, a distant descendant of the feared Khan Ho Tep. The Khan had the original Taj Mahal design enlarged by a factor of more than ten. That original building was beautiful, a true testament to love—nothing remains of that structure because the Khan had it slagged, wanting only this mausoleum to be remembered. This place is a memorial to wretched excess more than anything else."

"The location is . . . interesting," Harman said softly.

"Yes," said Prospero, pulling up his blue sleeves. "That bit of wisdom is as true about real estate today as it was in Odysseus' day—location, location, location. Come."

They walked into the center of the marble-screen maze, an empty patch of marble perhaps a hundred yards square with what looked to Harman to be a bright reflecting pool in the center. Prospero's walking staff made echoing taps as they walked slowly to the center.

It was no reflecting pool.

"Jesus Christ," cried Harman, stepping back from the edge.

It seemed to be empty air. To the left, just visible, was the vertical north face of the mountain, but beneath them—perhaps forty feet beneath the level of the floor—a steel and crystal sarcophagus seemed to be floating in midair, high over the jagged glacier six miles below. Inside the sarcophagus lay a naked woman. A narrow, white marble spiral staircase snaked down to the level of the sarcophagus, the last step appearing to hang out over that empty air.

It can't be open, thought Harman. There was no blast of the jet stream, no roaring of high-altitude wind up and through the opening in the floor. The sarcophagus had to be resting on *something.* By squinting, he could make out facets, a multitude of nearly invisible geodesics. The burial chamber was made up of some incredibly transparent plastic or crystal or glass. But why hadn't he seen this sarcophagus and stairway during their ascent in the cablecar or . . .

"The burial vault is invisible from the outside," Prospero said softly. "Have you looked at the woman yet?"

"The beloved Lias Lo Amumja?" said Harman, not all that interested in staring at a naked corpse. "Who left this transient world on whenever the hell it was? And where's the Khan? Does he get his own crystal chamber?"

Prospero laughed. "Khan Ho Tep and his beloved Lias Lo Amumja, daughter of Cezar Amumja of the Central African Empire—she was a stone bitch and a harpy, Harman of Ardis, trust me on this—were dumped overboard less than two centuries after they were entombed here."

"Dumped overboard?" said Harman.

"Perfectly preserved bodies unceremoniously dumped over the same wall you peered over thirty minutes ago," said Prospero. "Tossed overboard like yesterday's garbage from a tramp steamer. Successors to the Khan—each one more minor in his or her own way—liked to be buried here for all eternity . . . that eternity lasting until the next Khan-successor wanted the best possible mausoleum space."

Harman could picture it.

"That is, until fourteen hundred years ago," said Prospero, returning his blue-eyed gaze to the glass and wood sarcophagus four stories below them. "This woman was truly the beloved of someone in power and she has rested here for fourteen centuries, undisturbed. Look at her, Harman of Ardis."

Harman had been looking in the general direction of the sarcophagus but trying not to stare at the body. The woman was too naked for his tastes—she looked too young to be dead, her body was still pink and pale, her breasts were too visible—nipples looking rosy even from forty feet away—the short hair on her head one comma of black against white satin pillows, the rich triangle of hair at her groin another black comma—her dark eyebrows, strong features, broad mouth even from this distance, almost . . . familiar.

"Jesus Christ," cried Harman for the second time that morning, but this time loud enough that his shout echoed from the dome and bounced back from the mezzanines of books and white marble.

She was younger—much younger—hair black rather than gray, body firm and young rather than pulled into tired lines and folds by long centuries as Harman had seen with the skintight thermskin—but her face had the same strength, the cheekbones the same sharpness, the eyebrows the same bold slash, the chin the same firm set. There was no doubt.

It was Savi.

"So where *is* everyone?" asks fleet-footed Achilles, son of Peleus, as he follows Hephaestus across the grassy summit of Olympos.

The blond mankiller and Hephaestus, god of fire and Chief Artificer to all the gods, are walking along the shore of Caldera Lake between the Hall of the Healer and the Great Hall of the Gods. The other white-pillared god-homes seem dark and deserted. There are no chariots in the sky. There are no immortals walking the many paved walkways, illuminated by low, yellow-glowing lamps that Achilles notices are not torches.

"I told you," says Hephaestus. "With the Cat away, the Mice are playing. Almost all of them are down on the Ilium-Earth to be players in the last act of your petty little Trojan War."

"How does the war proceed?" asks Achilles.

"Without you there to kill Hector, your Myrmidons and all the other Achaeans and Argives and whatever you want to call them are getting their asses kicked by the Trojans."

"Agamemnon and his people are retreating?" asks Achilles.

"Aye. The last time I looked—only a few hours ago, just before I made the mistake of checking out the damage to my crystal escalator and getting into a wrestling match with you—I saw in the holopool in the Great Hall that Agamemnon's attack on the city walls had failed, yet again, and the Achaeans were falling back to their defensive trenches near the black ships. Hector was about to lead his army outside the walls—ready to take the offensive again. Essentially, it came down to which of us immortals were tougher than the others in a serious fight—it turns out that even with tough bitches like Hera and Athena fighting for Ilium—and Poseidon shaking the earth for the city, which is his thing, you know—shaking the earth—the pro-Greek team of Apollo, Ares, and that sneaky Aphrodite and her friend Demeter are carrying the day. As a general, Agamemnon sucks."

Achilles only nods. His fate now is with Penthesilea, not with Agamemnon and his armies. Achilles trusts his Myrmidons to do the right thing—to flee if they can, to fight and die if they must. Ever since Athena—or Aphrodite disguised as Athena, if the Goddess of Wisdom had told him the truth several days earlier—murdered his beloved Patroclus, Achilles' bloodlust has focused only on vengeance against the gods. Now—even though he knows it is just the result of Aphrodite's perfumed magic—he has two goals: to bring his beloved Penthesilea back to life and to kill the bitch Aphrodite. Without being aware that he is doing so, Achilles adjusts the god-killing dagger in his belt. If Athena was telling the truth about the blade—and Achilles believed her—this bit of quantum-shifted steel will be the death of Aphrodite and any other immortals who get in his way, including this crippled god of fire, Hephaestus, if he tries to flee or block Achilles' will.

Hephaestus leads Achilles to a parking area outside the Great Hall of the Gods where more than a score of golden chariots are lined up on the grass, metal umbilical cords snaking into some underground charging reservoir. Hephaestus climbs into one of the horseless cars and beckons Achilles aboard.

Achilles hesitates. "Where are we going?"

"I told you. To visit the one immortal who might know where Zeus is right now," says the Artificer.

"Why don't we just look for Zeus directly?" asks Achilles, still not stepping into the chariot. He has driven or been driven in a thousand chariots, but he has never flown in one the way he frequently sees the gods flitting to and fro above Ilium or Olympos, and while the idea does not actively frighten him, he's in no hurry to leave the ground.

"There is a technology known only to Zeus," says Hephaestus, "which can hide him from all of my sensors and spy devices. It's obviously been activated, although I'd guess by his wife Hera rather than by the God of Gods himself."

"Who is this other immortal who can show us where Zeus hides?" Achilles is distracted by the howling sandstorm and wild flashes of lightning and static discharge a few hundred yards above them as the planetary storm throws itself against Zeus's Olympos-girding *aegis* forcefield.

"Nyx," says Hephaestus.

"Night?" repeats Achilles. The fleet-footed mankiller knows the goddess's name—the daughter of Kaos, one of the first sentient creatures to emerge from the Void that was there at the beginning of time before the original gods themselves helped separate the darkness of Erebus from the blue and green Gaia-order of Earth—but no Greek or Asian or African city he knew of worshiped the mysterious Nyx-Night. Legend and myth said that Nyx—alone, without an immortal male to impregnate her—had given birth do Eris (Discord), the Moirai (Fates), Hypnos (Sleep), Nemesis (Retribution), Thanatos (Death), and the Hesperides.

"I thought Night was a personification," adds Achilles. "Or just an oxcart load of bullshit."

Hephaestus smiles. "Even a personification or load of bullshit takes on physical form in this brave new world the post-humans, Sycorax, and Prospero helped make for us," he says. "Are you coming? Or shall I QT back to my laboratory and enjoy the . . . ah . . . pleasures of your sleeping Penthesilea while you dither up here?"

"You know I'll find you and kill you if you do that," says Achilles with no threat in his voice, only cool promise.

"Yes, I do," agrees Hephaestus, "which is why I'll ask you one last time: Are you going to get aboard this fucking chariot or not?"

They fly southeast halfway around the great sphere of Mars, although Achilles does not know that it is Mars he is staring at, nor that it is a sphere. But he knows that the steep ascent above Olympos' Caldera Lake and the violent penetration of the *aegis* into the howling dust storm behind the four horses that had appeared out of nowhere at takeoff— and then the ride through the blinding dust storm and high winds themselves—is not something he would choose to do again soon. Achilles hangs on to the wood and bronze rim of the chariot and works hard not to close his eyes. Luckily, there is some field of energy around the chariot car itself—some minor form of the *aegis* or variation on the invisible body shields the gods use in combat, Achilles assumes—that protects the two of them from the hurling sand and blasting winds.

Then they are above the dust storm, black night sky above them and the stars shining brilliantly, two small moons visibly hurtling across the sky. By the time the chariot crosses the line of three huge volcanoes, they have passed south of the worst of the dust storm and features are visible far below them in the reflected starlight.

Achilles knows that the gods' home on Olympos inhabits its own odd world, of course—he has been fighting on the red plain between what his moravec allies had called the Brane Hole for eight months, watching the tepid, tideless waves wash in from some northern sea that was not any of Earth's—but he's never before considered that the Olympians' world might be so *large*.

They fly high above an endless, broad, flooded canyon and darkness is broken only by reflected starlight on water and a few moving lanterns leagues below that Hephaestus says are running lights on the Little Green Men's quarry barges. Achilles sees no reason to ask the cripple to elaborate on that cryptic description.

They fly above treeless and then forested mountain ranges and countless circular depressions—craters, the god of fire calls them—some eroded or forested, many showing central lakes, but most obviously sharp and severe in the moonlight and starlight.

They fly higher, until the whistle of air around the chariot's mini-*aegis* dies away and Achilles is breathing a pure air emitted from the chariot car itself. The oxygen content is so high that he feels a little drunk.

Hephaestus names some of the rocky, mountainous, or valleyed features unrolling far beneath them in the night. Achilles thinks the crippled god sounds like a bored bargeman announcing stops along a river's way.

"Shalbatana Vallis," says the immortal. And then, some minutes later—"Margaratifer Terra. Meridiania Planum. Terra Sabaea. That heavily forested area to the north is Schiaparelli, the foothills dead ahead are called Huygens. We're swinging south now."

The chariot car flying behind the four straining, slightly transparent horses does not swing south, it *banks* south, and Achilles hangs on for dear life even though the floor of the car always—impossibly—seems to be *down*.

"What's that?" asks Achilles a few minutes later. A huge, circular lake has appeared, filling much of the southern horizon. The chariot is descending and while there is no dust storm here, the air still howls.

"Hellas Basin," grunts the god of fire. "It's more than fourteen hundred miles across and it has a bigger diameter than Pluto."

"Pluto?" says Achilles.

"It's a fucking planet, you stupid hick preliterate," growls Hephaestus.

Achilles releases his death grip on the chariot rim, freeing his hands for action. He thinks he will pick the crippled god up, snap his back over his knee, and fling him down from the chariot. But then Achilles glances over the side of the car at the mountain peaks and black valleys still many leagues below and decides he'll let the gimpy dwarf land the vehicle first. The lake looms ahead of them, filling the entire south. Then they cross the arcing northern shoreline and begin descending over starlit water. Achilles realizes that what had seemed like a circular lake from just a few miles higher is really a small, round ocean.

"It varies from two miles deep to more than four," says Hephaestus, as if Achilles had asked or cared. "Those two huge rivers flowing in from the east are called Dao and Harmakhis. Our original plan was to put a couple of million old-style humans in the fertile valleys there, just let them fucking go forth and be fertile and multiply, but we never got around to turning the beam this way and de-faxing them. Actually, Zeus and the other Pantheon originals just forgot everything before they were gods—it seemed like a dream to all of us. Besides, Zeus was busy overthrowing his parents, the Titan first-generation immortals—Kronos and his sister-bride Rhea—and casting them down into the Brane-reached world called Tartarus."

Hephaestus clears his throat and begins to recite in a minstrel's voice that sounds to Achilles like someone sawing a lyre in half with a rusty blade—

> *"A dreadful sound troubled the boundless sea.*
> *The whole earth uttered a great cry.*
> *Wide heaven, shaken, groaned.*
> *From its foundation far Olympus reeled*
> *Beneath the onrush of the deathless gods,*
> *And trembling seized upon black Tartarus."*

Achilles can see only dark water to the right and left of them now, water hurtling by beneath at an impossible speed, the cliff-walled edges of the circular lake gone, below the rim of the horizons. To the south, a single craggy island appears.

"Zeus only won the war," continues Hephaestus, "because he went back to the post-human Brane-punching machines in orbit around the original Earth—the *real* Earth, I mean, not yours, not this fucking terraformed counterfeit—and brought in Setebos and his egg-born ilk to fight Kronos' legions. The hundred-handed monsters with their energy weapons and their hunger for eating terror out of the dirt won the day, although they were tough as shit stains to get rid of once the war was over. Also, one of the Titans' fucking kids—Iapetus' boy Prometheus—turned double agent. And then there was that lab-built hundred-headed clone monster named Typhon that came through the Brane Hole in the four hundred and twenty-fourth year of the war. Now *that* was something to see. I remember the day when . . ."

"Are we there yet?" interrupts Achilles.

The island—Hephaestus drones on as they continued descending—is more than eighty of Achilles' leagues across and is filled with monsters.

"Monsters?" says Achilles. He has little interest in such things. He wants to know where Zeus is and he wants Zeus to tell the Healer to open the rejuvenation tanks and he wants the Amazon queen Penthesilea alive again. Everything else is beside the point.

"Monsters," repeats the god of fire. "The first children of Gaia and Ouranos are misshapen fiends. But very powerful. Zeus allowed them to live on here rather than joining Kronos and Rhea in the Tartarus dimension. There are three Setebosians among them."

This fact holds no interest for Achilles. He watches the island grow ahead of them and notices the huge, dark castle on the crags at its center. The few windows in the upright slags of stone glow orange, as if the interior is on fire.

"The island also holds the last of the Cyclopes," drones on Hephaestus. "And the Erinyes."

"Those Furies are here?" says Achilles. "I thought they were a myth as well."

"No, no myth." The crippled immortal banks the chariot around and lines up the horses' heads with a flat, open space above a black-rock shelf at the base of the central castle. Dark clouds twist and writhe around the mountain and its keep. The valleys on either side are filled with furtive movement. "When they are released from this place they will spend the rest of eternity pursuing and punishing sinners. They are truly 'those who walk in darkness,' with writhing snakes for hair and red eyes that weep tears of blood."

"Bring them on," says the son of Peleus.

The chariot lands gently at the base of a gigantic sculpture set on a great ledge made of black stone. The chariot's wooden wheels creak and the horses flick out of existence. The strange glowing panel that the Artificer had been using to control the craft disappears.

"Come," says Hephaestus and leads Achilles toward the broad, seemingly endless stairway on the other side of the statue. The immortal drags his bad foot along on stone.

Achilles cannot help but look up at the sculpture—three hundred feet high at least, a powerful man holding the double-sphere of Earth and Heaven on his powerful shoulders. "This is a sculpture of Iapetos," says Achilles.

"No," growls the god of fire, "it's old Atlas himself. Frozen here forever."

The four hundredth step is the last. The black castle rises above, its towers and turrets and hidden gables lost in the roiling cloud. The two doors ahead of them are each fifty feet high and fifty feet apart from each other.

"Nyx and Hemera pass each other here every day—Night and Day," whispers Hephaestus. "One going out, one coming in. They are never in the house at the same time."

Achilles glances up at the black clouds and starless sky. "Then we've come at the wrong time. I have no business with Hemera. You said it was Night with whom we need to speak."

"Patience, son of Peleus," grumbles Hephaestus. The god seems nervous. He glances at a small but bulky machine on his wrist. "Eos rises . . . now."

Around the eastern rim of the black island grows an orange glow. It fades.

"No sunlight penetrates this island's polarized *aegis*," whispers Hephaestus. "But it's almost morning beyond. The sun will be rising over the Dao and Harmakhis Rivers and the eastern cliffs of Hellas Basin within seconds."

A sudden flash blinds Achilles. He hears one of the gigantic iron doors slam shut, then the other one creak open. When he can see again, the second door is closed and Night stands in front of them.

Always in awe of Athena, Hera, and the other goddesses, this is the first time that Achilles, son of Peleus and the sea goddess Thetis, finds himself in *terror* of an immortal. Hephaestus has gone to both knees and lowered his head in respect and fear for the terrible apparition facing them, but Achilles forces himself to remain standing. Yet he has to fight an overwhelming urge to unstrap the shield from his back and cower behind it, his short god-killing-blade in his hand. Torn between fleeing or fighting, he lowers his face in deference as a compromise.

While the gods can assume almost any size—Achilles knows nothing of the Law of Conservation of Mass and Energy and would not understand the explanation of how the immortals get around this law—gods and goddesses seem most comfortable at around nine feet tall: tall enough to make mortals feel like children; not so tall that they have to reinforce leg bones or become too awkward even in their own Olympian halls.

Night—Nyx—is fifteen feet tall, wrapped in a roiling, vaporous cloud, dressed in what seems like multiple layers of diaphanous black cloth, strips hanging down in scores of lengths, with either a black headdress that includes a veil over her face or perhaps a face that looks like a molded black veil. Impossibly, her black eyes are perfectly visible through the black veil and vaporous clouds. Before averting his face, Achilles saw that she was incredibly large-breasted, as if she would suckle all the world to darkness. Only her hands glow pale, long-fingered and powerful, as if the fingers are made of solidified moonlight.

Achilles realizes that Hephaestus is speaking, almost chanting.

". . . Fumigation with torches, Nyx, parent goddess, source of sweet re-
pose from woes, Mother from whom Gods and men arose, Hear, blessed
Nyx decked with starry light, in sleep's sweet silence dwelling ebon
night. Dreams and soft ease attend thy dusky train, pleased with length-
ened gloom and feastful strain, dissolving anxious care, the friend of
mirth, with darkling speed riding 'round the earth. Goddess of phan-
toms and of shadowy play . . ."

"Enough," says Night. "If I want to hear an Orphic hymn I'll travel
through time. How dare you, God of Fire, bring a mere mortal to Hellas
and the night-shrouded home of Nyx?"

Achilles shivers at the sound of the goddess's voice. It is the sound of
a violent winter sea crashing on rocks, but understandable nonetheless.

"Goddess whose natural power divides the natural day," Hephaestus
grovels, still on his knees, still bowing, "this mortal is the son of immortal Thetis and is a demigod in his own right on his particular Earth. He
is called Achilles, son of Peleus, and his prowess . . ."

"Oh, I know Achilles, son of Peleus, and his prowess—sacker of
cities, raper of women, and killer of men," says Night in her wave-
crashing tones. "What possible reason could compel you to bring this . . .
foot soldier . . . to my black door, Artificer?"

Achilles decides it is time he spoke. "I need to see Zeus, Goddess."

The dark wraith turns more in his direction. It as if she is floating, not
standing, and the large and huge-breasted form swivels without friction.
Her veiled face—or face with the meshed face of a black veil—peers
down at him with eyes that are blacker than black. The clouds roil and
broil around her.

"You *need* to see the Lord of Thunder, the God of All Gods, the Pelas-
gian Zeus, Lord of Ten Thousand Temples and Dodona's Shrine, Father
of All Gods and Men, Zeus the Ultimate King Who Marshals the Storm
Clouds and Who Gives All Commands?"

"Yeah," says Achilles.

"What about?" asks Nyx.

It is Hephaestus who speaks up. "Achilles seeks to bring a mortal to
the Healer's tanks, Mother of the first black germless egg. He wants to
ask Father Zeus to command the Healer to bring back to life the Amazon queen, Penthesilea."

Night laughs. If her voice had been a wild sea crashing against rocks,
Achilles thinks her laugh sounds like a winter wind howling off the
Aegean.

"Penthesilea?" says the black-garbed goddess, still chuckling. "That
brainless, blond, big-boobed lesbian tart? Why on a million Earths
would you want to bring that musclebound bimbo back to life, son of
Peleus? After all, it was you I watched run her *and* her horse through

with your father's great lance, skewering them both like peppers on a kebab."

"I have no choice," rumbles Achilles. "I love her."

Night laughs again. "You *love* her? This from the Achilles who beds slave girls and conquered princesses and captured queens as indifferently as others eat olives, only to cast them away like spit-out pits? You *love* her?"

"It's Aphrodite's pheromone perfume," says Hephaestus, still on his knees.

Night quits laughing. "Which type?" she asks.

"Number nine," grumbles Hephaestus. "Puck's potion. The type with the self-duplicating nanomachines in the bloodstream constantly · reproducing more dependency molecules and depriving the brain of endorphins and seratonin if the victim doesn't act on his infatuation. There is no antidote."

Night turns her sculpted veil-face toward Achilles. "I think that you are well and truly fornicated, son of Peleus. Zeus will never agree to rejuvenate a mortal—much less an Amazon, a race he thinks of rarely and thinks precious little of when they do come to his mind. The Father of All Gods and All Men has little use for Amazons and less use for virgins. He would see a resurrection of such a mortal as a desecration of the Healer's tanks and skills."

"I will ask him nonetheless," Achilles says stubbornly.

Night regards him in silence. Then the big-bosomed, ebony-ragged aparition turns toward Hephaestus, who is still on his knees. "Crippled God of Fire, busy artificer to more noble gods, what do you see when you look upon this mortal man?"

"A fucking fool," grunts Hephaestus.

"I see a quantum singularity," says the goddess Nyx. "A black hole of probability. A myriad of equations all with the same single three-point solution. Why is that, Artificer?"

The god of fire grunts again. "His mother, Thetis of the seaweed-tangled breasts, held this arrogant mortal in the celestial quantum fire when he was a pup, little more than a larva. The probability of his death day, hour, minute, and method is one hundred percent, and because it cannot be changed, it seems to give Achilles a sort of invulnerability to all other attacks and injury."

"Yessssssssss," hisses shrouded Night. "Son of Hera, husband of that brainless Grace known as Aglaia the Glorious, why are you helping this man?"

Hephaestus bows lower on the step. "At first he bested me in a wrestling match, beloved goddess of dreadful shade. Then I continued helping him because his interests coincided with mine."

"Your interest is to find Father Zeus?" whispers Night. Somewhere in the black canyons to their right, someone or something howls.

"My interest, Goddess, is to thwart the growing flood of Kaos."

Night nods and raises her veiled face to the clouds roiling around her castle towers. "I can hear the stars scream, crippled Artificer. I know that when you say 'Kaos,' you mean chaos—on a quantum level. You are the only one of the gods, save for Zeus, who remembers us and our thinking before the Change . . . who remembers little things like physics."

Hephaestus keeps his face lowered and says nothing.

"Are you monitoring the quantum flux, Artificer?" asks Night. There is a sharp and angry edge to her voice that Achilles does not understand.

"Yes, Goddess."

"How much time, God of Fire, do you think we have left to survive if the vortexes of probability chaos continue to grow at this logarithmic rate?"

"A few days, Goddess," grunts Hephaestus. "Perhaps less."

"The Fates agree with you, Hera-spawn," says Nyx. The volume and sea-crash timbre of her voice make Achilles want to clap his callused hands over his ears. "Day and night, the *Moirai*—those alien entities which mortal men call the Fates—toil at their electronic abacuses, manipulating their bubbles of magnetic energy and their mile-long coils of computing DNA—and every day the *Moirai*'s view of the future becomes less certain, their threads of probability more raveled, as if the loom of Time itself is broken."

"It's that fucking Setebos," grumbles Hephaestus. "Begging your pardon, ma'am."

"No, you are correct, Artificer," says the giant Nyx. "It's that fucking Setebos, let loose at last, no longer contained in this world's arctic seas. The Many-Handed has gone to Earth, you know. Not this mortal's Earth, but our old home."

"No," says Hephaestus, raising his face at last. "I didn't know that."

"Oh, yes—the Brain has crossed the Brane." She laughs and this time Achilles does clasp his hands over his ears. This is a sound that no mortal should be made to hear.

"How long do the *Moirai* say we have?" whispers Hephaestus.

"Clotho, the Spinner, says that we have mere hours left before the quantum flux implodes this universe," says Night. "Atropos, she who cannot be turned and who carries the abhorred shears to cut all our threads of life at death's sharp instant, says it may be a month yet."

"And Lachesis?" asks the god of fire.

"The Disposer of Lots—and she rides the fractal waves of the electronic abacus better than the others, I think—sees Kaos triumphant on this world and in this Brane within a week or two. Any way we cut it, we have little time left, Artificer."

"Will you flee, Goddess?"

Night stands silent. Howls echo from the crags and valleys beyond her castle. Finally she says, "Where can we flee, Artificer? Where can even we few of the Originals flee if this universe we were born into collapses into chaos? Any Brane Hole we can create, any quantum leap we can teleport, will still be connected by the threads of chaos to this universe. No, there is nowhere to flee."

"What do we do then, Goddess?" grunts Hephaestus. "Just bend over, grab our sandals, and kiss our immortal asses goodbye?"

Night makes a noise like the Aegean in mirthful storm. "We need to confer with the Elder Gods. And quickly."

"The Elder Gods . . ." begins the Artificer and stops. "Kronos, Rhea, Okeanos, Tethys . . . all those exiled to terrible Tartarus?"

"Yes," says Night.

"Zeus will never allow it," says Hephaestus. "No god is allowed to communicate with . . ."

"Zeus must face reality," bellows Night. "Or all will end in chaos, including his reign."

Achilles climbs two steps toward the huge, black figure. His shield is on his forearm now as if he is ready to fight. "Hey, do you remember I'm here? And I'm still waiting for an answer to my question. *Where is Zeus*?"

Nyx leans over him and aims one pale, bony finger like a weapon. "Your quantum probability for dying at my hand may be zero, son of Peleus, but should I blast you atom from atom, molecule from molecule, the universe—even on a quantum level—might have a hard time maintaining that axiom."

Achilles waits. He has noticed that the gods often babble on in this nonsense talk. The only thing to do is wait until they make sense again.

Finally Nyx speaks in the voice of wind-tossed waves. "Hera, sister and bride, daughter of Rhea and Kronos and incestuous bedmate to her divine brother, defender of Achaeans to the point of treachery and murder, has seduced Lord Zeus away from his duties and his watchfulness, bedding him and injecting him with Sleep in the great house where a hero's wife weeps and labors, weaving by day and tearing out her work at night. This hero brought not his best bow to do his bloody work at Troy, but left it on a peg in a secret room with a secret door, hidden away from suitors and looters. This is the bow that no one else can pull, the bow that can send an arrow straight through iron axe-helve sockets, twelve in line, or half again as many guilty or guiltless men's bodies."

"Thank you, Goddess," says Achilles and backs away down the staircase.

Hephaestus looks around, then follows, careful not to turn his back on the huge ebony figure in the flowing robes. By the time both men are standing, Night is gone from her place at the head of the stairs.

"What in Hades was all that about?" whispers the Artificer as they climb into the chariot and activate the virtual control panel and holographic horses. "A hero's wife weeping, hidden fucking rooms, axe-helve sockets, twelve in line. Nyx sounded like your babbling Delphic oracle."

"Zeus is on the isle of Ithaca," says Achilles as they climb away from the castle and the island and the growls and bellows of unseen monsters in the dark. "Odysseus himself told me that he had left his best bow at his palace on that rocky isle of his, hidden away with herb-scented robes in a secret room. I've visited crafty Odysseus there in better days. Only he can bring that huge bow to full pull—or so he says, though I've never tried—and after an evening's drinking, firing an arrow through iron axe-helve sockets, twelve in line, is the son of Laertes' idea of entertainment. And if there are suitors there seeking his sexy wife Penelope's hand, he would be even more greatly entertained to put his shafts through their bodies instead."

"Odysseus' home on Ithaca," mutters Hephaestus. "A good place for Hera to hide her sleeping lord. Do you have any idea, son of Peleus, what Zeus will do to you when you wake him there?"

"Let's find out," says Achilles. "Can you quantum teleport us straight from this chariot?"

"Watch me," says Hephaestus. Man and god wink out of sight as the chariot—empty now—keeps flying north and west across Hellas Basin.

50

"This isn't Savi."

"Did you hear me say it was, friend of Noman?"

Harman stood on the solid metal of the bier seemingly suspended above more than five miles of air a hundred yards from the north face of Chomolungma—staring despite his powerful urge *not* to stare at the dead face and naked body of a young Savi. Prospero stood behind him on the iron stairs. The wind was coming up outside.

"It *looks* like Savi," said Harman. He could not slow the beating of his heart. Both the exposure to altitude and to the body in front of him made him almost sick with vertigo. "But Savi's dead," he said.

"You are sure?"

"I'm sure, goddamn you. I saw your Caliban kill her. I saw the bloody remnants of what he ate and what he left behind. Savi is dead. And I never saw her this *young*."

The naked woman lying on her back in the crystal coffin could not have been older than three or four years beyond her first Twenty. Savi had been . . . ancient. All of them—Hannah, Ada, Daeman, and Harman—had been shocked at the sight of her—gray hair, wrinkles, a body that was past its prime. None of the old-style humans had ever seen the effects of aging before Savi . . . nor since, but that would all change now that the Firmary rejuvenation tanks were gone.

"Not *my* Caliban," said Prospero. "No, not *my* monster then. The goblin was his own master, sick Sycorax-spawn, a lost in thrall Setebos-slave, when you encountered it in yon orbital isle some nine months past."

"This isn't Savi," repeated Harman. "It can't be." He forced himself to stride back up the stairs toward the central chamber of the Taj Moira, brushing brusquely past the blue-robed magus. But he paused before passing up through the granite ceiling. "Is she alive?" he asked softly.

"Touch her," said Prospero.

Harman backed another step up the stairs. "No. Why?"

"Come down here and touch her," said the magus. The hologram, projection, whatever it was, now stood next to the crystal sarcophagus. "It's the only way you can tell if she is alive."

"I'll take your word for it." Harman stayed where he was.

"But I've not *given* you my word, friend of Noman. I've given no opinion on whether this is a sleeping woman, or a corpse, or merely a corollary of wax, wanting spirit. But I warrant you this, husband of Ada of Ardis—should she wake, should you wake her, should she be real—and should you then discourse with this waked and decanted spirit, all your most pressing questions will be answered."

"What do you mean?" asked Harman, descending the steps in spite of his urge to flee.

The magus remained silent. His only answer was to open the crystal top to the clear sarcophagus.

No smell of corruption came forth. Harman stepped onto the metal bier platform, then came around to stand next to the magus. Except for glimpses of hairless corpses in the healing tanks on Prospero's isle, he'd never seen a dead person until recent months. No old-style human had. But now he'd buried people at Ardis Hall and knew the terrible aspects of death—the lividity and rigor mortis, the eyes seeming to sink away from the light, the hard coldness of flesh. This woman—this *Savi*—showed none of these signs. Her skin looked soft and flushed with life. Her lips were pink almost to the point of redness, as were her nipples. Her eyes were closed, the lashes long, but it seemed that she could awaken any second.

"Touch her," said Prospero.

Harman reached a trembling hand and snatched it back before he touched her. There was a slight but firm forcefield above the woman's body—permeable but palpable—and the air inside the field was much warmer than that above it. He tried again, setting his fingers first to the woman's throat—finding the barest hint of pulse, like a butterfly's softest stirring—and then set his palm on her chest, between her breasts. Yes—the slightest beating of her heart, but slow—soft poundings far too far apart to be the heartbeat of a normal sleeper.

"This crèche is similar to the one your friend Noman sleeps in now," Prospero said softly. "It pauses time. But rather than healing and protecting her for three days, as Noman-Odysseus' slow-time sarcophagus does this very minute, this crystal coffin has been her home for one thousand four hundred and some years."

Harman plucks his hand back as if he'd been bitten. "Impossible," he said.

"Is it? Wake her and ask her."

"Who is she?" demanded Harman. "It can't be Savi."

Prospero smiled. Below their feet, clouds had swept in to the north face of the mountain and were curling gray around the glass-bottomed shelter in which they stood. "No, it can't be Savi, can it?" said the magus. "I knew her as Moira."

"Moira? This place—the Taj Moira—is named after her?"

"Of course. It is her tomb. Or at least the tomb in which she sleeps. Moira is a post-human, friend of Noman."

"The posts are all dead—gone—Daeman and Savi and I saw their Caliban-chewed and mummified bodies floating in the foul air of your orbital isle." Harman had stepped back from the coffin again.

"Moira is the last," said Prospero. "Come down from the p-ring more than fifteen hundred years ago. She was the lover and consort of Ahman Ferdinand Mark Alonzo Khan Ho Tep."

"Who the hell is that?" The clouds had enveloped the Taj platform now and Harman felt on more solid ground with the glass floor showing only gray beneath him.

"A bookish descendant of the original Khan," said the magus. "He ruled what was left of the Earth at the time the voynix first became active. He had this temporal sarcophagus built for himself but was in love with this Moira and offered it to her. Here she's slept away the centuries."

Harman forced a laugh. "That doesn't make any sense. Why didn't this Ho Tep whatshisname just have a second coffin built for himself?"

Prospero's smile was maddening. "He did. It was set right here on this broad bier, next to Moira's. But even a place as hard to get to as the Rangbok Pumori Chu-mu-lang-ma Feng Dudh Kosi Lhotse-Nuptse Khumbu aga Ghat-Mandir Khan Ho Tep Rauza will have its visitors over almost a millennium and a half. One of the early intruders pulled Ahman Ferdinand Mark Alonzo Khan's body and temporal sarcophagus out of here and tossed it over the edge to the glacier below."

"Why didn't they take this coffin . . . Moira's?" asked Harman. He was skeptical of everything the magus said.

Prospero extended an age-mottled hand toward the sleeping woman. "Would you throw this body away?"

"Why didn't they loot the upstairs then?" said Harman.

"There are safeguards up there. I will be happy to show you later."

"Why didn't these early intruders *wake* . . . whoever this is?" asked Harman.

"They tried," said Prospero. "But they never succeeded in opening the sarcophagus . . ."

"You didn't seem to have any trouble doing that."

"I was here when Ahman Ferdinand Mark Alonzo Khan devised the machine," said the magus. "I know its codes and passwords."

"*You* wake her, then. I want to talk to her."

"I cannot wake this sleeping post-human," said Prospero. "Nor could the intruders had they bypassed the security systems and managed to open her coffin. Only one thing will wake Moira."

"What's that?" Harman was on the lowest step again, ready to leave.

"For Ahman Ferdinand Mark Alonzo Khan or another human male descended from Ahman Ferdinand Mark Alonzo Khan to have sexual intercourse with her while she sleeps."

Harman opened his mouth to speak, found nothing to say, and simply stood there, staring at the blue-robed figure. The magus had either gone insane or had always been mad. There was no third option.

"You are descended from Ahman Ferdinand Mark Alonzo Khan Ho Tep and the line of Khans," continued Prospero, his voice sounding as calm and disinterested as someone speculating on the weather. "The DNA of your semen will awaken Moira."

51

Mahnmut and Orphu went outside onto the hull of the *Queen Mab* where they could talk in peace.

The huge ship had ceased setting off its Coke-can-sized atomic bombs upon passing the orbit of Earth's moon—they wanted to announce their arrival but not antagonize anyone or anything in the equatorial or polar rings into firing on them—and now the *Mab* was decelerating toward orbit under a mild one-eighth gravity using only its auxiliary ion-drive engines extended on short booms. Mahnmut thought that the blue glow "beneath" them was a pleasant alternative to the periodic smash and glare of the bombs.

The little Europan had to take care out in vacuum under deceleration, making sure that he was attached to the ship at all times, staying on the catwalks that ringed the ship, watching his step on the ladders that were everywhere on the thousand-foot-long spacecraft, but he knew that if he did something stupid Orphu of Io would come after him and save him. Mahnmut might be comfortable in full vacuum for only a dozen hours or so before having to replenish air and other requirements and he'd rarely practiced using the little peroxide thrusters built into his back, but this outside world of extreme cold, terrible heat, raging radiation, and hard vacuum was Orphu's natural environment.

"So what do we do?" Mahnmut asked his huge friend.

"I think it's imperative that we bring the dropship and *The Dark Lady* down," said Orphu. "As soon as possible."

"We?" said Mahnmut. *"We?"* The plan had been for Suma IV to pilot the dropship with General Beh bin Adee and thirty of his troopers—the rockvec soldiers under the direct command of Centurian Leader Mep Ahoo—in the dropship passenger nacelle, while Mahnmut waited in *The Dark Lady* down in the dropship's hold. When and if the time came to use the submersible, Suma IV and any other required personnel would climb down into *The Dark Lady* via an access shaft. Despite Mahnmut's misgivings about being separated from his old friend, there had never been any planning to include the huge, optically blind Ionian in the dropship part of the mission. Orphu was to remain with the *Queen Mab* as external systems engineer.

"So what is this 'we'?" Mahnmut asked again.

"I've decided that I'm indispensable to this mission," rumbled Orphu. "Besides, you still have that comfortable little niche for me in the sub's hold—air and energy umbilicals, comm links, radar, and other sensor feeds—I could vacation there and be happy."

Mahnmut shook his head, realized he was doing it in front of a blind moravec, realized then that Orphu's radar and infrared sensors would pick up the movement, and shook his head again. "Why should we insist on going down? Trying to land on Earth could jeopardize the rendezvous with the broadcasting asteroid-city on the p-ring."

"Bugger the broadcasting asteroid-city on the p-ring," growled Orphu of Io. "The important thing right now is to get down to that planet as fast as we can."

"Why?"

"Why?" repeated Orphu. "*Why*? You're the one with the eyes, little friend. Didn't you *see* those telescope images that you described to me?"

"The burned village, you mean?"

"Yes, the burned village, I mean," rumbled Orphu. "And the other thirty or forty human settlements around the world that seemed to be under attack by headless creatures that seem to specialize in slaughtering old-style human beings—*old-style humans*, Mahnmut, the kind that designed our ancestors."

"Since when has this turned into a rescue mission?" asked Mahnmut. The Earth was a big, bright, blue sphere now, growing by the minute. The e- and p-rings were beautiful.

"Since we saw the photos showing human beings being slaughtered," said Orphu and Mahnmut recognized the near-subsonic tones in his friend's voice. Those rumbles meant either that Orphu was very amused or very, very serious—and Mahnmut knew that he wasn't amused at the moment.

"I thought the idea was to save our Five Moons, the Belt, and the solar system from total quantum collapse," said Mahnmut.

Orphu growled low tones. "We'll do that tomorrow. Today we have a chance to help people down there."

"How?" said Mahnmut. "We don't know the context. We have no idea what's going on down there. For all we know, those headless metallic creatures are just killer robots that humans have built to kill each other. We'd be meddling in local wars that are none of our business."

"Do you believe that, Mahnmut?"

Mahnmut hesitated. He looked far, far down to where the ion-engines out on their booms lanced blue beams in the direction of the growing blue and white sphere.

"No," he said at last. "No, I don't believe that. I think something new is going on down there, just as it is on Mars and on Ilium-Earth and everywhere we look."

"I do, too," said Orphu of Io. "Let's go in and convince Asteague/Che and the rest of the Prime Integrators that they have to launch the dropship and submersible when we go around the backside of the Earth. With me aboard."

"Just how do you plan to convince them to do this?" asked Mahnmut.

This time, the Ionian's deep rumble was more in the amused spectrum of bone-rattling subsonics. "I'll make them an offer they can't refuse."

Harman tried to get as far away from the crystal coffin as he could. He would have returned to the *eiffelbahn* car but the winds outside were roaring—easily over a hundred miles per hour, enough to sweep him off the marble tabletop surrounding the Taj Moira—so he climbed through the spiraling levels of books instead.

The walkways were narrow and soon very high, each one a little farther out over the low-walled maze far below as the inside walls of the curved dome pressed the bookshelves and walkways farther in, and Harman would have been disturbed by the dizzying height beneath his feet on the open-iron catwalks if he hadn't been so eager to put distance between himself and the sleeping woman.

The books had no titles. They were of uniform size. Harman estimated that there were hundreds of thousand of volumes in this huge structure. He pulled one out and opened it at random. The letters were small and printed in pre-rubicon English, older than any book or writing he'd yet encountered, and it took him minutes to sound out and guess at the first couple of sentences he encountered. He slid the book back in and set his palm on the spine, visualizing five blue triangles in a row.

It did not sigl. No golden words flowed down his hand and arm to settle in his memory. Either the sigl function did not work in this place or these ancient books were impervious to sigling.

"There's a way you can read them all," said Prospero.

Harman jumped backward. He'd not heard the magus approaching across the noisy catwalk. He was just suddenly *there,* not an arm's length away.

"How can I read them all?" said Harman.

"The *eiffelbahn* car will be leaving in two hours," said the magus. "If you're not on it, it will be a while until the next one stops here at Taj Moira—eleven years, to be precise. So if you're going to read all these books, you had best start at once."

"I'm ready to go now," said Harman. "It's just too damned windy out for me to get to the car."

"I'll have one of the servitors rig a line when we are ready to leave," said Prospero.

"Servitor? There are working servitors here?"

"Of course. Do you think the mechanisms of the Taj or the *eiffelbahn* repair themselves?" The magus chuckled. "Well, of course, in a way they *do* repair themselves, since most of the servitors are nanotech, part of the structures themselves and too small for you to detect."

"All of our servitors at Ardis and the other communities quit working," said Harman. "Just . . . crashed. And the power went out."

"Of course," said Prospero. "There are consequences to your destruction of the Firmary and my orbital isle. But the orbital and planetary power grid and other mechanisms are still intact. Even the Firmary could be replaced if you so choose."

Harman was stunned to hear this. He turned and leaned on the iron railing, taking deep breaths, ignoring the long drop to the marble floor far below. When he and Daeman—with this magus's instructions—had directed the huge "wormhole collector" into Prospero's Isle nine months ago, it had been to destroy the terrible banquet table where Caliban had been feasting for centuries on the bodies and bones of Final Twenty oldstyle humans in the Firmary. Since that day, since the destruction of the Firmary and the knowledge that one would be faxed there after any serious injury and on every twentieth birthday, mortality had lain heavily on everyone's spirit. Death and aging had become a reality for everyone. If Prospero was telling the truth now, virtual youth and immortality was once again an option. Harman didn't know what he thought of this new option, but just the thought of choosing made him sick to his stomach.

"There's another Firmary?" he said. He had spoken softly but his voice still echoed under the gigantic dome.

"Of course. There's another on Sycorax's orbital isle. It merely needs to be activated, as do the orbital power projectors and automated fax systems."

"Sycorax?" said Harman. "The witch you said was Caliban's mother?"

"Yes."

Harman started to ask how they might get up to the orbital rings to activate the Firmary, power, and emergency fax system, but then he remembered that Savi's sonie they kept at Ardis could fly to the rings. Harman took long breaths.

"Harman, friend of Noman," said Prospero, "you need to listen to me now. You can leave this place when the *eiffelbahn* commences to run again in one hour and fifty-four minutes. Or you can go outside and leap to your death on the Khombu Glacier. All choices are yours. But it is as certain that night shall follow day that you shall never see your Ada again, nor return home to what is left of Ardis Hall, nor see your friends Daeman, Hannah, and the others survive this war with the voynix and *calibani,* nor ever again see a green Earth not turned blue and dead by Setebos' hunger, if you do not waken Moira."

Harman stepped away from the magus and balled both hands into fists. Prospero was leaning on his staff as if it was a walking stick, but Harman knew that one motion by Prospero with that staff would send him flying over the rail to his death on the jewel-encrusted marble walls hundreds of feet below. "There has to be another way to waken her," he said through clenched teeth.

"There is not."

Harman pounded the iron railing. "None of this makes any goddamned sense."

"Do not infest your mind with beating on the strangeness of this business," said Prospero, his words echoing under the high vault. "At picked leisure, which shall be shortly, Moira will resolve you of every one of these happened accidents. But first you must wake her."

Harman shook his head. "I don't believe that I'm descended from this Ahman Whatshisname Khan Ho Tep," he said. "How could I be? We old-styles were created by the posts centuries after Savi's people disappeared in the Final Fax and . . ."

Prospero smiled. "Precisely. Where do you think your DNA templates and stored bodies were taken from, friend of Noman? Moira can explain it all to you and more. She is a post-human, the last of her kind. She knows how you can read all these books before our *eiffelbahn* car leaves this station. She may well know how you can defeat the voynix— or the *calibani*—or perhaps even defeat Caliban and his lord, Setebos himself. But you will have to decide soon whether your Ada's life is worth one small infidelity. We now have one hour and forty-five minutes before the *eiffelbahn* starts running again. Fourteen hundred years of sleep and more cannot be shaken off in an instant. Moira will need some time to awaken, to eat, to understand our situation, before she will be ready to travel with us."

"She'd go with us?" Harman said stupidly. "On the *eiffelbahn*? Back to Ardis?"

"Almost certainly," said Prospero.

Harman gripped the railing so tightly that his knuckles turned first bright red, then white. Finally he released the iron and turned to the waiting magus. "All right. But you wait here. Or better yet, go back to the car. Out of sight. I'll do this thing, but I have to be alone."

Prospero simply winked out of existence. Harman stood on the high railing for a minute, breathing in the musty leather smell of ancient books, and then he hurried down the nearest flight of steps.

It was a ragtag, motley group of forty-five freezing men and women that made the seven-mile walk from Starved Rock to the fax pavilion.

Daeman led the way, carrying the pack with its glowing, occasionally squirming white Setebos Egg, and Ada walked by his side despite her concussion and cracked ribs. The first few miles through the forest were the worst—the terrain was rough and rocky, the visibility was poor, it had started snowing again, and everyone was braced for the attack of unseen voynix. When thirty minutes passed, then forty-five minutes, and then an hour with no attack—no sign of the voynix at all—everyone began to relax a little.

A hundred feet above them, Greogi, Tom, and the eight seriously injured survivors of Ardis filled the sonie. Greogi would flit ahead, circle high over the forest, and then come back, swooping low just long enough to shout information.

"Voynix ahead about half a mile, but they're retreating—staying away from you and the egg."

Through the pounding headache and the duller ache from her wrist and broken ribs—every breath pained her—Ada found little comfort that the voynix were only a half mile away. She'd seen them run at full speed, watched them leap into and out of trees. The creatures could be on them in a minute. The group had about twenty-five flechette rifles or pistols with them, but not many extra magazines of ammunition. Because of her broken right wrist and taped-up ribs, Ada didn't carry a weapon, which made her feel all the more exposed as she walked up front with Daeman, Edide, Boman, and a few of the others. The drifts were a foot or more deep here in the woods and Ada barely had the energy to kick her way through the clinging wet snow.

Even after they got out of the rockiest, thickest part of the forest, still heading southeast to intercept the road between Ardis and the fax pavilion, the group traveled with excruciating slowness because of those who were ambulatory but more seriously injured or sick, including some who'd been victims of hypothermia the last two nights. Siris, their other medic, was walking with them and she shuttled back and forth constantly, making sure that the ill and injured were getting help and reminding the leaders to slow their pace.

"I don't understand," said Ada as they came out into a wide meadow that she remembered from a hundred summer hikes.

"What's that?" asked Daeman. He carried the rucksack with the glowing egg in it ahead of him at arm's length, as if it smelled bad. In truth, as Ada had noticed, it *did* smell bad—a mixture of rotten fish and something sewerish. But it was still glowing and it vibrated from time to time, so presumably the little Setebos inside was still alive.

"Why do the voynix stay away while we have this thing?" said Ada.

"They must be afraid of it," said Daeman. He slipped the rucksack from his right hand to his left. He was carrying a crossbow in his free hand.

"Yes, of course," said Ada, speaking more sharply than she'd meant to. The throbbing in her head, ribs, and arms was making her short-tempered. "I mean, what is the connection between that . . . thing . . . in Paris Crater and the voynix?"

"I don't know," said Daeman.

"The voynix have been around . . . forever," said Ada. "This Setebos monster just arrived a week ago."

"I know," said Daeman. "But I feel that somehow they're connected. Maybe they always have been."

Ada nodded, winced from the pain of nodding, and trod on. There was very little talking in the rough ranks of the forty-five men and women as they trudged through another patch of thick woods, crossed a familiar stream that was now mostly frozen over, and headed down a steep hill of frozen high grass and weeds.

The sonie swooped low. "Another quarter mile to the road," Greogi called down. "The voynix have moved farther south. Two miles at least."

When they reached the road there was a stir among the survivors, urgent whispers, people clapping one another on the back. Ada looked west toward Ardis Hall. The covered bridge was in sight just before the turn in the road that ran up to the manor house, but there was no sight of the great hall, of course, not even a plume of black smoke. For a minute she thought she was going to be sick to her stomach. Black spots danced in front of her eyes. She paused, put her hands on her knees, and lowered her head.

"Are you all right, Ada?" It was Laman speaking. The bearded man wore only rags, including one wrapped around his right hand where he had lost four fingers during the battle with the voynix at Ardis.

"Yes," said Ada. She rose, smiled at Laman, and hurried to keep up with the small group at the front of the shuffling pack.

It was less than a mile to the fax pavilion now and all looked familiar, except for the unusual snow. There was not the slightest sign of voynix. The sonie circled above, disappeared in wider circles, and then swept back, Greogi giving them a thumbs-up as he dipped the machine low and then flew on ahead.

"Where are we going to fax, Daeman?" asked Ada. She heard the flatness and lack of affect in her own voice but was too tired and hurting to put any energy in her tone.

"I don't know," said the lean, muscled man who had once been the pudgy aesthete who'd tried to seduce her. "At least I don't know where to go for the long run. Chom, Ulanbat, Paris Crater, Bellinbad, and the rest of the more populated nodes have probably been covered with blue ice by Setebos. But I do know an unpopulated node I stop by from time to time—it's in the tropics. Warm. Nothing but an abandoned little town, but it's on the ocean—some ocean, somewhere—and has a lagoon. I haven't seen many animals there other than lizards and a few wild pigs, but they don't seem to be afraid of people. We could fish, hunt, make more weapons, take care of our injured . . . lay low until we come up with a plan."

"How will Harman, Hannah, and Odysseus-Noman find us?" asked Ada.

Daeman was silent for a minute and Ada could almost hear him thinking—*We don't even know if Harman is alive. Petyr said that he disappeared with Ariel.* But what he finally said was, "No problem there. Some of us will fax back here regularly. And we can leave some sort of permanent note at Ardis Hall with the faxnode code for our tropical hideout. Harman can read. I don't think the voynix can."

Ada smiled wanly. "The voynix can do a lot of things none of us ever imagined they were capable of."

"Yeah," said Daeman. And then they were silent until they reached the fax pavilion.

The fax pavilion looked pretty much as Daeman had seen it forty-eight hours earlier. The stockade had been breached. There was dried human blood everywhere, but the voynix or wild animals had carried off the bodies of those Ardisites who'd fought to the death trying to defend the pavilion. But the pavilion structure itself was still intact, the faxnode column still rising in the center of the open, circular structure.

The band of humans stood awkwardly at the edge of the pavilion floor, looking over their shoulders at the dark forest. The sonie landed and the injured were helped out or carried.

"Nothing for five miles," said Greogi. "It's weird. The few voynix I saw were fleeing south as if you were in pursuit of them."

Daeman looked at the milkily glowing egg in his backpack and sighed. "We're not pursuing them," he said. "We just want to get the hell out of here." He told Greogi and the others of his plan.

There was a brief spate of argument. Some of the survivors wanted to fax to familiar locations and to see if friends and loved ones were alive. Caul was sure that the Loman Estate node wouldn't have been invaded by this Setebos thing Daeman had told them about. Caul's mother was there.

"All right, look!" Daeman called over the rising voices. "We don't know *where* Setebos might be by now. The monster turned the huge city of Paris Crater into a castle of blue-ice strands in less than twenty-four hours. It's been more than forty-eight hours since I got back and I was the last person to fax in. Here's my suggestion . . ."

Ada noticed that the babbling stopped. People were listening. They accepted Daeman as a leader just as they had once accepted her leadership . . . and Harman's. She had to stifle a sudden urge to weep.

"Let's decide now if we're going to stick together for a while or not," said Daeman, his deep voice easily carrying to the edge of the crowd. "We can vote and . . ."

"What does 'vote' mean?" asked Boman.

Daeman explained the concept.

"So if just one more than half of us . . . votes . . . to stay together," said Oko, "then we all have to do what the others want?"

"Just for a while," said Daeman. "Let's say . . . a week. We're safer together than traveling apart. And we have people injured, sick, who can't defend themselves. If people all fax different directions right now, how are we ever going to find each other again? Do we let those who want to strike off alone carry the flechette rifles and crossbows, or do those stay with the larger group who wants to stick together?"

"What do we do in that week . . . *if* we agree to go with you to this tropical paradise?" asked Tom.

"Just what I said," answered Daeman. "Recuperate. Find or build some more weapons. Build some sort of defensive perimeter there . . . I remember a little island just beyond the reef. We could make some little boats, set up our homes and defenses on the island . . ."

"Do you think voynix can't swim?" called Stoman.

Everyone laughed nervously but Ada glanced at Daeman. It had been gallows humor—a phrase she'd learned sigling the old books in Ardis Hall's library—but it had broken the tension.

Daeman laughed easily. "I have no idea if voynix can swim, but if they can't, that island would be the perfect place for us."

"Until we breed so many children that we won't fit on it anymore," said Tom.

People laughed more easily this time.

"And we'll send reconaissance teams out from the faxnode there," said Daeman. "Starting the first day we arrive. That way, we'll have some idea of what's going on in the world and which nodes are safe to fax to. And after a week, anyone who wants to leave can. I just think it's better for all of us if we stay together until our sick people are better and until we all get a chance to eat and sleep."

"Let's vote," said Caul.

They did, hesitantly, with more laughter at the thought of raising their hands to decide such a serious issue. The vote was forty-three to seven to stay together, with three of the most seriously injured not voting because they were unconscious.

"All right," said Daeman. He approached the faxpad.

"Wait a minute," said Greogi. "What do we do with the sonie? It won't fax and if we leave it here, the voynix will get it. It's saved our lives more than once."

"Oh, shit," said Daeman. "I didn't think about that." He ran his hand over his dirty, blood-streaked face, and Ada saw how pale and tired he was under the thin veneer of energy he'd been projecting.

"I have an idea about that," said Ada.

The crowd looked at her, their faces friendly, and waited.

"Most of you know that Savi showed some of us how to use new functions last year . . . proxnet, farnet, and allnet. Some of you have even tried them yourselves. When we get to Daeman's tropical paradise, we call up the farnet function, see where the place is, and then someone faxes back here to fetch the sonie and fly it to our island. Harman, Hannah, Petyr, and Noman got to the Golden Gate at Machu Picchu in less than an hour, so it shouldn't take too long to fly to paradise."

There was some chuckling, much nodding.

"I have an even better idea," said Greogi. "The rest of you fax off to paradise. I'll stay here and guard the sonie. One of you fax back with the directions and I'll fly it there today."

"I'll stay with you," said Laman, holding up a flechette rifle in his good left hand. "You'll need someone to shoot voynix if they come back. And to keep you awake during the flight south."

Daeman smiled tiredly. "All right?" he asked the group.

People shuffled forward, eager to fax.

"Wait," said Daeman. "We don't know what's waiting for us there, so six of you with rifles—Caul, Kaman, Elle, Boman, Casman, Edide—you come with me to the pavilion node and we'll fax through first. If everything's good there, one of us will be back in two minutes or less. Then we should bring the wounded and sick through. Tom, Siris, could you please organize the stretcher teams? Then Greogi will supervise half a dozen of you back there with rifles to keep watch while the rest fax though. Okay?"

Everyone nodded impatiently. The rifle team walked to the star inlaid on the fax pavilion floor while Daeman poised his hand over the keypad. "Let's go," he said and tapped in the code for his uninhabited node.

Nothing happened. The usual puff of air and visual flicker as people faxed out of existence simply did not happen.

"One at a time," said Daeman, although faxnodes could easily handle six people faxing at a time. "Caul. Stand on the star."

Caul did, shifting his rifle nervously. Daeman faxed in the code again.

Nothing. The wind made a noise as it blew snow into the open pavilion.

"Maybe that faxnode doesn't work anymore," called a woman named Seaes from the crowd.

"I'll try Loman's Estate," said Daeman and tapped in the familiar code.

It did not work.

"Holy Jesus Christ Shit," cried the burly Kaman. He pushed forward. "Maybe you're doing it wrong. Let me."

Half a dozen people had a try. Three dozen familiar faxnode codes were tried. Nothing worked. Not Paris Crater. Not Chom or Bellinbad or the many Circles of Heaven code for Ulanbat. Nothing worked.

Finally everyone stood in silence, stunned, speechless, their faces turned to masks of terror and hopelessness. Nothing in the past year, none of the nightmares of the last months—not the Fall of the Meteors, not the failing of electricity and the fall of the servitors, not the early attacks of voynix nor the news from Paris Crater, not even the Ardis Hall Massacre or the hopeless situation on Starved Rock had struck these men and women with such a sense of hopelessness.

The faxnodes no longer worked. The world as they had known it since they were born no longer existed. There was nowhere to flee, nothing to do now but wait and die. Wait for the voynix to return or for the cold to kill them or for disease and starvation to finish them off one by one.

Ada stepped up onto the small base around the faxpad column so that she could be seen as well as be heard.

"We're going back to Ardis Hall," she said. Her voice was strong, brooking no argument. "It's only a little more than a mile up the road. We can be there in less than an hour, even in our condition. Greogi and Tom will bring those to sick to walk."

"What the fuck is at Ardis Hall?" asked a short woman whom Ada did not recognize. "What's there except corpses and carrion and ashes and voynix?"

"Not everything burned," Ada said loudly. She had no idea if everything had burned or not; she'd been unconscious when they'd flown her away from the flaming ruins. But Daeman and Greogi had described unburned sections of the compound. "Not everything burned," she said again. "There are logs there. Remnants of the tents and barracks. If nothing else, we'll pull down the stockade wall and build cabins out of the wood. And there will be artifacts—things that didn't burn in the ruins. Guns, maybe. Things we left behind."

"Like the voynix," said a scarred man named Elos.

"Maybe so," said Ada, "but the voynix are everywhere. And they're afraid of this Setebos Egg that Daeman's carrying. As long as we have it, the voynix will stay away. And where would you rather face them, Elos? In the darkness of the forest at night, or sitting around a big fire at Ardis, in a warm hut, while your friends help stand watch?"

There was silence but it was an angry silence. Some still tried tapping at the faxpad, then pounding the column in frustration.

"Why don't we just stay here at the pavilion?" said Elle. "It has a roof already. We can close in the sides, build a fire. The stockade is smaller here and would be easier to rebuild. And if the fax starts working again, we could get out fast."

Ada nodded. "That makes sense, my friend. But what about water? The stream is almost a quarter of a mile from the pavilion here. Someone would always have to be fetching water, risking exposure or voynix attack to get it. And there's no place to store it here, nor room enough for all of us under this pavilion roof. And this valley is *cold*. Ardis gets more sunlight, we'll have more building material to use there, and Ardis Hall had a well under it. We can build our new Ardis Hall *around* the well so we'll never have to go outside for water."

People shifted their weight from foot to foot but no one had anything to say. The thought of walking back down that frozen road, away from the salvation of the fax pavilion, seemed too difficult to contemplate.

"I'm going now," said Ada. "It will be dark in a few hours. I want a big fire roaring before ringlight sets in."

She walked out of the pavilion and headed west down the road. Daeman followed. Then Boman and Edide. Then Tom, Siris, Kaman, and most of the others. Greogi supervised loading the sick back into the sonie.

Daeman hurried to catch up to her and leaned close to whisper to her. "I have good news and bad news," he said.

"What's the good news?" Ada asked tiredly. Her head was pounding so ferociously that she had to keep her eyes closed, opening them only once in a while to stay on the frozen dirt road.

"Everyone's coming," he said.

"And the bad news?" asked Ada. She was thinking—*I will not cry. I will* not *cry.*

"This goddamned Setebos Egg is starting to hatch," said Daeman.

54

As Harman took off his clothes in the crystal crypt beneath the marble mass of the Taj Moira, he realized just how damned cold it was in that glass room. It also must have been cold in the huge Taj chamber above, but the thermskin he'd put on in the *eiffelbahn* car had kept him from noticing. Now he hesitated at the foot of the clear coffin with the thermskin peeled half down his torso, his regular clothes in a tumble at his feet and goosebumps rising on his bare arms and chest.

This is wrong. This is absolutely, totally wrong.

Other than a lifetime awe of the post-humans in their orbital rings and the almost spiritual belief everyone had that they would rise to the rings and spend eternity with the posts after their Final Fax, Harman and his people knew nothing of religion. The closest they had come to understanding religious awe and ceremony had come from the glimpses they'd received of the Greek gods through the turin-cloth drama.

But now Harman felt that he was about to commit something like sin.

Ada's life—the life of everyone I know and care for—may depend on me waking this post-human woman.

"By having sex with a dead or comatose stranger?" he whispered aloud. "This is wrong. This is *crazy.*"

Harman glanced over his shoulder and up the stairway, but, as he'd promised, Prospero was nowhere to be seen. Harman shucked out of the rest of his thermskin. The air was freezing cold. He looked down at himself and almost laughed at how contracted, cold, and shrunken he was.

What if this is all the crazy old magus's idea of a joke? And who was to say whether Prospero was lurking around under some invisibility cloak or other contrivance of his magusy ways?

Harman stood at the foot of the crystal coffin and shook. The cold was part of it. The unpleasantness of what he was about to do a greater part. Even the idea that he was descended from this Ahman Ferdinand Mark Alonzo Khan Ho Tep made him queasy.

He remembered Ada injured, unconscious, atop that place called Starved Rock with the pitifully few other survivors of the massacre at Ardis.

Who's to say that was real? Certainly Prospero could make a turin cloth transmit false images.

But he had to proceed as if the vision had been real. He had to proceed as if Prospero's emotional statement to him that he had to *learn,* to change, to enter this fight against Setebos and the voynix and the *calibani,* or all would be lost, was *true.*

But what can one man who's had his Five Twenties do? Harman asked himself.

As if to answer that, Harman crawled up over the edge of the massive crèche. He lowered himself carefully into the end of the thing, not touching the naked woman's bare feet. The semipermeable forcefield made it feel as if he were slipping into a warm bath through a tingling resistance. Now only his head and shoulders were out of the warmth.

The coffin was long and wide, easily wide enough for him to lie down next to the sleeping female without touching her. The cushioned material she was lying on had looked like silk, but it felt more like some soft, metallic fiber under Harman's knees. Now that he was mostly in the containment of the time crèche, he could feel surges and pulses of whatever energy field kept this Savi-lookalike young and perhaps asleep.

If I lower my head below the forcefield, thought Harman, *maybe it'll put me into a fifteen-hundred-year sleep as well and solve all my problems. Especially the problem of what to do next here.*

He did crouch lower, putting his face below the level of the tingling forcefield the way a timid swimmer might enter the water. He was now on his hands and knees over the woman's legs. The air was much warmer here in the crèche and he felt the vibration of energy from the sarcophagus machinery humming throughout his body, but it didn't put him to sleep.

Now what? he thought. There must have been some time in Harman's life where he had felt this awkward, but he couldn't recall it.

As with the absence of the concept of sin in Harman's world, so was there little incidence or thought of the idea of rape. There were no laws nor anyone to enforce laws in this now-vanished world of the old-style humans, but neither had there been aggression between the sexes or intimacy without permission by both parties. There had been no laws, no police, no prisons—none of the words Harman had sigled in the last eight months—but there had been a sort of informal shunning in their tight little communities of parties and cotillions and faxes to this event and that. No one had wanted to be left out.

And there had been enough sex for anyone who wanted it. And almost everyone had wanted it.

Harman had wanted it often enough in his almost-Five-Twenties. It was just in the last decade or so since he'd taught himself to read the strange squiggles in books that he had quit the fax-somewhere/bed-someone rhythm of life. He'd gained the odd idea that there was, or could be, or might be, someone special for him, someone with whom—for both of them—sexual intercourse should be an exclusive and shared special experience, separate from all the easy liaisons and physical friendships that made up the old-style human world.

It had been an odd thought. One that would have made no sense to almost anyone he would have told—but he told no one. And perhaps it was Ada's youth, she was only seven-and-First-Twenty when they first made love and *fell* in love, which allowed her to share his odd and romantic notions of exclusiveness. They'd even held their own "wedding" ceremony at Ardis Hall, and while the four hundred others had mostly humored them, accepting this excuse for yet another party, a few—Petyr, Daeman, Hannah, a few others—had understood that it meant much more.

Thinking about this is not helping you do what Prospero says you have to do, Harman.

He was kneeling naked above a woman who had been sleeping—according to the lying logosphere avatar who called himself Prospero—for almost a millennium and a half. And he was surprised to find that he was not ready for sex?

Why did she look so much like Savi? Savi had been perhaps the most interesting person Harman had ever met—bold, mysterious, ancient, from another age, never quite honest, shrouded in ways that almost no old-style human from Harman's age could ever be—but he'd never been attracted to her as a woman. He remembered her thin body in its skintight thermskin on Prospero's orbital isle.

This younger Savi was not thin. Her muscles had not atrophied with the age of centuries. Her hair—everywhere—was dark—not the black he'd first thought, not the jet black of Ada's beautiful hair, but very dark brown. The clouds had dissipated off the north face of Chomolungma and in the reflected bright light from the emerging sun, some of this woman's hair glowed coppery red. Harman could see the tiny pores in her skin. Her nipples, he noticed, were more brown than pink. The set of her chin had Savi's center crease and firmness, but the wrinkles he remembered on her brow and around her mouth and the corners of her eyes were not yet there.

Who *is* she? he wondered for the fiftieth time.

It doesn't matter who she really is, Harman's mind screamed at itself. *If Prospero is telling the truth, she's the woman you have to have sex with so she'll wake up and teach you the things you have to learn to get home.*

Harman leaned forward until his weight was partially on the sleeping woman. She was lying on her back with her arms at her side, palms down against the cushioned material, legs already slightly apart. Feeling every inch the violator, Harman used his right knee to move her left leg farther to the side, then his left knee to open her right leg. She could not have been more open and vulnerable to him.

And he could not have been less physically excited.

Harman raised his weight on his hands until he was doing a push-up above the supine form. He forced his head up and out of the only slightly buzzing forcefield and drew in great gulps of the freezing air there. When he lowered his head into the sarcophagus' energy field again, he felt like a drowning man going under for the third time.

Harman laid his weight upon the sleeping woman. She did not budge or stir. Her eyelashes were long and dark, but there was not the slightest flutter or sense of her eyes moving under their lids as he'd seen Ada's do so many times when he lay awake watching her sleeping next to him in the moonlight. Ada.

He closed his eyes and remembered her—not injured and unconscious on Starved Rock as Prospero's red turin cloth had shown, but the way she had been during their eight months together at Ardis Hall. He remembered waking up next to her in the night just to watch her sleep.

He remembered the clean soap and female scent of her next to him in the night in their room with the bay window in the ancient Ardis manor.

Harman felt himself start to stir.

Don't think about it. Don't think about now. Just remember.

He allowed himself to remember that first time with Ada, just nine months three weeks and two days ago now. They had been traveling with Savi, Daeman, and Hannah and had just met the reawakened Odysseus at the Golden Gate at Machu Picchu. They each had separate sleeping cubbies that night—the round, green spheres clinging to the orange tower of the ancient bridge like grapes on a vine, these hanging beneath the horizontal support strut some seven hundred feet and more above the ruins far below.

After everyone had gone to his or her own sleeping domi—everyone taken aback that the floors were as transparent as the crystal floor of this crypt—*No, don't think about that now*—Harman had slipped out of his room and knocked on Ada's door. She'd let him in and he'd noticed how lustrous her dark eyes were that night.

He'd actually gone to her room to talk to her about something, not to make love to her that night. Or so he thought at the time. He'd already hurt Ada's feelings once—in Paris Crater it was, he remembered now, at Daeman's mother's place, Marina's domi high on the bamboo-three towers at the edge of the red-eyed crater. And Ada had risked her life— or at least a fax to the orbital Firmary—by climbing from her balcony to his, teetering over a thousand miles of black hole crater to join him on his balcony that night. And he'd said no. He'd said "Let's wait." And she had, although certainly no man had ever turned down or turned away beautiful black-haired Ada from Ardis Hall before.

But that night in the clear-sided sphere-domi hanging from the Golden Gate at Machu Picchu, with the mountains he later guessed to be the rocky Andes rising around them and the haunted ruins a thousand feet below, he'd come to talk to her about . . . what? Oh, yes—he'd come to her room to persuade her to remain behind at Ardis Hall with Hannah and Odysseus while he and Daeman went on with Savi to that legendary place called Atlantis where there might be a spaceship waiting to take them to the rings. He'd been very convincing. And he'd lied through his teeth. He told young Ada that it would be better if she were to introduce Odysseus to everyone at Ardis Hall, that he and Daeman would certainly be gone just a few days. In truth, he'd been frightened that Savi would lead them into terrible danger—and she had, at forfeit of her own life—and even then Harman did not want Ada in harm's way. Even then, he felt that it would be his own flesh and soul sundered if harm came to her.

She'd been wearing the thinnest of short, silk sleeping gowns when she'd ordered the cubby door to iris open on the night she became his. The moonlight had been pale on her arms and eyelashes while he spoke so earnestly to her about staying at Ardis Hall with this stranger Odysseus.

And then he'd kissed her. No—he'd only kissed Ada on the cheek at the end of their conversation, the way a father or friend might kiss a child. It had been *she* who first kissed *him*—a full, open, lingering kiss, her arms going around him and pulling him closer as they stood there in the moonlight and starlight. He remembered feeling her young breasts against his chest through the thin silk of her blue nightgown.

He remembered carrying her to the small bed that lay against the curved, clear wall of the cubby. She'd helped him off with his clothes, both of them in a clumsy yet elegant hurry now.

Had the storm swept down out of the higher mountains and struck just as they began to make love on that narrow bed? Not long after, certainly. He did remember the moonlight on Ada's upturned face and the moonlight illuminating her nipples as he cupped each breast and raised it to his lips.

But he remembered the wall of wind hitting the bridge, rocking the cubbie dangerously, sensuously, just as they began to rock and move themselves, Ada under him, her legs rising around his hips, her right hand slipping down and finding him, guiding him . . .

No one guided him now as he stiffened and rose against the sex of this woman in the crystal crèche. *This won't work,* he thought through the surge of his own memories and renewed desire. *She'll be dry. I'll have to . . .*

But the rest of that thought was lost as he realized that she was not dry against his tentative probes, but soft and opening and even moist, as if she had lain there waiting for him all these years.

Ada had been ready for him—wet with excitement, her lips as warm as her warm sex, her arms insistent around him, her fingers arched on his bare back as he moved gently into her and with her. They had kissed until the kissing alone would have made Harman—he of the Four Twenties and nineteen years that very week, the oldest of the old that Ada knew or had ever known—almost swoon with a teenaged boy's lust and excitement.

They'd moved as the cubbie rocked to the wild gusts of wind—gently at first, forever it seemed, and then with increasing passion and less restraint as Ada urged him to lose restraint, as Ada opened to him and urged him deeper, kissing him and holding him within the powerful circle of her arms and squeezing legs and raking fingernails.

And when he'd come, Harman had throbbed in her for what seemed like long moments. And Ada had responded with a series of internal throbs that felt like tremors rising from some infinitely deep epicenter until he felt as if it was her small hand clenching the core of him tighter, releasing, then clenching again, rather than her entire body.

Harman throbbed inside the woman who looked like Savi and couldn't be. He did not linger but pulled out immediately, his heart pounding with guilt and something like horror even as he was filled with his love for Ada and his memories of Ada.

He rolled aside and lay panting and miserable next to the woman's body on the metallic-silken cushions. The warm air stirred around them, trying to lull him to sleep. Harman felt at that moment that he could sleep—could sleep for a millennium and a half just as this stranger had—sleep through all the danger to his world and to his friends and to his single, perfect, betrayed beloved.

Some small movement brought him up out of the fringes of his dozing.

He opened his eyes and his heart almost stopped as he realized that the woman's eyes were open. She had turned her head and was staring at him with a cool intelligence—an almost impossible level of awareness after being asleep so long.

"Who are you?" asked the young woman in dead Savi's voice.

55

In the end, it wasn't just Orphu's eloquence but a myriad of factors that decided the moravecs to launch the atmospheric dropship carrying *The Dark Lady*.

The moravec meeting on the bridge happened much sooner than the two hours Asteague/Che had suggested. Events were occurring too quickly. Twenty minutes after their conference outside on the hull of the *Queen Mab*, Mahnmut and Orphu were back on the ship's bridge conferring verbally in full Earth-standard sea-level atmosphere and gravity with the Callistan Cho Li, Prime Integrator Asteague/Che, General Beh bin Adee and his lieutenant Mep Ahoo, the ominous Suma IV, an agitated Retrograde Sinopessen, and half a dozen other moravec integrators and military rockvecs.

"This is the transmission we received eight minutes ago," said the navigator Cho Li. Almost everyone had heard it, but he played it back via tightbeam anyway.

The maser broadcast coordinates were the same as the previous transmission—from the Phobos-sized asteroid in Earth's polar ring—but there was no female human voice this time, only a string of rendezvous coordinates and delta-v rates.

"The lady wants us to bring Odysseus straight to her house," said Orphu, "and not fool around swinging around the other side of the Earth on the way."

"Can we do that?" asked Mahnmut. "Brake straight to her high polar orbit, I mean?"

"We can if we use the fission bombs again for a high-g deceleration the next nine hours," said Asteague/Che. "But we don't want to do that for a variety of reasons."

"Excuse me," said Mahnmut. "I'm just a submersible driver, no navigator or engineer, but I don't see how we're going to drop our speed anyway given the weak deceleration we're getting from the ion-drive engines. Did we have something special in store for the last bit of braking?"

"Aerobraking," said the many-limbed bulky little Callistan, Cho Li.

Mahnmut laughed at the image of the *Queen Mab*—all three hundred nine meters of bulky, girdered, crane-festooned, nonaerodynmic bulk of her—aerobraking through the Earth's atmosphere and then realized that Cho Li hadn't been joking.

"You can *aerobrake* this thing?" he said at last.

Retrograde Sinopessen skittered forward on his spidery silver legs. "Of course. We had always planned to aerobrake. The sixty-meter-wide pusher plate with its ablative coating retracts and morphs slightly to serve very nicely as a heat shield. The plasma field around us during the maneuver should not be prohibitive—we can even maser comm through it if we so choose. Our original plans were for a mild aerobraking maneuver at an altitude of one hundred and forty-five kilometers above Earth sea level with several passes to regulate our orbit—the difficult part will be passing through the busy artificial p- and e-rings, since they have nothing comparable to the debris-cleared F-ring Cassini Gap around Saturn—but those computations were easy enough. We just have to dodge like a sumbitch. Now, since we seem to have been ordered to make a command appearance at the lady's asteroid-city on the p-ring, we plan to dip to thirty-seven kilometers and burn off velocity much more quickly, establishing the proper elliptical orbit for rendezvous on the first attempt."

Orphu whistled.

Mahnmut tried to visualize it. "We'll be dropping to within a hundred-some thousand feet of the surface? We'll be able to see individual faces on the humans below."

"Not quite," said Asteague/Che. "But it will be more dramatic than we had planned. We'll definitely leave a streak in their sky. But the old-style humans down there are probably too distracted right now to notice a streak in their sky."

"What do you mean?" asked Orphu of Io.

Asteague/Che transmitted the most recent series of photographs. Mahnmut described the elements that Orphu could not get through the accompanying datametrics.

More images of slaughter. Human communities destroyed, human bodies left out for carrion crows. Infrared imagery showed hot buildings and cold corpses and the motion of equally cold humped and headless creatures who were doing the killing. Fires burned where homes and modest cities had been on the night side of the planet. All over the planet, the old-style humans seemed to be under attack by the gray-metallic headless creatures which the moravec experts could not identify. And on four continents, the blue-ice structures were multiplying and growing and now images appeared of a single, huge creature looking like a human brain with eyes, only the brain the size of a warehouse, then video—vertical images looking almost straight down on the thing scuttling on what looked like gigantic hands with more stalklike arms protruding like ganglia. Obscene proboscises extruded from feeding orifices and seemed to be drinking or feeding from the earth itself.

"I see the data," said Orphu, "but I'm having trouble visualizing the creature. It can't possibly be that ugly."

"We're looking at it," said General Beh bin Adee, "and we're having trouble believing what we're seeing. And it *is* that ugly."

"Is there any theory," asked Mahnmut, "about what that thing is or where it's from?"

"It's associated with the blue-ice sites, originally seen at the former city of Paris and the largest blue-ice complex," said Cho Li. "But that's not what you mean. We simply don't know its origins."

"Have moravecs ever seen an image of anything like that in all our centuries of observing the Earth through telescopes from Jupiter space or Saturn space?" asked Orphu.

"No." Asteague/Che and Suma IV spoke at the same time.

"The brain-hands-creature doesn't travel alone," said Retrograde Sinopessen, bringing up another series of holographic images and flat-plate projections. "These things are with it at every one of the eighteen sites we've seen the brain."

"Humans?" asked Orphu. The data was confusing.

"Not quite," said Mahnmut. He described the scales, fangs, overly long arms, and webbed feet of the forms in the images.

"And according to the datametrics, there are hundreds of those things," said Orphu of Io.

"Thousands," said Centurion Leader Mep Ahoo. "We've looked at images taken simultaneously at sites thousands of kilometers apart and counted at least thirty-two hundred of the amphibian-looking forms."

"Caliban," said Mahnmut.

"What?" Asteague/Che's softly inflected voice sounded puzzled.

"On Mars, Prime Integrator," said the little Europan. "The Little Green Men talked about Prospero and Caliban . . . from Shakespeare's *The Tempest*. The stone heads, you remember, were supposed to be images of Prospero. They warned us about Caliban. The thing looks and sounds like some versions of Caliban in the staging of that play over the centuries on Earth."

None of the moravecs had anything to say about that.

"There are eleven new Brane Holes on Earth since we began measuring this spike of quantum activity two weeks ago," Beh bin Adee said at last. "As far as we can tell, the brain-creature has generated—or at least is using—all of them for transport purposes. It and the scaled, amphibious-looking things you call Caliban. And there *is* a pattern to where they appear."

More holographic images misted into solidity above the chart table and Mahnmut described them on tightbeam, but Orphu had already absorbed the accompanying data.

"All battlegrounds or sites of ancient historical human massacres or atrocities," said Orphu.

"Precisely," said General Beh bin Adee. "You notice that the city of Paris was the first Brane quantum opening. We know that more than twenty-five hundred years ago, during the EU Empire's Black Hole Exchange with the Global Islamic Surinate, more than fourteen million people died in and around Paris."

"And the other Brane Hole sites here fit that category," said Mahnmut. "Hiroshima, Auschwitz, Waterloo, HoTepsa, Stalingrad, Cape Town, Montreal, Gettysburg, Khanstaq, Okinawa, the Somme, New Wellington—all bloodied historical sites from millennia ago."

"Do we have some sort of Calabi-Yau traveling intermemBrane tourist Brain here?" asked Orphu.

"Or something worse," said Cho Li. "The neutrino and tachyon beams rising from the spots this . . . thing . . . visits carry some sort of complex coded information. The beams are interdimensional, not directional in our universe. We just can't tap into the beams to decode the messages or content."

"I think the brain is a ghoul," said Orphu of Io.

"Ghoul?" asked Prime Integrator Asteague/Che.

Orphu explained the term. "I think it's sucking up some sort of dark energy from those places," said the big Ionian.

"That hardly seems likely," chirped Retrograde Sinopessen. "I know of no recordable . . . energy . . . left behind by the mere event of violent action. That is metaphysics . . . nonsense . . . not science."

Orphu shrugged four of his multiple articulated arms.

"Do you think the large brain creature might be something the post-humans or old-styles designed and biofactured during the dementia years after rubicon?" asked Centurion Leader Mep Ahoo. "And the Caliban-creature and headless robotic killer things as well? All artifacts from wildcat RNA engineers? Like some of the anachronistic plant and animal life reintroduced to the planet?"

"Not the big thing," said the tall Ganymedan, Suma IV. "We would have seen it before this. The brain creature with the hands came through Brane Holes from another universe just a few days ago. We don't know where the Caliban things came from, or the humpbacked creatures that are decimating the old-style humans. They might well be artifacts of genetic manipulation. We have to remember that the post-humans designed themselves right out of the human gene pool more than fifteen hundred standard years ago."

"And I've seen the holos of dinosaurs and Terror Birds and saber-toothed cats roaming this Earth," said Centurion Leader Mep Ahoo.

"The humpbacked metallic things have killed up to ten percent of the old-style population?" asked Mahnmut, who was a stickler for the proper use of that word "decimate."

"They have," said General Beh bin Adee. "Probably more. And just since we've been in transit from Mars."

"So what do we do now?" asked Orphu of Io. "Although if no one has an immediate answer, I have a suggestion."

"Go ahead," said Prime Integrator Asteague/Che.

"I think you should defrost the thousand rockvec soldiers we have in cold storage, fire up the dropship and the dozen atmospheric hornets you have onboard, load them to the gunwales with troopers, and get into the fight."

"Get into the fight?" repeated the navigator Callistan, Cho Li.

"Start by nuking that brain creature into radioactive pus," said Orphu. "Then get moravec boots on the ground and defend the humans. Kill those Calibans and the headless-humped things that are killing humans everywhere. Get into the fight."

"What an extraordinary suggestion," said Cho Li in a shocked voice.

"We hardly have enough information to decide on a course of action at this point," said Prime Integrator Asteague/Che. "For all we know, the brain creature—as we so respectfully call it—may be the only peaceful, sentient organism on Earth. Perhaps it's some sort of interdimensional archaeologist or anthropologist or historian."

"Or ghoul," said Mahnmut.

"Our mission was to carry out surveillance," said Suma IV in tones that were meant to be final. "Not start a war."

"We can do both things for the price of one," said Orphu. "We have the firepower aboard the *Queen Mab* to make a difference in whatever is going on down there. And although you haven't officially told Mahnmut or me, we know there must be a host of more modern stealthed moravec warships following the *Mab*. This could be a wonderful opportunity to hit that thing—all those things—and coldcock them before they even know they're in a fight."

"What an *extraordinary* suggestion," repeated Cho Li. "Absolutely extraordinary."

"Right now," said Asteague/Che in that odd James Mason voice that Mahnmut remembered from flatfilms, "our goal is not to start a war, but to deliver Odysseus to the Phobos-sized asteroid city in the polar ring as per the request of the Voice."

"And before *that*," said Suma IV, "we have to decide whether to go ahead with the dropship mission under cover of the aerobraking maneuver, or to wait until after rendezvous with the Voice's orbital city and delivery of our human passenger."

"I have a question," said Mahnmut.

"Yes?" Prime Integrator Asteague/Che was also a Europan, thus almost the same size as the diminutive Mahnmut. The two stared visor-plate to visor-plate while the administrator waited.

"Does our human passenger *want* to be delivered to the Voice?" asked Mahnmut.

There was a silence broken only by the hum of ventilators, comm reports to and from those 'vecs monitoring instruments, and the occasional bang of attitude thrusters from the hull.

"Good heavens," said Cho Li. "How could we have overlooked asking him?"

"We were busy," said General Beh bin Adee.

"I'll ask him," said Suma IV. "Although it will be embarrassing at this point if Odysseus says no."

"We have his garments all prepared," said the skittering Retrograde Sinopessen.

"Garments?" rumbled Orphu of Io. "Is our son of Laertes a Mormon?"

No one responded. All moravecs had some interest in human history and society—it had been programmed into their evolving DNA and circuits to keep such an interest—but very few were as immersed in human thinking as the huge Ionian. Nor had the others evolved such an odd sense of humor.

"Odysseus obviously has been wearing clothing of our design while he's been aboard the *Queen Mab*," chirped Retrograde Sinopessen. "But the clothing he will wear during the rendezvous with the Voice's orbital asteroid will have every sort of nano-sized recording and transmission device we could conceive of. We will all monitor his experience in real time."

"Even those of us who are going down to Earth on the dropship?" asked Orphu.

There was an embarrassed silence. Moravecs were not given to frequent embarrassment, but they were capable of it.

"You were not chosen for the dropship crew," Asteague/Che said at last in his clipped but not unpleasant tones.

"I know," said Orphu, "but I think I can convince you that the dropship mission *must* be launched during the *Mab*'s aerobraking and that I have to be on board. The little corner of the hold on Mahnmut's sub will serve me just fine as my passenger space. It has all the connections I need and I like the view."

"The submersible bay has no view," said Suma IV. "Except via video link, which might be interrupted if the dropship were to come under attack."

"I was being ironic," said Orphu.

"Also," said Cho Li, making a noise like a small animal clearing its throat, "you are—technically, optically—blind."

"Yes," said Orphu, "I've noticed. But beyond proper affirmative-action hiring practices—never mind, it's not worth the time to explain— I can give you three compelling reasons why I have to be included on the dropship mission to Earth."

"We haven't concluded that the mission itself should occur," said Asteague/Che, "but please proceed with your reasons for being included. Then we Prime Integrators must make several decisions in the next fifteen minutes."

"First of all, of course," rumbled Orphu, "there's the obvious fact that I will be a splendid ambassador to any and all sentient races we meet after landing on Earth."

General Beh bin Adee made a rude sound. "Is that before or after you nuke them into radioactive pus?" he asked.

"Secondly, there is the less obvious but still salient fact that no moravec on this ship—perhaps no moravec in existence—knows more about the fiction of Marcel Proust, James Joyce, William Faulkner, and

George Marie Wong—as well as the poetry of Emily Dickinson and Walt Whitman—than I do, therefore and ergo, no moravec knows more about human psychology than I do. Should we actually speak to an old-style human, my presence will be indispensable."

I didn't know you also studied Joyce, Faulkner, Wong, Dickinson, and Whitman, tightbeamed Mahnmut.

It never came up, answered Orphu. *But I've had time to read out there in the hard vacuum and sulfur of the Io Torus over the last twelve hundred standard years of my existence.*

Twelve hundred years! tightbeamed Mahnmut. Moravecs were designed for a long life span, but three standard centuries was generous for the average 'vec's existence. Mahnmut himself was less than one hundred fifty years old. *You never told me you were that old!*

It never came up, transmitted Orphu of Io.

"I did not quite follow all the logical connections there in the verbal part before you tightbeamed your friend," said Asteague/Che, "but pray continue. I believe you said that you had three compelling reasons why you should be included."

"The third reason I deserve a chair on the dropship," said Orphu, "figuratively speaking, of course, is that I've figured it out."

"Figured what out?" asked Suma IV. The dark buckycarbon Ganymedan wasn't visibly checking his chronometer, but his voice was.

"Everything," said Orphu of Io. "Why there are Greek gods on Mars. Why there's a tunnel through space and time to another Earth where Homer's Trojan War is still being fought. Where this impossibly terraformed Mars came from. What Prospero and Caliban, two characters from an ancient Shakespearean play, are doing waiting for us on this real Earth, and why the quantum basis for the entire solar system is being screwed up by these Brane Holes that keep popping up . . . everything."

56

The woman who looked like a young Savi was indeed named Moira, although in the next hours Prospero sometimes called her Miranda and once he smilingly referred to her as Moneta, which added to Harman's confusion. Harman's embarrassment, on the other hand, was so great that nothing could add to it. For their first hour together, he could not look in Moira's direction, much less look her in the eye. As Moira and he ate what amounted to breakfast as Prospero sat at the table, Harman finally managed to look in the woman's direction but couldn't raise his gaze to her eye level. Then he realized that this probably seemed as if he was staring at her chest, so he looked away again.

Moira seemed oblivious to his discomfort.

"Prospero," she said, sipping orange juice brought to them by a floating servitor, "you foul old maggot. Was this key to my awakening your idea?"

"Of course not, Miranda, my dear."

"Don't call me Miranda or I'll start calling you Mandrake. I am not now, nor was I ever, your daughter."

"Of course you are and were my daughter, Miranda, my dear," purred Prospero. "Is there a post-human alive whom I did not help become what they are? Were not my genetic sequencing labs your womb and your cradle? Am I therefore not thy father?"

"*Is* there another post-human alive today, Prospero?" asked the woman.

"Not to my knowledge, Miranda, dear."

"Then fuck you."

She turned to Harman, sipped coffee, sliced at an orange with a frighteningly sharp knife, and said, "My name is Moira."

They were at a small table in a small room—a space more than a room—that Harman had not noticed before. It was an alcove set within the booklined wall halfway up the inside of the great inward-curving dome, at least three hundred feet above the marble-walled maze and floor. It was easy to understand why he hadn't seen the space from below—the walls of this shallow alcove were also lined with books. There had been other alcoves along the way up, some holding tables like this one, others containing cushioned benches and cryptic instruments and screens. The iron stairways, it turned out, moved like escalators or it would have taken much longer for the three of them to climb this high. The exposure—there were no railings and the narrow marble walkways and the wrought-iron escalator steps were more air than iron—was horrifying. Harman hated to look down. He focused on the books instead and kept his shoulders against the shelves as he walked.

This woman was dressed much as Savi had been the first time he'd seen her—a blue tunic top made of cotton canvas, corded trousers, and high leather boots. She even wore a sort of short wool cape similar to the one he'd seen on Savi when they met, although this cape was a dark yellow rather than the deep red the older woman had worn. However, its complicated, many-folded cut seemed to be the same. The major difference between the two women—besides the vast difference in age—was that the older Savi had been carrying a pistol when they met, the first firearm Harman had ever seen. This version of Savi—Moira, Miranda, Moneta—he knew with absolute certainty, had not been armed when he first met her.

"What has happened since I first slept, Prospero?" asked Moira.

"You want a summary of fourteen centuries in as many sentences, my dear?"

"Yes. Please." Moira separated the juicy orange into sections and handed a section to Harman, who ate it without tasting it.

" 'The woods decay,' " intoned the magus Prospero, " 'the woods decay and fall,

> The vapours weep their burthen to the ground,
> Man comes and tills the field and lies beneath,
> And after many a summer dies the swan.
> Me only cruel immortality
> Consumes; I wither slowly in thine arms,
> Here at the quiet limit of the world,
> A white-hair'd shadow roaming like a dream
> The ever-silent spaces of the East,
> Far-folded mists, and gleaming halls of morn.' "

He bowed his balding and gray-haired head a bit.

" 'Tithonus,' " said Moira. "Tennyson before breakfast always makes my bowels ache. Tell me, is the world sane yet, Prospero?"

"No, Miranda."

"Are my folk all dead or changeling'd then, as you say?" She ate grapes and redolent cheese and drank from a large goblet of ice water the floating servitors continued to refill for her.

"They are dead or changeling'd or both."

"Are they coming back, Prospero?"

"God knows, my daughter."

"Don't give me God, please," said Moira. "What about Savi's nine thousand one hundred and thirteen fellow Jews? Have they been retrieved from the neutrino loop?"

"No, my dear. All the Jews and rubicon survivors in this universe remain a blue beam rising from Jerusalem and nothing more."

"We did not keep our promise then, did we?" asked Moira, pushing her plate away and brushing crumbs and juice from her palms.

"No, daughter."

"And you, Rapist," she said, turning to the blinking Harman, "do you have any other purpose in this world than taking advantage of sleeping strangers?"

Harman opened his mouth to speak, thought of nothing to say, and shut his mouth. He felt actively ill.

Moira touched his hand. "Do not reproach yourself, my Prometheus. You had little choice. The air inside the sarcophagus was scented with an aerosol aphrodisiac so potent that Prospero sent it off with one of the original changelings—Aphrodite herself. Lucky for both of us its effects are very temporary."

Harman felt a surge of relief followed by fury. "You mean I had no choice?"

"Not if you carried the DNA of Ahman Ferdinand Mark Alonzo Khan Ho Tep," said Moira. "And all males of your race should."

She turned back to Prospero. "Where is Ferdinand Mark Alonzo? Or rather, what was his fate?"

The magus bowed his head. "Miranda, beloved, three years after you entered the loop-fax sarcophagus, he died of one of the wildcat variants of rubicon that swept through the old population every year as surely as a summer zephyr. He was interred in a crystal sarcophagus next to yours—although all the fax equipment could do was keep his corpse from rotting then, since the Firmary tanks had not yet learned how to deal with rubicon. Before the vats could educate themselves, a score of Caliphate mandroids climbed Mount Everest, evaded the security shields, and began looting the Taj. The first thing they looted was poor Ferdinand Mark Alonzo's heavy coffin—throwing it over the side."

"Why didn't they throw me over as well?" asked Moira. "Or for that matter, finish their looting? I noticed all the agate, jasper, bloodstones, emeralds, lapis, cornelian, and other baubles were still in place on the walls and screen maze."

"Caliban faxed in and dispatched the twenty Caliphate mandroids for you," said Prospero. "It took the servitors a month to mop up all the blood."

Moira's head came up. "Caliban still lives?"

"Oh, yes. Ask our friend Harman here."

She glanced at Harman but refocused her attention on the magus. "I'm surprised Caliban didn't rape me as well."

Prospero smiled sadly. "Oh, he tried, Miranda my dear, he tried many times, but the sarcophagus would not open to him. Had the world bent to Caliban's will and member, he would have long since peopled this island earth with little Calibans by you."

Moira shuddered. Finally she turned to Harman again, ignoring the old man. "I need to know your story and your character and your life," she said. "Give me your palm." She set her right elbow on the table and held up one hand, palm toward him.

Confused, Harman did the same, but not touching her.

"No," said Moira. "Have the old-style humans forgotten the sharing function?"

"They have, actually," said Prospero. "Our friend Harman here can— or could until the *eiffelbahn* inhibited his access—call up only the finder, allnet, proxnet, and farnet functions. And those only by visualizing certain geometric shapes."

"Mother of Heaven," said Moira. She dropped her hand to the table. "Can they still *read*?"

"Only Harman and a handful of others he's taught in the last few months," said Prospero. "Oh, I forgot to mention that our friend did learn to sigl some months ago."

"Sigl?" Moira laughed. "That was never meant to be used to *understand* books. That was an indexing function. It must feel like glancing at a recipe in a cookbook and thinking you've actually eaten the dinner. Harman's people must be the dullest subspecies of *homo sapiens* ever to receive a patent."

"Hey," said Harman. "I'm right here. Don't talk about me as if I'm not even here. And I may not know this sharing function, but I can learn it quickly. In the meantime, we can talk. I have questions to ask too, you know."

Moira looked at him. He noticed the rich gray-green of her eyes.

"Yes," she said at last, "I have been rude. You must have come a long way to waken me—and you took that action against your will—and I am sure you would rather be elsewhere in the world. The least I can do is show you some manners and answer your questions."

"Can you show me how to do this sharing function you were talking about?" asked Harman. He was determined not to lose his temper with this woman who looked so much like Savi and spoke in her voice. "Or show me how to fax without faxnode pavilions," he added. "The way Ariel does it."

"Ah, Ariel," said Moira. She glanced at Prospero. "The old-styles have forgotten how to freefax?"

"They've forgotten almost everything," said Prospero. "They were *made* to forget. By your people, Moira. By Vala, by Tirzah, by Rahaba—by all your Urizened Beulahs."

Moira tapped the flat of her knife against her palm. "Why did you use this person to wake me, Prospero? Has Sycorax consolidated her power and freed your monster Caliban from your control?"

"She has and he is free," Prospero said softly, "but I felt it was time you woke because Setebos now walks this world."

"Sycorax, Caliban, and Setebos," repeated Moira. She drew in a long breath, hissing it between her teeth.

"Between the witch, the demidevil, and the thing of darkness," Prospero said softly, "they would control the moon and Earth, decide all ebbs and flows, and deal all power to their command."

Moira nodded and chewed her full lower lip for a moment. "When does your *eiffelbahn* car depart again?"

"In one hour," said the magus. "Will you be on it, Miranda dear? Or will you be sleeping in the fax-coffin of time again, allowing your atoms and memories to be restored in such a meaningless loop forever?"

"I'll be on your damned car," said Moira. "And I'll take from the update banks what I need to know about this brave new world I'm born into yet again. But first, young Prometheus has his questions to ask and then I have a suggestion on what he can do to regain his function status." She glanced toward the apex of the dome.

"No, Moira," said Prospero.

"Harman," she said softly, putting her soft hand on the back of his, "ask your questions now."

He licked his lips. "Are you really a post-human?"

"Yes, I am. That is what Savi's people called us before the Final Fax."

"Why do you look like Savi?"

"Ah . . . you knew her, then? Well, I will learn her health or fate when I call up the update function. I knew Savi, but more important, Ahman Ferdinand Mark Alonzo Khan Ho Tep was in love with her and she returned no love for him—they were of separate tribes, so to speak. So I took her form, her memories, her voice . . . everything . . . before coming here to the Taj."

"How did you take her form?" asked Harman.

Moira looked at Prospero again. "His people do know nothing, don't they?" To Harman she said, "We post-humans had reached the point where we had no bodies of our own, my young Prometheus. At least none that you would recognize as bodies. We needed none. There were only a few thousand of us, but we had bred ourselves out of the human gene pool, thanks to the genetic skills of the avatar of the cyberspace logosphere here . . ."

"You're welcome," said Prospero.

"When we wanted to take a human form—always a female human form, I might add, for all of us—we just borrowed one."

"But *how*?" said Harman.

Moira sighed. "Are the rings still in the sky?"

"Of course," said Harman.

"Polar and equatorial both?"

"Yes."

"What do you think they are, Harman Prometheus? There are more than a million discrete objects up there . . . what do your people think they are?"

Harman licked his lips again. The air here in the great temple-tomb was very dry. "We know our Firmary, where we were rejuvenated, was up there. Most of us think the other objects up there are the posts—your people's—homes. And your machines. Cities on orbiting islands like Prospero's. I was there last year on Prospero's Isle, Moira. I helped bring it down."

"You did?" She looked at the magus again. "Well, good for you, young Prometheus. But you're wrong in thinking that the million orbiting objects, most of them much smaller than Prospero's Isle, were habitats for my kind or machines serving solely our purposes. There are a dozen or so habitats, of course, and several thousand giant wormhole generators, black hole accumulators, early experiments in our interdimensional travel program, Brane Hole generators . . . but most of the orbiting objects up there are serving you."

"Me?"

"Do you know what faxing is?"

"I've done it all my life," said Harman.

"Yes, of course, but do you know what it *is*?"

Harman took a breath. "We'd never really thought about it, but on our voyages last year Savi and Prospero explained that the faxnode pavilions actually turn our bodies into coded energy and then our bodies, minds, and memories are rebuilt at another node."

Moira nodded. "But the fax pavilions and nodes are not necessary," she said. "They were simply ruses to keep you old-style humans from wandering in places you shouldn't go. This fax form of teleportation was staggeringly heavy on computer memory, even with the most advanced Calabi-Yau DNA and bubble-memory machines. Do you have any idea how much memory is required to store the data on just one human being's molecules, much less the holistic wavefront of his or her personality and memories?"

"No," said Harman.

Moira gestured toward the top of the dome, but Harman realized that she was actually gesturing toward the sky beyond and the polar and equatorial rings turning up there now against the dark blue sky. "A million orbital memory banks," said the woman. "Each one dedicated to one of you old-style humans. And in many of the other clumsy orbital machines, the black-hole-powered teleportation devices themselves— GPS satellites, scanners, reducers, compilators, receivers, and transmitters—somewhere up there above you every night of your life, my Harman Prometheus, was a star with your name on it."

"Why a million?" asked Harman.

"That was thought to be a viable minimum herd population," said Moira, "although I suspect there are far fewer of you than that today since we allowed each woman to have only one child. In my day, there were only nine thousand three hundred and fourteen of your subspecies of humans—those with nanogenetic functions installed and active—and a few hundred thousand dying old-old-style humans, those like my beloved Ahman Ferdinand Mark Alonzo Khan Ho Tep, the last of his royal breed."

"What are the voynix?" asked Harman. "Where did they come from? Why did they act as silent servants for so long and then start attacking my people after Daeman and I destroyed Prospero's Isle and the Firmary? How do we stop them?"

"So many questions," sighed Moira. "If you want them all answered, you will need context. To gain context, you need to read these books."

Harman's head jerked and he looked up and down at the curving inner dome lined with books. He could not do the mathematics on the square or cubic feet of books here, but he imagined—wildly, blindly— that there must be at least a million volumes on these shelves.

"Which books?" he asked.

"*All* of these books," said Moira, lifting her hand from his to gesture in a circle toward everything. "You can, you know."

"Moira, no," Prospero said again. "You'll kill him."

"Nonsense," said the woman. "He's young."

"He's ninety-nine years old," said Prospero, "more than seventy-five years older than Savi's body was when you cloned it for your own purposes. She had memories then. You carry them now. Harman is no tabula rasa."

Moira shrugged. "He's strong. Sane. Look at him."

"You'll kill him," said Prospero. "And with him, one of our best weapons against Setebos and Sycorax."

Harman was very angry now, but also excited. "What are you talking about?" he demanded, pulling his hand back when Moira threatened to touch it again with hers. "Are you talking about me sigling all these books? It would take months . . . years. Decades, maybe."

"Not sigling," said Moira, "but *eating* them."

"Eating them," repeated Harman, thinking, *Was she mad before she entered the time coffin or have the centuries of being replicated there, cell by cell, neuron by neuron, made her mad?*

"Eating them," agreed Moira. "In the sense that the Talmud spoke of eating books—not reading them, but eating them."

"I don't understand."

"Do you know what the Talmud is?" asked Moira.

"No."

Moira pointed toward the apex of the dome again, some seventy stories above them. "Up there, my young friend, in a tiny little cupola made of the clearest glass, there is a cabinet formed of gold and pearl and crystal and I have the golden key. Within, it opens into a world and a little lovely moony night."

"Like your sarcophagus?" asked Harman. His heart was pounding.

"Nothing like my sarcophagus," laughed Moira. "That coffin was just another node on your faxing merry-go-round, replicating me through the centuries until it was time to wake and go to work. I'm talking about a machine that will allow you to *read all these books in depth* before the *eiffelbahn* car leaves the Taj station in . . ." She glanced at her palm. "Fifty-eight minutes."

"Do not do this, Moira," said Prospero. "He will do us no good in the war against Setebos if he is dead or a drooling moron."

"Silence, Prospero," snapped Moira. "Look at him. He's already a moron. It's as if his entire race has been lobotomized since Savi's day. He might as well be dead. This way, if the cabinet works and he survives, he may be able to serve himself and us." She took Harman's hand again. "What do you most want in this universe, Harman Prometheus?"

"To go home to see my wife," said Harman.

Moira sighed. "I can't guarantee that the crystal cabinet—the knowledge and nuance of all these books that my poor, dead Ahman Ferdinand Mark Alonzo accumulated over his centuries—will allow you to freefax home to your wife . . . what is her name?"

"Ada." The two syllables made Harman want to weep. It made him want to weep twice—once for missing her, again for betraying her.

"To Ada," said Moira. "But I *can* guarantee that you will *not* get home alive to see her unless you take this chance."

Harman stood and stepped out onto the railingless marble ledge three hundred feet above the cold marble floor below. He looked up at the center of the dome almost seven hundred feet above but could see nothing except a sort of haze there where the last of the metal catwalks converged like black and almost invisibly thin spiderwebs.

"Harman, friend of Noman . . ." began Prospero.

"Shut up," Harman said to the magus of the logosphere.

To Moira he said, "Let's go."

"I quantum teleported us here according to your directions," says Hephaestus, "but where in Hades' Hell are we?"

"Ithaca," says Achilles. "A rugged, rocky isle, but a good nurse to boys who would be men."

"It looks and smells more like a hot, stinking shithole to me," says the god of fire, limping along the dusty, rock-strewn trail that leads up a steep slope past meadows filled with goats and cattle to where the red tiles of several buildings glare in the merciless sun.

"I've been here before," says Achilles, "the first time when I was a boy." The hero's heavy shield is strapped to his back, his sword secure in its scabbard on a belt hanging over his shoulder. The blond young man is not sweating from the climb or heat, but Hephaestus, limping along behind him, is huffing and pouring sweat. Even the immortal Artificer's beard is wet with sweat.

The steep but narrow trail ends on top of the hill and in sight of several large structures.

"Odysseus' palace," says Achilles, jogging the last fifty yards.

"*Palace*," gasps the god of fire. He limps into the clearing in front of the high gates, sets both hands on his crippled leg, and bends over as if he is going to be sick. "It's more like a fucking vertical pigsty."

The remnant of a small, abandoned fortress rises like a squat stone stump fifty yards to the right of the main house on the promontory overlooking the cliff. The home itself—Odysseus' palace—is made of newer stone and newer wood, although the main doors—open—are comprised of two ancient stone slabs. Terra-cotta paving tiles on the terrace are made of expensive tile set neatly in place, obviously the work of the best craftsmen and stone masons—although equally obviously not dusted or swept recently—and all the outside walls and columns are brightly painted. *Faux* painted vines filled with images of birds and their nests spiral around the white columns on either side of the entry, but real vines have also grown there, their tangle inviting real birds and becoming home to at least one visible nest. Achilles can see colorful frescoes gleaming from the walls of the shadowy vestibule beyond the main doors, which have been left ajar.

Achilles starts forward but halts when Hephaestus grabs his arm. "There's a forcefield here, son of Peleus."

"I don't see it."

"You wouldn't until you walked into it. I'm sure it would kill any other mortal man, but even though you're the fleet-footed mankiller with what Nyx called your singularity probability quotient, the field would knock you on your ass. My instruments measure at least two hundred thousand volts in it and enough amperage to do real damage. Stand back."

The bearded dwarf-god fiddles with boxes and corkscrewed metallic shapes hanging from the various leather straps and chest bands on his heavy vests, checks little dials, uses a short wand with alligator clip jaws to attach something that looks like a dead metallic ferret to some terminus in the invisible field, then links four rhomboid devices together with colored wire before pushing a brass button.

"There," says Hephaestus, god of fire. "Field's down."

"That's what I like about high priests," says Achilles, "they do nothing and then brag about it."

"You wouldn't have fucking thought it was fucking nothing if you'd walked into that forcefield," growls the god. "It was Hera's work based on my machines."

"Then I thank you," says Achilles and strides through the archway, between the stone slabs of the open doorway, and into the vestibule and Odysseus' home.

Suddenly there is a growling noise and a dark animal lunges snarling from the shadows.

Achilles' sword is in his hand in an instant, but the dog has already collapsed on the dusty tiles.

"This is Argus," says Achilles, patting the head of the prostrate and panting animal. "Odysseus trained this hound from a pup more than ten years ago, but told me that he had to leave for Troy before he ever took Argus hunting for boar or wild deer. Our crafty friend's son, Telemachus, was supposed to be his master in Odysseus' absence."

"No one's been his master for weeks," says Hephaestus. "The mutt has all but starved to death." It is true; Argus is too weak to stand or move his head. Only his large, imploring eyes follow Achilles' hand as the hero pets the animal. The dog's ribs stand out against his slack, lusterless hide like the hull timbers of an unfinished ship against old canvas.

"He can't get outside Hera's forcefield," mutters Achilles. "And I'll wager that there was nothing to eat inside. He's probably had water from the rains and gutters, but no food." He pulls several biscuits from the small bag he's been carrying with his shield—biscuits purloined from the Artificer's home—and feeds two to the dog. The animal can just barely chew them. Achilles sets three more biscuits next to the dog's head and stands.

"Not even a corpse to feed on," says Hephaestus. "What with the humans gone everywhere on your Earth now except around Ilium . . . just disappeared like fucking smoke. "

Achilles rounds on the limping god. "Where *are* our people? What have you and the other immortals done with them?"

The Artificer holds both palms high. "It wasn't our doing, son of Peleus. Not even great Zeus's. Some other force emptied out this Earth, not us. We Olympian gods need our worshipers. Living without our mortal grovelers, idolators, and altar-builders would be like narcissists—and I know Narcissus well—living in a world without mirrored surfaces. This wasn't our deed."

"You expect me to believe there are other gods?" asks Achilles, sword still half-raised.

"Big fleas have little fleas, and little fleas have littler fleas to bite 'em, and littler fleas have even smaller fleas, and so on ad infinitum, or some doggerel like that," says the bearded immortal.

"Be silent," says Achilles. He pats the now actively chewing dog on the head one last time and turns his back on Hephaestus.

They pass through the vestibule into the main hall—the throne room as it were—where Achilles had been received years earlier by Odysseus and his wife Penelope. Odysseus' son Telemachus had been a shy boy of six then, barely up to the task of bowing to the assembled Myrmidons and then hurriedly being led away by his nurse. The throne room is now empty.

Hephaestus is consulting one of his instrument-boxes. "This way," he says, leading Achilles from the throne room back across the brightly frescoed vestibule to a longer, darker room. It is the banquet hall, dominated by a low table thirty feet long.

Zeus is sprawled supine on the table, his arms and legs thrown akimbo. He is naked and he is snoring. The banquet hall is a mess—cups, bowls, and utensils thrown everywhere, arrows spilled out all over the floor from where a great quiver had fallen from the wall, another wall missing a tapestry that was bunched up under the snoring Father of the Gods.

"It's Absolute Sleep, all right," grumbles Hephaestus.

"It sounds like it," says Achilles. "I'm surprised the timbers don't collapse from the snores and snorts." The mankiller is stepping carefully over the heads of barbed arrows that are scattered on the floor. Although few Greek warriors admit it, most use deadly substances for poison on their speartips and arrowheads, and the only thing Achilles, son of Peleus, knows from the Oracle's and his mother Thetis's predictions of his own death is that a poisoned arrowhead piercing the only mortal part of his body will be the cause of his demise. But neither his immortal mother nor the Fates had ever told him exactly where or when he will die, or who will fire the deadly arrow. It would be too absurdly ironic, Achilles thinks now, to prick a toe on one of Odysseus' ancient fallen arrows and die in agony even before he can waken Zeus to demand that Penthesilea be saved.

"No, I mean Absolute Sleep was the fucking drug Hera used to knock him out," says the Artificer. "It was a potion I helped develop into aerosol form, although Nyx was the original chemist."

"Can you wake him?"

"Oh, I think so, yes, yes, I think so," says Hephaestus, pulling small bags and boxes off the ribbons laced to his leather vest and harnesses, peering into the boxes, rejecting some things, setting other vials and small devices on the tapestry-rumpled table next to Zeus's giant thigh.

While the bearded dwarf-god fusses and assembles things, Achilles takes his first close-up gaze at Zeus the Father of All Gods and Men, He Who Marshals the Storm Clouds.

Zeus is fifteen feet tall, impressive even as he sprawls on his back, spraddle-legged on the tapestry and table, heavily muscled and perfectly formed, even his beard oiled into perfect curls, but other than the minor matters of size and physical perfection, he is just a big man who has enjoyed a great fuck and gone to sleep. The divine penis—almost as long as Achilles' sword—still lies swollen, pink, and flaccid on the Lord God's oily divine thigh. The God Who Gathers Storms is snoring and drooling like a pig.

"This should wake him up," says Hephaestus. He holds up a syringe—something Achilles has never seen before—ending in a needle more than a foot long.

"By the gods!" cries Achilles. "Are you going to stick that into Father Zeus?"

"Straight into his lying, lusting heart," says Hephaestus with a nasty cackle. "This is one thousand cc's of pure divine adrenaline mixed with my own little recipe of various amphetamines—the only antidote to Absolute Sleep."

"What will he do when he wakes?" asks Achilles, pulling his shield in front of him.

Hephaestus shrugs. "I'm not going to hang around to find out. I'm QTing out of here the second I inject this cocktail. Zeus's response to being wakened with a needle in his heart is your problem, son of Peleus."

Achilles grabs the dwarf-god by the beard and pulls him closer. "Oh, I guarantee it will be *our* problem if it is a problem, Crippled Artificer."

"What do you want me to do, mortal? Wait here and hold your hand? It was your fucking idea to wake him up."

"It's also in your interest to awaken Zeus, god of one short leg," says Achilles, not relinquishing his grip on the immortal's beard.

"How so?" Hephaestus squints out of his good eye.

"You help me with this," whispers Achilles, leaning closer to the grungy god's misshapen ear, "and in a week it could be you who sits on the golden throne in the Hall of the Gods, not Zeus."

"How can that be?" asks Hephaestus, but he is also whispering now. He still squints, but suddenly there is an eagerness in that squinting.

Still whispering, still holding Hephaestus's beard in his fist, Achilles tells the Artificer his plan.

Zeus awakens with a roar.

As good as his word, Hephaestus has fled the instant he injected the adrenaline into the Father of the Gods' heart, pausing only to pull the long needle free and fling the syringe from him. Three seconds later Zeus sits up, roars so loudly that Achilles has to clasp his hands over his ears, and then the Father leaps to his feet, overturns the thirty-foot-long heavy wooden table, and smashes out the entire south wall of Odysseus' house.

"HERA!!!!" booms Zeus. "GOD DAMN YOU!"

Achilles forces himself not to cringe and cower, but he does step back while Zeus rips out the last of the wall, uses a timber to smash the overhanging chariot-wheel candle-chandelier to a thousand pieces, destroys the heavy, tumbled table with one smash of his giant fist, and paces wildly back and forth.

Finally the Father of All Gods seems to notice Achilles standing in the doorway to the vestibule. "YOU!"

"Me," agrees Achilles, son of Peleus. His sword is in its belt loop, his shield politely strapped over his shoulder rather than on his forearm. His hands are empty and open. The god-killing long knife that Athena had given him for use in murdering Aphrodite is in his broad belt, but out of sight.

"What are you doing on Olympos?" growls Zeus. He is still naked. He holds his forehead with his huge left hand and Achilles can see the headache pain throbbing through Zeus the Father's bloodshot eyes. Evidently Absolute Sleep leaves a hangover.

"You are not on Olympos, Lord Zeus," Achilles says softly. "You're on the isle of Ithaca—under a golden cloud of concealment—in the banquet hall of Odysseus, son of Laertes."

Zeus squints around him. Then he frowns more deeply. Finally he looks down on Achilles once again, "How long have I been asleep, mortal?"

"Two weeks, Father," says Achilles.

"You, Argive, fleet-footed mankiller, *you* couldn't have awakened me here from whatever potion-charm white-armed Hera used to drug me. Which god revived me and why?"

"O Zeus Who Marshals the Thunderheads," says Achilles, lowering his head and eyes almost meekly, as he has seen the meek do so many times, "I will tell you all you seek to know—and it is true that while most of the immortals on Olympos abandoned you, at least one god remained your loyal servant—but first I must ask for a boon."

"A boon?" roars Zeus. "I'll give you a boon you won't forget if you speak again without permission. Stand there and be silent."

The huge figure gestures and one of the three remaining walls—the one that had held the quiver of poison arrows and the outline of a great bow—mists into a three-dimensional vision surface much like the holopool in the Great Hall of the Gods.

Achilles realizes that he is looking at an aerial view of this very house—Odysseus' palace. He can see the dog Argus outside. The starved hound has eaten the biscuits and revived enough to crawl into the shade.

"Hera would have left a forcefield beneath my cloaking golden cloud," mutters Zeus. "The only one who could have lifted it is Hephaestus. I will deal with him later."

Zeus moves his hand again. The virtual display shifts to the summit of Olympos, empty homes and halls, the abandoned chariots.

"They have gone down to play with their favorite toys," mumbles Zeus.

Achilles sees a daylight battle in front of the walls of Ilium. Hector's forces seem to be pushing the Argives and their siege machines back to Thicket Ridge and beyond. The air is filled with volleys of arrows and a score or more of flying chariots. Thunderbolts and bright red beams lash back and forth above the mortal battlefield. Explosions ripple across the battlefield and fill the sky as the gods do battle with each other even as their champions fight to the death below.

Zeus shakes his head. "Do you see them, Achilles? They are as addicted as cocaine addicts, as gamblers at their tables. For more than five hundred years since I conquered the last of the Titans—the original Changelings—and threw Kronos, Rhea, and the other monstrous Originals down into the gaseous pit of Tartarus, we have been evolving our godly, Olympian powers, settling into our divine roles . . . for *WHAT???*"

Achilles, who has not been explicitly asked to speak, keeps his mouth shut.

"*DAMNED CHILDREN AT THEIR GAMES!!*" bellows Zeus and again Achilles has to cover his ears. "Useless as heroin junkies or Lost Era teenagers in front of their videogames. After this long decade of their conniving and conspiring and secret fighting though I forbid it, and slowing time so they can arm their pet heroes with nanotech powers, they simply have to see it all to the bitter end and make sure their side wins. *AS IF IT MAKES ONE GODDAMNED BIT OF DIFFERENCE!!*"

Achilles knows that a lesser man—and all men are lesser men in Achilles' view—would be on his knees screaming from the pain of the divine bellow by now, but the ultrasonic boom and roar of it still makes him weak inside.

"Addicts all," says Zeus, his roar more bearable now. "I should have made them all sign up for Ilium Anonymous five years ago and avoided this terrible reckoning which now must come. Hera and her allies have gone too far."

Achilles is watching the carnage on the wall. The image is so deep, so three-dimensional, that it is as if the wall has opened onto the crowded killing fields of Ilium itself. The Achaeans under Agamemnon's clumsy leadership are visibly falling back—Apollo of the Silver Bow is obviously the most lethal god on the field, driving the flying chariots of Ares, Athena, and Hera back toward the sea—but it is not a rout, not yet, neither in the air nor on the ground. The view of the fighting gets Achilles' blood up and makes him want to rush into the fighting, leading his Myrmidons in a swath of counterattack and killing that would end only with Achilles' chariot and horses scarring the marble in Priam's palace, preferably with Hector's body being dragged behind it, leaving a bloody smear.

"*WELL??*" roars Zeus. "Speak up!"

"About what, O Father of All Gods and Men?"

"What is this . . . boon . . . you want from me, son of Thetis?" Zeus has been pulling on his garments as he's watched the events on the vision wall.

Achilles steps closer. "In exchange for finding you and awakening you, Father Zeus, I would ask that you restore the life of Penthesilea in one of the Healing vats and . . ."

"Penthesilea?" booms Zeus. "That Amazon tart from the north regions? The blond bitch who murdered her sister Hippolyte to gain that worthless Amazon throne? How did she die? And what does she have to do with Achilles or Achilles with her?"

Achilles ground his molars but kept his gaze—now murderous— turned downward. "I love her, Father Zeus, and . . ."

Zeus bellows in laughter. "*Love* her, you say? Son of Thetis, I've watched you on my vision walls and floors and in person since you were a baby, since you were a snot-nosed youth being tutored by the patient centaur Chiron, and never have I seen you love a woman. Even the girl who fathered your son was left behind like excess baggage whenever you felt the urge to go off to war—or whoring and rape. You *love Penthesilea,* that brainless blond pussy with a spear. Tell me another tale, son of Thetis."

"I *love* Penthesilea and wish her restored to health," grits Achilles. All he can think of at this second is the god-killing blade in his belt. But Athena has lied to him before. If she lied about the abilities of that knife, he would be a fool to move against Zeus. Achilles knows that he is a fool at any rate, coming here to beseech the Father for this gift. But he perseveres, eyes still lowered but his hands balled into powerful fists. "Aphrodite gave the Amazon queen a scent to wear when she went into combat with me . . ." he begins.

Zeus roars laughter again. "Not Number Nine! Well, you are well and truly screwed, my friend. How did this Penthesilea twat die? No, wait, I will see for myself . . ."

The Lord Father moves his right hand again and the wallscreen blurs, shifts, leaps back across time and space. Achilles looks up to see the doomed Amazon charge against him and his men on the red plains at the base of Olympos. He watches Clonia, Bremusa, and the other Amazons fall to men's arrows and blades. He watches again as he casts his father's unfailing spear completely through Queen Penthesilea and the thick torso of her horse behind her, pinning her on her fallen steed's horse like some wriggling insect on a dissecting tray.

"Oh, well done," booms Zeus. "And now you want her brought back to life again in one of my Healer's vats?"

"Yes, Lord," says Achilles.

"I don't know how you know about the Hall of Healing," says Zeus, pacing back and forth again, "but you should know that even the Healer's alien arts cannot bring a dead mortal back to life."

"Lord," says Achilles, his voice low but urgent, "Athena cast a spell of no corruption, of no encroaching death, over my beloved's body. It might be possible to . . ."

"SILENCE!!" roars Zeus and Achilles is physically driven back to the holowall by the blast of noise. *"NO ONE IN THE ORIGINAL PAN-THEON OF IMMORTALS TELLS ZEUS THE FATHER WHAT IS POSSI-BLE OR WHAT SHOULD BE DONE, MUCH LESS SOME MERE MORTAL, OVERMUSCLED SPEARMAN."*

"No, Father," says Achilles, raising his gaze to the giant, bearded form, "but I hoped that . . ."

"Silence," says Zeus again, but at a level that allows Achilles to re-move his hands from his ears. "I'm leaving now—to destroy Hera, to cast down her accomplices into the bottomless pit of Tartarus, to punish the other gods in ways they will never forget, and to wipe out this in-vading Argive army once and for all. You Greeks—with your arrogance and your oily ways—really get on my tits." Zeus begins to stride for the door. "You're on Ilium-Earth here, son of Thetis. It may take you many months, but you can find your way home by yourself. I would not rec-ommend you return to Ilium—there will be no Achaeans left alive there by the time you reach that place."

"No," says Achilles.

Zeus whirls. He is actually smiling through his beard. "What did you say?"

"I said no. You *must* grant my wish." Achilles unlimbers his shield and sets it in place on his forearm, as if he is heading to the front. He pulls his sword.

Zeus throws his head back and laughs. "Grant your wish or . . . what, bastard son of Thetis?"

"Or else I will feed Zeus's liver to that starving dog of Odysseus' in the courtyard," Achilles says firmly.

Zeus smiles and shakes his head. "Do you know why you are alive this very day, insect?"

"Because I am Achilles, son of Peleus," says Achilles, stepping for-ward. He wishes he had his throwing spear. "The greatest warrior and noblest hero on Earth—invulnerable to his enemies—friend of the mur-dered Patroclus, slave and servant to no man . . . or god."

Zeus shakes his head again. "You're not the son of Peleus."

Achilles stops advancing. "What are you talking about, Lord of Flies? Lord of Horse Dung? I am the son of Peleus who is the son of Aeacus, son of the mortal who mated with the immortal sea goddess Thetis, a king myself descended from a long line of kings of the Myrmidons."

"No," says Zeus and this time the giant god is the one who steps closer, towering over Achilles. "You are the son of Thetis, but the bastard son of my seed, not the seed of Peleus'."

"You!" Achilles tries to laugh but it comes out a hoarse bark. "My immortal mother told me in all truth that . . ."

"Your immortal mother lies through her seaweed-crusted teeth," laughs Zeus. "Almost three decades ago, I desired Thetis. She was less than a full goddess then, although more beautiful than most of you mortals. But the Fates—those accursed bean counters with the DNA-memory abacuses—warned me that any child I spawned with Thetis could be my undoing, could cause my death, could bring down the reign of Olympos itself."

Achilles stares hate and disbelief through his helmet eyeholes.

"But I wanted Thetis," continues Zeus. "So I fucked her. But first I morphed into the form of Peleus—some common mortal boy-man with whom Thetis was mildly infatuated at the time. But the sperm that conceived you is Zeus's divine seed, Achilles, son of *Thetis*, make no mistake about that. Why else do you think your mother took you far away from that idiot Peleus and had you raised by an old centaur?"

"You lie," growls Achilles.

Zeus shakes his head almost sadly. "And you will die in a second, young Achilles," says the Father of All Gods and Men. "But you will die knowing that I told you the truth."

"You can't kill me, Lord of Crabs."

Zeus rubs his beard. "No, I can't. Not directly. Thetis saw to that. When she learned that I had been the lover who knocked her up, not that dickless worm Peleus, she also knew of the Fates' prediction and that I would kill you as surely as my father, Kronos, ate his offspring rather than risk their revolts and vendettas when they grew up. And I would have done that, young Achilles—eaten you when you were a babe—had not Thetis conspire to dip you in the probability flames of the pure quantum celestial fire. You are a quantum freak unique unto the universe, bastard son of Thetis and Zeus. Your death—and even I do not know the details of it, the Fates will not share them—is absolutely appointed."

"Then fight me now, God of Feces," shouts Achilles and begins to advance, sword and shield ready.

Zeus holds up one hand. Achilles is frozen in place. Time itself seems to freeze.

"I cannot *kill* you, my impetuous little bastard," mutters Zeus, as if to himself, "but what if I blast your flesh from your bone and then rip that very flesh into its constituent cells and molecules? It might take a while for even the quantum universe to reassemble you—centuries perhaps?—and I don't think it could possibly be a painless process."

Frozen in midstride, Achilles knows that he is still able to speak but does not.

"Or perhaps I could send you somewhere," says Zeus, gesturing toward the ceiling, "where there is no air to breathe. That will be an interesting conundrum for the probability singularity of the celestial fire to solve."

"There is no place outside the oceans with no air to breathe," snarls Achilles, but then he remembers his gasping and weakness on the high slopes of Olympos just the day before.

"Outer space would give the lie to that assertion," says Zeus with a maddening smile. "Somewhere beyond the orbit of Uranus, perhaps, or out in the Kuiper Belt. Or Tartarus would serve. The air there is mostly methane and ammonia—it would turn your lungs to burned twigs—but if you survived a few hours in terrible pain, you could commune with your grandparents. They *eat* mortals, you know."

"Fuck you," shouts Achilles.

"So be it," says Zeus. "Have a good trip, my son. Short—agonizing—but good."

The King of the Gods moves his right hand in a short, easy arc and the paving tiles beneath Achilles' feet begin to dissolve. A circle opens in the floor of Odysseus' banquet hall until the fleet-footed mankiller seems to be standing on flame-lighted air. From beneath him, from the horrific pit below filled with surging sulfurous clouds, black mountains rising like rotten teeth, lakes of liquid lead, the bubble and flow of hissing lava, and the shadowy movement of huge, inhuman things, comes the constant roar and bellow of the monsters once called Titans.

Zeus moves his hand again, ever so slightly, and Achilles falls into that pit. He does not scream as he disappears.

After a minute of gazing down at the flames and roiling black clouds so far below, Zeus moves his palm from left to right, the circle closes, the floor becomes solid and is made up of Odysseus' handset tiles once again, and silence returns to the house except for the pathetic baying of the starving hound named Argus out in the courtyard somewhere.

Zeus sighs and quantum teleports away to begin his reckoning with the unsuspecting gods.

Prospero stayed behind as Moira led Harman around the marble balcony with no railing, up a moving flight of open iron stairs, then around again, up again, and so until the floor of the Taj became a circle seemingly miles below. Harman's heart was pounding.

There were a few small, round windows set into the booklined wall of the endlessly rising and inward-curving dome. Harman had not seen them from below or from outside, but they allowed light in and gave him an excuse to pause for breath and courage. They stood in the light for a minute as Harman stared out at the distant mountain peaks shining icily in the late morning light. Masses of clouds had filled the valleys to the north and east, hiding the ripple-crevassed glaciers from view. Harman wondered how far he was looking beyond the peaks and glaciers and massing clouds to the dusty and nearly curved horizon beyond—a hundred miles? Two hundred miles? More?

"It's all right," Moira said softly.

Harman turned.

"What you did to wake me," she said. "It's all right. We're sorry. You really did have no choice. The mechanisms to incite you were in place before your father's father's great-great-grandfather was born."

"But what are the odds that I would be descended from this Ferdinand Mark Alonzo Khan Ho Tep of yours?" said Harman. He could not hide the regret in his voice—nor did he want to.

Surprisingly, Moira laughed. It was Savi's laugh—quick and spontaneous—but lacking the edge of bitterness Harman had heard in the older woman's amusement. "The odds are one hundred percent," said Moira.

Harman could only show his confusion in silence.

"Ferdinand Mark Alonzo made sure that when the next line of oldstyle humans were being . . . readied and decanted," said Moira,"that some of his chromosomes would be in all males of the line."

"No wonder we're feeble and stupid and inept," said Harman.

"We're all a bunch of inbred cousins." He'd sigled a book on basic genetics less than three weeks earlier—although it seemed like years ago. Ada had been sleeping next to him while he watched the golden words flow from the book down his hand, wrist, and arm.

Moira laughed again. "Are you ready to go the rest of the way up to the crystal cabinet?"

The clear cupola at the top of the Taj Moira was much larger than it had appeared from below—Harman guessed it was at least sixty or seventy feet across. There were no marble walkways here and the iron-stairway escalators and black-iron catwalks all ended at the center of the dome, everything glowing in the sunlight from the clear windows encircling the Taj's pointed cupola.

Harman had never been so high—not even on the tower of the Golden Gate at Machu Picchu seven hundred feet above the suspended roadway—and he'd never been overwhelmed by such a fear of falling. This platform was so high that he could look down and hide the entire circle of the marble floor of the Taj with his outstretched hand. The maze and the crypt entrance on the main floor were so far below that they looked like the microcircuit embroidery on a turin cloth. Harman forced himself not to look down as he followed Moira up the last stairway out onto the web of catwalks to the wrought-iron platform in the cupola itself.

"Is that it?" he asked, nodding toward a ten- or twelve-foot-tall structure in the center of the platform.

"Yes."

Harman had expected this so-called crystal cabinet to be another version of Moira's crystal sarcophagus, but this thing looked nothing like a coffin. It was faceted with glass and metal geodesic struts the color of old pewter. The word "dodecahedron" came to mind, but Harman had learned that from sigling rather than from reading and wasn't sure if it was the correct term. The crystal cabinet was a multifaceted, twelve-sided object, roughly spherical except for the flat faces, made of a dozen or so slabs of clear glass or crystal framed by thin struts of burnished metal. Scores of multicolored cables and pipes ran from the walls of the cupola into the black metal base of the thing. Scattered on the platform near the cabinet were metal-mesh chairs, odd instruments with dark screens and keyboards, and micro-thin slabs of vertical clear plastic, some five or six feet high.

"What is this place?" asked Harman.

"The nexus of the Taj." She activated several of the screened instruments and touched a vertical panel. The plastic disappeared as a holographic virtual control panel took its place. Moira's hands danced on the virtual images, there was a deep sound from the walls of the Taj, and a golden liquid—not yellow but liquid gold, apparently no thicker than water—began pouring into the base of the crystal cabinet.

Harman walked closer to the dodecahedron. "It's filling with liquid."

"Yes."

"That's crazy. I can't go in there now. I'd drown."

"No, you won't," said Moira.

"You expect me to be in that cabinet when it has ten feet of this golden liquid in it?"

"Yes."

Harman shook his head and backed away, stopping six feet from the edge of the metal platform. "No, no, no. That's too crazy."

"As you will, but it is the only way you can gain the knowledge of these books," said Moira. "The fluid is the medium which allows the transmission of the contents of these million volumes. Knowledge you will need if you are to be our Prometheus in the struggle against Setebos and his kind. Knowledge you will need if you are to educate your own people. Knowledge you will need, my Prometheus, if you are to save your beloved Ada."

"Yes, but if the water fills it—whatever the liquid is—it'll be ten feet deep or deeper. I'm not a good swimmer . . ." began Harman.

Suddenly Ariel was standing next to them on the platform, although Harman hadn't heard his steps on the metal floor. The small figure was carrying something bulky wrapped in what looked to be a red turin cloth.

"Ariel, my darling!" cried Moira. Her voice carried a tone of delight and excitement that Harman had not yet heard from her—nor even from Savi in the time he'd known her.

"Greetings to Miranda," said the sprite, removing the red cloth and handing Moira some sort of antique instrument with strings. Harman's people played and sang some music, but knew few instruments and made none.

"A guitar!" said the post-human woman, taking the oddly shaped instrument from the greenish-glowing sprite and touching the strings with her long fingers. The notes that issued forth reminded Harman of Ariel's own voice.

Ariel bowed low and spoke in formal tone—

"Take
This slave of Music, for the sake
Of him who is the slave of thee.
And teach it all the harmony
In which thou canst, and only thou,

> *Make the delighted spirit glow,*
> *Till joy defines itself again,*
> *And, too intense, is turned to pain;*
> *For by permission and command*
> *Of thine own Prince Ferdinand,*
> *Poor Ariel sends this silent token*
> *Of more than ever can be spoken."*

Moira bowed toward the sprite, set the resonating instrument on a table, and kissed Ariel on his green-glowing forehead. "I thank thee, friend, sometimes friendly servant, never slave. How has my Ariel fared since I went to sleep?" And said:

> *"When you died, the silent Moon,*
> *in her interlunar swoon,*
> *Is not sadder in her cell*
> *Than deserted Ariel.*
> *When you live again on earth,*
> *Like an unseen star of birth,*
> *Ariel guides you o'er the sea*
> *Of life from your nativity."*

Moira touched his cheek, then looked at Harman, then back to the sprite-avatar of the biosphere. "Have you two encountered one another before?"

"We've met," said Harman.

"How is the world, Ariel, since I left it?" asked Moira, turning away from Harman again.

Ariel said,

> *"Many changes have been run,*
> *Since Ferdinand and you begun*
> *Your course of love, and Ariel still*
> *Has tracked your steps, and served your will."*

In a less formal voice, as if concluding some official ceremony, the biosphere sprite said, "And how is it with you, my lady, now that you are born unto us again?"

Now it seemed to be Moira's turn to sound more formal and cadenced than Harman had ever heard in Savi's voice—

> *"This temple, sad and lone,*
> *Is all spared from the thunder of a war*
> *Foughten long since by giant hierarchy*

Against rebellion: this old image here,
Whose carved features wrinkled as he fell,
Is Prosper's; I Miranda, left supreme
Sole Priestess of this desolation."—

To his horror, Harman saw that both the post-human woman and in-human biosphere entity were openly weeping.

Ariel stepped back, bowed again, swept his hand in Harman's direction, and said, "This mortal man who's done no harm, despite all the contrary his name implies, has he come to the crystal cabinet to be executed?"

"No," said Moira, "to be educated."

The Setebos Egg hatched during their first night back at the ruins of Ardis Hall.

Ada was shocked to see the devastation at her former home. She'd been unconscious when flown away on the sonie the night of the attack and because of her concussion and other injuries had only partial memories of the horrible hours before. Now she saw the ruins of her life and home and memories in stark daylight. It made her want to fall to her knees and weep until she slept, but because she was leading the group of forty-four other survivors as they came up the last hill toward Ardis, the sonie hovering with eight of the most severely ill and wounded above, she kept her head up and her eyes dry as she walked past the scorched ruins, glancing left and right only to point out articles and remnants that could be salvaged for their new camp.

Her home, the great manor of Ardis Hall, two thousand years of her family's pride, was all but gone—only soot-blackened timbers and the stone remnants of the many fireplaces left—but there was a surprising amount to salvage elsewhere.

There were also the rotting bodies of their friends—at least bits and pieces of them—left in the fields.

Ada conferred with Daeman and a few others and they agreed that the first priority was creating a fire and shelter—first a rough lean-to and warm place for the ill and injured to be treated and brought to before the short winter day was over, a shelter large enough for all of them to make it through the night without freezing. While Ardis Hall was lost to them, segments of several of the barracks, sheds, and other outbuildings erected in the last nine months before the sky fell were partially intact. They might have crowded into one of these shacks, but they were too near the forest, too hard to defend, and too far from the well that had been right outside Ardis Hall.

They found heaps of kindling and dry wood and used what Ada thought was too many matches from their dwindling supply to start a large fire. Greogi landed the sonie and they unloaded the unconscious and semiconscious injured and made them as comfortable as they could on makeshift cots and bedrolls near the fire. A work detail kept carrying more firewood from the various ruins—no one wanted to go as far as the shadowy forest and Ada had forbidden such adventures for that day. The sonie took off and orbited in a mile-wide circle, the exhausted Greogi at the controls and Boman with his rifle, both men watching for voynix. One of the barracks—the one Odysseus built by hand for his followers months before—yielded a treasure trove of blankets and rolls of canvas, all smelling of smoke but usable, and in another tumbled but only partially burned shed near Hannah's burned-out cupola, Caul found shovels, picks, crowbars, hoes, hammers, nails, spikes, nylon rope, carabiners, and other former servitor tools that might now save their lives. With the unscorched wood from the barracks and logs scavenged from large parts of the former palisade, a work party began erecting a structure part tent, part log cabin around the deep water well next to the still-smoldering ruins of Ardis—a temporary shelter good enough for that night and a few more nights at least. Boman had more elaborate plans for a permanent lodge with a tower, gun slits, and close-in palisade, but Ada told him to help build the survival lean-to first and plan the castle later.

There still was no sign of the voynix, but it was only afternoon and night would be coming quickly enough, so Ada and Daeman assigned Kaman and ten of his best marksmen to set up a perimeter defense. Other men and women with flechette weapons—they'd counted twenty-four working weapons and one that seemed defective, with fewer than one hundred and twenty magazines of crystal flechettes— were detailed to provide guard closer to the fire and lean-to.

It took a little more than three hours to get the basic structure hammered together and raised—walls only about six feet high, made from palisade logs, a cobbled-together arched roof made of wood planks from the barracks, and a canvas roof. It was important to put something between the wounded and the cold ground, but there was no time to fit a floor, so multiple layers of canvas were laid down atop straw brought in from the former hay barn near the north wall. The cattle themselves had disappeared—killed by voynix or simply run off. No one was going into the forest hunting for them that particular afternoon and the circling sonie had its own duties to perform.

By late afternoon, the temporary lean-to was completed. Ada, who had been working on new buckets and ropes for the well and leading burial parties with picks and shovels digging shallow graves in the frozen earth, returned to inspect the structure and found it large enough for at least forty-five people to crowd in close together to sleep, the others presumably on guard duty outside, and for all fifty-three of them to crowd into for meals if necessary, although it would be crowded. Three of the walls were of wood, but the fourth wall—facing the well and two fires now burning—was only canvas, with most of it open to the heat. Laman and Edide had scrounged metal and ceramic from Ardis Hall to build a stovepipe, if not an actual chimney, for the lean-to, but that modification would have to wait for the next day. There was no glass for windows, only small openings at different heights on each of the wood walls with sliding wood slats and covering canvas. Daeman agreed they could retreat to the lean-to and lay down a withering field of flechette fire from those slits, but one look at the canvas roof and the canvas fourth wall told everyone there that the voynix could not be held off long once they leaped to the attack.

But the Setebos Egg seemed to be keeping the voynix at bay.

It was almost dark when Daeman took Ada, Tom, and Laman away from the warmth of the fires to the ashes of Hannah's cupola to open his rucksack and show them the hatching egg. The thing was glowing even more brightly, shedding a sick, milky light, and there were tiny cracks everywhere in the shell, but no openings yet.

"How long until it hatches?" asked Ada.

"How the hell should I know?" said Daeman. "All I know is that the little Setebos inside is still alive and trying to get out. You can hear the squeals and chewing sounds if you put your ear to the shell."

"No thanks," said Ada.

"What happens when it hatches?" asked Laman, who had been in favor of destroying the egg from the beginning.

Daeman shrugged.

"What exactly did you have in mind when you stole the thing from Setebos' nest in the Paris Crater blue-ice cathedral?" asked the medic Tom, who'd heard the whole story.

"I don't *know*," said Daeman. "It seemed like a good idea at the time. At least we could find out what sort of creature this Setebos is."

"What if Mommy comes looking for her baby?" asked Laman. It was not the first time that Daeman had been asked this.

He shrugged again. "We can kill it right after it hatches if we have to," he said softly, looking at the growing winter darkness under the trees beyond the ruins of the old palisade.

"*Can* we?" said Laman. He put his left hand on the many-fissured eggshell and then pulled it away quickly as if the surface were hot. All those who had touched the egg had remarked on the unpleasantness of the experience, as if something on the inside of the shell were sucking energy through their palm.

Before Daeman could answer again, Ada said, "Daeman, if you hadn't brought that thing back with you, most of us would probably be dead now. It's kept the voynix away this long. Maybe it will after it hatches as well."

"If it—or its mama-poppa—doesn't eat us in our sleep," said Laman, cradling his mangled right hand.

Later, just after dark, Siris came and whispered to Ada that Sherman, one of their more seriously wounded, had died. Ada nodded, rounded up two others—Edide and a still-portly man named Rallum—and they quietly carried the body out beyond the edge of the fire, setting it under lumber and stones near the tumbled barracks so that they could properly bury Sherman in the morning. The wind was cold.

Ada did a four-hour shift of guard duty in the dark with a loaded flechette rifle, the warming fire a distant glow and the nearest other sentry fifty yards away, her concussion causing her head to pound so fiercely she really couldn't have seen a voynix or Setebos if it had sat on her lap. Her broken wrist required her to prop the weapon on her forearm. Then, when Caul relieved her from duty, she stumbled back to the crowded, snore-filled lean-to and fell into a deep sleep stirred only by terrible nightmares.

Daeman awakened her just before dawn, bending to whisper in her ear, "The egg has hatched."

Ada sat up in the dark, feeling the press and breathing of bodies all around her, and for a moment she knew she was still in the nightmare. She wanted Harman to touch her shoulder and wake her into sunlight. She wanted his arm around her, not this freezing dark and press of strange bodies and flickering, fading firelight through canvas.

"It hatched," repeated Daeman. His voice was very low. "I didn't want to wake you, but we have to decide what to do."

"Yes," Ada whispered back. She'd slept in her clothes and now she slipped out of her nest of damp blankets and carefully picked her way over sleeping forms, following Daeman out through the canvas, past the low but still-tended fire, south, away from the lean-to toward another, much smaller fire.

"I slept out here away from the others," said Daeman, speaking in a more normal tone as they got farther away from the main lean-to. His voice was still soft but each syllable roared in Ada's aching head. Far overhead, the e- and p-rings whirled as they always whirled, turning and crossing in front of the stars and a fingernail moon. Ada saw something move up there and for a minute her heart pounded before she realized it was the sonie, orbiting silently in the night.

"Who's flying the sonie?" she asked dully.

"Oko."

"I didn't know she knew how to fly it."

"Greogi taught her yesterday,"said Daeman. They were approaching the smaller campfire and Ada saw the silhouette of another man standing there.

"Good morning, Ada *Uhr*," said Tom.

Ada had to smile at the formal honorific. It had not been used much in recent months. "Good morning, Tom," she whispered. "Where is this thing?"

Daeman pulled a long piece of wood out of the fire and extended it into the darkness like a torch.

Ada stepped back.

Daeman and Tom had obviously piled up palisade logs on three sides to cage the . . . thing . . . in the triangular space. But it was scurrying to and fro in that space, obviously ready and soon capable of climbing the two-foot-high flimsy wooden barricades.

Ada took the torch from Tom and crouched lower to study the Setebos thing in the flickering light.

Its multiple yellow eyes blinked and closed at the glare. The little Setebos—if that is what it was—was about a foot long, already larger in mass and length than a regular human brain, Ada thought, but still with the disgustingly pink wrinkles and folds and appearance of a living, disembodied brain. She could see the gray strip between the two hemispheres, a mucousy membrane covering it, and a slight pulsing, as if the whole thing was breathing. But this pink brain also had pulsating mouths—or orifices of some kind—and a myriad of tiny, pink baby hands beneath it and protruding from orifices. It scrabbled back and forth on those pudgy little pink fingers that looked like a mass of wriggling worms to Ada.

The yellow eyes opened, stayed open, and locked on Ada's face. One of the orifices opened and screeching, scratching sounds came out.

"Is it trying to talk?" Ada whispered to both men.

"I have no idea," said Daeman. "But it's only a few minutes old. I wouldn't be surprised if it's talking to us by the time it's an hour old."

"We shouldn't let it get an hour old," Tom said softly but firmly. "We should kill the thing now. Blow it apart with flechettes and then burn its corpse and scatter the ashes."

Ada looked at Tom in surprise. The self-trained medic had always been the least violent and most life-affirming person she'd known at Ardis.

"At the very least," said Daeman, watching the thing successfully trying to climb the low wooden barrier, "it needs a leash."

Wearing heavy canvas-and-wool gloves they'd designed at Ardis early in the winter for work with livestock, Daeman leaned forward and plunged a sharp, thin spike that he'd curved to form a hook into the solid band of fibers—corpus callosum, Ada remembered it was called—connecting the two hemispheres of the little Setebos's brain. Then, moving quickly, Daeman tugged to make sure the hook was secure, snapped a carabiner to it, and rigged twenty feet of nylon rope to the carabiner.

The little creature screamed and howled so loudly that Ada looked over her shoulder at the main camp, sure that everyone would come boiling out of the lean-to. No one stirred except one sentry near the fire who looked over her way sleepily and then went back to contemplating the flames.

The little Setebos writhed and rolled, running against the wooden barriers and finally clambering over them like a crab. Daeman tugged it up short on six feet of leash.

More tiny hands emerged from their folded state in the pink brain's orifices and pulled themselves along on elastic stalks a yard or more long. The hands leaped at the nylon rope and tugged at it wildly, other hands exploring the hook and carabiner, trying to pull them free. The hook held. Daeman was pulled forward for a second but then jerked the scrabbling creature back onto the frozen grass of its cage.

"Strong little bastard," he whispered.

"Let it wander," said Ada. "Let's see where it goes. What it does."

"Are you serious?"

"Yes. Not far, but let's see what it wants."

Tom kicked the low post-wall down and the Setebos baby scurried out, the baby fingers under it working in unison, blurring like some obscene centipede's legs.

Daeman allowed himself to be tugged along behind it, keeping the leash short. Ada and Tom walked beside Daeman, ready to move quickly if the creature turned toward them. It moved too quickly and too purposefully for any of the humans not to sense the danger from it.

Tom's flechette rifle was being held at the ready and Daeman had another rifle strapped over his shoulder.

The thing didn't head for the campfire or the lean-to. It tugged them twenty yards into the darkness of the west lawn. Then it scurried down into one of the former defensive trenches—a flame trench Ada had helped to dig—and seemed to squat on its spraddled hands.

Two new orifices opened at either ends of the little creature and stalks without hands, pulsing proboscises, emerged, wavered, and suddenly attached themselves to the ground. There came a sound that was a mixture of a pig rooting and a baby suckling.

"What the hell?" said Tom. He had the rifle aimed, the plastic-metal stock set firmly against his shoulder. The first shot, Ada knew, would slam several thousand crystal-barbed flechettes into the pulsing pink monstrosity at a velocity greater than the speed of sound.

Ada started shivering. Her constant, pulsing headache turned to a wave of nausea.

"I know this spot," she whispered, her voice shaking. "It's where Reman and Emme died during the voynix attack . . . they burned to death here."

The Setebos spawn continued loudly rooting and suckling.

"Then it's . . ." began Daeman and stopped.

"Eating," finished Ada.

Tom put his finger on the trigger. "Let me kill it, Ada *Uhr*. Please."

"Yes," said Ada. "But not yet. I have no doubt that the voynix will return as soon as this thing dies. And it's still dark. And we're nowhere near ready. Let's go back to your camp."

They walked back to the campfire together, Daeman tugging the reluctant and finger-dragging Setebos thing along behind them.

60

Harman drowned.

His last thoughts before the water filled his lungs were—*That bitch Moira lied to me*—and then he gagged and choked and drowned in the swirling golden liquid.

The crystal dodecahedron had filled only to within a foot of its multifaceted top while Harman had been watching the golden liquid flow into it. Savi-Moira-Miranda had called the rich golden fluid the "medium" by which he would sigl—although that had not been her term—the Taj's gigantic collection of books. Harman had stripped down to his thermskin layer.

"That has to come off, too," said Moira. Ariel had stepped back into the shadows and now only the young woman stood in the bright light from the cupola windows with him. The guitar was on a nearby tabletop.

"Why?" said Harman.

"Your skin has to be in contact with the medium," said Moira. "The transfer can't work through a bonded molecular layer like a thermskin."

"What transfer?" Harman had asked, licking his lips. He was very nervous. His heart was pounding.

Moira gestured toward the seemingly infinite rows of shelved books lining the hundred curved stories of inner dome-wall widening out below them.

"How do I know that there's anything in those old books that will help me get back to Ada?" said Harman.

"You don't."

"You and Prospero could send me home right now if you wanted," said Harman, turning away from the filling crystal tank. "Why don't you do that so we can skip all this nonsense?"

"It's not that easy," said Moira.

"The *hell* it isn't," shouted Harman.

The young woman went on as if Harman had not spoken. "First of all, you know from the turin and from what Prospero told you that all of the planet's faxnodes and fax pavilions have been shut off."

"By whom?" said Harman, turning back to look at the crystal cabinet again. The golden fluid was swirling to within a foot of the top, but it had stopped filling. Moira had opened a panel on the top—one of the multifaceted glass faces—and he could see the short metal rungs that would allow him to climb up to that opening.

"By Setebos or his allies," said Moira.

"What allies? Who are they? Just *tell* me what I need to know."

Moira shook her head. "My young Prometheus, you've been *told* things for the better part of a year now. Hearing things means nothing unless you have the context in which to place the information. It is time for you to gain that context."

"Why do you keep calling me Prometheus?" he barked at her. "Everyone seems to have ten names around here . . . Prometheus, I don't know that name. Why do you call me that?"

Moira smiled. "I guarantee that you *will* understand that at least, after the crystal cabinet."

Harman took a deep breath. One more smug smile out of this woman, he realized, and he might hit her in the face. "Prospero said that this thing could kill me," he said. He looked at the cabinet rather than the post-human thing in Savi's human form.

Moira nodded. "It could. I do not believe it will."

"What are my chances?" said Harman. His voice sounded plaintive and weak to his own ears.

"I don't know. Very good, I think, or I would not suggest you go through this . . . unpleasantness."

"Have you done it?"

"Undergone the crystal cabinet transfer?" said Moira. "No. I had no reason to."

"Who has?" demanded Harman. "How many lived? How many died?"

"All of the Chief Librarians have experienced the crystal cabinet transfer," said Moira. "All the many generations of the Keepers of the Taj. All the linear descendents of the original Khan Ho Tep."

"Including your beloved Ferdinand Mark Alonzo?"

"Yes."

"And how many of these Keepers of the Taj survived the cabinet transfer?" asked Harman. He was still wearing the thermskin, but his exposed hands and face felt the terrible chill in the air up there near the top of the dome. He concentrated on not shivering.

Harman was afraid that if Moira merely shrugged, he'd just walk away forever. And he didn't want to do that—not yet. Not until he knew more. This awkward crystal cabinet with its glowing gold liquid might kill him . . . but it might also return him to Ada sooner.

Moira did not shrug. She looked him in the eye—she had Savi's eyes—and said, "I don't know how many died. Sometimes the flow of information is simply too much—for lesser minds. I do not believe you have a lesser mind, Prometheus."

"Don't call me that again." Harman's freezing hands were tightened into fists.

"All right."

"How long does it take?" he asked.

"The transfer itself? Less than an hour."

"That long?" said Harman. "The *eiffelbahn* car leaves in forty-five minutes."

"We'll make it," said Moira. Harman hesitated.

"The medium fluid is warm," said Moira as if reading his mind. It was more likely, he realized, she was reading his shivers and shaking.

That may have decided the issue for Harman. He had peeled off the thermskin, embarrassed to be naked in front of this stranger with whom he had had a strange sort of sex less than two hours earlier. And it was *cold.*

He had quickly clambered up the side of the dodecahedron, using the short rungs for hand and footholds, feeling how cold the metal was against the bare soles of his feet.

It had been a relief when he lowered himself through the open panel and actually dropped into the golden liquid. As she'd promised, the fluid was warm. It had no scent and the few drops that landed on his lips had no taste.

And then Ariel had levitated from the shadows and closed and locked the panel above Harman's head.

And then Moira had touched some control on the vertical and virtual control panel where she stood.

And then a pump chugged to life again somewhere in the base of the crystal cabinet and more fluid began to fill the closed container.

Harman had screamed at them then—screamed at them to let him out—and then, when both post-human and biosphere non-human ig-nored him, Harman had pounded and kicked, trying to open the panel, trying to shatter the crystal. The fluid continued to rise. For some seconds Harman found the last inch of air at the top facet of the dodecahedron and he breathed it in deeply, still pounding on the overhead panels. And then the fluid rose until there was no more inch of air, no more air bub-bles except those escaping from Harman's lips and nose.

He held his breath for as long as he could. He wished that his last thought could have been of Ada and his love for Ada—and his sorrow for having betrayed Ada—but although he thought of her, his last thoughts while holding his breath until his lungs were afire were a confused jumble of terror and fury and regret.

And then he could hold his breath no more and—still pounding on the unyielding crystal panel above him—he exhaled, coughed, gagged, cursed, gagged more, breathed in the thickening fluid, felt darkness flowing over his mind even as overwhelming panic continued to fill his body with useless adrenaline, and then his lungs held no air at all, but Harman did not know this. Heavier without air in his lungs, his body no longer kicking, moving, or breathing, Harman sank to the center of the dodecahedron.

There had been a flurry of activity and tightbeamed conversation on the bridge of the *Queen Mab* as another masered message came in from the Voice on the asteroid city on polar Earth orbit, but it was only a repeat of the previous rendezvous coordinates and after five minutes confirming this and with no other message following, the principal moravecs met back at the chart table.

"Where were we?" said Orphu of Io.

"You were about to present your Theory of Everything," said Prime Integrator Asteague/Che.

"And you said you knew who the Voice is," said Cho Li. "Who or what is it?"

"I don't *know* who the Voice is," answered Orphu, vocalizing in soft rumbles rather than tightbeaming or transmitting on the standard in-ship comm channels. "But I have a pretty good guess."

"Tell us," said General Beh bin Adee. The Belt moravec's tone did not suggest a polite request so much as a direct order.

"I'd rather explain my entire . . . Theory of Everything . . . first and then tell you about the Voice," said Orphu. "It'll make more sense in context."

"Proceed," said Prime Integrator Asteague/Che.

Mahnmut heard his friend take in a full breath of O-two, even though the Ionian had weeks or months of reserve in his tanks. He wanted to tightbeam his friend the question—*Are you sure you want to go ahead with this explanation?*—but since Mahnmut himself had no clue as to what Orphu was going to say, he remained silent. But he was nervous for his friend.

"First of all," said Orphu of Io, "you haven't released the information yet, but I'm pretty sure you've identified most of the million or so satellites that make up Earth's polar and equatorial rings that we're so quickly approaching . . . and I bet that most of the objects aren't asteroids or habitations."

"That is correct," said Asteague/Che.

"Some of them we know to be early post-human attempts at creating and corralling black holes," continued Orphu. "Huge devices like the wormhole accumulator that you showed us crashing into that other orbital asteroid city nine months ago. But how many of those are there? A few thousand?"

"Fewer than two thousand," confirmed Asteague/Che.

"It's my bet that the bulk of the rest of the million . . . *things* . . . that the post-humans put in orbit are data storage devices. I don't know what kind—DNA, maybe, although that would require constant life support, so they're probably bubble memory combined with some sort of advanced quantum computer with some complicated post-human memory storage that we moravecs haven't discovered yet."

Orphu paused and there was a silence that seemed to stretch on for hours to Mahnmut. The various Prime Integrators and moravec leaders were not looking at one another, but Mahnmut guessed that they had a private tightbeam channel and that they were conferring.

Asteague/Che finally broke the silence—which had probably lasted only seconds in real time.

"They *are* mostly storage devices," said the Prime Integrator. "We're not sure of their nature, but they appear to be some sort of advanced magnetic bubble-memory quantum wavefront storage units."

"And each unit is essentially independent," said Orphu. "Its own hard disk, so to speak."

"Yes," said Asteague/Che.

"And most of the rest of the satellites in the rings—probably no more than ten thousand or so—are basic power transmitters and some sort of modulated tachyon waveform transmitters."

"Six thousand four hundred and eight power transmitters," said the navigator Cho Li. "Precisely three thousand tachyon wave transmitters."

"How do you know this, Orphu of Io?" asked Suma IV, the powerful Ganymedan. "Have you hacked into our Integrator comm channels or files?"

Orphu held two of his multisegmented forward manipulator arms out, flat palms up. "No, no," he said. "I don't have enough programming knowledge to hack into my sister's diary . . . if I had a sister or if she had a diary."

"Then how . . ." began Retrograde Sinopessen.

"It just makes sense," said Orphu. "I have an abiding interest in human beings and their literature. Over the centuries, I've paid attention to those observations of Earth, the post-humans' rings, and the data about the few humans left on the planet that the Five Moons Consortium has made public knowledge."

"The Consortium has never released public information on the memory storage devices in orbit," said Suma IV.

"No," agreed Orphu, "but it makes sense that's what those things are. All evidence fourteen centuries ago when they left the surface of the Earth was that there were only a few thousand post-human entities in existence, isn't that right?"

"That is correct," said Asteague/Che.

"Our moravec experts at the time weren't even sure these post-humans had bodies . . . not bodies as we think of them," said Orphu, "so they sure didn't need to build a million cities in orbit."

"That does not lead to the conclusion that the majority of the objects that *are* in Earth orbit are memory devices," said General Beh bin Adee.

Mahnmut found himself wondering what the punishment on this ship was for espionage.

"It does when you look at what the old-style humans have been doing on Earth for almost a millennium and a half," said Orphu of Io. "And what they *haven't* been doing."

"What do you mean, 'haven't been doing?' " asked Mahnmut. He'd planned to stay silent during this conversation, but his curiosity was too great.

"First of all, they haven't been breeding like human beings breed," said Orphu. "There were fewer than ten thousand of them for several centuries. Then that neutrino beam—guided by modulated tachyons, I understand from the astronomers' online publications—shot up from Jerusalem fourteen hundred years ago, a beam aimed at nowhere in deep space, and then, suddenly, there seemed to be no humans left. None."

"Only briefly," said Prime Integrator Asteague/Che.

"Yes, but still . . ." said Orphu. He seemed to lose track of what he was going to say, but then said, "And then, less than a century later, there were about one million old-style humans scattered around the planet. Evidently not descendants of those ten thousand or so who disappeared. No buildup of population . . . just wham, bang, thank-you-ma'am . . . one million people out of nowhere."

"And what did that tell you?" asked Asteague/Che. The formidable little Europan seemed privately amused, rather as a teacher might be when a student suddenly showed unexpected promise.

"It told me that these old-styles weren't born to begin with," said Orphu of Io. "They were decanted."

"Virgin birth?" asked Cho Li, the Callistan's odd voice dripping sarcasm.

"Of a sort," said Orphu, his easy, rumbling tones suggesting that he'd taken no offense at the sarcasm. "I think the post-humans have and had a million or so human memories and personalities and data on bodies stored in those orbital memory devices—who knows? Perhaps one satellite per human being—and they restocked the herd. Which leads to the explanation of why the population appears to have peaked at one million every few centuries, dropped to a few thousand, then jumped back to a million as if by magic."

"Why?" asked Centurion Leader Mep Ahoo. As with Mahnmut, the rockvec soldier sounded honestly curious.

"Minimum herd population," said Orphu. "The post-humans seem to have allowed the old-styles to breed only to half of replacement numbers . . . that is, one baby per woman. And then only when there had been a death. And I've read the conjecture that the old-styles live exactly one Earth century and then disappear. Enough to keep the herd going given climate changes or whatever, not so many they could overbreed or wander off the reservation, but the population drops rapidly. Then, every thousand years or so, they restock the herd to its maximum size of one million old-styles. Because women have only *one child*, the population begins dropping until the next restocking."

"Where did you read that old-style humans lived precisely a century?" asked Cho Li. He sounded shocked.

"In *The Scientific Ganymedan*," said Orphu. "I've had a broadcast subscription for more than eight centuries."

Prime Integrator Asteague/Che held up his very humanoid hand. "You'll have to pardon me, Orphu of Io, but while I congratulate you on your deductions about the purpose of the orbital devices and about the precise longevity we've observed of the remaining hundred thousand old-style human beings—at least until recent months, during which time there's been quite a drop-off in population due to these attacks by creatures unknown—you said that you could tell us why there are Greek gods on Mars, who the Voice is, how Mars was so miraculously terraformed, and what is causing the current quantum instability on both Earth and Mars."

"I'm getting to that," said Orphu. "Do you want me to condense it and put the whole Theory of Everything into a high-speed tightbeam squirt? That'd take less than a second."

"No, no need for that," said Prime Integrator Asteague/Che. "But perhaps speak more rapidly. We have less than three hours before we have to launch the dropship—or not—during the aerobraking maneuver."

Orphu of Io rumbled on the subsonic levels in a way that Mahnmut had long interpreted as laughter.

"The old-style humans are clustered around some three hundred localized habitation centers on five continents of Earth, correct?" said the Ionian.

"Correct," said Cho Li.

"And the populations around these nodes vary," said Orphu, "yet our telescopes have never picked up any signs of transport—no major roads in use, no aircraft, no ships—not even quaint sailing ships like the one Mahnmut and I traveled the length of Mars' Valles Marineris in— not even an occasional hot air balloon. So we assumed that the old-style humans were quantum teleporting, even though our moravec scientists could never perfect that mode of travel."

"It was a reasonable assumption," said Suma IV.

"Reasonable," agreed Orphu of Io, "but wrong. We know now because of the quantum data left by the so-called Olympian gods on Mars and on the otherdimensional Earth where the battle for Troy is still being fought what real quantum teleportation looks like. We know its footprint, and what the old-style humans were doing to get from Point A to Point B ain't it."

"If the old-style humans aren't quantum teleporting," said Centurion Leader Mep Ahoo, "then how have they been moving instantaneously from one place to the other on Earth for more than fourteen hundred years?"

"The old-fashioned idea of teleportation," said Orphu. "Storing all the data of a human being's body and mind and personality in code, breaking down the matter into energy, beaming it, then reassembling it elsewhere, just as in the old TV broadcast series from the Lost Era—*Star Truck.*"

"*Trek,*" corrected General Beh bin Adee.

"Aha!" said Orphu of Io. "Another fan."

The General clacked barbed killing claws in embarrassment or irritation.

"Our scientists long since determined that storing such incredible amounts of data would be impossible," said Cho Li. "It would require more terabytes of storage space than there are atoms in the universe."

"Evidently the post-humans found a way to build that memory storage," said Orphu, "because the old-style humans have been teleporting their butts off for centuries. Not true quantum-level teleportation of the kind our friend Hockenberry or the Olympian gods carry off, but the crude mechanical ripping apart of molecules and reassembling of them somewhere else."

"Why would they do that for the old-style humans?" asked Mahnmut. "Why such an incredible engineering project for a few hundred thousand people whom they treat almost like pets . . . like creatures in a zoo? We've seen no signs of new human engineering, city building, or creativity for more than that millennium and a half."

"Maybe the teleportation itself has something to do with that cultural retardation," said Orphu. "Maybe not. But I'm convinced that's what we're looking at down there. It's a case of 'Beam me up, Scooty.' "

"Scotty," corrected Retrograde Sinopessen.

"Thank you," said Orphu. To Mahnmut he tightbeamed, *That makes four of us.*

"You may well be correct that the old-style humans have been using a crude form of matter replication-transmission rather than true quantum teleportation," said Asteague/Che, "but that doesn't explain Mars or . . ."

"No, but the post-humans' obsession with reaching another dimensional universe does," said Orphu, not even noticing in his excitement and pleasure of the telling that he was interrupting the most important Prime Integrator in all the Five Moons Consortium.

"How do you know the posts were obsessed with getting to another dimensional universe?" asked General Beh bin Adee.

"Are you kidding?" said Orphu. Mahnmut had to think that the stern Asteroid Belt rockvec general had not been asked that question many times in his life or military career.

"Just look at the junk the post-humans left behind in orbit," continued Orphu, oblivious to the military moravec's taken-abackness. "They have wormhole accumulators, black hole accelerators—all early attempts at ripping through space and time, taking shortcuts out into this universe . . . or to another one."

"Black holes and wormholes don't work," the Callistan Cho Li said flatly. "At least not as transport devices."

"Yeah, we know that now and that's what the post-humans found out more than fifteen hundred years ago," agreed Orphu. "Then, when they had these incredible memory-storage satellites in orbit, plus the crude matter-replication teleportation portals for the old-style humans—who, I would wager, they were using as guinea pigs in all this experimentation—only *then* did the post-humans start messing around with Brane Holes and quantum teleportation."

"Our scientists and engineers have been . . . messing around, as you put it . . . with quantum teleportation and the generation of Calabi-Yau universe Membrane Holes for many centuries," said Retrograde

Sinopessen. The Amalthean was so agitated that he was almost dancing on his long, spidery, silver legs. "With no luck," he added.

"That's because we didn't have the one thing that allowed the post-humans to make their breakthrough," said Orphu of Io and paused. Everyone waited. Mahnmut knew that his friend was enjoying the moment.

"The million human bodies, minds, memories, and personalities that were stored as digital data in their orbital memory satellites," said Orphu. His deep voice was triumphant, as if he'd solved some long-pondered mathematical conundrum.

"I don't get it," said Centurion Leader Mep Ahoo.

Orphu's radar flickered over all of them, a feathery touch on the electromagnetic spectrum. Mahnmut thought that his friend was waiting for their reactions, perhaps for their shouts of approval. No one moved or spoke.

"I don't get it either," said Mahnmut.

"What is the human brain?" Orphu asked rhetorically. "I mean, all of us moravecs have a piece of one. What is it like? How does it work? Like the binary or DNA computers we also carry around for thinking purposes?"

"No," said Cho Li. "We know that the human brain is not like a computer, neither is it a chemical memory machine the way the Lost Era human scientists believed. The human brain . . . the mind . . . is a quantum-state holistic standing wavefront."

"Exactly!" cried Orphu. "The post-humans used this intimate understanding of the human mind to perfect their Brane Holes, time travel, and quantum teleportation."

"I still don't see how," said Prime Integrator Asteague/Che.

"Think about how quantum teleportation works," said Orphu. "Cho, you can explain that better than I can."

The Callistan rumbled and then modulated the rumbles into words. "The early experiments in quantum teleportation—done by old-style humans in ancient times, as far back as the Twentieth Century A.D.—worked by producing entangled pairs of photons—and teleporting one of the pair—or actually by teleporting the complete *quantum state* of that proton—while transmitting the Bell-state analysis of the second photon through regular subliminal channels."

"Doesn't that violate Heisenberg's principle and Einstein's speed-of-light restrictions?" asked Centurion Leader Mep Ahoo, who, like Mahnmut, had obviously not been briefed on the mechanisms by which the gods on Mars' Olympus Mons QT'd to Ilium.

"No," said Cho Li. "Teleported photons carried no information with them when they moved instantaneously from place to place in this universe—not even information about their own quantum state."

"So quantum teleported photons are useless," said Centurion Leader Mep Ahoo. "At least for communication purposes."

"Not quite," said Cho Li. "The recipient of a teleported photon had a one-in-four chance of guessing its quantum state—the quantum photon had only that many possibilities—and, by guessing, utilizing the quantum bits of data. These are called qubits and we've successfully used them for instantaneous comm purposes."

Mahnmut shook his head. "How do we get from quantum-state photons carrying no information to the Greek gods quantum teleporting to Troy?"

"The imagination may be compared to Adam's dream," intoned Orphu of Io. "He awoke and found it truth. John Keats."

"Could you try to be more cryptic?" Suma IV asked caustically.

"I could try," said Orphu.

"What does the poet John Keats have to do with quantum teleportation and the reason for the current quantum crisis?" asked Mahnmut.

"I suggest that the post-humans made their breakthrough in Brane Holes and quantum teleportation more than a millennium and a half ago precisely because of their intimate knowledge of the holistic quantum nature of human consciousness," said the Ionian, his voice serious now.

"I've run some preliminary studies on the ship's quantum computer," Orphu continued, "and when you represent human consciousness as the standing wavefront phenomenon it really is, factor in terabytes of qubit quantum date on the wavefront basis for physical reality itself, apply the proper relativistic Coulomb field transforms to these mind-consciousness-reality wave functions, you quickly see how the post-humans opened Brane Holes to new universes and then teleported there themselves."

"How?" said Prime Integrator Asteague/Che.

"They first opened Brane Holes to alternate universes in which there were points in space-time where entangled-pair wavefronts of human consciousness *had already been*," said Orphu.

"Huh?" said Mahnmut.

"What is reality except a standing quantum wavefront collapsing through probability states?" asked Orphu. "How does the human mind work except as a sort of interferometer perceiving and collapsing those very wavefronts?"

Mahnmut still shook his head. He'd forgotten about the other moravecs standing on the bridge, forgotten that they might be taking his sub and the dropship down to Earth in less than three hours, forgotten the danger they were in . . . forgotten everything except the headache that his friend Orphu of Io was giving him.

"The post-humans were opening Brane Holes into alternate universes that had come into being through—or at least been perceived by—the focused lenses of pre-existing holographic wavefronts. Human imagination. Human genius."

"Oh for the Christ's sake," said General Beh bin Adee.

"Possibly," said Orphu. "If you assume an infinite or near-infinite set of alternate universes, then many of these have necessarily been imagined through the sheer force of human genius. Picture them as singularities of genius—Bell-state analyzers and editors of the pure quantum-foam of reality."

"That's metaphysics," said Cho Li in a shocked voice.

"That's bullshit," said Suma IV.

"No, that's what's happened here," said Orphu. "We have a terraformed Mars with altered gravity and are asked to believe that such terraforming could be achieved in a few years. *That's* bullshit. We have statues of Prospero on a Mars where Greek gods live atop Mount Olympos and commute through time and space to an alternate Earth where Achilles and Hector are fighting over the future of Ilium. *That's* bullshit. Unless . . ."

"Unless the post-humans opened portals to precisely those worlds and universes earlier imagined by the force of human genius," said Prime Integrator Asteague/Che. "Which would explain the Prospero statues, the Calibanish creatures on Earth, and the existence of Achilles, Hector, Agamemnon and all the other humans on Ilium-Earth."

"What about the Greek gods?" sneered Beh bin Adee. "Are we going to meet Jehovah and Buddha next?"

"We might," said Orphu of Io. "But I would suggest that the Olympian gods we met are transformed post-humans. That's where the post-humans disappeared to fourteen hundred years ago."

"Why would they choose to change into gods?" asked Retrograde Sinopessen. "Especially gods whose powers come from nanotechnology and quantum tricks?"

"Why would they not?" asked Orphu. "Immortality, choice of gender, sex with each other and any mortal they choose to mate with, breeding many divine and mortal offspring—which is something the post-humans could not seem to do on their own—not to mention the decade-long chess game that is the siege of Troy."

Mahnmut rubbed his head. "And the terraforming and gravity change on Mars . . ."

"Yes," said Orphu. "It probably took the larger part of fourteen hundred years, not three years. And that was with the gods' quantum technology at work."

"So there's a *real Prospero* down there or out there somewhere?" asked Mahnmut. "The Prospero from Shakespeare's *Tempest*?"

"Or something or someone close to it," said Orphu.

"What about the brain-monster that came through the Brane Hole on Earth just a few days ago?" asked Suma IV. The Ganymedan sounded angry. "Is *it* a hero in your precious human literature?"

"Possibly," said Orphu. "Robert Browning once wrote a poem called 'Caliban Upon Setebos' in which the monster Caliban from Shakespeare's *Tempest* ponders his god, a creature called Setebos, which Browning had Caliban describe only as 'the many-handed as a cuttlefish.' It was a god of arbitrary power that fed on fear and violence."

"That's quite a reach in speculation," said Asteague/Che.

"Yes," said Orphu. "But so is the creature we photographed that looks like a giant brain scuttling around on giant human hands. An improbable evolution in any universe, wouldn't you say? But Robert Browning had an impressive imagination."

"Are we going to meet Hamlet down there on Earth?" asked Suma IV with an audible sneer.

"Oh," said Mahnmut. "Oh. Oh, that would be nice."

"Let's not get carried away," said Prime Integrator Asteague/Che. "Orphu, where did you get this whole idea?"

Orphu sighed. Instead of responding verbally, a holographic projector in the comm pod atop the huge Ionian's pitted and scarred carapace created an image that floated above the chart table.

Six fat books sat in a virtual bookcase. One of the books—Mahnmut saw that it was titled *In Search of Lost Time—Volume III—The Guermantes Way*—fluttered open to page 445. The image zoomed in on the type on the page.

Mahnmut suddenly realized that Orphu was optically blind—he couldn't *see* what he was projecting. It meant that he had to have all of Proust's six volumes memorized. The idea made Mahnmut want to howl.

Mahnmut read along with the others as the font floated in midair—

> *"People of taste tell us nowadays that Renoir is a great eighteenth-century painter. But in so saying they forget the element of Time, and that it took a great deal of time, even at the height of the nineteenth century, for Renoir to be hailed as a great artist. To succeed thus in gaining recognition, the original painter or the original writer proceeds on the lines of the oculist. The course of treatment they give us by their painting or by their prose is not always pleasant. When it is at an end the practitioner says to us: 'Now look!' And, lo and behold, the world around us (which was not created once and for all, but is created afresh as often as an original artist is born) appears to us entirely different from the old world, but perfectly clear. Women pass in the street, different from those we formerly saw, because they are*

Renoirs, those Renoirs we persistently refused to see as women. The carriages, too, are Renoirs, and the water, and the sky; we feel tempted to go for a walk in the forest which is identical with the one which when we first saw it looked like anything in the world except a forest, like for instance a tapestry of innumerable hues but lacking precisely the hues peculiar to forests. Such is the new and perishable universe which has just been created. It will last until the next geological catastrophe is precipitated by a new painter or writer of original talent."

All the moravecs by the chart table stood in silence, broken only by the ventilator hums, machine sounds, and soft background communication of the moravecs actually flying the *Queen Mab* at that critical moment as they approached the equatorial and polar rings of Earth.

Finally General Beh bin Adee broke the silence—"What solipsistic nonsense. What metaphysical garbage. What total horse manure."

Orphu said nothing.

"Perhaps it is horse manure," said Prime Integrator Asteague/Che. "But it's the most plausible horse manure I've heard in the last nine months of surreality. And it's earned Orphu of Io a ride in the hold of the submersible *The Dark Lady* when the dropship separates and drops into the Earth's atmosphere in . . . two hours and fourteen minutes. Let us all go prepare."

Orphu and Mahnmut were heading for the elevator—Mahnmut walking in a sort of daze, the huge Orphu floating silently on his repellors—when Asteague/Che called out, "Orphu!"

The Ionian swiveled and waited, politely aiming his dead cameras and eye-stalks at the Prime Integrator.

"You were going to tell us who the Voice is that we rendezvous with today."

"Oh, well . . ." Mahnmut's friend sounded embarrassed for the first time. "That's just a guess."

"Share it," said Asteague/Che.

"Well, given my little theory," said Orphu, "who would demand in a female voice to see our passenger—Odysseus, son of Laertes?"

"Santa Claus?" suggested General bin Adee.

"Not quite," said Orphu. "Calypso."

None of the moravecs seemed to recognize the name.

"Or from the universe our other new friends came from," continued Orphu, "the enchantress also known as Circe."

62

Harman had drowned but was not dead. In a few minutes he would wish he were dead.

The water—the golden fluid—filling the dodecahedral crystal cabinet was hyperoxygenated. As soon as his lungs completely filled, oxygen began moving through the thin-walled capillaries of his lungs and reentering his bloodstream. It was enough to keep his heart beating—start beating again, one should say, since it had skipped beats and stopped for half a minute during his drowning process—and enough to keep his brain alive . . . dulled, terrified, seemingly disconnected from his body, but alive. He could not breathe in, his instincts still cried out for air, but his body was getting oxygen.

Opening his eyes was a huge struggle and all it rewarded him with was a swirling vision of a billion golden words and ten billion throbbing images waiting to be born in his brain. He was vaguely aware of the six-sided glass panel of the flooded crystal cabinet and of a blurrier shape beyond which might have been Moira, or perhaps Prospero, or even Ariel, but these things were not important.

He still wanted to breathe air the correct way. If he had not been only semiconscious—tranquilized by the liquid in preparation for the transfer—his gag reflex alone would probably have killed him or driven him insane.

But the crystal cabinet reserved other means for driving him insane.

The information began pouring into Harman now. Information, Moira and Prospero had said, from a million old books. Words and thoughts from almost a million long-dead minds, more, because every book contained multitudes of other minds in its arguments, its refutations, its fervent agreements, its furious revisions and rebellions.

Information began to pour in, but it was like nothing Harman had ever felt or experienced before. He had taught himself to read over many decades, becoming the first old-style human being in uncounted centuries to make sense of the squiggles and curves and dots in the old books moldering away on shelves everywhere. But words from a book flow into the mind in a linear fashion at the pace of conversation—Harman had always heard a voice not quite his own reading each word aloud in his own mind after he learned to read. Sigling was a more rapid but less effective way to absorb a book—the nanotech function flowed the data from books down one's arms into the brain like coal being shoveled into a hopper, without the slow pleasure and context of reading. And after sigling a book, Harman always found that some new data had arrived, but much of the meaning of the book had been lost due to absence of nuance and context. He never heard a voice in his head when sigling and often wondered if it had been designed as a function for oldstyles in the Lost Era to absorb tables of dry information, packets of predigested data. Sigling was not the way to read a novel or a Shakespearean play—although the first Shakespearean play Harman had encountered was an amazing and moving piece called *Romeo and Juliet*. Until Harman had read *Romeo and Juliet*, he'd not known that such a thing as a "play" existed—his people's only form of fictional entertainment had been the turin drama about the siege of Troy, and that only for the past decade.

But while reading was a slow, linear flow and sigling was like a sudden tickling of the brain that left a residue of information behind, this crystal cabinet was . . .

> *The Maiden caught me in the Wild*
> *Where I was dancing merrily*
> *She put me into her Cabinet*
> *And locked me up with a golden Key*

This information Harman was receiving was not entering through his eyes, ears, or any of the other human senses nature had evolved to bring data to the nerves and brain. It was not—strictly speaking—passing into him through touch, although the billion-billion pinpricks of information in the golden liquid passed through each pore of his skin and each cell of his flesh.

DNA, Harman knew now, likes the standard double helix model. Evolution had chosen the double helix for a variety of reasons to carry its most sacred cargo, but primarily because it was the easiest and most effective way for free energy to flow—forward or back—as that energy determines the folds, joins, forms, and function of such gigantic molecules as proteins, RNA, and DNA. Chemical systems always move toward the state of lowest free energy, and free energy is minimized when two complementary strands of nucleotides pair up like a double Shaker staircase.

But the post-humans who had redesigned the hardware and software of Harman's branch of the old-style human genome had redesigned a sizeable percentage of the redundant DNA in his decanted species' bodies. Instead of right-handed twisting B-DNA, the post-humans had set in place left-handed Z-DNA double helixes of the usual size, about two nanometers in diameter. They used these Z-DNA molecules as keystones, lifting from them a scaffolding of more complex DNA helixes such as double-crossover molecules, tying these ropes of DX DNA together into leakproof protein cages. Within those billions upon billions of scaffolded protein cages deep within Harman's bones, muscle fibers, gut tissue, testicles, toes, and hair follicles were biological reception and organizing macromolecules serving still more complex caged clusters of nanoelectronic organic memory storage clusters.

Harman's entire body—every cell—was eating the Taj Moira's library of a million volumes.

> The Cabinet is formed of Gold
> And Pearl & Crystal shining bright
> And within it opens into a World
> And a little lovely Moony Night

The process hurt. It hurt a lot. Drowned and floating belly-up now like a dead carp in the golden liquid of the crystal cabinet, Harman felt the pain of a leg or arm that had gone to sleep and that was slowly, painfully coming awake again—the limb being pricked by ten thousand sharp, hot needles. But this was not just his leg or his arm. Cells in every part of his body, cells on every surface inside and out, molecules in every cell's nucleus and every cell's wall, were awakening to the data flowing the free energy route through the Yan-Shen-Yurke DNA circuits everywhere in the collective organism called Harman.

It hurt beyond Harman's ability to imagine or contain such hurt. He opened his mouth repeatedly to scream from the pain, but there was no air in his lungs, no air around him, and his vocal cords merely vibrated in the golden liquid in which he'd drowned.

Metallic nanoparticles, carbon nanotubes, and more complex nanoelectronic devices everywhere in Harman's body and brain, elements that had been there since before his birth, felt current, were polarized, rotated, realigned in three dimensions, and began conducting and storing information, each complex DNA bridge out of the trillions waiting in Harman's cells rotating, realigning, recombining, and securing data across the DNA backbone of his most essential structure.

Harman could see Moira's face near the glass, her dark Savi-eyes peering in, her crystal-warped expression expressing something—anxiety? Remorse? Sheer curiosity?

> Another England there I saw
> Another London with its Tower
> Another Thames & other Hills
> And another pleasant Surrey Bower

Books—Harman realized through the Niagral cascade of pain—were merely nodes in a near-infinite matrix of information that exists in four dimensions, evolving toward the idea of the concept of the approximation of the shadow of Truth vertically through time as well as longitudinally through knowledge.

As a child in his crèche, Harman had taken rare sheets of vellum and even more rare markers called pencils and covered the sheets with dots, then spent hours trying to connect all the dots with lines. There always seemed to be another possible line to draw, another two dots to connect, and before he was done the sheet of creamy vellum had become an almost solid smear of graphite. In later years, Harman had wondered if his young mind had been trying to capture and express his perception of the fax portals he had stepped through since he was old enough to walk—old enough to be carried by his mother, actually. Nine million combinations rising from three hundred known faxnode pavilions.

But this connect-the-dots of information to storage macromolecule cages was thousands of times more complex and infinitely more painful.

> Another Maiden like herself
> Translucent lovely shining clear
> Threefold each in the other closed—
> O what a trembling fear
>
> O what a smile! a threefold Smile
> Filled me, that like a flame I burnd
> I bent to Kiss the lovely Maid
> And found a Threefold Kiss returnd

Harman knew now that William Blake had made his living as an engraver, and not that popular or successful an engraver at that. [*Everything is context.*] Blake died on a hot and muggy Sunday evening—August 12, 1827—and on the day of his death, almost no one in the general public knew that the quiet but often angry engraver had been a poet respected by several of his better known contemporaries, including Samuel Coleridge. [*Context is to data what water is to a dolphin.*] [*Dolphins were a species of aquatic animal driven to extinction early in the Twenty-second Century A.D.*] William Blake quite literally considered himself a prophet along the lines of Ezekiel or Isaiah, although he held nothing but contempt for the mysticisms, dabblings in the occult, or theosophies so popular in his day. [*Ezekiel Mao Kent was the name of the marine biologist who was by the side of Almorenian d'Azure, the last dolphin, who died of cancer in the Bengal Oceanarium on the hot, muggy evening of August 11, 2134 A.D. The N.U.N. Applied Species Committee decided not to replenish the family* Delphinidae *from stored DNA but, rather, to let the species join all other* Delphinidae *and other great marine-cetacean mammals in peaceful extinction.*]

The data itself, Harman found as he stared, naked, out from the center of his own crystal, was tolerable. It was the constant nerve-web-expanding pain of context that would kill him.

> *I strove to sieze the inmost Form*
> *With ardor fierce & hands of flame*
> *But burst the Crystal Cabinet*
> *And like a Weeping Babe became*
>
> *A weeping Babe upon the wild*
> *And Weeping Woman pale reclind*
> *And in the outward air again*
> *I filld with woes the passing Wind*

Harman reached the limit of his ability to absorb such pain and complexity. He stirred his limbs in the thick, gold liquid, found that he had less mobility than an embryo, that his fingers had turned to fins, that his muscles had atrophied to weak rags, and that this pain was the true medium and placental fluid of the universe.

I am not a tabula rasa!! he wanted to scream at that bastard Prospero and that ultimate bitch Moira. This would kill him.

Heaven and Hell are born together, Harman thought and knew Blake had thought it first, knowing that Blake had thought it in refutation to Swedenborg's Calvinistic belief in Predestination:

> *Truly My Satan thou art but a Dunce*
> *And dost not know the Garment from the Man*

Stop that! Stop it! Please God

Tho thou art Worshiped by the Names Divine
Of Jesus & Jehovah: thou art still
The Son of Morn in weary Nights decline
The lost Travellers Dream under the Hill

Harman screamed despite the fact that there was no air in his lungs to form the scream, no air in his throat to allow the scream, and no air in the tank to conduct the scream. [*The naked device, one of six trillion, consists of four double helixes connected in the middle by two unpaired DNA strands. The crossover region can assume two different states—the universe often enjoys assuming a binary form. Rotating the two helixes a half turn on one side of the central bridge junction creates the so-called PX or paranemic crossover state.*] Do this three billion times per second and one achieves a purity of torture never dreamt of by the most fanatical designers of the Inquisition's most ingenious racks, clamps, extractors, and sharp edges.

Harman tried to scream again.

Fifteen seconds had now elapsed since the transfer had begun.

Forty-four minutes and forty-five seconds remained.

My name is Thomas Hockenberry. I have a Ph.D. in classical studies. I specialize in studying, writing about, and teaching Homer's *Iliad*.

For almost thirty years I was a professor, the last decade and a half at Indiana University in Bloomington, Indiana. Then I died. I awoke—or was resurrected—on Mount Olympos—or what the beings posing as gods there called Mount Olympos, although I later discovered it was the great shield volcano on Mars, Olympus Mons. These beings, these gods, or *their* superior beings—personalities I've heard of but know little or nothing about, one of them named Prospero, as in Shakespeare's *The Tempest*—reconstructed me to be a scholic, an observer of the Trojan War. I reported for ten years to one of the Muses, recording my daily accounts on speaking stones, for even the gods there are preliterate. I'm recording this on a small, solid-state electronic recorder that I stole from the moravec ship the *Queen Mab.*

Last year—just nine months ago—everything went to hell and the Trojan War as described in Homer's *Iliad* ran off the rails. Since then there has been confusion, an alliance between Achilles and Hector—and thus between all Trojans and Greeks—to wage war against the gods, more confusion, betrayals, a closure of the last Brane Hole that connected present-day Mars to ancient Ilium and that caused the moravec troopers and technicians to flee this Ilium Earth. With Achilles gone—disappeared on the other side of the Brane Hole on a now-distant Mars of the future—the Trojan War resumed, Zeus disappeared, and in his absence the gods and goddesses came down to fight alongside their respective champions. For a while it looked as if Agamemnon and Menelaus' armies had penetrated Troy. Diomedes was on the verge of capturing the city. Then Hector came out of sulking seclusion—interesting how that part of our recent story parallels Achilles' long sulk in his tent in the real *Iliad*—and Priam's son promptly killed the seemingly invulnerable Diomedes in single combat.

On the next day, I'm told, Hector bested Ajax—Big Ajax, Great Ajax, the Ajax from Salamis. Helen tells me that Ajax begged for his life but Hector slew him without mercy. Menelaus—Helen's former husband and the aggrieved party who started this goddamned war—died with an arrow in the brain that same day.

Then, as I'd seen so many hundreds of times before in my more than ten years here watching, the initiative of battle swung once again, the gods supporting the Achaeans led the counterattack behind goddesses Athena and Hera, with roaring Poseidon destroying buildings in Ilium, and for a while Hector and his men were in retreat to the city again. I'm told that Hector carried his wounded brother, the heroic Deiphobus, on his back.

But two days ago, just as Troy was on the verge of falling yet again—this time to a combined attack of infuriated Achaeans and the most powerful and ruthless gods and goddesses, Athena, Hera, Poseidon, and their ilk beating back Apollo and the other gods defending the city—Zeus reappeared.

Helen tells me that Zeus blasted Hera to bits, dropped Poseidon into the hellpit of Tartarus, and commanded the rest of the gods back to Olympos. She says that the once-mighty gods, scores and scores of them, in their flying golden chariots and in their fine golden armor, went obediently quantum teleporting back to Olympos like guilty children awaiting their father's spankings.

And now the Greeks are getting their asses kicked. Zeus himself, rising taller, Helen says, than the towering stratocumulus, killed thousands of Argives, drove the rest back to the ships and then burned their ships with bolts of his lightning. Helen says that the Lord of Gods commanded a huge wave to roll in, a wave that sank the blackened hulks of the ships. Then Zeus himself disappeared and has not returned since.

Two weeks later—after both sides lit corpse fires for the thousands of their fallen and observed their nine-day funeral rituals—Hector led a successful counterattack that has driven the Greeks even farther back. It appears that about thirty thousand of the original hundred thousand or so Argive fighters have survived, many of them—like their king Agamemnon—wounded and dispirited. With no ships for escape and no way to get their axemen to the wooded slopes of Mount Ida to cut wood for new ships, they've done the best they could—digging deep trenches, lining them with stakes, throwing up wooden revetments, digging a series of connecting trenches within their own lines, building up sand berms, massing their shields and spears and deadly archers in a solid wall around this dwindling semicircle of death. It's the Greeks' last stand.

It is now the third morning since my arrival and I am standing in the Greek encampment, a trenched and walled arc little more than a quarter of a mile around with the thirty thousand miserable Achaeans massed and huddled here by the smoldering ruins of their ships. Their backs are to the sea.

Hector has every advantage—an almost four-to-one ratio of men who have better morale and adequate food—the Greeks are beginning to starve even while they can smell the pigs and cattle roasting over the Trojan siege fires. Helen and King Priam had been sure that the Greeks would be defeated two days ago, but desperate men are brave men—men with nothing to lose—and the Greeks have been fighting like cornered rats. They also have had the advantage of shorter interior lines and fighting from behind fixed defenses, although admittedly these advantages will be short-lived with food running out, no permanent supply of water here since the Trojans damned up the river a mile from the beach, and typhoid beginning to spread within the crowded and unsanitary Achaean encampment.

Agamemnon is not fighting. For three days the son of Atreus, king of Mycenae, and commander in chief of this once-huge expeditionary force, has been hiding in his tent. Helen reported to me that Agamemnon had been wounded during the general Greek retreat, but I hear from captains and guards here in the camp that it was only a broken left forearm, nothing life-threatening. It seems that it was Agamemnon's morale that was critically wounded. The great king—Achilles' nemesis—had not been able to recover Menelaus' body when his brother was struck down by the arrow through the eye, and while Diomedes, Big Ajax, and the other fallen Greek heroes received proper funerals and cremations on their tall biers near the shore, Menelaus' body was last seen being dragged behind Hector's chariot around the cheering-crowded walls of Ilium. It seems to have been the last straw for the high-strung and arrogant Agamemnon. Rather than being enraged into a fury of fighting, Agamemnon has sunk into depression and denial.

The other Greeks have not needed his leadership to know that they have to fight for their lives. Their command structure has been sorely thinned—Big Ajax dead, Diomedes dead, Menelaus dead, Achilles and Odysseus both disappeared on the other side of the closed Brane Hole— but gabby old Nestor has led most of the fighting for the last two days. The once revered warrior has become revered once again, at least among the thinning ranks of Achaeans, appearing on his four-horsed chariot wherever the Greek lines appeared ready to give way, urging trench engineers to replace stakes and redig collapsed areas, improving the internal trenches with sand berms and firing slits, sending men and boys out as scouts at night to steal water from the Trojans, and always calling for the men to have heart. Nestor's sons Antilochus and Thrasymedes, who had few valorous moments during the first ten years of the war or during the short war with the gods, have fought splendidly the last two days. Thrasymedes was wounded twice yesterday, once by a spear and again by an arrow in the shoulder, but he fought on, leading his Pylian brigades to push back a Trojan offensive that had threatened to cut the defensive semicircle here in half.

It's just after sunrise here on the third day—quite possibly the last day, since the Trojans were moving, shifting forces, bringing up more troops, chariots, and trench-bridging equipment all during the night— and more than a hundred thousand relatively fresh Trojan troops are massing around the defensive perimeter even as I speak.

I've brought the recorder here to Agamemnon's camp because Nestor has called a council of his surviving war chieftains. At least those that can be spared from their fighting positions. These tired and filthy men ignore my presence—or rather, they probably remember that I spent much time with and near Achilles during the eight-month war with the gods, so they *accept* my presence. And the sight of this wafer-sized recorder in my hand means nothing to them.

I no longer know for whom I'm observing and recording these things—I imagine that I would be the ultimate persona non grata if I were to show up on Olympos and hand this recording chip to one of the Muses who sought to kill me—so I will make these observations and record this recording only as the scholar I once was, not as the slave-scholic they turned me into. And even if I am no longer a scholar, I can serve as a war correspondent in these last hours of the last stand of the Greeks and the end of this heroic era.

NESTOR

What is the news? And do you think your men will hold the line today?

IDOMENEUS

(Commander of the Crete contingent. The last time I saw Idomeneus, he had just killed the Amazon Bremusa with a spearcast. Moments later, the Brane Hole closed. Idomeneus was among the last to abandon Achilles.)

The news is bad from my part of the line, Noble Nestor. For every Trojan we've killed in the last two days, three more have taken his place in the night. They ready their trench-filling tools and spears for the attack. Their archers are still massing. It will be decisive today.

LITTLE AJAX

(As different as the Aeantes—the two Ajaxes—had been, they had been as close as brothers. I have never seen this Ajax of Locris look so grim. The grooves and wrinkles on his face are so outlined in mud and blood that they resemble a kabuki mask.)

Nestor, son of Neleus, hero of these darkest of times, my Locris fighters engaged the enemy through much of the night as Deiphobus' scouts tried to flank us on the north end of the perimeter. We fought them back until the surf ran red. Our section of trench is filling up with our own and the Trojan dead until they soon will be able to walk across on bodies heaped ten feet high. A third of my men are dead, the rest exhausted. Hector has sent new troops to replace his losses.

NESTOR

Podalirius, how goes it with the remaining son of Atreus?

PODALIRIUS

(The son of Asclepius is one of the last healers left to the Greeks. He is also co-commander, along with his brother Machaon, of the Thessalians from Tricca.)

Noble Nestor, Agamemnon's arm has been set in a splint, he has taken no herbs for the pain, and he is awake and rational.

NESTOR

Why is it then that he has not emerged from his tent? His corps is the largest left to our army, but they shelter in the center like women. Their hearts are gone without their leader.

PODALIRIUS
Their leader's heart is gone without his brother Menelaus.

TEUCER
(The master archer, half brother and dearest friend to the murdered Big Ajax.)

Then Achilles was right ten months ago when he confronted Agamemnon in all our sight and told the great king he has the heart of a fawn. (Spits into the sand.)

EUMELUS
(Son of Admetus and Alcestis, commander of the Thessalians from Phereae. Often referred to by the missing Achilles and Odysseus as "lord of men.")

And where is the accuser Achilles? The coward stayed behind at the base of Mount Olympos rather than face his death here with his comrades. The fleet-footed mankiller turned out also to have the heart—and hooves—of a fawn.

MENESTHIUS
(The huge captain of the Myrmidons, a former lieutenant of Achilles'.)

I'll kill any man who says that about the son of Peleus. He would never abandon us of his own free will. We all saw and heard the goddess Athena tell Achilles that he had been enchanted by Aphrodite's spell.

EUMELUS
Enchanted by Amazon pussy, you mean.

(Menesthius steps toward Eumelus and begins to draw his sword.)

NESTOR
(Stepping between them.)

Enough! Aren't the Trojans killing us quickly enough, or do we need to add to our own slaughter? Eumelus, step back! Menesthius, sheath your sword!

PODALIRIUS
(Speaking as the Achaean's last healer now, not as Agamemnon's personal doctor.)

PODALIRIUS *(cont.)*

What's killing us is the disease. Another two hundred dead, especially among the Epeans who are defending the riverbank to the south.

POLYXINUS
(Son of Agasthenes, co-commander of the Epeans.)

This is true, Lord Nestor. At least two hundred dead and another thousand too sick to fight.

DRESEUS
(Captain of the Epeans, just raised to the rank of commander.)

Half my men did not respond to muster this morning, Lord Nestor.

PODALIRIUS

And it's spreading.

AMPHION
(Another recently promoted captain of the Epeans.)

It's Phoebus Apollo's Silver Bow striking us down, just as it was ten months ago when the god-spread disease had corpse fires burning every night. It's what led to the first falling-out between Achilles and Agamemnon—it's what led to all our woes.

PODALIRIUS

Oh, fuck Phoebus Apollo and his Silver Bow. The gods—including Zeus—did their worst to us and now they're gone, and only they know if they're coming back. Personally, I don't care if they do or don't. These deaths, this disease, didn't come from Apollo's Silver Bow—I think it comes from the foul water the men are drinking. We're drinking our own piss and sitting in our own excrement here. My father, Asclepius, had this theory of origins of disease in contaminated water and . . .

NESTOR

Learned Podalirius, we will rejoice to hear your father's theory of disease at another time. Right now I need to know if we can hold off the Trojans today and what, if anything, my captains advise us to do.

ECHEPOLUS

(Son of Anchises)

We should surrender.

THRASYMEDES

(Nestor's son who had fought so valiantly the day before. His wounds are bandaged and bound up, but he appears to be suffering from them more today than in the heat of yesterday's long fight.)

Surrender, my ass! Who is in our circle of Argives that so cowers from fear that he suggests craven surrender? Surrender to me, son of Anchises, and I'll put you out of your misery as quickly as the Trojans certainly will.

ECHEPOLUS

Hector is an honorable man. King Priam used to be an honorable man, and may well still be. I traveled with Odysseus to Troy when the Ithacan came to reason with Priam, to try to get Helen back through talk to avoid this war, and both Priam and Hector were reasonable, honorable men. Hector will hear our surrender.

THRASYMEDES

That was eleven years and a hundred thousand souls sent down to Hades ago, you fool. You saw the extent of Hector's mercy when Ajax the Great begged and pleaded for his life, his long shield hammered into tin, snot and tears rolling down our hero's face. Hector severed his spine and hacked out his heart. His men probably won't be so merciful to you.

NESTOR

I know there has been talk of surrender. But Thrasymedes is correct—too much blood has been spilled on this Trojan soil to hold out any hope for mercy. We would have given the citizens of Ilium none, would we, had we but breached their walls to more success three weeks ago—or ten years ago? All of you here know that we would have killed every man old enough or young enough to lift a sword or bow, slaughtered their old men for spawning our enemies, raped their women, carried all their surviving women and children into a life of slavery, and put the torch to their city and their temples. But the gods . . . or the Fates . . . whoever is deciding the outcome of this war, have turned against us. We cannot expect from the Trojans, who suffered our invasion and our ten years of siege, more mercy than we would have granted them. No, tell your men, if you hear these murmurings, that it is madness to surrender. Better to die on your feet than on your knees.

IDOMENEUS

Better to not die at all. Is there no plan to save ourselves?

ALASTOR

(Teucer's commander)

The ships are burned. The food is running out, but we will all be dead of thirst before we starve. Disease claims more every hour.

MENESTHIUS

My Myrmidons want to break out—fight our way through the Trojan lines and make for the south—to Mount Ida and the heavy forests there.

NESTOR

(nodding)

Your Myrmidons are not the only ones thinking about breaking out and escaping, brave Menesthius. But your Myrmidons cannot do it alone. None of our tribes or groups can. The Trojan lines stretch back for miles and their allies' lines go deeper. They expect us to try to break out. They're probably wondering why we haven't tried it before this. You know the iron laws of combat with sword, shield, and spear, Menesthius—all Myrmidons and Achaeans know it—for every man who falls in shield-to-shield combat, a hundred are slaughtered while fleeing. We have no working chariots left— Hector's chiefs have hundreds. They'll run us down and slaughter us like sheep before we cross the dried bed of the River Scamander.

DRESEUS

So we stay? And die here today or tomorrow on the beach next to the charred timbers of our great black ships?

ANTILOCHUS

(Nestor's other son)

No. Surrender is out of the question for any man here with balls, and defense of this position will be untenable in a few hours—it may be untenable during the next attack—but I say we all try to break out at the same time. We have thirty thousand fighting men left—more than twenty thousand well enough to fight and run. Four out of five of us may fall, verily—be slaughtered like sheep before we reach the concealing forests of Mount Ida—but at those odds, four or five thousand of us will survive. Half that number may even survive the searches of the forest for us which the Trojans and their allies will carry out, like royalty pursuing a stag, and half that remaining number may find their way off this goddamned continent and cross the wine-dark seas to home. Those odds are good enough for me.

THRASYMEDES

And for me.

TEUCER

Any odds are better than the certainty of our bones bleaching on this fucking goddamned motherfucking shit-eating piss-drinking beach.

NESTOR

Was that a vote for breaking out, son of Telemon?

TEUCER

You're fucking goddamned right it was, Lord Nestor.

NESTOR

Noble Epeus, you've had no voice in this council yet. What do you think?

EPEUS

(Shuffling his feet and looking down in embarrassment. Epeus is the best boxer of all the Achaeans, and his face and shaved head show his years at the sport—cauliflower ears, a flattened nose, permanent scar tissue on his cheeks and brow ridges, countless scars even on his scalp. I cannot fail to see the irony in Epeus' position in this council and my own effect on his life and fate. Never famed for his battle prowess, Epeus would have won the boxing matches in Patroclus' funeral games—held by Achilles—and been the master builder of the Odysseus-conceived wooden horse if I had not begun screwing up the Homeric version of this story almost a year ago. As it stands now, Epeus is in the council of chieftains only because all his commanding officers—up to Menelaus—have been killed.)

Lord Nestor, when one's opponent is most confident, when he crosses the fighting space toward you with certainty in his heart that you are down for the count, unable to rise, that is the best time to strike him hard. In this case, strike him hard, stun him, knock him back on his heels, and run for our lives. I was at the Games once when a boxer did just that.

(Laughter all around at this.)

EPEUS
But it will have to be at night.

NESTOR
I agree. The Trojans see too far and ride their chariots too quickly for us to have a fighting chance in the daylight.

MERIONES
(Son of Molus, close comrade of Idomeneus, second in command of the Cretans.)

We won't have a much better chance in the moonlight. The moon is three-quarters full.

LAERCES
(A Myrmidon, son of Haeman)

But the winter sun sets earlier and the moon rises later this week. We will have almost three hours from the beginning of real darkness—the kind of darkness where you need a torch to find your way—and the rising of the moon.

NESTOR
The question is, can we hold through the hours of daylight today and will our men have enough energy left in them to fight—we'll have to concentrate our attack and hit hard to forge a hole in the Trojan lines—and enough energy left then to run the twenty miles and more to the forests of Mount Ida?

IDOMENEUS
They'll have the energy to fight today if they know they might have a chance to live tonight. I say we hit the Trojans right in the center of their lines—right where Hector leads—since he's concentrated his strength on both flanks for today's fighting. I say we break out tonight.

NESTOR
The rest of you? I need to hear from everyone here. It's truly all or nothing, everyone or no one in this attempt.

PODALIRIUS

We'll have to leave our sick and wounded behind, and there will be thousands more of these by nightfall. The Trojans will slaughter them. Perhaps do worse than mere slaughter in their frustration if any of us gets away.

NESTOR

Yes. But such are the vagaries of war and fate. I need to hear your votes, Noble Chiefs of the Achaeans.

THRASYMEDES

Aye. We go for it all tonight. And may the gods watch over those left behind and those captured later.

TEUCER

Fuck the gods up the ass. I say yes, if our fate is to die here on this stinking beach, I say we defy the Fates. Go tonight at fall of true dark.

POLYXINUS

Yes.

ALASTOR

Yes. Tonight.

LITTLE AJAX

Aye.

EUMELUS

Yes. All or nothing.

MENESTHIUS

If my lord Achilles were here, he'd go for Hector's throat. Maybe we can get lucky and kill the son of a bitch on our way out.

NESTOR

Another vote for breaking out. Echepolus?

ECHEPOLUS

I think we'll all die if we stay and fight another day. I think we'll all die if we try to escape. I for one choose to stay with the wounded and offer my surrender to Hector, trusting in the hope that some shards of his former honor and sense of mercy have survived. But I will tell my men that they can make up their own minds.

NESTOR

No, Echepolus. Most of the men will follow their commander's lead. You can stay behind and surrender, but I'm relieving you of your command and appointing Amphion in your place. You can go straight from this meeting to the tent where the wounded wait, but speak to no one. Your brigade is small enough and it is on Amphion's left on the line . . . the two can merge with no confusion or need to reposition troops. That is, I am promoting Amphion if Amphion votes to fight our way out tonight.

AMPHION

I so vote.

DRESEUS

I vote for my Epeans—we fight and die tonight, or fight and escape. I for one want to see my home and family again.

EUMELUS

Agamemnon's men told us, and the moravec things confirmed it, that our cities and homes were empty, our kingdoms now unpopulated—our people stolen away by Zeus.

DRESEUS

To which I say fuck Agamemnon, fuck the moravec toys, and fuck Zeus. I plan to go home to see if my family is waiting. I believe they are.

POLYPOETES
(Another son of Agasthenes, co-commander of the Lapiths from Argissa)

My men will hold the line today and lead the fight out tonight. I swear this by all the gods.

TEUCER

Couldn't you swear by something a little more constant? Like your bowels?

(Laughter around the circle)

NESTOR

It's agreed, then, and I concur. We'll do everything in our power to hold back the Trojan onslaught today. To that end, Po-

dalirius, oversee the serving out of all rations this morning except
for what a man can carry in his tunic tonight. And double the
morning's water rations. Go through Agamemnon's and dead
Menelaus' private stores, pull out anything edible. Commanders,
tell your men before this morning's battle that all they have to do
today is hold—hold for their lives, die only for their comrades'
lives—and we will attack tonight at true dark. Some of us will
reach the forest and—Fates willing—our homes and families
again. Or, failing that, our names will be written in gold words of
glory that will last forever. Our children's grandchildren's grandchildren will visit our burial mounds here in this accursed land
and say—"Aye, they were men in those days." So tell your ser-
geants and their men to breakfast well this morning, for most of
us will eat dinner in the Halls of the Dead. So tonight, when it's
true dark and before the moon arises, I will authorize our favorite
pugilist—Epeus—to ride up and down our lines, shouting
Ápete—just as they do to start the chariot races and footraces at
the Games. And then we'll be off to our freedom!

*(And that should have been the end of the meeting—and a rousing end
it was, for Nestor is a born leader and knows how to wrap up a meeting
with action items and energy, something my department chair at Indiana University never understood—but, as always, someone breaks the
perfect rhythm of the perfect script. In this case, that someone is Teucer.)*

TEUCER

Epeus, noble boxer, you never told us the end of your story.
Whatever happened to that Olympics boxer who stunned his opponent and then ran out of the arena?

EPEUS
(Who as everyone knows is more honest than wise)

Oh, him. The Olympics priests hunted him down in the woods
and killed him like a dog.

The Achaean chieftains have dispersed, gone back to their lines and
their men. Nestor has left with his sons. The healer Podalirius has put together a detail of men to sack Agamemnon's tent in a search for food and
wine. I'm left alone here on the beach—or at least as alone as one can be
when pressed cheek to jowl with thirty thousand other unwashed men
all reeking of sweat and fear.

I touch the QT medallion under my tunic. Nestor did not ask for my
vote. None of the Achaean heroes so much as looked at me during that

entire debate. They know I don't fight and they seem to like me no less for it—it's the way these ancient Greeks treat men who like to dress up in women's clothing and paint their faces white. There is no dishonor there in most of these men's eyes, only dismissal. I'm a freak to them, an outsider, something less than a man.

I know I'm not going to stay until the bitter end. I doubt if I'll stay during today's battle since the air here will grow dark with volleys of arrows in the next half hour. I don't have the morphing gear and impact armor that I had as a scholic—I haven't even donned the metal or leather armor that's so available from Achaean corpses all around me. If I stay, I doubt I'd last the day—the last two days have been a series of craven hours and timid cowering for me here, near the back of the line, near the tent where the wounded are dying. If I were to survive the day, my chances of surviving the attack on the Trojans after dark would be near zero.

And why would I stay? I have a quantum teleportation device hanging around my neck, for Christ's sake. I could be in Helen's chambers in two seconds, relaxing in a hot bath there in five minutes.

Why would I stay?

But I'm not ready to go. Not quite yet. I'm no longer a scholic and there may be no purpose to being a scholar here, but even as a war correspondent who will never be able to report his observations, this last glorious day of a lost glorious epoch is too interesting to miss.

I'll stay for a while.

The horns are blowing everywhere. No one's had time for those promised big breakfasts yet, but the Trojans are attacking all along the line.

64

To know that everything in the universe—everything in history, everything in science, everything in poetry and art and music, every person, place, thing, and idea—is connected, that is one thing. To experience that connection, even incompletely, that is quite another.

Harman was unconscious for most of nine days. When he wasn't unconscious, he was awake only briefly and then screaming in pain from a headache beyond all capacity of his skull and brain to contain it. He threw up a lot. Then he would lapse into coma again.

On the ninth day he awoke. The headache rolled over him, worse than any headache he had ever experienced, but no longer the scream-maker of his nine-day nightmare. The nausea was gone and his stomach was empty. He'd later realize that he'd lost more than twenty-five pounds. He was naked and lying in the bed on the second floor of the *eiffelbahn* cablecar.

The cablecar is designed and decorated mostly in art noveau, he thought as he staggered out of bed and pulled on a silk dressing gown that had been thrown over the arm of the overstuffed Empire-era armchair next to the bed. He wondered idly where in the world anyone was raising worms to make silk—had it been one of the servitors' duties these long centuries of human idleness? Was it being artificially created in some in-dustrial vat somewhere, the way the post-humans had created—recreated, actually—his race of nano-altered human stock? Harman's head hurt too much to ponder the thought now.

He paused on the mezzanine, closed his eyes, and concentrated. Nothing. He remained in the cablecar. He tried again. Nothing.

Staggering slightly, dizzy now, he went down the wrought-iron metal staircase to the first floor and collapsed into the only chair at the table near the window. The table was covered with white linen.

Harman said nothing as Moira brought out orange juice in a crystal glass, black coffee in a white thermidor, and a poached egg with a bit of salmon on the side. She poured the coffee into his cup. Harman lowered his head slightly to allow the heat from the coffee to rise against his face.

"Come here often?" asked Moira.

Prospero came into the room and stood in the brilliant and despica-ble morning light that was streaming in through the glass doors. "Ah, Harman . . . or should we call you New Man? It is a pleasure to see you awake and ambulatory."

"Shut up," said Harman, ignoring the food, sipping the coffee gin-gerly. He knew now that Prospero was a hologram, but a physical one—a logosphere avatar forming himself from microsecond to microsecond with matter being beamed down from one of the mass-fax-accumulators in orbit. He also knew that if he tried to strike or attack the old magus, the matter would turn to untouchable projection faster than any human reflexes.

"You knew that my chances of surviving the crystal cabinet were about one in a hundred," said Harman, not even looking at Prospero. The light there was too bright.

"A little better than that, I think," said the magus, mercifully drawing the heavy drapes.

Moira pulled a chair over and sat at the table with Harman. She was wearing a red tunic, but otherwise showed the same hardy adventure clothing she had been wearing in the Taj.

Harman looked unblinkingly at her. "You knew the young Savi. You attended the Final Fax Party in the New York Archipelago at the flooded Empire State Building, and you told her friends you hadn't seen her, but you'd actually visited Savi at her home in Antarctica just two days before."

"How on earth do you know that?" asked Moira.

"Savi's friend Petra wrote a short essay about their attempt—mostly hers and her lover Pinchas'—to find Savi. It was printed and bound up right before the Final Fax. Somehow it found its way into your friend Ferdinand Mark Alonzo's library."

"But how would Petra have known that I visited Savi before the New York Archipelago party?"

"I think she and Pinchas found something Savi had written when they went through her Mount Erebus apartments," said Harman. The coffee did not come back up on him, but it didn't help his throbbing headache much either.

"So you know everything about everything now, do you?" asked Moira.

Harman laughed and regretted it almost immediately. He put down the coffee cup and held his right temple. "No," he said at last, "I know just enough to know that I don't know much of anything about anything. Besides, there are forty-one other libraries sprinkled around the Earth whose crystal cabinets I haven't visited yet."

"That *would* kill you," said Prospero.

Harman wouldn't have minded at that moment if someone had killed him. The headache put a pulsing corona around everything and everyone he tried to look at. He sipped more coffee and hoped that the nausea wouldn't come back. The cablecar creaked along, although he knew that it was traveling at more than two hundred miles per hour. Its slight swaying back and forth did nothing to keep his stomach settled. "Would you like to hear all about Alexandre-Gustave Eiffel? Born in Dijon on December 15, 1832 A.D. Graduated from the École Centrale des Arts et Manufactures in 1855. Before coming up with the idea for his tower at the 1889 Centennial Exposition, he'd already designed the movable dome of the observatory at Nice and the framework for the Statue of Liberty in New York. He . . ."

"Stop it," snapped Moira. "No one likes a showoff."

"Where the hell are we?" asked Harman. He managed to get to his feet and shove back the drapes. They were passing through a beautiful wooded valley, the car moving along more than seven hundred feet above a winding river. Ancient ruins—a castle of some sort—were just visible along a ridgeline.

"We've just passed Cahors," said Prospero. "We should be swinging south toward Lourdes at the next tower switching station."

Harman rubbed his eyes but opened the glass door and stepped out. The forcefield deployed along the leading edge of the flat-sided cablecar kept him from being blown off the balcony. "What's the matter?" he asked back through the open door. "Don't you want to head north and visit your friend's blue-ice cathedral?"

Moira looked startled. "How could you possibly know about that? There was no book in the Taj with that . . ."

"No," agreed Harman, "but my friend Daeman saw the beginnings of that—the arrival of Setebos. I know from the books what the Many-Handed would do after he arrived in Paris Crater. So he's still here . . . on Earth, I mean?"

"Yes," said Prospero. "And he is no friend of ours."

Harman shrugged. "You two brought him here the first time. Him and the others."

"It was not our intention," said Moira.

Harman had to laugh at that, no matter how much it made his head throb. "No, right," said Harman. "You open an interdimensional door into darkness, leave it open, and then say 'It was not our intention' when something really vile comes through."

"You've learned much," said Prospero, "but you still do not understand all that you will have to if . . ."

"Yeah, yeah," said Harman. "I'd listen to you more closely, Prospero, if I didn't know that you're mostly one of those things that came through the door. The post-humans spend a thousand years trying to contact Alien Others—changing the quantum setup of the entire solar system in the process—and get a many-handed brain and a retread cybervirus from a Shakespearean play instead."

The old magus smiled at this. Moira shook her head in irritation, poured some coffee into a second cup, and drank without comment.

"Even if we wanted to drop by and say hello to Setebos," said Prospero, "we could not. Paris Crater has no tower—has not had one since before the rubicon virus."

"Yeah," said Harman. He went back in, but stood looking out while he lifted his own cup and sipped coffee. "Why can't I freefax?" he asked sharply.

"What?" said Moira.

"Why can't I freefax? I know how to summon the function now without the training wheels symbol triggers, but it didn't work when I got up. I want to jump back to Ardis."

"Setebos shut down the planetary fax system," said Prospero. "That includes freefaxing as well as the faxnode pavilions."

Harman nodded and rubbed his cheek and chin. A week and a half of stubble, almost a real beard, rasped under his fingers. "So you two, and presumably Ariel, can still quantum teleport, but I'm stuck on this stupid cablecar until we get to the Atlantic Breach? You really expect me to walk across the ocean floor to North America? Ada will be dead of old age before I get to Ardis."

"The nanotechnology that grants your people functions," said Prospero, his old voice sounding sad, "did not prepare you for quantum teleportation."

"No, but *you* can QT me home," said Harman, looming over the old man where he now sat on the couch. "Touch me and QT. It's that simple."

"No, not that simple," said Prospero. "And you're literate enough now that you must know that you cannot compel either Moira or me to submit to threats or intimidation."

Harman had accessed orbital clocks when he'd awakened and he knew he'd been unconscious for most of nine days. It made him want to smash the pot, cups, and table with his fist. "We're on the *eiffelbahn* Route Eleven," he said. "After we left Mount Everest, we must have followed the Hah Xil Shan Route up right past the Tarim Pendi Bubble. I could have found sonies there, weapons, crawlers, levitation harnesses, impact armor—everything Ada and our people need for their survival."

"There were . . . detours," said Prospero. "You would not have been safe if you had left the tower to explore the Tarim Pendi Bubble."

"Safe!" snorted Harman. "Yes, we must live in a safe world, mustn't we, magus and Moira?"

"You were more mature before the crystal cabinet," said Moira with much disdain.

Harman didn't argue the point. He set down his cup, leaned forward with both hands on the table, stared Moira in the eye, and said, "I know the voynix were sent forward through time by the Global Caliphate to kill Jews, but why did you posts store the nine thousand one hundred and fourteen of them and beam them into space? Why not just take them up to the Rings with you—or some other safe place? I mean, you'd already found the otherdimensional Mars and terraformed it. Why turn those people into neutrinos?"

"Nine thousand one hundred and *thirteen*," corrected Moira. "Savi was left behind."

Harman waited for an answer to his question.

Moira set down her coffee cup. Her eyes, just like Savi's, showed every rush of anger she felt. "We told Savi's people that they were being stored in the neutrino loop for a few thousand years while we cleaned up the untidiness on Earth," she said softly. "They interpreted that to mean the RNA constructs everywhere left over from Dementia Times—dinosaurs and Terror Birds and cycad forests—but we also meant such little things as the voynix, Setebos, the witch in her city up in orbit . . ."

"But you didn't clean up the voynix," interrupted Harman. "The things were activated and built their Third Temple on the Mosque of the Dome . . ."

"We could not eliminate them," said Moira, "but we reprogrammed them. Your people knew them as servants for fourteen hundred years."

"Until they started slaughtering us," said Harman. He turned his gaze on Prospero. "Which started after you directed Daeman and me on how to destroy your orbital city where you and Caliban were . . . imprisoned. All that to reclaim just one hologram of yourself, Prospero?"

"More the equivalent of a frontal lobe," said the magus. "And the voynix would have been activated even if you had not destroyed the controlling elements in my city on the e-ring."

"Why?"

"Setebos," said Prospero. "His millennium and a half of being denied—of being kept and fed on alternate Earths and the terraformed Mars—had come to an end. When the Many-Handed opened the first Brane Hole to sniff the air of this Earth, the voynix reacted as programmed."

"Programmed three thousand years ago," said Harman. "The old-styles of my people aren't all from Jewish descent like Savi's folk."

Prospero shrugged. "The voynix do not know that. All humans in Savi's time were Jews, ergo . . . to the weak mind of all voynix . . . all humans are Jews. If A equals B and B equals C, then A equals C. If Crete is an island and England is an island, then . . ."

"Crete is England," finished Harman. "But the rubicon virus did *not* come from a lab in Israel. That's just another blood libel."

"No, you are perfectly correct," said Prospero. "The rubicon was indeed the one great contribution to science that the Islamic world gave the rest of the world in a two-thousand-year stretch of darkness."

"Eleven billion dead," said Harman, his voice shaking. "Ninety-seven percent of Earth's population wiped out."

Prospero shrugged again. "It was a long war."

Harman laughed again. "And the virus got almost everyone but the group it was built to kill."

"Israeli scientists had a long history of nanotech genetic manipulation by then," said the magus. "They knew that if they did not inoculate their population's DNA quickly, they could not do it at all."

"They might have shared it," said Harman.

"They tried. There was no time. But the DNA for your stock was . . . stored."

"But the Global Caliphate didn't invent time travel," said Harman, not one hundred percent sure if this was a question or statement.

"No," agreed Prospero. "A French scientist developed the first working time bubble . . ."

"Henri Rees Delacourte," muttered Harman, remembering.

". . . to travel back to 1478 A.D. to investigate an odd and interesting manuscript purchased by Rudolph II, the Holy Roman Emperor, in 1586," continued Prospero without a pause. "It seemed a simple enough little trip. But we know now that the manuscript itself—filled with a strange, coded language and featuring wonderful drawings of non-terrestrial plants, star systems, and naked people—was a hoax. And Dr. Delacourte and his home city paid a price for the voyage when the black hole his team was using as a power source escaped its restraining force-field."

"But the French and the New European Union gave the designs to the Caliphate," said Harman. "Why?"

Prospero held up his old, vein-mottled hands almost as if he were giving a benediction. "The Palestinian scientists were their friends."

"I wonder if that rare-book dealer from the early Twentieth Century, Wilfrid Voynich, could have dreamt that he'd have a race of self-replicating monsters named after him," said Harman.

"Few of us can dream of what our true legacy will be," said Prospero, his hands still raised as if in blessing.

Moira sighed. "Are you two finished with your little trip down memory lane?"

Harman looked at her.

"And you, my would-be Prometheus . . . your dingle is dangling. If this is a one-eyed staredown contest, you win. I blinked first."

Harman looked down. His robe had come open during all the talking. He quickly sashed it shut.

"We'll be crossing the Pyrenees in the next hour," said Moira. "Now that Harman has something in his skull other than a pleasure thermometer, we have things to discuss . . . things to decide. I suggest that Prometheus go up and shower and get dressed. Grandfather here can take a nap. I'll clear the breakfast dishes."

65

Achilles is considering the possibility that he made a mistake in maneuvering Zeus into banishing him to the deepest, darkest pit in the hell-
world of Tartarus, even though it had seemed like a good idea at the
time.

First of all, Achilles can't quite breathe the air here. While the quantum singularity of his Fate to Die by Paris's Hand theoretically protects
him from death, it doesn't protect him from rasping, wheezing, and collapsing on the lava-hot black stone as the methane-tainted air fouls and
scours his lungs. It's as if he's trying to breathe acid.

Secondly, this Tartarus is a nasty place. The terrible air pressure—
equivalent to two hundred feet beneath the surface of Earth's sea—
presses in on every square inch of Achilles' aching body. The heat is
terrible. It would have long since killed any merely mortal man, even a
hero such as Diomedes or Odysseus, but even demi-god Achilles is suffering, his skin blotched red and white, boils and blisters appearing
everywhere on his exposed flesh.

Finally, he is blind and almost deaf. There is a vague reddish glow,
but not enough to see by. The pressure here is so great, the atmosphere
and cloud cover so thick, that even the small illumination from the per-
vasive volcanic red gloom is defeated by the rippling atmosphere, by
fumes from live volcanic vents, and by the constant curtain-fall of acid
rain. The thick, superheated atmosphere presses in on the fleet-footed
mankiller's eardrums until the sounds he can make out all seem like
great, muted drumbeats and massive footsteps—heavy throbs to match
the throbbing of his pressure-squeezed skull.

Achilles reaches under his leather armor and touches the small mechanical beacon that Hephaestus had given him. He can feel it pulse. At
least it hasn't imploded from the terrible pressure that presses in on
Achilles' eardrums and eyes.

Sometimes in the terrible gloom, Achilles can sense movement of
large shapes, but even when the volcanic glow is at its reddest, he can't

make out who or what is passing near him in the terrible night. He senses that the shapes are far too big and too oddly shaped to be human. Whatever they are, the things have ignored him so far.

Fleet-footed Achilles, son of Peleus, leader of the Myrmidons and noblest hero of the Trojan War, demigod in his terrible wrath, lies spread-eagled flat on a pulsing-hot volcanic boulder, blinded and deafened, and uses all of his energy just to keep breathing.

Perhaps, he thinks, *I should have come up with a different plan for defeating Zeus and bringing my beloved Penthesilea back to life.*

Even the briefest thought of Penthesilea makes him want to weep like a child—but not an Achilles' child, for the young Achilles had never wept. Not once. The centaur Chiron had taught him how to avoid responding to his emotions—other than anger, rage, jealousy, hunger, thirst, and sex, of course, for those were important in a warrior's life—but weep for love? The idea would have made the Noble Chiron bark his harsh centaur's laugh and then hit young Achilles hard with his massive teaching stick. "Love is nothing but lust misspelled," Chiron would have said—and struck seven-year-old Achilles again, hard, on the temple.

What makes Achilles want to weep all the more here in this unbreathable hell is that he knows somewhere deep behind his surging emotions that he doesn't give a damn about the dead Amazon twat—she'd come at him with a fucking poisoned spear, for the gods' sake—and normally his only regret would be that it took so long for the bitch and her horse to die. But here he is, suffering this hell and taking on Father Zeus himself just to get the woman reborn—all because of some chemicals that gash-goddess Aphrodite had poured on the smelly Amazon.

Three huge forms loom out of the fog. They are close enough that Achilles' straining, tear-filled eyes can make out that they are women—if women grew thirty feet tall, each with tits bigger than his torso. They are naked but painted in many bright colors, visible even through the red filter of this volcanic gloom. Their faces are long and unbelievably ugly. Their hair is either writhing like snakes in the superheated air or *is* a tangle of serpents. Their voices are distinct only because the booming syllables are unbearably louder than the booming background noise.

"Sister Ione," booms the first shape looming over him in the gloom, "canst thou tell what form this is spread-eagled across this rock like a starfish?"

"Sister Asia," answers the second huge form, "I wouldst say it were a mortal man, if mortals could come to this place or survive here, which they cannot. And if I could see it were a man, which I cannot since it lieth upon its belly. It does have pretty hair."

"Sister Oceanids," says the third form, "let us see the gender of this starfish."

A huge hand roughly grips Achilles and rolls him over. Fingers the size of his thighs pluck away his armor, rip off his belt, and roll down his loin cloth.

"Is it male?" asks the first shape, the one her sister had called Asia.

"If you wouldst call it so for so little to show," says the third shape.

"Whatever it is, it lies fallen and vanquished," says the female giant called Ione.

Suddenly large shapes in the gloom that Achilles had assumed were looming crags stir, sway, and echo in non-human voices, "Lies fallen and vanquished!"

And invisible voices farther away in the reddish night echo again, "Lies fallen and vanquished!"

The names finally click. Chiron had taught young Achilles his mythology, as well as his theology to honor the living and present gods. Asia and Ione had been Oceanids—daughters of Okeanos—along with their third sister Panthea . . . the second generation of Titans born after the original mating of Earth and Gaia, Titans who had ruled the heavens and the earth along with Gaia in the ancient times before their third-generation offspring, Zeus, defeated them and cast them all down into Tartarus. Only Okeanos, of all the Titans, had been allowed exile in a kinder, gentler place—locked away in a dimension layer under the quantum sheath of Ilium-Earth. Okeanos could be visited by the gods, but his offspring had been banished to stinking Tartarus: Asia, Ione, Panthea, and all the other Titans, including Okeanos' brother Kronos who became Zeus's father, Okeanos' sister Rhea who became Zeus's mother, and Okeanos' three daughters. All the other male offspring from the mating of Earth and Gaia—Koios, Krios, Hyperion, and Iapetos, as well as the other daughters—Theia, Themis, Mnemosyne, golden-wreathed Phoebe, and sweet Tethys—had also been banished here to Tartarus after Zeus's victory on Olympos thousands of years earlier.

All this Achilles remembers from his lessons at the hoof of Chiron. *A fucking lot of good it does me*, he thinks.

"Does it speak?" booms Panthea, sounding startled.

"It squeaks," says Ione.

All three of the giant Oceanids lean closer to listen to Achilles' attempts at communication. Every attempt is terribly painful for the mankiller, since it means breathing in and trying to use the noxious atmosphere. An observer would have guessed from the resulting sounds—and guessed correctly—that there is an unusual amount of helium remaining in the carbon dioxide, methane, ammonia mix of Tartarus' soup-thick atmosphere.

"It soundeth like a mouse that hath been squashed flat," laughs Asia.

"But the squeaks sound vaguely like a squashed mouse's attempt at civilized language," booms Ione.

"With a terrible dialect," agrees Panthea.

"We need to take him to the Demogorgon," says Asia, looming closer.

Two huge hands roughly lift Achilles, the giant fingers squeezing most of the ammonia, methane, carbon dioxide, and helium out of his aching lungs. Now the hero of the Argives is gaping and gasping like a fish out of water.

"The Demagorgon will want to see this strange creature," agrees Ione. "Carry him, Sister, carry him to the Demogorgon."

"Carry him to the Demogorgon!!" echo the giant, insectoid shapes following the three giant women.

"Carry him to the Demogorgon!!" echo larger, less familiar shapes following farther behind.

66

The *eiffelbahn* ended along the 40th Parallel, on the coast where the nation of Portugal had once existed, just south of Figueira da Foz. Harman knew that less than a couple of hundred miles southeast, the modulated forcefield templates called the Hands of Hercules held the Atlantic Ocean out of the dry Mediterranean Basin, and he knew exactly why the post-humans had drained the Basin and to what purpose they'd used it for almost two millennia. He knew that less than a couple of hundred miles northeast of where the *eiffelbahn* ended here, there was a sixty-mile-wide circle of the terrain fused into glass where thirty-two hundred years ago the Global Caliphate had fought its determining battle with the N.E.U.—more than three million proto-voynix pouring over and past two hundred thousand doomed human mechanized-infantry knights. Harman knew that . . .

All in all, he knew, he knew too much. And understood too little.

The three of them—Moira, the solidified Prospero hologram, and Harman still-with-the-headache-of-a-lifetime—were standing on the top platform of the final *eiffelbahn* tower. Harman was finished with his cablecar ride—perhaps forever.

Behind them were the green hills of former Portugal. Ahead of them was the Atlantic Ocean with the Breach continuing due west from the line of the *eiffelbahn* route. The day was perfect—temperature perfect, mild breezes, not a cloud in the sky—and sunlight reflected off green at the top of the cliffs, white sand, and broad expanses of blue on either side of the slash of the Atlantic Breach. Harman knew that even from the top of the *eiffelbahn* tower he could see only sixty miles or so to the west, but the view seemed to go on for a thousand miles, the Breach starting as a hundred-meter-wide avenue with low blue-green berms on either side, but continuing on until it was only a black line intersecting with the distant horizon.

"You can't seriously expect me to walk to North America," said Harman.

"We seriously expect you to try," said Prospero.

"Why?"

Neither the post-human nor the never-human answered him. Moira led the way down the steps to the lower elevator platform. She was carrying a rucksack and some other gear for Harman's hike. The elevator doors opened and they stepped into the cagelike structure and began humming lower past iron trellises.

"I'll walk with you for a day or two," said Moira.

Harman was surprised. "You will? Why?

"I thought you might enjoy the company."

Harman had no response to this. As they stepped out onto the grassy shelf under the *eiffelbahn* tower, he said, "You know, just a few hundred miles southeast of us here, in the Med Basin, there are a dozen post-human storage facilities that Savi never knew anything about. She knew about Atlantis and the Three Chairs way of riding lightning to the rings, but that was more or less a cruel post-human joke—she didn't know about the sonies and actual cargo spacecraft stored at the other stasis bubbles. Or at least these stasis bubbles *used* to be there . . ."

"They still are," said Prospero.

Harman turned to Moira. "Well, walk with me a few days to the Basin rather than send me on a three-month hike across the ocean floor . . . a hike I'll probably never complete. We'll fly a sonie to Ardis or one of the shuttles up the rings to have them turn the power and fax-node links back on."

Moira shook her head. "I assure you, my young Prometheus, you do not want to walk toward the Mediterranean Basin."

"Almost one million *calibani* are loose there," said Prospero. "They used to be contained to the Basin, but Setebos has released them. They've slaughtered the voynix that once guarded Jerusalem, have swarmed across North Africa and the Middle East, and would have covered much of Europe now if Ariel weren't holding them back."

"Ariel!" cried Harman. The thought of the tiny little . . . *sprite* . . . single-handedly holding back a million rampaging *calibani*—or even one—was totally absurd.

"Ariel can call upon more resources than are dreamt of in your philosophy, Harman, friend of Noman," said Prospero.

"Hmm," said Harman, unconvinced. The three walked to the edge of the grassy cliff. A narrow path switchbacked down to the beach. From this close, the Atlantic Breach looked much more real and strangely terrifying. Waves lapped up on either side of the impossible segment cut out of the ocean. "Prospero," said Harman, "you created the *calibani* to counter the voynix threat. Why do you allow them to rampage?"

"I no longer control them," said the old magus.

"Since Setebos arrived?"

The magus smiled. "I lost control of the *calibani*—and of Caliban himself—many centuries before Setebos."

"Why did you create the damned things in the first place?"

"Security," said Prospero. And he smiled again at the irony of the word.

"We . . . the post-humans," said Moira, "asked Prospero and his . . . companion . . . to create a race of creatures ferocious enough to stop the replicating voynix from flooding into the Mediterranean Basin and compromising our operations there. You see, we used the Basin for . . ."

"Growing food, cotton, tea, and other materials you needed in the orbital islands," finished Harman. "I know." He paused, thinking about what the post had just said. "*Companion*? Do you mean Ariel?"

"No, not Ariel," said Moira. "You see, fifteen hundred years ago, the creature we call Sycorax was not yet the . . ."

"That will do," interrupted Prospero. The hologram actually sounded embarrassed.

Harman didn't want to let it go. "But what you told us a year ago is true, isn't it?" he asked the magus. "Caliban's mother was Sycorax and its father was Setebos . . . or was that a lie as well?"

"No, no," said Prospero. "Caliban is a creature out of the witch by a monster."

"I've been curious how a giant brain the size of a warehouse with dozens of hands bigger than me manages to mate with a human-sized witch," said Harman.

"Very carefully," said Moira—rather predictably, Harman thought.

The woman who looked like young Savi pointed to the Breach. "Are we ready to start?"

"Just another question for Prospero," said Harman, but when he turned around to speak to the magus, he was gone. "Damn it. I hate it when he does that."

"He has business to attend to elsewhere."

"Yes, I'm sure. But I wanted to ask him one last time why he's sending me across the Atlantic Breach. It doesn't make any sense. I'm going to die out there. I mean, there's no food. . . ."

"I've packed a dozen food bars for you," said Moira.

Harman had to laugh. "All right . . . after a dozen days, *then* there's no food. And no water . . ."

Moira pulled a soft, curved, almost flat shape from the rucksack. The thing looked almost like one of the wineskins from the turin drama—but one that was all but empty. A thin tube ran from it. She handed it to Harman and he noticed how cool to the touch it was.

"A hydrator," said Moira. "If there's any humidity in the air at all, this collects it and filters it. If you're in your thermskin, it collects your sweat and exhalations, scrubs them, and provides drinking water that way. You will not die of thirst out there."

"I didn't bring my thermskin," said Harman.

"I packed it for you. You will need it for hunting."

"Hunting?"

"Fishing might be a better term," said Moira. "You can press through the restraining forcefields any time and kill fish underwater. You've been underwater in your thermskin before—up on Prospero's Isle ten months ago—so you know that the skin protects you from pressure and the osmosis mask allows you to breathe."

"What am I supposed to use for bait to get these fish?"

Moira flashed Savi's quick smile. "For sharks, killer whales, and many other denizens of the deep out there, your own body will do quite nicely, my Prometheus."

Harman was not amused. "And what do I use to kill the sharks, killer whales, and other denizens of the deep that I might want to eat . . . harsh language?"

Moira pulled a handgun from the rucksack and handed it to him.

It was black—darker and stubbier and much less graceful in design than the flechette weapons he was used to—and heavier. But the hand grip, barrel, and trigger were similar enough.

"This fires bullets, not crystal darts," said Moira. "It's an explosive device rather than gas-charged as with the weapons you've used before . . . but the principle is obviously the same. There are three boxes of ammunition in your rucksack . . . six hundred rounds of self-cavitating ammunition. That means that each bullet creates its own vacuum ahead of itself underwater . . . water does not slow it down. This is the safety— it's on now—press down on the red dot with your thumb to release the safety. It has more recoil than flechette weapons and is much louder, but you'll grow used to that."

Harman hefted the killing device a few times, pointed it at the distant sea, made sure the safety was still on, and set it back in his pack. He'd test it later—once he was out in the Breach. "I wish we could get a few dozen of these weapons to Ardis," he said softly.

"You can deliver this one to them," said Moira.

Harman balled his right hand into a fist. He wheeled on Moira. "More than two thousand miles across here," he said fiercely. "I don't know how many miles I can hike a day, even if I do catch these god-damned fish and if your hydrator thing keeps working. Twenty miles a day? Thirty? That could be two hundred days of hiking just to get to the east coast of North America. But that kind of progress is only if the land in the Breach is *flat* . . . and I'm looking at proxnet and farnet mapping right now. There are fucking *mountain ranges* out there! And canyons deeper than the Grand Canyon! Boulders, rock crevasses, great furrows where continental drift dragged entire landmasses over the ocean floor, larger gaps where tectonic-plate activity opened up the bottom of the ocean and spewed forth lava. This ocean floor's always re-creating it- self—it's *bigger, rougher, and rockier* than it used to be. It'll take me a year to get across, and once I get there I'll have almost another thousand miles to cover to get back to Ardis—and that's through forests and mountains infested with dinosaurs, saber-toothed cats, and voynix. You and that mutant cyberspace personality can quantum teleport anywhere you want to go—and take me with you. Or you could command a sonie to fly here from any of your post-human hidey holes where you've stashed your toys, and I could be home at Ardis helping Ada in a few hours . . . less. Instead, you're sending me to my death out there. And even if I survive, it'll be many months before I can get back to Ardis and odds are that Ada and everyone I know will be dead—from that Setebos spawn, or the voynix, or the winter, or starvation. Why are you doing this to me?"

Moira did not flinch from his fierce gaze. "Has Prospero ever spoken to you of the logosphere's predicators?" she asked softly.

"Predicators?" Harman repeated stupidly. He could feel the adrena- line filling his system beginning to drain away toward despair. In a minute, his hands would be shaking. "You mean *predictors*? No."

"Predicators," said Moira. "They are as unique—and often as dan- gerous—as Prospero himself. Sometimes he trusts them. Sometimes he does not. In this case, he has entrusted your life and perhaps the future of your race to them."

Moira pulled her hydrator from the rucksack and slung it over her back, shifting the flexible drinking tube so it lay along the side of her cheek. She started down the steep path toward the beach.

Harman remained at the top of the cliff for a minute. Shouldering the rucksack, he shielded his eyes and stared back through the morning glare at the black *eiffelbahn* tower rising high against the blue sky. The cablecar cables ran off to the east. He could not see the next tower from this vantage point.

Swiveling, he looked out to the west. Large white birds and smaller white birds—gulls and terns, his protein DNA memory storage told him—wheeled and screeched over the lazy blue sea. The Atlantic Breach remained a startling impossibility, its eighty-foot-wide cleft taking on scale now that Moira was halfway down the cliff face.

Harman sighed, tugged the rucksack straps tighter—already feeling the sweat soaking through his tunic where it met the cotton of the small backpack—and began following Moira down the trail toward the beach and the sea.

67

A lot was happening at once.

The *Queen Mab*—all one thousand one hundred and eighteen feet of her—began her close-encounter aerobraking maneuver, the ship's curved pusher plate draped across its derriere, both ship and saucer surrounded by flame and streaking plasma.

At the height of the ion-storm around the aerobraking spaceship, Suma IV cut loose the dropship.

Just as with the spacecraft that had first brought Mahnmut and Orphu to Mars, no one had gotten around to naming this dropship—it remained just "the dropship" in their maser and tightbeam conversations. But *The Dark Lady* was secure in the dropship's hold, and in his environmental control cubby, Mahnmut kept up a running description of video feeds—both from the dropship's camera and from the *Queen Mab*—as the stealth-shielded ovoid of the dropship thrust away from the flame-wreathed larger ship, spun through the upper atmosphere at five times the speed of sound, and finally deployed its stubby high-speed wings when their velocity dropped to a mere Mach 3.

Originally, General Beh bin Adee had planned to drop Earthward with the reconnaissance dropship, but the more imminent threat of the Voice's asteroid rendezvous made all the Prime Integrators vote that the general remain aboard the *Mab*. Centurion Leader Mep Ahoo was in the jumpseat of the passenger/cargo compartment behind the main control blister on the upper part of the ship, and behind him—strapped into their web seating, heavy energy weapons locked upright between their black-barbed knees—rode his command: twenty-five rockvec Belt troopers recently defrosted and briefed on the *Queen Mab*.

Suma IV was an excellent pilot. Mahnmut had to admire the way the Ganymedan guided the dropship down through the upper atmosphere, using thrusters so briefly that the ship seemed to be flying itself, and he had to smile when he remembered his own disastrous plunge with Orphu through Mars' atmosphere. Of course, his ship had been charred and broken then, but he could still give credit to a real pilot when he flew with one.

The data and radar profile are impressive, tightbeamed Orphu of Io from the hold. *What's the visual look like?*

Blue and white, sent Mahnmut. *All blue and white. More beautiful even than the photographs. The entire Earth is ocean below us.*

All of it? said Orphu and Mahnmut thought it was one of the few times he'd heard his friend sound surprised.

All of it. A water world—blue ocean, a million ripples of reflected sunlight, white clouds—cirrus, high ripples, a mass of stratocumulus coming over the horizon above us . . . . no, wait. It's a hurricane, a thousand kilometers across, at least. I can see the eye. White, spinning, powerful, amazing.

Our track is nominal, sent Orphu. *Coming right up from Antarctica crossing the South Atlantic toward the northeast.*

The Mab's *out of atmosphere and on the other side of the Earth now,* sent Mahnmut. *The communication sats we seeded are working fine.* Mab's *velocity is down to fifteen kilometers per second and falling. She's climbing back to the polar ring coordinates and decelerating on ion drive. Trajectory is good. She's headed for the rendezvous point the Voice gave us. No one's fired on her yet.*

Even better, sent Orphu, *no one's fired on* us *yet, either.*

Suma IV allowed atmospheric drag to slow them to less than the speed of sound just as they crossed the bulge of Africa. Their flight plan had called for them to fly over the dried Mediterranean Sea, shooting video and recording data about the odd constructs there, but instruments now told them that there was some sort of energy-damping field extending in a dome up to forty thousand meters above that dried sea. The dropship might fly into that and cease flying altogether. In fact, according to Suma IV, if they flew into that, all the moravecs on board might cease functioning. The Ganymedan banked the dropship east across the Sahara Desert, flying in a wide curve around to the south and east of the waterless Mediterranean.

The feed continued to flow in from the *Queen Mab*, carried around the blocking mass of the planet by a score of snowflake-size repeater satellites.

The large spacecraft had reached the coordinates beamed to it by the Voice—a small volume of empty space just outside the edge of the orbital ring some two thousand kilometers from the asteroid-city from which the Voice had broadcast its—her—messages. Obviously the Voice did not want a spaceship that was propelled by atomic bombs to come within shockwave proximity of her—its—orbital home.

Besides realtime data the dropship was uplinking, it was getting twenty broadband tightbeams of information flowing in: feeds from the *Queen Mab*'s many cameras and external sensors, comm bands from the *Mab*'s bridge, ground data from the various satellites they'd seeded, and multiple feeds from Odysseus. The moravecs had not only rigged the human's clothing with nanocameras and molecular transmitters, they'd mildly sedated Odysseus during his last sleep period and had started to paint cell-sized imagers on the skin of his forehead and hands, but had discovered to their shock that Odysseus already had nanocameras in the skin there. His ear canals also had been modified—long before he came aboard the *Queen Mab* they realized, with nanocyte receivers. The moravecs modified all these so they would send every sight and sound back to the ship's recorders. Other sensors had been installed around his body so that even if Odysseus were to die during the coming rendezvous, data about his surroundings would continue flowing back to the moravecs.

At that moment, Odysseus was standing on the bridge with Prime Integrator Asteague/Che, Retrograde Sinopessen, navigator Cho Li, General Beh bin Adee, and the other command moravecs there.

Suddenly Orphu and Mahnmut perked up as the *Queen Mab* relayed real-time radio data from the ship's comm.

"Incoming maser message," said Cho Li.

"*SEND ODYSSEUS ACROSS ALONE,*" came the sultry female voice from the asteroid-city. "*USE A SHUTTLE WHICH IS NOT ARMED. IF I DETECT WEAPONS ABOARD HIS SHIP OR IF ANYONE ORGANIC OR*

ROBOTIC ACCOMPANIES ODYSSEUS, I WILL DESTROY YOUR SPACECRAFT."

"The plot thickens," said Orphu of Io on the common dropship band.

The moravecs in the dropship watched with only a second's delay as Retrograde Sinopessen escorted Odysseus down to the number eight launch bay. Since all of the hornets were armed, only one of the three Phobos construction shuttles still aboard the *Queen Mab* would satisfy the Voice's requirements.

The construction shuttle was tiny—a remote-handling ovoid with barely room inside to squeeze in one adult human being and no life support beyond air and temperature—and as Retrograde Sinopessen helped the Achaean fighter squirm into the cable and circuit-board cluttered space, the moravec said, "Are you sure you want to do this?"

Odysseus stared at the spidery moravec from Amalthea for a long moment. Finally he said in Greek, "I cannot rest from travel: I will drink life to the lees: all times have I enjoyed greatly, have suffered greatly, both with those that loved me and alone; on shore, and when through the scudding drifts the rainy Hyades vexed the dim sea; I am become a name. . . . Much have I seen and known; cities of men and manners, climates, councils, governments, and myself not least, but honored them all; And drunk delight of battle with my peers, far on the ringing plains of windy Troy. . . . How dull it is to pause, to make an end, to rust unburnished, not to shine in use! As though to breathe were life. Life piled on life were all too little, and of one to me little remains: but every hour is saved from that eternal silence, something more, a bringer of new things; and vile it were for some three suns to store and hoard myself . . . close the goddamned door, spider-thing."

"But that's . . ." began Orphu of Io.

"He's been in the *Mab*'s library . . ." began Mahnmut.

"Hush!" commanded Suma IV.

They watched as the shuttle was sealed. Retrograde Sinopessen stayed in the shuttle bay, clinging to a strut so as not to be swept out in space as the bay dumped all its atmosphere, and then the ovoid shuttle moved out into space on silent peroxide thrusters. The egg-shaped thing tumbled, stabilized, aimed its nose at the orbital asteroid-city—only a glowing spark among thousands of other p-ring sparks at this distance—and thrusted away toward the Voice.

"We're coming up on Jerusalem," said Suma IV on the intercom.

Mahnmut returned his attention to the dropship's various video monitors and sensors.

Tell me what you see, old friend, tightbeamed Orphu.

All right . . . we're still more than twenty kilometers high. On the unmagnified view, I see the dry Mediterranean Sea about sixty or eighty kilometers to the west, it's a patchwork of red rock, dark soil, and what looks to be green fields. Then along the coast there's the huge crater that used to be the Gaza Strip—a sort of impact crater, half-moon-shaped inlet to the dry sea—and then the land rises into mountains and Jerusalem is there, in the heights, on a hill of its own.

What does it look like?

Let me zoom a bit . . . yes. Suma IV's doing an overlay with historical satellite photos, and it's obvious that the suburbs and newer parts of the city are gone . . . but the Old City, the walled city, is still there. I can see the Damascus Gate . . . the Western Wall . . . Temple Mount and the Dome of the Rock . . . and there's a new structure there, one not in the old satellite photos. Something tall and made out of multifaceted glass and polished stone. The blue beam is coming up from it.

I'm reviewing the data on the blue beam, sent Orphu. *Definitely a neutrino beam sheathed in tachyons. I don't have a clue as to what function that might have and I bet our best scientists don't either.*

Oh, wait a minute . . . sent Mahnmut. *I've zoomed on the Old City and it's . . . crawling with life.*

People? Humans?

No . . .

Those headless humpy organic-robotic things?

No, tightbeamed Mahnmut. *Would you just let me describe these things at my own speed?*

Sorry.

There are thousands—more than thousands—of the clawed, fin-footed amphibian things that you suggested looked like Caliban from The Tempest.

What are they doing? asked Orphu.

Just milling around, essentially, sent Mahnmut. *No, wait, there are bodies on David Street near the Jaffa Gate . . . more bodies on the Tariq el-Wad in the old Jewish section near the Western Wall Plaza . . .*

Human bodies? sent Orphu.

No . . . those headless humpy organic-robotic things. They're pretty torn up . . . a lot of them look eviscerated.

Food for the Caliban monsters? asked Orphu.

I have no idea.

"We're going to overfly the blue beam," Suma IV broadcast on the intercom. "Everyone stay strapped in tight—I need to get some of our boom sensors into the beam itself."

Is this wise? Mahnmut asked Orphu.

Nothing about this expedition to Earth is wise, old friend. We don't have a maggid *aboard.*

A what? tightbeamed Mahnmut.

Maggid, sent Orphu of Io. *In olden days, the old Jews—long before the caliphate wars and the rubicon, I mean, back when humans wore bearskins and*

T-shirts—the old Jews said that a wise person had a maggid*—a sort of spiritual counselor from a different world.*

Maybe we're the maggids, sent Mahnmut. *We're all from another world.*

True, sent Orphu. *But we're not very wise. Mahnmut, did I ever tell you that I'm a gnostic?*

Spell that, sent Mahnmut.

Orphu of Io did so.

What the hell is a gnostic? asked Mahnmut. He'd had several revelations about his old friend recently—including the fact that Orphu was an expert on James Joyce and Lost Era writers other than Proust—and he wasn't sure he was ready for more.

It doesn't matter what a gnostic is, sent Orphu, *but a hundred years before the Christians burned Giordano Bruno at the stake in Venice, they burned a gnostic, a Sufi magus named Solomon Molkho in Mantua. Solomon Molkho taught that when the change occurred, the Dragon would be destroyed without weapons and everything on Earth and in the heavens would be changed.*

"Dragons? Magus?" Mahnmut said aloud.

"What?" said Suma IV from the cockpit bubble.

"Say again?" commed Centurion Leader Mep Ahoo from his jumpseat in the troop transport module.

"Please say that again," came Prime Integrator Asteague/Che's British-accented voice from the *Queen Mab,* telling Mahnmut that the mother ship was monitoring their intercom chatter as well as their official transmissions. But not, he fervently hoped, tapping into their tight-beam conversations.

Never mind, sent Mahnmut. *I'll ask about the dragon and the maguses and such another time.*

On the intercom, Mahnmut said, "Sorry . . . nothing . . . just thinking out loud."

"Let's maintain radio discipline," snapped Suma IV.

"Yes . . . uh . . . sir," said Mahnmut.

Down in the hold, Orphu of Io rumbled in the subsonic.

Odysseus' construction shuttle slowly approached the brightly lit glass city girdling the asteroid. Sensors from the shuttle confirmed that the underlying asteroid was roughly potato-shaped and about twenty kilometers long by almost eleven kilometers in diameter. Every square meter of the asteroid's nickel-iron surface was covered by the crystal city, with the steel, glass, and buckycarbon towers and bubbles rising to a maximum height of half a kilometer. Sensors showed that the entire structure was pressurized at sea-level Earth normal, that the molecules of air inevitably leaking out through the glass suggested Earth-norm oxygen-nitrogen-carbon-dioxide mix atmosphere, and that the internal temperatures would be comfortable for a human who had lived around the Mediterranean Sea before the late Lost Era climate changes . . . some-one from Odysseus' era, for instance.

On the bridge of the *Queen Mab* a thousand kilometers away and holding, all of the command 'vecs monitored their sensors and screens more intently as an invisible tentacle of forcefield energy reached out from the crystal asteroid city, grabbed the construction shuttle, and pulled it in toward an airlock-like opening high on the tallest glass tower.

"Shut down the shuttle's thrusters and autopilot," commanded Cho Li.

Retrograde Sinopessen monitored Odysseus' biotelemetry and said, "Our human friend is fine. Excited . . . heart rate up a bit and adrenaline levels rising . . . he can see out that little window . . . but otherwise healthy."

Holographic images flickered above consoles and the chart table as the shuttle was drawn closer and then pulled into the dark rectangle of the airlock. A glass door slid shut. Sensors on the shuttle registered a forcefield differential pushing it "down"—substituting for gravity to within 0.68 Earth standard—and then the sensors recorded atmosphere rushing into the large airlock chamber. It was as breathable as the air at Ilium.

"Radio, maser, and quantum telemetric data is quite clear," reported Cho Li. "The glass of the city wall does not block it."

"He's not in the city yet," grumbled General Beh bin Adee. "He's just in the airlock. Don't be surprised if the Voice cuts off transmissions as soon as Odysseus is inside."

They watched on the subjective skin cameras—and so did everyone aboard the dropship some fifty thousand kilometers away—as Odysseus uncoiled from the small space, stretched, and began walking toward an interior door. Although wearing soft shipsuit clothing, the human had insisted over all the moravecs' protests on bringing his round shield and short sword. The shield was raised now and the sword was ready as the bearded man approached the brightly illuminated door.

"Unless anyone has any further need to study Jerusalem or the neu-trino beam, I'll set course for Europe now," Suma IV said over the inter-com.

No one protested, although Mahnmut was busy describing the colors of the Old City of Jerusalem to Ophu—the reds of the late afternoon sun on the ancient buildings, the gold gleaming of the mosque, the clay-colored streets and dark gray shadows of the alleys, the shocking, sud-den green of olive groves here and there, and everywhere the slick, wet, slimy green of the amphibian creatures.

The dropship accelerated to Mach 3 and headed northeast toward the old capital of Dimashq in what had once been called Syria or the Kahn Ho Tep Province of Nyainqêntanglha Shan West, Suma IV keeping a distance between the aircraft and the dome of nullifying energy over the dried-up Mediterranean. As they covered the length of old Syria and banked sharply left to head west along the Anatolian Peninsula over the bones of old Turkey, the ship fully stealthed and doing a silent Mach 2.8 at an altitude of thirty-four thousand meters, Mahnmut suddenly said, "Can we slow down and orbit near the Aegean coast south of the Hellespont?"

"We can," replied Suma IV over the intercom, "but we're behind schedule for our survey of the blue-ice city in France. Is there something along the coast up here that's worth our detour and time?"

"The site of Troy," said Mahnmut. "Ilium."

The dropship began decelerating and losing altitude. When it reached the crawling pace of three hundred kilometers per hour—and with the brown and green of the emptied Mediterranean approaching fast and the water of the Hellespont to the north—Suma IV retracted the stubby delta wings and unfolded the hundred-meter-long, multiplaned gossamer wings with their slowly turning propellers.

Mahnmut softly sang on the intercom—

> "They say that Achilles in the darkness stirred . . .
> And Priam and his fifty sons
> Wake all amazed and hear the guns,
> And shake for Troy again."

Who's that? sent Orphu. I don't recognize that verse.

Rupert Brooke, Mahnmut replied on the tightbeam. World War I–era British poet. He wrote that on his way to Gallipoli . . . but he never got to Gallipoli. Died of disease along the way.

"I say," boomed General Beh bin Adee on the common band, "I can't say much for your radio discipline, little Europan, but that's a cracking good poem."

On the crystal city in polar orbit, the airlock door slid up and Odysseus entered into the city proper. It was filled with sunlight, trees, vines, tropical birds, streams, a waterfall tumbling from a tall outcropping of lichen-covered stone, old ruins, and small wildlife. Odysseus saw a red deer quit munching grass, raise its head, look at the human approaching behind his shield with sword raised, and then walk calmly away.

"Sensors indicate a humanoid form is approaching—not yet visible through the foliage," Cho Li radioed to the dropship.

Odysseus heard the footsteps before he saw her—bare feet on packed soil and smooth rock. He lowered his shield and slid his sword into the loop on his broad belt as she came into sight.

The woman was beautiful beyond words. Even the inhuman moravecs in their steel and plastic shells, with organic hearts thumping next to their hydraulic hearts, organic brains and glands nestling next to plastic pumps and nanocyte servomechanisms—even the moravecs one thousand kilometers away staring at their holograms recognized how incredibly beautiful the woman was.

Her skin was a tanned brown, her hair long and dark but streaked with blond, the curls flowing down over her bare shoulders. She wore only the slightest two-piece outfit of glittering but flimsy silk that emphasized her full, heavy breasts and broad hips. Her feet were bare but there were gold bracelets around her slim ankles and a riot of bracelets on each wrist, silver and gold clasps on her smooth upper arms.

As she came closer, Odysseus and the staring moravecs in space and the staring moravecs circling above ancient Troy saw that the woman's eyebrows arched in a sensuous curve over her amazingly green eyes, that her lashes were long and dark, and that what had looked like makeup around those amazing eyes from three meters away resolved into normal shadows and skin tones as she approached to within a meter of the stunned Odysseus. Her lips were soft, full, and very red.

In perfect Greek of Odysseus' era, in a voice as soft as a breeze through palms or the rustle of perfectly tuned wind chimes, the beautiful woman said, "Welcome, Odysseus. I have been waiting for you for many years. My name is Sycorax."

68

On the second evening of his hike through the Atlantic Breach with Moira, Harman found himself thinking of many things.

Something about walking between the two high walls of water—the Atlantic was more than five hundred feet deep here, on their second day of walking, now almost seventy miles out from the coast—was absolutely mesmerizing. A bundle of protein memory stored in modified DNA helixes somewhere near his spine pedantically tugged at Harman's consciousness and wanted to fill in the details—(*the word mesmerizing is based upon Franz Anton Mesmer, born May 23, 1734, in Iznang, Swabia, died March 5, 1815, in Meersburg, Swabia—German physician whose system of therapeutics known as mesmerism, in which he affected sympathetic control of his patients' consciousness, was the forerunner of the later practice of hypnotism . . .*)—but Harman's mind, lost in labyrinths of thought, batted away the interruption. He was getting better at shutting down the nonessential voices roaring in and around his mind, but his head still hurt like a son of a bitch.

The five-hundred-foot-high walls of water on each side of the eighty-yard dry path were also frightening and even two days in the Breach hadn't fully acclimated Harman to the sense of claustrophobia and fear of imminent collapse. He'd actually been in the Atlantic Breach once before, two years earlier when he was celebrating his ninety-eighth birthday—leaving from faxnode 124 near the Loman Estate on what had once been the New Jersey coast of North America and walking two days out, two days back, but not covering nearly so much ground as he was with Moira—and the walls of water and deep gloom of the trench had not bothered him so much then. *Of course*, Harman thought, *I was younger then. And believed in magic.*

He and Moira had not spoken in several hours, but their strides easily matched each other and they walked well together in silence. Harman was analyzing some of the information that now filled his universe, but mostly he was thinking about what he could and should do if he ever did manage to get back to Ardis.

The first thing he should do, he realized, is apologize to Ada from the bottom of his heart for having left on that idiotic voyage to the Golden Gate at Machu Picchu. His pregnant wife and unborn child should have come first. Consciously, he'd known that then, but he *knew* it now.

Next Harman was trying to stitch together a plan for saving his beloved, his unborn child, his friends, and his species. This was not so easy.

What was *easier* with the million volumes of information that had been—literally—poured into him was seeing some options.

First of all, there were the reawakened functions his mind and body kept exploring, almost one hundred of them. The most important of these, at least in the short term, was the free-fax function. Rather than find nodes and activate machinery, the nano-machinery present in every old-style human, and now understood by Harman, could fax from anywhere to anywhere on the planet Earth and even—should the interdictions be dropped—from the surface of the planet to selected points in the

1,108,303 objects, machines, and cities in orbit around the Earth. Free-faxing could save them all from the voynix—and from Setebos and his loosened *calibani,* even from Caliban himself—but only if the fax machines and storage modules in orbit were turned back on for humans.

Second, Harman now knew several ways he could get back up to the rings and even had a vague understanding of the alien-witch-thing named Sycorax who now ruled the former post-human orbital universe up there, but he had no clue as to how he and others could overpower Sycorax and Caliban—for Harman was certain that Setebos had sent his only begotten son up to the rings to interdict the fax function. But if they *did* prevail, Harman knew that he would have to drown in more crystal cabinets before he'd have all the technical information he needed to re-activate the complicated fax and sensor satellites.

Third, as Harman studied the many functions now available to him—many of which dealt with monitoring his own body and mind and finding data stored there—he knew that it would not be a problem sharing his newfound information. One of the lost functions was a simple sharing function—a sort of reverse sigling—wherein Harman could touch another old-style human, select the RNA-DNA caged protein memory packets he wanted to download, and the information would flow through his flesh and skin to the other person. It had been perfected for the Little Green Men prototypes almost two thousand years earlier, and quickly been adapted to human nanocyte function. All old-styles had this nano-induced DNA-bound memory capability and all old-styles had the hundred latent functions in their bodies and minds, but it took one informed person to start the rekindling of human abilities.

Harman had to smile. Moira could be . . . no, *was* . . . annoying with her many little in-jokes and obscure references, but he understood now why she kept calling him "my young Prometheus." *Prometheus,* according to Hesiod, meant "foresighted" or "prophetic" and the character Prometheus in Aeschylus, and in the works of Shelley, Wu, and other great poets, was the Titan revolutionary who stole essential knowl-edge—fire—from the gods and brought it down to the groveling human race, elevating them into something almost like gods. Almost.

"That's why you disconnected us from our functions," Harman said, not even realizing that he was speaking aloud.

"What?"

He looked at the post-human woman walking next to him in the gathering gloom. "You didn't want us to become gods. That's why you never activated our functions."

"Of course."

"Yet all of the posts except you chose to go off to another world or di-mension and play at being gods."

"Of course."

Harman understood. The first necessity and prerogative for a god, small "g" or capital "G," was to have no other gods before him or her. He concentrated on his thoughts again.

Harman's thinking had changed since the crystal cabinet. Where it once centered on things, places, people, and emotions, it now was mostly figurative—a complicated dance of metaphors, metonymies, ironies, and synecdoches. With billions of facts—things, places, and people—set into his very cells, the focus of his thoughts had shifted to the connections and shades and nuances and recognition side of things. Emotions were still there—stronger, if anything—but where his feelings had once surged like some big, booming bass overpowering the rest of the orchestra, they now danced like a delicate but powerful violin solo.

Much too much murky metaphor for a mere measly man, thought Harman, looking with irony at the presumption of his own thoughts. *And an awful lot of alliteration from an anxious asshole.*

Despite his self-mockery, he knew that he now owned the gift of being able to look at things—people, places, things, feelings, himself— with the kind of recognition that can only come from maturing into nuance, growing into oneself, and in the learning how to accept ironies and metaphors and synecdoches and metonymies not only in language, but in the hardwiring of the universe.

If he could reconnect with his own kind, get back to any old-style human enclave, not just back to Ardis, his new functions would change humankind forever. He would not force them on anyone, but since this iteration of *homo sapiens* was very close to being eradicated from this post-postmodern world, he doubted if anyone under attack by voynix, *calibani,* and a giant, soul-sucking brain skittering around on multiple hands would object too strenuously to gaining new gifts, powers, and a survival advantage.

Are these functions—in the long run—a survival advantage for my species? Harman asked himself.

The answer, which came in his own mental voice, was the clear cry of a Zen master hearing a stupid question from one of his acolytes— "Mu!"—meaning roughly, "Unask the question, stupid." This syllable was often to followed by the equally monosyllabic "Qwatz!" which was the Zen master's cry simultaneous with leaping and striking the stupid student about the head and shoulders with the heavy, weighted teacher's staff.

Mu. There is no "long run" here—that will be for my sons and daughters and their children to decide. Right now, everything—everything—exists in the short run.

And the threat of being disemboweled by a humpbacked voynix

tends to focus the mind wonderfully well. If the functions were turned back on—Harman knew why the old functions, including the finder function, allnet, proxnet, farnet, as well as sigling, were not working—someone up there in the rings had turned off the transmissions as surely as they'd switched off the fax machines.

If the functions were turned back on . . .

But how could they be turned back on?

Once again, Harman studied the problem of getting back up to the rings and switching everything back on—power, servitors, fax, all of the functions.

He needed to know if there were others besides Sycorax up there, waiting, and what their defenses were. The million books he'd ingested in the crystal cabinet had no opinion on this crucial question.

"Why won't you or Prospero QT me up to the rings?" asked Harman. He turned to look at Moira and realized that he could just barely see her in the failing light. Her face was illuminated mostly by ringlight.

"We choose not to," she said in her most maddening Bartleby fashion.

Harman thought of the slug-throwing gun in his pack on the back. Would brandishing a weapon in her direction—and allowing her to read the sincerity in his face since the post-humans had their own functions for reading and understanding human reactions—would that combination convince her to quantum teleport him to Ardis or the rings?

He knew it wouldn't. She would never have given him the gun if it were a threat to her. She had some countermeasure built into the weapon—perhaps she could keep it from firing just by the force of her post-human thoughts, some simple brainwave circuitry built into the firing mechanism—or something equally as foolproof and bulletproof built into her.

"You and the magus went to all that trouble to kidnap me, ship me across India to the Himalayas, just to stick me in the crystal cabinet, drown me, and educate me," said Harman. These were the most words he'd strung together since they'd begun hiking the Breach, and he realized how banal and redundant they were. "Why did you do that if you don't want me to prevail against Setebos and the other bad guys?"

Moira did not smile again. "If you're meant to get to the rings, you'll find a way up there."

" 'Meant to' sounds like some sort of Calvinist predestination," said Harman, stepping over a low lump of desiccated coral. The Breach so far had been surprisingly easy—iron bridges over the few ocean-bottom abysses they'd encountered, paths blasted or lasered into rocky or coral ridges, gentle inclines for the most part and metal cables to help them descend or ascend where the going was steep—so Harman had not had to spend much time watching his feet. But it was hard to see detail in this falling light.

Moira had not responded or visibly reacted to his feeble witticism, so he said, "There are other Firmaries."

"Prospero told you that before."

"Yeah, but it's just sunk in. We old-styles don't *have* to die or rebuild medicine from scratch. There are more rejuvenation tanks up there."

"Yes, of course. The post-humans prepared to serve an old-style population of one million. There are other Firmaries and blue-worm tanks on other orbital isles in both the equatorial and polar rings. Surely this is obvious."

"Yes, obvious," said Harman, "but you have to remember that I have all the savvy of a newborn babe."

"I have not forgotten that," said Moira.

"I don't have specific data on where the other Firmaries are," said Harman. "Can you pinpoint them for me?"

"I'll point them out for you after we douse the campfire tonight," Moira said drily.

"No. I mean on a chart of the rings."

"Do you *have* a chart of the rings, my young Prometheus? Is that part of what you ate and drank back at the Taj?"

"No," said Harman, "but you can draw one for us—orbital coordinates, everything."

"Are you pondering immortality so soon after birth then, Prometheus?"

Am I? wondered Harman. Then he remembered his last thought before the realization that other Firmaries were in mothballs up there in the post-human rings—it had been of Ada, pregnant and injured.

"Why were all the operative fax-in/fax-out healing tanks on Prospero's isle?" he asked. Even as he asked the question, he'd seen the answer like a memory of a forgotten nightmare.

"Prospero arranged that to keep his captive Caliban fed," said Moira.

Harman felt his stomach lurch. Part of that was his reaction to having ever felt any friendly or forgiving thoughts toward the logosphere avatar magus. But most of the sudden surge of nausea came from the fact that he'd not eaten anything since two bites of that day's food bar before dawn that morning, and he'd forgotten even to drink from his hydrator tube in the past few hours. "Why are you stopping?" he asked Moira.

"It's too dark to walk," said the post-human. "Let's build our fire and cook our weenies and roast some marshmallows and sing camp songs. Then you can get a few hours' sleep and dream of living forever in the bright future of the blue-worm tanks."

"You know," said Harman, "you can really be a sarcastic pain in the ass sometimes."

Moira smiled now. Her smile was Cheshirecatlike, almost the only detail he could see of her in the Breach-trench darkness. "When my many sisters were here," she said, "before they all flew off to become gods—many of them *male* gods, which I thought was a demotion—they used to tell me the same thing. Now pull that dried wood and seaweed that we've been picking up all day out of your pack and start us a nice fire . . . that's a good little old-style."

69

Mommy! Mommmmeeee! I'm so scared. It's so cold and dark down here. Mommy! Come help me get out. Mommy, please!

Ada awoke just half an hour after falling asleep in the cold, early hours of the dark winter morning. The child-voice in her mind felt like a small, cold, and unwelcome hand inside her clothes.

Mommy, please. I don't like it here. It's cold and dark and I can't get out. The rock is too hard. I'm hungry. Mommy, please help me get out of here. Mommeeeee.

As exhausted as she was, Ada forced herself out of her bedroll and into the cold air. The survivors—there were forty-eight now one week and five days after their return to the ruins of Ardis—had made tents out of salvaged canvas and Ada now slept with four other women. The cluster of tents and the original lean-to next to the well formed the center of a new palisade, with the sharpened stakes set only a hundred feet out from the center of the tent city and the tumbled ruins of the original Ardis Hall.

Mommeeee . . . please, Mommy. . . .

The voice was there much of the time now and although Ada had learned to ignore it during most of her waking day, it kept her from sleeping. Tonight—this dark predawn morning—it was much worse than usual.

Ada pulled on her trousers, boots, and heavy sweater and stepped out of the tent, moving as quietly as she could so as not to waken Elle and her other tentmates. There were a few people awake by the center campfire—there always were, all through the night—and sentries out on the new walls, but the area between Ada and the Pit was empty and dark.

It was *very* dark; thick clouds had blocked the starlight and ringlight and it smelled like snow was on the way. Ada stepped carefully as she made her way to the Pit—some people still preferred sleeping outdoors now that they'd stitched together and lined better bedrolls and sleeping bags. She didn't want to step on anyone. Just in her fifth month of pregnancy, Ada already felt fat and clumsy.

Mommeeeeeeeeee!

She hated that damned voice. With a real child growing inside her, she couldn't tolerate the pleading, whining ersatz-child voice coming from that thing in the Pit, even if it was just a mental echo. She wondered if her own baby's developing neural system could pick up this telepathic invasion. She hoped not.

Mommy, please let me out. It's dark down here.

They'd decided to have one person standing guard at the Pit at all times, and tonight it was Daeman. She knew the thin, muscular silhouette with its flechette rifle slung over his shoulder even before she could make out his face. He turned to her as she came up to the edge of the Pit.

"Can't sleep?" he whispered.

"It won't let me," she whispered back.

"I know," said Daeman. "I can always hear it when it targets you with its pleading. Faint, but audible—a sort of tickling at the back of the brain. I hear the thing calling 'Mommeee' and just want to unload this magazine of flechettes into it."

"That's probably a good idea," said Ada, staring down at the metal grill welded and bolted into rock above the Pit. The grill was large, heavy, and fine-meshed—they'd taken it from the old cistern near the ruins of Ardis Hall—and the Setebos baby had already grown to the point where it couldn't get its stalk-wandering hands through the mesh. The Pit itself was only fourteen feet deep, but they'd hacked it and blasted it out of solid rock. And strong as the monstrous thing down there was—the many-eyed, many-handed brain part of it was now more than four feet long and its hands were stronger every day—it wasn't strong enough to tear the grill's bolts and welded, sunken rods out of the rock. Not yet.

"A good idea except for the fact that we'd have twenty thousand voynix on us in five minutes if we kill the thing," whispered Daeman.

Ada didn't have to be reminded of this, but hearing it said aloud made the coldness and chill of nausea creep deeper into her. The sonie was up now, in the cloudy dark, doing its slow reconnaissance orbits.

The news was the same every day—the voynix stayed away, in an almost perfect circle with a radius of just under two miles from what could be this last human encampment on Earth—yet the numbers kept growing. Greogi had estimated at least twenty thousand to twenty-five thousand of the dull-silvery things out there in the treeless forests yesterday afternoon. There would be more at first light this morning. There were more each day. It was as certain as the weak, wintry sunrises. It was as certain as the fact that the pleading, whining, insinuating mental voice coming up from the Pit would never stop until it got free.

And then what? wondered Ada.

She could imagine. Just the presence of the thing had cast a pall over the Ardis survivors. It was hard enough just to get through the days— building and expanding their little tents and shacks, salvaging what they could from the ruins, improving their hopeless little log fort, not to mention getting enough to eat—without the Setebos baby's evil whining in their minds.

Food was a serious issue. All the cattle had been driven away during the massacre and sonie outings had found only their rotting carcasses in distant fields and on the winter forest floor. The voynix had slaughtered them as well. And with the soil frozen and even the hope of gardens or crops or planting months away, and with the canned and preserved goods that had been in the basement of Ardis Manor now merely melted blobs under charred rubble, the forty-eight Ardis survivors depended on the hunters who went out in the sonie every day. There was no game within the four-mile circle of the voynix army, so every day two men or women with flechette guns risked a trip beyond the voynix—a longer trip every day as the deer and larger game fled the area—and every evening, if they were lucky, a mule deer or wild pig would turn on the spit above the central cooking fire. But they hadn't been that lucky recently—they didn't have fresh meat every day, and fewer hunts provided them an animal to kill within the increasing radius of their flights, so they preserved what they could with smoking and with the remaining precious salt salvaged from the storehouses, and they munched on their monotonously bad-tasting jerky, and they watched the voynix continue massing, and each day and night their moods grew darker with the Setebos baby constantly sending its white, clammy hands and tendrils of telepathy into their brains. Even while they slept. And like the game they hunted from the sonie, sleep grew increasingly harder to find.

"Another few days," Daeman said softly, "and I think it will be able to tear its way out of this cage." He took the burning torch from its niche several feet away and held it out over the Pit. The size of a small calf, its brain surface gleaming with moist, gray mucus, Setebos' baby was hanging from the grill. Half a dozen of its tendriled hands gripped the dark iron mesh. Eight or ten yellow eyes squinted, blinked, and closed at the sudden flare of light. Two of its feeding mouths pulsed open and Ada stared in fascination at the rows of small, white teeth in each.

"Mommy," it squeaked. It had been speaking for the last week, but its actual voice was nowhere near as human-sounding or childlike as its telepathic voice

"Yes," whispered Ada. "We'll call a general meeting today. Let everyone vote on the time. But we have to make final preparations for departure soon."

The plan pleased almost none of them, but it was the best they had come up with. While Daeman and a few others stood guard on the baby, they would begin evacuating materials and people to an island they'd scouted about thirty-five miles downriver from Ardis. It was not the paradise isle Daeman had wanted to fax to somewhere on the far side of the world, but this small rocky islet was in the center of the river, the currents ran fast there, and most important, the ground was defensible.

They all assumed that the voynix were faxing in somehow, from somewhere—although daily checks of the Ardis faxnode showed that it was still inoperable. That meant that the voynix could easily follow them, perhaps even fax to the island. But the forty-eight survivors could cluster and set their camp on a grassy depression on the center knob of the isle—hunt and bring in their food via sonie the way they were doing now—and the island was so small that the voynix would have trouble faxing in more than a few hundred at a time. They might be able to kill or drive off that many.

The last men and women to leave Ardis—and Ada fully intended to be the last woman—would kill the Setebos spawn. And then the voynix would flood over this hallowed place like frenzied grasshoppers, but the rest of the survivors would be on the island and safe. Safe for a few hours, Ada guessed.

Could voynix swim? Ada and the others had searched their memories for any instance of seeing one of their slave voynix swimming way back in the ancient history before the sky fell ten months earlier, before Harman and dead Savi and Daeman had destroyed the Firmary along with Prospero's isle. Before the end of their foolish world of parties and endless faxing and safety. No one could be sure if they had ever seen a voynix swim.

But Ada was sure in her own heart. The voynix could swim. They could walk along the bed of the river under all that water and in all that swift current if they had to. They would get to the humans on their little island once the Setebos baby was dead.

And then the survivors, if there were any, would have to flee again—but to where? Ada's vote was for the Golden Gate at Machu Picchu since she remembered well Petyr's description of the voynix massed there being unable to get into the green environmental bubbles clustered on the bridge towers and suspension cables. But the majority of the others had not wanted to go to the Bridge they'd never seen—it was too far away, it would take too long to get there, they'd be caught inside the glass structures high above nothing with voynix all around them.

Ada had told them how Harman, Petyr, Hannah, and Noman/ Odysseus had reached the Bridge in less than an hour, hurtling up into the fringes of space and then tearing back down into the atmosphere above the southern continent. She explained how the sonie still had that flight plan in its memory—how a trip to the Golden Gate at Machu Picchu would take only a few minutes longer than the ferry down the river to the rocky island.

But they still did not want to try that. Not yet.

But Ada and Daeman continued to make their plans for that long evacuation.

Suddenly there came a sound from above the dark line of trees to the southwest—a sort of rattling, hissing noise.

Daeman unslung his flechette rifle and held it ready, clicking off the safety. "Voynix!" he shouted.

Ada bit her lip, the Setebos thing at her feet forgotten for a moment, its mental urgings drowned out by real noise. Someone by the central fire was ringing the main alarm bell. People were stumbling out of the big lean-to and the other tents and yelling to wake others.

"I don't think so," said Ada, almost shouting so Daeman could hear her over the din. "It didn't sound right."

When the bell quit clanging and the shouts died down, she could hear it more clearly now—a metallic, rasping, mechanical noise—not like the sibilant leap and rustle of a thousand voynix attacking.

Then a light became visible—a searchlight stabbing down from the sky, only a few hundred feet up, the shaft and circle of light illuminating bare branches, frozen and fire-blackened grass, the palisade walls and the shocked sentries on the crude ramparts there.

The sonie did not have a spotlight.

"Get the rifles!" Ada shouted at the group milling near the central fire. Some people had weapons. Others grabbed them and readied them.

"Spread out!" shouted Daeman, running toward the clustered crowd and waving his arms. "Take cover!" Ada agreed. Whatever this thing was, if it had hostile intentions, there was no need to help it by clustering up like fat and happy targets.

The humming and rasping grew so loud that it drowned out even the warning bell that someone had redundantly and wildly begun ringing again.

Ada could see it now—something mechanical flying, something much bigger than their sonie but also much slower and more awkward, something not the sleek oval of their sonie but like two lumpy circles with the skittering searchlight stabbing out from the front circle. The thing bobbed and wavered as if it were ready to crash, but it cleared the low palisade walls—a sentry throwing himself to the ground to avoid protuberances on the flying machine—and then skidded roughly across the frozen grass not that far from the Pit, rose into the air again, and then settled heavily.

Daeman and Ada ran toward it, Ada running as well as her five months of pregnancy would allow her to and carrying a torch, and Daeman with the automatic flechette rifle raised and aimed at the dark shapes now clambering out of the landed machine.

The dark shapes were people—eight of them by Ada's quick count. She saw faces she did not recognize, but the last two out of the machine, the two who had been at the controls near the front of the forward metal circle, were Hannah and Odysseus—or Noman as he'd asked to be called the last few months before he was injured and taken to the Bridge.

And then Ada and Hannah were hugging, both of them weeping but Hannah sobbing almost hysterically. When they paused to look at each other, Hannah gasped, "Ardis Hall? Where is it? Where is everyone? What's happened? Is Petyr all right?"

"Petyr is dead," said Ada, feeling the flatness of her own emotional reaction to the words. Too much horror had happened in too short a period of time; she felt that her soul had been bruised. "The voynix attacked in force shortly after you left. They overran the walls, used rocks as missiles. The house burned. Emme is dead. Reman is dead. Peaen is dead . . ." She went down the list of those old friends who had died in the attack and after.

Hannah—who had always been thin but who looked much thinner in the torchlight—covered her mouth in horror.

"Come," said Ada, touching Noman's wrist and putting her arm around Hannah again. "You all look starved. Come to the fire—it will be dawn soon. You can introduce your friends and we'll get you some food. I want to hear all about everything."

They sat by the fire until the winter sun rose, exchanging information as unemotionally as they could under the circumstances. Laman cooked a rich morning stew and they had that and tin cups of almost the last of the thick, rich coffee they'd found in one of the only partially burned storehouses.

The five new people, three men and two women, were named Beman, Elian, Stefe, Iyayi, and Susan. Elian was the leader, a completely bald man who carried the authority of age and who might have been almost as old as Harman. All were bandaged or had been slightly wounded and as the others talked, Tom and Siris tended to their injuries with what medical supplies were left.

Ada very quickly filled in her young friend Hannah—who somehow did not seem so young any more—and the silent Noman on the saga of the Ardis Massacre, the days and nights on Starved Rock, the nonfunctioning faxnode, the massing of the voynix, and the hatching and containment of the Setebos baby.

"I felt the thing in my mind even before we landed," Noman said softly. While Hannah began her tale, the barrel-chested and gray-bearded Greek, clad only in his rough tunic even in the freezing weather, walked over to the Pit and stared down at its captive.

"Odysseus came out of his recovery crèche three days after Ariel took Harman away," said the dark-haired young woman with the lustrous eyes. "The voynix continued to try to get in, but Odysseus reassured me that they couldn't as long as the zero-friction field was on. We ate, slept . . ." Hannah lowered her eyes here for a minute and Ada knew that the two had done more than sleep. "We expected Petyr to return for us as he'd promised, but after a week Odysseus began work trying to assemble the fragments of sonies and other flying machines we'd seen in the garage—hangar—whatever one should call it. I did most of the welding. Odysseus did the circuitboard and propulsion system work. When we ran out of parts we needed, I scavenged through the rest of the Golden Gate bubbles and secret rooms.

"He got the thing to hover and fly a little bit within the hangar—it's made up mostly of two servitor-type flying machines called skyrafts, not made for long-distance travel—but we had trouble with the guidance and control systems. Finally Odysseus had to dismantle part of a lesser AI that operated some of the Bridge kitchen, leaving the cooking and recipe parts but lobotomizing it to handle navigation and attitude for the raft. It's not happy flying that clumsy machine—it keeps wanting to cook us breakfast and suggest recipes."

Ada and some of the others laughed at this. There were more than a dozen people listening, including Greogi, one-handed Laman, Ella, Edide, Boman, and the two medics. The five injured newcomers were now eating their hot stew and listening in silence. The snow that Ada had smelled hours earlier now came down lightly but did not stick to the ground. Sunlight actually peeked through the scudding clouds.

"Finally, when we felt sure that Ariel wasn't bringing Harman back and that Petyr or none of the rest of you were returning for us, we filled the raft with supplies—we brought more weapons that I found in another secret room—opened the hangar doors, and headed north, hoping that the repellors would keep us airborne and the crude navigation system would get us to the general vicinity of Ardis."

"Was this yesterday?" asked Ada.

"It was nine days ago," said Hannah.

Seeing Ada's shocked reaction, the younger woman went on. "This thing flies *slowly*, Ada, fifty or sixty miles per hour at top speed. And it had problems. We lost most of the food supplies when we actually went down in the sea where Odysseus says the Isthmus of Panama used to be. Lucky for us, he'd added the flotation bags to the raft so that it could act like a *real* raft for a few hours while we jettisoned weight and Odysseus hammered the flight systems into working again."

"Did you have Elian and the others with you then?" asked Boman.

Hannah shook her head, sipped more coffee, and huddled over the warm tin cup as if it was giving her necessary heat. "We had to stop along the coast once we crossed the Isthmus Sea," she said. "There was a faxnode community there—you've been to it, I think, Ada: Hughes Town. There was that tall plascrete skyscraper there with all the ivy."

"I went to a Three Twenty party there once," said Ada, remembering the view of the sea from a terrace high atop that tower. She'd been young, not quite fifteen. It had been around the time she'd first met her pudgy "cousin" Daeman and she remembered an awakening sense of sensuality from those days.

Elian cleared his throat. The man had livid scars on his face, forearms, and hands, and his clothing was more a mass of torn rags than anything else, but he carried himself with strong authority. "There were more than two hundred of us in the node community when the voynix attacked a month ago," he said in a soft but deep voice. "We had no weapons. But the primary Hughes Town Tower was too tall for them to leap onto easily, something about the outside surface of the tower made it hard for them to cling and climb there, and the overhanging terraces made defense easier than any other place else we could retreat to. We barricaded the stairways—the power for the elevators had gone off back during the Fall of the Skies, of course—and used whatever we could find for weapons: servitor tools, iron bars, crude bows and arrows made of metal cables and leaf springs from barouches and droshkies—anything. The voynix got most of us, half a dozen or so of us made it to the fax pavilion and faxed away for help before the fax quit working, and the five others and I were on the penthouse of the Hughes Town Tower with five hundred voynix occupying everything. We'd been out of food for five days and out of water for two when we saw Noman's and Hannah's sky-raft lumbering in over the gulf."

"We had to jettison more of the food and medical supplies and even most of the guns and flechette ammunition to make up for the extra weight," Hannah said sheepishly. "And we had to land three more times to work on it. But it finally got us here."

"How did its navigation system know how to find Ardis?" asked Casman. The thin, bearded Ardis survivor had always been interested in machinery.

Hannah laughed. "It didn't. It could barely find what Odysseus calls North America. He guided us here—Odysseus—following first one big river he calls the Mississippi, and then our own Ardis River, which he called the Leanoka or Ohio. And then we saw your fire."

"You flew on at night?" asked Ada.

"We had to. There were too many dinosaurs and sabertooths down in the forests south of here to risk landing for very long. We all took turns helping fly the thing while Odysseus caught naps. But he's been awake for most of seventy-two hours."

"He looks . . . well again," said Ada.

Hannah nodded. "The recovery crèche healed most of the wounds the voynix inflicted on him. We were right to bring him back to the Bridge. He would have died otherwise."

Ada was silent a minute, thinking of how that decision had taken Harman from her.

As if reading her friend's mind, Hannah said, "We looked for Harman, Ada. Even though Odysseus was sure that Ariel had quantum teleported him somewhere—that's like faxing, only more powerful somehow, it's what the gods did in the turin drama—even though Odysseus was sure that the Ariel-thing had QT'd him far away, we flew down and searched the old Machu Picchu ruins below the Golden Gate and even looked along the nearby rivers and waterfalls and valleys. There was no sign of Harman."

"He's still alive," Ada said simply. She touched her swollen belly as she said this. She always did—it was not only a part of her connection to Harman, but it seemed to confirm that her intuitive feeling was accurate. It was almost as if Ada's unborn *child* knew that Harman still lived . . . somewhere.

"Yes," said Hannah.

"Did you see any other faxnode communities?" asked Loes. "Any other survivors?"

Hannah shook her head. Ada noticed that her young friend's always-short hair had grown out some. "We stopped at two other nodes between Hughes Town and Ardis," said Hannah. "Small-population nodes—Live Oak and Hulmanica. They'd both been sacked by voynix—there were voynix carcasses and human bones left, nothing more."

"How many people do you think died there?" Ada asked softly.

Hannah shrugged and sipped the last of her coffee. "No more than forty or fifty total," she said with the unemotional lack of affect common to all the Ardis survivors. "Nothing like the disaster here." Hannah looked around. "I can feel something scrabbling at my mind like a bad memory."

"That's the little Setebos," said Ada. "It wants to get in our minds and out of its Pit." She always thought of the thing's hole as "the Pit" with a capital "P."

"Aren't you afraid that its mother—father—whatever that thing in Paris Crater was that Daeman saw, will come for it?"

Ada looked over to where Daeman was standing by the Pit, speaking earnestly to Noman. "The big Setebos hasn't showed up yet," she said. "We're more worried about what the little one will do." She described to them all how the many-handed thing seemed to suck energy out of the earth where someone had died horribly.

Hannah shivered even though the sunlight was stronger now. "We saw the voynix in the woods with our searchlight," she said softly. "Countless numbers of them. Row upon row of them. Just standing there under the trees and along the ridgelines, the closest about two miles out, I think. What are you going to do?"

Ada told her about the plan for the island.

Elian cleared his throat again. "Excuse me," he said. "It's not my business and I know I don't get a vote here, but it seems to me that a rocky island like that would put you in our position in the tower. The voynix would keep coming—and you have so many more around you here—and you'd die off one by one. Someplace like the Bridge that Hannah told us about seems to make more sense."

Ada nodded. She didn't want to argue strategies quite yet—too many of the listening Ardis survivors sitting around this circle would vote for the island. "You *do* get a vote here, Elian," she said instead. "Every one of you does. You're part of our community now—any refugee we find will be—and you get as much of a vote as I do. Thank you for your opinion. We're all going to discuss this at the noon meal and even the sentries will vote by proxy. I think you should get some sleep before then."

Elian, Beman, the blond Iyayi—who somehow had remained beautiful despite her scratches and rags—and the short, silent woman named Susan and the big, bearded man named Stefe nodded and moved off with Tom and Siris to find empty bedrolls under canvas somewhere.

"You should sleep, too," Ada said, touching Hannah's forearm.

"What happened to your wrist, Ada?"

Ada looked down at the rough plaster cast and grubby bandage. "I broke it during the fight here. It's nothing. I'm interested that the voynix disappeared from the Golden Gate at Machu Picchu. It makes me think we're fighting a finite number of the things . . . if they have to redeploy, I mean."

"A finite number," agreed Hannah. "But Odysseus thinks there are more than a million voynix, and fewer than a hundred thousand of us humans." She thought a second and added, "A hundred thousand of us before the slaughters began."

"Does Noman have any idea *why* the voynix are killing us?" asked Ada, holding Hannah's strong hand now.

"I think he does, but he hasn't told me," said Hannah. "There's a lot he keeps to himself."

That's the understatement of the Twenty, thought Ada. Aloud she said, "You look exhausted, my dear. You really should get some sleep."

"When Odysseus does," said Hannah, meeting Ada's gaze with something like the bashfulness, defiance, and pride of a young lover.

Ada nodded again.

Daeman stepped up to the fire. "Ada, could we see you a minute?"

Touching Hannah's shoulder, Ada rose awkwardly and followed Daeman back to the Pit where Noman stood. The man they'd once called Odysseus was not much taller than Ada, but he was so solid and muscular that he emanated power. Ada could see the curly gray hairs on his chest through the open tunic.

"Admiring our pet?" asked Ada.

Noman did not smile. He scratched his beard, looked down into the Pit at the strangely quiescent baby, and then returned his dark-eyed gaze to Ada. "You'll have to kill it," he said.

"We plan to."

"I mean quickly," said Noman/Odysseus. "These things aren't so much babies of the real Setebos as lice."

"Lice?" Ada said. "I can hear its thoughts . . ."

"And you'll hear them more and more loudly until the thing comes up out of there—it probably could already if it wanted to—and sucks the energy and souls right out of your bodies."

Ada blinked and looked down into the Pit. The baby's two-hemisphered brain-back was just a gray glow down there. It was on the floor of the Pit now, tendrils and hands reeled in, its motile hands tucked under its mucousy body, its many eyes closed.

"The eggs hatch and these things swarm out," continued Noman. "They're like scouts for the real Setebos. These things only grow to be about twenty feet long. They find . . . food . . . in the soil and then return to the original Setebos, I don't know quite how they travel so far, Brane Holes probably—this one's not quite old enough to summon a Hole—and when they report back, the big Setebos thanks them for the infor-

mation and eats them, absorbing all the evil and terror these . . . babies . . . have sucked up from the world."

"How do you know so much about Setebos and his . . . lice?" asked
Ada.

Noman shook his head as if that were too unimportant to deal with
now.

*And when are you going to start treating that sweet Hannah with the love
and attention she deserves, you male pig?* thought Ada.

"Noman had something important to tell us . . . ask us," said Daeman. Ada's friend looked worried.

"I need to take the sonie," said Noman.

Ada blinked again. "Take it where?"

"Up to the rings," said Noman.

"For how long?" asked Ada. She was thinking *You can't take the sonie!*
and she knew that Daeman was thinking the same thing.

"I don't know," said Odysseus in that strange accent of his.

"Well," began Ada, "it's out of the question that you take the sonie.
We need it to escape this place. We need it for hunting. We'll need it
for . . ."

"I have to take the sonie," repeated Noman. "It's the only machine on
this continent that can get me up there, and I don't have time to fly to
China or somewhere to find another. And the *calibani* will have made the
Mediterranean Basin unapproachable by now."

"Well," said Ada again, hearing the edge of rockhard stubbornness
that only rarely powered her voice, "you can't just take the sonie. We'll
all die."

"That's not so important right now," said the gray-bearded warrior.

Ada started to laugh but ended up only staring, her mouth partially
open in amazement. "It's important to *us,* Noman. We want to live."

He shook his head as if Ada had not understood. "No one on this
planet is going to live unless I can get up to the rings . . . and today," he
said. "I need the sonie. If I can, I'll bring it back or send it back to you. If
I can't . . . well, it won't matter."

Ada wished she had a flechette rifle with her. She glanced at the one
that Daeman carried—still unslung, he carried it casually. Noman
seemed to have no weapon on him, but Ada had seen how strong this
man was.

"I need the sonie," Noman said again. "Today. Now."

"No," said Ada.

Down in the Pit, the many-handed orphan suddenly began a wailing,
snorting, coughing sound that ended in a noise that sounded very much
like a human laugh.

70

A storm was raging far above them. The rings and stars had long since disappeared and lightning illuminated the vertical walls of water on either side and the obscenely pale slash of the Breach stretching away so far to the east and west that the lightning did not last long enough to show its immensity.

Now, however, the lightning flashes overlapped, thunder exploding and echoing down the hallway of energy-bound water, and, lying on his back snug in his silk-thin sleeping bag and thermskin, Harman could see the waves fifty stories above, rising and thrashing another hundred or so feet as the Atlantic Ocean threw itself into the frenzy of the storm. The whipping, writhing clouds were only a few hundred feet above the towering waves. And while the dark depths on either side stayed calm here more than five hundred feet below the surface, Harman could see the layers of agitation far above him. Also agitated were the funnel-bridges—he didn't have a good name for the transparent tubes and cones and energy-bound tunnels of water that connected the Atlantic south of the Breach to the Atlantic north of it, and Moira simply called them "conduits." There was such a funnel-bridge visible two hundred feet above the dry bottom of the Breach, visible when the lightning flashed at least, less than a half mile to the west of where they had camped and another a mile or so behind them to the east. Both water tunnels were broiling with activity, huge quantities of white water surging from one side of the Breach to the other. Harman wondered if more water was forced across the Breach during storms. Certainly there was more water falling on them now—the shifting energy walls kept the high waves from pouring over and drowning them, but the spray drifted down as a constant mist. Harman's outer clothes were tucked away in his rucksack, which was completely waterproof he'd discovered, as was the thinskin sleeping bag, but he'd left the osmosis mask open on his thermskin cowl and his face was damp. Whenever he licked his lips, he tasted salt.

Lightning struck the floor of the Breach less than a hundred yards from them. The percussion from the thunder shook Harman's molars.

"Should we move?" he shouted at Moira, who was in her own thermskin—she stripped naked and pulled on the thermskin right in front of him with no sign of embarrassment, almost as if they were lovers, which, he realized with a blush, they had been.

"What?" shouted Moira. His voice had been lost in the crash of wave and roars of thunder.

"SHOULD WE MOVE?"

She slid her sleeping skin closer and leaned over to speak close to his ear. She'd left her face exposed as well and was just lying on the sleeping bag, and the mist had soaked the outer layer of the skintight thermskin, showing every rib and rise of hipbone.

"The only place we can move to be safe," she said loudly next to his ear, "is underwater. We'd be safe from the lightning there at the bottom of the ocean. Want to adjourn?"

Harman didn't. The thought of stepping through the forcefield barrier into that almost absolute dark and terrible pressure—even if the magical thermskin would keep him from drowning or being crushed— was more than he wanted to deal with this night. Besides, the storm seemed to be letting up a bit. The waves up there only looked to be sixty or eighty feet tall now.

"No thanks," he shouted back to Moira. "I'll risk it here."

He rubbed his face dry and pulled the film-thin osmosis mask in place. Without the salt sting in his eyes and mouth, it was easier to concentrate.

And Harman had a lot to concentrate on. He was still trying to sort out his new human functions.

Many of these newly acquired—although "identified" would be a better word—functions had been interdicted along with his freefax abilities. For instance, Harman clearly saw how he could trigger access to the logosphere to acquire information or to communicate with anyone anywhere, but those functions had been interrupted by whoever or whatever was running the rings these days.

Other functions worked just fine but did not necessarily add to Harman's peace of mind. There was a medical monitor function that, when queried, told and showed Harman that his diet of food bars and water would lead to certain vitamin deficiencies if he continued it for more than three months. It also informed him that calcium was building up in his left kidney—resulting in a kidney stone in a year or less—that there were two polyps in his colon since his last Firmary visit, that his muscles were deteriorating because of age—it had, after all, been ten years since his last Firmary tune-up, that a strep virus was failing to set up a colony in his throat because of his genetic-cued defenses, that his blood pressure was too high, and that there was the slightest of shadows on his left lung that should demand immediate attention by Firmary sensors.

Great, thought Harman, rubbing his thermskinned chest as if the slight shadow that he was sure was lung cancer was already beginning to ache. *What do I do with this information? The Firmaries are a little out of bounds to me right now.*

Other functions served more immediate purposes. In the last few days he'd discovered that he had a replay function through which he could relive with amazing clarity—much more like experiencing something in reality than through memory—any point or event in his life, pinpointing the memory in a protein memory bundle rather than in his brain, uploading it, and timing the replay to the second. He'd already replayed a few minutes of his first meeting with Ada nine times (his memory couldn't have told him that she'd been wearing that light blue gown on the evening he met her at a fax-in party) and had replayed moments from the last time they'd made love more than thirty times. Moira had even commented on his fixed stare and robotic walk when he'd been replaying. She knew what he was up to, especially since neither his thermskin nor outer clothes had hidden his reaction.

Harman had enough sense to know that this function was addictive and that he must use it very, very carefully—especially while hiking across the bottom of the ocean—but he'd flashed back to certain dialogues he'd had with Savi to mine more data out of things she'd said about the past or about the rings or about the world—things that had seemed nonsensical or mysterious then, but made more sense now after the crystal cabinet. He also realized, with a great sadness, that Savi had been working from very incomplete information in her centuries of attempts to get up to the rings to negotiate with the post-humans, including her lack of knowledge of real spaceships stored in the Mediterranean Basin or the proper way to contact Ariel via Prospero's private logosphere connections.

Seeing Savi so clearly through replay vision also made Harman realize how much younger this Moira-iteration of Savi's face and body were, but also how much alike the women were.

Harman trolled through the other functions. Proxnet, farnet, and allnet were all down with the fax and logosphere functions—evidently everything internal worked; anything demanding use of the planetary system of satellites, orbital mass accumulators, fax and data transmitters, and so forth did not work.

But why did his internal indicators tell him that the sigl function was not working? Harman would have thought that sigling was as body-dependent as his medical monitoring, which worked all too well. Did the sigl function depend upon relay satellites in some way? His crystal cabinet data did not explain this.

"Moira?" he shouted. Only after he'd shouted did he realize that the storm had all but passed over and that except for the slide-crash of waves far above, the sound had abated. Also, he was wearing his osmosis mask with its inset microphones so poor Moira had heard his shout in her cowl earphones.

He pulled the osmosis mask free and breathed in the rich scent of the ocean again.

"What, oh mighty-lunged one?" replied Moira in soft tones. Her sleepingskin bag was about four feet away.

"If I use the touch-sharing function with my wife—with Ada—when I get home, will my unborn child receive the information as well?"

"Counting your fetus chickens before they're hatched, my young Prometheus?"

"Just answer the damned question, would you?"

"You'll have to try it," said Moira. "I don't recall the design parameters right now and I haven't ever touch-shared with preggoes, and we godlike post-humans *can't* get pregnant—nor did it help in that department that we were all female—so give it a try if and when you get home. I do remember though that there were safety nets installed in the genetic touch-share function. You can't pour harmful information to a fetus or a young child—replaying her own moment of conception, for instance. We don't want the little tyke in therapy for thirty years, now do we?"

Harman ignored the sarcasm. He rubbed his stubbled cheeks. He'd shaved before starting on this trip—the thermskin cowl was less than comfortable over a beard, he'd learned on Prospero's Isle more than ten months earlier—but two days of stubble rasped under his palm.

"You have all the functions you gave us?" he said to Moira, adding the rising inflection of the question mark at only the last instant.

"My dear," purred Moira. "Do you think we're fools? Are we going to give mere old-style humans some ability we lack?"

"So you have more than we do," said Harman. "More than this hundred you built into us?"

Moira did not answer.

Harman had discovered complex nanocameras and audioreceivers built into his skin cells. Some DNA-bound protein bundles could store this visual and auditory data. Other cells had been altered into bioelectronic transmitters—good for only short range because they were powered just by his own cellular energy, but easily strong enough to be picked up and boosted and retransmitted.

"The turin drama," he said aloud.

"What's that?" Moira said sleepily. The post-human woman had been dozing.

"I realize how you transmitted the images from Ilium—or your transvestite god-sisters did—and how we were able to receive them through the turin cloths."

"Well . . . duh," said Moira and went back to sleep.

Harman saw how he would no longer need a turin cloth to receive such transmissions. Between logosphere voice-over protocols and this multimedia connection, he could share both voice and full sensory data with any other human being who volunteered to uplink the input stream.

What would that be like, linked to Ada, while we made love? wondered Harman and then chided himself for being a dirty old man. *A horny, dirty old man*, he corrected himself.

Besides the logosphere function, there was another function he could trigger that offered a complicated sensory interface with the biosphere. Since it was satellite-dependent and interdicted at the moment, he could only guess how it worked and what it felt like. Was it like a chat with Ariel or did a person suddenly become one with the dandelions and hummingbirds? Could he communicate directly and at a distance with the Little Green Men that way? Feeling serious again, Harman remembered Prospero saying that Ariel was using the LGM to hold off the thousands upon thousands of attacking *calibani* along the southern fringes of Old Europe, and he immediately saw how he could use such a connection to ask the *zeks* for help fighting the voynix.

All this function-searching was giving Harman a worse headache. Almost by accident, he checked his medical monitor function and saw that indeed, his adrenaline levels and blood pressure combined was high enough to give him the headache he'd suffered with for two weeks now. He activated another medical function—this one more active than mere monitoring—and tentatively allowed some chemicals to be released into his system. Blood vessels in his neck dilated and relaxed. Warmth flowed back into his icy fingertips. The headache receded.

A teenaged boy could really use this function to chase away unwanted erections, thought Harman. He realized that he really *was* a horny, dirty old man.

Not so old, really, thought Harman. The medical monitor had told him that he had the physical body of an average slightly out-of-shape thirty-one-year-old man.

Other functions floated onto his mental checklist: figure-ground enhancement, enhanced empathy, another that he thought of as the beserker function—a temporary spiking of adrenaline and all other physical and strength-multiplying abilities, probably to be used as a last resort in a fight or if one had to lift a ton or two off one's child. Besides the already used and misused memory replay function, Harman saw that replay data inputted through someone else's sharing function. There was a function that would allow him to put his body into a sort of hibernation, a temporary slowing of everything to the point of stasis. He realized that this wasn't a quick way to catch a nap but designed to be used with something like the crystal coffin in the Taj Moira if one needed to remain alive but intert for long periods of time—in Moira's case, *very* long periods of time—without suffering bedsores, muscle atrophy, morning breath, and the other side effects of normal human unconsciousness. Harman saw at once that the real Savi had used this function many times in her time crèche on the Golden Gate at Machu Picchu and elsewhere to survive and thrive over the fourteen centuries of her hiding from the voynix and the post-humans.

There were many more functions—some of them intriguing beyond words—but the concentration necessary to explore them was bringing back Harman's headache. He shut down that part of his brain for the night.

Immediately more powerful sensory information flowed in. The surge of waves far above. A photoluminescent-phytoplanktonish glow in the upper strata of the Atlantic that looked like an underwater aurora borealis to his tired eyes.

The sky over the ocean was also alive with light—not air-to-sea lightning this time but internal cloud lightning, silent explosions showing the fractal complexity of the churning clouds as lit from within. These pulses and explosions of light were silent—not the slightest hint of thunder reaching his little sleeping bag on the bottom of the Atlantic Breach—so Harman crossed his arms behind his head and just enjoyed the light show, also appreciating the effect of the cloud lightning on the still-churning surface of the ocean.

Patterns. Patterns everywhere. All of nature and the universe dancing at the edge of chaos, reprieved by fractal boundaries and a billion hidden algorithmic protocols hardwired into everything and every interaction, but beautiful nonetheless—oh, so beautiful. He realized that there was at least one function he hadn't really explored that could sort out most of these patterns for him, far better than mere evolved human senses and sensibilities could, but it would probably be an interdicted function requiring ring-connections, and besides . . . Harman didn't need a genetically enhanced function to appreciate the pure beauty of this silent mid-Atlantic show that was being put on just for him.

He lay on the floor of the Breach, hands behind his head, and said a prayer for Ada and his possible son or daughter. (Her functions, when activated, would tell her which it was.) He wished he could be with her now. He prayed to the God he'd never really thought about—to the Quiet God whom Setebos and his lackey Caliban feared above all else according to what the monster had blurted out on Prospero's Isle—and he prayed only that his beloved Ada would remain well and alive and as happy as the terrible circumstances of these times and their separation across space would allow.

As he fell asleep, Harman heard the rasp and sawing of Moira's snoring. He smiled as he drifted off. A thousand years of post-human nanocyte and DNA-rearranging cleverness hadn't cured them from snoring. But, of course, it was Savi's human body that . . .

Harman fell asleep in midthought.

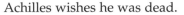

71

Achilles wishes he was dead.

The air is so foul and thick here in Tartarus, his lungs burn so fiercely, his eyes are watering and hurting so much, his skin and guts feel like they are ready simultaneously to implode and explode from the pressure, the Oceanids monster-woman is carrying him so rib-shattering tightly in her thigh-fingered fist, and his outlook for the future is so fucking dim, that he wishes that he could just die and get it over with.

But the quantum Fates will not allow him this option. That bitch of a goddess mother of his, that tart Thetis who'd professed love to his father—the man whom he'd always honored as his father, Peleus—and then lain with Zeus like the aquatic roundheels she was, had held him in the Celestial Fire and created a quantum singularity point for his death—to be reached only through the actions of the now dead and cremated Paris of Ilium—and that, as they say, is that.

So he suffers and tries to focus on what is going on outside his tight, rapidly imploding sphere of pain and discomfort.

The three Titan-giant daughters of Okeanos—Asia, Panthea, and Ione—are striding quickly through the poisonous gloom toward a brighter glow that might be a volcanic eruption, Achilles held tight in

Asia's huge, sweaty fist. When Achilles is able to open his burning eyes and catch glimpses of the landscape through his tears—tears from toxic chemicals in the air, not from emotion—he gets blurry views of high, rocky ridges such as the one the three Oceanids are now striding along, thundering volcanoes, deep chasms filled with lava and oddly shaped monsters, an escort of the giant centipede-things that must be related to the Healer on Olympos, occasional glimpses of silhouettes that must be other Titans crashing and bellowing through the gloom, and a sky filled with orange-limned clouds, wild lightning, and other electrical displays.

Suddenly the giantess Titan named Panthea speaks—"Is that the véiled form we seek who sits on that ebony throne?"

Asia, bitch-voice booming like boulders crashing down a rocky slope. (Achilles has not the strength to cover his aching ears with his acid-scalded hands.)—"It is. The veil has fallen."

Panthea—"I see a mighty darkness filling the seat of power, and rays of gloom dart round, as light from the meridian sun.—But the Demogorgon itself remains ungazed upon and shapeless, neither limb, nor form, nor outline; yet we all three feel it is a living Spirit."

The Demogorgon speaks then and Achilles buries his face in Asia's huge, rough palm in a vain effort to muffle the subsonic pain of that all-encroaching voice. *"ASK WHAT THOU WOULDST KNOW, OCEANIDS."*

Asia offers up her palm with the writhing Achilles on it. "Canst thou tell us what shape and manner of thing this is we have caught? It seems more starfish than man, and it writhes and squeaks as such."

The Demogorgon roars again. *"IT IS ONLY A MORTAL MAN, ALTHOUGH MADE IMMORTAL BY THE CELESTIAL FIRE'S MISTAKE. IT IS NAMED ACHILLES AND IT IS VERY FAR FROM HOME. NO MORTAL HAS EVER COME TO TARTARUS BEFORE THIS DAY."*

"Ah," says Asia, seeming to lose interest in her toy and roughly setting Achilles down on a burning-hot boulder.

Achilles feels the heat all around and when he opens his eyes, he can see farther because of the glow of lava and eruption, but is horrified to see that lava flowing past on both sides of his steaming boulder. When he looks up toward the Demogorgon on its throne—the throne a mountain taller than the erupting volcanoes, and the hooded and veiled non-shape on that throne seeming to rise up for miles and miles—the shapelessness of the Demogorgon makes him want to vomit. So he does. None of the Oceanics seems to notice his retching.

Asia asks the huge form, "What else canst thou tell?"

"ALL THINGS THOU DAR'ST DEMAND."

"Who made the living world?" asks Asia. Achilles has already decided that she is the most talkative, if not the most intelligent, of the three idiot Oceanids.

"GOD."

"Who made all that it contains?" persists Asia. "Thought? Passion? Reason? Will? Imagination?"

"GOD. ALMIGHTY GOD."

Achilles decides that this Demogorgon is a spirit-thing of few words. And fewer thoughts in its head, if it has a head. He would give anything if he could rise and pull his sword from his belt, unsling his shield from his back. First he would kill the Demogorgon and then the three Titan sisters . . . slowly.

"Who made that sense, which, when the winds of Spring in rarest visitation, or the voice of one beloved heard in youth alone," asks Asia in her crackly, booming voice, "fills the faint eyes with falling tears which dim the radiant looks of unbewailing flowers, and leaves the peopled world a solitude when it returns no more?"

Achilles throws up again. This time it is as an aesthetic statement more than a reaction to optical vertigo. He decides that he will kill the Oceanids first after all. He would like to kill this Asia bitch several times over. He visualizes hollowing out her skull and using it for a house, her eye sockets as round windows.

"MERCIFUL GOD," intones the Demogorgon.

There is no Greek word for "ditto," but Achilles thinks that the Demogorgon should coin one. It does not surprise the Achaean in the least that Oceanids and the formless spirit in the murk down here in Tartarus speak his form of Greek to one another. They're strange creatures, monsters really, but even monsters in Achilles' experience speak Greek. They're not barbarians, after all.

"And who made terror, madness, crime, remorse," continues Asia, her voice as relentless as the babble of a two-year-old who's just learned how to keep a conversation going with an adult by asking "Why?" a hundred times over. "Which from the links of the great chain of things, to every thought within the mind of man sway and drag heavily, and each one reels under the load toward the pit of death; Abandoned hope, and love that turns to hate, and self-contempt, bitterer to drink than blood. Pain, whose unheeded and familiar speech is howling, and keen shrieks, day after day; and . . ."

She breaks off.

Achilles hopes that it is some Tartarusian cataclysm that will end their world and swallow up Asia and her two sisters screaming like honey-covered appetizers at a Myrmidon feast, but when he forces his eyes open he sees that it is only a circle of bright light opening, pouring white brilliance into the red gloom.

A Brane Hole.

Something far from human is silhouetted against the light of that hole. It's shaped roughly like a man, but it is made up of metallic spheres—not only a sphere where the head should be, but spheres for the torso, spheres for the outflung arms, spheres for the staggering legs. Only the feet and hands—wrapped in some lighter-than-bronze metal—look even vaguely manlike.

The thing comes closer and two brilliant lights stab out from the smaller spheres that are its shoulders. A red light, thin as a javelin, leaps from its right hand and plays across the Oceanid Sisters, making their flesh sizzle and pop. The Titanesses stagger backward, wading through lava, evidently unharmed by the red beam but shielding their faces and eyes from the painful white light flowing out of the Brane Hole.

"Goddammit, Achilles, are you just going to lie there?"

It's Hephaestus. Achilles now sees the iron-sphere bubbles as some sort of protective suit, with iron-shod feet and heavily gauntleted hands emerging from the chain of globes. There is some sort of steaming, burping breathing pack on the back and the top bubble is clear as glass; Achilles can now make out the dwarf-god's ugly, bearded face in the reflected light from his shoulder searchlights and handheld laser.

Achilles manages a weak squeak.

Hephaestus laughs, the ugly noise amplified by the speakers in his pressure suit. "Don't like the air and gravity here, eh? All right. Get into this. It's called a thermskin and it'll help you breathe." The god of fire and artifice throws down some impossibly thin garment onto the boulder next to Achilles.

The hero tries to stir, but the air weakens and burns him. All he can do is wiggle and cough and retch.

"Oh, fuck me," says the crippled god. "I guess I'll have to dress you like an infant. I was afraid of this. Lie still, quit squirming. Don't shit on me or puke on me while I'm undressing you and tucking you into this thing."

Ten minutes later—with a tapestry of Hephaestus' curses now hanging in the air like glowing smoke from the volcanoes—Achilles is upright on solid rock next to Hephaestus, dressed in a gold thermskin under his armor, breathing easily through the thermskin cowl's clear membrane—the dwarf-god had called it an osmosis mask—brandishing his acid-etched shield and still-bright sword, staring up at the looming but still indistinct mass called the Demogorgon, and feeling invulnerable again and not a little pissed off. Achilles only hopes that the Oceanid named Asia will start asking one of her endless questions again so he will have an excuse to gut her like a fish.

"Demogorgon," calls Hephaestus, using the amplifier built into his fishbowl helmet, "we have met once before, more than nineteen hundred years ago during the Olympians' War with the Giants. I am called Hephaestus . . ."

"THOU ART THE CRIPPLED ONE," booms Demogorgon.

"Yes. How nice of you to remember. Achilles and I have come to Tartarus to seek out you and the Titans—Kronos, Rhea, all of the Old Ones—and to ask for your help."

"DEMOGORGON DOES NOT HELP MERE GODS AND MORTALS."

"No, of course not," says Hephaestus, his rasping voice amplified a hundred times by the speakers in his suit. "Shit. Achilles, do you want to take over? Talking to this thing is like talking to your own ass."

"Can that big mass of nothing hear me?" Achilles asks the little god.

"I HEAR YOU."

Achilles stares skyward, focusing on the roiling red clouds a little to the side of the featureless, veiled nonface of the nonthing looming above him. "When you say 'God,' Demogorgon, do you mean Zeus?"

"WHEN I SAY GOD, I MEAN GOD."

"You must mean Zeus then, for right now the son of Kronos and Rhea is calling all the surviving gods together on Olympos and is announcing that he—Zeus—is the God of Gods, the Lord of All Creation, the God of This and All Universes."

"THEN EITHER HE LIETH OR YOU DO, SON OF MAN. GOD REIGNS. BUT NOT ON OLYMPOS."

"Then Zeus has enslaved all other gods and mortals," says Achilles, his thermskin-speaker voice and radio broadcast echoing from the volcano's slopes and cinder ridges.

"ALL SPIRITS ARE ENSLAVED WHICH SERVE THINGS EVIL: THOU KNOWEST IF ZEUS BE SUCH OR NOT."

"I do know," says Achilles. "Zeus is a greedy immortal son of a bitch—no offense to Rhea if she's out there in the shadows somewhere listening. I think he's a coward and a bully. But if you consider him God, then he will reign on Olympos and in the universe forever and forever."

"I SPOKE BUT AS YE SPEAK, FOR ZEUS IS THE SUPREME OF ALL LIVING THINGS."

"Who is the master of the slave?" asks Achilles.

"Oh, that's good," whisper-hisses Hephaestus. "That's very good . . ."

"Shut up," says Achilles.

The Demogorgon rumbles. It is so loud that at first Achilles thinks the nearest volcano is in full eruption. Then the rumble modulates itself into words.

"IF THE ABYSM COULD VOMIT FORTH ITS SECRETS—BUT A VOICE IS WANTING, THE DEEP TRUTH IS IMAGELESS; FOR WHAT WOULD IT AVAIL TO BID THEE GAZE ON THE REVOLVING WORLD? WHAT TO BID SPEAK ON FATE, TIME, OCCASION, CHANCE, AND

CHANGE? TO THESE ALL THINGS ARE SUBJECT BUT ETERNAL LOVE AND THE PERFECTION OF THE QUIET."

"Whatever you say," says Achilles. "But as we speak, Zeus is proclaiming himself Lord of All Creation and soon he will demand that all of that creation—not just his little world at the base of Mount Olympos—pay homage to him and him alone. Goodbye, Demogorgon."

Achilles turns to leave, grabbing the sputtering god of artifice by his metal-bubble arm and pulling him around, away from the unformed mass looming above them.

"HALT! . . . ACHILLES, FALSE SON OF PELEUS, TRUE SON OF ZEUS, WOULD-BE AUTHOR OF DEICIDE AND PATRICIDE. WAIT."

Achilles stops, turns back, and waits with Hephaestus. The Oceanids are cowering, covering their heads as if from hot ashfall.

"I SHALL SUMMON THE TITANS FROM THEIR CREVICES AND CAVES, BRING THEM FORTH FROM THEIR COWERING CORNERS. I SHALL COMMAND THE IMMORTAL HOURS TO BRING THEM FORTH."

With a sound that makes all the other unbearable sounds seem small, the rocks around Demogorgon's throne cleave in the purple night, the lava glow grows deeper and broader, a rainbow of impossible colors arches through Tartarus' gloom, and chariots the size of mountains appear from nowhere, drawn by gigantic steeds that are not horses—nothing like horses, not even remotely like horses—some being whipped on by wild-eyed charioteers that are not men or gods, other steeds staring behind them with burning eyes filled with fear. The charioteers themselves are almost impossible for mortal eyes to look upon, so Achilles averts his gaze. He thinks that it would be unwise to vomit again while sealed behind this thermskin facemask.

"THESE ARE THE IMMORTAL HOURS WHICH THOU DIDST DEMAND HEAR THY CASE," booms the Demogorgon. *"THEY SHALL BRING KRONOS AND HIS ILK HERE TO THIS PLACE."*

The air implodes with a series of sonic booms, the Oceanids scream in fright, and the huge chariots disappear in circles of flame.

"Well . . ." says Hephaestus over the suit radio and does not go on.

"Now we wait," says Achilles, setting his sword in his belt and slinging his shield.

"Not for long," says Hephaestus.

The air is filling with circles of fire again. The giant chariots are returning by the hundreds—no, by the thousands—each one filled with a giant form, some human-looking, many not.

"BEHOLD!" says the Demogorgon.

"It's hard not to," says Achilles. He braces himself and slides his great and beautiful shield across his forearm.

The Titans' chariots come on.

72

Moira was gone when Harman awoke. The day was gray and cold and it was raining hard. The sea far above was churning and whitecapped, but not the violent surge of liquid mountain ranges he'd watched by lightning flash the night before. Harman hadn't slept well—his dreams had been urgent and ominous.

He rolled up the silk-thin sleeping bag—it would dry by itself, he knew—and set it into his rucksack, leaving his clothes in the waterproof bag, taking out only his socks and boots to wear over his thermskin.

They'd had a campfire the last night before the storm began—no weenies and marshmallows, of course, Harman only knew what those were through the books he'd absorbed at the Taj—but he'd eaten the second half of his tasteless food bar and sipped water while they sat by the flickering flames.

Now the ashes were drenched and gray, the Breach floor between the rocks and coral had turned to mud, and Harman realized that he was walking in circles around their campsite, looking for some last sign of Moira . . . a note perhaps.

There was nothing.

He hitched the rucksack higher, pulled the thermskin cowl lower so that the goggles were properly lined up, wiped the rain from them, and began hiking west.

Instead of growing lighter as the day progressed, the skies grew darker, the rain came down more heavily, and the walls of water on either side grew taller and more oppressive. He'd gotten used to the trick of perspective where it was never the ocean bottom going down, but always the vertical walls of water on either side growing taller. Harman trudged on. The Breach descended through path-blasted ridges of black rock, passed over deep crevasses on narrow, slippery black iron bridges with no railings, and climbed steeply up more rock ridges. Even though high ridges made the walls of water on each side lower—the ocean was no more than two hundred feet deep here, Harman guessed—the climbing was exhausting and even more claustrophobic than before, with the rock walls on either side of the narrow path making him feel as if there were walls within walls closing in on him.

By midday—which only his internal time-function announced since the sun was completely absent and the rain was falling so fiercely that he considered pulling down his osmosis mask over his nose and mouth—the Breach path had come out of the underwater mountainous country and stretched flat and straight ahead. That was something and it helped improve Harman's dark mood—but only a little.

He welcomed the rocky or coral sections of path now, since the ocean-floor bottom, which had a nice consistency of packed soil on the dry days, was become a squelching avenue of mud. Eventually he grew tired of walking—it was after noon at whatever local time it was there south of England—so he sat on a low boulder emerging from the forcefield-contained northern ocean and took out his daily food bar to munch on, while sipping cool water from the hydrator tube.

The food bars—one a day—left him hungry. And they tasted like he imagined sawdust must taste. And there were only four left. What Prospero and Moira expected him to do when the food bars ran out— assuming he had another seventy or eighty days of hiking ahead of him—he had no idea. Would the gun *really* work underwater? If it did, would it kill a big fish and could he haul it through the forcefield wall into the Breach? The dried seaweed and driftwood thrown down here from the sea above was already getting scarcer . . . how was he sup- posed to cook this theoretical fish? The lighter was in his pack, part of the sharp flip-knife, spoon, fork, multi-thingee, and he had a metal bowl he could morph into a pan by touching it in the right places, but was he really supposed to spend hours of his time each day fishing for . . .

Harman noticed another rock half a mile or so to the west. The thing was huge—the size of some of the more jagged ridges he'd passed through—and it protruded from the north wall of the Atlantic just before the dry bottom of the Breach dipped into another deep trench, but this rock or coral reef was strangely shaped. Instead of crossing the Breach with a path cut through it, this rock appeared to slant down from the water, disappearing in the sand and loam of the Breach itself. More than that, it looked strangely rounded, smoother than the volcanic basalt he'd been hiking through the last three days.

He'd learned how to activate the telescopic and magnification con- trols of his thermskin goggles and he did so now.

It was no rock. Some sort of gigantic, man-made device was protrud- ing from the north wall of the Breach, its snout sunk into the dirt. The thing was huge, widening back from a bottle-nosed-dolphin bow—

crumpled metal, exposed girders—to sinuous curves that widened like a woman's thigh and disappeared through the forcefield.

Harman put away the last of his food bar, pulled out the gun and attached it to the stik-tite patch on the belt of his thermskin, and began walking toward the sunken ship.

Harman stood under the mass of the thing—much larger than he imagined from almost a mile away—and guessed it had been some sort of submarine. The bow was shattered, exposed girders looked to be rusted by rainfall rather than the sea, but the bulk of the smooth, almost rubbery-looking hull appeared more or less intact as it angled back up through the forcefield and into the ocean's midday darkness. He could make out the silhouette of the thing for another ten yards or so in the ocean, but nothing more.

Harman stared at the large breach in the hull near the bow—a breach within a Breach, he thought stupidly, rain pounding down on his cowl and goggles—and was sure he could get into the submarine through that opening. He was equally sure that it would be pure idiocy to do so. His job was not to explore two-thousand-year-old sunken wrecks, but to get his ass back to Ardis, or at least to another old-style community, as quickly as he could—seventy-five days, a hundred days, three hundred days—it didn't matter. His only job was to continue walking west. He didn't know what was in this damned Lost Era machine, but something in there could kill him and he didn't see how anything in there could enlighten him any further than he'd been enlightened by his drowning in the crystal cabinet.

But still. . . .

It hadn't taken his enlightenment through drowning for Harman to know that—however genetically modified and nanocytically reinforced—his species evolved from chimps and hominids. Curiosity had killed countless of those noble, knuckled ancestors, but it had also gotten them up off their knuckles.

Harman stowed the pack some yards from the bow—the thing was waterproof but he didn't know if it was pressure-proof—pulled the ancient pistol from its stick-tite grip and held it in his right hand, activated the two bright searchlight patches on his upper chest, and squeezed his way past rended metal into the dark forward corridors of the dead machine.

73

The Greeks aren't going to make it to nightfall.

They aren't even going to make it to lunch at this rate. And neither am I.

The Achaeans are falling back into a tighter and tighter half circle, fighting like fiends, the sea at their backs and the surf running red, but Hector's attack is relentless. At least five thousand Achaeans have fallen since the attack began just after dawn, among them noble Nestor—alive but carried unconscious to his tent, struck from his chariot by a lance that pierced his shoulder and shattered bone. The old hero who'd tried to step in to fill in for the absent or dead giants—Achilles, Agamemnon, Menelaus, Big Ajax, crafty Odysseus—has done his best, but the spearpoint found him.

Nestor's son Antilochus, the bravest of the Achaeans these past few days, is dead, pierced through the bowels by a well-placed Trojan bowman's shot. Nestor's other captain son—Thrasymedes—is missing in action, pulled down into the Trojan-filled trench early on and not seen in the three hours since then. The trench and revetments are now in Hector's bloody hands.

Little Ajax is wounded, a nasty sword cut to both shins just aside the greaves, and was carried from the field to the non-safety of the burned boats just minutes ago. Podalirius, fighting captain and skilled healer, son of the legendary Asclepius, is dead—cut down by a circle of killers from Deiphobus' attacking legions. They hacked the brilliant physician's body to pieces and hauled his bloodied armor back to Troy.

Alastor, Teucer's friend and chieftain, who took over Thrasymedes' command during the terrible battle of the bulge behind the abandoned trenches, fell in front of his men—still cursing and writhing for minutes with a dozen arrows in him. Five Argives fought their way forward to retrieve his body, but they were all cut down by Hector's advance guard. Teucer himself was sobbing as he killed Alastor's killers, firing arrow after arrow into their eyes and guts as he fell back with the slowly retreating Greeks.

There is nowhere left to retreat. We're crammed here onto the beach, the rising tide lapping at our sandaled feet, and the rain of arrows is constant. All of the Greek horses have died loudly, except for those few whose owners, weeping, set them free and whipped them toward the advancing enemy lines. More trophies for the Trojans.

I'm going to be killed if I stay here. When I was a scholic, especially when I was Aphrodite's secret-agent scholic, all decked out in levitation harness, impact armor, morphing bracelet, stun-baton, the Hades invisibility helmet—and whatever else I hauled around then—I felt pretty invulnerable, even when moderately close to the fighting. Except for the arrows, which are deadly enough at astounding distances, there isn't much killing-from-afar in this war. Men smell their enemy's sweat and breath and are splattered with his blood, brains, and saliva when they shove steel—or in most cases, bronze—into the man's guts.

But I've almost been skewered three times in the last two hours: once by a cast spear that came over the lines of defenders and almost took my balls off—I leaped in the air to avoid it and when it buried itself in the wet sand here and I came down straddling it, the vibrating shaft smacked me in the gonads. Then an arrow parted my hair and a minute later another arrow, one of thousands darkening the sky and rising like a miniature forest out of the sand everywhere here, would have taken me square in the throat if an Argive I don't even know hadn't raised his round shield, leaned over, and deflected the barbed and poisonous shaft.

I have to get out of here.

My hand has touched the QT medallion a hundred times in the hours since dawn, but I haven't quantum teleported away. I'm not sure why.

Yes I am. I don't want to desert these men. I don't want to be safe in Helen's bathchamber or atop some nearby hill knowing that these Achaeans I've spent ten years watching and talking to and breaking bread with and drinking wine with are being slaughtered like proverbial cattle on this blood-dimmed bit of beach.

But I can't save them.

Or can I?

I grab the medallion, concentrate on a place I've been, twist the gold circle half a turn, and open my eyes to find myself falling down a long, long elevator shaft.

No, I'm not falling, I realize—realize too late since I've already screamed twice—I'm in free fall in the main corridor on the deck of the *Queen Mab,* or at least in the main corridor on the deck where I'd had my private quarters. But there had been gravity then. Now there is only this falling and falling, tumbling in space but not really falling, flailing to get to the cubby door or to the astrogation bubble twenty yards down—or up—the corridor.

Two black and chitinous Belt moravecs, the soldiers with the built-in black armor, barbs, and masklike heads, kick out of a nearby elevator shaft—there is no elevator car in it—and grab me by the arms. They shoot back toward the shaft and I realize that the rockvecs can move in this zero-g not just because they're used to it—it must be close to their native level of gravity in the Asteroid Belt—but because their carapaces have built-in and nearly silent thrusters that pulse expanding jets of what may just be water. Whatever it is, it allows them to move fluidly and quickly in this zero-gravity world. Without a word, they pull me into the shaft that runs the length of the *Queen Mab*—imagine jumping into an empty elevator shaft the height of the Empire State Building—so I do the only thing a sane man would do—I scream again.

The two soldiers jet me hundreds of feet up or down this echoing shaft—echoing to just my screams—and then pull me through some sort of forcefield membrane into a busy room. Even upside down as I am, I can recognize it as the bridge of the ship. I'd been on the bridge only once during my stay, but there was no mistaking this room's function—moravecs I'd never seen before are busy monitoring three-dimensional virtual control boards, more rockvec soldiers are standing by holographic projections, and I recognize General Beh bin Adee, the skittery spider 'vec—I can't think of his name right now—as well as the strange-looking navigator, Cho Li, and the Prime Integrator, Asteague/Che.

It's the Prime Integrator who effortlessly kicks through the zero-g bridge space to me as the two soldiers firmly set me into a mesh chair and tie me down so that I can't escape. No, I realize, they're not tying me down like a captive, merely attaching mesh web belts to hold me in place. It helps—just being stationary gives me a sense of up and down.

"Dr. Hockenberry, we didn't expect you back," says the little moravec who's roughly the same shape and size as Mahnmut, but made of different-colored plastics, metals, and polymers. "I apologize for the lack of gravity. We're not under thrust. I could arrange for the internal force-fields to exhibit a pressure differential that could simulate gravity for you—after a fashion—but the truth is we're station-keeping near Earth's polar ring and we do not want to exhibit a major change in internal energy uses unless we have to."

"I'm all right," I say, hoping that they haven't heard my screams in the elevator shaft. "I need to talk to Odysseus."

"Odysseus is . . . ah . . . indisposed right now," says Asteague/Che.

"I need to speak with him."

"I am afraid that this will not be possible," says the moravec who's about the same size as my friend Mahnmut, but who looks and speaks so differently. His voice actually has a soothing quality to it.

"But it's imperative that I . . ." I stop in midsentence. They've killed Odysseus. It's obvious that these half-robot things have done *something* terrible to the only other human being on their ship. I don't know why they would have killed the Achaean, but then I've never understood two-thirds of the things these moravecs do or don't do. "Where is he?" I ask, trying to sound in-control and authoritarian even while web-strapped into my little chair. "What have you done to him?"

"We've done nothing to the son of Laertes," says Asteague/Che.

"Why would we harm our guest?" asks the boxlike, spiderlegged 'vec whose name I can't remember . . . no, I do recall it now, Retrograde Jogenson or Gunderson or something Scandinavian.

"Then bring Odysseus here," I say.

"We cannot," repeats Prime Integrator Asteague/Che. "He is not on the ship."

"Not on the ship?" I say, but then I look at one of the holographic displays set into a niche in the hull where a window should be. Hell, for all I know it *is* a window. The full blue and white is turning below, filling the viewscreen.

"Odysseus went down to this Earth?" I say. "To *my* Earth?" Is it my Earth? I lived and died there, yes, but thousands of years ago if the gods and moravecs are to be believed.

"No, Odysseus has not gone down to the surface again," says Asteague/Che. "He has gone to visit the Voice that contacted the ship during our transit . . . the Voice which asked for him by name."

"Show Dr. Hockenberry," says General Beh bin Adee. "He'll understand why he can't talk to Odysseus right now."

Asteague/Che appears to ponder this suggestion. Then the Europan moravec turns to look at the navigator Cho Li—I suspect some sort of radio transmission has taken place between them—and Cho Li moves a tentacle arm. A six-foot-wide three-dimensional holographic window opens not two feet in front of me.

Odysseus is making love to the most sensuous woman I've ever seen in my life—except perhaps for Helen of Troy, of course. My male ego had thought that my lovemaking—well, sexual intercourse—with Helen had been energetic and imaginative. But thirty seconds of staring slackjawed at the coupling going on between the naked Odysseus—his body battle-scarred, tanned, barrel-chested but short, and the pale, exotic, pneumatic, sensous, and slightly hirsute woman with the incredible eye makeup—lets me know that my exertions with Helen had been tame, unimaginative, and in slow motion compared to what these erotic athletes are involved in.

"Enough," I say, mouth dry. "Turn it off."

The pornographic window winks out of existence. "Who is that . . . lady?" I manage to say.

"She says her name is Sycorax," answers Retrograde Somebody'sson. It's always odd to hear that solid voice coming out of that tiny metal box atop those long skinny legs.

"Let me talk to Mahnmut and Orphu of Io," I say. I've known those two 'vecs the longest and Mahnmut is the most human of all these machine-people. If I can convince anyone here on the *Queen Mab*, it will be Mahnmut.

"I'm afraid that won't be possible, either," says Asteague/Che.

"Why? Are they having sex with some female moravec babes or something?" I hear how stupid my attempted witticism is as it mentally echoes in the long seconds of censuring silence that follow.

"Mahnmut and Orphu have entered the Earth's atmosphere in a dropship carrying Mahnmut's submersible," says Asteague/Che.

"Can't you link up to them by radio or something?" I ask. "I mean, they could patch together radio calls like that way back in my Twentieth and early Twenty-first centuries."

"Yes, we are in contact," says Retrograde Whoever. "But at the moment their ship is being attacked and we do not want to distract them with unnecessary communications. Their survival is problematic at best."

I consider asking more questions—who on Earth is attacking my friends? Why? How?—but realize that such a dialogue would only distract me from my real reason for being here.

"You need to create a Brane Hole back to the beach near Ilium," I say.

General Beh bin Adee moves his black-thorned arms in a way that might suggest a question. "Why?" he says.

"Because the Greeks are being slaughtered to a man by the Trojans and they don't deserve to be wiped out that way. I want to help them escape."

"No," says the general. "I meant why do you think we have the ability to create Brane Holes at will?"

"Because I saw you do it once. You created all those Holes that you jumped through from the Asteroid Belt to Mars, then accidentally to Ilium-Earth. More than ten months ago. I was there, remember?"

"Our technology is not adequate to the effort of creating Brane Holes to different universes," says Cho Li.

"But you *did* it, goddammit." I can hear the whine in my voice.

"No, we did not," says Asteague/Che. "What we actually did at the time was . . . it is hard to describe and I am not a scientist or engineer, although we have many . . . what we did at the time was interdict the so-called gods' Brane Hole connections and tunnel some of our own into the quantum matrix they had created."

"Well," I say, "do it again. Tens of thousands of human lives depend on it. And while you're at it, you can bring back the few million Greeks and others in the Europe of Ilium-Earth who were disappeared—shot into space in a blue beam."

"We don't know how to do that, either," says Asteague/Che.

Well then, what the fuck good are you? I'm tempted to ask. I don't.

"But you're safe here, Dr. Hockenberry," continues the Prime Integrator.

Again, I want to shout at these plastic-metal things, but I realize that he—it—is correct. I *am* safe here on the *Queen Mab.* Safe from the Trojans at least. And perhaps the luscious babe boinking Odysseus has a sister. . . .

"I need to go back," I hear myself saying. *Go back where, you idiot? To the Greeks' Last Stand? Sounds like a baklava shop in L.A.*

"You'll be killed," says General Beh bin Adee. The large, dark, humanoid soldier-thing doesn't sound the least bit upset at the prospect.

"Not if you can help me."

The moravecs seem to be communicating silently with one another again. I can see one of the holographic window-monitors far across the bridge is tuned to Odysseus and the exotic woman still going at it like rabbits. The woman is on top now and I can see that she's even more beautiful and desirable than my first glimpse had suggested. I concentrate on not getting an erection in front of these moravecs. If they notice, and they tend to notice a lot about us humans, they might take it wrong.

"We will help you if we can," Asteague/Che says at last. "What do you desire?"

"I need to go somewhere without being seen," I say and begin describing the lost Hades Helmet and my old morphing bracelet to them.

"The morphing technology—at least as it applies to living organisms—is beyond our technological capabilities," says Retrograde . . . Sinopessen . . . I remember it now. "It manipulates reality on a quantum level we do not yet fully understand. We are far away from being able to create machines to alter that form of probability collapse."

"And we have no clue as to how this Hades Helmet proffered true invisibility," adds Cho Li. "Although if it is consistent with the Olympians'— or those powers behind the Olympians—other technologies, it probably involves a minor quantum shift through time rather than space."

"Can you whomp up something like that for me?" I ask. I realize that there's no compelling reason for these busy moravecs to do *any-thing* for me.

"No," says Asteague/Che.

"We could adapt some chameleon cloth for him," says General Beh bin Adee.

"Great," I say. "What's chameleon cloth?"

"An active-stealth camouflage polymer," says the general. "Primitive but effective if one does not move too quickly between widely varying backgrounds. Roughly the same material that your Mars ship was coated in, only more breathable and invisible to the infrared. The eyepieces are nanocytic, so there would be no interruption of the chameleon adaptation."

"The gods saw us and shot our Mars ship out of orbit," I say.

"Well, yes. . . ." says General Beh bin Adee. "There is that to consider."

"This chameleon cloth is the best you can do?"

"On short notice," says Asteague/Che.

"Then I'll take it. How long will it take your people . . . I mean your . . . moravecs . . . to fit me out in this chameleon suit and show me how to use it?"

"I ordered the environmental engineering department to begin work on such a suit the second we began discussing it," says the Prime Integrator. "We had your vital measurements on record. They should bring the finished product within three minutes."

"Wonderful," I say, wondering if it is. Where exactly am I going? How can I convince those where I'm going to help the Greeks escape? Where could the Greeks escape *to*? Their families and servants and friends and slaves have all been sucked up into the blue beam rising from Delphi. As if in anticipation of getting out of here, I begin playing with the gold medallion hanging around my neck, fingering the sliding circle that activates it.

"By the way," says Cho Li, "your quantum teleportation medallion does not work."

"What!?" I rip myself out of the straps and float in place. "What the hell are you talking about?"

"Our inspection when you were on the ship earlier has shown the disk to be effectively functionless," says the navigator.

"You're full of shit. You guys told me earlier that it just couldn't be replicated for your use, that it was keyed to my DNA or something."

Prime Integrator Asteague/Che makes a self-conscious noise that sounds amazingly like a human male clearing his throat in embarrassment. "It is true that there is some . . . communication . . . between the medallion around your neck and your cells and DNA, Dr. Hockenberry. But the medallion itself has no quantum function. It does not QT you through Calabi-Yau space."

"That's nuts," I say again, trying to curb my language. I still need these moravecs' help and lizard suit to get out of here. "I *got* here, didn't I? All the way from the universe of the Ilium-Earth."

"Yes," says Cho Li. "You did. With no help whatsoever from that hollow gold medallion hanging around your neck. It is a mystery."

A soldier moravec with the chameleon outfit appears from the open elevator-shaft doorway. The garment looks like nothing special. Actually, it reminds me of an oversized version of a so-called leisure suit I was foolish enough to own in the 1970s. It even had the same stupid, pointy collars and monkey-puke-green sheen to it.

"The collars extend into a full cowl," says Asteague/Che as if reading my mind. "The suit itself has no color. This green is merely a default setting so we can find the material."

I take the suit from the 'vec soldier and make the mistake of trying to pull it on. Within seconds, I'm tumbling out of control, spinning around my own axis in zero-g, hanging on to the useless garment as if I'm waving a flag, but achieving nothing else.

General Beh bin Adee and his trooper grab me, secure me—they seem to know just where to lodge their feet on the consoles to keep themselves from acting with an equal and opposite reaction—and then they unceremoniously stuff me into the chameleon outfit. Then they attach one of the chair straps to my suit, velcroing me to some patch I can't see. It keeps me in place.

I pull the collars up into a cowl and pull the cowl completely over my head.

It's not nearly as comfortable as just putting on the Hades Helmet and disappearing. For one thing, it is tremendously *hot* in this lizard suit. For a second thing, the nanowhatsits that allow me to see through the material in front of my eyes don't quite achieve cricital focus. An hour peering out of this thing and I'll have the worst headache of my life.

"How is it?" asks Prime Integrator Asteague/Che.

"Great," I lie. "Can you see me?"

"Yes," says Asteague/Che, "but only via gravitational radar and other bands of the nonvisible-light spectrum. To all visual intents and purposes, you have blended in with the background. With General bin Adee, actually. Will the personages where you are traveling be using gravitational radar, enhanced negative thermal imaging, or other such techniques?"

Would they? I have no clue. Aloud, I say, "There's one problem."

"Yes? Perhaps we can fix it." The Prime Integrator sounds solicitous, even actively concerned. My wife used to love James Mason.

"I have to twist the QT medallion to QT," I say, wondering how muffled my voice sounds to them. Sweat is rolling down my temple, cheeks, and rib cage by now. "I can't twist it without opening the suit and . . ."

"The chameleon cloth is tailored to be very loose," interrupts Beh bin Adee. The military 'vec always sounds slightly disgusted with me. "You can pull your arm inside the suit to touch the medallion. Both arms if you need to."

"Oh, yeah," I say, pulling my right arm out of the suit arm and into the suit, and with that as my final contribution to our conversation, I twist the medallion and quantum teleport away from the *Queen Mab*.

Does too work! I'm tempted to shout as I flick into solidity at the place in space/time that I'd envisioned. But then I remember that I forgot to ask the moravecs for a weapon. And some food and water. And maybe some impact armor.

But it wouldn't be a good time for me to shout anything.

I've appeared in the Great Hall of the Gods on Mount Olympos and all the gods seem to be here—all except Hera, whose smaller throne is wreathed in black funereal ribbon. Zeus looks to be fifty feet tall where he sits on his own gold throne.

All of the other gods seem to be here—more even than I'd seen at their last large conclave, which I'd crashed in my infinitely more comfortable Hades Helmet. I don't even know many of these gods, can't identify them even after ten years of reporting to Olympos daily with my voice stones and action reports. There are hundreds upon hundreds of gods here, easily more than a thousand.

And all of them are silent. Waiting for Zeus to address them.

Trying not to breathe loudly or faint from the stifling heat in this goddamned lizard suit, hoping that none of these Olympian Immortals is using deep gravitational radar or enhanced negative thermal imaging, I stand perfectly still, almost cheek to jowl with the mob of gods and goddesses, nymphs, Furies, Erinyeses, and demigods, and wait to hear what Zeus is going to say.

74

Even before Harman stepped through the gash in the hull into the bow of the derelict ship, he had a pretty good idea what the thing was. The DNA-bound protein data packets in his body had a thousand references of thousands of types of seagoing craft across ten thousand years of human history. Harman couldn't make a perfect match based only upon the damaged bow, the debris field around the bow, and by looking at the breached sheaths of elastic sonar-stealth material encasing the morphable smart-steel of the hull itself, but it was fairly obvious that he was stepping into a submarine from some century late in the Lost Era: possibly something from after the rubicon release but before the first post-humans had been genetically brought into being. Dementia times.

Once inside, making his way down an only slightly canted corridor and breathing through his osmosis mask even though this part of the sunken ship was dry, he was sure it was a submarine.

Harman was standing in a room that was listing only about ten degrees from vertical but the ancient impact with the ocean bottom here only two hundred feet beneath the surface of the sea—long before there was an Atlantic Breach—had crumpled metal and tumbled half a dozen long canisters off their racks. Harman wouldn't need the pistol he was carrying. Nothing lived in this hulk. He pressed the pistol against the stick-tite patch on his right hip and extended a bit of thermskin elastic over it, securing it as surely as if he were wearing one of the holsters he'd seen in books via the crystal cabinet.

He cupped his right palm against the rounded edge of one of these tumbled canisters, curious to find if his data-seeking function would work through the molecule-thin thermskin gloves.

It did.

Harman was standing in the torpedo room of a *Mohammed*-class warship submarine. The AI in the guidance system of this particular torpedo—"torpedo" being neither a word nor concept he had ever encountered until that millisecond—had gone dead more than two thousand years earlier, but there was enough residual memory in the dead microcircuits for Harman to understand that his palm was inches above a nuclear warhead tucked into the end of a thirty-four-thousand-pound high-speed, self-cavitating, hunt-until-it-kills-something torpedo. This particular torpedo warhead—"warhead" being another term he had never encountered until that instant—was a simple fusion weapon, packing only 475 kilotons, the equivalent of 950 million pounds of TNT detonating. The blast from the pearl-sized sphere a few inches beneath his palm would reach tens of millions of degrees within a millionth of a second. Harman could almost feel the lethal neutron and gamma rays crouching there, invisible dragon-eels of death, ready to leap in all directions at the speed of light to kill and infect every bit of human nerve or tissue they would encounter, tearing through them like bullets through butter.

He snatched his hand away and rubbed it against his thigh as if cleaning something filthy from his palm.

This entire submarine was a single instrument designed for killing human beings. His briefest encounter with the warhead's dead guidance AI had told him that the torpedo warheads were all but irrelevant to the machine and crew's real mission. But to understand what that mission was, he would have to pass out of the torpedo room, up the canted deck, through the wardroom and mess room, up a ladder and down a corridor past the sonar shack and integrated comm room, and then up another ladder into the command and control center.

But everything beyond the near half of the torpedo room was under water.

The beams of light from his chest lamps showed him where the north wall of the Breach began not fifteen feet ahead. The submarine had been lying here along this ocean ridge two hundred feet beneath the surface and fully filled with water for many centuries before whatever created the Breach had sucked the ocean out of these forward compartments, but nothing lived here anymore, not so much as a dried barnacle remained from the myriad of undersea life forms that must have thrived here for centuries, and there were no signs of human bones or other remnants of the crew. The forcefield that held back the Atlantic Ocean did not physically slice through the morphable metal of the submarine's hull or metal structure—Harman's lamps picked up the solid, uninterrupted line of deck overhead—but he could visualize the complete oval-slice of ocean inside the hull of the ship. The north wall of the Breach forcefield held back the sea in every open space, but a step beyond that . . . Harman could imagine the pressure down here at two hundred feet and see the wall of darkness ahead, his lamplights reflecting off it as if from a dark-burnished but still mirrored surface.

Suddenly Harman was filled with a sick and terrible terror. He had to clutch at the despised torpedo to keep himself from reeling, from falling onto the corroded plates of the deck. He wanted to run from this ancient warship out into the air and sunlight, to rip off his osmosis mask, and to be sick if he had to in order to get rid of this poison that had suddenly filled his body and mind.

It was a mere torpedo he was leaning against, designed for destroying other ships, a harbor at most, yet its thermonuclear yield was three times the full explosive power dropped on Hiroshima—another word and image that had just entered Harman's reeling mind—capable of destroying everything in a hundred-square-mile area.

Harman—always fair at judging distances and sizes even in his era that demanded no such skills—saw in his mind's eye a ten-by-ten-mile area in the heart of Paris Crater, or with Ardis Hall at the center of its bull's-eye. At Ardis, such a blast would not only vaporize the manor house and the new outbuildings in a microsecond, but blast away the hard-built palisades and roll its fireball to carry away the faxnode pavilion a mile and a quarter down the road less than a second later, turning the river at the base of the hills into steam and the forest into ash and fireball in an expanding circle of instant destruction ranging farther north than the Starved Rock he'd seen in his turin-cloth glimpse of Ada and the others.

Harman activated dormant biofeedback functions—too late—and received the message he dreaded. The torpedo room was filled with latent radiation. The damaged torpedo fusion warheads should have dropped beneath lethal leakage levels long ago, but in the process of doing so they must have irradiated everything in the forward part of the submarine.

No—the sensors told him that the radiation was worse straight ahead, aft of the torpedo room—the direction in which he would have to go if he wanted to learn more about this instrument of death. Perhaps the fusion reactor that had driven this obscene boat had been slowly leaking all these centuries. It was a radioactive hell ahead of him.

Harman knew just enough about his new biometric functions to realize that he could query the data monitors. He did so now, but only with the simplest question possible—*Will the thermskin adequately shield me from this radioactivity?*

The answer came back in his mind's own voice and was unequivocal—*No.*

It was insane to go forward. He also didn't have the *courage* to go forward through that black wall of water, into the maelstrom of radiation, through the rest of the submerged torpedo room, up through the dark and cold of the wardroom and mess room where ancient Geiger counters would have gone wild, needles pinned off their own dials, and then up again and down a corridor past the sonar and comm rooms, and then up another ladder that impossible, terrifying, bone-chilling, cell-killing distance into the submerged command and control center.

It was literally insane to stay in this malevolent hulk, much less to go deeper into it. It was death—death to himself, to the hopes of his species, to Ada's trust in his return, to his unborn child's need for a father in these most terrible and dangerous of times. Death to all futures.

But he had to know. The quantum remains of the torpedo warhead AI had told him just enough that he had to know the answer to a single, terrible question. So go forward is exactly what Harman did—one terrified step at a time.

After three days and nights in the Breach, this was the first time he had pressed through the forcefield wall. It was a semipermeable forcefield, just like the ones he'd passed through before on Prospero's orbital isle—and now Harman knew that the "semipermeable" meant that it was designed to allow old-style human beings or post-humans to pass through an otherwise impervious shield—but this time he was stepping through from air and warmth to cold, pressure, and darkness.

Harman trusted the thermskin to keep him alive from the effects of the deep if not from the radiation, and this it did; he refused even to call up data he knew he had on how the thermskin was designed, on what made it work. He didn't care how it worked to keep the ocean pressure away—only that it did.

His chest lamps automatically increased their brightness to deal with the reflections and dense, particle-filled water.

The submerged parts of the submarine were as thick with living organisms as the dry parts of the torpedo room had been sterile. Whatever lived here now not only survived in heavy radiation but feasted on it, thrived on it. Every metal surface had been hidden beneath layers of mutated coraled fungus and masses of green, pink, and gray-bluish glowing living matter, their frills and tendrils waving slightly in unfelt currents. Crablike things scuttled from his lights. A blood-red eel lunged from a hole in what had been the aft torpedo room hatchway and then pulled its head back, leaving only its rows of teeth glinting in the light. Harman gave it room as he edged through that encrusted hatch.

The dead warhead AI had given him a rough schematic of the ship—at least enough to lead him to the command and control center—but the ladder he had to take up to the wardroom and eating area was gone. Most of this submarine had been built from super alloys that would last another two thousand years, even here beneath the sea, but the ladder—*gangway* his protein bundles told him it had been called—had long since corroded away.

Sinking his fingers into the silt and waving fans on either side of the slanted stairwell, hoping that he wasn't putting his fingers into another eel's mouth, Harman laboriously pulled himself up through the green soup of the sea. Particles and bundles of radioactive living particles clung to his thermskin and had to be wiped from his goggles and osmosis mask.

He was close to hyperventilating by the time he reached the wardroom level. He knew from experience that the osmosis mask would keep feeding him fine, fresh oxygen, but this sense of pressure against every square inch of his body made him squirm. He didn't have to access memory modules to know that the thermskin would also protect him from the cold and pressure—the same type of suit had kept him alive in the zero-pressure of space—but outer space had felt *cleaner*.

I wonder if this slime coating my eyepieces was once part of the men and women who ran this boat?

He banished thoughts like that. They were not only ghoulish, they were absurd. If the crew had gone down with this boat, the ever-hungry denizens of the ocean had cleaned their bones in just a few years and then eaten and decomposed the bones themselves in not many more years.

But still—

Harman concentrated on making his way aft through the litter of overgrown and collapsed bunks. He could only know this had been a sleeping area for human beings through the schematic in the warhead's decaying memory molecules; now it looked like an overgrown crypt, its fungus-thick gray shelves harboring mutated crab-things and light-fearing eel-things rather than the rotting bodies of Montagues or Capulets.

I have to actually read *more of this Shakespeare person. So many things in the data packets connect to his thoughts and writings,* thought Harman as he passed through an open hatchway, brushing aside stalagmites of slime, floating into what had been an eating area. What had once been a long dining table for some reason reminded him of Caliban's cannibal table up on Prospero's Isle so many months earlier. Perhaps it was because the fungus and mollusks here had mutated to a bloody pink color.

At the far end of the pink dining cavern, Harman knew, he had to go up a vertical ladder—a real ladder this time, no slanted gangway—to the integrated comm room before he could go aft through the sonar shack to the command and control center.

There was no ladder. And this time the narrow tube of a vertical corridor was clogged with green and blue marine growth, reminding Harman of Daeman's description of Paris Crater turned into a blue-ice nest.

But this was Earth ocean life that had woven this web, however mutated, and Harman began ripping it apart, pulling out centuries of life's slow encroachment and advancement in great, grunting handfuls, wishing all the time he had an axe. The water around him became so filled with glop that he couldn't even see his hands. Something long and slippery—another eel? Some sort of sea snake?—slid along the length of his body and was gone below. He kept pulling away clumps and globs of thick, sludgy, radioactive stuff, fighting his way up through the blinding murk.

He felt as if he was being born again, but this time into a much more terrible world.

It was such a struggle that for several moments after he'd clawed his way up and into the comm room level, he didn't know he'd arrived. Tendrils of green hung everywhere, the water was so filled with floating particles that his own searchlight beams blinded him, and he lay in the primordial ooze too exhausted to move.

Then—remembering that every moment he spent in this death-hulk meant a greater chance of death to him—Harman got to his knees, pulled vines and tentacles of old plant growth away from his shoulders and back, and began to shuffle aft.

The comm room was still alive.

Harman froze with the knowledge of it. Functions in his body that he hadn't even catalogued yet picked up the pulsing readiness of machines hidden under the living gray-green carpet of this room to reach and communicate. Not with him. These comm AI's did not acknowledge his presence—their ability to interact with human beings had long since died away with the shifting quantum core of their computers.

But they wanted to communicate with *somebody*—most of all to receive orders from *somebody, something.*

Knowing that he would not find what he needed to know here in the integrated comm room, Harman half-walked, half-swam aft past the encrusted sonar and GPS shack. He didn't know why his bundle-memories wanted to call the little space a shack and he didn't want to know.

Had he ever thought about submarines, which he never had, Harman would have probably guessed that such boats were built for traveling under water—he knew that the AI warhead had preferred a translation of the word "boat" to that of "ship"—that such underwater boats would have been made up of many small compartments, each one shut off with a door, a hatch, watertight, separate. This sub was not. The spaces were large in comparison to the volume of the ship itself, not overly capsulized or compartmentalized. If the ocean found a way in—as it obviously had—the deaths of the men and women in this machine would not have been by slow drowning, gasping for air near the ceilings, but in a massive, implosive pressure wave, killing all in seconds. It was almost as if the humans who had worked here had preferred the choice of instant death in larger spaces to slow drowning in smaller ones.

Harman quit swimming and let his feet sink to the deckplates when he realized he was in the middle of the command and control center.

There was less marine growth here, more bare metal. From just the warhead AI's cartoon schematic, he could make out the torpedo launch and weapons' control centers—vertical metal columns that would have projected a myriad of holographic virtual controls when the ship was in combat. Harman moved around the space, touching metal and plastic with his thermskinned palm, allowing the dead quantum brains embedded in the material to speak to him.

There was no chair, seat, or throne for the captain. That man had stood here, near the central holgraphic chart table, directly in front of a display console—virtual under the proper conditions, projected from within LCD plastic panels if the virtual system were damaged—into which every one of the ship's many systems and functions were channeled and shown.

Harman moved his gloved hand through the green murk and imagined sonar displays appearing . . . *here*. Tactical displays to his left . . . *there*. Several yards back the way from which he'd come, gray-glob mushrooms were the stools where the crewman had crouched in front of constantly changing virtual displays controlling and reporting on ballast and trim, radar, sonar, GPS relay, drone controls, torpedo readiness and launch controls, physical wheels for controlling the diving planes. . . .

He jerked his hand away. Harman didn't need to know any of this crap. He needed only to know . . .

There.

It was a black metal monolith just aft of the captain's station. No barnacles, mollusks, coral, or slime had attached themselves to it. The thing was so black that Harman's lamps had not reflected back from it on his first several passes through that part of the command center.

This was the boat's central AI, built to interface in a hundred ways with the submarine's captain and crew. Harman knew that a quantum computer, even from this lost age, even one dead for more than two millennia, would be more alive at one percent capacity than most living things on the planet. Quantum artificial minds died hard and died slowly.

Harman knew that he would not have the codes to access the central AI's banks, perhaps not even the language to understand the codes he did not know, but he also knew that it didn't matter. His functions were developed and nanogenetically programmed into his DNA long after this machine had died. It would have no secrets from him.

The thought terrified him.

Harman wanted out of this flooded crypt. He wanted to get away from the radiation that must be pinging through his skin, brain, balls, guts, and eyes even as he stood here, frozen in indecision.

But he had to know.

Harman set his palm atop the black metal monolith.

The submarine was named *The Sword of Allah*. It had left its port on. . . .

Harman skipped the log entries, dates, reasons for the ancient war—he lingered only long enough to confirm it was after the rubicon release, during the Dementia years when the Global Caliphate was near its end, the democracies of the West and Europe were already dead, the New European Union a fiction of gasping vassal states under the rising Khanate. . . .

None of that mattered. What was in the belly of this submarine, as real as the fetus growing in the womb of his wife Ada, was what mattered.

Harman did pause long enough to listen to a fast-forward of the last testament of *The Sword of Allah*'s twenty-six crew members. The Mohammed-class ballistic-missile submarine was so automated that it required a crew of only eight, but there had been so many volunteers that twenty-six of the Chosen had been allowed to go on its last mission.

They were all men. They were all devout. They all surrendered their souls to Allah as their doom approached—a cordon of Khanate attack submarines, aircraft, spacecraft, and surface ships as far as Harman could tell. The men knew that they had only minutes to live—that the Earth had only minutes before its destruction.

The captain had given the launch command. The primary AI had seconded it and relayed it.

Why hadn't the missiles launched? Harman searched the AI to its quantum guts and could find no reason why the missiles had not launched. The human command had been given, the four sets of physical keys had been turned, the AI target-package coordinates and individual launch commands had been confirmed and relayed, the missiles had been denoted in the proper launch sequence, the switches—both virtual and literal—had closed. All of the massive-metal missile hatches had been successively opened by redundant hydraulics—only a thin, blue, fiberglass dome had separated the missile tubes from the ocean, and each of these launch tubes had been filled with nitrogen to equalize the pressure to keep that ocean from rushing in until the actual instant of launch. The forty-eight missiles should have been propelled out of their crèches by the nitrogen gas generators, a twenty-five-hundred-volt charge igniting the nitrogen discharge. The gas itself would have produced more than eighty-six thousand pounds per square inch of pressure in less than a second, sending the missiles hurtling upward within their own rising bubbles of nitrogen until they popped out of the sea like rising corks, and then the solid rocket propellant in each missile would have been ignited the second the missiles hit open air above. There were redundant and double-redundant launch and ignition initiators. The missiles should have roared and flown to their targets. The AI's launch indicators were all red. In each of the forty-eight missile silos back in the pregnant belly of *The Sword of Allah,* the sequence had proceeded properly from HOLD to DENOTE to LAUNCH to SUCCESSFULLY LAUNCHED.

But the missiles were all still sitting in their tubes. The dead and decaying AI knew that and communicated something like shame and chagrin through Harman's tingling palm.

Harman's heart was pounding so fiercely and he was breathing so raggedly that the osmosis mask had to lower the oxygen input so he wouldn't hyperventilate.

Forty-eight missiles. Forty-eight warhead-platforms. Each warhead was MRVed and carried sixteen separate reentry vehicles. Seven hundred sixty-eight actual warheads, all armed, primed, safeties off, set to go. They had been targeted at seven hundred and sixty-eight of the world's remaining cities, ancient monuments, and dwindling rubicon-survivors' population centers.

But these were no mere thermonuclear warheads such as carried in *The Sword of Allah's* torpedoes.

Each of the seven hundred sixty-eight actual warheads still aboard this sub carried a tenuously contained black hole. The human race's and the Global Caliphate's ultimate weapon at that point in time—*its ultimate detergent,* thought Harman with a noise that was part sob, part giggle.

The black holes in themselves were small. Each not much larger than what one of the dead crewmen had described in his urgent and religious farewell speech as "the soccer ball I grew up kicking around the ruins of Karachi." But when they escaped their containment spheres and dropped on their targets, the result would be much more dramatic than a mere thermonuclear weapon.

The black hole would plunge into the earth, creating a soccer-ball-sized hole in the center of whatever target city it arrived at. But the second it was exposed there would be a plasma implosion a thousand times worse than a thermonuclear explosion. The descending black hole, turning all earth, rock, water, and magma ahead of it into a rising cloud of steam and plasma, would also suck in behind it the people, buildings, vehicles, trees, and actual molecular structure of its target city and hundreds of square miles around it.

The black hole that had created the kilometer-wide hole in the center of Paris Crater had been less than a millimeter wide and unstable—it had eaten itself before reaching the Earth's core. Harman knew now that eleven million people had died because of that ancient experiment gone wrong.

These black holes were not meant to eat themselves. They were meant to ping-pong back and forth through the earth, reemerging into atmosphere, plunging back through the planet. Seven hundred sixty-eight plasma and ionizing-radiation surrounded spheres of ultimate destruction coring and recoring the Earth's crust, mantle, magma, and core again and again and again, for months or years, until they all came to rest at the center of this dear, good Earth and began eating the fabric of the planet itself.

The twenty-six crewmen's voices Harman had listened to had all celebrated this outcome to their mission. They would all be reunited in Paradise. Praise God!

Wanting only to be sick within his constraining osmosis mask, Harman forced himself to keep his hand on the black-monolith AI for another full, endless, eternal minute. There had to be some instructions here for finding some way to disarm these activated blackholes.

Their warhead containment fields had been very powerful, designed to last for centuries if they had to.

They had lasted for more than two and one-half millennia, but they were very unstable. Once one of the black holes escaped, they all would. It did not matter one iota whether they began their voyage to the Earth's core and beyond from their targets or from this place along the north wall of the Atlantic Breach. The outcome would be the same.

There were no procedures in the AI or anywhere in *The Sword of Allah* for disarming them. The singularities existed—had for almost two hundred and fifty of Harman's standard Five Twenties—and in a world where old-style humans' highest technology consisted of crossbows, there was no way to reset their containment fields.

Harman pulled his hand away.

Later, he had no memory of finding his way out of the submerged parts of the submarine, or of staggering out through the dry forward torpedo room, through the rent in the hull, out onto the sunny strip of muddy dirt that was the Atlantic Breach.

He did remember peeling off his cowl and osmosis mask, dropping to his hands and knees, and vomiting for long minutes. Long after he'd gotten rid of the little substance in his belly—the food bars were nutritious but left little residue—he continued dry retching.

Then he was too weak even to stay on his hands and knees, so he crawled away from his own vomitus, collapsed, and rolled onto his back, looking up at the long, thin blue strip of sky. The rings were faint but clear, revolving, crossing, moving like the pale hands of some obscene clock mechanism counting down the hours or days or months or years until the warhead containment spheres just yards from Harman decayed to collapse.

He knew that he should get away from the radioactive wreck—crawl west if he had to—but his heart had no will to do so.

Finally, after what must have been hours—the strip of sky was darkening toward evening—Harman activated the function to query his own biomonitors.

As he'd suspected, the dosage he'd received had been lethal. The dizziness he felt now would only grow worse. The vomiting and dry retching would soon return. Blood was already pooling under his skin. Within hours—the process had already begun—the cells in his bowels and guts would begin sloughing off by the billion. Then would come the bloody diarrhea—intermittent at first but then constant as his body began literally to shit his dissolved guts out into the world. Then the bleeding would become primarily internal, cell walls breaking down completely, entire systems collapsing.

He'd live long enough to see and feel all this, he knew. Within a day he'd be too weak even to stagger along between the episodes of diarrhea and vomiting. He'd be prostrate in the Breach, his stillness broken only by involuntary seizures. Harman knew that he wouldn't even be able to look at the blue sky or stars as he died—the biomonitors already reported the radiation-induced cataracts building on the surface of both his eyes.

Harman had to grin. No wonder Prospero and Moira had given him only a few days' worth of food bars. They must have known he wouldn't need even that many.

Why? Why make me Prometheus for the human race with all these functions, all this knowledge, all this promise to give Ada and my species, only to let me die alone here . . . like this?

Harman was still sane and conscious enough to know that billions of human beings no more elect than himself had hurled similar final thoughts toward the unanswering skies in the hours and minutes before their death.

He was also wise enough now to be able to answer his own question. Prometheus stole fire from the gods. Adam and Eve tasted of the fruit of knowledge in the Garden. All the old creation myths told versions of the same tale, exposed the same terrible truth—*steal fire and knowledge from the gods and you become something more than the animals you evolved from, but still something far, far below any real God.*

Harman at that second would give anything to rid himself of the twenty-six last personal and religious testaments by the madmen who crewed *The Sword of Allah.* In those impassioned farewells he felt the full weight of the burden he had been about to bring back to Ada, to Dae-man, to Hannah, to his friends, to his species.

He realized that all of the last year—the turin-cloth story of Troy that had been Prospero's little joke-gift to the old-humans, passed on through Odysseus and Savi, their various mad quests, the deadly masque on Prospero's Isle up in the e-ring, his escape, the Ardis Manor people's discovery of how to build weapons, fashion some crude begin-nings to society, discover politics, even grope toward some religion . . .

It had all made them human again.

The human race had returned to Earth after more than fourteen hun-dred years of coma and indifference.

Harman realized that his and Ada's child would have been fully human—perhaps the first real human being to be born after all those comfortable, inhuman, watched-over-by-false-post-human gods' cen-turies of stasis—confronted by danger and mortality at every turn, forced to invent, pressured to create bonds with other human beings just to survive the voynix and the *calibani* and Caliban himself and the Sete-bos thing . . .

It would have been exciting. It would have been terrifying. It would have been *real*.

And it all would have led, could have led, might have led, back to *The Sword of Allah*.

Harman rolled to one side and vomited again. This time the vomitus consisted mostly of blood and mucus.

More rapid than I thought.

Eyes closed against the pain—all the varieties of pain, but most espe-cially against the pain of this new knowledge—Harman felt on his right hip. The pistol was still secure there.

He undid the strap, pulled the weapon free of the stick-tite pad, used his other hand to rack the chamber the way Moira had shown him—chambering one of the shells—clicked off the safety, and held the muz-zle to his temple.

75

The Demogorgon fills half of the flame-filled sky. Asia, Panthea, and the silent sister Ione continue to cower. The rocks and ridges and volcanic summits nearby are filling with gigantic, looming shapes—Titans, Hours, monster steeds, monster-monsters, Healer-type giant centipedes, inhuman Charioteers, more Titans, all coming to their positions like jurors showing up for a trial on the steps of a Greek temple. The thermskin goggles allow Achilles to see everything and he almost wishes they didn't.

The monsters of Tartarus are too monstrous; the Titans too shaggy and titanic; the Charioteers and the things the Demogorgon had called the Hours aren't really possible to bring into full focus at all. They make Achilles think of the time he cleaved a Trojan's belly and chest open with a sword stroke and found a small human homunculus staring out at him, blue eyes seeming to blink at him through the shattered ribs and spilled entrails. It had been the only time he'd ever vomited on the battlefield. These Hour and Charioteer things were equally as difficult to look at.

As the Demogorgon waits for the monstrous jurors to sort themselves out and gather, Hephaestus pulls a slim cord from the helmet bubble of his absurd suit and clips the end of the line into the cowl of Achilles' thermskin.

"Can you hear me now?" asks the crippled dwarf-god. "We have a few minutes to talk."

"Yes, I hear you, but can't the Demogorgon also? He did before."

"No, this is a hardline. That Demogorgon is a lot of things, but not J. Edgar Hoover."

"Who?"

"Never mind. Listen, son of Peleus, we have to coordinate what we're going to say to this giant rabble and the Demogorgon. A lot depends on it."

"Don't call me that," growls Achilles with a glare that has frozen battlefield enemies in their tracks.

The god Hephaestus actually takes an alarmed step back, accidentally pulling tight the communications cord between them. "Call you
what?"

"Son of Peleus. I never want to hear that phrase again."

The god of artifice holds up his heavily gauntleted hands, palms outward. "Fine. But we still have to talk. We only have a minute or two before this kangaroo court commences."

"What is a kangaroo?" Achilles is growing tired of this mini-god's
double-talk. The fleet-footed mankiller's sword is in his hand. He has a
strong suspicion that all he has to do to kill this so-called immortal is
slash a gash in the bearded fool's metal suit, and then step back to watch
the god of fire choke to death on the acid air. Then again, Hephaestus *is*
an Olympian immortal, even without the big bug's Healing tanks back
on Olympos. So perhaps, as Achilles had, the impudent bearded cripple,
exposed to Tartarus' acid air, would just cough, gag, retch, and sprawl
around in pain for an eternity until one of the Oceanids ate him. It is a
powerful impulse in Achilles to find out.

He resists the urge.

"Never mind," says Hephaestus. "What are you going to say to the
Demogorgon? Shall I do all the talking for us?"

"No."

"Well, we need to get our stories straight. What are you going to ask
the Demogorgon and the Titans to do other than kill Zeus?"

"I am not going to ask this Demogorgon *thing* to kill Zeus," Achilles
says firmly.

The bearded dwarf-god looks surprised behind the glass of his head-
bubble. "You're not? That's why I thought we were here."

"I am going to kill Zeus myself," says Achilles. "And feed his liver to
Argus, Odysseus' dog."

Hephaestus sighs. "All right. But for me to sit on the throne of
Olympos—the deal you offered me and which Nyx agreed to—we still
need to convince the Demogorgon to intercede. And the Demogorgon is
insane."

"Insane?" says Achilles. Most of the monstrous shapes seem to be in
position now among the ridgelines, cindercones, and lava flows.

"You heard the thing going on about the God supreme, didn't you?"
says Hephaestus.

"I don't know which god Demogorgon speaks of, if not Zeus."

"Demogorgon is speaking of some single, supreme god of the entire
universe," says Hephaestus, his already raspy voice rasping even more
over the communications line. "One god with a capital 'G' and no others at all."

"That's absurd," says Achilles.

"Yes," agrees the god of fire. "That's why the Demogorgon's race exiled him to this prison world of Tartarus."

"Race?" says Achilles incredulously. "You mean there's more than one of these Demogorgons?"

"Of course. Nothing living comes in complete sets of one, Achilles. Even you must have learned that. This Demogorgon is as crazy as a Trojan shithouse rat. He worships some single all-powerful capital-G god and sometimes refers to him as 'the Quiet.' "

"The Quiet?" Achilles tries to imagine any god being a silent god. The concept is certainly something out of his experience.

"Yes," growls Hephaestus over the cowl earphones. "Only this 'the Quiet' isn't all of the single all-powerful capital-G god, but is just one of many manifestations of Him . . . capital H there."

"Enough with the capitals," says Achilles. "So the Demogorgon *does* believe in more than one god."

"No," insists the god of fire and artifice. "This big God just has many faces or avatars or forms, sort of like Zeus when he wants to screw a mortal woman. You remember once Zeus turned into a swan to . . ."

"What the fuck does all this have to do with the hearing that's going to start in about *thirty fucking seconds*?" shouts Achilles over his thermskin microphones.

Hephaestus claps his hands over his glass bubble where his ears should be. "Hush," hisses the dwarf-god over the intercom. "Listen, this has *everything* to do with our argument to convince the Demogorgon to release the Titans and the others here to attack Zeus, wipe out the current Olympians, and install me as the new king on Olympos."

"But you just said the Demogorgon is a prisoner here."

"I did. But Nyx—Night—opened the Brane Hole from Olympos to here. We can go back that way unless it closes before this goddamned hearing, trial, town meeting, whatever it is, gets under way. Besides, I think the Demogorgon can leave whenever it wants to."

"What kind of prison is it that allows you to leave whenever you want to?" asks Achilles. He's beginning to think that it's the bearded dwarf-god who's the lunatic here.

"You have to know a little about the Demogorgon's race," says the bubble-head on top of the iron-bubbled body. "Which is all anyone knows about them . . . very little. This Demogorgon is imprisoning himself here because he was told to. He can quantum teleport anywhere, any time . . . if he thinks it's important enough to. We just have to convince him it's important enough to."

"But we have the Brane Hole," says Achilles. "And what is Nyx getting out of this? You told me at Odysseus' home before I woke Zeus that Night would open the Hole and I believed you, but why? What's in it for her?"

"Survival," says Hephaestus and looks around. All the monstrous shapes seem to be in position. The court is in session. Everyone is waiting for the Demogorgon to speak.

Achilles can see this as well. "What do you mean, survival?" he hisses over the interphone. "You told me yourself that Nyx is the one goddess whom Zeus fears. Her and her goddamned Fates. He can't hurt her."

The glass bubble moves back and forth as Hephaestus shakes his head. "Not Zeus. Prospero and Sycorax and . . . the people . . . the beings who helped create Zeus, me, the other gods, even the Titans. And I don't mean Ouranos god of the sky mating with Gaia, mother Earth. Before them."

Achilles tries to wrap his mind around this concept of someone other than Earth and Night creating the Titans and the gods. He can't.

"They trapped a creature named Setebos on Mars and your Ilium-Earth for ten years," continues Hephaestus.

"Who did?" says Achilles. He is totally confused by now. "What is a Setebos? And what relevance can this have to what we have to say to the Demogorgon in one minute?"

"Achilles, you must know enough of our history to know how Zeus and the other young Olympians defeated his father Kronos and the other Titans, even though the Titans were more powerful?"

"I do," says Achilles, feeling like a child again, being tutored by Chiron, the centaur who raised him. "Zeus won the war between the gods and the Titans by enlisting the aid of terrible creatures against whom the Titans were powerless."

"And which was the most terrible of these terrible creatures?" asks the bearded dwarf-god through the intercom. His teacherly tone makes Achilles want to gut him on the spot.

"The *hundred-armed*," he answers, exerting the last of his patience. The Demogorgon will be speaking any second and none of this gibberish has helped Achilles know what to say. "The monstrous many-handed thing which you gods called *Briareous*," he adds, "but which early men called *Aigaion*."

"The thing called Briareous and Aigaion is really named Setebos," hisses Hephaestus. "For ten years this creature has been distracted from its hungry intentions, left to feed on your puny human war between Trojans and Achaeans. But now it is loose again and the quantum underpinnings of the entire solar system are coming unhinged. Nyx is worried that they'll destroy not only their Earth, but the new Mars and her entire dark dimension. Brane Holes connect everything. They're being too reckless, this Sycorax and Setebos, Prospero and their ilk. The Fates predict total quantum destruction if someone or something does not inter-

cede. Nyx would prefer me—the crippled dwarf—on the throne of
Olympos rather than risk such total quantum meltdown."

Since Achilles has not the least fucking clue as to what the dwarf-god
is babbling about, he remains silent.

The Demogorgon seems to be clearing his non-throat to silence the
last of the murmurs and movements in the crowd of Titans, Hours,
Charioteers, Healers, and other malformed shapes.

"The best news," hisses Hephaestus over his intercom, whispering
now as if the huge shapeless and veiled mass above them can hear them
despite the comm cord, "is that the Demogorgon and his god—the
Quiet—eat Seteboses for snacks."

"The Demogorgon is not the insane one here," Achilles whispers
back. "It's you who's crazy as a Trojan shithouse rat."

"Nonetheless, will you let me speak for us?" Hephaestus whispers,
urgency in every syllable.

"Yes," says Achilles. "But if you say something I don't agree with, I'm
going to hack your cute little suit into separate iron balls and then cut
your real balls off and feed them to you through that glass bowl."

"Fair enough," says Hephaestus and jerks the comm line free.

"YOU MAY BEGIN YOUR APPEAL," booms the Demogorgon.

They decided to vote on whether Noman could borrow the sonie. The
meeting was scheduled for noon, when the minimum number of sentries were posted and the bulk of the day's necessary chores were done,
so that most of the Ardis survivors—including the six newcomers and
Hannah, bringing their number up to fifty-five—could attend, but already the nature of Odysseus/Noman's request had got out to even the
farthest-posted sentry and already the consensus was dead set against it.

Hannah and Ada spent the rest of the morning catching up with
events. The younger woman was all but inconsolable over the loss of
their friends and Ardis Hall itself, but Ada reminded her that the Hall
could be rebuilt—at least some crude version of it.

"Do you think we'll live to see that?" asked Hannah.

Ada had no answer. She squeezed Hannah's hand.

They talked about Harman, about the details of his odd disappearance from the Golden Gate with the thing called Ariel and about Ada's sense that Harman was still alive somewhere.

They talked about small things—how food was being prepared these days and Ada's hopes to enlarge the camp before the voynix began massing as they had.

"Do you know why this Setebos baby keeps them away?" asked Hannah.

"None of us have a real clue," said Ada. She led the young sculptor to the Pit. The Setebos-thing—Noman had called it a form of louse—was at the bottom, hands and tendrils curled under it, but its yellow eyes stared up with an inhuman indifference much worse than mere malevolence.

Hannah grabbed her temples. "Oh my . . . oh God . . . it's clawing at my mind, wanting to get in."

"It does that," Ada said softly. She had carried a flechette rifle to the Pit and now she aimed it casually at the mass of blue-gray tissue and pink hands a few yards below.

"What if it . . . takes over?" asked Hannah.

"Begins to control us, you mean?" said Ada. "Turns us against one another?"

"Yes."

Ada shrugged. "We half expect that to begin every day, every night. We've discussed it. So far, we all can vaguely hear this Setebos baby calling to us—like a bad smell in the background—but when it comes strongly, as it just did with you, it's just one person at a time. If the rest of us hear it and feel it, it's like an . . . I don't know . . . an echo."

"So you think that if it takes control," said Hannah, "you think it'll be one of you at a time."

Ada shrugged again. "Something like that."

Hannah looked at the heavy flechette rifle in Ada's hand. "But if the thing starts controlling you right now, you could kill me—kill a lot of us—before . . ."

"Yes," said Ada. "We've discussed that as well."

"Did you come up with some plan?"

"Yes," Ada said again, very quietly, as she stood above the Pit. "We're going to kill this abomination before it comes to that."

Hannah nodded. "But you'll have to get all your people out of here before you can do that. I see why you don't want to loan Odysseus the sonie."

Ada had to sigh. "Do you know why he wants it, Hannah?"

"No. He won't tell me. There's so much he won't tell me."

"Yet you love him."

"Since that first day we saw him at the Bridge."

"You were under the turin cloth back when it worked, Hannah. You know that *that* Odysseus was married. We heard him speak to the other Achaeans about his wife, Penelope. His teenage son, Telemachus. The language they spoke was strange, but somehow we always understood it under the turin."

"Yes." Hannah looked down.

Down in the Pit, the Setebos baby began to scurry back and forth on its many pink hands. Five tendrils snaked up the side of the pit and other hands wrapped around the grill, pulling the metal until it seemed to bend. The thing's many yellow eyes were very bright.

Daeman was on his way back from the forest and headed toward the noon gathering when he saw the ghost. He was carrying a heavy canvas bag filled with firewood on his back and wishing that he'd been on sentry duty or hunting detail that day instead of having to chop and haul wood when a woman stepped out of the forest only a dozen yards from him.

At first he saw her only in his peripheral vision—enough to know that it was a human being, female, and therefore part of the Ardis community rather than a voynix—and for a few seconds he kept walking, flechette rifle in his right hand but pointed downward, eyes lowered as he hitched up the heavy pack on his back, but when he turned her way to call a greeting, he froze.

It was Savi.

He straightened up and the huge load of wood in his makeshift canvas rucksack almost toppled him over backward. It would not have been an overreaction. He could only stare.

It was Savi—but not the gray-haired, older Savi he'd watched being murdered and dragged off by Caliban in the caverns under Prospero's hellhole of an orbital isle almost a year earlier—this was a younger, paler, more beautiful Savi.

A resurrected Savi? No.

A ghost was Daeman's dual stab of thought and fear. His era of old-style humans did not even believe in ghosts, did not truly have the concept of ghosts; he'd never heard of ghosts outside mentions in the turin drama or heard a ghost story until he started sigling the ancient books in Ardis Manor the previous autumn.

But this had to be a ghost.

The young Savi did not seem completely substantial. There was something—shimmery—about her as she saw him, turned, and began walking straight toward him. Daeman realized that he could see through her, more even than he'd been able to see through the hologram of Prospero up on the orbital isle.

Yet somehow he knew that this was no hologram. This was . . . something . . . real, real and alive, even as he noticed the soft, pale glow her entire body gave off and the fact that her feet did not seem to be touching the ground with any weight as she strode through the high, brown grass toward him. She was wearing a thermskin and nothing else. Daeman knew from experience that thermskins—not as thick as a coat of paint—made one feel more naked than naked, and that's how she looked now as she began walking in his direction. Naked. The thermskin was a pale blue but showed every muscle working as she walked, emphasized rather than hid the slight bobble to her breasts. Deaman had grown used to Savi in thermskins, but where there had been slightly sagging breasts, slack buttocks, and floppy thigh muscles with the older Savi, this apparition showed high breasts, a flat stomach, and powerful, young muscles.

He freed his arms from the straps, dropped the load of firewood, and gripped his flechette rifle with both hands. Daeman could see the new inner palisade more than two hundred yards away and even a dark head moving above the line of logs, but no one else was in sight. He and the ghost were alone in this wintry field at the edge of the forest.

"Hello, Daeman."

It was Savi's voice. Younger, even more vibrant with life than the mesmerizing voice he remembered, but definitely Savi's.

Daeman said nothing until she stopped within arm's reach. Her very solidity seemed to flicker—one second complete, the next transparent and insubstantial. When she was substantial, he could see even the areolae around her slightly raised nipples. The young Savi, he realized, had been very beautiful.

She looked him up and down with those familiar dark eyes he remembered so well. "You look well, Daeman. You've lost a lot of weight. Gained muscle."

Still he did not speak. Everyone who went out into the forest carried one of the high-decibel whistles they'd dug from the ruins. His was on a lanyard around his neck. He had only to raise it and blow it and a dozen armed men or women would be running his way in less than a minute.

Savi smiled. "You're right. I'm not Savi. We've never met. I know you only from Prospero's descriptions and video recordings."

"Who are you?" he asked. His voice sounded hoarse, tight, tense, even to himself.

The apparition shrugged as if her identity were of little importance. "My name is Moira."

The name meant nothing to Daeman. Savi had never mentioned anyone named Moira. Neither had Prospero. For a wild second he wondered if Caliban could be a shapeshifter.

"What are you?" he said at last.

"Ah!" The syllable was launched in Savi's husky laugh. "A wonderfully intelligent question. Not 'Why do you look like my dead friend Savi?' but '*What* are you?' Prospero was correct. You were never as stupid as you seemed, even a year ago."

Daeman touched the whistle on his chest and waited.

"I'm a post-human," said the Savi apparition.

"There are no more post-humans," Daeman said. With his left hand, he raised the whistle slightly.

"There *were* no more post-humans," said the shimmering woman. "Now there are. One. Me."

"What do you want here?"

She slowly extended her hand and touched his right forearm. Daeman expected her hand to pass through him but her touch was as solid and real as that of any of the Ardis survivors. He could feel the pressure of her long fingers through his jacket. He could also feel an almost electrical tingle there.

"I want to come with you to watch the discussion and then the vote on whether Noman can borrow your sonie," she said softly.

How in the hell does she know about that? he wondered. Aloud, he said, "If you show up, there probably won't be a discussion and vote. Even Odys . . . Noman . . . will want to know who you are, where you're from, what you want."

She shrugged again. "Perhaps. But none of the others will see me. I will be visible only to you. This is a little trick Prospero built into my sisters when they went off to become gods and I decided to keep it for myself. It comes in handy from time to time."

He fingered the whistle with his left hand, slipped the index finger of his right hand into the trigger guard of the flechette rifle, and looked at her as she shifted slightly from full focus to transparency back to full focus again. There was too much in what she just said to allow him even to frame the proper questions right now. His intuition was that the best thing he could do was keep her around. He couldn't explain even to himself why that made sense. "Why would you want to come to the discussion?" he asked.

"I am interested in the outcome."

"Why?"

She smiled. "Daeman, if I can be invisible to the other fifty-five people there, including Noman, I could certainly have remained unseen by you. But I want you to know I'm there. We will talk about things after the discussion and after the vote."

"Talk about what things?" Daeman had seen the dead, brown, mummified corpses of what Savi, Harman, and he had thought were the last of the post-humans up in the thin, stale air of Prospero's dying realm. All female. Most of them chewed on by Caliban centuries ago. Daeman had no clue if this apparition was what she claimed to be. To him, she more resembled the goddesses from the turin drama he had watched only on occasion—Athena perhaps, or a much younger Hera. Not as beautiful as the glimpses he'd had of Aphrodite. Suddenly he remembered that almost a year ago, in Paris Crater, there had been word of street altars being set up to the gods from the Trojan War turin drama.

But everyone in Paris Crater now was dead, including his mother. Murdered and eaten by Caliban. The city buried in that blue-ice gunk by Setebos. If the people of his home city had ever prayed to the turin gods and goddesses, it had done them no good. If this was a goddess from the drama, he was sure that she would do him no good.

"We can talk about where your friend Harman is," said the spectral figure who called herself Moira.

"Where is he? How is he?" Daeman realized that he'd shouted.

She smiled. "We can talk after the vote."

"At least tell me why this vote is so important that you've come from . . . wherever you've come from to watch it," demanded Daeman, his voice sounding as hard as he'd become inside over the past year.

Moira nodded. "I came to hear it because it is important."

"Why? To whom? How?"

She said nothing. Her smile had disappeared.

Daeman released the whistle. "Is it important that we give Noman the sonie or important that we *don't* loan it to him?"

"I just want to watch," said the Savi-ghost who called herself Moira. "Not vote."

"I didn't ask that."

"I know," said the thing with Savi's voice.

The bell for the conclave rang. People were gathering around the central lean-to, tent, and cooking area.

Daeman was in no hurry to rush to it. He knew it might be less of a threat to lead a live voynix into their camp. He also knew he had a very short time in which to make his decision. "If you can view the meeting without being seen by anyone, why did you reveal yourself to me?" he asked, his voice low.

"I told you," said the young woman, "this was my choice. Or perhaps I'm like a vampire—I can only enter a place the first time if I am invited in."

Daeman didn't know what a vampire was but he didn't think that was important right now. "No," he said. "I'm not going to invite you into our safe area unless you give me a compelling reason to do so."

Moira sighed. "Prospero and Harman also said you were stubborn, but I couldn't imagine they meant *this* stubborn."

"You talk as if you've seen Harman," said Daeman. "Tell me something about him—how he is, where he is—something that will make me believe you've met him."

Moira continued to gaze at him and Daeman felt that the air around their locked gazes should be sizzling.

The bell quit ringing. The meeting had begun.

Daeman stood motionless, silent.

"All right," said Moira, smiling slightly again. "Your friend Harman has a scar through his pubic hair, just above his penis. I didn't ask him how he received it but it must have been since his last Twenty. The healing tanks on Prospero's Isle would never have left it there."

Daeman did not blink. "I've never seen Harman naked," he said. "You'll have to tell me something else."

Moira laughed easily. "You lie. When Prospero and I gave Harman the thermskin he is wearing now, he said that he knew exactly how to get into one—they're tricky to pull on, you know—and that you and he had worn them for weeks up on the Isle. He said that once you had to strip in front of Savi to pull your thermskins on. You've seen him naked and it's a noticeable scar."

"Why is Harman wearing a thermskin now?" asked Daeman. "Where is he?"

"Take me to the meeting," said Moira. "I promise I will tell you about Harman afterward."

"You should talk to Ada about him," said Daeman. "They're . . . married." The strange word did not come easily to Daeman.

Moira smiled. "I will tell you and you can tell Ada if you think it is appropriate. Shall we go?" She held out her left arm, crooked, as if he were going to take it to escort her into a formal dining room.

He took her arm.

" . . . so that's the beginning and end of my request," Noman/Odysseus was saying as he saw Daeman enter the circle of fifty-four people. Most were sitting on sleeping pads or blankets. Some were standing. Daeman stood apart, behind the standing survivors.

"You want to borrow our sonie—the one thing offering us a chance of survival here," said Boman, "and you won't tell us why you want it or how long you might keep it."

"That is correct," said Noman. "I might need it for only a few hours—I could program it to return on its own. It's possible that the sonie might not return at all."

"We'd all die," said one of the Hughes Town survivors, a woman named Stefe.

Noman did not reply.

"Tell us why you need it," said Siris.

"No, that's a private matter," said Noman.

Some of the sitting, kneeling, and standing people chuckled, as if the bearded Greek had made a joke. But Noman did not smile. He was as serious as his demeanor.

"Go find another sonie!" cried Kaman, their would-be military expert. He'd told others that he had never trusted the *real* Odysseus in the turin drama he'd watched every day for ten years before the Fall and was prepared to trust this older version even less.

"I would find another if I could," said Noman, his voice level, unagitated. "But the nearest ones I know about are thousands of miles from here. It would take too long for the cobbled-together sky-raft I built to get there, if the thing could get there at all. I need to use the sonie today. Now."

"Why?" asked Laman, absently rubbing his still-bandaged right hand with its missing fingers.

Noman remained silent.

Ada, who had remained standing near the barrel-chested Greek after her opening of the meeting and her introduction, said softly, "Noman, can you tell us how it might benefit us if we let you borrow the sonie?"

"If I succeed in what I want to do, it's possible that the faxnodes will begin working again," he said. "In just a few hours. A few days at most."

There was an audible intake of breath among the crowd.

"It's more possible," he continued, "that they won't."

"So that's your reason for using our sonie?" asked Greogi. "To get the fax pavilions working again?"

"No," said Noman. "It's just a possible side effect of my trip. Not even a probable one."

"Would your . . . borrowing of the sonie . . . help us in some other way?" asked Ada. It was clear that she was more sympathetic to Noman's request than the majority of those frowning among the ragged clump of listeners.

Noman shrugged.

Everyone was so silent for the next moment that Daeman could hear two sentries calling to each other more than a quarter of a mile away to the south. He turned—the spectral Moira was still standing near him, her arms crossed across her thermskinned breasts. Incredible as it was, no one who had looked up to watch the two of them approach the group—including Ada, Noman, and Boman, who had been staring at him since he passed through the palisade gate—evidently had been able to see her.

Noman held out his blunt, powerful hands, fingers splayed as if reaching for them all—or perhaps pushing them all away. "You want to hear that I will perform some miracle for you all," he said, his tone low but his powerful, rhetoric-trained voice still echoing off the palisade. "There is no such miracle. If you stay here with the sonie, you'll be killed sooner or later. Even if you evacuate to this island downriver you're thinking of fleeing to, the voynix will follow you there. They can still fax, and not just through the faxnodes you know about. There are tens of thousands of voynix surrounding you now, massed within two miles of here—while all over the Earth, the last few thousand human survivors are either fleeing or holed up in caves or towers or the ruins of their old communities. The voynix are killing them. You have the advantage that the voynix won't attack while this Setebos . . . *thing* . . . in the pit is your captive. But within days, if not hours, that Setebos-louse will be strong enough to rip its way out of the pit and into your minds. Trust me, you don't want to experience that. And, in the end, the voynix will come anyway."

"All the more reason to keep the sonie to ourselves!" shouted the man named Caul.

Noman turned his hands palms-up. "Perhaps. But soon there will be no place on this Earth for you to flee. Do you think you're the only ones with a Finder Function? Your functions have ceased to work—the voynix's and the *calibanis'* finder functions haven't. They'll find you. Even Setebos will find you when he's finished gorging himself on your planet's history."

"You don't seem to offer us any chance," said Tom, the quiet medic.

"I am not," said Noman, his voice rising now. "It is not for me to offer you a chance, although my trip may accidentally afford you one if I am successful. But the odds of my success are low—I won't lie to you. You deserve the truth. But if something important does not change, sonie or no sonie, the odds of *your* success—of your survival—are zero."

Daeman, who had sworn he would stay quiet during the discussion, heard himself shouting. "Can we go to the rings, Noman? The sonie would take us there—six at a time. It brought me home from Prospero's Isle on the e-ring. Would we be safe in the orbital rings?"

All faces turned toward him. Not a single gaze moved to where the shimmering Moira stood not six feet to his right.

"No," said Noman. "You would not be safe in the rings."

The dark-haired woman named Edide stood suddenly. She seemed to be sobbing and laughing at the same time. "You're not giving us a fuck-ing *chance*!"

For the first time—maddeningly, infuriatingly—Odysseus/Noman smiled, his teeth white against his mostly gray beard. "It's not for me to give *you* a chance," he said harshly. "The Fates will either choose to do that or decline to do that. It is up to you today to give *me* a chance . . . or not."

Ada stepped forward. "Let's vote. I think that no one should abstain in this vote, since everything may depend on it. Those in favor of allow-ing Odysseus . . . I'm sorry, I mean Noman . . . to borrow our sonie, please hold up your right hand. Those opposed, keep your hands down."

The city and battlefield of Troy—ancient Ilium—wasn't much to look at from five thousand meters up.

"That's it?" asked Centurion Leader Mep Ahoo from the troop carrier deck. "That's where we were with the Greeks and Trojans fighting? That shrubby hill and bit of land?"

"Six thousand years ago," said Mahnmut from his control room of *The Dark Lady* in the dropship's cargo bay.

"And in another universe," said Orphu from his corner of *The Dark Lady*'s own cargo bay.

"It doesn't look like much," said Suma IV from the controls of the dropship. "Can we move on?"

"One more circle, please," said Mahnmut. "Can we go lower? Fly over the plain between the ridge and the sea? Or the beach?"

"No," said Suma IV. "Use your optics to magnify. I don't choose to run that close to the interdiction field dome over the dried-up Mediter-ranean Sea or get that low."

"I was thinking of getting a little closer to allow Orphu's radar and thermal imaging to get better signals," said Mahnmut.

"I'm fine," rumbled the intercom voice from the hold.

The dropship orbited again at five thousand meters, the westernmost part of its circle above the ruins on the hilltop and still more than a kilometer from where the Mediterranean Basin began. Mahnmut zoomed his image from the primary camera feed, shut off other inputs, and looked down with a strange sense of sadness.

The rubble of the ruins of the ancient stones where Ilium had once stood lay on a ridge running westward toward the curve of Aegean shore—it was never really a bay, just a bend where ancient ships had tied up to stakes and stone anchors. And where Agamemnon and all the Greek heroes had beached their hundreds of black ships.

To the west then, the Aegean and Mediterranean had stretched forever—the wine-dark sea—but now, through the slight shimmer of the post-human-created interdiction field that would cut all the dropship's power in a millisecond if they flew into it, there stretched away only more dirt, more rock, distant green fields—the dry Mediterranean Basin. Also easily visible to the west were ancient islands that once rose from the sea—islands that Achilles had conquered before assaulting Troy: Imbros, Lemnos, and Tenedos, visible now only as steep, forest-covered hills with rocky bases meeting the sandy bottom of the Basin.

Between the now-dry Aegean and the ridge holding the ruins of Troy, Mahnmut could see a kilometer and a half or so of alluvial plain. It was a forest of scrub trees now, but the little moravec could easily see this plain as it was when he had been there with Odysseus, Achilles, Hector, and all the other warriors—about three curving miles of shallow sea fringed with marshes and sandy alluvial flats, the man-crowded beach, the sand dunes that had soaked up so much blood in the years of fighting there, the thousands of bright tents above the beach, then the wide plain between the beach and the city—wooded now, but stripped bare of all trees then after a decade of foraging for firewood for cooking fires and corpse fires.

To the north there was water still visible: the strait once called the Dardanelles, the Hellespont, dammed up by glowing forcefield hands of the same sort as between Gibraltar and Africa on the west end of the drained Mediterranean.

As if he were studying the same area with his radar and other instruments, Orphu said over their private circuit—"The post-humans must have built some huge drainage system underground or this entire area would be flooded now."

"Yes," sent Mahnmut, not really interested in the engineering or physics of the thing. He was thinking of Lord Byron and of Alexander the Great and of all the others who had made their pilgrimage to Ilium, Troy, this strangely sacred site.

No stone there is without a name. The words seemed just to appear in Mahnmut's mind. Who had written that? Lucan? Perhaps. Probably.

On the hilltop now, only a few gray-white scars of disturbed rock showed, a tumble of stones, all without a name. Mahnmut realized that he was looking at the ruins of ruins—some of those scrapes and scars probably dated back to the Troy-fanatic and amateur archaeologist Schliemann's careless digs and brutal excavations from when he first started digging in 1870—more than three thousand years ago on this true Earth.

It was noplace special now. The last name it had held on any human map was Hisarlik. Rocks, scrub trees, an alluvial plain, a high ridge looking north to the Dardanelles and west to the Aegean.

But in Mahnmut's mind's eye he could see precisely where the armies had clashed on the Plains of Scamander and the Plain of Simois. He could see where the walls and topless towers of Ilium had held their high place there, where the long ridge dropped down toward the sea. He could still make out a thicketed ridge in between the city and the sea— the Greeks had called it Thicket Ridge even then, but the priests and priestesses in the temples of Troy often referred to it as Mryine's Mounded Tomb—and he remembered how he had watched Zeus's face rise in the south as an atomic mushroom cloud not so many months ago.

Six thousand years ago.

As the dropship completed its last, high circling, Mahnmut could make out where the great Scaean Gate had held back the screaming Greeks—there had been no large wooden horse in the *Iliad* Mahnmut had seen firsthand, and the great, main lane inside past the marketplace and central fountains all leading to Priam's palace, destroyed in the bombing more than ten months ago in Mahnmut's time, and just northeast of the palace the great Temple to Athena. Where only rocks waited now and scrub trees grew, Mahnmut from Europa could see where the busy Dardanian Gate had been and the main watchtower and well just north of it where once Helen had . . .

"There's nothing here," said their pilot, Suma IV, over the intercom. "I'm leaving now."

"Yes," said Mahnmut.

"Yes," rumbled Orphu over the same commline.

They flew north, retracting the slow-flight wings and breaking the sound barrier again. The echo of the sonic boom went unheard on both sides of the empty Dardanelles.

"Are you excited?" Mahnmut asked his friend over their private line. "We'll be seeing Paris in a few minutes."

"A crater where the center of Paris used to be," answered Orphu. "I think that black hole millennia ago took out Proust's apartment."

"Still and all," said Mahnmut, "it's where he wrote. And for a while a fellow named James Joyce as well, if I remember correctly."

Orphu rumbled.

"Why didn't you ever tell me that you were obsessed with Joyce as well as Proust?" persisted Mahnmut.

"It never came up."

"But why those two as your primary focus, Orphu?"

"Why Shakespeare, Mahnmut? Why his sonnets rather than his plays? Why the Dark Lady and the Young Man rather than, say, *Hamlet*?"

"No, answer my question," said Mahnmut. "Please."

There was a silence. Mahnmut listened to the ramjet engines behind and above them, the hiss of the oxygen flowing through umbilicals and ventilators, the static emptiness of the main comm lines.

Finally Orphu said, "Remember my spiel up in the *Mab* about how great human artists—singularities of genius—could bring new realities into existence? Or at least allow us to cross universal Branes to them?"

"How could I forget? None of us knew if you were serious."

"I was serious," rumbled Orphu. "My interest in human beings focused on their Twentieth through Twenty-second centuries, counting from Christ. I decided long ago that Proust and Joyce had been the consciousnesses that had helped midwife those centuries into being."

"Not a positive recommendation, if I remember history correctly," Mahnmut said softly.

"No. I mean, yes."

They flew in silence for a few more minutes.

"Would you like to hear a poem I ran across when I was a little pup of a moravec, fresh from the growth bins and factory latices?"

Mahnmut tried to imagine a newborn Orphu of Io. He gave up the effort. "Yes," he said. "Tell me."

Mahnmut had never heard his friend rumble poetry before. It was an oddly pleasant sound—

Still Born

I.

Little Rudy Bloom, ruddy-cheeked in his mother's womb
Red light permeating his sleepy, unfocused watchings
Molly clicking long knitting needles as she weaves red wool for
    him
Feeling his small feet move against the inside of her
Tiny fetus dreams consume him, preparing him for the smell of
    blankets

II.

A man gently pats his lips with a red napkin
Eyes focused on a sea of clouds drifting behind high brick
    chimneys
Submerged in the sudden memory of hawthorn stalks rubbing
    together in a storm
Reaching small hands out towards fluttering pink petals
The scents of days long past curl into the low wings of his nostrils

III.

Eleven days. Eleven times the lifespan of a tiny creature emerging
    from a cocoon
Eleven hush-stained mornings of warmth and shadow creeping
    across floorboards
Eleven thousand heartbeats before night fell and the ducks
    abandoned the far pond
Eleven indicated by the long and short hands when she held him
    to her breast
Eleven days they watched his pink body sleeping in ruddy wool

IV.

Fragments of the novel were bound in his imagination
But loose pages drifted through the dark channels of his mind
Some were blank, others contained nothing but footnotes
Tediously he had suffered the contractions of his imagination
But once in ink, the memories never survived the night

When the Ionian rumble died away on the intercom, Mahnmut was silent for a short while, trying to assess the quality of the thing. He had trouble doing so, but he knew it meant a lot to Orphu of Io—the giant moravec's voice had almost trembled near the end.

"Who is it by?" asked Mahnmut.

"I don't know," said Orphu. "Some Twenty-first Century female poet whose name was lost with the rest of the Lost Era. Remember, I encountered this when I was young—before I'd *really* read Proust or Joyce or any other serious human writer—but this bit of verse cemented Joyce and Proust together for me as two facets of a single consciousness. A singularity of human genius and insight. I never quite got over that perception."

"It's rather like the first time I encountered Shakespeare's sonnets . . ." began Mahnmut.

"Turn on your video feed relayed from the *Queen Mab*," Suma IV ordered all hands aboard.

Mahnmut activated the feed.

Two human beings were copulating wildly on a broad bed of silk sheets and bright woolen tapestries. Their energy and earnestness was astounding to Mahnmut, who had read enough about human sexual intercourse, but who had never thought to look up a video recording of it from the archives.

"What is it?" asked Orphu over the private comm. "I'm getting wild telemetric data—blood pressure levels soaring, dopamine flowing, adrenaline, heartbeat pounding—some fight to the death somewhere?"

"Ah . . ." said Mahnmut. Then the figures rolled over, still joined and moving rhythmically, almost frenetically, and the moravec saw the man's face clearly for the first time.

Odysseus. The woman appeared to be the Sycorax person who had greeted their Achaean passenger on the orbital asteroid city. Her breasts and buttocks seemed even larger now, unfettered as they were, although at this particular instant, the woman's breasts were flattened against Odysseus' chest.

"Um . . ." began Mahnmut again.

Suma IV saved him.

"That input isn't important. Switch to the forward dropship cameras."

Mahnmut did so. He knew that Orphu was turning to the thermal, radar, and other imaging data he was still capable of receiving.

They were approaching the black-hole-cratered Paris, but just as in the images taken from the *Queen Mab*, there was no crater visible, only a dome-cathedral seemingly spun of webbed blue-ice.

Suma IV radioed the *Mab*: "Where is our many-handed friend who built this thing?"

"No Brane Holes visible anywhere we can see from orbit," replied Asteague/Che at once. "Neither our ship viewers nor the cameras on the satellites we seeded can find it. The thing seems to have finished feasting on Auschwitz, Hiroshima, and the other sites for the time being. Perhaps it's returned home to Paris."

"It has," said Orphu on the shared comm. "Check the thermal imaging. Something very big and very ugly is nested right in the center of that blue spiderweb, just beneath the highest part of that dome. There are a lot of thermal vents there—it seems to be heating its nest with warmth from the crater—but it's there, all right. You can almost see the hundreds of oversized fingers under the warm areas of the glowing brain in the deep-thermal imaging."

"Well," said Mahnmut over his private line, "at least it's your Paris. Proust's City of . . ."

Afterward, Mahnmut would never understand how Suma IV reacted so quickly, even while jacked into the dropship's controls and central computer.

The six bolts of lightning leaped upward from different points around the giant blue dome. Only the dropship's altitude and its pilot's instantaneous reflexes saved them.

The dropship shifted from ramjets to scramjets, hurtled sideways in a 75-g bank, dove, rolled, and then climbed toward the north, but the six streaks of billion-volt lightning still missed them only by a few hundred meters. The implosion of air and shock wave of thunder flipped the dropship over twice, but Suma IV never lost control. The wings retracted to fins and the dropship ran for it.

Suma IV banked again, rolled deliberately, triggered full-active stealth, popped flares, and blanketed the air above the Paris blue-ice cathedral-dome with electronic interference.

A dozen fireballs rose from the ice-buried city, hurtling skyward at Mach 3, seeking them, seeking them, accelerating, seeking them. Mahnmut watched the radar track with something more than casual interest and knew that Orphu, with his direct sensory radar feed, must be *feeling* the plasma-missiles closing on him.

They did not find the dropship. Suma IV already had them scramjetting at Mach 5 and rising above thirty-two thousand meters and climbing into the fringes of space. The fireball-meteors exploded at different altitudes below them, their shock waves overlapping like a dozen violent ripples on pond.

"Why, that fucker . . ." began Orphu.

"Silence," snapped Suma IV. The dropship rolled, dove, turned south, expanded its sphere of radar and electronic interference, and climbed again toward space. No fireballs or lightning came up from the city that was falling behind so quickly—six hundred kilometers below and behind already and getting smaller by the second.

"I guess our many-handed brain friend has weapons," said Mahnmut.

"So do we," came Mep Ahoo's voice on the comm. "I think we should nuke him . . . warm up his nest for him a little bit. Ten million degrees Fahrenheit would do for a start."

"Quiet!" snapped Suma IV from the cockpit.

Prime Integrator Asteague/Che's voice came over the common band. "My friends, we . . . you . . . have a problem down there."

"Tell us about it," rumbled Orphu of Io, still forgetting that he was still on the common radio link.

"No," said the Prime Integrator, "I am not speaking of the many-handed creature's attack on you. I'm talking about a more serious problem. And just beneath your current trajectory track. Our sensors might not have picked it up if they had not been following you."

"More serious?" sent Mahnmut.

"*Much* more serious," said Prime Integrator Asteague/Che. "And not just one serious problem, I'm afraid . . . but seven hundred and sixty-eight of them."

78

"*PROCEED WITH YOUR APPEAL,*" booms the Demogorgon.

Hephaestus nudges Achilles to signify that he will do the speaking, makes an awkward bow—a series of iron spheres and one glass bubble bobbling—and says, "Your Demogorgoness, Lord Kronos and other respected Titanisms, Immortal Hours, and . . . honorable other things. My friend Achilles and I come here today not to appeal, not to ask you for a boon, but to share essential information with all of you. Information you need to know and will want to know. Information which . . ."

"*SPEAK UP, CRIPPLED GOD.*"

Hephaestus forces a smile through his beard, grits his teeth hard, and repeats his preamble.

"*SPEAK THEN.*"

Achilles wonders if Kronos and the other Titans, not to mention the huge, indescribable entities surrounding them, things with odd names like the Immortal Hours and Charioteers, are going to take an active part in this meeting or if the Demogorgon has the floor until it—he—she—it—formally recognizes someone or something else to speak.

Hephaestus then surprises him.

From his bulky backpack—a clumsy iron and canvas frame holding what Achilles imagined must be tanks of air—the god of artifice pulls a brass ovoid studded with glass lenses. He carefully sets the device on the top of a boulder between him and the looming Demogorgon and fusses with various switches and settings. Then the dwarf-god says, shouting and amplifying his helmet speakers to the maximum, "Your Demogorgonoidness, most noble and frightening Hours, your most ma-

jestic Titans and Titanesses—Kronos, Rhea, Krios, Koios, Hyperion, Iapetos, Theia, Helios, Selene, Eos, and all others of Titan-persuasion assembled here—your many-armed Healernesses, rudely shaped
Charioteers—all honored Beings out there in the fog and ash—rather
than make my own case today, the case for removing the pretender Zeus
from the throne for attempting to usurp all divinity unto himself—asking you to depose him, or at least oppose him, for presumptuously
claiming all worlds and universes his own from this day forth to the end
of time, I shall allow you to see an actual event. For even as we huddle
here on this lava-riddled shitheap of a world, Zeus has called all the
Olympian immortals into the Great Hall of the Gods. I left my camera
concealed there but broadcasting live to a repeater station in Hellas
Basin—the immortal Nyx's Brane Hole allows us to receive this broadcast with less than a second of delay time. Behold!"

Hephaestus fiddles with more switches, throws a toggle.

Nothing happens.

The god of fire bites his lip, curses into his microphone, and fiddles
with the brass device some more. It blinks, whirs, flickers, and falls silent
again.

Achilles begins to slide his god-killing blade from its place in his belt.

"Behold!" cries Hephaestus, again using full amplification.

This time the brass device projects a rectangle almost a hundred
yards wide into the air above them all, in front of the Demogorgon and
the hundreds of hulking forms in the red lava-light and smoke around
them. The rectangle shows nothing but static and snow.

"Oh, fuck me," growls Hephaestus, each word quite audible over his
helmet speakers. He hurries to the device and wiggles some metal rods
which remind Achilles of the ears of a rabbit.

The huge image above them leaps into clarity. It is a holographic projection, very deep, fully three-dimensional, in living color, striking the
eye like a wide window into the actual Hall of the Gods itself. The visuals are accompanied by surround-sound—Achilles can hear the nearby
whisper of the hundreds upon hundreds of the waiting gods' sandals
scuffing softly on marble. When Hermes softly breaks wind, it is audible
to everyone here.

The Titans, Titanesses, Hours, Charioteers, insectoid Healers, unnamed monstrous shapes—everyone except the Demogorgon—gasp,
each in its own inhuman way. Not at Hermes' indiscretion, but at the
immediacy and impact of the still widening and encircling holographic
projection. By the time the band of light and motion closes around
them here, the illusion of being among the immortals in the Great Hall
of the Gods is very powerful. Achilles actually pulls his blade further
free, thinking that Zeus on his golden throne and the thousand

Olympian gods standing around them must certainly hear the noise in their midst and turn to see them all huddled here in the reek and gloom of Tartarus.

The Olympian gods do not turn. It's a one-way broadcast.

Zeus—at least fifty feet tall on his throne—leans forward, scowls out at the ranks upon ranks of assembled gods, goddesses, Furies, and Erinyeses, and begins to speak. Achilles can clearly hear the god's new-found ultimate self-importance in the archaic cadence of each slow syllable:

> *"You congregated powers of this Olympos, you who share*
> *the glory and the strength of him ye serve,*
> *rejoice! Henceforth I am omnipotent.*
> *All else has been subdued to me; alone*
> *the souls of man, like unextinguished fire,*
> *yet burns towards heaven with fierce reproach, and doubt,*
> *and lamentation, and reluctant prayer,*
> *hurling up insurrection, which might make*
> *our antique empire insecure, though built*
> *on eldest faith, and hell's coeval, fear;*
> *And though my curses through the pendulous air,*
> *like snow on herbless peaks, fall flake by flake,*
> *and cling to it, though under my wrath's night*
> *it climbs the crags of life, step after step,*
> *which wound it, as ice wounds unsandaled feet,*
> *it yet remains supreme o'er misery,*
> *aspiring, unrepressed, yet soon to fall:*

Zeus stands suddenly and the radiance flowing from him is so brilliant that a thousand immortal gods and one very mortal man in a sweaty chameleon suit—the stealth-suited man is quite visible to Hephaestus' camera and thus to everyone here in Tartarus—take a hesitant step backward as Zeus continues.

> *"Pour forth heaven's wine, Idaean Ganymede,*
> *and let it fill the Daedal cups like fire,*
> *and from the flower-inwoven soil divine*
> *ye all triumphant harmonies arise,*
> *as dew from earth under the twilight stars:*
> *Drink! Be the nectar circling through your veins*
> *the soul of joy, ye ever-living gods,*
> *till exaltation bursts in one wide voice*
> *like music from Elysian winds.*

*And thou
now attend beside me, veiled in the light
of the desire which makes thee one with me,
as I become God Ascendant, the single God to thee,
the one and true Omnipotent God,
Almighty God, true Lord of all Eternity!"*

Hephaestus shuts off the brass and glass projector. The huge, circular window binding Tartarus to the Hall of the Gods on Olympos flicks out of existence and everything returns to cinder, soot, stink, and red gloom. Achilles shifts his feet farther apart, hefts his shield, and holds his god-killing knife out of sight behind that shield. He has no idea what will happen next.

For the longest moments, nothing does happen. Achilles expects shouts, cries, demands that Hephaestus prove that the images and voices had been real, Titans bellowing, the big Healer bugs scuttling around on rocks—but there is no movement, no sound from the hundreds of gigantic figures still gathered around. The air is so thick with smoke, the red-lava glare so filtered by the ash in the air, that Achilles silently thanks the gods—or someone—for the thermskin goggles he's wearing that allow him to see what's going on. He sneaks a glance at the Brane Hole that Hephaestus had said Nyx—Goddess Night herself—had opened for him. The Hole's still there, about two hundred yards away, perhaps fifty feet high. If fighting starts, if the Demogorgon decides to eat both dwarf-god and Achaean hero as a snack, Achilles plans to make a run for that Brane Hole, even though he knows he'll have to hack his way through giants and beasties every foot of the way. He's prepared to do so.

The silence stretches. Dark winds howl over misshapen boulders and more misshapen sentient forms. The volcano burbles and belches but the Demogorgon does not make a noise.

Finally, it speaks—*"ALL SPIRITS ARE ENSLAVED WHICH SERVE THINGS EVIL. NOW THOU KNOWEST WHETHER ZEUS BE SUCH OR NO."*

"Evil??" roars Kronos the Titan. "My son is *mad*! He is the usurper of all usurpers."

Rhea, Zeus's mother, has an even louder voice. "Zeus rides the wreckage of his own will. He is the scorn of the earth and the bane of Olympos. He needs to suffer the outcast of his own abandonment. He must wither in destined pain and be hanged from hell in his own adamantine chains."

The Healer-monster speaks and Achilles is shocked to hear that its voice is very feminine. "Zeus reaches too far. He has first mimicked and now mocked the very Fates."

One of the Immortal Hours booms down from its rocky precipice— "Downfall demands no direr name than this—Zeus Usurper."

Achilles grabs the nearest shaking boulder, thinking that the volcano behind the Demogorgon is erupting, but it is only the muted rumble from the assembled Beings.

Kronos' brother, the shaggy Titan Krios, speaks from where he stands amidst a lava flow. "This pretender must sink beneath the wide waves of his own ruin. I myself will ascend to Olympos where once we ruled and drag this empty thing down to hell, even as a vulture and a snake outspent drop, twisted in inexplicable fight."

"Awful shape!" cries a many-armed Charioteer to the Demogorgon. "Speak!"

"MERCIFUL GOD REIGNS," echoes the shapeless Demogorgon giant's voice amid the Tartarus peaks and valleys. "ZEUS IS NOT ALMIGHTY GOD. ZEUS MUST NO LONGER REIGN ON OLYMPOS."

Achilles had been sure that the veiled Demogorgon was limbless, but somehow the limbless giant raises a robed arm that was not visible a second earlier, extends something like terrible fingers.

The Brane Hole two hundred yards behind Hephaestus rises as if on command, hovers above them all, widens, and begins to drop.

"WORDS ARE QUICK AND WORDS ARE VAIN," booms the Demogorgon as the burning red and still-widening circle of flame drops down around them all. "THE SINGLE SURE AND FINAL ANSWER MUST BE PAIN."

Hephaestus grabs Achilles' arm. The dwarf-god is grinning wildly, insanely, through his beard. "Hang on, kid," he says.

79

It was a desperate, almost insane, turn of events, but Mahnmut couldn't have been happier.

The dropship had hovered very low and dropped Mahnmut's *The Dark Lady* submersible into the ocean about fifteen kilometers north of the troublesome critical-singularity coordinates. Suma IV explained that he didn't want the splash setting off the seven hundred sixty-eight detected black holes—presumably on warheads in the the ancient, sunken sub also detected—and no one gave him an argument.

If Mahnmut had owned a human mouth, he would have been grinning like an idiot. *The Dark Lady* was designed and built for beneath-the-ice, black-as-inside-God's-belly, horrific-pressure exploration and salvage work on Jupiter's moon Europa, but it worked just fine in Earth's Atlantic Ocean.

Better than fine.

"I wish you could see this," Mahnmut said over their private comm. He and Orphu of Io were on their own again. None of the other moravecs had shown any great interest in approaching the seven hundred sixty-eight nascent but close-to-critical black holes and the dropship had already flown away on Suma IV's continued reconnaissance—of the eastern seaboard of North America this time.

"I can 'see' the radar, sonar, thermal, and other data," said Orphu.

"Yes, but it's not the same. There's so much *light* here in Earth's ocean. Even here below twenty meters depth. Even full Jupiter-glow never illuminated my oceans—if there was a lead, a bare patch, above—deeper than a few meters."

"I'm sure it's beautiful," said Orphu.

"It really *is*," burbled Mahnmut, not noticing or caring if his big friend had been speaking ironically. "The sunlight shafts down, illuminating everything in a dappled-green, glowing way. The *Lady* isn't sure of what to make of it."

"She notices the light?"

"Of course," said Mahnmut. "Her job is to report everything to me, to choose the right data and sensory feeds at the right time, and she's self-aware enough to note all this difference in light, gravity and beauty here. She likes it, too."

"Good," rumbled Orphu of Io. "You'd better not ruin it by telling her why we're here and what we're swimming toward."

"She knows," said Mahnmut, not letting the big moravec ruin his buoyant mood. He watched as the sonar reported a ridgeline ahead—the ridge the wreck was on—rising to a silty bottom less than eighty meters below the surface. He still couldn't get over how shallow this part of Earth's ocean was. There was no spot in the Europan seas less than a thousand meters deep and here a ridgeline brought the bottom of the Atlantic Ocean up to not much more than sixty meters beneath the surface.

"I've run the full program of the disarmament protocol Suma IV and Cho Li downloaded to us," continued Orphu. "Have you had time yet to study the details?"

"Not really." Mahnmut had the long protocol in his active memory, but he'd been busy overseeing *The Dark Lady*'s exit from the dropship and the submersible's adaptation to that beautiful, wonderful environment. His beloved sub was as good as new—better than new. The Phobos 'vec mechanics had done a wonderful job on his boat. And every system that had worked well on Europa before their devastating crash landing in Mars' Tethys Sea the previous year now worked better than well here in Earth's gentle sea.

"The good news about the disarming of each black-hole warhead is that it's theoretically doable," said Orphu of Io. "We have the tools aboard—including the ten-thousand-degree cutting torch and the focused forcefield generators—and in many of the necessary steps, I can be your arms while you're my visible-light spectrum eyes. We'll have to work together on every warhead, but they're theoretically disarmable."

"That is good news," said Mahnmut.

"The bad news is that if we work straight through, without coffee breaks or restroom stops, it's going to take us a little over nine hours per black hole—not per MRVed warhead, mind you, but for each near-critical black hole."

"With seven hundred sixty-eight black holes . . ." began Mahnmut.

"Six thousand nine hundred twelve hours," said Orphu. "And since we're on Earth and moravec standard time is *real* planetary time here, it's two hundred forty-seven days, twelve hours, *if* everything goes according to plan and we don't run into any real problems . . ."

"Well . . ." began Mahnmut. "I guess we deal with this factor when we find the wreck and see if we can get to the warheads at all."

"It's odd getting direct sonar input," said Orphu. "It's not so much like better hearing, it's more as if my skin had suddenly enlarged to . . ."

"There it is," interrupted Mahnmut. "I see it. The wreck."

Perspectives and visual horizons were different there, of course, on the so-much-larger Earth than the Mars he'd almost gotten used to, even more out of proportion to perceived distances on the tiny Europa, where he had spent all the other standard years of his existence. But sonar readings, deep radar, mass-detection devices, and his own eyes told Mahnmut that the stern of this wreck was about five hundred meters dead ahead, lying on the silty bottom just a little below *The Dark Lady*'s depth of seventy meters, and that the crumpled boat itself was around fifty-five meters long.

"Good God," whispered Mahnmut. "Can you see this on radar and sonar?"

"Yes."

The wreck lay on its belly, bow-down, but the bow itself was invisible beyond the shimmering forcefield that held back the Atlantic Ocean from the dry strip of land that ran from Europe to North America. What made Mahnmut stare in amazement was the wall of light from the Breach wall itself. Here at more than seventy meters depth, where even in Earth's sunlit oceans the bottom should be inky black, dappled sunlight illuminated the terminus of water and dappled the moss-green hull of the sunken sub itself.

"I can see what killed it," said Mahnmut. "Does your radar and sonar pick up that blasted bit of hull above what should be the engine room? Just behind where the hull humps up to the long missile compartment?"

"Yes."

"I think some sort of depth charge or torpedo or missile exploded there," said Mahnmut. "See how the hull plates are all bent inward there. It cracked the base of the sail and bent it forward as well."

"What sail?" asked Orphu. "You mean a sail like the triangular one on the felucca we took west up the Valles Marineris?"

"No. I mean that part that sticks up way forward, almost to the forcefield wall there. In the early submarine days, they called it a conning tower. After they began building nuclear subs like this boomer in the Twentieth Century, they started calling the conning tower a sail."

"Why?" asked Orphu of Io.

"I don't know why," said Mahnmut. "Or rather, I have it in my memory banks somewhere, but it's not important. I don't want to take the time to do a search."

"What's a boomer?"

"A boomer is the early Lost Era humans' pet name for a ballistic missile submarine like this," said Mahnmut.

"They gave pet names to machines built for the sole purpose of destroying cities, human lives, and the planet?"

"Yes," said Mahnmut. "This boomer was probably built a century or two before it was sunk here. Perhaps built by one of the major powers then and sold to a smaller group. Something sank it here long before this groove in the Atlantic Ocean was created."

"Can we get to the black hole warheads?" asked Orphu.

"Hang on. Let's find out."

Mahnmut inched *The Dark Lady* forward. He wanted nothing to do with the forcefield wall and the empty air beyond it so he never moved closer to that forcefield than the missile compartment of the wreck itself. He had *The Dark Lady* play powerful searchlights all over the wreck even as his instruments probed the interior of the ancient sub.

"This isn't right," he murmured aloud on their private line.

"What's not right?" asked Orphu.

"The sub is overgrown with anemones and other sea life, the interior is rich with life, but it's as if the sub sank here a century or so ago, not the two and a half millennia or so it would have to have gone down."

"Could someone have been sailing it just a century or so ago?" asked Orphu.

"No. Not unless all our observation data has been wrong. The old-style humans have been almost without technology the last two thousand years down here. Even if someone had found this sub and managed to launch it, who would've sunk it?"

"The post-humans?"

"I don't think so," said Mahnmut. "The posts wouldn't have used something so crude as a torpedo or depth charge on this thing. And they wouldn't have left the black hole warheads here ticking away."

"But the warheads are here," said Orphu. "I can see the tops of them on the deep-radar return, with the critical-one black hole containment fields inside. We'd better get to work."

"Wait," said Mahnmut. He had sent remote vehicles no larger than his hand into the wreck and now the data was flowing back through microthin umbilicals. One of the remotes had tapped into the command and control center's AI.

Mahnmut and Orphu listened to the last words of the twenty-six crew members as they prepared to launch the ballistic missiles that would destroy their planet.

When the testimonials and data flow were finished, the two moravecs were silent for a long minute.

"Oh, what a world," whispered Orphu at last, "that hath such people in it."

"I'm going to come down and get you ready to go EVA," said Mahnmut, his voice a dull monotone. "We'll look at this problem from close up."

"Can we look into the dry area?" asked Orphu. "The gap?"

"I'm not going near it," said Mahnmut. "The forcefield might destroy us—the *Lady*'s instruments can't even decide what the field is made of—and I promise you that this submersible of ours is no good in air and on dry land. We're not going near the breach."

"Did you look at the dropship's aerial photos of the bow of this wreck?" asked Orphu.

"Sure. I've got them on the screen in front of me," said Mahnmut. "Some serious damage to the bow, but that doesn't concern us. We can get at the missiles back here."

"No, I meant the other things lying around on the dry ground out there," said Orphu. "My radar data might not be as good as your optic images, but it almost looks like one of those lumps lying there is a human being."

Mahnmut peered at his screen. The dropship had shot an extensive series of images before it had flown off and he flicked through all of them. "If it *was* a human being," he said, "it's been dead a long time. It's flattened, limbs splayed wrong, desiccated. I don't think it was—I think our minds are just trying to see that shape amidst random stuff. There's quite a debris field out there."

"All right,"said Orphu obviously aware of their priorities. "What do I have to do to get ready here?"

"Just stay where you are," said Mahnmut. "I'm coming down to get you. We'll go out together."

The Dark Lady sat on its stubby legs not ten meters west of the stern of the wreck. Orphu had wondered how they would exit through the cargo bay doors set in the belly of the Europan submersible with the ship sitting on the bottom of the ocean, but that question had been settled when Mahnmut had extended the landing legs.

Mahnmut had entered the cargo bay through the interior airlock and tapped into direct comm contact with the big Ionian while the submersible pilot carefully flooded the hold with Earth ocean water, equalized pressures, and then opened the cargo bay door. They'd disconnected Orphu from his various umbilicals and the two had gently dropped to the bottom of the ocean.

As cracked and ancient as Orphu's carapace was, he didn't leak. When he showed curiosity at the pressure readings his shell and other body parts were reading, Mahnmut explained.

The atmospheric pressure up above, on a theoretical beach or just above the surface of the ocean here, held relatively steady at 14.7 pounds per square inch. About every 10 meters—actually every 33 feet, Mahnmut said, using the old Lost Era measurements with which Orphu was equally comfortable—that pressure increased by one atmosphere. Thus at 33 feet of depth, every square inch of the moravecs' outer integument would feel 29.4 pounds of pressure. At 66 feet, they would be under three atmospheres, and so forth. At the depth of this wreck—more than 230 feet—the sea pressure was exerting eight atmospheres on every square inch of *The Dark Lady*'s hull and the moravecs' bodies.

They were built to withstand far greater pressures, although Orphu was used to *negative* pressure differentials as he worked in the radiation- and sulfur-filled space around the moon Io.

And speaking of radiation, there was a lot of it around. They both registered it and the *Lady* monitored it and relayed her readings. It was not dangerous to moravecs of their design, but the feeling of the neutron and gamma rays pouring through them caught their attention.

Mahnmut explained that under this pressure, if they had been human beings and if they had been breathing tanked standard Earth air—a mixture of twenty-one percent oxygen with seventy-nine percent nitrogen—the multiplying and expanding nitrogen bubbles under eight atmospheres would be playing havoc with them, giving them nitrogen narcosis, distorting their judgment and emotions, and not allowing them to surface without hours of slow decompression at different depths. But the moravecs were breathing pure O-two, with their rebreathing systems compensating for the added pressure.

"Shall we look at our adversaries?" asked Orphu of Io.

Mahnmut led the way. As careful as he was climbing the curved hull of the wreck, silt rose around them like a terrestrial dust storm.

"Can you still see by fine radar?" asked Mahnmut. "This crap is blinding me on visual frequencies. I've read about this in all the old Earth-based diving stories. The first diver at a wreck site on the bottom or inside the wreck would get a view—all the others would have zero viz—at least until the silt and crud settles."

"Zero viz, huh?" said Orphu. "Well, welcome to the club, amigo. The detailed radar I use in the sulphur-mess vacuum near Io serves to probe through these little silt clouds just fine. I see the hull, the hump of the missile compartment, the whatchamacallit—the broken sail—thirty meters forward. If you need help, just ask and I'll lead you by the hand."

Mahnmut grunted and switched his primary vision to thermal and radar frequencies.

They drifted over the missile compartment, five meters above the warheads themselves, both moravecs using their built-in thrusters to maneuver, each being careful not to squirt any thrust in the direction of the tumbled warheads.

And tumbled they were. There were forty-eight missile tubes and forty-eight missile tube hatches wide open.

These hatches look heavy, said Mahnmut over their tightbeam. Everything they said and saw, of course, including tightbeam, was being relayed up to the *Queen Mab* and the dropship via a relay radio buoy Mahnmut had deployed from *The Dark Lady*.

Ophu had been gripping one of the huge hatches—its diameter as large as the Ionian—and now he said, "Seven tons."

Even after the crew had ordered the sub's AI to open the forty-eight missile tube hatches, the missiles themselves still had been covered by blue fiberglass domes that held out the sea. Mahnmut saw at a glance how the missiles—propelled to the surface by huge charges of nitrogen gas, their engines to ignite only after each missile reached air—would easily burst through those fiberglass covers.

But the missiles had not exploded from their tubes in rising bubbles of nitrogen, nor had their engines ignited. The fiberglass dome-covers had long since worn away; only brittle blue fragments remained.

"What a mess," said Orphu.

Mahnmut nodded. Whatever had hit the stern of *The Sword of Allah*, breaking its back just above the engine room, severing its propulsion jets, and sending the ocean rushing in through the length of the boomer as a wall of shock wave and seawater, had breached the various missile compartments and tumbled the missiles themselves. It looked like a heap of ancient straw. In some cases the warheads were still pointing vaguely upward, but in others the ancient, corroded rocket engines and their solid fuel were at the top and the warheads buried in silt.

Forget that easy six thousand nine hundred twelve hours of work, tightbeamed Orphu. *It'll take that long just to get to some of those warheads. And odds are overwhelming that any serious torch cutting or twisting on one will detonate another one.*

Yeah, said Mahnmut. There was no silt obscuring his view now and he looked at the tangled mess primarily on his optical frequencies.

"Do either of you have a suggestion?" asked Prime Integrator Asteague/Che.

Mahnmut almost jumped. He'd known they were being monitored by everyone on the *Mab*, but he had been so absorbed with studying the wreckage that the connection had almost slipped his mind.

"Yes," said Orphu of Io, switching to the common band. "Here's what we're going to do."

He described the procedure as succinctly and nontechnically as he could. Rather than try to disarm each warhead through the long proto-col the Prime Integrators had downloaded, the Ionian now planned for Mahnmut and him to do it the quick and messy way. Mahnmut would bring *The Dark Lady* right above the wreck, extending her landing legs to full length until she was squatting over the boomer like a mother hen on her nest. They'd use all the ship's belly searchlights to illuminate their work. Then Orphu and Mahnmut would separately use the torches to cut each warhead away from its missile, using a simple chain and pulley system to haul the nose cones directly up into *The Dark Lady*'s cargo hold and setting them in place in cargo baffles there like eggs in a carton.

"Isn't there a great chance of the black holes going critical during this rough and tumble process?" asked Cho Li from the bridge of the *Queen Mab*.

"Yeah," rumbled Orphu over the comm, "but the odds are one hundred percent that one of the black holes will activate if we spend a year or more futzing around with them. We're doing it this way."

Mahnmut touched one of the Ionian's manipulators and nodded agreement, sure that his nod would be picked up by Orphu's close radar.

Suma IV's stern voice broke in over the commlink. "And what do you propose to do with the forty-eight warheads with their seven hundred sixty-eight black holes once you get them loaded in your submersible?"

"You're going to pick us up," said Mahnmut. "The dropship will haul *The Dark Lady* and its bellyful of death into outer space and we'll send the holes on their way."

"The dropship isn't configured to fly out beyond the rings," snapped Suma IV. "And the leukocyte robotic attack drones in the e- and p-rings will certainly mob us on the way up."

"That's your problem," rumbled Orphu. "We're going to get to work now. It should take us ten to twelve hours to hack and cut these war-heads free and load them into *The Dark Lady*. When we break surface, you'd better have a plan. We know you have other spacecraft than the *Mab* up there on this mission—stealthed, out beyond the rings, what-ever. You'd better have one ready to meet the dropship in low Earth orbit and take this mess off our hands. We don't want to have come all this way to Earth just to destroy it."

"Acknowledge your transmission," said Asteague/Che. "Please be advised that we have a visitor up here. A small spacecraft—a sonie, I believe—is rendezvousing with Sycorax's orbital isle as I speak."

80

There was no ceremony surrounding Noman's departure. One minute he was in the hovering sonie and chatting with Daeman, Hannah, and Tom who were standing beside it, and the next second the sonie had tilted almost vertically, its forcefield pressing Noman into the mat, and then it shot skyward like a flechette, disappearing into the low, gray clouds in seconds.

Ada felt cheated. She'd wanted her last words with the friend she'd once known as Odysseus.

The vote to allow Noman to borrow the sonie had been decided by one vote. The last vote—the deciding vote—had been cast by a man named Elian, the bald leader of the six Hughes Town refugees who had come in with Hannah and Noman on the skyraft, not even one of the Ardis survivors.

The Ardis people who had voted against losing the sonie were furious. There were demands for a recount. Flechette rifles actually had been raised in anger, along with shouting voices.

Ada had stepped into the middle of the melee and announced in a loud, calm voice that the issue had been decided. Noman was to be allowed to borrow the sonie but would return it as soon as possible. In the meantime, they would have the sky-raft that Noman and Hannah had cobbled together in the Golden Gate at Machu Picchu—the sonie could carry only six; the sky-raft could haul up to fourteen people at a time if they had to make a run for the island. This matter was settled.

The flechette rifles had been lowered, but the grumbling continued. Old friends of Ada's refused to meet her gaze in the hours afterward and she knew that she'd used up the last of her capital as leader of the Ardis survivors.

Now Noman and the sonie were gone and Ada had never felt lonelier. She touched her slightly bulging belly and thought, *Little person, son or daughter of Harman, if this was a mistake that endangers you, I shall be sorry to the last second of my life.*

"Ada?" said Daeman. "Can I have a word in private with you?"

They walked out beyond the north palisade to where Hannah had once kept her scaffolded hearth working. Daeman told her about his meeting with the post-human who called herself Moira. He described how she looked exactly like a young Savi and how she was invisible to the rest of them as she stood near him during the meeting and the vote.

Ada shook her head slowly. "None of that makes any sense, Daeman. Why would a post-human appear in Savi's body—stay invisible to the rest of us? *How* could she? *Why* would she?"

"I don't know," said Daeman.

"Did she have anything else to say?"

"She promised—before the meeting—to tell me something about Harman after the meeting if she could attend."

"And?" said Ada. She felt her heart pounding so wildly that it might have been the child stirring within her, as eager as she to hear the news.

"All the Moira-ghost said afterward was 'Remember that Noman's coffin was Noman's coffin,' " said Daeman.

Ada made him repeat that twice and said, "That makes no sense either."

"I know," said Daeman. He looked crestfallen, shoulders slumped. "I tried to make her explain but then she was . . . gone. Just disappeared."

She stared hard at him. "Are you sure this happened, Daeman? We've all been working too hard, sleeping too little, worrying too much. Are you sure this Moira-ghost was real?"

Daeman stared hard back at her, his gaze as angrily defensive as hers was angrily doubtful, but he said nothing else.

"Remember that Noman's coffin was Noman's coffin," muttered Ada. She looked around. People were going about their early afternoon chores, but the work groups had now broken themselves into clusters of those who had voted the same. Neither side was speaking to the bald man Elian. Ada fought off the urge to sob.

Neither Noman nor the sonie returned that day. Nor the next. Nor the next.

On the third day, Ada went up in the wobbly sky-raft with Hannah at the controls, accompanying Daeman's hunting party out beyond the circle of voynix and trying to get an estimate of how many of the headless, carapaced killers were out there. It was a beautiful morning—no clouds at all, a blue sky and warmer winds promising spring—and she could easily see that the number of voynix pressing into their two-mile radius from the Pit had grown.

"It's hard for me to guess," Ada whispered to Daeman although they were a thousand feet above the monsters. "There must be three or four hundred just visible in that meadow. We never had to count large numbers of things growing up. What do you think? Fifteen thousand in the whole encircling mass? More?"

"More, I think," Daeman said calmly. "I think there are thirty to forty thousand of the things surrounding us now."

"Don't they ever get tired of standing there?" asked Ada. "Don't they have to eat? Drink?"

"Evidently not," said Daeman. "Back when we thought they were servant-machines, I never saw one eat or drink or get tired, did you?"

Ada said nothing. Those times seemed too remote to think about, even though they had ended less than a year earlier.

"Fifty thousand," muttered Daeman. "Perhaps there are fifty thousand here now, and more faxing in every day."

Hannah flew them farther west to find game and fresh meat.

On the fourth day, the Setebos baby in the Pit had grown to the size of a yearling calf—one of their yearling calves, now all slaughtered by voynix, of course, but a calf that was only a pulsating gray brain with a score of pink hands on its belly, yellow eyes, pulsating orifices, and more three-fingered hands leaping out on gray stalks.

Mommy, Mommy, whispered the thing in Ada's mind, in all their minds. *It's time for me to come out now. This pit is too small and I am too hungry to stay here any longer.*

It was early evening, less than an hour from twilight and another long, dark winter night. The group gathered near the Pit. Men and women still tended to stand near only those who had voted as they had on the loan of the sonie. Everyone now carried a flechette weapon, although crossbows were kept close to hand in reserve.

Casman, Kaman, Greogi, and Edide stood over the Pit with their rifles aimed at the large thing in the hole. Others gathered close.

"Hannah," said Ada, "is the sky-raft fully provisioned?"

"Yes," said the younger woman. "All of the first trip crates are aboard and still room for ten people on the first trip. We can get fourteen people aboard on every trip after that."

"And what time are you down to in rehearsing the trip to the island and the unpacking of the crates?" asked Ada.

"Forty-two minutes," said Laman, rubbing the stumps of his missing fingers on his right hand. "Thirty-five minutes with just people. It takes a few minutes to get people aboard or off."

"That's not good enough," said Ada.

Hannah stepped closer to the fire they kept burning near the Pit.

"Ada, the trip to the island takes fifteen minutes each way. The machine can't fly any faster."

"The sonie would have been there in less than a minute," said Loes, one of the angriest of the Ardis survivors. "We could all have been delivered there in less than ten minutes."

"We don't have the sonie now," Ada said. She heard the lack of affect in her own voice. Without meaning to, she glanced to the southwest, down toward the river and the island, but also toward the woods where fifty to sixty thousand voynix waited.

Noman had been right. Even if the entire colony of humans here escaped to the island, the voynix would be on them there in hours—perhaps minutes. Even though the Ardis faxnode was still nonfunctioning—they kept two people there at the pavilion day and night to keep testing it—the voynix were faxing. Somehow, they were faxing. There was nowhere on earth, Ada realized, that they would be free of the killers.

"Let's get back to making dinner," she called above the murmuring. Everyone could feel the Setebos spawn's clammy voice in his or her mind.

Mommy, Daddy, it's time for me to come out now. Open the grill, Daddy, Mommy, or I will. I'm stronger now. I'm hungry now. I want to come meet you now.

Greogi, Daeman, Hannah, Elian, Boman, Edide, and Ada sat talking late into the night. Above them the equatorial and polar rings whirled silently, turning as they always had. The Big Dipper was low in the north. There was a crescent moon.

"I think tomorrow, first light, we abandon the idea of the island and begin evacuating as many people as possible to the Golden Gate at Machu Picchu," said Ada. "We should have done it weeks ago."

"It would take weeks for this stupid sky-raft to get to the Golden Gate at Machu Picchu," said Hannah. "And it may break down again and never get there. Without Noman to fix it, the people on the sky-raft will be stranded."

"We're dead if it breaks down here as well," said Daeman. He touched Hannah's shoulder as the young woman seemed to slump. "You've done an amazing job keeping it working, Hannah, but this is a technology we just don't understand."

"What technology *do* we understand?" muttered Boman.

"Crossbows," said Edide. "We were getting damned good at building crossbows."

No one laughed. After a few minutes, Elian said, "Tell me again why the voynix can't get into the habitation part of this bridge at Machu Picchu."

"The habitation bubbles are like grapes on a vine," said Hannah, who had spent more time there than any of them. "But linked together. Clear plastic or something. It's late Lost Era technology, maybe even post-human technology—some sort of forcefield just above the surface of the glass. Voynix just slide off."

"We had something similar on the windows of the crawler Savi drove us in from Jerusalem into the Mediterranean Basin," said Daeman. "She said it was a frictionless field to keep the rain off. But it worked for voynix and *calibani* too."

"I'd enjoy seeing one of these *calibani*," said Elian. "And also the Caliban thing you described." The bald man's mouth and other facial features seemed always set to a show of strength and curiosity.

"No," Daeman said softly, "you wouldn't enjoy seeing either one. Especially the real Caliban. Trust me on this."

In the silence that followed, Greogi said what they had all been thinking. "We're going to have to draw straws . . . something. Fourteen get to go to the Bridge. They can carry weapons, water, and minimum rations, hunt along the way perhaps, so a full sky-raft load of fourteen can go. The rest of us stay."

"Fourteen out of fifty-four get to live?" said Edide. "Doesn't seem right."

"Hannah will be one of those who goes," said Greogi. "She flies the sky-raft back if the fourteen get to the Bridge on the first trip."

Hannah shook her head. "You can fly the thing as well as I can, Greogi. We can teach anyone here how to fly it as well as I can. I'm not automatically on the first trip and you know . . . you *know* . . . there won't be a second trip. Not with the shape the sky-raft is in. Not with the voynix continuing to mass out there in the dark. Not with the Setebos thing getting stronger every hour. Those fourteen short straws, long straws, whichever, will have a chance to live. The rest will die here."

"Then we'll decide as soon as it's light," said Ada.

"There may be fighting," said Elian. "People are angry, hungry, resentful. They may not want to draw straws to see who lives and who dies. They may rush the raft right away, or after they don't get a seat."

Ada nodded. "Daeman, take ten of your best people and have them surround the sky-raft—protect it—even before I call the council together. Edide, you and your friends quietly try to collect as many of the loose weapons as possible."

"Most people sleep with their flechette rifles now," said the blond woman. "They don't let them out of their hands."

Ada nodded again. "Do what you can. I'll talk to everyone. Explain why this is the only hope."

"The losers will want to be ferried to the island," said Greogi. "At the very least."

Boman nodded. "I would. I *will* if I don't get the right-sized straw."

Ada sighed. "It won't do any good. I'm convinced that the island is just another place to die . . . the voynix will be there minutes after we are if the Setebos thing isn't there to protect us. But we can do that. Ferry those who want to go, then let the fourteen head for the Bridge."

"It will waste time," said Hannah. "Put more stress on the sky-raft."

Ada held her hands out, palms upward. "It may keep our people from killing each other, Hannah. It gives fourteen people a chance. And the rest get to choose where they stand and die. That's something—an illusion of choice if nothing else."

No one had anything else to say. They broke up to head toward their own sleeping tents and lean-tos.

Hannah followed Ada and touched her arm in the dark before they reached Ada's sleeping tent.

"Ada," whispered the younger woman, "I have this feeling that Harman is still alive. I hope you're one of the fourteen."

Ada smiled—her white teeth visible in the ringlight. "I have this feeling that Harman is alive, too, my dear. But I'm not going to be one of the fourteen. I've already decided that I'm not going to take part in the drawing of straws. My baby and I are staying at Ardis."

In the end, none of their planning mattered.

Just after sunrise, Ada jerked awake to cold hands in her mind and within her womb.

Mommy—I have your little boy here. He's going to stay inside for a few months while I teach him things—wonderful things—but I'm coming out to play!

Ada screamed as she felt the mind in the Pit touching the developing mind of the fetus inside her.

She was on her feet and running, carrying two flechette rifles, before anyone else could fully awaken.

The Setebos baby had bent the bars of the grill back and was squeezing its gray brain-girth through the bent mesh and bars. Already the thing had tentacles flung out fifteen feet to a side, three-fingered hands sunk deep in the dirt. Three of its feeding orifices were open and the long, fleshy, trunklike appendages there were already drinking grief and terror and history from the soil of Ardis. Its many yellow eyes were very bright and as it rose out of the Pit, the many fingers on its large pink hands were waving like sea anemones in a strong current.

Mommy, it's all right, hiss-thought the thing as it pulled itself free of the Pit. *All I'm going to do is . . .*

Ada heard Daeman and others running behind her, but she did not look over her shoulder as she stopped, jerked down the flechette rifle from her shoulder, and fired a full clip into the Setebos thing.

It spun as thousands of crystal darts shredded part of its left lobe. Tentacles lashed toward her.

Ada dodged, slapped in a second magazine, emptied it into the writhing brain.

Mommmmmmmmeeeeeeeeeeeeeeeeeeeeeeeeeeeeeeeeeeeeeee

Ada dropped the first flechette rifle when the second magazine was empty, raised the second rifle, clicked it to full automatic, stepped three paces closer between the clawing tentacles, and fired the full magazine of flechettes between the yellow eyes at the front of the brain.

The Setebos spawn screamed—screamed with its real many mouths—and fell backward into the Pit.

Ada strode to the edge of the Pit, slammed in a new magazine and fired, ignoring the shouts and screams behind her. When that flechette magazine was empty, she slapped in another, aimed at the bleeding gray mass in the pit, and fired again. Again. Again. The brain split along its hemispheres and she blasted each pulped hemisphere as if smashing a pumpkin. The pink hands and long stalks spasmed, but the Setebos spawn was dead.

Ada felt it die. Everyone did. Its last mental scream—in no language except pain—hissed away to silence in their minds like filthy water going down a drain.

Everyone except sentinels came out from their shelters and stood grouped around the Pit, staring down, feeling the absence but not yet believing.

"Well, I guess I don't have to go gather straws after all," said Greogi to Ada, leaning close and almost whispering into her ear amidst the stunned silence.

Suddenly there came a noise from all around them—a whirring, whistling, humming, terrifying noise, distant yet growing louder, the whir and scrabbling noise echoing through the forest and from the surrounding hills.

"What in the hell . . ." began Casman.

"The voynix," said Daeman. He took Ada's rifle from her, slapped in a fresh magazine of flechettes, and handed it back to her. "They're all coming at once."

81

Here I am watching and listening as a god goes mad.

I don't know what help I thought I could get up here on Olympos for my besieged and dying Achaeans, but now I've trapped myself, just as surely as the Greeks on their beach with the Trojans closing in are trapped to the death, me standing here in my sweaty chameleon suit, cheek by jowl with a thousand immortals, trying to hold my breath to keep from giving myself away while watching and listening as Zeus, already king of the gods, declares himself the one and only Eternal God Almighty.

I shouldn't worry about being noticed. The gods around me are staring with their immortal jaws hanging slack, their godlike mouths hanging open, and their divine Olympian eyes bugging out.

Zeus has gone mad. And his dark eyes seem to be boring into me as he spittles on about his new ascendance to ultimate Godhood. I'm sure he can see me. His eyes have the self-pleasuring patience of a cat with a mouse between its paws.

I put my thick-suited hand on the QT medallion against my chest under the sticky chameleon suit.

But where to go? Back to the beach with the Achaeans means certain death. Back to Ilium to see Helen means pleasure and survival, but I will have betrayed . . . betrayed who? The Greeks haven't even noticed when I've walked among them, at least not since Achilles and Odysseus both disappeared on the wrong side of the closing Brane Hole. Why should I feel loyalty to them when they don't. . . .

But I do.

Speaking of Odysseus—and X-rated images pop into my mind when I do think of him—I know that I can QT back to the *Queen Mab*. That might be the safest place for me, although I really *have* no place there among the moravecs.

Nothing feels right. No move feels better than a cowardly betrayal.

Betrayal of whom, for Gods' sake? I ask myself, taking the Lord's name in vain even as the universe's new Lord and only Almighty God stares me in the eye and finishes his fist-pounding, spittle-flying rant.

Lord God Zeus did not end his speech with *"ARE THERE ANY QUESTIONS?"*—but he might as well have, based on the thickness of silence that now falls over the Great Hall of the Gods.

Then, suddenly, inexplicably—given the real-time terror of the situation—the undying pedant in me, the would-be scholar rather than the has-been scholic, is struck by a Miltonic line by Lucifer: *I will exalt my throne above the stars of God . . .*

Something rips the roof and upper floors of the Great Hall of the Gods clean away, revealing naked sky and a shapeless form. Wind and voices roar.

The wall crashes inward. Huge shapes, some vaguely human, smash in masonry, tumble pillars, flow down from the sky, and attack the assembled gods. Every immortal with any sense QT's away or takes off running. I am frozen in place.

Zeus leaps to his feet. His golden armor and weapons are stacked not twenty feet from where he stands, but that is too far away. Too many forms are closing too quickly for the Father of the Gods to arm himself.

He raises and pulls back his muscled arm to fling lightning, to guide the thunder.

Nothing happens.

"Ai! Ai!" cries Zeus, staring at his empty right hand as if it has disobeyed him. "The elements obey me not!"

"NO REFUGE! NO APPEAL!" booms a voice from the shifting thundercloud mass looming over the disassembled building and the warring gods and shapes. *"COME DOWN WITH ME NOW, USURPER. THOSE WHO REMAIN, LOVE NOT THRONES, ALTARS, JUDGMENT-SEATS, AND PRISONS, ALL THOSE FOUL SHAPES ABHORRED BY TRUE GOD AND MAN. COME, USURPER, TYRANT OF THE WORLD, COME TO YOUR NEW HOME STRANGE, SAVAGE, GHASTLY, DARK, AND EXECRABLE."*

For all its booming volume, the terrible voice is more terrible because of its calmness.

"No!" cries Zeus and quantum teleports away.

I hear the immortals fighting near me shout "Titans!" and "Kronos!" and then I run, praying that I remain invisible in my moravec chameleon suit, running out through the tumbling pillars, past the fighting forms, through literal lightning, out under the fire-rent blue skies of the Olympos summit.

Already some of the Olympian gods have taken to their flying chariots, and already they have been met and joined in battle by larger, stranger chariots and their indescribable drivers. All around the shores of the Caldera Lake, gods are fighting Titans—I see a form that can only be Kronos taking on both Apollo and Ares—while monsters are fighting gods and gods are fleeing.

Suddenly I am seized. A powerful hand jerks me to a stop, pins my right arm before I can reach for my QT medallion, and strips the chameleon suit off me like someone ripping Christmas wrap from a poorly wrapped package.

I see that it is Hephaestus, the bearded dwarf-god of fire, Chief Artificer to Zeus and the gods. Behind him on the grass are what looks to be a series of iron cannonballs and a goldfish bowl.

"What are you doing here, Hockenberry?" snarls the unkempt god. Dwarfish as he is to other Olympians, he's still taller than me.

"How did you see me?" is all that I can manage. Fifty yards away, it appears as if Kronos has killed Apollo with a huge cudgel. The stormcloud-being hovering above the roofless Great Hall of the Gods seems to be dissipating on the high winds that blow around the summit of Olympos.

Hephaestus laughs and taps a glass and bronze lens-thing dangling from his vest amidst a hundred other tiny gizmos. "Of course I could see you. So could Zeus. That's why he had me *build you*, Hockenberry. It was all supposed to lead to his ascension to the Godhead today being *observed*—observed by someone who could *fucking well write it down*. We're all postliterate here, you know."

Before I can move or speak, Hephaestus grabs the heavy QT medallion, rips it off me—breaking the chain—and crushes it in his massive, blunt-fingered, filthy hand.

OhJesusGodAlmightyno I manage to think as the god of fire opens his fist just enough to drop the crumbs of gold into a vest pocket he pulls out wide.

"Don't shit your pants, Hockenberry," laughs the god. "This thing never worked. See—there's *no fucking mechanism!* Just the dial you could ratchet around. This has always been your Dumbo Feather."

"It worked . . . it's always . . . I came from . . . I used it to . . ."

"No, you didn't," says Hephaestus. "I built you with the nanogenes necessary to quantum teleport—just like the big boys. Just like us gods. You just weren't supposed to know about it until the proper time came. Aphrodite jumped the gun—gave you the fake medallion to use you in her plot to kill Athena."

I look around wildly. The Great Hall of the Gods has collapsed. Flames lick up through the tumbled pillars. Fighting is spreading everywhere, but the summit is emptying out as more and more gods are flicking away to hide on Ilium Earth. Brane Holes are opening here and there and the Titans and monstrous entities are following the fleeing gods. The

Thundercloud Being that had ripped the roof and top three floors off the Great Hall is gone.

"You need to help me save the Greeks," I say, my teeth actually chattering.

Hephaestus laughs again, rubs the back of his sooty hand across his greasy mouth. "I've already vacuumed up all the other humans on that fucking Ilium-history Earth," he says. "Why should I save the Greeks? Or even the Trojans for that matter? What have they done for me recently? Plus, I'll need some humans down there to worship me when I take this throne of Olympos in a few days . . ."

I can only stare at him. "*You* vacuumed up the people? *You* put the population of Ilium Earth in the blue beam rising from Delphi?"

"Who the hell do you think did it? Zeus? With all his technical prowess?" Hephaestus shakes his head. The Titan brothers Kronos, Iapetos, Hyperion, Krios, Koios, and Okeanos are walking this way. They are covered with the golden-ichor blood of gods.

Suddenly Achilles appears from the burning ruins. He is fully clad in his gold armor, his beautiful shield also besmirched by immortal blood, his long sword out, his eyes staring almost madly from the slits of his streaked and sooted golden helmet. The apparition ignores me and shouts at Hephaestus. "Zeus has fled!"

"Of course," replies the god of fire. "Did you expect him to wait around for the Demogorgon to drag him down to Tartarus?"

"I can't find Zeus's location anywhere on the holographic pool locator!" shouts Achilles. "I forced Aphrodite's mother, Dione, to help me with the locator. She said it would find him anywhere in the universe. When she failed, I cut her to ribbons. Where *is* he?"

Hephaestus smiles. "You remember, fleet-footed mankiller, the one place Zeus had hidden from all eyes when Hera wanted to fuck him into an eternity of sleep?"

Achilles grabs the fire god's shoulder and almost lifts him off the ground. "Odysseus' home! Take me there! At once."

Hephaestus' eyes crinkle into unamused slits. "You do not command the future Lord of Olympos such, mortal. Singularity that you are, you must treat your betters with more respect."

Achilles releases his grip on Hephaestus' leather vest. "Please. Now. Please."

Hephaestus nods and then looks at me. "You come, too, Scholic Hockenberry. Zeus wanted you here for this day. Wanted you as witness. Witness ye shall be."

82

The moravecs aboard the *Queen Mab* received all the following live, in real-time—Odysseus' nano-imagers and transmitters were working well—but Asteague/Che decided not to relay it down to Mahnmut and Orphu of Io where they were working there beneath the ocean of Earth. The two 'vecs were six hours into their twelve-hour job of cutting free and loading the seven hundred sixty-eight critical black-hole warheads and no one on the *Mab* wanted to distract them.

And what was occurring now could qualify as distracting.

The lovemaking—if that was what the near-violent copulation between Odysseus and the woman who had identified herself as Sycorax—was in one of its temporary states of pause. The two were sprawled naked on the tousled cushions, drinking wine from large two-handled mugs and eating some fruit, when a monstrous creature—amphibian gills, fangs, claws, webbed feet—pushed aside curtains and flip-flop-walked its way into Sycorax's chambers.

"Dam, thinketh he yes that he must announce that as he was readying to melt a gourd-fruit into mash, when so Caliban did hear the airlock cycling. Something there is which has come to see you, Mother. Saith, it has all flesh-meat on its nose and fingers like blunt stones. Saith, Mother, and in His name I shall rend this work's tasty flesh from its soft-chalk bones."

"No, thank you, Caliban, my darling," said the naked woman with the purple-colored eyebrows. "Show our visitor in."

The amphibian thing called Caliban stepped aside. An older version of Odysseus entered.

All of the moravecs—even those who sometimes had trouble telling one human being from another—could see the resemblance. The young Odysseus sprawled naked on the silk cushions stared dumbly at the older Odysseus. This older version had the same short stature and broad chest, but more scars, gray hair and gray in his thicker beard, and bore himself with much more gravity than their passenger on the *Mab*'s voyage had.

"Odysseus," said Sycorax. As well as the moravecs' human emotion auditory analysis circuits could deduce, she sounded truly surprised.

He shook his head. "My name is Noman now. I'm pleased to see you again, Circe."

The woman smiled. "We have both changed, then. I am Sycorax to the world and myself now, my much-scarred Odysseus."

The younger Odysseus started to rise, his hands bunched into fists, but Sycorax made a motion with her left hand and the young Odysseus collapsed back onto the cushions.

"You are Circe," said the man who called himself Noman. "You were always Circe. You will always be Circe."

Sycorax shrugged very slightly, her full breasts jiggling. Young Odysseus was sprawled to her left. She patted the empty cushions on her right. "Come sit next to me, then . . . Noman."

"No, thank you, Circe," said the man dressed in tunic, shorts, and sandals. "I will stand."

"You will *come and sit next to me*," said Sycorax, her voice intense. She made a complicated motion with her right hand, her different fingers moving not at random.

"No, thank you, I will stand."

Again the woman blinked in surprise. Deeper surprise this time, the moravec facial-emotion analysts thought.

"Molü," said Noman. "I think you know of it. A substance made from a rare black root which bears a milk-white bloom out of the earth once each autumn."

Sycorax nodded slowly. "My, you have traveled far. But haven't you heard? Hermes is dead."

"That doesn't matter," said Noman.

"No, I suppose it doesn't. How did you get here, Odysseus?"

"Noman."

"How did you get here, Noman?"

"I used Savi's old sonie. It took me almost four full days, creeping from one orbital lump to the next, always hiding from these robotic intruder destroyers of yours or outrunning them in stealth mode. You need to get rid of those things, Circe. Or sonies need to include toilet facilities."

Sycorax laughed softly. "And why on earth would I get rid of the interceptors?"

"Because I ask you to."

"And why on earth would I do anything you ask, Odys . . . Noman?"

"I'll tell you when I finish with my requests."

Behind Noman, Caliban snarled. The human ignored the noise and the creature.

"By all means," said Sycorax. "Continue with your requests." Her smile showed how very little attention she was prepared to pay to these requests.

"First, as I say, eliminate the orbital interceptors. Or at least reprogram them so that spacecraft can move safely within and between the rings again . . ."

Sycorax's smile did not waver. Nor did her violet-eyed, purple-painted gaze warm.

"Secondly," continued Noman, "I would like you to remove the interdiction field above the Mediterranean Basin and to drop the Hands of Hercules fields."

The witch laughed softly. "What an odd request. The resulting tsunami would be devastating."

"You can do it gradually, Circe. I know you can. Refill the basin."

"Before you go on," she said coldly, "give me one reason I should do this thing."

"There are things in the Mediterranean Basin which the old-style humans should not have soon."

"The depots, you mean," said Sycorax. "The spacecraft, weapons . . ."

"Many things," said Noman. "Let the wine-dark sea refill the Mediterranean Basin."

"Perhaps you haven't noticed since you've been traveling," said Sycorax, "but the old-style humans are on the verge of extinction."

"I've noticed. I still ask you to refill the Mediterranean Basin—carefully, slowly. And while you're at it, eliminate that folly that is the Atlantic Breach."

Sycorax shook her head and lifted the two-handled cup to sip wine. She did not offer Noman any. The young Odysseus lay back glazed on the cushions, apparently unable to move.

"Is that all?" she said.

"No," said Noman. "I'll also ask you to reactivate all faxnodes for the old-style humans, all function links, and the rejuvenation tanks remaining on both the polar and equatorial rings."

Sycorax said nothing.

"Finally," said Noman, "I want you to send down your tame monster here to tell Setebos that the Quiet is coming to this Earth."

Caliban hissed and snarled. "Thinketh, time has come to pluck the mankin's sound legs off and leaveth stumps for him to ponder. Thinketh, He is strong and Lord and this bruised fellow shall receive a worm, nay, two worms, for using His name in vain."

"Silence," snapped Sycorax. She stood, looking more regal in her nakedness than other queens could in full regalia. "Noman, *is* the Quiet coming to this Earth?"

"I believe so, yes."

She seemed to relax. Lifting a clump of grapes from the bowl on the cushions, she carried them to Noman, offered them. He shook his head.

"You ask much of me, for an old and non-Odysseus," she said softly, pacing the space between the cushioned bed and the man. "What would you give me in return?"

"Tales of my travels."

Sycorax laughed again. "I know your travels."

"Not this time, you don't. This has been twenty years, not ten."

The witch's beautiful face twisted in something the moravecs' interpreted as a sneer. "Always seeking the same thing . . . your Penelope."

"No," said Noman. "Not this time. This time when you sent the young me through the Calabi-Yau doorway my travels in space and time—twenty years for me—were all in search of you."

Sycorax stopped her pacing and stared at him.

"You," repeated Noman. "My Circe. We loved each other well and have made love well many times these twenty years. I've found you in your iterations as Circe, Sycorax, Alys, and Calypso."

"Alys?" said the witch.

Noman only nodded.

"Did I have a slight gap between my front teeth then?"

"You did."

Sycorax shakes her head. "You lie. In all lines of reality it is the same, Odysseus-Noman. I save you, pull you from the sea, succor you, feed you honeyed wine and fine food, tend your wounds, bathe you, show you physical love of a sort you have only dreamed of, offer you immortality and eternal youth, and always you leave. Always you leave me for that weaving bitch Penelope. And your son."

"I've seen my son this twenty years past," said Noman. "He is grown into a fine man. I do not need to see him again. I wish to stay with you."

Sycorax returns to her cushions and drinks two-handed from the large goblet. "I am thinking of turning all your moravec mariners into swine," she said at last.

Noman shrugged. "Why not? You did that to all my other men in all these other worlds."

"What kind of swine do you think moravecs will make?" asked the witch, her tone merely conversational. "Will they resemble a row of plastic piggybanks?"

Noman said, "Moira is awake again."

The witch blinked. "Moira? Why would she choose to waken now?"

"I don't know," said Noman, "but she's in Savi's young body. I saw her on the day I left Earth, but we didn't speak."

"Savi's body?" repeated Sycorax. "What is Moira up to? And why now?"

"Thinketh," said Caliban behind Noman, "He made the old Savi out of sweet clay for His son to bite and eat, add honeycomb and pods, chewing her neck until froth rises bladdery, quick, quick, till maggots scamper through my brain."

Sycorax rose and paced again, coming close to Noman and raising one hand as if to touch his bare chest, then veering away. Caliban hissed and crouched, his palms on granite, his back hunched, his arms straight down between his crouched and powerful legs, his yellow eyes baleful. But he remained where she had told him to stay.

"You know I can't send my son down to tell his father Setebos about the Quiet," she said softly.

"I know this . . . *thing* . . . is not your son," said Noman. "You built him out of shit and defective DNA in a tank of green slime."

Caliban hissed and began to speak again in his terrible lisping rant. Sycorax waved him silent.

"Do you know your moravec friends are lifting more than seven hundred black holes into orbit even as we speak?" she asked.

Noman shrugged. "I didn't know that, but I hoped they would be."

"Where did they get them?"

"You know where they must have come from. Seven hundred sixty-eight black-hole warheads? There is only one place."

"Impossible," said Sycorax. "I sealed that wreck off inside a stasis-egg almost two millennia ago."

"And Savi and I unsealed it more than a century ago," said Noman.

"Yes, I watched as you and that bitch hurried around with your hopeless little schemes," said Sycorax. "What in the hell did you hope to accomplish with those turin-cloth connections to Ilium?"

"Preparation," said Noman.

"For what?" laughed Sycorax. "You don't believe those two races of the human species will ever meet, do you? You can't be serious. The Greeks and Trojans and their ilk would eat your naïve little old-style humans here for breakfast."

Noman shrugged. "Call off this war with Prospero and let's see what happens."

Sycorax slammed down the wine goblet onto a nearby table. "Leave the field while that bastard Prospero remains on it?" she snapped. "You can't be serious."

"I am," said Noman. "The old entity called Prospero is quite mad. His days are over. But you can leave before the same madness claims you. Let's leave this place, Circe, you and I."

"Leave?" The witch's voice was very low, incredulous.

"I know this rock has fusion-drive engines and Brane Hole generators that could send us to the stars, beyond the stars. If we get bored, we step through the Calabi-Yau door and make love across the whole, rich universe of history—we could meet at different ages, wear our different bodies at different ages as easily as changing clothes, travel in time to join ourselves making love, freeze time itself so that we can take part in our own lovemaking. You have enough food and air here to keep us comfortable for a thousand years—ten thousand if you please."

"You forget," said Sycorax, rising and pacing again. "You're a mortal man. In twenty years I'll be changing your soiled underwear and feeding you by hand. In forty years you'll be dead."

"You offered me immortality once. The rejuvenation tanks are still here on your isle."

"You *rejected* immortality!" screamed Sycorax. She picked up the heavy mug and threw it at him. Noman ducked but did not move his feet from where they were planted. "You *rejected it again and again!*" she screamed, tearing at her hair and cheeks with her nails. "You threw it in my face to return to your precious . . . *Penelope* . . . over and over again. You actually laughed at me."

"I'm not laughing now. Come away with me."

Her expression was wild with fury. "I should have Caliban kill you and eat you right here in front of me. I'll laugh while he sucks the marrow from your cracked bones."

"Come away with me, Circe," said Noman. "Reactivate the faxes and functions, drop the old Hands of Hercules and other useless toys, and come away with me. Be my lover again."

"You're *old*," she sneered. "Old and scarred and gray-haired. Why should I choose an old man over a vital younger one?" She stroked the thigh and flaccid penis of the seemingly hypnotized and motionless younger Odysseus.

"Because this Odysseus will not be leaving through the Calabi-Yau door in a week or month or eight years as that young one will," said Noman. "And because this Odysseus loves you."

Sycorax made a choked noise that sounded like a snarl. Caliban echoed her snarl.

Noman reached under his tunic and took a heavy pistol from where he had hidden it under his broad belt in the back.

The witch stopped pacing and stared. "You can't possibly think that thing can hurt *me*."

"I didn't bring it to hurt you," said Noman.

She flicked her violet gaze to the frozen younger Odysseus. "Are you mad? Do you know what mischief that would do on the quantum level of things? You're courting *kaos* by even contemplating such a thing. It would destroy a cycle that has been going on in a thousand strands for a thousand . . ."

"Going on for too long," said Noman. He fired six times, each explosion seemingly louder than the last. The six heavy bullets tore into the naked Odysseus, tearing his rib cage apart, pulping his heart, striking him in the middle of the forehead.

The younger man's body jerked to the impacts and slid to the floor, leaving red streaks on the silk cushions and a growing pool of blood on the marble tiles.

"Decide," said Noman.

83

I don't know if I teleported here via my own, medallion-less ability, or just came along with Hephaestus because I was touching his sleeve when he QT'd. It doesn't matter. I'm here.

Here is Odysseus' home. A dog barks madly at us as Hephaestus, Achilles, and I pop into existence, but one glance from bloody-helmeted Achilles sends the mutt whining back out to the courtyard with its tail between its legs.

We're in an anteroom looking into the great dining hall of Odysseus' home on the isle of Ithaca. Some sort of forcefield hums over the house and courtyard. There are no impudent suitors lounging in the long room at the long table, no Penelope dithering, no impotent young Telemachus plotting, no servants hustling to and fro dispensing the absent Odysseus' food and wine to indolent ne'er-do-wells. But the room looks as if the Slaughter of the Suitors has already taken place—chairs are overturned, a huge tapestry has been ripped off the wall and now lies thrown over table and floor, soaking up spilled wine, and even Odysseus' greatest bow—the one that only he alone could pull, according to legend, a bow so wonderful and rare that he decided not to take it to Troy with him—now lies on the stone floor, amidst a clutter of Odysseus' famous barbed and poisoned hunting arrows.

Zeus whirls. The giant wears the same soft garments he had been wearing on the Throne of Olympos, but he is not so gigantic now. Yet even shrunken to fit this space, he is still twice as tall as Achilles.

Beckoning us to stand back, the fleet-footed mankiller raises his shield, readies his sword, and steps into the dining hall.

"My son," booms the God of Thunder, "spare me your childlike anger. Would you commit deicide, tyrannicide, and patricide in one terrible stroke?"

Achilles advances until he is across the span of the broad table from Zeus. "Fight, old man."

Zeus continues smiling, apparently not the least bit alarmed. "Think, fleet-footed Achilles. Use your brain for once rather than your muscles or your dick. Would you have *that* useless cripple sit on the golden throne of Olympos?" He nods toward where Hephaestus stands silent in the doorway next to me.

Achilles does not turn his head.

"Just think for once," repeats Zeus, his deep voice causing crockery to vibrate in the nearby kitchen. "Join with me, Achilles, my son. Become one with the penetrating presence that is Zeus, Father of All Gods. Thus joined, father and son, immortal and immortal, two mighty spirits, mingling, shall make a third, mightier than either alone—triune together, Father and Son and holy will, we shall reign over heaven and Troy and send the Titans back down to their pit forever."

"Fight," said Achilles. "You old pigfucker."

Zeus's broad face turns several shades of red. "Detested prodigy! Even thus, deprived of my control of all elements, I trample thee!"

Zeus grabs the long table by its edge and flips it into the air. Fifty feet of heavy wood planks and posts flies tumbling through the air toward Achilles' head. The human ducks low and the table smashes into the wall behind him, destroying a fresco and sending splinters flying everywhere.

Achilles takes two steps closer.

Zeus opens his arms, opens his hands to show his palms. "Would you kill me as I am, oh *man*? Unarmed? Or shall we grapple barehanded like heroes in the arena until one fails to rise and the other takes the prize?"

Achilles hesitates only a second. Then he pulls off his golden helmet and sets it aside. He removes the circular shield from his forearm, lays the sword in its cusp, adds his bronze chest armor and greaves, and kicks all that to our doorway. Now he is clad only in his shirt, short skirt, sandals, and broad leather belt.

Eight feet from Zeus, Achilles opens his arms in a wrestler's opening stance and crouches.

Zeus smiles then and—in a motion almost too fast for me to perceive—crouches and comes up with Odysseus' bow and a poisoned black-feathered arrow.

Get away! I have time mentally to shout at Achilles but the blond and muscled hero does not budge.

Zeus goes to full pull, easily bending the bow that no one on Earth except Odysseus was supposed to be able to bend, aims the broad-bladed poison arrow right at Achilles' heart eight feet away, and lets fly.

The arrow misses.

It cannot miss—not at that distance—the shaft appears straight and true, the black feathers full—but it misses by a full foot or more and buries itself deep in the smashed table angled against the wall. I can almost feel the terrible venom, rumored to be originally gathered from the most deadly of serpents by Hercules, as it drains into the wood of the table.

Zeus stares. Achilles does not move.

Zeus crouches with lightning speed, comes up with another arrow, steps closer, notches, pulls, releases.

It misses. From five feet away, the poisoned arrow misses.

Achilles does not stir. He stares hate into the now-panicked gaze of the Father of All Gods.

Zeus crouches again, sets the arrow to the cord with careful precision, goes to full pull again, his mighty muscles now sheened in sweat, visibly straining, the powerful bow almost humming with its coiled power. The King of the Gods steps forward until the point of the arrow is not much more than a foot away from Achilles' broad chest.

Zeus fires.

The arrow misses.

This is not possible, but I see the arrow embed itself in the wall behind Achilles. It has not passed through Achilles, nor curved around, but somehow—impossibly—absolutely—it has missed.

Achilles leaps then, slapping the bow aside and seizing the twice-tall god by the throat.

Zeus staggers around the room trying to remove Achilles' powerful hands from around his neck, pounding Achilles with a god-fist half as wide as Achilles' broad back. The fleet-footed mankiller hangs on as Zeus thrashes, smashing timbers, the table, the doorway arch, the wall itself. It looks like a man with a child hanging from him, but Achilles hangs on.

Then the much larger god gets his own powerful fingers under Achilles' much smaller fingers and peels back first the mortal's left hand, then his right. Now Zeus crashes against, bangs onto, and smashes into things with a deadly purpose, holding Achilles' forearms in his own massive hands, the mortal man dangling as Zeus head-butts Achilles—

the sound echoing like two great boulders colliding—then rams his god-chest against mortal ribs, finally crashing both of them against the un-yielding wall and into the doorway opposite us, arching Achilles' back against the unyielding stone of the doorframe.

Five seconds of this and he will snap Achilles' back like a bow made out of cheap balsa.

Achilles does not wait five seconds. Or three.

Somehow the fleet-footed mankiller has got his right hand free for an instant as Zeus bends him backward, backward, spine grinding against vertical stone.

I see what happens next in retinal echo, it occurs so quickly.

Achilles' hand comes up from his own belly and belt with a short blade in his fist.

He rams the blade in under Zeus's bearded chin, twists the knife, rams it deeper, rotates it with a cry louder even than Zeus's scream of horror and pain.

Zeus stumbles backward into the hallway, crashing into the next room. Hephaestus and I run to follow.

They are in Odysseus' and Penelope's private bedchamber now. Achilles pulls the knifeblade free and the Father of All Gods raises both his massive hands to his own throat, his own face. Golden ichor and red blood both are pulsing into the air, flowing from Zeus's nostrils and open, gaping mouth, filling his white beard with gold and red.

Zeus falls backward onto the bed. Achilles swings the knife far back, plunges it deep into the god's belly, and then drags it up and to the right until the magical blade rasps on rib cage.

Zeus screams again, but before he can clutch himself lower, Achilles has pulled out yards of gray gut—gleaming god intestine—and wrapped it several times around one of the four posts of Odysseus' great bed, tying it off in a mariner's swift and sure knot.

That post is the living olive tree Odysseus fashioned this room and bed around, I think in a daze. The lines from *The Odyssey* come back to me from the Fitzgerald translation I first read as a boy, Odysseus speaking to his doubting Penelope—

> *An old trunk of olive*
> *grew like a pillar on our building plot,*
> *and I laid out our bedroom round that tree,*
> *lined up the stone walls, built the walls and roof,*
> *gave it a doorway and smooth-fitting doors.*
> *Then I lopped off the silvery leaves and branches,*
> *into a bedpost, drilled it, let it serve*
> *as a model for the rest. I planned them all,*

inlaid them all with silver, gold and ivory,
and stretched a bed between—a pliant web
of oxhide thongs dyed crimson.

Now more than the oxhide thongs are dyed crimson as Zeus struggles to free himself from the restraining tether of his own tied-off intestines, golden ichor and all-too-human-red-blood flowing from his throat, face, and belly. Blinded by his own pain and gore, Mighty Zeus feels for his tormenter by swinging his arms. Every step and tug in search of Achilles pulls more of his gleaming gray insides out. His screaming makes even the unflinching Hephaestus cover his ears.

Achilles prances lightly out of reach, dancing in closer only to slash and hack at the blind god's arms, legs, thighs, penis, and hamstrings.

Zeus crashes down on his back, still connected to the living olive tree bedpost by thirty feet or more of knotted gray gut, but the immortal being still thrashes and howls, spewing ichor across the ceiling in complicated Rorschachs of divine arterial spray.

Achilles leaves the room and returns with his battle sword. He pins Zeus's thrashing left arm with one battle-sandaled foot, raises the sword high, and brings it down so hard it strikes sparks on the floor after passing through Zeus's neck.

The head of the Father of All Gods tumbles free, rolling under the bed.

Achilles goes to one gory knee and seems to be burying his face in the giant open wound that had been Zeus's bronzed and muscled belly. For one perfectly horrible second I am sure that Achilles is eating the guts out of his fallen foe, his face largely hidden in the abdominal cavity—a man turned pure predator, a ravaging wolf.

But he was only hunting.

"Ahah!" cries the fleet-footed mankiller and pulls a huge, still pulsating purplish mass from the tumble of glistening gray.

Zeus's liver.

"Where is that goddamned dog of Odysseus'?" Achilles asks himself, his eyes gleaming. He leaves us to carry the liver out to the dog Argus cowering somewhere in the courtyard.

Hephaestus and I stand aside quickly to give Achilles room as he passes.

As the sound of the mankiller's—godkiller's—footsteps recede, both the god of fire and I look around the room.

Not a square inch of bed, floor, ceiling, or wall appears to have remained unsplattered.

The huge, headless corpse on the stone floor, still tethered to the olive-tree post, continues to twitch and writhe, its bloodied fingers flexing.

"Holy fuck," breathes Hephaestus.

I want to tear my gaze away but cannot. I want to leave the room to go vomit quietly somewhere, but cannot. "What . . . how . . . it's still . . . partially . . . alive," I gasp.

Hephaestus grins his most insane grin. "Zeus is an immortal, remember, Hockenberry? He's in agony even now. I'll burn the bits in the Celestial Fire." He stoops to retrieve the short knife Achilles had used. "I'll burn this god-killing Aphrodite blade as well. Melt it down and pour it into something new—a plaque commemorating Zeus, maybe. I never should have made this blade for the bloodthirsty bitch."

I blink and shake my head, then grab the hulking fire god by his heavy leather vest. "What will happen now?" I ask.

Hephaestus shrugs. "Just what we agreed on, Hockenberry. Nyx and the Fates, who have always ruled the universe—this universe, at least—will allow me to sit on the gold throne of Olympos after this mad second war with the Titans is over."

"How do you know who will win?"

He shows me his uneven white teeth against his black beard.

From the courtyard comes a commanding voice. "Here, dog . . . here Argus . . . here, boy. That's a nice pup. I have something for you . . . good dog."

"They don't call them 'the Fates' for nothing, Hockenberry," says Hephaestus. "It will be a long and nasty war, fought more on Ilium Earth than on Olympos, but the few surviving Olympians will win . . . again."

"But the thing . . . the cloud-thing . . . the Voice thing . . ."

"Demogorgon has gone home to Tartarus," rumbles Hephaestus. "It cares not the least fucking fig what happens now on Earth, Mars, or Olympos."

"My people . . ."

"Your pretty Greek friends are fucked up the ass," says Hephaestus and then he smiles at his own wit. "But, if it makes you feel any better, so are the Trojans. Anyone who stays on Ilium Earth will be in the crossfire for the next fifty to a hundred years while this war goes on."

I grab his vest harder. "You have to help us . . ."

He removes my hand as easily as an adult male would remove the clinging hand of a two-year-old child. "I don't *have* to do a goddamned thing, Hockenberry." He wipes his mouth with the back of his hand, looks at the twitching thing on the floor behind, and says, "But in this case I will. QT back to your pitiful Achaeans and your woman, Helen, in the city and tell them to get their asses out of all high towers, off the walls, out of the buildings. There's going to be a nine-point quake in old Ilium Town in a very few minutes. I need to burn this . . . thing . . . and get our hero back to Olympos so he can try to talk the Healer into waking his dead bimbo."

Achilles is coming back. He is whistling and I can hear Argus's nails scrabbling on stone as the dog eagerly follows.

"Go!" says Hephaestus, god of fire and artifice.

I reach for my medallion, realize it's not there, realize I don't need it, and QT well away from there.

Their estimated twelve hours of continuous work took a little more than eighteen hours. The forty-eight tumbled missiles and missile tubes were more trouble to sort out, separate, and cut up than either Orphu or Mahnmut could have guessed. Some of the metal warhead casings had cracked completely away, leaving only the plastoid-alloy MRV cradles and the containment fields themselves, each glowing blue from its own Cerenkov radiation.

The sight would have been interesting if anyone other than the silent moravecs on the *Queen Mab* had been watching: the submersible *The Dark Lady* crouching over the hull of the sunken death sub, its belly searchlights illuminating mostly a world filled with silt, fanning anemones, torn cables, twisted wiring, and lethal, greengrown missiles and warheads. Brighter than the dappled daylight coming in through the Breach wall, brighter than the super-halogen bright searchlights aimed on the work area, brighter than the sun itself were the fires of the 10,000-degree-Fahrenheit cutting torches that both the blind Orphu and the silt-blinded Mahnmut were wielding as delicately as scalpels.

Girders, winches, pulleys, and chains were all in place and now in heavy use as the two moravecs and *The Dark Lady* herself supervised the winching-up of each MRVed warhead as it was cut away from the missile itself. The cargo hold of Mahnmut's Europan submersible was never really empty; it was honeycombed with a programmable flowfoam that formed itself into fluted cathedral buttressings of internal bracing against terrible pressures when the hold was "empty" of cargo, but that could and did flow tight around any cargo—including Orphu of Io when he rode in the corner of the cargo bay. Now the flowfoam was adapting itself to cushion and support each ungainly lump of warhead as Mahnmut and Orphu ratcheted and cursed it into place.

At one point a little beyond halfway through the exhausting work, Mahmut pretended to pat the containment-field-glowing warhead itself as the flowfoam closed around it, as he said—

> "What is your substance, whereof are you made,
> That millions of strange shadows on you tend?"

"Your old friend Will?" asked Orphu as both moravecs dropped back into the confusion of agitated silt below to begin cutting away the next warhead.

"Yes," said Mahnmut. "Sonnet Fifty-three."

About two hours later, just after they had secured another blue-glowing warhead in the now-crowded hold—they were spacing the black holes as far apart as they could—Orphu said, "This answer to our problem is costing you your ship. I'm sorry, Mahnmut."

The Europan nodded, trusting his huge friend's deep radar to pick up the motion. As soon as Orphu had suggested this approach, Mahnmut had realized that it meant losing his beloved *Dark Lady* forever—there was no way they could take the chance of removing the warheads from the *Lady*'s flowfoam cushioned hull and putting them into a different cargo bay. The very best case scenario now was that the moravecs would have another spacecraft up there in low earth orbit that could boost *The Dark Lady* and her planet-lethal cargo out and away from Earth, into deep space, as gently but quickly as possible.

"I feel that I just got her back," said Mahnmut, hearing the pathetic tone in his own radio voice.

"They'll build you another someday," said Orphu.

"It wouldn't be the same," said Mahnmut. He had spent more than a century and a half in this little sub.

"No," agreed Orphu. "Nothing will ever be the same after all this."

At the end of the eighteen hours, after the last Cerenkov-glowing cluster of nascent black holes was loaded away, flowfoamed into place, and *The Dark Lady*'s cargo bay doors were shut, both moravecs were in a state of near total physical and nervous exhaustion as they hovered together above the wreck of the boomer.

"Is there anything we need to investigate or bring back from *The Sword of Allah*?" asked Orphu.

"Not at this time," sent Prime Integrator Asteague/Che from the

Queen Mab. The ship had been conspicuously quiet during the last eighteen hours.

"I never want to see the goddamned thing again," said Mahnmut, too exhausted to care that he was speaking on the common channel. "It's an obscenity."

"Amen," said Centurion Leader Mep Ahoo from the dropship circling above.

"Is there anything you guys want to tell us about what's been going on up there with Odysseus and his girlfriend over the last eighteen hours or so?" asked Orphu.

"Not at this time," said Prime Integrator Asteague/Che again. "Bring the warheads up. Be careful."

"Amen," said Mep Ahoo again, and there seemed to be no irony in the soldier 'vec's voice.

Suma IV was a damned good pilot, one had to grant him that—and Orphu and Mahnmut did. Suma IV actually hovered the dropship so that *The Dark Lady* remained fully submerged as the aircraft-spaceship's much larger bay doors closed under it. Then Suma IV slowly drained out the seawater, but only as the dropship's own flowfoam took the water's place, encysting the submersible and its blue-glowing cargo in another layer of wrapping.

Orphu of Io had already used dropcables to scramble and scrabble to the roof of the dropship before *The Dark Lady* was ingested, but Mahnmut left his enviro-crèche only at the last moment, allowing the *Lady* to steady and monitor herself during the delicate lifting and placement. Mahnmut felt that he should have some last words as he stepped off his ship forever more, but other than a tightbeamed and unacknowledged *Goodbye, Lady*, to the submersible's AI, he said nothing.

The dropship lifted out of the water, ocean streaming from its cargo venting tubes, and Mahnmut used the last of his strength—mechanical and organic—to haul himself up to the top of the dropship and then down through the smaller of two access hatches into the troop-carrier hold.

In any other circumstances, the confusion in the troop-carrier section would have been comic, but not that many things seemed humorous to Mahnmut at that moment. By retracting all of his manipulators and antennae, Orphu had just been able to squeeze through the larger of the two dropship hatches, but now the Ionian's bulk filled most of the space where the twenty rockvec soldiers had been perched on their web seating. The soldiers now spilled over into the narrow access corridor going forward to the cockpit itself, black-barbed rockvecs and their weapons sprawled everywhere, and Mahnmut had to crawl over their chitinous forms to join Mep Ahoo and Suma IV in the cramped cockpit.

Suma IV was flying the hovering dropship manually, using the omnicontroller constantly to balance the ship and its shifting contents, playing the thruster tabs the way human pianists must have once played their instrument of choice.

"No more tie-down straps," Suma IV said to Mahnmut without turning his head. "We used the last to harness your big friend into the troop-carrier space. Extend that last jumpseat and magtite yourself to the hull, please, Mahnmut."

Mahnmut did as he was told. He realized that he was too tired to stand again—Earth's gravity was terrible after all—and felt like weeping from the release of chemicals after the last eighteen hours of total effort and tension.

"Hang on," said Suma IV.

The dropship engines roared and they rose slowly, vertically, meter by meter, no shocks, no surprises, until Mahnmut saw out the main cockpit window that they had reached an altitude of around two kilometers, and then they began to pitch forward slightly—the engines moving from the vertical to forward thrust. He could never have imagined that a machine could be handled so delicately.

Still, there were bumps and at each bump Mahnmut found himself holding his breath, feeling his organic heart pound as he waited for the black holes in the belly of the hold of the dropship to go critical. It would only take one and all the others would collapse into themselves a millionth of a second later.

Mahnmut tried to imagine the immediate aftermath—the mini-black-holes immediately merging and plunging through the hull of *The Dark Lady* and the dropship, the mass accelerating toward the center of the Earth at thirty-two feet per second, sucking in all the mass of the two moravec ships with it, and then the air molecules, then the sea, then the sea bottom, then the rock, then the crust of the Earth itself as the black holes plummeted centerward.

How many days or months would the large mini-black-hole, comprised of all seven hundred sixty-eight warhead black holes, ping-pong back and forth through the planet, arcing up into space—for how far?—on each ping or pong? The electronic computing part of Mahnmut's mind gave him the answer even though he didn't want it, even though the physical part of his brain was too weary to absorb it. Far enough for the black holes to suck in all of the million-plus objects on the orbital rings in the first hundred ping-pongs through the planet, but not so far that it would eat the moon.

It would make no difference to Mahnmut, Orphu, and the other moravecs, even those on the *Queen Mab*. The dropship moravecs would be spaghettified almost instantaneously, their molecules stretched toward the center of the earth with the mini-hole as it fell, then farther, elasticating—was that a word? Mahnmut tiredly wondered—back through themselves as the black hole cut another swatch back up through the molten, spinning core of the planet.

Mahnmut closed his virtual eyes and concentrated on breathing, on feeling the dropship accelerate smoothly but constantly as it climbed. It was as if they were on a smooth, glass ramp rising to the heavens. Suma IV was *good*.

The sky changed from afternoon blue to vacuum black. The horizon bent like an archer's bow. The stars seemed to explode into sight.

Mahnmut activated his vision and watched out the cockpit window as well as via the dropship's imager feed via the umbilical connection at his jumpseat station.

They weren't climbing to the *Queen Mab*, that was obvious. Suma IV leveled out the dropship at an altitude of not more than three hundred kilometers—barely above the atmosphere—and tapped thrusters to roll the Earth into the overhead cockpit windows so that full sunlight fell on the ship's cargo bay doors. The rings and the *Mab* were more than thirty thousand kilometers higher and the moravec atomic spacecraft was on the opposite side of the Earth at the moment.

Mahnmut shut off the virtual feed for a second—feeling the zero-g as a physical release from the gravity of their work the last eighteen hours—and looked up through the clear overheads at the terminator moving across what had once been Europe, at the blue waters and white cloud masses of the Atlantic Ocean—the breach-gap wasn't even a thin line from this altitude or angle—and not for the first time in the last eighteen hours, Mahnmut the moravec wondered how a living species gifted with such a beautiful homeworld could arm a submarine—themselves, any machine—with such weapons of total mindless destruction. What in any mental universe could seem worth the murder of millions, much less the destruction of an entire planet?

Mahnmut knew that they were not out of harm's way yet. For all technical purposes, they might as well still be at the bottom of the ocean for all the good these few hundred kilometers did them. If any one of the black holes activated now, tripping the others into singularity, the ping-pong ripping-through-the-heart-of-Earth end of things would be just as certain, just as sure. Being in free fall was not the same as being out of the Earth's gravitational field. The warheads would have to be far away—far beyond the Moon's orbit certainly, since it was obvious the Earth's gravity still reigned there—millions of kilometers away before the threat to Earth was over. The only difference in outcome at this measly altitude, Mahnmut knew, would be that the moravecs' spaghettification ratio might grow a few percent in the initial minutes.

A matte-black spacecraft uncloaked—unstealthed, deforcefielded, came out of hiding—damn, Mahnmut had no word for it—*appeared* less than five kilometers from them on the sunward side. The ship was obviously of moravec design, but of a more advanced design than any spacecraft Mahnmut had ever seen. If the *Queen Mab* had seemed like some artifact from the Earth's Lost Era Twentieth Century, this just-appeared spacecraft seemed centuries ahead of everything the moravecs had now. Somehow the black shape succeeded in seeming both stubby and deadly sleek, both simple and impossibly complicated in its fractal-batwing geometries, and there was no doubt whatsoever in Mahnmut's mind that the ship carried awesome weapons.

He wondered for a few seconds if the Prime Integrators were actually going to risk the loss of one of their stealthed warships but . . . no . . . even as he wondered, Mahnmut saw an opening morph into being in the warship's curved belly and a long witch's broom of a device peroxided itself out into space, rotated along its own axis, lined up with the dropship, and used secondary thrusters on either side of an absurdly oversized engine bell to shove itself silently in their direction.

Orphu tightbeamed him. *Why are we surprised? The Prime Integrators have had more than eighteen hours to come up with something and we moravecs have always bred good engineers.*

Mahnmut had to agree. As the broomstick thrusted closer, slowing and rotating again as it came, putting on the brakes now, keeping the thrust bursts far away from the dropship's belly, Mahnmut could see that the thing was probably about sixty meters long along its axis with a small AI brain node hitched in the center of mass like a saddle on a skinny nag, lots of silver manipulators and heavy-metal clamps, and one whomping big high-thrust engine just forward of that huge engine bell, along with scores of tiny thruster quads.

"I'm releasing the submersible now," said Suma IV on the common band.

Mahnmut watched from the dropship hull cameras as the long cargo bays opened and *The Dark Lady* was floated gently out, propelled by the tiniest puff of gas. His beloved submersible began to rotate very slowly and since its own stabilization system had been shut off, she didn't even try to stabilize herself. Mahnmut thought that he had never seen anything so out of her element—again—as the *Lady* was here in space, three hundred kilometers above the bright blue evening ocean of Earth.

The broomstick robot ship didn't allow the submersible to tumble for long. The thing thrusted carefully, matched velocities perfectly, pulled *The Dark Lady* close to it with manipulator arms moving as gently as a lover after a long and tentative absence from his beloved, and then latched solid clamps in place—clamps built to lock into the submersible's docking receptacles and various vents. Again with a sort of loving care, the broomstick AI—or the moravec on the warship currently controlling it—extruded a bright gold-foil molecular blanket and carefully, carefully folded the crinkling thing around the entire sub. The engineers didn't want changes in temperature to trigger the black holes.

Quad thrusters fired and the praying mantis form of the robot ship and the foil-blanketed bulk of *The Dark Lady* moved away from the dropship, the robot aligning along its axis so that its engine bell was aimed *down,* toward the blue sea and white clouds and visibly moving terminator crossing Europe.

"What are they going to do about the little laser leukocytes?" Orphu of Io asked on the common band.

Mahnmut had wondered that himself—how were they going to keep the cleanup robotic laser attackers from triggering the warheads—but it hadn't been his problem so he hadn't tried to work it out in the past eighteen hours.

"The *Valkyrie,* the *Indomitable,* and the *Nimitz* are going to accompany the robot ship and destroy any approaching leukocytes," said Suma IV. "While our warships remain stealthed, of course."

Orphu actually laughed aloud on the common band. "*Valkyrie, Indomitable,* and *Nimitz?*" he rumbled. "My, we peaceloving moravecs are getting scarier by the minute, aren't we."

No one answered. To break the silence, Mahnmut said, "Which one is that . . . no, wait, it's gone." The matte-black fractal bat had restealthed, its presence not even suggested by a blotted-out patch of starfield or ringfield.

"That was the *Valkyrie,*" said Suma IV. "Ten seconds."

No one counted down aloud. Everyone, Mahnmut was sure, was counting silently.

At zero, the high-thrust engine bell was illuminated by the slightest blue glow, reminiscent to Mahnmut of the Cerenkov-radiation glow of the warhead nacelles. The broomstick-mantis began to move, began to climb—with agonizing slowness. But Mahnmut knew that anything under constant thrust long enough would achieve a horrific velocity soon enough, even while climbing up out of Earth's gravity well, and he also knew that the robot ship would be increasing that thrust as it climbed. Probably by the time the ship and the dead, thermal-blanket-wrapped hulk of *The Dark Lady* reached the empty orbit of Earth's moon, the package would have achieved escape velocity. Even if the black holes activated after that point, the singularities would be a hazard in space, no longer the death of Earth.

The robot ship soon disappeared against the moving ringfield. Mahnmut saw not the slightest hint of fusion or ion exhausts from the three stealthed moravec spacecraft that were presumably escorting the robot.

Suma IV closed the cargo bay doors. "All right, everyone, please listen up," said the pilot. "Some strange things have been going on while our two friends have been busy under the surface of the water-ocean down there. We need to get back to the *Queen Mab*."

"What happened to our reconnaissance mission . . ." began Mahnmut.

"You can download the recorded feed as we climb," interrupted Suma IV. "But right now the prime integrators want us back aboard. The *Mab* is leaving for a while . . . pulling back to lunar orbit at least."

"No," said Orphu of Io.

The syllable seemed to echo on the comm line like the single tolling of some huge bell.

"No?" said Suma IV. "Those are our orders."

"We need to go back down to that Atlantic gap, breach, whatever we call it," said Orphu. "We need to go back down now."

"You need to shut up and hang on," said the big Ganymedan at the controls. "I'm taking the dropship back to the *Mab* as ordered."

"Look at the images you shot from ten thousand meters," said Orphu and fed the image to everyone aboard via their umbilicaled Internet.

Mahnmut looked. It was the same picture he'd looked at before they began work on cutting the warheads free: the startling gap in the ocean, the crumbled bow of the submarine emerging from the north wall of that gap, a small debris field.

"I'm blind on optic frequencies," said Orphu, "but I kept manipulating the accompanying radar imagery and something's odd there. Here's the best magnification and clarification I could get on the visual photograph. You tell me if there's something there that deserves closer examination."

"I'll tell you right now that nothing we see there will make me fly the dropship back there," Suma IV said flatly. "You two haven't got the word yet, but the asteroid isle—that huge asteroid where we dropped Odysseus off—is leaving. It's already changed its axis and aligned itself, and fusion thrusters are igniting as we speak. And your friend Odysseus is dead. And more than a million satellites in the polar and equatorial rings—mass accumulators, the fax-teleport devices, other things—are all coming alive again. We're leaving."

"*LOOK AT THE GODDAMNED PHOTOGRAPHS*," bellowed Orphu of Io.

All the moravecs on board, even those without ears, tried to put their hands over their ears.

Mahnmut looked at the next photograph in the digital series. It had not only been magnified far beyond their original view, but the pixels cleared up.

"That's some sort of backpack sitting there on the dry floor of the breach," said Mahnmut. "And next to it . . ."

"A pistol," said Centurion Leader Mep Ahoo. "A gunpowder slug-thrower, if my guess is correct."

"And that looks like a human body lying next to the pack," said one of the black-chitinous troopers. "Something that's been dead a long time—all mummified and flattened."

"No," said Orphu. "I checked the best radar imagery. That's not a human body, just a human thermskin."

"So?" said Suma IV from his command chair at the controls. "The submarine wreck expelled one of its passengers or some of a human's belongings. They're part of the debris field."

Orphu snorted loudly. "And it's all still there after twenty-five hundred standard years? I doubt it, Suma. Look at the pistol. No rust. Look at the rucksack. No rot. That part of the breach-gap is open to the elements—including sunlight and wind—but this stuff hasn't degraded."

"It proves nothing," said Suma IV as he tapped in the rendezvous co-ordinates for the *Queen Mab*. Thrusters kicked the dropship into proper alignment for the burn and climb. "Sometime in the past few years some old-style human wandered out there to die. We have more important things to deal with right now."

"Look in the sand," said Orphu.

"What?" said their pilot.

"Look at the fifth image I blew up. In the sand. I can't *see* it, but the radar was good down to three millimeters. What do you *see* there—with your eyes?"

"A footprint," said Mahnmut. "A footprint of a bare human foot. Several footprints. All distinct in the muddy soil and soft sand. All leading west. Rain would wipe away those prints in a few days. Some human has been there in the last forty-eight hours or less—perhaps even while we were working on recovering the warheads."

"It doesn't matter," said Suma IV. "Our orders are to return to the *Queen Mab* and we're going to . . ."

"Take the dropship back down to the Atlantic Breach," commanded Prime Integrator Asteague/Che from thirty thousand kilometers higher on the opposite side of the Earth. "Our review of imagery we took hastily on the last orbit shows what may be the body of a human being in the Breach approximately twenty-three kilometers to the west of the submarine wreckage. Go and recover it at once."

85

I flick into solidity and realize that I've QT'd myself into Helen of Troy's private bathing chambers deep within the palace she used to share with her dead husband, Paris, and which she now shares with her former father-in-law, King Priam. I know I have only a few minutes in which to act, but I don't know what to do.

Slave girls and serving women shriek as I stride from room to room calling Helen's name. I hear the servants calling for the guards and realize that I may have to QT away quickly if I don't want to end up on the end of a Trojan spear. Then I see a familiar face in the next chamber. It's Hypsipyle, the slave woman from Lesbos whom Andromache had used as a personal minder for crazy Cassandra. This Hypsipyle might know where Helen is, since Helen and Andromache were very close the last time I saw them. And at least this slave isn't running away or calling for the guards.

"Do you know where Helen is?" I ask as I approach the heavyset woman. Her blunt face is as expressionless as a gourd.

As if in answer, Hypsipyle rears back and kicks me in the gonads. I levitate, grab myself, fall to the tiled floor, roll around in agony, and squeak.

She aims another kick that would take my head off if I don't dodge it, so I try to dodge, take the kick on the shoulder, and end up rolling into the corner, not even able to squeak now, my left shoulder and arm numb all the way down to the fingertips.

I struggle to my feet, hunched over, as the huge woman approaches with her eye full of business.

QT somewhere, idiot, I advise myself.

Where?

Anywhere but here!

Hypsipyle grabs me by my tunic front, tears the tunic, and aims a ham-fisted blow at my face. I raise my forearms to block the blow and the impact of her big-knuckled fist almost breaks the radius and ulna in both arms. I bounce off the wall and she grabs me by the shirt again and punches me in the belly.

Suddenly I'm on my knees again, retching, trying to clutch both belly and balls, no longer having enough wind in me even to manage a squeak.

Hypsipyle kicks me in the ribs, breaking at least one, and I roll to my side. I can hear the slap of the guards' sandals as they rush up the main staircase.

Now I remember. The last time I saw Hypsipyle she was protecting Helen and I sucker-punched her to drag Helen away with me.

The slave-woman lifts me like a rag doll and slaps me—first forehand, then backhand, then forehand again. I feel teeth loosen and find myself feeling glad that I'm not wearing the reading glasses I used to have to wear.

Jesus Christ, Hockenberry, rages part of my mind. *You just watched Achilles kill Zeus-Who-Drives-the-Storm-Clouds in single combat, and here you are getting the shit kicked out of you by one lousy Lesbian.*

The guards burst into the room, spearpoints raised toward me. Hypsipyle turns toward them, still holding my bunched tunic in one of her huge hands, the tops of my feet scraping the floor, and holds me out, offering me to their spears.

I QT the two of us to the top of the great wall.

A blast of sunlight around us. Trojan warriors yards away exclaiming and leaping back. Hypsipyle is so astonished at this instantaneous change of place that she drops me.

I use the few seconds of her confusion I have left to kick her heavy legs out from under her. She scrambles to all fours, but—still on my back—I pull back my legs, coil them, and kick her clean off the open rampart into the city below.

That'll teach you, you great muscled cow, teach you not to mess with Dr. Thomas Hockenberry, Ph.D. in Classical Literature . . .

I get to my feet, dust myself off, and look down from the rampart. The great muscled cow has landed on the canvas roof of a marketplace stall backed to the wall, has torn through the canvas, landed again in a heap of what look to be potatoes, and is currently running toward the stairs near the Scaean Gate to scramble back up to where I wait.

Shit.

I run along the rampart toward where I now see Helen standing with the other members of the royal family on the broad reviewing area of the wall, near Athena's Temple. Everyone's attention is firmly fixed on the battle on the beach—my Achaeans' doomed last stand, obviously in its last stages now—so no one interdicts me before I'm grabbing Helen by her beautiful white arm.

"Hock-en-bear-eeee," she says, marveling. "What is it? Why do you . . ."

"We've got to get everyone out of the city!" I gasp. "Now! Right now!"

Helen shakes her head. Guards have whirled and gone for their spears or swords, but Helen waves them away. "Hock-en-bear-eee . . . it is wonderful . . . we are winning . . . the Argives fall like wheat before our scythe . . . any minute now Noble Hector will . . ."

"We have to get everyone out of the buildings, off the wall, out of the city!" I shout.

It's no good. The guards are all around us now, ready to protect Helen, King Priam, and the other royal family members here by killing me or dragging me off in an instant. I'll never convince Helen or Priam to warn the city in time.

Panting, aware of Hypsipyle's heavy running footsteps coming down the rampart toward us, I gasp, "The sirens. Where did the moravecs put the air raid sirens?"

"Sirens?" says Helen. She looks alarmed now, as if my madness must be dealt with quickly.

"The air raid sirens. The ones that used to wail months ago when the gods attacked the city by air. Where did the moravecs—the machine-toy people—put the equipment for the air raid sirens?"

"Oh, in the anteroom of the Temple of Apollo, but Hock-en-bear-eeee, why do you . . ."

Keeping my grip firm on her upper arm, I visualize the steps of Apollo's Temple here in Ilium and QT us there an instant before the guards and one big, angry woman from Lesbos can grab me.

Helen gasps as we pop into solidity on the white steps, but I drag her up into the anteroom. There are no guards here. Everyone in the city seems to be on the walls or in a high place to watch the end of the war play out on the beach to the west.

The equipment is here, in the small acolytes' changing room next to the main temple anteroom. The air raid siren warning had been automatic, triggered by the moravecs' antiaircraft missile and radar sites—now gone—that had been stationed outside the city—but, just as I remembered, the moravec engineers had put a microphone with the other electronic gear here, just in case King Priam or Hector had wanted to address the entire Trojan population through the thirty huge air-raid-siren loudspeakers set around the walled city.

I study the equipment for just a few seconds—it had been made simple enough for a child to use so that the Trojans could manage it themselves, and child-simple technology is exactly the kind Dr. Thomas Hockenberry can manage.

"Hock-en-bear-eeee. . . ."

I flip the switch that says PA SYSTEM ON, throw the toggle that reads LOUDSPEAKER ANNOUNCEMENT, lift the archaic-looking microphone, and begin babbling, hearing my own words echoing back from a hundred buildings and the great walls themselves—

"ATTENTION! ATTENTION! ALL PEOPLE OF ILIUM . . . KING PRIAM IS ISSUING AN EARTHQUAKE WARNING . . . EFFECTIVE IMMEDIATELY!! LEAVE ALL BUILDINGS . . . *NOW!* GET OFF THE WALLS . . . *NOW!!* RUN FROM THE CITY INTO OPEN COUNTRY IF YOU CAN. IF YOU ARE IN A TOWER, EVACUATE IT . . . *NOW!!* AN EARTHQUAKE WILL HIT ILIUM AT ANY SECOND. AGAIN, KING PRIAM IS ISSUING AN EARTHQUAKE EVACUATION ORDER EFFECTIVE IMMEDIATELY . . . LEAVE ALL BUILDINGS AND SEEK OPEN SPACE *NOW!!*"

I echo on for another blaring minute, then switch off, grab the staring, open-mouthed Helen, and drag her out of the Temple of Apollo into the central marketplace.

People are milling and talking, staring at the various speaker locations from where my blaring announcement had come, but no one seems to be evacuating. A few people wander out of the large buildings that adjoin this central open plaza, but almost no one is running for the open Scaean Gate and the countryside as my announcement had commanded them to.

"Shit," I say.

"Hock-en-bear-eeee, you are very worked up. Come to my chambers and we shall have some honeyed wine and . . ."

I tug her along behind me. Even if no one else is headed through the open gate and out away from the buildings, I sure as hell am. And I'm going to save Helen whether she wants me to or not.

I slide to a stop just before entering the narrowing avenue at the west end of the huge plaza. What am I doing? I don't have to run like an idiot. I just have to visualize Thicket Ridge way out beyond the walls and QT us there . . .

"Oh, shit," I say again.

Above us, horizontal, seemingly miles wide, descending rapidly, is the kind of Brane Hole I'd seen above Olympos earlier—a flat circle rimmed by flames. Through the Hole I can see dark sky and stars.

"Damn!" I decide at the last second not to quantum teleport—the chances of us getting caught in quantum space just as the Brane Hole hits us is too great.

I tug the staring, horrified Helen a dozen yards back toward the center of the huge plaza. With any luck we'll be out of the range of the falling walls and buildings.

The hoop of fire falls around us past Ilium, falls past the surrounding hills, plains, marshes, and beaches for a circle of at least two miles, and the instant after it falls, we fall. There is a sensation of the entire city of ancient Troy being on an elevator suddenly cut free of its cables, and two seconds later all hell breaks loose.

Much later, the moravec engineers would tell me that the entire city of Ilium fell a literal five feet and two inches before landing on the soil of the present-day Earth. All of those fighting on the beach—more than one hundred fifty thousand struggling, screaming, sweating men—also suddenly dropped five feet two inches, and not onto soft beach sand, but onto the rock and tangled scrub brush that had taken the sand's place after the coastline had retreated almost three hundred yards to the west.

For Helen and me in Ilium's great city square, those last minutes of Ilium were almost our last minutes as well.

It was the topless tower near the wall beyond the southeast corner of that square—the same damaged, topless tower where Helen had stabbed me in the heart in what seemed like ages ago—that came falling over lower buildings, toppling and collapsing like some giant factory smokestack, crashing directly at us as we cowered in the open square near the fountain.

It was the fountain itself that saved our lives. The multistepped structure with its pool and central obelisk—no more than twelve feet tall—was just large enough to part the path of the tower's tumbling debris, leaving us coughing in a cloud of dust and smaller pieces, but sending the larger stone blocks careering elsewhere across the marketplace.

We were stunned. The huge paving stones of the plaza itself had been shattered by the five-foot fall. The fountain obelisk was tilting at a thirty-degree angle and the fountain itself had stopped forever. The entire city was lost in a cloud of dust that did not fully clear away for more than six hours. By the time Helen and I picked ourselves up and started dusting ourselves off, coughing and trying to clear our nose and throats of all the terrible white powder, other people were already running—most randomly, in pure panic, now that it was too late to run—while a few had even begun digging in the ruins and rubble, trying to find and help others.

More than five thousand people died in the Fall of the City. Most had been trapped in the larger buildings—both the Temple of Athena and the Temple of Apollo had collapsed, their many pillars cracking and flying apart like broken sticks. Paris's palace, now the home of Priam, was rubble. No one on the terrace of Athena's temple survived except for Hypsipyle, who was still hunting for me when her part of the wall collapsed. Many of the people had been on the main west and southwest ramparts, which did not collapse in their entirety, but which tumbled outward or inward in many places, sending bodies flying out and down to the rocks on the Plain of Scamander or into the city and down onto the rubble. King Priam was one of those who died that way, along with several other members of the royal family, including the ill-fated Cassandra. Andromache—Hector's wife and a survivor if ever there was one— survived without a scratch.

The city of Troy was as much in an earthquake zone in the ancient days as that part of Turkey is now, people knew how to react to quakes then much as they do now, and my announcement probably saved many. Many people did run to solid doorways or escaped to open spaces to avoid the collapsing buildings. It was later estimated that several thousand ran out onto the plain itself before the city fell, the towers tumbled, and the walls came down.

For my part, I stared around in stunned disbelief. The noblest of cities, this survivor of ten years of siege by the Achaeans and months more war with the gods themselves, was now mostly rubble. Fires burned here and there—not the omnipresent flames of a modern city of my era after an earthquake, for there were no ruptured gaslines here— but fires enough from braziers and hearths and cooking kitchens and simple torches in windowless halls that were now open to the sky. Fires enough. The smoke mixed with the roiling dust to keep the many hundreds of us milling in the plaza coughing and dabbing at our eyes.

"I have to find Priam . . . Andromache . . ." said Helen between coughs. "I have to find Hector!"

"You go look after your people here, Helen," I said between coughs. "I'll go down to the beach in search of Hector."

I turned to go but Helen grabbed my arm to stop me. "Hock-en-bear- eeee . . . what did this? Who did this?"

I told her the truth. "The gods."

It had long been prophesied that Troy could not fall until the stone above the huge Scaean Gate was dislodged, and as I pushed my way out with fleeing crowds, I noticed that the wooden gates had splintered and that the great lintel had fallen.

Nothing was as it had been ten minutes earlier. Not only had the city been destroyed in an instant of encircling fire, but the surrounding area had changed, the sky had changed, the weather had changed. We weren't in Kansas anymore, Toto.

I had taught the *Iliad* for more than twenty years at Indiana University and elsewhere, but I had never thought to go to Troy—to the ruins of Troy along the coast of Turkey. But I'd seen photos enough of the place at the end of the Twentieth Century and beginning of the Twenty-first

Century. This place where Ilium had crash-landed like Dorothy's house looked more like the ruins of Troy in the Twenty-first Century—a small area named Hisarlik—than like the busy center of empire that had been Ilium.

As I looked at the changed scenery—and changed sky, since it had been early afternoon when the Greeks were fighting their last stand, and it was now twilight—I remembered a Canto of *Don Juan* by Byron, written when the poet had visited this place in 1810 and had felt both the connection here to heroic history and the distance from it—

> *High barrows without marble or a name,*
> *A vast, untilled and mountain-skirted plain*
> *And Ida in the distance, still the same,*
> *And old Scamander (if 'tis he) remain;*
> *The situation seems still formed for fame—*
> *A hundred thousand men might fight again*
> *With ease; but where I sought for Ilion's walls,*
> *The quiet sheep feeds, and the tortoise crawls.*

I saw no sheep, but when I looked back at the toppled city, the ridge-line was much the same—although obviously five feet two inches lower where the city had just fallen onto the rubble of amateur archaeologist Schliemann's ruins. A memory struck me that the ancient Romans had sheared off yards of the top of that ridgeline to build their own city of Ilion more than a millennium after the original Ilium disappeared, and I realized that we'd all been lucky to fall just five feet two inches. If it hadn't been for Roman rubble on top of Greek ruins, the fall would have been much worse.

To the north where the Plain of Simois had stretched for many miles, a low grassland perfect for pasturing and running the famous Trojan horses, there now grew a forest. The smooth Plain of Scamander, the area between the city and the shoreline to the west, the plain where I'd watched most of the fighting take place during the last eleven years, was now a gully-riddled riot of scrub oak, pine, and swampy marsh. I headed for that beach, climbing what the Trojans had called Thicket Ridge without even recognizing where I was, but as soon as I reached the low ridgeline I stopped in amazement.

The Sea was gone.

It's not just the mile or so of receded shoreline that I knew about from the memories of my Twenty-first Century previous life, the *entire fucking Aegean Sea was gone*!

I sat down on the highest boulder I could find on Thicket Ridge and thought about this. I wondered not only *where* Nyx and Hephaestus had sent us, but *when*. All I could tell right now in the failing twilight was that there were no electric lights visible anywhere inland or along the coast and that the bottom of what should be the Aegean here was overgrown with mature trees and shrubs.

Toto, we're not only not in Kansas anymore, we're not even in Oz anymore.

The evening sky was completely covered over by clouds, but it was still light enough that I could see the thousands upon thousands of men packed together in a half-mile arc along what had been the beach just fifteen minutes earlier. At first I was sure that they were still fighting—I could see thousands more fallen on each side—but then I realized that they were just milling around, all lines of combat, trenches, defenses, communication, and discipline lost. Later I'd discover that almost a third of the men down there, Trojans and Achaeans alike, had broken bones—mostly leg bones—from the five-foot fall onto rock and into gullies that hadn't been there a second earlier. In places, I'd soon learn, men who had been trying to slash each other's guts and skulls to bits a few minutes earlier were now lying moaning together or trying to help each other up.

I hurried to get down the hill and to cross the mile of alluvial plain that had been so much easier to cross when it had been so worn-down and bare from battle. By the time I reached the rear of the Trojan lines— such as they were—it was almost dark.

I started asking for Hector immediately, but it was another half hour before I found him, and by then everything was being done by torchlight.

Hector and his wounded brother Deiphobus were conferring with the temporary commander of the Argives—Idomeneus, son of Deucalion and commander of the Crete heroes, and Little Ajax of Locris, son of Oileus. Little Ajax had been carried to the conference on a litter, since he'd been slashed to the bone on both shins earlier in the day. Also there conferring with Hector was Thrasymedes, Nestor's brave son whom I'd thought had been killed earlier in the day—he'd gone missing in the battle for the last trench and had been presumed dead down among the corpses there, but as I'd discover in a minute, he had only been wounded a third time, but it had taken him hours to dig his way out of the corpse-filled trench, then only to find himself among the Trojans. They'd taken him prisoner—one of the few acts of mercy this day or any day of the almost eleven years of war between the two groups—and now he was using a broken lance as a crutch as he negotiated with Hector.

"Hock-en-bear-eeee," said Hector, apparently and oddly happy to see me. "Son of Duane! I am glad you survived this madness. What caused this? Who caused this? What has happened?"

"The gods caused this," I said truthfully. "To be specific, the fire god

Hephaestus and Night—Nyx—the mysterious goddess who lives and works with the Fates."

"I know you were close to the gods, Hock-en-bear-eeee, son of Duane. Why have they done this thing? What do they want us to do?"

I shook my head. The torches were ripping and tearing at the night in the strong breeze coming in from the west—coming from the direction of what had once been the Mediterranean but which now bore smells of vegetation on the wind. "It doesn't matter what the gods want," I said. "You'll never see the gods again. They're gone forever."

The hundred or two hundred packed men around us said nothing and for a minute there came only the sound of the torches and the moans of the many injured in the dark.

"How do you know this?" asked Little Ajax.

"I just came from Olympos," I said. "Your Achilles killed Zeus in hand-to-hand combat."

The murmurs would have grown to a roar if Hector had not silenced everyone. "Continue, son of Duane."

"Achilles killed Zeus and the Titans returned to Olympos. Hephaestus will rule eventually—Night and the Fates have decided this already—but for the next year or so, your Earth would have been a battlefield on which no mere mortal could have survived. So Hephaestus sent you—the city, its survivors, you Achaeans, you Trojans—here."

"Where is here?" asked Ideomeneus.

"I have no idea."

"When will we be allowed to return?" asked Hector.

"Never," I said. I was sure of this and my voice reflected that certainty. I'm not sure I ever spoke two syllables with such certainty before or since.

At that moment, the second of the three impossible things of the day occurred—the first being, by my count, the falling of Ilium into a different universe.

It had been cloudy since the city landed on the ridgeline—solid clouds spread from east to west—and the twilight darkness had come more quickly because of the cloud cover. But now the wind that had borne the smell of vegetation was moving the entire cloud mass from west to east, clearing the early night sky above us.

We heard the men—Achaeans and Trojans both—exclaiming for long seconds before we realized that they were looking and pointing skyward.

I became aware of the strange light even before I looked up at the skies. It was brighter than any night under a full moon that I'd ever experienced and it was a richer, milkier, and strangely more fluid sort of light. I found myself looking down at our multiple, moving shadows on the rock beneath us—shadows no longer thrown by torchlight—when Hector himself prodded my arm to make me look up.

The clouds had all but passed. The night sky was still Earth's night sky; I could see Orion's Belt, the Pleiades, Polaris, and the Big Dipper low in the north, all more or less in their proper places, but that familiar late winter sky and the crescent moon rising above tumbled Troy to the east were paled to insignificance by this new source of light.

Two broad and moving bands of stars were moving and crossing above us, one band in our south and obviously moving quickly west to east, the other ring directly above us and moving north to south. The rings were bright and milky but not indistinct—I could make out thousands upon thousands of bright individual stars in each ring even as some long-lost memory from a science column in some newspaper reminded me that on the clearest night from most places on Earth, only about three thousand separate stars were visible up there. Now there were tens, perhaps hundreds of thousands of individual stars visible—all moving together and crossing in two bright rings above us, easily illuminating everything around us and giving us a sort of half-evening-light, the kind of half-light I'd always imagined they played softball by at midnight in Anchorage, Alaska. This may have been the most beautiful thing I'd seen in two lifetimes.

"Son of Duane," said Hector, "what are these stars? Are they gods? New stars? What are they?"

"I don't know," I said.

At that moment, with more than a hundred and fifty thousand men in armor rubbernecking, staring openmouthed and fearful at the amazing new night sky of this other Earth, men closest to the beach started shouting about something else. It took several minutes for us to realize that something was happening at the westernmost reaches of the mob of men, and then it took those of us at Hector's conference more minutes to make our way west to a rocky rise—perhaps the edge of the original beach here thousands of years ago in Ilium's day—to see what the Achaeans were still shouting about.

For the first time I noticed that the hundreds of burned black ships were still here; they had passed through the Brane Hole with us—the scorched wrecks near no water now, beached forever on the scrubby ridges here high above the alluvial marsh to the west—and then I noticed what the hundreds of men were yelling about.

Something black and inky but which reflected the turning starlight above us was creeping across the floor of the missing sea from the west, something moving silently toward us along the bottom of the dry basin, something flowing and sliding eastward with the subtle, slow, but sure certainty of Death. It filled up the lowest points as we watched, then encircled the wooded hilltops in the distance near the horizon—quite easily visible in the light from the new rings above us—and within minutes those hilltops had been surrounded by the dark motion until they ceased being hilltops and became the islands of Lemnos and Tenedos and Imbros once again.

This was the third strange miracle of this seemingly endless day.

The wine-dark sea was returning to the shores of Ilium.

Harman held the pistol to his forehead for only a few seconds. Even as his finger touched the weapon's trigger, he knew that he wasn't going to end things that way. It was a coward's way out, and however terrified he felt right then at the imminence of his own death, he did not want to exit as a coward.

He pivoted, aimed the weapon at the hulking bow of the ancient submarine where it emerged through the north wall of the Breach, and squeezed the trigger until the weapon stopped firing nine shots later. His hand was shaking so badly he didn't even know if he'd hit the huge target, but the act of shooting at it both focused and exorcised some of his rage and revulsion at the folly of his own species.

The soiled thermskin came off slowly. Harman did not even consider trying to wash the thing, but simply cast it aside. He was shaking from the aftermaths of the vomiting and diarrhea, but he didn't even consider putting on his outer clothes or boots as he rose, found his balance, and started walking west.

Harman didn't have to query his new biometric functions to know that he was dying quickly. He could feel the radiation in his guts and bowels and testicles and bones. The final weakness was growing in him like some foul homunculus stirring. So he walked west, toward Ada and Ardis.

For several hours, Harman's mind was wonderfully quiescent, becoming aware only to help him avoid stepping on something sharp or to lead him to the correct path through ridges of coral or rock. He was vaguely aware that the walls of the Breach on both sides were growing much higher—the ocean was deeper here—and that the air around him was much cooler. But the midday sun still struck him. Once, in midafternoon, Harman looked down and saw that his legs and thighs were still soiled, mostly with blood, and he staggered to the south wall of the Breach, reached his bare hand through the forcefield—his fingers feeling the terrible pressure and cold—and scooped enough saltwater out of the sea to clean himself. He staggered on toward the west.

When he did begin thinking again he was pleased to note that it was not just about the obscenity of the machine and its cargo of planetary death that were now out of sight behind him. He began to think about his own life, one hundred years of it.

At first Harman's thoughts were bitter—scolding himself for wasting all those decades on parties and play and an aimless series of faxing to this social event or that—but he soon forgave himself. There had been good times there, real moments even amidst that false existence, and the last year of true friendships, real love, and honest commitment had made up at least in part for all the years of shallowness.

He thought of his own role in the last year's events and found the capacity to forgive himself there as well. The post-human who called herself Moira teased him about being Prometheus, but Harman saw himself more as a sort of combined Adam and Eve who—by seeking out the one Forbidden Fruit in the perfect Garden of Indolence—had banished his species from that mindless, healthy place forever.

What had he given Ada, his friends, his race, in return? Reading? As central as reading and knowledge had been to Harman, he wondered if that one ability—so much more potentially powerful than the hundred functions now stirred to wakefulness in his body—could compensate for all the terror, pain, uncertainty, and death ahead.

Perhaps, he realized, it did not have to.

As evening darkened the long slot of sky far above, Harman stumbled westward and began thinking about death. His own, he knew, was only hours away, perhaps less, but what of the concept of death that he and his people had never had to face until recent months?

He allowed himself to search all the data stored in him after the crystal cabinet and found that death—the fear of death, the hope for surviving death, curiosity about death—had been the central spur for almost all literature and religion for the nine millennia of information he had stored. The religion parts, Harman could not quite comprehend—he had little context except for his current terror at the presence of Death. He saw the hunger there in a thousand cultures over thousands of years to have assurance—any assurance—that one's life continued even after life so obviously had fled. He blinked as his mind sorted through concepts of afterlife—Valhalla, Heaven, Hell, the Islamic Paradise that the crew of the submarine behind him had been so eager to enter, the sense of having lived a Righteous life so as to live on in the minds and memories of others—and then he looked at all the myriad versions of the theme of being reborn into an Earthly life, the mandala, reincarnation, the Wu-Nine Path to Center. To Harmon's mind and heart, it was all beautiful and as airy and empty as an abandoned spiderweb.

As he stumbled westward into the cold gathering shadows, Harman realized that if he responded to human views of Death now stored in his dying cells and very DNA, it was to the literary and artistic attempts to express the human side of the encounter—a sort of defiance of genius. Harman looked at stored images of the last self-portraits of Rembrandt and wept at the terrible wisdom in that visage. He listened to his own mind read every word of the full version of *Hamlet* and realized—as so many generations before had realized—that this aging prince in black might have been the only true envoy from the Undiscovered Country.

Harman realized that he was weeping and that it was not for himself or his imminent demise—nor even for the loss of Ada and his unborn child, who were never truly out of his mind—but it was simply because he had never had the chance to watch a Shakespearean play performed. He realized that if he were returning home to Ardis all hale and hearty, rather than as this bleeding, dying skeleton, he would have insisted that the community perform one of Shakespeare's plays if they managed to survive the voynix.

Which one?

Trying to decide this interesting question kept Harman distracted long enough that he did not notice the sky above fading to deep twilight hues, nor did he notice when the slice of sky became only starfields and ring movement and he did not immediately notice that the cold in the deep trench he was staggering westward in was seeping into his skin first, then flesh, then his very bones.

Finally he could go on no longer. He kept stumbling over rocks and other unseen things. He could not even see where the walls of the Breach began. Everything was terribly cold and totally dark—a pretaste of death.

Harman did not want to die. Not yet. Not now. He curled into a fetal position on the sandy bottom of the Breach, feeling the grit and sand rubbing his skin raw as the reality that he was alive. He hugged himself, teeth chattering, pulled his knees higher up and hugged them, body shaking, but reassured that he was alive. He even thought wistfully about the rucksack he had left so far behind and of the thermal-blanket sleeping bag in it and of his clothes. His mind acknowledged the food bars left in it as well, but his stomach wanted no part of that.

Several times during the night, Harman had to crawl away from the nest in the sand he had made with his curled body and shake on hands and knees as he retched again and again—but dry heaves only. Anything he'd had in his stomach yesterday was long gone. Then he would crawl back slowly, laboriously, to his little fetal-shaped gouge in the sand, anticipating the slight warmth he would find again when curled up there the way he once might have anticipated a fine meal.

Which play? The first he had ever read had been *Romeo and Juliet* and it held the affection of first encounter. Now he reviewed *King Lear*— *never, never, never, never never*—and thought it perfectly appropriate for a dying man such as himself, even one who had not lived long enough to see his son or daughter, but it might be too much for the Ardis family in their first encounter with Shakespeare. Since they would have to be their own actors, he wondered who among them could even play old Lear . . . Odysseus-Noman was the only face that seemed right. He wondered how Noman fared this day.

Harman turned his face upward and watched the rings turn in front of the stars, a beauty he had never appreciated as much as he did this terrible night. A bright streak—brighter than the rest of the ring stars combined—a bold scratch against black onyx, moved across the p-ring and moved between the real stars before disappearing behind the Breach wall on the south side. Harman had no idea what it was—it lasted far too long to be a meteor—but he knew that it was so very, very far away that it could have nothing to do with him.

Thinking of death and thinking of Shakespeare, not yet decided on which play to stage first, Harman encountered these interesting lines stored deep in his DNA. It was Claudio speaking, Claudio from *Measure for Measure*, as the character confronted his own execution:

> *Ay, but to die, and go we know not where;*
> *To lie in cold obstruction, and to rot;*
> *This sensible warm motion to become*
> *A kneaded clod, and the dilated spirit*
> *To bathe in fiery floods, or to reside*
> *In thrilling region of thick-ribbèd ice;*
> *To be imprisoned in the viewless winds,*
> *And blown with restless violence round about*
> *The pendant world; or to be worse than worst*
> *Of those that lawless and incertain thought*
> *Imagine howling—'tis too horrible!*
> *The weariest and most loathèd worldly life*
> *That age, ache, penury, and imprisonment*
> *Can lay on nature is a paradise*
> *To what we fear of death.*

Harman realized that he was sobbing—curled, cold, and sobbing—but not sobbing in fear of death or at the imminence of his own loss of everything and everyone, but weaping gratitude that he came from a race that could spawn a man who could write those words, think those thoughts. It almost—almost—made up for the human thought that had conceived, designed, launched, and crewed the submarine behind him with its seven hundred sixty-eight black holes waiting to devour all futures for everyone.

Suddenly Harman laughed aloud. His mind had made its own leap to John Keat's "Ode to a Nightingale" and he saw—he was not shown, but he saw on his own—the young Keats's nod in Shakespeare's direction with the lines to the singing bird—

> Still wouldst thou sing, and I have ears in vain—
> To thy high requiem become a sod.

"Three cheers for the alliance of Claudio's kneaded clod and Johnny's earless sod!" cried Harman. The sudden attempt to speak made him cough again and when he peered at his hand in ringlight, he saw that he had coughed up red blood and three teeth.

Harman moaned, curled again in his womb of sand, shook, and had to smile again. His restless brain could no more quit poking at Shakespeare than his tongue could quit probing the three holes in his gums where his teeth had been. It was the couplet from *Cymbeline* that made Harman smile—

> Golden lads and girls all must
> As chimney-sweepers come to dust.

He'd just gotten the pun. What kind of species of genius is it, wondered Harman, that can put such a childish, playful pun in such a sad dirge?

With that last thought, Harman slipped sideways into a cold sleep, insensate to the cold rain that had begun to fall on him.

He awoke.

That was the first marvel. He opened his blood-caked eyes onto a gray, cold gloomy predawn morning with the still-dark seawalls of the Breach rising five hundred feet or more on either side. But he had slept and now he waked.

The second marvel was that he could move, eventually, and after a fashion. It took Harman fifteen minutes to get to his hands and knees, but once there he crawled to the nearest boulder rising out of the sand and in another ten minutes managed to get to his feet and not quite fall again.

Now he was ready to walk west again, but he did not know which way was west.

He was completely turned around. The long Breach stretched away from side to side, but there was no clue to which way was east and which was west. Shaking, shivering, aching in ways he could never have imagined he could ache, Harman staggered in circles, hunting for his own footprints from the night before, but much of the seabed there was rock and the rain that had almost frozen him to death had wiped away any traces of prints of his bare feet.

Swaying, Harman took four steps in one direction. Convinced he was heading back toward the submarine, he wheeled and took eight steps in the other direction.

No use. Clouds hung low and solid above the Breach opening. He had no sense of east or west. Harman couldn't bear the thought of walking back toward the submarine with all that evil lying in its belly, of losing the distance he had made so laboriously yesterday toward Ada and Ardis.

He staggered to the wall of the Breach—he did not know now whether it was the north or south wall—and stared at his reflection in the slowly thickening predawn glow.

Some creature that was not Harman stared back. His naked body already looked skeletal. There were patches of blood pooled under the skin everywhere—on his sunken cheeks, his chest, under the skin of his forearms, on his shaking legs, even a huge mottle on his lower belly. When he coughed again, two more teeth were expelled. It looked in the water's mirror as if he had been weeping tears of blood. As if in an attempt to tidy himself, he brushed his hair to one side.

Harman stared at his fist for a long, empty moment. A huge swatch of hair had come away in his hand. It was as if he were holding a small dead creature made up completely of hair. He dropped it, brushed at his head again. More hair came loose. Harman looked at his reflection and saw the walking dead, already one-third bald.

Warmth touched his back.

Harman whirled and almost fell.

It was the sun—rising directly in the aperture of the Breach behind him. The sun, rising perfectly in the keyhole of the Breach, its golden rays bathing him in warmth in the few seconds before the clouds swallowed the orange sphere. What were the chances that the sun would rise directly down the Breach on this particular morning—as if he were a Druid waiting at Stonehenge for the equinox sunrise?

Harman felt so light-headed that he knew he'd forget which direction the sun had risen from if he did not act immediately. Aiming in the opposite direction of the warmth on his back, he began staggering west again.

By midday—the clouds parted between rain showers and gave hints of sunlight—Harman's mind no longer felt connected to his staggering body. He was taking twice as many steps as he had to, staggering from the north wall of the Breach to the south wall, having to set his hands lightly against the buzz-jolt of the forcefield itself to set himself moving again down the endless trough.

He was wondering as he walked at what the future might be—or might have been—for his people. Not just the survivors of Ardis, but for all the old-style humans who might have survived the vicious voynix attacks. Now that the old world was gone forever, what form of government, of religion, of society, culture, politics, might they have created?

A protein memory module nestled deep in Harman's encoded DNA—a memory that would not die until long after most of the other cells in Harman's body had died and come apart—offered him this fragment from Antonio Gramsci's *Prison Notebooks*—"The crisis consists precisely in the fact that the old is dying and the new cannot be born; in this interregnum a great variety of morbid symptoms appears."

Harman laughed aloud and the single bark of a laugh cost him another front tooth. Morbid symptoms, indeed. The slightest scan of the context of that fragment told Harman that this Gramsci had been an intellectual promoting revolution, socialism, and communism—the last two theories having died and rotted away less than halfway through the Lost Era, abandoned for the naïve bullshit they were—but the problem of interregnums certainly had remained and now here it was again.

He realized that Ada had been leading her people toward some sort of crude Athenian democracy in the weeks and months before Harman had stupidly left his expecting beloved. They had never discussed it, but he was aware of her recognition that the four hundred people in the Ardis community then—this was before the slaughter by voynix he'd seen via the red turin cloth on the *eiffelbahn*—turned to her for leadership, and she hated that role, even as she fell into it naturally. By deferring things to constant votes, Ada was obviously trying to establish the basis for a future democracy should Ardis survive.

But if the red turin had given him true images—and Harman believed it had—Ardis as a real community had not survived. Four hundred people made up a community. Fifty-four ragged, starved survivors did not.

The radiation seemed to have sheared off much of the lining of Harman's throat, and every time he swallowed now, he coughed up blood. This was a distraction. He tried to slow the pace of his swallowing to once every tenth step he took. His right hand, chin, and chest, he knew, were smeared with blood.

It would have been interesting seeing what social and political structures his race would have evolved. Perhaps the population, even before the voynix attacks, had—at a mere one hundred thousand men and women—never been sufficient to generate real dynamics such as politics or religious ceremonies or armies or social hierarchies.

But Harman didn't believe this. He saw in his many protein memory banks the examples of Athens, Sparta, and the Greek entities long before Athens and Sparta ascended. The turin drama—what he now clearly saw as Homer's *Iliad*—had borrowed its heroes from kingdoms as small as Odysseus' isle of Ithaca.

Thinking of the turin drama, he remembered the altar quickly glimpsed on their trip to Paris Crater a year ago, just after Daeman was eaten by a dinosaur—it had been dedicated to one of the Olympian gods, although he forgot right then which one. The post-humans had served, at least for the last millennium and a half, as his people's substitute for gods or a God, but what shapes and ceremonies would the future need for belief take?

The future.

Harman paused, panting, leaned against a shoulder-high black rock jutting out of the north wall of the Breach, and tried to think about the future.

His legs were shaking violently. It was as if his leg muscles were dissolving as he watched.

Panting, forcing breaths through his closing, bleeding throat, Harman stared ahead and blinked.

The sun was perched just above the cleft of the Breach. For a terrible second, Harman thought that it was still sunrise and that he had walked the wrong direction after all, but then he realized that he had been walking in a stupor all day. The sun had descended from the clouds and was preparing to set at the end of the long hallway of the Breach.

Harman took two more steps forward and fell on his face.

This time he could not rise. It took all of his energy to prop himself up on his right elbow to watch the sunset.

His mind was very clear. He no longer thought about Shakespeare or Keats or religions or heaven or death or politics or democracy. Harman thought about his friends. He saw Hannah laughing on the day of the metal pour by the river—remembered the specifics of her youthful energy and the glee of her friends as they poured the first bronze artifact created in how many thousand years? He saw Petyr sparring with

Odysseus during the days the bearded Greek warrior would hold forth with his long statements of philosophy and odd question-and-answer periods on the grassy hill behind Ardis. There had been much energy and joy in those sessions.

Harman remembered Savi's husky, cynical voice, and her huskier laugh. He perfectly recalled their cheering and shouting when Savi had driven Daeman and him out of Jerusalem in the crawler, with thousands of voynix chasing to no avail. And he saw his friend Daeman's face as if through two lenses—the pudgy, self-absorbed boy-man from when Harman first met him, and the lean, serious version—a man to be trusted with one's life—whom he'd last seen a few weeks ago on the day Harman left Ardis in the sonie.

And, as the sun entered the Breach so perfectly that its outer curves just touched the Breach wall—Harman smiled to think of a hissing steam sound rising and actually thought he heard one through his failing ears—Harman thought of Ada.

He thought of her eyes and smile and soft voice. He remembered her laugh and touch and the last time they had been together in bed. Harman allowed himself to remember how, when they turned away from one another as sleep came on, they also soon would curve against the other for warmth—Ada against his back, her right arm around him, himself later in the night against Ada's back and perfect backside, a bit of excitement stirring in him even as he drifted off to sleep, his left arm around her, his left hand cupping her breast.

Harman realized that his eyelids were so caked with blood that he could not really blink, could not really shut his eyes. The setting sun—the bottom of it already below the Breach horizon—was burning red and orange echoes into his retina. It didn't matter. He knew that after this sunset, he would never need to use his eyes again. So he concentrated on holding his beloved Ada in his mind and heart and on watching the last half of the sun's disk disappear directly to his west.

Something moved and blocked the last of the sunset.

For several seconds, Harman's dying mind could not process that information. Something had *moved into his field of vision and blocked his view of the last of the sunset.*

Still propped on his right elbow, he used the back of his left hand to rub some of the caked blood from his eyes.

Something was standing in the Breach not twenty feet west of Harman. It must have come through the Breach wall of water there on the north side. The thing was about the size of an eight- or nine-year-old child and was shaped more or less like a human child, but it wore a strange suit of metal and plastic. Harman saw a black visor where the little boy's eyes should be.

On the verge of death, as the brain shuts down from lack of oxygen, an unsummoned protein memory molecule prompted him, *hallucinations are not uncommon. Thus the frequent tales from resuscitated victims of a "long tunnel" ending in a "bright light" and* . . .

Fuck that, thought Harman. He was staring down a long tunnel toward a bright light, although only the top rim of the sun remained, and both walls of the Breach were alive with light—silver, bright, mirrored surfaces with millions of facets of dancing light.

But the boy in the plastic and metal red-and-black suit was real.

And as Harman stared, something larger and stranger forced itself out through the north wall of the Breach.

The forcefield is semipermeable only to human beings and what they wear, thought Harman.

But this second apparition was nowhere near human. It was about twice the size of the largest droshky, but looked more like a giant, robotic crab monster with its big pincer claws and many metal legs and its huge, pitted carapace now pouring water off it in loud rivulets.

No one told me that the last minutes before death would be so visually amusing, thought Harman.

The little boy figure stepped closer. It spoke in English, its voice soft and rather boylike, perhaps sounding much like Harman's future son might sound. "Sir," it said, "can you use some assistance?"

87

It was just after sunrise and fifty thousand voynix were attacking from all directions. Ada paused to look back at the Pit where the shredded corpse of the Setebos spawn still lay.

Daeman touched her arm. "Don't feel bad. We had to kill it sooner or later."

She shook her head. "I don't feel the least bit sorry," she said. To Greogi and Hannah she shouted, "Get the sky-raft up!"

Too late. More than half the survivors had panicked at the scuttling roar of the voynix attack—the creatures were still invisible in the forest but the two-mile radius must have been cut in half by now. They'd be at Ardis in less than a minute.

"No! No!" shouted Ada as thirty people, in their panic, tried to fit aboard the slowly lifting sky-raft. Hannah was at the controls, trying to keep it at a steady three-foot hover, but more people were trying to clamber aboard.

"Take it up!" shouted Daeman. "Hannah! Take it up now!"

Too late. The heavy machine let out a mechanical whine, dipped to its right, and crashed to the ground, sending people flying.

Ada and Daeman ran to the fallen machine. Hannah looked up with a stricken face. "It won't start again. Something's broken."

"Never mind," Ada said, her voice calm. "It would never have made even one trip to the island." She squeezed Hannah's shoulder and raised her voice—"*Everyone to the walls! Now!! Bring every weapon in the compound. Our best chance is to break their first charge.*"

She turned and ran to the west wall and a minute later the others began to do the same, choosing empty spots in the now-circular palisade. Everyone followed Ada's example of carrying at least two flechette rifles and a crossbow along with a heavy canvas bag of magazines and bolts.

Ada settled herself into a firing niche and discovered that Daeman was still beside her. "Good," he said.

She nodded, although she had no idea what he was really saying to her.

Working very carefully, in no rush, Ada slapped in a fresh magazine, clicked off the safety, and aimed the rifle at the treeline no more than two hundred yards away.

The rushing, hissing, clacking noise made by the approaching voynix grew deafening and Ada found she had to resist the urge to drop her rifle and cover her ears. Her heart was pounding and she was feeling slightly nauseated, almost the way she'd felt earlier in her pregnancy, but she did not feel afraid. Not yet.

"All those years of the turin drama," she said, not realizing that she was speaking aloud.

"What?" said Daeman, leaning closer to hear.

She shook her head. "I was just thinking about the turin drama. According to Harman, Odysseus said that he and Savi started that—distributing the turin cloths ten years ago, I mean. Maybe the idea was to teach us how to die with courage."

"I'd rather they'd given us something to teach us how to win a fight against fifty thousand fucking voynix," said Daeman. He clicked back the activation bolt on his rifle.

Ada laughed.

The little noise was drowned out by the roar as the voynix broke free of the forest—some leaping from tree branches even as others scuttled beneath the leapers—a gray wall of carapaces and claws rushing at them at fifty or sixty miles an hour. There were so many of them this time that Ada had trouble making out individual voynix bodies in the rising and falling mass. She looked over her shoulder and saw the same nightmare coming at them from all sides as the tens of thousands of voynix narrowed the radius at full speed.

No one yelled *Fire!* but suddenly everyone was shooting. Ada grinned in the grip of a sort of ferocious terror as the flechette rifle emptied its first magazine in a series of hard stutters against her shoulder. She let the ammunition clip drop free and slapped a fresh one in.

The flechettes struck by the thousands, crystal facets gleaming in the rising sun, but the hits seemed to make no difference. Voynix must be dropping, but there so many thousands still leaping, scuttling, jumping, running, scrambling, that Ada couldn't even see the wounded and dead ones fall. The gray-silver wall of death had covered half the distance from the woods in a few seconds and the things would be over the low palisade walls in another few seconds.

Daeman may have been the first to go over the wall—Ada couldn't swear to it, since it seemed to be an almost simultaneous decision. Grabbing up one weapon and screaming, he jumped from the parapet, vaulted over the tops of the logs, landed, rolled, and began rushing toward the voynix.

Ada laughed and wept. Suddenly it was the most important thing in the world to her that she join in that charge—the most important thing in the world to die attacking this mindless, vicious, stupid, programmed-for-murder enemy, and not wait here behind wood walls to be killed cowering.

Absurdly taking care because she was, after all, five months pregnant, Ada jumped, rolled, got to her feet, and rushed after Daeman, firing as she ran. She heard a familiar voice screaming to her left and she turned just long enough to see Hannah and Edide running not far behind, stopping to shoot, then running again.

She could see the humps on the gray-carapaced voynix bodies now. They were covering twenty or twenty-five feet at a leap, their killing claws extended. Ada ran and fired. She no longer knew that she was screaming or what words she might be screaming. Briefly, very briefly, she summoned an image of Harman and tried to send a message his direction—*I'm sorry, my darling, sorry about the baby*—but then she paid attention only to running and firing and the gray forms were almost on them, rising above them like a silver-gray tidal wave. . . .

The explosions threw Ada ten feet back and burned off her eyebrows. Men and women were lying all around her, thrown backward with her, too stunned to speak or rise. Some were trying to put out flames on their clothing. Some were unconscious.

The Ardis compound was encircled by a wall of flame that rose fifty, eighty, a hundred feet into the air.

A second wave of voynix appeared, running and leaping through the flames. More explosions erupted along this line of running gray-silver figures. Ada blinked as she watched carapaces and claws, legs and humps flying in every direction.

Then Daeman was pulling her to her feet. He was panting, his face blistered from flash burns. "Ada . . . we have to get . . . back . . . to . . ."

Ada pulled her arm free and stared up at the sky. There were five flying machines in the air above the Ardis clearing and none of them were sonies—four smaller, bat-winged devices were dropping canisters toward the tree line while a much larger winged machine was descending toward the center of their palisaded compound—the palisade walls mostly tumbled inward now from the multiple explosions.

Suddenly cables dropped from the bat-winged shapes and black, humanoid but not human shapes whizzed down the lines, hitting the ground faster than a human could and running to establish a perimeter. When some of these tall, black forms ran past Ada, she saw that they were not humans—nor even humans in combat armor of some sort—but taller creatures, strangely jointed, covered with barbs, thorns, and a chitinous ebony armor.

More voynix came through the flames.

The black figures between her and the voynix had gone to one knee and raised weapons that looked too heavy for human beings to lift. The guns suddenly exploded into action—*chuga-chink-ghuga-chuga-ghink*—sounding like some chain-driven cutting machine while pulses of pure blue energy raked the oncoming ranks of voynix. Wherever a blue pulse struck, the voynix exploded.

Daeman was pulling her back toward the compound.

"What?" she shouted over the din. "What?"

He shook his head. Either he couldn't hear her or didn't know the answer himself.

Another round of explosions knocked all the retreating humans down again. This time the mushrooms of flame rose two or three hundred feet into the cold morning air. All of the trees to the west and east of Ardis were burning.

Voynix leaped through the flames. The chitinous black soldiers shot them down by the score, then by the hundreds.

Then one of the black things was looming over her. It reached out a long, barbed arm and extended a hand that seemed more black claws than hand. "Ada *Uhr*?" it said in a calm, deep voice. "I am Centurion

Leader Mep Ahoo. Your husband needs you. My squad and I will accompany you back to the compound."

The large ship had landed next to the Pit. This flying machine was too large for the palisade and had knocked down most of the rest of the wooden wall on its landing. It stood on high, multiply jointed metal legs and some sort of bay doors had opened in its belly.

Harman was on a litter on the ground with several different creatures huddled around it. Ada ignored the creatures and ran to Harman.

Her beloved's head was on a pillow and his body had been covered by a blanket, but Ada had to thrust her palm in her mouth to keep from screaming. His face was ravaged, cheeks hollow, gums all but empty of teeth. His eyes were bleeding. His lips had cracked until they looked as if something had chewed them to bits. His bare forearms were visible above the blanket and Ada could see the pooled blood under the skin—red skin that was sloughing off as if he had received the world's worst sunburn.

Daeman, Hannah, Greogi, and others were huddled near her. She took Harman's hand, felt the slightest pressure in return to her soft squeezing. The dying man on the litter tried to focus his cataract-covered eyes on her, tried to speak. He could only cough blood.

A small humanoid figure wrapped in red-and-black metal and plastic spoke to her. "You are Ada?"

"Yes." She did not turn to look at the machine-boy. Her gaze was just for Harman.

"He managed to say your name and give us the coordinates for this place. We're sorry we didn't find him earlier."

"What . . ." she began and did not know what to ask. One of the machine-things nearby was huge. It was delicately holding an intravenous bottle that fed something into Harman's emaciated arm.

"He received a lethal dose of radiation," said the boy-sized figure in its soft voice. "Almost certainly from a submarine he encountered in the Atlantic Breach."

Submarine, thought Ada. The word meant nothing to her.

"We're sorry, but we simply don't have the medical facilities for human beings in this condition," said the little person-machine. "We called the hornets down from the *Queen Mab* when we saw your problems here and they brought painkillers, more intravenous bottles, but we can do nothing for the radiation damage itself."

Ada didn't really understand anything the little person was saying. She held Harman's hand with both of hers and felt him dying.

Harman coughed, obviously could not make the speech sounds he was trying to make, coughed again, and tried to pull his hand away. Ada clung but the dying man was insistent, pulling . . .

She realized that the pressure of her grip must be hurting him. She released his hand.

"I'm sorry, my darling."

Behind them, more explosions, farther away now. The bat-shaped flying machines were firing into the surrounding forests with that constant chain-rattling noise. The tall, chitinous troopers ran back and forth through the camp—some administering aid to slightly injured human beings, mostly for flash burns.

Harman did not pull his right hand back but held it up toward her face.

Ada tried to hold his hand again, but he batted her hand away with his left hand. She kept her hands still and let him touch her neck, her cheek—he laid the palm flat against her forehead, then used all of his strength to mold his hand to her skull, clutching at her almost desperately.

Before she could even think to pull away, it began.

Nothing, not even the explosion that had just thrown her ten feet backward through the air, had ever struck Ada as this did.

First there was Harman's clear voice—*It's all right, my love, my darling. Relax. It's all right. I must give you this gift while I can.*

And then everything around Ada disappeared except for the pressure from her beloved's damaged hand and bleeding fingers, pouring images in to her—not just to her mind, but filling her with words, memories, images, pictures, data, more memories, functions, quotes, books, entire volumes, more books, more memories, his love for her, his thoughts about her and their child, his love, more information, more voices and names and dates and thoughts and facts and ideas and . . .

"Ada? Ada?" Tom was kneeling over her, splashing water on her face while he gently slapped her face. Hannah, Daeman, and others knelt nearby. Harman had dropped his arm. The little metal-plastic person still fussed over Harman, but her darling looked dead.

Ada stood. "Daeman! Hannah! Come here. Lean close."

"What?" asked Hannah.

Ada shook her head. No time to explain. No time to do anything but share. "Trust me," she said.

She reached out her left and right hands, gripped Daeman's forehead with her left hand, Hannah's with her right, and activated the Sharing function.

It took no more than thirty seconds—no more than the time it had taken for Harman to share the functions and essential data with her, the data he'd spent the hours of his walk west in the Breach compartmentalizing, preparing for transmission—but the thirty seconds seemed like thirty eternities to Ada. If she could have done the next part alone, she wouldn't have bothered, wouldn't have taken the time—not even if the future of the human race depended on it—but she couldn't do the next part alone. She needed one person to continue the Sharing and one person to help her try to save Harman.

It was done.

All three—Ada, Daeman, Hannah—fell to their knees, eyes closed.

"What is it?" asked Siris.

Someone ran shouting into the compound. It was one of their volunteers at the pavilion a mile and a quarter away. The faxnode was working! Just as the voynix were closing in there, shouted the messenger, the faxnode had come alive.

There's no time for the fax pavilion, thought Ada. And nowhere to go among the numbered faxnodes either. Everywhere the humans were in retreat or under direct attack. There was no other place on a known node where her darling could be saved.

The large creature that looked like some sort of giant metallic horseshoe crab was rumbling in English. "There are human rejuvenation tanks in orbit," it was saying. "But the only tanks we know about for certain are on Sycorax's orbital asteroid, and it just passed the moon under full thrust. We're sorry we don't know any other . . ."

"It doesn't matter," said Ada, kneeling next to Harman again. She touched his forearm. There was no reaction but she could feel the last embers of life in him—his biomonitors speaking to her new biometric functions. She was madly sorting through all the thousands of freefax nodes, the freefax function procedures itself.

There were the post-human storage depots in the Mediterranean Basin—they had medicines even for such radiation death—but the depots were sealed in stasis and Ada saw from the allnet monitors that the Hands of Hercules had slowly disappeared, refilling the Mediterranean. She would need machines—submersibles—to get to the depots there. Too long. There were other post storage areas—on the steppes of China, near the Dry Valley in Antarctica . . . but all would take too long to reach and the medical procedures were too complicated. Harman wouldn't live long enough to . . .

Ada grabbed Daeman's arm, pulled him down next to her. The man seemed dazed, transfixed. "All the new functions . . ." he said.

Ada shook him. "Tell me again what the Moira ghost said!"

"What?" Even his stare was unfocused.

"Daeman, tell me again what the Moira ghost said to you on the day that we voted on letting Noman leave. Was it 'Remember . . .' Tell me!"

"Ah . . . she said . . . 'Remember, Noman's coffin was Noman's coffin,' " he said. "How can that . . ."

"No," cried Ada. "The second Noman was meant to be two words. 'Noman's coffin was no man's coffin.' Hannah, you waited while that sarcophagus at the Golden Gate at Machu Picchu cured Odysseus. You've been to the Bridge more often than any of us. Will you go with me? Will you try?"

Hannah took only a second to understand what her friend was asking. "Yes," she said.

"Daeman," said Ada, rushing not only against time, but against Death, who was already among them, who already was holding Harman in his dark claws, "you need to do the Sharing with everyone here. At once."

"Yes," said Daeman, moving away quickly, calling others to him.

The moravec troopers—Ada knew them all now by form if not by name—were still firing around the perimeter, still killing the last of the attacking voynix. Not one voynix had gotten through.

"Hannah," said Ada, "we'll need the litter, but if it doesn't freefax, put Harman's blanket over your shoulder, we'll use that if we have to."

"Hey," cried the small Europan morevac when Hannah roughly pulled the blanket off their dying human patient. "He needs that! He was shivering . . ."

Ada touched the little moravec's arm, felt the humanity and soul even through the metal and plastic. "It's all right," she said at last. She pulled its name—his name—from his cybernetic memory. "Friend Mahnmut, it's all right," she said. "We know what we're doing. After all this time, we finally know what we're doing."

She gestured for the others to stand back.

Hannah knelt on one side of the litter, one of her hands on Harman's shoulder, the other on the metal handle of the litter itself. Ada did the same on her side.

"I think we just visualize that main room—the one where we met Odysseus—and the coordinates come to us," said Ada. "It's important that we've both been there."

"Yes," said Hannah.

"On the count of three?" said Ada. "One, two . . . three."

Both women, the litter, and Harman winked out of existence.

Even though the dying Harman looked as if he weighed nothing, it took all of their strength for the two women to carry him and the litter from the main museum area of the Golden Gate Bridge at Machu Picchu, down several flights of stairs through the green bubble into the sarcophagus area, past Savi's old-time sarcophagus and down the final flight of curved stairs to Odysseus-Noman's coffin.

Ada's palm could find only the slightest flicker of living response when she set her hand against her beloved's ravaged chest, but she did not waste more time in searching for life.

"On the count of three again," she panted.

Hannah nodded.

"One, two . . . three."

They gently lifted the naked Harman out of the litter and lowered his body into Noman's coffin. Hannah pulled the lid down and snapped it shut.

"How do you . . ." began Ada in a panic. She could interrogate all the various machinery here, her new functions told her that, but it would take too long . . .

"Here," said Hannah. "Noman showed me after he revived." Her sculptor's fingers tapped a series of glowing virtual buttons. The old-style human functions interacted with the crèche controls.

The coffin sighed, then began to hum. A mist flowed into the sleeping chamber through unseen vents and hid most of Harman's body from view. Ice crystals formed on the clear cover. Several new lights came on. One winked red.

"Oh!" said Hannah. Her voice was very small.

"No," said Ada. Her tone was calm but firm. "No. No. *No*." She set her palm across the plastic control nexus of the coffin as if she were reasoning with the machine.

The red light winked, changed to amber, switched back to red.

"No," Ada said firmly.

The red light wavered, dimmed, switched to amber. Stayed amber.

Hannah's and Ada's fingers met briefly above the coffin and then Ada returned her palm to the glowing curve of the AI nexus.

The amber light stayed on.

Several hours later, as late afternoon clouds moved in to obscure first the ruins of Machu Picchu and then the roadway of the suspension bridge six hundred feet below them, Ada said, "Hannah, freefax back to Ardis. Get some food. Rest."

Hannah shook her head.

Ada smiled. "Then at least head up to the dining area and get us some fruit or something. Water."

The amber light burned all that afternoon. Just after sundown, as the Andes valleys were bathed in alpenglow, Daeman, Tom, and Siris freefaxed in, but they stayed only a few moments.

"We've already reached thirty of the other communities," Daeman said to Ada. She nodded, but her gaze never left the amber light.

The others eventually faxed away with promises to return in the morning. Hannah pulled the blanket around her and fell asleep there on the floor next to the coffin.

Ada remained—sometimes kneeling, sometimes sitting, but always thinking, and always with her palm on the coffin control nexus, always sending word of her presence and her prayers through the circuits separating her and her Harman, and always with her eyes on the amber monitor light.

Sometime after three a.m. local time, the amber light turned to green.

PART

4

88

One week after the Fall of Ilium:

Achilles and Penthesilea appeared on the empty ridgeline that rose between the Plain of the Scamander and the Plain of the Simois. As Hephaestus promised, there were two horses waiting—a powerful black stallion for the Achaean and a shorter but even more muscular white mare for the Amazon. The two mounted to inspect what was left.

There was not much left.

"How can an entire city like Ilium disappear?" said Penthesilea, her voice as contentious as always.

"All cities disappear," said Achilles. "It is their fate."

The Amazon snorted. Achilles had already noted that the blonde human female's snort was similar to that of her white mare's. "They aren't supposed to disappear in a *day* . . . an *hour*." The comment sounded like a complaint, a lament. Only two days after Penthesilea's resurrection from the Healer's tanks, Achilles was getting used to that constant tone of complaint.

For half an hour they allowed their horses to pick their way through the jumble of rock that stretched for two miles along the ridgeline that once had held mighty Troy. Not a single foundation stone was left. The divine magic that had taken Troy had sheared it off almost a foot beneath the earliest stones of the city. Not so much as a dropped spear or rotting carcass had been left behind.

"Zeus is powerful indeed," said Penthesilea.

Achilles sighed and shook his head. The day was warm. Spring was coming. "I've told you, Amazon. Zeus did not do this. Zeus is dead by my own hand. This is the work of Hephaestus."

The woman snorted. "I'll never believe that little bumbuggering bad-breathed cripple could do something like this. I don't even believe he's a real god."

"He did this," said Achilles. *With Nyx's help,* he mentally added.

"So you say, son of Peleus."

"I told you not to call me that. I am no longer son of Peleus. I was Zeus's son, no credit to him or me."

"So you say," said Penthesilea. "Which would make you a father-killer if your boasts are true."

"Yes," said Achilles. "And I never boast."

Both Amazon and her white mare snorted in unison.

Achilles kicked the ribs of his black stallion and led them down off the ridge, along the rutted south road that had led from the Scaean Gate—the stump of the great oak tree that had always grown there since the creation of the city remained, but the great gates were gone—and then right again onto the Plain of the Scamander that separated the city from the beach.

"If this sad Hephaestus is now king of the gods," said Penthesilea, her voice as loud and irritating as fingernails on a flat, slate rock, "why was he hiding in his cave the whole time we were on Olympos?"

"I told you—he's waiting for the war between the gods and the Titans to end."

"If he's the successor to Zeus, why in Hades doesn't he just end it himself by commanding the lightning and the thunder?"

Achilles said nothing. Sometimes, he had discovered, if he said nothing, she would shut up.

The Scamander Plain—worn smooth over its eleven years as a battlefield—looked as if the ground had not been sheared, there were still the prints of thousands of sandaled men here, and blood dried on the rocks—but all living human beings, horses, chariots, weapons, corpses, and other artifacts had disappeared even as Hephaestus had described it to Achilles. Even the tents of the Achaeans and the burned hulks of their black ships were gone.

Achilles allowed their horses to rest on the beach for a few minutes and both man and Amazon watched the limpid waves of the Aegean roll up on the empty sand. Achilles would never tell the wolf-bitch next to him this, but his heart ached at the thought that he would never see his comrades in arms again—crafty Odysseus, booming big Ajax, the smiling archer Teucer, his faithful Myrmidons, even stupid, red-headed Menelaus and his scheming brother—Achilles' nemesis—Agamemnon. It was strange, Achilles thought, how even one's enemies become so important when they are lost to you.

With that, he thought of Hector and of the things Hephaestus had told him about the *Iliad*—about Achilles' own other future—and this caused the despair to rise in him like bile. He turned his horse's head south and drank from the goatskin of wine tied to the pommel.

"And don't think I will ever believe that the bearded cripple god actually had the ability to make us married," groused Penthesilea from behind him. "That was a load of horse cobblers."

"He's king of all gods," Achilles said tiredly. "Who better to sanctify our wedding vows?"

"He can sanctify my ass," said Penthesilea. "Are we leaving? Why are we heading southeast? What's this way? Why are we leaving the battlefield?"

Achilles said nothing until he reined his horse to a halt fifteen minutes later.

"Do you see this river, woman?"

"Of course I see it. Do you think I'm blind? It's just the lousy Scamander—too thick to drink, too thin to plow—brother of the River Simois which it joins just a few miles upstream."

"Here, at this river we call the Scamander and which the gods call the holy Xanthes," said Achilles, "here according to Hephaestus who quotes my biographer Homer, I would have had my greatest *aristeia*—the combat that would have made me immortal even before I slew Hector. Here, woman, I would have fought the entire Trojan army single-handed—and the swollen, god-raised river itself!—and cried to the heavens, 'Die, Trojans, die! . . . till I butcher all the way to sacred Troy!' Right there, woman, do you see where those low rapids run? Right there I would have slain in a blur of kills Thersilochus, Mydon, Astyplus, Mnesus, Thrasius, Aenius, and Ophelestes. And then the Paeonians would have fallen on me from the rear and I would have killed them all as well. And there, across the river on the Trojan side, I would have killed the ambidexterous Asteropaeus, my one Pelian-ash spearcast to his two. We both miss, but I hack the hero down with my sword while he's trying to wrest my great spear from the riverbank to cast again. . . ."

Achilles stopped. Penthesilea had dismounted and gone behind a bush to urinate. The crude sound of her making water made him want to kill the Amazon then and there and leave her body to the carrion crows that roosted on the creosote bush's branches near the river. The vultures' daily feed of dead flesh evidently had disappeared and Achilles hated to leave them disappointed.

But he could not hurt the Amazon. Aphrodite's love spell still worked on him, leaving his love for this bitch coiling in his guts, as nausea-making as a bronze-tipped spear through the bowels. *Your only hope is that the pheromones may wear off in time,* Hephaestus had said when they were both drunk on wine that last night in the cave, toasting each other and everyone they knew, raising the big two-handled cups and confiding in each other in the way only brothers or drunks can do.

When the Amazon was remounted, Achilles led the way across the

Scamander, the horses stepping carefully. The water was no more than knee deep at its deepest. He turned south.

"Where are we going?" demanded Penthesilea. "Why are we leaving this place? What do you have in mind? Do I get a vote on this or will it always be the mighty Achilles deciding every little thing? Don't think I'll follow you blindly, son of Peleus. I may not follow you at all."

"We're hunting for Patroclus," Achilles said without turning in his saddle.

"What?"

"We're hunting for Patroclus."

"Your friend? That queer-boy fruit friend of yours? Patroclus is dead. Athena killed him. You saw it and said so yourself. You started a war with the gods because of it."

"Hephaestus says that Patroclus is alive," said Achilles. His hand was on the hilt of his sword, his knuckles white, but he did not draw the weapon. "Hephaestus says that he did not include Patroclus in the blue beam when he gathered up all the others on earth, nor when he sent Ilium away forever. Patroclus is alive and out there somewhere over the sea and we shall find him. It shall be my quest."

"Oh, well, *Hephaestus says*," jeered the Amazon. "Whatever *Hephaestus says* has to be true now, doesn't it? The runty crippled bastard couldn't be lying to you, now could he?"

Achilles said nothing. He was following the old road south along the coast, this road that had been trod by so many Trojan-bred horses over the centuries and followed north more recently by so many of the Trojan allies he'd helped to kill.

"And Patroclus out there alive somewhere *over the sea*," parodied Penthesilea. "Just how in Hades' name are we supposed to get over the sea, son of Peleus? And *which sea*, anyway?"

"We'll find a ship," said Achilles without turning to look back at her. "Or build one."

Someone snorted, either the Amazon or her mare. She'd obviously stopped following him—Achilles heard only his own horse's shoes on stone—and she raised her voice so that he could hear her. "What are we now, bleeding shipbuilders? Do *you* know how to build a ship, O fleet-footed mankiller? I *doubt* it. You're good at being fleet-footed and at killing men—and Amazons who are twice your better—not at building anything. I bet you've never built anything in your useless life . . . have you? Have you? Those calluses I see are from holding spears and wine goblets, not from . . . son of Peleus! Are you listening to me?"

Achilles had ridden fifty feet on. He did not look back. Penthesilea's huge white mare stood where she had reined her in, but it now pawed the ground in confusion, wanting to join the stallion ahead.

"Achilles, damn you! Don't just assume that I'm going to follow you! You don't even know where you're going, do you? Admit it!"

Achilles rode on, his eyes fixed on the hazy line of hills on the horizon line near the sea far, far, far to the south. He was getting a terrible headache.

"Don't just take it for granted that . . . gods damn you!" shouted Penthesilea as Achilles and his stallion kept moving slowly away, a hundred yards now. The bastard son of Zeus did not look back.

One of the vultures on the shrub-tree by the holy Xanthes flapped its way into the sky, circling the now-empty battlefield once, its kin-of-the-eagle eye noting that not even the ashes of the corpse fires—usually a place to find a midday morsel—remained.

The vulture flapped south. It circled three thousand feet over the two living horses and human beings—the only ground-living things visible as far as the far-seeing carrion bird could see—and, ever hopeful, it decided to follow them.

Far below, the white horse and its human burden remained unmoving while the black horse and its man clopped south. The vulture watched, hearing but ignoring the unpleasant noises the rearward human was making as the white horse was suddenly spurred into motion and galloped to catch up.

Together, the white horse trailing only slightly, the two horses and two humans headed south along the curve of the Aegean and—lazing easily on the strong thermals of the warming afternoon—the vulture followed hopefully.

89

Nine days after the Fall of Ilium:

General Beh bin Adee personally led the attack on Paris Crater, using the dropship as his command center while more than three hundred of his best Beltvec troopers roped and repellored down into the blue-ice-hive city from six hornet fighters.

General bin Adee had not been in favor of joining this fight on

Earth—his advice had been to choose no one's side—but the Prime Integrators had decided and their decision was final. His job was to find and destroy the creature named Setebos. General bin Adee's advice then had been to nuke the blue-ice cathedral above Paris Crater from orbit—it was the only way to be sure to get the Setebos thing, he'd explained—but the Prime Integrators had rejected his advice.

Millennion Leader Mep Ahoo led the primary assault team. After the other ten teams had roped down and blasted through the outer surface of the blue-iced city, establishing a perimeter and confirming it over tactical comm—the thing could not escape now—Mep Ahoo and his twenty-five picked rockvec troopers jumped from the primary hornet hovering at three thousand meters, activated their repellors at just the last second, used shaped charges to blow a hole in the roof of the blue-ice cathedral dome, and roped in—their fastlines anchored from pitons driven into the blue ice itself.

"It's empty," radioed Millennion Leader Mep Ahoo. "No Setebos."

General bin Adee could see that himself on the images sent back from the twenty-six troopers' nanotransmitters and suitcams. "Grid and search," he commanded on the prime tactical band.

Reports were coming in now from all perimeter teams. The blue-ice itself was rotten—a fist could collapse an entire tunnel wall. The tunnels and corridors had already begun to collapse.

Mep Ahoo's team returned to repellor flight and flew their grid search in the cavernous central place over the ancient black hole crater itself. They started high—making sure that nothing was hiding in one of the blue-ice balconies or high crevices—but soon were swooping low over the fumaroles and abandoned secondary nests.

"The main nest has collapsed," reported Mep Ahoo on the common tactical channel. "Fallen into the old black hole crater. I'm sending images."

"We see them," replied General Beh bin Adee. "Is there any chance the Setebos creature could be in the black hole vent itself?"

"Negative, sir. We're deep radaring the crater now and it goes all the way to magma. No side vents or caverns. I think it's gone, sir."

Cho Li's voice came over the common band. "It confirms our theory that the quantum event of four days ago was an opening of a final Brane Hole in the blue-ice cathedral itself."

"Let's be sure," said General Beh bin Adee. On the tactical command tightbeam, he sent to Mep Ahoo—*Check all nests.*

Affirmative.

Six rockvecs from Mep Ahoo's primary assault force checked the collapsed ruins of Setebos's central nest, then fanned out, repelloring above the collapsing cathedral floor to look at each decaying fumarole and sagging nest.

Suddenly there was a cry from one of the perimeter teams that had just penetrated to the central dome. "Something written here, sir."

Half a dozen other troopers, including Millennion Leader Mep Ahoo, converged on the point high on the south wall of the dome. There was a terrace there where the largest corridor entered the dome, and in the wall of the dome where the corridor widened into the so-called cathedral, something or someone had written in the blue ice, using what appeared to be fingernails or claws—*Thinketh, the Quiet comes. His dam holds that the Quiet made all things which Setebos vexes only, but He holds not so. Who made them weak, meant weakness He might vex. But thinketh, why then is Setebos here then vexed to flight? Thinketh, can Strength ever be vexed to Flight by Weakness? Thinketh, is He the only One after all? The Quiet comes.*

"Caliban," said Prime Integrator Asteague/Che from the *Queen Mab* in its new geosynchronous orbit.

"Sir, tunnels and caverns all checked and reported empty," came a Centurion Leader's report on the common tactical channel.

"Very good," said General Beh bin Adee. "Prepare to use the thermite charges to melt the whole blue-ice complex down to the original Paris Crater ruins. Make sure none of the original structures will be damaged. We'll search them next."

Something here, said Mep Ahoo on the tactical tightbeam. The images flowing into the dropship monitors showed the troopers' chest searchlights falling on a tumbled fumarole nest. All of the eggs in that nest had burst open or collapsed inward . . . all except one. The Millennion Leader repellored down, crouched next to the egg, set his black-gloved hands on the thing, then set his head against it, actually listening.

I think there's something still alive in here, sir, reported Mep Ahoo. "Orders?"

Stand by, barked General Beh bin Adee. On his tightbeam to the *Queen Mab,* he said, *Orders?*

"Stand by," said the bridge officer speaking for the Prime Integrators.

Finally Prime Integrator Asteageu/Che came on the line. "What is your advice, General?"

"Burn it. Burn everything there . . . twice."

"Thank you, General. One second, please."

There was a silence broken only by slight static. Bin Adee could hear the breathing of his three hundred and ten troopers over their suit microphones.

"We would like the egg to be collected," Prime Integrator Asteague/Che said at last. "Use one of the stasis-cubes if feasible. Hornet Nine should shuttle it up. Have Millennion Leader Mep Ahoo stay with the egg on Hornet Nine. We shall use the *Queen Mab* itself as a quarantine laboratory. The *Mab* has divested itself of all weapons and fissionable material . . . the stealthed attack cruisers will monitor our study of the egg."

General Beh bin Adee was silent a few seconds and then said, "Very well." He opened the tightbeam to Millennion Leader Mep Ahoo and relayed the orders. The team in the blue-ice cathedral already had a stasis-cube ready.

Mep Ahoo sent, *Are you sure about this, sir? We know from Ada and the Ardis survivors what their Setebos baby was capable of. Even the unhatched egg had some power. I doubt if Setebos left one viable egg behind by accident.*

"Implement the orders," said General Beh bin Adee on the common tactical band. Then he opened his private tightbeam to Mep Ahoo and sent—*"And good luck, son."*

Six months after the Fall of Ilium, on the Ninth of Av:

Daeman was in charge of the raid on Jerusalem. It had been carefully planned.

One hundred fully functioned old-style humans freefaxed in at the same second, arriving three minutes before four moravec hornets carrying a hundred more volunteers from Ardis and other survivor-communities. The moravec soldiers had offered their services for this raid months earlier, but Daeman had vowed a year ago that he would free the old-style humans locked in Jerusalem's blue beam—all of Savi's ancient friends and Jewish relatives—and he still felt it was a human responsibility to do so. They had, however, accepted the long-term loan of combat suits, repellor backpacks, impact armor, and energy weapons. The hundred men and women in the hornets—piloted by moravecs who would not otherwise join the fight—were bringing in the weapons too heavy to carry in during freefax.

It had taken Daeman and his team—humans and moravecs alike—more than three weeks to check and double-check the specific GPS coordinates of the old city streets, avenues, plazas, and junctions down to the inch in order to plot the hundred freefax arrival areas and designated landing sites for the hornets.

They waited until August, until the Jewish holiday of the Ninth of Av. Daeman and his volunteers freefaxed in ten minutes after sunset, when the blue beam was at its brightest.

As far as the *Queen Mab*'s surveillance and aerial reconnaissance could tell them, Jerusalem was unique of all places on Earth in that it was inhabited by both voynix and *calibani*. In the Old City, which was their target tonight, the voynix occupied the streets north and northwest of the Temple Mount, in areas roughly equivalent to the ancient Muslim and Christian Quarters, and the *calibani* filled the tight streets and buildings to the southwest of the Dome of the Rock and Al-Aksa Mosque in areas once called the Jewish Quarter and the Armenian Quarter.

From the spy images—including deep radar—they estimated there were about twenty thousand combined voynix and *calibani* in Jerusalem.

"Hundred to one odds," Greogi had said with a shrug. "We've had worse."

They faxed in almost silently, a mere disturbance in the air. Daeman and his team appeared in the narrow plaza in front of the Kotel . . . the Western Wall. It was still light enough to see, but Daeman used his thermal imaging and deep radar in addition to his eyes to find targets. He estimated that there were around five hundred *calibani* lounging, sleeping, standing, and milling just in the space and on the walls and rooftops immediately west of the plaza. Within seconds, all of his ten squad commanders had checked in over the combat suit intercoms.

"Fire at will," he said.

The energy weapons had been programmed to disrupt only living tissue—*calibani* or voynix—but not to destroy real estate. As Daeman targeted and fired, watching the running, leaping long-clawed *calibani* go down or erupt into thousands of fleshy pieces, he was glad for that. They didn't want to destroy this particular village in order to save it.

The Old City of Jerusalem became a maelstrom of blue energy flashes, *calibani* screams, shouted radio calls, and exploding flesh.

Daeman and his squad had killed every target they could see when he saw by his visor chronometer that it was time for the hornets to arrive. He triggered his repellor pack and rose to the level of the Temple Mount—Daeman was alone, this was no time to have the air full of people—and watched as the first two hornets swept in, landed, disgorged their people and cargoes, and then swooped out. Thirty seconds later, the last two hornets had arrived and the combat-suited men and women were spilling across the stones of the Mount, carrying their heavy weapons on tripods and repellor blocks. The two hornets swooped away.

"Temple Mount secured," Daeman radioed to all his squad leaders. "You may fly when ready. Stay out of the set lines of fire from the Mount."

"Daeman?" sent Elian from his position above Bab al-Nazir in the old Muslim Quarter. "I can see masses of voynix coming up the Via Dolorosa and bunches of *calibani* coming your way east on King David Street."

"Thanks, Elian. Deal with them as they arrive. The larger guns may engage as . . ."

Daeman was deafened by heavy weapons' fire from the Mount just beneath his feet. The humans all along the walls and rooftops there were firing in all directions toward the advancing gray and green figures. Between the vertical blue beam and the thousands of blue-flashes of energy weapon fire, all of Old Jerusalem was bathed in an arc-welding blue glow. The filters on Daeman's combat suit goggles actually dimmed a bit.

"All squads, fire at will, report any penetration in your sectors," said Daemon. He tilted on the hovering backpack repellors and then slid through the air to the northeast to where the taller, more modern blue-beam building rose just behind the Dome of the Rock. He was interested to find that his heart was pounding so wildly that he had to concentrate on not hyperventilating. They'd practiced this five hundred times over the past two months, freefaxing into the mock-up of Jerusalem that the moravecs had helped them build not far from Ardis. But nothing could have prepared Daeman for a fight of this magnitude, with these weapons, in this city of all cities.

Hannah and her squad of ten were waiting for him when he arrived at the beam building's sealed door. Daeman landed, nodded at Laman, Kaman, and Greogi, who were there in the soft twilight with Hannah, and said, "Let's do it."

Laman, working quickly with his undamaged left hand, set the plastic explosive charge. The twelve humans stepped around the side of the metal-alloy building while the explosion took the entire door off.

The inside was not much larger than Daeman's tiny bedroom back at Ardis and the controls were—thank whatever God might be out there—almost as they'd surmised from reviewing all Shared data available from the Taj Moira's crystal cabinet.

Hannah did the actual work, her deft fingers flying over the virtual keyboard, tapping in the seven-digit codes whenever queried by the blue-beam building's primitive AI.

Suddenly a deep hum—mostly subsonic—rattled their teeth and bruised their bones. All of the displays on the AI wall flashed green and then died.

"Everyone out," said Daeman. He was the last one to leave the beam-building's anteroom, and not a second too soon—the anteroom, the metal wall, and that entire side of the building folded into itself twice and disappeared, becoming a black rectangle.

Daeman, Hannah, and the others had backed down onto the stones of the Temple Mount itself, and now they watched as the blue beam dropped from the sky, the hum growing deeper as it died—painfully so. Daeman found himself shutting his eyes and gripping his hands into fists, feeling the dying subsonics through his gut and testicles as well as his bones and teeth. Then the low noise stopped.

He pulled his combat suit cowl off, earphones and microphone still in place, and said to Hannah, "Defensive perimeter here. As soon as the first person is out, call in the hornets."

She nodded and joined the others where they were facing and firing outward from the high Temple Mount.

At some time during the preparation for this night, someone—it might have been Ada—had joked that it would only be polite that Daeman and the other raiders should memorize the faces and names of all of the 9,113 men and women captured in that blue beam fourteen hundred years ago. Everyone laughed, but Daeman knew it would have been technically possible; the crystal cabinet in the Taj Moira had given Harman much of that data.

So over the past five months since they'd decided how and when to do this, Daeman *had* referred to those stored images and names. He hadn't memorized all 9,113 of them—he, like all the survivors, had been far too busy for that—but he was not surprised when he recognized the first man and woman to come stumbling out of that black-rectangle door from the neutrino-tachyon beam reassembler.

"Petra," said Daeman. "Pinchas. Welcome back." He grabbed the slim man and woman before they could fall. Everyone emerging from the black door, two by two like the animals from Noah's ark Daeman had time to notice, looked more stunned than sensible.

The dark-haired woman named Petra—a friend of Savi's, Daeman knew—looked around in a drugged way and said, "How long?"

"Too long," said Daeman. "Right this way. Toward that ship, please."

The first hornet had landed, carrying another thirty old-styles whose job was just to accompany and help load the long lines of returning human beings. Daeman watched as Stefe came up and led Petra and Pinchas across the ancient stones toward the hornet ramp.

Daeman greeted everyone coming down the ramp from the beam building, recognizing many on sight—third was the man named Graf, his partner who was also named Hannah, one of Savi's friends named Stephen, Abe, Kile, Sarah, Caleb, William . . . Daeman greeted them all by name and helped them the few steps to those others waiting to help them to the hornets.

The voynix and *calibani* kept attacking. The humans kept killing them. In the rehearsals, it had taken them more than forty-five minutes—on a good evening—to load 9,113 people onto hornets, even given only seconds between one hornet being loaded and leaving and the next arriving—but this evening, while under attack, they did it in thirty-three minutes.

"All right," said Daeman on all channels. "Everyone off the Temple Mount."

The heavy-weapons teams lugged their equipment into the last two hornets where they hovered near the east edge of the Mount. Then those hornets were gone—following the dozens of others to the west—and it was just Daeman and his original squads.

"Three or four thousand fresh voynix coming from the direction of the Church of the Sepulchre," reported Elian.

Daeman pulled his cowl on and chewed his lip. It would be harder to kill the things with the heavy weapons gone. "All right," he said over the command channel. "This is Daeman. Fax out . . . now. Squad leaders, report when your squads have freefaxed away."

Greogi reported his squad gone and faxed away.

Edide reported and faxed away from her position on Bab al-Hadid Street.

Boman reported his squad gone from their position on Bab al-Ghawanima and then Boman was gone.

Loes reported from near the Lions Gate and flicked out.

Elle reported from the Garden Gate and was gone.

Kaman reported his squad successfully faxed away—Kaman seemed to be enjoying this military stuff too much, Daeman thought—and then Kaman redundantly requested permission to freefax home.

"Get your ass out of here," radioed Daeman.

Oko reported her squad gone and followed them.

Caul reported in from below the Al-Aksa Mosque and flicked out.

Elian reported in, squad freefaxed home, and faxed himself away.

Daeman got his squad together, Hannah included, and watched as they flicked away, one at a time, from the growing shadows of the Western Wall Plaza.

He knew that everyone was gone, that the beam building had been emptied, but he had to check.

Tapping the repellor-pack's controls on his palm with his middle finger, Daeman flew up, circled the beam building, looked in the empty beam building's doorway to emptiness beyond, circled the empty Dome of the Rock and empty plaza, and then flew lower, wider circles, checking all the points in all four quarters of the Old City where his squads had held the perimeter while not losing a single human to the voynix and *calibani* attacks.

He knew he should go—the voynix and *calibani* were rushing in through the ancient, narrow streets like water into a holed ship—but he also knew why he was staying.

The thrown rock almost took his head off. The combat suit's radar saved him—picking up the hurled object, invisible in the twilight gloom, and overriding the backpack's controls, sending Daeman dipping legs and feet over ass, righting him just yards above the pavement of the Temple Mount.

He landed, activating all of his impact armor and raising his energy rifle. All of his suit senses and all of his human senses told him that the large, not-quite-human shape standing in the black doorway of the Dome of the Rock was no mere *calibani*.

"Daemannnnnn," moaned the thing.

Daeman walked closer, rifle raised, ignoring the suit's targeting system's imperative to fire, trying to control his own breathing and thoughts.

"Daemannnnn," the oversized amphibious shape in the doorway sighed. "Thinketh, even so, thou wouldst have Him misconceive, suppose this Caliban strives hard and ails no less, would you have him hurt?"

"I would have him *dead*," shouted Daeman. His body was quivering with old rage. He could hear the rasp and scrape of thousands of voynix and *calibani* scuttling and scurrying beneath the Mount. "Come out and fight, Caliban."

The shadow laughed. "Thinketh, human hopes the while that evil sometimes must mend as warts rub away and sores are cured with slime, yessssss?"

"Come out and fight me, Caliban."

"Conceiveth, will he put his little rifle down and meet the acolyte of Him in fair fight, hand and claw to hand and claw?"

Daeman hesitated. He knew there would be no fair fight. A thousand voynix and *calibani* would be up here on the Temple Mount in ten seconds. He could hear the scrabbling and scratching in the Western Wall Plaza and on the steps already. He raised the rifle and clicked the targeting to Auto, hearing the target-confirmed tone in his earphones.

"Thinketh, Daemannnnnn will not shoot, noo," moaned Caliban in the Dome of the Rocks' doorshadows. "He loveth Caliban and his lord Setebos as enemies too much to draw—O! O!—a curtain o'er their world at once, yesss? Nooo? Daeman must wait for another day to let the wind shoulder the pillared dust, to meet death's house o' the move and . . ."

Daeman fired. He fired again.

Voynix leaped to the walls of the Temple Mount in front of him. *Calibani* scrambled up the steps of the Temple Mount behind him. It was dark now in Jerusalem, even the blue beam's glow—constant for one thousand four hundred and twenty-one years—had gone out. The monsters owned the city once again.

Daeman didn't have to look through the rifle's thermal sites to know that he had missed—that Caliban had quantum teleported away. He would have to face the thing some other day or night, in a situation much less advantageous to him than today's.

Strangely, secretly, in his heart of hearts, Daeman was happy at this thought.

Voynix and *calibani* both leaped across the ancient stones of the Temple Mount at him.

A second before their claws could reach him, Daeman freefaxed home to Ardis.

Seven and a half months after the Fall of Ilium:

Alys and Ulysses—his friends called him Sam—told their parents they were going to the Lakeshore Drive-in to watch the double feature of *To Kill a Mockingbird* and *Dr. No*. It was October and the Lakeshore was the only drive-in movie theater still open since it had portable in-car heaters on the stands as well as speakers, and usually, or at least in the four months since Sam had gotten his solo driver's permit, the drive-in movie had sufficed for their passion, but tonight, this special night, they drove out through fields of harvest-ready corn to a private place at the end of a long lane.

"What if Mom and Dad ask me about the plot of the movies?" asked Alys. She was wearing the usual white blouse, tan sweater loose over her shoulders, dark skirt, stockings, and rather formal shoes for a drive-in movie date. Her hair was tied back in a ponytail.

"You know about the book *To Kill a Mockingbird*. Just tell them that Gregory Peck is good as Atticus Finch."

"*Is* he Atticus Finch?"

"Who else could he be?" said Sam. "The Negro?"

"What about the other movie?"

"It's a spy movie about some British guy . . . James Bond, I think the guy's name is. The president likes the book the movie is based on. Just tell your dad that it was exciting, full of shooting and stuff."

Sam parked his dad's 1957 Chevy Bel Air at the end of the lane, beyond the ruins and in sight of the lake. They'd driven past the Lakeshore Drive-in and around the oversized pond that provided the "lake" for the theater's name. Far across the water, Sam could see the small rectangle of white that was the drive-in movie screen and beyond that the glow of their little town's lights against the low October sky, and much farther beyond that, the brighter glow of the real city to and from which their fathers commuted each day. Once upon a time, probably back during the Depression, there'd been a farm at the end of this lane, but now the house was gone—only overgrown foundations remaining, those and the trees lining the driveway in. The trees were losing their leaves. It was getting chilly as it got closer to Halloween.

"Can you leave the motor on?" asked Alys.

"Sure." Sam started the engine again.

They began kissing almost immediately. Sam pulled the girl to him, set his left hand on her right breast, and within seconds their mouths were warm and open and wet, their tongues busy. They'd discovered this pleasure only this summer.

He fumbled with the buttons of her blouse. The buttons were too small and they went the wrong way. She let the loose sweater fall and helped him with the most troublesome button, the one under her soft, curved collars. "Did you watch the president's speech tonight on TV?"

Sam didn't want to talk about the president. Leaving the lowest buttons on her blouse buttoned, breathing rapidly, he slipped his hand inside her loose blouse and cupped her breast in its rather stiff little brassiere.

"Did you?" asked Alys.

"Yeah. We all did."

"Do you think there's going to be war?"

"Naw," said Sam. He kissed her again, trying to bring her back to the passion at hand, but her tongue had gone into hiding.

When they broke apart long enough for her to pull the tails of her blouse out of her skirt, dropping the shirt behind her—her body and bra pale in the dim reflected light from the sky and in the yellow glow of the dashboard radio and dials—she said, "My father says it could mean war."

"It's just a lousy *quarantine*," said Sam, both arms around her, his fingers fumbling with the still-strange hooks and eyes of her brassiere. "It's not like we're *invading* Cuba or anything," he added. He couldn't get the damned thing loose.

Alys smiled in the soft light, put her hands behind her, and the bra miraculously fell free.

Sam began nuzzling and kissing her breasts. They were very young breasts—larger and firmer than an adolescent girl's little bud breasts, but still not fully formed. The areolae were as puffy as the nipples; Sam noticed this in the light from the radio dial, and then he lowered his flushed face to nuzzle and suck again.

"Easy, easy!" said Alys. "Not so rough. You're always so rough."

"Sorry," said Sam. He began kissing her again. This time her lips were warm, her tongue was present . . . and busy. He felt himself getting more excited as he pressed her back toward the passenger door of the Bel Air. The front seat was wider and deeper and softer than the davenport in their parlor at home. He had to wiggle to get out from under the giant steering wheel and he had to be careful—even here at the end of Miller's Lane, he didn't want to accidentally honk the horn.

Lying half atop her, his erection pressing against her left leg, his hands busy on her breasts and his tongue busy finding her tongue, Sam became so excited that he almost ejaculated the first instant she set her long fingers on his corduroyed thigh.

"But what if the Russians *do* attack?" Alys whispered when he raised his face for a moment to breathe. The car was too damned hot. He turned off the ignition with his left hand.

"Stop that," he said. He knew what she was doing. She'd chosen the track and line. She wanted him thinking about which one it might be. He wanted only to appreciate what the boy-Sam was thinking and feeling.

"Ouch," said Alys. He had pressed her back so that her shoulders were against the large door handle. He was lowering his face toward her for more kissing when she whispered, "Do you want to get in the backseat?"

Sam could hardly breathe. That phrase had been their signal the last weeks for the serious stuff—not just getting to third base, which he had several times now with Alys, but going all the way, which they'd come close to twice but not quite achieved.

Alys went around her side—prissily pulling her blouse on, but not buttoning it again, he noticed—and Sam went around the driver's side. The overhead light came on until they'd secured both the rear doors. Sam rolled his window down a bit so that he could have some air—he still seemed to be having a problem breathing normally—and also so he could hear any car approaching down Miller's Lane in case Barney happened to come down here in his old black-and-white police cruiser left over from before the War.

The two had to get reintroduced all over again, but within moments, he had his shirt open to feel her breasts against his chest and Alys sprawled lengthwise on the wide seat, him half on her, half falling off, her legs partially raised and his bent strangely because they were both taller than the backseat was wide.

He slipped his right hand up her leg, feeling her own warm breath come more quickly on his cheek when he paused in kissing her. She was wearing stockings. Sam had never felt anything so soft. He felt the garter where the nylon stockings attached to the . . .

"Oh, come on," said Ulysses, laughing and speaking through the boy despite himself. "This has to be an anachronism."

Alys smiled up at him and he saw the real woman through the girl's dilated pupils. "It's not," she whispered, giving him the full length of her tongue now and sliding her hand down, rubbing his erection through the slightly dampened corduroy. "Honest," she said, still rubbing him. "It's called a panty girdle and it's what she wears. Pantyhose haven't been invented yet."

"Shut up," said Sam, closing his eyes as he kissed her and pressed his lower body against her playing hand. "Shut up, please."

He couldn't get the metal ring out from around the round snap-stud that she later explained was called the "garter"—it just wouldn't move. Sam kept moving his hand from between her legs—where the fabric was wet, he was sure he could feel her warming to him through the fabric— back to the goddamned sonofabitching garter thing.

Alys giggled. "I can take the whole thing off," she whispered.

As she did so, Sam realized that they needed more room. He opened his driver's side rear door—the light blinded them—

"Sam!"

He reached up and switched off the overhead light. For a minute neither of them moved, two deer blinded in headlights, but when he could hear the wind through the late-autumn leaves over the pounding of his heart, he leaned over her again.

The distraction had kept him from coming too soon. He tasted her lips, lowered his face to her breasts, and licked softly. She pulled his head closer. Her hand went lower, expertly undid his belt, unsnapped the top snap, and tugged the zipper down too quickly for his piece of mind.

He emerged unscathed and throbbing.

"Sam?" she whispered as he levitated into position above her. Her stockings and underpants were in a bunch under his knee. He almost panted as he shoved her skirt higher.

"What?"

"Did you bring . . . you know . . . a thing?"

"Oh, fuck *that*," he snapped through the boy's voice, not even pretending to be in character.

She giggled but he stopped that noise with an openmouthed kiss. His heart threatened to break through his ribs as he shifted his weight and she opened her legs to him. He caught a glimpse of her dark skirt riding up almost to her bare breasts, of her pale thighs, of the vertical rather than triangular floss of darkness there between her thighs . . .

"Easy," whispered Alys as she reached down and found him. She cupped his scrotum expertly, ran her fingers up the length of his penis, captured the glans with her fingertips. "Easy, Odysseus," she purred.

"I am . . . Noman," he whispered between pants. She was positioning him. The preseminal fluid at the tip of his penis was dampening her thighs as she maneuvered him to the best angle. He could feel the heat flow out of her.

She squeezed him—hard enough to make him gasp but not hard enough to make the sixteen-year-old him come. "How can you say that," she whispered into his mouth, "when *this* proves otherwise?"

Alys set the swollen head of his penis against her moist and tight labia, then moved her hand up against his cheek. Sam caught the scent of her excitement on her own fingers and that alone almost made him come. He hesitated this perfect second before continuing.

The flash came from directly ahead of the car, beyond the drive-in movie screen, and it was not brighter than a thousand suns, it was brighter than ten thousand suns. It turned everything in the musky darkness into a photographic negative—all black-blacks and pure whites. There was no noise, not yet.

"You *have* to be kidding," he said, poised above Alys as if he was doing push-ups, with only the tip of his erection touching her right now.

"The city's forty miles away," whispered Alys, pulling him down, trying to pull him. "We have a long time until the shock wave gets here. A *long* time." She gave him her mouth and set her hands solidly on his back and butt, pulling him closer.

He considered resisting. To what purpose? This boy-Sam was so excited that two or three thrusts in his beloved's perfect, virginal cunt would probably be all he could take before he exploded anyway. The incinerating shock wave and their youthful orgasms would probably arrive at the same instant. Which, he realized, was almost certainly just as his ageless beloved had planned it.

The light was fading some, still bright, bright enough to illuminate sixteen-year-old Alys's slight dusting of purple eye shadow, and seeing that made him lower his face to hers for a final hot kiss as he began thrusting forward and in.

92

One year after the Fall of Ilium:

Helen of Troy awoke just after dawn to a dream-memory of the sound of air raid sirens. She felt along the cushions of her bed, but her lover Hockenberry was gone—had been gone for more than a month now—and it was only the memory of his warmth that made her hunt for him each morning. She had yet to take another lover, although half the Trojans and Argives left here in New Ilium wanted her.

She had her slave-women, Hypsipyle included, bathe and perfume her. Helen took her time. These apartments in the rebuilt section near the Pillar House near the fallen Scaean Gate were no comparison to her former palace, but the amenities of life were beginning to return. She used the last of her well-rationed scented soap in the bath. Today was a special day. The Joint Council would be deciding on the expedition to Delphi. She had the slave girls dress her in her finest green silk gown and gold necklaces for the morning Council meeting.

It was still strange to see the Argives, Achaeans, Myrmidons, and other invaders in the Trojan council house. Both the Temple of Athena and the larger Temple of Apollo had crumbled that day of the Fall, but the Trojan and Greek masons had erected a new palace where the rubble of Athena's temple had once been, just north of the main avenue and not far from where Priam's palace had stood with its proud porches and pillars before the gods had bombed it into oblivion.

This new palace—they had no other name for their central civic building—still smelled of fresh wood, cold stone, and paint, but it was bright and sunny this early spring day. Helen slipped in and took her place near the royal family, next to Andromache, who gave her a brief smile and then turned her attention back to her husband.

Hector was getting some gray in his dark-brown curly hair and beard. Everyone had noticed it. Most of the women, Helen knew, thought it made him look even more distinguished, if such a thing were possible. It was Hector's place to open the meeting and he did so now, welcoming all the Trojan dignitaries and Achaean guests by name.

Agamemnon was here, still strange, occasionally giving everyone that long, unfocused gaze he had worn for so many months after the Fall, but he was lucid enough now to be heeded in the Joint Council discussions. And his tents were still full of treasure.

Nestor was here, but he had to be carried to the city—carried up from the tent-city of the Achaeans, undefended now on the beach—on a portable chair toted by four slaves. Wise old Nestor had never recovered the use of his legs after that final day of terrible battle on the beach. Also here from the Achaean camp—sixty thousand Greek warriors still lived, enough to demand a vote—were Little Ajax, Idomeneus, Polyxinus, Teucer, and the acknowledged, if not yet publicly acclaimed, leader of the Greeks—handsome Thrasymedes, Nestor's son. With the Greeks were several men whom Helen did not recognize, including a tall, gangly young man with curly hair and beard.

At his introduction and welcome by Nestor, Thrasymedes glanced in the direction of Helen and Helen lowered her eyes in modesty while allowing herself to blush slightly. Some habits died hard, even here on a different world and in a different time.

Finally Nestor introduced their emissary from Ardis—not Hockenberry, who had not yet returned from his trip west, but a tall, thin, quiet man named Boman. No moravecs were present this morning.

Having finished the welcomings, unnecessary introductions, and ritual words of assembly, Hector established the reasons for this council and what needed to be decided before they could adjourn.

"So today we must decide whether to launch the expedition to Delphi," concluded noble Hector, "and, if we do so, who shall go and who shall stay. We also have to decide what to do if it is possible to interdict the blue beam there and bring so many of the Argives' relatives back. Thrasymedes, your people were in charge of building the long ships. Would you tell the Council what progress has been made?"

Thrasymedes bowed, his knee raised slightly on a step and his golden helmet on his leg. He said, "As you know, our best surviving shipbuilder, Harmonides—literally 'Son of the Fitter'—has been in charge of the construction. I shall let him report."

Harmonides, the curly-bearded youth Helen had spotted a minute earlier, now stepped forward a few paces and then quickly looked down at his feet as if he wished he hadn't made himself so conspicuous. He had a slight stammer as he spoke.

"The . . . thirty long ships are . . . ready. Each can . . . carry . . . fifty men, their armor, and provisions adequate for . . . reaching Delphi. We are also close to . . . to completing . . . the twenty other ships . . . as commanded by the Council. These ships are . . . broader of beam . . . than the long ships, perfect for . . . for transporting goods and people should we find such . . . goods and people."

Harmonides quickly stepped back into the group of Argives.

"Very good work, noble Harmonides," said Hector. "We thank you and the Council thanks you. I've inspected the ships and they are beautiful—tight, firm, made with precision."

"And I wish to thank the Trojans for knowing where to find the best wood on the slopes of Mount Ida," spoke up the blushing Harmonides, but with pride this time, and no hint of a stammer.

"So we now have ships to make the voyage," said Hector. "Since the missing families on the mainland are Achaean and Argive, not Trojan, Thrasymedes has volunteered to lead the expedition back to Delphi. Would you tell us, Thrasymedes, your plans for that voyage?"

Tall Thrasymedes lowered his leg, holding his heavy helmet easily in one palm, Helen noticed.

"We propose to sail in the next week when the spring winds bless our voyage," said Thrasymedes, his low, strong voice carrying to the far ends of the large, pillared Council chamber. "All thirty ships and fifteen hundred picked men—Trojan adventurers are still invited if they want to see the world."

There was some chuckling and good humor in the room.

"We shall sail south along the coast past empty Colonae," continued Thrasymedes, "then to Lesbos, then across dark waters to Chios, where we shall hunt and lay in fresh water. Then west-southwest across the deep sea, past Andros, and into the Genestius Strait between Catsylus on the peninsula and the isle of Ceos. Here, five of our ships will break away and sail upriver toward Athens, the men crossing on foot for the last way. They will hunt for human life there, and if they find none—they shall march to Delphi on foot, their ships returning and sailing past the Saronic Gulf after us.

"The twenty-five ships remaining to me shall sail southwest past Lacedaemonia, circumnavigating the entire Peloponnese, braving the straits between Cytherea and the mainland if the weather allows. When we spot Zacynthros off our port bows, we will approach the mainland once again, then east-northeast and east again deep into the Corinthian Gulf. Just past Cyolain Locrians and before we reach Boeotia, we shall sail into harbor, beach our boats, and walk to Delphi, where the moravecs and our Ardis friends assure us the blue-beam temple holds the living remnants of our race."

The person named Boman stepped into the center of the open space. His Greek was horribly accented—much more so even than old Hockenberry's had been, thought Helen—and he sounded as much the barbarian as he dressed, but he made himself understood despite syntactical errors that would make the mentor of a three-year-old blush.

"It is a good time of year for this," said Boman, the tall Ardisian. "The problem is—if you do follow our procedures for bringing back the people trapped in the blue beam, what do you do with them? It's possible that the entire population of Ilium-Earth was coded there—up to six million people—including Chinese, Africans, American Indians, pre-Aztecs . . ."

"Excuse me," interrupted Thrasymedes. "We do not understand these words, Boman, son of Ardis."

The tall man scratched his cheek. "Do you understand the idea of six million?"

No one did. Helen wondered if this Ardisian was fully sane.

"Imagine thirty Iliums, when its population was at its height," said Boman. "That is how many people may come out of the Temple of the Blue Beam."

Most in the Council chambers laughed. Helen noticed that neither Hector nor Thrasymedes did.

"This is why we're going to be there to help," said Boman. "We believe that you can repatriate your own people—the Greeks—with little problem. Of course, the houses and cities, temples and animals are gone, but there's much wild game and you can breed the domesticated animal population up again in no time . . ."

Boman paused because most of the people were laughing or tittering again. Hector gestured for the Ardisian to continue, without explaining his error. The tall man had used the word for "fuck," as it applies only to humans, when he had talked of breeding up the number of domesticated animals. Helen found herself amused.

"Anyway, we'll be there and the moravecs will provide transport home for those . . . foreigners." He used the proper word, "barbarians," but he obviously wanted another one.

"Thank you," said Hector. "Thrasymedes, if all your many peoples are there—from the Peloponnese, from the many islands such as Odysseus' little Ithaca, from Attica and Boeotia and Molossi and Obestae and Chaldice and Bottiaei and Thrace, all the other areas your far-flung Greeks call home, what will you do then? You will have all those people in one place, but no cities, oxen, homes, or shelters."

Thrasymedes nodded. "Noble Hector, our plan will be to dispatch five ships back to New Ilium immediately to inform you of our success. The rest of us shall stay with those freed from the blue beam at Delphi, organizing safe trips for families back to their homelands, finding a way to feed and shelter everyone until order is established."

"That might take years," said Deiphobus. Hector's brother had never been a fan of the Delphi Expedition.

"It may well take years," agreed Thrasymedes. "But what else is there to do but attempt to free our wives, mothers, grandfathers, children, slaves, and servants? It is our duty."

"The Ardisian could fax there in a minute and free them in two," came the resentful voice from the couch where he sat. Agamemnon.

Boman stepped back into the open space. "Noble Hector, King Agamemnon, nobles and worthies of this Council, we could do as Agamemnon says. And someday you will also fax . . . not freefax as we . . . Ardisians . . . do, but fax through places called faxnodes. You're not near one here, but you will discover one or more back in Greece. But I digress . . . we could fax to Delphi and free the Greeks in hours and days, if not minutes, but you will understand when I say it is not right for us to do this. They are *your* people. Their future is *your* concern. Some months ago, we freed a mere nine thousand-some of our own people from another blue beam, and while we were grateful for the extra population, we found it difficult to care for even that few without much planning in anticipation. The world has too many voynix and *calibani* roaming in it, not to mention dinosaurs, Terror Birds, and other oddities you will discover when you leave the safety of New Ilium.

"We and our moravec allies will help you disperse the non-Greek population, if there is such in this blue beam, but the future of the Greek-speaking peoples must remain in your hands."

This short speech, although barbaric in its grammar and syntax, was eloquent enough to earn the tall Ardisian a round of applause. Helen joined in. She wanted to meet this man.

Hector stepped into the center of the open area and turned in a full circle, meeting almost every individual's gaze. "I call now for a vote. Simple majority rule. Those who agree that Thrasymedes and his expedition volunteers should leave for Delphi on the next good wind and tide, raise your fists. Those against the expedition, hold your palms down."

There were a little more than a hundred people in the Joint Council meeting. Helen counted seventy-three raised fists—including her own—and only twelve palms down, including Deiphobus' and, for some reason, Andromache's.

There was much celebration inside and when the heralds announced the outcome to the tens of thousands in the central plaza and marketplace outside, the cheers echoed back off the new, low walls of New Ilium.

It was outside on the terrace that Hector came up to her. After a few words of greeting and comments on the chilled wine, he said, "I want so badly to go, Helen. I can't stand the thought of this expedition leaving without me."

Ah, thought Helen, *this is the reason for Andromache's no vote.* Aloud she said, "You cannot possibly go, noble Hector. The city needs you."

"Bah," said Hector, swallowing the last of his wine and banging the cup down on a building stone that had not yet been set in place. "The city is under no threat. We've seen no other people in twelve months. We spent this time rebuilding our walls—such as they are—but we shouldn't have bothered. There *are* no other people out there. Not in this region of the wide Earth, at least."

"All the more reason for you to remain and watch over your people," said Helen, smiling slightly. "To protect us from these dinosaurs and Terrible Birds our tall Ardisian tells us about."

Hector caught the mischief in her eye and smiled back. Helen knew that she and Hector had always had this strange connection—part teasing, part flirting, part something deeper than a husband and wife's connection. He said, "You don't think your future husband will be adequate to protect our city from all threat, noble Helen?"

She smiled again. "I esteem your brother Deiphobus above most other men, my dear Hector, but I have not agreed to his marriage proposal."

"Priam would have wished it," said Hector. "Paris would have been pleased at the thought."

Paris would have puked at the thought, thought Helen. She said, "Yes, your brother Paris would be happy to know that I married Deiphobus . . . or any noble brother in Priam's line." She smiled up at Hector again and was pleased to see his discomfort.

"Would you keep a secret if I tell you?" he asked, leaning close to her and speaking almost in a whisper.

"Of course," she whispered back, thinking, *If it is in my interest to do so.*

"I plan to go with Thrasymedes and his expedition when it sails," Hector said quietly. "Who knows if any of us will ever return? I will miss you, Helen." He awkwardly touched her shoulder.

Helen of Troy set her smooth hand over his rough one, squeezing it between her soft shoulder and her soft palm. She looked deeply into his gray eyes. "If you go on this expedition, noble Hector, I will miss you almost as much as will your lovely Andromache."

But not quite so much as Andromache will, thought Helen, *since I will be a stowaway on this voyage if it costs me the last diamond and the last pearl of my sizeable fortune.*

Still touching hands, she and Hector walked to the railing of the Council palace's long stone porch. The crowds in the marketplace below were going mad with happiness.

In the center of the plaza, exactly where the old fountain had stood for centuries, the mob of drunken Greeks and Trojans, milling together like brothers and sisters, had pulled in a large wooden horse. The artifact was so large that it wouldn't have fit through the Gaean Gate, if the Scaean Gate still stood. The lower, wider, topless gate, hastily erected near the place where the oak tree had stood, had no problem swinging wide for this effigy.

Some wag in the mob had decided that this horse was to be the symbol for the Fall of Ilium and today, on the anniversary of that Fall, they planned to burn the thing. Spirits were high.

Helen and Hector watched, their hands still touching lightly— silently but not without communication to each of them—as the mob set the torch to the giant horse and the thing, made mostly of dried driftwood, went up in seconds, driving the mob back, bringing the constables running with their shields and spears, and causing the noblemen and women on the long porch and balconies to murmur in disapproval.

Helen and Hector laughed aloud.

93

Seven years and five months after the Fall of Ilium:

Moira quantum teleported into the open meadow. It was a beautiful summer's day. Butterflies hovered in the shade of the surrounding forest and bees hummed above clover.

A black Belt soldier moravec approached her carefully, spoke to her politely, and led her up the hill to where a small, open tent—more a colorful canvas pavilion on four poles, actually—flapped gently in the breeze from the south. There were tables in the shade of the canvas and half a dozen moravecs and men bent over them, studying or cleaning the scores of shards and artifacts laid out there.

The smallest figure at the table—he had his own high stool—turned, saw her, jumped down, and came out to greet her.

"Moira, what a pleasure," said Mahnmut. "Please do come in out of the midday sun and have a cold drink."

She walked into the shade with the little moravec. "Your sergeant said that you were expecting me," she said.

"Ever since our conversation two years ago," said Mahnmut. He went over to the refreshment table and came back with a glass of cold lemonade. The other moravecs and men there looked at her with curiosity, but Mahnmut did not introduce her. Not yet.

Moira gratefully sipped the lemonade, noticed the ice that they must QT or fax in from Ardis or some other community every day, and looked down and over the meadow. This patch ran a hilly mile or so to the river, between the forest to the north and the rough land to the south.

"Do you need the moravec troopers to keep away rubberneckers?" she asked. "Curious crowds?"

"More likely to interdict the occasional Terror Bird or young T-Rex," said Mahnmut. "What on earth *were* the post-humans thinking, as Orphu likes to say."

"Do you still see Orphu much?"

"Every day," said Mahnmut. "I'll see him this evening in Ardis for the play. Are you coming?"

"I might," said Moira. "How did you know that I was invited?"

"You're not the only one who speaks to Ariel now and again, my dear. More lemonade?"

"No, thank you." Moira looked at the long meadow again. More than half of it had its top several layers of soil removed—not haphazardly, as from a mechanical earthmover, but carefully, lovingly, obsessively—the sod rolled back, strings and tiny pegs marking every incision, small signs and numbers everywhere, trenches ranging from a few inches in depth to several meters. "So do you think you've found it at last, friend Mahnmut?"

The little moravec shrugged. "It's amazing how difficult it is to find precise coordinates for this little town in the records. It's almost as if some . . . power . . . had removed all references, GPS coordinates, road signs, histories. It's almost as if some . . . force . . . did not want us to find Stratford-on-Avon."

Moira looked at him with her clear gray-blue eyes. "And why would any power . . . or force . . . not want you to find whatever you're looking for, dear Mahnmut?"

He shrugged again. "It'd be just a guess, but I would say because they—this hypothetical power or force—didn't mind human beings loose and happy and breeding on the planet again, but they have second thoughts about having a certain human *genius* back again."

Moira said nothing.

"Here," said Mahnmut, drawing her over to a nearby table with all of the enthusiasm of a child, "look at this. One of our volunteers found this yesterday on site three-oh-nine."

He held up a broken slab of stone. There were strange scratches on the dirty rock.

"I can't quite make that out," said Moira.

"We couldn't either at first," said Mahnmut. "It took Dr. Hockenberry to help us know what we were looking at. Do you see how this forms IUM and here below US and AER and here ET?"

"If you say so," said Moira.

"It does. We know what this is now. It's part of an inscription below a bust—a bust of *him*—that, according to our records, once read—'*JU-DICO PYLIUM, GENIO SCORATUM, ARTE MARONEM: TERRA TEGIT, POPULUS MAERET, OLYMPUS HABET.*'"

"I'm afraid I'm a bit rusty on my Latin," said Moira.

"Many of us were," said Mahnmut. "It translates—*THE EARTH COVERS ONE WHO IS A NESTOR IN JUDGEMENT; THE PEOPLE MOURN FOR A SOCRATES IN GENIUS; OLYMPUS HAS A VIRGIL IN ART.*"

"Olympus," repeated Moira as if musing to herself.

"It was part of an inscription under a bust the townspeople had made of him, and set in stone in the chancelry of Trinity Church after he was interred there. The rest of the inscription is in English. Would you like to hear it, Moira?"

"Of course."

> "STAY PASSENGER, WHY GOEST BY SO FAST?
> READ IF THOU CANST, WHOM ENVIOUS DEATH HATH
>   PLAST,
> WITH IN THIS MONUMENT SHAKSPEARE: WITH
>   WHOME.
> QUICK NATURE DIDE: WHOSE NAME DOTH DECK y^s
>   TOMBE,
> FAR MORE THEN COST: SIEH ALL, y^tHE HATH WRITT,
> LEAVES LIVING ART, BUT PAGE, TO SERVE HIS WITT."

"Very nice," said Moira. "And quite helpful for your search, I would imagine."

Mahnmut ignored the sarcasm. "It's dated the day he died, the twenty-third of April, 1616."

"But you haven't found the actual grave."

"Not yet," admitted Mahnmut.

"Wasn't there some headstone or inscription there, as well?" she asked innocently.

Mahnmut studied her face for a moment. "Yes," he said at last. "Something cut into the actual grave slab set over his bones."

"Didn't it say something about—oh . . .'Stay away, moravecs. Go home?' "

"Not quite," said Mahnmut. "The grave slab is supposed to have read—

"GOOD FRIEND FOR JESUS SAKE FORBEARE,
TO DIGG THE DUST ENCLOSED HEARE:
BLESTE BE $_Y{}^E$ MAN ^T_Y SPARES THESE STONES,
AND CURST BE HE ^T_Y MOVES MY BONES."

"Doesn't that curse worry you a little?" asked Moira.

"No," said Mahnmut. "You're confusing me with Orphu of Io. He's the one who watched all those Universal flatfilm horror movies from the Twentieth Century . . . you know, *Curse of the Mummy* and all that."

"Still . . ." said Moira.

"Are you going to stop us from finding him, Moira?" asked Mahnmut.

"My dear Mahnmut, you must know by now that we don't want to interfere with you, the old-styles, our new guests from Greece and Asia . . . with none of you. Have we thus far?"

Mahnmut said nothing.

Moira touched his shoulder. "But with this . . . project. Don't you sometimes feel as if you're playing God. Just a little bit?"

"Have you met Dr. Hockenberry?" asked Mahnmut.

"Of course. I spoke to him only last week."

"Odd, he didn't mention that," said Mahnmut. "Thomas volunteers here at the dig at least a day or two every week. No, but what I meant to say was that the post-humans and the Olympian gods certainly 'played God' when they re-created Dr. Hockenberry's body and personality and memories from bits of bone, old data files, and DNA. But it worked out all right. He's a fine person."

"He certainly seems to be," said Moira. "And I understand he's writing a book."

"Yes," said Mahnmut. The moravec seemed to have lost his train of thought.

"Well, good luck again," said Moira, holding out her hand. "And do give my best to Prime Integrator Asteague/Che when you see him next. Do tell him that I so enjoyed the tea we had at the Taj." She shook the little moravec's hand and began to walk toward the line of trees to the north.

"Moira," called Mahnmut.

She paused and looked back.

"Did you say you were coming to the play tonight?" called Mahnmut.

"Yes, I think I will."

"Will we see you there?"

"I'm not sure," said the young woman. "But I'll see you there." She continued walking toward the forest.

Seven years and five months after the Fall of Ilium:

My name is Thomas Hockenberry, Ph.D., Hockenbush to my friends. I have no friends alive who call me that. Or rather, the friends who once might have called me that—Hockenbush, a nickname from my undergraduate days at Wabash College—have long since turned to dust on this world where so many things have turned to dust.

I lived fifty-some years on that first good Earth, and have been gifted with a bit more than twelve rich years in this second life—at Ilium, on Olympos, in a place called Mars although I didn't know it was Mars until my last days there, and now back here. Home. On sweet Earth again.

I have much to tell. The bad news is that I have lost all the recordings I have made over the past twelve years as both scholic and scholar—the voice stones I handed to my Muse with each day's observation of the Trojan War, my own scribbled notes, even the moravec recorder I used to describe the last days of Zeus and Olympos. I lost them all.

It doesn't matter. I remember it all. Every face. Every man and woman. Every name.

Those who know say that one of the wonderful things about Homer's *Iliad* is that no man died nameless in his telling. They all fell heavily, those heroes, those brutal heroes, and when they fell they went down, as another scholar said—I'm paraphrasing here—they went down heavily, crashing down with all their weapons and their armor and their possessions and their cattle and their wives and their slaves going down with them. And their names. No man died nameless or without weight in Homer's *Iliad*.

If I tried to tell my tale, I would try to do as well.

But where to start?

If I am to be the Chorus of this tale—willing or unwilling—then I can start wherever I choose. I choose to start it here, by telling you where I live.

I enjoyed my months with Helen in New Ilium while that city rebuilt itself, the Greeks helping after the agreement with Hector that the Trojans would help them build their long ships in return, once the city's walls were up again. Once the city lived again.

It never died. You see, Ilium—Troy—was its people . . . Hector, Helen, Andromache, Priam, Cassandra, Deiphobus, Paris . . . hell, even that ornery Hypsipyle. Some of those people died, but some survived. The city lived as long as they did. Virgil understood that.

So I can't be Homer for you and I can't even be Virgil telling the tale from the time of the fall of Troy . . . not enough time has passed for that part to become much of a story, although I hear that might be changing. I'll be watching and listening as long as I am living.

But I live here now. In Ardis Town.

Not Ardis. A big house has gone back up on the broad meadow far up the hill a mile and a half from the old fax pavilion, a big house very near where Ardis Hall once rose, and Ada lives there yet with her family, but this place is Ardis Town, no longer Ardis.

There are a few more than twenty-eight thousand of us here in Ardis Town now, according to the last tax census—taken just five months ago. There is a community up on the hill, scattered around Ada's new home of Ardis House, but most of the town is down here, spread along the new road that runs from the fax pavilion down along the river. Here is where the mills are, and the real marketplace, and the tanners' smelly buildings, and the printing press and paper, and too many bars and whorehouses, and two synagogues, and one church that might best be described as the First Church of Chaos, and some good restaurants, and the stockyards—which smell almost as bad as the tannery—and a library (I helped bring that into being) and a school, although most of the children still live in or around Ardis House. Most of the students in our Ardis Town are adults, learning to read and write.

About half our residents are Greek and half are Jewish. They tend to get along. Most days.

The Jews have the advantage of being fully functioned; that is, they can freefax wherever the hell they want to go whenever the hell they want to do it. (I can do that as well . . . not fax, but QT. It's in my cells and

DNA, you know, written there by whoever or Whoever designed me. But I don't QT as much any more. I like slower forms of transportation.)

I do help Mahnmut with his Find Will project, at least once a week if I can. You've already heard about that. I don't think he ever will find his Will, and I suspect he believes that also. It's become a sort of hobby for him and Orphu of Io, and I help out in the same spirit of "what the hell." None of us—not even Mahnmut, I think—believes that Prospero, Moira, Ariel, any of the Powers That Be . . . even this Quiet we keep hearing so much about . . . are going to allow our little moravec to find and recombine the bones and DNA of William Shakespeare. I don't blame the Powers That Be for feeling threatened.

The play is going on up at Ardis this evening. You've heard about that as well. Many of us in Ardis Town are going up the hill to it, although I confess the hill is steep, the road and stairs are dusty, and I may pay fivepence to ride up in one of the steam coaches that Hannah's company runs. I just wish the damned things weren't so noisy.

Speaking of finding and not finding someone, I don't believe I've told you how I found my old friend Keith Nightenhelser.

The last I'd seen of my friend, he'd been with a prehistorical Indian tribe in the wilderness of what would once be Indiana—say in three thousand more years. It was a hell of a place for him and I felt guilty because I'd put him there. The idea was to keep him safe during the war between the heroes and the gods, but when I went back to look for old Nightenhelser, the Indians were gone and so was he.

And Patroclus—a very pissed-off Patroclus—was wandering around there somewhere as well, and I suspected that Nightenhelser had not survived.

But I freefaxed to Delphi three and a half months ago when Thrasymedes, Hector, and his crowd of adventurers interdicted the Delphi blue beam and lo and behold, in about the eighth hour of people emerging stunned from that little building—it reminded me of the old circus act where a tiny little car would drive up and fifty clowns would climb out—about eight hours into the people, mostly Greeks, emerging from that building, here comes my friend Nightenhelser. (We always called each other by our last names.)

Nightenhelser and I bought this place where I'm sitting and writing this now. We're partners. (Please note—I mean business partners, and good friends, of course, but not *partners* in the strange Twenty-first Century use of that word when it came to two men. I mean, I didn't go from Helen of Troy to Nightenhelser of Ardis Town. I have problems, but not in that particular arena of confusion.)

I wonder what Helen would think of our tavern? It's called Dombey

& Son—the name was Nightenhelser's suggestion, far too cute for my taste—and it gets a lot of business. It's fairly clean compared to the other places strung along the riverbank here like shingles overhanging an old roof. Our barmaids are barmaids and not whores (at least not here or on our time or in our tavern). The beer is the best we can buy—Hannah, who is, I'm told, Ardis's first millionaire of the new era, owns another company that makes the beer. Evidently brewing was something she learned about when studying sculpture and metal pouring. Don't ask me why.

Do you see why I hesitate to tell this epic tale? I can't keep my story-telling on a straight line. I tend to wander.

Perhaps I'll bring Helen here someday and ask her what she thinks of the place.

But rumor has it that Helen cut her hair, dressed up like a boy, and went off on the Delphi adventure with Hector and Thrasymedes, with both men following her around like puppies after a bone. (Another rea-son I hesitate to begin telling this epic tale—I was never worth a damn with metaphors or similes. As Nightenhelser once said—I'm trope-ically challenged. Never mind.)

Rumor has it, hell. I *know* Helen is with the Delphi Expedition. I saw her there. She looks good in short hair and with a tan. Really good. Not like my Helen, but healthy and very beautiful.

I could tell you more about my place and more about Ardis Town—what politics looks like when it's in its infancy (just about as useless and smelly as an infant) or what the people are like here, Greeks and Jews, functioned and non-functioned, believers, and cynics . . . but that's not part of this tale.

Also, as I will discover later this evening, I'm not the real teller. I'm not the chosen Bard. I know that makes no sense to you now, but wait just a while here, and you'll see what I mean.

These last eighteen years have not been easy for me, especially not the first eleven. I feel as scarred and pitted psychologically and emo-tionally as old Orphu of Io's shell is physically. (He lives up the hill at Ardis most of the time. You will see him a little later, too. He's going to the play tonight, but he always has an appointment with the kids each afternoon. That's what tipped me off to the fact that even all my years as scholar and scholic did not make me the chosen one to tell this particu-lar tale when the time comes to tell it.)

Yes, these last eighteen years, expecially the first eleven, have been tough, but I guess I feel richer for them. I hope you do when you hear the tale. If you don't, it's not my fault—I abdicate in the telling, although my memories are free for anyone who wants to borrow them.

I apologize. I have to go now. The afterwork crowd is coming in—the daytime tannery shift is just getting off, can you smell them? One of my barmaids is sick and another has just eloped with one of the young Athenians who chose to come here after Delphi and . . . well . . . I'm short-handed. My bartender comes in for the evening shift in forty-five minutes, but until then, I'd better draw the beers and slice the roast beef for the sandwiches myself.

My name is Thomas Hockenberry, Ph.D., and I think the "Ph.D." stands for "Pouring His Draft."

Sorry. Humor never was, except for a few literary puns and belabored jokes, my strong point.

I'll see you at the afternoon storytelling, before the play.

Seven years and five months after the Fall of Ilium:

On the day of the play, Harman had business in the Dry Valley. After lunch, he dressed in his combat suit and thermskin, borrowed an energy weapon from the Ardis House armory, and freefaxed down there.

The excavation of the post-humans' stasis dome was going well. Walking between the huge excavation machines, avoiding the downblast of a transport hornet hauling things north, it was hard for Harman to believe that eight and a half years earlier he'd come to this same dry valley with young Ada, the incredibly young Hannah, and the pudgy boy-man Daeman in search of clues about the Wandering Jew—the mystery woman he discovered was named Savi.

Actually, part of the blue stasis dome had been buried directly under the boulder where Savi had left her scratched clues leading them to her home on Mount Erebus. Even then, Savi had known that Harman was the only old-style human on Earth who could read those scratches.

The two supervisors on the stasis-dome excavation here were Raman and Alcinuous. They were doing a good job. Harman went down the checklist with them to make sure they knew which gear was destined for which community—the bulk of the energy weapons were destined for Hughes Town and Chom; the thermskins were going to Bellinbad; the crawlers were promised to Ulanbat and the Loman Estate; New Ilium had made a strong bid for the older flechette rifles.

Harman had to smile at this. Ten more years and the Trojans and Greeks would be using the same technology as the old-styles, even using the pavilion nodes to fax everywhere. Some of the Delphi group had already discovered the node near Olympus . . . the ancient town where the Games were held, not the mountain.

Well, he thought, the only solution was to stay ahead of them—in technology and everything else.

It was time to go home. But first Harman had one stop he wanted to make. He shook hands with Alcinuous and Raman and freefaxed away.

Harman had come back to the Golden Gate at Machu Picchu, the place where he had been given his life back seven and a half years earlier. He freefaxed not to the Bridge itself, but to a ridgeline across the valley from the bridge and the high ruins on the terrace of Machu Picchu. He never tired of looking at the ancient structure, the green habitation globules hardly visible from this distance, but he'd come back not just out of sentiment.

He was to meet someone here.

Harman watched the early afternoon clouds shift up the valley from the direction of the waterfall. For a while, the sunlight turned the mists to gold, half obscuring the ruins of Machu Picchu, making them appear as half-glimpsed stepping-stones there beyond the old Bridge's span. Everywhere Harman looked, life was winning its anti-entropic battle against chaos and energy loss—the grass on the hillsides, the canopy of trees in the mist-shrouded valley, the condors circling slowly on thermals, the tatters of blowing moss on the suspension cables of the Bridge itself, even the rust-colored lichen on the rocks near Harman.

As if to distract him from thoughts about life and living things, a very artificial spaceship rocketed from south to north across the sky, its long contrail slowly breaking up in the jet steam high above the Andes. Before Harman could be sure of the make and model of the ship, the gleaming speck was gone over the northern horizon behind the ruins, trailed by three sonic booms. It had been too large and too fast to be one of the hornets hauling gear north from the Dry Valley. Harman wondered if perhaps it was Daeman, returning from one of their joint expeditions with the moravecs, plotting and recording the decreasing quantum disturbances between Earth-system and Mars.

We have our own spacecraft now, thought Harman. He smiled at his own hubris at even thinking such a thing. But the thought still made him warm inside. Then he reminded himself that we *have* our own spacecraft, but we can't yet *build* our own spacecraft.

Harman hoped he would live long enough to see that. This led his thoughts to the search for the rejuvenation vats in the polar and equatorial rings

"Good afternoon," said a familiar voice behind him.

Harman raised the energy weapon out of habit and training, but lowered it even before he'd fully turned. "Good afternoon, Prospero," he said.

The old magus stepped out of a niche in the rocks. "You're wearing a full combat suit, my young friend. Did you expect to find me armed?"

Harman smiled. "I'll never find you without weapons."

"If one counts wit as a weapon," said Prospero.

"Or guile," said Harman.

The magus moved his veined old hands as if in defeat. "Ariel said you wished to see me. Is it about the situation in China?"

"No," said Harman, "we'll deal with that later. I came to remind you about the play."

"Ah," said Prospero, "the play."

"You've forgotten? Or decided not to come?" said Harman. "Everyone will be disappointed except your understudy if you're not coming."

Prospero smiled. "So *many* lines to learn, my young Prometheus."

"Not so many as you gave us," said Harman.

Prospero opened his hands again.

"Shall I tell the understudy that he has to go on?" asked Harman. "He'll be thrilled to do so."

"Perhaps I would like to attend after all," said the magus. "But must it be as a performer, not as a guest?"

"For this play, it must be as a performer," said Harman. "When we do *Henry IV,* you can be our honored guest."

"Actually," said Prospero, "I've always wanted to play Sir John Falstaff."

Harman's laugh echoed off the crags and cliff face. "So I can tell Ada that you'll be there and will stay for refreshments and conversation afterward?"

"I look forward to the conversation," said the solid hologram, "if not to the stage fright."

"Well . . ." said Harman, "break a leg." He nodded and freefaxed away.

At Ardis House, he checked in his weapon and the combat suit, pulled on canvas jeans and a tunic, slipped on light shoes, and walked out to the north meadow where final preparations were going on at the play-house. Men were rigging the colored lights that would hang over the rows of freshly sawed wooden seats and over the beer gardens and in the trellises. Hannah was busy testing the sound system from the stage. Some of the volunteers were slapping a final coat of paint on backdrops and someone kept drawing the curtain to and fro.

Ada saw him and tried walking with their two-year-old, Sarah, but the toddler was tired and fussy, so Ada swept her up and carried her up the grassy hill to her father. Harman kissed both of them, and then kissed Ada again.

She looked back at the stage and rows of seats, pulled a long strand of black hair out of her face, and said, "*The Tempest?* Do you really think we're all ready for this?"

Harman shrugged, then put his arm around her shoulders. "It was next."

"Is our star really coming?" she asked, leaning back against him. Sarah whimpered and shifted position a little bit so that her cheek was touching both her parents' shoulders.

"He says he is," said Harman, not believing it himself.

"It would have been nice if he'd rehearsed with the others," said Ada.

"Well . . . we can't ask for everything."

"Can't we?" said Ada, giving him the look that had typed her as the dangerous sort to Harman more than eight years ago.

A sonie rocketed low over the trees and houses, sweeping low toward the river and the town. "I hope that was one of the idiot adult males and not one of the boys," said Ada.

"Speaking of boys," said Harman. "Where's ours? I didn't see him this morning and I want to say hello."

"He's on the porch, getting ready for story time," said Ada.

"Ah, story time," said Harman. He turned to walk toward the dell in the south meadow where story time usually took place, but Ada gripped his arm.

"Harman . . ."

He looked at her.

"Mahnmut arrived a while ago. He says that Moira may be coming to the play tonight."

He took her hand. "Well, that's good . . . isn't it?"

Ada nodded. "But if Prospero is here, and Moira, and you said you invited Ariel, although he wouldn't play the part . . . what if Caliban comes?"

"He's not invited," said Harman.

She squeezed his hand to show that she was serious.

Harman pointed to the sites around the playhouse, trellised beer gardens, and house where the guards would be posted with their energy rifles.

"But the children will be at the play," said Ada. "The people from the town . . ."

Harman nodded, still holding her hand. "Caliban can QT here any time he wants, my love. He hasn't done so yet."

She nodded slightly but she did not release his hand.

Harman kissed her. "Elian has been rehearsing Caliban's moves and lines for five weeks," he said. *"Be not afeard. This isle is full of noises,/Sounds and sweet airs that give delight and hurt not."*

"I wish that were always so," said Ada.

"I do, too, my love. But we both know—you better than I—that it's not the case. Shall we go watch John enjoy story hour?"

Orphu of Io was still blind, but the parents were never afraid he'd bump into something or hit anyone, even as the eight or nine boldest children of Ardis piled on his huge shell, climbing barefoot to find a perch. The tradition had become for the kids to ride Orphu down to the dell for the story hour. John, at a little over seven one of the oldest, sat at the highest point on that shell.

The big moravec proceeded slowly on its silent repellors, moving almost solemnly—except for the explosion of giggles from the children riding and the shouts from the other children trailing behind—carrying them from the porch down past the old elm to the dell between the bushes and the new houses.

In the shallow depression, magically out of sight of the houses and other adults except for the parents of some of those here, the children clambered off and sprawled on the banks of the grassy bowl. John sat the closest to Orphu, as he usually did. He looked back, saw his father, and waved but did not come back to say hello. The story came first.

Harman, still standing with Ada, Sarah snoring in his arms now—Ada's arm having almost fallen asleep—noticed Mahnmut standing near the line of hedges. Harman nodded but the small moravec's attention was on his old friend and the children.

"Tell the Gilgamesh story again," shouted one of the bolder six-year-old boys.

The huge crab-monster slowly moved its carapace back and forth, as if shaking its head no. "That story's finished for now," rumbled Orphu. "Today we start a new one."

The children cheered.

"This one is going to take a long time to tell," said Orphu, his rumble sounding reassuring and engaging even to Harman.

The children cheered again. Two of the boys tumbled and rolled down the little hill together.

"Listen carefully," said Orphu. One of his long, articulated manipulators had carefully separated the boys and set them gently on the slope, a few feet apart. Their attention turned immediately to the big moravec's booming, mesmerizing voice.

> "Rage—Sing, Goddess, sing the rage of Peleus' son Achilles,
> murderous, doomed, sing of the rage that cost the Achaeans
> countless losses, hurling down into Hades' Dark House so many
> sturdy souls, great fighters' souls, heroes' souls,
> but also made their bodies carrion,
> feasts for the dogs and birds, even as Zeus's will was done.
> Begin, O Muse, when the two first argued and clashed,
> the Greek king Agamemnon, lord of men,
> and the brilliant, godlike Achilles . . ."

Acknowledgments

I would like to thank Jean-Daniel Breque for his permission to use the details of one of his favorite walks down the avenue Daumesnil and the rest of that *Promenade Plantée*. A full description of this delightful walk can be found in Jean-Daniel's essay "Green Tracks" in the *Time Out Book of Paris Walks*, published by Penguin.

I also would like to thank Professor Keith Nightenhelser for his suggestion of the Renoir-as-Creator quote from *The Guermantes Way*.

Finally, I would like to thank Jane Kathryn Simmons for permission to reprint her poem "Still Born" as it appears on p. 571.

THE JOLLY ROGERS

THE STORY OF
TOM BLACKBURN
AND NAVY FIGHTING
SQUADRON VF-17

TOM BLACKBURN

Orion Books • New York

Published by Orion Books, a division of Crown Publishers, Inc., 225 Park Avenue South, New York, New York 10003

ORION and colophon are trademarks of Crown Publishers, Inc.

Design by Jake Victor Thomas

Manufactured in the United States of America

Library of Congress Cataloging-in-Publication Data

Blackburn, Tom (John Thomas)
     The Jolly Rogers/Tom Blackburn; introduction by James Stockdale.
     p.   cm.
   Bibliography: p.
   1. Blackburn, Tom (John Thomas) 2. World War, 1939–1945—Aerial operations, American.   3. World War, 1939–1945—Naval operations, American.   4. World War, 1939–1945—Campaigns—Pacific Area. 5. World War, 1939–1945—Personal narratives, American. 6. United States. Navy. Fighting Squadron VF-17—History.   7. Fighter pilots—United States—Biography.   8. United States. Navy— Biography.   I. Title.
   D790.B476 1989
   940.54/4973—dc19   88-12686
                                                                CIP

ISBN 0-517-57075-0

10 9 8 7 6 5 4 3 2 1

First Edition

For the Fallen . . .

JOHN KEITH

Missing in Action
November 1, 1943

THOMAS KROPF

Missing in Action
January 30, 1944

BRADFORD BAKER

Missing in Action
November 16, 1943

DOUGLAS GUTENKUNST

Killed in Accident
January 30, 1944

CHARLES PILLSBURY

Missing in Action
November 21, 1943

HOWARD BURRISS

Missing in Action
January 31, 1944

ROBERT HOGAN

Missing in Action
January 26, 1944

DONALD MALONE

Missing in Action
February 4, 1944

JAMES FARLEY

Missing in Action
January 26, 1944

PERCY DIVENNY

Missing in Action
February 4, 1944

THADDEUS BELL

Missing in Action
January 27, 1944

CLYDE DUNN

Missing in Action
February 17, 1944

JAMES MILLER

Missing in Action
February 17, 1944

Contents

Photographs appear following pages 78 and 174.

Introduction

This is the story of the fighting days of a naval officer who shaped my life. John Thomas Blackburn was forty-five or forty-six years old during the time I spent with him on the aircraft carrier *Midway* in the late fifties. He was, to be sure, that great ship's commanding officer, but to her four thousand officers and sailors, and particularly to her pilots, he was The Immediate Presence, the mentor, the guide—the man we all knew could do anything better than anybody aboard without half trying. He could turn the ship around on a dime in a narrow channel, take over from a boat coxswain in high winds and choppy seas, and make a flawless approach and landing at the accommodation ladder, or outfly the hottest fighter pilots with aplomb. He "had it" upstairs, at the tips of his fingers, in the seat of his pants. If ever a man was tailor-made to be an across-the-board role model and leader of men flying and fighting from ships at sea, it was Tommy Blackburn.

This book tells how he got that way. You get the feel of tension and drive as the young fighter pilot, son and younger brother of naval officers more comfortable with the peacetime Navy than he, taxes himself, subconsciously prepares himself for the crucial tests of World War II. He becomes a perfectionist in the techniques of getting masses of airplanes on and off aircraft carriers at sea, smartly. I was a lead fighter pilot on that carrier, *Midway*, in 1958 and 1959, and we all felt the teeth and sting of his perfectionism, but it wasn't until I read this story that I got the feel for how it was developed, or an appreciation of how it had paid off in his fighting days.

In November 1943, at the age of thirty-one, Tom Blackburn was commanding his second fighter squadron in combat. On New Year's Day of that year he had commissioned VF-17, the Navy's second squadron, to fly the F4U Corsair. By October the squadron had become the first to fight in the airplane, and on this November 11, in the predawn darkness, he was leading twenty-four of his Corsairs from the island of New Georgia toward Japan's primary fortress in the South Pacific, Rabaul. En route, they were to fly cover over a force of three carriers and nine destroyers from darkness into light, and then land aboard and refuel and rearm while the carriers' planes attacked Rabaul. Time was of the essence because VF-17 had to relaunch to face the horde of Japanese fighters that could be expected to follow the carrier planes back to their ships. In the early light, after shooting down a Japanese prowler over the ships in the dark, Tom picked up the "Prep Charlie" visual signal flashed from the carriers, and watching aircraft launching on the decks below, maneuvered his planes in radio silence to be at the ramp, landing gear and hooks down, ready to start landing the instant "Clear Deck" was signaled.

To know the man and his element is to appreciate the joy in Tom's heart as the ships, heading into the wind, sailing ever closer to enemy territory, received VF-17's planes, at tight interval, no wave-offs, quickly and silently. And these were the first carrier landings any of VF-17's pilots had made in over two months. (They had been based ashore for logistic, not operational, reasons.)

And yes, the squadron did launch in time to face one hundred or more inbound Japanese planes and, in the next hour that morning, they were credited with 18.5 kills (including another for the skipper). When I was serving in Blackburn's ship fifteen years later, I was making a pioneer deployment in the F4U Corsair's grandson, the F8U Crusader. In no small measure trading on Tom Blackburn's inspiration, I took the F8U Crusader through a squadron and wing command and introduced it into the war in Vietnam, in which it achieved the highest kill-to-loss ratio of any Navy, Marine, or Air Force fighter type in the conflict. But in the course of the whole war it shot down only as many planes as Blackburn's squadron shot down that morning of November 11, 1943.

Of course, we all know that World War II was the place to set kill records. The targets were plentiful, the closing rates were somewhat less, and the enemy planes were very vulnerable. But as the following pages will make clear, VF-17's combat record in the Solomons was unbeatable. That one squadron, in seventy-six combat days, had a confirmed kill score of 154.5 Japanese airplanes with a kill to loss ratio of over eleven. Thirteen pilots of VF-17 made ace in this period. This, by a factor of more than a third, exceeds the scores of the Black Sheep Squadron made famous in the modern television serial. True, Tom Blackburn was generally operating with a third more planes than his Marine counterpart, but even after applying this factor, his numbers still come out higher.

But inspiration is what I'm writing these few pages about, and that was the legacy that Tom left all fighter pilots. He saw his war in a heroic, go-for-the-jugular, romantic context. I think he's right when he suggests that destroying their fighter planes and pilots in air-to-air combat may have done Japan's self-confidence more violence than bombs. But it was his manner, his conviction, and his courage (including the physical kind, in a supersonic Crusader cockpit) that stuck with me from those days on the *Midway*. Perhaps it's no coincidence that I realized my greatest aspirations for service—mine in a North Vietnamese prison—when I was the same age as he was when his tremendous influence on me counted most: forty-five or forty-six.

James Stockdale
Vice Admiral
U.S. Navy (Ret)

Glossary

A/C aircraft

Acknowledge voice-radio directive: "If you understand and will comply with the order given, reply 'Wilco' "

Airflow spoiler a fitting or device to destroy lift when desired

AirLant Air Force Atlantic Fleet

Ammo ammunition (bullets)

Angels fighter direction code for altitude in thousands of feet

Anti-G suit rig to minimize blackout from gee (**see** G)

Anzac military man from Australia/New Zealand

ASAP as soon as possible

Augured in crashed, originally used with tailspin accidents

AvCad Navy rank, Aviation Cadet

B-24 Consolidated's Liberator; four-engine heavy bomber

B-25 North American's Mitchell; two-engine medium bomber

Back to battery return to normal

Bail out to jump out of an a/c

Bastille prison, jail, slammer, calaboose, hoosegow

Beach land area; opposite of "at sea"

Betty IJNAF land-based twin-engine bomber, appearance like Martin B-26

Black Shoes nonaviation Naval officers (aviators: brown shoes)

Bogey fighter direction code: unknown aircraft

Bomber One the main landing strip at Espiritu Santo

Boresight to align guns and sighting devices

Boresighted, he had me enemy in perfect firing position

Bought the farm fatal crash, usually associated with home base

Brain bucket crash helmet or hard hat

Bridge the topside control station of a ship

BT-1 Northrop monoplane dive bomber, prototype of SBD

Bulkhead nautical term for wall; also vertical panel in a/c

Bunker Hill CV-17, *Essex*-class carrier (36 F6F 36 SB2C 19 TBF)

CAG Carrier Air Group Commander

'Canal short for Guadalcanal

CarQual qualify for carrier flight operations (landings and takeoffs made under controlled conditions)

Cat catapult; also short for Wildcat; part of the capstan used in handling anchor chain

Cat, walk back the reverse a policy or dictum

Catwalk walkway just below flight deck level, providing shelter and fore and aft access

CAVU　Ceiling and Visibility Unlimited; weather

Chandelle　a steep climbing turn, usually started at high speed (*see* Zoom)

Charger　USS *Charger* CVE 29, small merchantman converted to flattop

Chennault's Flying Tigers　the American Volunteer Group in China pre-WW II

Chocked　wheel held in place by wooden blocks

Church key　beer can opener

CInCPac　Commander in Chief Pacific Fleet

Clocks　aircraft instruments, especially flight aids

Cockpit coaming　the rim

ComInCh　Commander in Chief (of the U.S. Navy)

ComAirLant　Commander Air Force Atlantic Fleet

ComAirPac　Commander Air Force Pacific Fleet

ComAirSols　Commander Air Forces Solomon Islands

ComAirSoPac　Commander Air Forces Southern Pacific

ComSoPac　Commander Southern Pacific Area (VAdm W. F. Halsey, USN)

ConForSols　Confederate Forces, Solomon Islands

CV　large aircraft carrier

CVE　small "escort" carrier, usually converted merchantman

CVL　"light" carrier, U.S. normally converted cruiser

Dauntless　*see* SBD

DD　destroyer

Echelon　aircraft formation with planes following on a single line of bearing from leader; level of command; ancillary unit

Essex　CV-9, *see* **Bunker Hill**, except VB: 36 SBD

ETA　estimated time of arrival

ETD　estimated time of departure

F2A　Brewster Buffalo, early monoplane fighter

F2F, F3F　Grumman biplane fighters

F4B　Boeing biplane fighter (AAF P-12)

F4F　Grumman Wildcat, small midwing monoplane, Vmax 325, standard equipment for all VF squadrons till early 1943

F4U　Vought Corsair, the Hog; also U-Bird; gull-winged, Vmax 400, Navy and Marine Corps Fighter and Fighter-Bomber squadrons

F6F　Grumman Hellcat, low square-tipped wing, Vmax 375; principal fighter in Navy squadrons, after F4F, until VJ Day

FW 200　German four-engine long-range recco

Fairey fulmar　British two-seater carrier-based "fighter"

Fam, fammed　familiarize(d)

Fan　propeller

Feathered　propeller blades aligned with flight path to reduce drag and stop rotation (*see* Windmill)

FFT　for further transfer (transportation)

Fifties　U.S. machine guns, bullet diameter 0.50 inch

Filled to the gunwales (gunnels) loaded to capacity

Fire-wall, fire-walled partition immediately aft of engine, hence throttle to max forward (open) position

Fish a torpedo

Five squared (5 by 5) voice radio: strength five (max); readability five; also "loud and clear"

Flak antiaircraft fire; also adverse criticism

Flat-hatting flying at very low levels, usually exhibitionistic

Flipper aircraft horizontal control surface; elevator

Fokker Dreidecker German triplane fighter of WW I (Richtofen)

Freeboard vertical distance from surface of water to gunwale (edge of boat)

Full bore maximum engine power

G, Gee force of gravity used as a measure of (usually) vertical acceleration or deceleration

Gauges *see* Clocks

GP bombs general purpose explosive (contrasts with incendiary, for example)

Hack, in officer's punishment: relieved of duty and restricted to quarters

Hamp Japanese fighter, square-wingtip version of Zero

Hand on the helm in command of

Heave around work hard; get busy at assigned task

Helen Japanese medium two-engine bomber, similar in appearance to B-25

Hellcat *see* F6F

High blower an engine supercharger setting used at high altitudes

High-side run a fighter attack pattern using steep dive from the side (*see* Overhead)

Hit the silk to parachute, or bail out

Hog *see* F4U

IJAAF Imperial Japanese Army Air Force

IJNAF Imperial Japanese Naval Air Force

Independence CVL-22, (24 F6F 9 TBF)

Island the superstructure above the flight deck of a carrier, incorporates bridge(s), mast(s), smokestack, etc.

Jeep carrier a CVE

JU-88 German two-engine medium bomber

Kate IJNAF torpedo bomber

Kiwi a New Zealander

Knucklehead U.S. strip in Russell Islands; someone not bright

LCI landing craft infantry; a small seagoing vessel for landing troops on beaches

LCT landing craft tank; a boat carried by ships of amphibious forces to land tanks, light artillery, and small numbers of troops

LSO   landing signal officer; the controller of aircraft on final approach to carrier landing

LST   landing ship tank; a 280-foot seagoing vessel to carry men and equipment to beachheads (also known as large slow target)

Lufbery (circle)   a horizontal ring of fighters for mutual defense (WW I)

Main mount   large wheel and tire of a/c

Maru   Japanese "ship"

ME-109   German fighter, principal equipage of *Luftwaffe*, Vmax 350

Meat wagon   ambulance portion of airfield crash crew

Mil(s)   gunnery term of angular measurement, 1 mil equals 1 foot of arc at 1000 feet

Milk up   raise gradually

Mosquito   British two-engine light bomber, designed for low level ops

NAAS   Naval Auxiliary Air Station; usually a small satellite field to an NAS

NAS   Naval Air Station

NJ   North American, fixed landing gear, the first U.S. monoplane trainer, prototype of SNJ

Nugget   a fledgling pilot

O'clock   relative bearing code using straight ahead as twelve, dead astern as six, etc.

Oleo, oleo struts   shock absorber(s)

One-eighty (180)   a turn of 180 degrees, course reversal

Oscar   obsolescent IJAAF fighter, fixed landing gear, Vmax 300.

Out   radio code: end of transmission, reply is neither requested nor desired, never used with "Over"

Over   radio code: end of transmission, but reply is requested

Overhead   aboard ship; the ceiling; aerial gunnery; a steep diving run from directly above target

P-38   Lockheed Lightning two-engine fighter, Vmax 350

P-39   Bell Aircobra fighter, Vmax 325

P-40   Curtiss Tomahawk; no further comment

P-51   North American Mustang, Vmax 400

P&W   Pratt and Whitney (Aircraft Engine Company), makers of high HP radial engines

Part brass rags   to sever connections with a close associate

PBY   Consolidated two-engine seaplane (and amphibian)

Photo recco   photographic reconnaissance

Plank owner   member of ship or squadron complement from date of unit's commissioning

Plebe   U.S. Naval Academy freshman

Plowback   school graduate retained as an instructor

Poilu   French common soldier

Pollywog   one who hasn't crossed the equator

Porpoised   as with torpedo broaching after initial plunge

Prep Charlie (PC)   prepare to land aboard (carrier)
Pri fly   aircraft carrier's flight operations nerve center (usually on aft end of island structure)
Princeton   CVL-23 (24 F6F 9 TBF)
PT   motor torpedo boat

Refam, refammed   refamiliarize(d)
Retread   officer with WW I service brought back to active duty from civilian life
Revetment   horseshoe-shaped embankment for protection from horizontal blast

SBD   Douglas Dauntless, divebomber; standard equipment for Navy and Marine VB squadrons 1941–43; wings did not fold
SB2C   Curtiss Helldiver (the Beast), divebomber, replaced SBD starting in late 1943
SB2U   Vought Vindicator, Navy's first monoplane divebomber, replaced by SBD prior to December 1941
SNJ   North American advanced trainer (USAF AT-6); the mainstay of U.S. military fighting training
Saddle position   astern of another aircraft in position for attack
Saratoga   CV-3, built on battle cruiser hull (36 F6F 24 SBD 18 TBF)
Scramble   launch a/c as fast as possible
Scuttlebutt   rumor, gossip
Seven-point-seven (7.7) mm   bullet diameter of Japanese machine guns (about 0.27 inch)
Shellback   a seafaring man who has crossed the equator
Sick bay   medical area aboard ship or Navy Base
Skip bombing   very low level bombing wherein bomb skips into target from water (or land) like a flat rock
Slipstream   the turbulent blast of air created by an a/c prop
Slot, the   New Georgia Sound, the passage between the Solomons from Bougainville to Guadalcanal
Snoop, snooper   to hang around a ship or force observing from a distance; surveillance
Sonar   device for submarine detection from sound reflection
SoPac   South Pacific; the command area embracing the islands from New Ireland to New Caledonia, including the Solomons
Spad   Allied WW I biplane fighter
Spin in   to crash, especially from a tailspin
Spitkit   (Nautical: spittoon) a small ship
Spliced   get married
Split-S, split-essed   a violent half roll to an inverted position; go as quickly as possible from level flight into a vertical dive
Spook   startle; scare off
Stall, stalling out   breakdown of smooth airflow resulting in loss of lift
Standard rate turn   a gentle turn of approximately 3 degrees per second

Tail-end-Charlie   the rearmost plane of a formation

TBD   Douglas Devastator; torpedo plane, the Navy's first service monoplane; replaced by TBF starting mid-1942

TBF   Grumman Avenger; torpedo plane, used also as glide bomber. Standard equipment for Navy and Marine squadrons after mid-1942

TBM   Avenger, built by General Motors

Tojo   IJAAF radial engined fighter; follow on to Zero, Vmax 400(?); never appeared in significant numbers

Tokyo express   high speed Japanese resupply and reenforcement by ship, especially through the Slot to Guadalcanal at night

Tokyo Rose   The English-speaking DJ on Radio Tokyo who broadcast propaganda and "seductive" messages in a honeyed female voice

Tony   IJAAF in-line engine fighter; no relative of, but looked like, Me 109; Vmax 350

Torpecker   torpedo plane or pilot

Turkey   an *affectionate* name for the Grumman TBF

Turkey shoot   a one-sided bloody aerial battle

Uncle Sugar   the U.S.A.; the U.S. government

V   true airspeed; Navy letter denoting heavier than air (VP = patrol plane, ZP = blimp, CA = cruiser, CV = aircraft carrier)

Vmax   sustained top speed in level flight

VAL   Japanese dive bomber; fixed landing gear

VB, VF, VF (N), VP, VT   aircraft type and squadron designators; bomber, fighter, night fighter, patrol, torpedo; when followed by number denotes unit

Washing Machine Charlie   Japanese high-altitude night heckler over Solomons beachheads

WestPac   almost all of Pacific area west of Hawaii except SoPac

Windmill   propeller rotating on dead engine

Zero, Zeke   Japanese fighter, principal VF equipment of IJNAF from 1940 on; Vmax 350

Zoom   a steep climb started at high speed for maximum altitude gain

Zoomie   Black Shoe equalizer term for aviators

Danny Boy

Bougainville
February 19, 1944

"Honest, Duke, this second Zeke did the same dumb thing. After Oc came in too fast, missed, and chandelled out, the Zeke pulled up in a forty-five-degree climb, straight ahead. He was just hanging there. I opened up inside two hundred yards, dead astern, led him about fifty mils. Just like the skipper keeps telling us: 'Get close before your shoot; you're never as close as you think!' I waited until he filled my whole windshield. I was right on. I squeezed the trigger and BLOOIE!—the biggest ball of fire I'll ever see. I went right through it; got a load of oil on my windshield. I think my first bullet flamed him. Couldn't have been more than a half-second burst. Jesus, those two poor bastards never knew what hit 'em. One minute they're fat, dumb, and happy; the next, they're exploded in the goddamnedest blossom of orange you ever saw.

"I lost Oc on this run . . ."

The official action report written that evening by the VF-17 air combat intelligence officer, Lt(jg) Duke Henning, is more laconic. By February 1944 Duke had heard many combat reports related by successful pilots still hyperstimulated by the mind-blowing pressures of air-to-air combat. While not unbelieving, Duke was obliged to expunge the hyperbole and reduce the tales to their reportable essentials:

"Lt [Oscar] Chenoweth and Lt(jg) [Daniel] Cunningham were the only F4Us to complete the mission. They arrived at the target area at about 1005, twenty minutes ahead of the bombers. They came in at 30,000 feet and circled, letting down to 24,000 feet. They saw six to eight Jap fighters over St. George Channel at 18,000 feet. Chenoweth made a firing run with Cunningham on his wing. Then Chenoweth followed the Zeke down to 12,000 feet (Cunningham stayed at 18,000 feet) and saw him crash on Cape Gazelle. He then climbed and rejoined Cunningham. The section made a second run. Chenoweth overshot, and as this Zeke pulled up he was an easy target for Cunningham, who burned him. The section recovered and

xvii

headed westward over Blanche Channel where they spotted Zekes below them on the same course. A section run was made, and Cunningham again caught a Zeke as he pulled up and set him afire. In both cases, the Zekes were slow and Cunningham used less than 75 mils lead. . . . As he made his kill, Cunningham lost Chenoweth.

"When Cunningham lost [sight of] Chenoweth he was over Simpson Harbor at 5,000 feet. He headed for Blanche Channel at full throttle. Spotting an F4U he turned north to join up, but the F4U also turned north in pursuit of another Zero. Cunningham spotted a second one coming down behind him. He turned hard into the Jap, but the latter evaded, going for the other Corsair. Cunningham closed and sent him down flaming. Recovering at 3,000 feet, he headed for Cape Gazelle, saw another single close to the covering fighters with our retiring bombers. Shooting from . . . 150 yards, he put a fourth flamer into the water. He then joined the bomber cover heading home."

Oc Chenoweth had joined VF-17 in January, another in a long line of castoffs from other squadrons. Danny Boy Cunningham was the squadron shorty; he could not properly operate the huge F4U's rudder pedals without a special rig. Had it not been for his plaintive "I *can* do it; give me a chance," he would have been banished. On February 19, 1944, Oc got 3 confirmed kills, bringing his total score to 8.5, and Danny Boy got 4, bringing his total score to 7. That day, VF-17 pilots scored 16 confirmed kills.

In all during VF-17's two combat tours under my command, we were credited with 154.5 Japanese airplanes destroyed, 27 probably destroyed, and 25 damaged. Until then, no U.S. Navy or Marine fighter squadron in World War II had done as well.

PART I

To War

1

My war began in January 1941 when I received orders to join the newly created instructional staff at Naval Air Station, Miami. NAS, Miami, or Opa-Locka, as the base was also called, was to be the Navy's finishing school for carrier-bound fighter, dive-bomber, and torpedo pilots.

To say that I was underwhelmed at being dragged out of an active carrier-based fighter squadron to play nursemaid to an endless stream of youngsters fresh out of primary flight training is putting too good a face on my feelings. I was incensed. My squadron, VF-2, the so-called Fighting Chiefs, was considered one of the best in the U.S. Navy, and being one of only several officers flying beside the finest enlisted naval aviation pilots (NAPs) was a singular honor. The blow was doubly hard to swallow because of the timing. Throughout 1939 and 1940, professional officers expected to be at war within days or weeks. Training new pilots to fill the Navy's burgeoning ranks was vital duty, I realized, but my entire ten-year Navy career had been focused on just one thing: preparing myself to fly a Navy fighter in combat. On the day the new orders reached me, and for many months thereafter, I just *knew* that I was to be cheated of an opportunity that could arise only once in a generation.

The fact was that instructing at Opa-Locka was an honor as well as an unparalleled opportunity to hone my skills and learn more about flying fighters than I could ever have learned in the Fleet during peacetime.

NAS, Miami, was still under construction when I reported aboard in March 1941. Essential structures had been completed and others were abuilding. Most of the concrete for the runways and working areas had been poured, but the runways had no shoulders, just the 8-inch drop-off to the sandy soil on which the base was being built. Going off the hard surface at any significant speed equaled a crash. There were no runway lights; necessary night operations were thus truly hairy because the torch pots provided confusing and erratic lighting of the runways and taxiways.

The station commander and director of the training program was

Cdr Jerry Bogan, a tough, feisty little man who, I found, had handpicked his subordinates. The command thus bore his indelible stamp. He demanded and got high performance. From the start, our unspoken motto was: Work hard, play hard, don't alibi, produce.

My immediate superior was Lt Joe Clifton—Jumping Joe. He graduated from the Naval Academy in 1930, three years ahead of me. His nickname derived from his days as a star 165-pound fullback. Joe was a fitness nut decades before most Americans heard of fitness, a dynamo of nervous energy, a man of enormous charisma. He was a natural leader, an activist, a born delegator of tiresome details of administration. As Joe's immediate subordinate, I not only found myself flying a lot, I made up and modified schedules for instructors and students, and worked up and superintended the ground phase of the training program. Not the least of my responsibilities was making certain that the mercurial Lieutenant Clifton arrived from his myriad other activities on time for hops and lectures.

Another standout staffer was Lt(jg) Roger Hedrick, a fine pilot and superb marksman. Cool, calm, and capable, Rog was to be my strong right arm. Much for what I have been given credit then and later in the war was Rog's doing. Unlike most of his superiors at the school and in naval aviation in general, Rog was not an Academy man. Rather, he was one of our direct links with most of the young pilots we would be training at Opa-Locka. Rog was an AvCad, a Naval Aviation Cadet who had been flying with the Fleet since completing flight school in 1936. This contrasts with my career pattern and, to a greater or lesser degree, those of all the Annapolis graduates in naval aviation; we had all been obliged to serve for two years in the Fleet before entering the flight-training program and earning our wings. Roger Hedrick's assignment to our staff was not only a personal triumph for Rog, it was proof positive that the AvCad program had arrived.

It is hard to say too much in praise of all the early AvCads on our faculty. The first AvCads to complete training had joined the Fleet in mid-1936 and most of them had elected to remain on active duty after the conclusion of their four-year contracts. This, despite the fact that they were not then officially ranked as officers and did not draw full officers' pay. All of our AvCad instructors—and all the Academy men—had extensive carrier service under their belts. The early AvCads were an exceptionally select group in that, at the inception of the program, only absolutely perfect physical specimens had been selected. As little as one dental filling led to disqualification, a consciously absurd criterion meant to limit access to the program from among a throng of Depression-age candidates. On the other hand, every one of them was a highly qualified college graduate who, in 1935, did not have the draft breathing down his neck. Thus, the early AvCads were highly motivated volunteers, willing to earn less status and less pay if only they could become naval aviators.

Our band of instructors steadily grew as our student load increased, for the flight schools at Pensacola and Jacksonville were really churning them out. Some of the new instructors, AvCads and Annapolis men, joined us from the Fleet, but many were plowbacks—selected students retained upon completion of their training, not only because they were excellent students with much promise but because they appeared to possess the temperaments of good trainers.

At the time we opened NAS, Miami, in mid-1941, Annapolis graduates had to serve two full years in the Fleet before being accepted for flight training. This, combined with the limited number of Regulars who could be spared for flight training, the virtual closure of the enlisted pilot program, and the burgeoning needs of the Fleet, stressed the importance of the Naval Aviation Cadet program in the job of building naval aviation manyfold its size while maintaining world-class standards.

By 1941 the AvCad program, which had undergone numerous changes since its inception in 1935, was accepting candidates with as little as two years of college, though we had our share of cadets with postgraduate degrees as well. In return for a guaranteed bonus of five hundred dollars a year, to be paid at the conclusion of a four-year contract, AvCads were trained to fly and commissioned in the Navy Reserve or Marine Corps Reserve upon earning their wings at Opa-Locka or at the Navy's multiengine training base.

By 1940 the physical entrance standards for the revived AvCad program had been relaxed to reasonable levels. This, because the objective was to churn out a great number of pilots from a much vaster pool of physically and mentally qualified applicants. Most of our students had been subject to the draft and had thus volunteered for the program under some duress. That is no reflection on them; our qualified candidates could have chosen from among a lot of easier, less dangerous jobs than flying combat aircraft. The people we washed out reverted to enlisted rank and were obliged to serve out the terms of their contracts, but I suspect that most of them eventually wound up with commissions, for they were still among the best young men our nation was producing.

In addition to the Academy men and AvCads we trained was a small number of Reserve officers who had served on active duty with the Fleet and were between the ages of twenty-five and thirty. For the most part, these were men who had graduated from civilian colleges after completing the Reserve Officers' Training Course (ROTC).

Paralleling our efforts to turn out competent fighter pilots were the scout-and-dive-bomber unit and the temporarily moribund torpedo unit. The sum of our efforts at Opa-Locka was to produce pilots for the burgeoning carrier and Marine air groups. This was not accomplished without setbacks, among which was the complete unavailability of even obsolescent torpedo bombers, a factor that obviated torpedo training per se.

The airplanes we did have at Miami were castoffs from the Fleet, which was itself only beginning to receive relatively modern new fighter and bomber types. Initially, we flew and trained in a mixed bag of obsolete Boeing F4Bs, Grumman F2Fs, Grumman F3Fs, and others—biplanes all—supplemented by several two-seat North American SNJ advanced trainers, our only monoplanes, and a half-dozen biplane basic trainers with which we taught techniques for recovery from inverted spins. Mercifully, I had no connection with aircraft maintenance, but we did have a dedicated band of mechanical miracle workers to undertake that unenviable job of keeping our ungodly mixed bag of a working aircraft museum airborne. As it was, a single day's flying might find an instructor belting up in any of several of the numerous types in our possession. Thus, the instructor's expertise was paramount, for our fledglings had to have example as well as precept. Moreover, whenever required by the student load of the moment, instructors were expected to switch between fighters and dive-bombers.

Although all our students had completed primary flight training at Pensacola or Jacksonville, they were anything but finished products. About all they had proved was that they could regularly take off, perform basic aerobatics, and safely land. As a finishing school for Navy and Marine pilots bound for operational Fleet combat units, our syllabus included ground school with the pilot's handbooks for both fighters and bombers, cockpit checkout, supervised touch-and-go landings at unpaved outlying fields, elementary formation work, and field carrier training—simulated carrier landings on a paved runway. Next, all student pilots learned air-to-air gunnery over the Everglades against towed target sleeves. If successful, they went on to dive-bombing, where it took three hits for five drops on a 50-foot circle to get an "up"—a passing grade. If the fighter student made it that far, he went on to dogfighting, which we called "grab-ass," and then on to aerobatics. The final leg was night-flying familiarization, mostly landings and takeoffs rounded out with some extremely tame night formation flying. I doubt if the total flight time for any Miami student of the day came to 150 hours.

We did no high-altitude work at Miami. Almost without exception, the highest we took our students was 12,000 feet, where oxygen was not needed unless we were going to stay up for a long time. Thus, the mysteries of high-altitude flying—particularly the problems encountered in the use of oxygen equipment—simply were not addressed during our training course. As with everything, it was a matter of not having the equipment, which was in short supply even in the Fleet.

Each student who completed this course—each in his own time, within reason—was commissioned a Navy ensign or a Marine second lieutenant, given his wings, and sent on to the Fleet. If a student could not cut it as a fighter or dive-bomber pilot, we could send him to multiengine school. Most of us—instructors and cadets alike—considered that to be a fate worse than death, a purgatory of disrespect. It was not really our job to wash pilots completely out of the program—the incompetents theoretically did not make it as far as advanced training—but we had to do so on occasion, mostly as a result of ongoing disciplinary problems or because a cadet lost his nerve. The surest ticket out of the program—one that was punched with astounding rarity, given our rickety equipment and frenetic pace—was being killed or maimed in an accident.

The gunnery training that we gave to students at Miami was high-deflection-angle shooting. The runs we taught were the overhead, the high-side, and the flat-side.

In the overhead run, one comes over the target on an opposite course and approximately 3,000 feet above it. At the right moment, the pilot goes into a half roll to the inverted position and pulls through in a very steep dive. At the point of opening fire, approximately 500 feet from the target, the ideal is to be in a vertical dive perpendicular to the horizontal target. This requires maximum deflection—lead—because the relative motion of the target is great-est. As the dive progresses, the angle of the dive decreases and, thus, the amount of deflection needed also decreases. If properly executed, a pass close aboard the target will find the attacker in about a 45-degree dive. With recovery beneath the target, the speed obtained in the dive is used to zoom back up to get ahead and in position for the next run.

The high-side run is somewhat similar to the overhead run, except that the dive starts about 1,000 feet to one side of the target. The attacker should be in a steep dive abeam of the target so that the shooting is done at a 45-degree deflection angle both in the vertical plane and at the four o'clock position or eight o'clock po-sition. (The target's nose is considered to be pointed at twelve o'clock.) The recovery is executed much as from an overhead run.

In the flat-side run, the optimum position for opening fire is 90 degrees to the course of the target. This narrows to a maximum deflection shot of 45 degrees as the attacker passes astern of the target and recovers.

These runs were designed to minimize the exposure of the at-tacking airplane to the flexible guns of bombers. They were ex-tremely effective once they were mastered in that they made for a very tough shot for the bomber's gunners.

During aerial gunnery instruction, the instructor flew above and to the rear of the target sleeve so he could observe the students during their runs. When the radios worked—not very often—the instructor could coach the students as well as be available to issue warnings in case of hazardous situations, as when two people tried to make their runs at the same time. The instructor kept notes on each run of every student for a postflight skull session—debriefing.

The hectic training schedule and rickety equipment claimed a few student lives, but the pace did not allow for much in the way of lamenting such loses. We replaced the dead bodies with live ones and the ruined equipment with whatever they sent us, and we went on in our mad race against history.

Throughout my tour at Opa-Locka, the training staff was starkly aware that our course was quite rudimentary when taken against what we knew our "nuggets" would need to know in combat. But we also knew that we were locked on the horns of competing dilemmas. In the first instance, the Fleet was crying for new pilots to fill new billets created by ongoing programs aimed both at expanding the size of existing units and creating new units altogether. In the second case, we were just a stopover in the pipeline between the primary schools and the Fleet; we had strictly limited facilities with which to train ever-increasing numbers of cadets flowing out of the two Florida-based primary schools. Acute equipment shortages in the Fleet prevented us from training our students in the actual models of airplanes they would be flying in the Fleet.

Our training program was essential, but it was by no means comprehensive. And we by no means suffered under the illusion that we were turning out Fleet-ready pilots, but we did teach them a lot and we did inculcate them with the spirit of self-confidence as well as transmitting to them the esprit de corps of naval aviation. If anything, our most important task, aside from the physical and mental skills we imparted, was to teach our students a brand of *perfectionism*. Indeed, this was the philosophical basis of all the training those young men received at primary and advanced flight-training schools. Ours was a truly high-risk business; a really elevated level of self-awareness and devotion to doing things perfectly were needed by these naval aviators to survive the rigors of simply flying high-performance airplanes in carrier operations—not to mention triumphing over adversaries flying other high-performance airplanes.

Our first cadre of instructors at Miami literally was in on the ground floor of the U.S. Navy's incredible, unprecedented growth toward its eventual full wartime strength. However, though much of what would come later was certainly in the air, our pace at the outset was not frenetic or tinged with a do-or-die mind-set. The senior staff, including Rog Hedrick and several of the other early AvCads, had been painstakingly trained over long years, and that is how we hoped to train our first flock of cadets. We well knew the shortcomings of the physical plant and we certainly heard the calls from the Fleet, but we were determined to impart all the skill and knowledge that we could in the few months allowed to us. As pressure from both sides picked up—as the Fleet yelled louder and as the primary schools churned out ever greater numbers of nuggets—we were obliged to speed things up, to cut some corners, to shave some of the fine points off our instructional program. This placed the burden of truly completing the training cycle upon the Fleet and initially left us feeling that we had not quite done our jobs. But even these feelings fell prey to the ever-increasing pressures the coming war imposed.

One event that relieved some of the pressure, albeit imperceptibly, was the commissioning of a new primary flight school at Corpus Christi, Texas. In the fall of 1941, as the new school was being created, we at Opa-Locka were called upon to train a cadre of experienced Fleet pilots who would set up an advance school there identical to our own. If nothing else, at least we did not have to take on the flow of Corpus Christi's primary school graduates ourselves.

2

Miami was by no means all work and no play. We had no officers' club at Opa-Locka, but we were welcomed at the Tatem Surf Club in Miami Beach. These luxurious facilities, including a huge pool adjacent to the surf, came to us at nominal cost. We flocked there on torrid summer afternoons at the conclusion of flight ops, and, until the pace picked up, practically lived there on weekends. My son, Mark, who was nearly four, was a real water rat and a great favorite of the young studs. To his mother's terror, they induced him to go off the high board and tossed him back and forth medicine ball fashion in the shallow end.

As a rule, we drank a lot, ate well, and danced up a storm. The few wives in attendance loved having slews of bachelors around, but I have no knowledge of extracurricular activities.

Two of our standout instructors were Lt(jg) Harry Harrison, a colorful if somewhat laid-back scion of the Philadelphia Main Line, and Lt(jg) Sam Silber, a former all-American lacrosse player from the University of Maryland. These two early AvCads delighted in playing practical jokes on our boss, Joe Clifton, primarily through the medium of Joe's prized new Buick. One day Harry and Sam jacked up a rear wheel so that the tire was just touching the ground, a fact that was obscured by the tall weeds growing in the parking lot. When Joe charged out to the lot a little late for a squash date in Miami, he characteristically jumped behind the wheel without looking, thrust the key into the ignition, and impatiently fire walled the gas pedal. A large audience that had unobtrusively gathered for the event witnessed Joe's frantic reaction to the engine's overrevving scream and the rubber smoke thrown up by the screeching tire. Another time, the two miscreants loaded several empty cartridge cases into one of the Buick's hubcaps. This produced a fearsome racket which disappeared at cruising speed. It took Joe some time to track down the source of the noise, but no time at all to decide who had planted the cartridge cases. Such high jinks helped relieve the tension of the job.

Instructors and students often enjoyed close personal associations that carried over into our off-duty hours. This close association was both a carryover from the days of an exceptionally small naval aviation service, when all of us formed a band of brothers, and a recognition of the rite of passage our course represented. On the other hand, however close we felt to our students, training time on the station—in the air or in classrooms on the ground—was marked by the strict adherence to military discipline and courtesy, for it was still our duty to inculcate our students into the rigors of the undemocratic, nonegalitarian military society for which they had volunteered. We did have mavericks to deal with from time to time, and we came down hard when they revealed themselves.

Lacking a war of our own, we followed the triumphs and travails of our British cousins as closely as we could, primarily in the press. No doubt, the Office of Naval Intelligence received a huge steady flow of information on tactics and equipment—Allied and Axis—but they did not deign to share it with any of us who might actually be able to use it. We were thus completely unaware of the appearance over China of the superb Japanese Zero fighter, a nimble airplane that was a full generation ahead of our most advanced Fleet-type monoplane fighter, the lamentable Brewster F2A Buffalo. The same held true in the case of the most advanced British Royal Air Force fighters; we were thus mystified by the Germans' inability to turn the Mediterranean into their own lake. Meantime, like us, the Royal Navy's Fleet Air Arm was struggling along with antiques of every type. This resulted in a criminal waste of resources and a vital need for pilots. Yet, somehow, the Fleet Air Arm gave the Germans and Italians stiff enough opposition to help keep the supply lanes to Malta and North Africa open.

Little did we know how closely our early war experience would parallel the Fleet Air Arm's in terms of such losses—and such closely run triumphs.

Through August 1941 we flew a five-day week. Then we flew six days. After December 7, flight-training operations were conducted every day, though instructors and students alike flew a staggered schedule so that all hands got one day off in seven.

News of Pearl Harbor came over the commercial radio as several of us were beering up at my house following a relaxed Sunday morning round of golf. We had no idea of the magnitude of destruction. Indeed, our initial reaction was one of satisfaction that the issue, so long a threat, was now joined. We assumed that our patrol bombers out of Hawaii would quickly locate the enemy task force and that our counterattack would be devastating. As the facts slowly emerged, however, we became as horrified as we were incredulous at the ineptitude of our Pacific commanders.

Withal, the commander in chief of the Japanese Combined Fleet, Adm Isoroku Yamamoto, was correct in opposing the Pearl Harbor attack while it was in the planning stage. He said, "No matter how successful it may be, it will wake the sleeping dragon." Unwittingly, the Japanese did us another service in addition to uniting our nation for the war; it was a favor that ultimately saved more lives than were lost at Pearl Harbor. By pure luck, none of our six precious fleet-type aircraft carriers were lost on December 7, 1941. Indeed, by crippling our battleship forces, the Imperial Navy forced the U.S. Navy to completely change over from a strategy based on a powerful surface fleet to one based on the employment of carrier air. The U.S. Navy was forced by its losses in battleships at Pearl Harbor to use the emerging carrier-based air arm as its primary offensive weapon from the onset of the Pacific War.

Of immediate use to us in the earliest weeks of the war was the Fleet's decision to scrap the Brewster F2A monoplane fighter in favor of the far better but still somewhat outclassed Grumman F4F Wildcat. As soon as more new Wildcats reached the carrier air groups and Marine squadrons, around the first of the year, Buffalos were released to the training command. The modern Buffalos were an invaluable supplement to the obsolete biplane fighters that we heaved around in, checking out ourselves and our students. While inadequate for combat, the F2As were ideal for our purposes, especially for approximating the level of engine power and flight characteristics our graduates would experience in the new Wildcat.

The introduction of the Buffalo at Opa-Locka temporarily boosted my prestige, for I was the only instructor who had flown it or any monoplane fighter in the Fleet, it having made its Fleet debut with VF-2 during my last year there. Of course, at the outset, my work load was increased, for I had to check out instructors after teaching them the vagaries of this quirky, hard-to-handle compromise airplane. Moreover, I had been VF-2's engineering—ground maintenance—officer when the Buffalo made its debut with

VF-2, so it also fell on me to help get the Opa-Locka maintenance staff up to speed on that dog's gremlins, which were legion.

After we had processed our first batch of students in the newly acquired F2As, Roger Hedrick and I were introduced to a new sort of teacher, LCdr Charles Evans, of the Royal Navy, a combat veteran fresh from the perils of flying the ghastly, inadequate Fairey Fulmar against German Messerschmitt Me-109s in Europe.

It would be an understatement to brand Lieutenant Commander Evans a mere "character." With a neatly cropped red mustache and beard—unheard of in the U.S. Navy—and a swagger stick in hand, this slight, handsome Britisher was the epitome of quiet self-confidence. He was unmistakable in his black silk scarf, octagonal-lensed goggles, and standard Royal Air Force leather flying helmet, which he wore in even the hottest weather. He was a superb, extremely skilled pilot and a warm, perceptive gentleman. With Lieutenant Commander Evans's arrival came news that Roger and I would receive as our next class a complement of Royal Navy trainees.

Once Evans had had a chance to study the pilot's handbook and receive a cockpit checkout in one of our F2As, he took off for a one-hour familiarization flight. Rog and I carefully monitored his ground-handling technique, takeoff, and final landing, and we saw that he handled the airplane expertly and smoothly. As Evans rolled up to the hardstand, Rog and I both knew what was coming next.

"Tom, I'd like to fly with you chaps. Can we take three of these aircraft out for a little formating?"

"Certainly, sir. We'll get our gear and be ready to go in fifteen minutes." As Rog and I turned to leave, we could not help grinning at one another, for we had both evaluated a lot of pilots just this way ourselves.

Rog and I followed Evans closely as we taxied out, and Evans looked briefly startled as we pulled into a tight vee for a formation takeoff. Routine climb-out, shallow dives, turns in each direction—Rog and I stayed locked in tight throughout. Next, Evans headed out over the cobalt Gulf Stream, eased down to about 30 feet above the whitecaps, and started a series of turns. The trick here is for the pilot on the inside to drop below the leader in order to keep formation; the tighter the turn, the lower he has to go. This is routine flying at most operating levels, but it gets a mite hairy when you know that your outboard wingtip, which you cannot watch, is getting ever closer to the water. You only snag once in that sort of situation.

After giving both of us a good trial by fire to see if we would clutch or sky out, Lieutenant Commander Evans pulled up, gave each of us a smile and a thumbs-up, and headed back to base to land. After that, whatever Rog and I did with the Brits was okay with him. This was most helpfully the case when one of the British students tried showing off for his girlfriend and augered in. I was sick but furious as I called all the Brits together and read them the riot act; I brusquely informed them that any more unauthorized flying at low level would be cause for immediate grounding and that Lieutenant Commander Evans would probably recommend that the offender be sent home in disgrace. The students groused a lot behind my back, but to no avail; Evans backed me all the way. We had no further discipline problems with the Brits, but they never forgave me for saying, "Your mate killed himself by his own stupidity."

Later in the war, when we led VF-17, Rog I invariably employed LCdr Charles Evans's low-level checkout technique with pilots who wanted to fly with us.

Our Royal Navy students were eager, dedicated young men to whom war was much more a reality than it was to their American counterparts. However, by early 1942, the Royal Navy was reaching fairly far down into the barrel for pilot candidates, and it is fair to say that these Brits were not of the same caliber as their American fellow sufferers at our hands.

Lieutenant Commander Evans wound up paying NAS, Miami, one of the finest compliments it ever received. In commenting on the quality of the Royal Navy students we were turning out, Evans said that they were better trained than those the Royal Navy was turning out for itself at home. This, from a combat veteran representing a service that had been at war for two years.

3

The CO, Cdr Jerry Bogan, made short shrift of my official January 1942 letter to the Navy Department requesting orders for sea duty. As soon as the letter reached Bogan's desk for an endorsement, I received the word, "Report to the commanding officer at once."

"You sent for me, sir?"

"You're goddamn right I did. I need you and all the other able-bodied instructors I can get for a long time to come. I will not so much as forward your request for sea duty recommending disapproval. Take it, get out of here, and don't waste my time again. Is that clear?"

"Yes, sir."

"Okay, Blackburn, shove off."

I was zero for two in my efforts to buck the system: My original assignment to Opa-Locka had stuck before there was a war, and my official request to get out of there had been turned back now that there was a war. Shortly after leaving Commander Bogan's office, however, I dropped a note to a personal friend working at the Aviation Detail Office, in Washington, and put in an unofficial request. Later still, I happened to be in Dallas picking up a new SNJ trainer to ferry to Miami when a recruiter for Claire Chennault's American Volunteer Group—the Flying Tigers—came through Opa-Locka. I was so frustrated at being kept from the war that I probably would have resigned my commission and signed on with Chennault if I had been home to see the recruiter.

But all was not lost.

"How the hell did you do this," Commander Bogan yelled as he waved a sheaf of official papers at me from behind his desk.

It was May 1942, long after I had given in to my sorry lot of being a beached fighter pilot playing nursemaid to tyros. I had no idea what the skipper was talking about, so it was no work at all adopting the look of honest, injured innocence I would have had on my face even if I had known what was going on.

The "this" turned out to be orders detaching me in June to travel to NAS, Norfolk, to form, commission, and command Escort Fighting Squadron 29 (VGF-29). Once formed, VGF-29 would report for duty aboard the new escort carrier, *Santee*. I was breathless and, for once, speechless.

Bogan cooled down a bit as he slowly came to realize that my look of surprise and delight was unfeigned. "Come on, Tommy, I've got connections you wouldn't believe, and *I* can't get sprung from here. You son of a bitch, how did such a junior lieutenant do it? Who do *you* know?"

I held my features deadpan as I rejoined, "Sorry, skipper, but that's classified information."

The skipper tried several unsuccessful approaches to get a clue, then finally growled, "Okay, shove off. Get back to work." As soon as I could, I sent a fifth of very good scotch to my friend at the Aviation Detail Office. It was the best investment I ever made.

When I picked up my orders from the skipper's office as I was checking out of Miami in June, I was flattered as well as touched to see that Jerry Bogan had penned in "with regret" after the standard typed-in phrase, "Detached this date."

July 1, 1942, was a typical blistering day at Norfolk when I read my orders aloud before twelve officers, eighty-plus sailors, and a handful of well-wishers: Escort Fighting Squadron 29 was formed and commissioned. Flight ops commenced several days later, as soon as we were equipped and checked out in a dozen factory-fresh Grumman F4F-4 Wildcat fighters

Two of my officers were combat veterans of the new war, and one had even flown and scored kills in the Wildcat in combat, albeit his fighter was the earlier F4F-3 variant. The F4F-4, which was just then making its way into the Fleet, was the first folding-wing fighter ever to be purchased by the U.S. Navy. The folding wings would prove to be a must aboard the cramped escort carrier to which VGF-29 was bound. The F4F-4 mounted a solid battery of six .50-caliber machine guns, three in each wing, and sported a good reflector gun sight. On the down side, the airplane was moderately underpowered and therefore quite slow in the climb, a compromise necessitated by the wing-folding mechanism, heavy armored seatbacks, and heavy ammunition load required for the six machine guns. About the best thing that could be said about the added weight was that it would help Wildcats get away from most

Japanese and German fighters while in a dive. Already proven at the Coral Sea and Midway, the Wildcat had a reputation for standing up to heavy fire and bringing its pilot home.

The Wildcat was a far better airplane than the transitional Brewster F2A Buffalo it replaced, but it had some weird quirks and terrible ground-handling characteristics. The powerful engine torque could cause an unwary or inexperienced pilot to ground loop to the left on takeoff, sometimes with fatal results. Also, its retraction mechanism for the main landing gear was a chain attached to a handle that the pilot was obliged to turn about twenty-seven times while he was doing all the other things required of him right after takeoff. Many an unwary or inexperienced Wildcat pilot sported painfully bruised shins after the handle got away from him while he was raising or lowering the landing gear. While no thoroughbred, the Wildcat was still the best, most powerful, most reliable production fighter the Navy had thus far put into service. I, for one, was glad to have it.

The training got off to an intense start, a holdover from my recent instructional duty. Within days, it became apparent that my exec, an old hand at flying multiengine patrol planes, was not making the grade as a fighter pilot despite a valiant effort on his part. He was unable to break ingrained habits and I was thus forced to send him back to multiengine flying. That left me with the job of choosing a new exec from between two experienced combat pilots whose squadrons had been lost when fleet carrier *Lexington* had been sunk in the Coral Sea in May. One, Lt(jg) Harry "Brink" Bass, was a 1938 Annapolis graduate who had earned a Navy Cross planting one of the bombs that sank the Japanese light carrier *Shoho* at Coral Sea. The other, Lt(jg) Bill Eder, was an ex-AvCad who had earned a Distinguished Flying Cross and whose score thus far in fighters was 1.5 confirmed kills and 1 probable. Brink, who had only just transitioned from dive-bombers to fighters, was senior to Bill, and fortunately a much better leader, so he got the nod despite Bill's combat record in fighters.

All the rest of the pilots under my command were fresh-caught ensigns right out of the advanced school at Corpus Christi. Rounding out VGF-29 was a sound, devoted ground staff. From the start, it was a happy, hardworking outfit.

Shortly after I formed the squadron, I was promoted to lieutenant commander. And shortly after that, we escaped the complications and strictures of a big-time base like NAS, Norfolk, and moved to our own operating base. Naval Auxiliary Air Station (NAAS) Pungo was in the boondocks 15 miles south of Norfolk, on the eastern edge of the Dismal Swamp. Pungo wasn't much, but it was mine, for I was the senior aviator present. With only our twelve Wildcats assigned to the station, we were free to set our own schedules and traffic patterns, and come and go as we pleased.

We came through our brief training at Pungo very well, though we lost one pilot who clutched and rode his Wildcat into the ground when he got into a spin trying to stream a towed target sleeve. In good time, all hands carrier qualified aboard jeep carrier *Charger*, a small converted merchantman, and we were all set to board Cdr Bill Sample's *Santee* when she completed conversion from fleet tanker to escort carrier in September. At that time, we joined the balance of the new escort air group, nine Grumman TBF Avenger torpedo bombers and nine Douglas SBD Dauntless scout-bombers. The bomber leader, LCdr Joe Ruddy, an old friend and comrade, was several years senior to me and thus filled in as air-group commander.

The very real German U-boat threat curtailed practice operations in the Atlantic, so we did our group workups while *Santee* remained in Chesapeake Bay. It was during the early part of the carrier work that I got caught with my pants at half-mast and made a beautiful comeback.

It happened when the fighter director, LCdr Red Gill, another *Lexington* survivor, called me by voice radio during one early flight: "Fighter Leader, this is *Santee*. My call sign is Romeo. What is yours? Over."

There followed a dismal pregnant silence. I had not thought about a call sign for the squadron; it had never occurred to me that we would be needing one. I had no response ready, but I had been taught as a plebe at the "trade school"—Annapolis—never to say "I don't know;" a dumb answer is better than no answer. I was not about to lose face over this one, not with the whole squadron and possibly the whole ship listening.

"Arrgh . . . Romeo, this is . . . Shillelagh Leader. Send your message. Over."

Our unofficial squadron insignia soon appeared on the left shoulder of our flight coveralls. It depicted a stylized Irish war club within a kelly green border.

*   *   *

Santee sailed for Bermuda in October 1942 as part of a task force bound for Operation TORCH, the invasion of North Africa. Of course, we had no idea what lay ahead, but we sensed that it was something of importance.

Our immediate group comprised one small fleet carrier and three CVEs, *Santee* and two other escort carriers converted from fleet tankers. Our flagship was *Ranger*, a small fleet-type carrier that was to have been the first of a line of many such economical carriers. However, *Ranger* had been found wanting because the lack of a third elevator between her flight deck and hangar deck that resulted in very slow launch and recovery operations. Though fleet carrier *Wasp* was really an updated *Ranger*-type carrier, the addition of a third elevator allowed her to participate in dangerous offensive operations. *Ranger* was not really up to taking part as a full partic-ipant in the strategically critical battles then raging in both the Pacific and Mediterranean, so she had been relegated to serving as an oversized escort and escort leader.

We conducted five days of intense warm-up exercises in Ber-mudan waters. It was a meager shakedown for new ships operating with new squadrons.

During the Bermudan interlude, one of my gang managed to wreck a Wildcat in a bad landing. Upon returning to the anchorage for a final resupply before heading east toward Africa, we received a message from the task force commander: "Replacement aircraft arriving aboard *Chenango* [on October 15]. All ships submit [air-craft] replacement requirements." Captain Sample called LCdr Joe Ruddy and me to his cabin and showed us the message.

"Captain, I recommend that we ask for two fighters. That'll improve the chances of getting the one we need."

The skipper nodded with a look that spelled "conniver," but he said, "Okay, Tommy, I'll do that."

The following day I was told to report to the captain's cabin "on the double." There, I found Bill Sample with a big grin on his coppery face. "Tommy, I just got word that *two* fighters will be arriving by barge this afternoon. That's thirteen planes for twelve pilots! I can't have a spare plane I can't use cluttering up my ship. You got us into this, so you go get us out!"

My mind was already at work. "Aye, aye, sir. Do I have your permission to go talk to the people aboard the flagship?"

"Yeah. Do whatever's needed. We don't have much time."

Once aboard *Ranger*, I headed straight for the cabin of the task group chief of staff, Capt John Ballentine. I told the unvarnished truth and saw the amusement in Captain Ballentine build to a great belly laugh. When I quit talking and he quit laughing, the captain asked, "Okay, Blackburn, what do you want from me?"

"Sir, I'd like to talk to your personnel people and see if somebody has a Wildcat pilot he can spare. If so, I'd like to get him temporarily transferred to us."

Unbelievably, the chief of staff bought the idea. This meeting with Captain Ballentine was to have a significant impact upon my future.

On our first day out of Bermuda, we had a mishap involving an SBD as it was being launched by catapult to take its turn on the antisubmarine patrol. As usual, the scout was armed with a 500-pound general-purpose bomb, fused so that its pilot could select the mode of detonation—upon high-speed impact with the surface or as a depth charge, 40 feet below the surface. As the Dauntless flew off, the suspension lug holding the bomb failed. We onlookers gawked with terrified fascination as the explosive device bounced and rolled down the flight deck and then fell over the bow.

The bomb went off as a depth charge—with a great roar and a mighty upheaval of water directly below the aircraft elevator. An optical rangefinder weighing 300 pounds toppled down upon the open bridge, narrowly missing the skipper and bruising several men before it came to rest. Word was instantaneously passed over the ship's public-address system that the explosion was from one of our own depth charges, and not a torpedo hit. This news came as an immense relief to all hands who had not seen what had happened.

It was immediately discovered that the aircraft elevator had been jammed in midposition, and that resulted in the damage-control party being called out. The damage-control people also learned in short order that the tough double tanker hull had apparently oil-canned, a remarkably fitting technical term meaning that it had first dished in and then had snapped back out. No leakage or apparent other damage was found. However, of direct interest to me and four other members of VGF-29, the detonation had fouled up our aircraft homing device, a malfunction that would not be discovered until it was too late.

4

The four small carriers and their meager screen of destroyers sortied from Bermuda on schedule on October 25 and joined with the rest of the North Africa invasion armada on October 27. TORCH, the first major American amphibious assault of the war in the European Theater of Operations, brought together in its U.S. component 102 ships of every type and size, from battleships to fleet tugs. The Navy's job was to get the Army ashore in French Morocco before the winter storms and soggy fields made the landing and breakout unacceptably risky.

On Halloween, at 0200, *Santee* came frantically alive with the clanging of the General Quarters alarm—a bugle blast and PA blatting, "General Quarters. General Quarters. All hands man your battle stations." As we ran through the hangar deck on our way to the squadron ready rooms, we felt the shock waves of depth charges transmitted through the steel deck and, seconds later, heard the loud *boom, boom, boom* of the detonations. Every one of us had seen tankers burning off the Atlantic coast, so we were all scared.

After a long hour in the ready room, we got the word that we had been the victims of a false alarm, that no submarine had been found and that a destroyer's sonar contact had apparently been erroneous. We had no quibble with being shaken from our sleep in such a manner; mistakes of this nature were common because the policy of the day—a good one—was to shoot first and ask questions later. We headed back to our staterooms, still nervous and upset by the rude awakening and the pensive hour in the ready rooms, but happy that nothing had come of it. In another hour, we would all be awakened again, routinely, for our daily predawn General Quarters stand-to.

Unbelievably, the U-boats made no contacts with the invasion armada as we followed a sinuous track to the objective. Naturally, the apprehension over a submarine attack grew as we ventured farther out into the Atlantic, closer to their favored killing grounds and closer yet to their bases. By November 6 we were plodding along within reach of German long-range land-based patrol bombers that might be flying out of the Moroccan bases we were being sent to seize.

*   *   *

On the way, we finally learned what we were facing. The TORCH operation started for us with the study of meager intelligence data pertaining to the southwest coast of French Morocco, particularly the area around Safi, a little port about 65 miles northwest of Marrakech. We were given time to pore over old charts of our objective area, but no aerial photos were available. We had zero data on the Vichy French air forces in the target area, and no clue as to how many, if any, Germans were positioned there or nearby. I do not believe any of us had enough experience or sense to be alarmed by how little we knew.

Everything was to start at first light on November 8. The SBDs and TBFs of our escort air group were loaded with general-purpose bombs and charged with dropping them on call in support of the landing force. Meanwhile, Fighting-29 was to attack the airfield at Safi and destroy any planes found there with our machine guns. Then we were to provide cover for the amphibious task force charged with landing the infantry. After completing our runs on the Safi airfield, my fighters were to report in by voice radio to the amphibious force commander and thereafter "operate as directed" by him.

The night takeoff was hairy, to say the least. To give my first division of six F4Fs an adequate takeoff run in the event there was no surface wind—there was none—and with *Santee* cranked up to her maximum speed of 19 knots, we needed all the deck run we could get. Thus, the seven remaining fighters, their wings folded, were lined up heading aft along the starboard side of the flight deck from abeam the island. The first group of six, which I led off, trundled down the lane between the folded-wing Wildcats and the port edge of the flight deck. When we reached a deck crewman holding a bright light to indicate when we had reached the end of the line of seven waiting fighters, each of us in turn eased over to the right so we could use the whole width of the flight deck—55 feet!—for the remaining 125 feet leading to the black hole beyond the bow. Farther out were two red mast lights, each marking the position of one of the two destroyers steaming 1,000 yards ahead of *Santee* and 30 degrees on either bow. Those lights were our "horizon." All this because safer, surer launch by catapult was deemed too slow.

Shortly after liftoff each of us turned on his running lights so we could rendezvous at 1,000 feet and about 5 miles ahead of the task group. It soon became apparent that only four of my clutch of five chicks had made it. After orbiting as long as we could, I doused my lights, and the others followed suit. Then we test fired our guns and turned for the coast.

We were at 10,000 feet and 10 miles north of Safi when the clear dawn broke. From there, we could easily see the landings in progress as well as the heavy fire from our surface warships and the light counterbattery fire from the Vichy French coastal guns. The airfield we had been sent to neutralize did not exist. We saw no antiaircraft fire nor any evidence of hostile air action. Thus, as ordered, I placed a voice-radio call to the task force flagship, but there was no response. I kept trying, but it eventually became apparent that something was awry, perhaps with my radio, perhaps with theirs. So we circled and observed the action, contributing nothing. It was a dreadful disappointment, and in brief radio exchanges with my formation I gathered we were all as angry as we were frustrated.

When our appointed time on station ran out, we headed for the barn. I had not kept notes of courses and times on the way out to our orbiting station because I anticipated no strain in spotting the ship and getting back aboard quickly and safely. However, by the time we quit our station, the weather had deteriorated from perfect to low overcast and numerous rain squalls. I could not see the carrier, but I did have another proven means for finding her and guiding myself and my fighter formation to sighting distance.

In bad weather and at night, we routinely relied upon the YE homing gear, more popularly known as the "hayrake" because of the shape of its antenna. Simply put, the YE transmitted a different signal—one Morse letter—in each of twenty-four directions, one letter to each 15-degree segment of a 360-degree circle. All a lost pilot had to do was hear a particular letter to know in which direction he should turn to find the ship. If a new letter came up, he had passed the ship and needed only to turn back. In addition, the signal grew louder as one closed, so that the pilot could approximate the distance to the ship. It was not a precise system, but it was nearly foolproof and by late 1942 it had brought many a plane back to our ships.

In addition to the YE receiver, each of us also had a four-channel VHF radio aboard, with frequencies accurately preset and automatic self-keying from transmit to receive modes and vice versa. Also, by late 1942, all of our ships had surface search radar and larger vessels such as carriers all had air search radars as well. Thus, the airplane's radio and the carrier's YE transmitter, combined with the air search radar, was a potent combination for bringing planes and ships into roughly the same area so that recoveries could be made. If there were a lot of planes in the air, and a ship's controller was not sure which was his, a particular pilot or pilots could stand out from the crowd by flying an expanding-square pattern while increasing altitude, a maneuver known as a "square dance."

When I turned my fighters for home—where I thought home should be—the hayrake signal was coming in loud and clear; I thus knew exactly which way to fly. However, long after the estimated time of arrival, we still saw only empty ocean. Also, the hayrake signal had changed to one that did not seem possible. Time for the radio.

"Romeo. This is Shillelagh Leader. Over."

"This is Romeo. Hear you five by five. Over."

"This is Shillelagh Leader. Do not have you in sight. If you hold me, request a steer. Over."

"This is Romeo. Do not have you on my gadget. Commence square dance and stand by for steer. Acknowledge."

"Shillelagh Leader. Wilco."

So we commenced the expanding-square pattern, climbing all the while. I was not completely relaxed, but I was still far from clutching.

At last, "This is Romeo. Hold you. Steer two-five-oh. Acknowledge."

"Shillelagh Leader. Steer two-five-oh. Wilco. Out."

At this point I had about thirty-five minutes of fuel left. I guessed that my four wingmen had less because they had been using more keeping station on me, a typical outcome of any formation flying. I gave it ten minutes on course 250, but no ship appeared. It was safe to bet that the fighter director had seen another target on his radarscope and had jumped to the conclusion that it was us.

"Romeo. This is Shillelagh Leader. I do not have you in sight. I am setting course for the beach. Over."

"This is Romeo. Roger. I no longer hold you. Good luck. Out."

As we swung to the northeast, my mind flashed to a bit of history from the Spanish-American War of 1898: Lieutenant Hobson stands alone of the deck of the burning collier *Merrimack*, which is fast aground in the channel of Santiago de Cuba harbor. Spanish artillery is zeroed in and the shore is lined with hostiles firing small arms. What to do? Stay aboard the ship and burn or swim for shore and be shot? Thus, Hobson's choice. (He swam, survived, and was acclaimed as a hero.)

We had about as attractive a choice. We could ditch in the frigid Atlantic though no one knew where to look even if they had the time or resources. Or we could try to get over the beach and make forced landings in or bail out over hostile territory.

For me, there really was no choice; I ran out of fuel before the others, which was unusual. As soon as my engine coughed, I patted the top of my head, pointed to my wingman, made a vertical chopping motion in the direction of the formation's heading, blew my wingman a kiss, and peeled off to head into the surface wind. The hand signals meant, "You have the lead, continue on your present course, good-bye."

As my four companions swiftly flew out of sight to the northeast, I went through the busy, hurried routine of preparing for a water landing: crank open the cockpit, unsnap my parachute harness, check the life raft lanyard fastened to my Mae West life jacket, cinch my seat belt and shoulder harness as tight as they would go, fully lower my landing flaps, drop my tail hook. I wanted to splash at minimum speed while heading straight into the wind, nearly at the top of an oncoming swell. The tail hook was down to help me find the surface; as soon as I felt it drag in the water, I let the nose drop slightly. And in we went.

Before the spray subsided, I tripped the seat belt–shoulder harness release, stood up, and dived straight over the windshield. My Wildcat, 29-GF-1, rapidly reared her tail up and sank. By then, I had already set the unconfirmed world's record for the 10-yard dash, freestyle, to avoid getting bashed in the head or taken down by the vertical fin as the fighter flipped over. I shucked off my chute, pulled the raft in front of me, and pulled the toggle hooked to the carbon dioxide bottle. As soon as it inflated, I climbed aboard. My watch said that it was 1030, November 8, 1942. My first thought was that I had racked up a brief, ignominious war record. Then I assessed my performance in terms most of my students at Opa-Locka had heard from time to time: "Dumb, dumb, dumb."

I took stock of my situation. I was clad in a lightweight summer flying suit over my skivvy pants, a lightweight flight jacket, Marine field shoes, thin leather gloves, a leather flying helmet with goggles, and a life jacket. There was thus precious little between me and the elements, and none of it was waterproof. I had a .45-caliber automatic pistol with seven tracer rounds, a large hunting knife in a leather sheath, a small flashlight, and two dye marker packets. The life raft's survival pack yielded a pint of water sealed in a soup-type can, two 3-inch by 12-inch "paddles," and nothing else. This was the standard issue of the day.

I estimated that I was 60 miles from the coast on a northwest-southeast line; the wind and swells were out of the northwest. As soon as I had inventoried my meager possessions, I tied a glove on a crude lanyard and dropped it over the side so I could clock the seconds it took the looped lanyard to extend fully. This old-time "speedometer," borrowed from the days of sail, gave me an approximation of my drift rate. If I was right about my position, I would reach shore in about six days. If the raft stayed afloat. If the wind held. If hypothermia did not kill me first.

I quickly hit rock bottom. I was lonesome and frightened and, the more I turned it over in my mind, overwhelmingly depressed by a stupid outcome to my big chance as a fighter-squadron skipper. I also knew that there was zero probability of anyone launching a search-and-rescue effort in my behalf; the forces were not available. As I plumbed the underside of self-pity, I conducted an internal conversation: Why go through an agonizing, futile effort to survive; why not just stick the pistol in my mouth; no one will ever know. But I lacked the courage.

Thankfully, the days were bearable, mostly sunny. The nights, however, were cold and wet, and they seemed of interminable length as I watched Cassiopeia and the Big Dipper inch their way across the cosmos until the sun's first warming glow appeared in the east. The little raft, which was snug at the hips and just long enough to sit in with my legs only slightly bent, perpetually had several inches of water in it. The freeboard of about 6 inches did little to stop the annoying spray kicked up by the blessedly steady wind that was propelling me toward the faraway shore.

After a long time at sea, as I was thinking about the baby goat I would slaughter and whose blood I would drink upon reaching shore, a grouper—three feet long—cruised up, looked me over, and decided that the flimsy raft was a good place to scratch his back. Things were not bad enough; now I stood to get my raft punctured by an itchy fish! What to do? Stab him with my knife? What if I only wound him; will he thrash around angrily and swamp the raft? If I kill him, will his blood attract a shark? Will waiting him out suffice? I have no idea how long he stayed around; my sense of time was gone. But he eventually left me and my good ship, *Lollipop*, making a leisurely, final, and welcome departure without causing any damage. His stay was the most agonizing part of the painful ordeal.

I spotted *Santee* and her two accompanying destroyers on November 10, hull down to the east. Several SBDs were tooling around in the distance as well. I knew damn well they were not looking for me; there were not adequate forces to undertake any searches. In any case, only the other four members of my formation had any clue as to my location, and their news was over two days old—assuming any of them had been rescued.

Santee and her consorts remained beyond sighting distance of me for the rest of the day, though maddeningly close. On November 11, after a pensive night, the task force came into sight again, dead to leeward. One of the destroyers came alongside the carrier to refuel while the other snaked back and forth ahead looking for the feared plume of a submarine periscope. It so happened that the second destroyer was heading straight for me. I silently coached him on, fearful of upsetting the balance of nature that had brought him this far along. Don't hurry, I pleaded, just hold your course and you'll steam right over me.

The tension was unbearable. I knew that from a destroyer's bridge a man in a raft can be seen—if the observer is looking for him—a mile away at most. If, as was the case this day, there were 10-foot swells running, then the raft was in sight of the ship only about 10 percent of the time, only when it was on a wave crest. I knew that the refueling operation would be rushed because the carrier and the refueling destroyer were extremely vulnerable as long as they were obliged to hold a steady course side by side in a straight line. While tethered by the refueling lines, they were a submarine skipper's dream target.

I saw the patrolling destroyer's bridge erupt in furious activity when she was still a half-mile from my position. Then signal searchlights started flashing messages among all three ships. Well, this was it; they had found me or they had found a submarine. Before I could wonder more, the lead destroyer swung toward me, backed down hard to check her way, and dropped a motor whaleboat. I even found it in my heart to admire their smart seamanship.

The pickup was anticlimactic. I was hauled into the whaleboat and motored back to the ship. I was a little shaky getting aboard; my legs and butt were cramped after three full days of sitting half-crouched in the watery bottom of the life raft. I had no feeling in my feet, but I declined proffered assistance. I am proud to say that I still had my whole pint can of water when I was picked up. I had kept my mouth moist by chewing a cud of chamois cut from the liner of my flight helmet. The water was for a *real* emergency. A smiling bluejacket gave me a little drink of water on the main deck of the destroyer and led me below for a divine hot shower. I sort of faded out and came to later, aware that I was buried in blankets and undergoing a gentle, continuous foot massage while the ship's doctor superintended the wolfing down of heavenly hot broth. My first words: "Doc, the foot rub hurts. More soup, please."

"No more just now. Soon, if you keep it down. You have an advanced case of immersion foot—prolonged soaking in cold water. I think we can restore the circulation, but another day of it and gangrene would have set in. You'd have at least lost your feet if that happened."

The news just made my sense of the pickup by my own little task group—by anyone—seem all the more miraculous.

With occasional awakenings for more light fare, I slept through a solid fourteen hours. I neither needed nor wanted the free medicinal booze that was offered at each awakening, a fact not everybody believed when I mentioned it.

Having gone into the drink while in top physical condition, I rebounded quickly and was "back to battery" the following day. I was thus transferred back aboard *Santee* by high line, riding in a coal sack. Having made such an ass of myself, I arrived feeling very hangdog. To my delight and amazement, the ship's exec was on hand to warmly greet me and present the skipper's apology for not being able to do so himself, what with the press of business on the bridge. However, I was invited to see the captain on the bridge as soon as I felt up to it. All this as well as the large welcoming committee of cheering shipmates which turned out to greet me.

As soon as I got my breath back, I asked about the four other members of my formation. Glum-looking countenances told me before words arrived that there was no news yet. There was still hope, but very little, even in spite of my own miraculous reappearance.

*   *   *

The next day, November 13, Brink Bass was scheduled for a solo flight to the Vichy French base at Marrakech to drop messages of amity along with cartons of American cigarettes. I quietly told Brink that I was taking the hop, and I suited up. At "Man planes," I proceeded to the flight deck by interior passageways and climbed right into the Wildcat positioned on the catapult, which was on the port bow of the ship. By boarding the plane from the port side, I was able to get into the cockpit unobserved by the skipper or anyone else on the bridge.

As I was getting hooked up and strapped in by the grinning plane captain, who of course had figured out what was going on, the flight deck bullhorn blared, "Do not launch that plane till Lieutenant Bass is in the cockpit. Lieutenant Commander Blackburn, report to the captain on the bridge immediately."

Skunked! It turned out that our dedicated and enormously competent flight surgeon had come topside looking for me so we could watch the launch together, and so he could see how I was doing on the psychological front. When he found Brink instead of me, he hotfooted it to the bridge and spilled the beans to the captain. I was extremely angry over being found out, and when I learned that the doctor had turned me in, I nearly alienated his friendship by calling him "Doc Fink" for several days, until I cooled down.

Summaries of our invasion efforts brought out that the amphibious part of the operation had been superbly run and totally successful, but that air ops had been a near disaster. Dive-bombers and torpedo planes, as well as fighters, had ditched because of the problem with the hayrake antenna, which had been jarred loose on October 26, when the bomb had gotten loose from the SBD. In all, VGF-29 lost five pilots missing in action—the four members of my formation and one out of Brink Bass's formation, the extra pilot we had picked up with the extra Wildcat in Bermuda. The latter flew into a cloud and was never heard from again. Against that sorry score, one of our pilots, Ens Bruce Jacques, shot down a Vichy fighter on November 10, the same day one of the *Santee* Dauntlesses got a Vichy dive-bomber.

The French soon capitulated and *Santee* was released to head west, for Norfolk. Almost as soon as we left station, good news caught up with us; all four of the strays from my D-Day formation were alive.

They had barely made it to the beach near Cape Blanco, well north of Safi, and had all made dead-stick—powerless—landings on fields and roads. Every one of the planes was totaled, but none of the pilots was injured. Astonished and irate locals rounded up the four at gunpoint and incarcerated them in the local bastille until the armistice was signed. They were turned over to the U.S. Army and started on the road back to Norfolk, where they arrived in early December, none the worse for wear and possessed of vivid sea stories.

Following a brief period of R&R—rest and rehabilitation—we reopened for business at NAS, Norfolk, in early December. We were just getting revved up, in fact, when orders for me arrived out of the blue: "As soon as relieved as CO of VGF-29, report to Commander, Air Force, Atlantic Fleet, on 1 January 1943 to form and commission Fighting Squadron 17 as commanding officer."

I was not entirely pleased with this unanticipated and unasked-for news of my rising fortunes. Obviously, it was a terrific assignment; I was to be the CO of a thirty-six-plane fighter squadron, part of the air group of a new first-line fleet carrier. But VGF-29 and *Santee* were going concerns that would certainly face new adventures long before the new carrier and her air group. Moreover, VGF-29 and *Santee* were congenial, happy outfits which had transitioned through the sweat and agony common to new organizations and their shakedowns.

I came up with a great idea and presented it to the people at ComAirLant: Wouldn't it be dandy to incorporate VGF-29 in toto as the working nucleus of VF-17? Unspoken: Let somebody else do the dirty work of setting up and starting a new outfit from scratch.

"Tommy," a senior AirLant staffer replied, "you must be out of your skull. Not only 'no,' but 'hell no!' The remaining VGF-29 people will remain there. However, we'll consider, but not promise, to get you the key pilots you request for VF-17."

I did succeed in getting Brink Bass fleeted up to skipper of VGF-29, even though he was considered very junior for the assignment. He filled the job with distinction and success. VGF-29 was expanded and became VF-29 toward the end of 1944. In Pacific combat under LCdr Bill Eder from November 1944 to April 1945, the squadron scored a highly commendable 113 kills, many of which were credited to the nucleus I had formed and trained.

PART II

Fighting-17

5

New Year's Eve, 1943, was more enjoyable than I had anticipated so I did not find my way home from the Norfolk
Officers' Club to the Bachelor Officers' Quarters until 0500. Precisely at 0800, wearing my best blue uniform, I was standing tall
before ten ensigns and eight bluejackets, reading from a piece of
paper in my hand. Fighting Squadron 17 was born.

I made no inspirational speech that first morning of 1943; just,
"Report for duty at 0800 tomorrow. Dismissed."

The AirLant staffers had promised to try to fill key squadron
billets with people I requested by name. Unfortunately, I was a
little late in drawing from the pool of extremely qualified instructors with whom I had served at Opa-Locka a year earlier. LCdr
Jumping Joe Clifton had recently commissioned Fighting-12, and
he had thus beat me to the same talent pool. Nevertheless, I was
able to snag LCdr Roger Hedrick as my exec, and some other
Miami talent was said to be on the way.

By the end of January, we had two combat veterans aboard,
Lt(jg) Johnny Kleinman and Lt(jg) Sunny Jim Halford. Both
had served with carrier-based fighter squadrons early in the Pacific War and then, in September and October 1942, land-based
at Guadalcanal's Henderson Field. Unfortunately, their squadron, Fighting-5, had been right at the forefront—literally the
first line of defense—during its tour at Guadalcanal, and the
experience had been brutal. Though Kleinman and Halford each
had had ample home leave and time to recover, both proved to be
a little shaky still when they reported aboard Fighting-17. In
truth, neither was overjoyed with the prospect of going out
again.

Six lieutenants joined us from various elimination bases, where
they had been instructors at the most basic level of the Navy's
pilot-entry program. They were all good pilots, but none had any
combat experience nor even any time in high-performance airplanes. We got one more lieutenant, who, along with a passel of
new ensigns, had only just completed advanced training. I was
shocked to learn that none of the newly bewinged pilots had any

time in fighters; the final phases of their flight training had been done, perforce, in trusty, undemanding SNJ trainers.

Blackburn, Hedrick, Kleinman, Halford and Lt(jg) Timmy Gile, one of my Miami plowback instructors—we were the only pilots in VF-17 who had ever set foot in a combat-type airplane. Everyone else had flown only trainers of various and sundry types.

When the dust settled, VF-17 totaled forty-two pilots—and no fighters. In addition to merely forming a new squadron, we were to receive and evaluate a hot new fighter type, the Vought F4U-1 Corsair. I quickly learned that the F4U was an airplane the Navy's own flight-test activities regarded with much trepidation and whose characteristics were cloaked in mystery and, to some degree, misinformation. Nevertheless, the squadron's lead pilots would have to get everyone checked out in the new fighter so we could oversee the transition by all hands. At the same time, on the run, it would be left to us to work out the bugs so the F4Us were ready to go into combat when we were. From this hodgepodge of raw material—new pilots, new fighter type—I had to weld a fighting machine of my own and then get it meshed with the two other squadrons of Air Group 17—another horde of grass-green pilots flying the Grumman TBF Avenger torpedo bomber and the new and unevaluated Curtiss SB2C Helldiver scout-bomber. As if this were not enough, the air group then had to be merged with a brand new fleet-type carrier, *Bunker Hill*, CV-17, which was still abuilding at Quincy, Massachusetts.

Our estimated time of arrival in the Pacific war zone was August 1943, a scant eight months hence.

The icing on the cake was the location of our training activities. There could have been a worse place to do them than NAS, Norfolk, in the winter, but choosing it would have been difficult.

I had been through most of this before, with Fighting-29. I had learned a thing or two about creating a new squadron, by doing things right as well as wrong. On the day Fighting-17 opened for business, I knew precisely what I wanted to do, what *had* to be done.

The first consignment of new Corsairs was not even *promised* until early February because the first batches of production F4Us were properly bound for Fighting-12 and several Marine squadrons that were scheduled to make their combat debuts in the hotly contested

Solomon Islands, at Guadalcanal, in the spring. Thus, my first order of business was to get some airplanes—fighters and several advanced trainers—so my eager tyros could log as much flight time as possible while we were waiting. I knew only too well that all pilots—especially fresh-caught pilots—lose their touch very quickly if they do not fly regularly. Moreover, I had to evaluate each pilot's abilities while there was still time to weed out the weak sisters and snatch good men from the pipeline leading to squadrons throughout the Navy's rapidly expanding fighter forces. I still had some good connections at the force material command, left over from my Fighting-29 days, and I went right to work latching on to ten SNJ trainers and eight F4Fs.

Transitioning inexperienced pilots from trainers to fighters is not as simple as it sounds. The wing-loading—the ratio of the area of the wings to the weight of the aircraft—is vastly different. Fighters, with their high wing-loading, are inherently more dangerous to fly than trainers. The difference manifests itself most obviously when the power plant shuts down; a lighter trainer will glide for a long distance while a heavier fighter tends to drop like a brick.

We started everyone off in the SNJs. Rog and I, who had learned many tricks of the trade at Miami, first wanted to see how each man handled himself aloft. The early flight time was equally important to the new men because many of them had not flown for several weeks, what with time off for Christmas and long leaves following graduation from flight training, plus the time it took us to get the SNJs. All we did at first was bore holes in the sky and shoot landings. This was time well spent in that it brought all hands up to speed.

As each pilot completed fifteen or twenty hours in our SNJs he was considered ready to transition into the F4Fs. Except for its egregious ground-handling characteristics, the Wildcat was really the ideal high-performance fighter of the day for transitioning new fighter pilots. It was a very nice, honest airplane to fly, an excellent intermediate step on the way to the Corsair.

We managed to stagger through the transition into the Wildcat without killing anyone. Working overtime in these welcome hand-outs, in lousy, cold, wet weather and operating from an extremely overcrowded field, Hedrick, Halford, Kleinman, Gile, and I went at it hammer and tongs. For the moment, I was not interested in training my pilots to fight in the Wildcat, merely to fly in it. By the end of January, everyone had at least soloed in the Wildcats. In addition to giving the troops needed experience, it allowed the squadron's front office to discover the standout pilots as well as to learn of the shortcomings in various people, those that could be corrected and those that could not. As a result of our early evaluations, five of the tyros were reassigned elsewhere, replaced with five new unknowns who then had to be brought through the entire process and fairly evaluated.

One gain from the transition period was the early tentative identification of candidates to lead sections and divisons within the squadron. Seniority usually played a role in such decisions, but there was no reason to adhere strictly to the rank criterion for there were natural leaders and better fliers of every rank. At this early stage, however, everything of the sort was tentative and everyone started even. If nothing else, the possibility of prestigious assignment as section and division leaders gave the youngest, least senior officers something to shoot for.

Training and evaluating aside, I let it be clearly known early on that I wanted no reluctant dragons in Fighting-17, that my door was always open to anyone who felt he could not cut the mustard or otherwise wanted out. I let it be known right away that anyone who asked would be transferred without prejudice, nor with even a pejorative entry in his record book. I am sure that every pilot who ever was in VF-17 while I was the commanding officer must have taken the time to think about whether he *really* wanted to be a fighter pilot. My open-door offer was meant precisely to make everyone think about whether he was tough enough or adventurous enough—or brave enough—for the job. There were pilots who did come in and discuss their doubts and second thoughts. If Rog Hedrick and I concurred, we eased the man out—hopefully without anyone else being the wiser. If the solution was less apparent, Rog and I had no qualms about consulting with the flight surgeon or other key older members of the unit.

This policy left me with a solid band of aggressive eager beavers, but I also had to make two exceptions in the cases of Johnny Kleinman and Sunny Jim Halford. Though both expressed their reluctance to relive the horrors of their Guadalcanal experience, the squadron would have been ill served by my allowing our only two combat veterans—Halford had 3.5 kills, including 1 at Midway, and Kleinman had a kill and a probable—to go elsewhere; the need to leaven the vast majority of tyros with experienced combat veterans overrode all personal considerations. Balancing their desires and interests with the needs of the squadron, I promised to release them from the squadron at the conclusion of our first combat tour if they still wanted out. This deal with them was agreed to by Rog Hedrick as well, in the event I did not make it to the conclusion of our first tour.

From the first day, Fighting-17 was not destined to be a spit-and-polish outfit. I had acquired a horror of the superstructured military unit in which the brass sets itself up as a corps of infallible *patrones* and treats the junior officers like *peones*. I made it as clear as I could from the outset that I was concerned not with form but with substance, that the accent was on self-discipline rather than the externally applied variety. I perhaps tolerated a little more spirit-edness than did other unit commanders, but the troops learned my limits in very short order; anyone who could not operate at the required level of self-governing needed to go through what we all faced together was as good as gone. My experience was that can-do pilots do not require rigid formalities; the ideal is the easy personal relationships formed in countless ready-room bull sessions, where a free exchange of ideas and comments move up the chain of command as well as down. And this is what I fostered.

My own days as a red-assed ensign in a battleship had started a decade before I formed VF-17. In *that* world, age and experience equated with brains. Furthermore, the Old Navy philosophy was, if it wasn't invented here it couldn't possibly be any good. Old Navy—that is exactly what the professional officer corps had to put behind us if we were to absorb and make proper use of the many thousands of wartime officers, the very best of whom found their way into the burgeoning air establishment. These were smart young men, many with degrees from great schools. Who could work with them and fail to notice that behind the temporary facade of youthful exuberance were the minds that would run the machine of our society, of our economy, indeed of our own Navy once we had won the war?

All this is not to say that I did not firmly establish my authority as Fighting-17's CO. When I made a decision, that was it; debate was done, over. I also made it clear that, as exec, Rog Hedrick was my alter ego, and that I would back *his* decisions to the hilt. Though Rog's natural reserve precluded overfamiliarity, he was soon simply

"Rog" to all the pilots. I allowed only "Skipper" or "Mr. Blackburn," the traditional greetings. When our prince of chutzpah, Ens Mel Kurlander, tried "Skip" out on me, he was quickly and firmly put back on the track by a few curt words and the cold stare our troops called the "inspection look."

We were military, but not *that* military. We started each work day promptly at 0800 with all hands mustered at quarters and dressed in clean, complete uniforms—khakis sans tie—faces groomed, shoes or boots shined. Hung over or healthy, everyone was expected to stand tall, ready to go. My predilection for half-Wellington "fighter boots," mirror shined, was soon emulated by most of the young tigers. Punctuality for all events was taken as a matter of course, and woe betide the man who was late for a scheduled flight. Other than that, and very little else, we saved our heavy discipline for work in the air, where it really counted for something.

I left nothing to chance in getting across to my men that VF-17 was a *fighter* outfit, charged with engaging the enemy and blowing him out of the sky. The trick, then, was to hone aggressive—indeed, predatory—instincts while building loyalty to the group and to the precepts of military discipine. I was facing nothing new in this regard; it had been part of the process of inculcating fighter pilots from the earliest days of the trade. I had been through the same program myself, and I had already run VGF-29 through the program, with good results, I think. What we needed was high-performance men to fly and fight in high-performance airplanes, to mesh the man and the machine and then to mesh both of them into cohesive units—two-plane sections of section leader and wingman, four-plane divisions of two two-plane sections each, flights of two four-plane divisions each, building to a complete squadron of up to thirty-six airplanes. I needed to make every man feel and act as a part of the team while instilling in each of them the sense that his personal contribution was vital. I needed to make every man interchangeable with every other man in such a way as both to hone individual skills and self-reliance *and* curb an overabundance of individuality.

To do the job, I was not above using any and all corny gimmicks to raise and maintain morale. We got to work early trying to stand out, a means for instilling group spirit and élan into the rough admixture that formed through January. We all flew with flight scarves for sensible reasons of comfort, particularly in cold weather. But while everyone else wore the beautiful standard issue white nylon items, Fighting-17 pilots sported flaming red ones. I also had to tolerate the odd personal totem because I had one of my own, albeit for practical reasons. I had learned upon reporting aboard my first Fleet squadron, Bombing-2, that the standard issue flight helmet was not tailored to my oversize, knobby head. Thus, since then, I had slit the center seam as needed to provide a reasonably comfortable fit. The result prevented headaches, but what the observer saw was a blond-plumed helmet.

More than red scarves and a few bland personal totems, VF-17 needed a squadron insignia around which a sense of group pride could coalesce. Striking eagles and pouncing tigers had long since been preempted and overworked. The anthropomorphic designs copying the Disney world were in vogue, so armed, threatening animals abounded. To us—me—they smacked of being too cutesy and thus utterly inappropriate for a tough combat fighter squadron. Flaming sword, flaming spear, sheaf of arrows, battle-ax, mailed fist—these were all tried in various combinations, but none really pleased me. My thought was that since we were to be a Corsair squadron we should have a piratical theme. Since I was the boss, my views took precedence over everyone else's. In short order, someone worked up a sinister black flag emblazoned with a stark white skull-and-crossbones insignia. Whoever approved such items up the line approved this one, which was a good thing inasmuch as it had appeared on our engine cowlings by then. Furthermore, the standard practice of painting insignia on the fuselage below the cockpit was not for us; we wanted that space reserved exclusively for flags denoting kills.

Once we had our Corsairs in possession, I ordered that the propeller spinner and first 18 inches of each blade be painted in bright colors to denote the part of the squadron to which that airplane was attached. For example, red denoted the two four-plane divisions of my flight, white denoted Rog Hedrick's flight, and so forth.

To help instill unit pride and create personal relationships, we had happy-hour get-togethers every afternoon. There was a lot of singing in addition to a lot of drinking—mostly beer. We were very fortunate in that we did not lack for talented and enthusiastic musicians. We had an excellent pianist in Ens Brad Baker, a great trumpeter in Ens Teeth Burris, and Lt(jg) Duke Henning and Lt(jg) Timmy Gile had been whiffenpoofs at Yale. I was known as the one who could not carry a tune but always remembered the words.

We always went to happy hour as a group and remained apart as an island within the ebb and fow of other enthusiastic drinkers, singers, and talkers. When the Corsairs arrived, we were further set apart by the fact that we were the only F4U squadron in residence at Norfolk, a rather telling distinction when we began encountering dangerous bugs that appeared not to quell our boisterous off-duty activities one iota. I quite consciously fostered the mystique of being a unit apart.

While working on the things that set Fighting-17 apart from other—run of the mill—squadrons, I was also quite concerned lest my fledglings miss a good grounding in the heritage of courage and devotion to duty that stood as the foundation for the U.S. Navy's fighting arms. It was my solemn duty and privilege to teach the uninitiated that, from the ancient days of sail, seafaring men have known that their lives and fortunes depend upon the bonds formed among shipmates. The teachings were embodied in oft-repeated aphorisms like "Never let your shipmate down," and "Never flee in the face of the enemy."

Our young pilots learned from the small cadre of professionals about all the brave men who had gone before them and why and when and where they had said, "Don't give up the ship; fight her 'til she sinks," and "Give me a fast ship, for I intend to go in harm's way." I wanted them to be especially mindful of the heroes and heroics of naval aviation, of LCdr John Waldron and his Torpedo-8, a squadron of slow, vulnerable, obsolete torpedo planes that, unsupported and in broad daylight, had bored through Japanese antiaircraft fire and Zero fighters to attack the Japanese carriers at Midway. Waldron and all but one of his pilots died in that attack, but they established with their blood and their lives a nonpareil precedent of devotion to duty. I did not expect my youngsters to die as the Torpedo-8 pilots and aircrewmen had died, but I did expect them to go down facing the enemy, if indeed they must go down. More important than merely dying with their boots on and thus providing us with an example of courage and devotion to duty, Torpedo-8 had sucked down the Japanese fighter cover and had thus allowed our dive-bombers to score numerous hits that started the decline of the Imperial Navy's hitherto unbeatable carrier air arm. *That* was the real contribution, the real lesson of Torpedo-8, the one I did expect my squadron to emulate—making our positive contribution to the final victory.

6

The long-awaited word arrived in mid-February—one new F4U-1 Corsair fighter was ready for delivery at Floyd Bennett Field, New York. I chose this auspicious moment to throw my rank around and so caught the first available flight. I was still clutching the pilot's handbook when we landed so I could get right down to the business of cockpit familiarization and checkout.

The airplane was huge, far bigger than any fighter I had ever seen. Most of it seemed to be engine. As soon as possible, I fired up the big bird and began going through the pretakeoff checks the moment the 2,000-horsepower engine was warm. At length, I gingerly taxied forward, cursing the extremely poor ground visibility of this and all Navy fighters of the day; with its long nose stretching an unprecedented 12 feet in front of my windshield, the F4U was the champ of champs in this regard. Sinuous forward movement was an absolute must if I wanted to see anything out ahead.

"Navy oh-two-three-oh-three cleared into position and cleared for takeoff."

"Oh-two-three-oh-three. Roger."

I went through a last minute cockpit scan and pushed the throttle forward to the stop as I began to roll. Habits die hard; I applied right full rudder, a must with the Wildcat. A snowbank on the right side of the runway loomed large, and then my overcorrection threatened to plow the Corsair into the left-hand snowbank. My zigs and zags, highly erratic at first, gradually damped out and I managed to lift off the center of the runway. The thermometer stood at 25 degrees, but I was bathed in sweat. I had already learned a few valuable lessons that needed to be imparted to my eager beavers at Norfolk.

By then, the Corsair had already earned a servicewide sobriquet. After finding the F4U more responsive to persuasion than dominance, Dog Ears Coleman, an ole country boy serving with VF-12, had remarked, "This plane is as cooperative as a hog on ice." Thus, the F4U was known for a long time as the Hog—a nickname the folks at Vought eventually worked through to replace with their favorite, the rather meek U-Bird.

As a crowd of the committed gathered in Norfolk's dank cold, ground crewmen nimbly painted the first Hog's official designator —17-F-1—on either side at midfuselage. Then the skull-and-cross-bones insignia was painted on either side of the engine cowl. Finally, "Big Hog" went on the vertical tail fin. I had been caught napping once; I would be ready the first time someone asked for my call sign this time around.

The early work in Wildcats paid handsome dividends as we received more Hogs. By mid-March, when we had a full working complement of thirty-six Corsairs, all hands were fully checked out. By then, also, we were well along in our carrier training.

The first step in getting all hands carrier qualified had been a thorough classroom indoctrination—or refresher, if that applied—for all the troops, many of whom had only a vague sense of what they were facing and how best to overcome it. Then it was off to begin field carrier training, the vital precursor to actual work aboard a ship. The exacting fieldwork required all hands to get "aboard" a simulated flight deck marked with flags on a portion of a much longer concrete runway. The work was by no means a breeze even for experienced hands like Rog Hedrick and I were; we had never done the job in Corsairs.

After about a dozen sessions of field carrier landing practice with our Landing Signal Officer (LSO), Lt(jg) Shailer "Catwalk" Cummings, I was ready to try Big Hog on the real thing. Of course, the Navy, in its infinite wisdom, had not seen fit to share any of the vital information gleaned from earlier activities conducted by Joe Clifton's VF-12. It was thus up to us to develop our own techniques from scratch.

My first actual carrier landing in a Hog went off on March 1, 1943, when I caught up with faithful old *Charger* in Chesapeake Bay. I rolled out of the approach turn about a hundred yards astern of the training carrier, hanging on the prop, indicating about 90 knots. Except for a lot of cold water, all I could see was Catwalk Cummings; the little ship was completely hidden by the Corsair's huge nose. Catwalk was giving me a "Roger"—both arms holding his colorful paddles straight out at shoulder level. This means, Okay, keep coming just as you are. Then I saw the paddle in Catwalk's right hand slice smartly across his chest and then back across his throat. This was the "Cut"—chop the power and land.

I dropped Big Hog's nose to get a view of the flight deck, but I went too far and set up a fearsome sink rate. I honked back on the stick and rotated the nose up so the Corsair would be in the perfect three-point attitude when it impacted—not landed, *impacted*—on the deck. The plane bounced what felt like a good 20 feet, but the tail hook caught the Number-1 arresting wire, and we slammed back into the deck. Both main tires blew as the Corsair and I came to an abrupt stop, both of us vibrating like harp strings. I shut down and climbed from the cockpit to go over the plane with the mechanics. Miraculously, we could find no structural damage; all we had to do was replace the wheels and tires.

My next four touchdowns and arrests—all I needed to qualify for carrier ops in a Corsair—were not as exciting. Indeed, each was progressively smoother. This was cause for some extra celebrating with Catwalk that night at Boys' Town, as we called the Norfolk officers' club.

VF-17 got through carrier qualifications with no personnel casualties. We busted a lot of wheels, blew a lot of tires, and totaled several of our airplanes, but everyone eventually made his five qualifying landings aboard *Charger*. When Ens Jack Chasnoff bounced higher than *Charger*'s masthead on his first landing attempt, he gave his Hog full power and flew the 35 miles back to Norfolk with wheels, flaps, and hook still down. It was a miracle that we suffered no personnel losses. In addition to working with a remarkably temperamental bird, most of our pilots had never seen a steamboat when they joined the squadron three months earlier. Moreover, *Charger* hardly qualified as a carrier; that spitkit rarely produced the 25 knots of relative wind over her flight deck that was considered the standard minimum for safe landing operations.

Even recognizing the remarkable performance of my grass-green tyros—they kept their cool and drove like old hands—most of the credit for our zero casualty rate must go to Catwalk Cummings. An LSO is not unlike a golf pro who can see what a student is doing right or wrong and who can coach the fledgling into fully utilizing his abilities. The typical flag-waver suffers enormous stress getting even experienced pilots aboard a carrier; our qualification program was as tough as it gets.

The Corsair appeared to be a superb fighting machine, but it was overengineered and thus hard to maintain. At the start of a typical day's ops, only about half of our full complement was safe to fly. By "secure," half of those could be expected to be "down."

The 2,800-cubic-inch engine was a monster to fire up after it had sat in subfreezing weather overnight. First, it took two strong men pulling on a prop blade to slowly accomplish the minimum revolutions needed to clear the lower cylinders of oil so the start-up could be accomplished in safety. Next, the engine had to be primed with raw gasoline. This touchy enterprise had to stop short of flooding and thus drowning the spark plugs and evade the obvious fire hazard while getting enough vaporized fuel into the cylinders to get the engine to cough to life. Some genius had equipped the Corsair with a shotgun starter in lieu of the heavy electric starter. When all was in readiness, the shotgun shell was fired. Sometimes it went *bang* and turned the prop through three or more revolutions. Mostly, however, it just went *poof* and the prop just twitched. Four abortive tries generally overheated the starter, and that resulted in a fifteen-minute stand-down for cooling. So much for geniuses.

Each of fourteen cowl flaps had its own baby hydraulic cylinder to open and close it. These tended to leak. In addition, until the maintenance crews became expert, the big radial engine tended to throw a lot of oil. The combination rapidly coated the windshield and seriously decreased the airplane's inherently limited forward visibility. We all became expert at quickly locating rain showers through which we could fly in order to wash away the oil.

The landing flaps had a protective device to prevent extension at airspeeds high enough to cause overstressing. This was a dandy feature—except that the flaps could and often did retract fully and without warning during the final stages of a landing approach. Of course, this resulted in a horrendous loss of lift and a rapid sinking. The pilot, ever alert for such mishaps, had to slam on full power to evade disaster. After too many narrow escapes, we got the "flap blowup" removed, it being our decision to risk tearing off a flap as against losing lift in this terrifying, dangerous manner. To my knowledge, no one ever did tear off a flap.

The Corsair's storage battery, which was located in the cockpit, had an unhealthy habit of boiling over. In one case, a battery exploded while the airplane was in flight. We later determined that it had been excessively overcharged, but the incident gave us one more in a long line of potential life-threatening problems to bear in mind while we were also trying to fly, and eventually, fight our irascible Hogs.

The enormous task of absorbing a new type full of hidden, potentially fatal, bugs was in no way enhanced by the Navy's decision to centralize repair and maintenance efforts. Through the first full year of the war, each Navy aviation squadron had had its own ground crew organization. However, as we were forming VF-17, the system was radically altered. A large, permanent carrier aircraft service unit (CASU) was established at each major base to perform the major portion of maintenance needs for all units flying out of that base. Similar, scaled-down versions of the CASUs were established for each carrier, organic to each ship's company and *not* organic to the air group or specific squadrons. This system certainly provided more flexibility to cope with the habitual steady flow of squadrons on and off bases and carriers, but it also adversely affected ground crew esprit de corps. The trade-off resulted in a general decline in the daily availability rate of aircraft in all units.

Fortunately, each squadron did retain a small cadre of senior petty officers, each a specialist in his field or in the specific aircraft type deployed with the squadron. Our little cadre, which was an organic part of the squadron, knew all there was to know about our Corsairs. They became infected with unit pride and, as much as possible, they rode herd on the less-senior pool maintenance people to whom our machines were consigned.

We lost four pilots killed in accidents during the early phases of our training at Norfolk, but none to the vagaries of the airplane. Two died in a midair collision while making simultaneous gunnery runs on a towed target. The other two died because they were unable to fly "basic instruments" when they became disoriented. The latter tragedies made Rog and me fully and painfully aware that our squadron's overall flying proficiency was poor, that the fledglings had received inadequate training in instrument flying in the press to get pilots out to Fleet squadrons.

Disorientation is a hazard that can overcome a pilot even on a perfectly clear day. Haze makes the surface blend in with the sky so that there is no apparent horizon. The pilot must lock his attention on the gauges. In its basic and most elementary form, this is "needle, ball, and airspeed" flying. The needle is the gyro-actuated turn indicator, an utterly reliable instrument that shows any turning movement proportionate to its rate; if the needle is centered, the airplane is holding to a steady heading even though the pilot's senses have him absolutely convinced that he is turning. The ball, which rides a curved path, infallibly tells the pilot if he is slipping or skidding; if the ball is centered, the plane is in balanced flight. The airspeed indicator tells the pilot whether the plane is in level flight or climbing or diving; fundamental familiarity with the airplane automatically tells the pilot what airspeed to expect at a steady power setting in level flight. So, if the pilot is at all unsure of his orientation, he only needs to center the needle and ball, then nose up or down to get the airspeed stabilized. Then, to figure out what is going on, he needs to check the view outside and the status of other instruments, such as the altimeter.

The unfortunate alternative to utilization of these basic flying skills and aids is the "graveyard spiral." The nose drops and the plane is turning even though the pilot's basic senses convince him that all is well or that the plane is turning the other way. Typically, when the disoriented pilot in the graveyard spiral sees the altimeter unwinding, he comes back on the stick. But instead of pulling the nose up, this merely tightens the turn. Conscious that the speed is building up, the disoriented pilot will whack off the throttle. But when the plane is already heading for the water or the ground, this action fatally increases the rate of descent. The pilot in such a predicament might hit the silk. If he does not, he will panic or black out. In all cases except the first, the next of kin need to be notified.

After the second incident in which both plane and pilot were lost in safe flying weather, with no "Mayday" or other transmission, we deduced that the problem was disorientation. This led to an intensive course in the six two-seater SNJs the squadron was allowed to retain after the introduction of our full complement of Corsairs. The "students" were placed "under the hood"—in the SNJ's rear cockpit, literally shrouded beneath a lighttight canvas canopy. There, they were utterly dependent on the clocks, albeit while being monitored by the safety pilot in the front seat. This added training paid enormous dividends; not only were there no more losses from disorientation, our guys got so good that we were able to fly day or night in weather so dirty that the multiengine lads were "aborting because of bad weather."

*   *   *

While it was not evident from my sorry display on D-Day in North Africa, I was a real enthusiast of fuel-saving techniques, which had been assiduously practiced by Lt(jg) Bill Eder when we were forming and training Fighting-29. Fuel conservation was an important part of Fighting-17's syllabus, and particularly so as word of my experience afloat off Morocco filtered through the squadron. It would be safe to describe my post-North African attitude toward fuel consumption as downright niggardly. The results of the intensive training were extremely satisfying and bound to stand us all in good stead when we started flying combat ops in the Pacific. In fact, we did so well that our techniques became the overall standard for all the Navy and Marine squadrons equipped with the F4U.

7

O ur job in Fighting-17 in early 1943 was to train the squadron to be thoroughly proficient in fighter-versus-fighter combat, to be able to defend friendly airfields and flight decks from enemy bombers and fighters, and to escort and protect friendly bombers and torpedo planes charged with attacking enemy ships and ground targets. It soon became apparent that Norfolk was not filling the bill as the ideal place to be learning our trade.

Of necessity, the NAS field operations people were conservative souls, to put it mildly. If the ceiling or visibility from the control tower was not above the prescribed minimum in *all* directions, the field was closed to landings or takeoffs, or both. It was frustrating to be obliged to sit on the end of the runway, wait-wait-waiting when there was bright sunlight in all quadrants except for a low-lying fog bank two miles to the east. If one landed before the plane ahead had completed its rollout and turned clear, there was hell to pay. Similarly, cutting in ahead of an airplane making a landing approach or passing someone on "final" was a rigidly enforced no-no. We seemed perpetually on the phone either hearing a bitch or pleading to get flight ops under way.

I did nothing to encourage grab-ass games in the operating areas—I did not need to!—but I did not frown on them either. My standard reply to some aggrieved squawk that an "F4U appeared from nowhere" to dust off a patrol plane or some such was, "Look, Jack, take an even strain. We're providing excellent training for you guys to keep a sharp lookout as well as an excellent practice opportunity for your tail gunners." For some reason, this reasoned response did not go over well with our brethren in the multiengine squadrons.

Instances of low-level flying—"Hey Ma! Look at me!!"—were not unknown. Needless to say, we aroused a great many beefs about our "flat-hatting," as this generally proscribed technique was known. No beef was ever as long or as loud as the one that resulted from Ens Teeth Burriss's encounter with a truck driver who aroused his ire. The road-bound miscreant in question was barreling down a two-lane road, forcing passenger cars to take to the shoulders or otherwise evade injury or death. Teeth flipped his Hog inverted and came at the big truck head-on below treetop level. The semi took evasive action right into a ditch.

What finally took the rag off the bush was an incident involving a dogfight between Ens Ike Kepford and an Army Air Forces P-51 right over Norfolk. The Army pilot was as enthusiastic as Ike, but not so the citizenry when the two inevitably got below 500 feet. ComAirLant himself, VAdm Pat Bellinger, had me on the carpet.

"Blackburn, I've been hearing reports on your squadron for some time, but this is *too much*. Either you get those hellions of yours squared away and stop this or I'll find someone who can. Is that clear?"

"Yes, Admiral."

"I want a written report from you by tomorrow telling me what you've done about it."

"Aye, aye, sir."

Ike was put in hack for ten days—grounded, forbidden to go ashore or even to Boys' Town. The pilots were assembled, and the riot act was read to them along with the sincere threat that the next one caught getting out of line would be banished to the limbo of a flying-boat squadron.

There were no tears shed—on either side—when we escaped or were banished from NAS, Norfolk, in early April. Our destination was Naval Auxiliary Air Station, Manteo, in the outermost boondocks of North Carolina, just southeast of Kitty Hawk.

It would have been difficult for the Navy to have found a more desolate place than the sand dunes just north of Cape Hatteras and 50 miles from any place bigger than a village. Quonset huts were the base's only structures. There were no fleshpots around Manteo either. Recreation consisted of listening to the radio and playing our deluxe model jukebox in our minimal O Club.

Together with our well-deserved reputation around Norfolk, the enforced isolation of Manteo brought us closer together. It also made for some serious, unobstructed attention to training.

Our gunnery range was available as soon as we reached altitude, for the station was immediately adjacent to the open Atlantic Ocean. We flew whenever we wanted to, in virtually any weather and at virtually any altitude, at whatever landing and takeoff intervals we decided to establish. The many uninhabited islets that dotted Currituck Sound had no wildlife and were thus ideal targets for our ground-strafing practice. There was almost no one else flying in our area; we had it virtually to ourselves and were thus free to undertake unlimited air-to-air dogfights and other grab-ass without worrying about other people and without the constraints of collision hazard.

On the other hand, night ops were difficult because the field lighting was inadequate, to say the least. That, however, did not stop us from doing a lot of night work. In fact, doing so appreciably increased our instrument proficiency.

The skipper of the station was an aged, conservative World War I retread who soon despaired of our wild ways and gave us a free hand. The locals were the uncorrupted descendants of the Elizabethans who once had lured passing merchantmen onto the shoals with lanterns hung from the necks of their horses—hence Nag's Head. They could not have cared less what we did as long as we minded our own business.

Most of our gunnery training and practice was conducted against flat banners 15 feet long by 3 feet wide. These were towed at 115 knots or more, flat to the ground or vertical, depending on the type of run we were working on. Of course, all the shooting had to be deflection from the side, above, or below to avoid hitting the tow plane.

We did an enormous amount of low-level work, over the water, at minimum altitude. Much of this work was in formations from two to thirty-six airplanes. Many detractors said we were just showing off. This was true to a degree, but my real purpose was to make all hands comfortable with working at high speeds at extremely low level so we could do this type of flying, day or night, with impunity. The ultimate objective was to allow us to achieve surprise against ship or shore targets. Such hair-raising—and eyebrow-raising—efforts off the North Carolina coast paid handsome dividends in the Pacific.

We also got into high-altitude flight ops and vigorously pursued them in order to reassure all hands that their oxygen equipment would keep them alive for long periods at and above 30,000 feet. This work also made everyone aware of the marked changes in performance characteristics the airplanes experienced at various altitudes up to 30,000 feet and beyond.

Another of the many things I stressed was target acquisition. All of the great fighter aces of World War I and the early part of World War II agreed that half the battle of being a successful fighter pilot is seeing the opponent before he sees you. The needed technique—habits, really—could be learned. Though it is axiomatic that some people have sharper eyes than others, it was important for me to get across the fact that the man who masters the basic target acquisition techniques could be a higher scorer than the man with the inherently better shooting eye. The technique is simple: The fighter pilot simply blocks off a small section of the sky, meticulously searches it with horizontal sweeps, and then moves to the adjacent section of the sky to do the same, and so forth. This simple technique needed to be absorbed as an invariable habit.

I also imparted a simple philosophy based on action. I encouraged all my pilots to try new things whenever possible, albeit within the constraints of the guidelines that had been clearly set forth. More to the point, all hands learned very early that a wrong action was much preferred to no action at all.

Further, I made it clear to all hands that the experienced people in the squadron—initially myself, Hedrick, Kleinman, and Halford—were available at any time to discuss any of the professional aspects of our job. In VF-17, there was no such thing as a dumb question. Nor was there a dumb idea; everyone's ideas were heard through and treated with respect. In fact, many ideas floated by the novices found a place in our standard procedures.

At the heart of it all was the task of getting these young men to have faith in themselves, to make their own moves when they were on their own with reasoned judgment and not too late—certainly not after wasting precious seconds trying to recall some instruction they had heard weeks or months earlier. It takes the utmost self-discipline for young men used to being subordinates to act on their own. Aside from the acquired mental and physical skills needed to fly a high-performance fighter in combat, it takes self-motivation, self-confidence, and self-discipline to survive and win.

In May, as part of a self-generated graduation exercise, we sent the following dispatch to all the squadrons in the Norfolk area: "Combat air patrol will be airborne over Manteo from 0800 until 1200 each weekday. Visitors welcome."

The response was marvelous. The poor, beleaguered CO of

NAAS, Manteo, nearly flipped his wig. Fighters, dive-bombers, torpedo bombers, even a few patrol types, swarmed in from all directions for some legalized grab-ass.

I have a vivid mental picture of a section of dive-bombers pulling out of their attack on the treetops at 300-plus knots with Corsairs, wingtips skyward, making 90-degree deflection attacks at their level.

We were busy. We never had more fun or better training.

The enormous amount of time we spent aloft was leavened with ample ground school opportunities focused upon every part of the airplanes; what all the surfaces were, why they were shaped the way they were, why they were constructed the way they were, their weaknesses, and their strengths. We put a lot of emphasis on power plant operation since it is the heart of the airplane. I made it a particular point to convince my young birdmen that the abused power plant sooner or later dumps its abuser into the drink, and that treating a high-power engine with tender loving care pays off in the clutch. Aircraft recognition was another course we ran all hands through at length. We had slides, silhouette books, and models aplenty, and we demanded perfection—for the sake of friends as much as anything else.

A great deal of our ground school effort was based on the things the more experienced pilots remembered needing in past jobs or whenever we noticed particular deficiencies in our tyros. The effort was not, alas, as comprehensive as it might have been, nor as thorough as it would become under organized auspices as the war progressed. We simply made do with what we had, and that prevented us from being as thorough in some areas as we would have liked. We were also facing a more or less finite deadline; the length of training time at Manteo would be determined by the availability of our ship, which was nearing completion in Massachusetts.

Our time at Manteo was when I really began to get a feel for the stronger characters and more talented pilots—when the squadron's distinctive personality began to emerge. Several of the conditional leadership appointments I had made early in the year were overturned, several by death and transfer, others based on talent and skill.

Our air combat intelligence officer (ACIO), a real gem, was Lt(jg) Basil "Duke" Henning, a 1932 Yale graduate and former history professor. Our only nonflying officer, Duke knew nothing about airplanes and hated even to be a passenger in one. Slim, dark, aristocratically handsome, Duke was low-key, highly intelligent, loved and respected by all. A good listener as well as very calm, very mature, and very discreet, Duke filled the bill as our father confessor. The young tigers got into the habit of unloading woes on Duke that they could not bring up to their CO or exec. He counseled them and, when necessary, brought certain matters before me or Rog Hedrick. He was a key asset from the start. In time, Duke's presence in the squadron was nearly as important as mine or Rog's.

Our senior lieutenant was Chuck Pillsbury, an AvCad whose only operational flying duty before he joined the squadron had been as an elimination instructor. As the senior officer after Rog and me, Chuck was assigned duties as the squadron operations and scheduling officer. Fortunately for us all, Chuck was a smooth coordinator and a strong leader. He also directly oversaw a flight of two four-plane fighter divisions, as did Rog and I.

Lt(jg) Butch Davenport emerged from the pack to take on duties as the squadron maintenance officer. His interest and aptitude for engineering were marked. His duties as maintenance officer brought him into a close relationship with Russ Clark, a talented civilian F4U project engineer, and with Ray DeLeva, our Vought Field Service representative. Between them, Russ and Butch developed and installed a small airflow spoiler which sharply decreased the Hog's nasty tendency at low speeds to stall without warning with the left wing whipping down. The benefit was that, at stall, the wings stayed more nearly level and thus more manageable. In refined form, the field expedient fabrication wound up being installed on all later production Corsairs.

Every military unit *needs* a scrounger if it is to stay in business. Fighting-17's chief scrounger—officially our material officer—was Ens Hal Jackson, a shrewd Texan and a formidable poker player. Hal never seemed at a loss in winning needed parts and spares from the Supply Corps misers. Frankly, I never dared inquire too closely into how that was done, lest I be hauled in as an accessory after the fact.

I had little curiosity regarding the backgrounds of my subordinates; other than their professional credits, I knew little about them. I was the product of a Navy household and my own years of service, and I had certainly followed the tradition of snobbishness and bigotry that characterized the prewar service. However, somewhere along the line—I am not sure where or how—I concluded that it literally took all kinds to forge a national war effort and that the only things that really counted in a combat fighter squadron were skill and desire.

Some of my pilots, like Lt Chuck Pillsbury and Lt(jg) Timmy Gile, came from backgrounds of wealth and prominence, though certainly neither had attained either in his own right. Others, like Lt Lem Cooke and Ens Ike Kepford, had outstanding records of athletic prowess. But all that cut no ice with me. I was not about to run either a democratic or an elitist military organization, but I did realize the truth of Napoleon's dictum that there is a field marshal's baton in the knapsack of every soldier. If this dictum is followed, the results can be astonishing. My watchword was "loyalty from the top down," and strict adherence paid handsome dividends throughout my tour as VF-17's CO.

Ens Danny Cunningham was short and stocky, strong and tough. He was shanty Irish, his face the map of Ireland, and he had all the traits—quick laughter, quick temper, affection, and loyalty nearly to a fault. He also had a classic fondness for spirits that cleanly wiped out all after-duty inhibitions. Danny was a handful. When the new Hogs had arrived in February, it had become obvious to all that Danny Boy could barely see over the cockpit coaming or reach the pedals with his feet. The Hog had a huge cockpit, and Danny was a small man.

After seeing him give it a try, I called Danny in to my office. "Dan, you're a good man, and we'll need scrappers like you, but that bucket just isn't built for you. I'll have to get you transferred. I can set it up so that you can go to a Hellcat squadron, or wherever you want. You can be sure you'll get a strongly favorable recommendation from me."

Tears welled up. "Skipper, give me a chance. I'll rig up with cushions and pillows—whatever it takes. This time tomorrow I'll demonstrate to you, statically and taxiing that jewel, that I can reach and operate anything and everything."

And so he did.

*   *   *

I did not take to Lt Lem Cooke, a 1939 Annapolis graduate who came across as a slow Southern good ole boy, content to follow the path of least resistance, still riding high on his reputation as an outstanding Academy football star. I grudgingly assigned Lem as a section leader following the division and flight lead of younger pilots junior to him in rank. Was I ever wrong. I am glad to "walk back the cat" in the combat area.

Ens Bobby Mims was our *enfant terrible*. Five-eight and with a classic middleweight's wide shoulders and trim hips, Bobby was a handsome man in the macho mold. The spoiled scion of a wealthy Dallas household, Bobby was perpetually belligerent. With a few drinks under his belt, which was about any time they were available, his ferocious temper all too often manifested itself as he erupted into a cloud of fists. Withal, Bobby Mims was a gutsy man and an outstanding pilot. Hedrick and many others in the squadron wanted no part of him. Once, after I had bailed Bobby out of yet another pointless scrape, Rog said to me privately, "Tommy, you're nuts to put up with him. Get rid of him before he gets you in a bind." I usually heeded Rog's levelheaded advice, but I had a feeling about Bobby, who was fiercely loyal to the squadron and who really thought the sun rose and set on me and his fellow Texan, Hal Jackson, our chief scrounger. Once all hands knew about Bobby, Hal or I could count on getting a storm warning as soon as Bobby got drunk and often before a brawl developed.

One fine morning, as my lead division swung back toward the field to complete the routine rendezvous with my flight's second division, we were horrified to see an orange ball of flame and a plume of black smoke near the end of the runway. On landing, I learned that Ens Sam Carlton, a very capable and promising pilot of whom we expected great things, had apparently lost power shortly after liftoff. Instead of continuing straight ahead with no greater problem than ditching in the swamp or Currituck Sound—more than doctrine, an ironbound commandment—Sam had tried to save the plane. As he honked back around, turning to try to get back to the field, he ran out of airspeed and spun in. Sam, our premier radio technical expert, was well liked and highly respected; his death was keenly felt.

One of the most distressful aspects of squadron command was

following the chaplain in consoling the bereaved. It is tough enough to handle the loss of close friends—an occupational hazard to which I never became inured—but it is even worse to lose a youngster who has been cast in the role of a son. Inevitably, the painful process of getting over Sam Carlton's death, and others, was tinged with feelings of guilt and the unending mental litany, What did I fail to teach him?

———— 8 ————

Though our time at Manteo was Fighting-17's halcyon days of independence, we were not entirely on our own while training there. Fighting-17 was one of three squadrons comprising Air Group 17, and we were obliged to coordinate our training with the others so that we would go aboard *Bunker Hill*, when the day arrived, as an integrated combat air group.

The air group commander, or CAG, was Cdr Michael "Bags" Bagdanovich, a 1929 Annapolis graduate who had been Joe Clifton's immediate boss at Opa-Locka. Bags, a giant Nordic type, had plenty of carrier squadron operating experience, but he fell into the trap of treating his position in Air Group 17 as a sinecure. This attitude was a holdover from prewar days, and it unfortunately ruined a lot of potentially useful CAGs during the war. Bags exercised only superficial supervision and did not even deign to master all the aircraft types employed by the group. He did not even check out in the F4U, nor, to my knowledge, in our dive-bomber type, the SB2C, but only tooled around when he had to in the TBF command plane assigned to him. We seldom even saw Bags in our squadron areas, which I felt was a mixed blessing since it provided the squadron COs with virtually complete freedom of action. On the other hand, there were times when Bags's experience and clout would have been useful in dealing with superior officers who did not quite see things our way. Word from the Pacific already warned us that the Navy carrier air groups had had a bad time during all the early carrier battles precisely because they had been unable to launch coordinated, mutually supporting group strikes. Indeed, a coordinated strike by as few as two groups had never come off.

Bombing-17's thirty-six Curtiss SB2C Helldiver dive-bombers were commanded by LCdr James "Moe" Vose, a 1934 Annapolis graduate. Moe was an extremely skilled combat flight leader who had led nearly two squadrons of SBD Dauntless dive-bombers which severely damaged a Japanese carrier in October 1942 during the Santa Cruz carrier battle. Now he faced the unenviable task of forging a new fighting force out of tyros like my own with the

misbegotten Helldiver, which was known universally and unaffec-
tionately as The Beast. Moe elected to undertake Bombing-17's
training work at Norfolk, a decision that was influenced in large
measure by his proximity to the supply center, good shops, and,
most important, the aircraft overhaul and repair facility. The Beast
was that bad; it required no end of changes and modifications to
remain operable.

Moe's Academy classmate, LCdr Frank "Silver Fox" Whittaker,
an immensely imaginative and capable pilot and leader, jumped at
the chance to train his eighteen TBF crews at NAAS, Chincoteague, Virginia, 50 miles north of Norfolk on the seaward side of the
Delmarva Peninsula. Chincoteague was as isolated as Manteo. The
Grumman TBF Avenger type with which Torpedo-17 was
equipped had made an unsatisfactory debut in very limited numbers at Midway, but it subsequently proved itself a superb airplane.
It was still experiencing some growing pains in early 1943, but it
and its virtually identical successor, the General Motors TBM, was
so good that, after Midway, it was the only torpedo type deployed
by the Navy and Marines in the war. The dynamic Grumman
people remained right on top of any problems Torpedo-17 encountered during its training cycle. The Silver Fox worked his batch of
nuggets hard and well, establishing a tough standard for later torpedo squadrons to emulate. Early on, this lifelong innovator
begged, borrowed, or stole several airborne radars, which he used
to develop foul-weather and night-attack techniques that eventually
won fleetwide acceptance in early 1944.

Air Group 17's composition—40 percent fighters, 40 percent
dive-bombers, and 20 percent torpedo bombers—reflected the painful lessons of 1942. The ratio at that time—25-50-25—had resulted
in high losses among the bomber types and extremely spotty fighter
cover over the carriers. The quandary of the planners was and
remained how much bomb- and torpedo-delivery capability needed
to be endangered or sacrificed in order to maintain an adequate
combat air patrol over friendly flight decks while protecting the
strike aircraft. The attempts at answering this basic question in four
carrier-versus-carrier battles between May and November 1942 had
had disastrous results wherever the fighters had *not* been committed. The 40-40-20 ratio appeared to be the best solution in 1943,
particularly inasmuch as more and somewhat better carriers were
coming on-line. Even in mid-1943, we were able to foresee that

decisions would be more easily reached as we were able to mobilize larger carrier task forces and learned to coordinate the efforts of multiple carrier air groups. However, there were no assurances as we awaited *Bunker Hill*; we had to assume that Air Group 17 would have to attack enemy targets and defend our own carrier without support from other air groups. We had to be independent and self-sufficient, just as many of the earlier carrier air groups had been.

As a senior fighter pilot, I was painfully aware of the shortcomings of the fighter squadrons in the early Pacific battles. This lesson was driven home with some force during a routine cocktail party and dinner hosted by Bombing-17 in March. One of the young wives, whose husband had been one of my favored students at Miami and who had gone on to fight some of the early battles, buttonholed me late in the evening and delivered a heartfelt plea. "Tommy," she started, the directness of her tone no doubt stiffened somewhat by alcohol, "I know that a lot of these guys, maybe my Joe, aren't going to come home from the war. We wives have to accept that. But I want you to promise me that your outfit will do its damnedest to see that they do."

Already mindful of the stories of early Wildcat units flying uselessly hither and yon, like Jeb Stuart's Confederate cavalry at Gettysburg, while the bombers fell prey to unchallenged Zero fighters, I did indeed promise what she asked, and I held to the pledge as I trained and inculcated my Fighting-17 troops. Thus, in addition to honing their predatory instincts, I had to instill in them a loyalty to the air group which might oblige them to stick scoreless with the bombers they were escorting rather than allow themselves to be sucked away by the allure of easy kills.

The entire air group was scheduled to be on target at 1000 one April day to make a simulated attack on a group of Amphibious Command transports and a new command ship boasting the latest in air search radars. The target ships were anchored in Chesapeake Bay at the mouth of the Potomac, about 100 air miles from Manteo. The weather at our base was marginal, and it got even worse as twenty-four of us stooged up the beach line. The cloud base dropped to about 200 feet, with occasional pockets up at 500 feet, and there was plenty of patchy fog as a result of lots of shower activity. As we flew north, it became obvious that Norfolk would be shut down, that the CAG and VB-17 would be grounded. Nevertheless, we closed up tight and forged ahead through the muck—taking advantage of the welcome opportunity to clean the oil from our windshields.

At 1002, as we finished dusting off the task group with pull-ups over their masts at the conclusion of our strafing runs, the Silver Fox led in all of his VT-17 Avengers from Chincoteague and simulated a perfect coordinated torpedo attack. The black shoes were crimson-faced as they scrambled topside from the flag mess and their various wardrooms. They had all been imbibing hot coffee, safe in the illusion that the brown-shoe fly-boys would never attempt the simulated attack in such weather.

For a change, ComAirLant was pleased with Fighting-17.

PART III

Bunker Hill

9

*B*unker Hill cleared the shipyard at Quincy, Massachusetts, in early June 1943. As the spanking new carrier arrived off the Capes on her way to Norfolk, Fighting-17 greeted her with a tridirectional strafing attack from steep dive angles that carried our Corsair flights right across her flight deck with only seconds of separation.

The long hours of practice and rehearsal paid a handsome dividend; the swish and roar of the first division arriving from out of the sun was the ship's company's first inkling of the mock attack. *Un*rehearsed was the follow-up by Lt(jg) Teeth Burriss, who roared straight up the flight deck from bow to stern at 25 feet—inverted. From that moment on, I was told, as far as *Bunker Hill*'s captain was concerned, Fighting-17 was *in*.

Following slow-paced, weeks-long warm-up operations in Chesapeake Bay, in which the ship and air group took each other's measure, Air Group 17 was hoisted aboard on July 15 and *Bunker Hill*'s bows were pointed south for a shakedown in the Gulf of Paria, west of Trinidad. By then, I had long since reported directly to the new carrier's skipper, Capt John Ballentine, the same officer from whom I had conned the extra pilot on Fighting-29's way out to North Africa. At our first meeting on *Bunker Hill*'s bridge, Captain John gleefully reminded me of the incident—as if I needed reminding—and thereby hinted that my quick ascension to the command of Fighting-17 might not have been a matter of luck, or even of skill.

Shakedown is an apt term for the always-difficult early operations of any new ship, but particularly during a war. The difficulties seem to increase in geometric proportion to the size of the ship involved. Learning the vagaries of a huge and complex physical plant is only one aspect of honing a cohesive crew from a body of more than 2,500 officers and men, 95 percent of whom have never been to sea. For *Bunker Hill*'s crew and Air Group 17, the added pressure of getting ready to go into action by a fixed date too near in real time was virtually unbearable at times.

The interaction between the air group and the ship in the basics of aircraft launch and recovery was vital, but it represented only a small part of the teamwork required of the pilots. The air department was a huge organization overseeing, among many other things, the maintenance and operation of the arresting gear and catapults, the fueling and arming of the airplanes, flight deck fire fighting, crash removal and salvage, and inspection and maintenance of the aircraft. Moreover, essential as it is as the heart of a carrier, the air department was only one of many large and complex departments that must work as a team. Engineering moved the ship and, among numerous other duties, maintained the airplane elevators. Navigation got us from place to place. Supply kept us stocked up. Gunnery was charged with defending the ship against attack in the event enemy warplanes fought through the fighter umbrella. Communications kept us in touch with the rest of the world. And so forth. The carrier was an immensely complex machine that was run by an immensely complex human community.

The transformation of a new ship with a raw crew into a cohesive operational unit, almost from scratch and virtually overnight, is an enormous undertaking. Schools ashore were essential for sending *Bunker Hill* the trained human material, but intensive practice at sea, painstakingly meshing the whole, was the only way to get the job done. Thus we faced days and weeks of intense drill and practice—endless, repetitious practice. In the end, the enormous responsibility for every detail of the transformation fell to the shoulders of the skipper. Possessed of the dedication of Saint Paul and the patience of Job, John Ballentine did a superb job. He was tough and uncompromising but always fair. Somehow, as we all stumbled along, he never lost his cool.

In our case, the "typical" insurmountable shakedown problems were disproportionately increased by Air Group 17's need to work the bugs out of two new, untried, and extremely recalcitrant types of aircraft, both entering Fleet service for the first time.

Our most basic need was to undertake enough daytime landings and takeoffs to teach all the air group's pilots to *safely* get on and off the steamboat in smooth and expeditious fashion. At the same time, we had to merge with and work out and perfect the symphonically complex evolutions of the air department.

Once the group was hoisted aboard, the plane handlers had to learn how, with tractors and human plane-pushers, to "spot" the airplanes in a "takeoff spot" on the hangar and flight decks. The primary tool of the trade is the "Ouija board," a scaled diagram of the hangar or flight deck on which are positioned flat cutouts of the various aircraft aboard the ship, one set of cutouts modeling planes with wings folded and the other with wings extended. The flight deck officer and the hangar deck officer are the key men, the conductors who must orchestrate positioning of the aircraft on the flight and hangar decks *and* the smooth flow of aircraft between the decks by means of the ship's three aircraft elevators. The trick is for the two supervisors to arrange and rearrange the cutouts on the Ouija board so that there is at least enough open deck space, particularly on the flight deck, to move other planes. A final requirement is for the flight deck officer to leave at least 415 feet of clear deck for the takeoff run of the first plane. Follow-on aircraft need enough room to taxi forward to the takeoff position, and that means their wings and propeller arcs must remain clear of all obstructions. A taxiing accident will not only inevitably destroy aircraft and possibly kill people, it will shut down the flight deck, which is literally the last thing anyone aboard or aloft above a carrier desires or needs.

With ninety airplanes aboard, the deck-spotting permutations were virtually infinite. However, once the most commonly used spots had been worked out, the various results were photographed and one-to-one-scale prints were made available for reference. The spotters, most of whom were school trained but new to the job, had to study the standard spots, committing each to memory. The trick was to be able to perform flawlessly in the dark or in the rain— perhaps even under enemy attack.

As the pilots are being briefed in the squadron ready rooms, the plane captains are running up the engines, checking them and other systems for proper operation. When the plane captains are satisfied that all is well, the engines are shut down. After the order "Pilots, man planes" is sounded in the ready rooms and throughout the plane-handling areas, the flight crews strap in and the engines are restarted.

The flight deck officer takes position off the right wingtip of the first plane to go, holds up his left hand with one finger extended and rotates his checkered flag slowly in a circular motion with his right hand. The pilot of the lead plane revs up to half power, checks his gauges and indicators, makes sure all the control surfaces can move freely, and, if satisfied, gives the flight deck officer a thumbs-up sign. The flight deck officer then holds up two fingers and rotates the flag more rapidly. The pilot applies full power while holding his feet on the brakes and the stick in his belly, the former to prevent a premature rollout and the latter to prevent a nose-up. When the pilot nods to signify "Ready," the checkered flag is swung out and down to point at the bow of the ship. Properly executed, all this happens in a matter of seconds. As the number one airplane starts its run, the flight deck officer is already signaling the number two into takeoff position.

The flight deck officer's chief assistant, the yellow-jerseyed director, moves with the grace and precision of a ballet star. His basic hand signals are universal: both hands held high with the knuckles toward the pilot gesturing "come on" to indicate "taxi straight ahead"; one hand held so and the other hand pointing toward a wheel means "keep moving and hold the brake indicated to turn"; hands with palms facing the pilot means "stop temporarily"; both fists clenched means "stop and hold the brakes locked until further orders." The director using these signals, with the pilot following them precisely, can move the plane with only a few inches of clearance if need be; he will be able to position the plane *exactly* where he wants it. The director's hand-signaled commands are mandatory. However, if a pilot does not understand a signal or feels that there is danger lurking—that he might swung his tail surfaces into the arc of the propeller behind him, for example—he stops dead in his tracks until the problem is resolved. While the airplane is taxiing to the takeoff position, the pilot extends and locks the wings and sets the wing and cooling flaps to their takeoff positions.

When the number two airplane is in the takeoff position, the director gives the pilot the hold signal, pats the top of his head, and points with both hands to the flight deck officer. Control of the airplane is thus passed. The flight deck officer, who has visually checked to see that the number one airplane has cleared the flight deck, turns and begins the final run-up sequence with number two. The desired takeoff interval is twenty to thirty seconds—less time for the faster-accelerating fighters, more time for the heavily laden bombers. This leaves no time for dillydallying. The entire sequence, including the rendezvous of various fighter and bomber units, was developed and standardized during the 1930s.

Once sent on his way by the flight deck officer's checkered flag, the pilot gets extremely busy, though all his motions from that point on are ingrained and should be automatic and smooth. Basic takeoff techniques include bringing the tail up enough to allow adequate forward vision, but no more than that; tail too high makes for extra drag, but it had to be well up in our long-nosed Corsairs. The pilot needs to hold a steady course right down the center of the flight deck—and he must do so using only the rudder and *never* the brakes. As the plane nears the bow, the pilot eases the tail down—that is, rotates the nose up—so the plane flies itself off the ship. The instant the plane clears the bow, the pilot turns smoothly 45 degrees to the right so the next man will not have to battle his slipstream *and* so he will not be in the ship's path in the event he loses power and has to ditch. Once airborne, the pilot promptly gets his wheels up—hydraulically, thank goodness, in the Corsair—and reduces to climb-out power (which causes the black exhaust smoke to disappear). Then it's a smooth, steady climb with no settling as the landing flaps are "milked up" to the fully retracted position.

During the shakedown period, every VF-17 takeoff was monitored by a two-man team of pilots, one to observe the takeoff and the other to keep detailed notes, including times and intervals. At the start of the work, Rog Hedrick or I usually monitored the monitors.

The monitors watched the performance of every move and noted any lapses while logging the minutes and seconds from the "go" signal. A group critique in the ready room followed every flight. The monitors' merciless comments in front of all hands had a salutary effect. As time went on, we shaved seconds from each takeoff and, thus, minutes from each takeoff evolution. In combat, those seconds and minutes could mean the difference between survival of our ship or others at the hands of a surprise enemy air strike. In all cases, seconds saved on the flight deck meant minutes more in the air, and more time in the air translated to more range or more time in a fight.

My personal refinements, while not made mandatory for the others, were naturally observed and sometimes imitated. Just be-

fore full-power turnup, I retracted the landing flaps to achieve a
more sensitive rudder response and to decrease drag for optimum
rate of acceleration. I extended the flaps again as I neared liftoff and
applied light back stick pressure. Halfway through the takeoff
run—daylight only—I angled toward the starboard corner of the
bow, thus completing part of the needed clearing turn before becoming airborne. As the ailerons became effective, I rolled the right
wing down to the horizontal. This resulted in no net loss of lift
while the added pressure of the right wheel on the deck obviated
any tendency to be drifted by a cross wind. In addition, a small
start was made into the right clearing turn. I had developed these
minutiae flying the Navy's first monoplane dive-bomber, the
Vought SB2U-1, from *Lexington* in 1939.

Once airborne, the flight followed the rendezvous patterns and
practices that had evolved in the Fleet before the war. This was all
old hat for VF-17 since we had been using the carrier-type rendezvous from the day we arrived at Manteo.

Following the clearing turn, the flight leader resumes the original
launch heading while holding at 1,000 feet of altitude at 150 knots
for thirty seconds multiplied by the number of aircraft in his flight,
up to a maximum of eight. He then makes a standard rate—
gentle—left turn to reverse course. Succeeding members of the
flight formate so that as the flight passes abeam of the carrier,
heading downwind, it is comfortably joined up, ready to orbit to
await following units or ready to proceed with the task at hand.

To routinely land aboard, a flight arrayed in right echelon passes
abeam the carrier's starboard side at 1,000 feet of altitude, tail hooks
down. After thirty seconds on this course, the flight leader breaks
left to take the downwind heading. (The carrier always operates
with her bow into the wind during takeoff and recovery operations.) Followers likewise peel off at thirty-second intervals. During
this phase of the recovery, the landing checklist is followed by the
pilot so that, when abeam of the ship's port side, he is ready to start
the 180-degree turn into the final landing approach. Once in the
final "groove" approximately 200 yards astern the ship, the plane
comes under the control of the LSO, who passes inviolable instructions by means of a pair of colorful paddles. He does everything
from correcting the speed and altitude of the approaching plane to
holding it steady on course or transmitting news of an oversight,

such as an undropped tail hook. At the last instant, the LSO either executes the cut, in which case the aircraft lands, or the wave-off, in which case the pilot must—absolutely must—apply full power and clear the area without landing.

Exceptions to the basic pattern are many. For example, a critically low fuel state or damage or mechanical trouble will get a particular plane cleared for an immediate landing—if the flight deck is clear and the ship is not under attack. If there is a problem, the pilot sets himself up to arrive in the groove by any means necessary—dive, right turn, whatever is quickest. In an emergency, all other airplanes in the landing circle must fend for themselves while maintaining the obligatory thirty-second intervals.

After touchdown, the plane decelerates rapidly as the tail hook picks up one of the eight arresting wires stretched tautly across the full width of the after flight deck. As the plane comes to a stop, power off, the alert pilot flips the hook control to the up position while two green-shirted deck crewmen come out from the edges of the deck to clear the wire from the hook. The yellow-shirted landing-area plane director appears ahead and to the right of the airplane and signals the pilot to stop the plane's backward roll with his brakes and to start revving up to taxi forward. As a matter of course, the director holds his left hand out with the palm down and jabs into it with the upraised thumb of his right fist. This means "hook up." As the wire drops clear, the director signals the pilot with an agitated "come ahead" signal to use full throttle to start rolling. Control is then passed to a second yellow jersey 100 feet forward along the flight deck. The director signals the pilot to continue ahead fast or—hands out at waist level, palms down with a patting motion—"come ahead, but slow down." As soon as the plane is out of the landing area and forward of the crash barriers, the throttle is set to idle, the brakes are applied lightly, and control is assumed by a third yellow jersey, who guides the pilot to the "landing spot" or sends him to an elevator to be struck below to the hangar deck. Done properly, the elapsed time from "hook up" to clearing the barrier is twenty seconds or less.

While watching the yellow jerseys, the pilot works the throttle with his left hand and, because the control stick is of no further use, his right hand accomplishes various housekeeping chores with practiced precision by feel alone. These include opening all the cooling flaps to wide, raising the landing flaps, unlocking the wings, and setting the wing control to "fold." All this while controlling the airplane with brakes and throttle, watching the yellow jerseys, and instantly responding to their commands.

Fighting-17's merciless monitors were at their posts for every landing, having positioned themselves so as to have a clear view to port and especially aft of the barriers right on up the groove. This system's net gain for all, in addition to making all hands sharp, heads-up carrier pilots, was the rapid buildup of the squadron party fund. In addition to often stinging criticism, an elaborate system of fines was imposed, no alibis accepted. It cost a dollar for a pilot-caused wave-off and fifty cents per second for a cut more than thirty seconds later than the preceding cut. Every second over twenty seconds between "hook up" and "clear deck" cost two bits. Lesser goofs cost less, but the standards applied to every move. Only perfection was free.

The ultimate fine was five dollars if guns were not set on "safe." This dumb error had killed innocent people on the decks of other carriers, but it did not happen on *Bunker Hill*. The threat was real. We almost always flew with ammunition aboard, and quite often with rounds in the breeches and gun switches on. It was to be expected that a pilot would inadvertently squeeze the trigger switch while clenching his hand during the tension of an arrested landing. The five-dollar fine was levied only once, and that without an accident. Amusingly, the culprit was our squadron gunnery officer, Lt(jg) Timmy Gile, who, characteristically, turned himself in.

10

The Gulf of Paria is a 70-mile-by-30-mile expanse of deep water bounded on the east by Trinidad. The only deep-water entrance is the Dragon's Mouth, at the northeast corner, while the only other pass, to the southeast, is through the foul ground of the shoals of the deltas of the Orinoco River. The passes were heavily mined by mid-1943, and meticulously patrolled by numerous surface vessels and aircraft. For *Bunker Hill*, the gulf was the perfect locale for a shakedown away from the danger of German submarines. For Air Group 17, the cruise to and in the gulf was the perfect opportunity to practice group and squadron tactics and to learn to mesh with the ship's company. We worked hard and played only aboard ship. We saw lusty, lively Port of Spain, home of "Rum and Coca-Cola," only from the air. Once embarked, it was all business. We got in an invaluable period of intensive operations without let or hindrance.

Air Group 17 flew seven days a week, undertaking simulated coordinated group strikes, bombing and strafing a towed sled target. No towed target sleeves or high-speed banners were available for Fighting-17, so we in the fighters got no opportunity to practice our aerial gunnery. However, the spectacular tridirectional coordinated strafing attack we had launched on *Bunker Hill* off the Capes was repeated unto perfection with all guns blazing a frothing, tracer-lit path on the surface of the gulf and enveloping the target sled at the rate of 1,600 .50-caliber rounds per second. Alas, when we started finding wing damage from spent shell casings ejected from the planes which had just crossed ahead of the target, Captain Ballentine reluctantly ordered, "Knock it off; save it for the Japs."

The most valuable work we did was in learning to coordinate our intercept work with the ship's Fighter Direction Officer and the Combat Information Center staff. As part of the intercept work, competition was keen among my eagles in the area of eyeball target acquisition. All hands vied to be the first one to holler, for example, "Tallyho! Eight bombers, two o'clock, down twenty degrees."

* * *

Despite the immense progress all hands were making on all operational fronts, our beloved Hogs were giving us and *Bunker Hill* fits. As if we were not sufficiently beleaguered by oil-coated windshields, exploding batteries, and other general cussedness, our Corsairs were beset by a series of mysterious barrier crashes following what appeared to be perfect landings. After touchdowns with not unreasonable bounces, several of our planes surged ahead undecelerated instead of being arrested. Hog after Hog, deployed in perfect three-point attitude, pranged into the barrier cables at around 60 knots. Almost every time, the runaway went up and over in the barrier, strewing expensive debris in all directions, often as not breaking in two at the engine mount. Miraculously, there were no pilot injuries.

At length, a sharp-eyed green-shirt spotted the problem. The F4U's arresting-hook point, for reasons known only to the Naval Aircraft Factory, had a cross section like an ax blade. Combined with the unseasoned and unweathered soft fir of *Bunker Hill*'s deck, the hook dug in and cut a furrow—something it had not done on *Charger*'s use-toughened planking. In most landings, the hook engaged an arresting wire, which lifted the hook clear off the deck. However, in those instances where the hook remained in contact with the deck, the hook point snagged on contact with a steel cross-deck drain channel and snapped off, typically flying over the stern. The plane continued undecelerated, of course, and the missing hook point was unnoticed in the twisted scrap pile of the totally demolished machine.

Urgent dispatches to the Bureau of Aeronautics produced the required information and approval. In short order, the supply system coughed up replacement hook points. The siege of barrier crashes was lifted as soon as the hook points were switched. But that was only one problem among scores that we got behind us.

Toward the end of the shakedown, Cdr Bags Bagdanovich and I were summoned to Captain Ballentine's sea cabin. Grave-faced, Bally showed us a dispatch from ComAirLant which offered to replace our troubleprone Hogs with new Grumman F6F Hellcat fighters. The question was whether we three felt comfortable deploying to the Pacific forward area in a fighter that many thought had not been suitably designed for carrier work. The dispatch indicated that we needed to make an immediate decision so that new Hellcats could be ready and waiting for Fighting-17 as soon as we returned to Norfolk.

The query was not unexpected. Vought had been heaving around to get numerous needed changes into the production line. These included, among many others, raising the cockpit, providing a semibubble canopy, perfecting zero-bounce oleo struts—shock absorbers—finding ways to get the tail higher in the three-point attitude, perfecting and installing our homegrown right-wing leading-edge spoiler, perfecting nonspray cowl flap actuators, and on and on. Russ Clark, the boss of the Vought civilian crew aboard ship, had kept messages flying to the factory with problem identifications and recommended solutions. The company clearly saw what was at stake, so promised, scout's honor, to have not less than a dozen F4U-1As waiting for us dockside at Norfolk upon our return on August 10. The balance of the thirty-six fighters allowed the squadron would be in our hands, they swore, by August 20.

Bags, who had not troubled himself with keeping abreast of our difficulties, begged the question. I had spent a great deal of time on the bridge observing flight ops and thus had had many opportunities to talk with the captain. I knew him pretty well, and he knew me. Above all, I knew that he kept himself well informed and was decisive to boot. He clearly expected the same of his subordinates, so Bags's waffling did not sit well. At length, Bally got fed up and turned to me. "Well, Tommy?"

I had done my homework. "We both know that Captain Eddie [Clexton, the AirLant material officer] is no dummy, that he has a real handle on the validity of Vought's replacement schedule. He concurs with you and me that the Hogs we have aboard are by no stretch of the imagination carrier ready. So, he's telling Admiral Bellinger, 'We can go either way. If Ballentine figures the better performance of the Corsair justifies the risks and operational nightmares, I recommend we go along. He knows he'll have to live with them.' "

Bally was all ears. He merely nodded into my break, so I went on. "What you're asking me is, do I believe these fixes for the Corsair are going to give us a combat-ready airplane. Right?"

"Right. I'm listening."

"Skipper, I'm so convinced, and so are my pilots, that I recommend in the strongest terms that we go forward with the Corsairs. Fighting-17 could make the switch to the F6Fs without even breathing hard. But we believe that that would be a cop-out and a serious mistake. The F4U is the better combat airplane."

Bally smiled. "I expected that answer, but not put in such positive terms."

"Captain, we'll be doing a lot of operating during the trip from Norfolk to San Diego. In addition to the crack-ups we've had, we've averaged one blown tire in every three landings. I'll bet you ten bucks that we'll not only have zero crashes, but we won't blow ten main mounts on the jaunt to San Diego—provided, of course, we're not demoted to the Hellcat."

"You've got a bet, Tommy. I'll tell ComAirLant that *Bunker Hill* strongly recommends deployment with the F4U."

It was my practice to cut all hands—enlisted as well as officers—into whatever I could tell them about dealings with outside commands and agencies. Needless to say, everyone had expressed vital interest in the resolution of the what-do-we-deploy-with question. Scuttlebutt—rumor—was rampant in the small-town environment aboard *Bunker Hill*, as in any ship, and I well knew that bum scuttlebutt can be damaging to morale.

The troops were delighted to know that Captain Ballentine had concurred with us and had gone up the chain of command with his pitch to keep us in the Corsairs. When I was able to announce a few days later that we had an unequivocal statement from on high that Fighting-17 would be deploying with F4Us, the cheers were long and loud.

Before the euphoria wore off, however, I put the truth to them in the bluntest terms possible: "This puts the heat on us when we get back to Norfolk. We'll have a month at the most before we shove off again. We've got a hell of a lot of work to do. There'll be intense bounce drill until Catwalk Cummings and I are satisfied that every man is completely ready to land aboard. There will be maximum gunnery practice on banners at two hundred knots. Intercepts and grab-ass at twenty-five thousand feet or more will be routine. I well know that you guys are way behind in your drinking and screwing—so am I. I expect you to play hard, but, by God, it better not interfere with getting this squadron's job done."

I let that last sink in, then went on. "We'll work a six-day week, from first light until dark. Then we'll do night-flying. Anybody who puts in for leave for anything other than a dire, *provable* emergency can expect to be put in hack. If you're not prepared to heave around flat out, let me know now and I'll see that you are promptly sent on your way to a patrol outfit."

I noted that not everybody smiled as I went on to the finale. "There's no knowing how much chance we'll have after this for training before we get into combat. It might not be much. The group, Captain Ballentine, and the ship are counting on us. They believe that you're as good as I think you are. We will not let them down. To paraphrase Henry the Fifth at Agincourt, we'll say to our grandchildren, 'I was there. I served with Fighting-Seventeen!'"

The Vought people proved as good as their word. As soon as *Bunker Hill* arrived at Norfolk, the new Hogs were picked up at Floyd Bennett Field. As I was making my check hop in the first of them—my new Big Hog—I got a radio call, "Corsair out of Floyd Bennett. This is LaGuardia Tower. Over."

"This is Big Hog. Go ahead La Guardia."

"Big Hog, we've got very little traffic. Can you make a low pass by the tower? There are a lot of people who'd like to see that thing."

Would I! Do fighter pilots like girls? "This is Big Hog. Can do. I'll come by downwind. I'll call you one minute out in case you need to wave me off."

"This is La Guardia. Roger. Standing by."

I pointed her down from 5,000 feet and came by, full bore, close aboard the tower at window level indicating 350 knots—403 miles per hour. I pulled up in a 45-degree climb, slow-rolled to the right, slow-rolled to the left, and leveled out at 10,000 feet from the half loop and half roll of the Immelmann, which put me on a heading back over La Guardia.

"Big Hog, this is La Guardia. Wow! I say again, Wow! Thanks."

"This is Big Hog. My pleasure. Any time. Out."

I did not tell the troops about this incident until we were safely on the way south from Norfolk a month later. Based on our past experience at Norfolk, all hands had been sternly notified that we would be ultrarespectable while concentrating on our transition work into the 1A Hogs; no unauthorized grab-ass with other fighters, no dusting off the heavies, and no—repeat, no—flat-hatting. We did not need any trouble with the front office.

Lt(jg) Tom Killefer—TK—had been one of my star pupils at Miami, a bright-eyed youngster with whom I had shared an extremely close father-son-type relationship before he was sent to help form a new escort fighter squadron. Tom's ship, escort carrier

Bogue, which had been dedicated to antisubmarine work for nearly a year, happened to be in Norfolk when *Bunker Hill* returned from her shakedown cruise in the Gulf of Paria. Thus, Tom was on hand to waylay me almost as soon as I set foot on the beach.

As soon as our first round was set before us on the Boys' Town bar, TK launched into his prepared speech. "Boss, I want to go out with you guys. This pushing a Wildcat around looking for subs is important work, I know, but I got some Hog time in with Jumpin' Joe and it won't take me long to get refammed. My CAG and I don't operate on the same wavelength, so he wouldn't be desolated to see me go elsewhere."

It was a masterful sales pitch. In just a few brief sentences, TK had volunteered responses to every objection I could possibly raise—had I had a mind to.

"Okay, Tom, let me see what I can do."

It just happened that one of our new ensigns was newly married and, while competent, he was no ball of fire. His reluctance to part with his buddies—and me—was tempered with a considerable urge to remain on the East Coast, where he would be able to see his new bride occasionally. He agreed to being part of a swap if I could set it up with *Bogue*'s CAG, LCdr Howard Avery, an AvCad I had known since he came to the Fleet in 1938.

Howard was a very competent, conscientious officer, absolutely straight-arrow, eternally serious, with no use for blithe spirits. After plying him with a few beers at Boys' Town, I opened my pitch. "Howard, I hear that you've got some trouble with Killefer. You probably don't know that he was a student of mine at Miami. I think I can straighten him out. We happen to have a very good pilot who just got spliced, and he would prefer Atlantic duty. He's car-qualled in the U, and he has some Wild-cat time, too."

By this time, *Bogue* and her little air group had set a superb pace in pioneering hunter-killer operations against Nazi submarines in the central North Atlantic. Howard's pilots had sunk four U-boats and damaged three, so Howard, who was quite properly riding high, could afford to be magnanimous. "Killefer," he responded, "is a fine pilot. I like him personally, but I find he's not my cup of tea. He's a bit much, if you know what I mean."

"I sure do, Howard. You've probably heard around Norfolk that VF-17 has a lot of prima donnas, including me. Killefer would fit

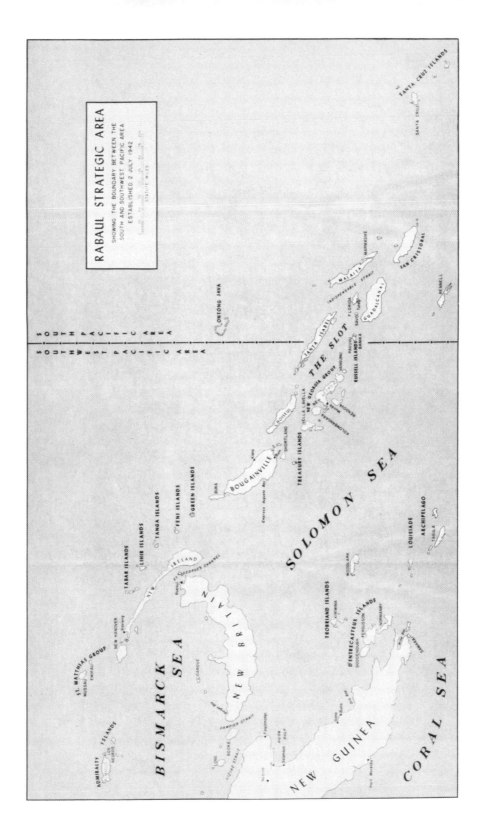

RABAUL STRATEGIC AREA

SHOWING THE BOUNDARY BETWEEN THE
SOUTH AND SOUTHWEST PACIFIC AREA

ESTABLISHED 2 JULY 1942

STATUTE MILES

SANTA CRUZ ISLANDS

SANTA CRUZ

SOUTH PACIFIC AREA
SOUTHWEST PACIFIC AREA

ONTONG JAVA

MALAITA

INDISPENSABLE STRAIT

SAN CRISTOBAL

FLORIDA
SAVO
ISLANDS
GUADALCANAL

RENNELL

SANTA ISABEL

THE SLOT

NEW GEORGIA GROUP
RUSSELL ISLANDS
NDI-
BANIKA

CHOISEUL
VELLA LAVELLA
KOLOMBANGARA
NEW

SHORTLAND
TREASURY ISLANDS

BUKA
BOUGAINVILLE

TANGA ISLANDS
FENI ISLANDS
GREEN ISLANDS

LIHIR ISLANDS
TABAR ISLANDS

NEW IRELAND
ST GEORGE'S CHANNEL

SOLOMON SEA

LOUISIADE
ARCHIPELAGO

WOODLARK

ST. MATTHIAS GROUP
MUSSAU
EMIRAU

NEW HANOVER

NEW BRITAIN

BISMARCK SEA

TROBRIAND ISLANDS

D'ENTRECASTEAUX ISLANDS
GOODENOUGH
FERGUSSON
NORMANBY

DAMPIER STRAIT

VITIAZ STRAIT

ADMIRALTY ISLANDS
LOS NEGROS

NEW GUINEA

PORT MORESBY

CORAL SEA

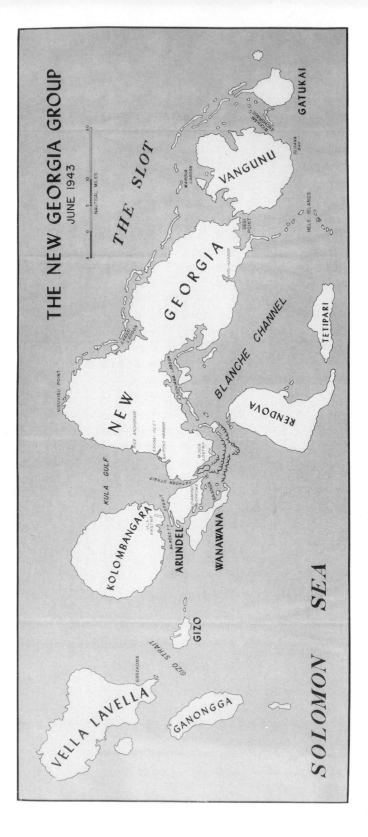

THE NEW GEORGIA GROUP
JUNE 1943

NAUTICAL MILES

THE SLOT

GATUKAI

VANGUNU

GEORGIA

BLANCHE CHANNEL

TETIPARI

NEW

RENDOVA

KULA GULF

KOLOMBANGARA

ARUNDEL

WANAWANA

SOLOMON SEA

GIZO

GIZO STRAIT

VELLA LAVELLA

GANONGGA

RABAUL AND ITS AIRFIELDS

JUNGLE GROWTH
PLANTATIONS
FARMS AND GARDENS
CONTOUR INTERVAL 500 FEET

BOUGAINVILLE

○   JAPANESE AIRBASE

ELEVATIONS IN FEET

0   1000   3000   5000 AND ABOVE

0   10   20   30   40 MILES

0   10   20   30   40 KILOMETERS

Green Is

TO TRUK
900 MILES

TO RABAUL
190 MILES

BUKA I

Buko Passage

BUKA

BONIS

BOUGAINVILLE

ISLAND

EMPEROR RANGE

Mt Balbi

Numa Numa
Ibu

TENEKAU

Mt Bagana

ROROVANA BAY

Kieta

KIETA

CROWN PRINCE RANGE

Cape
Torokina

EMPRESS
AUGUSTA
BAY

KARA

KAHILI

Buin

Erventa
Tonolei Hbr

Bougainville Strait

Fauro I

BALLALE

SHORTLAND

Faisi I

Poporang I

Alu I

S   O   L   O   M   O   N

Mono I

TREASURY IS

S   E   A

Stirling I

F. Temp

Cdr Tom Blackburn is re-
turned to USS *Santee*. November 1943.

Cut! Ideal attitude and position from which to land on a carrier deck.
USS *Bunker Hill*. August 1943.

This Corsair's tail hook has successfully captured the arresting wire and is about to make a passable landing aboard the USS *Charger* in Chesapeake Bay, March 1943.

A barrier crash. The pilot was shook up but not hurt.

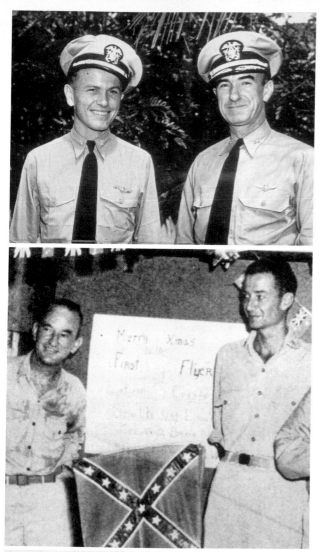

LCdr Tom Blackburn and RAdm John Ballentine. March 1944.

Fighter Command: Col Oscar Brice, USMC, and Lt Joe Bryan, USN.

Big Hog: Wharton, Gutenkunst, March, Blackburn, Killefer, Streig, Dr. Hermann, and Corporal J. M. Taylor, USMC. Ondongo, November 1943.

The twin Japanese airfields at Buka (*r*) and Bonis. November 1943.

Tom Blackburn poses in front of propeller blades depicting forty-three confirmed kills for the squadron. November 15, 1943.

"Oh, bullshit, Boss!" Tom Killefer speaks out during a postcombat brag session. *(from l to r)* Gile, Streig, Killefer, Gutenkunst, and Blackburn. Ondongo, November 1943.

right in. I think I can keep him pointed in the right direction. I'll be glad to take him off your hands."

"Thanks, Tom. I appreciate it."

"It's a deal. I'll fix it up with AirLant tomorrow."

The staff guys were cooperative, Howard was happy, the ensign and his bride were happy, TK was delighted, and I was smug. What I did not then realize—what I could not then have known—was that I had set the stage for VF-17 to become awash in castoffs from other squadrons. TK was the first of a boatload of extremely talented, albeit restive, chargers prone to partake of personality clashes, but hot to trot if the promise of battle was in the air. Why not? Having them aboard suited my spirit.

I updated Captain Ballentine almost daily on Fighting-17's status and progress. Capt Eddie Clexton's AirLant material office and Jack Hospers, the boss of Vought's service reps, could not do enough for us. The CASU maintenance people gave us top priority even though they were still wrestling with the bow wave resulting from the January shift from squadron maintenance units to the CASU's own centralized garage service. Notwithstanding the CASU's Sisyphean task of trying to satisfy the urgent demands of numerous temperamental squadron COs, they really came through for us. I suppose it helped that the CASU's skipper, LCdr Daniel "Dog" Smith, a top-notch naval aviator, was my old friend and long-standing golfing companion.

We went on getting acquainted with our new 1As with vigor and enthusiasm. Raising the cockpit and replacing the antiquated bird cage canopy with a bubble wonderfully improved the pilot's field of vision. Contrary to the gloomy predictions of some aerodynamicists, performance was not impaired. In fact, we noted a slight gain in maximum velocity with no ill effect, thus demonstrating once again that aircraft design is more an art than a science. But we did encounter new problems.

As part of our familiarization syllabus, each pilot had to climb to 30,000 feet, half roll to inverted, and let her go straight down. After checking out roll rates and control forces, the pilot was to level out at 20,000 feet. Lt Chuck Pillsbury, our operations officer, returned badly shaken from one of the first of these maneuvers. He told us that he had experienced some loss of elevator control and was thus unable to level out at anything like the expected rate. When we looked, we found that most of the fabric from his flippers—elevators—was gone.

I was alarmed, but I thought that Chuck had experienced an isolated failure ascribable to poor fabrication of that one new airplane. Nevertheless, I went up and repeated his maneuver in Big Hog, something I had already done with no ill effects. I was terrified when I felt the stick force lighten when it should have become heavier, and when I saw that I was only pulling two gees when I should have been pulling as many as four. As had Chuck, I arrived on the runway with my elevators tattered. I was not happy.

In bull sessions with flight-test people we had heard vague tales of "compressibility" and the magic numbers Professor Ernst Mach had developed with regard to flying at and above the speed of sound. As it turned out, portions of our 1As had been subjected to supersonic airflows. We eventually learned that several Army Air Forces P-38 fighters had been seen disintegrating in steep dives. In those cases, we were told, the dive angles had *increased* at the points pullouts had been programmed. Each time it happened, things got out of control so fast that the hapless pilots had not even been able to transmit, much less bail out. It would be some time before the scientists discovered that the compressibility phenomena were producing control reversal or "tuck-under."

We did not know what we had gotten into, but two deep scares—including my own—were enough to get me to ban vertical dives above 20,000 feet from that day on. Everyone who had completed the maneuver in the 1A had been just plain lucky. Other men in other Corsair squadrons died learning the lesson.

The intensive training period of bounce drill, gunnery, night ops, and other tactics and skills went forward without other notable incident. The Fighting-17 tigers were models of discretion in flight ops, and so there were no unpleasant sessions on ComAirLant's carpet, a fact that I am sure relieved him nearly as much as it relieved me.

On September 8, 1943, we taxied down to the Naval Operating Base's carrier pier and were hoisted aboard *Bunker Hill*. We shoved off to join the Great Adventure in the Pacific on September 10.

Well clear of the Virginia Capes, the big carrier swung into the wind and launched a small flight composed of all types aboard to begin refresher work for some of the air group and for the ship's company. I was on the bridge with Bally, who, pleased with the smooth takeoff, gave orders to start landings as soon as the flight deck was ready.

Because this would be Tom Killefer's first attempt at getting aboard a carrier in a Hog, he was first in the pattern in case he needed to go around more than once. With hook, wheels, and flaps down, Tom came up the groove, hanging on his prop at 90 knots. Catwalk Cummings picked TK up with a Roger and held the "okay" signal until it was time for the cut. The Corsair, which bore its typical resemblance to an old lady with her skirts at half-mast ready to go potty, touched down on three points without even the hint of a bounce.

Bally turned to me and answered my grin with one of his own. "He's qualified." Then the skipper turned to his phone talker, who had a hot line to all the essential stations in the ship. "Tell Pri Fly to have the pilot of that Corsair report to me as soon as he's parked."

Shortly, TK reported with a snappy, "Lieutenant Killefer, Captain. You sent for me?"

"Well done, Killefer. Any problems?"

With an absolute straight face, TK responded, "Thanks, sir. No sweat. It was like stabbing guppies in the toilet with a three-prong fork."

Captain John rolled his eyes heavenward as he turned to me, "Jesus, Tommy, are *all* these guys as outrageous as you?"

I was first aboard the next day and was pleased to be chalking up a smooth approach and landing when I heard and felt the right main tire blow out. Startled and horrified, I taxied forward, Big Hog thumping and clanking its way across the barrier to be parked by grinning directors who knew of my boastful bet with the captain regarding blown tires. As soon as I got to the bridge, Bally gleefully rubbed more salt into the wound with a lusty, "Looks like I'll have to buy you a drink with your ten bucks when we get to Panama." For a change, I had no rejoinder. I must say that the captain was as gracious as he was gloating, for he paid off the bet as soon as I put my hand out while we were tying up at North Island, in San Diego. My blowout was one of only five we sustained all the way from Norfolk to the West Coast, half the wagered number.

Transit of the Panama Canal was fascinating and effected with minimal damage to the ship. Some farsighted soul had decreed more than four decades earlier that the locks be 1,000 feet by 110 feet, even though battleships of the era stretched a mere 500 feet with an 85-foot beam. All of our fleet carriers were designed with the Canal in mind, so all could be shoehorned through. There was ample clearance fore-and-aft, but much squalling of tortured steel and scraping of unyielding concrete on both sides. While the waterline of the *Essex*-class carriers was under 100 feet, and the starboard side was nearly a flat vertical, the horizontal span at flight deck level exceeded 140 feet. Outboard of the fore-and-aft access and shelter catwalks were safety nets, which protruded another 8 feet. The port side bulged at frequent intervals with 20mm and 40mm gun tubs, and the deck edge elevator and its supporting structure protruded 20 feet even in the vertical, folded, position. Thus, concrete lampposts well clear of a lock's sides were regularly mowed down like tall weeds with each Fleet carrier transit.

We got in eight full days of flight ops between Norfolk and San Diego, a wonderful opportunity to prove out our new 1As and our ability to operate them. All hands were extremely pleased with the results. Captain Ballentine went out of his way to make sure that Washington, ComAirLant, and, especially, ComAirPac were fully apprised of our progress and ongoing success. We were all fully aware that there would be no further opportunities for training operations once we sortied from San Diego, bound for Pearl Harbor and the forward area. Carriers departing San Diego were filled to the gunwales with spare aircraft, trucks, and personnel—*Bunker Hill* carried four thousand passengers—so the decks were locked.

The sortie from San Diego on September 28 was exciting. We were on our way at last.

11

O ne evening, only a few days out of San Diego, I was summoned to Captain Ballentine's cabin. Something had to be
wrong.

"Tommy," he began, right off, "I just received a message I think
you ought to see right away."

Oh god, I thought as he handed me the message flimsy, which
read, "Upon arrival at Pearl Harbor, VF-17 detached from *Bunker
Hill*. Proceed by first available transportation to Espiritu Santo and
report to Commander, South Pacific, for duty. VF-18 will replace."

Typically, no explanation was given. I looked up at Bally, but he
just shook his head with a beaten air of finality; there was no sense
trying to squawk our way out of this one, the decision from on high
was obviously final. Bally and I had talked about the possibility of
something like this happening, and we both thought we knew why.
As the Navy's *only* carrier-based Corsair squadron, our place in the
supply system was ambiguous, to say the least, and troublesome.
All the other carrier-based fighter units were equipped with F6F
Hellcats or, in the case of smaller ships, F4F Wildcats. The hard
realities of the supply system, we guessed, had simply overwhelmed the front office's authentic desire to see us operating
Corsairs from the carrier. I suspected that the decision had been
made without emotion at AirPac headquarters, for they, after all,
would be the people who would have had to jump through hoops
to keep us supplied. Bally was later told by AirPac staffers at Pearl
that this was indeed the reason we were relieved, and not—definitely not—because the front office thought the airplanes were
unsuitable for carrier work. The decision and news, however, were
truly shattering. The fact that VF-18 had been formed by my
fellow Miami instructor, the redoubtable LCdr Sam Silber, was a
meager consolation. I wished Sam well, but I also wished he had
not found a berth aboard a carrier at our expense.

I called all hands to the squadron ready room as soon as I got
back from the bridge. I wish I could take back the words I had to
use to convey the situation to my mates. One moment, they were
fidgeting and fooling around in their seats, the next, they were

looking up at me with rapt attention, trying to determine if this was
yet another feeble attempt to put them on. And, a moment after
that, they were all sitting up in their leather-upholstered chairs
with terrible expressions on their faces. It was as if I had told them
that a bus containing all their relatives had gone off the road, killing
everyone aboard.

Suddenly, one of them demanded of me, "Where the hell is
Espiritu Santo?"

Good old Duke Henning waded right in to field that and a dozen
more questions concerning the hunting possibilities in the South
Pacific. Ah, the elasticity of youth; I am sure that they were
dreaming of new worlds to conquer.

We were off-loaded from *Bunker Hill* the day we arrived at Pearl,
October 2. Our first order of business was to bid farewell to a mate.
The night before we reached Pearl, the ineffable Bobby Mims
awoke with the granddaddy of all bellyaches. By the time the ship's
senior doctor could be persuaded to look, Bobby was in severe pain
and uncontrollably discharging from both ends. The medicos who
misdiagnosed Bobby's ailment and refused to operate, appeared
happy to see the last of him as he was rushed to Tripler General
Hospital aboard an ambulance that had been summoned to meet us
as the ship docked. Bobby was operated on at once for a ruptured
appendix. Of course, I closely followed Bobby's ordeal and soon
had word that he would not be returned to flight status for at least
a month. Sadness in the squadron was not universal when he was
permanently transferred. However, this was not the last VF-17 saw
of this scrapper.

As the squadron's gear was being off-loaded, I told our yeoman
to discreetly pack the typewriter that had been on loan to us from
the ship. After all the troops and impedimenta were ashore, I
started on my way up to the CO's cabin to bid Bally a fond farewell
and a regretful adieu. I was crossing the quarterdeck when I ran
into the exec of the ship, Cdr Swede Ekstrom. As I launched into
a syrupy good-bye, I could see that the genial Swede had gone all
flinty eyed. "Tommy," he interrupted with a peremptory wave of
the hand, "can it. You aren't leaving just now."

"Sir?"

"You will not leave the ship until that typewriter is back aboard."

"Typewriter?"

But Swede was not buying what I was trying to sell. In the end—it was a quick end—I had to send word to the dock to unload the stolen machine and return it to the exec with all possible speed. The squadron would have to make do with a flimsy portable on loan from one of the pilots. Of all the things we needed to run the squadron, a good office standard typewriter came in only one step behind aviation gasoline.

I had only just walked into the temporary quarters assigned to me at Ford Island when Lt Johnny Kleinman appeared at the door. "Skipper, I'd like you to meet two old friends of mine who just showed up. They'd like to talk to you."

The two impressed me at first sight. They were both smartly turned out in tropical worsted khakis, and their fighter boots gleamed as if ready for a Marine parade. "Sir," Johnny introduced, "Lieutenants March and Innis."

"Yes?" I decided not to fool around; I thought I knew why they had arrived at my door, and I was right.

There was no sparring, no time frittered away on inconsequential pleasantries. Characteristically, March was the spokesman: "Sir, we want to go back out with Fighting-Seventeen."

Even before I knew March's and Innis's credits, I was willing to give them any benefit of the doubt. "Any friend of Johnny Kleinman's starts with a strong recommendation."

The pair had been in Wildcats off carriers and land based at Guadalcanal—during the "dark days," as everyone who was there rightly called them. As a fresh caught ensign, Don "Stinky" Innis had bagged a Zero before being shot down and painfully burned on D-Day at Guadalcanal, August 7, 1942. Also an ensign on D-Day, flying off *Enterprise* with Fighting-6, Harry "Dirty Eddie" March had killed a Val dive-bomber, a feat he repeated at the Eastern Solomons carrier battle on August 24, 1942. Who wouldn't jump at the opportunity to get two blooded veterans aboard an unblooded fighter squadron? Both had lots of carrier time in Wildcats and Hellcats, but neither had ever set foot in a Corsair, a minor, eminently correctable flaw.

So what were they doing trying to get into Fighting-17? Like Tom Killefer, they did not march to the pace of their present CO's drum. Their visit with me was strictly aboveboard; their CO knew they were looking for a new home, and approved of the transfer if they could wangle it with me. We got the paperwork started through channels that afternoon. The two were on the flight schedule the very next morning.

They were a real Mutt-and-Jeff combination. Dirty Eddie March was tall and rangy, with the build of a track-and-field star. Despite his opprobrious nickname, he was extremely fastidious, a good-looking young man in the John Wayne mold. Stinky Innis was about five-eight, of medium build, and darkly handsome. Though warm and friendly, Stinky was by no means the effervescent extrovert his sidekick proved to be.

If not on personality alone, Dirty Eddie's popularity with his fellow pilots was quickly established. He had been at Pearl for some time and had made connections among the young ladies who manned the plotting boards at the Honolulu Aircraft Plotting and Tracking Center. To cap this enormous vote-getting asset, Dirty Eddie had the keys to a huge antique Buick touring car left behind by some departing pilot and thereafter passed from one transiting fighter squadron to the next.

We faced a busy week at Pearl. In addition to flying the socks off March and Innis to get each of them at least forty hours in the Corsairs, we all put in a full schedule with intercept practice at 25,000 feet, generally honing the sharp edge of our fighting abilities, for first combat could not be far ahead.

Meantime, we wasted no time establishing a beachhead in a suite at Waikiki's Halekulani Hotel. This magnificent, generally staid landmark adopted us with a live-and-let-live attitude. The open, honest approach of the Hawaiians toward sex had long stood in refreshing contrast to the hypocritical Victorian or absurd puritanical preachments that anything enjoyable was, ipso facto, sinful. This was, after all, the end of the second full year of the war, and Hawaii was the last jumping-off point for many thousands of sailors and airmen bound for life-threatening duty in the forward area. We were not vulgar or sloppy or brawling, but we sure were not angelic either. We all had wallets made fat by our days of isolation at Manteo and aboard ship, and these were matched by compelling urges and enthusiasms, all of which could be bought or otherwise paid for in the Hawaii of the day. We never had it so good, nor in such quantity. Bacchus and Eros beamed.

*   *   *

We left Pearl on Columbus Day, October 12, 1943, aboard the jeep carrier *Prince William*. The "Pee Willie," as she was universally tagged, was chockablock with our thirty-six Corsairs and an entire squadron of Army Air Forces P-40 fighters, miscellaneous other planes, trucks, jeeps, and bluejackets and Marines bound for the forward area. We plodded along at 15 knots under escort of one dinky little destroyer, which, we agreed, was present only so someone would witness our demise at the hands of Japanese submarine wolf packs. In fact, only six weeks later, that is exactly what happened to the Pee Willie's sister ship, *Liscome Bay*.

The passage was no joy. Only the small wardroom was air-conditioned, and the hot, sweaty bodies of the many officers aboard threatened to overwhelm the system almost from the first hour afloat. Only two events enlivened the crushingly boring eleven-day passage.

We were a few days out when the forenoon calm was split asunder by the clanging of the general alarm and the blatting of "General Quarters. All hands, man your battle stations," from the PA system. We apprehensively jumped to the conclusion that the tiny destroyer escort ahead had picked up a submarine contact on her sonar. Calm was shortly restored. My summons to report to the bridge soon followed. It turned out that Timmy Gile's maintenance boys had been working over a Corsair on the hangar deck when one of them somehow fired three .50-caliber rounds. The hangar deck was filled with airplanes fueled to capacity with an aggregate of thousands of gallons of volatile avgas. Moreover, the hangar's forward bulkhead was covered with torpedos, each mounting an impact sensitive Torpex warhead. One incendiary armor-piercing .50-caliber round was thus enough to torch or blow the entire ship and all who sailed in her. Those three ear-splitting bangs echoed and reverberated through the entire rest of the trip. Terror was palpable. Miraculously, the three half-inch bullets harmlessly plowed into the overhead.

The second main event was crossing the equator, which brought with it the traditional initiation of Pollywogs by Shellbacks. Neptunus Rex, complete with a flowing white beard festooned with seaweed, presided over judgment and punishment of all parties guilty of trespassing with our first incursion into his Imperial Domain. The horseplay, rough to a point just short of injury, consisted of a trip on hands and knees through a 30-foot "tunnel of love" which followed and preceded shellacking by torrents of biting salt water sprayed from high-pressure fire hoses. The tunnel was two 3-foot-diameter target sleeves filled with garbage, shredded paper, and malodorous butcher's scraps saved in warm storage for the occasion. Final indignities were meted out by barbers who randomly provided Mohawk haircuts or whacked off half a beard or mustache. The barber chairs had been hinged so as to flip Polly-wogs, ass over teakettle, into a seawater tank manned by frustrated fullbacks who ducked and reducked victims trying to make their final escapes so they could be proclaimed Shellbacks. Age and rank were not ignored; seamen second class got the lightest treatment, and officers got the works. The ship's exec, Cdr Dave Young, once my squadron mate in Fighting-2, and the Air Boss, LCdr Sammy Randall, with whom I had played water polo at Annapolis, were on hand to be sure that I got the royal works.

Each day saw all pilots dragooned into very vigorous calisthenics led by me for half an hour following the standard 0800 quarters for muster. The bitching was long and loud, but I was adamant.

Duke Henning filled our forenoons with skull sessions, preparing us for our imminent combat tour. Foremost was geographical orientation. To us, as was the case with most Americans, the Solomon Islands were terra incognita. Only Guadalcanal and Rabaul were by then household words, the former because of the grinding six-month-long first American offensive that had taken place there from August 1942 to early February 1943, and the latter because it remained the center of the Japanese war effort in the region. New Georgia, which the U.S. Army had invaded and seized between June and August 1943, only a few months before our arrival on the scene, was less well known. There were names of places we had never heard before: Choiseul, Kolombangara, Vella Lavella, and Bougainville.

I was astounded to discover that the charts upon which our charts were based had last been updated by the British Admiralty in 1852. Once I had that vital fact under my belt, there was no longer any need for Duke to explain why a close look revealed topographical information so vague as to be nonexistent. I had been exercised about the vagueness of charts relating to Morocco in 1942, but the meager offerings provided for our trip to this war front exactly a year later won the prize. As we would learn quite soon, for our purposes the key failings of these charts were life-threatening bum elevations and the mislocation of nearly all the peaks and ridges jutting up from those mountainous islands.

For survival purposes, Duke passed out small books filled with phrases in Pidgin, the universal glot of the islanders in the region to which we were heading. Phrases key to the downed pilot were, among others, "Gifim wara bilong dring," meaning "Bring drinking water," or "Balus bilong me im all buggerup," which informs the interested party that your plane had crashed. "Ouse pek-pek ware e stop" is the vital inquiry if one is in search of the nearest facility with a modicum of plumbing—a bush, perhaps.

Except for updates as to the general situation in the air war in the Solomons, I must say that, no fault of Duke's, I came away from the briefings with a sense of having retained my crushing ignorance.

At long last, October 25 found us standing by to be catapulted off Pee Willie, bound for the island of Espiritu Santo, our side's primary supply base in the New Hebrides, within easy one-way fighter range of fabled Guadalcanal. Even then, nearly a year after the air war at Guadalcanal had turned in favor of the thin Marine and Navy squadrons based there, that base was itself only a fighter's flight to the ongoing air battles over the Central and Northern Solomons. The main runway complex at Guadalcanal, Henderson Field, was still occasionally subjected to harassment raids by single Japanese bombers.

Almost everyone was happy to see me take the first catapult launch, just to see if Pee Willie's slingshot worked. A catapult shot makes for an easy takeoff, but it is not for the fainthearted; you *always* wonder if it is really reliable.

The flight in to the beach was brief. We set up a landing pattern at Bomber-1 and went in to experience a new thrill. The strip was "paved" with interconnected perforated steel plates known as Marston Matting. These provide quite a smooth surface, firm even on soft or sandy ground. The only shortcoming is that it tends to become glassy if wet. What raised goose bumps for us that day— our first time landing on the matting—was the ungodly loud banging and clanging that accompanied each touchdown and rollout. I was sure I had blown both main tires, and I believe everyone else thought the same. Only our four South Pacific veterans, Lieutenants Halford, Kleinman, March, and Innis, wondered what all the excitement was about.

My first official act after parking the planes was to jeep over to ComFairSouth headquarters to report us in and ready for duty. The Fair (Fleet Air) commands were basically support activities responsible for air ops and maintenance outside the combat areas. I had no sooner reported Fighting-17's presence than the ops guys told me, "Take off tomorrow morning for Guadalcanal. On arrival, report to ComAirSoPac for further orders. Your ground echelon and gear will go tomorrow, too." *Wham, bam.*

I quickly learned, also, that Cdr Jumpin' Joe Clifton was temporarily based at Bomber-1. His carrier-based Fighting-12 had recently transitioned under duress from Corsairs to Hellcats. By the time I made it back to the squadron from Fair headquarters, Jumpin' Joe and a bunch of his pilots were on our flight line drooling over our new 1As, the first to reach the forward area. The brightly painted prop hubs and the fierce skull and crossbones emblems on the cowls made a wonderful impression. With Joe leading the way, all hands repaired with alacrity to the O Club to swap lies, tell sea stories, exchange gossip, and so gird for the combat into whose face we were finally about to charge.

While at Bomber-1, I learned of the loss of destroyer *Strong* in one of the many hellish night surface actions that had marked the progress of our forces at Guadalcanal and, more recently, in the New Georgia Group. Among *Strong*'s dead, I learned, was her exec, my Naval Academy roommate and dear friend, LCdr Fred Purdy. So, I was not only headed "in harm's way," I was doing so with a personal score to settle.

PART IV

Cherryblossom

12

The morning of October 26, 1943, found us killing time at Bomber-1 while the local mechanics tried to revive two sick Hogs. There was no joy there, so I decided to proceed to Guadalcanal with the thirty-four available Corsairs, hoping the other two would join us late in the day or soon thereafter.

Takeoff commenced at 1130. We all joined on the R4D transport, which would serve as our navigation plane while also carrying Duke Henning and some of our small permanent ground crew complement. The gooney bird turned out to be a headache; its cruising speed obliged the fighters to poke along at 135 knots. In fact, it was uncomfortable for the fighters to fly so slow, so what we had to do was set up intricate weaving patterns to, in effect, slow our rate of forward progress. I had to fight the urge to leave the gooney and do my own navigating—I was quite capable of holding a heading over only 500 miles of water—but two things stayed my hand. Our own people were aboard the gooney, and that fat, slow transport was capable of orbiting over one spot for quite a long time in the event an F4U had to ditch because of mechanical difficulties.

Our first sight of the Solomon Islands was when we made landfall over San Cristobal, the first big island at the southern end of the chain, the closest to Espiritu Santo. I was immediately struck by the beauty of the war's venue. From the air, San Cristobal was spectacular—steeply rising green-clad mountains and ridges set out in the cobalt blue of the deep tropical waters. The ridges rose 2,000 to 3,000 feet to greet us, and we saw volcanic cones in among the higher peaks, some of which pierced the sky to elevations in excess of 7,000 feet. The higher peaks were obscured by what were described as permanent cloud cover. It was an altogether breathtaking introduction to a region we had heard was dotted by little more than stinking, swampy, rain-forested hellholes.

North of San Cristobal, and stretching northwest to Bougainville, the northernmost and largest of the Solomons, was a double chain of mainly long, narrow, rain-forested islands. Immediately ahead were Guadalcanal and Malaita, the latter to the east and the former to the west. The next pair were New Georgia, to the west, and Santa Isabel, to the east. Choiseul, to the west, slightly over-laps the northern reaches of the New Georgia Group, which includes Kolombangara, and points the way to Bougainville. The name of the natural sea lane between the double chain of the Solomon Islands appears on the charts as New Georgia Sound, but all the Americans who had fought or otherwise served in the region knew it only as the Slot. Stretching away to the northwest of Bougainville's northern cape is the crescent of the Bismarck Archipelago, with New Britain to the west and New Ireland to the east. Rabaul, the huge port and air-base complex that was the hub of the Japanese regional war effort, was at the eastern end of New Britain, virtually overlooking the western cape of New Ireland. The Australian-held eastern leg of New Guinea is due south of Rabaul.

Our immediate objective that day was fabled Henderson Field, named for Marine Maj Lofton Henderson, who died leading a dive-bomber raid—sans protecting fighters—against Japanese sur-face warships at Midway. The original runway had been started by the Japanese in June 1942 and was nearing completion when the U.S. 1st Marine Division struck on August 7, 1942. The field fell with little bloodshed ashore, but several tragic oversights combined to set up the surface fleet for a brutal defeat the night of August 8–9. Four Allied heavy cruisers—three U.S. and one Australian—were sunk against no Japanese losses. The tragic Naval Battle of Savo Island resulted in the virtual abandonment of the Marine division by the naval forces charged with protecting and—above all—resupplying it. Even at the time of our arrival little more than a year after the event, the Guadalcanal Campaign had achieved a legendary aura, and Henderson Field was a fitting first stop for modern pilgrims on their way to battle the Japanese only a little farther north.

Four of my lieutenants—Sunny Jim Halford, Johnny Kleinman, Stinky Innis, and Dirty Eddie March—had flown with the only Navy fighter squadron, Fighting-5, to be committed to the defense of Henderson Field during the "dark days." They had told us how it was because we would not let up on them until they did. Each of them had tasted Japanese blood with aerial victories.

The combined U.S. Navy, Marine, and Army force committed to the simultaneous land, air, and naval campaigns associated with the Guadalcanal Campaign had not so much defeated as worn down the Japanese land, naval, and air forces charged with wresting back control of Henderson Field and environs. In a plodding six-month campaign punctuated once a month during the first four months by massive but not overwhelming Japanese combined-arms offensives, the thin American forces had pushed the Japanese from Guadalcanal. In doing so, they had suffered grievous losses, but they had destroyed so many Japanese ships and Imperial Navy warplanes that the Japanese were forced to take a backward step for the first time in the Pacific War. Following the official conclusion of the Guadalcanal Campaign on February 9, 1943, the U.S. forces in the region had been hors de combat, unable to follow through right away. The Japanese used the breathing space to build and fortify several new bases along the Solomons chain.

The Russell Islands, 35 miles northwest of Guadalcanal's western cape, Cape Esperance, had been bloodlessly seized in mid-February. A fighter strip—Advance Base Knucklehead—was quickly built by Seabees on Banika, one of the two large Russell Islands. However, it took until June 30 for VAdm William "Bull" Halsey's U.S. South Pacific Command to muster a blow against New Georgia, where the Japanese had built up a major air-base complex at Munda. Marine fighter squadrons out of Knucklehead and Army, Navy, Marine, and New Zealand fighter and bombing squadrons out of Henderson had amply supported the June 30 landings at Rendova. In time, as the terribly mismanaged New Georgia Campaign reeled on to victory at Munda, the Seabees built a new advance fighter base at Segi Point, on New Georgia itself.

In addition to supporting the ground effort against Munda and, later, outlying islands, the squadrons based at Segi and Knucklehead spent an increasing amount of their time raiding farther and farther up the Solomons, against the Treasury Islands, the Shortlands anchorages in southern Bougainville, outlying bases on Choiseul, and a variety of targets in and around Bougainville. It was generally held that these raids—none of them very heavy—were designed to soften the way for yet more contemplated landings that would eventually pave the way to Rabaul herself. By the time we arrived on the scene in late October, Munda was a full-going operation, and so were Segi and several new outlying fields scattered through the New Georgia Group. It remained to be seen what the next amphibious target would be, but it was certain that there would soon be one.

*   *   *

We were all stiff as we climbed from our revetted fighters following the 3.5-hour flight from Espiritu Santo. The landscape I had seen during my approach and as I shook out my legs on the taxi apron still gave vivid indications of the savage fighting that had wound up nine months earlier. Several scarred and frondless coconut palms were still in evidence, the ground was amply pocked by shell and bomb craters, and twisted, burned-out airplane carcasses—many of them Wildcats—still littered the edges of the runway. The usual level of exuberance following a Fighting-17 group landing was muted to the point of sober, dumbstruck—I would even say reverent—silence. I cannot begin to imagine the depth of feeling my four Guadalcanal-blooded veterans were experiencing.

At length a jeep came out to carry me to a meeting with Capt Al Morehouse, the AirSoPac operations officer. After I reported us present for duty, Al escorted me in to make a call on VAdm Aubrey "Jakey" Fitch, ComAirSoPac himself. The admiral was an old friend of my father's, so the welcome was warm and personal, and it extended to a cordial invitation to dinner in the Flag Mess. I welcomed the opportunity to connect early and at a social level with the key players running the regional aviation effort.

AirSoPac, like its boss, Halsey's Noumea-based South Pacific Command, was multinational and multiservice in its staffing and operational components. Present at the first dinner on Guadalcanal were Australians and New Zealanders as well as Navy, Marine, and Army Air Forces officers. The same held for the command responsible for air operations in the Solomons, AirSols; it was multinational and multiservice, truly an Allied and allied effort.

At the conclusion of dinner, Captain Morehouse directed me to have Fighting-17 ready to go at first light. We would be proceeding direct to Ondongo, on New Georgia. On arrival there, I would be working for ComAirSols, MGen Nathan Twining, of the Army Air Forces, through his Fighter Command chief, Col Oscar Brice, of the Marines.

We were airborne and enroute to Ondongo by 0600, October 27. After an uneventful but watchful ninety minutes, I led the squadron into the landing pattern over our new home. Proud of its carrier training, Fighting-17 pulled off a precision carrier-style breakup over the coral strip. Carrier-type approaches were made with standard tight turns with the cross-wind leg over Diamond Narrows, whose half-mile width separated New Georgia from Kolombangara. Three-point touchdowns at thirty-second intervals, we expected, would be the envy of the Army P-39 and New Zealand P-40 pilots already operating out of the place. However, we soon learned that they thought we were merely nuts as we came in low and slow preparatory to stalling out and landing on the first 200 feet of runway. On the other hand, on this and ensuing days, we did not emulate their sorry record of hairy landings and crack-ups from overshoots.

Ondongo—which means Place of Death—was a scenic spot, to say the least. The strip had been carved from a gorgeous coconut plantation and was framed on the west and south by the steep tree-shrouded ridges of northern New Georgia and on north and east by similar ridges of southern Kolombangara. Farther off to the north were Kolombangara's twin extinct volcanoes, each stabbing the sky in excess of 5,000 feet. Kolombangara, roughly circular and 25 miles in diameter, is set like a dark green jewel in the cobalt waters of Kula and Vella gulfs, and is further accentuated, as are all shorelines in the region, by the apple greens and turquoises of shoals, coral reefs, and passes. Placid and beautiful on the surface, Kula and Vella gulfs had been floored by the gray steel of American and Japanese warships and carpeted by the bodies of American and Japanese sailors in a pair of ferocious night naval actions associated with the New Georgia Campaign.

Scenic as this paradise seemed to be at first glance, we soon learned that there were no golden beaches and no dusky, barebosomed maidens. The nearest nurse was at Espiritu Santo. What we got was clean, virtually bugless, free of snipers, and, above all, near the enemy.

As promised by AirSoPac, we were met by a complete and extremely competent ground crew organization, that of Marine Fighting Squadron 215 (VMF-215), whose pilot component had just been rotated to Australia for R&R following a full six-week combat tour. Not entirely fair, the ground crew organizations worked straight through each squadron's six-month tour of the war zone while the pilots alternately flew and rested in six-week increments until the tour was completed. This was a boon to the land-based Navy units, of which Fighting-17 was merely the first

Corsair entry, in that there was no CASU operating this far forward. The superb VMF-215 ground crew adopted us as their own literally from the moment we taxied off the strip following our first landing. Indeed, it is difficult to tell if they considered themselves part of VF-17 or us as part of VMF-215. Whichever the case—perhaps both—we meshed gears perfectly from the first moment.

After we were chocked and shut down in the revetments, we made our way to the good-sized Quonset hut that served as the ready room and squadron office. As soon as I stowed my flight gear, I got on the hand-cranked field telephone and negotiated my way through the manual switchboard to Fighter Command. "This is Lieutenant Commander Blackburn at Ondongo. May I speak to Colonel Brice?"

After a brief delay, "This is Colonel Brice. Welcome."

"Colonel, Fighting-Seventeen reporting for duty with thirty-four F4Us. Two more will be in tomorrow. Taussig Nineteen-Seventeen."

"We're glad you're here. What the hell is 'Taussig Nineteen-Seventeen?' "

"Sorry, Colonel, that's an old Navy catch phrase. When someone asks when you'll be ready to go into operation, it signifies 'we are ready now.' "

In April 1917 Captain Fightin' Joe Taussig commanded the first group of U.S. Navy destroyers to reinforce the valiant, weary British antisubmarine forces at Cobh, Ireland. Mindful that the spitkit American destroyers had just weathered a stormy North Atlantic crossing, the British admiral had signaled, "How many days do you need to refit for sea?"

Taussig had instantly responded, "We are ready now."

The good colonel took us at our word, for our phone jangled after only a brief wait following the end of my reporting-in conversation. The word was that a reinforced brigade of the 3rd New Zealand Division had begun landing in the nearby Treasury Islands at daybreak. Thus, Fighting-17 was ordered to launch a flight of eight Corsairs to patrol over the beaches. I claimed the honor of leading off Fighting-17's first combat mission, which launched at 1315. The flight lasted ninety minutes; we were back on the deck by 1445. Results were negative; there were no contacts. Eight more Corsairs were aloft from 1400 until 1625, with the same negative results.

And the third mission of only four Corsairs made a similar dry run between 1545 and 1810.

The Japanese made only one effort to get at the American flotilla and New Zealand landing force, but it was headed off well to the north by Army Air Forces and New Zealand fighters out of Munda. The scrap happened while one of our flights was on station, but the ship-based fighter director did not even tell our combat air patrol (CAP) there was a fight going on, and we did not learn of it until the following day.

During the squadron briefing that evening, I made two policy statements I probably should have announced earlier. First, I wanted official news only of enemy planes positively shot down; "probable" and "damaged" claims would not find their way into the Fighting-17 War Diary. Second, pilots returning from combat missions were not—repeat, not—permitted to execute victory rolls or other low-level aerobatics; violators would be relieved and sent to the rear in disgrace. My reasoning was that too many fighter pilots had bought the farm while performing stunts in airplanes that had suffered unperceived structural damage from enemy fire.

That evening, our first at Ondongo, we settled into our spartan permanent housing, a pair of large Quonset huts. We also had the dubious pleasure of our first meal at the Hotel Ondongo Mud Plaza, the Army-run officers' mess. When we heard that our own ground echelon was coming over by boat from Munda at 1845, four of us jeeped down to the dock to greet and assist them. As they debarked, Condition Red was sounded and everything blacked out as streams of red tracer filled the sky immediately overhead. We all bolted for cover while the Marines and boat crews remained in the open, cackling with laughter over our discomfiture. As we tried to recover our dignity, a lone Japanese twin-engine Betty medium bomber tooled around overhead and dropped the odd bomb into the jungle as searchlights tried to fix her meandering course. One of the boat crewmen muttered "Washing Machine Charlie," the generic name coined by Marines at Guadalcanal for such goings-on. Shortly, the lone Betty departed, the lights came on, and the All Clear was sounded.

The following day, October 28, Fighting-17 flew forty-four combat sorties, but we did not get shot at nor get any shots off. On October 29 several of our pilots were titillated by ground fire while escorting B-25s and PV-1s on a pair of morning strikes against the Buka-Bonis airfield complex at the northwest tip of Bougainville. No damage was sustained and no enemy aircraft were seen in a pair of what the AirSols Strike Command bomber boys aptly called "milk runs."

Our warm-up continued through the afternoon of October 29 when sixteen of us relieved tension with a barge-busting mission. Heavy, armored barges had become the Imperial Army's chief means for getting troops and supplies from place to place in the Solomons. This was a legacy of the Guadalcanal Campaign, when so many Japanese transports and surface warships had been lost or severely damaged trying to lift troops through waters dominated in daylight by our land-based fighters and bombers. Barges were cheaper, there were lots of them, and they were relatively more difficult to detect as they lay beached along tree-shrouded shore-lines during the day.

The October 29 operation began as a support hop for a P-38 photoreconnaissance flight to the Shortlands anchorage, incorporating the Shortland Islands and southern Bougainville. However, when the P-38 failed to show at our rendezvous, I led the other Corsairs to Bougainville and approached Tonolei harbor from the north. In repeated strafing runs, we destroyed three 80-ton cargo vessels and four landing barges full of troops. The AA was light and ineffective, though they got several rounds into each of several Corsairs. Not what we expected, but Fighting-17 had finally drawn some blood.

On October 30 we launched twenty-four Corsairs, but one had to abort. Thus, twenty-three of us joined with forty other fighters of various types to escort seventy-two SBD dive-bombers and twenty-four TBFs, the latter being laden with four 500-pound bombs apiece. The target, the airfield at Kara, also part of the Shortlands complex, put up no resistance, and no Japanese fighters appeared from anywhere else. Thus, with full loads of machine-gun ammunition still aboard, Fighting-17 once again beat up on Tonolei on the way home.

That afternoon, twenty-four VF-17 Corsairs and a dozen Ondongo-based P-39 fighters again shot up everything in sight at Tonolei. This attack was the charm, for we never again saw a worthy target at what had been a major Japanese anchorage until it fell within range of our fighters. This result more than justified all the low-level work the squadron had undertaken at Norfolk and Manteo. Despite the opinion of all the cookie pushers at the former base, low-level fighter ops were clearly a key part in our matrix of victory in the Solomons. That last week of October 1943, my pilots were comfortable and skillful while executing high-speed firing runs at negligible altitudes.

That evening, we got a real demonstration of guts under fire. Sunny Jim Halford led off a flight of seven F4Us assigned to cover a PBY on a "Dumbo" mission, as air-sea rescue ops were called. The twin-engine Consolidated PBY-5A Catalina flying boats were very slow and extremely vulnerable, but the Dumbo crews never-theless routinely kited straight into the teeth of enemy installations to pluck our downed pilots from danger. As Sunny Jim and the other Corsair pilots strafed the beach to suppress the enemy fire, the seemingly nerveless PBY driver made a straight-in approach and stopped while his crewmen reeled in an Ondongo-based P-39 pilot who had had to ditch during the afternoon strafing run. All this was done within range of shore-based weapons that would have blown the PBY away had they not been engaged to the hilt by the Corsairs. The fighter pilots knew, as did the PBY crew, that the whole operation was a dream opportunity for a high-speed diving bounce by Japanese fighters who could surely cream the Catalina and knock down one or more Corsairs. *We* would not have ne-glected such a silver-platter presentation. It was a keen lesson for us; we knew that there were people on our side who were willing to risk death to bring us home alive.

October 31 provided a series of what proved to be warm-up operations that resulted in no bloodletting whatsoever. Despite the raids on Tonolei, there had been grousing in the ranks because we had yet to be placed in a position to engage enemy aircraft. Little did we know that the curtain was about to ring up on the next major Allied landings in the region, at Bougainville. Fighting-17 was about to climb aboard the gravy train.

——— 13 ———

We knew there was to be another landing, but that is all we knew. We *assumed* it would be somewhere on Bougainville, which was obvious to anyone with access to a map of the region. But we had no idea as to the precise location of the effort, nor the exact date, nor the size and composition of either our forces or the enemy's. Our briefing on the evening of October 31 simply told us that the landing was to be made at dawn, November 1, at Cape Torokina, about midway up Bougainville's southwestern coast. VF-17 was directed to provide overlapping high-cover missions over Empress Augusta Bay—code-named Cherryblossom—with eight-plane flights on station as follows: 0730–0930, 0845–1045, 0945–1145, and 1345–1545 and a four-plane division at 1545–1745.

I led the first flight off at 0640. I had Lt(jg) Doug Gutenkunst on my wing, and Ens Jim Streig led my second section with Lt(jg) Tom Killefer on his wing. Lt Thad Bell led the second division with Lt(jg) Earl May as number two and Lt Ray Beacham as number three leading Ens Don Malone.

Adhering to our standard practice, we test fired our .50-caliber wing guns as we turned northwest well out over the Solomon Sea—a short *brrrp* from each pair of sequence, then a short burst from all guns together. Gun switches and reflector gun sights were left on. When we were 10 miles southeast of our assigned patrol station, I reported in by radio to the FDO—Fighter Direction Officer—who was aboard the command ship *George Clymer*: "Cocker Base, this is Gem One. Eight F4U, twenty-five miles southeast, angels twenty, climbing to twenty-five. Over."

I heard no reply. Since I had broken radio silence anyway, I decided to check in with my companions. I learned right away that my transmitter had malfunctioned. I could hear Cocker Base, however, and some other chatter, which turned out to be Joe Clifton's characteristic perpetual yakking. As it turned out, Jumpin' Joe's VF-12, off Fleet carrier *Saratoga*, was getting its baptism at Buka-Bonis along with the remainder of Air Group 12 and light carrier *Princeton*'s Air Group 24.

We went into a 10-by-3-mile racetrack orbit pattern at 25,000 feet and 10 miles north-northwest of the landing area. All throttles were set for "fast cruise," a relatively high setting from which we could go into action without delay. While we were orbiting, far from our sight, Navy transports were landing two reinforced regiments of the untested 3rd U.S. Marine Division at Cape Torokina. Unbeknownst to us, the Japanese had already begun launching their first aerial counterstrikes of the day. Over the past three or four days, the first Imperial Army fighters to enter this thus-far private Imperial Navy air war had staged into several of the Rabaul airfields, and the complete air groups of Japanese light carrier *Zuiho* and Fleet carriers *Zuikaku* and *Shokaku* had also arrived for land-based duty.

At about 0745, Cocker Base transmitted, ". . . Many bogies, course one-eight-oh, angels fifteen." I immediately sighted a good-sized formation about 15 miles to the east-northeast and about 10,000 feet below. They were heading south, directly toward the landing area. I fired a short burst to alert the flight, bent on full combat power, took a heading to intercept, and tried to convey by sign language that we were going in on an attack.

What a moment! First combat! The tension and concentration were almost corporeal. Thank god, I exulted, no buck fever. While we were in a great relative position to attack, the Val dive-bombers in the formation were perilously close to the pushover point above our transports. There was not an instant to lose.

The sun was at the ten o'clock position relative to them, elevation 45 degrees. This was the ideal spot for a high-cover group of Japanese fighters to be on station to clobber an attacking force— us—preoccupied with the main formation. The targets were eighteen Val dive-bombers at 14,000 feet escorted by a dozen Zeke fighters at 16,000 feet. This was a scant fighter force to protect so many vulnerable dive-bombers drilling into an area that simply *had* to be infested with U.S. fighters. The whole setup fairly screamed, Mousetrap! It wasn't.

We flew into the Japanese formation from five o'clock at a shallow dive angle, indicating 350 knots. I set up to shoot at the fighter leader. When I was 1,000 yards from my prey, all the Zekes dropped their belly tanks. Instantly, the leader, followed in quick succession by his three wingmen, honked his Zeke around in a tight, tight right climbing turn. This was a duck hunter's nightmare, the toughest shot in the book, nearly head-on with the flight direction rapidly changing. I opened fire at 500 yards and held the trigger down until I had to flick Big Hog's nose up to clear him as we roared past one another. I am sure I got rounds into him, but I sure did not nail him with the 220 .50-caliber bullets I fired.

Recovery from the run was in the form of a steep left chandelle into the sun, back up to more than 20,000 feet. Time had become meaningless, a typhonic Technicolor blur. I suddenly found myself coming up fast on the tail of a Zeke, holding fire until he filled my windscreen. The next thing I knew, I was flying through a fireball, emerging with a coating of his oil and hydraulic fluid. Wow! What a sensation!

As we made our initial run in, Doug Gutenkunst spotted a Val as it bugged out of the main formation to head back toward Rabaul. Doug left his position on my wing to go after the Val, and he fired at it from long range until he realized that he was being dragged farther and farther from help of his own. He wisely gave up the chase and turned back to the fight. He found me tooling around alone following my kill. We rejoined, but he left again when he saw a Zeke below us. He opened fire, and the Zeke shot back, during a head-on run. Suddenly, tracers from an unexpected direction alerted Doug that a second Zeke had joined the duel astern of his Corsair. Doug took violent evasive action and managed to duck into a cloud before sustaining any damage. After he stopped twitching, he climbed to 25,000 feet, from which he searched for the rest of us. After a fruitless twenty-minute search, Doug headed home alone.

Streig and Killefer, who initially trailed Gutenkunst and me, fired on the first pass, but also without success. They leveled out together at 17,000 feet and headed east before turning back into the fight. The pair next executed a high-side run on a Zeke on the left flank of the formation. The Zeke flamed and exploded and Streig and Killefer zoomed back to regain altitude. They spotted yet another Zeke as it headed north against the volcanic smoke plume of Mt. Bagana. Fire-walling their throttles, they caught up and opened fire simultaneously at 250 yards. The Zeke started burning and the Japanese pilot hit the silk. Certain that there was more prey ahead, the two continued northward and inconclusively fired at a third Zeke near Buka. With that, they wisely decided to turn back south while they still had some bullets left. By the time they returned to the scene of the fight, the sky was empty, so they flew straight back to Ondongo.

Thad Bell's entire division followed mine, but neither element—Bell and May followed by Beacham and Malone—spotted the Japanese formation until it was too late to set up and shoot. Swinging back after the chandelle, Bell and May simultaneously fired 45-degree deflection shots at one of the swirl of Zekes. As they broke clear, they saw a flash of flame abaft the target's cockpit. However, the flame died out as the Zeke went into a steep dive and disappeared. A second, quite similar, attack on another Zeke netted no observable results. The two tried to get back into the fight, but the sky suddenly appeared empty, so they returned to the patrol station at 25,000 feet until it was time to head home.

Following the first abortive pass, Ray Beacham spotted a pair of Zeros making gentle S turns below his port bow. A steep high-side attack on one of the Zekes produced no evidence of hits, but the Zeke rolled into a vertical dive. Ray followed in his heavier, faster-diving Corsair and fired a solid burst from 200 yards dead astern. The Zeke blew up at about 5,000 feet. We later determined this to be the squadron's first kill.

As Beacham recovered and headed back east toward the fray, he realized that his gyrations had shaken Don Malone off his wing. He was thus alone and unprotected, passing back up through 13,000 feet, when he was bounced by a pair of Zekes boring in head-on from out of the sun. The leader hit him and held his attention while the wingman headed for the saddle position astern. When Beacham realized that he was in the hands of solid professionals, he kicked his Corsair into a violent skid and flipped inverted. All he wanted was out of there. The Zekes followed Ray's vertical dive, but again the heavier fighter was able to pull away. When he thought he was free, he leveled off, but he remained at full power until he was 100 miles closer to home. A strine of 7.7mm bullets and several 20mm cannon rounds had chewed up his right wing beyond repair.

Don Malone and I wound up as a pair as soon as the brannigan broke up. All the time from the moment I had completed my first firing pass until Malone and I suddenly found the sky around us clear of all other airplanes was a swirling kaleidoscope of infrequent and disjointed recollectins. The rest was and is a surrealistic stream of intensely vivid sensory memories. Malone and I orbited at 15,000 feet, breathing easier, calming down, looking and hoping for the onset of more excitement. When it was time to head home, we turned south and eased on down to 8,000 feet so we could shed our confining oxygen masks and crack our canopies for some cooling air.

We were just tooling along, still getting our emotions under control, when I spotted, broad on my starboard bow and at only 1,000 feet of altitude, a lone Ondongo-based New Zealand P-40 fighter obviously going flat out to reach friendly skies before the Zeke a mile astern of his tail caught up. Even as we dived to set up on the Zeke, it was obvious that he would catch up with the P-40 long before Don and I could arrive. With nothing to lose, I pulled my nose up a tad and, with Don following my every move, fired a long burst in the slim hope that my tracers would spook the Zeke. We witnessed a miracle. The pursuer broke off into a 180-degree turn for home. As we closed on the Zeke at full bore from dead astern, Don moved out about 200 yards abeam to counter the expected evasive action. However, the Zeke just flew on, straight and level. It was unbelievable; he had to know we were there. I put out a brief burst from 200 yards and sent him flaming into the Solomon Sea.

All eight Corsairs from the initial November 1 mission made it home. Several of the airplanes had sustained varying amounts of damage, but all would be back in commission by the following morning. For no losses of our own, we had scored 5 Zeke kills—2 for Blackburn, 1 for Beacham, 1.5 for Killefer, and .5 for Streig. Unbeknownst to me, and against orders, Duke Henning also scored "damage" to 4 Japanese—2 Zekes damaged by Blackburn, 1 Zeke damaged by Bell, and 1 Val by Gutenkunst.

That evening, a Kiwi flight lieutenant buttonholed me and thanked me for saving his life. The best I could get out was a Jimmy Stewart imitation, "Aw, shucks."

Sunny Jim Halford led his flight of eight F4Us, our second of the day, to 28,000 feet over Empress Augusta Bay at 0845. As he and his companions flew their racetrack pattern, the weather worsened. Typical of many days that dawned bright and clear, the fierce heat spawned heavy cumulus buildups in the muggy air. At 1045, Lt Butch Davenport tallyhoed bogies 270 degrees from Cape Torokina, but the enemy flight apparently spotted the Corsairs coming on and ducked into cloud cover. No contact. Sunny Jim had trouble with his oxygen, so he led his division back to base early while Lt Lem Cooke remained on station with his division until relieved at 1045. On the way home, Cooke led his boys on an ad hoc strafing mission against the Japanese airfield at Ballale. This was well within the directives for fighters returning to base with sufficient ammunition aboard. I was never convinced that we did enough physical damage to warrant the risks, but I am certain our ongoing efforts inflicted deep psychological damage. Still, I am not sure that that was worth the deaths we sustained over the long run at the hands of their antiaircraft gunners.

Johnny Kleinman's flight of eight, which arrived on station punctually at 0945, strained eyes and nerves to no avail. They left at noon and also strafed Ballale.

Rog Hedrick led off our fourth mission of the day, timed to arrive on station at 1345. While still climbing away from Ondongo, Rog heard the shipborne FDO off Torokina report that a large Japanese raid had been reported on its way down from Rabaul. Eager to arrive in time to get a piece of the action, Rog immediately speeded up. On the way, Rog's generator went out, so he took his radio off-line to conserve power—there was no way he was going to turn for home at that juncture!

Once over the Treasuries and within sight of Empress Augusta Bay, sharp-eyed Rog spotted several specks in the distance to the north. Though he was intent upon getting over the Torokina beachhead, Rog felt he had to check out the bogies over the bay; he could not recall any news of friendlies being in that quadrant. Rog figured that the bogies, which appeared to be at 20,000 feet, could only be fighters, so he continued to climb in order to get above them while sweeping out to sea to gain the preferred up-sun position.

At length, Rog made out eight Zekes flying in two four-plane divisions similar to our own. These were the first Japanese fighters Rog had ever seen, but, even from a considerable distance, he recognized them for what they were.

Rog set himself up in a gentle, moderately slow high-side run aimed at coming down astern of the Zekes. As he progressed, he gave the rest of the flight the visual "Attack" sign by rocking his wings. His target was the leader of the second four-plane Zeke division. Just before opening fire, Rog rocked his wings again to let all hands know they were free to attack. What Rog did not know was that no one else in his formation had yet seen the Zekes, which were by then quite close.

As busy as he was, Rog could not help focusing upon the huge red meatballs on the Zekes' wings and fuselages; he could not help thinking that the path that had led him to this point had begun years before at Pensacola. Like all old naval aviators, Rog had lost good friends to airplanes sporting identical insignia. This was his first opportunity to pay back some outstanding debts, and he did not want to ruin the opportunity.

As Rog fired at the Zeke's wing root—a tactic aimed at flaming the vulnerable fuel tank on that side—the Japanese fighter instantly burst into flames. With that, the remaining seven Zekes all instantaneously snap rolled in split-Ss and streaked earthward in vertical dives. As Rog dived to give chase, and without his seeing it, his first target blew up. The only other member of the entire Corsair flight to open fire on that attack run was Hedrick's wingman, Lt(jg) Mills Schanuel, but with no observable results. Several of the others later admitted that they were slow arriving at the realization that these were enemy planes and thus fair game. Sad to say, this is a reaction to the reality of first combat more typical than Rog's.

The entire flight followed Rog into the dive, all the way to the deck, in hot pursuit of the lighter Japanese fighters. The Japanese pilots were obviously of a superior caliber and undoubtedly fresh. (Their formation of sections and divisions suggested as much, for the Imperial Navy had until then flown in squadrons of nine deployed in three vees of three.) The paired deployment of Hedrick's quarry worked as well as ours. Their basic technique was known as the vertical scissors. As one of a pair comes under attack, he rolls away into a dive. Meantime, his mate executes a tight level turn in the opposite direction and then reverses course to get on the attacker's tail. This maneuver takes guts as well as skill and discipline. It forced our guys into violent evasive action, typically in the form of frantic diving for the deck or into a handy cloud.

All hands in Rog's flight eventually made it home, unscathed but disappointed. In addition to Hedrick's confirmed kill, Lt Timmy Gile, the second-division leader, and Lt(jg) Danny Cunningham shared credit on a damage claim, and Mills Schanuel damaged a Val he dug up along the way. Damage to our fighters was nil.

Sunny Jim Halford returned for a second mission with his division at 1545. The two-hour patrol over Empress Augusta Bay was fruitless, so he led his troops down to strafe Ballale on the way home. For the first time that day, Ballale responded with intense antiaircraft fire. Lt(jg) Johnny Keith's Corsair was hit and, streaming smoke, Keith ditched about 5 miles southeast of the Japanese base at 1810. Keith's wingman, Ens Country Landreth, saw Johnny swim clear of the sinking fighter, but Keith did not deploy his raft. While Halford and his wingman ran for our base at Barakoma, on Vella Lavella, to make a personal appeal to get a Dumbo flight laid on, Landreth circled over Keith. By the time a PT boat and a PBY were both sent north to find Johnny, the sun had set and Country was obliged to head for Ondongo while he still had fuel aboard. The PT boat and PBY arrived in the vicinity of Keith's downed Corsair, but it was much too dark to see a thing and, thus, they had to pull out with no results. A renewed effort at first light produced no sign of Keith. His apparent loss—we were not ready to give up—more than muted the effects of our six confirmed kills that day.

We learned several valuable lessons on November 1. First, the Japanese were quick to spot and attack singles, so it behooved us to do everything we could to maintain our basic two-plane sections or, at least, for singles to join on other singles. I also had to admit that my personal fetish for absolutely minimal radio transmissions had proved to be counterproductive; I thus decreed that flight leaders *had* to broadcast what they saw, right up to the last instant before an attack commenced. We came up with no easy fixes on countering the newly unveiled vertical-scissors maneuver, but all hands got to work thinking of one, and we passed the word to other fighter units so they could get working. In time, once we caught on, the Japanese maneuver was effectively countered by our getting the second pair of an attacking division latched onto the lead target's wingman, thus breaking up the maneuver before it could get going.

November 1 was not to be Fighting-17's best day—not by a long shot—but it *was* the day we lost our virginity.

14

On November 2, the day following Fighting-17's leap onto the scorecards, I led off my eight-plane division in time to provide high cover over the Bougainville invasion force beginning at 0745. However, on the way, Lt Thad Bell's Corsair developed engine trouble and his entire division aborted with him. As I flew on, I realized that this was at least the second time we had lost the services of a full fighter division because of the division leader's need to abort. I made a mental note to find a solution—to see how other fighter units handled the matter—because I was not about to allow Fighting-17 to get the reputation of a unit that did not fully meet its commitments. (The solution, simple in hindsight, was to maintain a "ready" division on the field, ready to launch for whatever reason.)

I orbited with Gutenkunst, Streig, and Killefer at 23,000 feet, directly over the landing area, trying to make sense of the confused babble among three FDOs vying for space on the single fighter circuit. This was an old problem the Navy clearly had not yet worked out.

At 0815, a strike of eighteen Vals escorted by eighty Zeros went after our destroyer *Foote*, which had been damaged in a wild night surface action only five hours earlier. (The Japanese had lost a light cruiser and a destroyer sunk.) *Foote*, whose stern had been blown off by a torpedo, was under tow and escorted by four cruisers and seven destroyers commanded by RAdm A. Stanton "Tip" Merrill. In the confusion of conflicting orders and information, a mixed bag of only sixteen fighters—eight F6Fs, one F4U, three P-38s, and four New Zealand P-40s—got out from our strong covering force over the beachhead to intercept the Japanese formation. About all those fighters did was draw off some of the escorting Zeros. Fortunately, the heavy concentration of shipborne AA was able to cope. Nevertheless, light cruiser *Montpelier* sustained two bomb hits that wounded several sailors but killed no one. The rest of Merrill's Task Force 39, including damaged *Foote*, was able to evade the remaining Vals' bombs. The Zeros did not attempt to strafe our ship. Several of the Zeroes initially engaged by our fighters were destroyed, and so were several others during the Japanese retirement, but we of Fighter Command were nevertheless frustrated and humiliated by the precipitating communication breakdown.

During my division's routine beat-up at Ballale on the way home, Killefer caught a 20mm explosive round in the cockpit, and it blew up his oxygen bottle. Wounded, burned, and a bit overwrought, TK thought he had bought the program. Remembering the last words of the Royal Air Force hero, Paddy Finucane, TK calmly keyed his mike and muttered, "This is Tom. This is it, chaps." But TK did not go down; he made it home. After our flight surgeon, Dr. Lyle Herrmann, patched TK's wounds and fortified him with a little medicinal brandy, Killefer appeared in the ready room, where he got only a very mild measure of sympathy. TK remained sulky until it came out that the 20mm round had smashed his transmitter and thus prevented his cool, gallant farewell from being heard.

By the time I landed, I learned that the meticulous, thorough search for Johnny Keith had produced no results. I wanted to hold out hope—downed pilots were known to turn up weeks and even months after going in—but I knew that it was not fair to withhold the news from Johnny's family. That afternoon, I wrote the first of all too many heart-wrenching next-of-kin letters from the forward area.

November 2 was a busy but unproductive day for Fighting-17. We launched forty-seven airplanes that clocked an aggregate of 186.9 hours in the air, but we never saw the enemy.

November 3 began with a twenty-eight-plane mission escorting Marine SBDs and TBFs to the big Japanese air base at Kahili, in southern Bougainville, overlooking the Shortlands anchorages. No Japanese fighters rose to challenge us; it was yet another milk run. Next, as soon as our fighters were refueled, Lt Chuck Pillsbury and I led off our divisions for a barge-busting strike through lousy weather at Matchin Bay, just south of Buka, in northern Bougainville. We were all a little frustrated, so we sort of ignored Fighter Command's dictum against jousting with the Japanese AA batteries—that is, to make just one pass and scram. When I pressed the trigger during my second pass, only one of six wing guns responded. In the face of plenty of small-arms tracer and mushrooming 3-inch shell bursts, Big Hog's relative silence was deafening. I considered myself lucky to come away with a wrecked wing panel and a deep gouge in the Plexiglas canopy just over my head and in line with the bullet hole in my wingtip. On the other hand, we believed we destroyed four or five barges and a pair of small coastal steamers. At about the same time, Rog Hedrick's division was setting fire to a 120-ton coaster and a fishing schooner elsewhere along Bougainville's northern coast.

Although the first Japanese surface reaction to the Cape Torokina landings had been soundly defeated by RAdm Tip Merrill's Task Force 39 in the Battle of Empress Augusta Bay, the Japanese were determined to destory the Allied transport fleet by any means. In addition to ordering the Japan-based 12th Air Fleet to bolster the Rabaul-based 11th Air Fleet, the Japanese had already committed complete air groups from two fleet carriers and one light carrier. Also, Imperial Army squadrons were on the way. Then, over the dire predictions of the admiral who had overseen operations in the Solomons for more than a year, the Truk-based Combined Fleet committed the largest force of cruisers to be sent to the Solomons since the previous November. So, in addition to the local and defeated force of light cruisers and destroyers already at Rabaul, the Imperial Navy committed seven heavy cruisers, one light cruiser, and four destroyers to the job of annihilating the Cape Torokina amphibious force and its covering surface armada.

On November 2, the day the fresh Japanese surface force sailed from Truk, the U.S. Navy had but two battle forces capable of meeting it. The first, Merrill's Task Force 39, was both outnumbered and out of breath following incessant operations beginning with the Treasuries invasion on October 27. The second was a task force built around Fleet carrier *Saratoga* and light carrier *Princeton*. Commanded by RAdm Forrest Sherman, Task Force 38 was ordered by VAdm Bill Halsey to stage strikes against the combined Japanese surface force before it could sally from Rabaul. AirSols—also known as Task Force 33—was ordered to bolster the antishipping strikes and help protect the carriers from Japanese strikes. It was widely held, when the word got around, that *Saratoga* and *Princeton* could not possibly survive the inevitable Japanese countermeasures.

In fact, quite the opposite occurred. At 0900, November 5, Task Force 38 launched two full air groups from a point in the Solomon Sea only 57 miles southwest of Cape Torokina and 230 miles southeast of Rabaul. The committed everything they carried. Of the ninety-seven planes, twenty-three were TBFs, twenty-two were SBDs, and fifty-two were F6Fs. As the strike cleared the ships, land-based fighters from bases around New Georgia arrived on station to guard the carriers.

The carrier strike pounced on Rabaul through breaks in heavy cloud cover and, despite heavy ship- and shore-based antiaircraft fire, they severely damaged three heavy cruisers, two light cruisers, and two destroyers. The Japanese surface battle plan was aborted before it was even launched. In return, the Japanese downed five carrier bombers and five escorting fighters at a cost of fifteen Americans killed or missing. None of the five downed carrier bombers fell to the guns of Japanese aircraft because no Japanese aircraft penetrated the tight fighter protection, a fact duly noted and appreciated by the bomber pilots and crewmen. Altogether, over and around Rabaul, U.S. Navy fighter pilots and bomber gunners were credited with twenty-eight confirmed kills and nineteen probable kills, and they damaged another seventeen Japanese aircraft.

Later on November 5, New Guinea-based 5th Air Force B-24 heavy bombers and P-38 fighters kept the Japanese at Rabaul busy by hitting wharves and other installations.

Japanese reprisal strikes failed to locate or attack Rear Admiral Sherman's Task Force 38. Instead, they claimed a tremendous victory by misidentifying the three warships they did find and attack—a small LCT, a somewhat larger LCI, and a PT boat—as "one large carrier blown up and sunk, one medium carrier set ablaze and later sunk, and two heavy cruisers and one light cruiser and a destroyer sunk."

As far as is known, the PT boat, which shot down two of eighteen attacking Kate torpedo bombers, was the only one of its class ever to rate an aerial torpedo attack. The deadly missile penetrated her light plywood hull, but it did not detonate, and the boat was salvaged. The LCI, which also bagged several Kates, was also torpedoed, but it too was salvaged after being towed home by the LCT. (The congratulatory dispatch to the PT boat closed, "Fireplug sprinkles dog.")

Fighting-17's part in the stupendously successful November 5 action was guarding the carriers. Beginning at 0735 and ending at 1840, we committed three eight-plane flights, each of which was on station over the friendly flight decks for three hours. However, thankfully, there was no joy. The carriers turned south at 1300, after recovering both air groups, and made 30 knots through heavy weather until beyond Japanese strike range.

The next day, November 6, the Impeial Navy's Combined Fleet commander, Adm Mineichi Koga, ordered all his heavy fleet units to depart Rabaul for Truk. These were the last heavy Japanese warships to use Rabaul.

On November 6, while returning from escorting six B-25s to Buka, Lt Butch Davenport's division spotted a lone Betty medium bomber off Cape Moltke. Unfortunately, it took all four of Butch's Corsairs ten runs and 4,200 .50-caliber rounds to beaver the Betty out of the sky. In a way, I felt sorry for the Betty crew, given the prolonged agony those Japanese suffered. So they would never have to stop explaining their crummy marksmanship, I told Duke Henning to award Butch and his boys .25 kills apiece.

15

The twin Japanese airstrips at Buka and Bonis, in northern
Bougainville, remained serious potential threats to the Torokina beachhead throughout early November 1943. Although the
Japanese did not regularly base airplanes at either field, they meticulously patched runway damage after each bombing raid, and
they maintained heavy antiaircraft defenses around both runways.
The danger lay in the readiness of the runways, through which the
Japanese could, at any time, stage raids against the beachhead or
supporting bases farther south. Moreover, as long as both runways
remained operational, Japanese aircraft damaged in fights farther
south had a safe haven 165 miles south of Rabaul. A new dimension
to the problem emerged as the Japanese worked furiously on a new
strip at Chabai, just 5 miles south of Buka Passage near Matchin
Bay. In addition, Matchin Bay was a large, sheltered, deep anchorage well suited for transloading barges bound for the Torokina area
and points as far south as the bypassed but still active Shortlands
bases. These facilities—the airstrips and the anchorage—were only
55 miles north of Torokina but 200 miles from our nearest runway, at Barakoma, on Vella Lavella. Rabaul was 165 miles north-
northwest of Buka Passage, a night's easy round-trip for troop- or
supply-laden destroyer transports or an hour's flight for airplanes
out of Rabaul. If the Japanese managed to base Zeros or bombers
around Buka Passage, they would be within easy attack range of
our air bases.

Similarly, the Japanese air bases in southern Bougainville—Kara
and Kahili—and Ballale, in the Shortlands, provided serious potential threats to the security of our rear areas. So did Tenekau and
Kieta, midway up Bougainville's northern coast. All five of these
bases could be used as staging areas for raids farther south, and, as
long as they were properly maintained, all five provided safe havens
for damaged Japanese airplanes.

AirSols's main job, in addition to guarding the Torokina beachhead and providing on-call support for our carriers, was neutraliz-
ing all of the Bougainville-area air bases and as many barge facilities
as we could uncover.

*   *   *

We held our regular evening briefing in the large Quonset hut
which served as the squadron office and ready room at 1930, November 7. Lt(jg) Duke Henning, our ACIO, had the floor.

"The first operation tomorrow will be a twelve-plane escort for
nine B-25s making a low-level bombing and strafing attack on
Matchin Bay. It looks as if it will be essentially similar to the
November 6 strike. Primary targets are two medium-size cargo
ships and their escort, probably a destroyer but possibly a light
cruiser. Time on target is 0700. Air opposition is not expected. As
you know, the Japs won't night-fly with Zekes, except for late-
evening return to their base. You should be in and out before their
CAP gets there from Rabaul, in the event one is sent. For your
information, they have not sent a CAP down for about two weeks.
Planned approach is straight in from the southwest, on the water.
Cross the harbor, then take a forty-five-degree turn and cross Bougainville's northeast tip. Retirement is down the east coast, staying
with the B-25s until south of Kahili. Secondary target is the new
installation on the beach of Chabai, and, of course, any targets of
opportunity. Fighters are to provide cover, in and out. If there's no
air opposition, you're free to strafe the ships and AA positions
ahead of the B-25s. There is no heavy AA known, just light automatic weapons on the ships and along the coastline. You'll rendezvous with the strike aircraft over Baga at 0600. We'll review this
tomorrow morning. Any questions before I turn this over to the
skipper?"

There were no questions, so I took center stage. "Reveille's at
0330. We'll leave the mess hall at 0410. Man planes at 0500. Take
off at 0520. Pilot and plane assignments as shown on the blackboard." I pointed to the blackboard, which indicated three four-
plane divisions with Tom Killefer and Dirty Eddie March as leaders
of the second and third divisions. This was to be Killefer's first hop
leading a division, a debut he had earned.

"Departure from Baga at 0600," I continued. "Due west of Cherryblossom [the Torokina beachhead] at about 0640. Take close
cover position there: March's four thousand feet above the B-25s,
Killefer's at two thousand, my division at three thousand. If any
Jap fighters show, we'll hold these positions 'til we're well clear on
the retirement. If there are no bogies at five miles from the target,
March will move out on the port beam and attack shore batteries,

left to right. Killefer moves to starboard to strafe straight ahead. I'll swing out to the right on the run-in, above Killefer, and attack right to left, pulling out above March. The B-25s will be making skip-bombing runs and shooting with everything they've got. We need to get in and out fast so we don't screw them up or catch a stray arrow.

"I don't believe this B-25 outfit has done this before, so they'll be skittish as hell. Our cover must be close and tight or they might bug out. No matter how tempting an opportunity you spot, do not break the cover pattern unless you absolutely must. When we're well clear on retirement, we'll resume comfortable loose escort positions. As you have seen, these guys have the nasty habit of leaving any cripple behind to fend for himself. Unless the group is under attack, my division will stay with the wounded bird 'til he either ditches or gets to Munda.

"Surprise is the key element. We'll stay at the B-25s' level until assuming cover positions. As usual, radio silence except for urgent bogie reports or ditching.

"Questions?"

Breakfast was at the Hotel Ondongo Mud Plaza, which was overseen by our Army Air Forces neighbors. As usual, the meal consisted of coffee too long on the fire, grapefruit-flavored battery acid, boxed cereal caressed with milk coaxed from powder, scrambled powdered "eggs," and fried Spam. Capping this luxurious eye-opener was the rainstorm that stuck as we were settling in for our final briefing.

Flying with exterior lights set on full bright as we went into the racetrack pattern for rendezvous, we dodged between moderate showers and intermittent heavy squalls. I was on the clocks—instruments—almost as soon as I lifted wheels from the runway surface. It became obvious after ten minutes of orbiting that some of the guys were not going to join up. I was not overly apprehensive about them, but I was furious about what I considered to be a second-rate performance. My hope was that the missing birds—seven of twelve!—would appear when we joined on the B-25s at Baga.

Not only didn't my clutch show at Baga, neither did the B-25s. I waited around in cruddy weather until full daybreak, but no one new arrived to join my five Corsairs. The five of us set course to the north, cruising at 500 feet to remain below the turbulence yet high enough to be relaxed. We had plenty of fuel aboard, so I went to fast cruise, 200 knots. All the stooging around and waiting for no-shows had put us behind schedule and I did not want to throw away all the tactical advantages of an early arrival if I did not have to. We broke into clear skies halfway to the target, and it remained bright and sunny the rest of the way. I could not help thinking— and the others later concurred—that it would have been nice to have had the weather the other way around. CAVU—Ceiling and Visibility Unlimited—over the target could make for a rough show.

At 50 miles out, I led the others down to about 50 feet and signaled all hands to go to combat-power settings for the run-in. The primary target area at Matchin Bay was empty, so we came left 45 degrees to set up for strafing runs at Bonis and Buka, respectively 6 and 8 miles to the north. Dirty Eddie March and Ens Whit Wharton formed a loose vee with me and Jim Streig and Tom Killefer flanked us well out to starboard. No radio transmissions nor even hand signals were needed as we swung to the right to line up with the runways—my three bound for Buka and Streig and Killefer bound for Bonis.

A light transport plane was in the traffic pattern over Buka, turning on final approach. Dirty Eddie and I fired at the same instant at about 200 yards; we didn't even have to pull up in order to clear the flaming wreckage. The three of us flew straight in, kicking up a lot of dirt mixed with tracer sparks. Wharton concentrated on a parked Zeke and smoked it while Dirty Eddie and I took aim on the fifty-man reception committee still in parade formation for the newly deceased dignitary aboard the flamed transport. As we hauled ass out of there, one AA shell burst vaguely in our direction. Jim and TK were not as lucky; they had to content themselves with shooting up the Bonis tower and sundry antiaircraft emplacements.

We strafed Ballale on the way home, but TK picked up a large hole in his right wing from the 20mm reception. He really laid on a bitch because the students at this AA postgraduate school had blown one up in his cockpit only a few days before. TK theorized they had it in for him, personally.

As I taxied up to the revetments at 0845, I anticipated the Marine plane captain's standard first question by holding up one finger— "One!" As soon as Duke finished interrogating the five of us, he got on the hand-crank field telephone to Fighter Command. When he got off, the told me that the Fighter Command skipper and his ACIO wanted to talk with me, in person, as soon as I could fly down to Munda, approximately immediately.

At Munda, I was quizzed at length by Col Oscar Brice, Fighter Command's Marine skipper. Also in the room were Brice's ACIO, Lt Joe Bryan, and Cdr Pat Rembert, the somewhat stuffy skipper of a Hellcat squadron based at Segi. When I had finished relating my tale of glory, Pat got in the first word—"Fools rush in." Colonel Brice and Joe Bryan just looked at him. Subsequently, Brice and Bryan laid a lot of static on their opposite numbers at Strike Command and the AirSols Army Air Forces types about the bombers aborting because of foul weather which had not stopped *their* fighters.

My euphoria from the warm session at Munda evaporated as I taxied out to return to Ondongo. A B-25 with a full load of gas and bombs aboard was approaching the runway with one fan feathered. Less than a quarter-mile short of the strip, the B-25 ran out of airspeed and dropped into the rough ground. He bounced once, landing gear sheared off, and he slid on his belly in a great cloud of dust onto the end of the runway. The wreckage stopped less than 50 feet from me and torched off into a ball of flames. I got close enough to feel intense heat and, with Big Hog's tail toward him, revved up full blast in a desperate hope I could blow the flames clear enough for a least some of the five crewmen aboard to get out. As the crash trucks and meat wagons screeched to a halt 200 yards from the inferno, I got the message and had just rolled rapidly to a safe distance when the Mitchell's bombs started cooking off. There were only small bits and pieces to be seen when the smoke finally cleared.

Our second mission of the day was an eight-plane romp to Empress Augusta Bay to provide high cover for the fleet. Johnny Kleinman led off his and Chuck Pillsbury's divisions at 0730, the prelude to two fruitless hours of orbiting at 25,000 feet.

It was by then an old saw that combat flying is hours of complete boredom punctuated by moments of sheer terror. The sort of flying Kleinman's and Pillsbury's foursomes endured on the morning of November 8 was classic. No matter how much natural padding a pilot had, or how much he squirmed about in the relatively spacious Corsair cockpit, the parachute beneath his stern got harder and harder with each passing minute. We complained that our major ailment was Acute Aereo Asserosis.

As the two divisions started for home at the end of two unproductive hours, Torokina's FDO sent them to strafe four camouflaged landing barges. Seeing nothing, all the eight could do was
spray lead across the designated tree-shrouded beach. The results,
if any, were not apparent, so the mission was logged as "Patrol
negative." All planes landed without incident at 1135.

Rod Hedrick led off two divisions, his own and Lt Timmy
Gile's, at 0930 to relieve Kleinman over Empress Augusta Bay.
However, shortly after the flight formed, Gile's Corsair developed
engine trouble, so Rog released him and sent his wingman, Ens
Brad Baker, back as escort in case Timmy had to ditch. Thus,
Hedrick arrived on station with his four-plane division—himself,
Lt(jg) Mills Schanuel, Lt(jg) Andy Anderson, and Lt(jg) Jack
Chasnoff—plus Gile's second pair—Lt(jg) Paul Cordray and Lt(jg)
Danny Cunningham.

The six spent an hour repeating Kleinman's no-joy mission, but
the radio suddenly crackled to life at about 1100: "Gem Three.
This is Cocker Base. Many bogies. Vector two-two-oh. Buster.
Acknowledge." The meaning of this esoteric verbal shorthand:
"Numerous unknown aircraft are on my radarscope. You steer
220-degrees magnetic to intercept them. Proceed at high speed."

To which Rog replied as he fought down the adrenaline rush,
"Gem Three. Wilco. Out." Since Rog had no information as to the
enemy's altitude, he quickly swung to the assigned heading and
went into a high-speed combat-power climb. There were two separate layers of broken cloud overhead, but no solid overcast.

Minutes after turning onto the FDO-provided heading, hawk-
eyed Rog spotted the enemy gaggles—two of them—coming on in
standard vee-of-vees formation. He also spotted four P-38s coming
up on him from astern. Certain the Army fighters were going to
join his Hogs in the bounce, Rog decided to attack the far larger
enemy formation. However, as it turned out, that one backward
glance was the last he saw of the P-38s.

"This is Gem Three. Tallyho. Twenty-four fighters. Angels
twenty-two. Fifteen Vals. Angels twelve. Course one-one-oh. Gem
Three out."

Fearing that there might be more Zeros up-sun of him, Rog had
his trailing section—Cordray and Cunningham—make a 360 to
catch any bushwhackers he might not have seen. Then Rog dived

away in the lead of his division, thinking all the while, "Well, here's where we learn how good the Hog really is."

Rog was astounded; as soon as he hit the big Japanese fighter formation, the enemy fighters broke up into two huge Lufbery circles. This maneuver, purely defensive in nature, was employed in World War I by small formations under attack by large formations—and not the opposite, as it was being employed in response to Rog's four-plane attack.

As Rog set up his firing pass, he noted with grim satisfaction that all the Vals were turning north for Rabaul without having dropped their bombs. He never considered breaking off to go after them; there were plenty of other fighters in the vicinity to take on that job. Rog's immediate concern was attacking the Lufbery circles. For Corsairs with an initial altitude advantage, it was like ducks going 'round and 'round in a shooting gallery: Pick a target, dive on it, shoot, zoom clear, and set up another run.

Rog picked out a Zeke and opened fire on it from out of a high-side run. However, the Zeke dived straight into a cloud, albeit streaming avgas from a punctured fuel tank. Mills Schanuel, who had followed closely on Rog's wing, picked out another circling Zeke, opened fire from 100 yards, and flamed it.

Meantime, Rog's second section, Anderson followed by Chasnoff, fixed sights on a Hamp, a square-wing Zero variant. Anderson opened fire from 500 yards and bored in to 100, blowing off quick bursts all the way until the Hamp exploded.

The two initial firing runs broke up the bigger of the two circles. Anderson and Chasnoff recovered from the first attack and tried to get their sights on one solid target in the sky littered with Zekes and Hamps. The two stayed together through a total of six firing runs, but their only kill was Anderson's first Hamp. Anderson got full credit for it and for one damaged Zeke.

Meantime, Hedrick and Schanuel chased a loose confederation of six Zeros north toward Buka. The two Corsairs, barreling along at 15,000 feet, finally overtook the Zeros, which were at 12,000 feet, just a few miles southwest of the Japanese air base. Suddenly, quite unexpectedly, all six Zeros reversed course to meet the two Corsairs. For the next few minutes, Rog kept finding himself embroiled in one head-on run after another. Unbelievable to Rog was the apparent fact that, in three consecutive head-on runs, each approaching Zero withheld fire. On two occasions, as Rog pulled up to avoid running into his targets, he was certain he saw large objects fly through the engine cowls of his targets; these were possibly cylinder heads knocked loose by his bullets. Rog also saw at least two Zeros he nailed in tail chases going down streaming what he described as "big buckets" of gasoline from fuel tank punctures. However, neither flamed or splashed. When the dust settled around Buka, Rog found himself all alone. He reversed heading to rejoin his flight over Empress Augusta Bay. He could find none of the others, so he headed for the barn. Schanuel joined up just as Rog passed over Bougainville's southwest tip. Mill's Corsair had sustained engine damage, and he had to make a low-state emergency landing at Barakoma. He got down with only 7 gallons of fuel aboard. Rog touched down alone at Ondongo at 1330.

The fight also led Anderson and Chasnoff away toward Buka. The two split out to take on a group of Zeros they found crossing in front of them. As Andy fired without apparent effect on one Zero that was heading for a cloud, he was in turn jumped from behind by two Zeros. He instinctively flipped inverted and nosed straight down, but the Zeros followed. Chasnoff saw what was going to happen to Andy, so he came in astern of the two Zeros, but he was in turn caught by four others before he could open fire. The combined fire of the four Zeros on Chasnoff's tail shot away his rudder cable, but he evaded with a desperate vertical dive into a cloud. Anderson also somehow evaded the Zeros on his tail and found Chasnoff. The two tooled around the clouds until the heat was off and then headed southeast at full throttle, their seats all the way down, their shoulders hunched up to provide as much protection for their skulls as they could. They made it home without further adventures.

Cordray and Cunningham had peeled off from Hedrick's division at the start of the action to guard against an up-sun bounce by unseen Zeros. As directed, despite the heavy action below, the two then remained at 29,000 feet, ready to take on high-altitude attackers if there were any. In fact, six Zekes flew by right over their heads, but neither side attacked. Apparently, the Japanese leader did not see the Corsairs, and Cordray coolheadedly did nothing to attract the attention of the larger Japanese flight. With that, Cordray led Cunningham into the free-for-all below. By then, the Lufberys had broken up and there were Zeros everywhere. Cordray's opening dive brought him right down on a lone Zero. He smoked the Japanese bird, but he had too much speed on and had to pull up before the Zeke blew up. As Cordray pulled up, Cunningham opened fire on the smoking Zeke, which disappeared into a cloud trailing thick black smoke. Just as the two rejoined, they were bounced by a dozen Zeros. They went into an immediate, instinctive, and thankfully successful defensive weave, covering each other's tail while trying to get rounds into the attacking fighters. At length, they evaded the Japanese swarm and started for home. From an altitude of 18,000 feet, the pair spotted two Zeros heading by on their port bow and 3,000 feet below. Cunningham led the way down on an opposite-course run. Danny's .50-caliber rounds flamed the lead Zero just as Danny chandelled out of his pass. For no good reason, the two Corsairs followed the flamer down for several thousand feet. Satisfied that it was indeed a dead airplane, they headed for home, arriving just behind Hedrick.

The initial official tally came to a meager two kills—one each for Schanuel and Cunningham—and five damaged—three for Hedrick, one for Anderson, and one for Cordray. Fellow pilots from other squadrons who were flying low cover beneath the clouds subsequently put in reports that as many as fifteen flamers might have crashed into the water. This number was high, no doubt the result of multiple sightings. Rog was sure he had killed three and pretty sure he might have killed two others, and several of the others were convinced that they, too, had scored uncounted kills.

On the up side, Rog returned with the deep-seated conviction that the Corsair was a wonderful Zero-killing platform. Until that day's series of wing-wrenching actions, he had had his reservations. This fight was the first time any of us had tested the Hogs in maximum combat situations. Rog pronounced the Hog superior to the Zero in every respect except maneuverability.

When we tallied up the reports of all six pilots involved in the November 8 battle, we were universally mystified by the Japanese tactics. For example, we could not figure out why the fighters were stationed 10,000 feet above the vulnerable Vals. Certainly, by this stage of the war, the Japanese had figured out that unescorted Vals were dead meat if our fighters were around. The Val pilots sure knew it; they bugged out the moment Rog engaged the Zeros. And there was no way to explain the Lufbery circles. The deployment into the Lufberys by the main body of twenty-four fighters smacked of rehearsal, but certainly the Japanese trainers did not mean for their pupils to go defensive when they had a four to one advantage in numbers. The only explanation we could think of was that the large fighter formation was acting as a decoy for the six-plane division Cordray and Cunningham saw passing over them. If so, however, we could not figure out why six up-sun Zeros with the altitude advantage had failed to attack the Corsairs.

Even if the bulk of Japanese fighter pilots were rank amateurs—as seems to have been the case—surely they had some combat veterans along who were capable of putting on an aggressive show. Three of them who stood up against Rog Hedrick's determined head-on attacks apparently did not return Rog's fire, which was simply beyond our comprehension.

We knew by then that we were no longer always fighting the Japanese first team. The superb air groups of early and mid-1942 had been ground to dust over Guadalcanal and environs by the end of that year. We also had not yet learned that the fresh 12th Air Fleet was staging in from Japan. Perhaps the Zeros Hedrick's flight engaged on November 8 were just in from the home islands; perhaps that explains their rank amateurism. But hadn't the Japanese bothered to train those kids adequately, or even to tell them what to expect? The only pros in the bunch seem to have been the Val pilots; they knew exactly what to do. They ran.

The last squadron missions of November 8 were a pair of two-division CAPs over Empress Augusta Bay. Long before I led off the earlier of the two missions, I had all available hands on the carpet to "discuss" my feelings about going into action that morning with five of the twelve planes assigned. This sad showing was not repeated; the two divisions I led off—my division, and Killefer's—were fully manned.

We got off at 1320 and returned at 1745 without sighting any enemy airplanes. Similarly, Halford's and March's divisions were at full strength on our last mission of the day. They got off at 1510 and returned without incident at 1820.

By later standards, November 8 was a so-so day. But it was evident that the squadron was picking up the rhythm. The troops certainly seemed to have caught on to what they were supposed to do when they found enemy airplanes sharing their patch of sky.

16

Fighting-17 was changing before my eyes. In just twelve days of continuous flight operations beginning October 27, we had matured well beyond any point I thought possible for so short a break-in period.

Among many other matters, the tactical organization of the squadron had been in a state of ongoing flux from the start. The squadron was nominally organized into five flights of eight planes each despite the fact that we initially deployed only thirty-six airplanes for, at first, forty-one pilots. Given our one combat loss so far, plus damage to a number of airplanes, plus ongoing routine mechanical malfunctions, the number of airplanes we had available on any given day was moot. Usually twenty-six to thirty were up. Typically, only four missions of eight planes each would be scheduled on a given day, sometimes only three. This allowed one flight to stand down on a rotating basis, so pilots could get needed rest. Our neat plan of assigning planes with the same color-coded propeller hubs to a particular flight soon became a shambles as airplanes were juggled from flight to flight to meet pilot assignments. Nevertheless, despite maintenance problems and battle damage, our schedulers did everything they could to see that each pilot flew his own, permanently assigned airplane. This was because each Hog had its own quirks, which were best overcome by the man who knew them the best.

I had made no changes in flight leader assignments; the flight leaders were still Rog Hedrick, Sunny Jim Halford, Johnny Kleinman, Chuck Pillsbury, and myself. However, I had been playing around with division leader assignments, both in the face of lackluster performances and to give some of the more junior shining lights an opportunity to try leadership roles. Dirty Eddie March had earned a division assignment before we left Hawaii, and so had Lem Cooke, once I saw beyond my early misjudgment of him. Lt Butch Davenport and Ens Ike Kepford were coming along, though I had only just tried them without permanent assignment.

Tom Killefer was a special case whose abilities were not at first utilized to the fullest. Because of my longstanding personal friendship with TK, I was extremely sensitive to a negative reaction of other pilots if he, as "teacher's pet," got what might seem like preferential treatment. So, early on, he flew as tail-end-Charlie in my division. There was no need for discussion with TK; he knew what was going on and performed in exemplary fashion. However, by the end of the first week, his talents were needed at the head of a division, and we used him as such on a rotating basis.

We had also begun the process of weeding out the weak sisters. I must say that no one knows how he will react to being thrown into combat. Despite all my years of flying fighters, I had no idea how I would really do when faced with the real thing. I was certain I would engage the enemy when the moment of truth came, but not *absolutely* certain. I could empathize with anyone who had doubts, hence my open-door policy with respect to transfer requests. At the same time, I recognized that some people were going to need a little time and trial to find themselves, one way or the other.

It is almost an axiom that units and people entering first combat experience some hesitation having nothing to do with guts or instincts. No matter how intense the training or inculcation, the immediate shift from a lifetime of peace to the first moment of war is accompanied by an instinctive *disbelief*. This was manifested in all our early combat, as when I opened fire too soon at my first Zero target, or when Rog's entire flight, except for Rog, failed to open fire at the Japanese flight of eight they otherwise bushwhacked on November 1. It takes a special concentration to fire at another human being—the first time. This is the well-known "buck fever" of the tyro big-game hunter. I was aware of the possibility that, despite their best intentions, there were pilots in VF-17 who would never fire unless first fired upon. However, I was determined to identify them and get them over the hump or send them home. The funny thing is that there was no way to tell in advance who those people were—mainly because they themselves did not know before the moment of truth overtook them. Given the rather aggressive group ethos I had instilled, I doubted if many of my young men would turn themselves in even after accepting the truth. I had no animosity toward this live-and-let-live attitude; it simply had no place in a fighter squadron at war.

As I pored over Duke Henning's laboriously typed pilot accounts of each engagement—the few we had had—I noted with pride and relief that the ex-nuggets—and the old men—were opening fire at progressively shorter distances from the enemy. This takes awareness and determination. We had trained them to fire at the shortest possible ranges, but doing so against target sleeves and real enemy aircraft are two very different matters. As each pilot gained confidence in his leaders, his airplane, and his instincts, we were getting closer and doing more damage with fewer rounds. In fact, it was standard practice for squadrons to maintain records of rounds per kill, and that became the basis for competition among flights, divisions, sections, and individual pilots. The payoff was building a squadron that typically was able to stretch a finite number of bullets per airplane on more kills per sortie. The best proof we had so far that it could be done was Rog Hedrick's November 8 performance, in which he fired on no less than seven Zeros and might have destroyed as many as five of them. Gun reliability increases with avoidance of long firing bursts.

I also noted with great satisfaction that our two-plane sections were routinely remaining joined, even through some hairy combat episodes. Our early performance in this regard had been miserable; we had too many lone-wolf incidents. During Rog's November 8 engagement, I was pleased to note, every section remained intact throughout the fight.

Attainment of my ultimate goals still seemed to be in the future, but even a casual reading of early reports and statistics revealed that Fighting-17 was already trending toward realizing its potential as a very competent squadron.

Before we deployed to the forward area, Kahili was known as an inordinately tough nut heavily defended by swarms of fighters amply assisted by plenty of competent antiaircraft gunners. Many good fighter squadrons had risen to prominence as Kahili was made untenable for the Japanese by means of the unrelenting daily assaults. By the time VF-17 joined the fray, Kahili's fighters were gone, but her AA defenses were still formidable. Woe betide the eager beaver who opted to throw in a second strafing pass.

"Kahili Knock," as it had come to be known, was a natural phenomenon brought on by overdrafts of the imagination. Pilots bound for Kahili in its heyday often perceived unusual vibrations in their airplanes, brought on, as some claimed, by bargain-basement spark plugs. These and other imagined ailments often led to a steady stream of aborts for "mechanical reasons." After Kahili was more or less defanged, Kahili Knock was encountered by pilots on the way to other tough targets. In-flight malfunctions occurred, of course, but a pilot became suspect when he routinely aborted "mechanical" too often. When one fighter aborted, the flight or division became unbalanced; it was almost better to send an even number home, as Rog Hedrick had done on November 8 when Timmy Gile experienced a malfunction.

By the middle of our second week at Ondongo, one of our young ensigns had experienced more than his share of Kahili Knock. After his third consecutive abort, I called him in for a little heart-to-heart. The first thing I did was remind him of my open-door policy; if he felt he wanted out, I would grease a transfer in such a way as to save him embarrassment.

The ensign appeared authentically shocked at the mere suggestion that his aborts had been intentional. "Skipper," he pleaded, "you've got me wrong. Honest, it's not my fault. I've had rough-running engines."

While I did not want to encourage bug-outs, neither did I want anyone augering in because they insisted on maintaining face by flying along in authentically malfunctioning airplanes. He could have been on the level, so I decided to give him another chance. *One* other chance.

The next mission was his last with us. He returned early with a "bad engine," which I immediately turned over to the plane captain for evaluation. The Marine mechanic soon reported that the engine was "baby-butt smooth" on run-up. As soon as our squadron engineering officer, Butch Davenport, returned from the same mission, he also test-flew the ensign's Hog. "Boss," he reported, "it runs like silk."

Our reluctant warrior's immediate exit did not end the problem entirely, but I am sure it convinced those of ambivalent attitude to think hard before they succumbed to Kahili Knock.

17

The next day, November 9, passed with various flights and divisions fruitlessly circling over Empress Augusta Bay and escorting unopposed bombing missions to Kahili and Buka. But the next storm was building, as I learned when Duke and I were summoned to Munda late that afternoon to confer directly with ComAirSols, MGen Nathan Twining, of the Army Air Forces.

As always, Duke's jaunt to the regional command center was attended by wild-eyed protests. No wonder! While I blithely flew down in Big Hog, Duke reluctantly climbed into the tiny passenger compartment of a rickety, antique parasol-wing monoplane transport piloted by a frustrated fighter pilot. Since this gem had lost its passenger access door, poor Duke was obliged to hang on for dear life in the windswept cabin. As usual, following each jaunt, our Yale professor pronounced us and anyone else who flew to be candidates for the Funny Farm.

Major General Twining, who commanded the Army Air Force's 13th Air Force as well as AirSols, chaired the conference at headquarters. Leading off was the command intelligence officer, who gave a detailed brief on our situation at Bougainville and that of the Japanese at Rabaul. This was the heart of the briefing, and no punches were pulled. According to the best information available, the November 5 air strike by the *Saratoga* and *Princeton* air groups had severely damaged units of the Imperial Navy's 2nd Fleet. However, the Japanese force of light cruisers and destroyers remained a formidable threat to the invasion fleet off Cape Torokina. Moreover, significant other Japanese surface forces were still based at Truk, only thirty-six hours sailing time away. The medium and heavy bombers of MGen George Kenney's New Guinea-based 5th Air Force had been unable to do more than harass the Rabaul-based Japanese surface ships. The primary fear was that the Japanese were still of a mind to mount an all-out surface attack against our invasion fleet. If they did so soon, they could count on the support of whatever was left of the 270 combat aircraft known to have been based in the region on November 1. It was possible, the intelligence officer averred, that the combined strength of Japanese air and

naval forces could overwhelm our outnumbered cruisers and destroyers, crush our thin-skinned amphibious force, and thus be in
a position to support the defeat of our ground forces on Bougainville.

As all the terrible possibilities sank in, the briefers sprang the
master plan. Even as the November 5 carrier-based air strikes were
under way, Adm Chester Nimitz, commander in chief of all our
forces in the Pacific, was setting the master strategic stroke into
motion. Fleet carriers *Essex* and *Bunker Hill*, with light carrier *Independence* and nine escorting destroyers, had been diverted from the
upcoming Gilberts (Tarawa and Makin) invasion in response to
Admiral Halsey's urgent plea for assistance. Commanded by
RAdm Alfred Montgomery, this powerful fresh force was to hit the
Japanese surface warships at Rabaul from the Solomon Sea while
Saratoga and *Princeton* launched simultaneous strikes from due east
of the objective. The operation was set to go off on November 11,
one full day hence.

Among numerous other records, the combined force of five carriers was the largest thus far gathered by the U.S. Navy for a single
mission. If successful, this would be a classic case of the projection
of power by means of carrier-based aircraft where horizontal bombing had failed—precisely what the earliest innovators of carrier
warfare had envisioned.

The stakes were high. If the powerful preemptive strike did not
work as planned, our naval forces faced the possibility of being
defeated in detail. While a success would certainly pave the way for
overcoming Fortress Rabaul in 1944, a failure would certainly stall
our thrust up the Solomons chain toward that essential objective.
The worst possible scenario, the sinking of the bulk of our carriers,
would undoubtedly set the war effort back, perhaps as long as
several years. The tide in the Pacific, which had already turned
once, might well turn again.

In addition to mounting a heavy bomber raid against Rabaul,
AirSols was charged with providing fighter protection for the carriers while their own fighter squadrons escorted the carrier-based
bombers to Rabaul. To accomplish this most effectively demanded
supplementing the fighters based aboard the carriers. That task
came down to two land-based Navy squadrons, Lt John Kelly's
Segi-based VF-33—a dozen Hellcats—and twenty-four VF-17
Corsairs. Twelve land-based fighters were to land aboard each of

Admiral Montgomery's three carriers, and all were to be available at his discretion. In addition, thirty-two Corsairs from VMF-212 and VMF-221 and a New Zealand P-40 squadron were to provide overhead protection while our land-based carrier-equipped Navy fighters were refueling aboard the carriers following our initial hop out from our bases.

General Twining turned to face me. "Blackburn, your people haven't been aboard ship for some time now. The word we have is that you were sent down here because the F4U isn't carrier suitable. If need be, we can assign the two other Hellcat squadrons we have based at Segi." He held up his hand when he saw me instinctively lean forward to launch my knee-jerk protest. "Colonel Brice tells me that you're his first team. You now know how vital this mission is. We can't afford a mistake. Can you handle it?"

I was already wound up for my delivery, and I got right into it. "General, that story that our Corsairs aren't carrier suitable is hogwash. My guys cut their teeth at carrier work with the old F4Us on a little bitty slow escort carrier. An *Essex*-class ship with plenty of wind over the deck is a piece of cake." Then, remembering how our cotenants on Ondongo still laughed about our habitual carrier-type landings, I added, "Every landing approach we make is a simulated carrier pass. My people are good! It'll be no sweat, sir."

The general gave us the nod, so, at the conclusion of the meeting, I flew back to Ondongo to tell our engineering officer, Lt Butch Davenport, to have the ground crew reinstall the tail hooks and check their operating mechanism and antibounce dashpots. As soon as our ground crewmen broke out the hooks—which had been removed upon arrival at Ondongo to save weight and prevent accidents—the pilots began showing up to try to allay their curiosity with eager questions. Duke and I brushed off all the where and when questions; we could not afford a leak in the event someone was shot down and captured before the mission got underway.

November 10 was another nothing day; more fruitless hops to the invasion area, more dry milk runs with the bombers. The troops were doubly put out because they knew a big show was imminent.

Duke and I conducted the squadron brief after supper on November 10. Reveille was to be at 0200 and takeoff was to commence at 0400. Six divisions—Hedrick's, Kleinman's, Pillsbury's, Bell's, Gile's, and mine—were to proceed as one unit at 10,000 feet, set to arrive over Admiral Montgomery's Task Group 50.3 well before dawn. Upon reaching the task group, which was to be 190 miles southwest of Rabaul, we would orbit and do our best to conserve fuel. After landing to refuel at about 0900, we would operate as directed, probably to resume CAP coverage for the carriers and their escorts. Depending upon Japanese activity, we would use the carriers for refueling—and rearming, if necessary—through the day or until sent back to our bases. All this effectively increased the availability of the carrier-based Hellcats, every one of which was needed to escort the bombers on Task Group 50.3's two planned antishipping strikes.

I assigned Hedrick to go aboard *Essex* with a flight of twelve; I would take the other twelve Corsairs aboard *Bunker Hill*, and John Kelly would land with his twelve Hellcats aboard *Independence*. As usual, voice-radio transmissions were to be made only if the information was vital or the situation extreme.

As soon as the brief was over, I sent all hands straight to bed with the reminder that we were all facing at least eight hours of flight time and, probably, stiff combat.

We were on schedule and on course at 0420, November 11, but one member of my flight had to drop out because of a mechanical problem. The night was clear and pitch-black. Running lights were doused as soon as we turned out of the rendezvous, but the formation was maintained through use of the blue lights located atop the wings of each plane as well as the ubiquitous and unavoidable flame and glow from the exhaust stacks, which could be seen only from below.

We were five minutes past our estimated time of arrival over the carriers, and I was already having dank visions of my adventure off Morocco, when Chuck Pillsbury decided to break radio silence. "Skipper, this is Chuck. I hold Judah's hayrake [*Essex*'s homing beacon]. We passed directly over three minutes ago. Out."

Enormously relieved, I silently bless my operations officer for his sharpness, and for having the brains and guts to speak up. I immediately banked into a gentle turn to get into our holding pattern. There was no need for additional transmissions; the ships had doubtless held us on their radars from the time we were 100 miles out. This was standard; our cruise-out altitude had been selected for, among other reasons, their timely acquisition of us at an altitude at which it was minimally probable that we would be mistaken for an inbound Japanese strike.

We saw nothing beneath our wings, which was to be expected. "Darken Ship" had been passed at sunset, and no exterior lights were showing except for a few dim hooded red ones needed on the bridges and other topside control stations. Even during night flight ops, the carriers remained darkened; only the dimmest lights were used to aid topside activities, and all ships in the force showed single red masthead lights as clearance markers for the airplanes. Deck-edge lights required for night landings and takeoffs were screened so that they were not visible except at horizontal near distances, generally from one edge of the flight deck to the other.

The breaking dawn brought with it the unforgettable, unimaginably beautiful sight of the two carriers' flashing bow waves and white wakes as they arrowed on parallel headings a mile apart. The light carrier similarly brightened the sea as it brought up the rear, forming an equilateral triangle. The nine destroyers were arrayed in a precise circle two miles from the center of the triangle. The dark blue of the tropical sea was thus ribboned by the twelve brilliant white wakes churned out by the 30-knot run that was taking Task Group 50.3 directly "in harm's way."

We circled overhead in our holding pattern for about an hour. Suddenly, the silence was broken by a call from *Essex*. "Big Hog, this is Judah. Bogey. Angels one-five. Vector three-five-oh. Buster. Acknowledge." (That is, Big Hog from the *Essex* fighter director: One unknown aircraft, probably enemy, is at 15,000 feet. Steer 350 degrees, magnetic, and proceed at high speed.)

"Judah, this is Big Hog. Wilco. Out." (*Essex* fighter director from Big Hog: I understand and will comply. End of transmission.)

We all bent on combat power, swung to the 350-degree magnetic heading (roughly north-northwest), and began climbing to 18,000 feet. Shortly, sooner than I expected, I heard myself yelling on the radio, "This is Big Hog. Tallyho! One Tony, eleven o'clock, twenty degrees down. Out."

If I had not spotted the huge red ball on its wing, I never would have guessed that the airplane I saw was one of the newly deployed Imperial Army fighters. The Kawasaki Ki-61 fighter looked almost exactly like our own P-51 Mustang fighter, and nothing like any of the Zero variants that had dominated Japanese fighter operations in the region from August 1942 onward. If I had not spent long hours beside the troops poring over aircraft identification tables, I never would have known he was a Tony. I might have guessed that he was a Messerschmitt Me-109, a mistake other Allied pilots had made since the Ki-61 had entered combat over New Guinea in April 1943.

Rechecking—for the fourth time—that individual gun selectors and the armament master switch were on and that all my guns were charged, I dived to intercept the lone enemy fighter. The Imperial Army pilot—a completely unknown quantity—saw us coming and desperately slanted for a nearby cumulus head. But he had all the prospects of a mouse at a cat ranch. I flamed him just in time, barely an instant ahead of the enormous and bloodthirsty talent approaching from up my slipstream.

"Judah, this is Big Hog. Splash one Tony. Returning to station. Over."

"This is Judah. Roger. Out."

Well, that wasn't so hard. But neither was it a fair test of what the Imperial Army had to offer in the way of a challenge to our skills.

A short time after returning to the task group to circle overhead, we saw the formation of ships realign preparatory to turning into the wind. Then, with ballet precision, all the ships executed simultaneous turns to begin launch operations. If all went as planned, the carriers would be stripped of all their aircraft, the land-based Marine F4Us and New Zealand P-40s would arrive on station, and we could land to refuel and, in my case alone, rearm.

As soon as the launch was completed, the carrier formation reversed course. This was expected. The surface wind was at 15 knots from out of the north-northwest—bearing roughly from the carriers to Rabaul—so flight ops inevitably carried them ever closer, at 20 knots, to the enemy base. The task force was close enough for our purposes, certainly, but prudence dictated that they get no closer in the event the Japanese surface task force that was our primary strike target sallied to throw in a counterpunch.

At length, the two Marine F4U squadrons arrived on station to relieve us and VF-33, but the New Zealand P-40s did not. When we were set, the carriers turned back into the wind and their signal searchlights blinked out the message we had been awaiting:

| - - - - - | . - - . | - . - . | - - - - - | . - - . | - . - . |
| Attention | P | C | Attention | P | C |

which means, Attention, prepare to land aboard.

By then, the twenty-three Corsairs had formed into two flights led by Rog and me. As the searchlights blinked, Rog and I both rocked our wings to acknowledge and rapidly led our flights down to 5,000 feet, Rog's twelve toward *Essex* and my eleven toward *Bunker Hill.* John Kelly's twelve F6Fs were doing the same toward *Independence.* As the ships swung full into the wind, I led my troops down *Bunker Hill's* starboard side, the three divisions strung out in right echelon formation with hooks down. Before the carrier's lights could flash "Land Aboard" (- . - . or "C"), I was already on my final approach, well into the groove. Dead ahead, Catwalk Cummings was holding his arms and paddles straight out from his shoulders—"Roger"—indicating that I was heading for the stern ramp in perfect attitude, speed, and height. As I crossed over the ramp, Catwalk signaled "Cut." It was 0830, precisely.

Here, as on *Essex,* Fighting-17 provided textbook perfect landings—good tight intervals, no wave-offs, no hairy passes, no blown tires. I was proud. Most of my pilots had never even *seen* a steamboat until nine months before this, and none of us had landed on one for about two months. If ever there was a question about the Corsair's suitability for carrier ops—or ours—we laid it to rest that morning.

We received a measure more than a royal welcome aboard *Bunker Hill.* The flight deck crewmen were beaming as we taxied forward to park, and they gave us ebullient thumbs-up signs or clasped their hands over their heads. I received huge grins and fervent handshakes from Captain Ballentine and his exec, Cdr Swede Ekstrom. I did not even have to put the arm on the air boss, Cdr Kit Carson, to collect the ten-buck wager I had attached to a parting boast that Fighting-17 would see combat before any part of the *Bunker Hill* air group; Kit paid up as soon as he saw me. I doubt if anyone topside or on the hangar deck missed seeing or commenting on the red-and-white meatball flags painted beneath the canopy rails of many of our Hogs. Each flag denoted a kill. My kill of that morning was painted on while Big Hog was below getting checked out and refueled.

Hedrick & Company got an equally enthusiastic but less personal welcome aboard *Essex,* as did John Kelly's troops aboard *Indepen-*

dence. As soon as Rog landed aboard the flagship, he was summoned to the flag bridge to brief Admiral Montgomery and his staff. His final comment: "From what we've seen in our two weeks down here, you can expect that the Japs will throw everything they can get airborne into a counterstrike. My estimate is that they'll be here at 1300."

As it turned out, the enemy was thirteen minutes late.

We used the interval to lay below for dreamy hot showers, I in the skipper's in-port cabin, which came complete with a steward serving delicious, well-made coffee. Once clean, all hands were ushered to the wardroom for a deftly served repast of fresh grapefruit, steak, eggs (the real thing!) cooked to order, hot toast, and good coffee. All this and sparkling white tablecloths and linen napkins; courteous, smiling stewards; and seconds and thirds of everything. As we stuffed ourselves, ship's officers swarmed in to hear our best sea stories—some of which were even true. As I felt more and more like the country bumpkin just come from out of the hills to visit rich relatives, I found it increasingly hard to believe that I had been part of this friendly, well-off tribe until only two months earlier. Fantasy briefly suggested that some—maybe all—of our pilots would find reasons to stay aboard, and I briefly regretted that only twenty-three of us out of forty had been awarded this delightful respite.

Our fling with the good life came to an early but necessary end as we were ordered to man the fighter ready room. When we arrived, the teletype connected to the Combat Information Center clanked out the first message, a heart-warmer which read, "Welcome home, Fighting-17." Then we got down to business. The teletype hammered out the current tactical situation—clear radar screens, Marine fighters on station overhead, our launch time set at 1030. There was no word yet from the strike group, which we all took to be good news. A yellow-jerseyed flight-deck coordinator arrived with a diagram of our takeoff spot plus word from the flight-deck officer that all planes, which had been completely reserviced, rearmed, and mechanically checked out, were ready for takeoff.

All the ships of Task Group 50.3 were at Readiness Condition II—all battle stations partially manned, guns loaded with live ammunition, and plenty of ready-service ammunition on hand. The ships were also opened up to provide plenty of relatively cool fresh air to internal compartments. All hands who could be spared were eating hot meals, showering, changing clothes, doing what they could to relieve tension. Nevertheless, all the ships were within mere seconds of being at Condition I—full combat readiness, all guns and battle stations fully manned, and all spaces buttoned up tight for complete watertight and damage-control integrity.

The twenty-three VF-17 fighters and twelve VF-33 fighters were launched beginning at 1030. We immediately climbed to 25,000 feet to relieve the high Marine Corsair squadron while John Kelly's F6Fs relieved the other Marine squadron at 20,000. The Marine aircraft shoved off toward their bases in the islands.

I had no sooner gotten airborne than my previously troublesome radio transmitter crapped out again. I desperately wanted to retain control of my flight, but I now had no way to communicate anything except basic instructions by visual signals, and even that only when the formations were close aboard. As soon as we reached patrol altitude, I reluctantly passed the lead of my flight to Chuck Pillsbury. Also, as soon as we got on station, three of our pilots— Tom Killefer from my flight and two others from Hedrick's— reported by radio that they were experiencing mechanical or ordnance malfunctions. Chuck ordered the three back to Ondongo. Thus, together with the Hog that had aborted over Ondongo, we were down to two unbalanced ten-plane flights.

The weather, which had been beautifully clear, remained so in the carriers' operating area. As the morning wore on, the usual cumulonimbus buildups started forming to the north and west. By noon, some topped 35,000 feet with bases as low as 1,000 feet. They did not form a solid front; the gaps were wide open over what amounted to about one-third of the sky.

The friendly strike bombers and fighters began returning well after noon. There was to have been a second strike, as soon as the bombers and carrier fighters could be refueled and rearmed, but at the last minute Admiral Montgomery decided to concentrate on getting his fighters back up to challenge any possible Japanese counterstrike. The task group's Hellcats had been sent on ahead of the bombers as soon as the strike group was well clear of Japanese aircraft activity. Using their superior speed, the Hellcats arrived home early, landed, and were readied for relaunch on an urgent basis.

Meanwhile, we were very much on the *qui vive* for Japanese attack aircraft that might have followed them home, but neither we nor the ship-based radar found anything. Unbeknownst to us, however, Japanese snoopers were almost certainly at work in the cloud cover. These no doubt guided in the expected strong Japanese counterstrike, for at 1300, when about a quarter of our own strike aircraft had yet to land, the routine chatter on the radio was stilled by, "All fighters. This is Judah. Many bogies. Bearing three-five-oh. Angels three to twenty-five. Distance thirty, closing. Vector three-five-oh. Buster." Hedrick's estimate to Admiral Montgomery was only minutes off.

Apparently, interference from the thunderstorms had masked the radar returns from both the snoopers and the incoming strike. The counterstrike was right on top of us, only 30 miles out and closing fast at high speed. There was neither time nor adequate information for other than blanket fighter direction, no time to deploy to optimum advantage.

From 25,000 feet, the scene was idyllic, peaceful. A sparkling azure sea accentuated the bright white comet tails left by the twelve toy ships. As we fire-walled our throttles and swung north to intercept as far from the ships as possible, I looked down at the carriers and saw that all three were frantically catapulting fighters at minimum possible intervals. It made me feel great in the face of unknown opposition that the carrier F6F squadrons were topnotch. The three Hellcat skippers were good leaders as well as close friends—LCdr Flip Torrey, my old prep schoolmate, had *Essex*'s Fighting-9; LCdr Sam Silber, formerly of Opa-Locka, had *Bunker Hill*'s Fighting-18; and Lt Harry Harrison, another Miami alumnus, had *Independence*'s VF-22.

Pillsbury led our ten-plane flight to the east of the huge thunderhead that was between the ships and Rabaul, and Hedrick sheered left into the clear alleyway to the west of it. I lost sight of our ships as the first of their Hellcats steered north and slanted up, each trailing the distinctive faint black smoke of an engine running at full bore.

We were only a few minutes out from the carriers when the radio opened up with simultaneous sighting reports from Jim Streig and Teeth Burriss.

"This is Jimbo. Tallyho! Thirty Zekes, angels twenty. Twenty-five Vals, angels eighteen. Eleven o'clock."

"This is Teeth. Tallyho! Thirty-five Zekes, angels eighteen. Fifteen Kates, angels fifteen. Twelve o'clock."

These were about the last intelligible transmissions I heard since there was only one frequency in use and it immediately became jammed with other sighting reports, battle cries, war whoops, rebel yells, warnings, boasts, and other assorted junk transmissions.

I had a fleeting look at John Kelly's Hellcats boring in after the Vals while Pillsbury led our flight into the first enemy formation, a gaggle of about twenty-five Zeros.

As Pillsbury moved to set up a high-side run, I broke my three—me, Gutenkunst, and Streig—to port to gain position over the lead Zero foursome. I half-rolled inverted to start my dive and lined up directly on the formation leader. I was still out of range when he saw me and snapped into a split-S to his left. At the same time, his wingman honked around in a tight level right turn, setting up to nail me with a beautifully executed vertical scissors. The only throught that registered was, These guys are *good*! I kept after my target, ignoring the wingman, who expected to reverse his turn and get on my tail. This time, however, Gutenkunst and Streig peeled off from my wing to go after the wingman. Hah! Jimbo flamed him, our first kill of the afternoon. (Streig subsequently got another kill and damaged a Zeke and a Hamp.)

I was sure that I could easily bag the opposing fighter leader, so I left my wingmen behind and followed the Zeke down. He violently twisted and turned as we screamed out of the heavens. It was dogma that the Zeke's ailerons got unusually stiff at very high speeds, but I saw no evidence of that as the nimble fighter kept a step or two away from my gunsight pipper. To the contrary, at my own high speed, *my* ailerons overbalanced and I needed to maintain a light but firm touch to avoid going into an uncontrollable wing roll. I was making little progress catching up and I thought I might lose him altogether, so I fired a desperation burst from 500 yards. My passing tracer, which was not concentrated enough at long range, caused him to execute an abrupt radical pullout from his dive; his wingtips were streaming water vapor as he pulled six gees or more. I believed I was finally getting some rounds into him as I honked back hard to try to keep my pipper apace of the rapidly increasing deflection. However, his tighter turning circle pulled him out of my sights despite my own gut-wrenching pullout. He disappeared into the cloud, undoubtedly shaken but by no means defeated.

As I flattened out at 2,500 feet, I became extremely angry with myself. What an amateurish performance! Not only had I failed to

kill the Zero, I had allowed him to suck me out of the battle, and
I was all alone to boot. The old pro had really boobed it.

My windshield and canopy were densely fogged by condensation, a near-constant hazard of diving from cold high altitudes to
moist, warm low altitudes. I could see only to the sides and rear. As
I could not reach the windscreen to wipe the condensation clear
with my hands, I made a beeline for the nearest cloud, opened the
canopy, and stooged around in the murk until the moisture evaporated. All the while, my radio receiver gave out an absolute babble: "Look out, Joe!" and "Wow!" and "Where are you, Sam?" and
"Jeez, look at that flamer!"

When I finally stuck my nose out of the soup, my head was
swiveling in all directions. The first item of interest was a flight of
six Tonys at four o'clock. They were 5,000 feet above me and all
too close aboard. The leader immediately rolled to his left, starting
a dive in my direction. I convulsively flipped Big Hog left into a
tight, tight diving turn, a terrified effort to get back into the cloud
before he opened fire. I know I hunched my head into my shoulders
and pressed hard into the seatback, for I fully expected to hear the
impact of a sheet of final bullets. I did not release my breath until
I was long seconds into the protecting cloud.

I have no idea how long I circled inside the lovely cumulus, and
I cared not at all about who or what might be in there with me.
Eventually, I quit shaking and got my heart rate and blood pressure
back under control. Eventually, I decided that the Tonys had
certainly shoved off in search of another patsy.

Screwing up my courage, I eased the speed back up to 200 knots.
Then out I went, hopeful I would find no more threatening hostiles. Indeed! Two F4Us were close aboard at nine o'clock, right at
my level, about 300 yards out. At once, I saw gun flashes erupt at
the leading edges of the leader's wings.

BAM-BAM-BAM!

Anguish and concern written all over his face, Rog Hedrick
pulled up beside me to the left. After closely inspecting Big Hog,
Rog shook his head and passed a questioning thumbs-up sign—was
I okay? To my right, Mills Schanuel did much the same as I rapidly
actuated various controls and scanned the guages to check for damage. All apparently was okay. Rog later told me that he had shagged
an enemy fighter into the cloud seconds before I emerged at just the
spot he thought we would find his quarry. Rog's was a beautiful full

deflection shot; he had put three .50-caliber bullets just behind the armor plate behind my seat and three through the engine accessory section, between the engine and fuel tank. Fortunately, Big Hog had been inside the convergence distance of his guns. Otherwise, those six rounds would have gone through me.

The view from the surface on up to 25,000 feet was almost beyond belief. The whole hemisphere of sky was polka-dotted with black 5-inch shell bursts interlaced with colorful 20mm and 40mm tracer. Here and there, dark-tailed orange comets marked the passage of burning airplanes as they arced toward the cobalt surface. Around the twisting ships, bomb and shell spouts heaved up spectacular white geysers. Through it all, planes rolled and turned with sunlight glinting off their flat surfaces and contrails streaming off their wingtips as they executed maximum-gee high-speed pullouts, some right on the deck. The scream of overrevving engines and props was punctuated with the *whomps* of bombs, guns, and shells, plus the staccato *rat-a-tat* of machine guns. It was Technicolor bedlam, and then some.

An exchange of hand signals with Rog revealed that he, like me, had only 75 gallons of fuel aboard. Schanuel had about the same. I signaled that I was heading for home, and Rog signaled his smiling assent. We had tooled around for nearly three hours before the battle and had used up huge quantities of fuel during our high-speed jousting; we had enough for the flight home but too little to get in any more fighting. I had a kill, and so did Rog. Enough was enough.

As I peeled out of the original flight formation to go after the Zeros with my trio, Chuck Pillsbury had gone in way too fast and had thus thrown the rest of the formation out of balance. He missed his target, but his two wingmen, Ens Hal Jackson and Ens Bob Hogan, each flamed a Zero.

As soon as Teeth Burriss tallyhoed the gaggle of Kates and their formidable fighter cover, Rog Hedrick positioned his division—himself, Ens Mills Schanuel, Lt(jg) Andy Anderson, and Lt(jg) Jack Chasnoff—for a high-side run against the lead Zeke division's port quarter, which was holding course at Rog's ten o'clock. At the same time, Lt Timmy Gile—followed by Ens Danny Cunningham, Lt(jg) Paul Cordray, and Ens Brad Baker—crossed ahead of the Japanese formation to set up for a close follow-on from the enemy's starboard quarter. Also at the same time, Lt Thad Bell and his division—Ens Teeth Burriss, Ens Ike Kepford, and Lt Lem Cooke—slanted in to hit the Kates with a horizontal pass from the targets' port side. This all added up to a nice bit of unrehearsed headwork by the two division leaders following Hedrick's lead.

Hedrick scored an immediate kill against the first Zeke that turned up in his gunsight, and Anderson and Chasnoff—number three and number four behind him—opened fire so close together on another Zero that they were not sure which of them hit it. They thus shared credit for a damaged Zeke.

Timmy Gile's tigers, attacking from the starboard side, met with about the same success. Brad Baker registered a clean kill when his target exploded in midair. Paul Cordray saw his target shedding big chunks of metal, but, when last seen, the smoking Zero was still flying straight and level. Paul got credit for a damaged Zeke.

Of Bell's division, only Burriss connected, a natural follow-up on his early sighting. His target, a Kate, was sent spinning out of control, trailing a huge plume of oily black smoke. Doubtless, our master of unauthorized inverted flight was displaying the toothy, mirthless, nervous grimace that had earned him his nickname.

All the rest of the Kates successfully scrambled into the nearest thunderhead—still in perfect formation. This obliged Bell's division to reconnoiter for new targets. They headed into the AA show over the carriers and Bell bounced a group of diving Vals well before they released their bombs. Screaming up their tails, Thad quickly bagged one and then dived onto the tail of a second, which he sent skidding out of control. Score two dead Vals.

Burriss missed the Vals but he found a lone twin-engine Betty. He peeled off into an overhead run and blew off the medium bomber's port wing. Shortly, Teeth found a lonesome Kate as it dropped down to begin its torpedo run on one of the ships. As he set up his firing run, a Hellcat zoomed in from out of nowhere and went after Teeth's target. Their combined competitive fire sent the Kate cartwheeling across the surface, and so they each got credit for a half kill.

Lt Johnny Kleinman and Ens Windy Hill, who had briefly joined on Pillsbury's trio, were shaken loose by Chuck's abrupt initial attack, so they got no rounds off at the ample targets. As Johnny and Windy pulled up from this run, they saw the big black puffs of ship-fired 5-inch AA. Reasoning correctly that the ships would not be firing at empty air, the pair dived in that direction to get in on the action. Using the AA as a beacon, they soon spotted a flight of torpedo-armed Kates nosing down and deploying in a fanlike attack formation against one of the carriers—*Bunker Hill*. Kleinman and Hill caught up with the torpeckers just above the water plumes put up by erupting 40mm and 20mm rounds from the ships.

Hill broke away from Kleinman and latched onto the first Kate he could reach. He opened fire as he flew straight up the torpedo bomber's tail and saw flame sprout just before the Kate knifed into the water, torpedo and all. Then Windy wisely decided to remove himself from within the only marginally friendly AA umbrella.

After damaging his first Kate target, Johnny Kleinman also drilled into the welter of AA while chasing another Kate. According to Cdr J. C. Shaw, *Bunker Hill's* gunnery officer, "I saw a Kate about twenty feet off the water dart by the formation with a Corsair closing fast. Like a cowboy roping a wild steer, the Corsair sent tracers licking out, and the Kate went in with an awesome splash." Johnny killed the Kate, but in the process a friendly 20mm round exploded on contact with his heavy glass bullet-proof windscreen. Blood coursing from many painful facial wounds created a red mist before Johnny's eyes that made flying an extremely difficult chore. He had tiny cuts all over his face, but his goggles had saved his eyes. As soon as he thought of it, he regained his vision by pulling the goggles up to his bleeding forehead. Not unreasonably, Johnny pointed his Corsair's nose for home. And, not unreasonably, his plane captain registered a terrified grimace when first he saw Johnny grinning broadly through the bloody mess of his face. The wounds proved to be superficial, and all quickly healed without appreciably marring Johnny's good looks.

Timmy Gile also bounced the Kates at low level. He caught up with one of them just as it made a bad drop—the fish porpoised and veered sharply from its target. This loner flew doggedly for home just above waves foamed by bullets from Timmy's guns, many of which undoubtedly passed through the Kate. At length, the stubborn torpedo bomber dropped its nose and flew straight into the next wave.

With that, Timmy got his division joined and headed for home. A short distance from the carriers, Brad Baker handsignaled that his fuel state was perilously low, so Timmy set course for Empress

Augusta Bay, where there was a chance of finding friendly ships to pick Brad up in case he had to ditch. Timmy was able to raise Cocker Base, the Torokina fighter director, on his voice radio. The FDO alerted the local search-and-rescue forces. Brad's prop started windmilling when the division was still a good 20 miles from the beachhead. Timmy and the others were also getting low on fuel, so they only hung around until they were sure Brad was safely out of the ditched fighter. Within minutes, a PBY touched down and scooped Brad out of the water, good as new. He was flown to Munda, checked out by the medicos, and returned to Ondongo in time for supper.

Like Kleinman, Ike Kepford drilled right on through the intense friendly AA to burn a Kate just as it seemed ready to launch its fish only 1,000 yards from *Bunker Hill*. Unlike Johnny, however, Ike evaded the friendly fire. However, at the same moment he was killing the Kate, and unbeknownst to Ike, a Hellcat blew a Zero off *his* tail.

Ike emerged from the shoreward side of the AA umbrella and decided to call it a day because he was getting low on fuel. He shaped course for Ondongo and cracked his cockpit canopy so he could dry his sweat-soaked coveralls and enjoy a relaxing smoke. He was just lighting up when he happened to see an unchallenged flight of six Vals on course for Rabaul. Ike flipped his smoke over the side, closed and locked the canopy, and went to General Quarters. He flamed three of the slower dive-bombers in quick succession as the virtually helpless quarry stayed bunched together to share the meager protection of their rear-firing 7.7mm machine guns. Ike was scoring hits on the fourth Val when he expended the last of his ammunition.

As Ike broke away from the surviving Vals, he noted that his fuel gauge was bouncing on "Empty." Estimating he had less than thirty minutes flying time left, and 150 miles from the nearest runway, Ike felt that his only recourse was to get back aboard one of the carriers. Fortunately, by then, the extreme clutter on the fighter frequency had died down, so Ike called the *Essex*-based fighter director: "Judah, this is Ike in [airplane number] Seventeen Fox Twenty-nine. Do you read? Over."

"Ike, this is Judah. Five square. Send your message. Over."

"This is Ike. I'm low state. Request steer and immediate pancake. Over."

"This is Judah. Roger. Steer two-eight-oh. Distance twenty. You'll get 'Charlie' by flashing light from whoever can take you. Acknowledge."

"This is Ike. Thanks. Wilco. Out."

Quick translation: Ike had asked Judah if they could hear him and Judah had replied they could hear and understand him perfectly ("five square"). Then Ike had told Judah he was short on fuel ("low state") and had asked for a course and permission to land aboard ("pancake"). Judah had given him a course and distance to the ship (they had him on their radar) and had told him that he would get a flashed searchlight signal—letter *C* for "Charlie"—from the first carrier that could take him.

As promised, *Bunker Hill* trained one of her signal lights on Ike as soon as the Corsair hove into sight. The Charlie signal (- . - .) was repeated until Ike was in the groove, coming up the carrier's wake toward the stern ramp. When Ike shut down the Hog forward of the barrier, it had 5 gallons of avgas aboard.

Ike was treated to a huge hearty hello and welcome aboard from all hands as he climbed out of his smoke- and oil-stained fighter. As far as *Bunker Hill*'s crew was concerned, he represented all the brave land-based fighter pilots who had helped save their ship from the Japanese attackers. Ike was instantly escorted to the bridge, where a beaming Capt John Ballentine boomed, "Welcome home, Ike. *Bunker Hill* thanks you and the rest of Fighting-Seventeen. I doubt that we'd have made it without your help. Anything we have is yours. What would you like?"

This set Ike back on his heels. It was a real thrill, second only to the realization that he had scored four sure kills. The fact that he, a mere ensign, was getting the royal treatment from this venerable, respected four-striper was almost too much. "Er, I could use some coffee, sir." Seconds later, Ike accepted a steaming cup directly from the skipper's hand. Ike next asked that he be allowed to fly off to the beach to rejoin the squadron. Captain Ballentine eagerly assented and, after enjoying a relaxing half-hour respite, Ike catapulted off in his refueled, rearmed, and fully checked-out Hog. Ensign Kepford clocked the squadron's high score—four kills and one damaged—and the high flight time—eleven hours—for the day.

In all, VF-17 was credited with 18.5 confirmed kills and 7 damaged Japanese warplanes. However, our evening celebration was severely muted by the mysterious disappearance of Ens Windy Hill.

But Windy was far from gone. After scoring his first kill on the Kate and threading his way apparently untouched through Task Group 50.3's shower of steel, Ensign Hill found himself all alone on the east side of the battle. His gas guage indicated there was only enough fuel aboard to get him back to Ondongo if he used an economical power setting. As he turned for home, he was pleasantly startled to see Chuck Pillsbury's Corsair overtake him. Both pilots were happy to have company for a long and anxious reach for friendly territory.

Hill's engine started cutting out northwest of the Treasury Islands. He radioed Chuck that he was apparently out of gas and that Chuck should not be a damn fool and stick around. Chuck knew he could do nothing to help Windy, so he sensibly nursed his Hog to Ondongo, where refueling required all but three gallons of his Corsair's total capacity. Chuck reported the coordinates at which he believed Windy had had to ditch.

Hill stayed airborne for ten additional agonizing minutes. His engine kept cutting in and out, but he maintained enough lift to keep him aloft 20 miles farther toward the Treasuries. When his engine sounded its final cough, the islands were close aboard. Following the adventure of ditching and escaping from his rapidly sinking Corsair, Windy took stock of his situation as he bobbed mostly above the surface in his Mae West life jacket.

Windy knew of our October 27 invasion of the Treasuries, but he was by no means sure that the island near him was yet in friendly hands. Thus, he did not yet want to risk greater visibility from the beach by deploying his life raft, which remained reassuringly attached to his Mae West by means of a stout lanyard. Soon, however, he found that he was tiring rapidly from the weight of his survival gear, so he reluctantly inflated the raft and climbed aboard.

Minutes later, Windy saw a ragged-looking figure appear from out of the bush at the beachline. He was sure it was a Japanese soldier. The stranger spotted the raft and waved, but Windy lay doggo. The potential adversary waved both arms and then sent a message in semaphore: "Help is on the way."

It was, according to Windy, "The only time in my life I was able to read semaphore."

Shortly thereafter, a PT boat roared up and hauled our happy warrior aboard. Windy was turned over to the New Zealanders at Mono Island's Blanche Harbor, where he spent a recreational four days until he was picked up by a PBY on its way from the Torokina beachhead to Munda—with VAdm Bill Halsey aboard.

Somehow, word of Windy's rescue did not reach Ondongo. Of course, intensive searches the next day at Windy's last known position proved fruitless. We had sadly given up long before Windy walked into the squadron ready room. Windy's adventure made for a good story the first time he told it. It was even good the second time. But Windy gummed the tale literally to boredom and death until all hands began giving him a wide berth.

The Battle of the Solomon Sea, as the November 11 imbroglio came to be called, was a bag of mixed results in which the combined might of our carrier- and land-based air groups did more damage to Japanese powers of perception than it did, in fact, to Japanese planes and ships.

The original plan had envisaged an initial antishipping attack on Rabaul's Simpson Harbor by New Guinea-based 5th Air Force bombers, immediately followed by successive strikes from our two carrier task forces, immediately followed by a strike by AirSols B-24s.

Bad weather over New Guinea caused all but thirteen of the 5th Air Force B-24s to abort. The results of the leadoff strike were, if anything, marginal.

RAdm Forrest Sherman's superb Task Force 38—*Saratoga* and *Princeton*—arrived on station at the right time and lauched thirty-six F6Fs, twenty-three SBDs, and fifteen TBFs while several land-based fighter squadrons flew CAP over the ships. The strike group flew into bad weather over Rabaul, but that was the least of the problems, for the earlier B-24 strike had fully alerted the defenders. Antiaircraft defenses were at maximum alert. The bombers sighted only one light cruiser and four destroyers through holes in the cloud cover. The attack was conducted under the worst possible conditions; the air was full of antiaircraft rounds and the targets were obscured. Hits were claimed, but the extent of damage inflicted, if any, was neither adequately nor accurately observed.

The 165-plane strike from Task Group 50.3 arrived about an hour after the Task Force 38 strike departed. Once again, the weather at Simpson Harbor was rainy, and the antiaircraft fire was enthusiastic. This time, numerous Japanese fighters were vectored in to engage the attackers. A total of seven of our fighters, three of our dive-bombers, and three of our torpedo bombers were downed, but our bombers claimed two destroyers sunk and several other Japanese warships damaged, and our pilots and gunners claimed thirty-five Japanese aircraft downed.

The final element of the attack, forty-two AirSols B-24s, arrived on schedule, just as the Task Group 50.3 bombers were leaving. As before, the results of the high-altitude drop through heavy clouds were negligible, if that.

A second series of carrier strikes had been requested by Admiral Halsey, but Sherman's Task Force 38 was obliged to withdraw early because several of the escorting destroyers were low on fuel. Montgomery's Task Group 50.3 had been in the process of simultaneously recovering and refueling—and preparing to relaunch—strike aircraft when the Japanese counterstrike arrived. Frantic efforts to clear the carriers eventually got a total of sixty-four Hellcats aloft before the Vals and Kates arrived and obliged the carriers to take evasive action. Also, twenty-three TBFs from the first strike were aloft, their landings having been delayed by the Japanese attack. They merely flew out of range until the action died down.

Aerial combat, particularly over ships firing their own guns all out, is confusing, to say the least. And the results are confusing. Overzealous pilots tend to claim kills for every burst fired, and there is a marked tendency by each of the crews of competing warships to count shared kills as their own. For whatever reasons, claims of kills over embattled warships are usually inflated and, at best, should be taken with a degree of skepticism. In all on November 11, over Rabaul and over Task Group 50.3, our planes and ships turned in claims for 111 confirmed kills. Postwar searches through Japanese records turned up confirmation for less than 50, including several torpedo-laden Bettys knocked down by Task Group 50.3 Hellcats after dark. I nevertheless stand behind Fighting-17's claim of 18.5 kills.

Despite the mixed and questionable physical results of the November 11 raids and the wild defense of Task Group 50.3, the Japanese regional high command was severely shaken. Whether the losses they suffered in ships and planes were as high as we claim or as low as they recorded, the fact that we had five carrier air groups, numerous heavy bombers, and so many artfully employed land-based fighter squadrons to devote to a spoiling raid on their fortress-like main base came as an awesome shock. Their resolve fell away, utterly. Far from reinforcing Rabaul, the Japanese *withdrew* their carrier air groups, which had been all but obliterated in two weeks of constant action. The Imperial Navy also withdrew their Rabaul-based warships to distant, safer Truk Lagoon. The enemy never again used Rabaul as a base for his men-o'-war. Thus, the November 11 strikes, serving as the culmination of a two-week struggle for hegemony over the Torokina beachhead, resulted in a decisive capitulation of the Japanese to the will of the Allies. A step taken at great peril to our own forces and long-range plans resulted in the virtual evaporation of the means by which the Japanese could reverse the trend of defeat followed by defeat in the Solomons campaign. Moreover, the total price we paid in ships, airplanes, and lives for so complete a psychological victory was astoundingly, gratifyingly low. This was of major strategic importance, for it opened the way for the Allied thrust westward into the Marianas and beyond.

In all, between October 27 and November 11, the Japanese carrier squadrons based at Rabaul lost forty-three of eighty-two Zekes, thirty-eight of forty-five Vals, and thirty-four of forty Kates. This, in addition to numerous other losses among land-based Army and Navy squadrons. This destruction all but finished the job our carrier pilots had begun in the Coral Sea in May 1942. From then, through Midway in June, at Eastern Solomons in August, and especially at Santa Cruz in October 1942, our side had gutted the solid core of first-team professionals manning the Japanese carrier air groups. Along the way, over islands from Guadalcanal to New Georgia to Bougainville to Rabaul herself, our land-based fighters had destroyed the core of the Imperial Navy's land-based air groups. Beginning in early November 1943, we started to work on the Imperial Army's air force. We won no clear operational aerial victory during the Solomon Sea battle itself, but we certainly drove a long way toward capping the victory in our ongoing war of attrition, for we could replace our losses in men and airplanes while the Japanese could not.

We did not perceive it at the time—though we might have had we looked hard enough—but the Solomons air campaign had been decided. After November 11, 1942, the Japanese were unable—or unwilling—to wage more than a rearguard holding action, a meager attempt to put off the inevitable for . . . what? A miracle?

18

Fighting-17 had a lot going on besides flying and fighting. Our return from carrier duty after the Solomon Sea battle marked the end of our first two weeks in the forward area, a good time to assess the squadron's gains and losses.

On the loss side, so far, was one missing pilot, Lt(jg) Johnny Keith. He was never found. We had also lost several airplanes, all to enemy fire. That was all.

On the plus side of the ledger, we had received credit for destroying 28.5 Japanese airplanes and damaging 18 others. None of us had achieved ace status—5 confirmed kills—but several of us were closing on the mark. Ike Kepford and I were tied for leader with 4 kills each. Jim Streig and Teeth Burriss each had 2.5, and a handful had 2 apiece. Counting his 2 kills early in the war with Fighting-5, Johnny Kleinman had 3. Given the tempo of the action in late 1943—moderate—we were doing as well as or better than most other land-based fighter squadrons in the area.

In addition to the problem I had had with the reluctant ensign, it was becoming clear that the stresses and strains of our heavy schedule were wearing down several other pilots. One contributing factor, I believe, was that our mail did not catch up to us until around the time we got back from carrier duty. I was sure that that had an all-around negative effect, particularly on worried young men far from home for the first time in their lives. (We oldsters suffered, too. My wife had always been a lukewarm letter writer, at best, and getting just a few brief missives from her rankled. By way of comparison, I found many letters in that first batch from a young widow whose husband had been killed during our training period. I had never been a completely faithful husband, and the comparison under stress inclined to make me less so—as soon as I got the opportunity.)

One of our pilots who had done fairly well to that point somehow shot himself in the hand. This posed a rugged dilemma. Self-inflicted wounds occurred all too often in the armed forces, and they elicited draconian consequences—up to and including prison sentences—if intent was proved. In this case, I did much soul-searching and discussed the matter at length with Duke Henning and our flight surgeon—and ad hoc psychiatrist—Lyle Herrmann. Our consensus was that the wound indeed had been accidental, so we kept the matter in the family. This pilot did okay in our second combat tour.

One of the men who was not doing at all well by the two-week point was Sunny Jim Halford, who was hardly sunny any more. He and Johnny Kleinman had never been particularly hot on the idea of another combat tour, but they had performed well, no doubt helped by the promise that they could go home immediately upon the squadron's relief for our first R&R leave. (Typically, land-based squadrons flew for six-week intervals separated by a lengthy break in the rear area.) It must be said that neither of them broached the matter; they hung in there. But Halford became increasingly and noticeably grimmer with each passing day. Finally, he aborted a routine CAP hop with the complaint of extreme nausea. Dr. Herrmann could find nothing physically wrong with Jim, but I felt that a psychosomatic illness was no less real than an authentic bug. I decided to send Jim home as soon as possible. And, since I had made the same commitment to Johnny Kleinman, I felt that it would be only fair to send him, too. Johnny was never happy about being in the forward area again, but even after he returned with his horribly bloodied face on November 11, he insisted upon carrying his share of the burden; he led his division on the thirtennth, albeit on a milk run. Much as I admired Johnny, and wanted him to stay, I could not muster the gall to try to con him into staying while Jim went home. I sent both of them south to Espiritu Santo on November 17, and they were both home by mid-December. I never heard from or of Jim Halford again, but I enjoyed lively and frequent correspondence with Johnny until his death in a senseless Training Command crash the following spring.

Duke Henning's fertile brain, plus our mutual disdain for some of the sillier aspects of "security," produced a useful if somewhat illegal means for getting our personnel aboard transport planes with high priority. Duke would draft and our yeoman would type orders for my signature, each beginning with the magic clause, "In accordance with highly classified instructions which cannot be quoted herein, the bearer will proceed . . ." Of course, the "highly classified" was our cover for sending someone somewhere to get some booze or, nearly as often, a spare part we could not acquire through normal channels. No one ever questioned it. We used it to get Halford and Kleinman back to Espiritu Santo without their having to wait for "space available." I was afraid to pull this dodge to get them all the way back to the States without inordinate delays because their pay status depended on honest-to-goodness transfer orders.

One of my early edicts resulted in my publicly walking back the cat. In early November, via ACIO channels, we got word that the other squadrons in the area had heard of my order, "Claim only confirmed kills; to hell with 'probable' and 'damaged' garbage." It turned out that the word was going around that Fighting-17 would claim a kill for *every* enemy airplane we believed we had hit. Thereafter, we conformed to the accepted reporting system.

I was frequently summoned to Munda to work with the Fighter Command staff, so I soon developed rapport with the people who made things go in our bailiwick. The boss, Col Oscar Brice, was an honest-to-god Southern gentleman whose wrinkled leathery face and hawk nose had been dyed by liberal ingestion of corn squeezings over the years. Oscar's characteristic smile was incandescent, and his wrath was equally spectacular. The good colonel knew his business and was extremely tolerant of new approaches voiced by subordinates within his blue-ribbon command. On the other hand, he had the shortest fuse I ever witnessed when it came to alibis and pusillanimity.

Colonel Brice's right-hand man was his ACIO, Lt Joe Bryan, a Richmond native and scion of one of the First Families of Virginia. Joe's forebears had served with distinction in every American war since Braddock's March. Joe had a keen, incisive mind, a lightning sense of humor, and a handsome, aristocratic visage that was the antithesis of Oscar's. This pair always had a flagpole with the Stars and Bars in the wind to mark their headquarters as the CP of ConForSols—Confederate Forces, Solomons.

Nearly always on hand for our informal conferences was LCdr Gus Widhelm, an authentic, 24-karat dive-bomber hero now commanding VF(N)-75, the Navy's pioneer night Corsair squadron. In fact, Gus's Corsairs, which arrived at Munda in September, had been the first Navy land-based Corsair squadron to reach the forward area. No dissembler, Gus cultivated the image of a diamond in the rough. A stranger to social graces, rough as a dry corncob, he was in every way a fighting man's fighting man. He had distinguished himself early in the war at Midway and Santa Cruz, where he drove and led SBD dive-bombers. His exploits had earned him a well-deserved pair of Navy Crosses in the days before many medals lost prestige from overgenerous distribution. With a toddy or two under his belt, Gus would open a conversation with, "Did I ever tell you how I won my first Navy Cross?" From anyone else, this would have been obnoxious, but not from Gus. For him, it was like showing snapshots of the kids. VF(N)-75 spent a lot of time in "alert" status, sitting on the end of the Munda runway, so Gus and his guys frequently came over to Ondongo to fly with us and keep sharp. They were always welcomed for their skill and experience, albeit with the standing proviso that they flew the tail-end-Charlie slot—except for Gus, who flew wing on me.

To us veterans of two weeks combat, it seemed that nothing much happened in the days immediately following our exciting November 11 combat. On the twelfth, sixteen of our Corsairs were tabbed to fly close escort on a PBY carrying the South Pacific Area commander, VAdm Bill Halsey, on his first eyeball inspection of the Torokina beachhead. Also that day, thirteen of sixteen Corsairs scheduled for an escort hop rendezvoused with forty-two SBDs and twenty-four TBFs over Baga Island and escorted them on a bombing raid against Kara airfield. The mission encountered no enemy fighters, and there was not even any antiaircraft fire over the target. A milk run.

November 13, Johnny Kleinman's last day in the air with us, was used up on three negative eight-plane patrols over Empress Augusta Bay and three two-hour patrols over a damaged cruiser. We saw no enemy aircraft.

For most of us, November 14 was just as dull, with three eight-plane missions covering a small naval task unit and two eight-plane CAP missions over Munda. We also mounted a four-plane escort for a Dumbo rescue mission in the Treasury Islands. The only excitement of the day was encountered by an eight-plane flight as part of an escort for fifty-four SBDs and eight TBFs that flew through extremely bad weather to bomb antiaircraft gun positions and supply areas around Ballale. The AA opposition was intense, but none of our fighters was hit and none of the bombers was shot down.

On November 15, at the conclusion of a negative two-hour patrol over Empress Augusta Bay, Lt Chuck Pillsbury, leading his and

Butch Davenport's divisions, was directed to strafe ground installations around Chabai Plantation, off Matchin Bay. Chuck led the
fighters up Bougainville's coast and about 20 miles inland, flying
very low. All eight Corsairs swept across the target area in line-
abreast formation—always an impressive entrance—and sprayed
.50-caliber rounds at numerous antiaircraft positions and buildings
the pilots assumed were barracks and storehouses. At least two
buildings were left burning and at least two AA positions were
silenced. After leaving Chabai, Chuck turned his division north to
take on the Buka and Bonis defenses. Chuck's was the first plane
across Bonis. As he turned southeast across the runway, his Corsair
was hit in the left wing by a 7.7mm machine-gun bullet and, worse,
a 37mm shell. Chuck's wingman, Lt Wally Schub, also took a
37mm round through the fuselage of his Corsair, albeit without
serious damage. The two Corsairs following Chuck and Wally were
not hit and their pilots reported no observable results. Butch Davenport's division, which had turned back south after hitting Chabai, found a 60-foot tug off Kuriki Island. The craft was high and
dry on a reef, so was easy pickings for Butch's four Corsairs, which
easily set it afire.

Also on November 15, our ongoing good terms with the staff at
Fighter Command briefly came to a screeching stop.

I was stooging around over Torokina, leading my flight of eight
Corsairs at 20,000 feet on a typical, boring CAP. About midway
through the patrol period, we spotted a flight of a half-dozen twin-
engine bombers to our northwest; they were heading more or less
toward us.

The local fighter director had not yet alerted anyone, but it was
prudent to check it out, so we eased out for a closer look. It seemed
most unlikely to any of us that the Japanese would be sending out
unescorted horizontal bombers at this stage of the campaign. While
still some distance out, we all saw a Hellcat execute an overhead
run on the bomber formation. I also saw a formation of six or seven
other Hellcats holding altitude over the bombers. The whole show
was too far away for me to see precisely what was going on, but it
was by then clear that the bombers were B-25s. Nobody was
getting hurt, there was no need for us to be there, so I swung back
to resume our station. I could not help thinking about how dopey
it was for that Hellcat pilot to play grab-ass with the bombers;

someone might have gotten trigger happy and the result could have been fatal. Then I gave the matter no further thought.

At the conclusion of our mission, we were ordered to strafe Chabai, but the weather on the way up was lousy, so we cut across Bougainville to scour the northeast coast for targets of opportunity. Four of us strafed a known AA position at Arawa Bay from treetop height with no observable results, and the other division strafed a building at the end of the Kieta runway, also at treetop height and also without observable results. As the entire flight swung east over the water, we came upon a 40-foot barge which was just backing off Banaru Reef. We set it afire almost as an afterthought.

On our return home, I was diverted to Munda to "report immediately to Fighter Command." I found Colonel Brice in a lather. "Tommy," he began without his usually affable preamble, "your outfit had the escort job for the B-25s we sent to Buka this afternoon." This was true; while I was over Torokina with my eight, Dirty Eddie March had been undertaking his first truly responsible job of the deployment, escorting the Buka-bound B-25s as leader of another flight of eight. I nodded. "Well, Strike Command is raising hell. The flight commander of the B-25s reported by radio that the fighters peeled off much too soon after the bomb drop and that the bombers were left exposed to an attack over Bougainville by a flight of Hamps. Luckily, they escaped damage. Tommy, you know damn well I won't tolerate this kind of performance by our fighters. You go back to Ondongo and look into this. I want an immediate report on who was responsible and how come it happened."

"Aye, aye, sir. Will do!" I bade farewell to the colonel, Lt Joe Bryan, and the CO of an F6F squadron who was also present. I was by then quite literally sick to my stomach. VF-17 had never done anything even remotely resembling this fiasco. I was prepared to have Dirty Eddie publicly hanged, drawn, and quartered—for starters.

When I confronted Lieutenant March, he recoiled in amazement. "Not so, Skipper. We stayed with those guys 'till they were well into the Empress Augusta Bay area. I even saw you and our other CAP before we shoved off. There were no—repeat, *no*—Japs seen, no cries for help."

"March, I can't help that . . ." I was getting wound up, but my tirade was cut short by the jangling of the field phone.

"It's for you, Skipper."

I had the rime of extreme annoyance in my voice when I answered, "This is Blackburn. What is it?"

It was Joe Bryan. "Tommy, I just got word from one of the ACIOs. One of his F6F pilots reported at debriefing that despite their best effort to stop him, his squadron skipper made a firing run on a flight of our B-25s. You're off the hook. The colonel told me to apologize to you for him."

It was obvious that the B-25 flight commander had mistaken the square-winged F6Fs for the square-winged Zero variant we called Hamp. But that did not explain how the errant F6F CO had been able to stand by listening while Colonel Brice reamed me out.

"Why," I spluttered, "that crummy son of a bitch."

"Those were the colonel's exact words before he relieved him at once and ordered him home. Colonel Brice said, and I quote, 'If he dares show his face around here, I'll kill him.' Tommy, the Old Man wasn't kidding."

For once, it was a pleasure to walk back the cat as I made peace with Dirty Eddie.

November 16 was another busy, dull day. We flew four uneventful two-hour eight-plane CAP missions over a naval transport group, a division-strength CAP over Munda, and eight-plane Dumbo escort to Empress Augusta Bay, and a four-plane search around Elo Island looking for a downed P-40 pilot. The only near-action of the day fell to divisions led by Dirty Eddie March and Timmy Gile while they were escorting a flight of sixteen SBDs against ground targets near the Jaba River. This was our first authentic mission in direct support of the Marines on the Torokina beachhead. Unfortunately, none of our guys saw a thing as the dive-bombers made a total of six bombing and strafing runs against targets in the trees.

We were bored, bored, bored, yet tense in the ever-present face of potential combat. We know we could never afford to dope off. Between the big day on November 11 and November 16, no Air-Sols pilot shot down or even encountered a Japanese warplane in daylight. The only kill was a Betty claimed at 0420 on November 13 by the crew of a Marine twin-engine PV-1 night fighter. Of course, we had no way of knowing that the depleted Japanese air groups at Rabaul had been laying low, using the last few days to gear up for a new offensive effort. Fighting-17's honeymoon was about to end.

19

The redoubtable Rog Hedrick led the way into VF-17's next action of consequence, on November 17. His flight was composed of his own division (Mills Schanuel on his wing, as usual, and Jack Chasnoff on Andy Anderson's wing) and Timmy Gile's (Danny Cunningham on his wing and Brad Baker on Paul Cordray's wing). Every one of the eight had at least one confirmed kill to his credit.

The flight was on station at 0800, 25,000 feet above Empress Augusta Bay. At 0830, Hedrick was electrified by: "Gem Three, this is Cocker Base. Many bogeys. Angels one-five. Distance thirty from Cherryblossom [Cape Torokina]. Vector two-five-oh. Buster. Acknowledge."

"This is Gem Three. Wilco. Out."

The flight had barely turned to the new course and was angling down at 325 knots when Gile spoke up: "This is Timmy. Tallyho! Bandits at two o'clock, thirty degrees down. Twelve Zekes right over eight Kates. Over." For a change, someone had spotted some targets before hawkeye Hedrick.

"This is Rog. See 'em. Timmy, swing left forty-five. Hit Kates from high side right as soon as we're clear. Over."

"This is Timmy. Gotcha, Rog! Will do. Out."

With that, Hedrick and Schanuel hurtled in at the unalerted fighters. Rog immediately flamed the flight leader while Schanuel nailed his wingman. Both Corsairs pulled out in steep chandelles to get into position at the enemy's two o'clock—up-sun from the Japanese formation.

While Hedrick and Schanuel were delivering their attack, Anderson and Chasnoff dropped back slightly to gain some freedom for maneuver. Andy selected the left-flank fighter and opened fire just as it went into a diving turn to the left. This left Anderson mousetrapped in a horizontal scissors executed by a pair of gutty Japanese fighter veterans. His "target's" wingman sheered right and then reversed course right onto Andy's tail. Andy heard the awesome sound of bullets striking his Corsair, so he abruptly pulled up, the least likely maneuver when under attack by faster-climbing

Zekes. The Japanese pair did not follow and Chasnoff joined up to check Andy's fighter for visible damage, of which, apparently, there was nothing serious. The pair headed back into the melee, but as soon as Anderson got off a long burst at a moderately distant target, he saw that his left wing was burning. With the cockpit rapidly filling with smoke, Andy desperately attempted to slow to 300 knots so he could safely bail out. No joy there, so he flipped inverted, kicked free, bounced off the horizontal stabilizer, and fell to 1,000 feet before his chute blossomed.

Meantime, Chasnoff boresighted a Zeke coming down on Andy's tail. Trailing smoke all the way, the Japanese fighter commenced a vertical plunge all the way into the water. Without missing a beat, Jack went after Anderson's original target as soon as Anderson's burning F4U broke off. A quiet, studious, shy young man, Jack Chasnoff was transmuted into a berserker by the apparent loss of his friend. He coldly withheld his fire until he was so close to the Zeke that the cloud of slugs he transmitted simply shredded the fighter into an expanding puff of incandescent bits and pieces— nothing big enough to damage the Corsair as it barreled straight through the mess. Frigidly calm, Jack tilted his nose to see Andy splashing in, apparently uninjured.

As the lead Corsair team chandelled into the sun, Schanuel lost sight of Hedrick thanks to a badly oil-smeared windscreen. After sensibly peeling out to prevent a rear-ender, Mills found himself all alone in the great blue sky. This was a weird but typical outcome of high-speed maneuvering in combat; one second, the sky is filled with dodging, twisting airplanes, and the next it is completely empty. Following long moments of anxious, thorough scanning, Mills prudently turned for home, for, all alone, he was easy meat.

Meantime, Rog had seen the Anderson-Chasnoff brannigan and he, too, searached high and low for Schanuel. Fearing the worst— he had seen Anderson bail out—he dived past Chasnoff and sig- naled "Join up." By then, for them too, the sky appeared to be completely at peace. Heartsick and despairing of two apparent losses, the pair touched down at 1045. They found that Schanuel had gotten in minutes earlier, unhurt but also fearing the worst.

Timmy Gile's attack in the torpedo bombers was equally aggres- sive. Though Timmy and Danny Cunningham apparently missed on their pass, Paul Cordray, the second-element leader, blew his

Kate away with just a short burst. Both pairs lost sight of the evading Kates during their pullouts, so they climbed to 12,000 feet and headed north.

"Tallyho!" Cunningham had something! "Ten fighters headed this way at twelve o'clock, twenty degrees down."

Gile completed three overhead passes in quick succession and Danny, who somehow clung to his tail through strenuous maneuvering, counted three definite flamers. By the time Timmy came around for a fourth attack, the sky was empty and Cordray and Baker were out of sight. Timmy coolly led Cunningham back to their patrol station and circled over the bay for another hour. It's a wonder neither had a coronary due to the rapid deceleration from top-flight excitement to sheer boredom.

As Gile whistled into his first attack on the lead threesome of the six Zekes and four Tonys, Cordray and Baker went after a Tony on the west flank. Cordray missed and pulled up with a pair of Tonys on his tail. Brad Baker failed to materialize altogether. As Cordray climbed through 10,000 feet, the Tonys broke off and headed for Rabaul. They were apparently novices flying close formation without swiveling their heads. Cordray's F4U whipped down and Paul opened fire. The trailing Tony fell away burning and exploded on contact with the surface. Fully alert and eager to draw more blood, Paul spotted a pair of Marine Corsairs shagging several northwest-bound Zekes. He joined in what became a fruitless chase. The three eventually quit and headed back toward the beachhead. On the way, the trio spotted three Tonys, low on the water and heading toward Rabaul. Totally without communication, the Corsair pilots executed a coordinated attack from dead astern of the once-again unwary Imperial Army fighters. Paul's target took violent evasive action, but to no avail. Solidly hit, the Tony skidded right into the water and kicked up a huge splash. The Marines missed their targets and joined with Paul for the trip home, they to Barakoma and Paul to Ondongo.

Hedrick's flight had accounted for seven Zekes, a pair of Tonys, and a Kate. Timmy Gile's three kills had brought him even with the squadron leaders, Kepford and Blackburn, at four apiece.

On the other hand, Fighting-17 had suffered its first losses from the guns of enemy airplanes. We knew that Andy Anderson had gotten down, apparently in one piece, but we had no news on Brad Baker, who had simply vanished while Cordray was busy evading a pair of Tonys. Brad had been forced to ditch on November 11, on the way home from the fight over Task Group 50.3. We knew that if he was down in one piece and functional, he would know what to do, but that did not alleviate the worry.

Eight of us—my division and Butch Davenport's—got airborne at 0345 the next day, November 18. We were to be over Cherry-blossom in time to intercept a possible dawn low-level attack of the sort that had slipped through the beaten up on our transports for several days running. Then, depending on the outcome of our trap, we were to launch an early-morning attack on any barges we could find around Buka. If all went well to that point, we were to fly a routine CAP over Empress Augusta Bay while looking for signs of our two downed pilots and a Marine who also had been shot down on the seventeenth.

This mission marked the beginning of Butch Davenport's reputation and fame. Early on, it had been clear that Butch was a good pilot and a good leader. Moreover, in his capacity as squadron engineering officer, he had contributed mightily to the Hog's emergence as a viable carrier fighter. So far, on the scoring chart, Butch's only contribution had been a one-fourth piece of the Betty his division had downed after much effort on November 6. I expected great things of Butch, and he began to show his true colors.

My earphones came to life as we were nearing Empress Augusta Bay: "Big Hog, this is Butch. Believe I saw a light in the water. Request permission to break off and investigate. Over."

"This is Big Hog. Roger, Butch. Permission granted. Keep me posted. Big Hog out."

As Butch led his division down, my four proceeded to carry out the balance of the mission, which came to absolutely nothing.

The following is quoted from the Fighter Command intelligence report distributed to all the area's squadrons:

> *On the afternoon of 17 November 1943, Lt(jg) R. S. Anderson, USNR, VF-17, was shot down near Cape Torokina. His rescue the next morning is owed to the resourcefulness of Lt M. W. Davenport, USNR, of the same squadron. The pattern of Lt Davenport's procedure follows. It is one which all pilots can study to advantage.*
>
> *Lt Davenport's division of four F4Us took off from Ondongo*

for a dawn strafing attack against Buka. At 0425, while proceeding up the west coast of Bougainville, he sighted a steady light in the water. The division investigated with their landing lights from a low altitude and found an object which might be Anderson afloat. They abandoned their mission, and, while the division circled above, Davenport turned on his emergency IFF [Identification Friend or Foe, a transmitter carried by each plane which displays a distinctive signal on friendly radar] and asked Dane Base [the nearest fighter director station] to take a bearing. It was reported to him as 295 [degrees], distance 32 [miles]. Soon afterward, the light went out, so the division went on patrol over Dane Base, their tertiary mission. As soon as dawn broke they resumed their search for Anderson and found him on their second run over the given course. Dane Base was notified, but no rescue boat [or Dumbo] was available. The division continued to circle above Anderson until fuel shortage forced one section back to Barakoma. Davenport and Lt(jg) Freeman were able to stay on station. Davenport was using [extraordinarily economical engine power and flight technique]. A PT boat finally picked up Anderson at 0900.

Davenport's alertness . . . and skill . . . cannot be too highly recommended. . . . Remember this. . . . It may be a direct means of saving someone's life.

As Butch and his wingman, Lt(jg) Chico Freeman, circled at only 200 feet over Andy in precarious, perilous balance against the laws of physics, Chico decided to help Andy's spirits with a poem and a girly picture. He scrawled the missive on the pad of notepaper strapped to his knee and zippered the sheet and the photo into the canvas pouch with the red streamer pilots used to drop messages to ships under conditions of radio silence. Chico was not much of a poet, but he had a good eye and nearly beaned Andy with the weighted pouch.

When Butch landed, he still had 23 gallons of fuel aboard after 6.75 hours aloft. Such fuel stretching was the result of a lot of experimentation we had undertaken during the boring patrol flights. The news jolted a lot of people into investigating and further developing the Corsair's unrealized operational capabilities.

Adding immeasurably to the legend was one of Andy's comments during a group visit to the sick bay, where he was healing a broken ankle, fractured rib, and a badly wrenched back. When one of the awed troops commented, "Lucky you had that flashlight," Andy recoiled in surprise.

"Lucky I had that flashlight? *What* flashlight? I didn't have any flashlight!" He had somehow neglected to clip his small standard issue waterproof flashlight to his Mae West life jacket.

Unlikely as it seemed, we could only surmise that Brad Baker or the downed Marine had held the light Butch had sighted. Of those two, Brad and the Marine, nothing more was ever heard. Possibly, Brad's luck had simply run out; maybe one unscathed rescue after a ditching was his limit. I fervently prayed that our mate had died at the controls of his Corsair, for, more than most, I knew well the feeling of drifting upon a sea that could suck life's heat from the body. It was terrible to think that the unknown man with the light had heard and seen Butch's division make those first low passes— had clung to life thinking that rescue was only a short time away. There is the story of a miracle in this, and of the cruel balance nature and the Fates imp

We lost Andy to his injuries, for he had to be evacuated to the States to recuperate fully. But at least he was back. He was flying fighters again by the following summer.

20

The ups and downs—days of boring routine missions punctuated by literally only minutes of sudden deadly action—were hard to take. It was difficult to remain in top form so we could fight when we needed to when all we had to do was bore holes in the sky.

On November 19 Fighting-17 undertook five negative two-hour patrols—forty sorties—over Empress Augusta Bay and one negative two-hour patrol—eight sorties—over Munda. November 20 was only marginally more rewarding: four negative two-hour patrols—thirty sorties—over a transport group, a negative two-hour one-division CAP over Munda, and an eight-plane escort mission with a light-bomber strike over Bougainville. The only action on November 20 came when Lt Lem Cooke and Ens Beads Popp smoked a Betty they found on the ground beside the Kara airstrip on their way home. Lem took the incident in stride, but Beads, who had arrived at Ondongo on November 18 following some detached duty on Espiritu Santo, thought he had really found the war.

On November 21 Fighter Command again assented to our proposal that we launch our first CAP mission an hour early to try to catch Japanese raiders bound for a dawn strike against the ships off Torokina. On their way north by 0400 were eight Corsairs led by Butch Davenport. On arrival at Cherryblossom, as agreed to in advance by Butch and his second-division leader, Dirty Eddie March, Davenport's division circled at 3,000 feet between Cape Torokina and volcanic Mt. Bagana while March's flew a northeast-southwest racetrack over the bay at 10,000 feet.

Just as dawn was breaking, Dane Base ordered Dirty Eddie to "Steer two-six-oh, angels twenty." (Butch was having radio problems and did not hear the vector order.)

The division was clawing for altitude when the sun appeared behind them. They had flown 25 miles from their original position when they heard the dreaded, "Base under attack!" (Three bombs dropped by an unseen intruder had detonated in the water off the beach.) The Corsair pilots did not need the follow-on orders that urged them to get back there as fast as they could. Within seconds, Dirty Eddie's four Corsairs were eastbound and angling down at top speed. Suddenly, as March was leading the way through 13,000 feet, a lone Tony flashed into view. It was on an opposite-course heading and going all out. Dirty Eddie tried a snap shot at a closing speed that had to be way over 500 knots. This tough shot was almost always a miss, and he did just that.

In the meantime, Butch, who was leading his foursome in his bushwack position, spotted six Zeros coming in to the beachhead area, so he swung into action. He opened fire on the lead Zeke from four o'clock level. Butch clearly saw his bullets going in; the Zeke did not smoke, but the pilot bailed out. (The injured man, who was later picked up by our PT boats, claimed to have been sent down from Rabaul specifically to find out why so many of their planes were being lost on supposedly safe dawn strafing missions!)

Davenport chandelled out of his first firing pass and found a lone Zeke making a right-angle beam run on his Corsair from 1,000 yards out. Butch turned into the attack, but he passed below the Zeke and could not get his sights on. Butch completed a 360-degree turn preparatory to going after the missed target, which was climbing, but he saw that he could not catch him. He rolled over on his back and dived back into the main melee. At that moment, he saw a Zeke on the tail of his division's tail-end-Charlie, Ens Andy Gump Jagger. Butch instantly tried to get rounds into that Zeke—at least to scare him off. The Zeke pulled up and Butch lost him, but at least Jagger was off the hook. As Butch turned back into the fight yet again, he found a lagging single below at eight o'clock. Almost as soon as Butch opened fire, the Zeke began smoking and pitched violently downward to crash into the bay. Butch followed him virtually the whole way, just to make sure. By then, it was safe to do so; Butch's second kill was the last of the six Zekes.

Lt(jg) Chico Freeman, who was flying 200 yards off Butch's wing, set up his initial firing run on the number three Zeke, but he saw the number two Zeke open fire on Butch, so he shifted targets. A tough shot from three o'clock level produced hits through the Zeke's engine, and the Japanese fighter began an unambiguous final dive straight into the water. By the time the Zeke started its plunge, however, two other Zekes had opened fire from about 75 yards behind Chico's tail. Stomping full rudder, Chico skidded violently to the left. The closer Zeke slid past to port while the wingman broke to the right and climbed steeply away. Chico reversed course to follow the climber. At length, just west of volcanic Mt. Balbi, Chico opened fire from dead astern the Zeke, and his bullets started a fire in the cockpit. He saw a chute blossom from the open cockpit, but the shrouds caught on the tail before it deployed. The Japanese pilot rode the burning fighter all the way into the jungle below.

Lt Ray Beacham, Davenport's second-section leader, successively found his way into fights—several tail chases and one breathtaking head-on duel—but each of the Zekes evaded fatal damage through radical maneuvering. His bullets even sent a Zeke into a steep spiraling dive, but the Japanese fighter recovered. Finally, the Kittyhawk Kid found a Zeke low on the water, heading west. He gave his Hog full throttle and came up on the target's tail. Cutting his speed, Ray opened fire from 100 yards, and the Zeke flew straight into the water. On a hunch, Ray turned back over the floating wreckage of the downed fighter and, sure enough, he spotted a swimmer buoyed up by a black life jacket. He relayed a message through Butch Davenport to call out the local PT boats to grab the swimmer.

Ens Andy Gump Jagger was initially too far out on Beacham's wing when the action started, so he did not join right in. He quickly lost Beacham when the section leader chandelled out of his first firing pass, so he climbed and then dived into the Japanese formation by himself. He made several passes at four Zekes which had by then started to form a Lufbery circle, but all his bullets were wide of the mark. He tried to join another Corsair (Davenport's) that was making a left turn, but he was not yet in position when the other Corsair opened fire at a Zeke crossing his—Jagger's—path. Andy Gump's turn carried him right onto the tail of the Zeke, which had broken off to flee. Jagger instantly got his gunsight pipper on the departing Zeke and pummeled it into a tight, smoking downward spiral. Still 1,000 feet from the surface, the Zeke suddenly burst into brilliant flames and streamed a spectacular black plume until it arced in.

As the unflappable Chico Freeman joined on Davenport to begin the routine CAP that finished out the mission, he radioed Dane Base to put in a bid for the injured Japanese prisoner's gold teeth—in case the man died. Chico's laconic explanation: "I want to make a bracelet for my gal in LA."

The November 21 action blasted Butch Davenport to deserved prominence. He had minutely planned the bounce and had executed it to perfection; his flight had bagged six out of the six Zekes encountered. Equally satisfying was the perfect reformation of the flight for the routine ho-hum patrol that followed. First the Anderson rescue, and now this. Butch was noticed by the front office and marked as a comer.

Tragedy struck the squadron later in what we thought would be a triumphal day.

Six Corsairs under Chuck Pillsbury routinely relieved the midmorning CAP over Empress Augusta Bay, and they flew yet another butt-grinding noon-hour CAP mission until relieved in turn by the early-afternoon flight. All six of Pillsbury's F4Us were directed to strafe targets of opportunity along the Monoitu–Kahili Trail, over which the Imperial Army had been resupplying their ground forces arrayed against the Torokina beachhead. Lt Wally Schub's division was unable to find the Monoitu Mission itself, but the four did expend most of their bullets on bridges and huts along the trail.

Meanwhile, Chuck and his wingman, Ens Bob Hogan, flew an independent course up the jungle-obscured trail and managed to flame five trucks. At about 1300, just before the pair reached Kahili, Hogan idly cut to starboard to pass around 400-foot Kangu Hill. He saw Chuck swing left around the same prominence. Though Bob neither encountered nor saw any signs of antiaircraft fire, that was the last he saw of Chuck. Bob circled offshore and called Chuck on his radio, but there was no response. Bob was by then running low on fuel, so he called the next CAP flight leader, who sent a division up to look for Chuck. No joy.

Fully a quarter century later, Chuck Pillsbury's virtually intact Corsair was located, purely by chance, in the dense jungle near Kangu Hill. Our comrade's remains were still strapped into the cockpit. One .25-caliber rifle bullet had gone through him from below and lodged in his skull. No doubt, Chuck died instantly, before the crash.

The demanding, mostly enervating routine continued unabated for yet another week. We remained busy and alert for the occasional bombing-mission escort, which carried us to potentially livelier locales than Munda or Empress Augusta Bay had become, but no Japanese fighters ever rose to meet us.

It was plain for all to see that the air and naval campaign in the Northern Solomons had reached a successful conclusion. For the rest of November 1943, there were virtually no hostile contacts in the air over the Solomons or Rabaul by Navy or Marine squadrons. Certainly, there were no contacts resulting in claims for Japanese aircraft destroyed or damaged in the air. The only time we got to fire our guns was in the course of strafing missions, and our fighters did encounter some Japanese antiaircraft fire, particularly over the northern airfields.

On November 28 my eleven-plane flight completed a routine two-hour CAP and vectored out to strafe an alleged radio tower at Motupena Point, Bougainville. The target was given top priority for destruction, and all hands were under orders to rake the area around the tower even if no targets were apparent. We were unable to locate the tower—if there was one—but we obediently made numerous firing passes over the indicated coordinates. In the end, after we had expended nearly 1,200 rounds apiece, Doug Gutenkunst reported falling oil pressure, apparently from a hit by an infantry weapon. Doug nursed the ailing Hog with its bullet-riddled oil cooler out over the water in Wilson Strait and then made a dead-stick landing. Doug was picked up within minutes—safely and without injury—by a crash boat.

Ground-strafing missions over wooded terrain had by then become fairly commonplace. The results, however, were always impossible to observe. We rarely found anything that would burn, such as trucks or fuel farms, and, as in the case of the phantom Motupena radio tower, we rarely even precisely located the object of the mission.

Some weeks after Chuck Pillsbury's disappearance and Doug Gutenkunst's dunking, a Japanese infantryman captured near Cape Torokina revealed the probable cause of both losses. Infantry units deployed along trails or other locales that were being routinely strafed by our fighters were under orders to form ranks under cover of the trees and, on command, simultaneously fire their rifles and light machine guns vertically into the air. This shotgun tactic was a neat method for getting the troops to overcome the feeling that they were helpless in the face of our offensive fighter tactics. In the case of Chuck Pillsbury, Doug Gutenkunst, and others, it proved to be a cheap, effective means for swatting the occasional Allied airplane from the skies. As soon as Fighter Command got the interrogation report, all routine strafing runs over wooded terrain were discontinued.

I received word during the last week of November that Fighting-17 was scheduled to go on a slightly premature R&R leave to Australia. I was not about to argue with the bosses in light of the zero action we felt we had been seeing. On December 2 thirty-four of us took off from Ondongo in our own fighters while the rest of the pilots and organic ground personnel followed aboard several gooney birds.

Our first stop was Henderson Field, Guadalcanal, where we could begin to unwind in the comparative luxury of the famous and infamous Hotel de Gink, a pilots' eating and sleeping establishment that dated from the darkest days of the Guadalcanal Campaign. There, we gorged on good *Navy* chow before repairing to the flourishing O Club for drinks, and then on to the nightly movie. Most of us were not yet up to carousing, so we hit the sack early.

Once again, I had the privilege and pleasure of dining with VAdm Jakey Fitch and his staff. This afforded me the opportunity to shoot myself in the foot.

After we had enjoyed our martinis and repaired to the dinner table, Admiral Fitch himself asked a question I was sure he had designed to get The Word to his soft-living staff from a real, hardened combat vet. "Tom, what do the guys up in New Georgia want that we can provide and that they aren't getting?"

Truly serious, I replied, "Admiral, they want beer. Few want to get drunk, but almost everyone had trouble relaxing. Beer would help." Out of the corner of my eye, I saw a scowl on the face of a senior staffer sitting across the table. Did he really expect me to request Parcheesi sets?

"Fair enough," the admiral replied, "We'll see if we can't improve that. The beer we have is not very good, but we have warehouses full of it down in Espiritu. Anything else?"

Feeling that I needed to inject a little levity into the proceeding, I told the admiral that our photoreconnaissance and intelligence boys had pinpointed the location of a cathouse for high-ranking officers on a hill overlooking Rabaul. I allowed as how I would like an opportunity to take the place out as soon as possible after Fighting-17 returned from leave. I gilded the lily a bit by relating the factual data on how Royal Air Force Mosquito light bombers found sport shooting up similar facilities servicing German brass based in France.

ComAirSoPac took this trifle in the spirit in which it had been offered, and he joined in the general laughter that began long before I concluded my half-serious pitch. Not so the owner of that earlier scowl, a senior captain who had been appropriately tagged with the sobriquet, Lord Plushbottom. After dinner, this arrogant, verbose sycophant cornered me well out of earshot of the admiral. He looked at me with warmth akin to that generated by flatulence in a phone booth.

"Blackburn, your off-color remarks at the admiral's table were badly out of place. You and that hooligan squadron of yours are getting a lot of publicity Stateside." (This was news to me, but it turned out that the tireless aircraft publicity departments were pushing us along with their products, our beloved Hogs, their engines, and their propellers.) Plushy continued at full steam, "The headaches you gave Admiral Bellinger around Norfolk with your wild behavior are notorious. Now, what with bearded aces, nonreg attitudes, and despicable actions, you're hitting the headlines as Blackburn's Irregulars. This is painting a picture which reflects no credit on the U.S. Navy, and especially on this command. If you're really harboring ideas of a big publicity stunt like a strike on that alleged whorehouse—and I wouldn't put it past you—I'll see to it that you rue the day."

Plushy had given me more good news than grief, but I kept a straight face and answered, "I understand, Captain." I was neither terrified nor impressed by this prudish popinjay, but I knew that he could have me summarily relieved of my beloved command by making a case with the front office that Fighting-17's actions were the antithesis of those "in keeping with the highest traditions of the U.S. Naval Service." I knew that he would knife me if he could.

But could he? Most probably. We *were* nonreg and freewheeling if not quite the hooligans Plushy made us out to be. Our very real discipline was not apparent to traditionalists of the prewar Navy. Beards we had, in profusion, but they were legitimate per Navy regulations even though few commands tolerated them. Our reputation from the Norfolk days was indeed somewhat gamy, and a few known peccadilloes had been just a hair short of court-martial.

Activities that might not stand the light of day *had* been discreetly conducted. We had transported a significant supply of hard liquor from the States to Ondongo via *Bunker Hill* and *Prince William*, carefully packed in plywood cases labeled "Aircraft Instruments— Fragile." And there was a jeep in Espiritu Santo, complete with squadron insignia, that did not appear on the motor pool records. These were among the skeletons that could make us look unparagonical if they were ever uncloseted. On the other side of the coin, however, was our combat record: 2 small cargo ships destroyed, 11 barges destroyed, 2 Betty bombers destroyed on the ground, and 48.5 Japanese airplanes destroyed in the air. This substantial tally had cost us 3 pilots—still missing, but all in fact dead—2 aircraft downed by enemy aircraft, 3 aircraft downed by ground fire, and 2 aircraft lost in water landings brought on by excessive fuel consumption in combat. These numbers marked VF-17 as a winning team.

With these thoughts, I lost concern about Lord Plushbottom's stuffy reaction to our proper *joie de vivre* and headed for the shucks. In the morning we would take off for Espiritu and then ride out to immerse ourselves and our libidos in the fleshpots of beckoning Australia.

PART V

Fortress Rabaul

21

With no ill will whatsoever toward the wonderful women of Australia, I must say that "Down Under" perfectly describes our two-week bout of unwinding. However, by the time we arrived back at Espiritu Santo on December 15 and 16, all hands were quite ready to take up the profession of arms again.

The first business at hand was wading through the mounds of savored mail that greeted our return to Espiritu. Among the treasured words of our loved ones were reams of newspaper clippings describing exploits of Blackburn's Irregulars in lurid detail, some of which was factual. So, Lord Plushbottom had not misspoken after all; the aircraft companies' publicity flacks had been more than earning their keep the whole time we had been in the forward area. The fact that we all innocently thought the publicity was deserved made us more obnoxious than ever.

For the moment, we faced an uncertain amount of another type of R&R—this one being best described as Regroup and Rearm. Among other chores was the need to inculcate several new arrivals into the mysterious ways of Fighting-17.

One "new" guy we did not have to work over hard was Lt(jg) Bobby Mims, our former bad boy of Manteo and Norfolk. Bobby had sailed with us to Hawaii in October but had been felled by a burst appendix just as we got ashore at Pearl. None of us ever expected to see Bobby again—and many, not including me, were happy with the prospect. Bobby had other thoughts. As soon as he was released from the hospital, he began an all-fronts onslaught against all the regional powers, the object of which was to get himself reassigned to what he later described as "my beloved Fighting-Seventeen." Bobby was more than equipped to make himself a nuisance with which the various staff personnel people had to reckon or go nuts. They reckoned, and Bobby had marched into our temporary squadron office the day after the last of us had departed for Sydney. I was pleased to see Bobby, a superb pilot and a proven aggressive soul.

I was told shortly after my arrival that five new ensigns and jaygees, strangers all, had also reported in during our absence.

However, all had been temporarily shanghaied to help ferry new F6Fs up to the forward area. The five reported in on December 27, and several more reported in over the next four or five days.

We set off with a bang to recoup the finer points of our flying and fighting skills the long layoff had no doubt dulled. On the other hand, our sojourn at Espiritu was far from all work and no play—given the rather limited play facilities. First and foremost for all hands seemed to be the rapid accumulation of restful sack time, "restful" being a trait of sack time I am sure nearly all of us had pointedly eschewed in Australia. We also had no trouble providing ourselves with ample quantities of beer—not the world's best, but good enough. The beach was superb, the surf was perfect, and the weather was uniformly temperate. The local O Club, complete with snack bar, was open every evening, and open-air movies were offered nightly. Feminine companionship was simply not available, but we managed to accept that one shortfall, all the time realizing that most male denizens of the base were years at a time between women.

Tons of fruitcake and shattered cookies—and no end of affection described in a mountain of letters—did not suffice to make Christmas 1943 a happy one. Fortunately, it was a busy time for me. Endless reports had to be churned out and turned in to describe and analyze the combat and other operational actions of our first combat tour. And I had a big hand in bringing up to speed and evaluating all the new kids who continued to dribble in through the latter half of December. I got completely off booze during this period as it had in it the potential for too much self-pity. The hurt from the loss of Johnny Keith, Chuck Pillsbury, and Brad Baker still seared, and the possibly foolish thought, "Where did *I* fail them," kept surfacing.

We made many personnel and leadership changes during our layover in Espiritu. Among the changes was one set off by the unexpected visit of Lt Oc Chenoweth, a plowback instructor at Opa-Locka and, at the time of our reunion, the exec of a small, rather unexcelling Hellcat squadron that had operated out of Segi. I knew what I was in for almost as soon as Oc flashed a forced smile, not at all his own, in my direction one evening at the O Club.

I was fully wired into the scuttlebutt network by then, so I all but perfectly anticipated Oc's opener, once he got around to it:

Ready Room: Schub, Davenport, Chasnoff, March, Kepford, Blackburn, Wharton *(kneeling)*, Kurlander *(kneeling)*, Streig, Hogan.
Odongo, November 15, 1943.

LCdr Roger Hedrick.   Lt Butch Davenport.

Lt Timmy Gile.

R.I.P.: Doug Gutenkunst's grave on Bougainville.

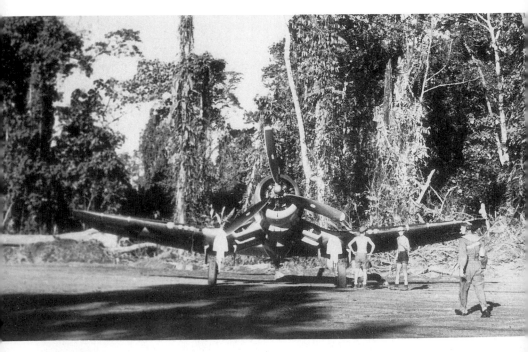

Manning a Hog. Piva Yoke, January 1944.

Ike Kepford and his bent bird. Note the flaps burned by exploding ammunition cans. Piva Yoke, January 31, 1944.

Happy Hour: (standing, l to r) Wharton, Hill, Mims; *(sitting, l to r)* Bitzegaio, Freeman. Piva Yoke, January 1944.

Ens Andy Gump Jagger after a hot mission. Piva Yoke, January 1944.

Crude facilities, gorgeous s roundings. Fighter Pilots' Car Bougainville, January 1944.

Ready to Go: (standing, l to March, Gilbert, Schub; (knee ing, l to r) Wharton, Jagge Bitzegaio. VF-17 Ready Roon January 1944.

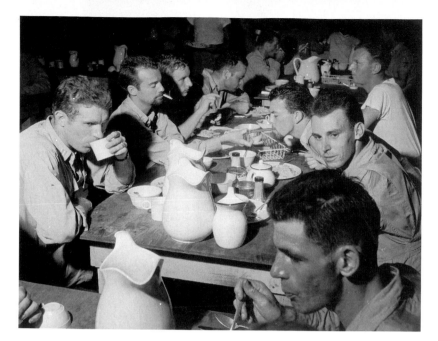

Pilot's Mess: (l to r) March, Henning, Bitzegaio, Meek, Dr. Hermann, Freeman *(with cigar)*, Peterson, Gile. Bougainville, January 1944.

"Honest, Duke!" In typical fighter-pilot fashion, Danny Cunningham relates details of his killingest mission to Duke Henning. Piva Yoke, February 19, 1944.

"Ike's Back!" Ike Kepford returns from his epic tail chase after downing three Japanese fighters. Piva Yoke, February 19, 1944.

F4U Bomb Rig: This model, similar to the one developed by VF-17 in late 1943, was first used by Marine Corsairs in the Marianas in March 1944.

Top Gun: Lt (jg) Ira C. Kepford the first US Navy pilot to sco sixteen confirmed kills.

Fighting-17. Espiritu Santo, October 1943. *Front Row:* Schub, Wharton, Gile, Killefer, Kropf, Jagger, Cordray, Davenport. *2nd Row:* Burriss, Baker, Jackson, Kleinman, Hedrick, Blackburn, Hogan, Bowers. *3rd Row:* Cooke, Anderson, Meek, Malone, Chasnoff, Schanuel, Ellsworth, Beacham, Freeman, Cunningham, Kurlander, Hill, Keith, Landreth, Bell. *Top Row:* Dunn, Gutenkunst, March, Halford, Gilbert, Henning, Kelley, Kepford, Streig, Pillsbury, May, Hall, Popp. *Missing:* Innis. Of the forty-three pilots manning the squadron prior to first combat, ten were killed while serving with VF-17.

Simpson Harbor, Rabaul, just after the attack of November 5, 1943. Moments after this picture was taken the photographer was killed when this TBF was attacked by a Zero.

The skull-and-crossbones insignia of VF-17 is still aloft in today's Navy.

"Tommy, I want to talk with you about a problem we're having in the squadron."

I nodded, perhaps a touch wearily, for him to go on. "We have a good bunch of guys, but we can't take our son-of-a-bitch skipper any longer. He bugs us day and night. He lays our lack of combat success on the people flying with him, but we all know bloody well who screws up. God, I hear talk of shooting him down before he gets one of us killed. Will you talk to Fighter Command for us?"

I was in full accord with Oc, but Fighting-17 was not directly affected. I thus felt that I would be way off base if I got directly involved. "Oc, I know it isn't kosher, and you might get your butt fried for it, but I recommend that you go see Colonel Brice. Tell him privately what you just told me. The colonel is a square shooter and will respect your guts. I'm sure he won't put your head on the block for doing what you feel is best for the troops and the war effort. But I have to warn you; if Brice sees fit to can your skipper, he's going to can you, too—make a clean sweep before putting in a new man. I'm sure he won't fleet you to command the squadron. If he gets that far, you tell him that you've spoken with me and I will be more than pleased to have you in VF-17."

And that is exactly the way it happened, with one pretty major addition: Colonel Brice asked me to recommend a replacement CO for the F6F squadron. Rog and I concurred that Lem Cooke was a natural. Lem and I had never become close, but I had come all the way around in my respect and admiration for his flying and leadership skills. It was a good choice; the unhappy outfit was completely rehabilitated with Lem's warm but firm hand on the helm. And we benefitted by enrolling another "castoff."

On the debit side of the ledger was the special case of Lt(jg) Jack Chasnoff. I was fond of this gentle man, a highly proficient, gutty pilot, but the loss of his dear friend and alter ego, Andy Anderson, during the November 17 air battle had left Jack a shaken, chastened man, and he had been going downhill physically since. I convened an informal board to discuss his future. Rog, Duke, and Dr. Herrmann unanimously agreed with my assessment that we would all benefit if he went home. I called Jack in for a heart-to-heart. As expected, he was understandably reluctant to leave, but I eventually brought him around to our view, and he agreed to take the Stateside Training Command assignment I proposed to him. Above all, I assured him that the transfer was no reflection on his courage or integrity, as heartfelt a bit of news as ever I uttered.

While disdainful of the Army Air Forces in general and their horizontal bombing in particular, we had noted with great admiration the development by 5th Air Force B-25s of the technique known as "skip bombing." This consists of a high-speed run, with all the forward machine guns blazing, at masthead height—or below—and the release of bombs just as the bomber pulls up to get over the target. Just as a flat stone skips off the surface of a lake, the bomb skips off the surface of the ocean to impact against the target vessel's side. As a further refinement, the bombs were equipped with delayed-action fuses so they would breach the hull of the target before detonating and after the attacker has flown clear. The accuracy rate was phenomenal; apparently, the bombs sometimes missed, but getting them to do so was not easy.

We had first heard of the skip-bombing technique around the middle of our first combat tour. Immediately, our heads filled with sugarplum dreams of nailing a fat Japanese tanker. Thus, during our last days at Ondongo, Butch Davenport, Timmy Gile, and I spent a good deal of time devising a way for our Hogs to lug bombs. At length, we settled on a modification of the catapult-hook structure.

All carrier aircraft have catapult hooks, which are attachment points for the loops of heavy wire that comprise the catapult "bridle." The bridle is the connector to the "shuttle," the business portion of the slingshot arrangement which accelerates the airplane from 0 to 80 knots in a few short feet. Manifestly, the cat hooks have to be attached to the main strength members of the airplane.

As with our tail hooks, we had no use for the cat hooks on land. So we unbolted the starboard hook of a spare old-model Hog and replaced it with a substantial steel plate. To this, our metal benders attached a standard bomb rack plus unstreamlined but adequate steel pipe for sway bracing. The ordnance gang worked up the arming and release rig to and in the cockpit.

Timmy and I both found the installation completely successful during several test hops, and we ordered up a total of eight bomb racks. However, the project went on a back burner for lack of potential targets within reasonable reach of Ondongo. While we were at Espiritu, however, we dusted off the jury-rigs and began further testing with the expectation of developing a surefire technique for scoring bomb hits from our Hogs.

While eight of our Hogs were being retrofitted with the new water-injection version of our standard Pratt & Whitney engines, Cdr Emerson Fawkes, the local Aircraft Overhaul and Repair Facility boss, heard of our homegrown bomb rack rigs. His first reaction was, "Tommy, it ain't safe," but I managed to talk him into taking a personal interest. He agreed to get eight good adapter rigs designed and built, then pushed the project with the Fleet Air operations section, and won an early approval. The eight jury-rigs thus were replaced in short order by a like number of properly engineered versions. We flight-tested the new ones and, when they had proven out, we had them preserved and packed to take with us on our return to the forward area.

A lot of fighting was in progress up the line, and we were both ready and eager to get in on it. Since we had no word about our next deployment by the end of the first week of January, I grabbed Doug Gutenkunst to accompany me on a quick hop up to Henderson Field so I could learn more or begin my politicking, whichever applied. I was greeted at AirSoPac headquarters by Capt Al Morehouse, who heard me out before launching his own typically patient pitch: "Tom, we know you're rarin' to go and I wondered when you'd show up squalling. We're as anxious to get you back to work as you are to be back, but we're in a big state of transition. Flight ops are moving up to Bougainville. Right now, we only have the little emergency strip the Seabees put in at Torokina, but they're at work on a big bomber strip and an adjacent fighter strip. We except to have both of the new strips running in a few weeks, and we will be moving squadrons in beginning January 24. We have Fighting-Seventeen slated to be among the first squadrons to operate off the new fighter strip. In fact, we're about ready to issue formal orders." Then, with a renewed, knowing smile, "I guess I don't have to ask if you'll be ready. Huh?"

We had about two weeks to get fully up to speed again. The time went by in a whirlwind of activities too varied and numerous to recall. We experienced a high and annoying level of personnel turbulence during the period, with all sorts of new blood joining

and departing. I must admit to being the prime source of the
departures. We had no way of selecting rookies other than trying
them out and retaining or detaching them based on admittedly
hurried assessments of their aggressive traits and flying skills. The
result was that we did get rid of a few tyros we thought would not
cut it, but we also wound up taking a few such back to the forward
area because they arrived late and were not adequately evaluated.
Fortunately, all the newcomers arrived with experience in cast-off
old-model F4Us that had found their way to Training Command.

We lost two of our fighters which were totally destroyed in
training accidents, but neither of the pilots was severely injured.

Fortunately, the comings and goings—except for the Cooke-
Chenoweth trade—had zero impact on my flight- and division-
leader assignments. Unlike many squadrons, the operational
leadership jobs were not assigned in strict conformity with seniority; rank was, at best, secondary. Thus, the five other flight leaders
were Rog Hedrick, Butch Davenport, Dirty Eddie March, Timmy
Gile, and Thad Bell. The division leaders were Tom Killefer, Oc
Chenoweth, Earl May, Paul Cordray, Ike Kepford, and Wally
Schub. Several of these division leaders could easily fleet up to lead
flights, and there were several section leaders who could certainly
get their shots at being division leaders.

The last truly important piece of business before our January 24
departure was the headache we had given ourselves by amassing
148 cases of beer in the giant Quonset hut I shared with Rog
Hedrick. How in the world were we going to get the cache from
Espiritu to Bougainville?

We had had ample luck during our Ondongo tour at transporting
the odd case of hard booze. Typically, camouflaged cases would be
marked "Electronics Equipment—Fragile," and we got them delivered with no difficulty. But 148 cases of beer was too much to even
think of masking within that scheme, and we *knew* that sending it
aboard a ship would result in a total loss.

At virtually the last minute, our great Supply Corps outwitter,
Lt(jg) Hal Jackson, arrived on my doorstep with a catbird grin—
and a solution.

"Skipper! Rog! I got it! I got it!"

What is this jaygee doing here? "Got what?"

"How to get the beer to Bougainville!"

I was all attention. "Bless your bones, you crook. How?"

With rather studied indignation, Hal stared me down, "I am not a crook!" But the catbird grin came on again. "I'm just alert."

"So give!"

"Well, the most planes we've ever had in one flight in the forward area was twenty-four. And we did alright. Right?"

"Hal, press *on!*"

He did, with great fervency. "The flight going up to Bougainville will be the whole squadron. We'll never in God's world get jumped. But if we do, wouldn't four guns per plane and two hundred rounds per gun be plenty?"

"Jackson," I beamed as I saw his ploy, "I apologize for calling you a crook. You're a bloody *genius!* I'll have Duke write you up for a Legion of Merit."

That very day—within minutes, actually—we were out on the flight line figuring out the best and safest way to stow the beer cases in the huge ammunition cans. It was clear after a quick trial that we had room for all 148 cases.

On January 24 we flew the last hour to Bougainville at 25,000 feet. As we shut down on our hardstands at our base, each pilot solemnly handed a new church key to his Marine plane captain and bade him fetch and open two ice-cold cans of beer from one of the ammo cans in the wings. What an attention getter!

—————— 22 ——————

The air war in the Solomons had taken a dramatic and decisive turn during Fighting-17's seven weeks in the rear area: The Japanese had gone over to an all but totally defensive mode. Moreover, their goals were extremely limited; they had given up the defense of their surviving bases on Bougainville in favor of conserving their declining resources for the defense of Rabaul against our inevitable direct onslaught.

By December 1943, the campaign in the Solomons had taken on a completely predictable pattern: As we seized or built new air bases, we launched progressively larger air assaults against those Japanese bases that came within our newly extended reach. They responded with aerial counterthrusts which we eventually and inevitably overcame. At length, we launched a new amphibious assault aimed at winning ground for yet new air bases. They attacked the new beachhead, and we proceeded to beat them at sea and in the air. This vital "stepping-stone" strategy had thus far carried us from Guadalcanal to the Russell Islands, to the New Georgia group, to Bougainville. Based on past performance, everyone—we and they—reasonably assumed that Rabaul would be softened up for the inevitable direct amphibious assault.

In late 1943 or very early 1944, it was firmly decided to cordon off Rabaul and employ it as a focus upon which the Japanese could expend irreplaceable ships, planes, pilots, and, indeed, ground-combat forces. Rabaul was not to be assaulted by our ground forces because the cost would inevitably be enormous and the strategic gain minimal. Maintaining the mere *threat* of imminent assault would do the job. In fact, the same principle applied to the remaining Japanese bases on Bougainville; they would be assaulted only from the air. They and Rabaul would, in the words of the Commander in Chief of the U.S. Fleet, Adm Ernest King, be left to "wither on the vine." Unfortunately for many pilots and aircrewmen, a credible threat could be maintained only by means of an unremitting air offensive.

Our side used December 1943 and most of January 1944 to build up its air-assault force. Not coincidentally, perhaps, the lull in which we had found ourselves in late November had deepened until only the occasional Japanese snooper or night bomber was tracked by our radar and sent burning into the sea by target-hungry fighter jocks. The pickings were slim because the Japanese temporarily had no air assets to do more than harass our buildup on Bougainville. At the same time, until we could move adequate light bombers and fighters up to Bougainville, Rabaul—the only target the Japanese would surely defend in strength—was out of range to all but our medium and heavy land-based bombers. Our only other possible means for effectively hitting Rabaul—the carriers—were busy farther north, striking blows against shipping, airfields, and support facilities in the Marshall and Caroline island groups.

On December 10 our new Torokina fighter strip got its first permanently based air unit, the seventeen Corsairs of VMF-216, a fresh and unblooded unit. Within the week, as fuel and ordnance stocks were built up, hundreds of fighter missions were flying from or staging through the Torokina strip to undertake strikes and sweeps to the north. In addition, the Corsair night fighters of LCdr Gus Widhelm's VF(N)-75 were moved from Munda, as were the twin-engine three-man PV-1 night fighters of VMF(N)-531.

The establishment of the new Bougainville air bases gave rise to a new command echelon, Aircraft, Northern Solomons (AirNorSols), a direct subordinate of AirSols. While we were gone, the command of AirSols had passed from Army MGen Nathan Twining to Marine MGen Ralph Mitchell. ComAirNorSols was also a Marine, BGen Field Harris; he set up shop at Torokina as soon as our transports could land there. Working directly under General Harris were the old Fighter and Strike Command teams, including my boss, Col Oscar Brice. They also moved forward to Bougainville and set up shop at Torokina pending the completion of the new light-bomber and fighter strips—Piva Uncle and Piva Yoke, respectively.

While Rabaul itself was never to be directly assaulted, the Allies did have several amphibious assaults scheduled to go in elsewhere on New Britain. The first of these went off on December 15, when a reinforced U.S. Army regiment landed at Arawe, far to the east of Rabaul, on New Britain's southern coast. Interestingly, the Arawe landings were seen by our side as being an extension of Gen

Douglas MacArthur's New Guinea offensive, and not as a contin-
uation of the Solomons campaign. In any case, the landings at
Arawe understandably drew some Japanese attention away from
Rabaul's immediate plight.

The Arawe landings and the main show—a landing by 1st Marine Division at Cape Gloucester, New Britain's western cape, on
December 26—were supported exclusively by the New Guinea-
based 5th Air Force and associated Allied air units. AirSols had no
part in the two New Britain landing operations, but we benefited
from them in that the Rabaul-based 11th Air Fleet (Imperial Navy)
and 4th Air Army (Imperial Army) were temporarily sucked out
west to oppose them. Whatever losses the Japanese sustained over
western New Britain naturally accrued to the advantage of the
AirSols forces.

The first Bougainville-assisted strike against Rabaul took place on
December 17, when a large fighter force took off from several New
Georgia-area bases to stage through Torokina. The flight leader
was Marine Maj Greg Boyington, the twenty-kill ace commanding
VMF-214. His strike group comprised thirty Marine Corsairs,
twenty-three New Zealand P-40s from Ondongo, and twenty-
three Navy Hellcats. This was strictly a fighter sweep; no bombers
were included. As similar missions had done over time at Kahili in
mid-1943, this and future fighter sweeps over Rabaul were aimed at
demoralizing the enemy by destroying his fighter force.

The Japanese had radar coverage of the approaches to Rabaul,
plus radio-equipped spotters in the hills overlooking our Bougainville runways. Nevertheless, apparently they were caught completely unaware. The only opposition the raiders found airborne
over the target was a lone Rufe, a single-float Zero variant. It and
two of forty scrambling Zekes were blown out of the sky. In all,
during the forty minutes Boyington's fighters remained over Rabaul, the Japanese got seventy of their fighters airborne, but the
Japanese pilots largely evaded the smaller Allied fighter force. It
was said that Boyington even taunted the Japanese on a radio
channel he knew they used, but to no avail. In all, the New
Zealanders got five Zekes, a VF-33 pilot got one, and a Marine got
credit for the Rufe. On the other hand, three of the P-40s were
downed with the loss of two pilots killed.

The tempo and strength of our new AirSols offensive against
Rabaul picked up over the remainder of December and on into

January. Our losses were heavy, but so were our gains. At length, the Japanese again stripped their carriers of aircraft, mainly fighters, and built up to a high of about three hundred operational aircraft deployed around Rabaul's five airfields. They were able to maintain that number more or less through the period by stripping replacements from operational squadrons throughout the Pacific and, indeed, from the home islands themselves.

On December 24 several of our cruisers and destroyers directly bombarded the Buka-Bonis complex in northern Bougainville. As a result of this and a similar earlier bombardment, the Buka-Bonis complex was written off by the Japanese.

On Christmas day *Bunker Hill* and light carrier *Monterey* launched all available strike aircraft against Kavieng, the big air-base and shipping complex at the northeastern end of New Ireland which served as a stepping-stone for warplanes transiting between Rabaul and Truk. Succeeding carrier strikes against warships based at Kavieng—on January 1 and 4, 1944—met with heavier opposition and less positive results, but they did have the effect of drawing off at least 10 percent of the fighters that would have met our land-based strikes over Rabaul. After the January 4 strike, however, our carriers departed for the Central Pacific, and Kavieng was not further molested.

The first land-based light-bomber strike against Rabaul staged through Torokina on January 5, but it aborted in the face of a solid wall of heavy weather over the target. A repeat effort on January 7—the first to stage through Piva Uncle—met a similar fate and also aborted. There was some fighter action over Rabaul, and twelve enemy fighters were claimed against the loss of three Hellcats. Two of the SBDs crashed on the way back to their base.

The first successful light-bomber strike took place on January 9, when twenty-three Munda-based SBDs and sixteen Munda-based TBFs staged through Piva Uncle to hit Tobera airfield. The forty Japanese fighters launched to intercept the raid hung back until after the bombers had gone in, and they were engaged by the sixty-two-fighter escort. Our fighters claimed thirteen kills against the loss of one F6F and two P-40s. Only seven bombers were damaged, all by ground fire, and only one of those ditched.

The January 9 strike—rated a success by all interested parties on our side—set the pace for most of the rest of the air offensive against

Rabaul. Coordinated dive-bombing and glide-bombing missions were undertaken just about every other day by one or two squadrons each of Marine SBDs and TBFs armed with 500-, 1,000-, or 2,000-pound bombs. On intervening days, Rabaul-area targets were hit by Munda-based B-25s and Munda- or New Guinea-based B-24s dropping 500-, 1,000-, or 2,000-pound bombs from high and medium altitudes.

All bombing raids were escorted by large forces of Allied fighters. In all cases, about a dozen New Zealand P-40s provided "very low" cover right over the bombers—mainly because they demonstrated execrable performance characteristics above around 14,000 feet. Most of the cover—stacked above the hapless P-40s—was provided by fifty or sixty Corsairs and Hellcats. Sometimes, P-38s accompanied B-24s from New Guinea bases. If so, they provided "very high" top cover. The only thing we saw of the P-38s was an early shower of their belly tanks. I don't know that any Japanese fighters were downed in any such debris storms, but they almost bagged me a few times.

The Corsairs and Hellcats were normally stacked in three flights of up to twenty each at 1,000- to 3,000-foot intervals above the bombers—low, medium, and high cover. On the approach to the target, as the entire mass of fighters and bombers neared an area that might be covered by enemy fighters, all the fighters accelerated from the cruising run-in speed of the bombers to 160–70 knots or more. This provided greater maneuverability and made it easier for the fighters to get to maximum speeds if need be.

The large increment of speed the fighters had over the bombers was compensated by a sinuous pattern of S-turns and weaves which allowed the fighters to keep proper position relative to the slower airplanes they were defending. The weave was a development of the familiar Thach Weave by which pairs of fighters and elements defended one another in combat—our analog of the defensive vertical scissors employed by Japanese fighters when they were under attack. Thus, in addition to slowing our relative speed as against that of the bombers, the weave also protected the vulnerable rear hemisphere of the fighter group. In addition to its other contributions, the continuous weaving vastly increased our visual scanning capabilities in our never-ending search for oncoming enemy fighters.

As the SBDs rolled into their dives and the TBFs angled down to begin their glides, the low and medium Corsair or Hellcat flights went down slightly ahead and so provided some measure of flak suppression by long-range strafing. At the same time, the high cover maintained its relative position about 4,000 feet above the strike bombers.

The best part about the entire strike technique was that it had been refined and proved effective earlier in the war, over Kahili and Buka. That knowledge increased everyone's faith in the outcome.

The early AirNorSols bombing raids against Rabaul, undertaken in the weeks before we returned to the fray, pointed up a stupefying weakness in the Japanese pattern of defense. From the outset—Boyington's December 17 fighter sweep—the fighters charged with defending Fortress Rabaul had been generally unwilling to accept the challenge of our fighters. So doing, they did not bother the relatively vulnerable light bombers during the run-in. After dropping their payloads, the bombers were usually strung out, scattered, and lacking tight fighter cover; they and the fighters were most vulnerable at this point, seemingly easy meat for the waiting fighters. Thus, most of the action occurred after the strike groups passed over the target and left the major portion of the AA fire astern. However, the Japanese proved to be base-bound—that is, they almost never followed our departing bomber formations much beyond the coastline—not even to bag easy kills against damaged, unescorted stragglers. Hundreds of our bomber pilots and crewmen owed their lives to this last oversight, for even a ditched crew had an excellent chance of getting home alive aboard an unmolested, closely escorted Dumbo.

We studied the emerging action from afar, using the closing weeks of our rest period to pore over reports and question veterans who happened to be passing through. We drew some early conclusions and concocted an innovation or two, but, for the most part, we wanted to get a strike or two under our belts before making up our minds.

On January 24, as promised, thirty-four of us took off from Espiritu and flew our Hogs to Guadalcanal to refuel. We all arrived safely at Piva Yoke by 1700 and, after sharing some of our beer, left the Hogs to our Marine ground crewmen while we went off to inspect our new home.

One of the first new experiences we had to get used to was the frequent *boom-swish* of outgoing artillery fire. The Torokina beach-head was enclosed in a 10-mile-diameter perimeter because the landings had never been intended to sweep the Japanese from all of Bougainville, but merely to provide room and protection for the Torokina and two Piva runways. Thus, as we soon learned with some trepidation, the active ground war still ebbed and raged only a few miles from our new home. Well, as long as the unsettling artillery eruptions were all outgoing . . .

The first contingent of our ground echelon was flown in the next day, January 25. On that day, also, we were told that thirty-two of us—nearly the entire squadron—were scheduled to accompany a mixed SBD-TBF strike against Lakunai airfield, overlooking Rabaul's Simpson Harbor, the next morning, January 26.

23

We expected our January 26 debut over Rabaul to be rough. The Japanese did nothing to disappoint us.

The SBDs made their run-in from the east at 14,000 feet, across the southern tip of New Ireland and on to a position just to the northeast of Lakunai airfield. The attack was delivered from approximately north to south, and the SBDs retired down the channel to a rally point five miles east of Cape Gazelle. VF-17 provided medium and high cover, that is we were positioned in two sixteen-plane flights at about 16,000 and 19,000 feet during the run-in. The Japanese interceptors, mostly Zekes and numbering fifty to sixty, initially were positioned from 15,000 to 21,000 feet.

As we crossed over St. George Channel to Crater Peninsula, we transitioned from the high tension of anticipation to the frantic activity of a one-legged man in an ass-kicking contest.

My division, which was part of the medium cover, was not jumped before the dive-bombers turned their noses down 60 degrees and hurtled groundward. As was standard procedure, we dived with the SBDs but remained slightly ahead of them so we could do our bit to help suppress the murderous AA rising from around the airfield. We started shooting as we passed through 8,000 feet, and we kept pouring out bursts until we leveled off at around 4,000 feet. The stream of SBDs dropped their bombs from 2,000 feet and recovered at about 1,000 feet as they headed for the rally point 10 miles to the south.

We encountered our first defender north of Rapopo airfield, a lone Zeke that made a head-on run at our level. My bullets hit him, first in the engine and then apparently in the wing root. He passed under me smoking and splashed in off Matupi Island.

I was an ace, Fighting-17's first.

After exchanging several unsuccessful snap shots with several other Zekes, Doug Gutenkunst finally nailed one of the Imperial Navy fighters from dead astern as it tried to get in among the SBDs. As Doug followed his flamer, another Zeke tried to set up on Doug with a low-side run. Doug was quick to discern the danger and honked his Hog around into a violent vertical bank. This put him in position to make a beautiful deflection shot at no more than 100 yards. The victim blew up. As Doug and I rejoined to assume position above the Dauntlesses, we saw that the opposition was keeping its distance from us.

Tom Killefer's four, which were flying as my second division, had a far rougher time. They dived down with us ahead of the SBDs, but almost immediately as soon as the AA on the ground opened fire, I saw a Corsair lose a wing to the intense fire. Several of our guys saw Bob Hogan's chute blossom, but no one was able to follow him down. Bob was never seen again. Hogan's wingman, Andy Gump Jagger, was caught by a pair of Zekes. He took a 20mm explosive round in his wing but survived by means of some very fancy maneuvering. He managed to rejoin the reforming group, and his tattered Corsair carried him home, albeit with some difficulty.

TK and Lt(jg) Jim Farley, one of the more promising new pilots, were jumped by six Zekes during the retirement over Blanche Bay. Tom missed a Zeke that was making a steep firing pass on the pair. The Japanese fighter followed through and hit Farley's Corsair, which crashed. The Zeke pilot erred when he pulled out into a vertical climb. TK had anticipated the maneuver, and he nailed him before joining on Doug and me.

Rog Hedrick was leading the top-cover flight at 19,000 feet when the SBDs and lower fighter flights began the attack. During the final approach phase, Rog's flight was jumped by eight Zekes screaming down from 22,000 feet. However, those Imperial Navy pilots did not press their attack. Even hawk-eyed Rog was unable to score discernible hits with a brief long-range burst.

Minutes later, as Rog's flight passed through 16,000 feet in concert with the dive-bombers, Windy Hill's Corsair took several 20mm hits which chewed up its left aileron and most of its tail surfaces. Windy spun down to 9,000 feet, recovered, and headed home alone. When he arrived, he had to make a high-speed, no-flaps landing. The wounded bird got away from him a moment after touchdown and flipped. The plane was totaled and Windy wound up in the hospital with a severe head gash. He was flying again the following week.

Minutes after Hill was shot out of the formation, Rog Hedrick suddenly found himself all alone. As he headed for the rally point, he encountered three single Zekes in quick succession. Each of them shot at Rog, and missed. Then, as Rog approached the SBDs, three more Zekes crossed ahead of his nose, setting up to hit the rendezvousing dive-bombers. Rog tailed in, but the Zeke pilots saw him and all three sharply pulled up. Rog coolly opened fire on the leader at the top of the latter's climb, then followed the burning debris most of the way to the deck. As soon as the Zeke crashed, he climbed back up, joined a Marine loner, and took up station above the retiring bomber gaggle. That was Rog's fourth *official* kill, but most of us believe it was his seventh *real* kill—at least.

Paul Cordray's division, which was the second in Rog's flight, was attacked by the same gaggle of Zekes that had initially feinted at Rog's division. Paul missed his first target, and a Zeke got solid hits into Cordray's wingman, Lt(jg) Jamey Miller. Jamey, who was superficially wounded, spun out and fell to 6,000 feet before recovering while Cordray stayed right with him all the way down. The two found themselves in clear sky, so they headed for the rally point. On the way, just north of the rendezvous, the two were challenged by eight Zeros. Cordray flamed one of the Zekes with a clean tail shot and followed through with a head-on pass at a second, although with unobserved results. As Paul opened fire on the first Zeke, Jamey got another in his sights and sent him down in flames. Meantime, Paul chandelled out of his second firing run and worked into a nice set-up from six o'clock high on another Zeke. His bullets drew smoke and flame, but the Zeke pulled clear by means of a violent evasive maneuver. When last seen, he was smoking but flying back toward the base. With that, Cordray and Miller rejoined the bombers.

Timmy Gile's flight of eight, part of my medium-cover group, came under fire from six Zekes as it started down with the SBDs. Timmy's troops successfully evaded the intrusion with no ill effects and leveled out at 7,000 feet. As Timmy led his entire flight straight into the widening melee over Rapopo, he missed each of three successive targets, but he set the fourth afire. Next, a dozen Japanese fighters bored right in after Timmy, and one of them got ample rounds into his wingman, Ens John Malcolm Smith. Gile turned in to Smitty's attacker, who broke off his pass and headed home with his mates in train. Smitty's hydraulic system was destroyed, but he managed a safe extremely exciting landing at Piva Yoke.

*   *   *

By all standards, January 26 was Fighting-17's grimmest day so far, an understandable but nonetheless sad outcome of our first tangle over Fortress Rabaul. We had two pilots missing, but neither ever turned up. One pilot, Miller, had been slightly wounded and another, Hill, was in the hospital with head injuries. We lost three airplanes, and five others had sustained repairable damage.

On the plus side, our mission had been a success in that none of the SBDs charged to our care had sustained any damage. In addition, we got credit for eight confirmed Zero kills, one probable kill, and one Zeke damaged.

The loss of two comrades on our first day back shook Fighting-17 to its core. Our rather gloomy happy-hour conversation revolved around variations on the same theme: We faced six weeks in the forward area, and most of our flight time would be spent on missions to Rabaul; if we continued to lose two a day, we would all be dead in only nineteen more days; if we averaged "only" one loss per day, one of us would survive to tell the tale.

I kept thinking that it couldn't possibly be as bad as all that. In the first place, Farley had been a new guy on his first combat hop; at least in part, his inexperience had surely contributed to his death. Hogan, an old hand, a steady if not spectacular pilot, had been downed by a freakish hit that sheared his right wing. That sort of thing was always a possibility in the face of intense ground fire, but it had to be realistically classed as a random event. Or was I kidding myself? Were we locked in a game of attrition we could not possibly overcome?

The good news was that everyone appeared to have made all the right moves. Sections and divisions maintained cohesion as well as they could, or regained it. Everyone knew where the rally point was, and everyone but Hill, in his critically damaged Hog, rendezvoused there. All the training and experience were clearly paying off.

It remained to be seen if our adversaries would get their defensive act together. After enduring fighter and bomber strikes for nearly six weeks, the opposition was still clearly reticent to challenge us in any meaningful way. They certainly could outnumber us over the target on any given day, but they chose to launch interceptors in numbers roughly equal to our cover flights, and to deliver piecemeal or incomplete attacks. Everything I had heard on the subject before the January 26 mission was seen to be true by one or another of us that day. One new and potentially dangerous twist I thought I perceived on January 26 was a hitherto unreported willingness on the part of some Japanese formations to risk being hit by their own AA as they delivered unswerving attacks on our diving bombers and fighters. This could be accounted for by the well-recognized ongoing piecemeal commitment of new units to the defense of Rabaul; clearly some of the new units were better trained, more aggressively led, or less demoralized than the norm. If we found many more such over the next few weeks, than we really did face a serious prospect of heavy losses.

I had some solutions, some innovations, some thoughts I wanted to try out, but one mission hardly embraced a trend. As I had before leaving Espiritu, I decided to hold off on anything new until we had more experience.

After this mission, we did the usual debrief while wetting our whistles with some of the beer we had flown in from Espiritu. Just what we needed to simmer down from the extreme tension of a tough combat flight. We were still hot and sweaty from the hop as we tooled out to the jeep for the mile-plus ride from our ready room Quonset hut to the fighter pilots' camp.

I took the wheel as nine more piled on—four inside and five manning the rear bumper, running boards, and hood. We were still pretty wound up and eager to strip down for a long, cold shower, change into fresh khakis, get some chow, and hopefully catch a nap.

The road crossed the south end of the fighter strip, so someone carefully checked for aircraft before I proceeded at the overloaded jeep's best speed. As I slowed to eyeball the runway-approach airspace, we were confronted by a very young Army MP in crisp, starched khakis, MP brassard, nightstick, police whistle on a lanyard, and *white* gloves. We were all gaping at this specimen when it held up a gloved hand in an imperious "Stop" signal. I braked and leaned out. "Hi! What can I do for you?"

"Sir, you can't proceed with more than four people in a jeep. This is the limit allowed by regulations. Carrying more than four is not safe. All these extra officers will have to dismount and walk."

All the guys aboard the jeep were big. Many had fearsome beards. We were all lean and mean. A lot of us habitually carried .45-caliber pistols at all times. Four of the bearded ruffians wordlessly dismounted and advanced on the 5'6", 125-pound representative of law and order. The soldier paled visibly, but stood his ground. Though annoyed, I was concerned that the pilots would dismember him, so I quickly and loudly hollered, "Hey! Knock it off! Get back aboard. Now!"

As the pilots backed off, I turned to the shaken doggie. "Son, this jeep is the only transport we have. I know that you have your orders, but, as your superior officer, I'm countermanding them for now. We're going to proceed as before. I'll take it up with the provost marshal."

"Okay, Commander, but I'll have to report you for the violation."

"Certainly, son, you do that."

I never heard a peep from on high, and we were never bothered again.

Early on January 27, twenty-four of us, forty-five Marine Corsairs, and twelve New Zealand P-40s took off to escort twenty-four B-25s to Lakunai. The medium bombers were to hit in two equal squadron waves from 12,000 feet.

Japanese fighter interception of the lead bomber squadron was desultory. Wally Schub was leading his four just above the P-40s, which were in close-cover position with the bombers. About twenty of the Marine F4Us were stacked in divisions to 19,000 feet. Only one Zeke pilot had the temerity to press home an attack against the bombers. He flew right into Schub's sights and acquired crippling hits that blew off large parts of his fuselage. However, the Zeke did not burn or smoke and, since it appeared to fly from the sight under its pilot's control, Wally properly claimed a probable.

The second B-25 squadron and its escorts bore the full brunt of the Japanese reaction. Immediately after "Bombs away," sixty to eighty Zekes and Hamps attacked with a hitherto unknown ferocity.

Thad Bell's division—Lt(jg) Hal Bitzegaio on Bell's wing and Ens Beads Popp on Lt(jg) Earl May's wing—were at 19,000 feet, the top of the heap. The Zekes hit them first.

Bitz, who was on his maiden combat hop, countered well. He flamed a Hamp and shot up two Zekes in quick succession. By then, Bell was leading all hands through a climbing turn to get at a dozen Zekes he had spotted as they positioned themselves overhead. One of the Zekes caught Bitz's Corsair in the right wing with a 20mm explosive round that blew up the contents of one ammo can. Bitz spun out through a half turn, but recovered. As he did, a Zeke came straight up his tail. Bitz yelled, "This is Bitz. Help! Somebody get this Zero off my butt."

Most of our guys heard the "cavalry" respond. "Bitz from Ike. See you. I'll get him."

Miraculously, Ike Kepford arrived in time and indeed did "get" the Zeke. Bitz managed to join on some friends and nurse his shredded bird home to a safe landing.

As Bitz was being saved by Ike, Beads Popp, the division tail-end-Charlie, saw Thad Bell's lead Corsair go straight up in a convulsive vertical climb and then fall away. Though Beads did not see a Zeke jump Thad, nor any rounds going into the division leader's cockpit, he was sure that Thad had been struck and possibly killed instantly by Japanese bullets. Whatever happened, when the dust settled, Thad had disappeared. No one ever saw him again.

Shortly after Bitz was culled from the division, May and Popp went into a vertical dive to deliver an attack on three Zekes that were dogging the tail of a lone P-40. May led Popp into a beam run from four o'clock on the nearest Zeke and opened fire. His target half rolled and dived straight in. The pair recovered at about 5,000 feet and rushed the bombers.

Kepford's division went into the fight just below Bell's and was jumped at the same time as Bell's. A skillful riposte against six Zekes 5,000 feet below them brought one Zeke into Ike's sights at seven o'clock level; it was destroyed. Ike's wingman, Ens Don McQueen, a new guy on his maiden combat hop, also bagged a Zeke, this one at ten o'clock high. Danny Cunningham, who was in the number three slot behind Ike, got in a well-planned shot from astern and above his target, which was destroyed. Kepford's foursome, which was still hanging together, was just pulling back up to 19,000 feet when the elements split up to deliver spoiling attacks on a gaggle of about twenty Zeroes. Nothing much was accomplished until Ike heard Bitz's plaint. After Ike saved Bitz, he and McQueen again climbed. Kepford spotted a Zeke chasing another F4U and executed a beam run from three o'clock. He opened fire early from middle range, more to rattle the Zeke pilot than to kill him. Still, he was credited with a probable. A great deal of chasing and shooting ensued down to 8,000 feet, at which point Ike and McQueen rejoined the bombers. The tireless duo then went on to repel two consecutive and uncharacteristically determined fighter attacks on the retiring B-25s. There were, however, no discernable results beyond chasing the Zeros off.

In the meantime, Danny Boy Cunningham, trailed by his wingman, was attacked by a Zeke from above. They split-essed away and, going to full power, got back above the bombers at the rally point. On the retirement, Danny saw a Zero formation to the south, over Cape St. George, and he headed straight for it. He was still far from the objective when he chanced to see a lone Zeke well below him. He executed a textbook high-side run, and the Zeke rolled away smoking, his propeller windmilling. Danny saw the Zeke strike the water, his second kill of the day and his third overall. With that, he led his wingman back to rejoin the bombers. (Had there really been a time when I felt that I had to transfer Danny because he literally did not measure up to a seat in a Hog?)

Though I have absolutely no direct recollection of this action, the records show that my flight of twelve got involved in a wild, swirling dogfight in which I suppose neither I nor Doug Gutenkunst found a target. On the other hand, my second section—Jim Streig leading Bobby Mims—initially dived away and lost the Zekes but found them again when they rebounded to 14,000 feet. The two pulled right up onto the tail of a Zeke which was in a chandelle away from the growing action. The two shared the kill with simultaneous bursts right into the Zeke's belly. They next spotted four Zekes overhead and two or more above and astern. Before our pair could respond, the two Japanese groups joined and came down to gang up on Streig's tail. Bobby turned in on one Zeke, came in from dead astern, and flamed him with a solid burst. Streig used Mims's attention-getter to escape by breaking left and diving away. In the process, however, he lost track of Mims, but he did find a lone Zeke at 3,000 feet. The Zeke was dispatched with a solid burst delivered from Jim's high-side run; it burned and crashed. Streig pulled out to 5,000 feet, but dived away when he saw a burst of tracer pass close aboard his fighter. He recovered at 1,500 feet without damage and again climbed back to 5,000 on a heading for Cape Gazelle. There, he saw seven or eight Zeros climbing away from the Rapopo runway. They were at 1,500 feet when Jim went for the nearest one. He delivered a firing run from abeam and watched the Zeke fall away to the right, all the way to the ground just outside the runway perimeter. Jim put on full power and headed out to overtake the retiring bombers. When he found them, he was making 310 knots at 1,000 feet.

After shooting the Zeke off Jim Streig's tail, Bobby Mims found eight or ten gray-painted fighters he was unable to identify but which he attacked nonetheless. He swung onto the tail of one of the gray fighters and put in a burst that sent it straight into the water. With that—2.5 kills in a matter of minutes on his second combat hop—Bobby chased after our retiring bombers. Eventually, Jim Streig joined on his wing for the trip home.

At the back of my formation, Dirty Eddie March's wingman, Lt(jg) Carl Gilbert, caught an arrow that blew a big hole in his wing. He nevertheless recovered and flamed a Hamp. When Gilbert began looking for Dirty Eddie, he saw nothing but a sky filled with Zekes, so he dived down to the water and turned for home. He was just getting abreast Cape Gazelle when four Zekes set up on him. However, the four disengaged when Carl turned in to meet their challenge. Seconds later, his Hog was hit again by rounds from a Zeke that crept up on his tail. In Carl's words, he was "scared skinny" by the time he joined a pair of P-40s over the bombers. And he was "still twitching" when he finally got home.

Teeth Burriss and Andy Gump Jagger, March's second section, were nearly swept away by six Japanese fighters, one of which put rounds through the accessory section of Teeth's Hog, just aft of the engine and just ahead of the cockpit. Teeth dived away and came out on the tail of a Zeke, which jinked forward and down. Teeth stayed on him, ripped off short bursts down to only 50 yards, and watched the target smoke and dive into the water. Meantime, Jagger latched onto the tail of the Zeke that had shot Teeth up. The Zeke rolled away, but Jagger stayed with him and fired one burst after another until the Zeke began smoking. It looked as if the Zeke was a goner, but Andy Gump could not wait around to see him go in as he was anxious to rejoin Teeth. However, as Teeth was recovering from his kill, he saw Jagger's target go all the way in. Jagger was unable to rejoin on Teeth before Teeth's oil pressure went went to zero and his Hog's propeller stopped as the engine seized up 120 miles from home. Teeth angled down for the surface and neatly skimmed in across an 8-foot swell. He got out of the sinking fighter without difficulty and waved to several friends who had already arrived.

During the early retirement, Lt Oc Chenoweth's section, which was the second part of Tom Killefer's high-cover division, was weaving 2,000 feet above the bombers when Oc spotted six late-arriving Zekes. The enemy fighters, which were coming in from the direction of Rapopo, were already well into their dives from overhead. Before Oc could act, the Zero leader made a run on his wingman, Ens Jim Dixon, but the Japanese pilot did not open fire. When tracer from another Zeke went by his own wings, Oc split-essed to the left and picked up the Zeke from out of the turn. Both fighters were on their backs when Oc opened fire from dead astern. Oc saw his rounds go in, and the Zeke began to smoke. At that moment, however, Oc had to kick up to the right to avoid several P-40s. When next he looked, the Zeke was cutting through the wave tops on its way in. By then, Dixon was long gone so Oc called him on the radio and arranged to rejoin over the bombers. They subsequently joined on a pair of Marine F4Us for the ride to Piva Yoke.

I circled over Teeth with three other Corsairs until a Dumbo Tom Killefer called out from Torokina arrived to pick him up. The wait seemed interminable. As I stooged around at 200 feet and 150 knots, I kept thinking, "Surely the Japs know we do this. Surely they'll send six or eight fighters out as a cleanup detail. We're easy meat, and the Dumbo will be easy meat when it gets here. I can't believe they're letting us get away with this!" However, Teeth was safely on his way home within an hour of ditching.

Our tally for the January 27 morning strike was impressive: sixteen Japanese fighters definitely downed and five probably downed. None of the B-25s was touched by enemy fighters. Our losses were Thad Bell missing and presumed killed and Teeth Burriss downed but rescued. Four of our fighters were slightly damaged and two were lost. The apparent death of Thad Bell was a severe blow to me—not that it was ever easy. I was closer to him as a friend than to most of the guys, and he had been one of the stalwarts from the first days—a good, solid leader who had *earned* command of a flight of eight.

Eight of us took part on an afternoon strike by fourteen B-24s, also against Lakunai. The Japanese put up a bunch of fighters, but none got close enough to be engaged. Even the AA opposition was meager. On the other hand, after sauntering through absolutely clear skies, the bombers put every one of their bombs into the water off the airfield. "Disgusted" does not begin to describe our feelings.

While not unaware of the high kill ratio we amassed in our first two days—twenty-four of them to three of us killed and five Hogs destroyed—we were still deeply concerned. As far as I could tell, the pattern had been established, so I alerted the wiser heads to get to work on solutions that would prevent us from being nearly decimated every time we went out. Out of the ensuing skull session came "Roving High Cover," perhaps our single best tactical contribution to the war effort.

24

When the day's ops drew to a close on January 27, I called my brain trust—Hedrick, Henning, Davenport, Gile, and March—to the Pilots' Mess for a skull session. Over some beers and potions of Black Death whiskey, we six started off with an attempt to assess the causes of our combat losses: What could we do to continue to accomplish our mission of getting strikes safely in and out without getting so badly chopped up ourselves?

The Japanese had shown well before our return that they would not try to counter fighter sweeps. By opposing only bomber raids, they could operate solely as hunters against the AirSols fighters tied to the bombers. This was a familiar ploy; AirSols fighters had done more or less the same over Empress Augusta Bay during our entire first tour. Alerted by their ground observers on Bougainville, they had a full report as to what was coming, and when. To obtain maximum results, their fighters could be guided on station by their radar, ready to take us on as we flew into the target area. As we had done throughout November, they usually pounced from higher up and out of the sun. I was certain that this tactic had culled Thad Bell from our ranks, just as several of us had culled Japanese flight leaders in November. Aggressively pursued with coordinated effort, these tactics could provide the Rabaul defenders with ample opportunities to attrit us with diminished risk to themselves at a rate that would make the losses of our first two days seem like a picnic.

Not unexpectedly, Rog Hedrick provided the basis for our thinking: "If we can hit them before we start our attacks, we could disrupt their plans and formations."

"Yeah," I rebutted, "that's great. But hit 'em with what? Fighter Command is going to schedule us to capacity in cover assignments. They're not going to hold still for any increase of exposure of the bombers."

Butch Davenport, in his capacity of maintenance officer, got the drift of Rog's premise and chimed in: "With our own mechs, plus the topnotch work of the Marine crews, we're averaging almost twenty-five percent better availability than other Corsair squadrons here. In effect, if we're committed to the cover assignments at the same rate as other outfits, we can still field as many as six fighters above and beyond our proportionate share, maybe more."

More mental lights started clicking on; I could feel the intellectual tension rise. What we began putting together was a tactic as old as war itself. It is not uncommon in ground warfare to detach a small unit to lurk well away from the main body so that it will be free to strike the enemy while his attention is focused upon the main action. Awareness of the Japanese tactics virtually led us to the obvious conclusion arising out of Butch's claim that he could provide extra airplanes.

As always, there was a down side. A small unit with no support was clearly vulnerable to being wiped out if the larger enemy force refocused even part of its ample power.

We were not treading new ground. I had been especially fearful of such a tactic going into our very first action over Bougainville on November 1. On that day, we had first—and only—seen twelve Zekes supporting eighteen Vals. I had immediately jumped to the conclusion that this was a bait run, that more Zekes were lurking in the up-sun position, ready to pounce as soon as we had committed ourselves to the obvious targets. The Japanese had not set up the trap as I had feared, but I never quite got over the sense that we could have been in a bad place if they had done the right thing.

Here was our opportunity to do the right thing.

While those of us who considered ourselves tactical geniuses blathered on at great length, Duke Henning quietly jotted down the notes that would soon form the basis of our formal proposal. When he thought enough had been said, Duke cut in. "Skipper, you know that Colonel Brice thinks we're tops. He'll listen to you and probably buy any reasonable proposal you make."

After reviewing Duke's notes, I jeeped over to the colonel's tent. "Good evening, sir."

His usual "Hi, Tommy" was immediately followed by a shrewdly assessing pause. "Oh boy! I can see by the gleam in your eye that you've got a bright idea you want me to find favor with. Well, at least this is better than the goddamn phone calls from Ondongo you used to raise the dead with at night. Have a beer, and hold your latest brainchild until I get some protection for my flanks."

While I absorbed some of the colonel's beer, he called out his

ACIO, Joe Bryan. As soon as the colonel replaced my empty beer bottle and he and Joe had opened theirs, he nodded, "Okay, Tommy, let's have it."

I explained our problem as we saw it, and what we thought the inevitable outcome would be. I pointed out that even our best and most aggressive pilots were not immune to the inexorable statistics, that the outstanding Maj Greg Boyington—then tied for the U.S. record of twenty-six kills—and his wingman had both disappeared without a trace on January 3. I cut it short when I saw signals from the colonel that he was only too well aware of our combat losses.

"Colonel Brice, we'll continue to meet all our flight assignments as laid on for us by your people. And we'll have ready fighters to cover aborts. Then, if we still have several planes and pilots ready to go, I'd like to use them at my own discretion. We'll keep you informed, of course."

The good colonel snorted. "What you mean, Tommy, is that you'll let me know what you did after you've done it!"

"Well, er, yes, sir. Uh, sort of."

The colonel leveled a knowing glare in my direction. "Maybe. Why don't you tell me exactly what you've cooked up now?"

I plunged on with the philosophical pitch Duke had cooked up— every squadron should have a Yale prof aboard—and concluded, "We'll send in four or six experienced guys, led by our best, at high altitude—say thirty or thirty-two thousand—about ten minutes ahead of the strike. They'll jump the Japs as they're forming up at altitude, before they're ready to begin attacking our incoming main formation."

At that point, Joe Bryan alertly chimed in, "What keeps the Zeros from figuring out what you're up to and ganging up on your unsupported dribble? They could shoot your asses off."

"Joe, damn little. This has occurred to us, too. My guys are willing to accept that possibility. Until we come up with a better answer to that question, I guess it's up to us to vary the timing and positioning patterns so we can keep 'em guessing."

After a brief, heavy silence, the colonel gave a brief, sharp nod. "Okay. *But* it's your responsibility to make damn sure you're not throwing away your best pilots and good aircraft. When do you want to try it out?"

"How about tomorrow morning?"

Bryan gave me a stare and a shake of his head, "Tom, you're out of your mind. Good hunting!"

Thus was the birth of Roving High Cover, or RHC. The official name came in as soon as Duke wrote up the first action report, the very next day. However, our guys quickly got to calling it the Gravy Train. Even the top Zero ace of the time, Lt Tetsuzo Iwamoto, wrote of us as "wolves . . . who pounce on the unsuspecting Zeros."

I led off twenty Corsairs at 0640 on January 28, 1944, and joined with eleven from VMF-211 and eight from VMF-215. The mission was to cover seventeen TBFs making a glide-bombing attack with 2,000-pound bombs on Tobera airfield. Well before we reached the target area, Rog Hedrick climbed to 32,000 feet and stormed ahead of the pack with five other Corsairs in tow; fittingly, he was to lead our first RHC bounce.

Based on their radar readings of the main body's approach, the Japanese launched fifty to seventy Zekes.

The RHC contingent approached the target area at 30,000 feet. As the bombers began their attack (there was another, separate formation of SBDs and their cover in on this, too), Rog spotted twelve Zekes in loose formation approaching at 24,000 feet from seaward. Typically, this bunch began breaking off to deliver loosely coordinated attacks in singles and pairs. As soon as the Zekes were committed to their attacks, Rog's six pounced from out of their own loose column of pairs.

Rog made three quick initial firing passes, but only one of his six machine guns responded each time, so the results were negligible. Worse, following the third pass, a Zeke got on Rog's tail as Rog zoomed up to regain altitude. Just as the Zeke appeared on the verge of stalling out, Paul Cordray, who was leading the second section, came up behind him and poured in a long burst with all six of his guns. The Zeke caught fire and fell away.

Hedrick made one more one-gun firing pass, also with no results, and finally got his whole battery working. At that point, he was 10 miles astern the by then retiring bomber formation, which was at 4,000 feet. He decided to close on the bombers but was arrested when he spotted a lone Zeke two miles off and slowly closing on the bombers. Suddenly, the Zeke pointed its nose down at an F4U flying close to the water. Rog fired at long range and missed, but the startled Zeke pilot pulled up in an Immelmann, and Rog followed. Rog cold-bloodedly closed to within 100 yards and fired all his guns into the Zeke's wing root and engine. The Zeke's canopy slid back and the pilot hurtled into the slipstream just before the plane caught fire. Rog strafed the chute, but his shots probably only bracketed it.

After blowing the Zeke off Rog's tail, Cordray and his wingman, Lt(jg) Jamey Miller, recovered and made several passes at several Zeros, all without observable results. Miller clung to Cordray through his first kill and several subsequent firing passes. When a Zeke Paul never saw set up a high-side run on Cordray's Corsair, Jamey turned into him to commence a head-on firing pass. He saw many pieces of the Zeke's engine fly off under the impact of his guns, and the Zeke eventually nosed down. As Miller rejoined on Cordray and the pair nosed down to follow the plunging Zeke, they spotted five more Zekes. Paul selected one of the Zekes, which was 300 feet below him, and set up a beam firing run which sent that fighter into a flaming dive all the way in. That was Paul's second kill of the day, his sixth overall. Score Fighting-17 another new ace! Miller's Zeke rolled away, but Jamey got in a deflection shot from astern. He saw his tracer going into the Zeke's belly, and then the Zeke blew up. With that, the pair joined up on the bombers for the ride home. Miller's first kill, which no one saw go in, was scored a probable.

Hedrick's wingman, Ens Fatso Ellsworth, lost Rog at the very start of the action. He shot at a Zeke, but missed, so climbed back to 20,000 feet, where he found another Zeke climbing. Fatso turned up into the enemy fighter and got a long burst into its engine. The Zeke staggered and fell away smoking and tumbling, but could only be scored a probable. That was more than enough for the lone fatman, so he headed for the rally point, where he joined on a Marine Corsair's wing for the retirement.

The third RHC pair, Lt(jg) Hal Jackson and Ens Don Malone, went down with Hedrick on the first firing pass. One of four passing Zekes pulled up right in front of Hal, too good a target to pass up. Hal put a long burst right into the cockpit, and the Zeke erupted in flames. Hal rolled away from the blast and was on the verge of joining on Cordray and Miller when he spotted a Zeke making a firing pass on Malone's tail. As Hal came down, the Zeke broke off and dived away. Malone rejoined on Hal's wing and the pair flew to the rally point to begin a protective weave over the retiring bombers. However, Malone's plane had been badly damaged in the fracas and Hal's was very low on fuel. The pair broke away from the formation and headed straight for the barn. They landed early without further incident.

Maybe it was the RHC plan, and maybe it was superb flying skills, aggressiveness, or a hundred other variables, but the six RHC Corsairs bagged a total of four unambiguous Zeke kills, plus two probables.

Perhaps it was our RHC attack, perhaps it was other factors, perhaps it was in the eye of the beholders—whatever lay behind it, the Japanese main effort was disorganized, nearly inchoate. Only thirty or forty of the fifty to seventy airborne Zeros closed on our bomber formations, and not one of them got any rounds into any of the bombers. The fourteen Fighting-17 Corsairs providing medium and high cover had one of our best days so far: Dirty Eddie March, Tom Killefer, Doug Gutenkunst, and newcomer Ens Percy Divenny each creamed two Zekes; Bobby Mims scored 1 full kill, shared another with a Marine, and scored a probable; Ens Bill Meek, another rookie, scored a definite kill; and Lt(jg) Carl Gilbert got a probable. Together with the RHC total, that comes to 14.5 definite kills and 4 probables, virtually as good as our November 11 turkey shoot over the carriers. Moreover, though we had three planes badly shot up and two more holed, we lost no pilots and, in the end, none of our fighters. Our Marine coworkers got 15.5 confirmed kills and 4 probables.

Though extremely successful, our RHC mission of January 29 took a turn I had feared it might.

Led by Rog Hedrick, sixteen of our guys launched to escort twenty-four SBDs to Tobera along with a like number of Marine Corsairs and a dozen low-cover New Zealand P-40s. On the way, our formation had two aborts, both of them Corsairs that were to have been in on the RHC bounce. Despite the 50 percent operational attrition, the two remaining RHC pilots—Kepford and Burriss—elected to complete the bounce. By this time, Ike had 6 kills and Teeth had 3.5. They were big boys, but, like all boys, they were bound to step a little beyond the bounds when no one was looking. I later had cause to question their judgment, but I could not openly reproach them in light of the results.

While the bombers ground along into the approach at 14,000 feet—we had seven Corsairs at 15,000 and seven at 16,000—Ike and Teeth climbed to 30,000. The approach was made over Cape St. George and south of Duke of York Island. As the final approach was being completed, Ike and Teeth spotted a dozen Zekes below them, at about 24,000 feet over Cape Gazelle. They both climbed slightly and then dived right away at the Zekes.

The RHC pair did everything right. Trading the lead after each firing run, the two maintained perfect cohesion in one textbook attack after another. In ten minutes of continuous high-side and overhead firing passes, with sharp chandelles in between, they accounted for four Zekes apiece. Moreover, not only was the personal score of each pilot superbly enhanced, there is no question that they broke the spirit of the Japanese. Only fifteen Zekes challenged the retiring bomber formation from above in a series of uncoordinated, half-hearted attacks. The two Zekes that got through to the bombers were shot down by their gunners, and our guys got a total of two kills (Timmy Gile and Earl May) and three probables (Oc Chenoweth, Ens Jim Dixon, and Ens John Malcolm Smith). Lower down, the Marines had quite a battle on their hands with Zekes, Hamps, and Tonys climbing into the strike formation. Their Corsairs got eleven kills and five probables.

At the debriefing, a proud and pleased Rog Hedrick let down his reserve long enough to bellow, "This one was really a piece of cake! It was great—and then some—to see the burning Zekes raining down as we came in on Tobera."

Overall, the squadron's morale soared after these two sensational days, and Fighter Command was elated. But I found myself possessed of a concerned fatherly rage over the reckless temerity evidenced by Kepford's and Burriss's ill-advised though manifestly successful showboating.

Ike and Teeth came away from the January 29 mission as our high scorers, Ike as a double ace and Teeth with 7.5. There was no jealousy evidenced by any of my other tigers; they just wanted to be sure their turns came up for the Gravy Train. It was all just as I had hoped—and just as I had feared.

At the pilots' meeting that evening, before the preflight briefing for the January 30 mission, I decided to lay down the law. "We've turned things around, and you men are showing all hands in Fighter

Command the kind of stuff you've got." I paused for a moment to allow silent cheers and mental backslapping. "*But*, . . ." all eyes were back on me, "don't you *dare* get overconfident. There is no surer way of getting your ass in a sling. We will have *no stars* in this outfit! As I told you before we came up here, if I see anybody—*any*body—who shows signs of getting Zero Happy, I'll ground him, maybe for a while, maybe forever. That includes Rog. And he'll lay it on me if he thinks I've been bitten by that bug. There will be no contests for record individual kills in Fighting-Seventeen. That sort of thing only gets people killed."

I let that sink in and turned to another problem we were just beginning to experience; I was sure it was a direct outgrowth of the nascent Zero-Happy problem. "Hereafter, if you're late getting off because of a mechanical problem, you're more than welcome to try to catch up to the flight and finish out the assignment." It had always been thus, with good results. "However, if you're not joined up by the time you get within twenty-five miles of Cape St. George, you will turn around and return to base. It doesn't matter if you get it into your head that there are no Japs around. Always keep in mind Blackburn's First Rule of Survival: 'It's the guy you don't see who's most likely to cream you.' As we all know, they're superaggressive when it comes to bouncing singles. Separate pairs will not go in either below thirty thousand feet. No exceptions."

25

The morning liftoff on January 30 comprised twenty VF-17 F4Us as part of the cover for a small flight of B-25s bound for Tobera. The operation was routine in all its parts, and the results were well within the norms we had established in just a week: Hedrick scored another kill while his wingman, Ens Fatso Ellsworth, scored his first definite air-to-air victory. Probables were scored by Lt(jg) Hap Bowers, Ens Jamey Miller, Ens John Malcolm Smith, and Ens George Keller. One Corsair brought back a wing chewed up by a Zero, but none of the bombers was molested directly.

After lunch and a nap, Doug Gutenkunst and I went down to the beach by the mouth of the Torokina River. Though a godsend for us, Bougainville's beaches will never put Waikiki out of business; the sand is coarse and coal black—the detritus from lava from the volcanic Franz Josef mountain range, which forms the big island's spine. Except on very stormy days, the surf runs at all of 6 inches.

Doug and I got along perfectly despite the difference in our ages and backgrounds. We were more brothers than colleagues, more trusted friends than commander and subordinate. My only real bitch about my wingman's superb fighting skills was his marked tendency in combat to sky out and take on the Imperial fighters on his own.

As we lolled and relaxed in the surf, the normal noise levels of engines being turned up for testing and the occasional bursts of fire from the nearby front lines suddenly altered drastically. Soon, all other noise was subordinated to the unmistakable throaty roar of numerous high-power engines.

"What's up, Skipper? I didn't know there was a launch scheduled for this afternoon."

"Me neither, Doug. May be a scramble."

We soon saw Corsairs lifting off from Torokina and Piva Yoke, while Turkeys—as we now called the TBFs—were climbing out of Piva Uncle to form up overhead. Doug and I did not exchange so much as a word as we hustled into our clothes and ran for the jeep. Minutes later, we screeched up to our line-shack, ready-room tent at the strip. By then, I learned later, seventeen of our hastily assembled pilots had climbed aboard any old Hog and gotten airborne on the run, in a catch-as-catch-can organization.

Doug and I whipped into the Marine cotton coveralls we preferred for our tropical flying and donned boondockers—the heavy Marine combat shoes that were the best footgear available in the event we had to bail out over land. As we grabbed our Mae West life jackets, cotton flying helmets, sheath knives, and pistols, Duke Henning briefed us on the run: "Some recon plane just radioed in that a Jap carrier is approaching Rabaul along with a small escort force."

The contact report had come in around 1500. While no time was wasted getting planes away to snoop the enemy task force, MGen Ralph Mitchell, ComAirSols, had by no means hit the panic button. He had gotten on the horn to Fighter Command, then to Strike Command, and had ordered them to "Scramble whatever fighters you can with a maximum of the ready Turkeys with fish. Get the flattop."

By 1640, the time Doug and I taxied out, more than twenty TBFs—half loaded with torpedoes and half loaded with 1,000-pound bombs—and forty Navy and Marine Corsairs were a half-hour out, barreling north-northwest at the best speed the laden bombers could make. Odd flights of bomb-laden SBDs were also on the way. Our seventeen VF-17 fighters were under Oc Chenoweth.

There was no carrier, so the strike went after the small game it could find at Simpson Harbor. The Japanese reacted to the unexpected incursion with a meager thirty Zekes and several flights of Imperial Army fighters, mostly Tonys. However, the AA barrage was fierce, as if the gunners deeply resented the breakup of their late afternoon sake hour.

As Doug and I came boiling in at full throttle in high blower, the scene over Rabaul was spectacular. The heavy AA was laying a thick carpet around the Turkeys, which were approaching at 14,000 feet. Just slightly lower down was an equally lethal array of tracer from the lighter AA. AirSols fighters were all over the sky, sending down burning Japanese fighters. Here and there, one or another of our fighters plummeted earthward trailing long plumes of thick black smoke.

Doug and I turned out to be a delayed version of the RHC as we

came in out of the westering sun to surprise some of the enemy
fighters preoccupied with the brouhaha below. I spotted six Zeros
in loose formation of three pairs as they flew through a gentle turn
at 20,000 feet. All of them seemed to be enjoying the show farther
down; certainly none of them imagined our approach. I hit the
number two man in the lead pair from a steep dive, a beam run that
ended astern as he blew up under the impact of my rounds.

As we chandelled out of the attack, I spotted another pair setting
up on a high-cover F4U. Doug and I got there in time and I set up
a low-side run on the wingman. He dived away in a spiral, but I
managed to get on his tail and stay there. Repeated hits set the Zero
afire, and that forced the pilot to bail out. At least I did not have to
follow the wreck to earth to claim a definite kill. However, I did
have to recover from my attack. The tight turn pulled more gees
than I expected, and I was on the ragged edge of blacking out. As
the gray fog evaporated, I spotted the recently blossomed parachute. I swung back to finish off the Japanese pilot; if I didn't, I
reasoned, he probably would be up to meet us the next day—
smarter, and looking for me. Unbelievably the harness was empty.
A closer look at the dangling straps revealed that they had burned
through. At that moment, it was not at all pleasant to think about
the Japanese pilot's 18,000-foot unarrested dive to the surface.

Doug had stayed with me all through the gyrations topping off
the two successful attacks. As a reward, I turned the lead over to
him. As we eased on down to about 10,000 feet to find a slot in the
high-cover formation above our bombers, Doug made a high-side
attack from four o'clock against a single Zero. When the target spun
out it was smoking and apparently out of control. Next, about a
dozen Zekes and Hamps jumped us, but we took violent evasive
action and shook them off. As we recovered and rejoined over the
bombers, Doug set up on a pair over the bombers and cut loose at
the wingman, who split-essed to safety. Instantly, Doug shifted his
attention to the element leader. I clearly saw Doug's round going
in, but the Hamp disappeared into a cloud.

Having had an opportunity to lead two attacks, Doug graciously
turned the lead back to me. As we again took station over the
outbound bombers, I saw a Zero about 2 miles astern and boring
straight in. I swung away, and Doug followed. I managed to set up
a full-deflection shot that staggered the Japanese fighter and started
a fire in the cockpit. Just as I stopped firing, however, the flames

died out. I shot again, and the Zeke glided away. When last seen as I led Doug back to the bombers again, the Zero was in a 30-degree dive and heading down through 1,000 feet.

The rest of the Fighting-17 team did very well. Ike Kepford bagged a Zeke and a Tony, and Butch Davenport got a pair of Zekes. Oc Chenoweth got two Zekes and shared a third with his wingman, Ens Jim Dixon, a new guy. Mills Schanuel got a single, his third definite kill.

The victory—ten confirmed kills—was not without cost. Lt(jg) Tom Kropf disappeared without a trace, and Lt Ray Beacham's Corsair was badly shot up. Ray got the damaged Hog home, but by then his hydraulic pressure gauge read zero. He thus had no flaps, and the CO_2 emergency gear-extension system got only one wheel down. Making matters hairier, Ray reported that he had about 5 inches of avgas sloshing around in his Hog's belly right below the cockpit, the result of a busted fuel line. It was getting dark, and Ray prudently elected to make a water landing. The splashdown was rough; the one wheel violently slewed the F4U upon contact with the water. The crash boat pulled Ray from the water in seconds. He was briefly hospitalized with a broken nose, but he and we all knew he had fared well.

A Tony had nearly creamed Kepford; an ammo can in his right wing exploded from a 20mm hit. There was a big fire raging in the wing for a while, but Ike doggedly kept on course for home. The fire soon burned itself out, but at the cost of vital controls. The result was that Ike came in for a high-speed, one-wheel touchdown. The Hog violently ground looped and piled up, a total loss. Blessedly, it did not burn. When the crash crew yanked Ike from the wreckage, our high scorer was physically okay but a mite shaken in the emotion department.

Ens Beads Popp also washed his plane out on landing. Unbeknownst to him, he came in on a flat tire. The Hog pulled a spectacular ground loop that turned into a magnificent cartwheel. The pilot was unhurt, but he was naturally exuding giant beads of sweat on his nose, the unique personal reaction to high stress that had led to his nom de guerre.

Doug and I were among the last fighters in. By the time we got over the field, it was nearly dark and the crash and salvage crews were overwhelmed by the busted birds piling up on Piva Yoke. We were therefore diverted to Piva Uncle, the bomber strip. Its traffic pattern was saturated with a mix of F4Us, TBFs, and SBDs. Further, by then, the radio discipline no longer existed; the tower's control frequency was hopelessly jammed with competing high-tension chatter. Efforts by the tower personnel to handle the traffic by means of red and green signal searchlights were ignored. It was all too evident that getting on deck in one piece was going to take some doing.

At length, I spotted a good-sized hole in the circle of planes on the downwind leg of the landing pattern and I decided to go for it. I gratefully slid in, and Doug followed at a thirty-second interval as I made our standard turning carrier-type approach. I laid on a perfect three-point landing as far down the strip as possible so I would spend the least amount of time getting off the runway. As I completed my rollout, I checked my rearview mirror to see if it was safe to turn. To my horror, all I saw was a huge ball of orange flame at the downwind end of the runway. I *knew* that Doug was in it.

Also in the inferno rising intensely against the black night sky was what had been a badly shot-up Corsair that had been driven by a seriously wounded Marine major. With neither lights nor radio, nor an operable hydraulics system, the Marine had been guided back to the field by his squadron mates, who had lined him up to the runway for a necessary straight-in approach. The Marine Hog was barely controllable. With no landing flaps available, it came in extremely fast. Moreover, blood from his head wound had left the major virtually blind. He and Doug collided at low altitude, right over the end of the strip. Neither pilot had a chance. It was nobody's fault; some malign fate had brought these two brave men into a space big enough for just one of them.

All hands in both squadrons were devastated. Combat losses were hard enough to take, but we could accept them, of necessity. This freak grisly accident was too much. Compounding the unacceptable was that the wounded major was seconds away from what would otherwise have been an epochally miraculous safe return.

I was wiped out. My beloved friend and loyal protector was a charred corpse. The final flight had been joyous, a successful scrap in which our team of two had come very much into its own.

On January 31 sixteen of us were assigned low and medium cover above the TBF component of a Piva-launched light-bomber strike against shipping in Karavia Harbor. The total loss of five of our aircraft the previous afternoon prevented us from mounting the usual RHC mission.

There was nothing worth taking on in Karavia Harbor, so the bomber leader diverted all his birds to Tobera. They made their approach over Cape St. George, up St. George Channel, over Duke of York Island, and then south over Londip Plantation. As the bombers made a right turn toward the target, we were approached by approximately forty Zekes and what looked to Chico Freeman like three Imperial Army Ki-44 "Tojo" fighters. There were not supposed to be any Tojos deployed around Rabaul—so the official records say—but the type's barrel-shaped P-47-like silhouette was absolutely unmistakable. In fact, Marine great 1st Lt Butcher Bob Hansen had been credited with two Tojo kills during the previous day's afternoon strike.

As so often happened, the interceptors stooged around until after the bombers had completed their drops and were retiring over Kabanga Bay. Even the typically aggressive AA defense was meager this day, and the heavier guns ceased firing altogether as the dive-bombers pushed over on the Tobera runway. The Japanese fighters began their runs from around 24,000 feet, but they were singularly unaggressive. Elements of three Marine Corsair squadrons flying top cover intercepted and got five kills and four probables, and one TBF gunner got a kill. However, during the run-in and early retirement, not one of the enemy fighters got as low as 14,000 or 15,000 feet, where we were tied down.

Well into the retirement, I saw a steeply diving Zeke slanting down on Teeth Burriss's fighter, which was number three behind my second-flight leader, Dirty Eddie March. I keyed my mike and yelled, "Teeth! Break hard right! Now!" But Teeth apparently did not hear my warning, for he continued in the gentle turn of his weaving pattern. The Zeke nailed him and followed through before any of our guys could get a shot off.

Teeth left the formation trailing smoke. His wingman, Andy Gump Jagger, followed him down until another single Zeke jumped them. Andy turned hard into this attacker, but the Zeke took violent evasive action and got away. When Andy turned back to his previous retirement course, Teeth was nowhere to be found.

We were able to send off a search mission on February 1 across the Solomon Sea to St. George Channel, straight up the track we thought Teeth might have followed as he limped home. We saw a submarine that dived before we got close enough to identify it, but nothing else was out there—no debris, and no raft.

We never learned Teeth's fate. Andy Jagger, who was miserable, had not been able to get close enough to Teeth's wounded Hog to check the extent or nature of the damage, or to see if Teeth was hurt. We all hoped Teeth had lived to make a water landing—he was one of our most skilled pilots and could have managed it if anyone could—but he could as easily have crashed. Though we marked him as missing, we well knew that Teeth Burriss was dead.

January's totals were 60.5 enemy fighters destroyed in the air—in only six days! However, we had also lost 5 pilots shot down and killed and 1 pilot killed in a midair collision. Altogether, 13 of our Hogs had been destroyed, 5 directly by enemy aircraft, 4 in crack-ups after being shot up by enemy aircraft, 3 in operational landing crashes, and 1 in the midair collision.

26

Though we got a search mission off after Teeth Burriss, the February 1 game was called on account of rain—a huge frontal system that totally shut down everything from Rabaul to Empress Augusta Bay. The rain was so bad that no one gave much thought to Hal Jackson's report that he had seen a drainage ditch filled with drowned frogs. Any flat place was calf-deep in mud, and the 10-foot-deep ditches the Seabees maintained on either side of all roadways were dangerous swift-moving streams. The entrance to my tent, a 5-foot-square area paved with empty beer cans, was maddeningly musical. By the second, even the gulls were walking.

The two-day respite was most welcome. In a mere week since we had taxied onto Piva Yoke's hardstands beneath the towering mahogany trees, we had had six consecutive days of furious, mind-numbing action. Six of our number were dead—one a day.

The living conditions at Piva Yoke were good—screened tents on wooden decks and plenty of showers with cool, sparkling water from jungle streams—but the down side had us all on edge. We often heard and sometimes saw tanks clanking down the main road running past the field, and we were treated constantly to the *boom-swish* of (thankfully) outgoing artillery fire. So far, each and every night, and most days, had been filled with the odd withering bursts of gunfire from the all-too-near front lines. We were constantly assured that there was zero chance of our being overrun, that two entire veteran Army divisions were dug in along or engaged in expanding the perimeter around us. The assurances would have been more credible without the sounds of gunfire. We all made sure our pistols were in easy reach and that we had plenty of ammo on hand. We begged, borrowed, or stole carbines until each of us had his own.

The bug population had been all but wiped out. There appeared to be no mosquitoes, but we all choked down our daily dose of vile, yellow-skin-producing antimalarial Atrabine. The only insect life that seemed impervious to the Seabees' DDT showers were the *giant* centipedes. We all learned to stow our shoes upside down and high off the ground at night, and to shake them out before donning them in the morning. One day shortly after our arrival, I unfolded my washcloth at the shower and found myself being stared down by a huge unfriendly looking specimen.

Thankfully, the Navy supplied and prepared our food. The fighter pilots' mess was adequate in every way. We even had plenty of refrigerated fresh food. I cannot give the facility four stars, but it was light-years better than the Army-run Hotel Mud Plaza at Ondongo.

Recreation was primarily based on our own resources. Card games never ended, though the cast changed from time to time, and everyone spent hours listening to Armed Forces Radio and Tokyo Rose. The former was considered okay, but all hands preferred the latter's better selection of good jazz records larded with the highly comedic Japanese propaganda. Beer was the favored beverage, but we maintained a decent supply of Black Death whiskey and Lejon brandy, which was tolerable if mixed with grapefruit juice.

When flight operations resumed on February 3, Butch Davenport led off twelve of our remaining twenty-four Corsairs. His job was to help escort a flight of B-24s bound for Lakunai. Only twenty-eight Japanese fighters were counted in the air over the target. As far as Butch's flight could see from their low-cover position, only seven Zekes actually engaged. Of these, Kepford got one and Chenoweth got a probable. Marines from two squadrons assigned to medium cover did a little better with five kills and four probables. There were sixteen P-38s along flying top cover, but I have no idea how they fared.

It was becoming obvious that the Japanese defense over Rabaul was crumbling. Individually, their few truly aggressive fighter pilots had been getting better at air-to-air tactics, but the overall effort had been in a deepening slump since we arrived. The pressure had dropped off to almost nothing on January 31, and it showed no signs of reemerging on February 3.

I led off twenty of our Corsairs on February 4. Once again, our charges were B-24s, this time bound for Tobera. I had a newly arrived lieutenant on my wing, a solid-seeming senior pilot I wanted to check out before moving him up to lead a section, or even a division.

Only twenty Zeros and ten Tonys appeared to challenge us. On the approach, however, Ens Perce Divenny, who had joined us in Espiritu but who already had two kills under his belt, made a really dumb mistake. Instead of opening the valve that released CO_2 into the Corsair's wing-purging system, he opened the adjacent valve, which actuated his emergency landing-gear system. Once down by this means, there was no way to get the wheels back up while in flight. We were by then too close to the target to allow Perce to abort, so, as soon as I saw the reason why he was dropping back, I radioed to tell him to tuck in beneath the heavy bombers. If Perce understood and did exactly what he was told—and stayed put—he would have it made; the Zekes would never be able to get at him.

We were retiring from the bomb-drop point when, to my utter horror, I saw Divenny's Corsair slowly dropping behind the B-24s. We could never figure out what happened; Perce was a cool hand, so the only theory that held was that his Hog suffered some sort of engine-power loss. In any case, by this time, the Zeros were nipping at our flanks, looking for an opening so they could get at the Liberators or bounce exposed fighters. Our job was to protect the B-24s, and we all had our hands full doing that, so I made the brutal decision to withhold cover for Divenny. Naturally, the Zeros—at least eight of them—pounce on Perce. As they started in, Earl May broke from his position in the bomber cover and led his wingman, Beads Popp, to the rescue. The two got to Divenny's lagging fighter, and they did get their talons into one of the Zekes. Earl got credit for an assist and Beads got full credit for the kill. However, the rest of the Zeros bore down on them and May and Popp had to dive to safety. A Zeke came down on Perce's tail and hammered him into a fatal dive.

As the retiring bombers were clearing the coast, six Zekes hit the formation from 500 feet above the low-cover flight. Attacking from the rear, these Zekes put in a series of aggressive high-side runs. The rear division, under Lt(jg) Paul Cordray, turned back to take on the Zekes, and the Zekes broke contact. However, when Paul turned again to rejoin the bombers, two Zekes slipped in and set up a firing pass at the rear element, Lt(jg) Hal Jackson followed by Lt(jg) Don Malone. Jackson was well behind Cordray and his wingman, and Malone was lagging even farther behind Jackson.

Cordray gave a frantic "Close up" zooming signal, and Jackson promptly moved in. Malone, who had a long history of lagging in formation, did not respond to the unmistakable series of short dives and zooms, nor even to "Don! Don! Close up! Close up," which Paul frantically broadcast by radio. When the Zekes pulled up at the conclusion of their single firing run, Malone's Corsair was burning and falling away. Attracted by Cordray's vain warning, several of us saw Don's chute blossom. We hoped he would get down safely, but we had to leave. No one ever saw Don again.

As soon as we landed, I confronted Earl May at the ready room and let him have it with my fury. I had been literally sick to my stomach when I saw Divenny going down, but I had made the painful decision to carry out our responsibility to defend the bombers. I had determined that we could not do that and cover Divenny, too. It was, in my mind, a tough fact of life that Perce had been lost because he had been unable to stay under the heavy bombers. The only thing that kept me from grounding Earl was the lucky fact that no enemy fighters had attacked through the hole his departure had left in our formation.

"Get this straight, Earl. Nobody has ever questioned your courage. You don't have to prove yourself like some show-off schoolboy. You had no goddamn business breaking out of your cover position with Beads to take on all those Japs. For what? Sure, you and Beads flamed one, but you damn sure didn't help Divenny. You were lucky as hell you and Beads didn't get it, too. You *know* that if the enemy hadn't muffed their chance they'd have had three easy kills instead of just one. Worse than that, you exposed the rest of us and the bombers. Our job is to get those klunkers in and out in one piece. I'm *proud* that we haven't lost one yet. They *depend* on us. This is a team operation. There's no place for some wild-ass who shoves off to be the heroic White Knight riding to the rescue. I will not tolerate this kind of shit. Is that clear?"

Earl was angry with me—his body language said as much—but he was wrong and I was right, and he knew it. I got a sheepish, "I understand, Skipper."

"If you weren't such a good man who's always done a top job before, I'd throw your ass out. As it is, you're no longer a division leader. You'll fly wing, where I can keep my eye on you."

I was so obviously angry for the rest of the day that no one got within 10 feet of me if he could help it.

*   *   *

My overall reaction and anger over the two losses might seem unreasonable, but both were firmly grounded in my lifelong perception of how duty must come before my personal feelings for my subordinates, strong as they were. All hands—even late arrivals like Perce Divenny—knew that our responsibility was to guard the bombers *at all costs*.

In part, however, the display of anger was a mask for my profound grief. The two unnecessary losses were almost more than I could bear. I privately judged myself at least a little culpable in both cases.

With respect to Perce's fatal lapse, I allowed the wing-purging and emergency landing-gear CO_2 bottles to remain side by side even though I easily could have gotten Vought or even our own mechanics to relocate one safely away from the other. The potential for error was *so* obvious! Amazingly, Divenny's gaffe had been the first of its sort in hundreds of combat sorties.

Malone's loss was a little different, and I bore more direct responsibility. All hands knew that Don had a marked propensity to lag. Maybe I should have ridden him harder, or moved him forward from the definitely vulnerable tail-end slot. We knew that the Imperial pilots, like us, were quick to spot and nail a laggard.

Worst of all was my conviction that I had seen both situations developing. I had certainly seen Divenny fall behind, and I am sure I had seen Malone do so earlier in the mission. In Divenny's case, I *could* have taken the chance and gone back or sent help, but I deliberately chose not to. In Malone's, Cordray could have gone to help, but Paul knew—and accepted—my thinking, so he did not dangerously expose his division and put others at risk, as May had done.

These were two more painful examples of the loneliness of command. I found, after a long search through my soul, that I would not have acted differently in either case. But I had contributed to Malone's death by being too lenient; I should have grounded him because of his inability to correct a long-apparent problem. It was a bomb that had ticked away—that I had heard ticking—until it blew up in Don's face.

27

On February 5 twelve of our F4Us led by Dirty Eddie March were assigned as part of the SBD cover on a joint SBD-TBF strike against Lakunai. On the approach over Duke of York Island and Crater Peninsula, the SBDs flew at 12,000 feet and our fighters flew low cover at 13,000 feet.

Right between Duke of York Island and Crater Peninsula, the formation was approached by a dozen brown-painted Zekes coming in over a volcano called The Mother. Five of the Zekes executed overhead runs against the SBDs just before the dive-bombers pushed over on the Lakunai main runway. As they did, and without ever losing his place in the formation, Butch Davenport, who was leading the rear division, depressed the nose of his Hog and caught one of the Zekes with a 40-degree deflection shot. The Zeke burned all the way in. It was Butch's fifth full kill; he was an ace. None of the attacking Zekes laid a glove on the Dauntlesses.

On the retirement—straight out directly over St. George Channel—six to eight Zekes were spotted over Tobera at about 6,000 feet. Probably, they had just taken off and were only just forming up. A pair of the new arrivals attempted to put in a low-side run against Lt Wally Schub's middle F4U division. However, Lt(jg) Country Landreth, the leader of Schub's second element, dived at one of the attackers and got a good, solid burst into the target's engine. This Zeke went down in flames. At the same time Country was swatting his Zeke, Schub spotted yet another Zeke diving into his formation. The Japanese pilot turned away prematurely as Schub angled up to meet him. Wally got in a great belly shot from eight o'clock. The Zeke caught fire and fell all the way into the water. With that, the rest of the Zekes backed off and our formation was not molested during the remainder of the retirement.

Our only other mission of the day was a Dumbo-escort hop east of Buka. I turned the lead of my division over to the new lieutenant who was my temporary wingman. I happened to be the one to spot the life raft first, but I was pleased with the new officer's leadership, and I mentally noted that he was nearly ready for some unsupervised section-lead flying.

I led off sixteen of our guys early on February 6, but we had two early aborts. We were assigned to fly high cover over a formation of twenty-seven B-25s out of the Treasuries. Also along for the ride were twenty-four New Zealand P-40s, twenty-four Marine Corsairs from two squadrons, and eight F6Fs from Lem Cooke's squadron, out of Vella Lavella. The target was Lakunai again. As we got close, I turned the lead over to Wally Schub and peeled off for RHC along with my wingman and a section composed of Bobby Mims leading Hal Bitzegaio.

In absolutely clear skies, the B-25s approached Lakunai at 12,000 feet in reverse of the usual pattern, from south of Duke of York Island and north of Gredner Island before turning right to get in over the runway. Retirement was to be over the tip of New Ireland's East Cape.

At least forty Japanese fighters were spotted; sixteen were forming up over Tobera and the rest were over Rapopo. I decided to pile in against the Tobera bunch and timed my arrival from 25,000 feet for just before Bombs Away.

The first firing run was made from out of the sun at four or six Zekes which were still over Tobera but heading in the direction of the bombers from 22,000 feet. I lined up on the first Zeke I saw and dived in at a 25-degree down angle from the five o'clock position. A very short burst instantly caused the Zeke to explode—a clean kill. As I was getting my Zeke, Bobby Mims flamed one of his own.

I recovered in a right chandelle and flew up through the expanding ball of debris of my kill at 23,000 feet. The entire division came out of the pass as a complete unit. As I leveled off, I saw another group of Zeros heading away to the northwest to intercept the bombers.

We caught up with the Zeros and dived to catch them at 20,000 feet, right over Lakunai. I led my division in and made an immediate high-side run from the left. My target started burning after I had fired only a short burst. Bitz also got a Zeke on the pass. Mims bored right up to the tail of what he later swore was a Tojo and, after nearly rear-ending the oddity, fired a short burst that sent the bottle-shaped Imperial Army fighter down in a shower of flames and debris. That was Bobby's fifth kill (including two half kills), so he, too, was an ace. Moments later, he got his sixth, another Zeke. He also scored two probables in this wild and woolly melee.

Meantime, before I completed my recovery from the first firing pass, another Zeke flew straight into my sights. I instinctively opened fire as I followed him into a tight diving turn. I kept putting out bursts until, at about 4,000 feet, I was on the verge of blacking out. I began to ease out of the spiral at just the instant my wingman saw my target flare up into a huge ball of fire. I continued to recover to my left and led my wingman up in a climbing spiral.

On the way up, I spotted a mixed bag of four Zekes and Hamps above me, but I declined to get into a fight without a sure altitude advantage. I poured on all my power and fought for altitude, but they never even approached. When I got to 22,000 feet, the four Zeros were still circling obliviously where I had left them, so I turned back down to get at them. As I was approaching, two of the Zeros vanished and the other pair dived away in opposite directions. I followed one Zeke into a radical dive, but it looked like he was going to get away, so I pulled out in a right chandelle. As soon as I gave up the chase, the Zeke turned sharply to the right and zoomed back up in a vertical climb.

This was an *old* trick. As the two planes are reaching the top of the climb, but well before the U.S. fighter is close enough to get in a killing shot, both begin running out of flying speed. Since a Zero was more maneuverable at low speeds than any of our fighter types, it could usually pull through the loop onto the tail of the attacker. We lost scores of airplanes and pilots to this maneuver earlier in the war, and I suppose we were still losing tyros to it over Rabaul. I was no tyro, so I put in a disquieting burst at long range and broke off as soon as I saw what the play was going to be. I saw my tracer fall right on the Zeke, but I was unable to observe any obvious damage before I had to go.

I was amazed and gratified to see how quickly the division again reformed on my lead. We had been running like a single piece of machinery all morning. I expected good things of Mims, who was one of the old Norfolk and Manteo hands, but I also got great performances out of the newcomers on our wings. I was particularly happy with my wingman, who, though he scored no kills, was proving out as an excellent pilot. As we headed out to join on the retiring bombers, Bobby flew up alongside to tell me via hand signals that he was getting low on oxygen. I signaled back, directing him and Bitzegaio to return to base immediately.

As my wingman and I were nearing Cape St. George, still following the retiring bomber group, we picked up a lone Hamp tooling along in straight and level flight at moderate speed. Talk about a death wish; this guy had clearly secured from General Quarters a mite too soon. We closed up his tail to within about 50 yards and never got a glimmer of reaction. The Hamp blew into a million pieces as soon as I began squirting rounds at him. My wingman's windshield was doused with oil and fuel, and he heard chunks of debris hitting his Hog as I led him through a fireball for the second time that morning.

The Roving High Cover ploy did *exactly* what it was meant to do; it broke the spirit of the welcoming committee before most of the airborne Japanese fighters could go after the bombers. Nevertheless, there were attacks on the main group.

Those Japanese who managed to stay out of the clutches of my RHC division attacked the standard high-cover fighters as the bombers were turning over Lakunai for the drop. This was the ideal spot for the interception because many of our fighters had to swing wide to stay with the bombers. The object was to pick off the outside fighters while they were most vulnerable.

As the B-25s turned, Wally Schub's second section—Lt(jg) Country Landreth leading Ens Clyde Dunn—went too wide to the outside. Then, as the bombers straightened out, Landreth and Dunn were sucked in behind their assigned position. Two or three Zekes at 17,000 feet—2,000 above our errant pair—pounced from dead astern just as the two Corsairs came right to cut back inside the bombers. At almost the same instant, Schub and his wingman, Ens Whit Wharton, were attacked by two or three other Zekes. This was the best example of a coordinated bounce we had experienced at Japanese hands in many a day.

Schub's section turned obliquely to the right—Wally said it was 135 degrees—and arrived in time to meet the second Zeke coming down on Landreth's section. Wally got a good burst in from two o'clock and below, and the Zeke fell away burning. He then led Wharton straight down to evade the trio of Zekes that had been closing on him all the while. Wally's intervention temporarily scared off the survivors of the team that had bounced Landreth and

Dunn, but at least two pairs of these superb Japanese pilots managed to get in several high-side and overhead attacks in very rapid succession. Schub's and Wharton's Hogs were hit by 20mm rounds, but neither was disabled. At length, the Japanese withdrew and our two sections were able to rejoin. They scissored over the bombers the whole rest of the way home.

I was extremely proud of the manner in which my makeshift division had flown during the flight. All attacks were made in pairs that never came unglued, and the pairs smoothly reformed immediately at the conclusion of each individual fracas. Every attack was made from an altitude advantage, and all of us had the opportunity to decline to join with Japanese fighters that started out over our heads—just as it should be done. In fact, the entire action and all its parts had been executed exactly as prescribed in Blackburn's Unwritten Rules for Fighter Pilots. I do not believe any VF-17 foursome had ever attained that level of air discipline before. The results were gratifying: Mims emerged with three fresh kills and two more probables on his tally; Bitz had another Zero kill, his second; and I had bagged three Zekes and a Hamp, plus two more Zekes damaged.

I was elated with my temporary wingman, and I was all set to tell him that he had earned a trial slot as a section leader. When he approached me following the debrief back at Piva Yoke, he had a "look" on his face, and I thought he was going to ask for the lead assignment I had decided he had coming.

"Skipper, you're nuts! I want out of this. Now!"

I was more than just miffed; I felt betrayed. My startled immediate response was an inadequate "So?" Then I recovered and told him to go pack, that he could fly out to the rear before sunset. However, the last thing I said to him was from the heart: "I *am* sorry to lose you."

28

We tried something altogether new and exciting on February 7. Our choice, the sum of numerous evening skull sessions, was dubbed the Statue of Liberty Play, after its resemblance to the well-known football tactic.

In the playing field version, the quarterback stands with his arms cocked to throw a pass down the left side. The left end swings back and runs behind the quarterback, grabs the ball, and runs ahead to the right. Theoretically, the defense is focusing on the possible pass receivers, so the ball carrier is in the clear.

The basis for our flying version of the play was the base-bound strategy of the Japanese defenders around Rabaul. I could well imagine where that stupidity came from. No doubt, some staff cookie pusher had come to the brilliant conclusion that if their pilots did not fly past Point X their losses beyond Point X would be sharply reduced. He no doubt sold the idea to his boss in the plush, secure surroundings of a headquarters office, complete with maps and statistical tables keyed to validate the conclusion. If there were any Japanese pilots like us—folks who realized they were expendable to the whims of their leaders—they probably commented in terms to the effect, "Holy Fujiyama! Look at the latest order from headquarters: 'No pursuit, under any circumstances, beyond Point X!' Those staff jerks must be out of their minds."

To which another veteran would certainly add, "Never mind that, Ichi, look who *signed* the order." And there they were: base bound and losing their butts.

Our caper was to stay with the bombers until they had dropped their loads and were well out to sea, safely on their way home. Eight of our F4Us whose pilots had ample combat experience *and* plenty of fuel aboard would dive to the deck at moderate power and head away north, well out to sea. On reaching a point well to the northeast of the target, the Hogs would turn due west. On approaching New Ireland's east coast, the flight leader was to open his throttle to 95 percent of full power (in order to leave the other planes some reserve power to prevent lagging). Then it would be up and over New Ireland, right at treetop level, and then back down on the waves—so low that each Hog trailed a white wake. A final 90-degree port turn would set the Hogs up for a final run-in. At the last moment, the second division would split out abeam the lead division and the eight Hogs would rattle windows as they roared in just over the rooftops of Rabaul.

The theory was that we would achieve total surprise over the Japanese birds as they leisurely flew into the Lakunai traffic pattern. There would be *one* firing pass, all forty-eight .50-caliber machine guns blazing a path of destruction. Recovery would be straight ahead, and, still on the deck, we would retire over Cape St. George.

There were several caveats. If the Japanese anticipated the play— or were forewarned by observers or their radar—we stood a good chance of getting creamed by their fighters with an altitude advantage. There is no place to dive out when you are already hugging the deck. If that happened and there were enough of them, we would be lucky to get anyone out alive.

I had made my initial presentation to Colonel Brice on rainy February 2. I had lots of credibility in view of our ongoing RHC successes, so I had turned on the charm and let the new idea rip. When the colonel and Joe Bryan had heard me out, the colonel had shaken his head in amazement. "You nut! Down on the runway at twenty-five feet? You'll probably get shot to ribbons by their light AA even if the Zekes don't nail you." He paused and eyed me with the shrewdest stare. "I suppose you're going to lead this." It was not a question.

"Of course, sir." There had been some give and take—to be sure!—but I left with the desired permission.

The February 7 strike was the usual midmorning call for twenty-four of our Corsairs taking part in covering the SBD component of a mixed SBD-TBF strike against Vunakanau. The remainder of the top-cover force was the customary mixed bag of Marine Corsairs. Eight of Lem Cooke's F6Fs plus eight Torokina-based New Zealand P-40s were low cover. For some reason, only sixteen of the scheduled twenty-four Hogs got to Rabaul. I thus had to call the four-plane RHC contingent down to beef up the high-cover group.

The formation closed on Vunakanau without incident, but we found the target closed in by a localized weather front. The bomber leader thus turned to his secondary target, Tobera, which was attacked from west to east.

The Japanese launched about forty Zekes, Hamps, and Tonys, which put in pathetically desultory attacks—less aggressive than usual. About all most of that gaggle did was try to impress us with an aerobatics display far out of range. However, several braver souls did try to throw in determined attacks, and several actually succeeded in pushing through the high-side and overhead runs on our formation.

Lt(jg) Earle Peterson, a member of Paul Cordray's division, was scissoring around in the number four slot, on Hal Jackson's wing, when he nailed one of about six Zekes making a concerted overhead run on the bombers. Peterson's firing run, which was from five o'clock below, produced solid hits in the target's cockpit and right wing root, and the Zeke flared up. Just as the burning Zeke rolled away, however, Peterson's Hog was drilled from dead astern by numerous 7.7mm machine-gun rounds and one 20mm shell, which exploded in the cockpit. Wounded and barely able to see through a shattered windscreen, Peterson rolled out, recovered, and started looking around for the rest of his division. Unable to find *any* friends, he flew directly to the rally point over Kabanga Bay, but there was no one there except a bunch of Zekes. He managed to skirt the area and set a course for home, but a lone Zeke found him and made a swift, surprising overhead run before pulling up directly in front of the wounded Hog's nose. Peterson opened fire, but he was unable to see the results. As he was passing New Ireland, he was joined by several Marine Corsairs, which escorted him back to Piva Yoke. We kept Peterson on the books for several weeks, hoping for a complete recovery from his wounds, but he never made it back to us.

Wally Schub's division, which was flying at 16,000 feet as part of Cordray's flight, was also attacked by the Zekes just as the bombers were turning into Tobera. Schub saw the Zekes, but he continued his weave over the bombers. This decision led Wally and his wingman, Whit Wharton, away from the Zekes, but Wally expected his second section to cover him. Unbeknownst to Wally, his second pair—Landreth and Dunn again—had been sucked back during the turn—an exact repeat of the previous day's error—and was not in position to cover Wally's pair. Wally's F4U began acquiring hits from one and maybe two of the attackers. A little later than Wally would have hoped, Dunn, the tail-end-Charlie, came around, saw what was going on, and thumped a snap shot at one of the Zekes. Miraculously, his rounds hit the Zeke and pried loose a stream of debris. The Zeke ran. Country Landreth also came around and joined in, executing a slightly belated high-side run on the Zeke that was putting rounds into Schub's Hog. Country's bullets hit the target; the Zeke's cockpit exploded and the Imperial Navy fighter went down burning.

Chico Freeman, who was taking a turn leading the second section of Rog Hedrick's medium-cover division, also came under attack during the turn into the target. The Hog was not hit and the attacker pulled away. Seconds later, Chico managed to get in a beam run on another Zeke. He closed to within 40 yards and saw the Japanese fighter fly right through his stream of tracer. A piece of the Japanese fighter was blown off, but the plane successfully evaded.

As aggressive as this little bunch of Zeke pilots had been against our fighters, it did not escape our attention that they made no effort whatsoever to get in among the bombers. If anything, we were seeing the result of some inspired thinking on the part of a very few aggressive Japanese who had figured out where the medium-cover fighters were most vulnerable.

The entire formation retired down St. George Channel. Much to my disgust, the majority of rather unaggressive Zekes, Hamps, and Tonys followed us much farther than was their custom, nipping and feinting along a 20-mile track. The Marine Corsairs and Lem Cooke's Hellcats took these guys on, and they bagged a few. I was despairing of running the planned Statue of Liberty, but the Japanese eventually turned back, so the bombers no longer needed maximum cover.

The composition of the Statue of Liberty group was to have been two full divisions, eight Hogs in all. However, the two ironclad requirements—experienced pilots with plenty of fuel aboard—netted us only six participants in all: Earl May on my wing, Clyde Dunn on Country Landreth's wing, and Windy Hill on Chico Freeman's wing. We stayed with the bombers for about ten minutes after the Japanese fighters left, then dived away to the deck and proceeded up the east coast of New Ireland.

The adrenaline was flowing freely; we would know how well we had planned within the next half hour. I signaled all hands to fire a test burst from each gun followed by a salvo from all six guns. We would need all the firepower we could get, so it was prudent to check. Further exchanges of hand signals established that each Hog had at least 150 gallons of fuel aboard, more than enough for the minimum twenty minutes of full-power flight, plus cruise requirements and a prudent reserve.

We saw neither shipping nor any other planes until we recrossed the shoreline just north of Rabaul, blowing sand all the way. I was mindful that we had no idea if we were being observed by ground-based lookouts or radar; I tried to keep such thoughts from my mind.

My pulse was racing, my throat was parched, my nerves were taut as we pulled up to skim over the ridge and then dropped away to the rooftops. We were doing about 320 knots in roughly line-abreast formation—my pair in the center, Chico's on the right, and Country's on the left.

We saw no traps or ambushers, but we did see four or six Zekes and Hamps in the traffic pattern over Lakunai—their number one field. Was that all?!? But I had long since realized that our late start away from the bombers would mean fewer juicy targets. Obviously, most of the Japanese interceptors had already landed there or at any one of the other three operational fields.

There was nothing in the air dead ahead of my gunsights. Much as I would have liked to turn into the Zekes in the traffic pattern, we all had to fly pretty much straight ahead to avoid mutual interference, so I fired at several fighters on the taxiway, straight ahead. As soon as I started shooting, Earl May followed suit. We both saw chunks of debris and lots of dust kicked up by our streams of bullets, but we started no fires.

Country was in a better position to score. He got his talons into a Hamp that was climbing out of a missed approach with its wheels still down. Dunn squarely hit two Zekes in the parking area and smoked a third that was still airborne at the south end of the field. Country got credit for a kill because his hits had produced flames, but Dunn only got two probables and one damaged because none of his targets burned.

On the right, Chico and Windy roared down the west side of the strip, blazing away as they came. Chico's two airborne targets, a Zeke and a Hamp, were seen trailing black smoke and losing altitude, but no one saw them crash. Score two probables. Against orders, Windy pulled up to 1,000 feet to take on a Zeke in the approach pattern. However, the Zeke pilot was alert enough to take radical evasive action.

We were all clear of the field, still going flat out on the deck, before any of their guns got a round off in our direction. We throttled back to cruise power as we exited St. George Channel and then climbed to a cooler, more relaxing 3,000 feet for the run home. I cracked my canopy for a relaxing smoke and saw that some of the others had done the same. There were smiling faces everywhere I looked.

The ploy had clearly been successful, but far short of what we had hoped for. We all had expected to leave Lakunai littered with burning enemy fighters. Be that as it may, our intrusion could not have helped Japanese morale.

29

We were rained out again on February 8, which worked out okay. The troops needed a day off and I had to steel myself to the dreaded duty of writing letters to the next of kin of our departed comrades. The only one I knew was dead for sure was Doug Gutenkunst; all the others were properly classified as missing in action. So all the letters except for those to Doug's mother and fiancée could be leavened with words of hope and encouragement. By hideous coincidence, my letter to Doug's mother never got to her, nor did the Navy Department's telegram. In the heart-wrenching sequence that ensued, Mrs. Gutenkunst's first inkling that her son was dead arrived in the form of a phone call from a sobbing woman, Doug's fiancée, who had just received my letter to her. Part of the fallout eventually reached me in the form of a reprimand. What a sad and unfortunate close on a very deep friendship!

Our February 9 cover mission was more of the same against diminishing odds. Oc Chenoweth and Earl May scored a solid Zeke kill apiece, and Mills Schanuel damaged a Hamp from his RHC leadership position.

On February 10 sixteen of our F4Us under Oc Chenoweth accompanied a B-25 strike to Vunakanau while I and six others escorted a simultaneous B-24 strike against Tobera. The opposition was meager, but we scored three kills: one Zeke apiece by Davenport and Ellsworth over the B-24s and a shared Zeke kill over the B-25s by Bitzegaio and Jagger.

As the bombers were departing, I detached my entire flight from the B-24s and picked up two extra airplanes from Oc's B-25 group. The objective was a low-altitude sweep up along the coast well to the north and west of Rabaul in search of multiengine airplanes we thought might be hiding out there. It had only just dawned on one of my geniuses that we had seen absolutely no transports or bombers of any sort since the start of our second tour. Reason dictated that the Japanese, who we knew were forewarned of incoming strikes by ample radar and observer coverage, were sending their bombers and whatever transports they had out early. We were certain they still had bombers based around Rabaul, for there were plenty of large, well-maintained revetments in evidence at several of the larger fields. It stood to reason that a careful search would eventually reveal the location at which they were orbiting while our bombers were hitting the fields.

The search produced none of the expected results, none of the easy kills we eight had been contemplating all morning. My report, which made its way through channels, drew an eventual response from our side's intelligence wizards. It turned out that we had seen no bombers or transports because everything except fighters had been pulled out of Rabaul in early January. It was nice of our guys to tell us.

On the way up the coast that day, we did stumble upon a very small ship—a 100-ton, 125-foot wooden schooner—tied up to a dock in an out-of-the-way harbor. We worked out all our frustrations on that meager target, and I wrote it up in my report almost as an afterthought. Strangely, this routine dustup was treated as a very big deal by the higher-ups, and it was even cited in the text of one of my two combat awards. It is galling that the things I felt were my really major contributions—the RHC ploy and, above all, the fact that my squadron never lost a bomber it was charged with protecting—were to be officially ignored.

Nothing at all happened on February 11. We undertook escort duties for two bombing missions to Tobera and one for a Dumbo that plucked an entire B-25 crew from the water southwest of Buka. One of the Tobera raids drew out some Japanese fighters, but they never got close to the bombers and were handled by our Marine compatriots, who failed to score.

February 12 was another dull day. We sent twenty-two F4Us with the day's B-25 mission to Tobera, but no enemy aircraft were sighted.

Danny Cunningham finished off a Zeke on February 13, and one of our F4Us was damaged when gunfire from another Zeke blew up the ammunition cans in its right wing.

Again, for us, nothing of note occurred on February 14. The B-25s we escorted made it in and out over Vunakanau through meager and inaccurate heavy-caliber AA and no fighter opposition.

We saw no action on February 15, but it was a red-letter day nonetheless. Elements of the 3rd New Zealand Division went ashore in the Green Islands, four tiny, flat islands 117 miles east of

Rabaul. We flew a total of seven two-hour patrols over the islands and the transport force, but we never saw an enemy airplane. More of the same ensued on February 16. The thing that made the duty so nice was that one of the islands was slated for conversion to an emergency airstrip for our wounded birds. It would be half the distance from Rabaul than our closest existing bases, on Bougainville.

We experienced several amusing incidents during the week-long dry spell. Or, perhaps we only remember them because we had the time and leisure to file them away in our memories.

On one return hop from the Green Islands, Tom Killefer led a low-level reconnaissance over Tuli Island, 60 miles northeast of the Greens. When TK and the others got home they *officially* reported seeing many beautiful, big-breasted, cocoa-colored women infesting the place. Sure.

The premier performance was made by Ens George Keller, an eager young new guy who had already been through some heavy action with us. Georgie was tabbed to go back to Guadalcanal to ferry a brand new TBF up to Piva Uncle. The way it worked was that the squadron was asked to make a pilot available—a routine headache—and Georgie was sent because he had originally trained as a Turkey pilot. In fact, we looked forward to these ferry missions because it provided us with the means for major booze purchases. The fact that the airplane in question was a TBF—with huge storage spaces—made this mission all the more worthwhile. Ensign Keller was entrusted with a rather large bankroll and very explicit instructions, the breaking of which, we assured him, would certainly mean his life. The central admonition was that he was not to leave the plane under any circumstances from the moment the booze was loaded until it was safely turned over to a senior squadron officer. (We were not above stealing another squadron's hooch if given the opportunity, and we would not blame another squadron for bagging ours. However, we *would* blame the youngster into whose care the booze was consigned.)

Duly briefed, Georgie bravely set forth. Unfortunately, he left with incomplete advice, for it had dawned on none of the old hands that Georgie was new to the area and that this was to be his first trip alone over the bypassed little fortresses in the Shortlands.

Our man accomplished his mission in stellar fashion at Guadalcanal. Affecting the air of a complete rube, Georgie used his engaging charm to drive extremely hard bargains. He wheeled into the wind at Henderson Field with the Turkey's bomb bay loaded down with a dozen cases of rotgut whiskey, six cartons of brandy, and thirty cases of canned beer. We who awaited him would have been proud of how well he had eked out the booze fund had not fate and inexperience intervened in the proceeding.

Georgie was motoring along at 5,000 feet, plump, inattentive, and content as he approached the venue of the Ballale Postgraduate School for Frustrated Antiaircraft Gunners. Before Georgie knew quite what was happening, he was shaken from his reverie by the flash-*crack*-and-black-puff signature of heavy-caliber AA. Before he could react, he heard a giant *kebang* and felt the new Turkey's airframe shiver violently.

As Georgie later told us, "I thought it was the end of the world." For him, as far as we were concerned, it might as well have been.

Now fully alert, our dashing hero of the air reflexed admirably with a violent push-over into a steep diving start of some extremely radical evasive action. Sensing that a great deal was amiss, Georgie cool-headedly leveled off at the first opportunity and dropped his main gear before all the hydraulic fluid bled out of numerous holes in the system. As soon as he was clear of Ballale, he called in for clearance for a deferred emergency landing.

Safely tucked away in a Piva Uncle revetment thirty-five minutes after the shooting incident, Georgie shakily shut down the Turkey's engine and went to examine the damage. It was almost total. The new torpedo bomber smelled like a saloon on New Year's morning and the beat-up bomb bay doors were dripping beer suds. Georgie felt they might as well have been dripping his life's blood. He called for help as soon as he found a lucid moment.

When the welcoming committee got into the bomb bay, we found scarcely an intact bottle; only a welter of sodden cardboard and broken glass. Beer was still trickling from three hundred ruptured cans.

As if the loss of our booze were not adequate punishment, Strike Command informed me that they did not appreciate receiving this mint TBF in its diminished condition. It needed a major rework— following cleanup and deodorizing. They added that they thought I would like to know that fragments from a bursting 37mm AA shell had started a fire as they severed gasoline and hydraulic lines and shorted out wiring. I heard them out to that point and then tartly rejoined that I had heard that the flames, fed by the flammable fluids and alcohol fumes, had not destroyed the bomber only because they had been quenched by the foam and carbon dioxide from the gushing beer—that maybe this was an idea worth pursuing for installation in all their light bombers.

We did not, as threatened, take Ensign Keller's life, but we did apply a new nickname that would immortalize the incident. In the air, his radio call remained Georgie, but on the deck he was known only as Dumbo.

30

For reasons beyond our ken, the air war over Rabaul picked up again on February 17, when I led twenty VF-17 fighters to help protect a mixed SBD-TBF strike against shipping in Simpson Harbor. For the first time in about two weeks, the Japanese challenge force was composed of up to fifty fighters—Imperial Navy Zekes and Hamps and Imperial Army Tonys and Oscars. Some of the desperation of the defenders could be seen in the commitment of the latter type, the inferior and easily downed Nakajima Ki-43.

The approach was made over St. George Channel and Credver Island, where the bombers started letting down through the overcast. The Japanese fighters intercepted our formation just as it turned left over Keravia Bay. We were stacked between 14,000 and 16,000 feet, but the leading wave of Japanese made their approaches from about 12,000, through broken clouds that made it extremely difficult for us to engage.

Ens Clyde Dunn, who was making his first hop as a section leader, shot down a Zeke during the initial attack. Moments later, during the bombers' final run-in, four Tonys ganged up on Dunn's wingman, Dumbo Keller, who had radioed Clyde to begin scissoring with him. Dunn did not respond; even a burst fired beneath his wings by the understandably concerned Ensign Keller brought no response. As Dunn flew on straight ahead, Dumbo was forced to dive away, the first step in his ultimately successful struggle to evade the Tonys. Keller later reported that he saw no enemy planes on Dunn's tail, but Dunn was never seen again.

Ens John Malcolm Smith, who was flying wing on Timmy Gile, spotted at least a dozen Zekes climbing into the fight from over Blanche Bay. He warned the others in his division, and all four turned back the way they had come to prevent the Zekes from getting onto the tails of the bombers. Moments after the opposing forces deployed to engage, Smitty lost track of Gile. As he recovered from a chandelle, he saw a Zeke approaching from port at his altitude; it looked to Smitty like the Zeke was trying to join up on his wing. Smitty turned into a quick beam attack, fired a long burst, and watched the Zeke spin down in flames. After recovering,

Smitty looked around for some F4Us to join, but there was no one around. He did see the bombers nose over into their dives, so he dived to 8,000 feet. There, as he had hoped, a Zeke was setting up on the vulnerable SBDs. Smitty damaged the Zeke in a beam attack, but the Japanese fighter rolled over and dived away. Certain he had done a day's work, Smitty flew toward the rally point off Cape Gazelle. Before he got there, however, he spotted an Oscar slightly below and heading in the same direction. A stern run brought Smitty to within 1,000 feet of the Oscar, and a good if distant burst sent the Imperial Army fighter diving away with gas streaming from holes in its wing tanks. Smitty declined to follow the Oscar; rather, he climbed away with the intention of continuing on to the rally point. Still well short of the objective, he was bounced from dead astern by a Zeke. The Japanese pilot had Smitty's Hog perfectly boresighted; numerous 7.7mm rounds holed both wings and sent Smitty diving away in radical elusive twists and turns. He managed to shake the Zeke and rejoin the rest of us at the rally point. He was given credit for one Zeke downed, one Zeke probably downed, and one Oscar damaged.

The AA barrage over the target was meager this day, but it was not inaccurate. Lt(jg) Jamey Miller's plane was hit 10,000 feet over the target, and about 5 feet of his right wing was blown off. The airplane spun down to 5,000 feet before Jamey got out. When last seen, he was in one piece, and he even waved to his wingman before the latter was forced off by more fire from the ground. As with all our parachuting pilots over Rabaul, Jamey Miller was never heard from again.

After the bombers were safely on their way home, I led off another six-plane Statue of Liberty sweep. Staying above the overcast, we zoomed back in over Kabanga Bay from the direction of New Ireland. The Japanese should have been returning to their roosts by then, but we saw absolutely nothing. I led the crew to Blanche Bay, but there was nothing there either. We saw several fighters climbing out over distant Tobera, but there was no time to go after them. We left in a hurry, fearful their fighters might be waiting to pounce from out of the clouds.

On February 18 while Dirty Eddie March led off sixteen Corsairs to escort the first of two B-24 squadrons bound for Vunakanau, Rog Hedrick moved eight of our fighters into position for an

RHC bounce. As the bombers flew in at 20,000 feet, and heavy-caliber AA burst above and below them, only about twelve Japanese fighters made a direct challenge, and only two of those seriously attempted to make firing runs. Portions of our high-cover divisions turned to meet the attack, but the Japanese declined to engage. It looked to Dirty Eddie and his crew like it was going to be another humdrum milk run. For them, it was. But for Hedrick's eight, February 18 was a big day.

The bombers were scheduled to arrive at 1115, so Rog had timed his arrival for 1040. The RHC approached from the south over Wide Bay at 32,000 feet and made a wide circuit of the area. As they circled, the two divisions split apart, Rog's going to 29,000 feet and Timmy Gile's going to 26,000.

As Timmy got over Blanche Bay, he spotted eight Zekes deployed in two four-plane divisions; they were at about his altitude in a climbing turn. Certain that his division had been spotted, Timmy tried to climb to an altitude advantage, but the Zekes kept climbing, too. Nevertheless, the Hogs got to 30,000 feet before the Zekes, and from there Timmy led his birds in to undertake successive section runs on the opposition. The Zekes dived away and the action developed into a running fight. Finally, over Keravat and following repeated unrewarding firing passes, our guys cut off one Zeke at about 25,000 feet. The Zeke split-essed, but the entire Corsair division threw in a pass from five o'clock and set the Japanese plane afire. The Zeke, which spun all the way in, was fully credited to Timmy Gile.

Suddenly, two Zekes appeared on John Malcolm Smith's tail. Smitty coolly followed Timmy into a tight 180-degree turn and on into a flat dive. The Zekes turned back and Gile chandelled after them. Smitty mistook Gile's initial turn-back for the opening part of a scissors, so he crossed beneath Timmy and turned back on the opposite course, thus losing Timmy altogether. As Smitty started a climb over Cape Gazelle, he saw a fighter approaching in a slight left turn and on an opposite heading. Our young hotshot turned to join on the other fighter's wing and saw that the other fighter was turning to join on his. Eventually, Smitty woke up to the fact that he was getting overly friendly with a Zeke pilot as confused as himself. Our man recovered first, within 1,800 feet of the other fighter, and set up perfectly astern of the Zeke. He coldly held his fire until the range had closed to 800 feet. The Zeke never varied from its course and a long burst sent it spinning down. Smitty recovered from his reflexive chandelle and followed his target down, pouring in bullets until the Zeke started burning.

Meantime, after losing Smith, Gile was attacked by a Zeke that climbed straight up on his tail. Timmy put his fighter into a 30-degree dive and rocketed from 20,000 feet to 10,000. He finally shook the Zeke as he was crossing over Cape Gazelle, where, lo and behold, Smitty appeared and joined up. The two shaped a course for home and arrived without further incident.

As Gile and Smith maneuvered to evade the two Zekes on their tails, Gile's second section—Earl May flying wing on Paul Cordray—went down into a high-side beam run on two other Zekes. May missed both targets, but Cordray sent one of them spinning out of control and smoking. Our pair, which never broke formation, turned toward Vunakanau to join on the bombers, but they got into a running fight with eight Zekes on the way. Still hanging together, they threw in a section run at all eight Zekes, but three of the Japanese fighters ganged up on Cordray, who dived into a layer of clouds at 16,000 feet. May had it all figured out; he called Paul to tell him to zoom back up into the clear so he, May, could shoot the Zekes off his tail. Paul did not hear the call and continued to dive. He eventually evaded the three Zekes and joined our retiring high-cover divisions.

Meantime, Earl May decided he did not like being alone, so he turned east again to chase the bombers. On the way, he came up behind a Zeke, which slow-rolled just as Earl was about to open fire. The Corsair followed the Zeke into the roll and put out rounds that flared the fuel tanks in both wing roots. The Zeke stalled and fell in. Earl continued on over the coast of New Britain and crawled up the tail of another Zeke single he found. This Zeke also slow-rolled when Earl opened fire, and Earl again followed his quarry through the roll. Once again, the Zeke went down in flames. Suddenly an ace, Earl was also suddenly out of targets. He joined on the retiring bombers.

Rog Hedrick made his first contact in the fight Gile's division had picked with the first eight Zekes it had found. His division began picking up the pieces south of Vunakanau at about the time Timmy's formation was breaking up. Rog and his wingman dived in from 29,000 feet and Rog caught a Zeke in a stern run at 18,000 feet. The Zeke burned. As Rog recovered, he spotted another Zeke below him, so he set up another stern run. This Zeke pilot saw him coming and dived away, but Rog stayed on his tail and blew him up with a short burst at 12,000 feet. By then alone, Rog turned back to Cape Gazelle. He was circling there when he saw a loose column of eight Zekes climbing through 15,000 feet a few miles east of Tobera. True to form, Rog waded in and came down astern the lead Zeke. As usual with Rog, a brief burst produced flames. As the Zeke fell away, Rog prudently withdrew before the other seven Japanese fighters could engage him. He joined up on the B-25s, which were well into their retirement.

Our box score for the day was three Zekes downed by Hedrick, two Zekes downed by May, one Zeke downed by Gile, one Zeke downed by Smith, and one probably downed by Cordray. That's seven, and probably eight, for no losses.

Eight of our planes were involved in escorting an afternoon SBD strike against the radar station on Cape Gazelle. The mission was completely unopposed.

Many an evening, the opposition sent over a twin-engine heckler at very high altitude. On the evening of February 18, the invader outwitted our two Torokina-based night-fighter squadrons and flew inland toward the Piva complex. Silhouetted by searchlights, Washing Machine Charlie circled and loosed an occasional bomb. Typically, the bombs fell into the jungle. The routine had become such old hat that no air raid condition was set. All hands went about their business and no one even bothered to douse the lights. As on most such nights, the higher-ups gave our AA boys an opportunity to relieve the ennui of their duty.

The bursts of 90mm rounds, the sweeping searchlight beams, the red gobs of 40mm rounds—it all made a fine show. As on many previous nights, TK and I stood in the open, drinking beer from cans, admiring the fireworks display, and debating some weighty philosophical point. Suddenly, from the beach area—close and to the west—there came a giant *WHUMP*, unmistakably an exploding bomb. Seconds later, and much closer, we heard *and saw* the second *WHUMP*. There were no foxholes nearby, so TK and I leaped toward the nearest tent, where the only possible cover was the floorboard. Unfortunately, I got there first. Even TK's solid 190-

pound frame and considerable momentum were unequal to the task of driving either of us through the 6-inch clearance between the boards and Mother Earth. Nearby, Big Jim Streig remained sane enough to remember that he recently had dug a foxhole outside the opposite wall of his tent. From a prone position on his cot, Jim levitated over the intervening table and bunk and went straight through the side of the tent, taking with him the two-by-four framing timber. In the process, he managed to graze and daze Lt(jg) Hap Bowers, who had somehow slept through the racket going on outside.

The stick of bombs ran out just as the unexpected and unopposed low intruder—a lone Judy torpedo bomber—reached the edge of the pilots' encampment. All we saw of him were the blue flames of his exhaust stacks as he hauled ass back out to sea. What was this, a new wrinkle in the Statue of Liberty play?

31

We approached Rabaul on February 19 in the throes of great anticipation. We hoped that the Japanese, who had been showing a renewed enthusiasm for jousting, would send up even more fighters than they had on the two previous days.

Twenty-four of us were assigned high cover for the TBFs and high and medium cover for the SBDs, and we had four planes tabbed for RHC. On the way to the target, however, we had four aborts, so I pulled in two of the RHC Corsairs, leaving only Oc Chenoweth and Danny Boy Cunningham for the Gravy Train.

While the rest of us stayed close to the slow-movers bound for Lakunai, Oc and Danny roared ahead and arrived at 1005, almost twenty minutes ahead of the main strike force. They came in at 30,000 feet, circled, and let down to 24,000, at which point they located six to eight Zekes 18,000 feet above St. George's Channel. Oc instantly selected one of the Zekes for his target and led Danny into the run-in. The Zekes saw our pair coming on and broke in all directions. Oc's target dived away, and Oc followed him to 12,000 feet while Danny broke off to cover him from 18,000 feet. The two Corsairs were vastly outnumbered and thus extremely vulnerable. Oc dispatched his Zeke, which Danny saw as it crashed on Cape Gazelle. Oc then climbed back up to rejoin Danny, and the two made a team run on another lone Zeke. Oc overshot the target, but as the Japanese fighter pulled up to get in what he thought would be an easy belly shot at Oc, Danny burned him with a solid burst.

The Corsair element recovered and headed for fresh hunting grounds to the west, over Blanche Bay. On the way, both pilots saw several Zekes below and on the same course. Once again, Oc led Danny down. Once again, Oc overshot. Once again, the target pulled up to shoot at Oc. And once again, Danny Cunningham blew the Zeke away. This was Danny Boy's fifth kill.

Unfortunately, the F4Us became separated during the recovery from this run. Oc spotted a lone Zeke and made a stern run, but only one of his machine guns responded, so the Zeke got away. Oc turned out of the fight to get all his guns working, then headed for a group of Zekes he saw hovering at 10,000 feet between Duke of

York Island and Rabaul, right over the arriving bombers. He made a stern run on the nearest Zeke and set it afire. As soon as the Zeke pilot bailed out at 4,000 feet, Oc turned back toward Cape Gazelle, where he saw a group of Tojos sneaking up on the bombers from low on the water. As Oc turned into a pair of the Tojos, the wingman snap-rolled to avoid him and flew into the water before Oc fired a shot. Oc was given credit for the kill, his third and last of the day, a total of 8.5 overall.

Danny was at 5,000 feet near Simpson Harbor when he lost Oc. He went full throttle and blasted off for Blanche Bay. On the way, he saw another F4U, assumed it was Oc, and turned to join up. However, the other F4U turned north in pursuit of a Zeke. As Danny roared on to catch up, he saw another Zeke coming down astern the other Corsair, so he turned hard into him. The Zeke saw Danny coming, pulled through his dive, and again attempted to close on the tail of the other F4U. Danny stayed on the Zeke and closed to within range. A single burst sent the persistent but stupid Zeke pilot to his death in a burning airplane.

After recovering at 3,000 feet, Danny climbed away in the direction of Cape Gazelle to join the bombers. As he approached, he saw a single Zeke loitering outside the bomber screen and a little above it. Almost routinely, he came up astern the unsuspecting Imperial Navy fighter and opened fire at 150 yards. The Zeke instantly burst into flames and went all the way down in an uncontrollable turning dive. Danny rejoined the bombers, a seven-kill ace, richer this day by four. Nothing in the world could have better justified my early decision to let the little scrapper stay with the squadron.

Though the Japanese were thought to have launched upward of fifty fighters, the strike group was not molested much on the run-in; only a few Zekes made feints in its direction. On the retirement, however, the Zekes became intensely aggressive. Six of our F4Us guarding the TBFs were directly challenged by a large contingent.

Lt(jg) Mills Schanuel and Ens H. B. Richardson were all that was left of their division, the division leader and his wingman having aborted. Mills spotted seven of the oncoming Zekes at 19,000 feet, 3,000 feet overhead and on the port quarter, so he led Richardson around and tried to pull up into the enemy fighters. The effort was cut off when all the Zekes pitched over and came on at our pair.

One of the Zekes got right onto Richardson's tail and opened fire. This brand-new rookie levelheadedly dived away. When he got to 3,000 feet, the Zeke pulled out of the chase, but not before shooting off Richardson's tail wheel and somehow blowing off the doors off his main-gear wheel wells. Schanuel had been able to follow the chase, albeit outside of firing range, so he was on hand as Richardson recovered. He led his wingman directly back to Piva Yoke for a safe landing,

Timmy Gile's leading high-cover division had to fight its way through a group of Zekes and several Tojos which had interposed themselves in Timmy's path. Timmy's wingman, Ens John Malcolm Smith, caught a Tojo at 14,000 feet and set it afire with a neat stern-quarter shot. Immediately after recovering from this run, the section made a similar run on another Zeke. This time, Timmy was the first to fire. A long burst started the Zeke burning and spinning down. It was seen to crash, thus giving Timmy his eighth confirmed kill. By then, the rest of the Japanese fighters had withdrawn, so Timmy and Smitty climbed back to rejoin the retiring bombers.

In the meantime, Gile's second section—Earl May followed by Beads Popp—had initiated a run against the same cloud of Zekes and Tojos. Earl dived on a Zeke and engaged him in a head-on run in which the Zeke vaporized into a ball of flame and metal. The pair recovered at 3,000 feet and headed toward Cape Gazelle. The Japanese fighters, mainly Zekes, were all over the sky, and a bunch of them joined to attack May and Popp with successive stern firing runs. Our pair not only managed to repulse the attacks by going into the standard protective scissoring mode, they shot down a total of three—two for May and one for Popp. The action suddenly ended when all the Zekes simply vanished from the arena. Breathless and sweating, our wolves pulled up and gingerly rejoined the bombers.

The only other action of the day was one for the history books. For me, it started just as the Japanese fighters began working on us over St. George Channel, when I heard a cry for help from one of my little lambs: "Skipper! Skipper! This is Ike! Ike! Three have me boxed. I'm headed north."

"This is Big Hog. Roger Ike. Good luck." I had no idea where Ike was. We were totally committed to our escort assignment; there was nothing I could do except sweat and face the pain of the probable loss of yet another comrade.

Ike had started the mission as leader of the high-cover division that had included Schanuel's and Smith's element. When Ike's wingman had developed engine trouble and turned back near Buka, Ike had stayed with the TBFs until the strike reached Cape St. George. The cover at that point appeared adequate, so Ike decided he should turn back in consideration of the fact that he had no wingman.

As Ike began an easy turn to the right, however, he saw "something" low on the water off Cape Siar. He went down to investigate and found a Rufe single-float Zero heading north at 1,000 feet. Unable to resist such an easy kill, our high-scoring ace settled down on the Rufe's stern and set it afire with a short burst.

Just as the seaplane fighter hit the waves, Ike saw big trouble coming: at least twenty Zekes were letting down through a huge cloud 16,000 feet over New Ireland. Four of the Zekes were coming right at Ike in a loose column. The Zeke leader caught up with the lone Corsair from dead astern and opened fire. Ike popped his flaps to dump speed and then pulled up as the Zeke unavoidably overran him. The timing was perfect and Ike got in a good belly burst that sent the Zeke leader crashing in flames.

When Ike recovered, he was at 1,000 feet and making a rather meager 200 knots. The other three Zekes were in line-abreast formation. Two were on his starboard quarter, preventing him from turning east toward the Green Islands, and the one to port stood between him and Bougainville. After screaming for help, Ike did what he had to do. He turned his nose north, put his Corsair into a shallow dive, and shoved the throttle forward to the firewall. Ike also had a new asset at his disposal, 250 horsepower not previously available. Ike was flying one of the squadron's eight Corsairs that had been retrofitted in Espiritu Santo with Pratt & Whitney's new water-injection system. As Ike roared north, he wound the engine up to 2,750 rpm and 62 inches of manifold pressure. There were few aircraft in the world that could match that performance. With a speed advantage Ike estimated as being about 10 knots, he slowly pulled ahead and nosed over to put some nearby New Ireland hills between himself and the enemy. His Corsair's nose no sooner crossed the beach than the water-injection system faltered and the engine missed. Ike pulled back the throttle control and frantically pushed it forward again. The water injection caught, then died, and the engine missed again. The chase was only four minutes old.

What to do? Ike's Hog was indicating 305 knots. His water injection fluid was used up, but his engine seemed to be running okay at the normal combat-power setting. He decided to stay on course to the west-northwest, and did so for fifteen or twenty minutes, until his fuel was down to about 160 gallons. The Zekes were hanging on, so Ike had to go for broke. He made an ultraviolent turn to the left, just off the wavetops, in hope of getting away to the south past the three trailing Zekes. The Japanese fighter on his left tried to turn inside Ike's radical turn, but, too eager, he dug his left wing into the water and cartwheeled to destruction. The two fighters on Ike's right were caught flat-footed and got sucked wide. They gave up the chase as Ike crossed New Britain at Open Bay. Ike kept up his run for home at full speed for ten minutes after the pursuit ended, then slowly throttled back.

Ike was late getting home—so late that we believed we would never be seeing him again. The last anyone had heard, he was being chase north by three Zekes. Despite our universal exhaustion, all hands remained out on the flight line, not far from Ike's hardstand. We conjectured aimlessly about what might have happened after that last plaintive radio call. We all feared the worst.

We literally could not believe our eyes when the single Hog marked "29" taxied in. We streamed out to the hardstand as the huge prop stopped and the grinning mechanics chocked the wheels. A pale and exhausted pilot wearing a sweat-soaked flight suit struggled out of the cockpit with the plane captain's help. When Ike held up three fingers, we went into a frenzy. He had been in the air for 4.2 hours and returned with less than 40 gallons of avgas aboard.

Ike's three kills—including the self-destructing Zeke—brought his total to sixteen. Other pilots had been awarded the Congressional Medal of Honor for less. Ike, however, got the Silver Star.

Fighting-17's February 19 total was thirteen Zekes, two Tojos, and one Rufe.

Three of our divisions escorted a B-25 strike to Lakunai the next day, February 20. We saw no Japanese fighters. Indeed, we never saw a Japanese fighter again—or any Japanese airplane. As we soon learned, the Japanese had withdrawn every flyable airplane they owned from Rabaul beginning at dawn, February 20. There was nothing flyable left by the time our morning strike arrived overhead. Coincidentally, then, the Air Battle of the Solomons and Bismarcks ended eighteen months to the day after the first Marine fighter squadron arrived to defend the skies over Guadalcanal's newly won Henderson Field.

When the full breadth of the Allied aerial victory at Rabaul was revealed in the form of ongoing nonopposition in the air, we felt that ComAirSols, especially Fighter Command, had won it. And well we might have. But the totality of the victory had as much to do with large events outside our ken as it had to do with the months of aerial combat culminating in the daily grind over Fortress Rabaul.

By early February, AirSols was able to mount daily attacks—weather alone interfered—aggregating as many as two hundred bombers and fighters. The Japanese were willing to take on our strikes, but they lost airplanes and pilots at a tremendous rate. The combination was crushing, for, though they were able to replace the airplanes with others of more-or-less similar quality, the only fresh pilots they had to spare were rank novices drawn from the flight contingents of three of their carriers.

The clincher came in February in the form of numerous strategic blows, some quite far afield. By then, the Allied Central Pacific Offensive was well under way, having begun in late November 1943 with the amphibious strike into the Gilbert Islands, at Tarawa and Makin. During the first week of February 1944, the successful leap into the Marshall Islands, at Kwajalein Atoll, effectively outflanked the Truk anchorage from the north and provided the commander in chief of the Imperial Navy's Combined Fleet with the first intimations that Truk itself might be the next target. In a way, he was right. For two days, February 17 and 18, VAdm Raymond Spruance's Fast Carrier Task Force—*nine* carrier air groups— subjected Truk to withering air strikes. Among other accomplishments, carrier pilots downed seventy Japanese fighters and bombers in the air and damaged or destroyed numerous others on the ground. Unfortunately, we had tipped our hand as early as February 4, when an extremely gutsy long-range Marine photoreconnaissance bomber overflew the anchorage. Thus, the main target, the bulk of the Combined Fleet—the main strength of Japanese surface naval power—had withdrawn permanently to the home islands on February 10. Nevertheless, the Japanese were extremely shaken by the power and fury of the great Truk Raid, and they immediately made the decision to abandon Rabaul to what appeared to be its imminent fate—a direct amphibious assault. On the night of February 17–18, Japanese paranoia was further influenced by twin bombardments undertaken by our destroyers at Rabaul and Kavieng. At the former, five of our destroyers sailed right up St. George Channel and delivered—the hard way—3,868 5-inch rounds against shore installations at Praed Point and throughout Rabaul town.

Virtually as soon as the last of our strike aircraft left the scene on February 19, all their airplanes were ordered to prepare to fly to bases out of our reach in the rear. Only about thirty damaged and grounded fighters and reconnaissance types were unable to make the mass morning exit. All that remained at Rabaul was a powerful infantry defense force, a formidable artillery array, and all the AA batteries we had been facing for months. These Japanese remained vigilant for a direct amphibious assault that never came and, as Admiral King predicted, they withered.

Postwar estimates revealed that only about 70 Japanese fighters were withdrawn on February 20, though some Japanese claimed there were up to 120. Further, it appears from incomplete and contradictory Imperial Navy records that our virtually daily attacks over a two-month period had destroyed at least 250 Japanese fighters in the air. No Imperial Army records of the Rabaul defense were ever located. Our records, quite possibly inflated, reveal 789 kills. Between December 17, 1943, and February 19, 1944, AirSols lost 151 warplanes of all types. The Japanese claimed 1,045 kills. It is doubtful that accurate statistics—or anything nearly accurate—will ever be determined. Whatever the real numbers, we won and they lost. Our victory was complete, for we accomplished exactly what we had set out to do.

What "exactly" we had set out to accomplish turned out to be news to me well after the event. While it was going on, we all saw our Rabaul missions in the context of assisting the bomber forces in their ongoing efforts to wear down the Japanese, to make their continued use of the airfields as difficult and resource-consuming as possible. In our eyes, the daily destruction of Japanese fighters was secondary to getting the bombers safely in and out.

Our perception was exactly backward. As crass and cold-blooded as it seems now, the only reason we had bombers along was because the Japanese had demonstrated an unwillingness to commit their fighters to challenging our fighter-only sweeps. They had done so in December, at the outset of the Rabaul offensive, and had had their butts broken. Thereafter, they only launched responses against our bombers. So, unbeknownst to us worker ants, our bosses sent the bombers mainly as a means to provide us, the fighters, with ample targets. Any damage the bombers themselves inflicted was considered a bonus.

The beauty of this strategy was that it worked so well. Fewer than twenty-five Allied bombers were lost as a result of damage sustained over Rabaul. Fighting-17 lost *no* bombers entrusted to our care, and we accounted for 106 confirmed kills. Moreover, solely because of our direct aerial offensive against all of Rabaul's air bases, not one of our ships nor any of our shore installations came under meaningful enemy air attack after November 1943. The only exceptions were periodic night nuisance raids by Washing Machine Charlie.

For all that, Fighting-17 was not quite out of the war.

32

W e continued to escort strikes into Rabaul. It remained twitch-
producing work both because we did not yet know for a
certainty that the Japanese air groups had permanently abandoned
the place, and because of the usual worrisome but ineffective AA
opposition over the targets. Combat air patrols over the newly
occupied Green Islands were truly a bore—aimless circling that
produced nothing but acute aero asserosis.

After two days of facing clear skies over Rabaul, it seemed like a
good idea to go see Colonel Brice about an idea that had been
brewing since before we completed our first combat tour. I jeeped
to the boss's tent after the February 21 mission, and, following the
usual amenities, I got down to the cases: "Colonel, I'd like your
permission to go see Peggy O'Neill"—Marine Col David O'Neill,
the chief of AirSols Strike Command.

"Holy cow, Tommy, what are you cooking up now?"

I grinned. "Sir, you'll remember that we cobbled up some bomb
rack adapters last November. Well, as you may remember, we
flight-tested them with five-hundred-pound bombs, then put them
on the shelf. Our thought has always been that they would be handy
in case of no air opposition, which is what we seem to be seeing now."

The boss had a pained look. "Yes, I do remember," he answered,
with more than a hint of resignation in his voice. "I'll admit it really
slipped my mind, but a light is dawning. Go on."

"Well, sir, when we got back to Espiritu in December we demonstrated the bomb racks for the FairWing ordnance guys. They
were appalled by the Rube Goldberg rig; the consensus was 'Great
idea, but they ain't safe.' So, they designed and manufactured
properly engineered adapters for the F4Us. We brought eight sets
with us when we rejoined them in January. We want to put them
in operation."

"Maybe. What's Strike Command got to do with this?"

From his expression, I knew that we were about to be in business. "Matter of protocol. I figure we're sliding into Strike Command's territory. I don't want Peggy pissed off at us enough to kill
our baby. Secondly, we need material support from his outfit. We

jury-rigged the racks last fall with moonlight requisitioning. We have eight bomb racks, but for starters we'll need fifty five-hundred-pound bombs and fuses. And we'll need some of his ordnancemen for a few days. Our troops are red-hot with fifty-caliber machine guns, but even the best of them is rusty in the bomb department."

"Commander Blackburn, you're a devious schemer!"

"You know, Colonel, a very attractive lady in Sydney used those exact words not long ago!"

We went together to Colonel O'Neill's digs beside neighboring Piva Uncle. Oscar Brice gave him a rundown, adding that he posed no objection.

Colonel O'Neill started off with, "Tommy, your guys are getting bored, and you want to stir up some excitement. Right?" I shrugged and nodded. "That doesn't surprise me, but no jousting with AA batteries! Okay?"

In my best Waikiki beach-boy pidgin I answered, "Nevah hoppen!"

Peggy smiled. "No shit? Well, in that case, I'll issue instructions to my people to give you whatever you need."

The installations were rapidly completed and exhaustively ground tested. Then Timmy Gile and I took off, each with a live bomb, and made individual low-level bombing runs. Each observed the other from a respectful distance as we made runs on a beached barge hulk from 25 feet. The releases worked perfectly. The five-second delay fuse in the tail of the bomb enabled us to get well clear before the great eruption of water, sand, and barge bits blossomed.

The bombs were the standard General Purpose (GP) type designed for use against conventional surface targets. They could withstand moderately severe impact without breaking up. The explosive was relatively stable; it would not blow up unless activated by a detonator or subjected to prolonged high heating. The detonator was touchier, but, theoretically, it would not explode until "armed," a process effected by release of a multibladed fan-type device that spun a fixed number of turns during flight subsequent to release. The fan was kept from spinning prior to release by a wire that went between two of its blades, and the wire was held in place by a pair of clips not unlike ladies' bobby pins. If the pilot wanted to jettison a bomb not meant to explode, the "arming wire" stayed in place on the fuse as the bomb was released. When a detonation was desired, the arming wire was held tightly by the pilot-controlled latch on the bomb rack. If so, as the bomb fell away the wire pulled free of the arming fan, shedding its clips. The fan then spun so that the fuse could function on impact. With the fuses we were using, the bomb did not detonate until five seconds after first impact. Taking off and flying with the arming control in the cockpit set on "safe" meant the pilot could reasonably expect no disaster in the event a bomb fell off as a result of an arrested or hard landing. However, the pilot did have to remember to change the control from "safe" to "arm" prior to release. Many "dud" bombs were merely the result of pilots forgetting to arm them. After landing, the ordnancemen routinely checked to see if the wire was still there; if so, the pilot had irrefutable evidence that he had at least done his part of the job properly.

As soon as I returned from my mission to Strike Command, I went to see Duke Henning, who had been supervising the nuts and bolts of flight scheduling since we had lost Chuck Pillsbury in November. This, in addition to his formal assignment as ACIO.

"Duke, dig us up some targets in the Rabaul area that are free of AA coverage. I'm looking for bridges, warehouses, and the like. While you're looking, I want the following pilots to have made two successful live drops before the twenty-fifth: me, Gile, Hedrick, Killefer, Freeman, Landreth, May, and March. Also Kurlander and Ellsworth are to make at least one drop each. I'll explain later."

"Aye aye, sir. Sounds like a roll call of the squadron's leading studs."

"Never mind." Duke was right on the mark, but I did not want him to know that yet. My problem was that the squadron did not lack for highly competent, gutty pilots. I picked this team because I knew its members were the squadron's leading girl chasers. It seemed appropriate to the mission I really had in mind.

The preliminaries proceeded with the expected growing pains— bombs that would not release without coaxing, duds, early drops, belated drops, you name it; they all cropped up. The bugs were squared away in due course and the mystified-but-eager bomb droppers grew confident that they had mastered their new craft. The ordnance experts agreed.

Several days after my first visit, I took Duke to a return engagement I had set up with Colonel Brice and his ACIO, Lt Joe Bryan. "Colonel, we're set to go on that project I first discussed with you and Joe at Munda. As you recall, Joe had some aerial photos of Rabaul town. You'll recall that we discussed the nature of the target in great detail." I was jerking the skipper's cord, but I really did want to see if he would remember on his own.

Joe caught on first. "Ah! You mean that you're finally ready to strike a blow for morality and clean living?"

"Precisely, Joe. We'll be known for our punishment of wickedness and vice. We'll earn a well-deserved accolade as the Galahads of the South Pacific. However, there's a—excuse the word—*hooker* from another quarter. A certain captain on Admiral Fitch's staff has vowed to see me hung from the yardarm if we pull this off and it gets publicized. He ain't kidding. I have to ask that this caper remain very closely held info: just General Mitchell,"— ComAirSols—"Peggy O'Neill, and yourselves. I won't tell my pilots anything they don't have to know until the mission has been successfully completed. Even then, if asked by the wrong people, I'll lie about its ever having happened. With the colonel's permission, I don't even think we should turn in an after-action report if no one gets hurt."

The colonel went for the whole scheme and invited me out for a drink while Bryan briefed the still-mystified Henning on the precise nature of the target and provided him with the necessary charts and photographs. When it was all over, we had permission to bomb what appeared to be the official cathouse for the Rabaul region's senior officer contingent.

The weather for the Rabaul area for the morning of February 26 was forecast to be free of rain squalls. Perfect, for I would not consider taking the added, unnecessary, risk of flying at night at low altitude into that area without excellent visibility. Many good pilots had been lost in the South Pacific when clouds had rock linings instead of silver ones. I ordered our ordnancemen, now fully up to speed, to hang a 500-pound GP bomb on each of eight F4Us. The eight primary pilots, plus the two in reserve, were routed out of their sacks *very* early and assembled in the ready room at 0400.

The scheduling blackboard that greeted the enormously curious pilots read:

```
CHATTE FLAMBÉE
TAKEOFF: 0500

17-F-1 Blackburn          17-F-7 Hedrick
    -8 May                    -21 Landreth
    -25 March                 -23 Gile
    -5 Killefer               -31 Freeman


Standbys: Kurlander, Ellsworth
```

After the necessary preliminaries by Duke regarding weather, radio calls, and survival data, I took over the briefing.

"In my fractured French, this caper is *Chatte Flambée*. I'll translate when we get back. For your protection, I won't explain the purpose of the mission until after we get back here. If it works as I think it will, the Japs are going to be very, very mad. If you get knocked down, and are taken prisoner, honest lack of foreknowledge might save your skin.

"I'll use seventeen hundred rpm at twenty-eight inches manifold pressure, in automatic lean [fuel mixture] for cruise. Our run up there will use up the fuel in the wingtip tanks [unprotected integral tanks, purged with carbon dioxide before combat]. Full fuselage tanks will provide us with more than enough gas for any foreseeable needs. With these eggs aboard, that power setting should give us one hundred ninety knots [indicated air speed] at three thousand feet. The run-in will be very similar to the Statue of Liberty to this point [indicated on the wall chart] ten miles north of the center of Rabaul. My division will make an easy one-eighty [degree turn] to come in on the target west to east. Rog, you'll do a three-sixty and then come in from the northwest. Cross over the target one minute behind us. The lead division will retire straight ahead on the deck 'til halfway across the channel. Then we'll make an easy one-eighty to the left, climbing to five thousand feet. The second division will make a hard ninety left immediately after bomb release, then join up on me. We'll swing back well clear of heavy AA range to see what we can before coming home.

"On the final leg to drop point, fly a regular loose vee of four. Intervals of about one hundred feet. Division leaders will give a 'Stand by' at about five seconds, then 'Drop.' In the event you don't hear 'Drop,' pull the chain when you see the division leader let his bomb go.

"We'll strafe on the last part of the bombing run.

"I know it sounds goofy, but the object is eight near—*very* near—misses on the center building. We'll put bullets into the structure, and I expect that our bullets will torch off any vehicles parked close aboard. If we blow up the main target, that's just the way the highway squirrel squashes.

"Obviously, the closer to line abreast and at your division leader's level the wing planes are at bomb release, the healthier it will be. Rog and I, as usual, will use power settings of twenty-five-fifty rpm at forty-four inches of manifold pressure. Wing planes have three-hundred-twenty-five horses in reserve at full bore. But if you're caught in a trailing position, for God's sake don't be a hero. Break clear to the left and abort your run. Even if an earlier bomb blast doesn't get you, the flying debris you can't see will!

"Certainly, there are lots of questions on your minds, but unless they are strictly on what I've told you, I won't answer them 'til later. I'm asking you to buy a pig in a poke. We've got two spare pilots standing by to replace anybody who has the good sense to think this is a nutty operation." Silence greeted this remark. "If there are no questions, let's go! Down with *sin*!" The guys looked at me, clearly thinking The old bastard has really lost his marbles. I did not elaborate.

Before climbing into our birds, each of us performed an operation in addition to the routine preflight inspections—such as kicking the tires; we tried to shake the bomb to be sure it was tightly held by its rack and sway braces, and inspected the arming wires for security and proper installation. The ground crewmen had decorated these ugly weapons with chalked graffiti such as "This one's for you, Tojo" and "Last Rising Sun, Watanabe-san."

We made the standard carrier-type join-up and doused all the lights except the blue ones on top of each wing. These lights, which were visible only at short range and from above, supplemented the exhaust flames for formating purposes. We headed southwest for 20 miles at 1,500 feet to deceive Japanese observers on Bougainville, then we swung northeast to keep well clear of all the islands.

Steady on course at 3,000 feet at cruise power, I lit a cigarette and relaxed. As always at night, I was flying on instruments.

Closing one eye during the Zippo lighter's brief flare kept my night vision acute. The cockpits glowed faintly from the red instrument lighting; I could barely make out Earl May on one wing and Dirty Eddie March on the other. Turning the master gun switch from "safe" to "fire" activated the dim yellow light of the aiming crosshairs, circles, and pips of the gunsight reflected in the center of the windscreen. I actuated the gun-charging controls to "fire," thus putting a live round in each of the six gun breeches. Then I fired a short burst from each pair of guns: inboard, center, and outboard. Finally, I set all three gun switches to "on" and followed with a few rounds from all six guns at once. The tracers arcing ahead crossed the line from my eyes through the crosshairs and then the firefly cone expanded as it curved off and down into the blackness. Finally, I put the master gun switch back to "safe"—all ready to shoot as soon as that all-important control was reset to "fire." The other seven planes followed suit in accordance with our long-established doctrine.

As dawn broke, we dropped to 50 feet off the water and turned west to approach New Ireland. We climbed just enough to safely clear the treetops as we crossed the beach. On the other side of the island, we eased back down to minimal altitude and increased to combat power and speed as we approached our initial point due north of the town of Rabaul. The sea had gone from invisible to gray to deep blue flecked with whitecaps indicating a surface wind of 15 knots. As expected, the whitecaps and the wind streaks showed that the wind was southeasterly and steady. We would not have a problem with lateral drift from a strong crosswind on our bombing runs, and there would be minimum turbulence from the wind spilling over the ridge on which the target sat.

With the sun about to break over the jungles of New Ireland, we had ample light to see our objective clearly. Coming in from the darker semicircle of the west minimized the possibility of early visual acquisition by an alert Japanese coast watcher.

Amazingly, the attack went precisely as planned. Rog's division had to hit the easternmost of the three buildings; as he later reported, he could not see the center structure at the last minute because it was blanked out by smoke and dust.

No gunfire from the ground was seen until we were effecting rendezvous of—blessedly—all eight unscratched airplanes. The AA that we saw as we were leaving was wild and uncoordinated.

There were no "hung" bombs; all the bombs had released at the target. Postflight inspection revealed an arming wire still dangling from the shackle on each bomb rack, clear evidence that every plane indeed had made a "live" drop.

As we tooled back to eyeball our handiwork, the main building was still standing but smoking. Flames and black smoke rose from several vehicles parked beside it. Rog's division had flattened the eastern building.

An hour later, we were all back on the deck at Piva Yoke, ready for debrief. All hands were very excited and pleased. There were smiles galore. I was immediately beset by pilots shouting "Hey Skipper! How about that?" and "Did you see?" and on and on. The ground crewmen were beaming too, though they didn't know exactly why.

"Please! Let me talk! Quit shouting questions at me!" When all had settled down, I went on, "My fractured French, pronounced 'shot flombay,' very roughly translates as 'singed pussy.' See, that center building used to be the British Officers' Club. The Japs renamed it The House of Flowers. Until this morning it was a spo'tin' house for Jap officers, the centerpiece for the maintenance of their morale. You can reasonably say that those samurai bastards came for a little ass, but lost much face instead. Well done!"

I reported the results direct to Colonel Brice, received a hearty pat on the back, and then filed a completely bogus after-action report for the benefit of the prudes up the chain of command.

In addition to getting the target, Fighting-17 started up a whole new industry for fighters. Beginning within the month, Corsairs throughout the Pacific were routinely bombing Japanese targets. We were aware that this development would have occurred anyway; however, we took pride in the fact that the crude rigs we fabricated at Ondongo in November 1943 were the first. By war's end, the Navy and Marines were fielding whole squadrons—mainly Corsairs—designated as fighter-bombers.

Epilogue

A fter two weeks of utterly boring no-results missions, Fighting-17 flew for the last time on March 6, 1944. Butch Davenport led fourteen Corsairs in a barge hunt along the west coast of New Ireland and the northeast coast of New Britain and left six small barges and a 125-footer smoking. Later, eight of our Corsairs escorted an SBD strike against Lakunai, and in the very last mission, eight Corsairs escorted three TBFs against shipping in Simpson Harbor.

We were officially relieved by VF-34 on the afternoon of March 7. Beginning at 0615, March 8, our thirty-five airworthy Corsairs began lifting off from Piva Yoke. The last man off, Lt(jg) Country Landreth, heard a thrilling new sound as he was taxiing out to the runway—the *swish-boom* of incoming artillery fire. As Country lifted his wheels from the runway, he saw two TBFs burning fiercely in their revetments at Piva Uncle. The next day, we heard, the Japanese mounted a major ground assault against the Torokina beachhead. They never penetrated to the airfields—as we had long feared—but they put up a stubborn fight that lasted several weeks. Our nonflying personnel and several extra pilots were safely lifted out of Torokina by transport on the tenth. By then, the Piva runways had been closed because of the incoming artillery. Two of our ground crewmen who came out on that flight had been slighty wounded by shrapnel only moments after Country Landreth had lifted off.

Our return to the rear area was marked by a deafening silence from the headquarters of ComSoPac, Admiral Halsey. No sayonara—much less "Well done"—when we departed. Then and later, recognition by most higher headquarters of our status as, by far, the top scoring squadron—Navy or Marine—to date was niggardly, to put the best face on it.

My fantastically successful tour as a pilot and as CO—including seven of my eleven confirmed kills—was memorialized by the award of a second Distinguished Flying Cross. Since by then the USAAF was awarding the DFC to most any pilot who became airborne twenty-five times west of Hawaii, I declined the honor. In

1947, following a servicewide review of wartime awards by the Navy's Board of Medals and Awards, I was summoned to the office of Secretary of the Navy James Forrestal, who pinned a Navy Cross on my number one blue uniform just below my golden wings.

The stellar Ike Kepford, who, with sixteen kills, was the Navy's leading ace of the day, initially received a Silver Star and a DFC. All the services, including the Navy, had been and were later awarded the Congressional Medal of Honor for a lot less. Depending on whom you use as authority, at war's end Ike ranked sixth or seventh in the list of Navy and Marine aces. Eventually, he received two Navy Crosses—one basically for his superb performance in the defense of the carriers on November 11, 1943, and the other covering his overall perforamnce.

Not so fortunate were the distinguished Hedrick and Gile. Rog's nine kills and 250 combat hours, Timmy's eight and 200 hours "earned" each of them a pair of DFC's. These minimal awards were never upgraded.

It is my belief that the aircraft companies' balls-out campaign via the press earned VF-17—emphasizing "Irregulars," "castoffs," and other nicknames—the enmity of many seniors who, like Plushbottom, saw us as a bad destabilizing influence on "good order and discipline."

Our recognition, then and subsequently, has come from our contemporary peers, from the Navy and Marine pilots who came on later, and from objective authors. It is heartwarming forty-plus years later to be admired as having been a member of *the* Fighting-Seventeen—near or at the top of any listing of Navy or Marine Corps fighter squadrons.

We were flown back to Pearl shortly after parting with our Hogs at Espiritu. After the warmest of receptions—well publicized—by Commander Air Force Pacific, we were turned loose on Waikiki for super R&R. Not me, for long. I was summoned back to Washington for grueling skull sessions with the high brass and the aircraft companies. It afforded me the privilege and joy of early reunion with my wife and family. On the negative side were sessions with reporters, complete with unnerving flashbulbs destroying my shaky composure at random intervals. Prior to heading back to the West Coast, I was assured by the Detail Office of immediate assignment as Air Group Commander (CAG) aboard a big new Fleet carrier. This was not to be, but that's another story.

On April 10 all hands—who'd come back to CONUS aboard, of all ships, *Prince William*—mustered at quarters at NAS, Alameda. I tearfully read the official orders decommissioning Fighting Squadron Seventeen. Some months later, a new F6F squadron was commissioned under that designation. I am happy to report that our heirs performed with immense distinction and success until VJ Day. The skull-and-crossbones insignia is still flying: It, under various numerical designations, has served proudly in Korea, in Vietnam, and most recently off the coast of Libya in 1985.

The decommissioning ceremony was followed by an uninhibited party to end all parties, hosted by Chance Vought Aircraft at the Mark Hopkins Hotel "atop Nob Hill in San Francisco." Then the Jolly Rogers scattered to the winds to begin their well-deserved month's shore leave before reporting to new duty stations.

For many of us, the combat action, if not the war, was over. Not so for the redoubtable Hedrick, by far the best fighter pilot with whom I ever served. He returned to the headaches and heartaches of forming a new squadron—this time as CO of VF-84, one of the many by now with Corsairs. They got into combat in late 1944 flying from *Bunker Hill*. In February 1945, following the combat death of his air group commander, Rog was fleeted up to CAG. Among Rog's Fighting-84 pilots were several VF-17 alumni— Chico Freeman, Fatso Ellsworth, and John Malcolm Smith. Rog scored three more aerial victories, Chico ran his total from two to nine, and Smitty fulfilled his early promise by adding seven to his Rabaul total of three. Unfortunately, *Bunker Hill*'s deployment was cut short by two kamikaze hits on May 11, 1945. One of the suicide planes vaporized inside VF-84's ready room. Among the many fighter pilots burned to a crisp was that nifty guy Chico Freeman.

Rog retired in 1958 with the rank of Rear Admiral. He subsequently prospered as a residential building contractor in Southern California.

Timmy Gile, Country Landreth, and Danny Cunningham returned to combat in F4Us in early 1945 as members of VF-10, aboard *Intrepid*. Unfortunately, none of the three scored further kills. However, Paul Cordray scored his seventh while flying from the same ship with VBF-10, also in the bent-wing bird. Timmy wound up as a VP with the financial giant Morgan Stanley. Paul died young—in bed—in 1963.

Country knocked himself down in March 1945. He was strafing an ammo dump on Honshu that blew sky high as he was making his pullout. It fatally wounded the lube oil system, forcing him to ditch. He was picked up by the locals, grilled (fortunately they never discovered that Country knew a lot about the upcoming Okinawa operation), and thrown into a POW labor camp. He there saw Greg Boyington, who everybody thought was long since dead. Landreth was the only "missing" VF-17 pilot or alumnus to be repatriated at war's end. He went on to a long and distinguished Navy career.

Following their month at home, Dirty Eddie March and Tom Killefer were sent to Florida to instruct in the Advanced Training Command. Soon after reporting aboard, they were joined by Lem Cooke. Their boss during this tour was Jumpin' Joe Clifton. By astonishing coincidence—it must have been that!—these three *and* Duke Henning plus Bob Anderson were among the Plank Owners when Air Group 74 (*Midway*) was formed and commissioned in May 1945 with me as CAG and Lem as CO of the thirty-six-plane fighter-bomber Corsair squadron. Air Group 74 had finished training and was ready to go into combat when VJ Day changed our world.

In early 1946 Dirty Eddie, who'd been training for the NCAA decathlon and thus was in superb physical condition, was killed off in a week by a mysterious, violently virulent flu bug. TK was mustered out in late 1945, and after a year as a Rhodes scholar in England, earned his degree at Harvard Law School. He was a VP at Chrysler but amicably parted brass rags with them before that company's great bailout by Uncle Sugar. He went from there to be president of a prestigious New York bank. Cooke left VBF-74 to join one of the Navy's experimental test units. He was killed in 1949 when the jet fighter he was wringing out developed a control malfunction and took him in. Earl May got it also, flying at the Naval Air Test Center in 1951.

The Navy kept Kepford busy in nonflying activity until after VJ Day. He was underdecorated but overworked making appearances and speeches to sell War Bonds and urge plant personnel to produce. As a civilian, he started out as a soda jerk in a Rexall drug store. In 1956 he became president of the company.

Butch Davenport resigned his commission in 1949 after a final tour at the NATC, flight testing our early jet fighters. He went to work for a small manufacturing company and helped build it into the now much larger and very prosperous firm of which he became president. Butch is the only VF-17 member still driving an airplane regularly. (Remember shy, studious Jack Chasnoff? This most successful corporation lawyer and his wife tour the country—still—on a big Harley-Davidson motorcycle.)

I served in a variety of challenging and rewarding assignments, including that of CO of the big carrier *Midway* on which I had made the first landing and served as CAG thirteen years before. By mid-1962, the Navy sensibly decided that it didn't need an Admiral who could not handle his booze. Thus, twenty-nine years after graduating from the Naval Academy, I retired as a Captain and began growing wine grapes and raising blue-ribbon golden retrievers in California's Napa Valley. Following harrowing years of battling alcoholism—endless recoveries followed by ignominious relapses—I was finally reprieved from that hideous squirrel cage at the outset of 1981.

Other squadrons later surpassed our record of 154.5 kills, but in our day, we were the Navy's top guns. A lot of that had to do with lucky timing and positioning—and because Vought and our Navy and Marine mechs kept us equipped with a full complement of well engineered and maintained hogs. But the lion's share of the credit is due the pilots—all of them, living and dead—not just me nor Rog, but *all*. We were a cohesive superbly successful *team*. It is for them, then, that I grant Big Hog "permission to leave the ship" with a quote from Shakespeare's *King Henry V*. Herewith Henry's exhortation to his troops the night before their stunning victory in 1415 over the French at Agincourt:

> *He that outlives these days and comes safe home will stand a tip-toe when these days are named. . . . He that sees old age will strip his sleeve and show his scars. . . . This story shall the good man teach his son. . . . And gentlemen who were then abed shall think themselves accurst that they were not there, and hold their manhoods cheap whiles any speak that fought with us.*

Appendix

Roster of Fighting-17 Officers
October 1943–March 1944

NAME	NICKNAME(S)	NOTES
Anderson, Robert S.	*Bob, Andy*	Det. 11/24/43
Baker, Bradford W.	*Brad*	MIA 11/17/43
Beacham, Sheldon R.	*Ray*	
Beeler, Edward E.	*Ed*	Det. 2/4/44
Bell, Thaddeus R.	*Thad, Juggy*	MIA 1/27/44
Bitzegaio, Harold J.	*Bitz*	
Blackburn, J. Thomas	*Tommy, Tom*	Ace
Bowers, George F.	*Hap*	
Burriss, Howard M.	*Teeth*	Ace, KIA 1/31/44
Chasnoff, Jack W.	*Jack*	Det. 12/10/43
Chenoweth, Oscar I.	*Oc*	Ace
Cole, Marvin, W.	*Ace*	
Cooke, Lemuel D.	*Lem*	Det. 1/10/44
Cordray, Paul	*Paul*	Ace
Cunningham, Daniel G.	*Danny*	Ace
Davenport, Merl W.	*Butch*	Ace
Diteman, James E.	*Dite*	
Divenny, Percy E.	*Perce*	MIA 2/4/44
Dixon, James C.	*Jimmy*	
Dunn, Clyde R.	*Clyde*	MIA 2/7/44
Einar, Robert W.	*Ine*	
Ellsworth, John O.	*Fatso*	
Farley, James	*Jim*	MIA 1/26/44
Fitzgerald, Louis A.	*Lou*	
Freeman, Doris C.	*Chico*	(*Ace* in VF-84, '45)
Gilbert, Carl W.	*Gibby*	
Gile, Clement D.	*Timmy*	Ace
Gutenkunst, Douglas H.	*Doug*	KIA 1/30/44

NAME	NICKNAME(S)	NOTES
Halford, James A.	*Sunny Jim*	Det. 11/22/43
Hedrick, Roger R.	*Rog*	*Ace*
Hill, Robert H.	*Windy*	
Hogan, Robert R.	*Bob*	KIA 1/26/44
Innis, Donald A.	*Stinky*	
Jackson, Robert H.	*Hal*	
Jagger, Frederick A.	*Andy Gump*	
Keith, John H.	*John*	KIA 11/1/43
Kelley, Louis M.	*Lou*	Det. 11/22/43
Kepford, Ira C.	*Ike*	*Ace*
Killefer, Tom	*Tom, TK*	
Kleinman, John M.	*Johnny*	Det. 11/22/43
Kropf, Thomas F.	*Kropf*	KIA 1/30/44
Kurlander, Melvin M.	*Mel*	
Landreth, William L.	*Country*	
Malone, Donald T.	*Don*	KIA 2/4/44
March, Harry A.	*Dirty Eddie*	*Ace*
Matthews, Marvin	*Matty*	
May, Earl	*Earl*	*Ace*
McQueen, Donald R.	*Mac*	
McQuiston, Louis T.	*Cue*	Det. 2/6/44
Meek, William P.	*Willie*	
Miller, James	*Jamie*	KIA 2/6/44
Mims, Robert	*Bobby*	*Ace*
Peterson, Earle C., Jr.	*Pete*	Det. 2/19/44
Pillsbury, Charles A.	*Chuck*	KIA 11/21/43
Popp, Wilbert P.	*Beads, Peter*	
Richardson, Harold B.	*Rich*	
Schanuel, Mills	*Mills*	
Schub, Walter J.	*Walt*	
Smith, James M.	*Smitty*	(*Ace* in VF-84, '45)
Streig, F. James	*Jim*	*Ace*
Wharton, Whitney C., Jr.	*Whit*	

Bibliography

Boyington, Gregory. *Baa Baa Black Sheep*. New York: Bantam Books, 1977.

Hammel, Eric. *Guadalcanal: Starvation Island*. New York: Crown Publishers, Inc., 1987.

———. *Guadalcanal: The Carrier Battles*. New York: Crown Publishers, Inc., 1987.

Lord, Walter. *Incredible Victory*. New York: Harper & Row, 1967.

Miller, John, Jr. *Cartwheel: The Reduction of Rabaul, U.S. Army in World War II: The War in the Pacific*. Washington: Department of the Army, 1959.

Mondey, David. *Concise Guide to American Aircraft of World War II*. London: Temple Press, 1982.

———. *Concise Guide to Axis Aircraft of World War II*. London: Temple Press, 1984.

Morison, RAdm Samuel Eliot. *Breaking the Bismarcks Barrier*, Vol. VI, *History of United States Naval Operations in World War II*. Boston: Little, Brown & Co., 1950.

Okumiya, Masatake, et al. *Zero!* New York: E. P. Dutton & Co., Inc., 1956.

Olynyk, Frank J. *USMC Credits for the Destruction of Enemy Aircraft in Air-to-Air Combat in World War II*. Aurora, OH: Frank J. Olynyk, 1982.

———. *USN Credits for the Destruction of Enemy Aircraft in Air-to-Air Combat in World War II*. Aurora, OH: Frank J. Olynyk, 1982.

Shaw, Henry I., Jr., and Mjr Douglas T. Kane. *Isolation of Rabaul*, Vol. II, *History of U.S. Marine Corps Operations in World War II*. Washington: Marine Corps Historical Branch, 1963.

Tillman, Barrett. *Corsair: The F4U in World War II and Korea*. Annapolis: U.S. Naval Institute Press, 1979.

———. *Hellcat: The F6F in World War II*. Annapolis: U.S. Naval Institute Press, 1979.

Documents

"Fighting Squadron Seventeen Log," Basil Henning, *10/27/43–2/16/44, 2/17/44–3/7/44*

"VF-17 War Diary," *9/28/43–3/31/44*

"VF-17 Action Reports," *10/27/43–11/29/43, 1/26/44–3/5/44*

Acknowledgments

If I hadn't learned it in many hard ways before, this writing would have convinced me fully that "no man is an island."

The quintessential Virginia gentleman and Unreconstructed Rebel Joe Bryan of Richmond, Virginia, suh, has been patient, tolerant, encouraging, and infuriatingly right over the many gestatory months. Thanks, Colonel.

Other talented professionals in the wordsmith field who have given unstintingly include Barrett Tillman, Adm Chris Cagle, Sallie Coolidge, Carl Solberg, and the Stockdales—Sybil and Jim. I'm truly grateful.

For aid in the military and aeronautic aspects I've been shamelessly and successfully crying MAYDAY. Rescuers have been squadron mates Rog Hedrick, Butch Davenport, Country Landreth, Windy Hill, Tom Killefer, and, the pearl beyond price, Basil Duke Henning. Boone Guyton, Bob Dosé, and Marvin Harper have fleshed out and squared away recollections wasted by forty-odd years. I hope you approve of your foster child.

The light of my life, Jamie, continues to be my delightfully unobjective instructive critic.

Finally, last but most, my deepest appreciation goes to the brave men, living and dead, who *did it* so that there is a tale to tell.

Tom Blackburn
Jacksonville, Florida

Index